First Edition April 2004

Published in the UK by
Poison Pixie Ltd

ISBN 0-9546115-0-0

A catalogue record for this book is available from the British Library

Cover illustration by Max Scratchmann
The publishers have made every attempt to identify copyright holders for the found images incorporated therein.

Printed and bound in Finland by WS Bookwell Ltd

DANNY

Volume One

Chancery Stone

Poison Pixie

For John and Danny
Who loves you baby?

"What of the very handsome boy, seeing himself in mirrors, hearing people comment on his beauty?.... Like the adolescent girl who must walk more slowly and be less, the boy must give up knowing too consciously what his beauty buys him. How very twisted."

Nancy Friday *The Power of Beauty*

"Research shows that when sibling bonds are intense and exert a formative influence on the development of personality... these siblings use each other, much as other children use their parents, in a search for personal identity.

It should not surprise us, then, that violence between siblings is more common than violence between parent and child or violence between spouses. Sibling violence is the most overlooked form of domestic violence. Knives or guns are used by one sibling toward another in three out of a hunderd cases of sibling violence."

Jane Goldberg *The Dark Side of Love*

"If you cannot get rid of the family skeleton you may as well make it dance."

George Bernard Shaw

Danny was sitting in the kitchen waiting for the bathroom when his mother came in. She passed behind his chair, pausing to look at the back of his neck. "You're peeling again."

Danny flinched away from her. He heard the fridge door open and close, the sound of a milk bottle. He did not turn. "Tell me about it."

He rubbed his stinging neck, trying to ease the stiff nettling pain, then dropped his hand in disgust and took a swig of beer from the can on the table. He didn't even know whose it was.

He heard the kitchen door open and close as his mother went out again, the television babbling briefly in the front room, playing to no-one in particular. He stood up and crossed to the dresser, picking up a piece of pie crust from the dish. It tasted unpleasantly salty. He threw it back on his plate and sat down again heavily.

The dog wandered into the kitchen and lapped noisily at his water bowl then fell into the doorway in an undignified heap, trying desperately to catch the slightest stirring of air through the open door.

The kitchen door opened yet again, with a suddenness that made Danny look up. John came in, wrapped only in a towel. His dirty brown hair, bleached with the sun, curled wetly on his neck. He looked twice as naked as anyone else would have done in similar circumstances.

Their eyes met briefly, away again. John pulled the towel tighter about his waist before saying, "Plenty of hot water left."

Danny nodded. He heard the glass cupboard door behind him open and close. He got up with a noisy scrape of his chair and went out quickly before John could say anything else.

The bathroom window stood wide open, letting in the last of the evening light. It was a pink room and the red setting rays of the sun deepened the roseate light. The large mirror above the basin streamed with long streaks of condensation and odd sworls where the others had attempted to clear it to shave.

Danny undid his jeans and peeled them off, throwing them in the wash basket, then his shorts. He turned on the shower and stepped under the sharp scalding spray. He could almost feel the weariness seeping out of his bones and running down into the shower tray. He lay back against the wall and turned his face up into the spray, running his hands up slowly over his chest. He jumped guiltily when someone pounded on the door.

"Don't be all bloody night in there."

"Oh fuck off," he whispered fiercely, turning his back to the door and scrubbing water from his eyes.

"You hear me?" More pounding.

"I hear you!" he yelled back.

Nothing. Silence. He let his forehead drop against the wall and closed his eyes.

After a moment he straightened up and took the soap and washed down, careful not to linger or rub too hard. He shampooed his hair and rinsed.

The towel was rough and dry and he got a masochistic pleasure out of rubbing his sunburn. He could not see himself in the mirror to shave and did not try. He moved to

the bathroom window, letting the air blow dully on his damp skin. It felt shivery and cool and vaguely disturbing.

The bathroom faced onto the back yard. He could see the tractors parked below, looking oddly desolate and abandoned, John's parked awry as usual.

He wondered briefly if anyone could see him up here.

He turned away abruptly, feeling that odd prickling sensation of arousal again.

He went to the sink and brushed his teeth with a punishing enthusiasm that left his mouth numb. His mother always bought the same clear bright green toothpaste that blew your mouth off. He couldn't feel his tongue afterwards. Maybe he ought to scrub his prick with it.

"Danny!" The door thumped again.

"Alright, alright! I'm coming." He grabbed a towel and knotted it round his waist then opened the door.

"Don't know what the hell you find to do in here." His father pushed past him, slamming the door in his face before Danny could even frame a reply.

He stood there for a moment, staring blankly at the door, then stuck his tongue out with an intense childish pleasure.

He turned away and went along the hall to his room.

He pushed the sash window up a little higher and stood looking out onto the village green. The sky was noticeably darker at this side of the house, but the breeze was still poor and dull. Danny stood at the window and ran his hand through his damp hair. It always formed a thick tangle of curls when it was wet. Time-it-was-cut season again. Well they could fuck that.

He could see the vague forms of people moving about on the green below, hear the odd murmur of conversation. He felt restless and irritable. He was over-tired and his hair was wet. He hated sleeping on wet hair, but it never had a bloody chance to dry because that lot never let him have first shower, fucking...

Rab banged suddenly on his door. "Put that down and get to sleep."

He heard John's low laugh, could almost see his smug smile. "You probably woke the bugger up."

Danny gave them the finger but did not answer them.

"Night Danny," Rab called but Danny still did not answer. He heard them laughing together then their doors closing in succession.

After a minute or two he heard the toilet flush and then the bathroom door open and his father shouting something down to his mother. She, too, finally came upstairs. He could hear his father's muttered replies until their door, too, clicked shut.

Danny lay down with a sigh and immediately felt his wet hair cold and unpleasant against his neck. He sat up with a jerk, cursing under his breath, and reached for a cigarette.

He lit it and sat watching its glow ebb and flow as he smoked. He wasn't supposed to smoke in his room.

Well she can fuck that too, he thought irritably, defiantly letting the smoke stream out of his nostrils.

After he finished the cigarette he realised he was thirsty.

He went out of his room carefully, stealing past his parents' room, wishing he'd put something on. All he needed was someone to bump into him wandering around the house like a bloody nudist.

Downstairs the dog thumped his tail lethargically on the kitchen floor but did not bother to get up.

"Don't blame you dog," he whispered, pouring himself a glass of cold milk and

shoving the fridge door shut with his foot.

He wandered back upstairs, glass in hand. On the landing he nearly spilt the lot.

"*Danny?*" The figure was peering at him. It was John. "What the hell are you doing?"

"Getting something to drink. What does it look like?" They were whispering.

"Well since you ask..."

He could feel John looking down at him. He blushed, glad of the darkness. "I didn't expect to bump into anyone, did I?"

"You say." He could see John's teeth glint in the gloom.

"Oh, fuck off John."

He made to pass him, but John was already turning away, pushing open the bathroom door. He whispered back suddenly over his shoulder, "Watch or your mother will hear." There was no laugh.

Danny gave him the finger and slammed back into his room.

TWO

That night Danny had the same dream.

He was wrapped deep in a pile of straw, just like usual. It was dusty, suffocating. It was high summer, very hot and pitch black. No light at all, like he was blind.

At this stage it wasn't threatening. There was no sense of menace in the darkness, only a kind of doped paralysis. He could smell the hay, feel its weight on his body, but his breathing was easy and deep, as if at some level he knew he was safely asleep.

Abruptly he realised he was in the old hayloft at Jerrett's and with the knowledge came a peculiar shifting of the light, as if he'd come into the darkness after being outside, his eyes slowly adjusting, becoming aware of hazy red silhouettes, of objects swimming slowly, and with a faint hint of menace, into focus. Then the weight on him shifted and he realised that someone, or something, was lying on top of him.

He tried to lift himself off the floor and couldn't, but now it was not that doped paralysis that prevented him, it was whatever was on top of him pinning him down. Then the weight shifted again and became, unmistakably, a person. A man. He could smell fresh sweat from him, feel their skins sticking together as if they were both barechested.

"*Danny…*"

The voice seemed to call from a long distance away. He *knew* that voice, but he was still blinded, struggling to see.

"*Danny…*"

The man was somehow closer, hotter. He could feel breath on his face now, like a draught of hot air. He struggled again to get up and it was as if the man suddenly came into his own body much as Danny had, as if he too had been paralysed up to that point.

He felt the unmistakable sensation of the man's face close to his, his cheek brushing against his as he turned his head. He felt a sudden and immediate panic. But now he was gripped, as if the man held his head rigid in two massive hands.

He was going to kiss him. Danny knew it before the man even moved.

Then his lips were there, horribly cold and wet in that heat, as if the man were dead or frozen.

The man's mouth moved off, trailing across his cheek. He felt heavy and drugged under the odd icy burning trail of that mouth. He was aware of a bitter metallic taste on his lips, like snail-slime. He felt poisoned, slowly dying.

"Danny."

The voice was suddenly right in his ear. No longer disembodied, but breathless and urgent, close.

Danny could feel a sudden excitement. The man had not touched him, there was nothing sexual in that cold kiss, and yet Danny had gone from nowhere to the point of no return in seconds.

The man was suddenly thrusting against him. He could feel his tongue, a horribly cold thick thing, trying to push between his lips. And yet, somehow, he was still saying Danny's name, over and over again, in that low urgent voice.

Danny felt himself surge up as the man's tongue finally pushed into his numb mouth. It felt huge, thrusting down his throat, coated in that same thick poisonous slime. Danny gagged convulsively, body jerking up. He groaned and twitched as the man's smell seemed to engulf his head. Salty, sweet, exotic - horribly familiar.

"Wake up Danny. For Christ's sake, wake *up*."

Danny's eyes jerked open, body half upright, panting with fright, as someone shook him.

He found himself held there, staring at John, half-dressed, frowning down at his pale face.

He blinked stupidly and dropped back down onto the bed as John let him go, defensively pressing his fists to his sticky groin. "What is it?"

John's frown deepened, eyes going from Danny's glistening chest to his face before he said, "It's time to get up. What did you think, fire drill?" There was a pause that felt a hundred years old before he added, "What was all the groaning and moaning for?"

Danny blinked again, eyes suddenly somehow focusing on John's, then he blushed the dull brick red of all redheads. "Nothing, bad dream."

John smiled disbelievingly, his eyes flicking down the bed to where the unmistakable shape of an erection showed through the thin summer blanket.

Danny tugged over onto his side, curling up, face flaming. "Why don't you fuck off and let me get up?"

John smiled a small smile. "Seems to me you're up already." He stood up slowly and moved to the door. "And you've overslept half an hour."

"Alright, al*right*. If you'd piss off I'll get up."

"Don't worry about me." He opened the door. "I've seen it before, remember?" And he went out, closing the door behind him.

Danny lay there for a second or two, fists clenched, eyes tight shut, then he sat up and jerked the sheet back, trying to dry up the mess as best he could.

His cock was still standing to attention as if it had some kind of depressing intention of never going down. He could still feel his skin crawling with the unpleasant sensation of the man's skin against his, the crushing weight. He felt repulsed by his own arousal.

Stuffing his ill-disciplined member inside his trousers, he pulled on the rest of his clothes and went downstairs.

Rab was standing with Ian in the yard. He turned round when Danny came out the kitchen door. "Well, well, look who's at the cow's tail."

Danny said nothing. John stuck his head round the kitchen door. "He got lost in a dirty dream. Couldn't tear himself away."

"Oh yeah? Who was it then? Anyone we know?" Rab climbed down off the tractor at the possibility of a new point of attack.

John came out the back door, wiping his hands. "Won't say. Obviously a big girl though, you should have seen the size of his hard-on."

Rab laughed, too loudly, but Ian only ran a hand through his lank hair. He smiled though. That twisted smirk that served him for a smile. Oh, Ian was happy enough.

"Practising for the big day maybe." John was suddenly close up behind him, making Danny spin round at his nearness.

Ian laughed sourly. "What big day? He hasn't got a cherry left to lose - unless it's with a sheep."

Danny pushed past him aggressively. "Are we going to do any work this morning or are we just going to fuck about?"

Rab winked at John over his shoulder. "Tetchy, tetchy."

"Must be love," John answered softly, no smile at all.

Danny stopped and turned and thought he had never realised before just how irritating his brother's face could be.

"Come on you lot, get a move on!" Their father came out, slamming the back door,

shattering the moment.

Another day had started.

They came into the kitchen in dribs and drabs at one o'clock. The tractors were hot and creaking in the noon sun. Already Danny could feel yesterday's sunburn playing up, although he'd kept his T-shirt on for as long as possible.

Rab and Ian were already at the table. His mother was ferrying cold food over from the fridge. "Eat," she said to him. "Before it gets hot."

Danny pulled his shirt off and sat down, well away from the sun slanting in the back door.

Rab leaned back in his chair and smiled his dirty smile. "Well Don Juan?"

Danny gave him a warning look.

His mother looked up at him from the plate of ham she was cutting. "Don Juan?"

"He's taking the piss," Danny said, trying to divert her attention.

"I've told you before about that expression." She slapped ham on his plate. "Why Don Juan? What have you been up to?"

"Nothing." He concentrated on cutting his meat, trying to hide his irritation. He didn't know why he was bothering.

Rab and Ian exchanged malicious glances.

"Leave him alone you two," she said flatly, and went into the living room in search of missing glasses.

Ian immediately sat forward, body bent over the table, elbows spread wide. "Think our Daniel's left his mother any dirty evidence?" He made a small noise like he was sucking his teeth.

Rab sat back again, laughing abruptly, too loudly, just like he'd done that morning in the yard.

Ian's body bent further forward, so far he had to tilt his head in order to look up into Danny's face. "Oh, he's a dark horse our Daniel. Wouldn't know it to look at him, would you?"

He dropped his cheek suddenly onto his hands, like a small child falling asleep, then began tracing a pattern on the table with his fingertip. He whispered so softly that Danny barely heard him, "Bet I can guess who it was about…"

Danny jerked up out his seat. "Why don't you fucking shut up?" His face was scarlet.

"Here, what's the language in aid of?" His father came in, shaking out his shirt. "Well?" he demanded, looking from one to the other.

Danny was standing at the table glaring. Ian sat back with an odd satiated, boneless movement. It was Rab who answered. "He's just getting upset at nothing as usual."

"Tell them to leave off me," Danny demanded.

His father turned to him. "Who the hell are you shouting at? You go and eat outside if you can't control your temper."

"Don't worry, I'm going." And he grabbed his plate and stalked out the door.

"You two want to…"

But Danny didn't hear the rest of his father's sentence.

Outside the sun hit everything squarely black and white. He crossed the yard and dropped down into the shade of the henhouse and ate his second roll, not tasting a mouthful.

He saw John go into the house. He was raging thirsty, almost thirsty enough to

contemplate yelling across to him to bring him out some beer, but he'd be damned if he would. This was all his fucking fault anyway. And he wasn't going back in there either. He'd die of thirst sooner. Fuck them.

He lay back against the warm gritty paintwork of the henhouse wall and closed his eyes.

"Here." John's voice spoke suddenly out of his darkness. He opened his eyes and squinted up against the light. John was standing there, a red-rimmed silhouette above him. Danny hesitated then took the offered can from his outstretched hand.

"Look," he said, sitting down beside him, "I even brought you a glass."

Danny took it and muttered a grudging thanks. What was he, a fucking mind reader? He filled the glass slowly so it wouldn't foam up and put the can deep in the shade. He took a mouthful.

Suddenly John reached over and patted his stomach. "You'll need to watch your belly, drinking all that beer."

Danny flinched away, pushing his hand off. "Don't."

"Don't what?"

"Just don't." He could feel his face burning.

John only raised his eyebrows as if to say, Touchy, then leaned back against the shed again and closed his eyes.

Danny looked at him surreptitiously. His belly was hard and flat, his chest broad and muscular. He had definitely lost weight this summer.

Danny looked down at his own stomach. It was flat enough, but he was never going to have John's washboard muscles, or his lousy tan for that matter. "Are you saying I'm getting fat?" he demanded abruptly. He looked down at himself again. From this angle it did look a bit podgy.

"What?" John sounded dopey. He didn't move.

"Are you saying I'm getting fat?" Danny scowled at him irritably. He sat up further to flatten his stomach out. He even tried pulling it in.

John opened one eye, turning his head to him. "Mm?"

"For Christ's sake. Fat John. Me. Is that what you're saying?"

John opened both eyes, considered him. "You look alright to me." He closed his eyes again and turned his face up to the sun adding, "So far."

Danny felt more irritated than ever. They were silent for a while, Danny taking covert glances at John's body. His jeans were so tight it kept drawing your eyes down to his crotch. That had never been his style before, but now whatever Rab did...

Suddenly he realised John was watching him through deceptively half-closed eyes. He blushed violently, just like he always did.

"Well?" John's lazy drawl.

"Well what?" Danny took another swig of beer and glared over at the house, studiously not looking in his direction.

"Have you seen enough?"

How the hell was he supposed to answer a question like that? *I was only comparing sizes?*

He continued to glare silently at the house, blushing harder than ever. He heard John climb to his feet, brush his hands on his jeans. His body moved level with Danny's eyes, blocking his view, but Danny didn't lift his head.

"Danny..."

He could hear the smug smile in the fat rat's voice. He lifted his eyes slowly to look up at him. John grinned down at him for a moment then blew him a silent little kiss.

Danny turned his head away with a violent jerk. "Fuck off."

John reached out and rumpled his hair. "Only joking Danny-boy. Only joking."

Danny could hear him chuckling all the way across the yard.

They had been baling hay all afternoon, until the tractor had finally overheated.

"No water in the fucking radiator," John said, slamming the hood back down. "Ian, you can be today's hero - go and get some. Take your time. It needs a chance to cool down."

Ian looked up at the hay wagon as if to say, Why not him? then turned abruptly and began walking towards the pick-up.

Danny dropped exhaustedly onto the hay bales and stretched out luxuriously, covering his face with his T-shirt.

After a minute or two he heard the pick-up roar off.

Almost a full minute passed before John called up to him, "Danny?"

He didn't reply. After a second or two he felt the wagon rock, followed by the rustling sound of John crawling across the hay towards him, then the weight of his body settling next to his. "Not talking?"

He said nothing. He could feel John stretching out beside him, feel his skin sticking against his bare shoulder.

Under the shelter of his T-shirt he felt suddenly blindfolded, abruptly afraid. He wished he could take it off to see what John was up to. He lay tense and unhappy. All his nerves felt rubbed raw. An insect tickled over his chest. He jumped and brushed it away. A second or two later he felt it on his stomach. He brushed it off again. A second later it was worming its way under the waistband of his trousers. He threw off the T-shirt and shot upright.

John was lying beside him, lazily playing with a piece of straw. "Something biting?"

"Yeah, a six foot blonde horsefly."

"*Blonde?*" John's laugh was incredulous. "Either I'm improving or you're going blind. And that's six-*three*." John gave him an unsettling look then added, "Of course, maybe you're just mixing me up with Rab."

Danny flushed and threw himself on his stomach. After another minute the tickling started again. "Fuck off John," he said without turning.

The tickling continued with exactly the same irritation as a fly. "I said, fuck off John. Are you deaf?"

"Me? I'm not doing a thing. Just lying here, minding my own business, going slowly blonde."

"Like fuck you are." Danny jerked his elbow in, blocking the straw's path to his armpit. It withdrew.

After a few moments it started again. Danny saw red. He flung himself over and on top of John's body, knocking him flat and pummelling his sides with his fists before John could stop him. It took several seconds and too many hard blows before John came to his senses. But he outweighed Danny by more than two stones and outstripped him by at least four inches. He threw his arms around him in a tight bear hug, effectively pinning his flailing arms down.

They lay breathlessly locked together for a second or two, panting heavily, stupefied by the violence of the skirmish. Danny became aware of the scent of hay and sweat, a faint hint of something else. John's soap? No, it was the stink of Rab's fucking cigarettes. And then he realised. In the dream. That was the strange exotic smell in the dream.

It *couldn't* be.

He was trapped tight in John's arms, pinned down in the hay, the stink of him invading his nostrils. Suddenly he was tired beyond all reason, emotionally exhausted. He felt himself go limp. He didn't care anymore. "Let me go," he said numbly.

"Why? So you can beat fuck out me?" John's voice was ugly with damaged ego

and fright.

"I won't touch you," Danny said dismally. It was the wrong thing to say, inferring as it did that John had nothing to fear from him. It wasn't what he'd meant.

"Too fucking right you won't," John said savagely and rolled him onto his back, pinning him down with his weight. The smell of his sweat, with that faint hint of spice, seemed to rise out of the hay itself. Their skins were stuck together, their hair soaked with sweat. Danny felt panicked. All he could see was John's dark silhouette, outlined in red. He couldn't read his face at all. His eyes watered with staring up at him.

"Let me go, you shit." He tried to push up, but his exhaustion and the soft base of hay gave him no leverage at all. John sensed the rising panic in him and his anger fed on it.

"You look like a girl, know that?"

Danny could feel tears of frustration begin to form in his eyes. "I said, let me go."

John rammed his shoulders down as he tried to lift himself. *Dream on.*

Danny jerked his head away, feeling a drop of sweat run down into his mouth, filthily salt. He licked his lips feverishly, straining his head to one side.

John saw the tongue darting over his dry lips. They looked swollen, cracked. Another drop of sweat dripped from his forehead onto Danny's cheek. Danny scrubbed it furiously against the hay, eyes tight shut all the while. In that one movement, petulant, skittish, he really did look like a girl.

John brought his face close. "Come on then, give us a kiss."

Danny struggled violently, suddenly galvanised with something very like terror. *"Don't."*

But John pressed his mouth down on his.

Danny tasted of salt. His lips, not cracked at all, moist and open with shock under his own.

It was all he had intended to do, humiliate him. But the thing felt surprisingly good. Danny groaned beneath him, still struggling, making things worse for himself. John kissed him again, hungrily, enjoying his struggles and, he realised dimly somewhere in his overheated brain, enjoying the kiss.

"Hello?!" A door slammed. "John?!"

"Christ." John sprung off him as if he had been stung. Ian. Christ, the little shit must have fucking raced it. *Shit.*

"John?!" Querulous now, full of suspicion.

"Here!" John's voice sounded shaky. His face was white.

Danny lay flat on his back, his eyes blank with shock, his face streaked with sweat and dirt.

John crammed his fist into his pocket and yanked out his handkerchief, pushing it at him. "Here, clean yourself up for Christ's sake." He turned away, sitting up and dragging his hands through his hair.

The wagon rocked. John yelled, "Hang on, I'm coming down," and scrambled quickly over to the edge. He swung his body over then paused to check his footing. He looked up, for one second right into Danny's eyes, then whispered furiously, "Move Danny. No-one's fucking raped you," he looked down over his shoulder to judge his distance then back up into Danny's face "...yet."

And then disappeared from view.

That night Danny was afraid to go to bed. He stood hanging onto the chill satin of the curtains. The breeze stirred coolly through his wet hair. He hadn't eaten, just grabbed a sandwich, pleading a headache.

John had ignored him solidly for the rest of that day. At supper his mother had said

he looked ill and God knows by then he felt ill, ill enough for Ian to let him shower before him at any rate. Be thankful for small mercies.

He had watched John go across to the pub an hour ago while he had been waiting on Rab finishing up in the bathroom. He'd paused at the pub door and suddenly turned and looked back up at the house, right up at Danny's bedroom window. Danny had dived back behind the curtain then began cursing himself.

"What the hell am I doing?" he'd hissed, but his heart still pounded with fright, as if he'd been caught doing something he shouldn't.

He lay on his bed now, watching the clock, careful to keep his hair off the pillow. Half eleven.

The back door banged. Danny closed his eyes.

After a minute or two he heard them come up the stairs together, talking and laughing. So he was ordaining to come home tonight? Big of him.

He listened as each went into the bathroom then their doors closed for the night. The silence was absolute.

Christ, he would never sleep tonight. He hadn't even undressed yet. He got up and went to the window again and sat by the chair.

He didn't hear the door open, only the click of the door closing. He turned, only half-curious at the odd noise, not yet realising what it was. When John spoke his stomach plunged as if he had been handling a knife that had slipped.

"Still up?"

John was leaning back against the door, both his hands behind him, holding the door handle. His voice was quiet, to Danny menacing.

Danny stood up. His legs felt like rubber. "No, I'm asleep. This is my astral projection. What do you want John?"

"Only to talk." He pushed himself up off the door and came towards him, hands open, palm outwards, as if to say, Look no tricks. "Only to talk, baby."

Danny could see the moonlight on his face, the deep-set black eyes, the wide curving mouth, the high broad planes of his face, the oddly bleached hair, so much brighter than he ever remembered it going before. He thought his brother had never looked more thuggish or more persuasively charming.

He stopped his advance. He'd hardly moved any distance at all Danny realised. He stood with his hands on the headboard of Danny's old bed, unmistakably leaning on it. Danny realised abruptly he was drunk. John, who was always so careful, so in control, was *drunk?* He felt an immense surge of gratification. His fucking great ugly lump of a brother was drop-dead drunk.

John sat down heavily on the bed then patted it like a large clumsy uncle. "Why don't you come sit beside me?"

"I'm fine where I am."

John looked up at him. He grinned. It looked evil in the dark moonlight. Nothing drunk about his dirty rapacious grin. "Promise I won't *rape* you." The emphasis was unmistakable, the voice mocking.

"I'm fine where I am John. Get on with it."

John got up, almost creakily, leaning on his knees. He came towards him until he was suddenly close, uncomfortably close. Danny backed away until he was pinned against the window. He wished now he had sat on the bed. He felt out-manoeuvred. John's breath was close enough to smell. He smelt of spirits, not beer. He smelt like his father.

"You stink." Danny jerked his face away. He turned back in time to see John's face tighten. He felt perversely pleased with the reaction.

He stepped to one side, intending to move round him, but John's hand shot out indecently fast and grabbed his shirtfront, jerking him up against him. "Don't get

fucking smart with me. It was a joke." He shook Danny slightly for emphasis. "A *joke*."

Danny pulled out of his grip and walked towards the door. "Sure."

Suddenly he was spun round by his hair. He felt as if his scalp was being torn off.

John pushed him down on the bed then caught hold of Danny's shirtfront and lifted him again. "You started it."

Danny felt the sweat of anxiety immediately soak the armpits of his shirt. He felt suddenly soiled, as if he'd never bathed. As if he'd come straight from the hay baler to here. As if John had been with him all along, just a continuation of the same scene, the scene that had somehow started that morning, in his room.

"Lying there pretending you were asleep, your dick twitching, moaning my name."

"You fuck off, you liar." But Danny's voice was a weak whisper.

John let him go suddenly, with a little push, and he fell back. Danny struggled up onto his elbows, staring up at him. "You liar," he said again. It had more force now.

"Keep your voice down. Christ knows, we wouldn't want your mother to hear."

"You're lying, you scumbag, I wouldn't suck your dick for mon..." Danny stopped, realising too late what he'd said. He saw John's white teeth glimmer in a carnivorous smile.

"No? Why don't you prove it?" He leaned forward and pulled Danny up against him, a sharp aggressive tug. The smell of soap was strong on his body. It felt hot and hard, dry as a lizard. No sweat now. "You're awake now. Let's see you prove it."

Danny prised him off, succeeded in half-sliding off the bed, but John caught his legs in a tackle, grunting with effort. Danny lashed out with a stream of low hissed invective. The bed thumped against the wall. Suddenly his parents' room door opened, flooding the floor of his room with light.

"*Shit*," John's voice hissed in the dark.

Danny went limp. John had one arm round his neck, the other locking his arm behind his back. They sat there like that, a tableau, neither daring to move.

Whoever it was went into the bathroom. Slowly, John eased his stranglehold.

Whoever it was came back out and went back into their room. The light went out.

Their bodies came apart like something coming unstuck. Danny was aware of John's weight lifting off the bed. There was a silence, no sense of movement. It went on too long, too unnaturally quiet, as if he stood there in the dark, waiting. Finally the door opened, a barely perceptible click, then John's voice whispered, "Next time baby."

THREE

Twice Danny woke in the night, convinced he heard the door handle rattle. He woke washed in cold sweat, his chest suffocated with holding his breath, and listened.

Only the creaking silence of the house, the distant tick of the old downstairs clock.

He woke finally to his mother banging on the door. "Danny? Come on, you're late again. Shake a leg."

He mumbled a reply and struggled up into a sitting position. He felt like a limp rag. He was sticky with sweat. His face felt stiff and sore.

His mother banged on the door again. "Did you hear me Danny?" The handle rattled irritably.

"I'm up. Just give us a bloody minute, will you?"

There was a pause then he heard her moving off down the hall, ominously silent.

When he got down to breakfast the rest had already gone out.

His mother looked at his face. His white skin took on a bruised look when he was tired or ill. He had it now. "I take it your headache hasn't cleared up?" She cut him some bread.

He shook his head. "Couldn't sleep. Too hot or something." He didn't look up at her. It seemed to hurt his eyeballs just to move them.

She stopped what she was doing and looked directly at him, then she came right out with it. "Why was your door locked?"

Danny immediately flared up, "I'm allowed to lock the bloody door. That's what the fucking key's for."

"I will not stand for that language Danny. I asked you a civil question."

"Well here's my civil answer..." He pushed up out of his chair, facing her furiously. "I am *nineteen* years old. I'll lock my bloody door if I want to."

She turned away sharply to the kitchen sink, her back speaking volumes. Danny glared at her, daring her to say another word, then turned and slammed out of the kitchen.

Danny spent the whole day by himself clearing rubble down by the copse of trees that grew by the river.

Ian came down at half one and wanted to know why he hadn't been up for lunch. "You're in deep shit little brother."

"So I'll swim." Danny hefted another boulder onto the trailer.

"You'll more likely have to eat it."

"Wouldn't be the first time."

Ian raised his eyebrows, smiling faintly, then simply turned and walked away up the hill.

Danny spent the late afternoon building up a bonfire with the cleared wood, tyres, and general flotsam that always seemed to build up down here. He arrived home late for tea. Only his father and mother were still in the kitchen.

"Where were you at lunchtime?" his father demanded without greeting.

"Down the back field, where you sent me." Danny sat down at the plate his grim-faced mother put in front of him.

"If you don't intend to come home for meals you tell your mother in future."

Danny said nothing. He began eating.

"I'm talking to you, boy."

"I heard you."

"Well you bloody well answer me then. And before you disappear upstairs, you're helping John clean out the old hayloft tomorrow so you make sure you've got your arse in gear."

Danny stopped eating. "What? Jerrett's?"

His father scowled at him. "You heard me."

"But I haven't finished the bottom field yet. You said..."

"Well now I'm saying different. You're helping John."

"Ian could do it. Why not Ian?"

"Ian's doing fences with Rab until the weather breaks again."

"I could do the fences."

His father slapped his hand flat on the table, making them both jump. "You do what you're bloody well told." He pushed his chair back and stood up, jabbing a finger at him. "And tomorrow you be up on time. This isn't a bloody holiday camp." He left the room, slamming the door behind him.

His mother looked at him as much as to say, Now look what you've done, and started clearing up the dinner dishes. Maybe she thought he'd engineered this. Went with the door being locked.

He pushed his meal away half-eaten and went up the stairs to wash.

He could not remember, could not pinpoint the precise moment, when he realised he was crying, but somehow he found himself standing there with his face pressed to the wet tiles, water streaming down his back, and the taste of salt in his mouth. He was glad he couldn't see himself.

He turned and leaned back against the wall, hugging himself, shivering even in the hot water, and cried till he was dry, nothing else to cry.

That night he fell into bed, oblivious even to his wet hair, and plunged into a deep and dreamless sleep.

FOUR

The alarm roused him slowly from the depths.

When he finally surfaced he wasn't sure if he had actually heard it. He peered at the clock's face. Six am. It had gone off then. He got up and dressed slowly and heavily. His fingers felt numb.

He went down the stairs, still tucking in his shirt. When he opened the kitchen door he saw John was alone in the kitchen. He lifted his head and stared at Danny with a fixed unreadable expression, then bent his head and went on eating.

His mother came in behind him. "Made it this morning, I see."

Danny took his hand off the door handle and moved into the room. He sat down as far away from John as possible. He said nothing. It seemed there never was anything he could say. Every time someone spoke to him it was only offering him rope to hang himself.

His mother banged his plate down.

He wolfed his food like a starving man. He hadn't known he was hungry till he tasted it. His mother refilled his cup without comment.

John pushed his plate away then took out a battered cigarette, idly watching Danny mop up his plate.

"John, if you actually intend to smoke that filthy thing you can do it outside." His mother jerked her head in the direction of the door. He got up without speaking and sauntered out.

Danny looked up at her. She did not meet his eyes. "I don't know what's wrong with everyone this week. Let's hope it's the weather." And she stuck her head out into the hall. "Ian?! Where are you?!"

There was an indecipherable reply.

"You said that ten minutes ago. I'm not calling you again. You can answer to your father next time."

Danny stood up and went out.

Jerrett's Farm had been acquired, part and parcel with fifty acres of land, before Danny had even been born. There had been a time when they had actually used the old hayloft, but not now. Now they used only the ground floor level, mainly for storing surplus animal feeds and the general junk that there never seemed anywhere else to put.

Danny didn't like the hayloft. In fact, just looking up the ladder gave him the creeps.

John was already inside, wearing thick work gloves and pulling plastic feed sacks across the lower floor. He didn't turn when Danny came into the building. It was deeply shadowed inside. What little light there was shone in from the open doors; one up, one down. The tiny windows were so grimy they barely let in any light at all.

It took his eyes a moment or two to accustom themselves to the change before he could discern the white of John's T-shirt moving in the dark.

"Fucking rats. Place is over-run with them." Another came bolting and squeaking from under a sack as John pulled it free. He turned and pulled something from his pocket. "Here."

Danny caught it on reflex. John had his back to him again. "Gloves. You'll need them."

One by one they pulled the sacks out into the yard. By eleven o'clock they were exhausted, soaked with sweat.

They went outside and sat down in the shade of the tractor, each smoking a cigarette. The sun beat down just beyond them, already fierce in its heat, although the rain had not been off twenty minutes.

They had been sitting talking for almost half an hour when John looked up at the sky and made some quip about the weather. Danny laughed. It felt almost strange, everything suddenly washed over with normality. Maybe his mother was right, maybe it was just the heat.

John stood up, stretching. "Come on. We better check out the loft before we get this lot onto the trailer."

Danny squinted up at him. "There's nothing up there, is there?"

"I don't think there's ever been anything up there, other than some hay out the ark, but we'll check just in case. You know what he's like. Come on." He offered his hand to Danny to pull him up.

Danny pretended he hadn't seen it and scrambled to his feet, hitching up his jeans.

John looked at him shrewdly. His face seemed to metamorphose from that rather perverse handsomeness he owned into something sharp and vindictive. "Don't overestimate yourself. Just because you like boys doesn't mean we're all tarred with the same brush."

"I never.."

But John cut him off, turning away as if the conversation had suddenly bored him. "Oh come on, let's get this over with."

Danny followed him with a heavy heart.

His eyes took longer to adjust this time. He could see John's bare torso going up the ladder ahead of him. He always had to strip his bloody shirt off, just to show him that real men could take a little sun. That long slope of back kept catching his eye, and the front was worse, the mat of hair on his belly tailing off into his waistband. Why not buy new jeans if he'd lost the button? Fact was he liked flaunting it. Another bad habit he'd picked up from Rab, fucking conceited pig.

He followed him up the ladder, trying to concentrate on hating him, and not on the sudden paralysing fear he could feel leadening his legs.

He hoisted himself up through the hatch with weak arms and straightened up. It was brighter up here; bigger door and skylights in the roof. The light streamed down in shafts, dancing with dust from where John had disturbed it opening the hatchway.

"John?" Danny realised he couldn't see him. He felt panic dance through him ridiculously.

"Over here."

Danny spun round, feeling the hairs stiffen all down his spine.

John was standing in a shaft of sunlight at the other side of the hayloft. The light lit his hair from within like a glowing halo. The same bright light washed his features clean, bleached him of detail. The lines of his chest seemed curiously blurred, making him look even broader, more powerful. Danny blinked.

"Over here," he said again as if Danny couldn't see him. Or was it a command?

Danny walked over to him, his skin crawling unpleasantly. It was suffocatingly warm up here. He sneezed, both hands to his face.

John smiled, that lazy sinister smile that always seemed to make his face a malcontent's. "It happened just here." He gestured at the floor with a nod of his head.

Danny stared at him, feeling his stomach slowly roll over.

"Old man Jerrett."

Danny pressed his hands to his stomach.

"This is where he finally lost it and topped himself."

Danny looked down at the floor. There was a dark stain on the floorboards, black in this light. He dragged his eyes back up to John's face. "You're kidding me."

John shook his head. "He had a weakness, liked little boys." And he looked at him in a way that Danny didn't want to understand, that could have meant anything - but definitely didn't.

Danny could hear his own breath grunt out of him as he lunged forward, hitting John straight in the gut.

John folded and went back into the drifts of mouldering hay. Danny flung himself on top, flying into him with both fists. John pushed the heel of his hand up under his chin.

Danny kept punching, kneeing, trying to gouge out his eyes. They grappled fiercely, rolling over each other.

"You little..." John grunted. He managed to twist a hand in Danny's hair and pull.

At first Danny felt nothing, the adrenaline was too strong, then he began to feel a dreadful red-hot pain right down his neck. John was still pushing against his chin, trying to get leverage to push his weight off.

Danny suddenly went with the pull on his hair. He lay on his back where he had fallen, abruptly winded, his eyes filling with pain. Inside he felt nothing.

John sprang over him and slapped his face with a broad, flat-handed slap. Danny felt his head jar with the impact of the blow. John kneeled panting above him, his hair wild, his lip bleeding. "What the fuck is *wrong* with you?"

Danny said nothing.

John sat down heavily on the floor. "I was only telling you for Christ's sake. *Chat*."

Danny didn't believe him. Danny didn't trust him. He said nothing.

John felt his ribs tentatively and winced. "You stupid little cunt. I think you've broken something." He stood up shakily. "You know something? You're sick in the head."

He walked unsteadily to the hatchway and started very carefully to climb down. "I'm going to get those fucking sacks loaded. You've got two minutes."

And he disappeared.

FIVE

"You were winding me up yesterday, weren't you?"

John looked up from rolling a cigarette. There was something awkward about it. Not clumsy, John was never clumsy, he just didn't look right doing it. He never would.

"What?"

"I said, you were winding me up yesterday, weren't you?"

John shaded his eyes with his hands, squinting up at Danny against the light. Danny had the advantage and knew it. He pressed the point. "Weren't you?"

John dropped his hands. They lay in his lap, palm upwards, the half-rolled cigarette held delicately between thumb and forefinger. "About what?"

"You knew I didn't know about Jerrett. That's why you took me up there. You weren't interested in whether there was anything up there, other than that."

John looked sideways down at the floor then he lifted his head, licked the cigarette, and sealed it. He put it in the corner of his mouth and patted his pockets, just like Rab always did.

Danny could feel the anger as if it were changing colour. What had started as a tight blue knot of anxiety in his stomach was flowing out redly through his veins with every moment that John studiously wasted. He felt his skin come alive like a cramped limb flooded with blood. A warm flush, almost like pins and needles, began to cross his skin.

John levered himself up into a standing position and felt in his hip pockets. Still his eyes were veiled. He was thinking, much faster than his hands were moving.

Danny held on like a terrier. "Why John? What was it all for? Just to annoy me?"

That made him smile. Danny could see the tension ease out of him. *He thinks I'm stupid.*

John found his matches and held a light to his face.

"Or were you leading up to a confession?"

The hand flinched, the flame wavered in the gloom for a second, then he lit the cigarette and threw the match in a long arc out into the concrete yard. Finally he spoke. "What d'you want me to say? Something revealing that you can go tell Mummy?"

"No. Why? You got a burden you're aching to share?"

That brought him round. "I've got nothing I need to share."

"No? Then what was it about?"

"I told you. It was just idle conversation. I had forgotten all about the dirty old bastard. Being up there reminded me, that's all."

Danny moved towards him, no clear intention, other than perhaps to force some kind of reaction out of him. Any kind. "Like hell you had."

John looked out the shed door as if the conversation was suddenly boring him, but he didn't make a move to go. His face looked set, his eyes bright and evasive. Now was Danny's moment. He said, "Maybe it's because Jerrett's not the only one who's had problems with little boys."

He got his reaction.

John swung on him, his mouth white with fury. He grabbed Danny's face, his powerful fingers digging into his cheeks. "You just shut the fuck up or I might just break your fucking neck." And he let him go with a push, as if he was an irritating insect.

The red began to flare into Danny's head. He felt as if it would burst out from behind his eyes. He could feel his face burning up with it. "Oh, you'd like that, wouldn't

you? You've always been dead fucking keen for me to shut up. Well not this time. I'll fucking tell her. Then what?"

John turned away with a jerk, putting distance between them. He grabbed one of the tractor's wing mirrors with both hands, as if he didn't trust himself. He spat out his cigarette and ground it underfoot, still hanging there.

Suddenly he lifted his head. The tension in him seemed to have undergone some kind of wonderful transformation, as if an unexpected light had just illumined his darkness. "You go for it Danny-boy. After all *what* exactly are you going to tell her? That will surprise her I mean."

"I'll tell her about you coming into my room, for one. As it is she's just burning up to know how you got that fat lip yesterday. Maybe I'll just tell her."

John suddenly grinned. If a grin could look venomous this one did. "Go ahead, tell her that you attacked me for no reason. She'll go running off to the old man trying to convince him you're not the sick little bastard she really knows you are. Me one, you nil. Just remember, you might have her fooled, but he isn't queuing up for your fan club."

"Don't try shoving it back on me. I'll tell her alright. You see if I don't. You just get off my fucking back John."

They stepped towards each other, a hairsbreadth from each other's throats, when Ian's yell unexpectedly shattered the tension. "John?! You out here?! You're wanted!"

John gave him one last poisonous look then turned on his heel and left.

Danny's mother had told him about Jerrett, surprised and a little uncomfortable with the subject.

"Why do you want to know?"

He didn't see any reason to hide it. "John showed me the spot where he's supposed to have done it."

"John?" She managed to sound surprised and unsurprised at once.

Danny nodded. "We were working up there yesterday."

There was a silence. She turned her back to him, fiddling with something at the counter.

Danny waited a beat then cleared his throat and said, "So it is true?"

"Oh, it's true enough." She became suddenly brisk about her work.

Danny wet his lips and pushed, "So he did? I mean, he was... messing about with kids, I mean?"

"Boys," she said emphatically. Her voice was clipped. "He was even charged with it once. He couldn't have been more than forty. I think everybody liked to think he'd stopped it. Maybe some of them even believed it. He hadn't of course. They never do."

Danny was silent. His mother slammed a cupboard door. "Right, that's enough. Finish that up, I'm waiting for the dish."

And so Danny knew the subject was closed. But he was still sure it was no coincidence. If he had compromised himself by attacking John in the hayloft, then John had at least done as much up on the hay wagon. Now it was quits. He wasn't going to become a butting post for John's frustrations. Let him use Rab if he was so fond. He could just leave him alone.

For good.

22

SIX

August rode on, hot and relentless.

The weeks passed in the same endless pattern. Everybody felt burnt out with the heat. Even Ian was unduly waspish.

It was the end of one of those fortnightly cycles; two weeks of blazing sun followed by two days of muggy rain.

Danny stood in the doorway of the tractor shed enjoying the smell of the rain, the sound of it on the galvanised roof.

John drove into the courtyard and manoeuvred the tractor, reversing it into the shed. The vehicle's windscreen wipers slapped to and fro in the silence after the engine was cut, then they too stopped. John got down from the cab and came over to where he stood.

Danny was leaning against the door jamb, staring out into a yard mystically transformed by the grey hissing veil of water.

Theirs had been an uneasy silence. Neither caring to be in each other's company, they had avoided each other as much as possible.

Danny could smell the faint aniseed that clung to John's damp clothes as he moved to stand beside him. He felt that familiar prickling sensation of awareness and animosity he always felt with him.

John went through his already familiar parody of Rab's pocket patting. "No matches," he said finally.

Danny reached into his pocket and took out a lighter. He flicked it on for him.

John bent his head over it, steadying Danny's hand with his own. It took a massive effort of will not to flinch from those rough, dry fingers.

John took a long drag then pulled his T-shirt from his jeans, waving it to and fro to let air into his body. Danny caught the faint hayish smell of him with his familiar soap. They stood for a moment in the grey scented silence, both soporifically relaxed by the enveloping hiss of the rain.

"I've never heard it so quiet." John's voice was soft. The tractor creaked massively behind them as it cooled.

Danny licked his lips and shifted his shoulder more comfortably against the frame. He looked down at the puddle at his foot then said, "You were bullshitting me that night in my room, weren't you?" He could feel John's instantaneous tension beside him. The air seemed to snap around him.

"When?"

He could still redeem the moment, make up something, but he said, "When you said I was saying your name."

Now it was out. What was it? A fortnight? Three weeks? Every night he was afraid to go to sleep. Every morning he woke with dread. He went over every detail obsessively. The dream, his waking, John's face. And now here he was letting John see how much it had bothered him. A monster in his brain made real.

"Come again?" John was looking at him. Not frowning, but his eyes were alert, so fucking sharp and bright. Oh, he knew. John knew alright. John knew everything.

Danny looked at him, flushing to the roots of his hair. "You know when. The night you came to my room drunk." He gave John the chance to reply, but John was going to sweat it out of him. He was enjoying this, the motherfucking sadist. "You said I was calling out your name while I was asleep."

John threw his cigarette out into the rain half-smoked. "Yes, Danny-boy. That's

your answer."

Danny's heart sank.

"Yes, I remember and yes, I was bullshitting you." Danny stared at him. He could see the corners of John's mouth turn up a tiny flick. His tongue flicked a strand of tobacco off his lip. "You never uttered a single word."

Danny knew he was lying. He was lying to him when he must have known the truth was much worse.

Danny hung onto the cross-spar of his window and bumped his forehead against his hands. Why? Why? *Why?*

He turned away and threw himself on his bed. He hadn't even bothered to wash tonight. He smelt of salt and his skin was sticky. He was so restless he could have smashed everything in the room. He should've been in bed an hour ago. Half of him was dog tired and the other half wide awake, going over and over it, looking for the loophole. Why would he lie to him? Just to torture him? He could have done that just as easily with the truth. There was always something more to John, some refinement of cruelty that Danny could never comprehend.

He sat up and reached for his jeans, pulling them on violently and very nearly ripping the button off. He had to get some air.

He moved out onto the landing stealthily, pulling the door shut behind him with the barest click.

He padded downstairs and into the kitchen. He looked for the dog then realised he would probably be outside on a night as hot as this. He hated the kitchen in the heat. He opened the fridge door. The white ghostly light lit up the whole room eerily. He reached for an unopened carton of orange.

"What's wrong? Can't sleep?"

He dropped the orange carton on the floor, his heart in his mouth.

"There's an open one in the door." John gestured with his glass to where the fridge was yawning wide. "I've got vodka in mine," he dipped his head to indicate the bottle on the table, "but you can keep yours healthy."

Danny bent to pick up the carton. "You might have spoken sooner. You nearly gave me a fucking heart attack."

John smiled and took another drink, his eyes watching Danny over the rim.

Danny poured himself a glass, leaving no room for vodka, and closed the fridge door. He stood a moment, accustoming himself to the dark, then walked to the table. He put the glass down and pulled out a chair. "What about you? Can't you sleep either?" He gestured to John's drink.

"Bad dreams, Daniel. Bad dreams."

Danny thought it best to leave that one alone. John was becoming clearer as his eyes grew used to the dark. He could see his black eyes staring at him unblinkingly.

John stretched his hands behind his head and pushed the chair back onto two legs. Danny could see the thick dark hair under his arms. "Do you have to spread yourself out like that?" he said irritably. "You're as bad as Rab." *Shit.* His bloody stupid tongue. He could see John smiling at him.

"I didn't know I was. It bothers you?" The 'bothers' was cut out from his reply as if it was painted in neon letters, pregnant with significance.

Danny snapped back, "Yeah, it bothers me. It bothers the hell out of me."

"In that case I'll stop it." And he dropped his arms and the chair simultaneously with a clatter.

Danny hissed, "*Shhh*... for Christ's sake. You'll wake the whole fucking household."

John poured more vodka into his glass. He did not bother to top up the orange. He

held the bottle above Danny's drink with a query, but Danny put his hand over the glass.

"Ever the good virgin, my little brother." And he put the bottle down again.

Danny wished he had a cigarette. In fact, he was wishing he'd simply stayed in bed. John was still watching him with that unblinking gaze. "Have you got a cigarette?" he said, as much to break John's gaze as anything else.

John stood up and pushed his hand in his pocket. He had to breathe in to do it.

"Doesn't Rab get sick of you copying him?" Danny asked sourly.

John paused, hand jammed in his pocket, and looked at him.

"Wear them any tighter and they'll castrate you."

"Would you be sorry baby?"

"Oh fuck off."

John pulled his hand out with a short derisive laugh and sat down again.

Danny looked away from the expression in his eyes.

John pushed the roll-up tin across to him.

Danny looked at it. "I can't make those fucking things up. What was wrong with your old cigarettes? Even that menthol crap was better than this shit."

"Give it here." John took the tin back and began to make up a cigarette surprisingly deftly, his big fingers moving surely in the dim light. He licked it long and slow, watching Danny all the while, his eyes blacker and blacker, more unreadable, as the moon moved slowly behind the clouds.

Danny took the offered cigarette and felt the faint touch of moisture on the paper. He pushed it between his lips with a shiver of repulsion. He could taste the liquorice almost immediately. He pulled it out again. "God, how do you smoke these things?"

"Inhale, exhale. Easy."

Danny made a contemptuous noise, but said nothing. He watched John make up another. The grandfather clock chimed. "Half twelve," he said.

John got up to get a light from the gas pilot. Danny could feel him behind his chair like a tangible force. When something brushed against his back he jumped.

"Hey, be calm Danny-boy." John sat back down. "You are safe from mutant invasion here in your own home."

"Christ, you're a fucking cheap sadist, know that?"

"Can't afford to be anything else baby. Have some?" He gestured with the bottle.

"Yeah, sure, why not? Go on." And he pushed his glass over. He wasn't going to have any more references to virgins. Anyway, maybe it would help him sleep.

"Good man." And he sloshed it in.

"Hey, whoa."

"No point in drinking in moderation Daniel, won't have any effect at all. Look at me."

Danny wasn't sure if that was an argument for or against moderation so he said nothing.

They drank in silence for a moment or two, their cigarettes winking in the dark. The moon had completely disappeared behind the clouds, leaving the room in darkness. Only the dull fluorescence of the pilot light and their cigarettes lit it up.

Danny drained his glass and decided on another. He'd lost count of how many John had had. The clock struck again. He jumped as if he'd been dozing. What time was it? Had he been asleep? Christ, he should really go to bed, but he felt too heavy to move.

"Danny?" John's voice sounded different. I think I'm drunk, Danny thought.

"Mm?"

"Ever had a girl?"

Oh fuck. No-win question time. But it wasn't enough to prompt him into a fight. "None of your business," he said shortly.

John chuckled. It sounded sarcastic. "Yeah, right, stupid question."

Danny loured across at him, his expression rendered impotent by the dark. He watched John stub out a barely smoked cigarette, could see the vague movements of him making up a new one. Christ, he wasted them just the same, effort or no.

"Give us a light."

Danny drew on his cigarette then held it out to him. John took it, holding his hand an age while he lit his cigarette. Danny hated the sight of that dark curly head bent over his hand. He looked away, watching the light spreading over the shed roofs as the moon emerged again.

"Know the best part?"

"How could I?" Danny slopped more vodka into his glass, and all but spat it out again when he took a mouthful. He added more orange juice.

"When you're on the point of coming. Your dick's like a ramrod wedged up her cunt and you daren't breathe, then she lifts herself to get it in further, impaling herself on it like she's in pain, aching for more and less at the same time - she doesn't know what she wants - and you just ram it home. You can feel it, I swear, come right out from the top of your head."

There was a silence. Danny moved uncomfortably. No sex please, I have enough trouble keeping it down as it is.

"Danny?" John's voice came out of the dark again.

"What?"

"Ever get desperate..." he paused as if he was searching for the right word, "ever get so desperate you'd fuck a sheep or something?" He laughed and said before Danny could answer, "You know, they make jokes about farmers and sheep, but sometimes I think, when the fuck do we have time to get anything else? When do we have the energy? Grabbing a sheep between one crop and the next is probably a better idea than they realise. I've seen some pretty sexy sheep." He laughed again, that same joyless grunt, and Danny heard the bottle clink, could see the vague movements of his hand.

They were silent again.

"It's the heat I can't stand. That and the fucking monotony. Up and down, every fucking day, six till ten, dawn till dusk, seven days a week, sweating your guts out, and for what? You know, I get so raw with it I ache for somewhere to shove it, just to ease that bloody nagging ache. Every night it's the same, I'm exhausted and still I can't sleep. I feel so hot and restless all the time."

Danny saw his cigarette flare deeply as he dragged on it, smelt the smoke come out rich and sweet as he exhaled. He could visualise the two thick dragon-like streams, so typical of Rab. He'd always thought it showing-off.

"I swear I'd fuck anything that moved if only that dull, hot, fucking ache would leave me alone."

The clock chimed suddenly. The fridge whirred into life. They could hear the dog scratching outside the door.

"You ever feel like that?"

Danny hesitated then gave a soft affirmative grunt. John's laugh was complicitous, like there were no secrets between them. "Yeah, like all the time."

Danny did not reply. He saw John sit forwards, leaning across the table. "What was the dream?" His voice was almost a whisper.

Danny stubbed out his cigarette violently. "You fuck off John."

John's hand shot out and grabbed him by the wrist, holding him down. "No, come on, I'm serious. It's the night for confessions, can't you feel it?"

"Let go my hand."

"No problem." John let him go.

Danny sat back down slowly then said, "I'm in the old hayloft..." He stopped, dragged on his cigarette, already feeling the suffocating anxiety of the dream, then said, "There's this weight pressing down on me. I can't see, but I know where I am. I just can't move. At first I don't know why then I realise someone's on top of me. I feel him move, that's how I know. He's heavy, really heavy." He stopped.

John urged him, "Go on."

"At first I don't realise what he's doing." Danny heard the embarrassment in his own voice and got it over with. "But he's hard, y'know?" He stopped again, searching for his drink, finding it empty.

John's voice sounded rough in the dark, uneven. "Then what?"

"Then I get turned on too. You know the way you do in dreams? Just instant, no build-up?"

John made a small noise that indicated he did know.

"Well, like that, and he's calling my name all the time like he's trying to get through to me or something, and I can't hear him. I recognise his voice, but I can't see who it is. Then I can feel his breath on my cheek, burning, really close, and he starts rubbing up hard against me. Then I come."

He delivered it flatly, trying to deaden the embarrassment of telling it.

"What does he do to you?"

Danny was thrown. "What do you mean? I just told you."

John's voice was soft, furry with drink or sleep. "No. What does he do to make you come?"

"Nothing."

"Oh come on. In real life, in dreams, there's always something that pushes you over the edge. What is it?"

"I told you, it just happens."

"Come on." His voice lowered. "What is it?"

"Alright," Danny snapped. "He sticks his tongue in my mouth, like he's trying to fucking rape me with it, and I go off firing on all cylinders - that satisfy you?"

"His *tongue*..."

His dirty whispering voice. Danny felt engulfed in waves of revulsion. *I hate that dirty, insinuating voice. I hate every fucking thing about him.* He pushed up from the table. "I'm going to bed."

"No, wait..."

Something not right about that voice, and I've had too much to drink. But Danny got up. John was round the table and in front of the kitchen door before Danny had even thought of it. Dimly he was surprised at his agility. Still fast as a cat even after all that drink. He was suddenly tired, burnt out of all emotion. "Don't fuck me about John," he said wearily, without animosity.

"Danny."

Just that and no more. It could have meant anything. Danny squinted at his face, trying to read it in the dark. He couldn't see anything at all.

"Let me out."

"No way." Definite, without malice or arrogance, just absolute. Danny could hear his smile rather than see it. What the hell was going on?

"What?"

"I said, no way."

"Get out of the way John." Danny felt no fear, not even anger, only an irritation that everything seemed to be sliding through his fingers. He didn't understand any of this. John said nothing. His smile had faded like a brief flowering.

"You're drunk John. Now let me past, I want to get to bed." He pushed in behind him, trying to get at the door handle, but John's body blocked him.

Suddenly John was up close against him, Danny's face in his hand. "Then get to bed... with me."

Danny's stomach dropped right into his bowels in one instant liquid movement. "Oh no, don't start."

John said nothing.

"No more of your fucking jokes. You're really getting on my tits with this. Grow up."

"Who's joking?" The grip on his face tightened.

Danny felt himself go hot and cold like he'd heard it told. "Are you completely off your head?"

"You said it yourself once, take it where you can get it. Well you can get it here, what's the problem?"

"In your bed, I suppose?" Danny hung onto anything that made it ordinary, avoiding the realities, obsessing the detail.

"Here in the fucking kitchen if you like."

Danny jerked his head free. "No." He shook his head. "Definitely, categorically no. You're going to regret this in the morning."

"Not as much as you will if I let you go out that door."

"What the hell's that supposed to mean?"

"We all know what your bad dreams are, want to know mine?"

"No, I fucking don't." He began to cajole, fighting the first twitchings of panic. "Come on John, let me out." He had to get out. On the heels of that thought came the realisation that there was more than one way to do it.

He slid out from under John's body like an eel from under a rock and ran for the back door, unlocking it and almost falling over the dog before John realised what he'd done.

He ran across the yard, making for the tractor shed. The milking shed would be better, it had a back door, but it was often locked and tonight would be the night. He didn't risk it.

He dived into the darkness and ran behind the cover of the tractors. He stood there watching the doorway, breath rasping, trying to conceal it. Maybe John wouldn't follow.

But he did.

He saw John's body silhouetted in the doorway. He pressed himself back against the wall, trying to blend further into the darkness.

"Danny?" John's voice was low and carrying in the night's stillness. It sounded almost uncertain. Danny pressed himself further back. The shed was hot and airless from the day's sun pounding on its tin roof. The tractors were pungent with hot diesel.

John stepped into the dark. Danny darted behind the wheel of the nearest tractor. It was almost as tall as his head.

"Danny, you here?"

Danny held his breath. He could feel the oily dirt beneath his fingers. He pressed his face to the tractor's side, trying to become smaller.

"Come on Danny." John sounded as if he were smiling. "Forget it. It was a bad joke anyway."

Danny didn't move. He couldn't trust him, didn't dare. He heard John's foot hit something, oil can maybe, prowling.

When he spoke next Danny jumped, his skin breaking out into a cold sweat. He was closer, much closer, and moving this way. "Come on baby. I'm sorry."

Danny panicked and darted forward. He heard John's grunt behind him and turned, desperately trying to place him, and ran full tilt into the wing mirror. It knocked him back, clutching his head, hissing, "*Shit*."

John grabbed him round the neck, hauling him back towards the tractor. Danny gurgled like a baby, scrabbling at John's hands. He couldn't breathe. He was thrown

hard against the back wheel. The wind came out of him in a grunt. "Don't ever try that again." John's breath was sour from too many cigarettes.

Danny tried to squeeze out a reply, but nothing would come.

John grabbed his chin, jerking it up, banging his head against the wheel. "Don't you ever run away from me again."

"John..." he croaked. But John was up against him and suddenly he could feel his hands on his bare chest, his thumbs, rough and calloused, deliberately insistent, brushing purposefully over his nipples.

His head came forward, equally deliberately, but Danny yanked his face away and the kiss landed on his cheek. But the contact was enough. John pressed against him, forcing him back against the hub of the wheel. Danny lost his footing, tried to regain it. John's mouth hovered over his ear. He was whispering his name, as if he was trying to somehow make the whole thing more real. He took Danny's hand and pressed it against the front of his jeans. "Feel that?"

Danny pulled his hand back as if it had been burnt. "John, don't, for fuck's sake."

But he might never have spoken. John's hands slid down Danny's body and began working at his belt.

Danny grunted, "Don't." But John undid his trousers, dragging them down to his thighs. Danny had no underpants on. He felt John's hand grip him tight then unmistakably begin to masturbate him.

Danny tried pleading, begging. He didn't even know what he was saying. He wasn't listening. "John don't, don't do this, John... please." Incoherent, useless.

John whispered against his face, "What's this I feel?" He was pressing himself hard against Danny's side, tugging Danny's cock as if it was made of rubber. "Christ, you have got an itch, haven't you?"

Danny tried not to listen, but John's mouth was against his ear, the words burning right inside his head. And he was right. Danny had an itch alright, an itch he couldn't scratch, was desperate to scratch. God he'd never wanted to satisfy an itch so bad in all his life. John's hand was pulling, teasing, drawing him out.

Danny didn't answer. Instead every muscle in his body suddenly went limp. He let his head roll back against the wheel. He closed his eyes. He didn't need to answer. He was no longer resisting. Danny had said yes. He wanted it.

The relief of it was immense.

"Oh boy..." There was elation in John's voice now. His weight eased off him, knowing that he was captive, pathetic, enslaved to his own need.

Danny spread his arms out wide against the wheel, pressing himself up towards him, thrusting towards the relief of John's hand. John moved off him just long enough to pull his own belt out of the buckle and drag his clothes down, then the feel of his erection pressed hard against Danny's thigh, hot and sticky, long and hard, already humping against him, spreading his legs for better leverage. He groaned, "Christ..." then he began to keep time, his body moving to the rhythm of his hand. Masturbation in synchronisation. "Christ..."

Danny trembled, hovered there, already, already. "Don't. I'm going to... *John*."

John's hand gripped his shoulder, slid round his neck. Danny lifted his hands bonelessly to fend him off. John pulled him to him, humping harder, fiercer, hurting him and kissed him full on the mouth, pushing his tongue in deep.

Danny grunted, hands grabbing at John's blindly, sucking on his tongue like a starving infant and felt it all come up. It was like vomiting. He could no more have stopped it once it started than become God.

He came, John's semen spurting hot over his leg, lubricating his thrusts, his own boiling over John's fingers.

That was all it took. It was over in seconds. Like a bomb going off. And after that

there was only their ragged breathing and the slow drip of semen on the shed floor.

SEVEN

There is always a day after. There always has to be.

Conveniently, Danny could not remember getting to bed. Inconveniently, he could remember everything else. Everything around him seemed to trigger images: the dog scratching, a glass of orange juice, the smell of Rab's cigarettes. Worst of all was the shed. As soon as he went in the smell of hot diesel brought everything up in glowing Technicolor. He was spared only one thing; his father had gone out early in the morning, taking John with him, and they would not be back for lunch. That meant he would not have to face him till tea-time.

By four o'clock he had burnt himself out, working twice as hard, trying to distance himself from his own thoughts and the knowledge that he would have to face John shortly. By five he was chain-smoking cigarettes and feeling emotionally and physically exhausted.

At six o'clock they went home, Danny delaying until the last. But his mother was alone in the kitchen, no John, and he wasn't going to ask. "Where's John?" he heard himself say with a kind of horrified disbelief.

"I told you, out with your dad somewhere. They won't be back till late."

She'd omitted that part earlier. If it was possible to be elated and miserable at once he was it.

After dinner he went up to bed and lay on the covers. His mind turned everything over endlessly. He felt hot and restless.

He threw himself on his stomach, punching the pillow up with his fist.

This was worse, pressed against the bed. He threw himself on his back again. He tried to go limp. *Relax Danny*.

He slid nervelessly back into his thoughts. His brain, suddenly unfettered, ran everything through like a film, but this time he didn't fight it. John kissing him on the hay wagon, John's thumbs rubbing his nipples, John unzipping, pushing himself on his leg.

The touch of his own fingers electrified him. He looked down at himself and felt the tight coil of excitement in his belly. He suddenly felt huge with his own potency, dying to show it off, full of strutting macho.

The idea came to him to do it at the window. A thrill of excitement at the possibility of being caught made his cock charge up harder. He could see the head of it, peeled back, massively distended. He got up and went to the window "Look," he urged under his breath.

He pressed the shaft down into his body, making it longer, harder. "There's a big one for you girls. How would you like a bit of that?" And he frigged it hard, grunting, watching himself.

He came immediately, his knees buckling as his penis jerked under his hand. He arched his body out, trying to shoot it as far as possible. He saw it splat against the window like thick white phlegm. He moaned in ecstasy at his own marvellousness as he pulled his orgasm out harder, making it last, milking himself dry.

When it was finished he dropped down onto the seat by the window, his legs like jelly, breathless. The come slid down the glass. "What the fuck...?" he said, incredulous at his own madness.

He wiped himself with shaking hands and zipped up then did the best he could with the window. It was on the fucking curtains. Christ that was going to be a neat one to explain. What if someone had seen him? Anyone could have looked up and seen him.

What had possessed him?

As soon as he had his breath back he went along to the bathroom and got a wet facecloth and wiped the window. He tried ineffectually to dab it off the curtains. "Oh boy..." he whispered.

He went back to the bathroom to rinse the cloth out and heard the bang of the back door. He heard his father's voice. His stomach dropped.

He ran back to the bedroom and closed the door, locking it, heart pounding.

He lay listening for a lifetime. The time dragged by like two nights, three. He heard Ian come up the stairs, Rab, his mother and father and then, finally, John. Did he pause at his door? No. He passed by and went on to his room.

Danny lay on his bed, heart thumping.

When half an hour had passed and the house had begun to tick with its midnight cooling he knew John wasn't going to come.

He got up and stripped off his clothes. He climbed under the single sheet and watched images of himself in the shed. When his cock came up he ignored it. "Let it burst," he whispered. And he fell into a tearful and hallucinatory sleep.

EIGHT

Danny woke the next morning with a kind of heavy dread, nameless, indefinable. Ian knocked him up. "Come on beautiful, rise and shine."

Danny mumbled something incoherent and swung out of bed. His usual morning erection repulsed him, sticking out of his groin like some obscenity. He felt like a dirty old man.

He pulled his shorts and jeans on quickly to hide it and caught himself on the zip. "Fucking hell," he hissed.

It made his day.

The kitchen was full, everybody there at once. John was at the end of the table wearing jeans and a white singlet. His hair might almost have passed for dark blonde. Danny caught his steady expressionless eyes once then looked away quickly, colouring up.

Everybody grunted at each other, a ritual that passed for good morning. He ate his breakfast, keeping his head down. His father handed out his instructions. "You finish up that bottom field," he said to Danny. "John, you help him out. I want that dead tree down. Take the chain-saw and see and make a good job of it."

John nodded and looked at Danny. Danny pushed up out of his seat and went out to the shed.

He drove the tractor out into the yard and was coupling up the trailer when John came out and climbed into his own vehicle.

He was already revving up the saw when Danny got down there.

They could say nothing over the sound of the saw. Danny was secretly relieved, but it didn't make him any less aware of him. He found himself staring when John pulled off his singlet. The dark hair under his arms was slick with sweat.

John wiped the singlet over his chest and under his arms. "Fucking hot Daniel, old son." He squinted up at the sky. "Take five minutes out, shall we?" He looked at Danny for the first time. "Underneath the spreading chestnut tree, where I fucked you and you fucked me." Something very like a smile quirked at the corner of his mouth.

Danny turned away angrily and moved off towards the tree. Carefully he lowered his back against the bark. His sunburn just kept peeling and burning, peeling and burning. It never seemed to stop hurting.

John sat down beside him, mopping his face with his shirt. He lifted his hair up to let the air under. Out of the corner of his eye Danny was aware of those dark spikes of hair in his armpit again and the heavy sweet smell of fresh sweat from him.

John leant his head back against the tree and closed his eyes. Thick dark lashes like Danny's own, remarkably similar in colour.

"Penny for them, Danny-boy." John's eyes had opened and were watching him slant-wise.

Danny blushed immediately and then hated himself for his transparency.

"Oho, dirty thoughts?"

Danny turned his head away. John sat up a little and began rolling a cigarette. "Want one?"

Danny barely shook his head.

John lit his cigarette and inhaled deeply. He turned to Danny and leaned over him, smiling. "Here, share mine," and he covered Danny's mouth with his own.

Danny, taken completely by surprise, did nothing except grunt with shock, allowing the smoke to invade his mouth. He tasted the strong aniseed of the rich sweet tobacco, and then John himself, that wide curving Cheshire cat mouth hot and searching, pushing his tongue into his mouth,.

Danny broke away, coughing and pink. "You dirty bastard."

John laughed. "Do you good. Stop you growing too big."

He leaned back against the tree again as if nothing had happened. Danny glared at him. John closed his eyes. "No good glaring Daniel. I refuse to kiss you again."

Danny was flustered, outraged. He scrambled to his feet. "You fucking..."

But words failed him.

The rest of the afternoon passed in a frigid silence on Danny's part and an incredibly irritating amused one on John's. How could he be so relaxed? Did nothing ever worry him? It was all one big fucking joke to him.

Danny sat on the back of the trailer watching him dismantle the chain saw. All that talk about desperation. He'd been drunk and horny and seen a way of getting his rocks off. The fucking hypocritical...

Danny watched him with mounting fury. John finished up and picked up his T-shirt, clambering over the cut logs to the trailer. "That's us, lad." Then he looked up at him. "God, look at its face, what's wrong with you?"

Danny jumped down from the trailer and turned his back on him. "Why don't you fuck off?"

"Just going to," John said, climbing into the cab, and did precisely that.

Danny got into the house last. He was at the end of the queue for the shower again.

He slammed around the kitchen, collecting cold meat and some salad that had been left for him. He ate his meal rigidly, as if he could barely open his teeth to let it in.

Rab came in and spoke to him, but was chased by his grim expression. Ian took one look at him and didn't even bother.

Finally John appeared, wrapped only in a towel as usual, and had the gall to smile at him. "Your turn Daniel."

Danny glared at him.

Suddenly John whipped his towel open like a stage magician. He laughed, the funny that isn't funny, then pulled it shut again saying, "Now you can toss off in the shower." But he couldn't seem to hold his gaze. He turned abruptly and went out.

Danny looked down at his hand. He'd crushed the piece of bread he was holding. He threw it on his plate and went up to the shower.

Danny tried to watch television, but couldn't concentrate. He went over for a quick drink before closing time only to find John secreted in the back with a couple of girls.

He left the drink half-finished and went home.

He felt as if he could hardly get his feet up the stairs. He unbuttoned his shirt and dropped it on the chair. He peered through the gap in the curtains. No sign of him. Probably poking one of the stupid cows out the back of the pub. He dragged the curtains shut.

He pulled his clothes off and climbed under the sheet. For the first time in his life he wished he could cry.

The back door slammed. Danny held his breath. But it was only Rab. He recognised the whistling as he came upstairs.

He must have dozed, although he could not comprehend how he managed it. He was startled to hear the toilet flush and the bathroom door bang. His mother? No, whoever it was came down the hall and went into John's room, banging the door again. Pissed by the sound of it.

Danny peered at his clock. 12:34. Where the hell had he been till this hour? Christ, he *had*. The dirty bastard had been fucking some bitch behind the pub. Where was 'desperation' now?

Danny punched the pillow and buried his face in it. Finally he was crying, tears of humiliation and rage.

Carried away with his own melodrama, he cried till he hiccuped and then hiccuped till he was sore. "Shit," he hicced again and swung upright, scrubbing at his itchy face. Christ, what a dickhead. He needed a drink.

He crossed the floor, opening the door carefully, and was pushed violently back into the room. He didn't even grunt. He staggered back and sat down plump in the chair by the window.

John closed the door quietly. His white shirt was unfastened to his waist, but still tucked in. He was barefoot. He looked as if he had been disturbed undressing. "Hello, baby."

Danny stood up, then sat down again, realising he was stark naked.

"Ready for me, I see." John began to pull his shirt out from his trousers.

Danny stared at him in disbelief. He had to be joking.

John began to unbuckle the heavy belt on his jeans.

"You've got to be kidding," Danny finally blurted out. "You go off fucking some bitch behind the pub and then come up here..."

"Quiet Danny. Mum's next door, sleeping but lightly."

Danny glared at him and went on in a low voice, "You come up here expecting... expecting..." But he couldn't say it, couldn't put it into words.

John raised his eyebrows. "Go on, expecting what?"

Danny clamped his lips shut, would say nothing more. John finished unbuckling his trousers, undid the button, and then stopped. "Expecting to fuck you too? Oh baby, have some faith. I can manage two in one evening. No sweat."

Danny was immediately furious. "Don't you dare..."

John laughed suddenly, richly, as if he were genuinely amused. "Just like his mother, listen to him." He mimicked, "Don't you *dare*." He laughed again. "I'd like to see you stop me."

Danny hurled himself at him, head down, knocking him flat onto the bed, pummelling him with his fists. The bed thumped against the wall.

John grunted with surprise. Every fucking time this little bastard caught him on the hop. He got a hand free and punched Danny in the kidneys with low, short, hard jabs.

Danny flinched away, trying to avoid the blows, and at that moment John pushed him. He fell onto the floor, flat on his back, the impact knocking all the wind out of him.

John scrambled off the bed and knelt on his chest, pulling his head back by the hair, and hissed, "That's it, wake the whole fucking house then we can be rolling around the floor naked, at one in the morning, with plenty of explanations, and every one a winner." He pressed down sharply with his knee. Danny winced, gasping for air, then lay quiet, exhausted of everything.

John got up and sat on the edge of the bed. He started searching his pockets for a cigarette. Danny lay on the floor, unmoving.

"Get up." John nudged him with his foot.

Danny remained immobile.

"I said, get *up*." He reached down and yanked Danny up by the hair, dragging him up onto the bed.

Danny wouldn't cry, not again, not in front of him.

"Here." John thrust the cigarette into his mouth. Danny took it between numb lips. "Inhale," John said. "You know, suck."

Danny lifted a shaking hand and inhaled the cigarette, passing it back to him.

"Good boy." John fell back abruptly on the bed. "Now I want you to see something."

Danny turned his face away.

"You're going to look, whether you like it or not. Now turn around."

Danny half turned, glancing over at him. He jerked his face away again.

John yanked him round by the arm. He was lying there, jeans undone, crammed down tight under his balls, squeezing them up fatly, his cock red and angry, sticking up his belly.

He grabbed Danny's hand, wrapping his fingers round the sticky head, pushing himself up into it, squeezing the fingers tight round himself, thrusting into it. "Feel how stiff that is? Know how it gets that stiff?"

He gave Danny's arm a yank, pulling him down onto his lap as he fell back. He grabbed Danny's hair and shoved his face into his groin, levering his hips up into his face. "Think this is what I want?" And he laughed unpleasantly, grinding Danny's face against his erection. "*You* want this."

And he pressed his fingers into Danny's jaw, and forced his mouth wide open.

NINE

It was September.

Where had August gone? Flamed and incandescent, as ephemeral as a match.

They had started refencing the fields to be in good time for the winter. They had all gone out in a group; Ian, Rab, John and him. They had been working down the back pasture for the entire morning, even eating their lunch down there. It was the first time he had worked with John in a fortnight.

Come two pm they had run out of fence wire. Danny had been sitting watching John work with something close to hate. It felt odd and flat inside, as if something within him had died. He felt at that moment as if he had hated him all his life.

Occasionally John would wink at Rab as if they shared some great joke. Maybe they did. Maybe he was saying, 'Guess what I got Danny to do last time I was pissed?'

And he'd flex that thick right arm of his, John's powerful wanking arm - bring you off in four seconds that arm, he'd timed him - and they'd laugh some more and wink some more, just like they were doing now.

"Well, we're out of it then, aren't we?" John ran a hand through his hair, exasperated. Ian waited patiently for instructions.

John turned to Rab "You're no fucking use with that hand. You stay here with boy-beautiful." He didn't even look at Danny when he said it. "Ian, you can come with me." He looked at Rab again. "Give you a good excuse to fart about Hardman."

Rab laughed, giving him the finger. Oh, they loved each other these two.

Ian and John drove off. Rab turned and smiled at him. It looked almost sheepish. He was picking at the bandage on his left hand. He'd cut it yesterday on the wire cutters. "Might as well sit down."

They sat down on the empty bobbins and lit up cigarettes.

"Hot?" Danny asked him unexpectedly. Rab looked at him, but he was looking out over the fields disinterestedly. He uh-huhed cautiously, aware of something tenuous hiding in the question.

"Me too." And Danny gave him an odd look, odd enough to make Rab colour up. He'd been doing this for the past two weeks, a million dirty little hints just like this one. He'd tried to read nothing into it, but the tone of Danny's voice said different. Rab realised he was holding his breath. His heart was thumping uncomfortably in his chest.

Danny threw his cigarette down and trod it into the grass as if he'd come to a decision, then he looked away again as if his mind had detached itself once more, off at yet another tangent. "Want to do it then?" he said abruptly, standing up.

"What?" Rab blinked up at him, shading his eyes against the sun.

Danny shrugged one shoulder as if to say, I don't know then said, "Whatever you want."

Rab still wasn't grasping. "I don't get you..."

"Sex. Whatever you want. And don't say you don't know what I'm talking about, I've seen you watching me." Danny looked at him steadily. It was almost challenging.

Rab wet his lips then managed to croak, "Here?" then realised what he was saying. "Are you nuts?" he added, infusing more annoyance into his tone, then he spoiled it again by saying, "They'll be back in a minute."

Danny smiled for the first time. It was soft, secretive. It was a beautiful smile, seductive. It made you understand just why he was considered one of the best looking boys in the village - if you'd been dense enough to miss it in the first place.

"I may not last a minute, so who's sweating?" The smile slid away. His eyes seemed to grow darker, like John's did when he was angry. "Come on Rab, don't make me beg." He cocked his head and said very softly, "You never know how long you'll have to wait till next time."

Rab looked away, his face flaming. "Christ. I thought I was imagining this. I never really believed... not you. Anyway, I wasn't looking at you. Why should I have been looking at you?"

"Last chance Rab."

Rab looked up at him.

Danny smiled.

Rab stood up quickly, not looking him in the eye. "If you tell anyone..." He was mortified by Danny's cold-bloodedness, his own willingness.

"Up on the lorry," Danny commanded

Rab climbed up and sat on the edge.

Danny smiled up at him, shaking his head. "Over there." Danny hoisted himself up and stood beside him, reaching out his hand. "Up against the cab."

Rab took it and let himself be pulled up. "What? Standing up?" He looked around him. "But we can be seen up here. It's like being on a fucking stage."

Danny came up against him, edging him backwards with his body until he was up against the back of the cab. "That's the whole idea." He watched Rab's face intently. "It's supposed to be a turn-on, exhibitionism, you know?" And his smile had something malevolent about it. His hand was at Rab's belt, undoing his clothes.

Rab caught at his hands. "But what if they come back?"

Danny tugged his hands away. "Well, you'll have to be fast, won't you baby?"

Rab could feel his hand slide inside his jeans then he was squeezing, groping. "What, not stiff?" He sounded as if he was amused, not irritated.

"What d'you fucking expect, stuck up here?" Rab looked round him nervously.

"Maybe you don't want it then?"

Rab felt suddenly angry. "Yeah, maybe I don't." And he tried to re-fasten his trousers, but Danny yanked them down with a sudden jerk, pulling his T-shirt up into a bunch under his chin.

He stood exposed to all the world, naked from neck to thigh, his cock flaccidly white in the bright light. "What the fuck...?" He tried to cover himself with his hands, but Danny pushed his body in the way.

"Very nice." It was breathy, excited. "I don't think I've ever seen you naked before."

Rab followed the direction of his eyes. He looked back up into his face, flushed and almost vindictive, and felt the sudden volte-face of lust. Abruptly his cock fattened, lengthened. He felt his face grow hot with shame.

Danny stood back, still holding his bunched-up shirt. "I see you've changed your mind."

Rab's cock stood out straight from his body. He said nothing.

"Oh well, maybe not." And Danny let his shirt go and turned from him.

Rab called, "Danny, wait..." before he could think.

Danny turned slowly. Rab slowly lifted his T-shirt in offering, but Danny stood where he was, hands in his pockets. Suddenly Rab wanted this more than he had ever wanted anything in his life.

"Ask nicely," Danny said.

"Please."

"Please what? "

Rab groaned and closed his eyes. "For pity's sake Danny, just do it, will you?"

Danny stepped forward and touched his cock lightly. His hand felt incredibly cool. "You only had to ask baby." And then, incredibly, Danny kissed him, slowly,

poisonously, like a drug.

Rab felt himself liquefy underneath the feel of his mouth. His lips travelled down Rab's neck, onto his chest. Danny got down on his knees.

Rab felt himself tauten with excitement. For two weeks Danny had been dangling the possibility of this before him; waiting until they were alone, then shamelessly flirting with him until Rab couldn't believe he was actually seeing it. Not Danny. Never in a million years. For years he'd secretly nurtured this fantasy. Only now could he confess it to himself. He still couldn't believe it. Yet here he was, kneeling before him, his white skin pale and cool against Rab's brown belly.

Danny spread his hands against the cab at either side of Rab's body and kissed the head of his cock. Rab closed his eyes, unable to bear the sight of him nuzzling him.

Danny sucked the head in slowly, using only his mouth, keeping his hands firmly pressed to the cab. Rab thought he would die. He made no noise, his eyes opening with the unbearable tension of it. In the dark he was alone with him, and he couldn't stand that. But it was no good. He couldn't see the fields, feel anything, register anything but that intensive suckling. He wanted to come, now, but it was too soft, too pulling. He needed friction.

Harder, harder, for Christ's sake.

But Danny just kept gently mouthing his glans, teasing it right out to the tip, letting it come out of his mouth, then softly sucking it right in again.

Rab thrust into his mouth, trying to move it faster, but Danny simply pulled his head away, letting him fall out every time he attempted it. So he stood still. It was torture to stand still, just as Danny intended it to be, but he stood like a statue, his knuckles whitely gripping his T-shirt, the metal brace bar digging into his back. He watched Danny's mouth, full and lascivious, wrapped around his cockhead, his eyes half-closed, and knew he was going to die. He wasn't going to come, he was going to die. He could see faint lights popping at the corners of his vision.

"Please Danny..." He tried to thrust again. Danny let him go then used his teeth to gently pull him back into his mouth.

"*Harder*..." he whispered.

He could feel a dull ache right round from his anus to his shaft. He felt as if his bowels were being sucked right out of his cock. Then he saw the van, the little green jolly-van, flashing through the hedgerows before it came to the gate. How long till it came to the gate? His heart stopped beating.

"Oh no, shit, Jesus..." He jerked forwards. Danny's hands pushed him back violently, teeth closing on his cock like a vice, only there was no pain at all. Instead Rab felt it go through him like a match in a bale of hay. He grabbed Danny's head to him as the van nosed through the gate.

This time Danny let him thrust his cock deep in his mouth, urging his head forwards as if his throat had opened right up and he intended to swallow him right down it.

Rab watched the pick-up bump over the cattle grid as he impaled Danny's head on his body. "Oh no, oh God, oh no..." and he came just as John looked up and saw them standing there.

"How often?" John demanded.

"What's it to you?"

John grabbed his shirt front and lifted him bodily off the bed. "You watch your lip, you little fuck, or I might just march into her room right now and drop you right in it. If you think I'm going to spend all my fucking life fishing a squalid little faggot like you out the shit..."

Danny ripped his hand off fiercely, dropping back onto the bed with a jolt. "*I'm* a faggot? It's not me who's re-enacting some fucking gay-boy fantasy out a wank mag." Danny scrabbled back, hissing at him, "Still hide them under the bed John? Still..."

But he didn't get to finish it. John was on the bed and had backhanded him savagely before Danny could move. John's hand was round his neck gripping, choking him. Danny scratched at it feebly.

"Touch him again and I'll fucking kill you."

Danny managed to whimper something, a noise.

Slowly, so slowly, John's hand loosened.

Danny fell back against the wall, trapped under John's crouched body, their faces inches apart, and everything in the room suddenly seemed to go slow, become languorous; the soft whirr of the clock, their breathing, life itself.

John backed off, got up. He looked odd, unsettled. When he spoke next he wouldn't meet his eyes. "I'll be watching you."

Danny just stared up at him, trying to understand, watching John leave.

The door shut. Danny let himself slide down the wall onto his back. He stared up at the ceiling, letting his arms drop above his head. He whispered suddenly, "Every step you take, every move you make..." He paused for a long moment, then said, "Yeah, but who knows what you're going to see John?"

TEN

John did watch him. As Danny's elder and better he maintained an absolute authority over him outside his father's jurisdiction, and he used it to make sure he never worked alone with Rab. If anyone noticed they put it down to diplomacy. After all, Rab and Danny had never got on. It was typical of John to act as a buffer between them, nothing unusual in that.

September had settled into rain, weeks of it at a stretch, as if it was trying to make up for the long hot summer. But it was a warm sweaty rain, making everything wet and uncomfortable and changing the landscape into a perpetual grey. It was as bleak and unrelieved as Danny felt.

On the twentieth his father woke with toothache. He was irritable and pig-headed because he would have to go to the dentist and they would be short-handed. He appointed Danny to mucking out with Rab and it was more than John could do to cross him in this mood. Nevertheless he stood behind his father in the kitchen while he was giving out his orders and stared at Danny over his shoulder. His face was a lecture, full of implied threats.

Danny ignored them all.

Rab closed the byre doors and turned to him. It was intensely dark inside, just as it always was on wet days, and it smelled pungently of cattle. They did not put on the lights.

"He did see." Rab looked at the remains of the bruise on his cheek.

Danny nodded.

"Warned off?" he asked, then laughed softly, a small huff of sound. "Who am I kidding? Of course you were." He barked a laugh, joyless, heavy with cynicism, then began patting his pockets. "And we all know why."

Danny stared at him.

Rab looked up at him from rolling a cigarette. Even in the dark he managed it elegantly. "Nothing to say?"

Danny was silent, his mind racing. His stomach felt like lead. A cold sweat began to prickle down his spine.

Rab smiled, watching him. The end of his cigarette glowed faintly in the dim light. He laughed sourly and scratched his chest through his T-shirt. Danny watched him uneasily. "You're not in any rush to contradict me Danny."

"It's bullshit," Danny said flatly.

Rab laughed then reached forward with a quick nervous movement and pulled Danny's T-shirt up, sliding his hand up inside, watching his face for a reaction.

Danny grabbed his hand. "What's Ian been saying?"

Rab laughed again. Relief, nerves, it was difficult to say. "The usual crap. You and John, joined at the hip, blah-de-blah-de-blah. He's been saying it as long as I can remember." Rab looked at him. "Okay, so he's a dipstick but it had you going, didn't it?"

Danny dropped his hand. His stomach seemed to slowly thaw inside him. He felt as if his guts were melting.

Rab moved up closer, boldly pulling Danny's shirt out completely, pushing his hands down the front of his jeans. He breathed heavily in his ear, "I can, can't I? This is what you meant, isn't it?"

Danny nodded. "But don't piss me off with any more of Ian's crap, okay?"

Rab said, "Okay." But his mind was already on other things. He let it go because he didn't care, because he didn't believe it. He never had, and he never would.

Predictably John came to his room that night, but he found the door locked. Danny stood at the window and listened to him outside. John's voice was whispering and urgent. "Danny?... Open the door."

Danny did not answer.

"Danny... open the bloody door." His voice was full of repressed anger.

Danny said nothing.

John rattled the doorknob violently. "Open this door you little cunt or I'll..." But he got no further. They both heard his father's steps on the stairs, his heavy tread carrying clearly in the silence of the hall.

John must have moved away from the door. When Danny heard him next he sounded as if he was standing outside the bathroom. He was talking to his father.

After a while the conversation died. John did not come back.

ELEVEN

It was three days after that before John finally caught up with him. He bumped into him, literally, working alone in the milking shed at seven in the evening. Danny involuntarily took a step back.

John's eyes immediately narrowed. Danny smiled with a tight mouth and tried to push past him.

"Oh no you don't." John's hand shot out, grabbing his shoulder and pulling him half round. Danny looked at the hand then at John's face. It was transformed by anger into something ugly. "What did you do with him?" It had all the vehemence of a long speech whittled away by time into one all-consuming question.

"Who?"

Danny was spun round to face him. "Don't give me that."

Danny jerked his shoulder free. "You've got a one track mind John."

John shoved him back against the corrugated iron wall with a thump. The pail he was carrying clanked against it. "What did you do with him? And don't bother to lie to me. You were practically licking your lips, you little queer." John shouldered him back again.

Danny's ribs felt as if they cracked with the impact. He hissed with pain. "You want me to tell you?" He saw John's lips compress furiously, but he went on, hating him so intensely he no longer cared what he said, "I know what you want John. I know what this whole fucking thing has been about right from the start." He felt John's body jerk back off him like a kicked dog.

Danny looked into his face, utterly thrown by the reaction. John was still furious, but there was something else darting in his eyes now and Danny had known too much of it in his life to mistake it. With some barely understood need to twist the knife he said, "Funny that what's one big fucking joke with me becomes deadly serious when he's involved. What exactly *is* your problem? So I sucked his root. I've sucked yours. Where's the difference? Tasted the same to me."

John lunged at him, running him back against the wall with a ferocity that made Danny slump. His hand clamped tight over Danny's mouth, covering the whole lower half of his face. Already he was struggling for air. "You want to die?"

He clawed at John's hand, but it was like an octopus smothering his face.

"You *want* to die?"

He began to see coloured spots. Areas of grey faded in and out of his vision. He felt himself grow weak. His hands seemed to pull at John's like empty gloves, without force. He could hear John saying it again and again, like an incantation, a man in shock. "You want to die?" His eyes were dilated, unseeing.

Danny slid away, thinking vaguely that it was a fucking crappy thing to die for.

It was the third such injury in so many weeks. Black eyes, fat lips, swollen jaws, and now this.

"What the hell is wrong with you?" Danny's father glared at him across the table.

Danny said nothing.

"Right," his father said, getting up, pushing the chair back. "This is the last. One more fight, one more 'I walked into the tractor Dad', and I'll expect explanations from the lot of you." He pointed at Danny as though he bore the singular blame. "This is the last, I mean it." And he slammed out the door.

Danny looked at the back door sullenly. He felt a dull diffuse resentment well up in him. This was John's fault. Where was his lecture? John had nearly fucking killed him for Christ's sake. Danny battered his eggshell to a pulp with his spoon. When Ian spoke to him he jumped.

"Nice collection of bruises. Gives you that well-worn look." He moved over to the toaster and pushed in two slices of bread. He turned and leaned against the counter, letting his eyes travel over Danny's body: the long slim legs, the narrow hips, the white skin emphasised by the dark T-shirt, his hair so long it was curling down over his collar, the sheer abundance of it intensifying the outrageous colour, a deep unearthly red. Danny had everything, was everything that Ian wasn't.

He realised abruptly he was staring. He straightened up and crossed the room.

Danny glowered up at him blackly as he pulled out a chair.

"What's this? Fear and loathing in Hope House Farm?" Ian sat down and began buttering his toast. "'Twas not I that marred that beauty." His gaze swept over Danny's face, taking in his fine etched brows, the thick dark lashes, his wide sensuous mouth. Poor used Danny.

Danny enunciated slowly and clearly, voice heavy with dislike, "Go *fuck* yourself."

Ian laughed uproariously, as if he had cracked an amazingly funny joke. He slapped his thighs, he choked, he coughed. "Oh boy..." He laughed some more. "Oh boy, that's rich..." He sobered abruptly, as if he had never laughed at all. His face looked thin and pinched, like a mask. "Really rich, coming from someone like you. It's all you know, isn't it? Fucking yourself."

Danny jumped up angrily and grabbed the front of his shirt. "Don't you fucking start. I've had you right up to here."

"Take your hands off me."

Danny bunched his fist up tighter.

Suddenly the door opened. John came in, stopping short when he saw them. Ian looked over at him. "Boy thinks he's had me up to here John." He looked back slowly into Danny's eyes. "You haven't had *me* up anywhere, baby. *Way* too crowded for me."

And he moved easily out of Danny's grip and went out of the door.

TWELVE

October moved in and with it came the first tinglings of cold. Rab felt it close in around him with a depressing sense of suffocation.

He had barely spoken to Danny since the day of his uncle's toothache. Past a fortnight now. Christ, it felt as if the entire year had moved in fortnights.

The enforced distance between them had produced a raging unmitigated ache in him that he blankly refused to name. He couldn't eat, he couldn't sleep. His only comfort was that John at least seemed to be suffering as much as he was.

It wasn't his imagination that John had lost more weight. Nor was it his imagination that the old man was determinedly keeping the three of them apart. He always seemed to be watching them from a distance, as if they were potentially dangerous animals.

Only Danny seemed to remain somehow untouched, isolated in that detachment of his. He found himself constantly drawn to him, watching him till it felt like a parasite living inside him, feeding off him. At mealtimes he would push his plate away, his meal barely tasted, unable to concentrate with Danny sitting so close, John taciturn beside him, eyes ever watchful, refusing food without explanation.

On the evening of the fourth Rab went into the living room and found Danny sitting alone in the dark watching TV. It felt like an act of God.

Danny looked round briefly then smiled and looked back at the TV saying, "Ill met by moonlight proud Titania."

Rab closed the door and leaned against it. He felt as if his entire hunger grew in his chest. *God, I feel like a wolfman, a monster. I feel like ripping him apart.*

He looked at Danny smiling there, his face planed into dark shadows and sharp blue angles by the shifting light, and croaked hoarsely, "I could eat you. You look so fucking..." Words failed him.

"Try sexy." Danny smiled some more then opened his legs, sliding down the settee to spread them wide. He gestured with his head. "Come on then, what're you waiting for?"

Rab swallowed. His voice when it came out sounded strangled, barely above a whisper. "Here?"

Danny looked around him then spread his arms along the back of the sofa. "Looks good to me."

Rab licked his lips. He could feel his hard-on pounding like it had a heart of its own. "The door..." He was still leaning against it. It was a glass door, frosted with leaves.

"No-one can see."

"They might... I mean anyone might..."

"They won't, trust me."

Rab let go the door's support like a man launching himself off a pier. He reached out a hand to Danny's hair just as the door opened.

"Did I leave my knitting in here?"

His aunt came in and began lifting cushions off her armchair. The colour swept into Rab's face like a tidal wave. Guilt and relief both. He was never more glad of the dark in his life.

Danny remained exactly where he was, sprawled indecently across the settee. His aunt looked at them both, aware suddenly of the unnatural silence. Her eyes swept over Danny's splayed body. Rab saw him look at her, his eyes half-closed, sleepy, lecherous with intent. His aunt looked away abruptly, talking to herself.

Rab thought, He did that deliberately. He embarrassed her deliberately. And he knew Danny had done it before, knew with a sudden intuitive knowledge that his aunt's thoughts were not as wholly pure and innocent as she would have them believe, and that Danny knew it and played on it.

"Ah, at last, found it." And she went from the room, not looking at either of them. The door closed with a bang.

Rab stood looking down at him, wondering what went on in his head. He was like an iceberg, always three-quarters under the water.

Danny reached over and lifted a packet of cigarettes from the chair arm and put one in his mouth. He lit it with one hand and placed the other back on the back of the sofa. "Come on, sit down."

Rab hesitated. He had had a bad fright, and something about Danny's performance made him wary, but the very act of standing there watching him smoke, his cheekbones in stark relief every time he drew on the cigarette, was acting like an aphrodisiac.

Danny grinned, "She won't be back, relax." He sounded like he could guarantee it.

Rab licked his lips, glanced at the door. Danny said, "Come on Rab, you want, you don't want, which is it to be?"

Rab sat down beside him and put his hand flat on Danny's stomach all in one gesture. As a statement of how he felt and what he wanted it couldn't have been more explicit.

Danny looked down at his hand then up into his eyes. "You got something in mind?"

Rab shook his head. His mouth was watering indecently. He swallowed convulsively.

"Well then, how about taking your clothes off?"

To Rab, who had been thinking more in terms of a quick hand-job out the fly of his jeans, it acted like a douse of cold water. He withdrew his hand. "Are you nuts? Your mother's upstairs. Ian's..."

Danny interrupted with a smile. "Who cares? What's the worst that can happen? Anyway she's on her way out."

As if on cue they heard the back door slam. Danny said, "See?"

Rab shook his head.

Danny smiled and slid a little closer. He lifted a hand and slid it round the back of Rab's neck, under his ponytail. "You're never chickenshit?" His voice was low and insidious.

"Ian..." Rab began.

Danny laughed. "Ian? The cat's a bigger threat."

Rab looked at him, frowning. Was he serious? But he seemed to be.

Danny's other hand was undoing his trouser button, pulling the zip down. "Come on, take your clothes off. I want to see you."

It acted like the mythic Magic Words. Danny wanted to see him. Oh, no problem then, Rab would simply have to oblige. And he did, scrambling out of his clothes with indecent haste until he stood before him naked, cock up like a peg.

Danny lay there, still sprawled, looking up at him. "All that platinum and tan." He looked up into his eyes. "Blonde all over, eh?" He smiled almost unpleasantly. Rab realised dimly somewhere inside that this surreptitious nasty streak in Danny was part of what excited him.

Danny stood up and walked round him like a buyer inspecting a carcass. He stopped behind him and said, "Kneel on the couch then."

Rab hesitated then got on the couch. Danny corrected him as he made to kneel sideways. "No, hands on the back. Look at the wall, back to me."

Rab did it, feeling a prickle of apprehension. The room was warm enough, but his skin was still covered in gooseflesh.

He jumped when Danny touched his thighs murmuring, "Spread them then." Rab did it, looking down at his own cock, the head a few inches away from the back of the sofa.

He grunted with surprise when something warm and soft tickled his anus. Warm, soft and wet. A tongue. Oh God, Danny was licking him out. He spread his legs wide, sticking his arse out, moaning softly. Danny pulled his buttocks apart with his hands, tongue pushing in deeper.

Rab grabbed his cock and began masturbating, squirming on the couch as Danny's tongue worked into his anus.

Abruptly it stopped. Rab hung there on the point of orgasm, quivering with closeness, part relieved because it had been too fast and part pissed off because he had been so close to the big one.

His head was resting on the back of the sofa. He lay there limply, heart pounding, and dimly heard Danny's zip then felt his legs against the backs of his knees. What was he doing?

It didn't take long to find out.

Rab felt the blunt unmistakable nudge of something at his anus, very hard and very insistent. Danny's knuckles dug into his balls while his other hand tugged at his right buttock as he tried to force it in.

Rab jerked his head up. "What are you doing?" He tried to see over his shoulder.

Danny pushed him down, none too gently. "Fucking you." It was flat, emphatic.

"What?"

Danny didn't answer.

"I don't want to..."

Danny cut him short. "Don't fuck me about. Where did you think this shit was leading if it wasn't leading here?"

Rab didn't answer.

"If you think I'm playing kids' wank games forever think again."

Rab tried to struggle round as it pushed painfully at his anus, nosing in. "No, wait, don't."

Then Danny did something odd, suddenly spreading his hands round Rab's chest and jolting him back. The head of his penis went in, lodged an inch inside Rab's sphincter, effectively impaling him. Rab swore.

"Good?" Danny whispered in his ear. He lay down over his back, but there was nothing slack or relaxed about it, rather the opposite, as if he was poised for resistance, anticipating it.

"No, don't."

But Danny jolted in again. He followed it immediately with another and Rab realised he must already have about half his length up there although it felt like more. The little bastard was raping him.

Suddenly Danny began to fuck him, a steady rhythm, cock sinking in deeper with every thrust. It was deep intrusive agony. Rab's erection had long since disappeared.

"Now we'll see..." Danny grunted, "what all the fucking magic is about."

Rab dropped his forehead against the sofa, clutching the back of it. Danny was slamming uncomfortably into his body. Rab could hear his thighs slapping against the back of his legs. Every jolt pushed him further upright, closer to the back of the settee.

Danny was in deep now, hardly withdrawing, just making small jerking movements, getting more and more rapid. Rab could feel him close in on his own orgasm. He felt a sudden excitement at the idea of Danny coming inside him. That, combined with the fact that his movements were now less aggressive, brought his erection back with a

bang. He looked down at it then realised suddenly that Danny was pacing himself, as if he knew.

Rab began to masturbate himself furiously. He was there, out of nowhere, and he'd never felt anything so intense. He tried to spread his legs, urging Danny to push up harder. "God..." he cried out. "*God.*" And he pulled his foreskin back tight and rammed his engorged glans against the stiff velvet of the sofa, smearing his come over the fabric as Danny helped jolt him into it, forking his body up into his.

And saying nothing at all.

THIRTEEN

"Hello Rab."

Rab's head shot up, banging himself on the engine hood. "What the...?"

Ian smiled at him, unobtrusively, like a good librarian. Rab rubbed the top of his head with his arm. "Fucking creeping about..." His eyes took in the dry clothes. It was pouring outside. "Where the hell have you come from?"

"In here."

Rab looked at him. "Since when?"

But Ian only smiled, offered no information.

Rab picked up a rag and wiped his hands. He shoved the rag in his pocket saying, "You know, I've never told you this before Ian, but I'll let you into a secret. You fucking bug me." Ian smiled some more and pushed his hands into his pockets. "And for the last two weeks you've really been fucking bugging me. What gives?"

Ian looked out into the yard. The rain was growing faint, drizzling. Soon it would be over. The light shone on everything with a sharpening glare. He answered without looking at him. "And I thought we were allies too."

"Did you now?" Rab's voice was sarcastic. He pulled a dog-end of cigarette out his pocket and began patting for matches. "Allies in what precisely?"

"The war against Danny." Ian looked at him steadily.

Rab managed to tear his eyes away, aware that his colour was betrayingly high. He struck a match and lit his cigarette, taking a deep drag and letting it out slowly down his nose.

Ian continued to look at him steadily, then he moved a little closer and said in a low voice, like one imparting a birthday secret, "I know about you and Danny."

Rab stared at him, waiting for what came next, because there was a next. It was written all over his face in capital letters.

But Ian said nothing, simply smiled that irritating little smile of his. What a grudging little spastic he was. That suety little face, like John without the strength or beauty.

"Well Ian, what's next? Am I supposed to give you a badge of merit or something?"

Ian laughed. "What a comedian."

Rab grew impatient. "You've waited a long time for this. You should get a badge for perseverance at any rate." He took another drag on his cigarette then looked out at the rain. This was beginning to bore him. Let the little git spit it out. "What do you want?"

Ian looked at him. He was still smiling. That is, an eighth of an inch of his teeth showed in a thin yellow line. It was the most of his smile the stifling little creep ever spared anyone. Rab saw it and thought, I've never realised before just how much this little bastard hates me.

"You."

Rab's surprise came out of him in a sort of soft grunt, then he laughed. "What exactly? My head on a platter?"

Ian was still smiling, as if the damn thing was painted on. "What the hell would I want with your head?"

He paused just long enough for the insult to sink in. "What I want out of you won't even fill a teaspoon." And Rab saw his eyes move over his face hungrily.

"Mealy-mouthed to the last. Why don't you just say it? You want to suck my dick."

"No, you're going to suck mine."

Rab turned his face away from him, pinching out his cigarette and tossing it out

into the dying rain. "You stupid little prick." He turned back to him. "I wouldn't look at you if I had been blind for half a century. You seriously think I'd give you anything, you grudging little fart?" He suddenly pushed Ian's shoulder, making his smile falter for the first time. A dull, angry colour crept into his face.

"My mother isn't going to like finding some queer mauling her favourite son, especially, when after all this time, it turns out to be you."

"Some queer? She doesn't have to look far for queers in this family. Besides, she wouldn't listen to you if you told her the barn was on fire. As far as she's concerned you're somewhere below the fucking dog. But don't let me stop you. You go tell her. I don't get many laughs around here." He turned away from him again. "Now fuck off, your face gives me a headache."

Ian smiled again, suddenly, like a peach bursting under the sun. The ugly, nail-paring little grin split his pasty face in half. He reached up his hand and brushed his thumb over Rab's cheekbone. Rab flinched away angrily, grabbing his hand and throwing it away from him. "Keep your fucking hands off me."

Ian shook his head. "No. I've paid years of lip service for this and now it's reward-time. You see, I know a little something else about you, and it's wicked not to share."

Rab's face stilled, his last fleeting expression held there like a snapshot. Ian played his trump card. "I know all about the *girls*." He watched the tan pale, become yellowish. "I know exactly where you went and what you did…"

Rab moved his head robotically. He looked out the door without seeing. Ian could see his mind racing. *Think you've got life stitched up Rab? Well, just you watch it come undone.*

Rab lit a cigarette. He put it in his mouth, going straight to his matches without preamble. It was curious to see how like John he looked when he did it. He spoke to Ian without looking at him. "You're full of little surprises, aren't you?"

Ian simply smiled.

Rab played his own trump card, knowing it was expected it of him, knowing it was a losing card anyway, doomed to failure. It pleased Ian to see it there, held out to him. "Why should she care? It's nothing to do with her."

"Who says I'm taking it to her?"

Rab turned and looked at him slowly, his eyes black, his mouth white. "Is that meant to scare me?"

Ian smiled, and for the very first time it looked genuine, as if there was a tiny hint of pity there. "You tell me."

Rab turned away. Ian watched him take another cigarette out then throw it away unsmoked. He watched him rub his palms on his shirt, hugging his body as if he was suddenly cold. He waited, everything on one throw of the dice. Rab was skewered between his needs and his wants. On the one hand Danny, on the other John. But John was old news, Danny was here and now. Still, he was quite capable of throwing everything away on some desperate and pointless act of vanity.

Ian gave one final jerk on the wire. "Of course," he added, "I haven't told him yet about what I heard in the living room last night."

Rab's body went limp. He said wearily, "What do you want?"

Very slowly and with infinite care Ian said, "Just what the rest get."

Rab looked at him.

Ian smiled his sickly smile. "And now seems as good a time as any." And he reached up again to stroke the contour of Rab's cheek.

FOURTEEN

It was going to be a solid gunmetal day, grey and heavy. Danny lay on his bed wide-awake. Ten minutes more and he would have to climb out into the cold.

His alarm went off unexpectedly, causing a reaction in him not unlike a bomb going off. He beat the clock senseless then lay there for a second or two trying to regain his composure. He took a deep steadying breath then climbed out of bed and into his work clothes.

In the hall he bumped into John coming out of his room. Danny nodded curtly, but John only looked him up and down and did not reply. Fuck you, Danny thought.

Downstairs the others ate their breakfasts in sullen silence. Only Rab, his hair a bright white under the fluorescent light, surprised him by winking at him over his spoon. Danny was equally surprised to find himself smiling back. Outside the rain began to fall in heavy, greasy drops.

"Well, that settles that," his father said, staring out the window in irritable resignation. "John, Ian, you come with me." He turned to Rab. "You take him and finish that whitewashing. Christ knows, it isn't fit for anything else today."

Rab smiled slowly at Danny. Danny felt his own smile answer back. John looked at them with something indecipherable in his expression. Only Ian's gaze was easy to read. Unfortunately no-one was looking.

The tool shed was the original stone barn attached to the house, laughably small now. Every couple of years they whitewashed the interior. They tended to do the job piecemeal between other jobs so, since May, it had been sitting half-painted, the tools piled on the floor, aggravating anyone who attempted to find anything in the shambles.

They went in, leaving the door open for light. There was no electricity in here.

"Now or later?" Rab asked, beyond being able to pretend.

"Have they gone?" Danny asked, already tugging his shirt out.

Rab managed to nod.

"Then now," Danny said, pulling his shirt over his head.

Rab looked at him, standing there half-naked. Where had Danny the boy gone, the one he'd fought a cold war with for years? He felt abruptly afraid. It was too much too soon. He wanted to ask him, Why are you doing this? As if that made any difference. As if Danny would tell him the truth. As if he really wanted to know. He didn't. He wanted this too much to risk anything that might stop it.

He felt Danny's hard chest move up against his, the feel of his mouth, surprisingly cool and aggressive, pressed to his throat. How had he come to be in this situation? To find this so heady? So intoxicating? How long had it been? Two weeks, three? When had he stepped over the line from expediency into want and then into need? He'd let him rape him for Christ's sake. Not even a murmur. How could it have happened so quickly?

Danny slid his hand down the front of Rab's jeans. He was quiet and determined, but his breathing was ragged and shallow. He was pushing against him, silently asking for relief. But Rab did not touch him, too taken with the sensation of Danny's hand groping inside his pants.

Danny pushed again, insistently. He kissed Rab's mouth, obviously trying to incite him. Let him wait, Rab thought. He wanted to savour this. He never knew when he would have him next. Even if there would be a next.

"*Rab.*" Danny's voice was irritable, demanding.

Rab opened his eyes, watching Danny's deep russet hair as he bent his head to his chest. Danny took a nipple between his teeth, hand gripping Rab's penis fiercely. Everything he did was charged with that same threat.

Rab groaned, dropping his head back against the wall, letting his eyes roll open blankly, seeing nothing, and there was John, standing in the doorway, watching them.

He clutched Danny's head to his chest with a jerk of fright, some dimly understood need to hide him.

"Rab," Danny demanded, breaking free and squashing Rab's thigh between his legs to grind against it. "Will you fucking *do* me?"

Rab stared at John, standing there stock still, utterly unmoving, and suddenly knew he wasn't going to do anything. He was just going to stand there and let it happen.

He wanted to scream at him, Making you stiff, you pervert? Turning you on, you fucking freak? But instead he grabbed Danny's head and kissed him deeply, sliding his hand down inside his trousers.

Danny broke free, like a child held against his will, and demanded, "Are we having sex or what?" And he undid his own jeans, yanking them down, shoving Rab's hand on his penis. "Now *do* it."

He felt Danny's hand pull on him fiercely, urging him to get on with it. He saw John still standing there, immobilized, like a great stupid animal. He wanted to yank Danny round and masturbate him in front of him, let him see his precious baby brother's prick jerking and twitching like a marionette. But he held him tight, crushing him against him, letting his eyes do the talking, making John feel it.

"I love you," he said, eyes holding John's. And out of nowhere he came, while John just stood there and watched.

John was waiting for him in his room after dinner that evening. Danny didn't even close the door. "Forget it John - out."

"I just want to talk. Can't a man even talk to his own brother?"

Danny looked at him, surprised at his quiet level tone. Even the sarcasm hardly passed muster. But John was against the window, hiding his face, so how could you be sure what you were really seeing, or hearing? He closed the door sighing, "Okay, so talk."

"Let's go out for a drive."

"Are you nuts? It's pissing down. Besides, it's past half ten and I'm shagged. Anything you've got to say, say it now or get out."

John turned his head to the window, showing a different profile against the dark, streaming glass. "Come on Danny, a favour. When do I ever ask you for a favour?"

"You're *asking*?" Danny didn't even bother to keep the incredulity out his voice.

"I'm asking."

"Oh wow." Danny looked at him a moment longer. John turned to face him fully as if to show he had nothing to hide. Danny said impulsively, "Okay. Why the hell not?"

They went downstairs, Danny leading, John following, always in shadow, like something elusive. They stole out of the back door like thieves and took the pick-up.

John pulled out into the road and drove in silence. The windscreen wipers snicked to and fro. Only the lights from the dashboard showed.

Danny looked at his profile staring straight ahead. There was something odd about his face. He looked... he groped for the word ...feverish, that was it, like he was coming down with flu or something.

"Where are we going?" he asked, taking a packet of cigarettes from the glove compartment.

"You'll see." John clicked the indicators on and the pick-up swung right across the oncoming traffic and onto a dirt track.

Danny had been watching John, not where they were going. He peered out the window now, cupping his hands to see better, but the rain was torrential and he could make nothing out.

They swung onto gravel, obviously some kind of a yard. It looked momentarily familiar, but John cut the lights before he could make out where he was. Danny rolled down the window as John cut the engine. He could hear nothing but the rain singing. Suddenly he recognised something about the squat building up ahead. He rolled up the window. He looked calmer than he felt. "Why have you brought me here?"

"Something I want to show you." And now Danny realised there was something odd about his voice too.

"Forget it. I've seen it already, remember? What is this? Some kind of pilgrimage to cure my sickness? Bring me to the scene of the crime, show me how I'm going to end up if I don't mend my ways? Well maybe you've got a hold of the wrong person John. Maybe you should take yourself for a walk round the grounds. I'm going home."

Danny made a move for the door handle, but John stopped him. "When was the last time I touched you?"

Danny turned to look at him. "What?"

"I said, when was the last time I touched you?"

Danny looked at him blankly, hand sliding off the handle.

"More than a month ago Danny. I can tell you the exact date. Now can we go into the house and talk?"

Danny gave him a look, irritation, confusion, then said, "Oh, for Christ's sake..." and slammed out the door. He darted across the yard to shelter under the stupid little corrugated plastic porch. He pressed back against the door - a futile move in this rain - and watched John locking up the van and crossing towards him. He turned to face the door as John drew close.

John took a key out his pocket and unlocked the door then pushed it open. Danny did not move. He was still thinking about John bothering to lock the van.

"Get in then," John said, nodding his head at the open doorway.

Danny hesitated, searching his face for a moment, then stepped over the threshold.

It felt as if he was instantly plunged into subterranean darkness. The door slammed to and the black became impenetrable. "John?" he said uncertainly. The silence was absolute.

"Right here." His voice was very soft behind him. "Upstairs."

Danny immediately balked. "No."

"Danny..." John began.

"I am not going upstairs."

"And why not? Believe me Danny, the only thing you have to fear up there is your own black soul. Now get upstairs."

Danny let out a sigh of irritation then stepped through the stair doorway. A faint light showed through it. The stairs themselves proved to be horrifically narrow, boxed in on both sides with wood panelling. They creaked badly.

There was a window on the tiny landing, which at least let in enough light to see by. Danny's heart was pounding uncomfortably. He felt claustrophobic and anxious in a way he could hardly identify.

When they turned off the landing Danny stopped dead, something huge paralysing his legs. John said softly behind him, "Don't worry, it's locked," and gave him a gentle push down the hallway and into the first door.

Danny went in thinking, *What's* locked? He was aware that he could hear his own

breathing. He looked round the room nervously.

When the door slammed he jumped, swinging round in time to see John latch it then lean against it. The moon came out abruptly and John's face became almost daylight clear after the intense darkness.

Danny backed away to the double bed that stood under the dormer window and sat down.

John said, "Good." Which could have meant anything but seemed only to indicate he was satisfied with the arrangements thus far. He settled himself more comfortably against the door before saying, "I saw you in the tool shed this morning. Quite a performance."

Danny looked up at him belligerently. No surprise, no confusion. "So that's why I'm here. So you can beat fuck out me without anyone interfering."

"Quite possibly." It was completely flat, unemotional, and somehow much more worrying because of that.

"What I do is my business," Danny asserted angrily.

"I don't think so."

Danny jumped to his feet. "Look John, don't bother threatening me again, I don't give a fuck any more."

"Sit down." It was perfectly level.

"Fuck you," Danny said sharply.

John was across the room and had shoved him flat on the bed before Danny could even move. He stood above him, waiting for Danny to struggle upright before he said, "You sit when you're told to sit."

Danny said nothing, just stared up at him, panting with fright. Suddenly he realised what it was he'd been seeing in him all evening and had not been able to identify. Rage. A huge icy rage that had all but eaten him up. John's superficial calm was a tiny tinfoil lid on a huge furnace of rage.

And John proved it. He moved away from him and went to stand back against the door again, as if he did not want to be within striking distance. It was such an uncharacteristic move Danny sat there utterly intimidated by it, waiting for whatever it was he had to say.

"I've been waiting for this a long time." John looked at him. "No surprise? Not even a, What the fuck are you talking about John?" He smiled. "Well, that doesn't surprise me. Nothing about you surprises me. Do you remember the day we went swimming?"

Danny took a while to shake his head.

"Well, I take it all back, now you do surprise me. Let me refresh your memory. We went swimming. I've been thinking about this. It has to have been a Saturday. And let's be more accurate while we're about it, me and Rab decided to go swimming, you invited yourself along. Then, for a reason that could only be apparent to your oversexed little brain, you decided to skinny-dip. Ring any bells?"

This time Danny nodded.

John smiled again, just barely. "And you remember what happened?"

"You got in a fight."

John lifted a brow. "And?"

"You thrashed the living daylights out of me."

There was another pause and then he said, "That's odd, you know, I don't remember that."

Danny pressed his palms to his cheeks.

John folded his arms and said, "It's a funny thing how memory cheats you. I can remember things about you and me that would probably surprise you. At least surprise you."

Danny said nothing, although John paused to let him.

54

John went on, "I even have a distant memory that we were friends once."

Danny laughed sourly. "Oh *yeah*."

John let his arms drop. They hung loosely against the door. "Maybe you're right. Maybe friend's not the right word."

Danny said nothing.

John sighed then said, "It seems pointless to warn you off again, you haven't listened so far. What if I make a deal with you instead?"

Danny frowned angrily. "You're forgetting something John. I don't have to do what you say any more. I'm no longer your little brother."

John threw his head back. A soft dry laugh escaped his mouth. "Wrong Danny. You are very much my little brother and ne'er the twain shall part. Didn't your near death experience teach you anything?" His voice, soft as it was, still managed to drop further when he said, "Believe me, if you don't leave him alone, next time it *will* be death."

Danny sat there breathing through his mouth, aware of all the hairs standing up on his arms at the sure, cold conviction in his voice. "I'm not scared of you," he managed and was surprised at how well it came out.

John laughed, a little soft thing. "Oh we know that, we've seen that. Trouble is, I'm not trying to scare you. You're not fucking Rab and that's that."

"Oh *right*," Danny said furiously. "Nobody fucks Saint Rab but you. That's what's wrong, isn't it? You're just aching to get it up him yourself."

John laughed again, more genuinely this time. "I fucked Rab senseless for six years. Been there, done that, I think."

Danny stared at him.

"Come on Danny, I don't believe Ian would have let that one slip by."

"Six *years*...?"

"You heard me."

"You shit."

John laughed again. "Ian would be proud of you."

"You dirty shit."

"I think maybe he's the dirty shit. He started it."

"I don't believe that."

"Why? Because your big brother told you different? Well, let me disinform you. I was fifteen, he was twelve. He came into the toilet one day while I was in the bath and we were fixed for mutual masturbation for life. Only it didn't last that long, although it did get more inventive."

"I don't believe you."

"You don't want to believe me."

"You dirty bastard."

"Consider this good advice. Leave him alone."

"I'll do what I damn well like."

"Fine, but just bear this in mind - I can do the same."

"Meaning what?"

"Use your imagination."

Danny looked at him just long enough then shook his head, shook it again more violently, getting to his feet and crossing the room away from him. This time John did not stop him. Danny stood with his back to him, facing the far wall, arms braced against it, palms flat, head down. John crossed silently to stand behind him and whispered in his ear, "You can stop it any time."

Danny swung round to face him, dropping back against the wall as if he was exhausted. "What am I John, some kind of toy you don't really want but can't stand to share?"

John looked at him for a long moment, his face subtly changing. He moved closer,

putting a palm on the wall at either side of Danny's head, fencing him in. He said softly, "What d'you want to hear? That you're important to me?"

Danny flushed bright red and turned his face away, but John brought him back round, forcing him to look at him again. "The big admission, is that what you're waiting for?"

Danny said nothing, closed his eyes against the expression in his eyes, closed his ears to that tenderness in his voice - oh so convincing.

John suddenly moved close, his body lightly touching his, his cheek barely skin to skin with his, and whispered, "What if it was true? Have you looked at yourself recently? You're barely human. There isn't a man, woman or child in the district who wouldn't do it with you if you asked. You're a god in human form. What else could possibly have lured Rab off the straight and narrow? What more reason could I need?"

Danny shook his head.

"Is that a refusal, disagreement, what?"

"I don't believe this, I just don't."

"Why not?"

Danny pushed him off, warnings forgotten. "Because I'm your fucking brother John, remember that?"

"And he's your ruddy cousin. You've got a fucking weird set of distinctions."

"All my life you've drummed into me..."

"That it's not right. Yeah, and all my life I've worked on this lousy farm, but that doesn't mean they weren't both mistakes. I love you Danny."

He said it so easily, so casually, just tacked on the end like he hadn't said anything at all. Danny simply slid down the wall and sat down.

John hesitated a moment then carefully hunkered down beside him as if he was afraid of startling him. He reached out a hand and gently lifted Danny's face, cupping his chin in his palm. "You don't believe me, do you?"

"Don't *believe* you?" Danny could hardly get the words out. He slapped his hand away. "You want some kind of exclusive rights to... to..." he racked his brain for a way of saying it and only came up with, "to use me any time you're drunk enough, to shove me in between one cunt and the next like some kind of light relief, and for that I'm supposed to be grateful or something, supposed to cut out what little life or free will I have left and hand it over to you, and all you can think about is whether I believe some crap you dredge up about loving me."

"It's not crap," John said flatly. "But even if it was it wouldn't matter. And don't harbour any notions of your free will either. You haven't got any free will. You haven't had any free will since you were six years old. You gave it away and you don't get it back, not from me. I don't care about what you think, or feel, or want. I don't care about anything except keeping your dick in your pants. It's not public property, and that includes Rab. He isn't even properly related."

"Jesus *Christ*, and that makes it *better*? Suddenly you being my brother makes it *better*?"

"Me being your brother makes it the only thing there is. Me being your brother makes it blood, not just something you lift and leave. A brother is for life not just for Christmas. Me being your brother is all there is."

Danny struggled up onto his feet. "Cut it short John. What does all this mean?"

"It means I want you to leave him alone, and that my reasons are none of your business. You feel free to believe what you like, but believe this, if you're going to be sucking anyone's dick it isn't going to be his."

"It'll be yours?"

"I can oblige baby."

"What? Sober?"

John slapped him. It made a huge crack in the room. It hurt like hell. John shoved his body up against his. "Sober, drunk, any way I like. You're so fucking keen to get down on your knees then fine, but you can fucking forget him."

"And the deal?"

"We just made it. Weren't you listening?"

Danny said, "Right, sure. Till the next time you're drunk enough then." And he pushed past him and went out the room.

When they came into the kitchen Rab was waiting for them, sitting in the dark, only the tip of his cigarette glowing.

John closed the door silently, trying to keep it quiet. Danny stood like an animal waiting to be moved. He was numb with emotional exhaustion.

"The wanderers return."

"*Shit.*" John dropped the key, slamming the door on reflex.

"Rab," Danny said dully, without inflection.

"The very same." An empty bottle sat on the table in front of him. It looked like there were things Rab needed to get drunk to do too.

"What are you doing here?" John demanded. "Why aren't you in bed?" His voice was sharply aggressive, the same old John of old.

"I might ask you the same question, more even, like where the fuck have you been?"

John looked at him sharply. "None of your fucking business."

"Oh but it is John-boy," Danny saw him push back his chair, saw the difficulty he had getting to his feet, "because that's my property you've got there and I don't recall giving you permission to take it anywhere."

"*Your* property?" The words came out as if something had choked all the power out of them. "Let's hope you're drunk Rab. Let's hope you're really, really drunk."

"Not drunk enough."

"I don't know. Right now it's saving your neck."

"Bet it didn't save his arsehole…"

Danny heard the impact, Rab grunting like a poleaxed animal. There was a rumbling crash as the heavy kitchen table was knocked back under their combined weight.

He walked to the kitchen door and left the room.

FIFTEEN

Ian stood in the dark again like Ian had so many times before. Ian had learned to be neither seen nor heard and it had given him just rewards.

They had been fighting over Danny again last night. He had not been able to catch much of it, but it had definitely been about Danny. When was it not?

The door slammed suddenly. Ian straightened up.

The front light flickered on, then the wall heater. He peered round from behind the trailer. Rab was struggling into a blue boiler suit, a cigarette hanging out the corner of his mouth. He didn't fasten it. Once, in the height of summer, he'd worn it with only his underpants underneath. He'd fastened it then, to just below his navel, decent and no more.

Ian closed his eyes, seeing the image again. The thick pale hair coming up his hard flat belly, the golden skin strongly reminiscent of John's.

He squeezed himself briefly through the lining of his pocket then opened his eyes again. Rab had rolled himself under the jacked-up car.

He walked over noiselessly. "Hello."

Rab's hand slipped, skinning his knuckles. He cursed and turned to see Ian's unmistakable boots, oddly laced, tight as corsets. He pushed himself back out. Ian leaned against the side of the car, looking down at him.

Rab got up to his feet slowly. "Well, if it isn't Mickey fucking Mouse. This is a surprise."

Ian flushed. "I'm getting tired of the way you talk to me."

"Like I'm getting tired of your face."

"I've come for what you owe me."

"You think I'm paying you anything for that fiasco last night?"

Ian stared at him for a long moment. "Well, I suppose even Danny can stand a few more truths before disillusionment sets in."

"What's that supposed to mean?"

"He was out with John last night. I doubt if they were discussing farming."

Rab grabbed the front of his jacket. "You don't know anything, you stirring little bastard."

"No? It was enough for you to start a fight with him last night."

Rab glared at him then pushed him away.

Ian went on, voice soft, curiously placating, "Come on. You think Danny likes to hear himself discussed as property, even if he knows damn well he is? Then there's all that unfaithfulness," he clucked, "and with John."

"That was long before he was around."

"Of course, and I'm sure he'll forgive you in the fullness of time, but he still has illusions about you. It would be a shame to shatter them now."

"Christ, I ought to wring your scrawny little neck."

Ian laughed. "You know you should really drop the macho shit. Living with John doesn't make you him. If it did you wouldn't be having any problems with Danny, believe me."

He stood watching Rab fume silently under the insult then said, "I think maybe you should start to think in terms of long term pleasure. After all, you never know what I might be able to push your way - when John's not looking." He smiled at him, just enough promise, just enough threat, so that Rab could not be sure which was uppermost, then slid his hand inside Rab's shirt.

Ian could feel the instant flush of revulsion goosepimpling his skin, but he bore his touching stoically, his head averted.

"Now, if you were to take off all your clothes and put the boiler suit back on I think I could have a very nice time, considering."

Rab spat out his cigarette and stood on it. After a moment he began to unfasten his shirt.

Danny was afraid.

He sat up, his heart hammering, and listened. There it was again. That same low insistent sound. Someone knocking at his door. He climbed up onto his knees and looked at it. The handle turned slowly. First one way, then the other.

Silence.

He looked at the clock. 3:36 am. Somehow that made the fright worse.

The knock sounded again, a little louder, then a whisper, as if whoever it was had their mouth pressed to the crack of the door. "Danny..."

Danny got up, wetting his lips nervously. He stood against the door frame and whispered back, "Who is it?"

"Rab."

Rab? What the hell did he want? A hundred things went through Danny's head as he reached down and unlocked the door. "Hold on."

He opened it a fraction. Rab pushed in and rolled him back against the wall, slapping a hand over his mouth as if he expected him to scream. The door was closed and locked all in seconds.

Danny smelt him before he actually realised. He knew that smell better than his own.

It was John's eyes that met his own over his hand, John's bulk that leant against him. "I'm going to take my hand away. No screaming hysterics, okay?"

Danny managed a tiny nod. John took his hand away.

"What the hell do you want?" Danny demanded immediately.

John jerked him up against him and kissed him hard on the mouth, pushing his tongue in deep. Danny struggled violently, but only succeeded in freeing his mouth. John's grip was iron-fast on his upper arms.

"What can you taste?" John was whispering against his mouth as if he intended to kiss him again.

"What?"

"I said, what can you taste? Want me to do it again?"

Danny pulled his head back sharply. "What d'you mean, what can I taste? Have you gone nuts?"

John yanked him forwards and kissed him again, harder this time, hurting his mouth. Danny didn't break away this time, John let him go. He stood there breathless, disorientated, blinking stupidly. John still gripped his arms. It felt as if he was being held by a machine.

"Well? What do I taste of? How drunk am I?"

Danny looked into his eyes. It was a slow thing, a dawning understanding. John tasted of a hundred half-smoked cigarettes, nothing more. He heard himself whisper, "You're not."

"That's right, I'm not."

Danny swallowed, wet his lips, and said in a low voice that sounded very young, "What do you want John?"

"You."

There was a long silence then John said, "I'm admitting it, alright? I want sex with

you. Here, right now, stone cold sober. Is that good enough? Do I finally earn you?"

Danny shook his head gently. It wasn't meant to be gentle, it just came out that way because he was stupid with broken sleep, pure incomprehension.

John said, "What?" as if he couldn't believe what he was seeing, and that made everything clear.

"I said no John, because there's just one little snag - I don't want to have sex with you."

It was John's turn to shake his head. "I don't believe you."

"Too bad."

John shook him violently. "I don't believe you, you little shit."

Danny looked at him levelly. He felt completely calm. More than calm. He felt dead. "It's true."

"What is this, some pathetic punishment because I took without asking? Because I wouldn't let you indulge your adolescent itch with Rab? Christ, I'm giving you what you want. I'm sick of hiding it. I'll deal with it. You've got my word."

Danny laughed. He heard himself with a kind of wonder. "What a spoilt, conceited bastard you are. How could I ever have imagined I felt anything for you, even as a stupid little kid?"

John stared at him then said in a voice so low it sounded barely there, "And you don't now? Think you don't need me any more?" John pulled him to him again, that same remorseless grip on his upper arms. "Kiss me. Let's see you keep the self-delusion going."

Danny shook his head.

John barked a small laugh. "What's wrong, think you can't get through it?" He suddenly let go his arms. "Look, I'm not even holding you. You kiss me Danny and let me hear that you never loved me, that you don't love me still. You can't do it. You know you can't." John shoved his face in his. "You can't fucking do it because you're a pathetic little faggot that can't resist a bit of rough, not even your own fucking brother."

Danny slapped him as hard and viciously as he could. John grabbed him and kissed him savagely, pushing him back against the wall.

They broke apart again. John grabbed his head in both hands as if he intended to kiss him again. Suddenly he kneed him hard in the groin.

Danny went down with a grunt, and was slammed back against the wall. John immediately dropped forward at the knees, pinning him there by the shoulders. He jerked Danny's head back by the hair and hooked his fingers into his open mouth, pulling it wide, his free hand scrabbling at his zip. He tugged his penis out into his hand and shoved it into his stretched mouth like someone cramming forcemeat into a body cavity, all the time hissing, "...Kiss this baby. See what this does for you. Give me the best blow job of my life. Do it like only a little brother can. Take me right back there. Cry, plead, make it real. Suck the life right out of me. That's what you want, isn't it? What you've always wanted? You *loved* it. You loved every crumb I ever... oh God, shit, *fuck*... you *love* me."

And John came.

SIXTEEN

Danny packed his bag with one eye on the clock. It was 5:35. He had barely half an hour left. At the outside. He closed his bedroom door quietly and went down the stairs. He lifted his jacket from the hall and shrugged into it. The leather felt cold and clammy to the touch. In the kitchen he lifted his mother's bills money from the dresser drawer and her agency money from behind the clock. The dog whuffed at him softly. He shushed it, bending down to stroke its head. It lay down again, its tail thumping gently in the dark.

Danny lifted his bag from the floor and crossed to the door, unlatching it quietly. He took the Fiat's keys from their hook and slid out, letting the latch fall to gently behind him.

There was no moon, but the sky was beginning to lighten in a false dawn. That meant it was going to be a nice day.

He crossed the yard and went into the tractor shed. His money was stashed under the seat of his tractor. An adolescent leftover. His 'getaway fund' he'd always called it. His security blanket in case he ever got too bored. He laughed mirthlessly, his breath puffing out before him. *Bored.*

He swung up onto the tractor and opened the door. The corpse was sitting bolt upright in the seat, staring at him. "Hello Danny."

Danny all but fell back out, only managing to pull himself upright by hanging onto the door.

"Going somewhere?"

Danny climbed back down unsteadily, feeling his knees buckle slightly as he reached the ground.

"Gave John a good time tonight. You should've known better than to open the door." Ian climbed down from the tractor, forcing Danny back a step.

Danny stared at him. "You heard," he said stupidly.

"I was listening."

I was listening, Danny thought, like it was entertainment. He pushed him. "Get out of my way."

He clambered into the tractor and jacked up the seat. He ferreted around inside. His heart dropped. Where was it?

"It's not there." Ian's voice came out of the dark, lazily full of Ian's inimitable brand of self-certainty.

Danny jumped down and grabbed him. "What have you done with it?"

"How beautiful you are when you're angry."

Danny hit him with both hands. A push that was intended to floor him. A spontaneous outburst of frustrated rage. Instead Ian flew back across the short space and folded up against the side of the other tractor. The blow knocked the wind from him, badly jarring his back. It was not something he had accounted for.

Danny pulled him up, sending pain jolting through him. "Where is it?" He shook him in desperation, aware of time sliding through his hands.

Ian hissed through his teeth, feeling icy-sharp jabs shoot out from his spine into his ribs, "Where you can't get at it."

Danny grabbed his hair with both hands, shaking his head like you might a dog by its ears. "I'll fucking kill you Ian, where is it?"

"In John's room." Even breathless as he was a deaf man could have heard the gloat in his voice.

Danny repeated it stupidly. "In John's room?"

Ian said nothing. He could save his breath. He didn't need to verify it. Danny didn't even have the strength to accuse him of lying. He knew it was the truth. After all, where else would Ian pick to put it? It was the safest bank in the world against Danny.

He made his decision. He had no time. Screw it. He had enough money. He turned and moved quickly through the shed. Ian's shout cut through the air. "Where are you going?"

Danny ignored him. He opened the door and passed out. He crossed the yard quickly and opened the car. The door caught as he pulled it shut behind him. Ian was hanging onto it.

"Fuck off," Danny snarled at him, pulling the door to.

Ian tugged it back and pushed himself between it and the car. "You can't leave." His face was almost afraid now. This wasn't in the script.

"Just watch me."

"I'll tell him you took the car."

"I doubt if you'll need to."

"She'll send the police after you."

Danny laughed. "I said, fuck off Ian." And he kicked out at him with both feet. But Ian threw himself on top of him, knocking him back half onto the passenger seat. They lay trapped by their own weight under the steering wheel. Danny squirmed underneath him, filled with sudden anxiety. He could see the time blinking on the dashboard, ticking away. "Get off you stupid bastard."

He tried to get leverage with his feet and found they didn't reach the ground. Nor could he raise his legs sufficiently to get them into the car. Ian's body was like a log across them.

Then he felt Ian's hands pawing at his chest. Perhaps it was something about their snuffling movements, or the sound of his breathing, but he felt a sudden claustrophobic revulsion. He doubled his efforts, grasped Ian's hands and held them off. They squirmed in his hands like oiled snakes, sweaty and elusive. He pulled free and began pawing again. His head was buried in Danny's chest, but he was slowly inching himself up Danny's body. His head moved up onto Danny's neck. Danny felt his mouth clamp onto his skin.

He jerked away, pulling at Ian's hair. He felt as if he was caught in some outrageous nightmare. He almost laughed.

Ian said nothing. He pulled frantically to get back. Danny could feel the insistent rubbing against his hip. He could smell the feverish sweat come off him in waves. He had succeeded in worming a hand inside Danny's shirt. His silence was dreadful, intense. There was no passion in him. He was like a dog over-excited by the scent of a bitch in heat. He panted in Danny's ear, his breath hoarse and raw. Danny felt his stomach heave.

Suddenly there was a shout across the yard, feet running, and then Ian was being dragged off. There was a noise that could have been a slap.

Danny lay there a moment then levered himself up onto his elbows.

"Get back into the house." His mother's voice was angry, but Danny could hear no shock in it. He could see her dressing gown, pale in the feeble light.

He sensed Ian's reluctance, but it was impossible to see his face from down here. They were just two headless bodies. He struggled up. His mother's face appeared in the doorway. Her eyes ran over his face, searching. He heard the kitchen door slam shut.

"You were taking my car," she said. It wasn't a question.

Danny nodded, letting his eyes slide away from hers. But she didn't ask him why. She didn't ask him anything. She turned away for a moment, then back, as if she had

made a decision. She reached across him and picked up his bag, throwing it in the back, then she looked him in the eye. "Give me the money."

Danny reached into his pocket and reluctantly returned it to her.

"Stay here. I'll be ten minutes, no longer. Promise me you'll wait here."

Promise? What the hell did he have to lose now? "I'll wait," he said.

She turned and went back across the yard and into the house.

Danny timed her. She was back in exactly eight minutes. She was dressed and carrying her shoulder bag.

She climbed into the passenger seat and handed Danny the key. "You drive."

She turned in her seat and put her bag in the back next to his.

Danny hadn't even noticed that she had taken the key, to make sure he wouldn't go anyway.

He turned on the ignition and pulled down into the access road. It was exactly 5:58. There was no traffic. He didn't have to wait long for his mother to speak.

"This is about John, isn't it?"

Danny slowed the car, aware of the way his foot had pressed down on the accelerator, but he didn't have time to frame a reply before she said, "If you expect me to help I expect some answers."

He said tightly, "It's about getting out of here. Period."

"And away from John."

Danny turned to her. "Listen, I was leaving. No clear ideas, no burning ambitions, just getting out - before you and Ian decided to rewrite the script, that is. And I don't expect your help. I don't expect anything from you. This was your idea."

"You were stealing my money."

"He stole mine."

"Is that why you were fighting?"

"I was fighting, he was doing something quite different."

She chose not to hear that. "How much was it?"

He shrugged. "£400 maybe."

She clucked at the sum then said, "And what's he done with it?"

"Who knows?"

"Didn't you ask him?"

"Of course I bloody asked him, this is Ian."

His mother looked away abruptly. "Slow down, we're turning next right."

Danny slowed, frowning at the road ahead. "Jerrett's?"

"That's right."

Danny braked to a standstill. "No way."

"And why not?"

"I'm not going to Jerrett's."

"Then where are you going?"

Danny didn't answer her.

"Well, if I was you I'd consider going there now."

"No."

"Fine. Then perhaps you'd like to go back home and we can ask John what this is about?"

Danny said nothing.

"Look," his mother's voice had changed gear, gone into what Ian called her cruel-to-be-kind mode, "you've got no money, no job and nowhere to go. I'm prepared to offer you free accommodation until you sort yourself out."

"Sort myself out?" Danny turned on her furiously. "Maybe you ought to give that

speech to John."

As always he realised too late what he'd said. He could see the self-satisfaction on her mouth. She was the one person in the family where you could see a real resemblance to Ian. That tight unforgiving mouth, something manipulative about it.

"So it is about John?"

"What if it is?" he demanded belligerently.

"It's not news to me, you know. Think I don't know what's been going on?"

"Oh, give it a rest." He ran a hand through his hair, turning away from her angrily.

"Danny, I am trying to help you."

Danny swung on her. "Then give me the money."

She took a breath, let it out again, mouth already a disapproving line. "Running away from him isn't the solution."

"Oh, isn't it? You'd know I suppose?"

A dull colour crept into her face. She retorted more sharply than normal, "More than you'd think. You're not unique in his obsessions."

Danny tore his eyes away from hers to look at the sill, then the dashboard, then the steering wheel and, finally, out of the side window so that he needn't see any part of her at all. He said quickly, "So I go to Jerrett's, then what? What if one of them turns up?"

"They won't. That's why you were sent to clean out the hayloft. I've finally managed to talk your father into letting it as a holiday home. And I've changed the locks, so John won't be paying it any more nocturnal visits either, I can assure you."

Danny looked at her. Did she know about John dragging him up there the night before? But she offered no further explanations so he asked, "How do I live?"

"I'll take care of that."

Danny stared at her. "Why are you doing this?"

"Because it's long overdue. John should have been sent packing long ago."

"You'll have a job convincing Dad of that."

"I won't need to convince anyone, John will leave."

"John? You're joking. You couldn't winkle him out of there with a crowbar. He's in for life."

"John will leave," she said again, emphatically.

Danny looked at her for a long moment then turned away. "So what about me? It still doesn't account for my day. Am I to stay there forever being kept by you as the mysterious holiday lodger?"

"You can come back home."

Danny looked at her. "After John's left?"

"That's right."

"You're nuts."

His mother coloured up. Danny spoke quickly, before she could. "What makes you think I'd want to? I was leaving, remember?"

"With no money?"

Danny stared at her. She went back into her persuasive headmistress mode. "You can come home, establish your savings again, then do as you see fit, only this time there will be no John..." She stopped. Danny was unsure whether she was looking for some elusive word or had stopped herself short of saying something she shouldn't. He couldn't resist it.

"No John prowling around the house looking for somewhere to shove it?" he offered.

His mother looked at him. She was hot-faced, but there was something hard and uncharacteristically unflinching in her eyes. "That doesn't shock me Danny. I'm just surprised you want to talk about it - now."

Danny turned his face away. "I don't."

"Fine. Then I suggest we get to Jerrett's before one of your brothers comes down this road and catches us."

Danny glanced at the dashboard clock, then at his mother, then started the car.

Danny followed his mother into the living room. She pulled open the thick curtains with a grating scrape of metal on metal. Danny could see the clouds of dust boiling through the air. "That's probably the first time they've been open in fifteen years," she said.

He looked around the room. It was bare except for an ugly old sideboard and a rusty red sofa that matched the curtains. The grate was full of soot and the ash of burnt paper.

Danny had never even seen into this room from the outside. The exterior of the building had always presented that same blank, closed-up face. All its curtains shut. Nobody home.

"Well?" his mother asked.

Danny pushed his hands in his pockets. "What can I say?"

"There's a Calor gas heater upstairs. You can use that until I get the chimney swept."

Danny nodded.

"And you'll find the bed in the room upstairs is made up. You can thank your brother for that too." His mother's voice was full of distaste, her John-tone as Ian called it.

Danny turned to look at her, but she had moved off into the kitchen saying, "The back bedroom's locked - I seem to have lost the key - but as I recall it's a poky little hole anyway. You're better off in the big room." He heard cupboard doors bang. "We'll need to get some food in for you."

She went on, but Danny wasn't listening. His mind was still struggling with the made-up bed, the heater.

His mother came back into the living room. "...I'll get it this afternoon, that'll be safer."

Danny wanted to ask, 'Than what?' but didn't.

"Right, I'm off." She smiled her rare tight smile. "I must be at the breakfast post, keep everything normal."

"What are you going to tell them?"

"Just the truth, that you've left."

Danny shook his head. "They won't just accept that."

They both knew he meant John wouldn't accept it, but neither said so.

"I have my persuasive side too Danny."

She turned away and picked up the car keys. "Fine, I'll see you about three then. There's a brush and so forth in the kitchen - should you wish to start clearing up." And she almost smiled at him again, then was gone.

She had an hour till they came in for lunch. She had decided on a slight change of plan and had gone shopping for Danny that morning. She'd left her purchases locked in the boot of the car.

She began making the meal, tidying the wreckage from the kitchen, evidence of her absence. She could read the confusion and disruption in the half-eaten bits of toast, the half-drunk teacups. What had Ian told them? Not that he had been caught clambering over Danny like a randy dog, of that she was sure. But he had

unmistakably been trying to stop him. It surprised her. Ian had no love for Danny, despite their years of plotting in corners, so why go so far as to take his money away from him? Assuming, of course, that it was actually intended to stop him and wasn't just spite.

And there was still John to deal with. There was always John, like a second shadow, dangerous, unpredictable, pregnant with ugly possibilities, repellent and seductive at once, utterly incomprehensible to her. Her heart sank at the thought of the ensuing battle.

And Robbie, how would he take it? Time was she could have been sure of that. Robbie and Danny were enemies, it was that simple. But new images niggled at her mind. That evening in the living room. Another when she'd walked into the kitchen and caught them standing close together, something about Robbie's stance giving everything away. Only she wasn't sure what it was he had given away.

"Where is he?" The door slammed just as she was taking the pie from the oven, startling her into burning her hand. She wheeled, sucking her injured wrist. John Jackson Moore, her husband, stood there.

"Well, where is he?"

"Who?" she said stupidly.

"Danny, who the hell else?"

"He's gone." She turned back to the oven, picking up the dish and placing it carefully on a raffia mat on the table.

"Once again." He shook out his jacket irritably and hung it up. Was it raining? She looked out the window.

"So where has he gone this time?" He pulled out a chair and sat down.

She began dishing up his meal. "I don't know."

"So where have you been then?"

"Shopping."

He looked at her. "Is this to be one of his twenty-four hour jobs?"

"I wouldn't know."

"Is that right?" He pulled his plate across to himself, looking up at her. "I'm short-handed now, you realise that?"

"I'm sure he didn't mean to inconvenience you."

"Didn't mean doesn't get the work done." He took a mouthful of pie. "So what's his excuse this time?" He was no longer looking at her, as if Danny's reasons were an afterthought, not as relevant as his actual absence.

"You make it sound like he does this every day of the week."

He ignored that.

She said, "I should imagine he was fed up."

That made him jerk his head up. "Fed up? When I've got a hundred acres just sitting there waiting for him to grace them with his royal presence? He picks the times."

"I can't imagine being fed up goes by the clock."

"Nothing about him goes by the clock, or ever has."

He began eating again, fiercely, seemingly absorbed in what he was doing. "That bloody face of his will get him into serious trouble one of these days."

She looked at him. He looked back at her, lifting his head in exactly the same way as John, Danny too, if she was forced to admit it. It was an unnerving gesture in all of them.

"All his life that face of his has been getting him into trouble, and it isn't going to get any better, not until somebody rearranges it for him, or he loses his looks altogether."

"Are you saying he's to blame for the way other people see him? That's nonsense."

She got up out of her seat on the pretext of moving a pot off the ring.

"Is it?" His hand was arrested, fork pointing at her. "Looks like his are as much trouble in a boy as they are in a girl. More. There's no-one to settle them down. No-one to come along and knock them up and knock it out of them. You never can knock it out of the likes of him."

She looked at him, the disgust evident on her face.

"Call it all the names you like," he said sharply, "all that one's suffering from is the two minutes boredom he has to endure catching his breath after he diddles with himself. He's being led by his prick, and he always will be, because the whole world's feeding it, wanting their hands about him. Christ knows, I've tried to control him, give him some discipline, but you've undermined every effort I've ever made with him. You'd change your tune if you'd seen what I've seen. He's bad, rotten. It's in his blood."

He didn't seem to see anything incongruous in the statement. She wondered exactly whose blood he had in mind, resisted the temptation to tell him that whoever's it was, at least it wasn't hers.

He had fallen silent. She dropped down onto the chair opposite him, caught by the arresting sight of his hand. It was trembling.

"You know," he said abruptly, "when Robbie first came here I thought, He's going to be exactly the same. But he's not the same breed, even though there were days I saw him just as restless, not minding his work. It never went anywhere. It always passed. But that dirty little brat is a different class of animal. It's beyond his looks, it's something rotten in his blood."

The door banged suddenly, making Margaret jump. Ian came in. His face looked tight, as if his skin hurt, or he had an ache about him that was just waiting to turn vicious.

"Your brother has disappeared." His father began eating again. "And don't waste your breath asking where he is. We don't know. Man of bloody mystery."

Margaret served Ian without looking at him. He, in turn, seemed jumpy with her, looking at her edgily, like a child afraid he is to be reprimanded later after company has gone.

John and Rab came in together. John was silent, tense, eyes immediately fixed on hers.

"He's gone," his father said, shovelling food in. "And we've no idea where, only that the fragile soul was fed-up."

"You don't know where?" John asked his mother directly, as if his father hadn't spoken. There were deep grey shadows under his eyes.

"No. Man of bloody mystery," his father answered before she could speak.

"Did you take him?"

His father looked up. Rab looked up. Everyone looked up.

"I gave him a lift to the station," she admitted. She got more food from the stove, began putting it out.

"The station?" His father was staring at her. "I thought you said you'd been shopping?"

"I was, after I took him to the station."

"You took him," he said flatly.

"He wanted to go."

"So you took him. Jesus Christ." He pushed his plate away and got up from the table, striding across the kitchen. He snatched his jacket off the peg. "Jesus Christ," he said again, yanking it on. "He always could wheedle his fucking way round you."

He yanked the door open savagely. "You lot. Out in half an hour. We're short-handed now thanks to your bloody mother."

And he went out, slamming the door hard enough to rattle the crockery.

The rest of the meal was eaten in uncomfortable silence. Margaret felt as if every man in the room would have spoken volumes if they had been alone with her. Only Rab seemed comfortable, or at least simply bemused.

Their father's restriction on thirty minutes seemed to have dampened any possibility for conversation. They ate like prisoners, silent and tense.

They got up and left in the same tense silence they had come in. John was the last to go. "I'll see you later," he said. His voice seemed inflectionless, without any special meaning or significance, but somehow it still sounded like a threat.

John came into her room that evening. She had escaped briefly to think, to organise, but she didn't get a chance. He came in without knocking.

"You might knock first." She watched him close the door carefully, stand against it.

"I might," he agreed.

She closed her wardrobe door. John continued to watch her, unspeaking, unmoving, except for his hand inserting and removing a cigarette - you couldn't call it smoking.

She felt as if her skin became itchy under his gaze. She sat at her dressing table and studied him in the mirror. "Well?" she said finally.

He took the cigarette out again. "I might ask you the same thing."

"What do you want John?"

"What are you offering?"

She banged down a jar that she had only lifted to cover her nervousness. "Don't play stupid games. What d'you want?"

He pushed off the door and crossed to the foot of the bed. He sat down and studied her face at closer range in the mirror. "Tell me where he is."

"I don't know where he is. You heard me at lunchtime." She began rummaging in a drawer. She tried to inject anger into her voice, but it sounded shallow, almost apologetic.

"Like fuck you don't." His voice was brittle, without humour or good-nature. She looked up at him, stupidly startled at the abrupt change.

"Why do you want to know?" She stared at him.

He stared back. "Why do you want to hide it?"

"I thought you'd be glad to be rid of him. Now you've got no reason to stay in a place you so obviously despise."

"Well you thought wrong. Where is he?"

"I told you, I don't know," she repeated, this time with more conviction.

It gave her a strange pleasurable sense of power to cross him. Not for a long time had she actually held anything he might value.

Slowly, purposefully, he dropped his cigarette onto the carpet and ground it in. Her mouth opened in protest, a dull flush of anger stained her skin. "Of all the dirty..." But she could go no further.

He was smiling again, unperturbed. "I'll wait Margaret, I'll be patience itself, because sooner or later you're going to let it slip."

He stood up and walked to the door then he turned back. "But let's hope it's sooner rather than later, because waiting bores me, and you know how destructive I can get when I'm bored."

She glared at his retreating back in the mirror, willing him to trip and break his neck, but he simply shut the door quite quietly, without any sign of temper, leaving Margaret

and her reflection completely alone.

SEVENTEEN

Danny prowled around the house irritably. He must have been mad to agree to this. The place gave him the creeps. Besides, he wasn't used to sitting around idle.

He heard a car drive into the yard and looked out the window. At last, the cavalry. His mother climbed out of the car with two large cans of paint. He went out to meet her. "What the hell's all this?" he asked.

"What does it look like? Here." She handed him the keys. "The other stuff's in the boot, bring it in."

"Other stuff?" he asked her retreating back, but she didn't answer. Danny sighed and crossed to the car and began relaying the strippers and fillers, papers and pastes, into the living room.

"Sweep's coming tomorrow," she said, pushing the front door shut behind him as he brought the last lot in. She followed him into the living room.

"Listen," he said as he dropped the rolls of paper on the floor. "I can't stay here, I'll go off my head. I need to get my money."

She looked at him, eyes familiarly flinty. "Suggestions?"

"For what?" Danny said blankly.

"Your money."

"Ian's got it."

"You think."

"No. I know where it is."

"And?"

"Well, I need you to get it for me, don't I?"

"So where is it?"

"John's room."

"*John's* room?" She stared at him.

Danny nodded, keeping his eyes on hers.

"Why in goodness' name would he put it in John's room?"

"Because he's Ian."

She looked at him for a long moment then turned away. "And you expect me to search John's room, on an off-chance?"

"You know when he's out. It's safe enough."

She turned her head to him. "It's obvious you haven't seen him recently."

"Why?"

His mother turned back to him, looking at him so long Danny coloured up, saying aggressively, "So I want to know he's suffering. I think I'm entitled to a little revenge."

She said nothing to that saying instead, "So I find it, supposing your premise is correct, then what?"

"I go."

"Where?"

"That's my business."

His mother looked at him. "And if I refuse?"

"I'll go back and get it myself."

She nodded, still watching him, then said, "Well, I suppose I don't have any option. As I have no intention of standing back and letting you endanger your life, I might as well endanger mine."

Danny laughed, "Oh come on..."

His mother didn't smile.

He said, "He's hardly likely to..." his smile sliding away. He never finished it.

"He's unbalanced and totally unpredictable. He always was, even as a small boy. He was overindulged and self-seeking as a child and as an adult he's forty times worse. He's completely ungovernable, thanks to your father. He thinks he can do anything he likes. Well, he's about to find out that he can't."

Danny wanted to say, Can't he? But he said nothing.

His mother turned away and became suddenly brisk. "Right, in the meantime you can start earning your keep. This place needs redecorated and you've nothing else to do."

"Fine," he said, relieved somehow at the change of subject.

"And you can unpack the groceries."

"Okay." Danny took them through to the kitchen, putting on the light. Christ, this place was dingy. He would start the decorating in here. Not that it mattered, he wasn't staying that long.

His mother came through, carrying cleaning materials.

"When will you look for it?" he asked, packing tea and coffee into a cupboard he'd just brushed free of mouse droppings.

"What?"

"The money." Danny glanced over his shoulder at her.

"In a day or two."

"What?" Danny turned to her.

"Danny," she put down the large blue bottle she was holding, "do you want John to find you?"

It took him a minute to answer. He shook his head, colouring up. "What the hell are you saying that for?"

"Because you seem to have some foolish notion that since you've walked out the door you're out of sight, out of mind as far as he's concerned. He's practically checking the cupboards for you. He's grilled me, your brother, even Robbie, although he has no suspicions whatsoever about them. He knows it's me. He's already threatened me. And what do you think he'll do if he finds me searching his room, or even suspects that I've searched it, or is *told* that I've searched it?"

Danny shrugged and looked away.

"Exactly. In short, John's deeply suspicious and Ian's happily feeding that suspicion. Now will you let me handle this my way?"

Danny nodded and turned away.

They went on unpacking in silence for a little while longer then his mother banged the cupboard door under the sink and straightened up. "Right, I need to get back. You're on your own until tomorrow. I'm not sure when I'll be round, but you've got plenty to do."

Danny nodded, feeling a sinking of the heart at the prospect of a night alone in the place.

He followed his mother out to the hall and stood at the open door with her. "It's in a Golden Virginia tin," he reminded her, "the money."

She nodded and zipped up her jacket, pulling her shoulder bag on. "Tomorrow then."

Danny nodded.

His mother left.

Rab could feel him standing there in the dark. He switched on the front light and pulled the door closed. He hung up his jacket. Maybe he ought to take out his dick and wiggle it around a bit like live bait for a worm.

He shrugged into his boiler suit. "Come on out Ian. I don't plan on jerking off for at least an hour. You'll get rheumatics hanging around that long." He sat down on the tractor step and began the process of rolling up.

Ian emerged silently from the shadows. Rab didn't look up until he was on the point of sealing his cigarette. When he did Ian was watching his tongue lick along the paper with a grim-faced avidity.

"Looks even better now Ian, doesn't it? When you can't have it any more."

"I could still tell," Ian said with a barely resigned hostility.

"Sure you could," Rab began patting, standing up to reach down inside the boiler suit into his jeans pocket. Ian watched his hand like a dog expecting to be presented with a biscuit. Rab withdrew his hand, lit his cigarette and sat down again. "Only what would be the point? Nothing to gain, everything to lose."

"You conceited bastard. D'you think I'd give a fuck if I never saw you again?"

Rab inhaled deeply and released the smoke through his nose. "What's wrong? Doesn't it feel so good this way round?"

"What makes you think it felt good at all?"

"Oh don't make me laugh. You'd take it any fucking way you can get it, just like the rest of your stinking family."

Abruptly Ian smiled. "What's wrong? Ditched you, has he?"

"Fucking shut up."

"What a shame. You'll just have to stick to screwing his big brother then. He's the only one who even remotely resembles him."

Rab smacked him. Hard. Full in the face. Ian stumbled back into the workbench, caught the small of his back and went down with an almost comic abruptness.

Rab stood back, shocked at himself, listening to Ian's hoarse breathing.

When he spoke it was rough, as if talking hurt him. "I kissed him before he went, and you know..." he stopped, taking a careful breath, "I'd have done a lot worse if he'd let me."

He looked up at Rab, his face a pasty white. He was neither gloating nor smug, just stating facts. "First time I think I ever truly understood the fascination. He even smells good."

"Oh Christ," Rab said running his hands through his hair, "I don't believe I'm hearing this."

Ian dropped his head back wearily, looked up at the ceiling. "Poor Rab. You know, I think confession must be in the air, I've heard that expression a lot recently."

He looked at Rab again, suddenly intent on him. "I didn't have the slightest intention of doing it. I don't think I could even call it a snatched opportunity, that's what makes it so weird. At best it was what my mother would call 'inappropriate behaviour'."

"Shut up, you're making me sick."

Ian looked at him and smiled. It was the first time in as long Rab had seen his natural smile. Perversely, it looked worse than his usual imitation. "But it's true. Just because it makes you sick doesn't mean it isn't true."

He was thoughtful for a minute or two then he pushed himself up more carefully against the bench. He held his back as if it was fragile.

Rab sat down heavily, dropping his head onto his hands.

"He was horrified, completely panic-stricken, but you know..." He stopped, listening to his mind sorting words. Rab was still, expectant, knowing what he was going to say before he said it. "I think he was enjoying it somewhere inside, just like he enjoys it with John. He can't help enjoying..."

"I think you should shut the fuck up, before I knock your teeth down your throat." Rab fixed him with a tight stare. "And I think you should get out while you can still walk."

Ian smiled again. Rab could see the old Ian surfacing, sly, destructive. He got up slowly, as if he was made of glass, and walked over to the door, then he stopped and looked back at Rab thoughtfully. "You know, I think you've suspected it all along. Even when you first took him on you knew nothing had really changed, only you were so desperate for it you didn't care."

Rab jerked upright in one convulsive movement. "Get out, before I wring your poisonous little neck."

And that made Ian smile some more, before he turned and went out the door.

Margaret closed the door carefully, wondering why she felt like tiptoeing. She was quite alone in the house and in no danger of being surprised.

She stood in John's room, feeling how unfamiliar it was. She came in here once a week to pick up dirty linen, and deliver clean, and that was it. Sometimes John beat her to it and she didn't even do that much. John didn't like anyone in his room and that suited her fine.

She began with the chest of drawers. She was filled with a sense of urgency. She must find the money before Ian tried to recover it, or worse still, John came across it by accident. The money was Danny's sole means of escape and she could not afford to let it fall into the hands of a third party, or to alert John to the possibility that Danny had not gone far.

Where would Ian put such a thing? She tried to see the place as Ian saw it, but she shared nothing in common with him. After all, who was Ian? She was his mother and she didn't know.

She opened the wardrobe and felt in John's jacket pockets. No, too risky, he would never put it there.

She stood back, closing the doors quietly, and peered up onto the top of the wardrobe. Nothing.

She got down on her knees and peered under the bed. A pile of pornographic magazines lay there, thick with dust. She stood up and dusted herself down with distaste.

She heard the back door slam. She stood still for a moment then crossed to the door and slid out into the hall. The door slammed again. She held her breath, listening. She heard the pick-up start up in the yard and let her breath out. One of them back for keys, that's all. She went back into the room, still alert to the slightest sound, but the house was completely still and silent.

She crossed the floor to the small cupboard under the sink. Not enough room to hide a measle in here, but nevertheless...

She looked inside. There was something, curled around the waste pipe. She pulled it out gingerly and carefully uncurled it. More pornography. But there was something different about these magazines. There were two of them, and they both featured young men on the covers.

She began leafing through them, studying each page almost minutely, her stomach clenched and nauseous, like a betrayed woman finally finding her husband's love letters, the damning evidence, far too important and long-imagined to be dealt with summarily. They were hardcore, filthily erect, everything red and hard and slavering like so much meat.

It was when she got to the centrefold that the photos fell out. She let them fall to the ground barely noticed because she was still staring at the boy spread widely across the pages. He was Danny's double, his doppelganger. She turned the page. There were maybe a half dozen more images of him, all equally obscene. She couldn't believe her eyes. Never in her wildest imaginings had John sunk this low. This was

proof.

The boy was older, she could see that now, and his hair was dyed, and there was something both harder and more effeminate about him, but he was unmistakably some kind of attempt at recreating Danny. It was then her brain registered the photographs lying at her feet. She bent down and picked them up, turning them over.

They were poorly exposed, as if they had been taken in inadequate light, but they were still clear enough. Three Polaroid photographs of a young man asleep in bed. Genuinely, deeply asleep, like a child sleeps. The blankets had been pulled down off his body to his thighs, just far enough to show him off. He was indescribably beautiful and, like the boy in the magazine, very busily erect. He was also unmistakably Danny. The real Danny.

The door clicked shut with a dreadful finality. "Find what you were looking for?"

Margaret stood open-mouthed, the photographs clutched convulsively in her hands, her face ashen.

John looked at her, at the two hectic spots of colour on her cheeks, back to her hands again, rapidly adding up. "You shouldn't have been looking." He made it sound like a threat, like Bluebeard and his little room.

"I..." I what? she thought hysterically, "I wasn't looking for this."

"No? Well you found it all the same." He waited like a headmaster, as if she was the one guilty of the crime. She felt a sudden fury at the cheek of him.

"And what have I found exactly?"

He laughed. A short, sharp bark more like a shout of derision. "What do you think?"

"Did you take these?"

He simply looked at her, head cocked to one side, waiting for her to catch up with him. Waiting for the inevitability of her conclusions.

"Why?" she demanded.

He looked at the ceiling, then licked his lips as if he were considering. Then he studied the carpet thoughtfully. Finally he said, "How about for a practical joke?" His head came up again, studying her, challenging her.

She shook her head without answering.

"Then you tell me."

"Because you're a filthy..." but she couldn't control the words. They stopped, stifled by the possibility of what she might say. He was looking away from her, smiling contemptuously, like a roué amused by a virgin's gaucherie. She found herself saying, "They've been taken at different times."

"One this year, two last summer." Then he smiled at her, an ugly smile. "And there's more, going further back. Would you like to see those too?"

"How did you get them?" she demanded.

"You don't really want to hear the answer to that. What you really want to hear is an excuse, something that shows a proper shame, a proper remorse." He shook his head as if she sickened him. "Well that's too bad, because I don't feel any remorse. I don't feel any shame. Sad, isn't it?"

"Have you been interfering with him?" It sounded preposterous even as she said it, like something some sad old family uncle might do, not John.

This time his smile was genuine. It looked somehow worse than anything else that had gone before. "Have I been *interfering* with him? Do you mean did I touch him up, feel his private parts?"

She grew hotter, angrier, under his sarcasm.

"Not as much as I would have liked, believe me. Not nearly as much as I would have liked."

"You're disgusting. How could you? Your own brother..." She petered out, lost in her own revulsion.

"Believe me it was easy. I doubt if even Jesus Christ himself could have resisted it. Danny is a very special taste."

"What did you do to him?"

"Why do you want to know?" The question felt loaded, his eyes narrowed with suspicion.

"I'm his mother, if I needed a reason. And don't think I won't take these to your father. Maybe now he'll believe me."

His eyes seemed to suddenly accuse her, as if he could see things beyond what she could see herself. She felt as if Danny's image burned into her fingers. He said softly, almost consideringly, "No, I don't think you will."

"I'm going to your father," she asserted.

John reached out and pulled the photographs from her hand as easily as if she had no power in her fingers at all. He looked at them carefully, fanning them out like a card sharper, then pulled one out and offered it back to her. "Here, have this one. I'm keeping the others." He looked at her insolently. "Since I no longer have the real thing these will have to do." His mouth smiled, but it did not reach his eyes.

She yanked it out of his hand and marched to the door. "I'm going to show this to your father right now." She pulled the door open. She sounded as if she was trying to convince herself, not him.

"No," he said again, making no attempt to stop her, "I don't think you will."

Her heart was suddenly racing, full of air, feeling in the pit of her stomach exactly what he was about to say, knowing the truth of it before she even heard the words.

He moved close beside her, and whispered in her ear, "You wouldn't want to share him with anyone else, would you?"

She slapped him. Hard. A huge satisfying smack that brought weals up on his face. He grabbed her hand, crushingly tight around the wrist, his face an ugly mask of anger - and then his expression changed, softened, almost like some saintly possession, some religious extreme of forgiveness, and he bent his head and lingeringly kissed the palm of her hand. "Poor Margaret, you probably want him more than all the rest of us put together."

His mother wrenched her hand free and slammed out the room.

EIGHTEEN

It was eight o' clock, and already it looked like a winter's evening. It was going to be a long cold winter. She could feel it in her bones. No autumn, just straight into cold and damp and howling winds.

The rain began to spit viciously, almost like sleet, just as she turned up the road to Jerrett's. She felt as if she was escaping. The house had become impossible, charged with an oppressive atmosphere of suspense. Everyone seemed to be watching her, waiting for her to make a mistake. At first she'd been confident that only Ian suspected she knew where Danny was, but now she felt as if they all did, despite the fact that Ian almost certainly hadn't passed his knowledge on. If he had she'd have known about it, John would have made sure of that.

The house was all lit up, looking curiously festive. Smoke was swirling in the damp air as she climbed from the car. It was like coming home.

Danny opened the door and grinned impulsively. "Welcome, fair damsel, to my palatial mansion." It felt like years since she'd seen him smile like that. The house smelt of paint, fruity and heady with fumes.

"I've had the windows open all day, but it still stinks."

"Doesn't matter, it smells fresh and clean."

"Come and see the living room." Danny pulled her arm.

He had finished the walls and was working on the woodwork. The fire was sharp and hot, roaring away in the grate.

Danny followed her eyes. "I feel as though that's the first heat I've had in ten years. I feel almost human again."

She looked at him. "Well, I'll make your day then." She held up the bag she was carrying. "Chinese take-away."

"Hey, great." His enthusiasm was infectious. "I'll get plates. I only had beans on toast for tea." He turned and grinned at her. "Not used to cooking for myself." And he laughed as he disappeared into the kitchen.

He brought plates back and they pulled the sofa closer to the fire. Danny sat on the floor and dished up. Margaret had brought a bottle of wine in from the car saying, "To celebrate your freedom." And Danny had smiled easily and gone to get glasses.

Now they sat before the fire and listened to the rain beating against the windows. The paint fumes were heavy in the heat and conspired with the wine to make them sleepier.

Danny stretched out beside her on the carpet and closed his eyes. She had moved down onto the floor at his suggestion and was leaning back now against the sofa. Such relaxed behaviour felt hugely unfamiliar to her. She shifted her weight, looking down into his face, and said, "We must get you some furniture."

"Mm." No protests, but then he didn't really seem to be listening.

Margaret looked down at him again and realised he looked just like he did in the photograph, half asleep, drifting.

She looked away. How could she have forgotten the photograph? For that matter why had she remembered?

She looked back down at him. It was no use. Now that the image had leapt into her head it was going to sit there, leering at her. She studied his face, thrown into half-shadow by the firelight, his hair turned molten red in the golden light, the long stretched length of his body. His breathing was regular, heavy. He'd fallen asleep.

She felt the quickening of an impulse, only dimly understood, and which she did

not stop to examine. She reached out a hand and stroked his hair.

He didn't move. His breathing was still deep. His body looked slack and relaxed, his lips very slightly parted. She ran a fingertip over his mouth.

He folded his lips as if they itched. She held her breath, but he still did not wake. She smiled, but it was an edgy thing, full of anxiety and tension. There was something compelling in this urge to touch him. She was not a tactile person, she disliked being touched herself, but Danny had always provoked this odd response in her. He was like some kind of beautiful but dangerous animal that you stroked at your peril. It was still alien enough to make her heart thump and her skin crawl, even after all these years.

He had his shirt open, as if he'd taken it off at some point and just carelessly pulled it back on, stuffing it inside his trousers rather than bother fastening it. She slid her hand inside. Her head thumped as if she had a headache coming on. The fire shifted suddenly in the grate, dropping ash. Her hand jerked, but Danny slept on. She pushed her hand more purposefully inside. His chest felt solid with young muscle, like his father's had once been. Her face flushed. She pulled her hand out.

His skin was beautiful, soft and plush, like a peach. How could anyone looking at her, dark and earthbound as she was, possibly believe that she had borne this boy? He was like a stranger to her, as if someone had stolen her child and replaced him. She felt robbed of her motherhood. She couldn't connect herself with him. She felt no protectiveness, no tenderness. He was alien flesh.

She let her hand pull the shirt out from his trousers. Gently. He had his hands behind his head and the shirt fell immediately in soft folds at the sides of his body, exposing his chest. She could see the fine hair seam running up to his belly button from below the waistband of his trousers. He looked older than he did in the photograph. She supposed he was, although surely not enough to make a difference? His nipples were very small and brown. She pressed her hand flat on his belly. She left it there, surprised at the warmth of him, the tautness, the odd blankness of his beauty.

She slid the tips of her fingers under the waistband of his jeans. He was stretched out. It was an easy thing to do. She felt the narrow seam of hair, thicker, glossier, but not that sickening mat of his father's. This was somehow childish, not threatening. It lay sleek on his belly, like a soft pelt. Her hand was squeezed slightly with every breath he took. She slid it in further and felt the waistband of his shorts. It stopped her as effectively as barbed wire. She did not have the conviction of her innocence to pass that elastic, no matter how much she'd had to drink.

She let her hand lie there, unmoving. Danny breathed in and out easily, without effort. His face was completely relaxed. She watched it, hypnotically running her eyes over its contours again and again. Gradually her hand did what it wanted to do without her knowing anything about it. It eased her neat short nails under the waistband. Past the knuckles it could reach in quickly and easily to the hot, slightly damp darkness. The hair here was thick but still not wiry, and deep in its coils lay a sleeping snake. Her hand brushed it. She moved her head slightly but still watched Danny's face. Her fingers walked it into her palm, wrapping around it, holding it there. Her heart thudded dully, as if it was slowed by an excess of drink.

She felt it stir.

It felt like a dream, an imagining. You wanted it to happen, were afraid it might happen, and so you thought it did happen. But this wasn't a dream, it did move in her hand, slowly at first, and then with sickening speed.

It grew corpulently fat. As it emerged from inside its skin she could feel the sticky touch of its swollenness adhere to her fingers.

Within seconds he was erect. To her he felt hugely erect. She saw his eyes move behind their lids as if he were dreaming. She let go, pulling her hand out slowly, rigidly,

like someone withdrawing from a scorpion poised to strike.

She freed her hand and looked down at him. Her breathing was rapid. She could see it, large and hard beneath the fabric of his jeans. She wiped her hand on her sweater and turned her head away. She began buttoning his shirt, carefully, from the neck down, not looking lower than his navel, but she knew it was still there, lurking just outside her vision, like a summonsed demon that would not return to its resting place without the taste of blood.

She wanted to tuck in his shirt, but she couldn't bring herself to put her hand back in there again. She sat there staring at his face.

If she was to unzip his trousers right now she'd see him just as he looked in the photograph, just as John had seen him.

Her hand reached out and pulled at his zip.

Danny's hand wrapped itself around her wrist. His eyes were open, looking at her from under his lashes. "What are you doing?" His voice was thick, heavy with sleep or drink.

"I..." She didn't know. She didn't have a clue what she was going to say because she didn't know what she had been doing. She'd forgotten as clearly as a waker from a dream forgets everything that has passed before.

Danny didn't move. He still held her hand, eyes half-closed, watching her like a drugged cat, half-dangerous, half-indifferent.

She looked at him, held by his eyes, hand clamped to his belly, barely touching the head of his erection. She could feel the slight swell of it under her pinkie.

He moved her hand down over it with a slight firm pressure, as if he was guiding her over its contours. She looked at him and didn't know him. She recognised the features, but couldn't recognise the face. He was hard and masculine, years older than his body, filled with indefinable urges and longings. She was feeling the erection of a strange man. I'm drunk, she thought wildly. She felt his penis jump beneath her hand. It was rock-hard, straining.

"You shouldn't have touched me," he said. "Now it won't go away."

"Don't talk nonsense." But her voice was tremulous. I sound afraid, she thought.

He shook his head, tiny shakes, barely perceptible. His eyes closed like a man drifting back into sleep. "Do it," he said. His voice was a whispered command. He lifted his hand from hers, freeing it. There was no uncertainty in him.

She snatched her hand back convulsively. She held it to her chest as if imprisoning it.

"Finish it," he whispered. She wasn't sure if he had actually spoken. He lay still, seemingly asleep, except his breathing was wrong.

She wasn't even sure what he meant, could only assume he meant she should finish what she had started, and what she had started was a desire to see him as John had, to be his equal, to see him naked.

She undid his belt, slowly, uncertainly. When she had done that she wiped her hands on her skirt as if to rub off the feel of the thick leather, the heavy warmth of it. She lifted the zip and pulled it down. It seemed to drag like a ton weight, resisting her. She pulled his trousers open and saw the huge ugly shape of it under the loose cotton of his shorts. She could smell the rich salty smell of him, like juicy meat. She felt her mouth water and felt sick.

She pulled the waistband of his shorts up and away from his body then tugged it down. His erection sprung out, peeled back and obscene. The colour was all wrong. He was as red and hard as his father was dark and swarthy. An image of John flashed through her head.

"Touch me."

She shook her head. She *wouldn't* touch him, not in that state, not with that filthy

78

thing... she wouldn't even say it.

"It hurts me." Danny's voice was whispery, without substance. "Touch me."

She lifted her hand - she could see it shaking - and pressed it gently along the length of him.

He groaned. A low, soft groan like a man easing a cramped leg, massaging an aching muscle.

She jerked her hand away, suddenly understanding what he was doing. But he caught her hand, horrifically fast, totally at odds with the incredible languor in his body. He pressed her fingers around his penis, holding them there, applying a subtle pressure to the swollen head as if he was trying to squeeze some of the blood back out, ease his distress.

"No," she whispered, trying to pull it back. But he began to masturbate in her hand, easing it up and down slowly, tightly. She could see the tension spread out into his body. She saw lines like pain form on his face. His free hand dug into the carpet. His erection became slick, sliding easily inside her hand, although the head grew harder, rounder, fatter, with every stroke.

He pushed his head and shoulders back down into the carpet as if he was trying to lever his hips further up. He started pumping her hand faster, reaching his other hand down between his own legs and gripping his testicles, pulling them down, making the skin drag against her palm so that she could feel the little string of flesh on the underside of his penis catch and pull on her fingertips like the raised underside of a tongue.

His eyes shot open suddenly. "Make me..." But he never finished it. He threw his head forward with a jolt, eyes riveted on her hand.

She watched, fascinated, as the milky fluid spurted out of him, splashing down the back of her hand, hot and gelatinous, pumping under her fingers like an animal's cut throat.

He watched it with glazed eyes, fascinated with his own performance, desperate for his own relief.

He slumped back as suddenly as he had come, letting her go, arms falling to his sides, his erection still huge and dripping, his face flushed.

She looked at her hand in horror, the trail of slime running and dripping down the side of his belly, then squirmed backwards like a crab and bolted from the room.

NINETEEN

She did not go back the next day, or the next. She could not face him. She could barely face herself. It was as if the simple act of being given that one photograph had poisoned her very thinking. Which was exactly what John had intended. He was trying to prove to her that she was as prey to the perversity and depravity he'd cultivated in Danny as all the rest of them. Well, he was wrong. And it was now imperative that she found the money.

They were all working long hours trying to cover Danny's work. In spite of their father's speeches, he had not attempted to hire anyone to replace him. Perhaps John had had a hand in that too, no doubt sure that Danny would be back. Well he was going to be wrong this time.

She worked as hard as they did, her time consumed with the myriad extra chores which now fell to her. But she made time to search John's room. Fifteen minutes here, half an hour there. She could find nothing.

She decided to try Ian's room. No longer needing to hide it from Danny, and suspecting that Danny had told her where it was, he'd make sure she would not be able to find it. That much was Ian, she was at least sure of that.

His room was tidy, familiar. She searched drawers, wardrobe. No tin, no pornography, no surprises. Ian's room was like Ian himself, meticulously unrevealing, giving nothing away.

On impulse she looked under his pillow - for years he'd kept a diary under here - and there it was; one Golden Virginia tin, one packet of liquorice cigarette papers. The papers threw her. She opened the tin nervously, half fearing it would contain tobacco, but it didn't. It contained forty-two £20 notes. She stared at it. More than eight hundred pounds. Twice what he'd said. She counted it again. No mistake. How had he...?

This time she heard no warning click. She just knew he was there. She turned slowly, not bothering to hurry, and found herself smiling. Maybe it was the only option left to her. "I wouldn't make much of a burglar, would I?"

But Ian didn't smile back. "I've been waiting for you to find it. I expected you sooner actually. After all, you've ransacked John's room. There can't be anything secret left to him."

She lifted her head, ready to deny it, face him down, but he smiled at her.

"You had him over a barrel. No money, no car, of course he'd tell you. He had to, because that's the only way you'd give him the money to get away. Only now you had to find that to stop John realising you must know." He nodded his head at the tin in her hand. "And sooner or later you put two and two together and realised I'd have to move it because I couldn't afford to let John know either." And he smiled at her again, a revolting little smile that she must have seen before only she couldn't remember it. Who is this man? she thought. Where have my sons gone? The house is full of strange men and I don't know any of them.

"...I want you to tell me."

She looked at him blankly, realising she hadn't heard what he'd said.

He repeated it. "You know where he is and I want you to tell me."

"What?" She tried that without conviction.

"Oh, come on."

"I can't tell you."

"I think you better, otherwise I could start telling tales out of school. Danny, John, so *good* looking. I wonder what happened to me?"

"What?"

"Pretty, alike. Pretty alike even." He smiled at his own joke.

"Shut up." She said it without conviction. She just didn't want to be sick. She didn't want to throw up on the carpet because she'd only have to clean it up. There wasn't anyone else to clean up sick. That was her job, end of the line.

"Even I wasn't allowed that." His hand snaked out and clutched at her breast, squeezing it viciously. "What about them?"

She slapped his hand away. "Don't touch me."

He laughed, a sniggering little sound. "Famous last words in this house. Everyone says them, but who means them?"

"What do you want?" She stared at him angrily, suddenly back inside herself, jolted out of her shock.

"I told you, all I want to know is where he is."

"Why?"

"Let's call it peace of mind."

"You're going to tell John."

He smiled again, ingratiatingly. "I'm not going to tell anyone, least of all John. The further Danny stays from here the better as far as I'm concerned." He smiled again. "Don't you find John's much more tractable when he's not around?"

He watched her swaying, wanting an ally, wanting to protect herself. He swung it the way he swung everything, by lying through his teeth. "Come on, you can trust me." He got high on the words, felt horny just saying them. He looked at her, all pretences dropping. "Where is he?"

"At Jerrett's." Her eyes were on his, very intent.

His eyes widened, his mouth twitched. "You're joking."

She shook her head, mouth a thin line.

He laughed suddenly, genuinely. "Oh Jesus, that's perfect." His amusement dropped away. He looked suddenly angry, vindictive. "What are you going to do, fuck him in John's leftovers? Think it'll get a better performance out of him?"

She slapped him, but it was weak, diffused by shame and guilt.

He suddenly gripped her breast again. "Maybe you've already been there. Well Mother, got into Danny's pants yet? Seen the queue?"

She slapped his hand away again, more violently this time. Her face was flaming. "Don't you *dare*. Don't you forget who I am Ian, and don't you forget that maybe your father has no idea about your shenanigans with John, but *I* do. Don't you *ever* threaten me." And she gave him a long furious look then slammed out the door.

John came into the kitchen last, tired and aching in his bones. She looked at him properly for the first time in days. He looked drawn, his face sharp. Already his tan was fading. He looked yellowish in the grey light of the kitchen. She smiled at him. She didn't know where she dredged it up from. Some genuine warmth? Some half-remembered tenderness? No, there never had been any.

John did not smile back.

"I have to talk to you," she said.

"Then talk." He took off his jacket, hanging it over the back of his chair.

"Ian knows something. I mean about..." She stopped, aware of the ridiculous melodrama in what she was saying, but she still couldn't bring herself to actually voice it.

He looked at her for a long moment, to be sure he understood her, but there was no surprise in him, only perhaps a quickening of his interest. "So?"

"What do you mean, So? Don't you realise what this means?"

John sat down and began searching in his pockets. "It means he spends too much time listening at keyholes."

She dropped down beside him. "You don't seem to care."

"Why should I?" He tapped a cigarette on the table. She realised it was one of the old type he used to smoke. She tore her eyes off it as if it meant something.

"What if he tells Danny?"

John laughed. "Don't be so fucking stupid, he's not going to tell Danny." He looked at her. "Besides he'd have to find him first, wouldn't he?"

She ignored that, flushing angrily at the way he casually insulted her. "What makes you so sure? Danny believes everything he tells him."

John laughed. "Much as Danny reveres the ground his brother walks on, he'd see Ian in Hell first before he believed anything as far-fetched as that particular fairy-tale. It's a fucking soap opera." He inhaled deeply. "Talk sense."

She looked at him, realising the truth of what he said with a strange sinking defeat.

He smiled lazily. "Now, hadn't you better tell me what you told him?"

"What?" She was buying time again, pathetically.

"Don't 'What?' me. I've been patient with you, very polite, then Ian comes along with a story so thin you could glaze windows with it and you tell him everything."

"I've told you, I don't know where Danny is. How many times do I have to repeat myself?" She sounded hysterical, even to herself.

John leant across the table as if he were about to tell her something in confidence and slapped her hard across the mouth. She flew back against the chair, her teeth jarring, her eyes wide with shock.

"Where is he?"

"What do you want with him?" Her lips felt numb.

"Where *is* he?

"Tell me what you want with him!" she yelled, holding her hands to her face, warding off blows, hiding her face. She didn't know herself.

John smiled. He looked down at the table then back up at her. "Just the same as you - his long life and happiness."

"You're lying."

"Well, you tell me then. You're the one with the theory."

She said nothing. Her face burned. Anger, the slap - she didn't care. Her mouth set stubbornly.

"You know, your suspicions are beginning to bore me. It's none of your business anyway. It never was. Now where is he?"

"I'm not telling you."

He slapped her again, so suddenly that she would have sworn he never moved.

She cried out on reflex. He was up out his seat, holding the front of her sweater. "Your face could be an awful mess at this rate. *Where?*"

Her temper flared up, instantly unleashed. "You want sex with him, don't you?" Her face was white with fury. The handprint stood clear against it, red on white. She couldn't see his face. She could see nothing but her own blinding rage. "It was you I heard in his room. The same old bullying and threats. He's been running away from you all his life. Well, he doesn't need to run anymore. He's safe now, where you can't get him."

"*I* want sex with him? *I* do? Who practically had to have it explained who he was until he was twelve years old - and who hasn't been able to keep her hands off him since?"

"That's a dirty lie."

"Oh no it isn't. It's absolutely spot on."

"You're the one who can't keep his hands to himself. I heard you in his room."

"Doing what?"

She looked at him blankly.

"Well? Doing what? You obviously have some idea."

"I know what you were doing, he told me so himself."

John laughed. "What? That I was bullying him? Is that what we're calling it today? Let's get this ugly fuck out into the open once and for all. I was *screwing* him. There, how does it feel to finally hear it?"

"I don't believe you."

"Oh, that's nice. After all these years it's a comfort to know you've never really believed bad of me."

She stood shaking her head. "You've been forcing him to have sex? All this time you've been forcing...?"

John laughed again. "Oh Christ, let's drop this routine, shall we? You know and I know the reason he's not half a mile from here right now is Danny *likes* it. In fact, Danny *needs* it, that's why he keeps that stiff little cock of his permanently in both hands. That masturbatory grip on himself is the only kind of grip he can keep on reality at all - and you know damn well that's the truth."

"I'm not listening to this." And she covered her ears with her hands.

But he pulled them off, holding her arms down. "He needs it, and I, poor besotted bastard that I am, am just obliged to see that he gets it. It's the least a brother can do. I'm the victim here, and all I get is the blame. But what the hell, I love him, so I just go on sacrificing myself. That's my role in life. He wants me to find him, you know he does, so why don't you help him out?"

"I won't tell you." She tried to wrench free.

"I'll just have to go to Ian then. I'm sure he'll tell me everything I need to know."

"Ian?"

"You didn't believe him, did you? Even you should know better than that."

"God, you're..."

"Yes?" he prompted her. "Don't stand on ceremony now, we've no secrets left. Your whole life has been vindicated, please don't hold out on me now."

"You're despicable."

He laughed, pulling on his jacket. "You don't know the half of it."

And he went out the door, slamming it shut like a tomb.

John sat in the shed and waited. He did not have to wait long. Outside he heard the Fiat's engine start up. He got up and looked out. Margaret driving off in a fury. He went back inside and sat down. Eventually Ian came in, closing the door silently behind him, as silently as he did everything. "No, don't put on the light," John said as he saw him reach for it.

Ian walked over to him carefully. John stood up. "I know where he is," Ian said.

John heard the suppressed excitement, the jubilation. He was surprised for a moment to feel a nudge of pity for him under everything else. It evaporated like water on a hot stone. "I know you do."

Ian didn't seem surprised. "I want a promise."

"My promises are worthless."

"I'll risk it."

John didn't look at him. He could see Ian's feet as two vague shapes on the floor, standing before him. He could hear his breathing, rapid, unnatural. "Alright Ian, a promise."

There was a pause then Ian brought his mouth to his ear. The words came out low and fast, getting it out in a rush. When he was finished John withdrew his head and

said, "What makes you so sure I want him that much?"

"You don't want to hear me telling you that, do you?"

"No, I don't think I do." He stopped again, moved his feet.

"Well?" Ian demanded. His voice was urgent, charged with suspense.

"His mother is itching to spill the beans. She does and you'll be somewhere lower than I am, and I'm dog-shit numero uno. Your guarantees wouldn't buy my spit then. Everything would be right through your hands like sand."

"Life's full of risks. What's one more? Now, do you want to know or don't you?"

"You know, sometimes I almost like you."

Ian smiled in the dark. His heart lit up with exhilaration. "It won't last John-boy. It never does."

"That's what I thought, I was just too polite to say so." He paused again. Ian's hands came out of the dark and lay against his chest. Like a woman's hands, loving him the same way.

"I don't suppose," he asked, feeling Ian's body move imperceptibly closer, "there's any point in asking you for the information now?"

"Oh no John-boy, payment in advance. I insist. Better safe than sorry."

"I promised."

"Your promises are shit."

"You know Ian, this could seriously be your last time. I don't like you so very much after all."

"Could be. They're so rare anyway, who cares?"

Ian made no further moves. John lifted his hands off him. "We don't touch. That's not on offer, savvy?"

Ian smiled, backing off. "Absolutely."

John nodded. "Shall we go then? I take it we are going somewhere?"

"Of course, always discreet with my big brother."

John patted his cheek. It was almost warning. "That's what I love about you Ian, you make the shit taste so good. Lead on."

Margaret drove the car through a blur of water. She wasn't sure if it was tears or rain.

There were no lights on in the house. The living room curtains were closed.

She let herself in, heart sinking. *He's gone. He's grown tired of waiting and gone.* "Danny?" she called. Her voice was soft, as if she feared he might be asleep. "Danny?" she called again, louder this time.

"Up here."

She peered up the stairs, following his voice.

"Up here," he called again.

She could see him now, silhouetted against the tiny stair window. "Why are you in the dark?"

"I felt like it. Come on up." His voice was low. He sounded...

She couldn't place the word.

Then it sprang suddenly into her head, unbidden.

Dangerous.

She shook herself like a dog, full of dread.

She climbed the steep stairs. He didn't move back. He seemed larger, darker, ominous in his featurelessness, his stillness. She stopped a few steps from the top, unable to walk on into him. Why wouldn't he move? "What's wrong?" she asked.

"Why haven't you found my money?"

"I've told you, I looked. What else can I do? I can't make it appear." She wondered

how much of her face he could see in the dark.

"Come up."

"I can't, you're in the way."

He moved back a step then turned and disappeared. She followed him down the passage and into the room. There was only one panel burning on the gas fire. He turned and looked at her as she came in. "Close the door."

She pushed it shut and faced him again. His hair seemed purple in the blue light from the fire. His face looked cold, sinister, in the almost undersea colours.

"You looked in John's room?"

"I told you I did. I told you that last time I saw you. Against my better judgement, I might add. It was you that insisted." He wasn't quite meeting her eyes. She could feel his gaze like two points of pain in her right cheek.

"What did you find?"

"Nothing, I told you. Is there any point in going over this again Danny? Am I under some kind of suspicion?"

There was a silence, a long silence, heavy with the hiss of the fire. Fresh bursts of rain threw themselves at the windowpane.

"On the bed."

Danny's voice made her jump. "What?" Her heart stopped, hung motionless for seconds.

"Look on the bed."

She looked at him, same unwavering stare. She crossed to it. There in the middle lay the photograph. Oh God. "Where did you get that?" she said, desperately thinking, trying to remember. It had been in her bag, the one place no-one ever went, sacrosanct. Mother's bag was always sacrosanct.

"Never mind where I got it. Where did *you* get it?"

She turned. He was standing, hands in his pockets, his eyes still watching her, always watching.

"It's John's," she said. "John took it."

He said nothing.

"Why don't you say something?"

"What should I say?"

"Your own brother has been taking obscene photographs of you and you're not shocked, not even surprised?" She could hear the disgust coming out in her voice and she couldn't stop it, couldn't stem the tide.

"My own mother carries an obscene photograph of me about with her, but that doesn't surprise me either."

She crossed the room in two strides, slapping him furiously, the whole body of her fear and anger coming out in one huge rush. "You've seduced them all. Him, Robbie, even..." she stopped.

"You?"

"You're filthy. You disgust me. You're no son of mine."

He shook his head. "Sorry, no amount of wishing will make that one come true."

"How dare you." She slapped him again.

She stood glaring at him, panting. He swallowed carefully, moistening his lips. He was looking somewhere over her shoulder, not meeting her eyes, like some insolent schoolboy reprimanded, punished and unrepentant. "I want my money." His voice was distant, uninvolved.

"I haven't *got* it."

"Then I'll go without it."

"You can't." Her voice was flatly emphatic.

He didn't answer her.

"If you would just learn some patience. Though God knows why I should help you, after the way you've behaved."

"Why don't you want me to leave?"

"It's not a question of you leaving."

"You've lied to me."

"I've lied to you? How dare you..." But she ran out of words. His eyes took all the words away.

"Why?" he repeated.

She shook her head. "The same reason as all the rest, is that what you're thinking?" Her voice was unsteady. "Something's happened to you Danny. Somewhere along the line you've become someone else. I used to think this was all John's fault, but I'm not so sure any more. I don't seem to be able to remember who you were, all I can see is what you are now, this filthy hunger you bring out all around you. They're sniffing around you like a pack of dogs, all biding their time."

She took a deep breath, let it out again. Her voice was steadier. "I have never wanted anything from you, no matter what you believe." She looked at him, knowing what he knew, giving him a chance to condemn her, but he said nothing. His face remained immobile, unrevealing. She pressed on, more confident now. "I took that photograph to show your father, that's all. I wanted to give him his proof, but the more I thought about it the more I realised how futile the whole thing was. He wasn't going to believe me. I knew what he'd say, I knew who he'd blame, and John would get off scot-free all over again."

Danny turned his back to her.

"Danny..." She gripped his upper arms.

Danny looked into the darkness. How long was it since she'd been here last? It was getting shorter. Like a drug it was getting shorter all the time. Why didn't he care?

He turned slowly, meeting her eyes, holding them. She let her hands slide off bonelessly. He caught hold of them, took them to his chest with both hands, like a Victorian beseeching his beloved, then he pressed the palms flat and slowly guided them down over his chest, down over his belly, then down.

He took his hands away, leaving her holding him. She stood there. She did not know what to do. Her face burned. She felt frozen by his gaze. Was it always like this? Did he get an erection as soon as anyone touched him?

She let go carefully, trying not to draw attention to it, trying not to do anything that might make him react, but she was unprepared for what he did do.

He turned away, his face set in hard lines. "Get out."

"What...?" Her confusion was absolute.

"Go on, get out." He began unbuttoning his shirt, back firmly turned against her.

"I know where your money is," she said before she could stop herself. She was bargaining, only she didn't know anymore what she was bargaining for.

He turned slowly. All she could see was his chest, flat and hard. "Then why didn't you bring it?"

"I couldn't, Ian's got it."

He studied her face.

He thinks I'm lying, she thought.

Slowly he peeled off his shirt then began unbuttoning his trousers. He stopped. "What are you going to do, watch?"

She quickly turned her back, her face colouring up. She could hear him pulling off his trousers.

"When will you bring it?"

"As soon as I can get it."

"Tomorrow?" His voice was soft again, almost inviting, as if he was making a date.

"Tomorrow," she agreed limply. She felt used, like a dirty old rag. She had gained nothing at all.

"You can turn around." His voice came out of the dark, heavy with intent. Suddenly she was afraid again. She did not want to turn around.

"Come on Mum, turn around."

She turned slowly.

He was standing there, stark naked, obscenely erect. He wasn't quite smiling, but it hovered there, like a suggestion around his mouth. "The real thing."

"*Danny…*" Her voice was numb, flat with shock. She felt her face flame.

"This was what you wanted, wasn't it? To see if I looked just the same? Don't you think it's better? In the flesh?"

She looked away, tearing her eyes off him, turning her body away. "Get dressed."

He laughed, low. "Come on, have another look. No charge."

She turned quickly, some dim notion of facing him down, but her mouth dried up at the sight of him.

"Why don't you touch it?"

She looked at his face, trying to read his expression. She didn't know who he was anymore. "No," she said in a whisper.

"Why not? Not moral scruples surely? Where were they two days ago?"

Her hand flew to her mouth like a comic book heroine.

"Another feel won't hurt, will it?"

She shook her head.

"She says no, but she means yes. Come on, be brave."

He jerked it. There, in front of her eyes, he made it jerk, flexing it like a muscle. It caused it to peel back on itself, revealing the head fully. "Look, he likes you. It would only be kind to give the boy a pat."

She saw his feet walking towards her. "No," she said to them, but they weren't listening. Then she smelt him, that same smell that had made her mouth water.

"That's it." His hand reached out to take hers. "There now, that was easy, wasn't it?"

She held it unmoving, huge in her hand, feeling the red heat come scalding off it. The veins were swollen so hard it felt inflamed.

"It actually physically aches." Although he was looking down at where he held her round himself it was obvious he wasn't talking to her. His voice was curiously flat, detached. It sounded as if he was talking about the affected limb of some fictitious patient on an operating table. "You don't know what that feels like, do you? You've never ached for anything in your life. What kind of a freak has a dick that comes up but won't go down? That can be tossed off six times in a row and still aches for more? Squeeze it," he grunted. "Really squeeze it." He pressed her fingers tight then said, "Sometimes I would even run cold water over it, rub it on the windows, trying to cool it on the glass. I used to sneak downstairs and rub ice cubes over it. Standing down there in the kitchen, this great red lump of meat sticking out in front of me, rubbing it all over with ice cubes. Bone weary, tossing off into a fistful of ice-cubes in the dark and crying afterwards because it was nothing, just a great big empty void of nothing. You talk about hunger. You don't know what that word means. You don't even *begin* to know what that word means."

She looked at his face in horror. *He doesn't even know what he's doing or who I am. There's no part of him functioning beyond his hand and that thing*. And suddenly she wanted to get it over with, see his face go slack as a stunned animal's, see him again as he had been two nights ago, spread out on the floor, helpless under her hands. She wanted that power over him, to see him destroyed by his own need.

She pulled his hand off hers and took hold of him. He said, "Oh Jesus," flatly, as if

he had dropped a cup or made some unforeseen error. She took a firmer grip on him and her mind flickered instantly to John, feeding this need in him, cultivating it for his own ends.

"Oh Jesus," he said again as she inexpertly attempted to masturbate him. Already she was panicking, wanting it finished.

"Oh, Danny." The voice was deep, filled with angry pain. She whirled round in fright. She stood there holding Danny by the penis as if she was leading him by it.

"This has *got* to be your all time low." John lay back against the door, shaking his head slowly from side to side.

"John," she said meaninglessly, like she could explain something. But he didn't even seem to see her. His face was white. He'd lost so much weight so quickly he looked almost gaunt. He looks like him, she thought hysterically. He *can't* look like him.

"Why do you do it Danny?"

Danny said nothing.

"John..." she said again, beginning to panic.

He looked at her suddenly, as if seeing her for the first time. "Let go of him."

She looked at her hand, half in surprise, and snatched it away, rubbing it furiously on her sweater, trying to wipe away the sticky feel of him.

"Why do you do it Danny?"

She turned quickly to Danny and saw his face. It was grotesque, his expression full of an intense itchy-white excitement. It was like some curling filthy smile consuming his whole face. "Danny...?" she said, but it didn't reach him. She felt suddenly irrelevant, as if neither of these men even knew she was in the room. She had simply ceased to be.

John began to walk towards him, slowly, his face eaten alive by some ancient emotion.

Margaret turned back to Danny frantically. He seemed blind to his own danger, like some automaton locked into a totally inappropriate response, utterly unable to function correctly.

She stepped in front of him, barring John's way. He looked at her as if he didn't know who she was. "Move it."

"Leave him alone."

"I said, move it." And his whole hand clutched her face, pushing her aside as if he were crumpling paper.

"*No!*" she screamed, catching at his arm.

He didn't even bother to shake her off, instead he elbowed her savagely in the chest, sending her flying back to hit the floor, flat on her back, and bang her head sickeningly on the tiled hearth.

She felt nothing but a single jolt that broke her neck.

He slapped Danny twice, lightly, only leaving the vaguest of marks. "Now you can't do it again."

"Cunt," Danny said, enunciating it as if he'd lived for the moment. John looked down between his legs and smiled. It looked wolfish on his thinned face.

"Unfinished business, that's all this is for you. Even on the Day of Judgement you'll be standing up there looking for some poor lost angel just aching for a way to fall." He slapped him again, harder this time. "Anybody at all." He smiled again. "Well, I can oblige baby."

He looked up at his face, eyes searching his intently, then he licked his lips. "Ask me then." John's hand slid round him, wrapping itself around his penis like a boa

constrictor. He gripped it fiercely.

Danny shook his head slowly, his breathing rapid. Sweat stood out on his forehead, a slick oily film.

John looked at him steadily. He still held Danny's cock, now inconceivably larger, as if it had somehow inflated itself still further to combat the crushing pressure of John's hand. "It calls you a liar Danny."

"No."

"It calls you a fucking desperate liar."

"No."

"You remembered, didn't you?"

Danny said nothing.

"That's why you came back here."

"You wish. You were fucking replaying it. You've been replaying it for months."

"Not all of it."

"I never did anything."

"No? That's memory and its tricks again for you. You were a little slut. Only six years old and already you were a little slut. Think he didn't know? Think he wasn't right? Look at you now."

"You told him it was the first time."

"Are you saying it wasn't?"

"It's you in the dreams. You chewed those fucking liquorice sticks all summer. That's why you took up smoking his filthy cigarettes, sticking your tongue in my mouth. To make me remember."

"Right to at least two. But that doesn't mean everything your diseased imagination dreams up is true."

"You liar."

"It's the truth. Rab was twelve, I was fifteen, you were six. He tried it out on me, I tried it out on you. The only major difference is we got caught. So it was no more baths, no more putting you to bed, and not because Dad didn't trust me either. After all what six year old kid do you know would tempt his big brother into a blow job?"

"You took those lousy photographs."

"You really think so?"

"You bastard."

"Why? I could have done worse. Christ knows you'd have let me. Come on Danny, be a little Christian."

Danny began to cry. The tears began to slide down his face effortlessly. "You greedy vicious cunt."

"Not me. They're the greedy ones. I only want what's mine."

"Fuck off."

John nodded his head as if he was encouraging a mental sub-normal. "We had a pact, you and I. Time the deal was well and truly sealed." He pushed Danny back against the bed. It caught him in the back of the knees, making him sit down. John climbed on, pushing him back. "Here..." he reached down between their bodies, lifting himself slightly, undoing his clothes "...want to see?"

Danny jerked his head away.

John pulled himself out with a grunt of satisfaction. "Used to fascinate you, the sheer fucking size of it, all that hair. Come on Danny, take a look."

Danny looked. And suddenly it was all back. In perfect detail. The smell of liquorice, the taste of salt, John making him take it in his mouth, the panic, but still, through it all, that pulsing excitement, knowing he'd get his reward in the end.

John showed it off, pulling it down, making it bigger. "Like it?"

Danny tore his head away.

John laughed, squeezing his penis. "Always did give you away." His voice changed. "Always was too bloody easy to make you stiff." His hand gripped Danny's jaw. "You know that it's me you've wanted all along, don't you?"

Danny shook his head again, fiercely.

John's hand gripped his face, hurting. "Say yes Danny." And he pulled Danny's head up and down. "That's better." He eased himself over Danny's leg. "Much better." He made a low grunting noise like a man easing himself into a chair. "There." And he began to move against him, their genitals sandwiched together under his weight. He looked down into Danny's face. Danny tried to close his eyes, but he couldn't, because suddenly it was all there in John's eyes, naked for him to see. He felt his own response, huge, monstrous, worse than ever.

John whispered, "Your mother's lying dead on the floor, and what are we doing?" He was watching Danny's face avidly. Danny knew what he was watching for.

Fuck him... *no.*

"Come on Danny, don't fight it." He whispered again, mouth close to his ear, "She's lying there dead. We haven't even checked. What does that say about us Danny?"

"No, " Danny said fiercely, trying to struggle free.

John smiled, a smile of triumph.

"No," Danny pleaded, desperation making him beg.

John smiled, nodded, as if Danny was being very good. Danny was being splendid.

"John..." Danny moaned. He heard it, appalled, felt it come straight from his cock to his mouth - the need in his gut, his very soul, out there for everyone to hear.

"Come on Danny," John whispered. "You know what we're doing."

Danny shook his head again violently, pressed his eyes tight shut, opened them again, the words trapped in his throat.

"Say it Danny."

He moved against him slowly, tormenting him with that dreadful grinding friction and Danny knew it was no good. He felt it build up in him, better than it ever was before, better than it ever had been, his whole body alive with it. And John saw his face, read it there, and brought his mouth against his lips whispering, "You say it Danny. Who do you love? I can make you say it. *Say* it."

Danny pressed his head back. "You cunt." But John followed his mouth, letting his lips just barely touch his, as if he wanted to feel the very vibration of the words when they came. Hearing them wasn't enough, not for John. And Danny knew he had to say it, there was no way round it, because he wasn't signing a pact and John knew it. He was acknowledging that his signature was already on it and had been for years. He was lying. He was telling the truth. It didn't matter, and John knew that too. All that mattered was he was going to do it. John had won, that was what mattered.

He closed his eyes and said it, a tense, gasped confession, so desperate it sounded real, trembling with false emotion - an orgasm masquerading as an oath - and John received it with his eyes sliding closed, mouth sinking onto his, becoming suddenly languorous in his thrusts. "Had to be Danny. Had to *be*..."

And he came.

TWENTY

Rab lay on his back and looked at the ceiling. It was late. The house was unnaturally hushed. He could hear Ian's breathing, heavy in the dark. His arm had gone to sleep. He pulled it out slowly, taking care not to wake him, and replayed the conversation again.

"He got exactly as far as Jerrett's."

"*Jerrett's?* But why?"

He'd been naive enough to expect Ian to say something about him, but Ian had only said, "You don't expect him to leave his big brother, do you? Besides, this way he's got his mother exactly where he wants her..." And he'd laughed and said, "On the end of his dick."

Rab had turned away, sickened by his dirty mouth, and then lain awake wondering about it.

The chances of his aunt indulging in anything incestuous with Danny was about as likely as... well, whatever. What was it about Ian's needling that made it work so well? You knew it was shit yet he still had you lying awake half the night wondering.

No, the more he thought about it the more he became convinced Danny's half-hearted escape must have been for his sake. Okay, it sounded conceited, but what was left? Unless, of course, it *was* Margaret. He smiled grimly to himself at the notion.

He lay there, aware of a slow growing excitement in himself. What if Danny really was at Jerrett's, waiting for him to show? It had been too fucking good, brief as it was, not to know. And if Danny wasn't there, if he'd just upped and gone, he might as well know that too. What did he have to lose any more? "Fuck it," he whispered and slid down the bed, easing himself over Ian's legs.

He picked up his clothes and sidled out the door, closing it silently behind him and going down the hall to the bathroom. Christ the place was quiet. Where was everyone tonight? Margaret still not back? And where was John if it came to that?

He stood under the shower, scalding himself awake, trying to scrub the smell of Ian off his skin. He stood, face turned up to the water, letting it run out of his mouth, washing out the taste, thinking about Danny.

Well, if nothing else Danny would get a surprise tonight. Danny and Margaret both according to Ian, but he couldn't get his brain around that picture. No, it said very definitely, not Danny and Margaret both. But inside a little contrary voice said, Oh yes, very probably Danny and Margaret both, and it won't be Margaret's doing either. He couldn't understand why it was festering in his imagination like this.

When he was finished he got dressed, went downstairs and put his boots on in the kitchen, then went to the keyboard for the pick-up's keys.

No keys. Where the hell were they? Had John come back after all, then gone out again in the pick-up? *Shit.* That left only the old man's Range Rover, or a tractor, and he'd be fucked if he was taking off in a tractor.

He lifted the Range Rover's keys, then unlatched the door carefully, letting it drop gently to behind him. The dog didn't even stir.

There was a heavy mist coming down that looked almost like fog. The road was quiet. Rab felt the warmth from the car's heater begin to make him sleepy, in spite of the shower. He looked at the dashboard. After one, no wonder he was tired. He tried not to think about what he'd find at Jerrett's, but pictures of Danny pushing into his

mother, face carved in sweaty ecstasy, kept creeping into his head. Damn Ian and his putrid insinuations.

He turned off the heater and opened the window. He almost missed the turning when it came. A hare dashed across the track, riveted for a second in the headlights. Rab turned them off, watching the hare come to life again and disappear into the mist.

He drove up the track slowly, in absolute darkness. There were no lights on in the house. He parked the car and cut the ignition. It was then the realisation hit him - no fucking key. How the hell was he supposed to get in? Just knock on the door? Hi guys, thought I'd drop in. Sorry to get you off your mother at such short notice.

He got out the car, closing the door carefully with a dull click. He left the keys in the ignition, although he had no idea why. Margaret's Fiat was up against the house, the pick-up blocking its exit. John? Here? Fuck. And why no lights?

The more he stood there, the damp seeping into his bones, the more he felt a horrible conviction that this was already a mess.

He walked up to the window and peered in. The curtains were closed and all he could see through the chink was the dying embers of an old fire lit hours before.

He moved over to the door. He wondered if a window might be open at the back, then he saw the key was in the lock.

Well fuck me, here's a nice thing. Stupid bastard's left the key in the lock.

He turned it and pushed in. The vestibule was in total darkness, except for a square of dull violet light where the stair door stood open.

He ignored it and carefully pushed open the living room door. But there was nothing, just a grate full of ash. He closed it again. Had to be upstairs. But why so quiet? Fighting, tears, even the sounds of some indecent three-way shafting he could have coped with, but the silence was unnerving.

He climbed the narrow stairs slowly. They creaked. Every second or third goddamn stair creaked. He hoped they weren't listening, although how they could miss it in that hush God alone knew.

He could see the bedroom door now. It was open, a bright lozenge of light falling on the hall carpet. And then John's voice called out softly, "Come on in Rab, join the party."

Rab let his breath out and dropped his shoulders. He walked down the hall and turned into the room, closing the door behind him over-carefully, like a nervous man going into the dentist's.

Danny was there alright, sitting behind John on the bed. Rab could only see the naked line of his back, a little of his hair. He had dropped his head onto his raised knees. His face was hidden. He did not look up. John began tucking his shirt in without getting up. He did it slowly, deliberately, with hard emphasis. Rab could not remember ever having hated anyone as much as he hated John right then. It was an odd moment to make a profound discovery, but Rab discovered that previously he had only ever felt dislike. This was hate - a hard, empty, brittle knot where his stomach used to be. "Where's Margaret?" he asked. He was amazed to hear how normal he sounded - good old normal Rab.

"There." John nodded his head into the gloom. He pulled a cigarette from his pocket.

John very seldom smoked and when he did it was like other men passed you over in conversation, studied, practised. Rab could hardly bear to tear his eyes away from the movements of his hands. But he did, turning, wanting to fix her to the point of his hidden hate like a butterfly. But she wasn't there.

He frowned, losing for a moment his twine-cut hold on the helium of emotion that floated his head. He felt himself deflate slightly, the edges of normal monotonous life eroding his high. Anger shot through him in a burst. How dare they try to unsettle him

now? Tonight he could kill them all with the sheer force of his hate and they still played secondary school games with him. *Love me, hate me, look who's on the floor now.*

And she was.

That's exactly where she was.

Like he'd known all along she would be - there, dead on the floor, her eyes filled with a glassy blue light, her skin stained to the floor as if she was fixed with dark glue, tar, varnish. Her head sat up at an angle as natural and happy as a broken blue poppy.

He turned back. John was smiling. No, not quite smiling, not *yet* smiling, just showing the faintest suggestion of his teeth. So many teeth, like an alligator. For years an alligator had been giving him head and suddenly it was going to bite off his dick. Mr Puppy turns quite mean.

"Danny did it for you, saved you the bother."

"Danny?"

"Of course. You didn't think I'd done it?"

"I don't believe you." *Christ, what a fatuous remark Rab.*

"Of course you don't, but you know it's true."

Rab stepped to one side, looking past John's body. "Danny?"

No answer.

He tried again. "Danny." But Danny would not even raise his head.

Rab attempted to cross the last few steps towards him, but John stood up with a sudden coiled movement. His lips drew back almost like a dog's snarl. "Don't touch him." His voice was low. He shook his head so imperceptibly he might have been doing nothing more dangerous than clearing his sinuses.

Rab stopped short and looked into his face and could see nothing but a blank mirror of his own hate, only John's hate was enough to murder legions.

He stepped to one side so that they stood almost side by side. "Danny," he said again. "Danny, are you listening to me?"

"Of course he's listening. What he's not doing is talking, can't you hear?"

Rab jerked his head round to face him. They were face-on now, their bodies still flat, like two Egyptian hieroglyphics. "Why don't you go crawl up your own arsehole?"

A long liquid moment slid past then John said, no smile, "He isn't going to answer you. He may never answer you again."

Rab spoke to Danny again, continuing to outstare John like a man outstaring a mad dog. "Danny, get up, come on, we're going."

John laughed, a small derisory huff of genuine amusement. "Think you can persuade him? Be my guest."

"He's not going to hang around here and take the rap for you."

"Nobody needs to take the rap for anybody. We're all going to live happily ever after. Don't you understand the concept of happy endings?"

"Nobody's going to believe he did it."

"Why shouldn't they? My loopy little brother. But it doesn't come to that, because you're not going to open your mouth."

Rab felt the first hair-stirring of fear and stood on it. He had to hang onto his anger. Anger was the only thing that could protect you. Anger was your weapon. "You wouldn't dare." *Another fatuous remark Rab, well done.*

"Dare? What's dare got to do with it? One word out of line and I'll break your neck. You're not in one of your cutesy fantasy books now Rab, this is real life, planet Earth."

"You're playing it like a fucking book John. Tell me the master plan."

"You don't listen, do you? We get rid of that." He gestured vaguely with his hand. "Then we all live happily ever after. That is, *we're* going to live happily ever after - you get to watch." Clear? his tone implied.

"Very clear," Rab answered as if he had actually said it. "Only why the hell should

I?"

"Because you don't want to die."

"You're going to kill me too?" Rab realised too late the unintentional irony in his own sarcasm.

John shrugged. "It's all or nothing now Robbie. Do you think anything else would stop me?" He smiled again.

Nothing else would stop him Rab knew, and he wasn't prepared to die for Danny. Not without some sign. "Danny..." he said, turning to him. It was supposed to be a question - where was the question mark?

Danny finally lifted his head, but he stared straight ahead, straight at the footboard of the bed. Then he turned slowly and looked him full in the face and Rab saw it there, clear as day, and he tasted a resentment as tangible as bile in his mouth. He said, "Okay. Sure. Why not? Anything you say John. Who am I to upset your plans?" And he turned his back on him. Let the mad dog bite him now while he knew nothing about it. But the silence went on so long he finally had to say, just to break it, "So what do we do now?"

"We get rid of that," John said again, only this time his voice was even more bland, as bland and flavourless as rice. "And then we go home."

And this time when Rab turned round John was smiling.

They took the body to the car. Rab took the feet because he couldn't bear to touch the head. John picked her up from under the shoulders, allowing her head to loll back. It fell back bonelessly, an ugly lump appearing in the throat. Rab stared at it in a kind of fascinated horror. "The head... lean her head against you."

"Why?" John asked, a smile beginning to move about his face, looking for somewhere to rest.

"Because if you don't I'll throw up and when they find her I don't want them identifying my puke on her legs."

John shifted her head against his stomach, resting it so it sat unnaturally upright and stared at him. It stared at him all the way downstairs. Even on those tight, steep, dark stairs he felt that stare break out on him like a cold sweat. You wished it on me, she stared at him.

They threw her in the back seat of her car like a sack of potatoes and locked it. Back upstairs Danny was dressed and pulling on a sweater. He would not look at either of them.

"What else is hers?" John asked him.

Danny gestured at her handbag.

John picked it up. "Anything else?"

Danny shook his head.

"Right, come on."

Rab stood aside to let Danny pass through the doorway then moved to follow him.

"Forget it." John pulled his arm and slid past him sidewise, getting between them. "I know you in the dark."

They passed out of the house quietly. Danny climbed into the Fiat's driving seat, John as his passenger. Rab took the pick-up.

They drove onto the coast road at a quiet pace, exciting no interest. They passed a sawmill lorry going the opposite way, and an ambulance without lights.

Rab watched the Fiat sitting at the traffic lights ahead. He could see John's profile turned towards Danny. Danny's face remained rigidly forward.

The lights changed and the car moved forward. They passed a police van sitting by the roadside. The policemen were eating sandwiches. They looked up and

watched the two cars with detached interest. Rab saw one of them pick up the radio receiver.

Oh great.

The road swung down closer to the water, where it was pinned between the grey shapes of an industrial belt and the black mass of the sea by a railway. Every once and a while they passed a railway bridge, half-lit by orange light and fading into nothingness on the seaward side.

Rab opened the window, but smelt nothing but the vague scent of burnt coffee and rubber. He could not smell the sea, nor hear it. The wind was blowing the wrong way.

The Fiat slowed and the left indicator came on, a bright orange flashing on-off, on-off. His own indicators ticked along with it. Both cars turned.

Behind high mesh two dogs employed by Bayhauser & Rutger hurled themselves at the wire.

The Fiat turned right. Rab followed.

The other side of the chemical factory was unprotected. There were no dogs. Huge cabless container lorries sat like headless insects in the car park. Their tarpaulins flapped violently in the wind. A towering blue-white worklight lit up the whole area and washed the colour from his hands. They looked like dead things on the wheel.

The Fiat turned left again. Rab bumped along behind them, down the empty track, then they swerved slightly to the left again. The Fiat pulled in. Its stop lights showed as two red points in the dark, then were extinguished. Rab's headlamps picked out the council signs bolted and rusted to the gate.

YARDHOLM BIRD SANCTUARY

PERMIT HOLDERS ONLY BEYOND THIS POINT

PERMITS AVAILABLE FROM........

But the name was missing. The plastic sign was broken in half. SLOW 5 MPH another sign read. *Ducks crossing*, someone had scribbled underneath.

Rab cut the lights, then the engine, and climbed out. John was already out, his head to the wind like a dog scenting its prey. Here the wind whipped up the trees into a high noise. They were ugly uniform black conifers, unnatural, man-made, regimented, like the bird reserve itself.

"Is it locked?" Rab asked.

"No." John stood with his hands in his pockets, unmoving.

"Well, what the fuck are you waiting for, your next message from God?"

"Rab..." His voice was quiet, confidential. It said, Let me give you some advice here; next time you talk to me like that I'll use your own teeth to carve out your tonsils. Or maybe all it said was, Did you know you die here too? That's what God's telling me, you die here in the car with Margaret, only you'll still be breathing when you go down into the dark. What he actually said was, "Come here."

Rab stepped forward, aware of the fear hanging about himself. Another new one, this fear. But John continued to look into the dark, seemingly unperturbed.

"If you touch him, even once, for whatever reason, I'll cut off your balls and feed them to you." He stopped, as if thinking about that. Was it really quite satisfying enough? Perhaps something a little more forceful? He went on, "When we get home..." He paused again.

He sounds as if we've been out for the day, Rab thought. *Our day out at the bird reserve where we dumped our mother.*

Rab began to sense it building in him. *He's standing there calm and relaxed and*

his feet are glued to the ground with cold rage. He felt that if he touched him right now he'd leave the skin of his hand frost-burnt to John's face.

John went on abruptly, "When we get home you don't look at him, you don't speak to him, but most of all..." and this time he did move, but it was to turn away from him, offering him his back, *Jump me now so I can wipe your face across the earth as one last red smear*, "...you don't touch him." *Come on, jump me so I can kill you. I want to kill you.*

Rab could see his shoulders, huge with the desire to do it. "No problem," he said and watched John's rage double just like that. *Not what you want to hear John? Oh shucks, my heart bleeds.*

He heard the Fiat's door open. Danny was walking towards them, appearing out of the darkness. He stopped just in front of John, but he was watching Rab, looking at him intently, listening to what he was saying.

"You've earned him," Rab said, "eat and enjoy."

John's hand shot out and slapped Danny so hard it sounded like a tree limb cracking.

Rab groaned. It came out involuntarily as a grunt, but it was whipped away and lost in the wind.

John said, "I told you to stay in the car." Danny blinked stupidly, stunned by the sudden violence of the attack, then jerked away. But John caught at his arm, pulling him back. "Get in the pick-up, and this time stay in the fucking pick-up."

Danny lowered his head, pulling his arm free, and walked towards the van, passing Rab without speaking.

It was John who returned to the Fiat.

When its engine started up again Rab moved forward to open the gate.

The Fiat, windows open, doors locked, had sat for one long moment, immovable, trapped in thick icy mud, before they managed to shift it.

Rab felt sure it would not be deep enough, but it was. It moved forward and slowly tipped over the shelf. It hung nose-down for a moment, until enough water had poured in the windows, and then sank into the ugly black water with a burp and disappeared without trace.

Rab had left his shoes on because he could not bear the thought of that cold dirty mud on his skin. John had left his on because he didn't care. Their trousers were soaked through.

Rab climbed out of the water with feet like lead, weighted down with mud and weed. He tried not to think of John pushing him under the water, but he could feel the heavy silence of him beside him in the dark, knowing he was feeling his death in his fingertips.

He watched John make his way back to the pick-up. He could see Danny sitting behind the wheel like a wax dummy. Rab closed the gates and thought about the tracks they'd left. Even going through the grass anyone could see a car had been there. Well, let's hope no-one came there for a while. Let's hope it rains. Let's all get down on our knees and pray.

John had moved into the driving seat. He switched on the headlamps. Suddenly the engine sprang into life. He revved it up and swung the headlamps on Rab, dazzling him.

He's going to run me down. Christ, I never realised before how many ways of dying there were.

But he managed to get out of the beam and round to the cab without dying. He made a move to open the door.

"Get in the back." John's disembodied voice came out of the window.

Rab straightened up slowly. "You're joking."

"Get in the fucking back or walk."

Danny stared straight ahead. His hands were folded in his lap like a schoolboy's.

Rab got in the fucking back. He was barely in before the pick-up swung round and pulled out. Everything seemed to happen in reverse. He sat with the wind cutting through his clothes like knives. John drove quickly, full of suppressed anger. The railway bridges shot backwards. The dogs had not even had time to bark. They looked up, heads together, like two men surprised plotting. Rab could see them standing there forlornly at the gates, mystified by life's injustices.

They waited at the other side of the traffic-lights. The police car was gone. Rab moved his feet tentatively, but could no longer feel them. His teeth began to chatter. He realised that there was no fog, no mist. There had been one earlier, hadn't there? He rubbed his head.

They pulled away from the lights past another saw-mill lorry. He wanted to scream, '*Dead woman in your pond!*' But he only clutched his knees tightly, trying to stop the shaking.

They pulled back into Jerrett's yard. John got out first. He spoke to him without looking at him. "Get some papers and cover the Rover's seat and carpet. You're in it."

Rab looked at him for a delicate moment, thinking how much he really did want to oblige those shoulders, but he decided he'd like to live for another day longer, just to see if there really was a God.

He managed to do as he was told, even though he could hardly feel his fingers. John startled him as he straightened up from covering the last patch of floor. "Get going."

Rab climbed in without speaking and pulled down the lane. He could see the pick-up behind him in the rear-view mirror.

When he reached the farm he killed his lights and dropped his speed. He pulled up into the yard and parked the Rover where it was always parked. He reached round for his bag and opened the door. The pick-up idled in alongside and disappeared into the darkness. He got out carefully and removed the papers. He flicked the light on and off again to check everything. He locked the door and lifted his bag.

Inside the back door he encountered John in his underpants, soiled jeans in one hand. Rab had an irrational desire to laugh. He fought the smirk that threatened to consume his face.

"Take your jeans off. And wash them out yourself, don't put them in the basket." John went on out into the hall, pushing Danny ahead of him.

Rab listened, but could not hear them moving upstairs. Who would he put them in the basket for now anyway?

He pulled off his boots and socks and peeled off his trousers with difficulty. He walked upstairs as quietly as he could. He heard John in the bathroom.

He went into his room and switched on the light. It made him feel wonderful, the act of switching on a light, of seeing things not built out of darkness.

He locked his door.

He dumped his clothes on the lino, well away from everything. He looked at his feet and saw a fat piece of pondweed clinging to his ankle like a slug. He tried to brush it off with his hand and realised it was alive, and attached. A leech. A thick black leech clinging onto his leg and feeding off him. All this time, since the pond, inside his clothes.

He stood up and picked up a cigarette from the packet on the window ledge. He lit it, holding his hands together to keep them steady. He drew on it twice, three times, until it was hot, then he pressed it to the leech's body.

It sizzled revoltingly and fell off. It left an ugly hole in his leg, red and bruised and oozing blood.

He crossed to the wash-hand basin and threw up. He threw up until he could hardly breathe, until he had nothing left to give and his ribs ached. His face was covered in salt tears, he was gasping.

He cleared the vomit then washed his face in hot water and soap, lots of strong scented soap, then he crossed to the leech and picked it up with a paper hankie. He rolled the hankie up and battered it with the book beside his bed. He opened the window and hurled the tissue out as far as he could onto the green. He closed the window and washed his feet and legs at the sink, carefully inspecting them. He found nothing. He scrubbed his hands twice. He rubbed his feet with a stiff dry towel until he could feel the heat start up in his toes. Finally he brushed his teeth then took a piss in the sink, letting the cold water run it away, then he opened the window wide to wash away the stink of sick, mud and fear.

He climbed into bed, smelling and feeling more like himself. He pulled the blankets up, soft and warm round his neck, and remembered suddenly, and with all the full clarity and perversity of memory, how Margaret's hair used to smell of pie-crust on warm days.

It was a long time since he'd last cried himself to sleep. If only he'd been crying for her.

TWENTY-ONE

"Why?" The old man looked at him with a face that was carved into thousands of hard furrows, all going nowhere.

"What d'you mean, why? Because it's his home. Why else? Where would you expect him to go?"

"I mean, why has he come back?"

"What's it to you? He's back, you're no longer short-handed. What more do you want?"

The old man got up to face him. "Don't cheek me. You're not the boy to do it, big and ugly as you are. I don't want him in this house, and you know why."

John smiled, slowly. "He stays." He smiled some more. "I've got a double bed, time I used it." He watched the old man's face go white then a dull red.

"Not under my roof."

"No, and not in your bed either. Too bad, Dad."

The old man punched him. It had no real power, only enough weight to irritate him. John floored him, swift and sure as he always was.

The old man hit the stone flags with a clatter of chairs. He lay winded, his face the colour of putty.

"Get up."

The old man got up slowly. He moved oddly, hunched, pulling his strength up.

"Forget it," John said quietly. He watched the threat sink home, watched him back off grudgingly. "Turn a blind eye Dad. I'm sure you can manage that. What you don't know can't hurt you. "

"Obscene." The old man said it low, lips curling, as if the word itself was an obscenity.

John laughed. "Get out. Go on, before I throw up in your face."

His father walked to the door stiffly.

John said to his back, "He'll be back at work tomorrow."

The old man stopped, his back rigid, listening.

"Be nice to him. After all, he *is* your son."

John Jackson Moore Senior slammed the door hard behind him.

Danny tried the door again. He needed to pee. If John didn't let him out soon he'd piss out the fucking window.

The door opened almost under his hand. He shot back as if he was guilty of something. John came in smiling. "Hungry?"

"I need to take a piss."

John stepped back to let him pass. Danny made himself as small as he could to slide by him. He followed Danny to the bathroom. Danny tried to shut the door, but John pushed his shoulder into the room, grunting a negative.

"I need to pee John."

"Go ahead."

"Not with you here. What d'you think I'm going to do, escape down the drainpipe?"

John smiled indulgently, but said nothing.

"Get out," Danny said.

"No."

"Why not?"

"I'm going to watch." John pushed him back into the room and closed the door.

"What the hell for?"

"Because I can."

Oh shit, this is not the time, Danny thought desperately, just take a leak and get out before it runs down your leg.

He turned his back on him, going at it sideways, expecting every minute that he would walk round for a better view, but he didn't. He stayed where he was, content to know he was humiliated.

Danny finished up and crossed the floor back to the door, but did not get too close. Let John move out of the way first.

John smiled. "You haven't kissed me today."

Danny looked at him.

"Come on Danny." John's face began to lose all the happy smiles, leaving that familiar monochromatic face. White skin, black eyes. No grey in John's life, or in his view.

"No," Danny said.

"Why d'you keep saying that to me?"

Danny said nothing, watched the whites get whiter, the blacks get blacker.

"You know it annoys me. Why are you always trying to annoy me?"

His tone changed suddenly to one of incredible patience, a reasonable man. "Now, let's try that again. Here Danny, now." His tongue came out, twitching gently at his lower lip, like a man threading a needle.

Danny shook his head. It was the best he could do. Like refusing a cigarette at his own execution.

John's eyes looked at the floor, glancing here, there, his head cocked as if he was listening. He came up off the door with his head down, still thinking. This was a man deep in thought. Oh God, Danny thought.

John punched his face, repeatedly. Not hard enough to break things, just hard enough to hurt.

"Learn to say yes," John said. "Learn good and sharp and fast." He was breathing heavily, but not with exertion. John's power was like an independent force charging up his body. He didn't break sweat to spend it. Something else made his breathing ragged. "Now, Danny..." he stood back a pace and Danny heard him take a steadying breath, "...kiss me."

He had not struck Danny's mouth. The bruising would not be on his lips. He could hardly see out of one eye, but the mouth was still beautiful, untouched.

Danny moved forward blindly, his head ringing, and pressed his lips against John's. He felt them hard and cold as steel under his mouth, unyielding. He tasted his own blood.

"Again." And this time John's voice was coming apart, his breathing like a man drowning.

Danny kissed him again. This time John's mouth came alive out of its hard lines. Danny recoiled, but John's arm pulled him closer until Danny could feel his teeth hard under his lips.

John let him go abruptly and led him to the sink. There he gently washed his face and carefully treated the cuts to his cheek and brow. He pushed the damp hair off Danny's face and said, "I love you."

Danny heard it and smiled.

After all, we all needed to be loved.

"He's back, isn't he?" Ian watched Rab shovelling stuck grain down towards the

hatch.

Rab went to the cab and set the hydraulic higher before he bothered to reply. "Yes," he said, coming back.

"You never left to bring him back."

"I never left to bring him back," Rab agreed and began the process of rolling up. "Want to hear something really dirty?" He turned to Ian and smiled suddenly. A fast edgy little smile. A man smiling quickly to get something unpleasant over with.

Ian nodded, although he wasn't sure that he did.

"I went to get him back but he didn't want to be got. Tragic, isn't it?"

"I'm crying," Ian said, his voice dry.

"What's wrong? Jealous?"

"Nothing to be jealous of. You didn't drive him away and you didn't bring him back."

Rab looked away. He took a long drag on his cigarette then passed it to Ian while he climbed up into the back of the trailer. "Finish it."

"You know I don't smoke." Ian put it in his mouth, but did nothing with it.

Rab stood with one foot on the tailgate, the other against the floor of the trailer. He pushed the last of the grain down through the hatch with the shovel. He stopped and looked down. "Inhale Ian. Suck. You know how to do that."

Ian inhaled, then coughed. Tears came into his eyes. His lips tasted strongly and sweetly of liquorice syrup, the dark flavoured Spanish tobacco.

Rab climbed back out and turned off the vacuum. "Give it here."

Ian handed it back. "What are you going to do?"

Rab splayed smoke down his nose in two deep angry vents. "Smoke it."

"Very funny." Ian waited.

Rab shrugged and said finally, "What can I do?"

"You could leave."

Rab looked at him tightly. "This is a change of heart."

"No," Ian answered, but he didn't elaborate. Suddenly he smiled his tight smile. "Never mind, just be glad it's not me or you he loves. Great man to be loved by."

Rab looked at him again and felt his chest tighten miserably.

Ian smiled slowly, his eyes narrowed, hard as flint.

Rab spat on the ground then abruptly climbed up into the tractor, lowered the trailer, and drove away.

"We'll have to get a replacement," the old man said across the table.

Rab stopped eating, fork poised. "A *replacement?*" What was she, a fucking spare part?

"You heard." The old man fixed his eyes on him, challenging. *Go on, let's hear it.*

But John spoke first, bringing his father back round. His voice was lazy, amused, as if the whole thing was vastly entertaining. "You don't even know where she's gone." He looked at Rab and smiled.

Ian watched and said nothing.

"I don't give a fuck where she's gone," the old man said, keeping his head down and shovelling food into his mouth. John tilted his head and raised an eyebrow at Rab as if to say, Listen to this. "Or why," he went on abruptly. "Just so long as I don't have to eat corned beef every night."

"She wouldn't just disappear," Ian said finally. "She's never done anything spontaneous in her life." He looked at John, let a nicely judged pause go by, then said, "Maybe something's happened to her." *There's your challenge John.*

John looked at him. "You're right Ian." He smiled. *Back to you.*

Rab felt a cold, sick anxiety in his stomach. Two days missing, two days dead, and

they've only just brought her up in conversation. Here every day for the past twenty years of her life and they're behaving as if she went in and out like a fucking tomcat.

"We'll have to report it to the police." Ian dropped it in nicely like everyone had just been waiting to hear it.

The old man's head came up, a dull flushed red. "I'll break every bone in your body if you even think about it. I've had enough of people walking out on me. She won't be coming back…" Rab saw John's lopsided smile, watched him turn and look out of the window, "…not into this house," the old man finished and pushed up from the table. "She's left. You can tell anyone who asks just that. Run off with her fancy man."

Ian watched him, incredulous. He's scared shitless. He doesn't want to know.

He stomped out of the room. They heard the television come on in the front room, a distant babble of tragedy and reserved calm, the evening news.

Ian looked at Rab. He looked as if he'd like to do a little murder himself. He turned to John and came face to face with John watching him. His eyes were fixed, that strange cold black way they went whenever he concentrated intensely on anything. John never normally looked at him. He didn't like the way he was watching him now. What had she threatened him with that was bad enough to make him kill her? He looked away quickly from his steady gaze.

Rab was still staring at nothing, his nostrils pinched.

Danny came in, startling their silence. Ian looked at the bruises for a second time that day. Their colour was even uglier under the kitchen light. His beauty was marred by one closed eye, livid, barely closed cuts.

Rab looked at him once and a muscle twitched in his cheek as if he had clamped his teeth shut too long. Danny looked at Rab and nothing moved in his face at all.

John heard Rab hesitate as he got up to leave the room. "Get out Rab," he said without turning.

Rab went out and Danny came in and sat down.

Ian watched him slice himself some corned beef, cut himself bread, then help himself to some tomatoes. He looked self-contained, detached, just like he always did.

"We're getting a replacement Danny," John said, carefully prising a biscuit from the folds of its wrapper. Ian wondered what he intended to do with it. He poured himself some tea. His hands always looked huge round cups, holding food. "A replacement for your mother," he clarified.

Danny stopped spreading his bread. He looked like a lightweight boxer after an ill-matched fight; edgy, angry, only half-beaten.

"Your daddy doesn't reckon she'll be back. Your daddy doesn't even *want* her back." John dunked the custard cream and looked up suddenly into Ian's face. Ian swallowed convulsively, with an audible noise. "Ian thinks we should tell the police. Ian reckons, I reckon, that she's been done away with."

Danny began to slice his tomatoes with extreme care and arrange them like a mosaic on his bread. He overlapped them carefully so that no bread showed through.

"Ian has an over-active imagination…" John was still looking up at him, his face now devoid of colour, his lips almost as white as the rest of him. The uneaten biscuit lay in a soggy mass on his plate where he'd pushed it. "…and too many eyes."

The knife snicked down suddenly. John pulled away, but not fast enough. The knife caught the side of his hand and sliced through it cleanly. Blood appeared instantly, and in quantity, all over the table. The knife was imbedded, point down, into the wood.

Ian had jumped back on reflex. Now he stood up slowly, on legs with rubber muscles. He looked at the knife.

John held up his hand. He seemed fascinated by the blood curling in a long snake down his arm, soaking into the pulled-up sleeve of his sweater. "Little bastard," he said, utterly without inflection.

Christ, this is it, Ian thought and watched in disbelief as Danny pressed his sandwich together carefully and began to eat it. He bit it in small bites on the other side of his face, away from the closed eye, as if his jaw hurt him.

John took a hankie from his pocket and wrapped his hand in it. Ian still stood in the middle of the floor, one hand on the chair-back, poised halfway in flight.

"Beat it," John said, looking up at him. Danny ate his sandwich slowly without looking up.

Ian couldn't move.

"Go on, get out." John flicked his head in the direction of the door. "Moosh."

Ian got out. The last thing he saw was Danny reaching across the table to pour himself a cup of tea and John's good hand coming out to meet him.

John held the knife in his other hand. The blade had a thin coat of blood down one side, like clear red varnish. Already it was changing colour. "You love me Danny?"

Danny took another step back and came up hard against the fridge. John held the knifepoint pressing into his good cheek, under his clear eye. The point hurt. It was sharp and hot against the skin-tight feeling of his face.

"Course you do." John dropped the knife hand and stepped back. "Upstairs."

Danny moved forward and went out the kitchen door. They went upstairs. John gestured with the knife. "Your room."

Danny opened the door.

"Move everything out that's yours, your clothes, everything personal..." he paused, Danny looked at him, "...into my room. I want all of you, everything of you, in my room. I'll be waiting." He went out. "And keep this door open."

Danny heard him walk along to his room. He heard the sink tap running. He moved to the wardrobe and felt a heavy numbness settle in his cheeks. It wasn't the stiff pain of earlier, it was worse. It felt as if his face had died.

John's voice came down the hall. "Get moving Danny."

Danny opened the door and scooped out an armful of his clothes, hangers and all. He walked along to John's room.

"Dump them on the bed." John was trying awkwardly to patch his hand, but the cut was too deep and still bleeding profusely. John looked up at him. "Come and hold it."

Danny crossed to the window where John leaned against the ledge and wiped his hands on his jeans.

"Press the two sides together." John watched his face. It was very close to his own.

Danny held his hand, pressing the wound shut. John placed his own fingers alongside and squeezed it shut, holding it in place. "Right, take that." He gestured at the reel of tape with his head. "Put plenty on."

Danny taped it up then bandaged it tightly in an attempt to prevent it re-opening. The knife lay on the sink top. John saw him seeing it. Neither of them spoke. "Get the rest of your stuff."

Danny went back down the hall to his room. John sat on the window ledge and waited.

Danny went to and fro, to and fro. Finally he brought back nothing but a handful of paperbacks. "That's it," he said.

"Good." John was putting a cigarette awkwardly into his mouth. He didn't try to light it. "Put your stuff away. There's room in the wardrobe."

Danny moved across the room.

"Shut the door first."

Danny shut it.

"Lock it."

Danny locked it.

"Good," John said again.

Danny hung up his clothes, put some bits in the unoccupied drawers of the tallboy, and squeezed his books onto the window ledge. Now they would fade in a different place.

"Light this," John said, nodding his head to his left-hand pocket to indicate his matches.

Danny slid his hand into his jeans. They were new, loose on him. The thin fabric of the lining conveyed the heat of his body instantly. There was nothing in the left-hand pocket. "It's empty," he said, trying to keep it out of his voice. He withdrew his hand, looking up at his face.

"Then try the other."

"Fuck you," Danny said, not moving. John stared at him. Finally Danny slid his hand in quickly, but it made no difference. He could feel every vein on its heavy body as he dragged the matches out. He felt it surge with excitement against his fingers. He could still feel it after he held the matches clear in his hand. Danny stared at him, feeling the colour burn in his face.

"Light it."

Danny took a match out and struck it, holding it up with a rock-steady hand. Nevertheless John took his hand and held it while he drew on the cigarette, then he took the cigarette from his mouth with his injured hand and pressed the glowing tip down into Danny's palm.

Danny pulled his hand back sharply, crying out, but John caught it in a vice-like grip.

John let him go and stubbed his cigarette out in the sink. Danny plunged his hand under the cold tap. "You cunt," he cursed.

"Thank Rab for that one. He was my inspiration."

Danny turned his back to him and held his hand under the tap until it was numb.

John lifted his hair gently and kissed the back of his neck. Danny felt goose-pimples cross his body like the touch of a cold breeze. He turned the tap off and picked up the towel, trying to step sideways out of John's reach. Suddenly he found himself pinned. "Say yes Danny."

"To what?"

"Just for the sake of it."

Danny said it.

"Sounds good." John moved back unexpectedly. "Keep practising, I'm going to take a shower."

Danny didn't turn round until he left the room and when he did it was only to hear the lock click in the door.

"Rab?"

Rab sat up in the dark. He was lying fully-dressed on the bed. "What is it?"

"It's me, Ian."

"What do you want?"

Ian came in and closed the door. He sat down on the bed without replying. As if I didn't know, Rab thought. He lay down again.

Ian could just make out his face in the dark. The tip of his cigarette glowed then faded. "He's moved Danny in with him."

Rab said nothing. What was there to say?

Ian watched the tip glow again, brighter this time. He felt his eyes start to nip. The air in here was like the fugues of Hell. He must have smoked at least fifty cigarettes

to produce this lot. "Hurting?" he asked quietly, but not quietly enough that Rab couldn't hear the edge of satisfaction hidden in it.

"Why don't you fuck off Ian?"

Ian spread his hands. "Sorry."

"Like fuck you are."

They sat quiet for a couple of minutes. Rab began to grow tired of being watched. Worse, he could feel something beginning to crawl into the dark beside them, something misallied from his pain and Ian's lust.

"I can make it better," Ian said. How often had Rab heard that voice in the dark saying a thousand variations of the same thing? How many ways can you buy souls anyway?

"No you can't." Rab shifted himself up the bed into a more upright position, kill a few loose ideas, maybe even some of his own.

"I listened."

"What?"

"I've been listening outside the door."

"Whose door?" But Rab knew whose.

"Oh guess Rab. Go on, try."

"This time it isn't a suggestion Ian, do it. Fuck off."

"Don't you want to know?"

"No, I don't."

"Danny tried to kill him tonight."

"*What?*"

"He tried to kill him."

"When?"

"In the kitchen, after you left."

"You're lying." Rab sat up and tried to read his face in the dark.

"No I'm not. He took a swipe at him with a knife."

"A knife? What fucking knife?"

"The paring knife."

"I don't believe you."

"Why not?"

"Because you're you." Rab sank down again. The cigarette came back to life.

"Okay. You take a look at John's hand tomorrow."

"His hand?"

"He got his hand."

"Trying to kill him? I suppose he missed?" Rab's voice was heavy with sarcasm.

A silence fell again. Ian moved irritably. "He's got plenty of reasons to kill him," he said.

"Plus some," Rab agreed.

"Why don't you believe me then?"

"Because John wouldn't let him get that far, that's why." Rab paused and dragged on his cigarette again. "What's this for Ian?"

"What?" Ian said evasively.

"What really happened?"

"I don't know."

Rab hadn't expected that answer. He sat up. "What do you mean you don't know? Weren't you there?"

"I was there alright. I saw everything. One minute Danny was slicing tomatoes, next he'd brought the knife down on John's hand. John's reflexes were fast, faster than mine would have been, but Danny still got him." Ian licked his lips. "He bled like a stuck pig."

"Oh boy."

"He sent me out of the kitchen. I thought, This is it, he's going to kill him, but nothing happened. I hung around in the hall until they came out and went upstairs. Then I hear Danny trucking his stuff to his room. First he stabs him then he moves in with him. You tell me."

"He's moved him in with him?"

Ian nodded.

"What did he say?"

"I thought you didn't want to know?"

Rab sighed ostentatiously.

"You owe me, you know. I..."

"Look," Rab swung up against him, pressing his arm against his chest, "I don't have to take this shit off you every time. I'm buying, okay? Tell me what you heard then we can get our dicks out and everybody'll be happy, especially you. I don't need this shit."

Rab let him go and moved back. He stubbed out his cigarette in the ashtray beside the bed. Everybody breathed nicely. Ian's hand slid across his thigh. Rab caught it and stopped it in its tracks. "Later. What did you hear?"

"This..."

John had come back, dressed, then taken Danny to the bathroom. He had sat like a prison warder, watching Danny's blurred outline through the frosted glass of the shower, watching it the same way he watched everything, with a cold detachment that never quite reached his eyes. The eyes have it, Danny thought, trying to remember where he'd read that.

They had bumped into Ian on the way back. He seemed more surprised to see Danny in one piece than to see him escorted from the bathroom. Danny was pleased to see how easily everyone accepted his new status of boy on a rope. *That's because you accept it yourself Danny-Boy.*

Back in John's room Danny turned his back and pulled on clean shorts, expecting at any moment to hear John's command to leave them off, but John said nothing. He climbed into bed and lay down, and immediately felt his hair wet against the pillow. He tried to lie still but couldn't. He sat up.

John looked at him.

"My hair's wet."

John didn't even acknowledge that he had spoken, he simply began to take off his clothes. Danny shut his eyes, but he felt his face burn as if he were still watching. Couldn't he do this in the fucking dark?

Danny's burnt hand throbbed. *Eye for an eye, tooth for a tooth John?* It was probably a good job he'd missed.

The bed moved. Danny opened his eyes in surprise He'd forgotten him for an instant. John had one knee on it, and he hadn't even made the pretence of putting on pyjamas.

Danny's face went red again. He turned his head away. He felt John climb in and lie down. He felt the slight down-pull of his weight on the old mattress. He might look like a half-starved jackal, but he still out-weighed Danny by plenty. Danny kept his body tight and far away from his. *What are you going to do Danny, lie awake all night so you don't touch him?*

"Put out the lights."

"What?"

"Put out the lights Danny... up there on the ceiling."

Danny got up and crossed to the door.

John watched him, one arm under his head. He watched him walk round the bed and flick the switch. And by the light of the bedside lamp he watched him walk back.

Danny stopped at the foot of the bed. "Are you going to watch me all my life? Every waking moment?"

"Maybe."

"You can't be there all the time."

"Try me."

"I intend to."

"Is that a threat?"

Danny didn't say anything.

"That's twice you've threatened me today. First the knife, now this."

Danny still didn't say anything.

"Get in the bed." John's head jerked sharply. When Danny didn't move John's face started to set like fast-drying concrete, turning grey and heavy. Soon it would be dry and white, set hard, eyes fixed forever on Danny's face.

Danny felt a surge of anger. "You're fucking nuts John." His hands were a dead pallor on the bed-end.

"I said, get in the bed." John raised himself on one elbow.

"You can't keep me locked up forever."

John stared at him for a long moment then smiled slowly, oddly. "Do you love?" The words dropped into the sudden silence of the room. Danny felt goose-pimples spring up all along his arms.

"What?" His voice sounded dull-witted, boneless.

"I said, do you love Danny?"

"I don't understand."

John smiled, wider this time, "No you don't, do you?"

He lay back down suddenly, as if his arm was exhausted from supporting his weight. He pushed the blankets down his chest, low onto his belly, like a parody of seduction. "Come here." And now his smile was as light and spacey as his eyes.

Danny moved round the bed as if mesmerised.

"You're on the raft Danny and the oil slick will get you in the end."

Danny stared at him. *What?*

John threw back the blankets. "Get in."

Danny hesitated.

"Don't worry, I've got to wait till you get really cold and hungry first, until there's nothing else for you to do but dive in and swim for it..." he paused "...and *then* I get you."

Danny climbed in and waited for him to pounce. But nothing happened, only John's hand brushing lightly over his face, skimming its contours with his fingertips. They slid over it minutely, callused and rough. Danny looked at the ceiling, lying rigid on his back, hardly daring to breathe.

Eventually it stopped. John's hand dropped exhaustedly on Danny's pillow, the back of his fingers resting against Danny's cheek. Danny could hear his breathing, light and erratic, like a man running, but nothing else.

They lay there poised in the silence, absolutely still, for a long time.

Eventually Danny fell asleep, the light still on, and slid immediately, like something abandoned, into a dream of panting dogs.

Rab enjoyed it.

He was cold and empty inside, and Ian had all the fervour of a long-lost lover, all

the hunger of someone who thought he was never going to eat again. Rab was the prodigal returned and his body was the fatted calf. Ian fed on him until it burnt the pain out of his body and he forgot.

Rab got an erection. In warmth, maybe even in gratitude.

Ian discovered it with wonder, tasting a satisfaction so intense it nearly blinded him. He handled Rab with a fragile touch that was heart-breaking to watch.

And Rab enjoyed it.

He lay there feeling it come up out of him, burning a path of heat through the numbness, and wanted it again, like a drunk, or an addict. He looked at Ian and said, "Take it in your mouth."

Ian looked at him, not even daring to understand.

"Come on, quickly," Rab said, feeling the heat begin to ebb. Ian heard the urgency and did as he was told.

He had never tasted him before, cold and salt. He relished it.

It happened again, a second time. Rab came up, just as hard, just as hot. He lay on the bed with Ian's head between his legs and thought about nothing, and this time Ian tasted it hot and fresh and bitter salt, scalding down his throat.

The taste of power.

TWENTY-TWO

It was the last week of September. All the Cropstores were filled, everything was on schedule.

Five mornings a week a local woman washed their clothes, made their beds and prepared their meals. On the Saturday she went shopping with Rab, just as he had formerly done with Margaret. He seldom even spoke to her.

She knew that Margaret Jackson Moore had gone off leaving her family in the lurch. She also knew that the eldest and youngest sons shared a room while one sat empty, but placed no special significance upon the fact. After all, their father intended to fill it soon with hired help.

She was working in the front parlour, dusting. They could hear her faintly in the kitchen, singing to herself tunelessly. John sat at the table crumbling a cracker into fragments. When Rab came in Danny moved automatically to get up.

"Sit down." John's voice was sharp.

Danny's lips compressed, but he sat down again. His hands found something on the table to occupy themselves with. Safely.

Rab looked at John and John looked at Rab. Ian went on eating carefully without looking at anyone.

Rab went to the cooker and helped himself to food. When he sat down he broke a chunk off the loaf. The bread knife was lost somewhere behind the cooker.

Ian kept eating.

One side of Danny's face was a faint patchwork of colour. A pale sickish yellow, a dull purplish green, two fine brown scars. His eyes were clear again, their usual vivid green. The old bruises lent him a kind of piratical charm.

Ian found himself studying him, trying to see what was left of the boy in him. He would be twenty soon. He had an odd disturbing mix of age and youth to him. The smoothness of his skin, his slightly boyish leanness, and then those old, old eyes. Give him five years John and it'll be a demon you take to your bed instead of a lover. Give him ten and he'll eat you for breakfast. Ian looked again at the ghosts of John's blows on his cheek. If he lives that long, he thought.

He looked at Rab, then away again quickly when he saw John was watching him. Rab looked at his dinner, Danny stared out the window, and Ian wanted to laugh. He bit it down. It was an unhealthy idea.

John stood up slowly and walked round behind Danny's chair. His eyes were fixed on Rab, very intent.

Rab looked up.

Danny's head turned slowly, meeting Rab's eyes. John moved in closer behind his chair.

Ian licked his lips as John brought one hand to rest on Danny's shoulder. Danny's head jerked slightly towards it. John's other hand slid briefly down over Danny's hair then onto his cheek and, very gently, down over his mouth, cupping his chin. John's thumb brushed across his lips, stayed there. Danny's eyes were unreadable. Rab turned his head away with a jerk, as if he had been slapped.

John smiled.

Ian put down his knife. He would have liked to have slit Danny open from his throat to his bowels and watched him bleed to death.

"Come on," John said.

Danny got up from the table, shrugging out of John's hands as if they itched him.

Rab stared at the empty seat. Danny walked out of the room stiffly, like a man walking on hate. John closed the door quietly as if he were leaving a sick room.

Rab picked up his glass and hurled it across the room. It smashed against the wall, showering the cooker in glass and beer. It sizzled on the stove top, filling the room instantly with its rich malty smell. Foam ran down the wall.

He picked up the salt cellar, unscrewed the top, and emptied it into his food.

He began mashing it in with his fist, pounding pie, potatoes, gravy, everything, into a slushy brown mess. He picked up the plate and got up. He crossed to the stove and pressed it hard into the wall above it, grinding it in its face. When he let go the plate held a moment then fell off, breaking cleanly into two halves on top of the cooker. He went out of the door without looking back.

The food dripped slowly off the wall in greasy lumps. Ian sat quietly listening to the sizzle of spilt beer and breathing in the thickening smell of burning food.

Danny sat down on the bed.

John closed the door and locked it. He crossed to the window and stood looking out.

"Why do you do that?" Danny asked.

"Do what?" John half-turned from the window to look at him.

"Why do you lock the door? Not one of them would dare to come in here, so why do you do it?"

John smiled. "Why do you think?"

Danny didn't think, Danny knew. "Fucking faggot," he said.

John laughed softly and turned round to face him, pushing his hands further into his pockets. His outline seemed to get sharper every day. Not solid-packed as it had been before, but wide and menacing, like a tiger taking form out of a mass of darkness. He never finished a meal. Food didn't feed him. He looked at Danny and chewed on his lip. "Eight days Danny."

Danny looked up at him from under his brows.

"Bet that's the longest you've ever gone without it in your whole life." John paused. "Hungry yet?"

Danny dipped his head again and studied the floor.

"Rab thinks you take it up the arse every night." John laughed, then the smile went out like a light. "Maybe it's time you did." He turned his back again, once more looking out the window.

Rain began spitting down, gradually at first, then picking up momentum until it beat upon the glass in streams. The room changed colour, sank under water.

"Come here." John's voice was quiet, without force.

Danny stayed where he was.

"I'm sick of asking you for everything twice Danny," he said in the same soft tone. "Come *here*," he snapped suddenly.

Danny jumped up and crossed to the window before he could change his mind.

John reached for his arm and pulled him in front of him. He wrapped his arms around him, pinning him back against his chest. Danny's thighs were pressed hard against the window ledge as John leaned against him. John laid his face against his hair. Danny looked out into the rain, grey in a violet sky, and tried not to feel anything.

"*Danny*..." John whispered. It was almost a question. His arms were strong and tight around him.

Danny let himself go limp. A voice in his head said desperately, Don't *do* that.

Eight days, Danny whispered back.

"Danny?" John said again, and this time it *was* a question. He was rubbing his

cheek against his hair.

Danny shifted his head slightly. Don't *do* that, the voice hissed.

Christ, eight whole days.

"Love me Danny." It wasn't a question this time. John's mouth felt soft against his ear.

Danny dropped his head back to let John's mouth in against his skin.

John pulled him round to face him, pressing his mouth against his. It could have been called a kiss, except it was too frantic for that.

Danny held onto him as if he was drowning. John's hands tugged at his clothes, gripping his head, kissing him again. *Rab*, Danny thought blindly. But it was nothing but a name. It had no magic any more.

John was pulling him to the bed, pulling his clothes off. Danny lay there watching him as he undressed. He was magnificent; rangy, raw, filled with rage. Danny's mouth went dry. Little Red Riding Hood about to be eaten by the wolf.

John lay down beside him in the half-light and ran his hands over his body. He looked in Danny's eyes. "Do you want it?"

Danny shut his eyes, his mouth, *everything*, tight.

John's hand tightened like a vice on his face. He felt the pain shoot from his cheek to his eye. "*Look* at me."

Danny opened his eyes.

"Do you want it?"

Danny didn't move.

"Do you want me?"

There was no reply.

"Do you?" His grip tightened.

Danny let his eyes slide closed. *Twice Danny*.

John bent his head and kissed his mouth gently, then looked at him again. His voice was like melting sugar. "Do you love?" he whispered.

No, Danny thought. That was three times. There should be a cock's crow here. Where was the cock?

But he already knew where it was. Exactly where it belonged. Strangle-hold tight, right in his hand.

Rab had slept fitfully for an hour or two. He had woken finally at quarter to three, pinned onto his side, with sweat streaming down his chest and soaking the sheet beneath him. His hair clung to his neck in wet strands.

He pushed up out of the bed and urinated in the sink. "Bad habit," he muttered, leaving the tap to run while he rolled a cigarette.

Ian had come to his room earlier, but he had sent him packing. He had locked the door, managed to sleep eventually, and this was the end result: only half the night gone and the worst part to be faced alone. He didn't like the sound of that either.

He stood up and turned off the tap. He looked out of the window and shivered. The sweat was chilling on his skin. He rubbed the back of his neck with a towel. Outside the wind was picking up. Occasionally a fitful burst of rain hit the window like a smattering of gravel. November soon. It already felt like bloody winter.

He climbed back into bed, back into his own residual heat. The sheets felt slightly damp, but they comforted him nevertheless. He pushed his pillow up the bed a little and lay there thinking half-thoughts that didn't lift up too many stones. Nothing too serious. Nothing that would commit him to doing anything.

He felt half-drowsy and found his hand, cigarette still lit, lying on the quilt. He shook himself and leaned over to stub it out. "More bad habits," he muttered.

He sat still suddenly and listened. Someone was outside his door. Ian? But the door handle didn't move. Rab listened again, but could hear nothing. He felt sure the person was just standing there, listening. He felt a mad desire to sing, recite poetry. He got up quickly, without giving himself time to think, and unlocked the door.

John stood there looking at him. Rab couldn't begin to fathom his expression. There was only the faint light from his bedside lamp, a hopeless item, so thickly enclosed in pink silk the light was subdued to the point of idiocy. John's face looked cavernous in the darkness of the hall. Only the broadest bones of his face were illuminated, the rest of him was nothing but darkness. He didn't speak. Rab wondered for an instant if he was sleepwalking, but he was wearing jeans. Did sleepwalkers bother to dress? Even half-dress?

Rab became aware of his own nakedness. He felt fragile against the sheer size of him. John's flesh had been pared down in the last few weeks, leaving nothing but the muscles roped onto his broad bones. His neck ran thick into massive shoulders; his jaw seemed heavy as an animal's; his mouth wide and inhumanly dangerous. Rab felt like a peeled prawn.

"What do you want?" It seemed an odd question as soon as it came out. Why not, 'What are you doing here?' Or even, 'What the fuck are you doing here?'

"I had a dream," John said. His voice was slow, careful, as if he were considering the words.

What? Rab thought. *Was* he sleepwalking? He began to feel cold and irritated. "What do you want John? It's past three in the morning."

"I saw your light," John said in the same considering voice. His body stood completely relaxed but totally unmoving, like a puppet at rest.

Rab turned back into his room and pulled his trousers from the chair. He yanked them on, buttoning them up with his back to him. When he turned back he found John had come into the room noiselessly and closed the door.

Quite suddenly he didn't want visits from John in the middle of the night. He didn't like the way John spoke to him, or the fact that John was between him and the door. He decided to roll a cigarette because if he had something in his hands they couldn't do anything else. And when he had a cigarette in his mouth he wouldn't be able to smartmouth anybody. They all seemed like perfectly good ideas, but before he could get the fucking thing where it belonged he looked at John and said, "You had a dream and decided that since I was up you would come and tell me about it. Why not Danny? Or do you only fuck it and not talk to it?"

I knew it, he thought. I knew I needed this cigarette.

He shoved it in his mouth and lit it before he could say anything else. He watched John over the flame, waiting for the first sign, but all John said was, "Remember the last time?"

"What last time?" Rab watched his chest warily, the slow heavy fall of his breathing. Should I be able to see that? he wondered.

"Last time we did it."

Rab looked at him, feeling something shift under the question. He would have liked to sit down, but he didn't want to risk being any smaller than he already was.

John closed his eyes abruptly and leaned his head back as if he were weary, like a man confessing, a man tired of lying. "Last time you *let* me do it." His voice was only just sarcastic, as if he was too tired even to be cynical.

His eyes opened slowly. For the first time Rab could see them, the slash of them under his lashes, caught in his tipped-back head.

Rab looked away, fixing his eyes on the sink. "No," he said.

"I do."

Rab wasn't sure what he was supposed to say to that other than maybe, Tell me

all about it John, let's reminisce. So he said, "Clap, clap." But he still kept his eyes averted.

He sensed John getting up off the door and crossing the room. He had to fight the desire to bolt past him and out the door. Instead he moved sharply away towards the bed and sat down. A bad move, but better than letting John near him. Now, at least, he was closer to the door than John was.

John filled the gap between the bed and the chair and looked down at him. He pushed his hands into his pockets. Rab looked at his feet. They were good feet. Like his body. It was a good body too. Shame about the face. "I'm not going to hurt you."

More sarcasm, less weary this time.

"Fuck off," Rab said, jumping up. It was too close to the truth and it seemed to drag his own cowardice up and shove it in his face.

"You're never scared of me?" John said and this time he was smiling faintly. When he smiled he looked vaguely like Danny, or was it simply a trick of the light?

"Terrified," Rab said. It was supposed to be sarcastic, but like everything else he'd said it seemed to peel away in his hands leaving nothing but naked truth behind it.

John's smile broadened. "Sit down."

Rab glared at him and caught it again, that touch of Danny, just there. How had he never seen it before? How could it be there in this great ugly bastard?

Rab sat down, eyes on his face.

"What do you see?"

Rab wet his mouth. What was he, a fucking mind reader? Suddenly he felt tired. He washed his face with his hand, pinching the bridge of his nose. His cigarette had gone out. He reached across the table for a light. When he spoke there was nothing left in his voice. "You came to tell me about a dream, right?"

"No, I came to tell me why I didn't kill you." John's voice was sharply cold.

Rab's hand jumped, but he steadied it and lit his cigarette. He inhaled it deeply, licking the strong sweet taste of liquorice off his lips as he blew smoke down his nose. "I already know why. It's not news."

John's smile glimmered again. "Tell me," he said.

"Security. In case Danny wouldn't play ball."

"Think he cares that much?"

"Maybe." It was the best he could do.

"But more than he cares for me?"

Rab looked up. "More than he hates you."

"Does he? Hate me?" John looked down at him, smiling.

Checkmate. Nothing was sure. We're playing games with an unknown quantity, both bluffing, both hoping like hell the other doesn't know how insecure we feel. Rab took a drag on his cigarette again, studied the carpet.

"I dreamt..." John paused and the pause went on too long.

Eventually Rab looked up. John was holding him with his eyes. "Do you find him *very* beautiful?" And it was dripping with sarcasm again.

Rab felt himself blush, half in anger, half in embarrassment.

"Go on, Mr Macho, let it go. Only me to hear." John was smiling again.

"Yes." He bit it out. Fuck you John.

"Do you still want him?"

"What do you think?" Rab wanted to gouge his eyes out.

"I don't think, I know." He showed his teeth this time. "But I like to hear you say it."

"Why? Can't you fuck him without it? Need to gloat to get it up?"

"No," John said, smiling harder than ever, so hard Rab knew that whatever it was he had to say it was going to hurt, "that was only with you."

Rab heard himself snap, like an audible breaking of his back. He closed his eyes.

"Don't cry Robbie." John's voice was low, sweet, almost promising.

Rab jumped him with a determination to do some damage. John took the blows in deadly silence. It was like punching a wall. When John finally hit back Rab felt the impact of his blow like a sledgehammer.

Everything stopped.

They stood facing each other. Rab panting, badly out of breath. "Some day," he grunted.

John wiped blood away from the corner of his mouth. His smile when it came was lopsided. His teeth looked pink, washed with blood. Maybe it was only another trick of the light. "Maybe I should finish this with Danny." He seemed to take a shaky breath, or perhaps it was a laugh. "This makes me so mean and hard."

"Don't," Rab said. It was supposed to be threatening, but it sounded like pleading.

"Why not? He's a big boy, time he learnt to fight back." He wiped again at his mouth, but the blood trickled on.

"You know he won't fight you." Rab winced at the breath forcing through his chest.

"You mean he's chickenshit."

"Yeah, just like the rest of us. Don't touch him," Rab finished, trying to keep his breath shallow. One of his ears was ringing alarmingly. Shooting pains went up the side of his head.

"You've got nothing to threaten me with Rab. Why don't you try bargaining for a change?"

Rab looked at him, trying to read his face. The blood was hardening at the side of his mouth, making it look wider, carved into the stone of his face. "Bargain? I've got even less to bargain with."

"Try me." John shifted his weight, holding one arm away from his body slightly and rubbing his shoulder as if it pained him.

Rab wiped his cheek and forehead upwards with the heel of one hand.

John moved towards him. His voice, when he spoke, was warm and quiet, barely above a whisper. "I dreamt that once you kissed me, remember that?"

Rab lifted his head to look at him, trying not to move too much. He shook his head. He didn't even know he'd done it.

"I want to feel that again."

Rab looked at him. "Why?" he said, only it came out as a croak.

John moved closer, close enough that finally Rab could see his eyes, but all he could see was crowded out with blackness. "Because I want to know just how low you can crawl." And he inclined his head, waiting.

Finally Rab lifted his face to his and their mouths touched briefly. John's lips were closed, sealed against him, like an enemy's. He looked into his eyes and could see nothing but that black.

John moved back. He smiled, but he said nothing.

Rab watched him, waited, but still John said nothing. The ultimate revenge.

He left the room, taking his truth with him.

Danny felt him come back into bed. He had been dimly aware of him leaving, but had no conception of how long he had been gone. John lay on his side until Danny began to slide back into sleep then he clicked on the lamp. Danny woke up, blinking hard against the light. He shaded his eyes with his hands. "What's up?" He was blinded. All he could see was John's dark shape against the light.

"I am." John was staring down at him. He took Danny's hand and pushed it between his legs.

Danny lay for a moment, numbed by the idiocy of sleep, then he groaned in

protest, trying to pull his hand away. "For fuck's sake, you're joking, what time is it?"

"Who cares? Do it."

"No." Danny pulled his hand back again.

John put his hand around Danny's throat, spreading it neatly across his Adam's apple. Already it was uncomfortable. Danny came further into wakefulness. He swallowed awkwardly. Suddenly he saw John's face. "What happened to your mouth?"

John caught his hand and pushed it back between his legs. "The same thing as will happen to yours if you don't start pulling me."

Danny could hear the anger. He was like a pressure cooker coming up to steam. What the fuck had he been doing? "No," he said, just to try the sound it.

John grabbed his pubic hair and twisted viciously. Danny hissed a breath in between his teeth.

"Now look, you've made me break my promise." He smiled briefly down into Danny's face then dropped his eyes like a veil. "For the last time, do it." He put his hand back down over Danny's throat. The pressure was faintly heavier. It made his throat ache like unspent tears.

"Alright," he said thickly.

John pushed the blankets down to his thighs. "I want you to watch."

Danny sat up slightly, trying not to shiver in the chill air. John propped his hands under his head and studied the curve of Danny's back, the hair curling down his neck. It needed cut, as usual. He watched Danny's white hand, the faint red-gold hair on his wrist catching the light as it slid up and down his cock. He read Danny's profile, saw the set expression of his mouth. He hates me, he thought.

Danny blinked his eyes rapidly, fighting to keep awake. John reached out and touched his hair, making him jump. "Faster."

Danny worked him harder, marvelling as he always did at the size of him. John was never anything less than monumentally erect. No half-measures for John-boy.

John watched Danny's eyes close gradually under the stroking of his hand on his hair. He pulled it viciously. "*Awake*, Danny."

Danny's eyes flew open and glared round at him. John smiled and nodded his head down at himself. "Keep looking."

Danny held his eyes for a moment longer then did as he was told. John waited. Sooner or later it would happen. He watched Danny watching. "Slowly," he warned.

Danny slowed.

"Harder." He ran his hand over the curve of Danny's shoulder then down into his armpit. Danny shifted slightly. John looked at his mouth… *there*. He felt a surge of excitement. Danny's tongue ran over his dry lips, a faint flush stole into his cheeks. His mouth seemed to decompress, the lips become full. He was watching his own hand covering up, then slowly unpeeling the plummy head of John's penis.

John watched him and knew that if he uncovered him now he would be erect. He said his name. Danny's shoulders stiffened. He didn't turn or reply, but John knew he was listening.

"Kneel between my legs," John ordered.

He didn't move at first, then slowly he began to get up.

"No tricks Danny-Boy."

Danny moved slowly, delaying the inevitable. John's legs slid apart and Danny climbed between them. He still held John in his hand. The new position forced his dick upright, like a totem pole.

"Up on your knees Danny-boy."

Danny got up. His mouth was pressed hard together again, his eyes glittered angrily, but it was there nevertheless. "*Oh yes*," John whispered. He swallowed

carefully then said in a raw voice, "Go on."

Danny took him hard in his hand, watching John's face watching him. He couldn't wank him easily or well in this new position, but it didn't matter. It never mattered. John had what he needed.

"Oh *yes*…" he said again, this time on a long drawn-out sigh. And he began to jerk and tremble in Danny's hand.

TWENTY-THREE

Danny woke with a splitting headache. When he tried to lift his head off the pillow lights came up out of his temples and hit him behind his eyes like blows from a sledgehammer. He laid his head down, carefully supporting the back of his neck, because he couldn't bear the touch of the pillow.

"Come on Danny-boy, rise and shine." John spoke to him over his shoulder as he opened the curtains.

Danny wasn't sure if he replied or not. John turned towards the bed. Somewhere in the house a door slammed. He heard Ian shouting in the hallway.

"You're late as usual." John walked over to the bed, saw his face then asked, "What's up?"

"My fucking head."

"What about it?"

"I feel as if a horse kicked it."

John looked at him. "Sit up."

Danny tried, but it made him feel outrageously sick.

John sat on the edge of the bed. "Too many late nights Danny-boy."

Danny looked at him, suddenly hating the way his eyes were always hidden, the way his mouth seemed set in a perpetual sneer. "Don't call me that."

John bent his head forward, still smiling, and kissed his mouth.

Danny pulled his head away, sending seasick waves of pain through his skull. He felt as if his eyes would burst. "Oh Jesus," he muttered, dropping his head back against the pillow.

"You are in a bad way, aren't you?"

Danny said nothing.

"Kiss me again and I'll let you stay in bed."

Danny opened his eyes. They looked like bruises in his white face.

John didn't let his smile slip. *What black dreams built this Danny?*

"I can't even think of anything ugly enough to call you John."

"Don't try, just kiss me." John bent his head and pushed his hand down under the blankets. He kissed him and mauled him until Danny felt suffocated.

John pulled away and looked at him, his eyes slowly travelling over his face. He followed Danny's brow with his thumb, eased his cheekbones out towards his temples, then he bent his head and kissed him again.

"Enough," Danny said, pulling his head away.

"No," John said, looking at the unnatural red of his mouth against the pallor of his skin. He pulled Danny's head back again to meet him.

"Leave me alone."

"One more."

"I feel sick John."

"Just one."

"No!" Danny snapped it in sudden temper. He felt as if the top of his head would come off. "Leave me alone." Two spots of colour appeared on his grey face.

John slapped him once, only once, making his head fall off onto the floor and explode. After he had picked it up and screwed it back on John lifted his hand and pressed his lips to his wrist, kissing it softly, telling him he loved him. Tears dripped off Danny's face. He knew they weren't supposed to be there, he knew he had his eyes closed to keep them in, but they seeped out anyway. John kissed his palms and told

him again how much he loved him. He even sounded as if he meant it.

Eventually he left. He went out, closing the door quietly, and Danny settled down in the bed. He pulled John's pillow under his head to try and make his own softer, curling into the comforting scent of his hair. The wind whistled shrilly round the house, throwing rain at the windows.

Danny fell back into sleep like a man falling off a cliff.

The wind tore at everything like a full-blown winter gale. The sky was so dark that it looked like five in the afternoon instead of ten in the morning. John sent Ian on an errand and then he and Rab tried to make headway in the bottom field. It was still only half-cleared from summer.

It was an exercise in futility. The wind slowed them down so much it felt like trying to move under water. John shouted above the roar, but the wind took the words out of his mouth. He gestured to the huge chestnut tree in the dip of the field. Rab joined him on the leeward side. They stood close together, miraculously out of the wind behind its broad trunk.

"Jesus." Rab pulled his hair back and squeezed it out.

John wiped his face down then looked at him. "It looks darker when it's wet."

Rab patted his pockets, wondering what chance he had of rolling a cigarette in this gale. "Hair's always dark when it's wet."

"Danny's looks like blood when it's damp."

Rab gave up. There wasn't any point in trying to roll a cigarette in this. "I know."

John offered him a packet. "Here have one of mine."

Rab took it and said, "Suddenly you're back on the hard stuff?" He looked up at him from lighting the cigarette.

"Suddenly I'm nervous."

Rab laughed, a short bark. "You?"

John took the packet back without making a reply. Rab inhaled deeply, coughing violently. It lasted long enough for John to shift in closer and the wind to bring a loose branch down.

"What's wrong with Danny?" Rab asked as soon as he got his breath back.

"Headache."

Rab looked at him. "Must be some fucking headache."

"It is." John took a cigarette out and lit it.

"You actually do smoke them then?"

"Well, I don't stick them up Danny's arse and eat them out, if that's what you mean."

Rab looked at him for a moment, then looked away, taking another long draw. This time he coughed only once, dry and hard. He could feel the heat of John against his arm. John's shoulder was only three inches or so higher than his own, but it felt as hard and vast as the tree they stood against. Rab could smell the fresh waxing on his jacket, oily and sweet from his body-heat. He looked up at the sky. "I think the rain's going to come back on." He strained his head up to look through the branches. "Think we should...?" But the question dried up in his mouth. John had swung round in front of him, his arms fencing his body in at both sides. His face, still slick with moisture, was inches from his own. "Want to try it properly this time?"

"Eh?"

John smiled, that tiny malicious curve. "Chickenshit."

Rab swallowed.

"What's wrong, nervous?" John was still smiling.

Rab said nothing.

"Want to try it again? Make your dreams come true. Look..." And he moved his eyes in a parody of scanning the landscape. "No-one to see us, just you and me under a howling sky. Want to try it again Rab, or are you too chickenshit?" And now the smile was showing just enough white teeth. Inside John there were lots of white teeth. His face came closer. Rab could feel his breath on his face. "*Chickenshit.*"

Alright, Rab thought, alright. He leaned his head back against the tree and waited. Finally John's weight shifted against him. It was like being crushed by a boulder. His mouth came down over his and this time the lips were soft and yielding. Rab's mouth opened under them, letting go.

Not chickenshit, no.

The wind tore at the tree around them, shaking it. Rab felt John press harder against him, his mouth exploring, so many teeth. Rab kept his hands against the tree. John kept his at the side of Rab's body.

Finally John pulled away. Rab opened his eyes and forced himself to look at him. They both stood with their mouths slightly parted. Rab's breath was coming slow and hard. His face was flushed.

"Now tell me I dreamt it."

Rab looked away. Suddenly he scrubbed his mouth with the back of his hand.

John's voice was harsh. "Come on Rab, tell me I dreamt it."

Rab turned towards him. John's eyes were narrowed, cat-green in the light. "You dreamt it." He spoke slowly and with emphasis. John stared at him, mouth tightening. "You dreamt it every time."

John's eyes searched his face. "You fucking chickenshit..."

Rab could see it building up in him, ready to charge right down and out of his arm, ready to charge into his face, wipe Rab clean away.

"Don't..." Rab started to say, hand coming up defensively, when suddenly there was a blinding flash and they were lost under a burst of thunder and a shattering curtain of rain.

Rab sat alone in the living room. He had turned the sound off on the television and sat now in the silence, watching the performers gesticulating like wordless lunatics.

He lay out full-length on the sofa with two cushions behind his head. The fire made him drowsy. Outside the wind still howled around the house. John had disappeared without a word - no threats, no warnings - so Rab put himself out of temptation's way. He sat alone in the living room, watching the explosions of silent colour on the ceiling.

Danny sat at the kitchen table with his feet up on the opposite chair, off the cold stone flags. Occasionally he threw the dog some of his food. He had eaten his way through a bowl of cornflakes and two rolls and cold meat. He sat now, peacefully dunking custard creams in his tea. Never had custard creams tasted so good. He ate slowly and was careful not to move his head too suddenly, but otherwise he was left only with a tender scalp, gritty tired eyes and a ravenous appetite. After another cup of tea he began to feel more human.

The house was quiet, only him and the dog. The wind rattled the door suddenly, making him jump, but no-one walked in.

He got up and put his dishes in the sink. First a seat by the fire, then wash up and back to bed. He looked at the clock. It could be an age before John came back.

He washed and dried his hands and hung up the towel then went out into the hall. He stopped in his tracks. Someone was in, watching television. Why no sound? Had the stupid bastards gone out and left it on?

He opened the door quietly and saw the blonde head lying against the cushions, one hand behind his head, the other lifting a cigarette. The smoke rose in a soft blue

coil into the air.

The open door pulled air through the hallway, the draught stirring the air like a cold stream. Rab turned his head awkwardly to look over his shoulder, then swung his feet to the floor and looked at him. Danny saw him checking his face. Looking for marks, he thought. Didn't John tell him I had a headache?

Rab smiled, "Hello stranger."

Danny smiled back, slowly at first. "A'reet?" he asked.

"A'reet," Rab conceded.

But Danny didn't move from the door and Rab didn't ask him to. "I thought you'd gone out with John," Danny said.

"He took Ian."

"He never..." Danny stopped, frowned.

Rab laughed. "No, nor me either. I think he's set us up. Joke," he added when he saw his expression. He looked at him keenly. His face was smudged with old bruises, his skin almost translucent white. In actuality Rab had a pretty good idea why John had slinked off and it was a fair guess that now he was too absorbed to care about what they were up to. Rab hoped. "Come on in."

Danny shook his head.

"I doubt if he'll be back much before eleven. Come on, come and sit down."

Danny looked away, as if he was listening for something, then he walked over swiftly, holding Rab's eyes. He sat beside him and watched an odd slow veil of reflected colour drop over his face, his hair slowly dyeing with the same eerie green glow. Rab's green hand took the black cigarette from his mouth and threw it in the fire. His green face came floating slowly out of the darkness to press his green mouth against Danny's own.

They fell back under their own weight onto the sofa. Rab climbed on top of him, kissing his eyes, his mouth, his cheeks. They were pressed together tightly, leg between leg. Danny felt dizzy. He was talking, but he didn't know what he was saying. Rab kissed his hair, his neck, then came up for air. He looked down at him and said, "Watch, no hands." He pushed slowly against Danny's thigh, a strange fixed smile on his face.

Danny pulled his mouth down to meet his. He knew exactly how deep that smile went. He felt Rab's groan like a growl in his throat. He felt his own skin flush up with sweat.

Rab dragged slowly against him, moaned again, broke free. He whispered into Danny's ear like a man who had been running hard, "I want to feel you." He undid their jeans, keeping his mouth down, exploring, tasting.

Danny lifted his backside and Rab eased his clothes down, then his own. When he lowered his body again their skins met like hot metal, welding them together.

Rab cursed, lying still, burying his face in Danny's neck.

But Danny wasn't waiting. He pressed Rab's hips down with his hands, grinding himself up against him. "Come on," he urged. He pushed up hard, bucking, grinding.

"No," Rab whispered, but it was too late. "Oh fuck." He thrust himself forward, crushing his cock hard against Danny's pelvic bone. "Fuck," he said again, then Danny dragged his mouth down onto his, smothering whatever else he might have said in silence.

Rab pressed him against the shower wall, letting the water run down his back. It streamed from his hair into their faces and into their mouths. He could feel and see nothing but Danny, hot and wet under his hands. Danny's hair was coiling like dark wine down his neck. He looked at his closed eyes, the long eyelashes spiked with

water, the incredible beauty of his face, and knew he must say it, just once. It was like a weight pressing on his heart. He bent his head and kissed Danny's neck, a hairsbreadth from biting him. "I love you," he whispered, letting the words escape from his mouth into the veil of hissing water.

Rab locked his bedroom door. He listened to Danny going back into John's room. He threw the towel on the floor ill-temperedly and climbed into bed. He felt an anger so intense that he closed his eyes to ease it. He reached blindly for a cigarette, lighting one from the packet without looking. At the first taste his eyes shot open. John's fucking mild menthol shit. *Teach me to steal fucking fags*. He stubbed it out, his anger flaring up again. The cigarette was supposed to calm him.

Rab heard the door slam. He listened. There was an ugly hacking cough. The old man. He lay and listened to the noise of the fire being riddled below - Margaret's job. Carefully he wiped the image of her from his mind. Slowly he pushed her back under the water. *See? Easy.*

He threw the blankets back violently and crossed to his jeans. Somewhere in here…

He found the tin and took it back to the bed. He rolled the cigarette, licked and sealed it, then placed it carefully in his mouth. He picked shreds of tobacco off the counterpane, then struck a match and lit the cigarette.

He listened to the old man thumping drunkenly up the stairs. Him and Ostler hitting the bottle again.

Eventually he made it into his bedroom. Rab brought his alarm clock under the lamp. Ten past eleven. *We could have had an extra ten minutes Danny*. He felt his feet itch with irritation. He wondered suddenly what he was doing. *You're in bed. Why don't you sleep you stupid bastard?*

He never heard the back door. The dog barked. He heard Ian's voice telling it to hush. No grand entrances. Ian had come in first, that was all. Was Danny sitting rigid like this? Sitting up in the dark trying to keep his wet hair off the pillow?

He heard Ian come up the stairs. The old man came back out his room and immediately started badgering him. Something about the Fiat. Rab's heart stopped. No it was the tractor, not the fucking car. *Back under the water Margaret.*

"Why not Danny?" the old man was grumbling, his voice carrying clearly, but Rab couldn't hear Ian's reply. The doors closed. Rab realised he was holding his breath. He let it out slowly.

Where the hell was John?

John locked the back door and pulled open the fastening on his jacket. The fucking zip was stuck again. He wrenched it apart, loosening it another quarter inch from its moorings. He threw it over the back of the chair then sat down to pull off his boots.

Ian stuck his head round the door. "John…"

But John cut him short, waving him away irritably. "Not now."

Ian backed off and went upstairs. John rubbed his eyes. Overhead he heard the old man come out of his room to intercept him. He could hear his hectoring tone from here. "Oh give it a rest," he muttered between gritted teeth, looking up at the ceiling.

The old man's voice fell silent as if by magic. A door slammed.

John sighed and let himself slide down in the chair.

He picked at the edge of the plaster on his hand. It was dirty again. It didn't take long for them to dirty here. He'd probably have a scar. *Thank you Danny, one I owe you.*

He rubbed his eyes again and wondered briefly if anyone had locked the tool-shed, but he didn't care enough to go out and see. It was dry now, but rain clouds were threatening. The tool-shed could go to hell. It wasn't worth getting wet for.

He looked at the kitchen clock. Twenty past eleven.

Why aren't you in bed John?

"I said, give it a *rest*." He slammed his cut hand against the edge of the table. He felt the wound scream in protest. The pain wiped out everything else.

He got up slowly and went out into the hall. He could smell soap, the wet plaster smell of the bathroom. He looked up the stairs. Someone had taken a shower in the last half hour.

He went into the living room and opened up the fire. He threw back the curtains and looked out at the green. The wind was dropping, but the clouds still scudded across the moon like a film set. He closed them again. He picked the tongs up and began to throw coal onto the fire. Upstairs Rab listened to the thunk, thunk as each lump hit the fire-back. John crouched there for a moment longer, his face lit demonically by the firelight, then he straightened up and dropped onto the sofa. He saw the cushions piled to one end. He picked a long blonde hair off the top-most cushion as carefully as if he was a forensic scientist clutching the only clue. He found another. He coiled them around his finger abstractedly until they formed a tight white line biting into his flesh. He picked the cushion up, buried his face in it, but he could smell nothing. In the ashtray there were only branded stubs, none of Rab's. He pressed the cushion to his chest. He uncoiled the hairs carefully and laid his head back against the sofa. He rubbed them softly between his finger and thumb. He breathed carefully through his mouth. He pushed the hairs into the breast pocket of his shirt and held the cushion tighter.

Someone took a shower.

Maybe it wasn't.

Wasn't what?

Maybe it wasn't some *one*.

"*Together...*" He whispered the word out into the silent room. The fire sank a little. Rain began tapping at the window. His eyes opened, but they saw nothing.

He looked suddenly at the cushion. It was old-fashioned, the cover carefully tacked shut where it would be unpicked for washing, and now he saw the dark hairs, not quite as long, coiled in soft spirals. His own hair curled like that.

Carefully he picked them off and held them up. In the firelight they looked red. He looked again at the cushion then he pressed his thumb-nail into the seam until the thread snapped. He inserted his fingers into the small split and when he had enough leverage he inserted the fingertips of both hands and ripped the cover open. He continued to tear it apart until it was completely split into two halves, then he began to snap threads, worrying at the fabric.

Eventually he had utterly destroyed it. It lay on his lap in a small pile of tatters. It was then that Rab came into the living room.

Rab looked at the odd pile of shredded fabric, at the naked cushion thrown to the floor, and closed the door. He went over to the fire and piled some more coal on. He could feel John's eyes on him, watching every move. He turned and looked at him. If John's eyes blinked Rab couldn't see it. He crossed to him and lifted the pile of fabric, letting it run through his fingers. "If thy right cushion offend thee..."

John's hand came down on his like a vice. Rab looked down into his face, but he had dropped his head and was looking at Rab's hand. Rab felt him start to flatten it around the curve of his thigh. He pulled his hand free with a jerk. He took a step back,

closer to the fire. John gathered the shredded fabric in one hand and began to work it convulsively, like a worry ball. He watched his own hand as if fascinated by a strange animal's industry.

This was a mistake, Rab knew it with a sudden and absolute clarity. He wondered if it was too late to backtrack and go back to his room. John had been in control until he had come in, only the cushion had been destined for destruction tonight, but now it was something else. *Well, you can just fucking ride out the storm Rab, it's your baby.* "Why don't you go to bed?" he said, just to say something.

John said nothing, he just kept watching that alien hand squeezing and releasing, squeezing and releasing.

Come on Johnny, Rab thought, talk to me. He tried to think of something to say but nothing would come. He stood looking down at the dishevelled hair, exactly like Danny's, except it was precisely the colour of shit. He remembered the old man saying that once and now he could never see it any other way.

John spoke suddenly. "First in here..." It was not quite a statement, but there was practically no question in it.

"What?" Rab said. His voice sounded calm, but guilt tripped through him like fright.

"...then in the shower." This time the little edge of question was missing. It was just a statement, plain, bald.

Oh Jesus, maybe he watches you through a hole in the wall... or maybe he just knows you. "No." The lie fell like a stone in the grate.

John looked up slowly and searched his face, but only briefly. He looked at his mouth, his eyes, like he knew exactly where to look. The hand had stopped. Somehow it was worse when the hand stopped.

Rab's eyes slid away guiltily. He knew he was going to do it but couldn't stop himself.

John made a sound in his throat like a man accepting death, a mixture of affirmation and distress. He laid his head back and shut his eyes. Rab looked at him and suddenly saw that his face was wet. The fucking ugly bastard was crying. "John..." he said.

But John never moved. The tears dripped off his face slowly. There was no emotion there. It was like watching a statue cry.

Rab began to feel unnerved. He wanted to touch him, but he was afraid to get any closer. "*John...*" This time he crossed to him and gripped his arm. It was like grabbing the limb of a tree. It felt unpleasantly hard and warm under the fabric. He hunkered down beside his legs. "Listen John, you've got to let him go."

The eyes came open with startling swiftness. "Oh no," he said, and he began shaking his head slowly from side to side. "The only way you'll ever get him will be as dead meat." His mouth seemed to taste the words. "Nothing but dead meat."

Rab felt a spurt of anger. "Like her?"

"Much slower."

Rab had expected him to deny it, perhaps try and pretend it had been an accident, but not to admit it. He stood up. "You meant to do it?"

John said nothing.

"Why?"

John's face became pinched and white. His eyes were black holes in his face. "Why do you think?" His voice dared him. No holds barred Rab. You scared or what?

Rab looked at him for a long moment. The silence seemed to go on forever. He felt a pulse pounding in his neck.

John looked up at him, and then all the tension seemed to go out of him. He laid his head back again as if he was incredibly tired. He smiled. "Of *course*... for *you.* Hasn't it always been for you?"

Rab went out of the room, leaving that mocking question floating in the air behind him like a grinning Cheshire Cat.

TWENTY-FOUR

When John came down to breakfast the next morning he had not shaved. Rab glanced up at him and saw the deep shadow on his face. Danny had come down immediately before him and had been in the act of seating himself at the end of the table when John had stopped him and sent him out. Danny left the house without a word and without breakfast.

Ian came in and sat down at the table opposite Rab, but Rab did not look up at him.

John pushed his plate away untouched and stood up. Rab watched him drain his tea like a Norseman downing lager. He shrugged into his jacket. "Get a move on, I'll be outside."

Rab raised his eyebrows as the kitchen door slammed.

"He wants you to go to Jerrett's with him," Ian offered.

Rab's head came round sharply. "What for?" He dropped his eyes again and popped a piece of bread in his mouth as if the answer wasn't terribly important, but Ian had already seen it.

"The old man wants to let it."

Rab nodded as if it didn't matter. Ian watched him until he gave up and pushed his meal away unfinished. He stood up and went out.

John saw him come out the back door. He broke the unsmoked cigarette in half and climbed into the driver's seat. Rab knocked on the window and pointed at the lock. John leaned over and opened it.

Rab climbed in, still shrugging into his jacket. He lifted his hair out and lifted his hips to tuck his shirt in at the back. John watched the fabric pull tight across his thighs. "We going?" Rab asked.

John turned away and started the engine. They backed out then pulled in an arc out of the yard and down into the road. John drove slowly with one arm out of the window. It was still dark but the wind had lightened. John drove without headlamps, but Rab didn't say anything. He turned his collar up and wished silently to himself that John would close the fucking window. A driver going the opposite way tooted and pointed at his lights. John switched them on without comment.

They pulled up into the yard. John cut the engine but made no move to get out. Rab looked at the sun struggling over the horizon, aware of John out the corner of his eye. Eventually he turned. "You got the keys?"

John got out the van without answering and went up to the door. Rab waited until he had unlocked it then followed him out. Even under the heavy leather of his jacket he felt chilled.

John was standing in the hall looking at the doorway to the upper stairs. Rab pushed past him into the living room. If they were going to be there all day he might as well light the fire. "John?" he called, "Do you want me to..."

"I'm here."

Rab turned sharply at the nearness of his voice. "Do you want me to light the fire?" he said again, lowering his voice. You creepy bastard, he added silently.

John nodded.

Rab turned back to the fire and began raking it out. What the fuck was wrong with him? He could feel him moving about behind him, tried to ignore him.

He went out to get coal. The back yard was completely overgrown. An old half-dismantled ploughshare sat right in the middle. The coal-house was full at any rate.

Rab went back in and made up the fire. The sticks were good and dry. At least the shed was watertight.

The sticks exploded like firecrackers, causing the whole structure to shift down in the grate. The fire caught quickly, sending thick plumes of grey-white smoke up the chimney.

"Come upstairs."

Rab straightened up, but didn't turn to him. He didn't like the sound of his voice, low, toneless. "Why?" he said, putting his hands in his jacket pockets.

"Please." It was equally flat, nothing in it.

Rab turned to him and looked at him. "Please from John. What's wrong? Scared to go up by yourself?"

But John wouldn't answer.

Rab turned away again. "What do you want to go up for anyway?"

"It's got to be done."

Done? Done could mean anything. Cleaned, decorated, or just faced up to. He said, "Go on then, you lead."

John went out and across the hall with Rab following. On the stairs, dark even in the daylight, Rab felt an instant of claustrophobia. He tried not to remember. They reached the upstairs passage. The bedroom door was closed. Who had closed it? Danny coming out? John? Who had been last in it? He couldn't remember.

John stopped and leaned against the door-jamb. "Go on."

"Why don't you? Think she'll be lying on the floor?"

"Shut up and get in."

Rab opened the door and walked in.

Everything looked normal, tidy. Someone had moved the Calor gas heater into the corner and folded the bedding neatly on top of the tallboy. The mattress had been stripped, exposing it, new and idiosyncratic, in the old room. The door closed and John leaned against it. John always liked to stand between people and doors.

"Very good John." Rab saw him smile. His head was lying back easily against the door, his eyes visible for once, revealed by the light from the window. They were intent, watching him from under the heavy brows. "You've already been back..." Rab paused and ran his eyes round the room, "and tidied everything away nicey-nicey." He looked back at him. "Lovely piece of play-acting. Just watch you don't wake up one day and find you've forgotten who the fuck you really are."

John turned his head and studied the wallpaper, still smirking like an insolent adolescent.

Rab was stuck. Move to the door and be within reach, stay where he was and be herded back against the bed. He didn't know what the exercise was for, but he wasn't going to give John any scope for experiment. He crossed to the fireplace. The hearth gave him room to manoeuvre. He didn't look at it and he didn't think about it. He stood silently watching John, waiting for the first move.

John shifted his eyes from the wall to Rab's face in one movement, belatedly answering him. "And who am I?"

It took Rab a second to understand, to say, "Did I say who? I meant what." John said nothing, did nothing. Rab went on, "And while we're about it let's get something else straight. I don't know what the fuck you think you're doing here, but I'm not part of it. No games, no threats, no bargains - nothing." He looked at him. "Right, now it's your turn."

John's eyes kept shifting about his body, never looking at his face, like Rab was just meat. He kept on smiling that irritating little smile. "I don't know," and his eyes

finally flicked up for a moment to meet his. "I'm making this up as I go along."

"Oh Jeez-us." Rab dragged his hair back in exasperation. Fuck it, fuck the whole bloody thing.

He went to the window and glared out across the fields. He could see a distant grey strip of sea smeared along the horizon. When John's hands gripped the tops of his arms he almost jumped out of his skin. "Or maybe not..." John breathed in his ear.

It wasn't feasible for any man so big to move so quickly, and wasn't that how he did it? Because they all underestimated him, all the time.

Rab's first impulse was to elbow him in the ribs, but he still didn't know what game he was playing. Anyway, he'd watched John provoke people into hitting him too often. Beside John Ian was an amateur at manipulation.

The hands kneaded the leather of his jacket, fingers digging in too deep. The lips were close to his ear, but not touching. Rab knew he was waiting, but what was he waiting for?

They went on kneading, bruising. Rab could feel his breath on his cheek. He felt himself come up in goose-pimples. He waited until he couldn't stand waiting any longer. "What do you want?"

"A compromise." The answer came back quickly, right on cue.

"What kind of compromise?"

"The kind that keeps more people alive than I want or need." His voice was clipped. He had moved his head away and was now talking behind his back, unseen. "But then, isn't that what all compromises are about, winning some and losing some?"

"Be specific."

"I don't slowly beat Danny to death..."

"And?"

"Nothing." John breathed it out quickly. He had pulled himself against Rab's back and now Rab could feel his chest moving against him. John was always breathing too fast, always running inside himself.

"How nothing?"

"You don't touch him," he paused, "and you can have me."

"No." Rab shook his head.

John went on as if he hadn't spoken. "You don't want him any more than he wants you, so why don't you give him a break?"

Rab pulled away from him, but he never moved an inch. He heard John's whispery laugh, hot in his ear. "Think about it."

Rab shouldn't have said it, but he did anyway. It blurted out of his mouth. "Tied up to you like a fucking dog, what do you think I am?"

"You see to it, I'll see to you."

"No." Rab shook his head, and then more vehemently, "No." He pulled away suddenly and turned to face him. John's mouth was already setting in a hard line.

"Then I'll kill him." His face was white, bloodless.

"You couldn't," Rab said, but even he could hear the conviction draining out of it.

"Just watch me." His eyes seemed blacker than any black could be. He stepped up to Rab and, without any intention showing on his face, punched him in the stomach. Rab folded with the suddenness of the blow. He sat back heavily on the window ledge, holding his stomach, trying not to heave up on the floor. "And in case you forget, that's how it feels."

And John walked out of the room and down the stairs.

Danny and Ian had taken the herd in and out again and then spent the morning shifting earth. The old man was excavating for a new out-building. Moving their own

earth was cheaper. That way they only needed to hire the excavator.

They were finished by lunchtime and the old man disappeared off with the vet while Danny and Ian sat in the kitchen. Danny looked at the clock. If John intended to come back for lunch it wasn't going to be in his time. He lit another cigarette. He felt like a hop-head. Anxiety was inflating him until he felt he might float away. It could only be a temporary reprieve, the lull before the storm. John was simply nurturing it like a plant, to make it grow.

"What's eating you?"

Danny jumped. "What?"

"I said, what's eating you?"

Danny seemed to see him for the first time. Ian, on the other hand, felt as if he had been watching Danny all his life.

"Nothing's eating me."

Ian made a puddle of breadcrumbs and then slowly and carefully wrote his name in it with his fingertip. When he spoke he was looking at the table. "You shouldn't play mouse when he's away, then you wouldn't have to worry about what he's going to do when he comes back."

Danny looked at him, more carefully this time. Ian lifted his eyes to meet his gaze. He was smiling, but it wasn't reaching his eyes. It wasn't even talking to his mouth.

"What's it to you?" Danny asked.

"Not even bothering to deny it?"

"I don't know what I'm denying yet."

"Screwing Rab, that's what." His mouth split apart like something coming unstuck. Underneath he showed a thin line of yellow teeth. "Or was it just a cosy game of cards?"

Danny kept looking, but he still wasn't sure what he was seeing.

"Was it as good as John? Or do you need a little violence to bring you off? Maybe you can't get up there without being punched about first."

Danny looked out the window then back at him. "I think if anybody's being eaten up inside it's you, not me."

Ian felt himself flush. The anger seemed to sweep over him in a tide. "I hope he flattens you. I hope one day he really loses it and wipes the floor with your pretty fucking face."

"I love you too Ian."

Ian pushed himself back out of his chair and leaned across the table, palms down, pushing himself in Danny's face. "Wondering where he is? Maybe he's out on one of his little wanders."

"Why don't you shut up Ian? Don't make a bigger cunt of yourself than you already are."

"Me? It's not me that's so fucking pathetic I sit at home pretending I don't know where he is or what he's doing. And what about his little predilection for shit-poking, where do you suppose he goes for that? Because he sure as fuck isn't getting it off you, is he?"

Danny felt himself tightening up with anger. "I said, why don't you shut up you whining little shit."

"You're looking at it Danny. Are you getting my message?"

Danny could feel his heart trip-hammering along. "He wouldn't fuck you if you paid him."

Ian laughed, suddenly. He almost clapped his hands. "No? Why don't you ask him?"

Danny looked at his face and saw the malicious gleam of triumph. Right is might, truth is in our camp. There wouldn't be any need to ask him - he did.

Danny looked at the table because there wasn't anywhere else to go.

Rab stood at the window and watched John through the open doorway. He was pacing about the kitchen, ostensibly calculating paint coverage, but every move was filled with repressed violence. His right hand was clenched by his side as if he was in constant readiness to take a swipe at something.

Rab had expected him to walk out on him, but he had been downstairs, stripped of his jacket, working. He had spoken to Rab in monosyllables, not looking at him. The more he watched him pacing the more he wondered about what he had done. Everything that happened to John was like stoking a boiler; it just kept going in and nothing came out until it blew.

Rab saw the right hand flex again. John cracked the knuckles. How much was bluff, how much real rage, and how much show to scare the shit out of him? Well, it's working John, the shit is well and truly on the move.

John came through the door. Rab turned away quickly then turned back to him casually, as if he had been standing there idly bored, not watching. "Finished?"

John nodded.

"Let's go then."

Rab went out and waited by the van for John to open up. He climbed in and looked at his watch. Three o'clock. The sun came out in skidding bursts of white between heavy grey clouds. More rain due. Rab felt John's hand brush his thigh. He looked down. Only moving the gearstick. John was reversing out, watching the road, feeling nothing, or at least showing nothing.

Rab's stomach rumbled. No lunch. Maybe the bastard was trying to starve him to death, or did he simply not notice? Rab looked at him covertly and decided he had just forgotten. He seemed to eat in bursts, just feeding the animal, then he would forget all over again. What happened to the boy that used to eat everything that was put in front of him - twice? He looked at him again.

"Reconsidering?" John clicked on the indicators, kept his eyes on the road.

Rab was annoyed to feel himself blush. "No."

John glanced in the mirror then turned to him. "He doesn't need you."

"Concentrate on your driving."

"He'd fuck anything."

Rab kept his mouth shut.

"Think if you had him you'd keep him? Want to hear what he was doing with his mother?"

"No."

"I'll bet you don't."

Rain spattered on the windscreen. John flicked the wipers on. The noise of them seemed to scrape along Rab's skin. *Bet you don't*, they said. *Bet you don't*. And they kept on saying it.

"Don't you ever wonder what he gets out of me?" John said.

"I don't need to wonder, I can see the marks of it on his face."

John laughed sourly. "Think that's my fun? That half pound of meat between his legs is *it*. If he's got any thought in his head at all it's just where to shove it next. Why don't you wake up?"

"Why don't you drop dead? You're full of fucking crap John, know that?"

John swerved violently into the side of the road, slamming his foot on the brake. A lorry pulled out from behind them by the skin of its teeth, its horn sounding a long blare of outrage. Rab watched the spread of its tail-lights disappear into the rain. The windscreen wipers went on and on and on.

John pushed both hands against the steering wheel as if he was trying to brace himself into his seat. Suddenly he pounded his fist on the wheel. "What is it *about?*"

Rab said nothing.

"Because he moves like an angel, touches like a dream? Is that it? Some kind of fucking poetic vision?"

Still nothing.

"*Tell* me."

"No, not because of that."

"His looks will fade, the hair will turn to something grey and dead as you watch."

"I said no, didn't I?"

"Then why?"

Rab folded his mouth shut tight. He turned his face away so that John couldn't read it, but he could feel John staring at him. He waited and he waited. John turned the windscreen wipers off. They were trapped together under a thick green waterfall of rain. John's hand took his chin and pulled it round to face him. Rab pushed his hand off and met his eyes.

"You think you're in love with him." John looked at him incredulously. "You think you're in love with that stupid, cock-obsessed little whore." He shook his head slowly. "I don't believe I'm hearing this."

"You're not hearing it." Rab's face was tight.

John nodded, "Oh yes I am, loud and clear. What happened to the stud Rab? What happened to Mr Macho who gave it all up because he wanted cunt? "

"You're handing me this shit? What about you?"

John threw back his head and laughed. The sound was huge and unexpected in that small space, but it was short-lived. "You really want to know?"

Rab shook his head. *No.*

"Think I'm in love with him?" Rab could see it come up into his eyes like something living. All day the anger had been building in him and this is where it blows.

Rab pulled back, but to where? He felt the far edge of the seat, the door. There wasn't anywhere to go.

John hit him like a felled ox. He was as effectively trapped as an insect under a rock. John's mouth was everywhere it shouldn't be. His hands were worse. *Christ, I'm going to be raped in the front seat of a car at the side of a major trunk road.* He lay there, not even struggling, because he couldn't think how to. John's hands were inside his shirt. Rab felt the buttons wrench and give. He kept turning his mouth away, but John kept chasing after it. The rain came down on the roof in a fresh burst, like stones dropping from the sky. Then somebody knocked at the window, loudly, insistently. After all, they were getting wet out there.

"Jesus," John hissed, body jerking off his.

They rattled the door handle. Rab could see them wiping the glass, cupping their hands, peering in. He saw the regulation waterproofs.

John struggled up, stuffing his shirt inside his trousers.

Rab squirmed upright. His belt was undone, his zip half down. He pulled them together hastily. His shirt was completely fucked, but he pulled his jacket shut to cover it. John was rolling down the window.

"What goes on here?" The policeman was drenched, the water pouring off his slicker in a stream. "You broken down or what?" He peered inside, looked at Rab, looked at his clothes. He'd seen alright. "You've no hazard lights on."

"Sorry." John muttered it.

He sounds as if it's choking him, Rab thought. "We stopped to check a noise," he said quickly. "We could hear it here in the cab, under the floor."

John looked straight ahead, face rigid.

"That's why you were rolling around on the seat together then, trying to find a funny noise?" Oh, he'd seen alright. John said nothing. Rab ran a hand through his hair.

"Consider it your lucky day it's fucking pissing down out here." His eyes met Rab's and held them for a moment then he pulled back out. "On your way," and he thumped the roof twice with his hand and stepped back. John started the engine without even bothering to close the window and took off like a bat out of hell.

The policeman watched them go and remembered suddenly where he'd seen that white-blonde head before.

Danny stood in the milking shed doorway and watched the rain coming down in sheets. *Come on, I've got to get the fucking cows in in half an hour. Rain's one thing, but this is a joke.*

Just then a blur of green came bumping up into the yard. They took the rise too fast and the front wheels came down with a crash over the cattle grid. Danny couldn't see who was driving, but he could guess. The driver's door slammed and John stalked off across the yard, his face white and set. Oh good, make my day, Danny thought as he watched him.

Rab swung the door open without attempting to get out, then saw him standing there. He made a dash for it. He came in shaking his hair. "Oh boy." He shook out his jacket.

Danny looked at him. "What happened to your shirt?"

Rab opened his mouth, then closed it again. "It's a long story." He wouldn't meet his eyes.

"Try me."

"Forget it." Rab's voice held a hint of warning.

There was just a nice length of silence, long enough to let Danny turn everything over. "Tell me something," he looked out at the rain, "is there anyone in the house you haven't fucked?"

Rab didn't look at him but he coloured up. "Who's been talking to you?"

"You aren't answering my question."

"And I won't, till you tell me who it was."

"Is John an on-going concern then? I mean, whose lies should I swallow first, his or yours?"

"What d'you mean, on-going concern?"

"Oh Christ Rab, my head doesn't button up the back. And speaking of buttons..." He looked again at Rab's torn shirt.

"I told you, we had a fight."

"You seem to forget I know John's fights. They might start out with him punching you so hard you wonder how many parts he can break with one blow, but they always end up with him shoving his dick in your face. Which kind did you have?"

"A fight's a fight, clothes get ripped, what's it to you? I don't hear you fighting him off every night. Or your own mother for that matter. How often did you shag her?"

Danny's face flushed.

Rab said sourly, "Oh, forgive me, as if he would. Let's hear it for Saint Daniel's holy purity, dragged screaming to his brother's bed nightly."

"You think I'm not?"

"Sorry, am I supposed to think you are? " *Shut up Rab, that's enough.* But he found he liked the taste of it. *Oh yes, nice to air the little worms of jealousy. Old worms eating your guts away.*

Danny stared at him, his breath coming fast and light, his face pale. Rab thought he was going to hit him, but he turned instead and unexpectedly stepped out into the

waterfall of rain like a man walking into the sea.

It took Rab a moment to realise before he shouted after him, "Danny!" But Danny had disappeared round the side of the shed, going down to the back pasture.

Rab ran after him. "Danny, wait!" He grabbed his arm, but Danny shook him off. "I'm sorry." He grabbed him again, tighter this time. "I'm sorry, please..."

Danny stood there looking at him, the rain turning his hair to dark blood, soaking his shirt, streaming down his face.

"Danny..." Rab said, looking at his mouth, that full beautiful mouth.

And that was all it took.

John watched them from the kitchen window. He had heard Rab shouting Danny's name. Until that moment he had completely forgotten that Danny must be out there, getting ready to bring the herd in. He had made another stupid mistake. He was making a lot of stupid mistakes and Rab took advantage of every one. Maybe he had forgotten that you could see right down to the pasture from this window, maybe in the heat of the moment.

John rubbed the condensation from the glass. It was difficult to see out, but not so difficult that he couldn't see how close they were, just one figure standing motionless in the rain. Mr Macho ran to some very high passions when Danny-boy was around. Mr Macho seemed to forget all about cunt when he saw that pretty face. And Danny... well, Danny was always ready for it. In the rain, up the arse...

"You stupid bastard," John whispered, leaning his head against the glass, closing his eyes against the sight of them. "You stupid fucking bastard."

Rab came into the kitchen and shook off his jacket. He was soaked through. He took the towel from the stove and rubbed his hair.

John sat watching him. "Where's Danny?" he asked finally.

"Gone to get the cows."

Of course, that's twice you've forgotten John. Remember the cows? You only milk them twice a day every day of the fucking year - you ought to remember the cows.

"Without his coat?"

"No, he's got..." Rab stopped and turned to him. "He got a waterproof from the shed."

John's eyes were as brittle as glass. "Bit late, wasn't he? I should think he must be already soaked through."

"You were watching."

"Maybe I was meant to."

"Go take a flying fuck John."

"Kissing in the rain... you're a born romantic Rab."

Rab felt himself flush.

"What's wrong, don't you like the idea of yourself as a romantic?"

Rab threw the towel down on the chair and crossed the room to go upstairs.

"Rab..." John's voice was low, arresting. Rab stopped, hand on the door. "I just want you to think about what that kiss is going to cost you."

Rab waited in silence, but John was going to make him ask anyway. "What do you mean?" he surrendered finally. He didn't turn. He didn't look at him.

"You're going to pay for it in blood... his. Maybe next time you'll think about it first."

Rab turned back and stalked over to him. "Don't even consider it."

"Why? Who's going to stop me? *You?* Don't threaten what you can't carry out Robbie."

132

Rab felt consumed with impotent fury. "I'm warning you John."

"I'm trembling."

"Don't push me too far."

John laughed. "Too far? What's too far for you? I'd really like to know."

Rab licked his lip, wanting to hit him, *needing* to hit him.

"Go on, why don't you?" John's voice was even lower. His eyes were steady, watching, waiting.

Rab turned quickly and went out of the room.

"*Chicken...*"

The word burnt the air behind him like a brand on his skin.

It started as soon as Danny came into the room. He stood for a moment, silhouetted by the light from the hall, his hand groping inside for the light-switch, when John's voice came out of the dark. "Leave it off."

Danny stood immobilized. He had not heard him come upstairs. There had been no warning, no black looks, no terse instructions, nothing. But now he was going to pay for last night's session with Rab. Now.

"Come in and shut the door."

Danny shut it. He wasn't told to lock it.

"Come here."

Danny crossed to him slowly, wondering if it would be over quickly. He tried to gauge his mood.

"Closer."

Danny stood in front of him. John was sitting in the chair by the window. Danny could see half his face lit clearly by the sharp moonlight. The other half was in total darkness. The sky behind him was that crystalline deep black that can only follow heavy rain, like night reflected in water.

John stood up and reached for his hair. Danny could feel the blunt fingers tangling themselves in his curls. "Still damp." John bent his head and lifted Danny's head up to meet his mouth. Danny could feel the tip of his tongue gently between his lips. "You always taste nice. How does an evil little bastard like you always manage to taste so nice?"

Danny felt his heart turn to lead in his chest. It was going to be a long, slow night. As long and slow as John could make it.

John's hand pulled on his hair. "Answer me."

"I don't fucking know," Danny snapped.

John let him go with unnerving suddenness. Everything changed tempo again. "You like kissing in the rain?"

Oh shit.

"Like doing it in the shower, is it? Full of erotic charge, all that water?" His thumb started rubbing gently along Danny's jaw. "You're not saying much Danny. Another headache?" Suddenly his hand dug into Danny's cheek, just as Danny knew it would. "Why don't you answer me, you two-faced little cocksucker? Did you like doing it in the shower with your cousin? Or did you prefer it on the sofa? That's where you had him first, isn't it? *Isn't* it?"

"No."

The hand tightened. "That's what I want to hear." And John's fist struck him low in the stomach.

Danny winced, the breath coming out of him in a grunt. But it wasn't a killer, it was just a nice little warm-up.

"Now let's start again, only this time let's not waste any time. Did you enjoy doing

it in the shower?"

Danny made to shake his head, but John held him rigid. "Now," he paused warningly, "think about it Danny. Think before you speak. Did you enjoy rubbing against him naked in the shower?"

"Yes," Danny said quickly.

John let out a long breath as if he had been holding it. "Very good. And that nice scene kissing in the rain, how did that feel? In your own words now."

Danny didn't know how it felt, couldn't have cared less how it felt.

"We're all waiting."

"I don't know."

"You don't know? Kissed by the man you love in the rain and you don't *know*?" Suddenly Danny's zip was yanked down and John's hand was gripping the thick hair of his crotch. "Now..." Danny could see his tongue licking his upper lip. He could smell the faint sweat coming off him, knew he was getting high on this. "Let's try again. Use your imagination, just let it rip. How did it feel to have him kiss you out there in the rain?"

"Cold."

The hand twisted in his pubic hair.

"*Jesus*," Danny hissed before he could stop himself.

"Not funny Danny. Not even vaguely amusing. Try again."

"I don't know. It was cold and wet. I wasn't thinking about it."

Suddenly John gripped his penis, pinching the head uncomfortably tight. "Okay, let's try the living room. What did you do in the living room?"

"You know."

"No, I don't. I can guess, but I don't *know*. That's for you to tell me."

"I can't remember."

John grabbed his balls and squeezed, so hard Danny felt as if he had been kicked in the stomach. He grabbed John's hand and tried to pull him off.

"Hands by your sides."

Danny let go, fighting panic, breathing like he'd run a marathon. John eased his grip. Danny's balls began to ache. John took hold of his penis again and tugged it towards him almost as if he was trying to lift him by it. Danny felt pain stinging his eyes.

"Stupid little bastard, aren't you? Right, this time let's hear what you did on the couch."

"We rubbed off." Danny said it quickly on an aching breath.

John gave a sharp upwards pull, making Danny rise off the floor. "I want *details*. Who was on top?"

"Him."

"How long?" John demanded.

Danny was thrown. "What?"

"How long did it last? From start to finish? From the moment you got your sweaty little hands on him, how long did it take you to come?"

Silence.

"I asked you a question Danny." The hand was pulling tighter.

"I heard you."

"Then *say* it. Say you love him."

Danny's mouth closed tight.

The hand yanked viciously. "*Say* it."

Nothing.

Again the pain went through him, worse this time. Danny moaned. *Please don't let me be sick.*

134

"Take your time, get your breath back and say it."

"I love him." It was a raw, angry whisper.

"I'm sure he'd be very happy to hear that." John let him go and stood looking at him. "Get undressed." He sat down on the armchair. "Back a bit, where I can see you… not too far," he warned and he stretched out, crossing his ankles.

Danny took his clothes off until he was standing naked before him.

"Jerk off."

"I can't." He felt too sore even to breathe.

"Of course you can, just think about kissing your cousin in the rain."

Danny took hold of himself gingerly. He saw John unzip his trousers. He dragged his eyes away.

"Look at me."

Danny turned back to him slowly.

"You look lovely by moonlight." Danny could see the glimmer of his teeth against the solid black of him. "See how lovely you look?" John held his penis up. Its shape was outlined in the silver moonlight that slanted in from behind his chair, making his erection show clearly against the dark of his body. Danny let go of himself.

"Kneel down," John said.

Danny knelt down carefully. John was still holding his cock up, sliding the foreskin up and down. His fingers looked silver against it. "It always makes you stiff, doesn't it?"

Danny said nothing. He didn't look at himself. He didn't touch himself. The pain was ebbing and he wanted it back.

"No matter what I do to you."

Danny sat with his palms on his thighs, watching him.

"He couldn't get a hard-on like this if you fucked him with it, but you don't care, do you?" He went on as if he didn't expect a reply, "No, you don't. And when you're gazing at him you don't care about this, do you?" He lifted his penis up till it stood perpendicular to his body. "Whoever is holding your gaze, they're everything in that moment, aren't they?"

There was a silence. Danny heard the clock ticking in the hall. He heard the old man cough in his room.

"Look at yourself Danny. Go on, be brave."

Danny looked down slowly.

"What do you think he'd say if he could see you now? Think he'd still love you?"

Danny kept looking at it, stuck out at right angles to his body, poking up between his legs, glossy in the light.

"What if he's listening right now? He can probably *hear* that hard-on. He can probably *smell* it." John paused. "Touch it."

Danny took it gently round the shaft.

"Wank."

Danny began to squeeze the bruised flesh.

"You thinking about him?"

Danny didn't answer. He heard John shift in his chair, heard the breathless urgency of his words. "You ready to come?"

Danny lifted himself off the floor, pulling himself up by the penis, pointing it towards his brother.

"You could come right now, couldn't you?"

Danny jutted his hips out towards him, inching closer.

"You're going to come, aren't you?" John's voice was choked and breathless, his hand full of the sticky sound of it.

Danny crawled forward, pelvis still obscenely thrust towards him, penis like a

magnet twitching North.

John slid down in his chair, unfastening his belt and pushing his jeans and pants down to his knees, then down round his ankles, spreading his legs wide apart. "Come on…" He pushed his penis down cruelly. Their cocks touched.

John massaged the heads together until he couldn't tell what was his own flesh, what was Danny's. He worked them insistently, as if he was trying to force together something badly glued, something about to come apart any second. He felt the sudden paroxysms of Danny's body, pinched the eye of his penis tight, as if he could prevent it, but it was too late. He felt the white sweat force its way out, felt his own ooze and weep as Danny gasped, moaned, shook.

They hung there, John slumped forward, Danny leaning over him, arms trembling, until John pulled his head round and rubbed his salt fingers over his lips whispering, "Taste my tears."

And then he kissed him.

TWENTY-FIVE

John stood behind the old man in the kitchen and listened. It was a fucking weird time to pay a social call and he looked like nothing that had ever ventured past the gate of a farm before.

"…tall, slim with very blonde hair."

"Could be Rab, I suppose."

"And where might I find him?"

"I don't know." The old man turned to him. "John, where's Rab?"

John came forward, his body filling the doorway, forcing the old man to one side. "Who wants to know?"

The blue eyes looked at him. There was a faint smile he didn't like. There was a lot of things he didn't like about him.

"I do. Who are you, his minder?"

John wondered briefly what it would be like to sink his fist into that loose little mouth. He jerked his head. "Over there, in the shed, the green one. You'll find him under a pick-up."

The man's eyes shifted suddenly, looking beyond John's shoulder. They narrowed. He looked suddenly familiar. John turned to see what he was looking at so intently. Danny was standing in the doorway tucking in his shirt. John turned back to face him. He decided he liked the face even less.

"Your brother?" the man said, still watching Danny. John gave him something that might have been a nod, if he'd let his head move.

The man smiled with the bottom half of his face. There was too much white and red, as if his mouth had been bleeding. He finally looked back at him. "He looks like you." And then he simply turned on his heel and walked over to the shed.

Rab was lying under the pick-up when the shed door trundled back. He looked out, squinting against the bright morning light, but he couldn't make out who it was. He pushed his head and shoulders out. The door closed again. Who the fuck was this?

He pulled himself out completely and got to his feet, wiping his hands on his overalls. The man was wearing a petrol blue sweater and grey trousers; knife-edge crease, shiny shoes, black scraped hair and a tiddly little moustache. His eyes were a cold flat blue. The man was smiling at Rab's close scrutiny.

"What's wrong? Don't you remember me?"

"The eyes yes, but I can't place the face." I can't place it, he thought, and I don't like it.

"We met yesterday. You and your… friend," there was a faint pause before the word friend and a faint sneer to go with it, "were looking for funny noises."

"Yes," Rab said, placing him immediately. He couldn't think of anything else to say.

"You don't look pleased to see me."

Rab shrugged then waited.

The policeman looked around then walked along to the tractor, pressed its massive wheel as if he was testing its pressure, and then leaned against it. "Don't you want to know why I'm here?"

"I'm rupturing a gut just thinking about it."

The policeman smiled. "Not only is he pretty but he has a smart mouth too." He looked at Rab with eyes like little pips. "Why was he taking your clothes off?"

Rab didn't say anything.

"It's not a private place, the A596, that makes it a prosecutable offence."

Rab still didn't say anything. The policeman raised an eyebrow. "Strong and silent with it. Doesn't it worry you?"

"It won't worry me till I hear it."

"And shrewd too." He paused. "You're a nice looking boy."

"It's beginning to worry me."

"Maybe I just want to be friends."

"Forget it."

"Forget that I saw two homosexuals committing an offence on the A596 in the front seat of a car in broad daylight?"

"I'm not a homosexual."

"Tell it to the marines."

"And that was yesterday. You should have booked us yesterday."

"Maybe I forgot my little black book."

Rab said nothing.

"Funny, you don't look like a queer-boy."

"I'm not queer."

"It didn't look that way to me."

"It wasn't my idea."

"I didn't see you struggling."

"You didn't see my feet either, but they were there."

The policeman took a deep breath. He let it out slowly. "Okay, then let's try this for size. Green Datsun pick-up, registration HGF 738K, in the name of John Jackson Moore. Mr Moore I've met."

"Jackson Moore."

"Jackson Moore. What's Big-boy's relation to him?"

"Son, eldest son."

"Good. On the 8th of October at 3:03 am, white Fiat, registration MJM 382A, in the name of Margaret Jackson Moore, passed through the junction at Kuyper Street and Ferris Lane, Ellenport followed by that very same green Datsun driven, this time, by you. Big-boy, as I recall, was in the Fiat."

Rab stared at him.

"Now we're making headway." The policeman smiled, showing a fine display of small white teeth against the unnatural red of his mouth. "Where were you going?"

"I don't remember."

The policeman shook his head. "What time do you boys get up in the morning?"

"Around six."

"And you don't remember what you were doing out at that hour? Pull the other one, it's got bells on it."

Rab said nothing.

"Well, just to refresh your memory I've got a little story to tell you. It's one of those amazing coincidences you read about in the Sunday papers. Bayhauser and Rutger have been broken into three times in two weeks, the two weeks immediately prior to the eighth. That same night, at roughly 3:20 pm, two vehicles passed under their work-lights and were spotted by the security guard. No numbers, that would be too good, but he reported it anyway. The dogs' barking had alerted him. The vehicles were a blue, or possibly green, pick-up and a white 'woman's car', 'a little run-around'. The vehicles were going down a road that leads only to Yardholm Bird Sanctuary. Now isn't that something? Just for the record, nobody cares because, as yet, nobody knows..." he paused just long enough, "except me, of course."

"It doesn't mean anything."

"Doesn't it? What were you doing at Yardholm? Fairy circle, was it? Jerking off in the round? There was another passenger, wasn't there?"

Rab nodded.

"Who?"

"Youngest brother."

"Yours?"

"John's."

"John? That Big-boy?"

"Yes."

"You're no relation?"

"Cousin."

"And your name?"

"Rab."

"Rab." He turned it over slowly in his mouth. "And your second name?"

"Hardman."

The policeman laughed. "Robert Hardman. It suits you. Well Robert, I think I'd like to get to know you better. Why don't you come round to my flat some evening? Say tonight at eight?"

"I can't. This is a farm, we don't just finish up at nice civilized hours to pay social calls."

"When will you finish?"

"It's usually about nine, just now about half past."

"Well then, we'll make it half nine."

"I've got to sleep. I get up early. I work."

"Well you shouldn't gad about at three in the morning then, should you?"

Rab glared at him, tight-lipped, but said nothing.

"I'll expect you. Ferrimans Court, the harbour redevelopment. It's the only block finished, number six." The policeman pulled open the door. "And have a bath first, I don't want the place stinking of shit."

The door closed behind him as Rab brought his fist down on the pick-up's roof.

John still stood in the kitchen doorway. He'd watched the shiny black shoes stepping very carefully over the muck then go into the shed and close the door. He didn't like that either. Now he was just standing staring at the shed, waiting for him to come back out.

Danny came up behind him. "Who's he?"

"I don't know."

"What does he want?"

"I don't know that either." John turned to look at him, then looked past him. The old man met his eyes, held them for a moment, then went out, slamming the door. John pulled Danny to his side, pushing his leg between his, and kissed his mouth thoroughly. He let him go. "Now fuck off."

Danny wiped his mouth with the back of his hand. John held up a hand. "Don't tell me, I'm a cunt."

Danny pushed past him, grabbing his jacket, and disappeared round the side of the house.

John could still feel the adrenaline of the kiss burning in his belly. He put his hand in his pocket and adjusted himself absently, concentrating his attention back on the shed. What was taking the little greaseball so long? And what was so familiar about him?

He rubbed the back of his neck and shifted his weight. When the shed door finally

opened again he stepped back into the shadow of the kitchen and pulled on his jacket. He waited until the shiny black shoes had disappeared round the corner, then he went out across the yard, shutting the door with a bang.

Rab was leaning against the pick-up with his head on his arms. He did not look up. "Who was that?"

"The police."

And then John remembered where he'd seen the face. "He isn't going to charge us now?" It was nervous, bitten, betraying.

"He wasn't trying."

"Then what? Community policing on the dangers of sexually transmitted diseases?"

"No." Rab lifted his head and looked at him as if it was his fault.

"Then what?" John demanded again.

"He wants to suck my dick."

"Yeah, right."

"I'm serious. Women have gone out of fashion around here, hadn't you noticed?"

"A bent policeman? Didn't you tell him you're absolutely straight?"

"I did."

"But?"

"He saw you crawling all over me. He was difficult to convince."

"If he's not pressing charges, then what?"

"He's got other little tricks up his sleeve."

"Like what?"

"We were spotted dumping Margaret's body."

John looked as if someone had just punched him in the gut.

Rab looked at him for a long moment then said carefully, "He saw us going through the town lights. He recognized me. He traced the cars. He saw you in the Fiat, me in the pick-up."

"Christ, I thought..." Colour came back into his face. "You said dumping the body."

"Same difference. We were spotted by some dog-fucker at Bayhauser and Rutger and from that he's deduced we could only have been going to Yardholm. So far, so fucking wonderful."

"So nobody actually saw anything. That lot as it stands doesn't mean shit."

"Doesn't it? What if he asks questions, wants to know where Margaret is, the car? What if he asks the old man? What then? He's going to ask questions John. If I don't go along he is *going* to ask questions."

"What d'you mean go along?" John picked it up with an unerring instinct.

"You heard the first time."

John stared at him.

"Looks like you've got another enemy to add to your list John-boy."

TWENTY-SIX

Rab was back under the pick-up the following day. John's voice came in from behind the rumble of the door. "If you want any lunch you better move your arse."

Rab pulled himself out. "What time is it?"

"Almost one." John was lighting a cigarette.

"Nervous again?"

John shook out the match without answering.

"Well, you're not alone. If I don't get this finished this afternoon PC Plod will have to find somewhere else to stick it."

"It isn't funny."

"Am I laughing?" Rab peeled the overalls down and leaned against the engine-hood while he tugged them off over his boots.

"What time does he want to see you?"

"I've told you about fifty times, half nine."

"What does he want to talk to you about?"

Rab's face was long-suffering. "He doesn't want to *talk* to me, he wants to get to *know* me."

"What kind of shit is that?"

"Police shit, it's cleaner than our stuff."

John stubbed out the cigarette barely smoked. Rab looked at it lying on the floor. "All they're doing is costing you money."

John ignored him. He said abruptly, "Listen..."

"I'm listening," Rab prompted when he didn't go on.

"There's nothing he can do. He can't even be sure it was us he saw that night."

"They're the family's cars John, it seems reasonable the family might be driving them."

"It's still his word against ours."

"Don't talk shit, it's recorded in his little black book. Come in Panda four, three men and their corpse off to mow a meadow."

"Why the fuck was he taking our numbers anyway?"

"I don't know. Maybe we had a harassed look that caught his eye."

"Don't..." John stopped again.

Rab looked at him curiously. "Don't what?"

John hit the door with his clenched fist, the noise thudding round the shed. "Just *don't*, okay?" He slumped back suddenly against the wall and said in a low voice, "You know what this is about, don't you?"

Rab stared at him. "I don't believe this." He shook his head. "Some little creep with the moral principles of an alligator wanders in here and threatens us with fuck knows what and all you can worry about is whether he wants to suck me off or not. You killed her John, and I'm worrying my arse off. It's you who should be worrying."

"What's there to worry about? He's nothing."

Rab shook his head. "Policemen are never 'nothing', so you can forget that pronto. And don't think I give a fuck about you, or what happens to you. What worries me is that when you go, we go with you."

John looked at him levelly, but his face kept saying the same thing.

"Don't threaten me John, it's not you the crawling little faggot's got his claws into. I don't need any more shit from you. Now get out of my way."

But John stayed where he was, barring the door. "I'm warning you, if you start

anything with him I'll finish it. I'll finish him, with his smart black shoes and his fucking bar-boy moustache."

"I said, get out of my way."

"I mean it."

Rab reached behind him and pulled the handle back, but John covered his hand with his own, crushing his fingers to the metal. "Leave him be."

Rab pulled the door open and squeezed out. "Drop dead."

John watched him cross the yard, his hair flaring out in darts of white light as the wind whipped at his head.

John was waiting for him in the kitchen when he came down. Rab's head was a slick pale ochre, like wet otter's fur. The tips lay dark on his back, dripping water from the ends. He took a towel from the stove and squeezed his hair into it.

Danny watched him moving about the kitchen. He looked at John's hand on the table top, breaking and rebreaking matchsticks, destroying one cigarette after another.

Rab sat down and began fastening up his shoes.

"It's only nine o'clock," John said finally.

"So?" Rab grunted, straightening up. He bent down again to fasten the other shoe.

"I thought you said half nine?"

Rab straightened again. "I'm going to be early, aren't I?"

Danny wanted to ask where he was going, but John's face was set in the familiar colourless lines. He didn't dare.

"What's the point in being fucking early?" John's hand had stopped breaking up cigarettes and instead picked up a knife and began picking into the table top. Pick, pick, pick.

Rab crossed to the coat-rack. "It gets it over faster."

"Or makes it last longer." And the knife went in deeper, digging little grooves in the wood.

Rab walked back to the table and hunkered down beside him as if he were cajoling a sulky child. He was too close to the knife, much too close. "Why don't you just relax John, and shut your trap?"

John's hand stopped. Danny could feel the slicing movement of the knife as it came down off the table.

But it never happened.

Rab stood up and pulled on his jacket. His crotch was almost level with John's face. "Here's piss in your eye John," he said.

And then he stepped out into the dark.

The road was quiet but Rab drove slowly, delaying the inevitable. The wind was picking up again. He turned the heater up full. *Come on, it's fucking frozen in this box.*

He passed Jerrett's access road without looking, then the hotel, the school, the abattoir.

He stopped at the first set of lights even though they had only just turned amber and nothing was waiting. He passed through the second set on the same green sequence. He went through the town and turned down into the new harbour road. It bypassed the open coal mine. It bypassed anything that connected the old with the new. The harbour development was upmarket. Upmarket office space, upmarket flats. Rab wondered where the hell they were going to find upmarket people to put in them. Imports probably, like PC Plod.

He passed a rash of architectural boards listing men with names that were as alien

in this part of the country as Rastafarians. All the boards had trees on them and words like Rural Development, or Enterprise Corridor. More boards, more names. He drove slowly in case he missed his turning. He saw the masts and funnels of the tugs and clicked on the indicators. He drove slowly, but still left a plume of white dust behind him from the loose aggregate. The truck bumped slowly along the road. He pulled slantwise onto the concrete of the harbour basin, nose against the capstan. He stopped the engine.

He sat for a moment, watching someone move about in the tiny lit cabin of a boat. It sat down low in the water. The tide was out and the dock wall was at least ten or twelve feet above its head. A lobster creel hung off the radio mast. A lone red rubber glove stuck up on the cabin roof like a bloody hand waving.

He got out of the pick-up and locked it. The flat blocks were low-density, only three floors high, in dark red brick. Each block had the same architectural detail; one large porthole-shaped plaque, blank, waiting for the date to be filled in. The first two blocks were complete. The other two were still boarded up, the ground around them scattered with bricks and large sheets of flapping polythene. Only the last block was still being roofed. They looked like children's toys.

Rab could see two, no three, lit windows in the first block. He walked across the loose road surface, the grey-white stones hurting his eyes under the over-bright lights. They were replica ships' lanterns filled with a blinding blue-white light. He pulled up his collar. He could hear the sea very distantly, as if it were miles away instead of ten feet beyond the wall.

The flat had an entry-phone. Rab had never used an entry-phone before. He pushed the button for number six. It was answered straight away. He opened the door when the buzzer sounded as instructed. The whole procedure unsettled him.

Inside, the building smelt of half-dry emulsion and petroleum solvents. Everything was painted in pastels. Pastel blue, pastel pink, even pastel grey. Rab wasn't sure how they could create a pastel grey.

There were two flats to a floor and Plod was on the top.

The door was ajar when he got there. He knocked anyway. The door swung open. Rab stuck his head round.

"Come in." He was standing in the entrance to the living room. Rab could see the large expanse of dark window behind him. "Shut the door."

Rab pushed it shut.

"Well come in then, don't just stand there."

He didn't move out of the doorway, making Rab walk through between him and it. Rab was careful not to touch him.

He was wearing a cream woollen sweater with a golfer on the breast, the same grey trousers, and those dinky little moccasins designed for driving. A blue regulation shirt collar showed over the top of his sweater. He stank of expensive aftershave. It had to be expensive because it smelt so cheap. He closed the door behind him and said, "You're early."

"I finished early." Rab looked round the room. It was dominated by two long sofas forming a broken 'L' against the wall. They were made of soft cream leather, or what looked like leather. There was no fireplace. The windows were floor to ceiling and ran the length of one wall. They were clad in colourless vertical slat blinds that looked as if they belonged in an insurance brokers. They were drawn back fully, exposing the window.

There was only one picture in the room, a poster size black and white photograph of a muscular nude male torso cradling a tiny baby. In one corner stood a small fortune in entertainment technology. Two triple speakers were mounted on the wall.

"Your hair looks different."

Rab turned to him. "It's wet."

"Give me your jacket." He held out his hand.

"I'm happy where it is."

"I'm not. Give me your jacket."

Rab took his jacket off reluctantly. The policeman crossed and took it from him. He disappeared back into the hall.

Rab looked at the carpet. It was a thick cream shag-pile. It covered the whole floor. He hunkered down and brushed it with his hand.

"One hundred per cent pure wool."

Rab straightened up. "Bully for it."

"And the settees are one hundred per cent Brazilian hide."

Rab looked at him.

"And in the kitchen there's a Swiss ceramic hob, a real Italian cappuccino machine, and a full size American cabinet-fridge, double doors with a drink dispenser... oh, and a New York toaster."

"What the fuck is a New York toaster?"

"A toaster I bought in New York."

His face was completely humourless. Rab wasn't sure if he was supposed to applaud or just worship in silence.

"Aren't you going to tell me it's a lot of money for one lousy copper to earn?"

"I never even thought about it."

"No accusations about running the local drugs ring, taking back-handers?"

Rab watched him, trying to read what was on his mind. "I doubt if anything much stronger than aspirin passes through this place."

"If you're referring to this flat not even that, but you're not going to tell me you're not curious how I paid for this lot?"

"I don't give a monkey's fuck if you stole this lot."

"I own a share in the family business." He looked at Rab as if daring him to laugh. "We makes kilts."

Rab didn't laugh. He could just see him in a kilt. Ten to one he'd been sent to school in a kilt. "You're Scotch."

He winced as if Rab had stood on his foot. "Scots."

"Not much of an accent."

"Good Edinburgh families don't have accents."

And now he drives around in a dinky little police car in a semi-rural no-man's land. How are we supposed to add that one up?

He looked at Rab for a moment, as if he was wondering if he'd said too much. "Come into the kitchen."

Rab followed him through a door that looked almost wet with varnish.

The kitchen was covered in black studded rubber like the stuff they put on shower-room floors. It was on the floor, the walls, even the ceiling. The whole room was black; the cupboard doors, the venetian blinds, even the fridge. Rab looked at the fridge. "*Is that a fridge?*"

The policeman was leaning back against the work-surface beside a round inset sink with a high swan-shaped tap. It was bright red. He nodded. "Go on, open it."

Rab opened the doors and looked inside. It appeared to contain bottled beer and apples and not a lot else.

"Day before I get my shopping."

Rab closed the doors and nodded - as if he cared. The policeman turned and opened the cupboard doors above his head. The entire cupboard was filled with spirit bottles. "What would you like?"

"I'd rather have a beer."

"Help yourself then."

Rab took a beer out of the fridge and undid the wire top. The policeman handed him a glass. Rab poured the beer and watched the policeman fill a tumbler with whisky. He didn't put anything else in it.

Rab looked at the pots hanging on the rack, the knives, the kitchen scales. Everything was bright red on black.

"A designer did it for me. I showed him the kind of thing I wanted and he did the whole house. One of the advantages of moving into a new building."

"And of having a lot of money."

"And of having a lot of money." He met Rab's eyes. "Do you want to see the rest?"

"No."

"What's wrong, doesn't interior design interest you?"

"Does it look as if it might?"

"It seems to."

"That's just the novelty value."

"The design's not that good."

"I was referring to the money."

There was a silence. Rab took another mouthful of beer and watched as the policeman filled up his glass. No wonder he had that red scrubbed look.

"Who's the angel-faced boy with the red hair?" He had his back to Rab, but the voice was too casual.

Rab placed the palm of his other hand under his glass. "Which?"

The policeman turned round. "You know which." The eyes were narrow again.

"Danny."

"It was him in the car that night?"

Rab shook his head. The policeman smiled. "Don't lie to me. Think I can't read lies on people's faces? That wouldn't make me much of a policeman."

"You're not much of a policeman anyway."

"You've got a cheeky little mouth son." The accent came up loud and clear when he was angry. He took a mouthful of whisky, watching Rab over the rim.

Suddenly Rab needed a cigarette very badly. "Can I smoke?" he asked.

"Smoke?" Henderson echoed as if he wasn't sure what was being asked of him. He looked at Rab's fingers. "It's a dirty habit."

"Can I or can't I?"

He folded his arms like a schoolmarm but he nodded his head.

Rab took out his tin and placed it on the nearest counter. He began rolling up a cigarette.

"Christ, rolly-ups at that." The policeman wrinkled his nose as if the idea offended him.

Rab rolled three and put one in his mouth. He put the other two carefully in the tin and then the tin back in his pocket. He began patting his pockets for matches.

"Here." The policeman threw him a box.

Rab lit his cigarette and looked for a bin. The policeman swung open a cupboard door. The bin was attached to the rear. Rab put the spent match in without comment.

There was another silence then the policeman sniffed. "What the hell is that, couch grass?"

"Tobacco."

"I never smelt any tobacco like that before."

"It's Spanish. Old Cured Anise. They flavour it with aniseed."

"I thought you had to smoke that kind of stuff in a pipe?"

"You learn something new every day."

"It smells like a laxative."

There was no answer to that. Rab took another drag and held the smoke in his lungs for a long moment, then he expelled it slowly down his nose. He began to feel slightly unnerved by his unblinking stare. "Do you have an ashtray?"

The policeman looked momentarily blank then he pushed up from the counter, turning to the cupboard. "It'll have to be a saucer."

"That'll do."

He handed him a saucer and leaned back against the counter again. Rab fought the urge to look at his watch. He took another drag then tapped the ash off.

"What goes on between Angel-face and his big brother?"

Rab put his saucer down carefully before replying. He picked up his glass again. "What d'you mean?"

"I got the impression today that Big-boy wanted to wrap my legs around my throat when he saw me looking at him."

"Maybe he didn't like the way you were looking."

"I was looking." That's all, his eyes added warningly.

"He's like that, very territorial."

"That's a new name for it."

"It would've been the same if you'd looked at the dog."

"Got the hots for the dog too, has he?"

Rab studied the floor then he drank a little more beer. "You've got a very dirty mind," he said carefully.

"Maybe." There was another pause. "What were you doing with him in the car?"

"We were having an argument."

"Do you always undo your trousers when you're arguing?"

"Maybe we were arguing over him borrowing my belt, or about what colour my shorts were, or whether my dick was bigger than his."

"And is it?"

Rab ground his cigarette out with short jabs. "You're really beginning to fucking annoy me Mr Policeman."

"And your lies are beginning to annoy me sonny-boy."

"I'm not your sonny-boy, you're lucky if you've got ten years on me."

"Consider it my privilege as a police officer."

"At this moment you're not a police officer, you're a fucking gay boy trying to get into my pants. Why don't you tell me what you want and we can get down to business."

"I don't need to buy my sex."

"Then what the fuck am I here for?"

"I told you, I just want to be friends."

"Friends? Oh for..." Rab banged his glass down and stormed out of the room.

The policeman caught up with him as he passed out into the hall. He grabbed his arm and pulled him round. Rab jerked his arm away, grabbing his jacket. "Screw this..." he pulled open the door, "and screw you."

The policeman caught him again, saying in a low voice, "I'll be seeing you."

"Not if I fucking see you first." And he went down the stairs three at a time and slammed the pick-up back out the harbour under a towering cloud of white dust.

John was waiting up for him. It wasn't late but Rab had the feeling everyone had been packed off out of his way. Or maybe they were just sick of the sight of John's scowling face. "You're all I need," he said, hanging up his jacket and crossing to fill the kettle.

John was swinging his chair on its two back legs. His feet were braced against the

146

table. "Have a nice time?" His smile was about as convincing as a two-year-old's painting.

Rab banged the lid on the kettle. "Why don't you come sniff me, see if you can smell where he's been?"

John's feet slammed down on the floor as the chair came down with a bang. Rab looked at his heavy, dark face then stalked across to him, unbuckling his belt and unfastening the button. He pulled his shirt out, dragging it up. "There, go on, any strange scents? Any sticky patches?" He started to stuff his clothes back in. "We didn't fucking do anything, okay?" He watched John visibly relax, and somehow that made it worse.

Rab slapped him a back-hander that made John's head bounce. He felt the pain shoot up his wrist. The skin on his hand felt numb with the impact. An angry red stripe appeared instantly on John's face.

Rab stood looking at him, flabbergasted, wondering how he had ever had the nerve.

John reached out slowly and took the hand that had hit him and curved the palm of it to his mouth. He had kissed it before Rab realised what he was doing. He jerked it away.

"Only cause I love you, baby." John was smiling, just barely.

Rab covered his ears with his hands. "I've had about as much of this as I can stand. You don't fucking own me John."

John stood up swiftly and grabbed him as he made to move off. "But I do. You might as well give in to it."

"Let go."

"I can make it hard for him." He smiled as if he had said something incredibly witty. He gripped Rab's shoulders tighter. "Want me to make it hard for you?"

Rab pushed his hands up between John's arms, levering him off. "Go to..." But he couldn't seem to think of anywhere bad enough. He said bonelessly, "You're a pile of shit John, a fucking great stinking pile of shit."

John's tongue flicked over his mouth. "You want it baby."

Rab turned his back on him abruptly, moving away. "I don't hear you John."

"Oh you hear me alright. You'll be listening, just like you do every night, and you'll be aching Robbie, just fucking aching."

But Rab had already closed the door.

Rab went straight upstairs and into John's room.

Nothing.

He went back down the hall and knocked on the bathroom door. He tried to keep it quiet but he couldn't make himself heard above the shower. The door was locked. *Hurry up Danny*. The shower went off. He knocked again.

Down the hall Ian got up off his bed and opened his door a notch.

Danny opened the bathroom door. He looked at Rab as if he didn't know who he was.

"Get your clothes," Rab said.

"What?"

Rab pushed him. "Just get your clothes."

Danny went back inside and grabbed his clothes off the chair. Rab took a hold of his arm and pulled him across the hall into his room. He took Danny's clothes and pushed them in a bundle under the mattress. He grabbed the towel off his waist.

"Hey!"

But Rab was already gone. Finally he came back in and locked the door. Danny

stood there shivering, wrapped in a blanket. "Have you gone off your fucking head?"

"Shh..." They heard John come up the stairs.

"*Fuck*," Danny whispered. Rab held a finger to his lips. They stood like two statues in the middle of the floor. John went into his room.

Rab switched on the bedside lamp then crossed the floor and turned off the overhead light. He checked the door again, half turning the key so that it could not be pushed out, then he lifted his bedside rug and laid it along the foot of the door. "On the bed. It'll take him a while to realise you aren't going to materialise."

"What the hell are you doing?" They spoke in whispers, as though John could hear them clearly through two walls and a hallway. Nevertheless Danny climbed on the bed and pulled the blanket tight about him. He pulled his legs up under him. Rab took the towel from the sink and sat behind him on the bed. He began to dry Danny's hair.

Danny flinched away from him.

"Sit still." And he pulled him back.

After a minute he stopped rubbing and took the towel away. He kneeled round in front of him and ran both hands through Danny's hair, untangling the knots, then he looked at his face. He ran his thumb slowly over his mouth.

"What..." Danny began, but they both froze at the sound of John's door opening again. "*Shit*," Danny whispered, pulling the blanket tighter. Rab moved behind him again and pulled him back against him. They leaned like that against the wall and listened to John opening the bathroom door.

"Danny?"

What the fuck is he calling his name for? Rab wondered. Can't the stupid bastard see he isn't in there? They heard the bathroom door shut and the sound of John's feet going downstairs.

"Let me up. Christ, he'll crucify me."

Rab held him. "He won't know."

John's feet came back up. They heard him go into the old man's room, then he came back along the corridor and into Ian's. They heard the murmur of voices. Eventually he stopped outside Rab's door.

"Rab..." John's voice was low. It wasn't a query.

"Fuck off John." Rab's voice sounded loud in the room. Danny shut his eyes and covered them with his hands.

"Send him out."

"I said, go away John."

"Send him out."

"He isn't in here. You think I'm off my fucking head? Try the bathroom."

"He isn't there."

"Maybe he escaped down the drainpipe."

"Rab..." And this time the door handle rattled. Danny flinched. Rab lifted his hair and kissed his neck, holding him tightly when he tried to pull away.

"I said, fuck off John."

"I know he's in there. Send him out or I'll break the fucking door down."

"Try it. You're a fucking paranoid bastard. Now, for the last time, clear off."

There was a moment's silence.

"He'll have to come out some time. I'll be waiting."

"You do that John. Don't forget your ray gun."

"I'm going to kill him. You think about that Rab."

"Good luck to you."

Suddenly the door buckled under the weight of a tremendous blow. Danny jerked as if he'd been kicked. Rab covered his mouth with his hand. "*Easy*," he whispered.

"I'm going to kill you Danny, you hear me?"

There was another silence, so intense it felt like thick elastic wrapping around them, then John's door slammed with finality.

"*Christ.*" Danny struggled round furiously to face him.

"He's nothing but noise. He's not even sure you're in here."

"Like fuck. Where the hell would I go at this time of night? Where else *could* I be?"

"You'll see," Rab smiled.

Danny looked at him. "What the fuck's that supposed to mean?"

"Later, it can all wait. Come on, smile."

And he took Danny's face in his hands.

TWENTY-SEVEN

Rab ran his fingertip over Danny's lip. "Come on Danny, wake up."

Danny shook his head as if he was shaking off a fly.

"Come on." Rab kissed his mouth. Danny moved restlessly. Rab kissed him again and felt his mouth move under his own. He began to get hard. He pulled back. "Come on Danny, wake *up*." He shook Danny's shoulder.

Danny scowled in an unconscious imitation of John and tried to pull the blanket over his head.

Rab pulled it back. "I've never met anyone could sleep like you." He pinched the skin over Danny's ribs. "Wake up you little fucker." He pulled the blankets off in one sweep. Freeze the little sod out.

Danny lay there, half-erect, in the glow from the lamp. Rab looked at him and felt the hair stand up on the back of his neck. He ran his finger down Danny's belly. Danny became fully erect. Rab traced his hand over it lightly, feeling the heat of it. He pulled his hand away. "Come *on* Danny." Then he saw Danny's eyes were open, half-lidded, watching him. "You little bastard," he whispered.

Danny stretched, pushing his pelvis up off the bed. His mouth was curved very faintly.

"No," Rab said, beginning to smile.

Danny pushed it up again, then he ran one hand down his belly and caught his cock in the fork between his fingers, making it lift up into the air. He looked at Rab and wet his mouth.

"We haven't time."

"Come on." Danny's voice wasn't quite like anything Rab had ever heard before. He felt the amusement drain out of him. It was replaced by something odd - half fear, half excitement. He shook his head.

"Have a taste." Danny's eyes seemed slick with knowledge, ancient. There was no hesitation, no doubt, no asking.

"We've no time." Rab felt as if his voice belonged to someone else.

"My boy lollipop," Danny said.

Rab bent over him awkwardly. As soon as he was close enough Danny thrust it up towards him. Rab felt excitement rip through him like a raging infection. He felt as if every hair on his body stood on end. His lips brushed the head. It was sticky, salty. Danny's hand came down on the back of his neck, tightly, holding him, then pushing him. "Suck it."

Rab took him in his mouth, holding the shaft tight. Danny's hand pulled him back off sharply, tugging his hair. "Know what I'd like?" His voice was odd, out of key. "I'd like to see him stuffing that big fat prick of his right down your smart little throat." He grabbed him suddenly and shoved. "Like *this*." He pushed him down savagely, body curving up to do it, saying, "He was up your arse every other day, wasn't he?" Now his fingers were digging into Rab's neck, his breathing heavy. "See? That's is the thing about loving, it always seems to involve a lot of pain. I always hear 'I love you' most when he's hitting me hardest." He laughed an odd little laugh then said abruptly, "Want to see a little trick?" He pulled Rab's head back sharply by the hair, holding him there awkwardly, straining against the pain of the pull.

Rab struggled to look up at him, his heart thumping with an uncomfortable anger. "Is this something else he taught you?" He wiped his mouth with the back of his hand.

Danny let him go. "Get between my legs." It came smiling out of that angel's face

like some kind of blasphemy.

Rab felt the colour drain from his face as if someone had unexpectedly slapped him. "Fuck off."

"Yeah, right," Danny laughed. "The human tent pole. *Go* boy."

Rab stayed where he was, willing his erection to go away, anything to prove him wrong, but the more he looked at him spread out self-enraptured beneath him the more he wanted him.

"Come on Rab, you want to see it, don't you? You'll really fucking appreciate it."

Rab moved between his legs, hating himself.

"You know," Danny's voice was casual, almost conversational, "you always remind me of those primary school pictures of young Greek gods. Icarus, that's you. Too smart for his own good. Okay. Now... let's see you pull a big load out of that. One to make John's mouth water."

Rab swallowed, but could do nothing.

Danny reached down and did the trick with his hand again, making his cock stand up. "Come on, itchy boy needs your lubrication." He was so swollen that the foreskin had peeled back tight against the shaft, unable to move. Danny opened his legs wide, dropped one foot to the floor.

Rab pushed his knees in, tight between his thighs, began stroking himself with one hand. Danny lay there watching him, his eyes half-shut. He was completely still, holding his cock up like bait. Rab began working it harder, wanting to finish it and wipe out the image of Danny beneath him.

"Tell me you love me." Danny's voice was thick.

"I love you." Rab gritted it out.

"Oh come on, you can do better than that. Say, I love you Danny."

"I love you Danny." And Rab felt it happen suddenly, out of nowhere. He said it again, without prompting. "I love you." And it came up in head-splitting bursts from somewhere deep in his bowels. "Oh Christ, I love you."

And he watched as Danny's cock jerked beneath him, untouched, with nothing but his face showing its pleasure in a twisted smile.

They cleaned up in silence. They put on their clothes in silence. Finally Rab spoke to him without turning. "What d'you want of me Danny?"

"What do you want of me Rab?"

Rab turned to him. Danny's eyes were bright, unreadable. When Rab didn't answer he said, "Well? Don't you know, or can't you say it?"

Rab turned away again. "Forget it."

"It's already forgotten."

Rab tried not to hear that. He looked at the clock. "Christ, we've left it a bit neat."

"It doesn't matter."

Rab looked at him. What didn't matter?

Danny held the look, said nothing.

Rab opened the door and looked out. The silence was heavy, unbroken. Danny followed him out into the hall and down the stairs.

"You can get a jacket from the shed." He was whispering. Danny nodded absently as if he didn't give a fuck. They stood in the kitchen. Only the vaguest hint of the false dawn came in through the window.

"It would be best if you went and rolled about in the hay a bit." Rab managed something like a smile. "Authenticity."

"Don't worry, I intend to. I intend to be fast asleep when he finds me. I could do with some sleep." He looked at Rab. "You know he's never going to fall for this."

"Why not? Those clothes have enough creases in them for four nights in the rough." A door banged upstairs. "Shit. Go on, move it." Rab pushed him out the door.

Danny went out round the front of the house. He daren't cross the yard; John's room was at the back and overlooked it. He would go down the lane, skirt round the shed, and up behind into the barns. He climbed over the front gate and looked down onto the road.

The white car was sitting across the road almost as if it had been placed there to watch the house. Danny's heart leapt. At first he thought it was the Fiat, his mother's Fiat, then he saw the police light on the roof. A speed trap maybe. The car door slammed and a policeman came across the road towards him. He was wearing a bright yellow banded jacket. Already it had a faint luminosity, even in the half-dark. Danny stood and watched him, waiting for him.

He probably thinks I've been breaking in. What if he decides to knock up the whole bloody house?

The policeman came up to him. Danny couldn't make out his face under his hat. The policeman looked at him for a long time then said, "Morning Danny."

Danny frowned. Was this someone he knew? "Morning," he mumbled, trying to see the man's face.

"Running away from home?"

Danny couldn't tell if he was joking or not.

"Come inside, I'd like to talk to you."

Danny thought for a moment he meant into the house, but the policeman started moving back towards his car. Danny followed him.

He opened the passenger door and ushered Danny in as if he was a criminal being escorted to the station. He closed the door. Danny heard the lock click shut. No escape.

The policeman walked round to the driver's side and climbed in. "Perishing cold. Brass monkey weather." He pulled the door shut and threw his hat onto the back seat then turned to face him.

Danny felt a cold trickle of anxiety run down his spine. It was the prick in the sweater.

"Recognise me now?" The policeman flicked the interior light on. The engine turned over, idling. The heater blew warm air up round Danny's feet.

"You came to see Rab."

The redhead's voice was unexpectedly deep, far older than his face. It was unsettling. The policeman reached his hand out and pulled Danny's collar away from his neck. "Wild night, Angel-face?"

Danny's hand went up to his neck. *Oh shit.*

"Didn't know it was there, eh? She always draw blood like that?"

Danny didn't say anything. His mind was racing. How the fuck would he keep it from John?

"Where's the girl then? You were coming out of the house, so where's she?"

Danny's mind went blank.

"Maybe it wasn't a she, that right?"

Danny's face coloured up immediately.

"Keep it in the family, do you?"

Danny looked out the window, biting his lip. *Shit. Shit.*

The policeman was silent for a long time. Danny wondered if he had forgotten about him. He glanced up at him covertly.

"Oh I'm still here, don't worry. What do Blondie and your big brother get up to in cars?"

It took Danny a minute to realise what he'd said. Panic flared up in him like fright.

A huge juggernaut thundered past, rocking the car and spraying the windows with dirty water, breaking the forty mile limit, but the policeman didn't seem to notice, or care. "Well?" he prompted.

"I don't know what you mean." Danny's voice was a deep croak.

"Don't you?"

"No." Danny's face coloured again.

"Do you know what gay-boys do together?"

"Yes..." Danny said it hesitantly, shooting him another glance. He felt as if he had been caught up in the middle of someone else's conversation.

The policeman studied his face for almost a full minute then said, "Have you got any of them on your shoulders?"

Danny stared at him. "What?"

"Bite marks. Have you got any on your shoulders?"

"No, I haven't. Why should I?" Danny couldn't follow any of this. What the fuck did he want?

"In homosexual killings the corpse often has bite marks on the shoulders." The policeman paused, letting this sink in. "That's because they do it up the arse."

Danny turned on him. "I don't know what you're getting at. What do you want?"

The policeman shook his head, raising his eyebrows innocently. "Just to talk, angel, that's all."

"About what?"

"You..." he paused "...and your big brother." He licked his lip. "And Blondie. Do you do it together? Get in a monk's circle and jerk off?"

"No, we fucking don't."

"No need to swear sonny, we're just talking. Nice girl, is she?"

Danny didn't say anything.

"What does she look like?"

"None of your business."

"Let me see... I'd say about six foot four, very broad, with a face like an orang-utan. That right? How does it feel, getting it up the arse?"

"I don't." It came out breathlessly, deflated by panic.

"Take your shirt and jumper off."

"What?"

"You heard me. Take them off."

"Fuck off."

"You want me to take you away in this nice car?" His eyes were so small they looked like little holes in his face.

"I haven't done anything."

"Then you don't need to worry, do you? Take them off."

Oh please God, don't let him have marked me. But Danny couldn't remember if Rab had bitten him or not, he had been too intent on other things. He pulled his sweater off over his head. Sparks of static crackled in the tiny space. He pulled it the right way out, delaying it.

"Hurry it up." The policeman looked at his hair.

Danny pulled his shirt out and unbuttoned it, then stopped. He looked straight out through the windscreen. Another truck went past. The policeman slid his hand inside his shirt, pushing the two halves open. For a long moment he stared at Danny's chest then he said, "Turn round."

Danny turned his back to him. He felt the hands pull at his collar then tug at the shoulders, pulling the shirt down. Goose-pimples came up over his back and arms. The policeman lifted his hair, brushing it up with the flat of his hand. He let it lie there, feeling the texture of the hair under his fingers. He took his other hand and began

probing Danny's shoulders, like a doctor feeling for broken bones. Danny's back was flawless. Only a fine dusting of red-gold hair followed the trail of his spine. There were no marks.

"You've been a dirty boy, angel."

Danny sat rigid, feeling his stomach turn to stone inside him.

"It's illegal for nice young boys like you to do things like that." The policeman's hand kept moving, testing. Danny could feel each mark on his skin like a bruise.

"Who was it angel? Big brother? Maybe we could charge him. Did he force you?" The hand slowed, stopped, then the thumb of the hand holding up his hair started stroking the nape of his neck. The other hand was kneading his shoulder now, but the thumb went on stroking under his hair. "No? You did it willingly? You wanted it? That disgusts me. Did it feel good?"

"I didn't do anything."

"Maybe I should run you in, for your own sake, a young boy like you. How old are you?"

"I'm almost twenty."

Such a deep voice. "Only nineteen. How long has he been doing it to you? We're very keen on child abuse in the police force."

"He's never touched me."

"Tell me the truth, angel. I can't help you if you don't tell me the truth."

Stop pawing me, Danny thought desperately.

"Come on angel." Both hands gripped his shoulders.

Suddenly Danny yanked his shirt up, shrugging his hands off violently. "Stop *pawing* me!"

The policeman was no longer smiling. "What did you say?"

"I said, stop pawing me."

"Dear, dear..." The policeman shook his head as if Danny had distressed him. "You're not suggesting I've got a sexual interest in you?"

Danny stared at him. It was like watching a vicious snake contemplating which part of you to bite.

"I'm a married man, sonny. I don't need to play dirty little boys' games. Get out."

"The door's locked." Danny kept his eyes on him, his hands fumbling blindly at his buttons.

"No it's not. Go on, get out."

Danny felt for the handle without taking his eyes off him. The door opened. He slithered out, grabbing his sweater.

"Oh, and angel..." Danny stopped, holding the door, wanting to slam it in his smarmy little face, "save me hanging around. Tell Blondie I'll be seeing him tonight, nine o'clock sharp." He pulled the door shut, yanking it out of Danny's hand.

Danny watched the car pull away meticulously and carefully, driving like a proper policeman should.

Rab threw open the curtains and hauled up his bedroom window. The place stank like a brothel. He stuck his head out and took a deep breath. It only got halfway into his lungs. He pulled his head back with a jerk, moving back against the curtains as if they might conceal him. He crossed quickly and put the room light out, then the lamp. He went back to the window.

The car was parked on the other side of the green, half up the pavement. The door opened and a policeman got out. Rab couldn't make him out, only the bands of his coat. He crossed the road.

He came up towards the house and disappeared beyond the edge of Rab's vision.

What time was it? He can't be coming here at this time. Rab looked at the clock. Six twenty-one, no, twenty-seven. Maybe it was just some officious bastard checking the place out. Why park carefully up out the way then?

He listened. He should be at the gate by now. He looked back out the window.

Danny was coming down the lane with him, following in his footsteps. The policeman opened the door and ushered him inside. He went round and got in the driver's seat. A second later the interior light came on. Rab could see the black half-shaved head, an arm. Fuck, it was him. Now what? But he couldn't see Danny. Rab watched until his eyes nipped. He blinked rapidly, making his eyes water. When they cleared he realised the policeman had moved. He could only see the back of his neck and part of his back now. What was going on? The policeman moved again, further forward.

Rab's door opened, slammed shut. He spun round. John was standing there, a flat black shape. "Where is he?"

"Down there," Rab said, turning back to the window.

"Don't fuck me around."

Rab grabbed his arm, pulling him over beside him. "There, see the pretty police car? He's in there with Dick Tracy, our man on the ball."

"What?" John said blankly, staring out almost sightlessly.

"I'm telling you, Danny's in there with the cunt in blue."

"I thought he was with you."

"I told you he wasn't. Look, he's coming out."

John followed his gaze, someone was climbing out the door. "Is it Danny?" His voice was low.

"It's not Dougal the Dog."

Danny got out. They watched him go to slam the door, then he stopped. In the morning silence they could hear the policeman's voice.

"What's he saying?"

Rab shook his head. "I can't make it out."

The door was yanked suddenly out of Danny's hand. It slammed shut. The car moved off slowly.

"He drives like someone's aunt."

"He probably fucks like one too." John's voice was dry, hard. "Come on."

They went downstairs and into the kitchen. John had pulled on his boots before Rab could even find his. He was already out the back door. "Danny!" He managed somehow to make it sound like a roar without really raising his voice.

Danny stopped dead. John was coming across the yard towards him in gut-wrenching strides. "Where the hell have you been?"

Danny opened his mouth, but nothing came out.

Rab came out behind him at a trot. "We saw you from upstairs. What did he want?" He was trying to talk to him with his eyes. *No sweat Danny, take it easy.*

"Well?" John demanded.

Rab could see him getting ready to lift him off the ground. "Why the fuck are we standing out here in this bitter cold?" he interrupted. " Let's get in." He turned, giving them no option but to follow.

They went back into the house. John closed the door and repeated himself all in one gesture. "Well? What did he want?"

"He wanted to see Rab."

Rab could see his hands moving as if they wanted to do something but he wouldn't let them.

"What, at this hour? Not even six-thirty? What kind of loopy bastard is he?"

"No... I mean, he was waiting to see him to tell him to..." But Danny wasn't sure if

that was right. He rephrased it. "That he would see him at nine o'clock sharp." He emphasized the word, just as the policeman had done. The hand jerked again. It was the left hand and the right moved as if to block its path. Both hands subsided again.

"What took him so long to tell you that?" John was cooling down. The irritation had slid from his voice to be replaced by a heavier, more dangerous, suspicion. Rab darted a look at him. He was looking at the buttons on Danny's shirt. Rab followed his eyes. They were misbuttoned. He was carrying his sweater.

There was an incredible silence in the room. They heard the toilet flush upstairs. The cockerel crowed in the yard, three times, like strangulated hiccups. It was John that spoke. "What went on in the fucking car Danny?"

Slowly Rab watched Danny's left hand go up to his neck, finally completing the gesture. He held it there protectively.

"What went on in the fucking car?" John's face was heavy and white as carved marble.

Danny stood there like a rabbit.

"Your shirt Danny... you've buttoned it up *all* wrong."

Danny looked down.

"Take you hand away."

Danny didn't move.

John stepped forward and yanked his hand off, pulling the collar back. His hand bunched in Danny's shirt, pulling it up out of his jeans, almost lifting Danny off the floor. "Couldn't get it off one so he got it off the other."

Rab pushed in between them. "Leave him alone."

John snarled at him, inches from his face, "*Fuck off.*"

Rab dug his nails into John's cheek, all five, like a claw. John swore, pulling back. Rab's hand came away, each nail heavy with skin as if he had been peeling oranges. John's cheek oozed pinkish from the semicircles under his eye. His smile was broad and ugly, almost a grimace. The pain seemed to make no impression on him.

"How d'you like that? Two minutes in the car and there he is, sitting in the middle of the village green giving the old police gearstick some head." He looked past him again to Danny. "I can just see you, shirt all undone. Very seductive. Like the moustache Danny? Ticklish?"

Rab walked in front of him, blocking his view.

"What's wrong? This come as a surprise? Show him your neck Danny." He was staring directly into Rab's eyes. "Show Rab the bite on your neck." He watched it sink in, watched Rab digest it.

Rab turned slowly and looked at Danny. His eyes were as empty and expressionless as glass. Slowly he looked at his neck. He could see a tiny edge of red.

"Go on, open his shirt and take a good look."

Rab turned slightly and lifted Danny's shirt away from his neck. Danny didn't stop him, his eyes didn't move. He reminded Rab of the pictures he'd seen of men in death camps lined up for roll call.

"Tell us what he did Danny." John's voice was crawling with something indefinable. He sounded like a man playing with himself, telling dirty stories under the blankets. It made Rab feel as if he had looked into a tin of maggots. "Should we look further down? Any strange scents? Any sticky patches?"

Rab turned on him. John was looking directly at him again, his expression malicious. "You seem to have been more successful than your cousin here. Maybe he prefers redheads."

"Pack it in John."

"Or?"

"I'm going to break your fucking neck."

"That's what I like to hear." John began flexing his fingers as if he could already feel the pleasure of hitting him. "But let me give you a *real* reason. Let me tell you what he really likes. Better still, let me show you. Danny..." He turned back to look at Danny.

There was a silence. Rab turned round.

"He's gone." John laughed suddenly. "The little fucker's gone."

They were quite alone in the room.

After breakfast Rab was sent off with Ian to repair fences. They had left John to the vagaries of their daily woman whose non-stop conversation always drove him to distraction. Danny was still locked in the bathroom where he had retreated earlier. Maybe he intended to stay there all day.

"Good, was he?"

Rab was startled to hear Ian's voice in the driver's seat beside him. He had almost forgotten him. He reached up and pulled the sun visor down, but he didn't reply.

"Three times by my calculations." He clicked his tongue. "I almost missed the morning one. That was the best. All that humiliation, heady stuff."

"You're a cruddy little bastard Ian."

"You mean I'm not as pretty as he is."

"No, I mean you're a cruddy little bastard."

"His looks won't last. Nothing lasts."

"I've heard this argument before, and from someone who looks as much like a pig's arse as you do. If you haven't got it, don't knock it."

Ian's face mottled with anger. Christ, Rab thought, he couldn't even get angry gracefully.

Ian swung the van onto the verge. Rab got out to open the gate then climbed back in. They bumped across the field and over the crest. The sea spread out in a long strip beneath them. Ian stopped the van. The sun disappeared abruptly behind a heavy grey cloud. The landscape changed colour as if a filter had been placed across it.

"Why have you been avoiding me?"

"Don't tempt me Ian, I might just tell you." Rab began patting his pockets.

"You can't just dump me, you..."

Rab interrupted, "If you even think about saying I owe you I'll push your fucking face through the windscreen."

Ian slapped his hands on the steering wheel. "Okay, then I tell Danny. Let's see you lie your way out of this one."

"You *tell* Danny? From what I hear you've already told Danny. At least threaten me with something new."

"I never said a word to Danny. Christ you're as thick as John, aren't you?"

Rab said nothing.

"What about his mother then?" Ian demanded. "He still doesn't know about you and his legendary mother."

"I said something new Ian."

"You want me to tell him?"

Rab turned to him. "No, I don't want you to tell him, but I don't want to suck your dick either, so it's six and half a dozen, isn't it?"

"You come." Ian threw it at him like a final vindication of all his arguments.

Rab laughed. "I come in my sleep sometimes, but that doesn't mean I'm in love with the mattress."

"Think I won't make trouble for you?"

"You've already done that."

"This?" Ian laughed. "Just wait till I tell John exactly what you did last night."

"Why should I care? John believes exactly what he likes. Whether it's true or not doesn't matter." But Rab could feel an edgy anxiety creeping in. He tried not to look at him.

"If you say so."

Rab gave in and took a long drag on his cigarette. Ian saw his hesitation, the worm of doubt. He said softly, "It's not much to pay for one less aggravation, is it? He's not going to like you buggering my beautiful baby brother."

Rab stared at him.

"A wine glass, it actually does work."

"You mean you sat there all night with your ear stuck against a fucking wine glass?"

Ian smiled. "Every word, every grunt, every pissy little kiss and cuddle of you dinky little lovebirds."

Rab shook his head. "You really are a cruddy little bastard."

Ian smiled some more.

"Why d'you do it?" Rab asked. "No, don't answer that, I don't want to know."

They were silent, the skies grew steadily darker, then Rab spoke again. "Okay, but you don't touch me and I don't kiss you."

Ian's face tightened.

"No, just shut up, there's more. If you so much as breathe one word to Danny I'll stuff your head right up your arse. And don't talk to John about *anything*. Think you can manage that? You shut up and I suck your dick. Strikes me you're the one getting a good deal."

"You conceited bastard."

"If you'd ever sucked your own dick you'd change your mind."

Ian turned on him, face livid. "I don't know why I put up with this shit from you. I don't know why I don't..."

"Do you want me to suck your dick or not?"

Ian stared at him: the black eyes, the white hair, the long fingers always holding one of those stinking cigarettes, one foot braced against the dashboard, the tight crotch. No matter what Rab was always up there flaunting it, saying, Look but don't touch. He was saying it right now.

"You're such a faggot," Ian said.

Rab laughed suddenly, and once he started he couldn't seem to stop.

"What's so fucking funny?" Ian demanded.

It took Rab two attempts before he could get out a reply. "I was just thinking..." he coughed on a fresh burst of laughter, "you're such a refreshing change."

Ian muttered, "Dickhead."

Softly it began to rain.

"Where's Danny?" Rab asked.

John sat with his back to him, steadily feeding. That's what it was like, watching a conveyor belt shovel food into a hatch.

"I've no idea. He disappeared with our Mrs Ostler at lunchtime and I haven't seen either of them since." He just kept on shovelling.

Rab raised his eyebrows. *Very laid-back John, but you aren't fooling anyone.* He could see the tense grip of his hands, even the way he was jabbing the food into his face. He was good and ratty and Danny would probably get it all when he finally showed up.

Rab sat down at the end of the table and began eating, but the food tasted like sawdust. He looked at the clock. 8:10, not long.

"You going to him again?" John was taking a piece of sponge pudding from the oven and spooning custard over it. Rab watched him, intrigued to see what he was going to do with it. He never touched sweet stuff.

"Uh-huh," he replied, looking away quickly as John caught him watching. He heard John's bowl bang on the table. "If I don't go there he'll only come here," he added.

John said nothing. He began stabbing into the pudding with his spoon as if he was delving with a spade. Rab wondered if he intended to eat the chips of bowl along with his food. Suddenly it no longer amused him. John's obsessions no longer amused him. He pushed his plate away. "I'm going to take a shower," he announced.

A grunt was John's only answer.

Rab took the road slowly again, only this time it was because it was raining. It was raining so heavily that the windscreen wipers seemed to cut swathes through the water. God, what a bloody wet dog's arse of a year. A few weeks of stifling heat and then nothing but fucking rain.

He pulled up at the traffic lights, watching the colour run down the windscreen like paint. The fan blew warm air into the cab that felt as if it scalded his lungs. He turned it off. Almost immediately he began to feel chilly. *Fuck it.*

Don't speak too soon.

He drove even slower, approaching the entrance to the new harbour road, watching for the turning. He crawled past the architects' boards and turned onto the loose road surface of the harbour. The white lamps were haloed with aureoles of hissing, singing light. He parked where he stopped, not trying to nose it onto the concrete. Probably drive right into the fucking water. He opened the door and made a dash for it, not bothering to lock the van. Anybody brave enough to steal anything in this weather deserved it.

He stood in the entrance, shaking himself like a dog, half-hypnotised by the singing white lamps and their rainbows of rain. He could hear the sea tonight alright, hurling itself against the outer harbour wall.

The buzzer went suddenly in his ear. A tinny voice said, "Come on up."

The cunt had been watching for him. He must have fucking 20-20 vision to see through that rain. Rab pushed against the door.

The smell of emulsion was stronger. The damp seemed to lift it out of the walls. There was an odd new smell about the place that reminded him of new office buildings. What the hell was it? Rab looked down and saw the grey marl spreading ahead of him. Last time the floor had just been plain grey concrete. He felt better dripping on that carpet.

He went upstairs. The door was open again. This time he was waiting for him in the hall.

"Come in, take your shoes off. Go on, you're not walking on my carpet in those filthy things."

Rab took his shoes off. When he stood up he felt the policeman's hands on his shoulders. He swung on him.

"I only want your jacket."

"Next time ask."

The policeman said nothing. He just stood waiting. Rab took his jacket off and handed it to him.

"Go on in."

The living room was too warm. The blinds had been pulled right back and the window created a huge mirror against the intense black of the sky. Rab watched him come in behind him, saw his eyes travel down over his back, then saw him realise he

could be seen.

"Nice colour." He gestured at Rab's shirt. "Suits you."

"I know."

"Conceited bastard, aren't you?"

"So they keep telling me."

The policeman shut the door. "Take a seat."

Rab sat down on the sofa facing the opposite wall. He sank into it as if he had been enveloped in marshmallow. He knew it would be a hell of a chair to get back out of. He saw the policeman watching him.

"Drink?"

"Okay."

"Same as last time?"

Rab nodded.

When he left the room Rab swung his feet up and lay down on the sofa. Better than his bed. He lay staring up at the ceiling, feeling the soft heavy warmth of the leather with his fingertips.

"Like it?" The policeman was standing above him holding two drinks; Rab's beer and something dark that looked like flat Coke.

Rab swung himself up. "Beats ours." He took the proffered drink, watching the policeman to see where he'd sit. But he sat on the other sofa so they could see each other. He could also watch Rab in the window.

"You've got a Greek profile. That aquiline nose, very Adonis."

"Wow, Icarus and Adonis in one day. You know, for a straight you do a lot of curvy talking."

The policeman took a mouthful of the black stuff. "I see you haven't improved your dirty mouth."

"You haven't improved your technique."

There was a silence. Rab wondered if he dare smoke. Tonight Plod was got up in a banana ensemble. Banana coloured V-neck in fine wool - this time with an eagle on the tit - same colour polo shirt underneath. The shirt was open a button or two and Rab could see a thick mat of intensely black hair right up to his neck. He noticed his hands were just the same, thickly covered right up to the first joint of his fingers.

"You know, someone ought to warn Big-boy that his young brother's underage... amongst other things."

Rab tore his gaze away from his fingers. "What?"

"He's been doing the vampire on Angel-face, biting his neck. Sucking his neck, to be more accurate. Who knows what else he's sucking."

Rab felt himself flush a dull angry red. "It was you who'd been at his fucking neck." *Very subtle Rab, nicely handled.*

"Me?" The policeman looked genuinely surprised. "He told you *I'd* done it?"

No, Danny hadn't, had he? Danny hadn't said anything. Rab felt everything shift into perspective. "Why d'you have his shirt off?"

"Just looking."

"Mr Straight Guy was taking a *look?*"

"Looking at the *marks* sonny-boy. I don't have to explain myself to you. I suspected he was being abused by his brother."

"What's wrong, jealous?"

Rab expected him to take off but all he said was, "Tell Big-boy it's illegal, and I'll have him for it if he doesn't watch out."

"You're supposing a lot, aren't you, from one mark?"

"Not just one mark."

"One mark plus a look at John's piss-off face."

The policeman drank his drink.

"What is that fucking stuff?" Rab asked.

"O.V.D. Old Vatted Demerara."

Rab looked blank.

"Black rum. My parents send it to me."

"Lucky you," Rab said absently, his mind still on that mark. It had been his, he'd done it, yet he'd stood in the kitchen and looked at Danny and really believed... let's put a lid on that one.

"What's in it for you?" the policeman asked.

"What?"

"I said, what's in it for you? You know what's going on yet you keep quiet. Why do you want to protect him?"

"I don't."

"You sure he was forcing you?"

Rab slammed his drink down.

"Mind my carpet."

"Fuck your carpet. What is this all about? I mean, even supposing John fucked every member of the household why should you care?"

"Because he's breaking the law."

"Bullshit. You don't give a fuck about the law, other than how you can bend it. What is it with you? Vicarious thrills? Picking up boys, getting them to tell you about the things they do? What d'you do, lie in bed and play with yourself thinking about all the things you've heard?"

The policeman leaned back in his sofa and said nothing. Then he said, "Why don't you drink some beer and relax?"

"I don't want to drink your goddamned beer."

"Well, bearing everything in mind from the fact that there's no Fiat to no Mrs Jackson Moore, and that your cousin is humping his young brother, I should drink it anyway."

"Fuck you."

"The name's Henderson and would you like to?" He studied Rab in the window lazily, insultingly. "You're a nice-looking boy. Maybe I could grow to like it."

"Your dick's fucking hanging out for it."

"Watch your mouth."

"Sure," Rab said, leaning back. He took another drink of beer then finished it. The policeman got up and took his glass, disappeared into the kitchen. Rab ran his hands through his hair. Henderson came back in.

"Here."

Rab frowned up at the dark glass.

"It's just the same as mine." He waved a frosted bottle. "There's Coke if it's too strong for you. Go on, try it."

Rab took a mouthful, coughed.

The policeman smiled, showing all his white teeth. "Not such a big mouthful next time. Like it?"

Rab nodded consideringly. "It's okay."

"I'm sure the firm will be pleased." The policeman pulled up his sleeves.

Rab saw the same thick black hair, like a silky mat on his arms. It lay flush across his skin as if it was painted on.

"Turn you on?"

Rab lifted his eyes to his face.

"Hairy men turn you on?"

"I told you," Rab bit each word out, "men don't turn me on, period."

"No wonder Big-boy gets frustrated then. Is that why he reams Angel-face, because he can't get you?"

Rab said nothing. He took a swig of rum that nearly choked him.

"I told you to go easy. Here, put some Coke in it if you're going to drink it like that."

Rab put his hand over the glass. "Fuck your Coke."

The policeman shrugged and put the bottle back down. "Want to hear some music?"

"No."

"What's wrong, don't you like music?"

"I hate music."

"Why?"

"If you ever had to sit in a tractor going up and down a field all day with nothing but the radio for company you'd hate music too. Music gives me vibrations in my legs."

"Alright, so you don't like music. How about a video?"

"I've got to go home."

"Not until I say so."

"What are you going to do, hold me prisoner?"

"If you like."

Rab looked at him. "You're really nuts, know that? It scares the shit out of me to think they let you in the police force."

"I'm one of the nice ones."

"That's what worries me."

"So, you want to watch a video?"

"Sure. Fuck it. Why not? It's better than your face."

The policeman got up and crossed to the large section of shelving facing Rab's chair. "What kind of thing do you like?"

"Something with lots of cunt in it."

The policeman turned and looked at him. "Really?"

Rab stared back at him. "Really."

"Alright."

The policeman walked out of the room and came back with a tape. Rab couldn't make it out. He slotted it in and switched on. The TV screen was large and flat, the colour perfect. He went to the room lights and faded them out. He saw Rab's expression. "Dimmer switch."

"Of course."

The film came on, imaginatively titled, 'Fuckin' & Suckin'. Paradoxically, it was expensively produced, bizarrely Hollywood.

"It's American."

Rab was startled to hear Henderson's voice beside him. He'd moved to the same sofa, presumably to see better.

"You can't play American videos on British machines," Rab said shortly.

"Alright then, it's a Dutch tape of an American video." He got up suddenly and disappeared into the kitchen. He came back with a bottle and filled up their glasses.

The cast consisted of one girl and two men. It wasn't long before everybody had their clothes off. The bodies were beautiful, brown and plastic. All-over tans; the girl big-breasted; the boys well-endowed. It was a hardcore movie, the fucking authentic. Rab found himself with a hard-on. This, he thought, closing his eyes to blot out the sight of the graphic penetration, was a bad mistake.

He could hear nothing from Henderson beside him. The drinking hand moved steadily, neither faster nor slower. Rab took another drink.

One young man held the girl's legs up wide in the air while the other fucked her until she made a lot of noise that was assumably intended to be a climax. Rab had

162

never seen a porn video before, but he'd heard that the men always withdrew to ejaculate on the girls so you could see it was authentic. He assumed that's what the young man would do now.

He did withdraw, but instead of doing what Rab expected, the two men began kissing and then the one who'd been watching went down on the one who'd been fucking the girl.

Rab blinked. *Shit*. Then the girl joined in, three-way sucking. Rab spoke without turning, "What the fuck is this?"

"It's a bisexual movie." Henderson's drink went to his mouth, his eyes stayed on the screen.

"You're having me on."

"No."

Rab looked back at the screen. The man was gobbling him now. His cock, both their cocks, were enormous. They were really enjoying it. Rab's erection didn't go away. "Turn it off." He put his glass down on the floor.

"Why? Don't you like it?" Henderson's voice was lazy.

"No, I don't."

Henderson kept watching the screen as if the conversation wasn't important. There was a lot of grunting. Rab turned back in time to see one of the men come in the other's face, holding his head tight, spurting it everywhere.

"Turn the fucking thing off Henderson."

Henderson got up slowly and stood in front of him. "Okay." He put his hands in his pockets and Rab saw it, just as he had been meant to see it; Henderson's erection, large and obvious in the looseness of his 'slacks', not flattened or concealed by punishing jeans.

He turned away and stopped the tape. He put it on to rewind. "What d'you want to see then?" he asked, keeping his back to Rab.

Rab sat there, livid, swallowing down his anger. "Anything that isn't about sex."

Henderson laughed. It was the first time Rab had ever heard him laugh. He sounded almost human.

Danny passed through the kitchen and out into the hall. The living room door stood open. John sat at one end of the settee, facing the door, waiting for him. "Well, well, the wanderer returns."

Danny got as far as the second stair.

"In here Danny. Right now."

Danny turned back down the stairs and went into the living room. He shut the door without being told. John was watching a film where everybody shot everybody else. The sound of guns was incessant.

"Sit down."

John had been smoking. Half a dozen half-smoked cigarettes lay in the hearth where they had landed. More lay stubbed out and broken in the ashtray. Danny sat down.

"Where've you been?"

"In town."

"Town shut hours ago."

"I went back to her place for a meal."

"You're joking."

"Does it sound like it?"

"Did you have to sing for your supper?"

"No."

"Bit old for you, isn't she? But I'm forgetting, if it's still kicking Danny'll fuck it."

Danny did not bother to reply.

"You think you can just dump your work any time you feel like it?"

Danny didn't answer that either.

John picked a cigarette up, broke it in half. He looked at him suddenly. "You fuck her?"

"Don't be so fucking stupid."

John slapped him in one explosive movement then he sat back heavily and said softly, "Alright." He reached over and pulled Danny along to him, touching softly where he'd slapped. "I missed you baby."

Danny sat with his hands pressed flat against the cushions.

"Where were you last night?" He undid Danny's zip and slid his hand in.

Danny closed his eyes. "In the barn."

"I don't want to slap you again..."

Danny kept his eyes shut. "I told you."

"Now why would you want to do a stupid thing like that?"

"I wanted to be by myself."

"You were with Rab, weren't you?"

Danny said nothing. John pulled his cock out his trousers. "Well, surprise, surprise, Danny's stiff."

Danny watched the men shooting each other and jumping in and out of cars.

"How many times did you do it with him?"

Danny kept watching the cars.

"Making up for lost time. A whole night alone. I bet you went at it like little rabbits. And now look, you can still get stiff for your big brother. Isn't love wonderful?" He was taking long slow pulls on him, squeezing the head. Danny kept his mouth shut.

"You ever come on this carpet Danny? I'm sure you must have." There was an odd note in his voice. Danny turned his face away.

"Maybe you'd like to get down there in front of the TV and do it in Steve McQueen's face?"

Danny laid his head back slowly and closed his eyes again because you could only pretend for so long that it wasn't going to happen, that you weren't part of it, after that you only made it worse. The longer you held out the more it satisfied him, so you let it just carry you along.

"An angel at the ecstasy of Christ." John's voice was a raw whisper.

Then the door opened. Danny didn't hear it, but he felt the cold air come past him. He kept his eyes closed. Tightly, tightly closed.

John's hand gripped him in surprise, then the pressure eased - no threat. "Hello Dad."

The door closed. Danny put his hands over his eyes. He wanted to know if he was in the room with them, but he couldn't bring himself to look. Then he heard someone thump heavily into the armchair.

"Open your eyes Danny, your Daddy's come to see you. Pissed out his head, but come to see you anyway. Open your eyes."

But Danny wouldn't look.

"Doesn't want to see you Dad. But you want to see him, don't you?" And John's hands began undoing Danny's shirt.

Danny grabbed at him. "Don't." His eyes shot open. He tried to keep his eyes on John's, but his head turned in spite of himself. His father was sitting there, perched forward on the edge of his chair as if for a better view.

John shrugged him off sharply. He pulled his shirt open like the policeman had done, but with a savage jerk. "Sit up, lift your arse."

Danny shook his head.

John grabbed his hair. "I said, lift it."

Danny lifted himself and John pulled his clothes down to below his knees. He pushed Danny's thighs open. "There Dad, now you can see the real thing. With Danny everyone always appreciates seeing the real thing. Danny's one of the few things in life where the real thing's better than the dream, isn't that right?" John looked down at him again, but his eyes came back up with a quick dart, his expression uncertain.

Danny was heavily flaccid. John's hand moved as if to touch his face, stopped, dropped away. He said Danny's name. It was a whisper, a question, meant only for his ears.

Danny opened his eyes in answer. John held his gaze then reached out and began to masturbate him, but it was soft-handed, almost reticent. Danny shook his head once, tried to, never completed the gesture. He tore his eyes away and saw his father looking at John's hand, watching intently, mouth open, face red.

Danny pressed his cheek against the settee with a small hopeless noise, closing his eyes again. He could feel the heat begin to climb in him again, worse because of the interruption. He could feel his breathing become difficult. He let his lips part a little.

John's hand tightened on him painfully. "Want to take a turn old man?"

Danny's head shot round towards him. John's eyes were black, as bottomless and cold as ice on the seabed. Danny turned away from him, looked at his father, and saw it all over his face. He was going to do it. John was going to sit there and let him do it. He was *asking* him to do it.

"Might be your last chance, and God knows you're drunk enough. You can always blame it on the drink. Do it then forget it. You know that one off by heart. Come on old man, come and get him on your hands."

Danny watched him drop down and crawl over on his knees because he was too fucking drunk to do anything else. Drunk on an offer he finally couldn't refuse.

Danny's nails dug into the cushion. He watched the old man drag himself up using his legs, pulling up over his knees, his thighs, then he pushed himself forward into Danny's crotch. He dropped his head between Danny's thighs and begun nuzzling his face in his pubic hair, butting him, drooling over him, like a baby blindly seeking the nipple.

It looked as if he was being eaten. The old man made little snuffling noises. He was licking and suckling at anything he could reach, crushing his face into his balls. He finally found Danny's cock and began cramming it into his mouth. He was salivating so heavily it felt like being dowsed in warm water.

Danny eventually got the words out. "Stop him."

John looked up at him. He moved back abruptly. "You stop him."

Danny looked down at his father's head. He put his hands up behind his head, gripping the back of the settee, bracing himself, trying to keep as much of his body away from him as possible. It looked odd, as if he were offering himself to him.

John lunged forward and punched him in the side of the mouth. Danny felt his teeth come down on his tongue. The pain was intense, instant, obliterating. He moaned. His mouth began to water, salt and pungent, almost immediately. He could taste the blood in it. His lips began to swell as if they'd been stung. The old man went back to his feasting as if nothing had happened.

Danny laid his head back began to cry, slowly and without expression.

"That's it old man, suck him off." And John got up with an awkward jerky movement and crossed to the window, turning his back on them.

He stood there, hands crammed in his pockets, listening to the noise of his father fellating his little brother.

Rab woke with a jerk. He blinked at the strange room, the coloured lights. "Jesus, I've got to go." He tried to get up, but subsided uselessly. "What time is it?" He could feel Henderson's thigh and arm against his. Why so close on an eight foot sofa?

"Half one."

"Half one? Fucksake."

He struggled again. Henderson caught his arm. "Stay here."

"What?"

"I said, stay here. You can sleep on the sofa. I'll wake you at six."

"No, I've got to go home."

"You're too tired to drive."

Rab tried to lever himself out of the settee.

"I said, you're too tired to drive." Henderson's hand was against his chest. "And too drunk. That's official."

"Sounds more like blackmail."

"My speciality."

Rab lay back. Henderson picked up the remote and the TV flickered out. There was nothing he wanted more than to just pass out on the settee.

Henderson got up. Rab marvelled at him. He seemed perfectly sober. He came back with a pillow and a couple of blankets. The pillow had a black satin pillowcase. Rab took it with raised eyebrows.

"Something bothering you?" Henderson asked.

"Not me."

"Will there be enough?"

"Plenty." The room was still overly warm. "I need to take a piss though. Where's your bathroom?"

"Through here." Henderson led him through the other door that led to the bedroom. There was another small hall with three doors off. He pushed one open and pulled on a light cord. They were reflected, standing there together, a hundred times over.

"Jesus," Rab said.

"All done with mirrors."

"Wouldn't like to take a shit in it."

"Charming."

Rab went in and closed the door. "Wow," he muttered, watching himself displayed from every angle. He relieved himself, keeping his eyes firmly down, then washed his face. He felt a little better. The towels were black to match the bathroom suite. They were monogrammed J.H. *J for John, Joseph, Jehoshaphat. Oh yes, definitely Jehoshaphat.*

He went back to the living room, but Henderson wasn't there. He came out of the kitchen.

"What's the J stand for?"

Henderson looked blank.

"On the towels."

"James."

"Jimmy Henderson. Sounds like a footballer."

"Don't call me that."

"What, Jimmy?"

"Neither Jimmy nor James, stick to Henderson."

"Okay, who gives a fuck?" Rab began making up his bed.

Henderson went back out. A few minutes later he returned with a toothbrush in his mouth and minus his shirt and jumper. He was completely covered in hair; shoulders, chest, belly, right up his arms. It lay in thick swathes on him like whirlpools, not wiry

166

but silky, long, brushable.

"You look like a fucking werewolf."

"So I've been told." Henderson turned round, showing Rab his back. It swept across his shoulder blades. Two belts of it came up from his hips and stopped about six inches above his waistband. The bare patches between shoulder and waist looked unnatural, a dead-white against that black hair. He turned back and lifted his arms.

"Masses of the fucking stuff," Rab said.

Henderson dropped his arms again. "Want to see the rest?" He was smiling.

"No way, I've seen enough." Rab turned his back. He heard Henderson wander back out of the room, the water running in the bathroom, the toilet flushing. He took off his shirt and trousers and climbed in. He left his socks and shorts on. A passion-killing combination. His insurance policy. The leather felt warm against his skin.

Henderson came back in. "Alright?"

"Yeah, do us a favour though, turn out the lights."

Henderson crossed the floor and dimmed the light completely. He finally closed the blinds across the window. Rab watched him in the light from the hall. Jesus, he was hairy.

Henderson came over and stopped beside him then sat down. Now what? Rab felt pinned under the blankets. He pulled his arms out and tucked them under his head. He saw Henderson looking at the dark hair in his armpits. He brought his arms back down.

"Want to feel it?" Henderson asked.

"What?"

"My body hair."

"Fuck off."

"No seriously, no strings. Go on, have a feel. Everybody ends up doing it sooner or later. Everyone at the station has had a go."

"I'll bet."

"Go on. You want to, don't you?"

He was right, he did. It looked so fucking weird, like animal fur.

Rab reached out his hand and felt his chest. He followed the pattern of it across his left breast. *Jesus.* "It really does feel as weird as it looks."

"Told you."

It was like stroking a cat, a hard cat. Rab could feel the muscle underneath. Our Mr Henderson worked out. He fucking would.

"Have another go."

"No thanks."

Henderson stood up. "Look." He began unbuckling his trousers.

"No." Rab almost shouted it. "Don't go any further."

"Don't panic, I just want you to see something." He stood there, his zip half down.

Rab subsided onto the sofa. "Okay, but let's get this over with, eh? I'm tired."

"Sure."

Henderson finished unfastening his trousers then pulled them open. He wore conventional brief-type underpants. They were the same banana yellow as his shirt had been. They were also low-slung. The hair on his belly was even thicker, so dense it appeared solidly black. It, too, grew in swathes. The two sides grew towards each other, meeting in an up-turned wave. It created a heavy silky curl like a seam down the middle.

"Feel it."

Rab could see the shape of his dick through his pants. It wasn't stiff. That made him feel both better and worse. He didn't analyse the feeling.

Rab felt it to get it over with. He didn't brush the hair with his hand, just in case.

Instead he ran his fingernails through it, feeling the depth of it.

"Nice, isn't it?"

"I'm a conceited bastard?"

"It is though, isn't it?" Henderson seemed very proud of it.

"If you like that sort of thing."

"And you don't?"

Rab took his hand away but didn't reply.

"Does it repulse you?"

"No."

"But you don't like it?"

"I'm indifferent. It's just weird, freaky, like having an extra joint in your finger."

Unexpectedly the policeman laughed. He fastened his trousers. "Now it's your turn."

"What?"

"I showed you - now you show me."

"Give over, I grew out of that bicycle shed stuff a long time ago."

"Fair's fair."

"I never asked you to show me anything."

"You wanted to see it. Now I want my turn."

Rab was never going to get any sleep at this rate. "Your turn at what?"

"I want to see your pubic hair."

"Get stuffed."

"Come on," Henderson cajoled. "Faster you do it, faster you can get to sleep."

Rab threw back the blankets. "This is fucking crazy, know that?" He tugged his shorts down low as he could without giving the greedy little bastard a free show. The thick blonde hair curled over his pubic bone and onto his belly.

The policeman stared at it. "White."

"What did you expect, green?" Rab made to pull up his shorts, but Henderson stopped him.

"Lift your arms."

Rab sighed and put his arms behind his head.

"Two different colours."

"So?"

The policeman nodded then reached out his hand. Rab grabbed it. "Oh no you don't." He pulled his shorts back up single-handed. "Right, get out, that's enough show and fucking tell tonight."

The policeman stood up without saying anything and left the room. Rab heard the door click shut. Almost immediately he fell fast asleep.

Henderson woke him at six as promised. He was in a pair of silky black pyjamas. "Want anything to eat?"

"No."

"Bath?"

Rab shook his head. "I've got to go." Christ, he felt like shit.

Henderson watched him get dressed. "You always sleep in your socks?"

"Only when there's a queer in the next room."

Rab sat down abruptly. Henderson had pushed him.

Rab looked up at him. "Closet gay movies, wanna see my willy, you're a nice-looking boy. Why don't you just come out Henderson and get it over with?"

"I'm not gay." Henderson's face was flushed with anger.

"Then what's it all about? Why all the interest in Danny?"

"I just want to be friends."

"You've got a funny way of making friends."

"Only way I know."

Rab stood up again and fastened his jeans. "I can see that. Where the fuck are my shoes?"

"In the hall."

Rab went out and levered his shoes on. Henderson followed him out. "I won't see you for a couple of days," he said. "I'm on night duty."

"Shame."

"Come over Saturday."

Rab pulled on his jacket. "What if I say I don't want to?"

"Then I'll come and get you."

"I wouldn't like to be your enemy if this is friendship."

Henderson shrugged - take it or leave it. "Same time," Henderson reminded him. "Nine o'clock."

Rab had his hand on the door.

"Bring the boy."

Rab stopped, turned. "No way. Uh-uh. No way."

"Why not?"

"Not to you."

"Is it me or him you don't trust?"

"I'm not bringing him. What d'you think I am, a pimp?"

Henderson grabbed the front of his jacket, shoving his face up close. "That's once too often, sunshine. Just bring the boy."

Rab stood, heart pounding, waiting for him to let go. The moment seemed to go on forever, then Henderson dropped his hand. "I'll expect you on Saturday - both of you."

"You can expect."

"Be here."

Rab glared at him then swung out the door, slamming it hard enough to wake every resident in the place.

Danny turned in time to see a silver Mercedes swing into the yard. He pushed the sack he was moving upright against the wall with his foot and squinted into the light. The car drew up beside him, forcing him to take a step back. The door was pushed

open. "Just the man I want to see."

Danny bent down slightly. It was him again. "What d'you want?"

"Not even a hello?"

"I'm busy."

"Well you can get un-busy. Go and change your clothes. You're not getting into my car in that lot."

Danny frowned at him. "I'm not going anywhere with you, I'm working."

"Oh yes you are angel, unless you want me to get difficult." The policeman outstared him. Danny pushed his hands into his pockets. "Good boy, now go and change your clothes."

"What am I going to tell my brother?"

"Tell him to go fuck a banana. Come on, shift yourself."

Danny walked across the yard and into the house. At least he was half in luck, only the old man. Danny didn't look at him, but he felt the old man's eyes on him all the way across the floor.

He locked his bedroom door and changed his clothes. Five minutes later he went back downstairs.

"Where are you going?" The old man was already slurring slightly.

"Out."

"Out where?"

"None of your fucking business."

Danny slammed the door and went across to the car. The policeman was revving the engine.

Danny had barely closed the door before he took off. Danny glanced at him. He looked different in civvies; an ox-blood leather jacket cut like a blazer and a navy jacquard sweater. The socks matched. Navy trousers. Danny saw his watch as his hands moved on the steering wheel, its strange woven gold strap. *Jesus, what hairy hands.*

"What's so interesting?"

Danny flushed and looked away.

"Well?"

"I was just looking at your watch."

"Omega."

The name meant nothing to Danny.

"The strap's real gold, if that's what you were wondering. Eighteen carat."

Danny said nothing. "Where are we going?" he ventured after a moment or two.

"You'll see."

Danny began to feel nervous when he saw they were staying on the coast road, bypassing the town centre, then they turned off down to where they were redeveloping the harbour.

"What happened to your mouth?"

Danny's hand went up to his face. "Cow."

"What?" The policeman looked at him quickly then back at the road.

"Cow kicked me."

"I didn't know cows kicked."

Danny nodded. The policeman said nothing.

They swung onto the road that led down to the harbour itself. They bumped across the loose surface and stopped in front of a garage beneath a flat block. The policeman got out and opened the door then came back and drove the car inside. "Right, out."

Danny got out and the policeman began locking the doors. Danny wandered out into the sunshine. Half a dozen tiny yachts bobbed between the old tugs and the revamped Clyde puffer.

"Come on."

Danny swung round and followed him into the building. The place smelt rubbery new. It made Danny sneeze. The policeman stared at him.

"It's the carpet," Danny explained.

They went on up the stairs.

"You live here?"

"Well I'm not breaking in." The policeman opened the door and gestured Danny in ahead of him.

Danny went into the living room and stopped dead. The whole place was covered in thick cream carpet, huge cream leather settees. It looked like something out of an advert.

"Well go in then. Give me your coat."

Danny took off his jacket and handed it to him. The policeman held it as if it might contaminate him. He disappeared. He came back in a moment later and said, "You can sit down. They won't melt."

Danny perched on the edge of the chair as if he was ready to bolt at any moment.

"Want a drink?"

"It's only three o'clock."

The policeman looked amused. "So?"

Danny blushed. "Okay."

He disappeared again.

Danny looked around him. He was studying the poster print when the policeman returned.

"Like it?"

"It's a bit odd."

"How?"

"A man with a baby."

"They help you know." The policeman was looking amused again.

"That wasn't what I meant."

"You mean men don't have babies so they shouldn't be photographed holding them."

"No..." Danny floundered, "I..."

"Well?"

"Never mind."

The policeman handed him his drink. Danny looked at it. "What is it?"

"Rum."

Danny stared at it some more, as if it was a dangerous volatile substance likely to go off at any moment.

"Believe me, your dick won't fall off if you drink it."

Danny flushed again and took a swig. He coughed until he was red in the face.

"Jesus, does no-one in your house know how to drink?"

Danny's coughing subsided.

"Next time, drink it slower." He moved across the room. "Want something in it? Coke or something? I promise I won't tell."

Danny nodded.

"Come on through."

Danny followed the policeman into the kitchen. He stared around him.

"Like it?"

"Not really."

"Well, you're honest. In the fridge. There, that black monster."

Danny pulled open the door and took out a Coke. "Funny fridge."

"Thank you."

"I didn't mean that." Danny flushed again.

"I know what you meant. Here." The policeman took the glass bottle and opened it.

"I didn't know they still made these."

"I prefer them."

Danny added some to his drink.

"Want anything to eat?"

"No thanks."

The policeman turned and looked at him. "Mouth sore?"

"I bit my tongue."

The policeman nodded. "Well excuse me if I eat, I'm on duty at five. This is my late lunch."

Danny watched him as he made himself a sandwich. He pushed his sleeves up, the hair once more catching Danny's eye. Was he hairy? Jesus.

"What relationship is Blondie to you?"

Danny tore his eyes away. "Cousin." He drank carefully from one side of his mouth.

"Your big brother got the hots for him?"

Danny looked at the floor, feeling himself redden. He was going to start this again. He felt like a man standing on paper-thin ice. "No."

"That's not what Blondie says. He says that your brother was trying to force him to have sex."

Danny stared at him.

"In the front seat of your pick-up. Sound likely?"

Danny transferred his stare to his feet.

"Well?"

"I don't know." He muttered it.

"You mean that it's possible, you wouldn't like to swear he wasn't? And before you answer, Blondie had his trousers undone, and if Big-boy wasn't dry-humping him I'm a WPC."

Danny's head came up sharply. "Dry-humping him?"

"Rubbing off on his leg."

"I know what it means."

"Do you?" The policeman's tone was suggestive.

Danny said nothing but took a quick gulping drink. His hand jerked slightly as he did it.

"Why so uncomfortable?"

"I'm not."

"Your hand's shaking."

"You keep accusing us of..." Danny stopped.

"Yes?"

"You know what. What am I supposed to do, be glad?"

"D'you think it's true?"

"What?"

"Your brother's got the hots for Blondie."

"I told you, I don't know."

"Oh come on, take a guess. Has he got a girlfriend?"

Danny shook his head.

"Ever had one?"

Danny shook his head again.

"How old is he?"

"Twenty-eight."

"And he's still a virgin?" The policeman moved in front of him and lifted his face

172

with his hand.

Danny pulled his head away.

"How about you then?" the policeman went on. "Has big brother got the hots for you?"

"No."

"What about the love-bite?"

"Get stuffed."

"Why is everybody in your family so keen to protect him?"

Danny said nothing.

"Know what I think? I think he's screwing you both."

Danny said nothing.

"And you don't want it to stop."

Danny still said nothing.

"What's wrong, cat got your tongue?" The policeman pinched Danny's face, catching his cheek and wounded lip.

"*Shit*," Danny hissed.

"Now, how about a little truth for a change? Is your big brother screwing you?"

Danny shook his head. The policeman tightened his grip. Danny winced and felt the blood start afresh in his mouth.

"Come on, angel, you can do better than that."

"What are you going to do?" Danny squeezed the words out.

The policeman smiled slowly, his fingers easing. "I'm not going to *do* anything. Live and let live, that's what I say."

"That's not what you were saying yesterday."

"Yesterday I was putting the wind up you."

Danny could taste the blood, salt in his mouth.

"Is he?" The policeman was watching him intently. "Come on, angel, I'll keep this up till Doomsday if I need to. Dragging you away from your work, harassing you. I can think up plenty of things, and a simple yes or no will stop it all. Is he screwing you?"

"No."

The policeman grabbed his jumper, banging his spine back against the counter. "Wrong answer." He pushed himself away, letting Danny go. "I see him pissing round you, marking you off. He bites your neck, punches your mouth, and I'll bet he does worse. D'you think I'm stupid or something? What's he got on you?"

Nothing but my life, Danny thought. Nothing you'd consider important.

"Alright." The policeman took a deep breath. "In that case maybe it's time we did something about Mrs Jackson Moore and her Fiat."

Danny could feel the blood draining from his face. A pulse started throbbing in protest in his temple.

"Want to change your mind?" The policeman was watching him. "Or shall I go ahead and start procedures to find Mrs Moore's car, Mrs Moore herself maybe?"

"Jackson Moore," Danny corrected automatically.

The policeman did not acknowledge the correction. He stood waiting. "Maybe we should start looking at Yardholm."

Danny put one arm protectively across his chest.

"I'll ask you for the last time…" the policeman raised his voice almost theatrically, "…is your big brother screwing you?"

Danny put his glass down as if the weight hurt him. "Yes," he said simply.

He felt an intense desire to laugh. Henderson had asked for it, but now he had it he looked as if it had jumped up and bit him. "Yes, he's screwing me." He watched it sink in.

The policeman's tongue, very red, came out over his equally red lips. "Jesus," he

said, as if he couldn't believe it.

Danny looked at him, waiting for his next move.

"What does he do?"

It always came down to this, a nice attention to detail. What do you do little boy?

"You don't need details from me."

"You mean...?"

Danny did not hesitate. "Yes."

"My God," he said again. He hadn't really wanted to know the truth, only to hear a yes. It was a fantasy for him, a game. Now he didn't know what to do with it.

Danny smiled as only Danny could smile. "Want to try it?"

"What?" Henderson said. He sounded almost panicky.

"I said, want to try it? No pain to me."

"No," he replied, too quickly.

"I'll deny it if you try and charge him."

"No," the policeman said again. No, he didn't want to? Or no, he wasn't going to charge him? Which?

Danny looked at the kitchen clock. "Only 3:30, plenty of time." He smiled again.

The policeman looked at him in perplexity, but Danny only smiled. He kept on smiling. For the first time he looked relaxed, confident, in control. Danny in his own territory.

The policeman looked at him. "You're committing incest."

Danny shrugged.

"With your own brother."

Danny resisted stating the obvious. He waited, watching the clock's second-hand sweep round.

"That great ape queer. I can't believe it."

Danny looked at the floor then looked up. "How old are you?"

The policeman frowned. "Thirty-six."

"Thirty-six and still a virgin." Danny's beautiful mouth smiled lopsidedly, wolfishly. "Well, well."

"I'm not a..." But he stopped, suddenly understanding.

"My brother's way ahead of you." Danny's eyes looked neon-green under the fluorescent light, his hair electric-red, artificially coloured. It reduced his red shirt to the colour of rusted blood. He robbed it of its colour.

"I don't want..."

Danny nodded.

"I'm not..."

Danny nodded again.

The policeman came over slowly, only three or four feet, crossing it like miles, until he stood before him.

Danny did not move. He could see the thick hair showing above the neck of the man's sweater, a tiny slick curl like a wisp of ponytail. He waited to see where the policeman's hand would touch him first. He could smell his aftershave, strong, pungent. He could see the tiny stubby eyelashes, freakishly bald amongst all that luxuriant hair. The mouth was very full and moist.

The hand came down on his belly, on top of the warm brushed cotton of his shirt. He began pulling Danny's shirt out until it was free of his trousers. He licked his lips, his eyes not daring to meet Danny's own. "You've no hair."

"Not there," Danny said, slowly pulling out his belt then pulling his zip down half way, the invitation clear.

The policeman put his hand inside. The skin went from smooth to thick tangled curls almost as dense as his own pubic hair. "Jesus," he said, his eyes flicking down

hungrily then back up again. But only as far as Danny's navel.

"Why don't you look?" Danny's voice was one Rab would have recognised. The policeman felt goosepimples come out along his spine at the sound of it.

He stood back a little and pulled the front of Danny's shorts down, just enough to see the hair. But Danny tugged them out of his hand, making his cock spring out like an ironing board. He stood, legs braced, leaning back against the counter, forcing it up towards him.

The policeman stared at it. Danny could see his clothes start to itch him like an animal dressed in human clothes.

"Take them off," Danny said.

The policeman shook his head.

"Go on." That same old, insidious voice. "Then you can see them together, yours against mine."

The policeman shook his head again, but began to pull his sweater over his head, then his shirt. He undid his trousers then stopped.

Danny reached out his hand and pulled him closer. The policeman stared at his cock. Danny pulled the policeman's trousers open then pulled down his briefs. He eased the whole lot down over his hips, then did his own. They stood facing each other with their trousers round their thighs.

He ran his hand over the man's belly. His cock was short and thick, thicker than any Danny had ever seen. The hair grew down well onto the shaft. He pulled him against him.

The policeman made an odd noise and grabbed him suddenly, running his hands feverishly up and down Danny's back.

The policeman began to move himself against him. Danny felt his hairy pelt sliding over his skin. The hair smelt strongly of soap. He was soaking with sweat. He moaned suddenly, "I can't."

"You already are," Danny answered, squeezing his buttock. It was heavy with muscle. The crack of his backside was slick with hair and sweat. The policeman tensed at the feel of his fingers.

"Relax," Danny said. He fingered him gently.

The policeman rocked against him, burying his face in his neck. "I'll come."

"That's what you want," Danny said, letting one finger tease his anus.

"Not so soon," the policeman whispered in his ear, and then there was an odd moment of tension in his body followed immediately by the feel of his heavy lips against Danny's neck. He could feel the brush of his moustache.

Danny moved his head to let the mouth in. The lips kissed him this time, a slow definite kiss.

Danny eased off his finger. They kissed him again.

Danny pressed his head. The shaved hair felt like thick velour. He pressed it gently, just enough.

"Oh God," the policeman moaned. "You're beautiful."

Danny smiled at the kitchen clock.

"You're so beautiful." He kissed him again, his mouth wet, trailing over the hollows of his neck, along his jaw.

Danny pressed his cock up against him. He began easing his finger into his crack again. He could feel his own cock coming up for it - the friction, the policeman's hunger.

Danny pushed his finger in.

The policeman stiffened.

Danny pulled his buttocks open with his other hand. "Keep kissing me." He pushed his finger in with a slow definite pressure.

"No, don't."

"Go on." *Here it comes.*

The policeman bucked against Danny's leg urgently, the fur of him sliding over Danny's skin, friction burning. His mouth finally found Danny's own. It only had time to touch his briefly, a wet clinging moment, before he pulled away, crying out, rutting against Danny's leg.

Danny pushed his finger in hard.

The policeman cried, "No!" once.

After that Danny stopped listening.

Danny stood, hands resting on the counter again, jeans still round his thighs, watching the policeman dry himself with kitchen towel. He offered the roll to Danny without looking at him.

Danny shook his head. He smiled at the way the policeman wouldn't meet his eyes. He could see him flushing as he put the roll back down, still keeping his back to him. And now he was pulling on clothes. "I never meant..." he began.

"Forget it," Danny said.

The policeman finally turned and looked at him. "You really are beautiful."

Danny smiled.

The policeman reached out his hand, hesitated.

"Go on," Danny said.

He felt Danny's chest, then his belly, finally he slid his hand down over Danny's cock. He felt the slick wet of the head. He still wouldn't meet Danny's eyes. "I want to do it again."

"Now?"

"No, I mean..." He hesitated again. "Will you come here again tomorrow?"

"I can't," Danny said.

"Then let me come to you."

"No."

"You want to?" The policeman looked at him, insecure.

"Are you asking me?"

"Yes."

"And if I say no?"

"I'll keep asking you."

"Then you have your answer."

The policeman searched his face, trying to be sure of what he meant. "When?"

"Whenever you like, as long as it's in the evening. And you'll have to pick me up, because no other way will my brother tolerate it."

The policeman nodded.

"Don't underestimate him," Danny said. "He doesn't love you." He smiled again, that same wolfish feel to it.

"I told Blondie to bring you on Saturday."

Danny dropped his head, watched the policeman's hand fondling him. His cock hung down, still swollen, but not stiff. He said abruptly, "You want to fuck him?"

The policeman looked at him.

"You want to know how to do it?"

"Are you serious?" The policeman held him in his hand, reading his face. "God, you're doing it with him too, aren't you?"

Danny looked down at his stilled hand, not answering.

The policeman gripped him tightly. "I never guessed."

"You want him or don't you?"

176

"That hair..." He offered it like some kind of excuse.

"Of course. You do what I say, you'll get him."

"Don't you care?"

Danny lifted his eyes. "What about?"

"That I might lay him."

Danny smiled. His cock came up slowly. The policeman felt it stiffen in his hand. He wet his mouth, looked down at it.

Danny's voice sounded low and deep in his ear. "Want to learn how to give head?"

Danny walked into the kitchen at 4:25. Only Rab was there.

"Where the fuck have you been? John's been going spare. What happened to your mouth?"

Danny took off his jacket. "With your policeman, that's just too bad, and a cow kicked it."

Rab stared at him. "Who?"

"A cow."

"No, who were you with?"

"You heard."

"What did he want?"

"To make sure I came along on Saturday." Danny sat down and undid his shoes.

"The bastard. What did you tell him?"

"That I'd be there, what else?"

"Did he threaten you?"

"What do you think?"

Rab looked at his mouth. "I can't even kiss you."

Danny didn't smile. "Why don't you try?"

Rab hunkered down beside him and kissed the good side of his mouth. He stiffened. "You stink of him."

Danny didn't even blink. "Do I?"

"You stink of his bloody cheap aftershave."

"Well, well."

Rab grabbed his wrist. "What did he do to you?"

"Just what everybody else does." Danny looked at Rab's hand gripping his wrist.

Rab let it go, reluctantly. He stared at him for a moment then said, "He wants you, doesn't he?"

"No, he's had me. Now it's your turn."

Rab shook his head. "You little..."

"Try whore, everyone else seems to like it."

They stared at each other, hate something tangible and ugly stalking round the room.

Rab spoke first, his voice low and hard, his eyes dark with anger. "If you were drowning, you bastard, I wouldn't lift a finger to save you."

Danny stood up to move past him. "Yeah, I know. You might have to take it out my arse first."

And the door closed quietly behind him.

Rab didn't come in for his evening meal. First Ian, then John both asked where he was.

"I've no idea," Danny said both times, and he didn't.

He went upstairs at eight o'clock, washed and went to bed. Half an hour later John

came up. He sat on the edge of the bed and turned Danny's head to examine his face. "Still hurting?"

"What do you think?"

"Too sore to give head?"

Danny shook his head free.

"Only asking. Maybe it'll keep you out of mischief. So where were you?"

"With the policeman."

John's face changed. "*What?*"

"He came and took me to his house."

"I'll..."

"Forget it," Danny interrupted. "It's not me he wants, it's Rab."

"Like fuck."

"Believe me, it's Rab."

John subsided a little. Danny could see the colour come back into his face, slowly. "I'm going to see him again."

"What?" John stood up this time.

"You heard."

"I thought he didn't want you?"

"He doesn't, but he likes to look at my pretty face."

John stared at him, at the way he lay there, his hands under his head, his broken mouth. "Are you threatening me?"

"No, he is. He knows about the body."

John sat down again.

Danny pulled his arms out from under his head, leaned up on one elbow. "He just wants a little company in exchange for a lot of silence John."

"Fuck him."

"I probably will."

John's hand lashed across his face. Danny fell back, felt the wound open again.

"One thing then another, what are you *doing* to me?"

Danny said nothing.

"No." John's voice was categorical.

"You can't stop me." Danny pressed his mouth with his fingertips.

"No?"

Danny struggled up, grasped his arm. "Screwing me he's up to his eyeballs in it. It's insurance John. This way he can't touch us."

"I *knew* it. The greedy little bastard. I ought to ram his cocksucking head up his arse."

"Leave him alone John."

"Don't tell me what to do."

"Leave him and you can have anything you want. *Anything*," Danny urged. "Just what he takes and the rest for you."

John laughed. "You, promising fidelity? You forget I can take you when I want. You're worthless."

Danny struggled up onto his knees to face him. "And don't you just *love* it?" He shook his head. "You don't fool me John - no way. Think about it."

John looked at him for a long moment, smile evaporated under his fury. He looked in Danny's eyes and saw something there he thought he'd never see again, had begun to wonder if he'd ever really seen at all.

He reached his hand under the blankets. His mouth was dry. "Convince me Danny-boy."

TWENTY-NINE

Rab went to his flat immediately after lunch the following day. He had to ring the doorbell two or three times before he replied.

"Who is it?"

"It's me, Robert Hardman." He felt odd saying his own name.

There was a silence then Henderson said, "Come up."

The buzzer went and Rab went in and up the grey stairs. He had to knock on the door this time. Henderson opened it wearing a paisley-patterned dressing gown over the black silk pyjamas. This time he took him into the flat, but did not invite him into the living room. They stood in the dark hallway. "What d'you want?" He spoke in a subdued voice.

"To talk to you."

"What about?"

"Danny."

The policeman flushed, his eyes shifting away, and Rab knew it was true. He grabbed Henderson's dressing gown. "You're not queer, eh?"

Henderson prised his hand off. "Keep your voice down."

"Why?"

"My wife's here."

Rab stared at him. "Your *wife?*"

"You heard."

"Since when did you have a wife?"

"I told you I was married. We're separated."

"Where is she?"

"In the bedroom."

Rab pushed his hands into his jacket pockets. "Let me get this straight. You're separated, but your wife's in the bedroom?"

"That's it."

"You're separated, but you're still fucking her?"

"That's it," Henderson said again.

"Sex with your ex?"

"Uh-huh." Henderson's voice was smug.

"Jesus, what a shit-bag."

Henderson flushed angrily. "You watch your mouth."

"Maybe I should tell her about this thing you've got for boys."

"Shut up."

"Maybe I should tell her about your fun and games with Danny."

"I said, shut up."

"Maybe it would pay you to leave him alone."

"Don't you threaten me."

"Why not? What's good enough for you is good enough for the rest of us."

Henderson laughed shortly. "Who was it said he was no homosexual while he's been screwing his pretty little cousin all along? You're a fucking homo, that's what you are."

Rab stared at him. "He told you that?"

"Yes, he told me." Henderson was suddenly leering. He moved closer and whispered thickly, "He likes to do it, doesn't he? Really goes at it. And *big...*"

Rab swiped at him, but Henderson sidestepped the blow and caught the thick

weight of Rab's hair in his hand. "Just don't try it sonny-boy, it's more than your life's worth."

Rab stood still, waiting for him to let go, but Henderson stood there holding him in the dark, breathing heavily in his ear. The words came out in a hot, moist rush. "I'd like to wrap my cock in this."

"Fuck off." Rab squirmed, but Henderson's hand pulled tighter in his trapped hair.

"I'm going to have him here every night."

"And what's your wife going to say to that?" Rab grunted.

"I don't see her more than once a month. Plenty of time for angel. Unless you'd like a few inches of course. Maybe I could spare you an inch or two."

"Go crawl up your arse-hole." He winced as the hand pulled his head back. He could feel Henderson's body up against his.

"You can push him out the picture."

Rab said nothing, but Henderson knew he was listening.

"Just say the word."

"You heard me the first time." Rab bit the words out.

"Think about it. You want to save him for yourself, then think it over." His hand loosened slightly. Somewhere in the house a door banged. Henderson let him go. A woman's voice called out his name. "Get out, go on," Henderson hissed.

Rab opened the door. Henderson caught at his arm, whispering up close again, "I'll see you on Saturday... both of you. You can let me know what you've decided."

"The answer's no."

Henderson smiled. Rab wanted to knock those white teeth down his red gullet. "I live in hope," he said, and shut the door in Rab's face.

THIRTY

Saturday evening was filled with the smell of burnt toast. Rab sullenly scraped it into the sink while Danny ostentatiously fed his to the dog.

John watched them with a feeling of dangerous satisfaction. Dangerous because in reality the whole thing was held together with old, dry sellotape.

He speared a piece of butter with his knife and threw it to the dog.

Danny went upstairs to change and Rab went off with Ian. Ultimately the hour rolled round.

Danny climbed in beside him.

The rain was coming down in earnest now. The pick-up had broken down again. They used the Range Rover.

Rab pulled out into the evening traffic. The car was spacious inside, but he could feel Danny sitting there beside him as if he was touching him skin to skin. "Are we going to go through this evening in absolute silence?" he asked.

"If you like."

"I don't like."

"Then don't," Danny said flatly.

Back to the start of the board, men. Rab tried again. "Listen, I don't care what you did with him, or why, just..." *Just what?* He shot forward in a burst of speed, overtaking the car in front by the skin of his teeth. The car's horn blared. "Just forget it," he snapped.

Danny never moved or changed. Rab might never have spoken.

He did not slow down till he was stopped by the traffic lights. They waited, watching the red lights bleed down the windows. He could see Danny out the corner of his eye, his hair almost purple in the reflected light, his mouth dark and stained. He sat low down in his seat, hands resting in his lap. He looked tense under that superficial calm.

"It's green." Danny's voice seemed to float out of nowhere. A car tooted behind them.

Rab started and the car shot forward.

They almost overshot the new harbour road, but Rab took it on a wide sweep, almost running them into a Caravanette. "Fuck," he muttered.

Danny slid further down in his seat.

He slowed right down, driving carefully past the boards then turning right into the harbour. The lights once again threw their dazzling white rainbows into the night. Danny shaded his eyes, then rubbed them before he sat up. Rab parked the Rover as close to Henderson's block as he could get.

Danny climbed out first. Rab watched him run through the white needles of rain like a dart of colour, then he climbed out, locking the door and bolting for it himself.

Danny stood panting in the doorway, hair covered in a thousand beads of water, lips parted. He looked as exquisite and as false as a photograph.

"You press it?" Rab didn't even look at the row of bells as he asked it, he just kept watching that image in fascination. It wasn't even really Danny.

Danny shook his head, eyes as deep as the sea. Rab knew what he was doing. He'd seen him do it too often to mistake it.

Danny leaned back against the glass wall and waited. Rab lifted his hand to press the buzzer. It was as if he was watching sand ticking through an egg-timer, whispering

a million gritty little provocations. *Will you? Won't you? Can you fight it?*

He never made it.

He put his hand on the icy-cold glass, palm flat beside Danny's face, close enough to feel the heat from Danny's cheek. Just one hand, enough to let him roll away. He bent his head so slowly that any fool could have run round the block and back and still been there for touchdown.

When he pressed his mouth finally on his he felt nothing but a cool, soft moisture under his own. It was like eating apricots on a hot day - fleeting, ecstatic, irreplaceable.

The door opened suddenly and two middle-aged women came out. They had watched the boys kissing, open-mouthed with shock and fascination. When Rab lifted his head the first woman's voice was stilled. The look on the boys' faces was so corruptly languorous she could not find what she had been going to say. Rab, then Danny, passed her and walked upstairs before either she or her companion could utter a word.

Henderson met them in the corridor. He looked at them with his hard little eyes. "What kept you?" Of course, he had seen them run across the forecourt. "Why didn't you buzz?"

"Your neighbours let us in." Rab was turning his collar down, shaking the rain off. Danny stood watching Henderson with unblinking eyes.

"Neighbours?" Henderson pushed open his door and let them pass before him.

"Two old dears wearing matching coats."

Henderson closed the door then said, "I'm surprised they let you in." He looked at Rab's face as he took his jacket.

"So am I."

Henderson stopped and looked at him questioningly, but Rab only crossed to the radiator and parked his rear end on it.

Danny crossed to the window and stood looking out. Rab watched him, seeing himself watching him in the huge black mirror of the window.

The stage was set for seduction. Henderson had the lights at half-mast. Some strange electronic music played quietly around the room. Rab looked round. There must be more speakers somewhere else.

Henderson came back in and stood between them like a victim. Rab was gratified to see him look discomfited. He muttered something about drinks and went into the kitchen.

Danny left the window and sat down on the sofa. He pulled his feet up and sat cross-legged. He did not take off his shoes.

Rab looked at him speculatively, but could not read what he was thinking. Let's see how Henderson takes this one.

He came in and said, "Take your bloody shoes off," before he even put down the drinks.

Danny uncurled his feet without speaking and undid his shoes. He had not said a single word since he'd come in. Henderson picked them up and threw them out into the hall.

For an instant Rab saw John that evening, just before they'd left, throwing his boots into the corner of the room, filled with silent rage, his eyes burning in his head. Henderson's face was merely irritated.

"What about yours?" Henderson demanded.

"No sir. I'm keeping mine on the floor sir." Rab smiled a cardboard smile.

"You're a shithead." Henderson glared at him.

"Yes sir."

Danny had already picked up his drink. He was adding Coke to it. Not much.

Henderson added nothing to his. He inclined his head at Rab, a question.

"No, I'll take mine macho-straight."

"Shithead," Henderson repeated.

He sat down beside Danny, not too close, but not too far away either. His hand moved too quickly, drinking even faster than normal. Danny laid his head back and looked at nothing in particular through half-lidded eyes. His hair was rich in the half-light, heavily emphasised against the cream leather, almost as if he knew it. But then, how much of him was ever natural and how much affected?

Henderson poured himself another drink. The rain flurried against the window. Rab was beginning to burn on the radiator. He moved to the opposite sofa and sat down. He could see the whole room clearly in the window.

The silence was horrific. Henderson finally had what he wanted and didn't know what to do with it. He was even dressed for seduction, all in black, even his socks, even different moccasins.

"Jesus," Rab said. He didn't realise he had spoken out loud till Henderson looked at him.

"What?"

"The rain... some rain," he improvised.

Henderson made a noise he would not have been able to define himself.

Christ look at him itch, Rab thought. Four days and he's been hanging out for it sixty minutes an hour, twenty-four hours a day. Look out Danny, he'll burn you up.

Danny handed him his glass for a refill without speaking.

Rab smirked. *Look at that boy go. That's it Henderson, get him drunk. You'll be in his pants in no time.*

Henderson passed his drink back with an unsteady hand.

Rab filled his own.

Henderson jumped up suddenly, as if he'd been shot, and went off into the kitchen.

Rab looked at Danny. "He's got a hard-on."

"I know." Danny's voice slid out into the dark, already deepened.

Oh boy, Rab thought. Do you know what you're doing Henderson? Do you now?

Henderson came back in with the inconceivable burden of sandwiches, crisps and full etceteras on a tray.

"Well, well, we *are* being entertained."

"You don't need to eat it," Henderson snapped.

"Yum, yum, I can't wait." Rab took a sandwich and bit it. It was good, some kind of meat and pickle. He didn't recognise it.

"Salt beef," Henderson offered.

"Nice," Rab said, taking another bite.

Danny didn't eat any. He just drank slowly and steadily. Henderson wolfed sandwiches down as if he hadn't eaten. Rab suspected that he probably hadn't been able to, he was so highly strung.

The music stopped. Rab expected him to get up to change it, but he didn't. Another disc slipped into place. Of course.

Henderson took more drink.

Rab grew suddenly tired and swung his legs onto the sofa.

"Feet."

He swung them back down again and took his shoes off, then lay down. He stared at the ceiling, hands behind his head. He was dimly aware of Danny and Henderson on the other couch. He patted his pockets. "Mind if I smoke?" he said to the ceiling.

"No." Henderson sounded choked.

"How about an ashtray?"

"I'll get one."

Rab smiled at the ceiling.

Henderson went out.

Rab lay there, half-sleepily listening to the rain. "Still there Danny?"

"Mm."

"He's going to get in your pants."

"Mm."

"And mine?"

There was a pause this time, slight but real. "You tell me."

Henderson came back in. He looked down at Rab and licked his lips. "Here."

Rab took it and balanced it on his stomach. He took a cigarette out his breast pocket and lit it. He took a deep drag and stared at the ceiling again. He let the smoke down through his nose. It curled down across his chest, blue and shadowy. The smell was heady, drug-like.

Henderson said, "Not the rolly-ups again."

Rab smiled. He heard Henderson pour himself another glass. "Danny," Rab said. Danny murmured in reply.

"What are we doing here?"

"I don't know."

Rab could feel Henderson listening, waiting. "You think Mr Henderson wants to see two boys making it?"

"Wouldn't surprise me." Danny's voice was low and heavy. He sounded half-asleep.

"Us?"

"Could be."

Rab heard the glass again. *Faster and faster Henderson.* Rab was quiet. He took another drag on his cigarette, closed his eyes, let the smoke out. When he spoke next the words went into the silence like a man talking in a deserted room, as if there could be no other noise. "Mr Henderson wants to come in my hair."

"What are you playing at?" Henderson's voice sounded almost afraid.

"Not us," Rab said. "You're the one playing games."

There was a silence then Danny spoke. Rab could picture him perfectly: charcoal-grey denims, steel-grey denim shirt, white socks, red head leaning back on the settee, cheekbones that would make your heart bleed, eyes the colour of green stones, mouth that a starving man would pay to eat, lying there like a cat waiting to be stroked, invitation in every line.

"Want it?"

Rab felt his pulse quicken just at the sound of the words, not even asked of him but he could still feel it all come up there panting. *Oh yes, we want it.*

Henderson said nothing, but Rab heard him shift, then he heard the press-studs on Danny's shirt. He could see Henderson in his mind's eye, bent over him, pulling his shirt open, aching to kiss his mouth, but no courage. No courage at all. He heard Danny's buckle clink, then the zip.

"Jesus," Henderson said.

Rab felt the goosepimples come up along his neck, his arms, even his fingers. He felt as if he was being slowly chilled. He lifted his cigarette and drew on it for heat, holding it tight inside himself until Henderson said it again.

"Oh Jesus."

And then he let it out.

He watched it curl towards the ceiling, listening. A rustle, silence. It began to eat at him. He wouldn't look. But it began to gnaw. He *couldn't* look. The silence went on. Then Henderson groaned, catching his breath at the end like desperation.

Rab climbed up slowly onto his elbows.

It wasn't Danny's belt or Danny's zip. It was Henderson's. Danny's head was in Henderson's lap. Henderson had one hand deeply immeshed in his hair. He was looking at Rab with eyes as hot and blue as dry ice. His face was flushed. Rab could see a fine film of sweat on his upper lip, at the sides of his moustache. His mouth looked almost like wet blood.

Rab couldn't make out where his clothes stopped and his body started, except for the thick red of his cock sticking out from the blackness like the stamen of a black orchid. Danny was sliding his tongue along the length of it, keeping his head to one side so that Rab could see it. Henderson's eyes were on him like magnets, like something stuck to his skin. His eyes were beginning to water. He blinked.

Danny took his cock back in his mouth. Henderson swore. Rab watched him push his hips upwards, trying to get in deeper. His hand moved feverishly in Danny's hair, but his eyes watched Rab.

Rab sat there like a hypnotised rabbit. He pulled himself up and embraced his knees. He was waiting for Henderson to speak. He felt sure he wouldn't be able to come without it.

Henderson's tongue came out slowly, lingeringly, as if tasting the trickle of salt from his moustache. Rab saw his other hand take Danny's head and push it on to him. His eyes flicked over Rab's face. "Let me kiss you."

Rab could feel those tactile hands trapping his hair in handfuls, catching his head with raping fingers. He shook his head. Let him do without. Let him dry-heave, be unsatisfied. Danny moved, kept moving.

"Let me feel your hair..." His face was growing darker, suffused with blood. Rab watched his hands go white with tension, digging into Danny's head.

He surfaced again. His eyes looked drugged. "I'd like to come in your hair," he whispered, his hands kneading Danny's head. "I want to come in your...oh..."

He began to push himself up. His eyes rolled shut, finally lost in his own visions.

"Oh fuck... fuck... fuck..." He grunted it up out of himself, pushing it into Danny's face, his hands tugging his head down. He jerked like an amputated limb, then stopped.

He lay there breathing heavily, his hands gradually loosening then falling away from Danny's hair.

Danny lifted his head. Rab saw him wipe his mouth with the back of his hand.

He got up without looking at him and left the room. Rab heard the bathroom door close.

Henderson opened his eyes and looked at him. He lay there, spread-eagled, with his red cock still stiff and shiny on his black belly. "Fantastic," he said hoarsely. His smile was fugitive, wavering.

Rab nodded.

"He's beautiful." The smile lost itself, disappeared.

Rab nodded again. *I know that too.*

"I want to see you do it to him."

Henderson's cock was not going down. He was still wanting, and this was what he wanted.

"Why?"

Henderson couldn't say it with his eyes open so he closed them. "I want to watch." He opened his eyes again, accusing, "You do it already anyway, don't you?"

"Why should I do anything for you?"

"Because it would be stupid not to."

"You've just had him."

Henderson smiled, a small uncracked smile, never reaching the corners of his mouth. "Don't be stupid."

185

Rab was thrown, but he still managed to say, "He doesn't give me anything different."

"Don't lie to me. You can hear it even in the way he talks to you."

Henderson was fondling his own cock, squeezing what he could from the head, rubbing it in. Rab tried not to watch him. He said, "Once you have one thing you'll want another. It will never be enough for you."

"So?"

So indeed. Good question.

"Wouldn't you rather make it with him than me?" Henderson asked.

Rab didn't answer.

"Do it with him and you'll be free."

"Free?"

"As free as you can be. Fuck him, that's all you have to do."

"And after you've had your jollies you'll fuck him too?"

"Why not?"

"It isn't much of an offer. Heads you win, tails I lose."

"You don't know what losing is yet." He was rubbing his cock now, rubbing it with serious intent.

Danny came back into the room. His hair was damp where he had washed his face. He looked at Henderson then closed the door and stood there leaning against it.

Henderson kept looking at Rab. "Make it with him."

Rab did not take his eyes from Henderson's face. He began to feel everything slide under his feet.

"Kiss him," Henderson said to Danny.

Danny crossed to Rab and sat down beside him, kneeling against his thighs, and turned Rab's head to meet his. Rab felt like stone. He couldn't yield with Henderson sitting there watching, wanking off on it. Danny released him. His smile was a sneer. Look, Rab can't handle it.

"Take his clothes off. I want to see him naked."

Danny began unfastening Rab's clothes, that same smile plastered all over his face. He undid Rab's shirt then started on his trousers. Rab caught at his hands.

Danny's smile was wider. "Chicken," he murmured under his breath.

Rab could hear Henderson's breathing. He was masturbating vigorously and the show wasn't even started. "Come on," he said, half-cajoling, half-irritated.

"No," Rab said, this time voicing it. "I'm not providing cheap thrills for this dick."

"They're not cheap, they're coming very expensive," Henderson said. "Look what they're costing you."

"Yeah, and look what they're costing you."

Henderson laughed. "Life's like that."

"Tough shit, the answer's still no."

"He's good enough to sell, but not you."

Rab felt Danny, still as death, beside him. "He sold himself." He regretted the words as soon as they were out, but there was no taking them back.

"Well, it's not enough. I want you both." Henderson was masturbating again. He was excited by the barter, high on his own trading skills. "Or I go the whole hog. The car, Yardholm, his mother - everything."

Rab sat, trapped.

"It was good enough for you at the start. You were willing to make bargains at the start. Now, suddenly, you've got scruples. You don't mind doing it with him, but not in front of me. Don't tell me you're shy?"

Danny was watching him with an incredible stillness, as if he were listening to his

thoughts. He felt his face burn as if he'd been caught red-handed and guilty.

"What's the problem?"

Rab didn't know, that was the problem.

"Kiss him angel. Give him a little encouragement."

Danny kissed him again, harder this time, his tongue tipping between his lips. Rab felt a surge of excitement.

"That's it." Henderson eased the words out slowly.

Danny kissed him again. This time he came up on his knees, holding Rab's head with one hand, pressing him back. Rab slid round till his back was against the sofa, his feet on the floor. Danny knelt between his legs, still kissing him. Slowly Rab lifted his hands and held Danny's head. Danny began to undo the buckle on his belt.

"*Danny*," Rab whispered. Only an incantation.

Danny undid his trousers and took him out. He did it flagrantly, letting Henderson see. Rab knew it and didn't care. He reached into Danny's trousers and did the same. Danny was as swollen and beautiful as Danny always was.

Rab pulled him up tight against his chest, feeling his erection press painfully against him. He squeezed Danny's buttocks, urging him on. Danny leaned his head on the wall, looking down at himself, watching his cock rub on Rab's chest. Rab kissed his stomach, revelling in the taste and scent of him. Danny spread his legs for better leverage, forcing Rab's legs wider. Rab felt his cock strut out huge and taut, arching, then he felt something else - hands on his thighs and a hot mouth sliding down over his cockhead. Hands snagged on his pubic hair, trying to worm under his balls.

He pushed Danny's body aside with a small grunt. Henderson was going down on him. He tried to push Danny off, but he wouldn't budge.

"Get off. Henderson, get off me."

Danny held him down, pressed him hard against the sofa.

He looked up at Danny, but whatever he was going to say dried up in his mouth. Danny was smiling down at him. Rab had never seen a smile quite like it.

Henderson was sucking on him greedily, grunting like a man in pain.

"You set me up..." It was barely a whisper. He felt Henderson's cock bruise against his shin, sliding off the bone time and again, fighting the awkward angle. "All along you were setting me up."

Danny pushed against him with an insolent slowness.

"Why?" Rab demanded. Henderson was digging his nails into his belly, his throat working. He made noises like an animal. "Why Danny?"

Danny pushed himself against him in long teasing strokes, watching Rab's face, eating up his expression. He licked his lips, pushed harder, "Because..." and Rab saw the change come over his face.

He managed to say, "Just because..." once more before he came, spurting up Rab's chest onto his chin, nothing in him showing it except that twitching mouth and his hard-glazed eyes.

Rab went home alone. He could not remember what Henderson threatened him with, only Danny smiling.

He carefully reversed the Range Rover out and onto the new harbour road. He did not turn the car homeward, instead he headed out onto the coast road.

There was plenty of petrol in the tank.

Danny watched Henderson's face. Henderson looked at him slowly. "You fucked that up."

Danny said nothing.

"You could have set him up and hooked him, but you wanted to fuck it up, didn't you?"

Still Danny said nothing. He lay there, one leg up, clothes still unfastened. Henderson looked at him. "You're so bloody *big*," he said, reaching out to touch it as if he couldn't help himself.

"Not as big as my brother." Danny watched him.

Henderson's hand dropped away abruptly. He turned away then said, "He meant it, didn't he?"

"What?"

"When he said he didn't care what I did. He won't come back, will he?"

Danny shook his head.

"Why did you do it?"

Danny shrugged.

Henderson looked at him again. "Move in with me."

Danny looked startled.

"At last, something reaches you."

"I can't."

"You mean you won't."

"You can't either." Danny sat up. He pulled his shirt closed as if he was suddenly cold.

"Just a friend sharing, being helped out."

"It's impossible."

"Only because you want it to be." Henderson sat down beside him. "I could make you."

Inexplicably Danny smiled, shook his head.

"What makes you tick?" Henderson asked, exasperated. "You didn't come here tonight because I threatened you, did you?"

Danny smiled his irritating little smile. Henderson grabbed him. "You've run rings round me. What d'you want?"

Danny went limp beneath his hands. Do what you like, his body said. Go on, do it.

The policeman let him go. "You're a creepy little bastard. I don't know what goes on inside your head." He reached over and poured himself what was left of the bottle. He took a swig, watching Danny in the window.

He swallowed the rest of the drink down then said, "Move in with me." He spoke to the empty glass.

"No." Danny rubbed his smooth belly as if entranced by the feel of his own skin then looked up at him from under his brows, almost slyly. "Why are you asking me when you really want him?"

"I don't know."

"Greedy," Danny said and smiled again.

"You make me greedy."

"No, you were greedy to start with. You just kept it hidden."

"You brought it out."

"No, I just gave you the excuse."

"You're a vicious little bastard."

Danny looked at him. "Want to wash me?"

Henderson felt as if his anger had walked into a wall. "What?"

"All those mirrors." Danny rubbed his belly again. "Think of it."

Henderson did. He saw it perfectly. A hundred million Dannys, slick and wet, his heavy black hands moving over him. *Sweet Jesus.* "Move in with me."

Danny shook his head.

"At least think about it."

Danny shook his head again. "Forget it."

"Why?"

Danny looked away.

"Why did you do it then? I don't understand you."

"You don't need to understand me to fuck me."

Henderson jumped up with irritation. "I want to understand you."

"No you don't. You only want to know so you can use it to get what you want."

Henderson's face flushed. "You've got a nasty little mind."

"Because I understand you?"

Henderson glared at him impotently.

Danny stood up, tucking himself in but fastening only the button of his jeans. He moved in front of him. "I'm going to take a bath. Why don't you come and watch?"

Henderson banged his glass down. "You're really sick, you know that?"

"Let's see how long my sickness keeps you away." Danny turned and went out.

In the event it was two minutes and eighteen seconds. Danny had not even finished running the bath when he got there.

Rab fought a morbid desire to go to the bird sanctuary. He could see himself standing there in the solid black, listening to the rain hissing on the water, watching her come out of it, green and rotten, dragging him under, the cold water in his eyes, leeches crawling over him like icy phlegm.

He slammed on the brakes, the car skidding to a halt.

He clicked on the indicators and swung the car round and up the opposite pavement. He bumped back down. The wipers whacked at the rain venomously.

Slowly. Drive slowly.

He pulled out, feeling the sea-wind pull at the car.

Rab looked at his watch then turned off the engine. Only just gone twelve. It felt like three in the morning.

He got out of the car and ran for the house without bothering to lock it.

He shut the door and turned on the light. Ian blinked at him, shading his eyes in the sudden glare.

"What are you doing up?" Rab took off his jacket.

"Bad dreams."

Rab laughed, a small dry sound.

"I dreamt my mother drowned."

Rab looked at him. "That's not funny."

"It was a nightmare, it wasn't meant to be funny."

Rab sat down and began unfastening his shoes. He kept his head down. "You really dream that?"

"Yes."

Rab put his shoes by the stove and pulled a chair over. He opened the fuel feed a little then put his feet up on the towel rail.

"Did my mother drown?" Ian asked.

"No." Rab took out his tin and put his last made-up cigarette in his mouth. He lit it slowly, curling his toes against the stove. His feet felt like ice.

"Where's Danny?" Ian asked.

"With Henderson."

"So that's his name?"

"Mm."

"He spending the night there?" Ian tried to sound casual but even he could hear the pitch of excitement in his voice.

"It looks like it."

Ian stood up. "You want some coffee?"

"I'd rather have tea."

"Tea it shall be." Ian felt excitement singing through him. There had definitely been a falling out, no mistake.

He put the kettle on and stood against the sink watching Rab's profile. His face was white. He looked half-fed. He smoked his cigarette too quickly, huddled into himself as if he was cold.

Ian rinsed the teapot then crossed over to him. He put his hand on Rab's shoulder, waiting for the flinch. Nothing. He laid the other hand on gently, like stroking a sleeping cat, waiting for it to start with surprise. All was quiescent.

Rab's hand came up to his mouth, went down again, a little slower now.

Ian stroked his hair, with its heavy gloss of wet over its shifting dry warmth underneath; the hair of a man who had dashed through rain. He rubbed it between his fingers like money.

Rab moved his head under him, accommodating his hands. His cigarette slowed further. The kettle began to boil. Ian could hear it, cursing its loud intrusive noise. Suddenly Rab ducked his head. "How about that tea?"

Ian let him go and moved across the kitchen. His heart thumped with frustration and resentment. He made the tea, standing by it, glaring at the pot as if he could somehow make it brew faster. He looked at Rab's profile again. He looked warmer, his hand moved more slowly, but he did not blow the smoke down his nose, a sure sign that he was still too tense.

Ian poured the tea. He brought it to the table and milked it. He handed Rab the mug.

"Thanks." He put his two hands round it, hugging the cup. He drank it in silence, alternating with his cigarette. Eventually he put the cup down. "Christ I'm tired." He looked at his cigarette, wondering if he could smoke it any further. He swung his feet down and put what was left of it inside the stove. He turned round and looked at Ian, and Ian could see it in his face. He was cold and afraid and he needed somebody, no questions asked.

Rab got up and turned away.

Carefully, with infinite joy, Ian followed him up the stairs.

And into his room.

Rab stirred in his sleep in the dead of night, somewhere between half-waking and half-sleeping. He'd had a wet dream. He could still feel it pulsing in him, stronger than normal.

Henderson.

He opened his eyes.

Ian was holding him, still rubbing him, his body sweaty against his. Rab heard him say something about John clearly and distinctly before he realised Rab was awake.

"Jesus." Rab wriggled away from him. "What are you *doing?*" He wasn't even sure what he was accusing him of.

"I'm sorry," Ian said, and he was, because now he had a raging hard-on that would be unappeasable, because Rab was angry and would give him nothing. "I'm sorry," he said again, trying to get closer.

Rab could feel him crawling over him. He shook himself free and climbed over his

body.

"Where are you going?" Ian's voice was urgent.

"To wash." He made it sound as if he was contaminated.

Rab went into the bathroom without putting on the light. He had a pee, flushed the toilet, then filled the wash-hand basin. It over-filled and slopped onto his feet. "*Fuck.*" He pulled on the shaving light above the mirror.

Behind him, reflected in the incandescent glow of the striplight, he saw a pair of feet in the bath.

He jumped, whirling round, "*Shit.*" His heart leapt uncomfortably in his chest. That fucking drunken old sot.

"Get up you stupid bastard." He stalked over to drag him out. He was bollock naked, his eyes wide open. He was staring up at Rab from under four inches of water. He had a huge white tongue sticking out of his mouth like a horrific gargoyle.

Rab backed away.

It was a bar of soap. He had a bar of soap crammed in his mouth.

Rab backed out of the room.

He went back into his room. "Ian..." He hardly croaked it out.

Ian was awake. He sat up, alerted by the tone of his voice. "What?"

When Rab didn't answer he pulled himself up and looked at him over the headboard. "What is it?"

Rab was leaning against the doorjamb. He made a vague gesture with his hand. "Through there... the old man... in the bath."

Ian looked at him for a long moment then got up and went through. He walked right into the room, right up to the bath, stood there looking down at him.

Rab stayed in the doorway, leaning against the jamb as he had done in the bedroom. He watched Ian's back then said abruptly, "Where's John?" His voice was suddenly taut.

Ian looked back at him sharply. "In his room." He turned fully. "You don't think..." Christ, I sound like a TV drama, he thought. He had to fight a hysterical giggle escaping his mouth.

"No, I don't think, I know." And now his voice was angry.

He went out and along to John's room. Ian followed him. The room was empty, the bed still made up. "He's never even been in it. When did you last see him?"

"About half ten. He said he was going to bed."

"Where was the old man?"

"No idea. I assumed he was drinking in his room as usual."

"Let's see if he's been there."

They went next door and found John lying out across his father's bed. He was lying on his stomach. Rab shook him. "John, wake up."

He didn't stir. The floor was littered with bottles. Rab looked at them. "He can't have drunk all this in one night."

"I don't know."

Rab shook him again. "John... come on... wake up." John grumbled as Rab pulled him over, trying to pull away.

Rab slapped him.

John's hand came up and caught his with a stomach-wrenching snap. "Don't." He said it quite clearly. His eyes weren't even open.

Rab took a deep, steadying breath and said, "Wake up John." John was still

holding him by one wrist.

John opened one eye. "Rab?" His voice sounded cottony.

"Yes, for Christ's sake wake up."

John let him go and sat up on his elbows. "What time is it?"

"Half three."

He sat up properly and put his head in his hands. "I feel like shit."

"Join the club. The old man's dead in the bath."

"I really feel like shit."

Rab grabbed his sweatshirt and almost pulled him, big as he was, off the bed. "Your father's dead in the fucking bath."

John stared at him.

Rab let him go and said in a low voice, "How the fuck did it happen?"

John's eyes narrowed. "Don't ask me."

"Don't play games John. One's a trial run, two must be easy."

Ian watched John while John watched Rab. "Shut your mouth Rab. I didn't touch the old bastard. I haven't seen the stupid old shit since dinnertime and now I'll never need to look at him again. Hoo-bloody-rah."

"Then who?"

"Sure it wasn't an accident? I assume he was pissed?" John got up slowly as if he was a hundred years old. "Fuck, I feel like shit." He ran his hands through his hair and went out the door unsteadily, bouncing off the door frame. They followed him.

He looked in the bathroom door and put on the overhead light. He crossed to the bath, leaving the other two in the doorway. "Soap's a nice touch. Wash your mouth out old man." He turned. "Where's Danny?" He seemed to see Rab properly for the first time. His eyes travelled over his body. Rab and Ian were both standing there naked.

"With Henderson." Rab grabbed a towel and wrapped it round his waist.

"I'll get dressed." Ian left the room. Neither of them seemed to have heard him.

"When did you come in?" John asked.

"About twelve."

"You didn't stay long."

"John, your father's dead in the bath, what the fuck difference does how long I stayed make?"

"Could've been you."

"What?"

"Could have been you who killed him. I didn't get in till two so you had a head start on me."

"You were out?"

John nodded.

"Ian said you went to bed at half-ten."

"Ian's a liar. I went out about half an hour after you and Danny."

"How could you? We had the car."

"I travelled by foot. You should try it sometime. Whoever the corpse in the bath belongs to he isn't mine."

Ian came back into the room. Rab turned on him. "Why did you lie to me?"

"What?"

"You lied about John going to bed, why?"

Ian looked at John. "You said you were going to bed."

John shook his head. He looked as if there was a smile hovering, just aching to get out.

"He did." Ian looked at Rab, face flushing. "He *did*."

Rab looked at them both. *Shit*.

John turned back to the bath. "What are we going to do about him?"

Rab followed his eyes, looked away again quickly. "Could it look natural?"

"You mean if we took the soap out?"

"Something like that." Rab looked at the door, the window, anywhere but at the bath.

"I don't know. If we could convince the doctor, maybe. But if not he might want an inquest or something, and then they check the body, don't they? I don't know what they'd find. We'll have to get rid of him."

"Rid of him?" Rab was looking from John to the bath, not quite making it.

"That's right, rid of him. Unless you want the police crawling all over here."

He went to the bath and pulled out the plug. He touched his father's foot. "He hasn't hardened up."

Rab felt sick. He looked at the sink. "How? How will we do it?"

"Fuck knows, all suggestions on a postcard please." John watched the body slowly emerging from the water. "We'll have to take that soap out." He bent over the body and tried to pull it out, but it wouldn't shift. "The fucker's teeth are embedded in it. Either he bit down on it himself or someone shoved his head down on it."

"I'm going to be sick," Ian said in a curiously flat voice.

John didn't even turn. "You're helpful. Rab, give us a hand, hold his mouth open."

"I can't."

John straightened up and rounded on them. "For Christsake! You all want to end up in jail or something? Wake up for Christsake and give me a fucking hand."

Rab crossed to the body. He watched John prise the mouth open. "There, see if you can unlatch the damn thing."

Rab worked it from his teeth, hating the feel of them, cold and hard on his fingertips. The soap was soft and oleaginous from lying in the water. It had almost been stuffed down his throat.

Ian was not sick. He stood there unmoving, watching them.

It came out finally. It lay on the side of the bath in two halves, severed neatly with a curving bite.

"Would've been easier if he'd had false teeth."

"For fuck's sake John." Rab wiped his hands on the towel with a shiver of revulsion.

John smiled grimly. "Keep cheerful Rab. Don't let the old bastard grind you down."

"What are we going to do with him?"

"I don't know. Let's get him out of the bath."

"Why?"

"In case he catches cold, why else?" John pulled the body up by the armpits, "Christ, he's cold as a trout," he said, then pushed him upright. He fell, slumped to one side. John stared at him. "What if the old bastard simply died of a heart attack?"

"With a bar of soap in his mouth, half-way down his fucking throat?"

"Maybe he put it there himself. Guilty conscience." John laughed strangely. "Maybe he was fantasising it was something else." He looked at Rab.

Rab flushed. "Shut up John."

"Of course Rab."

Ian watched it all and kept silent.

"How about the sea?" John suggested. "The Scar? Everything goes out there and it can take a week or more for the tides to bring it back in. By then he'll be soap himself."

Rab shook his head. "Too risky."

"Well let's hear your suggestion."

"We bury him."

"Bury him? You any idea how long it takes to dig a nice big hole for a body? They

use excavators nowadays y'know."

"So will we."

John looked at him.

"You're hiring one, aren't you?" Rab said. "For the bottom field?"

John nodded. "It's already hired. Tuesday."

"Then we keep him till Tuesday. Dig the hole during the day, put him in it at night, cover it up. The following day level off the land..."

"And plant it," John finished.

"Pasture," Rab said.

"It wasn't going to be pasture."

"Well it is now."

John stared at the body. "Alright," he nodded. "Okay." He looked at Rab. "Where we going to put him while he's waiting?"

"Jerrett's," Rab said.

John began to laugh softly.

He was still chuckling when they carried his father downstairs and into the car.

THIRTY-ONE

Henderson woke at 5:45, when the alarm went off. "Fuck," he muttered, his hand fumbling to destroy its insistent whining. Someone beside him tugged the quilt and grumbled. Henderson blinked and rubbed his face.

Danny.

He turned on his side. He could only see the top of his head. The rest of him was curled up into a ball, tight against the world. He reached out his hand and felt the warm skin of his back then dropped back down on the bed.

He'd shared his bed with another man. Somehow it made everything else seem childish, sex-in-the-shed. Actually getting into bed with one...

Well, at least he hadn't fucked him.

He lay there.

Let's face it Jimmy, you want to fuck him. Only a minute ago you felt the curve of his arse and thought, I could put it up him now, while he's asleep.

Why don't you ask him?

His hand crawled over to Danny's backside. He remembered soaping the crack of it last night while watching Danny in the mirror. Swollen, heavy, half-erect.

He sat up suddenly and shook Danny's shoulder, or as close as he could get to his shoulder through the hump of bedding. Danny shrugged him off violently.

"Wake up."

Nothing.

"Come on, wake up, it's almost six."

Danny grumbled and pulled the quilt over his head. Henderson sat up properly and tugged the slippy fabric. The satin slid out of Danny's hands, pulling down past his shoulders.

Henderson could see him at last, rumpled, frowning sourly. "Fuck off," he mumbled, pushing his face into the pillow.

Henderson clicked on the bedside lamp. Danny's hair seemed to come alive with colour, rich against the black sheen. His skin looked almost deathly white.

Henderson shook him roughly, jolting him.

Danny threw himself on his back, his eyes opening instantly, no half-awake. "What time is it?"

Henderson blinked. Danny's eyes looked glassy in the yellow light. "Almost six." Henderson kept drowning.

"S'alright." Danny stretched, yawned.

Henderson's eyes flicked to the edge of the quilt. It lay across Danny's stomach. Not far enough, he couldn't tell. He looked back. Danny was watching him, his face still, almost hard. "Wondering?"

"What?" But Henderson flushed.

"If I've got a hard-on."

"Have you?" Henderson felt a pulse throb under his arm. He moved restlessly, attempting to relieve it.

"Have you?" Danny asked.

Henderson looked at the foot of the bed. "Yes."

Danny was silent. Eventually Henderson looked back at him. "Well?"

"Well what?"

"You little bastard, you know damn fine what." Henderson sat, grim-faced, staring at him.

"Ask me again."

Henderson shook his head once, folding his mouth in a tight line.

"Then you'll never know."

Henderson glared at him.

"It would be easier if you just asked me. Why suffer?"

Henderson made a grab for the quilt, but Danny got there first. "Uh-uh. Ask me."

"*Have* you?" Henderson spat it out like an accusation.

"Yes," Danny smiled. Henderson's heart began to beat uncomfortably. "Ask me some more."

"Do you..." Henderson swallowed. "Do you always...?"

Danny smiled. That was all.

"Every day?" Now Henderson could hear the avidity in his own voice.

"How can you doubt it?"

There was a silence. Henderson looked at the quilt, cursing its fluffy, well-padded luxury. He could see nothing.

"Come on Henderson, you can do it." Danny's voice was crawling with insolence.

Henderson felt it score against his skin like an insult. He kept looking at the quilt. "I want to see," he demanded.

"Ask." There was a long silence.

"Please let me see." His voice ran out of him.

Danny lifted his hands, lazily tucked them behind his head. "Go ahead officer."

Henderson pulled the quilt down.

And there it was.

Henderson drove Danny home slowly, making it last. "I want to see you again tonight."

"Okay." Danny's voice was flat, disinterested. He was staring out the window.

"What time?"

"We finish earlier on a Sunday. This time of year, about seven."

"If I come at half past?"

"Whatever."

"Danny..."

"Mm?" Danny tried to feel a sense of the car moving, but it simply glided, soft as silk, nice.

"Will you think about it?"

"What?"

Henderson tried not to lose his temper. "Moving in with me."

Danny looked at him suddenly. "How much money do you have?"

Henderson took a quick look at him then back to the road. "Are you offering to be bought?"

"Are you willing to buy me?"

Henderson thought about it. "Yes, how much?"

"I like it." Danny settled back in his seat again.

"I don't understand." Henderson's face was flushed.

"I like the fact that you're willing to buy me. It pleases me."

Henderson slowed the car right down and looked at him. "You're weird."

"Why? Because I like to know I'm worth as much as an Italian leather sofa?"

Henderson stopped the car. "You're worth more."

Danny looked at him. "You know, you don't behave much like a policeman."

"I don't feel much like one any more."

They drove in silence until they reached the farm. "You're late," Henderson said,

looking at his watch.

"Fuck them," Danny answered.

Henderson pulled in on the opposite side of the road. "I already tried that."

Danny looked at him again. "Disappointed?"

"Wouldn't you be?"

Danny smiled at him. It was lascivious and old.

Suddenly Henderson wanted him out. He leaned across him to open the door and just as suddenly he wanted to hold on to him. "Think about it," he urged.

"How much?"

"What?"

"How much would you be willing to pay?"

"As much as you wanted."

"You're lying."

Henderson shook his head. "No I'm not. Anything you want. Will you?"

Danny laughed and opened the door. "No way."

Henderson caught his arm. "Don't play games with me."

Danny pulled his arm free and got out.

He slammed the door shut and was gone before Henderson could even say goodbye.

The kitchen was deserted when Danny went in. He looked around the room in perplexity - it was like the Marie Celeste - then he remembered the cows. "How could you forget the cows?" he muttered to himself.

"How indeed?" John came in from the hall. "I thought I saw Dick Tracy driving off. Nice time? Walk up and down the room a bit. Let's see if you can still move."

Danny took off his jacket and hung it up. "Any tea?"

"It'll be cold. Tell you what, why don't you go take a shower, or better still a nice hot bath, and I'll bring you a cup. How about that?"

"I don't want a bath, I've had one." Danny had his back to him, but John could see the tension in it.

"Put the kettle down Danny."

Danny stood there a moment then put the kettle down.

"We found the old man in the bath last night."

Danny stood still as a statue.

"I'm talking about dead, not pissed, but maybe you already know that."

"Where is he?" Danny's voice was calm, only curious.

"He's at Jerrett's Farm. You've got Rab to thank for that inspiration. We're going to bury him on Tuesday. You're invited to the funeral."

"Who found him?"

"Your cousin."

Danny nodded.

"Ian was there too. Why not ask me about Ian? We were all there. Quite a party. Shame you missed it." He looked at Danny. He could see something like desperation in him. "Don't worry, it's the great unsolved mystery." He looked at Danny's hands. "I'd have thought he'd have fought."

Danny didn't answer.

"So did you do it Danny? I'm curious."

"Did he tell you to ask John? I'm curious."

It took John a minute to realise what he meant, *if* it was what he meant. "Are we talking about Ian?" he said, hedging his bets, hoping Danny would give him some further clue.

But he didn't, all he said was, "You tell me."

"What is this, riddles?"

Danny said nothing.

John brought the subject back to safe territory. "Well, how are you going to play it?" he asked. "Shocked surprise? Blasé indifference? Tears? Tears would be nice."

"You've already told me John. Shocked silence should do it."

"Very good. Little Hard-as-Nails triumphs again." John came over to the sink. "You've got come on your jeans... just there." He pointed to Danny's thigh. Danny looked down and John's hand slapped the side of his head. It jarred his neck. Fool, he thought, you should have seen it coming.

John stroked his cheek. "Why d'you never hit me back?" His hand rubbed Danny's face gently, ran over the outline of his jaw.

"You know why."

"Afraid I'd kill you?"

"You know the answer to that too."

"I wouldn't kill you, I love you." John touched his mouth gently. "How many times?"

Danny's eyes slid away, became slightly glazed. There was, of course, no answer. He didn't give one.

"Delaying tactics Danny. How often?"

"Three times."

John pulled his shirt open. The poppers went with a kind of rip, like Elastoplast, all in one go. He picked the vegetable knife off the draining board. Danny tried not to look at it.

The knifepoint cut into his chest. It felt icy-hot. He sweated with the immediacy of fright at the sharp pain of it. "John..." he said.

John did it again then said, "Only one more."

Danny stood still. It was beginning to hurt.

The last was worst. John turned the knife with a little twisting motion. Danny grabbed at his hand.

"Let go," John said, keeping the knife pressed down.

Danny let go. The knife slid out. The wounds began to sting and burn. He closed his eyes. John bent his head to Danny's chest.

Ian came into the room. Danny opened his eyes and saw him standing inside the doorway, watching.

Danny's face was white, filmed with sweat. John straightened up and turned round. There was blood smeared across his mouth. Ian saw the cuts welling fresh blood on Danny's chest. John was still holding the knife.

Ian's face was filled with something that might have been revulsion. "You're fucking obscene John."

"What d'you want Ian?" John's voice was clipped. He could have been saying, We're in conference, do you mind?

"Nothing," Ian muttered, his eyes fixed on Danny's chest, and he went back out the way he came.

John turned back to him, brisk, business-like. "We better patch you up Danny-boy, before you bleed to death."

He crossed to the dresser and pulled open the drawer. He came back with a roll of tape. "Nasty mess." He wiped the wounds with wet kitchen towel then taped them. Danny could feel them still bleeding beneath the plasters. "But there'll be no disfiguring scars. Still pretty, once they've healed." He went on with hardly a pause for breath, "What did you do?"

This time there was no hesitation. "Sucked him off."

"Then?"

"Hand job in the bath and another in the morning."

"Three's your lucky number, isn't it?"

Danny said nothing.

John grabbed his face. "*Isn't* it?"

"Yes."

John nodded approvingly. "How big is he?"

"Short but thick," Danny paused, "...very thick."

"You like that?"

Another no-answer question. So truth or lie? "Yes."

"Oh boy, you're really something. So what else?"

"He's hairy."

"You like that too?"

"I'm not sure."

"Not sure *yet*. Plenty of time to find out." He was working up to it again. "Isn't that right?"

Danny nodded.

John's fist came into his stomach like a swung weight, completely without malice.

Now you know why I had no breakfast Henderson. My brother will only punch it up again.

Danny laid his head on John's shoulder. They looked like drunken boxers leaning on each other for support.

John took Danny's hand away from his stomach and rubbed it across his groin. "Good enough for you after Dick Tracy?"

Danny nodded into his shoulder.

"I can't hear you."

"I said yes."

John stood back suddenly, pushing him upright. "Get moving then."

Danny walked slowly ahead of him, still holding his stomach. Half way up the stairs he saw that the blood from his chest was soaking through his shirt. He felt like crying. It was his very best shirt.

THIRTY-TWO

John stood with his head pressed against the window.

"They'll see you."

"Who cares?"

Rab stretched his legs out and reached over for John's cigarettes. "You mean you want them to see you."

"That's right."

"Think it threatens him?"

"Which one?"

"Henderson."

"It ought to."

"It won't."

John shut the curtains with a jerk and walked round the sofa. He pushed Rab's legs off and sat down with a thump. Rab pulled himself up against the arm of the settee, drawing his knees up against his chest. "I can't figure you out."

"Smoke your own fucking cigarettes." John took the pack back.

"Why so jealous?"

"Who says I'm jealous?"

"What else would you call it?"

"I don't like that greasy little spastic."

"That's what I mean. Here you are alone with me, the man of your dreams, and you're pissing yourself over Danny."

John looked at him slowly. "Is that an offer?"

"No, just an observation. You're a liar incarnate John. You've got it so bad even you don't know when you're telling the truth anymore."

"I run this house." John looked at him. "I keep what's in it."

"You're as greedy as he is. You want both."

"That's right."

"You ever had an urge to see Danny and me together?"

"No."

"Don't shit your pants, I just wondered."

"Don't even think it."

"Alright, forget I asked."

John threw his cigarette in the fire unsmoked. Rab looked at it but said nothing. He blew some smoke down his nose then said, "You know what amuses me?"

John grunted.

"The way we kill people in this house and nobody asks questions."

"What's to ask?" It was a growl.

Rab laughed sourly. "Who did it? Why?"

"Who cares? We're too busy being happy that the fucker's dead."

"And you don't want to know?"

"Why should I? When did you last worry about why you threw something away? You don't care how it's done, you're only glad it's done at all."

"Somebody must have killed him."

John looked at him then slowly took another cigarette out of the packet. "Why should you care? You didn't love him."

"Oh come on John."

John laughed. "You want to clear your own team in case the whole thing blows up,

then you can shift the shit." He began systematically shredding the cigarette in his fingers. "You want to make sure it was me."

"No I don't."

"Yes you do, because then it won't be Danny." John was smiling slightly, the beginnings of a smile. He stood up and flung the shredded cigarette into the fire open-handed. "What d'you think - me or Danny?"

"Not Danny."

"Why not?"

"It doesn't fit."

"You don't want it to fit. You don't want him to be as loopy as his big brother." John stood over him and lifted his chin lightly with his hand. "That right, gorgeous?"

Rab pulled his head away. "Leave off."

"Why, too close for comfort?"

Rab reached over the arm of the settee and stubbed out his cigarette. John watched him for a moment then sat down again. He nodded his head at the television. "Why d'you watch it with the sound off?"

"I can't think with it on."

"You're not supposed to be thinking." John took another cigarette out and lit it this time. He laid his head back. Rab, catching the gesture, saw an echo of Danny in it. Not the first. The similarities always disturbed him. Like getting erections at naked children or pregnant women, you knew it was faintly indecent, but knowing didn't make them go away. Even his profile was similar, the firelight casting a reddish glow on his hair.

"Pass me a cigarette." Rab's voice was hoarse.

"Smoke your own." John never opened his eyes.

"They're upstairs."

"Lazy bastard." John threw the packet over then said, "Why don't you go over the road?"

Rab looked away from him. "Same reason you don't."

"I doubt it," John said flatly.

John's answer irritated him. "Why do you doubt it?"

"You're sitting here feeling sorry for yourself. I'm making up invoices."

"Invoices?"

"Monies due. Ways to make him pay." John turned his head, eyes half-open.

"You're a cheap sadist."

"No, I'm a real sadist. You're the cheap one."

Rab felt the smoke nip his eyes. He held the cigarette away from his face, trying to read John's expression. He was afraid to ask him what he meant.

John leaned his head back. His face looked suddenly heavy with weariness. Rab saw him take a deep breath and let it out slowly. Rab leaned his head forward and rested it on his knees. He closed his eyes.

John broke the silence. "Still imagine you're in love with him?"

Rab opened his eyes and looked down between his knees. He studied the raised velvet of the settee. Not a question he could answer. Not an answer there to give it. Not anything he could bear to hear. "Don't you imagine you are?" he returned. Answer a question with a question. Make the world move faster longer.

"Me? I've never been in love with him."

Rab lifted his head, looking at him in surprise. John's eyes were open. He was gazing at the ceiling. He was holding a lit cigarette in front of his face, watching the smoke spiral upwards.

"I'm not in love with Danny any more than I'm in love with you."

John threw the cigarette into the fire without looking. It spurted into flame and was

gone. "Actually, I hate him." He paused, folding his hands across his stomach. "I hate him because he doesn't love me, because I'm beginning to suspect he never has loved me, and he never will. There, now you know everything. A full insight into my great brain, my divine motivations."

He lifted his head slowly and looked directly at him. A smile spread out across his face, like a slow melting of ice, until it was almost a manic grin. "Only I could be lying." And he laughed. "What was it you called me? A liar incarnate. Here I am, The Liar Incarnate." He was still smiling. "Nothing to say?"

Rab licked his lip, shook his head.

"Hardman speechless - make a note of the date."

Rab straightened up, took another deep breath and flexed his shoulders. Too tense.

There was a long silence. The room filled with green. The fire settled then John spoke. "Jesus, listen to that rain. I swear it's the flood. I've never known it rain as much as it has this year."

It hurled at the windows like hail. They listened to it in silence then John spoke again. "Just think, out at Jerrett's the old man's spread out naked on the bed, listening to that cold, dark rain beating at the windows, turning blue and starting to rot already, and are we thinking about him? No, we're not. He's dead because we wanted him dead, just like we wanted her dead. They're dead, we forget about them. No, I'll tell you who we're *really* worried about. He's safely tucked up in a warm bed giving head to a bent copper, but that's all we can think about. Not about death or guilt or even tomorrow's dinner, just what he's doing now, and the real big one, does he like it? How *much* is he liking it? When is he going to walk over that fine line to liking it *too* much? That's what we're really worried about."

Rab lit another cigarette from the one in his hand. He threw the stub into the fire and said, "He sleeps on black satin sheets."

John looked at him then began nodding his head slowly. "Thank you. Thank you so much."

Rab laughed dryly. "Why should I suffer alone?"

John looked at him again, then he laughed too. "He would have black sheets."

"Black *satin* sheets."

"Of course, satin sheets."

"His house is crawling with money."

"Where does an ordinary copper get money?"

"Not the way you think, family income."

"Inherited?"

"I don't know. I didn't ask. They're in business."

"What business?"

"Kilts."

John laughed. "Christ, I can just see him in a kilt." He was serious again. "I wouldn't have thought there was that much money in kilts."

Rab shrugged.

"Why isn't he something higher up?" John asked.

Rab shrugged again. "Fuck knows."

"Everything about him stinks."

"No, he's straight."

John looked at him. "How the hell can he be straight?"

"He hasn't done it before. It's new territory, fantasy, wish fulfilment."

There was a silence again. John got up slowly as if his bones hurt. Rab saw him rub the back of his thigh. He's had sex, he thought. When Danny came home this morning he took him upstairs and did him, that's why he's aching. He felt a spasm of

revulsion.

John put more coal on the fire then sat down again. "I thought it was you he wanted."

"He does." Rab's voice was tight.

John looked up curiously at his tone. "What happened?"

"Why don't you ask Danny?"

John studied his face, his eyes narrow, flat, hard, then he said, "In order to make Danny tell the truth I have to beat it out of him, but I'll ask him if you like." He paused then said, "You're a cheap sadist, like I said."

Rab flushed. He felt it hit home like an arrow in his heart. Tonight was the night for ugly truths. "Nothing happened."

"You sound like Danny." John's voice was sarcastic.

"No, seriously... nothing happened. I left, came home," he finished lamely.

"Why? Did you do a deal? Give him Danny in exchange for your freedom?"

Another ugly truth. Rab shook his head.

"Let me guess then. Danny's taken a shine to him and you've been pushed out the picture. He's decided he likes hairy men."

Rab looked at him. "How do you know he's hairy?"

"He also has a short thick cock, right?"

Rab looked at him for a long moment then said, "What d'you do, get turn-ons out of him telling you?"

John's smile was lopsided. "Maybe he does."

Rab shut up. Maybe he did. Danny was capable of anything. John's voice cut into his thoughts. "What time is it?"

Rab looked at his watch. The clock had stopped. "Quarter to nine."

"What'll they be doing now?"

Rab shot him a sour glance. "How the hell should I know?"

John sighed and laid his head back again. He pulled his shirt out and scratched his stomach. Rab saw it, flat and hard, covered in the same shit brown hair.

"Why don't we fuck?"

Rab looked at him sharply. He looked relaxed, his eyes closed, as if he'd suggested a game of draughts.

"No."

"You're just saying no without thinking about it." John was smiling faintly.

"No."

"Listen..." John was still relaxed, eyes still closed. Rab watched the blunt, powerful fingers rubbing his belly. "For one night you can do what Danny thinks you're doing anyway. You've nothing to lose. We imagine him with Henderson. What do you think he imagines you're doing?"

Reaming you, it was on the tip of his tongue to say, but he snapped it down.

"For old time's sake. It's been how long? I can't remember."

"I've changed," Rab said dryly.

John turned his head. "I've noticed." His lips were parted slightly, inviting, just like Danny.

Rab looked away. "No."

He heard John sigh again. Rab watched him lay his head back once more, his hands resting on his lap again. His shirt was still awry. Rab looked at his stomach, the buckle of his belt.

"And why not?" John asked suddenly.

Rab turned his face away with a guilty start. "Because you murder people."

John laughed. "Good old Rab, always on the front line with a bit of melodrama. Okay, let's start again. We'll pretend you never said that, it'll only embarrass you later.

Why not?"

"I don't like you," Rab said shortly.

"That doesn't stop you elsewhere."

"I told you, the answer's no." Rab could hear his voice rise in pitch. He took a breath, dragged his hand through his hair. He swung his legs to the floor and stretched them out in front of him. Now they sat like a matching pair.

The rain opened a fresh onslaught against the window. Rab could see the colours of flame and erratic movement on the ceiling. The news - more men shooting each other.

"Maybe you just want me to want harder, is that it?"

Rab wouldn't answer him.

"Think I don't want you enough? Maybe you want me to bleed for it."

It wasn't a question. John could think what he liked.

"Six years is a long time." John's voice was mildly ruminative, as if he had forgotten everything he had just said. "It was something more than an adolescent crush to last six years. It had to be."

"Was it?"

John sucked air in through his teeth. "So sharp he'll cut himself."

There was another silence, more rain.

"I'll do you a deal then."

"I'm not interested."

"Listen first, then decide." He waited. Rab didn't contradict him. He went on, "Tell me the truth to one single question and I'll tell you the truth to one of yours."

Rab was silent for so long John looked at him to make sure he hadn't fallen asleep, but he was awake, eyes open, face edgy. "No," he said.

"Why not?"

"It's too expensive. I lose too much."

"You lose nothing. All you're giving me is a tiny piece of information."

"You can do anything with information."

"Only some information."

"I know what you're going to ask me."

"Then it's even easier for you."

"No."

John watched him. He knew it was too big a temptation. He could see Rab's long fingers scratching at his hand, nervy, edgy, too good to miss. His hand stilled suddenly. "Alright."

John felt his heart thumping. One step closer. "Why won't you fuck me?" And before Rab could reply, "The truth."

Rab pressed his eyes shut with his fingertips. "Because you look like him."

"Because..." John stared at him. He pulled himself upright. "Because I look like who? *Danny?*"

"You heard." Rab's voice was sharp.

"That's absurd. I don't look anything like Danny." He was silent a moment. When he spoke next his tone was unmistakable, gloating. "You're afraid."

Rab rubbed his forehead.

"You're afraid of yourself."

"You said one fucking question and you got one fucking answer." Rab glared at the ceiling then he brought his head down. "Now it's my turn. Did you kill the old man?"

John was smiling faintly, as if he already knew the question in advance. "No."

Rab felt the colour drain from his face. "The truth John."

"It is the truth. I didn't kill the old man."

"Did Danny?"

"One question, one fucking answer Rab." His smile was open now.

"I knew it. I knew it was a loser for me. Anything from you is always a fucking loser."

John shrugged. "You pays your money..."

Rab moved to get up. "I'm going to bed."

"No, don't." John caught at his hand.

"I'm tired John." Rab sat on the edge of the settee, waiting for him to let go. John still held his wrist. He wanted to pull his hand free but fought the urge, knowing the irritation it would cause. He didn't want to fight. He was too tired to fight.

"So? You can always sleep on the sofa. Stay with me. Just a while."

Rab looked at him. His eyes were green too. Sometimes you forgot. Maybe because they were so deep-set they looked black. Or maybe because they were always hidden.

"Alright," Rab sat back again, "for a while."

John got up, smiling suddenly, and heaped more coal on the fire. He turned the television off, plunging the room into a dull brown darkness. He opened the draught in the fire. Slowly it brightened. Rab felt sleepy in the extra heat, but it was nice. He was loath to change it.

"Put your head in my lap."

Rab frowned at him. "I thought you weren't going to try anything?"

"I'm not. You're tired. Stretch out and put your head in my lap."

Rab swung round, half-amused by the ridiculous notion of having his head in John's lap.

John's thigh was broad and hard under his head. Rab fidgeted some more, put his feet on the arm of the sofa, eased the crotch of his jeans.

"Comfy?"

"Just about." Rab closed his eyes, listened to the rain. "Pass me a cigarette."

John lit one from his own and put it between his lips. "Last one, make it last."

Rab nodded. They were silent again.

"Know what the worst thing of all is?" John said suddenly.

"What?" Rab's voice was sleepy.

"The empty bed. Isn't that a real heart-breaker? Henderson's got him in his bed while mine's empty, that's the worst."

Rab nodded.

"Maybe I should kill him for that. How would it sound in court? I killed Henderson because he was sticking it in my brother when my brother should've been home in bed being stuck by me. Think it would win me any votes?"

Rab shook his head.

"No, me neither." John started stroking his hair, soporifically fanning it out over his thigh. He stroked it gently, listening to the rain.

Rab lay there half-asleep and felt the hand fanning his hair out. *I want him to try it*, he thought.

John ran his finger nails along the length of the hair, spread it out like a child's drawing of the sun's rays, thinking, Christ, what a girl he is.

Rab felt his heart thumping. *I want it. Why doesn't he?*

John brushed his hand across Rab's forehead, then put the other hand down inside the neck of his shirt. He pushed the top button out of its buttonhole and slid his hand in flat against Rab's chest. He felt it move beneath his hand. He could feel his heart. Everything was too rapid; his breathing, his heartbeats. He looked at Rab's face. *Christ, he couldn't even say no for money right now.*

He sat up and bent his head down to Rab's mouth. Rab opened it to kiss him. Their tongues met somewhere upside down in a confusion of heat. Rab curved up almost like a snake, pulling himself round. John practically hauled him up against him, their

mouths still glued together.

Rab could feel the fullness of John's mouth, the hugeness of his head, the vastness of his body. It was like being crushed by a stone man.

John surfaced first, breaking to whisper in his ear, "I'm going to fuck you. That's what you need, a good hard fucking."

Rab found his mouth again, felt John's hands at his jeans, pulling them open, then down. He felt the warmth from the fire on his naked skin, then John was pulling his own down. It was Rab's turn to break away. "Let me see," he demanded.

John took his head and pressed it down against his chest as Rab knelt up to face him on the couch. "There," he said. He held his head with both hands, as if he was guiding him in the right direction.

He was huge, massively erect.

Rab stared at it.

But John had no time for that, his hands were already pushing him round. "Hold the back and spread your legs." He tugged Rab's jeans right down off his feet, but he left his own at half-mast. "Wider," he insisted.

Rab leaned forwards over the back of the settee. He felt John get between his legs. He could feel the jeans somewhere around his thighs. Rab heard him pull his own shirt open, then he tugged Rab's off completely.

John pressed against him, chest to back. His hands slid over Rab's belly, caught hold of his cock. He was leaning into his shoulders, his cock wedged hugely into the cleft of Rab's arse. He wasn't moving, just holding, squeezing. "So this is what he wants, this meat here." He pulled Rab's cock painfully tight.

He didn't prepare him, he simply pushed him forward. He spread his cheeks with both hands and put the head of his penis against his anus. "You're going to feel this, you bone-hungry cunt."

Rab's cock jerked at the words. John's hand came round again, wrapping tightly around Rab's shaft. "Tell me when you're near," he warned, then he began masturbating him lightly, fast. He never moved his own cock an inch. It sat there like a dangerous threat waiting to rip him open.

Rab grabbed suddenly at John's hand. "Stop," he gasped. His heart was pounding already.

John put one hand under his balls to keep his penis in place and pushed. Rab buckled slightly under his weight, but John kept pushing. It was dry and dragging, tugging on the hair.

It went in. It was painful enough to make Rab cry out. He clenched instinctively.

"Feel it," John whispered harshly. He began to work Rab's cock again, slowly withdrawing his penis until it was out - right out.

"Oh Jesus," Rab groaned, wanting it back in again.

"He likes that."

Rab nodded.

"Want more?"

Rab nodded again.

"Say it."

"I want more."

John lifted his cock and placed it against him again. Rab tightened in anticipation. John squeezed Rab's cock, peeled it, squeezed it again. He pushed again, hard, suddenly, going up with a vengeance.

Rab squirmed forward, crying out, but John pushed in until he was pinned against the back of the sofa. John had his legs riveted open. "Feel it shoving your shit now?" His voice was edgy with aggression. He stabbed into him in small upward thrusts, both hands pulling his backside open. Rab grunted under his weight. John pulled his pelvis

back towards him, pushing his legs further apart with his knees. He went further up, harder, wider.

Rab squirmed.

John gripped him remorselessly. "I'm going to have you spitting your own turds in a minute." He kept pushing until finally there wasn't any more to go in. He stopped.

There was a sweaty stillness. He held Rab tight against him like a limp doll, supporting his weight. He had his chin hooked over his shoulder. "All ten inches fully inserted," he hissed into his ear. "You aren't going to sit down for a week. Maybe two. Oh Rab, you waited too long baby." Rab could feel wet against his face. Sweat or tears?

"I should kill you now, in the perfection of the moment, at the point of orgasm, just bite out your throat." He bit into Rab's neck, let him go again, unable to hold anything past seconds. "Then I won't have to share."

Rab could feel the dull throbbing in his anus, rammed open, held rigid. The throbbing in his cock matched it, pound for pound.

"Sooner or later I'm going to kill one of you. Kill one, keep one, life is a knitting pattern. Christ Rab, why him? Couldn't it have been anyone other than him? Maybe I will kill you. God knows I should kill you. Christ knows I want to."

Rab felt sweat trickle down his sides. He felt his erection dry-throbbing against the velvet of the settee. He wanted it to go away. He was afraid of him, what he might do, and underneath all that, above all that, he was loving it, high on John's passions, the all-consuming intensity of what John felt, throwing life and death about as if it was so much theory. He knew how Danny felt listening to those words.

"Fuck me," he whispered. "You said you were going to fuck me. Why don't you fuck me?"

John lay still against his back. "Why should I give you anything?"

"I don't want you to give me anything. I want to feel your big prick up my arse." Rab stuck his backside out, offering, demanding. He felt the slight movement of that thick wedge inside him. It was as delicious as the clutch of pleasure immediately before an orgasm. He moaned.

"Alright." John said it slowly. "You want it, you'll get it."

"Put it all in." Rab kept pushing back at him. John gripped his shoulders. Rab braced himself against the settee.

John pulled out long and slow. Rab felt every inch of it on its way. His cock came up so hard he thought it would burst. Like the world's most beautiful shit. Oh yes.

Then John went in again, just as slow, right home, then a hard shove, as if to get it in an extra inch. Then again, out slowly, but this time he only withdrew so far, sinking back in deep. And again, not so far out, slightly further in. And again, withdrawing just barely and deeper, faster in. Only their breathing, the rain.

"Now," Rab said urgently, a low deep noise from somewhere inside himself. "*Now*."

John began plunging into him, pulling him up to meet it, watching his own cock, slick, pistoning, disappearing in and out of him.

Rab tried to speak, let it out, but all that came out was a long drawn out growl that dissolved in his mouth into a cry of elation. He pushed his arse out to meet him. "Up me... up me... up me..." he urged blindly as it spurted out, white-hot, forced out of his bowels, each thrust spreading it oily and wet over the velvet.

John's nails dug into him. John's teeth bit down on his back. John grunted like an animal until Rab felt him come inside him, ploughing him up, filling him with the bitter salt of it, hating him with every inch he had. "*Danny...*" he grunted.

It was quiet.

But not quiet enough.

"He looks as if he'd like to dismember me."

Danny fastened his seat belt. "You're a prat."

Henderson looked at him, irritated already and he wasn't two minutes in the car. "What the fuck's that supposed to mean?"

"You think he's funny. Anyone who finds him funny is a prat."

"You don't find him funny?"

"I live with him. Are we going or not?"

Henderson started the car, sliding it out into the traffic carefully as he always did.

"I love the way you drive."

Henderson shot him a quick suspicious glance. "What about it?"

"You drive like someone's grandmother."

Henderson flushed. "My car's worth more than all yours together."

Danny laughed. "I should have realised it was the fucking car."

Henderson scowled, but said nothing. He clicked the windscreen wipers on. "More bloody rain."

"I like driving in the rain."

"You want to?"

Danny looked at him. "What?"

"Go driving in the rain."

"Okay..." Danny said it slowly. "Cut down to the coast road. Don't go through the town."

The big silver car slid down into the dark, out of the village, away from the traffic. They passed through a smattering of houses, past the parish church, and down finally onto the coast.

Henderson slid into the junction. "Right or left?"

"Right."

He clicked on the indicators and swept round. Only a trickle of Sunday visitors were on the road, accompanied by a few homeworking joiners and builders finishing up. A large Dutch flower lorry overtook them, casting fine arcs of spray over the windows. Its back was a mass of red and orange lights diminishing ahead of them.

Danny peered out between his cupped hands, but couldn't see the sea. He wound the window down a fraction, but couldn't smell it either. He closed it again, wiping the moisture off his face.

"Want the radio on?" Henderson asked.

"No."

"Not you too?"

"Me too what?"

"Blondie says he hates music. Gives him vibrations in his legs."

Danny laughed quietly but said nothing.

Henderson glanced at his profile. He could smell his wet washed hair and the faint smell of animals that always clung to his jacket. It made his stomach warm. "You smell like a barn."

Danny turned to him quickly. "There's a limit to what soap and water can do. I work in barns."

"Hey, I wasn't getting at you. I like it."

Danny stared at him.

"I mean it, it's a nice smell. It's only faint anyway."

"You like it? What about the upholstery?"

Henderson laughed. "Okay, so I was tactless. I'm sorry."

Danny rested his head back again.

"Where d'you want to go?"

"Just keep going along the coast."

"We'll end up in Scotland."

"Well you can take me to meet your mum and dad."

Henderson laughed then after a moment said, "Would you like that?"

Danny looked at him. "What are you doing now, proposing marriage?"

"I wish I could."

Danny looked away. "Don't talk like that, it pisses me off."

There was a silence. Danny was still looking out the window. Henderson could see the tightness of his jaw. "I was serious about going to Scotland."

"We can turn back before we get that far if it worries you."

"No, I mean we could go there. I own a house there. On the West Coast. We could go there."

"Talk sense, I can't leave the farm."

"You mean you don't want to."

Danny swung round in his seat. "No. I mean I *can't*. It needs all hands. I work on it, seven days a week, and even if I could get away John wouldn't let me. You don't seem to understand him, or you don't want to."

Henderson's face was set, lit eerily by the dashboard lights. "You could leave. Permanently."

"With you." It wasn't a question.

"With me," Henderson agreed.

"A regular little live-in gay couple." Danny could see his face change colour.

"You live like that with them. I bet you even share their beds."

"Yeah, a different one every night, even the dog's. And what do I do when you get tired of me?"

"I won't."

"You say."

"I'll give you money. You can bank it. You'll be independent."

"What utter shit. A policeman with his live-in boyfriend. I'm not a fucking queer."

"Oh no? You look like one to me."

"Only because you want to see me as one."

"And what's all the cocksucking then?"

"Sex. Just sweet fucking sex. And, in case you haven't guessed it, I'd do it with anyone; male, female, animal or vegetable. Just ask my brother."

"I see."

"I doubt if you do."

The car rocked momentarily as the wind hit it broadside. Henderson slowed his speed. He was driving too fast. They were sweeping out round a point towards the sea.

Danny opened the window again. A cold gust of air brought salt rain in against his face, stinging his eyes. He could smell it now, driving head into it.

"Shut the fucking window," Henderson said tensely.

Danny wound it back up then said, "Turn around, let's go back."

"To the flat?"

"Yes."

"Why?"

Because there I can shove my dick in your stupid face and shut you up, Danny thought. "Because I want to."

"Okay, we'll turn at the next lay-by."

They drove on round the point, the rain slashing at the windows, the visibility about four feet. The lay-by had been cut through a dune to provide shelter from the strong winds. They pulled into it like a boat into harbour. The noise changed, seemed to float

outside them, above their heads, like a noise beyond a wall.

"Let's sit a minute, see if it abates," Henderson said. He left the engine running, the heater blowing air into the car. He clicked off the windscreen wipers. The rain ran down the windows like a waterfall; grey, solid, impenetrable. "Danny?"

"What?"

"Why do you do it?"

"What?"

"Have sex with me. You didn't do it because I threatened you, and you say you're not gay, so why?"

Danny didn't answer.

"It turns you on. I've seen you. You can't fake that."

"So it turns me on. Maybe that's why I do it."

"But you're not gay?"

"I told you, everything turns me on. I could ream a sheep. It doesn't mean anything."

"Then why?"

"Why not? You wanted it - I like doing it. Why not?"

"Then why not permanently? He punches you around, doesn't he?"

"Maybe I enjoy that." Danny turned and looked at him squarely for the first time since they'd stopped. "That never occur to you? Maybe it's not Rab, or the farm, or a fear of losing my independence. Maybe I'm hooked on him. How about that for size?"

"I don't believe you."

"Believe what you like."

"Alright then, what if I carry out my threats? It's my bet that if anybody in the family knows anything about your mother's disappearance it's your big brother. If you care about him so much maybe you'd want to protect him. Maybe you'd come with me to stop him being put inside."

"Maybe I'd tell you to go suck yourself."

Henderson grabbed his sweater fiercely. "Don't overdo it. I won't sit here indefinitely putting up with mouthy shit from you. You're the one in trouble, not me."

"Oh no, if we go, you go with us. I've got plenty of dirt on you."

"It won't wash."

"No, but it won't wash out either. Once it's been flung it sticks, no matter what. You'll be the queer cop, the one who can't keep his sticky fingers off the boys."

Henderson stared at him. "That *is* why you're doing it. That's why you've been doing it all along. An insurance policy, money down for future protection."

Danny laughed. It sounded like a puff of breath coming out against his will.

"Isn't it?" Henderson demanded. "That's why you're doing it, to protect yourself."

"I told you, believe what you like."

"You dirty little..."

"Oh no," Danny interrupted. "You started it. You were willing to do anything to lay hands on me. You're not so fussy, so don't come playing bleeding hearts and telling me I'm cheap. What about you, *officer* Henderson?"

Henderson punched him squarely in the face. Danny heard the crack and felt the immediate hot flood of blood down his nose. The pain moved across his face like a hot poker held against his skin. Sooner or later someone was going to break something in him. It had to be my nose, he thought.

Danny put his hand to his face, spreading his fingers as if to hide it. Henderson only hit him once. He was staring at him, at the blood which seemed to cover everything. "Oh Christ," he was saying uselessly. Danny wondered if it was the first time he had ever hit anybody. The strangest fucking policeman in boots.

He moved finally, giving Danny a hankie, taking a box of them from the glove

compartment, wiping his face. "I'm sorry," he said.

Danny shook his head to ward him off. Don't let him start apologising for fuck's sake.

They soaked dozens of hankies, one after the other, throwing them out into the rain.

"I think my nose is broken." He sounded as if he had a heavy cold.

"Shit, let me see."

Danny took his hand away. "Don't touch it," he said as Henderson reached out.

"How can I tell if it's broken if I don't feel it?"

"I don't care, just don't touch it."

Henderson put on the light. Danny blinked. Henderson shook his head. "I don't know, it's already so fucking swollen I can't tell. You want to go to a hospital?"

Danny shook his head.

"What if it is broken though?"

"Tough tits, they can't fix them anyhow."

"They can do something."

"Forget it."

Henderson flexed his hand and winced. "My finger's out of joint. I think I've staved it. It's swelling up as badly as your nose."

"Good," Danny said sourly. He rolled the window down and held a wad of hankies out in the rain. He brought them in after a moment and washed his face with them, then his neck, taking the worst of the blood off. His sweatshirt was soaked with it. It would wash off the leather of his jacket, he hoped. The pain was appalling. His eyes felt as if they were being pushed out his head. His cheekbones seemed to be bursting with fluid, as if he could press a cheek and blood would burst out afresh. "I need to go home."

"I'm sorry," Henderson said again hopelessly.

"Just drive."

Henderson started the car and swung out onto the road. The wind was still high, but the rain had eased temporarily. "Want to come back to the flat?"

"No."

"You'll be comfy there."

"Christ." Danny held the top of his head as if it might come off. "What are you going to do, make me give you head?"

"No... I..." Henderson felt the anger burst up in him again. He stopped. "I'll take you home," he said resignedly.

"Thanks." Danny's voice was scathing.

Henderson drove him right up into the yard this time. Danny moved to get out, but Henderson caught his arm. "Look, I'm really sorry..."

"Forget it." Danny tried to pull free. "I'm used to it."

Henderson looked at him for a moment then went on. It came out all of a rush and Danny realised he'd been steeling himself to say it all the way home. "I want to go on seeing you. I don't care why you come to me, or what you want, just let me..." he ran out.

"Fuck me," Danny finished. He felt as if the whole of his body was dead. Only his face was alive, alive and making up for the rest of him.

"If you want to put it like that." Henderson sounded sulky.

Danny looked at him but said nothing.

"Will you?" Henderson asked.

Danny nodded very slowly, very fragilely. "Of course. I've got to keep up my

insurance payments otherwise the policy expires."

Henderson gritted his teeth. "Thank you. Thank you so much."

Danny swung out the car. "Don't mention it, and thank *you* for the broken nose." And the door closed softly behind him.

Danny went into the kitchen and straight through the hall and up the stairs.

He tugged on the bathroom light and looked at the bath before closing the door. He didn't lock it. He put the light on above the mirror. There was no sound in the house.

He looked in the mirror. Christ, what a fucking mess. He only hoped it would save John the bother. He took his jacket off and hung it over the chair then pulled off his sweatshirt and stuck it in the bucket under the sink. He took it to the bath and filled it with cold water. He didn't look at the bath, or think about it. He left the bucket in the bath.

He ran the water, lukewarm, in the sink and washed his face carefully. He wanted to blow his nose to unblock it but was afraid to. He touched his face gingerly. He could feel nothing but sponginess and drunken pain. He ferreted behind the mirrored doors of the cabinet and found aspirin. He took three without reading the dosage. He closed the doors, looked at himself and said "Christ" again.

He sponged his jacket. It was black, so the blood didn't show, but it seemed to come off. He wiped it till the sponge ran clear. He put a dry towel round his shoulders and sat down on the cork-topped basket, leaning against the towel rail. He looked at the bath. He sat there waiting for the aspirin to work and thinking about nothing.

Nothing at all.

John lifted his head. "What the fuck was that?"

Rab listened. "It must be Danny. It's too early for Ian."

"Danny?"

"Yeah, you must remember Danny?"

John levered himself off him unceremoniously. He stood up, pulling his jeans up. "My legs are like fucking jelly." There was no panic in his voice, only irritation.

"Where are my jeans?" Rab looked for them frantically. He felt panicked enough for both of them.

John turned his head, scanning the floor, then picked them up from the side of the settee. He straightened up then stilled. "Shh..." He held the jeans in one hand, arrested.

Rab sat down heavily on his calves, making no attempt to take his trousers. Danny came out the kitchen and passed by and up the stairs. Rab let out a breath.

John threw him his trousers. "Get dressed."

He picked his own shirt off the settee and pulled it on, tucking it half-fastened into his jeans. Rab fished his shorts out of one leg and pulled them on. He realised he was shaking slightly. He straightened up to see John watching him. He was smiling.

"All brown and white stripes, like a cat. You're better than I remember."

Rab pulled his clothes on with a slow, dreadful disgust building inside himself. *Lots of years ahead to think of an excuse for this one Rab.*

John took his arm. "I'll go up first, you wait a while."

Rab nodded. He felt leaden. His arse hurt, a dull itchy throbbing.

John bent and kissed him suddenly.

Rab pulled back.

John looked at him, licking his mouth. "Back to the status quo already? Trouble is

you've spoilt me now, I've got the taste for you again. What *am* I going to do?"

"That's your problem." Rab wouldn't look at him.

John laughed, a nicely judged sound. "Oh no, I'll bet it's going to be yours."

And he passed out quietly into the hall.

John went into the bathroom unfastening his jeans. He was surprised to find the light on. When he saw Danny he jumped. "You scared the fucking life out of me. Christ, what's happened to your face?"

Danny was sitting on the linen basket. He was smoking a cigarette. It wasn't easy. His face was red, the nose and cheeks swollen and already purpling. His eyes were bloodshot and half-closed. He was wrapped in a huge pink towel.

"I got punched on the nose. You know, like in comics."

"Henderson?" John's voice was incredulous.

"Henderson."

"What for?" John lifted his face, looking at both sides on profile.

Danny pulled away. "Don't touch it."

"What for?" John said again.

Danny looked at the ceiling. "I was giving him cheek." His eyes looked up at John through a watery mist.

"I'll bet you were, like you're giving it now."

Danny said nothing.

John suddenly gripped his head under one arm, pressing it back. He probed the bridge of Danny's nose quickly and efficiently. Danny roared and lashed out at him. John let him go with a terse, "It's not broken."

Tears of pain were running down Danny's face. "You fucking bastard..."

"What are you worried about? It's not broken. The bone's fine, straight as a die. Your professional whoring can go on a little while longer."

Danny pressed his eyes into the towel, cradling his face.

John crossed to the toilet and unzipped. Danny's face was buried in the towel. It stayed there.

John finished up, flushed the toilet, then washed his hands. Anything else would have to be washed later. Danny was placing the cigarette carefully between his lips again. His hand was shaking.

"Why don't you go to bed?" John said, drying his hands. "It'll be a nice novelty for me to find you there."

Danny shook his head. "I want to sit here a while longer. I'm waiting for the aspirin to take effect."

"How many did you have?"

"Three."

"Hang on..."

John disappeared out and came back with a half-drunk bottle of whisky. He poured some into a toothmug. "He isn't going to finish it now. You might as well have it." He offered him the glass.

"On top of aspirins?"

"Only way to go."

Danny took it from him and took a mouthful. He coughed, sending bolts of pain up his nose, through his head.

"Slowly." John slapped his back. "No-one ever teach you how to drink? Take some more, sips this time."

Danny sipped it.

The door opened. Rab came in. Danny saw him look at John, then him. His face

213

was flushed. When he spoke it sounded almost theatrical, like a rehearsed line. "God, what happened to you?"

"Police brutality." John took the glass from Danny's hand, rinsed it, then filled it with cold water. He crossed the floor and sat down on the edge of the bath, holding the glass between his legs. He was watching Rab with that crawling expression Danny knew. Rab looked even more uncomfortable. Danny felt something sinking in his stomach.

"Why did he hit you?" Rab was looking at him, but he wouldn't meet his eyes.

Danny shrugged.

"He refused to take it up the arse," John volunteered from the bath. Rab looked over at him, his mouth tightening. John smiled. "That right Danny?"

Danny said nothing, just watched them playing games.

Rab looked back at him, still not meeting his eyes. "Is it broken?"

"No," John offered again. "His beauty will not be marred."

"It feels fucking broken." Danny spoke for the first time, in his thick suffocated voice. "I heard it crack."

"If you heard anything crack it was probably your brain coming loose. It isn't broken, feel for yourself."

"No thanks."

John smiled a little wider. "Daniel has a low pain threshold." He drank the glass of water in one belt then put the glass down where the bitten soap had been. Rab looked at the glass, then away again quickly.

"How you feeling now Danny-boy? Any lighter?"

"Numb. Numb and half-suffocated."

"That's the stuff. Time for beddy-byes." John got up and lifted him by one arm.

Danny felt as if his head was floating away. He saw red lights at the corners of his eyes, then his head began to throb. "I feel sick," he said.

"It's just the movement. Into bed and you won't feel a thing, come on." John led him past Rab and out into the hall. Rab closed the door on their voices. He locked it then stripped off his clothes. He turned the shower on hot and climbed in, wincing slightly and cooling the water before he got back under.

He washed everything twice. His backside felt as tender as if he'd just let rip after a month's constipation. He leaned, palms flat against the wall, and banged his head on it softly. Why, oh why, had he done it? What a stupid thing to do.

He pressed up suddenly and turned the water off. Danny had gone off wrapped in the bath towel so he had to improvise with the hand towel. He dried the rough off and nipped out to the linen cupboard for a proper towel.

John was coming out of the bedroom. He looked Rab up and down before speaking. "All tucked up with an extra pillow and half-asleep already."

Rab put the towel around his waist, rubbing his hair with the hand towel. "Such brotherly solicitude, it becomes you."

"Someone has to look out for him. Wouldn't do if he lost his looks, would it?"

"You make it sound like a threat."

John smiled suddenly. "Maybe it is. Maybe I ought to try that. Am I scaring you?"

"You always scare me."

"Good, that's what I like to hear." John reached up and patted his face. "Night-night sweetheart." He went into the bathroom.

Rab pushed the door open again before he could close it. "Chuck me out my clothes first."

"Chuck us in a towel," John returned.

Rab fetched another and they exchanged bundles. John winked at him and closed the door. He didn't lock it. John didn't need to lock the door against anyone.

THIRTY-THREE

Danny woke when John put on the bedside lamp. He groaned. He rubbed his eyes, sucking air in between his teeth when his fingers made contact. "Jesus, I feel as if a horse kicked me."

He heard John's dry laugh. He could see his dark shadow moving about beyond the light. "Aren't you coming to bed?" he asked.

John laughed again, louder this time. "I'm getting up Danny. The horse kicked you harder than you thought."

"Up? What time is it?"

John paused, squinting into the half-light. "Six 'o' six precisely."

Danny climbed up onto one elbow. John pushed him square in the chest. "Lie down, stay in bed, my treat."

"The cows..."

"I think I can manage. I've done it before. It doesn't take the whole family."

Danny lay back down. "What are we going to tell them, about Dad?"

"Who? The cows?"

"People. The dairy, his friends, the fucking coalman... everybody."

"We'll tell them he fell in the silo. Anyway, he didn't have any friends."

"Be serious."

"I am being serious. If he fell in there we'd have to wait till next summer before he surfaced again."

Danny groaned in exasperation, "*John...*"

"Relax, let me worry about it. That's what I'm here for, to see that we get away with murder. Anyway, we've got the law on our side. Unless, of course, the nose means it's all over between you." John sat down on the bed. "*Is* that what it means?"

Danny shook his head. John was a black shape glowing yellow in outline, like an apparition of the Lord, an avenging angel maybe. Danny squinted against the light. "He wants me to go and live with him. He keeps pestering me."

John searched his face. "You're not even thinking about that, are you?"

"No."

John put his hand under the blankets and laid it flat on his stomach. He rubbed his thumb to and fro. "Is that what the fight was about?"

"Yes and no."

"Yes...?"

"He wanted me to go with him and I wouldn't."

"And no...?"

"He didn't like the idea that I might just be screwing him to protect myself."

"And are you?" John's fingers spread like a starfish.

"Maybe."

John looked at him consideringly. "An almost broken nose makes you very brave. I don't like maybe answers."

Danny kept his mouth shut.

"I could hit it again, finish the job." He had the pleasure of seeing Danny's face pale. He stood up suddenly, giving Danny's pubic hair a vicious twist. "But as I love you I won't." He moved out of the light, back into being a black shape. "Stay in bed till I come and get you, okay?"

"Okay."

"No Rab."

"Okay."

"I mean no nobody but me Danny, you understand me?"

"Yes."

"Good. Get well soon." He moved to the door. "You owe me a lot of head."

And he went out.

Ian was last in for breakfast after milking, but he seldom had anything cooked anyway.

John shoved the cereal packet at him. "I'm going into town." He spoke to Rab. "I'll take the Rover. You and Ian take that seed barley over the way, and the grass seed down to the bottom pasture. No flowers please, by request." He laughed at his own joke. "After that you can get on with the creosoting."

"Where are you going?" Rab was mopping up with a bit of bread.

"Armstrong's."

"What for?"

"What's this, an inquisition?"

Ian looked up at him.

"I just wondered," Rab said. "I thought you were going to see Ostler."

"I was but I've changed my mind. Is that alright or should I ask in future?"

"Don't piss yourself."

"I never piss myself over people your size."

John got up and took his good jacket from the peg. "Danny's staying in bed. He doesn't require the comfort of your touch, or the solace of your eyes, understand?"

Rab didn't turn to look at him. Ian watched his face. It was white and angry. He was pushing a bacon rind round his plate with his fork. "Welcome back to the good old days," he muttered.

"They never went away Rab, you just let them slip your mind."

"Yeah."

"See you later." John closed the door behind him.

"So fucking long," Rab said to his plate and speared the rind on his fork.

John had no idea whether he'd be in or not, but it was a simple matter to go back again if he wasn't, and to keep going back.

It looked different in the daylight. He pulled into the harbour. About one hundred and eight school kids were filing out of a minibus and into the puffer. The teacher seemed to be counting them off.

John parked the car carefully. He couldn't see the Mercedes anywhere, then he saw the garages underneath. Of course he'd keep it in a garage, otherwise it might get wet.

He got out, rubbing his leg, and locked the door. This was where the problems started. He should've asked Danny last night when he was doped up. What the fuck, he should have asked him period.

He looked at the entry phone. This was worse than he thought. He looked at the panel of buttons. They looked back at him. Start at the top and work your way down. If a woman answers, forget it. If it's a man ask him if he's Henderson. Simple. Yeah, only he had to get in after that.

He pressed the first button. Nothing. No sound, no bell. Had the fucking thing rung at all? Suddenly a tinny voice spoke to him, "Yes?"

Was that a man or a woman? He felt stupid talking to no-one. "Mr Henderson?" he ventured.

"Yes."

John was silent. Beginner's luck alright.

"Who is that?" the voice demanded.

"Danny." He said it on impulse.

There was a silence then a loud buzzer went beside him. John stood for a moment, nonplussed, then he pushed tentatively at the door. It opened. "Well, well," he murmured, "isn't science wonderful?"

He went up the stairs looking at the carpet. A window looked out over the harbour at every landing. He made a face and kept going. What number had he pushed? He'd forgotten already. It was at the top, but which one was the top?

Henderson opened the door and looked out into the corridor.

"Ah, Mr Henderson, I presume?" John smiled at him, a deep wolfish smile that never reached his eyes.

"You're not Danny."

"I can tell you're a policeman." He was face to face with him now. He matched them up. A little shorter than Rab, although he was better built, but still no competition, none at all.

"What d'you want?" Henderson demanded.

"Forceful too. I want to talk to you. You don't want your neighbours listening to everything I have to say, do you?"

Henderson stood back, jerking his head back inside.

John passed him and went into the living room. The blinds were drawn across the huge window, but they were open, paper thin slats of plastic fracturing the view. The harbour looked grey and cold. It was dry, but rain clouds moved like dirty scum across the sky.

"What d'you want?" Henderson said again behind him.

John turned around, looking round the room, taking his time about it. "I told you, to talk to you." He looked at the settees. "Do I get to sit down?"

Henderson realised he looked a lot bigger in this room than he did on his farm. The scale was all wrong for him. *Remember, he doesn't love you*. Henderson didn't find him so funny this morning. He nodded brusquely.

"I like the pyjamas, they match the sheets."

Henderson looked at him, startled. John smiled at his expression. "We're a close family, we tell each other everything."

"I'll bet." Henderson pushed his hands in his dressing gown pockets, using the gesture to pull it a little tighter around himself.

John felt the leather under his fingertips. He moved his fingers very delicately for such big hands. In fact, he was singularly unclumsy for such a big man. "You like everything very nice, don't you?"

"I don't like it stinking of shit if that's what you mean."

John winced exaggeratedly. "The unkindest cut of all." He smiled again, briefly. "Are you trying to start a fight Mr Henderson? Because if you are you've already lost it."

"For the last time Moore, what d'you want?"

"Jackson Moore," John corrected.

Henderson waited. He did not acknowledge the correction.

"I don't like you handling the merchandise. I especially don't like it rolling home with a broken nose." The pretence at good humour had peeled away from his voice, leaving it cold and sharp.

Henderson sat down. This wasn't good. It wasn't even anything he'd seriously considered and that made it worse. He tried to relax. He leaned back. "Are you threatening me?"

"Oh..." John seemed to consider for a moment then said, "yes, I think so."

"What with?" Henderson paused then added, "Exactly?"

"You know, I don't really know, I hadn't really considered it. Death, possibly."

He was smiling again. Henderson wasn't sure if this was his cretinous idea of a joke. He began to wonder seriously for the first time what this gorilla was really all about.

"I can see you don't believe me. Maybe I ought to convince you." John looked out of the window, then at his shoes. He could see muck on the carpet where his feet were. It pleased him immensely. "You ever been ass-reamed?" He looked at the policeman suddenly, with a quick upward glance.

"Why don't you get out?" Henderson's face had gone blotchy red with anger.

"Answer my question and I'll think about yours. No, on second thoughts, don't bother. Who cares if you have or not? I'd like to do it anyway. I think I'm developing a taste for it."

"I said, get out." Henderson stood up.

John looked up at him. "Come on now, it's better than having your nose broken, isn't it?"

"You are talking to a police officer."

John laughed. "Look at it, standing on its dignity, all five foot eight of it." He laughed again, softly, then said, "Let's be accurate. I thought accuracy was important in your profession, getting the facts right? I'm talking to a police officer who offered to withhold criminal evidence on condition he got to sodomise my brother - who is underage. He has since had sex with him several times and added assault to his list of infamies." He took a deep breath, although he seemed perfectly calm. "Now, why don't you sit down again and rest your policeman's feet?"

Henderson sat down.

"Good. Now where would you like it, in here or in the bedroom? I rather fancy the bedroom myself, I've never done it on black satin sheets." He pursed his mouth. Henderson saw how like Danny's it was, that same curving shape, only his was wider, hungrier, filled with dangerous teeth.

"What's wrong? Don't you fancy me? Think I'll be too big for you? Don't worry, a bit of spit and it will slide in nicely. Unless, of course, you'd prefer to leave Danny alone. If you leave him alone I'm sure we can forget today's agenda. And Rab, of course, you must count him out too. No blowflies infecting my meat, however indirectly. What d'you think?"

"I think you can forget it."

"Fighting words."

"That's right."

"You know, I'm changing my mind about you. It would probably be faster if I just killed you. You're going to be difficult. I can spot a difficult bastard at fifty paces."

"You wouldn't dare." Henderson's smile was smug, confident.

"Oh don't say that. Every time somebody says that to me it brings out the worst in me."

"Your threats don't impress me."

"I can see that."

"And something you seem to forget Moore, if it comes to it I'm only risking being thrown off the force for improper sexual conduct, you're risking jail."

"How d'you make that out?" John was frowning, attentive, as if he were trying to catch some elusive logic.

Henderson blinked then said, "What?" confusedly.

"How am I risking jail?"

"For assaulting a police officer." Henderson was frowning now.

John laughed. "Christ, I'm not going to assault you, I'm going to kill you. Hasn't anybody given you a class on it yet?"

Henderson looked at him and began to worry. For the first time he didn't look right. Not just a bully-boy with too much brawn, he was something much more treacherous.

The door buzzer went. Henderson jumped. He got up and answered it before John had even registered what it was. "Yes?" He heard the quaver in his own voice.

"It's me, Robert..." Rab seemed to think better of it and said simply, "Rab."

"Come up." And Henderson pressed the buzzer to let him in.

John laughed, palms spread out flat on the settee. "Saved by the bell."

Henderson let him in. Rab could see the sweat on his upper lip. He ought to let that moustache grow right over, it would hide his emotions better.

"Hello Robbie." John didn't look up as he came through the living room door. "Fancy you showing up here, the knight errant saving our good policeman's neck. Not, of course, that I'd have harmed a hair on his little velvet head."

Henderson looked at him, his smile, and didn't know where he was. Was this man a master of deadpan or a psychotic lunatic? He looked at Rab. "He ought to be fucking locked up."

"Yeah, well, he got out his cage. Come on John-boy, time to go home."

John stood up. He smiled peaceably, all shucks-guys-I'm-licked, but when he got in front of Henderson his hand shot out, bunching his dressing gown up under his chin like so much paper. Henderson squeaked audibly. His hands came up uselessly. He could feel John's fingers like knotted chains beneath his own. "Next time, blowfly..." It was a hung threat. His fist tightened. "Don't come near him again or I'll take that moustache and wipe your arse with it."

He let him go, brushing him down with exaggerated care. Henderson watched his hands with a peculiar breathless stillness.

Rab was glaring at him. "Come on Godzilla, you're frightening everybody."

John walked up to him and patted his cheek amiably. "Remind me to kick your head in."

He went out. Rab could hear him whistling as he went down the stairs. He turned to Henderson angrily. "You stupid bastard, what did you let him in for?"

Henderson seemed stupefied. "He said he was Danny."

"And you believed him?"

"His voice is alike, I didn't think."

"Don't let guilt run your arse off."

Henderson was re-knotting his dressing gown abstractedly. "He threatened to kill me," he said. He seemed faintly outraged, as if John had slandered the family name.

Rab ran his hand through his hair. "Christ, I'm surprised they let you out in a uniform. How come you haven't been killed before now?"

Henderson didn't seem to hear that either. His face set suddenly, as if the slight had just registered. "He actually threatened to *kill* me."

Rab looked at him. "You can't touch him, not without dragging us in too."

Henderson looked back at him. His eyes were steady. "He's not going to get away with this."

"Thanks." Rab went to move out, but Henderson stopped him.

"Not you. Not you or Danny, just him." His face was oddly ecstatic.

"Then you'll take his place, eh?"

Henderson looked at him as if he was speaking a foreign language. Suddenly he smiled. He'd just found the translation in his phrasebook. "Then I'll take his place," he confirmed. He was nodding in rapid little jerks.

When Rab closed the door he was still standing there, looking into some far inner distance, his arms wrapped tightly around his own body.

John was leaning against the pick-up when Rab came down. The rain had already started. It was faint, tiny needles of wet on his face. John was holding a lit cigarette. He wasn't smoking it. "Don't do that again."

Rab took the cigarette from his hand and put it in his own mouth. John yanked it back out and threw it away in a wide arc. It fell at the school teacher's feet. She was herding the children back out again. She looked up at them, startled.

Rab's mouth tightened.

"Don't follow me around, don't tell me what to do, and don't *irritate* me." John split the irritate into hard, separate sounds.

The teacher watched them.

Rab pressed two fingers to John's mouth. "Not so loud."

John slapped his hand away. "Fuck you." But he had lowered his voice. The school teacher pretended she wasn't watching.

"You can't do this John." Rab moved his body round slightly, as if sheltering him from view. "You can't threaten him. You can't even *think* about threatening him. Tell me you don't think about it."

John just stared at him. The teacher made a show of quietening the children.

Rab moved a little closer. "Leave him alone John, he could make so much trouble."

"He doesn't even know what trouble is. They didn't teach it at the academy."

"He only wants to fuck him, for God's sake."

"*Only?*" John stared at him for a long moment then turned away savagely. "For your information he wants to live with him, fucking him's the least thing on the agenda."

The teacher was watching openly again.

"Danny won't go with him."

"I admire your confidence." John was still turned away from him.

"Leave him alone John," Rab pleaded.

"Fuck off."

Rab put his hand on John's face, pulled it round. "*Please.*"

John looked at him then dipped his face into Rab's palm, kissed it. The teacher's children had all gone but she didn't seem to notice. He turned his face away again. "Not even for you sweetheart."

Rab dropped his hand. "You're a stupid, pig-headed cunt. You're going to land the whole fucking lot of us in it."

"That's right." John turned back to him. He was smiling.

"Christ, I believe you'd like that, you really would."

John just kept on smiling. "Why don't you go home Rab and do a day's work for a change?" He pushed himself up off the pick-up.

Rab moved in front of him. "Where are you going?"

"Armstrong's, like the man said." He moved past him.

"See you make it there this time," Rab said to his back.

John swung back, grabbing his arm, almost wrenching it from its socket. "Get off my fucking back." It was a hiss. Then he smiled, broad, toothsome, terrifying. "Or I'll break you in half."

He threw Rab's arm back at him and climbed into the Rover. Rab watched him drive away. The school teacher watched Rab. He looked at her, slicked down the thighs of his jeans then gave her a big smile.

By the time he'd climbed into the pick-up and driven off she still hadn't realised she was standing there quite alone.

Danny woke up.

He felt someone sit down on the bed. The room was in deep gloom, the curtains drawn. "What time is it?" He fought to open his eyes.

"Eleven."

"Am or pm.?"

"Am."

There was something odd about the voice. He sat up on one elbow groggily. "John?" His head thumped.

"Ian."

Danny squinted at his shadowy shape, trying to make him out, then reached over and clicked on the light. "What do you want?"

"Charming. You could say hello."

"I could, but I don't think I'll bother." Danny pulled himself further up and reached over for a paper hankie. He blew his nose, wincing at the pain. It took him three blows to shift even a little of it. The hankie was full of a dark mess. He didn't look at it. Eventually he could breathe a little. His head thumped, but he could breathe.

"I heard you telling your big brother that he wants you to live with him."

Danny tried to think but he couldn't remember Ian being there. "Where were you?"

"Outside the door." Ian said it without blushing.

Danny wondered *which* door, but didn't disadvantage himself by asking, not Ian.

"Why don't you go?" Ian urged.

Danny looked at him.

"John couldn't touch you if you were with him. Automatic police protection. Why don't you go?" he said again.

"I don't know why you bother Ian, he doesn't even notice you."

Ian was instantly furious. "You greedy little bastard. Him, Rab, this policeman, you've got them all hot for you."

"Watch Ian, your envy's showing."

"You *greedy* little bastard."

Danny watched him curiously, wondering why he was winding himself up, then Ian dived at him, making a grab for his face. The pain reminded Danny of those dreams where you fall from a great height. He felt his stomach turn over. This nose was going to be broken even if God himself had to come down and do it.

Sheer resentment made him fight back. He felt the plasters on his chest catch on Ian's shirt as they grappled.

He succeeded finally in pinning Ian down. Ian was panting, staring up at him. Blood oozed from Danny's chest in a thin dark line. He felt it itch and burn, throbbing slightly.

He climbed off him shakily and got up off the bed. Ian just lay there watching him. Danny pulled the plasters off and went to the sink. He washed the blood away, dabbing at the cuts, trying to stem the flow. His nose had not bled again, but it throbbed viciously.

Ian went on lying there, watching him. When he spoke his voice was calm, easy, as if he were discussing the weather. "He keeps you marked. You realise that, don't you? He keeps you perpetually disfigured, one thing after another, nothing permanent, except that it's always there. He does everything he can short of maiming you and they're still queuing up. How does it feel to have indestructible beauty?"

"Like shit."

Ian looked at him, momentarily nonplussed. He swung up into a sitting position. "I don't believe you." He sounded as angry and hostile as a small boy being told that Santa Claus didn't really exist.

"Why don't you piss off?" Danny said wearily.

"I don't believe you. You love it. It's food and drink to you."

"Yeah." Danny's voice was flat.

Ian's face began to get worked up again. "Somebody fucked up when they gave you that angel's face, because inside you're as rotten and black as..." Ian stopped cold, his voice choked on his own fury. He looked at Danny leaning against the sink, just leaning there, his face disfigured, waiting for him to finish. He looked tired, bored, indifferent, and all the time even the way he stood was exquisite. He was a living cliché, the world's first Pre-Raphaelite farmhand. He was a joke in bad taste, an anachronism. Why was nobody laughing?

"You should look ugly," he said bitterly. "Your nose is broken. You're standing there tired and sweaty, your chest raw, your face a mess. Why don't you look ugly?"

Danny looked at him, startled out of his sick weariness by his vehemence. "I don't know," he said cautiously, listening to himself. "I didn't know I wasn't."

And Ian realised he meant it. He never even thought about being beautiful. He couldn't see it himself. Danny didn't care. Danny didn't care at all.

Ian stood up. "I wish you were dead."

Danny nodded.

"I really wish you were dead."

Danny nodded again. "I know you do."

And he said it as if he understood perfectly.

John came into the room seconds after. Danny was still standing at the sink.

"Don't tell me you're adding Ian to the list?" His voice was too casual. He walked past him and opened the curtains then looked at Danny's face. "What the fuck have you been doing?"

"Ian decided he wanted to have a go at winning the prize."

"What prize?"

"The prize for breaking my nose."

John grinned abruptly. "First Henderson, then Ian. What's this, the year the worm turns?" He stopped grinning. "What were you fighting about?"

"I wasn't fighting, *he* was fighting."

"What about?" He moved closer and circled Danny's wrist lightly with his fingers, keeping his eyes on his face.

"He's decided I'm too beautiful."

John took a step back without letting go his hold. "What *is* this Danny?"

"I'm telling you, he came in to beat me up because I'm too beautiful. It's a theory everybody has that if they hit me often enough I'll go away."

John yanked his arm. "I don't know where you picked this habit up, but drop it. When I ask you a question I expect an answer. What did he want?"

"*You.*"

John let him go.

Danny didn't look at him. At that precise moment he wanted to unwrite that one word more than he'd ever wanted anything in his life.

"Is this a change of subject or what?"

Danny didn't answer. He couldn't.

John turned away. He pushed his hands into his pockets. "In what way?" He kept his back to him, asking it like an examiner asking the key question, waiting for you to make a damning mistake.

Danny felt himself begin to sweat. At last God had sent his avenging angel - target, his nose.

"In what way Danny?" John demanded.

"I don't know." *Why am I risking my nose for Ian's sake?*

John turned and Danny saw that black and white face. John Stone, Man of Marble. He shook his head slowly. "Not with your face like that Danny. Don't be stupid."

He's right, don't be stupid Danny, not with your face like that. "Ask Ian," he said. *Good idea, let Ian fight his way out of it.*

John walked over to him. "I'm asking you." He started rubbing Danny's belly as if he was feeling for the softest part to hit, but his eyes were looking at his face, thinking about his nose.

Danny chewed his lip. He ran his hand through his hair. It was damp with sweat. He could smell himself, stale and afraid. "He wants me out of the way," he said quickly.

"You said that. Give me specifics."

"I don't know."

"Danny we're talking round this. Now I'm content to go round here all day but in the end..." John looked down at his feet. He looked back up as if he had reached a decision. *Ah, but you knew all along John, you don't fool me.* "...I'm going to mash your pretty nose right across your face."

"You've been up his fucking arse." Danny could hear his breath coming out fast. His stomach was filled with water. He was suddenly bursting for a pee.

"I've *what?*"

Danny nodded.

John shook his head. "I don't think so."

Danny shut his eyes. He felt suddenly limp with anger. His eyes flew open again. "No? Well, what about this? He's been fucking Rab right under your fucking nose, you conceited shit."

"*Rab?*"

"You heard me."

"He wouldn't."

"No? Maybe he doesn't love you as much as you like to think."

John ignored that, saying instead, "Why would he do something like that?"

"Because you're a crap fuck?"

John turned and sat down on the bed as if he was suddenly too heavy for himself. "So I'm a fully paid-up member of the I've-fucked-Ian team."

"Aren't you?" Danny's voice had little hard-baked edges.

John looked up. "The only thing I've ever wanted to do to Ian's arse is kick it."

"You said the same about Rab."

John cocked his head.

"You said it was finished with Rab," Danny insisted.

"And what makes you think it isn't?"

"All the eye-play last night."

"I'm surprised you can remember it."

"I remember enough."

"And what if we were?"

Danny looked away angrily, but didn't answer.

"What's it to you?"

Danny said nothing. How did he get started on this?

"Think you're in love with him? Or do you just like the way he wields his weapon?"

"I don't love anybody."

John looked at him. "No, you don't, do you? Now why is that?"

"I'm not queer." Danny's voice was tense, his face pink.

John stopped breathing. For a split second everything was still about him, then he laughed. "You think love comes with a set of instructions, an identikit picture? How the fuck would you know anyway? You can't even be sure you're *not* queer. After all, who

the hell have you ever fucked and meant it?"

"Oh, and you have?"

John looked at him for a moment. Then he smiled and reached out a hand and ran it over Danny's hair. "You're right. But what if I said I'd set my heart on who I wanted years ago and people like me don't change? The only way I could set myself free now is by dying. It's like that Shakespeare thing where they drop the potion in the lovers' eyes." He ran his hand over Danny's hair again. "You could have an asses' head and I'd still love you."

Danny turned his face away, straining against John's hands although he wasn't restraining him. "I don't know what the fuck you're on about."

John went on calmly, as if he hadn't spoken, "You really believe that if you lived my life it would cure you? You think because you can get hot over tits and cunt you're never going to itch to touch another cock?"

"I know it."

"Well, I've got news for you - it doesn't work."

"No? You keep trying."

There was a huge silence, everything falling into it. Danny waited for the blow, but it never came. Instead John said, "Jesus, I forget how young you are." He seemed to study Danny's face as if he'd never really seen it before, then his fingers brushed his cheek. "We've made you old before your time. Your head's still full of adolescent shit."

"I know what I want." But Danny was horrified to hear how uncertain his voice sounded.

"You don't even know yourself."

"And you do I suppose?"

John smiled. Danny wanted to hit him. More than he'd ever wanted anything in his life.

John turned away suddenly as if the subject bored him. "Get dressed. Our woman-on-the-spot's cleaning out the hen-house for us after lunch. Give her a hand."

He crossed over to the door. "But take it easy, we're planting Daddy tomorrow, all hands on deck." And he left.

THIRTY-FOUR

They shifted the rubble, the tree trunks, the dismantled silo, that had sat there for six years. They dug the hole. They stood in the rain and put planks down across the pit, then a thick sheet of chipboard.

That night, at exactly one am, John and Rab brought the body in the Range Rover and rolled it into the hole. It was already several inches deep in water. He splashed when he fell in. He lay face down in the muddy water, drowning all over again.

Rab shivered. John pulled the planking back and covered it over, then drove the excavator over the top, effectively sealing the hole.

They got into the Range Rover. John turned the engine on and gave Rab a cigarette.

"It scares the shit out of me, him lying there in that hole in the middle of the field for anyone to find," Rab said.

"It's only till tomorrow, and they'd have to move the digger off first, in the dark, on private land, in the rain." John looked out. "And the wind. Who gives a fuck? Not a bastard out there you can bet."

"She was wanting to know where he was today."

John looked at him. "Tell her to fuck off."

Rab laughed. "As an idea it's appealing but unrealistic."

"What did you tell her?"

"What you said. Away visiting."

"Yeah, Australia."

"It's not good enough John. I mean, Christ, who has he got to visit? What are we going to tell them?"

"Just keep telling them he's away, disappeared. It's none of their business."

"That's not going to stop them."

"You'd be surprised. If you tell them straight, looking them in the eye, they won't question anything. It's not the first time he's disappeared on a drunk. They don't care."

"Let's hope you're right."

"You know I am. You should drop the guilt, it doesn't suit you."

Rab swung on him. "I never killed him."

"That's what I mean."

Rab flushed and shut up.

John rolled down the window and threw the cigarette out into the rain. He closed it again. "His drinking was getting worse. All you've got to do is hint. People always want to believe the worst. With him it'll be easy, they'll enjoy it. Spread a little happiness, that's what I say."

Rab looked at him again. "Are you sure you didn't kill him?"

"Why should I?"

"Why should Danny?"

John looked at him curiously. "You really want to know that?"

Rab nodded and threw away John's cigarette. He felt his pockets for his tin and started rolling one of his own. He needed it, his heart was thumping uncomfortably.

John watched him for a moment or two then said, "The old man was after him."

"After him?" Rab could feel his throat dry up, but he looked up and held his gaze.

John fixed his eyes on him, gauging his thoughts. "I warned you."

"Yeah but..." Rab stopped rolling, the whole confection held delicately between his fingertips. "Well, he never *did* anything."

"No?" John paused, smiled. "Maybe he only took you on because he got stuck at incest." He seemed to find the idea amusing.

Rab swallowed. "How do you know for sure? Danny tell you?" He began rolling again. It wasn't easy.

"You're joking." John's voice was dry. "No, I found a stash of dirty photographs."

"Photographs?"

"You're beginning to sound like a parrot. Yes, photographs, of Danny, taken over the years. He must have been going into his room and photographing him while he was asleep."

"I don't believe that - no way."

"Well, maybe you should. Looking was always alright, so why should a few lousy photographs bother him? Maybe he got drunk and horny looking at them and came chasing after you."

Rab said, "Look, nothing happened... I was a kid... you always dramatise everything at that age." He paused then said quickly before John could question him, "He did ask me once what he looked like naked, just a few weeks ago, but he was blotto."

"Who?"

"That's what I said, but if he was talking about Danny then he already knew what he looked like naked."

John smiled. "Maybe he meant slick and naked, up and ready for it, eyes open and begging. He must've thought you knew."

"Don't overdo it."

"Well, you do know, don't you?"

"So do you."

"Then we're quits."

There was a silence.

"So what did you do when you found out?" Rab asked.

"Do? What was there to do?" John smiled to himself. If it was possible for a smile to look forcedly vindictive that one did. "I took the best photographs for myself, of course."

"You're sick."

John's smile was twisted. "Not as sick as his mother. She kept one in her handbag."

Rab looked at him. "Oh, you *are* kidding."

"You're too squeamish Rab. For someone that's fucked every bastard in the house you're much too squeamish." Rab didn't like the sound of his voice. There was more. This was just the warm up. He took a drag on his cigarette and waited. "For someone who can let Ian crawl all over him you're *much* too squeamish."

Rab looked out the window. "Who told you?"

"I hardly needed to be told, but Danny as it so happens."

"Thank you Danny."

"Right, it's not your fault for fucking the little weasel in the first place. What was it? Another little 'sacrifice' to rub in Danny's face?"

Rab screwed his eyes up tight and ran both hands across his hair, the palms dragging on it. His cigarette stuck out his face like a pin. "Oh shut up." He spoke round it, weary, angry, thoroughly fucking fed up. "Let's get out this fucking field before he climbs back out and gets us."

John reached over and turned on the ignition key for him again. "Such a guilty conscience."

They were half-way home before John spoke again. "I haven't seen Our Man at the Yard recently."

"He'll be on night duty. You'll see him soon enough."

"You think so?"

"I know so."

"Maybe he thinks I make empty threats."

"No, he just doesn't think, period."

"Maybe he needs convinced."

Rab stopped the car. He stopped it slowly and carefully because otherwise he'd have crashed it. "John, what do I have to do to convince you to leave him alone?"

"How about a little of what Ian gets?"

Rab waited a second or two because he wasn't really catching this. "Am I understanding you correctly?"

"If you understand that you take Danny's place in my bed when he's with Henderson then you're right on cue."

"Fully interchangeable fucks."

"You're the one telling me to leave Henderson alone, the least you can do is compensate me for the loss."

"Of Danny?"

"No, of kicking that greasy little fucker's head in."

"Let me think."

"Take all night."

Rab sat for a moment, hands braced on the steering wheel. The engine ticked over, cars passed them, the wipers swished, the heater cut out on its thermostat. There was a neat-stitched silence. He filled it. "I come to you when Danny's with him and you don't upset the apple-cart."

"That's right."

"That simple?"

"That simple."

"Why after all those dramatics do you change your mind?"

"I haven't changed it, I've just made it up."

"To go with the tide?"

"That's right."

"It doesn't wear very well."

"Shame."

"You won't tell Danny?"

"He thinks we're doing it already."

"But you won't say anything?"

"Of course not."

Rab looked at him. "Oh do me a favour, there's no 'of course' with you. You lie like other people eat."

"Then why ask me?"

Rab breathed out, said nothing.

"Well, is it a deal? You fuck me and I won't fuck with him." John's hand came round his thigh. There was some more silence. "You *do* like the way I touch you, don't you?" He said it with a kind of satisfied amusement.

Rab said nothing.

"Come on, be honest, I didn't dream it, did I? You *do* like it."

Rab made a defeated noise in this throat.

"Oh boy," John said. "It's my lucky night."

Rab said uncomfortably, "You were the first. You were bound to influence my tastes."

"Oh boy," John said again. "You're going to enjoy this 'sacrifice' then, aren't you?"

"Christ." Rab pushed his hand off. "Can't you leave anything alone? You've always

got to rip it open to see how it works."

"Oh don't cry Robbie, you're too old for romance."

Rab slammed the car into gear and shot forward. A passing car screamed at him.

John laughed. "You'll die young, just don't take me with you."

"When I go, you go, you ugly bastard."

John laughed again. "A man after my own heart."

Rab pressed down on the accelerator and shut him up.

Ian was in the kitchen when they went in. His turn to wash up.

"Where's Danny?" John asked.

"Living room." He kept his back to them. Rab wondered if John had already started on him. *Look out Ian, you're on the list. Any more deaths John and the whole house of cards comes down.*

Rab went out into the hall and heard John talking. He was standing in the living room doorway. "Hello baby, miss me?" There was a pause then his voice deepened a little, lost its sarcastic edge. "There's enough hot water for a bath, if you want one."

Rab had heard this before, in that same slick tone. He could almost imagine that 'bath'. He had never followed them upstairs, but he doubted if Danny was in the bathroom and John in his room.

Danny came out and caught his eye. His face was still a mess. The swelling was down a little, but it was turning some spectacular colours.

He walked past them and went upstairs. John followed. Rab stood there and listened. Only one door shut. He wanted to go up and listen, but he didn't want to hear. He put one foot on the stair then turned back quickly and went to talk to Ian.

John turned on the taps and said over his shoulder, "Go take a pee."

"I've just been."

"Well go again."

Danny did as he was told, and a fat lot of pleasure that dribble might bring the perverted bastard. He flushed the toilet, crossed over to the bath.

John straightened up, slid his hand inside his fly and felt the head of his penis briefly, almost clinically, as if he was checking to make sure he'd actually urinated. He withdrew his hand and began undressing him. He did it meticulously, tugging off each garment carefully and folding it over the chair. When Danny was naked he ran his hands down his flanks once, like someone checking a horse. Danny fought an urge to whinny.

John turned the taps off, feeling the water carefully, adding a little more cold. "In you get."

Danny climbed in and stood there.

"Turn round."

Danny turned to face the wall. John began washing his legs, slowly and methodically. He talked as he washed. He washed Danny's buttocks almost perfunctorily, then his back, his arms, his shoulders. "Turn round."

Danny turned again. He was half-erect. When John bent to wash the fronts of his legs he was almost face to face with it. Danny looked down at him, washing round it, never touching it, the hands dark and rough on his skin. He became fully erect.

John picked the jug up and began pouring water down his body, sluicing the soap off. It was an old ritual. Danny had just got taller, stronger. Suddenly he wanted to blow it apart, make him admit what was going on. He said, "Wash my dick."

John paused, surprised. He looked up.

Danny nodded. "Go on then."

John did it, no comment. It stung like hell.

John rinsed him down, leaving his penis peeled back because it was too distended to ease the skin down again. "Get down so I can wash your hair," he said as if nothing had happened, but his voice was thick, and he wasn't looking at him.

Danny knelt down in the water. John pulled out the plug. He used the taps, filling each jugful and testing it before using it. Gradually the bath water drained away. Danny couldn't see it - his eyes were closed tight against the suds - but he could feel his skin cooling like a slow unveiling. He could feel his cock emerge, then his calves, his feet.

John finished rinsing his hair. "Up you get." His voice hadn't lightened any.

Danny stood up again and was given a final rinse with clean water. John got a towel and began drying him, following exactly the same pattern as before, finishing between his legs. He wrapped the up-curve of his penis in a handful of towel and slid it up gently, this time managing to ease the foreskin up.

Danny made a little grunting noise.

John only hesitated for a second then succumbed to doing it again. Danny watched him. That was a mistake. He stopped John's hand before he could do it a third time. "I wouldn't," he said.

John looked up at him, marvelling at his voice, always somehow that bit deeper. His face pulped and yet still conveying that same erotic corruption.

John let go. Danny climbed out beside him and dropped his head, waiting compliantly. John began drying his hair. Danny watched his own cock as it swayed in front of him, occasionally brushing John's body with the vigour of his movements. He could see John's erection through his trousers, inches away from his own. He reached out and touched it, tracing it lightly, not caring what he thought.

John stopped rubbing his hair. "My, my, I *am* privileged tonight." It was supposed to sound facetious, but it didn't come out quite right.

Danny pulled the zip down.

"Better and better," John said and this time it came out worse, sounded as if he meant it.

Danny took his penis out and held it, feeling the heat and size of it.

"Somebody wants it tonight. Not afraid that makes you a queer?"

Danny ignored him, felt it with both hands, then pulled him closer and pressed his own against the length of it.

"When you've got your dick in your hand nothing else worries you, does it?" John's voice was still low and thick.

Danny went on sliding one against the other.

John bent his head and kissed his hair, tasted the wet cleanness of it. He took a strand into his mouth and sucked the water from it. He slid his hands under the towel and felt Danny's shoulders. He let the hair run out between his teeth. "When you've got your dick in your hand you can't even *think* about anything else, can you?"

Danny finally looked up, coming out from under the towel. A slow smile moved across his mouth, the only part of his face that seemed untouched. "Why don't you shut up John?" His voice was deep, velvet, *corrupt*. That word kept coming up. There was no other that could describe him. *Too old, too fast. He sees everything the wrong way round.*

John looked into the green eyes. "Rab says I look like you."

Danny looked back at him, but kept his hands moving out of sight, coupling them, pressing them tightly together like obscene Siamese twins.

"It doesn't surprise you?" John asked when he didn't answer.

Danny kept watching him, holding them tightly together in an unbreakable grip

somewhere miles below.

"It doesn't outrage you, beautiful as you are, to be compared to me?"

Danny finally shook his head.

"Why not?" John could feel his heart race. Already he was too close.

"Because you're beautiful too."

John tried to speak, caught Danny's hand, stopped him. The spasm subsided. Danny still held his eyes.

"You're taking the piss, I'm not beautiful." John's voice was cracked.

"If you say so." Danny began squeezing again.

"*Danny...*" It came out on a gasp.

There was a breath-held pause. Danny was still looking into his eyes. "I'm listening," he prompted.

"Say you love me."

Danny's smile stayed where it was, but this time his eyes dropped. *Secretive, always fucking secretive.* John felt a spurt of anger. "Say it." His voice was hard.

Danny looked up again. His mouth was fixed in an unpleasant smile. There was nothing but contempt in his voice. "I love you." And yet, somehow when he said the words they sounded so real, so heartfelt, his voice suggesting one thing, the words another. John felt his skin crawl.

Danny was squeezing their glandes together insistently, his head dropped again, his throat working as if he was dry-swallowing, his lips parted in concentration... or excitement.

John gave into it, and caught his mouth to his with a swift dive, like a striking bird. They were held like that for a moment, connected at two points, then John broke free again. He wanted to hear it again, a poor man's meal, slops and dirty water. "Say it again."

Danny didn't hesitate. "I love you." His hand gripped him with a sudden convulsive movement. John's eyes opened in a start of surprise, then closed quickly like someone trying to cheat pain or death. He caught Danny's head, thrusting his cock suddenly against his.

"I love you," Danny whispered again and suddenly John was sending it shooting up over his belly.

"Danny," he grunted. "Oh Jesus, Danny...." He dropped his head onto Danny's shoulder.

Danny smiled beyond him into space. He was thinking about nothing.

Nothing at all.

THIRTY-FIVE

They didn't see Henderson until the end of the week. The old man had been duly covered in eight feet of rubble and dirt. He had been smoothed down, ploughed and planted. John remarked that he'd finally got what he wanted - Danny had just ploughed his arse. Rab tried not to laugh.

Rab began to feel that he and John had never had the conversation about Henderson, sealed the deal. Outwardly nothing had changed. Every night John took Danny to bed and Rab sat up alone, downstairs, where he couldn't hear. Danny's face began to look vaguely like Danny's face again.

And the rain went on.

And on.

And then Henderson turned up on Friday night at nine o'clock. He was lucky because John was just on the point of going up to bed. Rab wondered how he would've reacted to having Danny physically removed from his arms.

The three of them were sitting in the living room. John and Danny on the couch, Rab in Margaret's armchair.

Fifteen minutes before Rab had seen John's hand move onto Danny's leg. Danny had slid down slightly to meet it. It lay there, curved round his thigh, a bare inch away from the softness of his crotch. Occasionally the thumb would rasp on the fabric, back and forth, back and forth. Rab watched the TV, trying not to watch the hand.

Danny lay there, eyes half-closed, and let John touch him.

Eventually John stood up and stretched, arms high above his head. Danny did not move. Danny never did. He was like a well-trained dog, or a disobedient one. Rab never knew which.

"Bed," John said, and just then the car horn sounded outside.

It was Rab who sat up, but John who dropped his arms saying, "Who's that?"

Rab lifted his head towards the window.

John went over and looked out between the curtains. "The boys in blue." His voice was muffled behind the fabric. He came back in. "Your lover has returned Daniel, giving you just enough time to heal your wounds."

Danny had shifted imperceptibly with John's rising. Now he got up in one fluid movement. He went out without speaking.

They could hear him moving around in the kitchen, then the back door closed. John stared at the fire. "You look." His face was drawn.

"Harder than you thought?"

"Just look, fuck you."

Rab looked out the window. He saw Danny, still adjusting the collar of his jacket, come down the lane. He looked carefully before crossing the road. He went round the car and climbed in. He never looked up at the house.

Rab closed the curtains again, not waiting to see the car pull away with all Henderson's precious caution.

"Well?" John demanded.

"Well what?"

John laughed suddenly, pressing his hand on the cushion. "I don't know."

Rab stood in front of the fire, watching him.

"Turn that fucking thing off." John was staring at his knees.

Rab turned the television off. Sound and light went together. Suddenly they could hear the clock ticking in the hall. John's voice startled him when he spoke. "He does

it all so smoothly. Nothing sweats him."

"Danny?" Rab asked confusedly.

John didn't answer that. "He doesn't register surprise, anger, not even pleasure. He's like a fucking robot." His voice was hard, despairing. "I don't think he feels anything at all, except lust and fear. Lust when I fuck him and fear when I hit him." He stopped suddenly and looked up at him. "How about you?"

"I don't get anything at all, remember?"

John laughed. "Poor soul, what *did* you get?"

"Why the fuck should I tell you?"

John smiled at him bitterly. "Think of the kick you'll get gloating over me."

"I've nothing to gloat about."

"You sound bitter."

"Then that's two of us."

John's eyes searched his face. "You want him to *love* you." The 'love' was sarcastic.

"So do you," Rab snapped.

"Yeah, like wanting to win the pools." He seemed to consider a moment. "The odds are probably higher on the pools."

Rab turned his back on him and stared into the fire.

John's voice cut into his thoughts. "Are you looking forward to it?"

Rab looked at him blankly.

"Making it with me."

"Jesus John, you've got some technique."

John laughed. "God, look at him, he's blushing. You're the only person I know who fucks anything that moves and still suffers from a becoming modesty."

Rab's mouth twisted in irritation, but he held his tongue.

"In my bed, all night." John drew the 'all' out long. "I like it."

Rab looked up at him, startled. "In your bed?"

"Well, I'm not fucking doing it in yours, I need room."

"But what if Danny comes back?"

"Then he'll get a surprise."

"No way," Rab said vehemently.

John sighed abruptly, his mouth straightening. "You're being tiresome. The deal was you take his place in my bed. You're going to *be* in my bed."

Rab stared at him angrily. "You're doing this deliberately."

"It makes it taste better."

"Christ, your mind's got more twists than a basket full of snakes. You want him to catch us."

"Could feel really nice."

"Not for me."

John licked his lip, studying his foot, swinging it slowly. "Who gives a fuck about you?"

Rab's anger felt like nausea. "You never miss a trick. Every single time you exact your revenge, another pound of flesh. It always has to hurt somebody. It's what you live for. It's your single, solitary impulse."

John raised his eyebrows mockingly. "A closet psychoanalyst."

"Better than a closet sadist."

"Oh, not in the closet, not that."

"You make me sick."

"So you've said."

"Why shouldn't I leave you to go to hell in your own way?"

"Because you're too *noble*."

Rab ignored the sarcasm. "Do you know what the truth sounds like John?"

That brought a big grin. He stood up. "Time we were going." He jerked his head at the door. "You go first, I like to watch your arse going up the stairs."

"You're a cunt."

"I love you too." And he slapped Rab's backside to get him moving.

Henderson shot him a surreptitious glance. It was difficult to tell in the dark, but his face looked better than he would have expected. "Your brother said it was broken."

Danny looked at him quickly. "John?"

"He paid me a social call, threatening to kill me."

Danny laughed. "I wonder why he changed his mind?" He seemed to give it serious thought then said, "It isn't broken."

Henderson looked at him. "You don't like him much, do you?"

"He's my brother."

Henderson wasn't sure how to go from there. During the long week away from him he'd had plenty of time to think about their last conversation and he had begun to wonder if he really was hooked on him in some perverse way.

His hand brushed against Danny's thigh as he changed gear. It felt hard and taut under the fabric. He glanced down. Danny's hands lay loosely linked in his lap, cradling his balls. It made his mouth go dry.

He looked out the windscreen and put on his indicators. The rain had settled into a steady vertical downpour. It came straight from the skies in a drop. It seemed to hang around the lamps like a thick mist.

Danny was waiting patiently for him in the doorway after he had put the Mercedes in the garage.

Henderson was dressed in maroon and black with some kind of overgrown anorak that looked as if it belonged on the ski slopes. He was watching Danny, the rain sparkling on his hair.

"We going in?" Danny asked.

"You look lovely."

Danny looked out into the rain, his irritation palpable.

Henderson opened the door and Danny walked in ahead of him. They passed the two sisters on the stairs. Henderson saw the odd look they gave Danny and then him. What was biting them? When they got to the door he saw Danny was smirking. "What's so funny?"

"Nothing."

"What happened the day they let you in?"

Danny smiled. "They caught Rab and me kissing in the doorway."

Henderson felt a flush of excitement, rapidly followed by a mixture of jealousy and irritation. "Christ, that's all I need."

"Why? It wasn't you they saw."

"They'll still wonder." Henderson opened the door. "No, correction, they'll assume."

"Fuck them." Danny went in.

"No thanks."

The door closed behind them.

The living room looked the same. Henderson put the lights on low. Danny could see him reflected in the window, moving behind him in the hall. He sat down and took his shoes off, then, on impulse, his socks. He curled his toes in the carpet.

Henderson came in and closed the door, smiling at him. "Feel good?"

Danny nodded then asked, "Ever fucked on it?" He enjoyed watching Henderson blush.

"No."

Danny didn't say anything else.

Henderson did what he always did and went into the kitchen to get drinks. Danny wondered if he could do it sober, if he would be different. He followed him into the kitchen.

Henderson could feel him watching him. He'd sat down on the small kitchen table and was watching his every move. Finally he gave in. "What is it?"

"What?"

Henderson turned to look at him. "Why are you sitting staring at me like that?" He handed him a drink.

Danny put it down behind him untasted. Henderson was already knocking his back. Danny pulled his sweater off and put it on the chair.

Henderson took another drink, watching him.

Danny undid his belt and pulled his T-shirt out then pulled it off too. He smiled.

Henderson looked at the tight muscles, the narrow wiry chest, the flat white stomach, the tiny dark nipples.

Danny undid his trousers completely then picked up his drink. He held it between his legs, watching him. Henderson put one hand in his pocket nervously. Danny saw the surreptitious adjustment he made.

Henderson took another drink. The glass was almost empty already. "You're not very subtle."

"Who needs it?"

"I do." He lifted the glass, drained it. He went to pour himself another.

"Try it without it."

"I can't." Henderson wouldn't look at him.

"How d'you know till you try?"

Henderson put his glass down slowly and turned to him. Danny was still smiling at him, his face full of lascivious invitation, his own particular brand. "Come on."

Henderson came over, stood in front of him.

"Closer."

Henderson moved up till his thighs were between Danny's legs, against the table.

"Go on then."

Henderson looked at him.

"Do what you want." Danny's voice was low. "Everybody *wants* something, just do what you want."

Henderson bent stiffly and kissed him. It was small-mouthed and dry, but Danny could feel the excitement in it. He kissed him carefully, precisely, like he drove his car. Danny felt the moustache, strange and coarse against his mouth. He could smell his aftershave, feel the rasp of his heavy facial shadow. Henderson had his own brand of excitement. Everybody brought their own, flavoured to taste.

Henderson kissed him again, this time holding his shoulders, pressing his mouth more firmly. Danny moved his head slightly, keeping his nose out of the way. He felt Henderson's hands slide fractionally as he pulled him nearer. Danny slid obligingly forward. But not too close. No need to make it easy for him.

Henderson slid one hand down his arm and then his thumb slid into his armpit. His breathing changed as he felt inside. He slid the other hand down quickly and felt the other armpit.

Danny smiled and Henderson kissed his mouth again. This time his tongue pushed in. Danny pulled his head free with a jerk. Henderson's hands came down over his chest and stomach, quickly and incisively. He pushed both hands inside Danny's

shorts.

Danny felt them plunder everything, quickly, exhaustively. It felt like he had six pairs.

Henderson pulled him closer, burying his face in his hair, breathing him in. "I love the smell of you."

Danny laughed. "Shit?"

Henderson laughed too, breathlessly. "Shit and shampoo. It makes me feel drunk." He kissed Danny's face, lightly at first, and then more urgently.

Danny timed him. *Any minute now*. Henderson clung to him, then began kissing his throat. *Now*, Danny thought.

"Touch me," Henderson said. It was charged with urgency.

Danny laughed softly. "Had to wait a long time, haven't you?"

"Please."

Danny put his hand out and unzipped his trousers. He could see the maroon underpants, the thick black hair. He put his hand in and felt the hand-stretching thickness of him. He took him out, feeling the stickiness, smelling the different smell.

Henderson groaned seriously.

"You have waited too long, haven't you?" Danny smiled at him. "You might as well get it over with. You aren't going to last anyway."

Henderson swallowed convulsively, not disagreeing.

"Let's have it quick and hard." Danny held him lightly, squeezing infrequently, not using any friction. "Want to touch my hair?" He smiled as he felt Henderson's cock swell further. "Why don't you kiss me?"

Henderson gave him small tight kisses. Danny kept his mouth closed, not kissing him back, frustrating him. He began to rub Henderson's cock lightly. He could feel him tightening with it, but knew it wasn't enough to bring him off. The kisses were just making him hotter. He was thrusting, trying to relieve himself, trying to make Danny kiss him back. His hands were tangled in Danny's hair.

Suddenly Danny pressed his mouth to his, holding it. He began to masturbate him in earnest. Henderson moaned, pushing frantically into Danny's hand, then Danny pushed his tongue in his mouth. It felt to Henderson as if it went, hot and probing, right down his throat. It filled him with an intense excited revulsion. It blew every ounce of self-control he had. He didn't even need to move.

He grunted once then it was boiling out over Danny's hand. Henderson heard himself moaning, felt the hot liquid splash on his stomach. His legs buckled beneath him, and still Danny kept digging down into his body and dragging more out of him than Henderson would have thought possible.

It was then he knew one single thing for an absolute truth. He had strived his entire life to reach this moment.

And he would probably spend the rest of it trying to reach it again.

John didn't lock the door. Rab looked at him but said nothing. It was a long time since he had seen the room lit like this, just with the lamps. He felt a growing excitement in his stomach that horrified him. He tried to damp it down, thought about Danny, but that only made it worse. In the half-light John seemed to resemble him at every turn.

John nodded at the left-hand side of the bed. "That's his side. You can probably smell him off the sheets."

"Jesus," Rab said, his mouth twisting in disgust, but he said nothing more.

"Take your clothes off."

"You're going to watch, right?"

"Right."

"How did I guess?"

John sat and watched him until he was naked.

"Can I get into bed now?" Rab said.

"Untie your hair first."

Rab reached back and untied his hair. He saw John look at his armpits and realised why he'd asked him to do it.

"I love your stripe, right up your belly. Makes me stiff."

"Oh goody."

John got up. Rab climbed into Danny's side and buried his face in the pillow.

"Not going to watch?"

"Fuck off," Rab said, then he realised he *could* smell him. He found himself inhaling deeply, sick with longing. It was instant, irrefutable. He wondered where it had come from with such force. He felt John get in beside him.

John pulled him round onto his back and leaned over him. His face was cavernously broad and ugly, sculpted by the light into blanks and shadows. He kissed him. It was intense, silent. It was like being ravaged. He seemed to put whole speeches into it, a day's worth of feelings, maybe a lifetime's. Rab didn't kiss him back, didn't do anything, because what he did didn't matter, this was John's show.

When he stopped it was sudden. He rolled off and lay on his back, breathing heavily. Rab lay by his side, vast with excitement, his head obliterated. He was thinking nothing, feeling everything.

Eventually John got up and straddled his body, still in deadly silence. He climbed right up the bed until he was above Rab's face, dangling it there, letting him see. He was a huge, ugly bastard, scaled-up, Neanderthal, too big to be beautiful. But here where it mattered, when all the clothes were off, the disguises, he wiped the floor with everybody. He was magnificent.

He peeled his cock back slowly, as if to say, Look, better than you remembered, the new improved model.

Rab moistened his lips. His voice seemed to bring everything in the room into focus. "It was meant for fucking women."

"Yep." John was sliding it up and down slowly, watching Rab watching it.

"And that's the closest you'll ever get to admitting it, isn't it? So what about now? Danny taking up all your time now?"

"Could be..."

"Oh come on John, I'm not stupid, I know what went on behind my back. You telling me he's reformed you? Has he?" he asked abruptly, as if it had really only just occurred to him. He moistened his mouth again and went on quickly, not giving John the chance to answer, "You know, you were always so hot for it I even half-expected you to try it on with Margaret."

"Maybe I did."

Rab kept his eyes on his penis, forcing himself to watch it. It would have been easy at any other time. "Did you?"

"You mean did I try it on with my own mother? Still looking for motives Doctor Freud?"

Rab flushed, looking up quickly, then back down between his legs.

John peeled it back down again. Rab watched the eye ooze as he squeezed it back up. He obviously wasn't going to say anything else so Rab filled the silence. "I caught her watching you once."

John's hand stopped. Rab spoke quickly, keeping his eyes down between John's legs. "You were working in the back pasture. She must have come down to see the old man and you were taking a pee rather than walk a hundred and fifty yards to the

toilet. I had come out the barn behind her. I was just about to speak to her when I realised she was watching you. She turned and saw me. Her face was a study." Rab paused. "I bet she fucked like a rabbit that week. I bet she got off thinking about you." He looked up at him, couldn't resist it.

"What planet are you on?" John smiled fleetingly, but the smile was too quick for Rab to understand. Rab didn't try to hide his surprise.

"Are you saying that does nothing for you?"

"Nope."

"It's a waste." Rab watched him intently as he said it.

"Why? You're getting it."

"I always felt you fancied her."

"Nope." John was masturbating again, unchanging in his pace. It drew Rab's eyes back remorselessly.

"Never wanted her, not even a little?" he asked.

"What d'you expect me to say, you sick bastard?"

Rab was silent. He flicked his tongue out suddenly and licked the tip of John's penis, then dropped his head back again as if he were exhausted.

John smiled slowly and kept his hand working.

"I always thought..." Rab was looking at him again. "I thought... well, you were always going on about her, even in the middle of it sometimes. I was sure you were getting off on it."

"Does it matter?"

"Never worry that you're queer? I mean, you and Danny..."

"Does it matter?" John said again, a little meaninglessly.

"The old man was. And Ian probably is," Rab persisted.

"No probably about it, runs in the family, that what you're driving at?"

"If I was?" Rab was watching him closely now. "Danny might be. Think he is?"

"You sound as if it would please you if he was. Would it please you?"

"No."

John stopped for a second. He brushed Rab's hair back off his face with his fingertips, then he started again. "It would only satisfy you if he loved you *and* he was queer. That's a bit greedy, isn't it?"

Rab watched the rhythm of his hand, perfect, relentless. He seemed completely unexcited. Only the tense line of his muscles, the grip of his hand, betrayed him.

"What about you, you're not greedy?"

"I want him just as he is."

Rab looked up at him quickly. "That's a lie. You can't handle how he is at all. The way he really is breaks you up."

"And you." John's voice was hard.

A hit, a palpable hit. Rab went limp.

John was watching him with a strange intentness now. His hand was slower. He cradled his balls with his other hand, spreading his legs a little wider, bringing his cock a little closer. "What if I was to tell you what I do to him?"

Rab said immediately, "I don't want to hear."

"Like hell you don't. That's what this is all about. You want the low down on how I kiss him, fuck him, *finger* him. Just in case he's getting more than you."

"Shut up."

"How I fill that tight arse right up."

Rab looked at him. "You don't."

John smiled. "Oh no?"

"You don't."

"No? I used to fill yours alright. Just because Danny tells you I don't doesn't mean

237

I don't."

"You're a lying cunt."

"Is that all?" John's hand was slower than ever, but painfully hard, punishing himself.

"A fucking lying cunt."

Rab saw him hold it tight for a second, then the hand cradling his balls came into Rab's hair, tangling in it. He dropped lower, spreading his legs still wider. His cock looked inflated so close to Rab's face. His balls brushed Rab's chin when he moved. "Say that again."

"With pleasure. You're a fucking lying cunt."

His hand tightened in Rab's hair. Rab looked at his face and realised too late what he was doing.

"Again."

Rab closed his mouth tight, shook his head against the pull of his hand.

"Oh Rab, you've got a mean spirit." John whispered the words out. His hand was still moving, but it was getting faster, lighter. "I'm going to shoot my load in your face about now."

"You dirty bastard."

"That's it, get it out your system."

Rab shut up, bottled down his anger.

"Think about what I do to your baby cousin. You haven't heard the latest." The words were coming out fast and breathy, the hand slicking. "I actually cut him open with a knife."

Rab tensed.

"I made this neat little hole in his chest then I sucked his blood..." He closed his eyes briefly. He was breathing through his mouth. He opened his eyes again, looking straight into Rab's face. "That's got to make you jealous. "

"You're an ugly bastard." Rab's voice was low, intense. "Inside and out."

John was smirking, infuriating him. Rab wriggled suddenly, trying to free himself, but John's weight came down on him, his cock shoved into his face, the hand gripping his hair. "God, that feels good."

He was grinding it down, sticky against his eyelids, against his cheek. When Rab turned his face aside he rubbed it in his hair. *Henderson would love this. He'd really flip over this one.*

"Come on Robbie, say it."

"Fuck off."

"Say you hate me. Let it all hang out." He pushed himself hard against Rab's mouth. Rab could taste it, oily and salt. He let it push into his mouth, then sank his teeth into it.

John slapped him immediately, like a man smacking a dog to make it drop a stick. He was smiling, almost like he'd been waiting for it. Rab wondered if he'd even felt the bite at all.

He soothed his cock, feathering it where Rab had bitten it, stroking it delicately. He was almost purring. "That was satisfying..." He was brushing it with his fingertips. "Surprisingly..." The first spurt caught Rab by surprise. He felt a splash on his face, blinked stupidly. John said, "Deliciously..." and Rab felt more land on his mouth. John's face was rapt. He wasn't looking at himself or Rab. His eyes were glazed. "*Satisfying*..." And Rab felt another gob of it hit him.

He swore violently, finally giving voice to his outrage. But John didn't hear him.

John wasn't listening.

John wasn't even there.

Danny was lying in the bed watching Henderson hang clothes on a hanger. Henderson always hung up his clothes.

Danny could see himself in the mirrored wall that was the wardrobe. Henderson was wearing the paisley dressing-gown. Danny was wearing nothing. He looked incredibly white against the black sheets. He hated Henderson's bedroom. He hated the sheets most of all. "It's my birthday soon," he said.

Henderson looked up at his reflection. "When?"

"Halloween."

Henderson smiled. "Seriously?"

"Seriously."

Henderson finished with his clothes and closed the door. "Why don't you lie down properly? You look very uncomfortable."

"I hate lying on wet hair."

Henderson sat down beside him. Danny let him get involved then said, "Do I get a present?"

Henderson looked up quickly, but Danny was smiling. "What d'you want?"

"If I don't want money?"

"What?"

"Never mind." Danny looked at himself in the mirror, wondering who the fuck he was. "I'd like to meet your wife," he said to his reflection. He saw Henderson's back straighten up.

"How d'you know about my wife? Did Blondie tell you?"

Danny looked at him. "Rab? No, you told me yourself. You said you were married."

"But I don't live with her."

Danny smiled. "I guessed as much." He made himself more comfortable. "I thought you were lying to me, then I saw her photo in your wallet. It is her, isn't it?"

"When did you see in my wallet?"

"Last time I was here. You left it on the bedside table."

"Do you always look in people's private property?"

"Only when I think they might have secrets."

Henderson got up abruptly and leaned his backside on the chest of drawers. He watched Danny intently. "Why d'you want to meet her?"

"I don't meet many women."

"How many's many?"

"Alright, at the moment I don't meet any."

"I'm not running a dating agency." Henderson's voice was ratty.

Danny sat up, hugging his knees with his arms. "I'm not asking you to make a date."

Henderson got up and paced past the bottom of the bed. "And how would I explain you to her?"

"What's to explain? I'm a friend. She must have met friends of yours before."

Henderson stopped. "I haven't *made* friends before."

"Well now you have." Danny watched him pacing. "What's up, does she suspect you're queer?"

"No." Henderson's face was flushed.

Danny smiled at his feet. No denials this time. "Well then, what's the problem?"

Henderson sat on the bottom of the bed. "I don't trust you, that's the problem."

Danny looked past him into the mirror. "Don't trust me to do what?"

"I don't trust what you want."

"I only want to meet her."

"Why?"

239

"I told you. I haven't changed my reasons since then."

Henderson watched him for a moment, his hands picking at the quilt, then said, "And what if I say no?"

Danny looked at him. "There's nothing I can do."

"But?"

"No buts."

"Oh come on, be honest, let's hear the but."

"No buts."

Henderson got up again. "She's due back in ten days."

"Due back?"

"She's in the States, visiting relatives."

Danny nodded.

"She'll be here for two or three days."

"Staying here?" Danny asked.

"Yes." Henderson was looking at him.

"She sleep with you?"

He nodded, almost reluctantly.

Danny smiled. Henderson could feel it crawling over his skin. "She's in for a disappointment then, isn't she?"

"And what the hell's that supposed to mean?"

Danny just kept smiling.

"You're a sadistic little bastard."

Danny shrugged.

Henderson got up suddenly and banged his fist on the wardrobe door. The mirror bent under the impact, sending the room and Danny into a shimmer, then it was still again. Henderson glared at him without speaking. Danny turned on his stomach, bunching the pillow under his head.

Henderson looked at the long white line of him, the dark blood-red hair. He looked like an alabaster sculpture. Henderson had never seen anyone that colour before. He doubted if he ever would again.

Danny felt his hand move down his back and come to rest on his buttock.

"Okay."

Danny smiled quietly into the pillow.

"Since it's your birthday." And Henderson buried his face in his back.

"He even looks good taking a piss."

Rab shifted in the dark. He could make out John's features as vague areas of light and dark. "I thought you were asleep."

"Well, you were wrong."

"You watch him taking a *piss?*"

"Mm."

"Aren't you a bit old for that kind of game?"

"You're never too old. You should try it."

"No thanks."

"It's good."

"No, I'm past that."

"Watch him and see, you might not be as far past it as you think. People never are."

Rab put his hands under his head. "Is this why you wanted me here, so we can talk about Danny, compare notes?"

"No, it was to fuck. You want to fuck?"

"No, let's talk about Danny."

John laughed. Rab flinched when his finger ran down his forehead onto his nose. "What are you doing?"

"Admiring your profile."

"I'm surprised you can see it in the dark."

"I can see enough. You've got a distinctive profile."

"I know, people keep telling me."

They were silent again.

"I wish I could smoke," Rab said.

"Why don't you?"

"My cigarettes? You're joking, he'd smell them as soon as he walked in the door."

"Have one of mine."

"That fucking menthol crap? Your cigarettes wind me up. They're *supposed* to be relaxing."

They heard the clock chime in the hall. "Three o'clock," John said.

"Jesus, I'm going to feel like shit in the morning."

This time the silence was longer.

"John?"

"Mm?"

"You want to fuck?"

Rab could feel him looking at him in the dark. "This is so sudden." His voice was smiling.

"Maybe it'll take my mind off it."

"Think I can take your mind off Danny?"

There was another small silence.

"Yes."

"I'm flattered."

John was silent again. It was a tense silence, pregnant. A trap door silence. With John you felt them all the time. After a while he said, "What's your excuse Rab?"

Rab said nothing.

"Because we go way back, first loves and last loves? Or is it because I remind you of him? Or what? Is it the mystery 'what' Rab?"

"I don't know."

"You mean you don't want to know."

"Maybe."

They were silent again, not touching. Rab was holding his breath. He felt as if the whole room was holding its breath.

"This has been a bad move for you." John's voice was too smooth, too much sleek knowledge all going in bad directions. "You should have said no."

"And have you murder Henderson?"

John shifted beside him, scrutinising him in the dark. "How you love to have someone else to take the blame."

"Like you wouldn't kill him - that what you're saying?"

"What I'm saying is, I'll kill him if I want to, no matter what you or anyone else says, and you know it." There was a thumping silence in the air, hanging between them. "You know it, don't you?" John persisted.

Rab pulled his arms under the blankets and threw himself on his side. But John's hand pulled his shoulder round. He loomed up over him. "You know it and you *want* to be here, don't you?"

"No I *don't*."

John let him go suddenly, lying back down, but like a cat lets go a rat's tail. "Liar."

Rab turned on his side again and pulled the covers up so he couldn't hear.

"You always were a lousy liar."

"Danny?"
Nothing.
"Danny?"
"Mm."
"You asleep?"
"I was."
"Sorry. Can I ask you something?"
"Mm."
"What d'you feel about your brother?"
"Ask me another question."
"What d'you feel about Rab?"
"I don't like that one either."
"What about me?"
"I like your dick."
"Is that all?"
"That's all."
"You're honest."
"Mm."
"Danny?"
"Mm?"
"You're right, I am queer."
"Mm."
Is that all you can say?"
"Hurrah."
"I once had a crush on a boy I arrested." Henderson was silent, waiting for Danny to say something. When he didn't he went on, "Know what I arrested him for?"
"What?"
"Selling blow-jobs in a public toilet."
Danny was silent.
"I caught him in the act, no lock on the door. He had long blonde hair. For months after that every time I masturbated I imagined it was him. Know what I imagined last time?"
"What?" Danny was awake now, listening.
"You and Rab."
"You still like the idea?"
"You must look beautiful together."
Danny was silent.
"Why d'you want to meet her?" Henderson asked. He heard Danny sigh, felt him tug over irritably.
"I told you."
"You're lying."
"Then don't bother."
"No, I will. I'd just like to know the truth."
"I'm not going to make trouble, if that's what worries you."
It was Henderson's turn to be silent. Danny turned back towards him. "What d'you think I'm going to do?"
"I don't know. Are you going to *do* anything?"
"No."
"Then what?"

"Oh for Christsake, give it a break." Danny hurled himself round.

Henderson waited a few moments then pressed himself against him. "I'm sorry."

"Get off me." Danny shrugged him free.

Henderson kissed his shoulders.

"I said, get off." Danny shrugged him off more violently.

"Danny listen..."

Danny came round elbow first, whamming it in just below Henderson's ribs. His hands came down on Henderson's throat, pressing it hard. Henderson was caught off-guard. He gurgled, already feeling the distress of asphyxiation. He grabbed at Danny's hands instinctively, forgetting everything he had been told about self-defence. He felt his chest begin to hurt. There was a singing in his ears.

Danny let go as suddenly as he had attacked him. "Take me home."

Henderson was panting, unable to draw breath. Danny was getting out of bed, telling him to take him home like he was a chauffeur or something.

"I'll be fucked if I will." He could hardly get the words out.

"Then I'll walk." Danny already had his jeans on. He was pulling his T-shirt over his head. He looked around for his sweater. Maybe still in the kitchen. He went out of the bedroom without speaking.

The light came on in the black kitchen with a flicker. Everything seemed to reflect dully at him. It hurt his eyes. He hated the kitchen too. Nothing but filthy red splashed all over the black.

He found his sweater on a stool and pulled it on.

Henderson was waiting for him in the living room. Danny looked at him once then sat down and began pulling on his socks and shoes.

"I'll run you home."

Danny said nothing.

"I'll get dressed."

Danny went out to the hall and got his jacket then returned to the living room and stood by the window, waiting. A full moon shone down on the water. It looked icy cold and black as a murderous rage. There was no wind. For once there was no rain either.

"Okay?"

Danny turned and went out ahead of him.

It was bitterly cold outside. There was a faint breeze off the water. It seemed to be made of frozen salt. Danny shivered inside his jacket, waiting for Henderson to get the car out.

He climbed into the icy car and sat with his hands between his legs until Henderson got in. He looked at the clock on the dashboard. 3:15. Hardly worthwhile going to fucking bed.

Henderson got in, letting a blast of cold air in with him. The engine started first time. "You've got a vicious temper." He was swinging out into the town road, slowly and carefully as ever, even though there was nothing else there.

Danny said nothing.

"You want to watch, some day you'll kill someone before you know what you're doing."

"What is this, a police lecture?"

"No, a word of warning."

"You're alive, aren't you?"

Henderson looked at him. His tone was hard, incisive. He felt a cold chill run down his back.

The car ate up the short distance effortlessly. They stopped opposite the farm. Danny went to get out. Henderson stopped him. "When will I see you again?"

Danny turned to him. "When your wife's here let me know."

Henderson frowned. "I've got to see you before then."

"Too bad."

"I can't wait that long."

"Why not? Use your hand. Think about me and Rab."

Danny was out of the car before he had a chance to stop him. "Danny!" he called out after him.

But Danny was already gone, disappearing into the dark like a wraith.

Rab woke with a start, trying to decide what he'd heard, if he'd heard anything at all. He felt his pulse beating in his ear.

"Danny." John's voice came out of the dark, relaxed, matter of fact.

"Shit." Rab struggled up, leaning on one elbow. John lay there listening.

"You sure?" Then Rab heard the kitchen door. "Christ, he's coming up." He threw the blankets off and sat up. *Please Danny, go to the toilet, go anywhere, don't come in here.*

"Forget it." John's voice was lazy. "You'll never make it."

"Where are my fucking clothes?" Rab couldn't make out anything in the dark. He didn't even know where the bedside lamp was.

He got up and was standing half-way across the floor when Danny came in. Danny came to a halt, said uncertainly, "John?" He sounded very young.

"Here Danny." John's voice came out of the dark, reassuring.

Danny stood for a moment, eyes adjusting, looking at the tall white shape, then he came in and shut the door and leaned against it.

Rab stood there watching him, utterly unable to see anything of his face.

"Oh boy." Danny's voice was low again, adult, familiar.

"We were lonely without you baby." John's voice was slow and amused.

"I'll bet."

Rab knew he was watching him. He began to get dressed, feeling on the chair for his clothes.

"Please, don't bother getting dressed Rab, not on my account. Stay the night. John can make it last forever, believe me."

"He was just going."

"Why? You bored with him already?"

"So sharp he'll cut himself." John still sounded amused.

Danny spoke again. "Why don't you stay and I'll join you, then my big brother can have everything he wants. One big happy family."

There was a silence with an edge in it sneaking into the room. John said nothing.

Rab pulled on his jeans, then his shirt. Danny still stood there. Rab waited a moment and knew he wasn't going to move. He crossed to the door. Now he could see Danny's face. Now Danny could see his.

"Not going so soon?" Danny's voice was quiet.

"Let me out Danny."

John listened to the low plea in it. There was no other sound in the room. He could see their two shapes; one tall and fair, the other leaner and darker.

No movement.

"Let him out Danny," he said, no amusement in it now.

No movement at all.

Then John saw Danny reach out and pull Rab towards him.

Rab had never tasted anything as liquid as his mouth. It felt like ice melting, as if his body had been frozen and come to life. He was drinking him down, feeling the instantaneous ignition of excitement.

John grunted out Danny's name. He came across the room at them, tearing them apart, yanking Rab off and punching into Danny all in one movement. He must have hit him three or four times before Rab realised what he was doing.

He moved forward, pulling at John's arm, saying his name, but he might have been a fly. John just kept punching into him like a sledgehammer. He could hear Danny's dreadful grunts every time a blow landed.

Rab renewed his attack, yanking at his hair. John came back in a swearing heap, sitting down abruptly on top of him on the bed. Rab wriggled up, but was too slow. John was already up on his feet again, but this time he was pulling Danny away from the door, pushing him towards the bed. He landed beside Rab in a heap, curled up like a foetus, holding his stomach.

"Danny..." But Rab had hardly spoken before John had grabbed him and hauled him up. Rab swung at him, the blow landing Christ knows where. He heard John curse. It seemed to trigger him off. He kept up a steady stream of low, vicious swearing. He flung Rab out the door and slammed it shut.

Rab rattled the door handle. "John!" But it was locked. He pressed his ear against the door, but all he could hear was the low, steady stream of John's invective going on and on.

Of Danny he could hear nothing at all.

John prised him open like uncurling a prawn. "You vicious little bitch."

Danny was smiling.

"I ought to break your neck."

"I'm going to be sick."

John picked him up half-bodily and walked him to the sink. Danny threw up. John turned the cold tap on. Danny threw up again. After a moment John asked, "Can you stand?"

Danny nodded. John let him go then walked over and put the bedside lamp on. He went back. Danny was dry retching. He took a cloth and washed his face in cold water. He swirled the edges of the vomit away, letting the tap run to help clear the smell.

Danny hung onto the sink like an old man. "One day you're going to kill me."

"Just try me."

John pushed him back towards the bed and started peeling his clothes off. He pushed him under the blankets and looked down at him. His face was a pasty grey. His eyes looked bruised. He pulled one of the plasters off his chest, making Danny wince. "How would you like me to open these again?"

"Any way you like." Danny was still breathing through his mouth. John could read the dull black glitter of his eyes like words written in asphalt. Hot, pungent, deep with secrets.

"Still a sharp little bitch."

The cuts were beginning to heal. They were red-raw and angry looking. John reached over to the drawer and pulled it open. Danny's eyes never left his face. He heard the click of the knife, John's envied flick-knife, almost twenty years old. "I've got a better idea." And he took the knife and pressed it against his own chest.

Danny watched the point go in, the blood held contained by the knife's shape, then it moved, parting the skin pinkly, the blood welling up immediately. The cut was deep and short, like a narrow mouth.

"Suck it," John said, lowering it to his mouth.

Danny closed his eyes as the slippy blood salted his lips. He sucked the wound as John had his, pushing his tongue in, wanting to make it bleed. He could feel John grow hard against his leg.

"*Suck it...*" John whispered, pushing against him.

Danny suckled harder, drawing more blood.

"When you die I'm going to bury you face down so they can ream your arse without turning you over." John moved against him, slowly, taking his time. "I missed you." Suddenly his voice was different. No softer, no harder, only different. "I really missed you."

Danny bit the wound, felt the sharp pain freeze him.

John drew his nail over the sores on Danny's chest, making them burn and itch. "Why don't you believe me?" He pulled himself up abruptly, looking down at his face. Danny's mouth was red with blood. It began to well up on John's chest, trickle down. He looked like a gargoyle of Christ.

"You went to see him," Danny accused.

John stared at him. "So?" He watched his tongue lick the blood off his lips.

"He says you threatened to kill him."

"So?" John said again.

"Why didn't you?"

John looked at him. He was serious. He took Danny's face in one hand, tried to read those flat eyes. "You *want* me to kill him?"

Danny said nothing.

John lay down on top of him. Danny felt the blood slick across his chest, sticking them together.

John kissed him. Danny closed his eyes, letting it happen, letting the heat burn him up. John consumed his mouth, giving him everything, taking everything away. When he stopped Danny could feel his cock throbbing. He could feel John's, like hot lead, digging into his belly.

"Tell me what you want Danny... tell me what you really want." John's eyes were black, no green at all. Danny's eyes reflected back exactly the same, just like a mirror.

Danny waited until they were both there, waited for the final stroke before speaking. "Kill him," he said on a gasp, trapped under John's weight, his eyes wide open and looking into his brother's. "*Kill him...*"

And then he was flooding their stomachs with sperm.

THIRTY-SIX

Danny found Rab in the barn. He stood watching him in the half-dark.

Rab didn't see him at first. After a few moments he straightened up and turned, feeling that infallible instinct of being watched.

Danny could see him frowning into the dark, knowing that he could only see his bottom half.

"Danny?"

Danny laughed but did not move. "How did you know it was me?" His voice sounded low in the dark, not quite his own and never anyone else's.

Rab sat down on the sacks and rubbed his forehead with the back of his hand. "Your natty line in wellingtons."

He took his tin from his pocket where it was disfiguring his chest. He began rolling a cigarette, doing it by touch. Danny continued to watch him silently, but Rab didn't find it unnerving. It was exciting him, alone in the dark with him, not knowing what he was thinking, and that he'd sought you out, the keenest edge of all.

The damp air became laden with the smell of liquorice.

"John's favourite smell. I always felt that was why you smoked them." Danny's voice was still as water, everything dropping into it, disappearing. Rain began to patter on the huge tin roof. A unique sound, never the same twice.

"Want one?" Rab's voice sounded so normal, so casual, it surprised him, but Danny didn't reply. "Aren't you risking it after last night?" Rab asked.

"He can only kill me once," Danny answered.

Rab felt his stomach turn at the words, said so casually, with such dead-faced conviction. "He wouldn't," he said involuntarily, and was horrified to hear a hint of question in it.

"Do you want me to reassure you or ease your conscience?"

Rab stared down between his knees at the cigarette. The smoke coiled distantly, like a ghost in the darkness. The rain was heavier. The sound changed in pitch. "Have you come to start a fight?"

"If you like. Why were you fucking him?"

Rab lifted the cigarette to his mouth. "He promised to stop threatening Henderson."

Rab heard Danny shift and looked up. He'd sat down opposite him. Now Rab could see his chest, his hands held loosely together, but still not his face.

"Did you do it every time I left the house?"

"Does that matter?"

"It might."

"We were never an item, trust me."

Danny was silent. Rab looked at him again, but could not discern his face. He waited, listening to the sound of the rain.

"I think it's time you understood something about me and John." Danny's voice was deeper still, low underneath the rain, like stones tumbling beyond hearing under the surface of a stream. Rab felt a prickle of warning across his skin, knowing that whatever he was going to hear he didn't want to hear it, knowing he would listen anyway.

"I may hate him," it was a heavy whisper in the dark, "but he's like a needle buried in my flesh, grown over, causing me pain, irredeemable, part of me."

Rab heard it with a kind of despair. He wanted to pick him up and smash him against the wall. "You're full of *shit*."

Danny said nothing. He sat there as if he were listening to something else Rab was saying but that he couldn't hear himself. Suddenly he laughed and said, "He had me too."

Rab stared at him, not wanting to understand, wanting to pretend stupidity, but he heard himself saying, "No." Then, "That is a *lie*."

Danny just went on looking at him.

"I don't believe you. He wouldn't. You were a *kid*."

"Yeah, learning everything you taught him."

"*I* taught *him*? I never taught him anything. Believe me, John could've taught the sodomites how it was done."

"He told me you'd started it, when you first came here."

"What, at twelve? Get real Danny, he was *fifteen*." He laughed sourly. "Oh nice try John. Reverse that and you've got the picture. John taught *me*, believe me."

"In the bathroom?"

"Come again?"

"Was the first time in the bathroom?"

Rab paused, thinking, remembering, then he nodded. "I needed to pee and he wouldn't let me in. I think he got some kind of perverted kick out of it. By the time he let me I was ready to wet my pants. Half way through I looked up and there he was with this fucking thing sticking out. John's erections were memorable even then." He paused then said in an odd low voice, "*He* taught *me*."

They were silent, then Danny spoke again. "He killed the old man."

Rab jerked his head up as if he'd been stuck by a pin. "What?"

"Ian saw him."

"That's crap."

He sensed Danny's nod.

Rab gave in. "Okay, why?"

Danny hesitated then said, "The old man wanted to give him head."

Rab felt his stomach turn. Even his skin felt queasy. "No *way*. Christ, that's gross, even for Ian."

Danny didn't answer.

"What happened?"

Danny's voice came out low. "John was in taking a bath. Ian had gone in to see him about something."

Yeah sure, Rab thought.

"John hadn't locked the door and the old man wandered in. He was blotto, weaving about. Ian said he was staring at John like he'd never seen him before." Danny stopped as if waiting for him to say something, but Rab couldn't think of anything to say.

"Ian called him over, told him down to get down on his knees, close his eyes and open his mouth. He didn't expect him to do it, but he did, so he shoved the soap in his mouth. He's hanging onto the bath, choking, and suddenly John just leans on his head and pushes him under." Danny stopped again, abruptly, as if he was exhausted.

Rab saw him drop his head down onto his knees. His hair came into the darkness like a flame. "And then?" Rab prompted him.

"The old man was kicking up a tidal wave. John's just holding him there. He roars at Ian to fuck off." Danny's voice was muffled.

"And he went, just like that, and John... what? Undressed him? Heaved him in the bath, with a bar of soap in his mouth? The world's most bizarre suicide. Is he *nuts?*"

When Danny didn't answer he said, "Who was supposed to find him?"

"I don't know. Ian didn't think he'd go through with it. He thought he was just getting rid of him so he could let the old man go, save face. The only way he could finish what

he'd started."

Rab put his cigarette in his mouth then threw it away. It was out. He lit a new one, took a deep drag. "How d'you do it Danny? How do you stay so calm?"

Danny's head lifted. He got up stiffly and crossed to where Rab was sitting. Now Rab could see his face plainly. There was a cut on one cheek. A small clean cut, like one made by a knife. "What's wrong, do you want to see me cry?"

Rab looked away. He handed Danny his cigarette. Danny sat down beside him and took a long drag. He coughed it all out again then handed the cigarette back.

"He do that with a knife?" Rab asked.

Danny looked perplexed.

"Your face."

Danny nodded absently.

Rab looked away and said, "How old were you when he first did it?"

"However old I was when he started with you."

Rab said, "That would be seven.... no, six... you must've been six. Christ, what was he *doing* to you?"

Danny shrugged. "He got me to suck him off once, I remember that, because that's what we were doing when we got caught."

"You got caught?"

"The old man caught us up in the loft at Jerrett's."

"Christ, the head shaving. Was *that* what it was about?"

Danny nodded. "He made me eat it."

"*Eat* it?"

"It wasn't much, just enough to make me remember." Danny laughed shortly. "He always hated me, for corrupting his favourite son."

"Or because you got there first," Rab said sourly.

Danny looked at him sharply.

Rab flushed and rubbed his face. After a moment he said, "He keeps going on about killing Henderson."

"I know."

"You don't think he means it, do you?"

"I don't know."

"Can't you stop seeing him?"

Danny looked at him. "Why? You want to go instead?"

Rab looked back. "Now you *are* kidding."

"It's not me he wants, you know."

Rab kept looking at him. "And you think John will be any happier with me there? You think you matter more to him than I do?"

Danny smiled. "What's this? Jealous?"

"And if I said I was?"

"I'd ask who of?"

When Rab didn't answer Danny turned away and said abruptly, "Henderson has to get drunk to get it up."

Rab looked at him for a long moment. "So?"

It was Danny's turn not to answer. Rab said, "You don't like him, do you?"

"Do you?"

"No, but I feel sorry for him."

"Well please him then, give him what he wants."

Rab shook his head. "He'd get no pleasure out of me."

"Try it, you might surprise yourself."

"No way."

"You sound afraid. Scared in case he proves you wrong?"

Rab looked at him. "You can be a vindictive little shit sometimes."

"No, I just hate liars."

"I'm not lying."

"What about John then?"

Rab looked away. "What about him?"

"He turn you on?"

"No."

"You're missing out." Danny was smiling.

"Are you saying he turns you on?"

Danny said nothing.

"The way he treats you?"

Danny looked at him, his mouth curving. "Maybe it's *because* of the way he treats me."

Rab shook his head in disgust. "Anyone who enjoys being cut up is sick."

Danny nodded, unperturbed. "Not like you of course, nothing touches you, not even John." He stopped smiling. "You really think I'm that stupid? You really think I believe you sacrificed yourself to save us all? What are you going to do Rab, give him up for Henderson?"

Rab looked at him. His face was sharp, his eyes hard and black, and this time he could see John in Danny, that same flat unmoving rage. "You're getting to be as two-faced as he is. What is *wrong* with you?"

Danny laughed. "Oh go on, ask me what happened to my sweet nature."

Rab stared at him, filled with a sudden repulsive conviction. "Christ, you're jealous. Not of him, of me. You want him for yourself."

Danny's face was implacable.

"You sick fuck," Rab said.

Danny stood up. "If you tell him any of this I'll deny it all."

"You sick fuck," Rab said again, and he kept saying it, even as he watched Danny go through the doorway into the rain.

"Where've you been?" Water was running down John's face. He was rubbing his hair with a towel. He handed it to Danny then pulled him tight between his legs, holding him around the waist, squeezing the breath out of him.

"With Rab." Danny ran the towel over his hair awkwardly.

John's arms grew tighter. Danny grunted.

"You never learn, do you?"

"We were talking."

John kissed him, tasting his mouth. "What were you talking about?"

"You... Henderson."

John shifted him to one hip, Danny's leg between his. He wanted him to feel him. "I *am* in good company. You still want me to kill him?" He was smiling, looking into Danny's eyes.

"Why? You still scared?"

"You've got a big mouth."

Danny said nothing.

John watched him. "Frightened to admit you got carried away last night? Or am I supposed to believe you're a latent psychopath?"

"I *told* you," Danny said angrily.

"Oh, I know what you told me." He kissed Danny again, slowly. "But I never believe what you tell me on point of principle. And I can taste his cigarettes off your mouth."

Danny said nothing.

"Love me Danny." It wasn't a question.

Danny did what he was told.

Henderson was sitting outside the field when Rab came over the crest of the hill. He watched him drive the Mercedes slap bang across the gateway. He was tempted for an instant to run the tractor over the top of it. Instead he stopped just short.

Henderson got out and looked at the space. "Bit neat, aren't you?"

"That's the idea."

"I want to see you." Henderson wouldn't meet his eyes.

"You've seen me."

"Properly. I need to talk to you."

"I'm working, this is called a tractor."

Henderson looked at him now, his face mottling. "I want to see you tonight, after work."

"What's wrong, they thrown you off the force?"

Henderson looked perplexed, then he realised what he meant. "I'm just on my way to work, that's why I'm in uniform."

"Oh, I thought you just put it on to harass people."

"I'll come for you at seven-thirty."

Rab folded his arms. "Will you indeed? And what makes you think I'm going to be there?"

"I want to talk to you about Danny."

"I don't get to fuck Danny any more, you're wasting your time."

Henderson's mouth grew tight, his eyes hard. "I'm serious, I've had about as much of you lot as I'm going to take. Either I see you tonight or fuck the lot of you." Henderson dared him to disagree.

"Okay." Rab turned and got back in his tractor. He left Henderson standing there, nonplussed by the speed of his agreement.

He waited while Henderson got into his car and pulled onto the road, then he pulled out after him and went in the opposite direction.

"I'm going out," Rab announced.

Danny looked up. John said, "Where?"

"What's it to you?"

"I have a deep sense of familial responsibility."

"To Henderson's."

Danny was watching him now, so was Ian.

"Why the sudden interest?" John asked.

"He asked me."

"When?"

Rab put down his cup and threw the rest of his biscuit to the dog. "None of your fucking business."

John leaned one arm back over the chair. "Have a nice time."

Rab got up. The dog nuzzled him for more biscuit. He pushed it away. "I will."

He went upstairs to wash.

Henderson was as neat and meticulous as ever. The charcoal slacks, the gold watch, the black moccasins. A navy jacquard sweater, navy jacquard socks - probably navy jacquard underpants. Rab saw that he had added a heavy gold identity bracelet.

251

It looked startling against the dark hair of his arms.

"Want a drink?"

He needs a drink to get it up.

"Okay."

"Beer?"

"Fine." Rab sat down and saw that the blinds were closed. It made the room warmer, more intimate. Maybe this was a seduction after all.

Henderson came back in and handed him his drink. He was back on the whisky again.

"Rum ran out?" Rab asked.

Henderson looked at his glass. "Danny drank it all."

Rab was surprised. "Danny?"

"He's got a taste for it."

Rab lifted his eyebrows, but said nothing more.

Henderson downed his glass and refilled it. Rab wondered how much he drank a week, wondered if anyone had ever thought to breathalyse him. He must be well over some mornings after the nights before. Maybe that's why he always drove like a lamb.

"He's never even had a parking ticket."

Rab focused on him, startled, wondering if he had been talking to him and he hadn't heard. But he hadn't.

"His big brother," Henderson said, seeing his blank expression.

"John," Rab said to remind him.

"Yes, John." Henderson repeated the name as if it might poison his mouth.

"So?"

"So nothing. He's clean as a bone."

Rab looked at his glass. "What did you expect to find? Murder? GBH? Child molesting?" He's done all three, Rab thought. That would surprise you.

"No, but I thought someone that aggressive might have been in trouble before. It seemed likely."

"What makes you so sure he's aggressive?"

"Come off it."

"It could be all bluster. On big people the slightest threat looks menacing."

Henderson looked at him. "Still trying to cover up for him?"

"I'm not."

"Yeah, like Danny isn't. He won't even contemplate charging him."

"Charging him?"

"With underage rape."

"I didn't know there was an age of consent for rape."

"You know what I mean," Henderson said irritably.

Rab took a drink before replying. "You mean you asked him to charge John with rape?"

"You got a problem with that?"

"Yeah, what makes you so sure he did?"

Henderson looked at him, then away again quickly and Rab knew he wasn't sure.

"No-one in their right mind would have sex with a gorilla like him."

"Why not? He has things to recommend him."

"Like?" Henderson was watching him intently.

"He's hung like a horse."

Henderson flushed.

Christ, he's embarrassed, Rab thought. Or excited. He wasn't sure which.

"How do you know?" Henderson asked. He wasn't looking at him directly.

Rab chased the urge to say, Because he was rubbing it in my face last night.

"Moments come when you spot these things."

Henderson looked almost disappointed. Maybe that was excitement after all.

"You think Danny likes to do it with him?" He still wouldn't look at him.

"I wouldn't know. What does he say?"

"Oh everything." He filled his glass again. "He says he hates him, then he says he's hooked on him. You can't believe anything he tells you."

It made Rab uncomfortable, hearing it come back at him from another source. All Danny's truths, and everybody so quick to call them lies. Rab took another mouthful of beer. "You want him to give you something to nail John with."

"Of course." Henderson said it without hesitation, the same way Ian confessed to listening outside doors.

"It never occurred to you that straightforward loyalty might stop him?"

"I don't understand what you're getting at."

"You really don't, do you?" Rab looked at the floor then asked, "Are you an only child?"

"No, why?"

Rab laughed. "Another theory up the spout. What have you got?"

"Brother."

"Just like Danny."

"Hardly, my brother is a lawyer, a successful lawyer."

"So? John's a successful farmer. They probably earn about the same."

"I doubt it."

The conversation ground to a halt. Rab took some more beer and lay back. He ran his finger over the frosting. Always perfectly chilled at Henderson's house.

"You always sit with your legs open." Henderson's voice was thick, like he needed to clear his throat.

Rab looked past his glass at him. "Does it bother you? Or does it just excite you?"

Henderson put his glass down. "You know, for someone who's at great pains to defend his sexuality you flaunt it a lot."

"Are you suggesting I'm trying to excite you?"

"Yes."

Rab laughed. "Then I'll let you into a secret, if you promise not to cry. My trousers are so fucking tight I can't cross my legs. *That's* why I always sit with my legs open."

"Sure, nothing to do with showing off your balls."

"Nothing at all. That's also why I'm always half-lying down. They cut me in half as well. Sad, isn't it?"

"Why d'you wear them so tight then?"

"I like the discomfort. Everybody has a touch of masochist, that's mine. What's yours? Falling in love with Danny?"

Henderson stared at him as if he'd read his mind. Rab felt his smile falter. Not another one. He'd said it as a joke and look at his face. *Oh great.*

"I can't get him with his brother there."

"Please, don't give me any true confessions. I meant that as a joke."

Henderson didn't even look up. "It's true, there's no point in trying to hide it, he fascinates me."

"Oh he fascinates everybody, don't worry about it."

But Henderson was well away.

"I didn't really believe I was queer until I met him."

"Don't you mean fucked him?"

Henderson flushed. "Alright, fucked him."

"And now you think it's love?"

"I know it."

Rab took a drink to stop his laugh from coming out. "You're just infatuated."

"No, I've been infatuated before, it's different."

"Don't tell me, you want to marry him."

Henderson looked up. "I would if I could."

Rab laughed this time.

"I don't see anything funny about it."

"I'm sure you don't. Unfortunately I do. I have a distasteful sense of humour."

"If only I could get rid of his brother."

Rab put down his glass. "Look, talk sense. Danny wouldn't come to you even if his brother wasn't there."

"I suppose you think he'd stay with you?"

"No, I don't. I just know he wouldn't come to you. He isn't queer. The rest of us might say it, pretend it, but he isn't."

"He's a virgin."

"Sorry?" Rab said, puzzled by the change of direction.

"He's almost twenty and still a virgin, yet he's fucked you, me, his brother. If he's not queer, then neither am I."

"I don't know where you got the idea he's a virgin. I think you'll find he's managed, in spite of the fact his choice has been pretty much limited to his mother or our seventy year old daily help." And he would have had his mother if he could, Rab thought.

"So how do you know he isn't queer then?"

"I just know it."

"How?"

Rab shrugged. "I do."

"Bullshit."

Rab picked up his glass, cradled it. He laid his head back, closed his eyes. *You could be right Henderson. Maybe it is all bullshit. After you with the 'I Want Danny' T-shirt, and like you I want him in my own image.*

"He wants to meet my wife."

Rab opened his eyes. "When did he see your wife?"

"He hasn't. He saw a photograph."

"Why does he want to meet her?"

"He says," Henderson's voice was scathing, "because he doesn't get to meet many women."

"That's true."

"I'm sure it is, but I don't believe it."

"Why not?"

"Do you believe it?" Henderson asked.

"No."

"See?"

The conversation stopped, killed by absoluteness.

Henderson refilled his glass. He pulled off his sweater. He had a white close-fit T-shirt underneath, like US Army issue. Probably a police vest. It looked very brilliant against the black body hair. He smoothed back his hair as if there was enough there to ruffle. He kicked his slippers off. His face was flushed. "You said you don't get to fuck him any more, that true?"

"Mm." Rab took a drink, cautious.

"His brother?"

"What do you think?"

Henderson swore. "A real little Hitler."

"He's not little."

"Why d'you let him push you about?"

Rab put his glass down carefully. "How would you like a punch in the mouth?"

Henderson looked startled. "No, I mean, I wouldn't have thought you were the type, that's all."

"Forget it," Rab said irritably.

"Sorry."

"I said, forget it." Rab finished his beer. "You got any more?" He lifted his empty glass.

"I'll get some." Henderson struggled to get up.

Rab stood up. "No, let me. You lie there and be comatose."

He went into the kitchen and got another from the fridge. He broke off a piece of cheesecake that was lying half-finished inside and stuck it in his mouth. He went back into the living room. "Nice cheesecake."

Henderson looked up at him from far away, his eyes focusing slowly. "Take some."

"I already have."

Henderson smiled. The teeth were as white as his T-shirt. He probably used an electric toothbrush.

"You use an electric toothbrush?" Rab asked, sitting down again.

"Yes, why?"

"No reason, I just like to be right occasionally." Rab lay down on one elbow, watching him.

"D'you miss him?" Henderson wasn't looking at him when he asked it.

"I see him every day."

"I'd have thought that was worse."

Rab was brought up short. "Yes… it is."

"So the brother's got some big magic to keep you away?"

He wasn't going to let up, drunk or not. You could see why he had become a policeman.

"No, just big fists."

"More bullshit."

"I didn't see you laughing when he threatened you."

"He hasn't scared me off either."

Rab was quiet. *Have another drinkie Henderson. Pass out and give us all peace.*

"What's he got?"

"I told you, a big dick."

Henderson looked at him suddenly, eyes shrewd, as if he hadn't touched a drop. "Whatever you did that night, it's his Sword of Damocles, isn't it?"

"What, his dick?"

"Oh come on. He's like the centre of a whirlpool, drawing everything into him. What did he do?"

"You should have a lamp in my face."

"What did he do?"

"Fuck off Henderson." Rab's voice was chilled.

Henderson blinked, then relaxed. He poured some more into his half-full glass and drank it. "I feel suitably mellow."

"I'm not surprised."

"Want to fool around?"

Rab looked at him, raising one eyebrow. "Not exactly the faithful type, are you?"

Henderson laughed. "And he is to me?" He looked away, no longer smiling.

Rab said, "He's hardly away from John's side, so who are you grudging him?"

Henderson looked at him suddenly, as if an idea of incredible magnitude had just penetrated. "They're in a relationship?"

Rab laughed. "You could call it that."

He sat up. "A serious relationship?"

Rab frowned. "He sleeps with him."

"In the same bed?"

"Well, not on the floor."

"Jesus Christ, I never… the filthy bastard."

"Hang on, you take turns you know. The outrage doesn't suit you."

"I'm not his *brother*."

"So? He can't get pregnant. Who does it hurt?"

"Him, being forced to have sex with his brother."

"You're really mad about this force part, aren't you?" Rab fell silent, wondering where the force began and ended, wondering how much force John really used, wondering how much they all accepted as normal, wondering what that made him, being there, riding it out, letting it all happen.

He sat up and took a long drink of beer, half-finishing the glass. He lay back down again. Let Henderson worry about it. Danny didn't want him anyway.

Henderson asked, "What are you thinking?"

"Fuck the little bastard."

"Who?"

"Danny."

There was a pause then Henderson said, "I'd like to."

"Yeah, so would I."

"He's in our way."

Rab looked up at him. "Danny?"

"His brother."

"He's like that. It's a hobby with him." Rab lay down again. The other way this time, Henderson behind him.

"Sure you don't want to fool around?" Henderson asked.

"Sure. You always get randy when you're drunk?"

"Always."

"You shouldn't drink so much then. It'll get you into trouble some day."

"How?"

"You'll make a pass at the wrong person."

"Like you?"

"No, not like me."

"Does that mean you'll *consider* fooling around?" Henderson asked.

"No."

"Not even if I shower you in expensive gifts?"

"Ah, that might be different," Rab conceded.

"What would you like?"

"A Porsche."

"You've got it."

Rab lifted his head to look at him, rising up on one elbow. "You haven't got that much money."

"Oh, I have."

"Maybe I should have let John kill you."

Henderson looked at him slowly. "Did you stop him?"

"Maybe."

"Why?"

"It's stupid to kill policemen."

"Very," Henderson said. He looked at him a while longer before saying, "That the only reason?"

Rab lay back down. "Yes."

There was a small silence then Rab asked, "How much money do you have - exactly?"

"Are you planning to bump me off?"

"No, I just like to talk about money."

"Well I don't." Henderson's voice was hard, categorical.

"Why?"

"It's never done me any favours."

Rab raised himself again. "Ha ha."

Henderson shrugged. Believe what you like. Rab lay back down.

"If Big-boy was going to kill me how would he do it?" Henderson asked.

"With his bare hands. He enjoys the feel of it."

"Has he done it before then?"

The air was suddenly electric.

"No," Rab said shortly.

"You said he enjoys the feel of it."

"I also said I'd like a Porsche."

"It doesn't matter. What could I do?"

"I don't know, what *could* you do?"

"Nothing."

"Then why ask?"

"Curiosity."

"It killed the cat."

"I'm not a cat."

"To John you're not even as valuable."

"What about you? What does he get out of you?" Henderson demanded.

"I don't know."

"He fucks you, doesn't he?"

Rab was silent then said, "And if he did?"

"What does he do, put all three of you in bed together?"

Rab laughed. "He'd rather stick pins in his eyes."

"So what then?"

"Strict rota. Danny to you - me into bed."

There was another of those little silences, only this one was different, then Henderson asked, "He just fills in the space he leaves, with you?"

"Yes." Rab could feel the tension. He climbed round to look at him again. Henderson was either livid or turned-on. It was difficult to tell which.

"Jesus, what a greedy bastard."

Rab laughed. "You'd do it if you could."

"Why won't you do it with me?"

"I don't want to."

"You can do it with that ugly bastard, why not me?"

"Maybe you're not ugly enough."

"You're in it up to your necks, aren't you?"

Rab sat up slowly and reached for the bottle. Henderson put his hand over the top of his, held it there. His hand was dry, surprisingly rough. "Aren't you?" he demanded.

"Yes."

"And if he goes?"

"We all go."

"His father's missing too now."

"How d'you know?"

"It would surprise you. And you've no idea where he is?"

Rab lifted the bottle, pulling his hand out, and poured some in his empty glass.

"None whatsoever. He was a drunk."

"Is that a warning?"

"Just an observation."

"He's walking a thin line. How many others are going to 'disappear'?"

"It's nothing to do with him."

"Still protecting him."

"Protecting me."

Henderson let him take another drink. "What would you do for your Porsche?"

"What d'you want me to do?"

"Murder?"

Rab rested the glass on his knee. "No."

"What did you do it for before then? A share in the farm?"

He put the glass down. "I haven't done it before."

"Then why not take it up? He's in your way, get rid of him."

"*No.*"

"Why not?"

"Murder him just so you can lay hands on Danny? I'm not stupid."

"We could do it together, then Danny can choose."

Rab laughed shortly. "Stop fantasising. With John dead he'd up and go."

"Not if he was incriminated."

Rab rubbed his forehead. "Fuck, this gets worse."

"You want to see the Porsche?"

"What?"

"My other car's a Porsche, like the sticker says. Want to see it?"

Rab looked at him suspiciously. "Where?"

"Downstairs. Second garage."

"What kind of kilts do your family make?"

"Tartan. The kind that goes onto expensive leather goods in Florida. They own a chain in the US. Some more at airports in Japan, Saudi Arabia, France. My father owns shares in firms with household names. My brother's an investment broker, plays the stock markets. I live off the fat of my invested money. We're one of the seven per cent who owns eighty-four per cent of the wealth. Want to see the Porsche?"

"Yes." Rab was nodding, half-stupefied. "Yes, I'd like to see the Porsche."

"Then kiss me first."

Rab leaned over and kissed him. He held Rab's head, but that was all. His mouth was heavy with whisky, his moustache surprisingly coarse. He let him go easily and said, "Let's go."

Rab got up and pulled on his shoes, tying them quickly.

The rain was off temporarily and a large moon scudded in and out the clouds. The second garage was further away.

"The only one I could get," Henderson said.

Rab shivered without his jacket.

"Come in."

They went in. Henderson brought the door down behind them, flicking on the light. It was a huge, flat, red car. Ultra-modern. So sleek it looked futuristic.

"Christ, I didn't think people actually owned these things." Rab ran his hand over it.

"Want to go out in it?"

Rab looked at him. "We're drunk."

"So?"

"Policeman of the month."

"Do you want to or not?" Henderson demanded.

"Yes, I want to."

"Open the garage door then."

Henderson got in and reversed the car out as soon as Rab had opened the door. It moved like an animal. He swung the passenger door open. "Get in."

"Aren't you going to lock the garage?"

"Get in."

Rab got in.

"Where do you want to go?"

"Anywhere we can go fast. Christ, the dashboard looks like a fucking cockpit."

Henderson laughed. "State of the art. The more you pay, the more confused you get."

The lights came on like searchlights.

"Wow… I'm impressed."

"You ain't seen nothing yet."

They went fast. They went fast enough to scare the living daylights out of him.

"Christ, here I am hurtling around the countryside at a hundred miles an hour, being driven by a drunk millionaire policeman."

"Who said I was a millionaire?"

"You're driving like one."

Henderson laughed and slowed down. "We've killed about forty rabbits."

"We should go back and get the tails."

"Sadist."

"No, just trying to prove I did it."

"High?" Henderson asked.

"As a kite."

"Where to now?"

"Anywhere. Let's cruise, nice and civilised."

"Wish we'd brought some whisky," Henderson said.

"Stop and I'll get some. It's early yet."

They stopped at an off-license. "Make sure you park in front," Rab said. "I want everyone to see."

Henderson laughed. "Okay, I'm your chauffeur."

Rab went in and bought a full bottle and some beer.

"Well, did they see?" Henderson asked as he climbed back in.

"You bet, jaws hanging wide open."

Henderson laughed again. "Give us a drink."

"Not here, wait till we're out of the town."

"Fuck 'em." Henderson took the bottle and took a deep swig, wiping his moustache on his hand. "That's better. Now, let's go."

He took off in a pit-stop start with a squeal of rubber. Rab laughed. "Christ, what are you going to do when they arrest you?"

"Plead innocent."

Rab laughed again. "God, I must be drunk."

Henderson looked at him. "You've hardly drunk anything."

"I'm drunk on speed."

They stopped and bought chips, then Henderson drove them down to the water, parking on the grass lot overlooking the sea. The rain began to spatter down again. Rab felt half-asleep, full of food and drink, exhausted by exhilaration. Henderson

passed him the bottle. He took a mouthful.

"Enjoy it?" Henderson asked.

"A1," Rab agreed.

"Worth the kiss?"

"Easy."

"Give me another then."

Henderson bent over him and kissed him. Rab let him. This time it was long and slow, explorative. He came off him reluctantly. Rab lay back, looking at him through half-closed eyes.

"Not so bad?" Henderson asked him.

"Not so bad."

"You wouldn't kill him for it?"

"The kiss or the car?"

"The whole package."

"What about Danny?"

"We could live without Danny."

Rab looked at him. "He was right about you. He said you didn't care which of us you had. You don't, do you?"

"No."

"That's not very flattering."

"On the contrary, it's immensely flattering. I'd really rather have you both."

"What the hell would you do with both?"

Henderson made a long drawn-out noise in his throat. "You couldn't begin to imagine."

"You know," Rab said, "at the back of my mind I have the sneaky feeling you wouldn't really be content with just one of us."

Henderson smiled. "I'm spoilt, always had what I wanted."

"That's why John bugs you so much. No Porsches, no money, and he still has the two things you want most. At least," Rab clarified, "as at this moment."

"That's right." Henderson's hand was on his leg. It wasn't bothering Rab, yet.

"And you think we'd kill him just to transfer allegiance to you?"

"Much more luxurious. No work, no punching you around."

"There's more than one way of imprisoning someone." Rab paused then asked, "Did you give Danny this speech?"

"No."

"Why not?"

"Don't be stupid, you know why not."

"You think he's loyal and I'm not?"

"I think he's afraid and you're not."

"Well the answer's still no."

"Think about it," Henderson urged.

"No."

Henderson smiled suddenly. "Why do you wear your hair tied back like that?"

"It gets in my way."

"Untie it."

Rab smiled at the eagerness in his voice. He lifted his arms and untied it. He shook his head slightly to loosen it.

Henderson said, "It's too long."

"I thought you liked it."

"I do, but as a policeman I'm obliged to say it's too long." Henderson reached up and touched it, rubbing it between his fingers. "I still want to come in it."

"I'll bet you do."

Henderson buried his face in it, the hand on his knee sliding up to Rab's crotch. Rab held his hand where it was, stopping its upward momentum. "I think we better go home officer."

"Just when I'm having fun."

"Let's go."

Henderson was kissing his neck. "What if I said screw or walk?"

"I'd say walk and shove you out, so let's move on, shall we?"

"Don't you want to fuck in a Porsche, add it to your experiences?"

"Maybe, but not with you."

"Who then? Danny?" He was holding Rab's shirt collar down, nuzzling into his hair.

"That's my secret, come on." He pushed Henderson off.

"You're killing me with frustration."

"It'll make you a better policeman."

"I don't want to be a better policeman."

"You ought to. Come *on*." Rab reached over and turned on the ignition.

"One last kiss," Henderson pleaded.

Rab let him kiss him. This time it was passionate, smacking of desperation. Rab pushed him off finally. "You'll cream in your fucking pants if you keep that up."

Henderson's hand groped at his crotch. "You're not hard." He sounded surprised.

"Top marks."

Henderson sat back heavily. "You don't fancy me."

"I wouldn't have been so rude myself but no, I don't."

Henderson was touching him again. "It doesn't make any difference, I still want you. Let me make love to you."

Rab pushed his hand off. "No."

"You're really a closet prude, you know that?" Henderson said, suddenly angry.

"If you say so."

"Always strutting your stuff then not giving out."

"Watch it, you're beginning to sound like a bitchy gay."

Henderson shut up. He slammed the car into gear and reversed violently, sending a shower of gravel up behind him.

He drove back in silence. Rab expected him to go back to the flat, but he didn't. He drew up opposite the farm.

Rab opened the door and got out. He had just closed the door when he remembered suddenly that he'd left his jacket behind, but Henderson had already snarled away. He watched the tail lights disappear before he remembered he had also left the pick-up.

Rab heard John just as he turned onto the landing. Perfect timing. Had he heard him come in? He wouldn't put it past him.

He was making it last, giving it his all. They probably heard him half-way across the village. It was incoherent with passion or excitement, violent, like living through an avalanche. Every night Danny must walk that edge. You would have thought Henderson would be a relief, a rest-cure, a fucking holiday. Maybe he was.

Rab slammed his door, and immediately regretted it. If the performance was for his benefit, well, he'd just applauded. Murdering John suddenly seemed like a very *nice* idea.

He took off his shoes and threw them under the bed. He dropped his clothes where he stood and climbed into bed. It was cold. He curled up to get warm, turning his face to the wall and pulling the blankets over his head.

Like all good clichés, the evening seemed like a dream, everything faintly unreal.

The car, Henderson, the talk. Never-really-happened-time.

He heard the door click. He was just in the mood for a nocturnal visit. Ian hell bent on suicide, the old man's ghost maybe. He didn't turn round. Maybe they'd stab him in the back. Good luck to them. Were they going to stand there all night? "Well?" he demanded without turning.

"Move over."

He struggled round furiously as he felt the bed dip. John climbed in beside him, half on top in the narrow bed.

"What the fuck...?"

John was smiling down at him. "I heard you come in." He frowned suddenly. "Jesus, what have you been drinking?"

Rab pulled out from under him, pressing back against the wall. "Get out the fucking bed John."

"Why?"

"Because I don't want you in it. Isn't one enough?"

"Never." John was smiling, but not trying anything. "Actually, I just want to talk, but it's cold out there."

"Talk and be quick."

John settled down, hands under his head as if he was there for the night. Rab could smell sweat off him. He could still feel the initial touch of him, clammy, pliant, satiated. He kept his back against the wall. John's face looked odd in the pink light, softened, different. "What did Henderson want?" he asked.

"My body."

"Did he get it?"

"Of course."

John looked at him. "You're lying."

"How can you be so sure?"

"You don't fancy him."

"So? I don't fancy Ian either." He paused then added harshly, "Or you."

John smiled, but said nothing. "Are you going to see him again?" he asked.

"I've no idea."

"He didn't ask you?"

"We didn't part friends."

"Why not?"

"I came without him."

John looked the other way. "Oh, someone's in a mood tonight." He looked back. "What's the matter, he only want to hump Danny?"

"He'd hump anything. He'd hump you."

John laughed. "I doubt it. Last time I offered he didn't want to know."

"It was probably the *way* you offered."

"Just the way I usually do."

"That's what I mean, one arm up his back."

"He looked like a masochist to me."

"They all look like masochists to you. It's your sadist's idea of supply and demand."

John was leaning up on one arm now, looking at him. "Are you sure it wasn't you that didn't get to come?"

"Positive."

"Want to come now?"

"I doubt if you could manage another."

John sucked air in between his teeth and said softly, "Jealous."

"Of who?"

"That's what I'd like to know."

Rab looked at him for a moment. "How about you getting out John? Like now."

"No." He lay back down. "Talk to me."

"Why don't you talk to Danny?"

"You said it - I don't talk to Danny, I fuck Danny."

"Christ, you're a pig."

"Thank you. Now talk to me."

Rab sighed. "What d'you want to talk about?"

"Why you fucked my mother."

Rab looked at him. John looked right back. "Problem?"

Rab shook his head.

"Okay, we'll deal with the sheer improbability issue in a moment. Did you fancy her?"

"No."

"Then why?"

"It was Ian's idea."

John said, "And was it his idea to drop me?"

"I think you dropped me John. Anyway, I was too old for it."

"At eighteen? You were too old for it at sixteen, why not then?"

"Margaret hadn't offered then."

"Margaret never did offer. You just wanted to hurt me, prove you weren't a homo."

Rab could feel his face burning, but he said nothing.

John laughed. "You're not going to give in, are you? Well, was she good? Did you enjoy my mother more than me?"

Rab answered reluctantly. "No."

"So what did it prove?"

"That I wasn't a faggot."

"Like I kept saying you were?"

"You wanted it John, so why the fuck do you keep going on about it? What's the problem?"

"Maybe I didn't know what I wanted."

"Then I'll tell you. You wanted it finished. That was reason enough."

"I was twenty-one."

"You obviously had a delayed childhood, didn't you?"

"Don't be flippant."

"What d'you want me to do, apologise?"

"Yes."

Rab looked at him. "You seriously want me to apologise for something I did when I was eighteen?"

"No, I want you to apologise for something you *pretended* to do when you were eighteen. I want you to apologise for going behind my back and hatching up pathetic plots with Ian." John's eyes were hungry again, no longer flat, disinterested. "I want you to apologise for pretending to be straight when you were as bent as a nine pound note."

"Get stuffed."

John's hand came up from under his head. In it he held the knife.

Rab looked at it then said slowly, "I didn't see it."

"You weren't looking for it."

"You never did fight fair."

"No-one fights fair when they think they might lose. Get down Rab."

Rab didn't move. His eyes were on the knife. "I remember that," he said in the same slow voice. "Your father took that off you years ago. Where did you find it?"

"In his desk drawer." John shook his head. "This isn't going to help. You're only

making it last longer."

"Alright by me. I've got a scar from that knife across three fingers of my right hand."

"You shouldn't have grabbed it."

"Not while you were holding it anyway."

John laughed. He put the point against Rab's throat. "Not while *anyone* was holding it. Want to fight Rab? Want to fight with a knife in the game?"

"No."

"Then get down." His eyes flicked down, directing him.

Rab slid down slowly. John lay on his back, pushing the pillow under his head. The narrow space forced Rab between his legs. John reached down and pulled his hair to one side so that he could watch him take it in his mouth. He lay the knife against his neck. "Can you taste him?" He was smiling.

Rab didn't answer. The knife pressed into his throat. He freed his mouth. "Yes," he admitted.

John's body relaxed.

Rab slid him back into his mouth.

"I get a big kick out of this. First you, then Danny, both at knifepoi..." He stopped abruptly, the knife digging in sharply. "Don't get smart with me."

Rab stopped what he was doing.

John dropped back again. "You know, you should be grateful for small mercies. Danny doesn't always fare so well. I think secretly he enjoys being punished." John laughed. "Or is that just my sadist's idea of supply and demand?"

He was silent a moment, watching Rab's head, his own cock. "Know what I think? I think you stopped fucking me because you were afraid. It wasn't anything to do with me or my mother. It was because you were getting to like it too much, and you were so goddamned scared, that right?"

Rab kept on. The knife dug in again. "I asked you a question."

Rab withdrew his head. "Yes," he said. He lowered his head again.

John stopped him. "Look at me and say that again."

Rab sat up, wiping his mouth on the back of his hand. "I was scared." And as he sat there looking at John, voluptuous in his own potency, he could feel it happening. He didn't try to hide it, didn't care. Fuck him, that's what he wanted to hear, then let him hear it. That's what he wanted to see, then let him see it.

John looked at him. "You do." He was smiling Danny's evil smile. "You always have."

"Yes." Rab felt tired. His heart was beating with a dull, heavy thump.

John closed the knife. The noise and movement was sudden. "Then I'm asking you Rab."

Rab looked at him. "And if I say no?"

"You'll break my heart, but I can't force you."

Rab's eyes hardened. He felt elated with the power of it. "Then the answer's no."

John smiled slowly, his eyes sharp, alive, thriving with it. Rab heard the click and felt the knife pressed against his leg. "I lied."

Rab bent his head as he felt the knife run up his thigh.

Danny looked up at him as he came in. He came in smiling, as Danny knew he would.

"Still awake?" John's voice was casual, amiable, as if it was the last thing he expected.

"What do you think?"

John climbed in and put out the light. He lay on his back.

Danny shifted to give him room. "Was he good?"

"You know he is, why ask?"

Danny closed his eyes against the dark. If six months ago anyone had said, Soon you'll be lying in bed with your brother asking him if he's enjoyed fucking your cousin right after you. Your mother will be dead, your father will be dead, but first they'll both have sex with you. The police will be after you, but will be quite content to have sex with you too. What d'you think of that Danny? Sound like a good plot?

Ha ha. Ha, fucking, ha.

"Why so quiet?" John asked.

"What's there to say?"

"Say you love me."

"Why?"

"I like the noise it makes."

"I love you." Danny's voice was weary, defeated.

John grunted and rolled over to face him. "Want to taste him?"

Danny pulled away violently.

John laughed. "He didn't want to taste you either." His hand began tracing Danny's face in the dark. "Tired?"

"Yes." *Dog-fucking tired, John. Right out of my mind.*

"Shame." But John didn't make any move. Instead he asked, "What would you do for me?"

"How d'you mean?"

"If I killed him what would you give me?"

"What do you want?"

John lay there thinking, trying to clear it in his head, define it. "I've got the farm, the money, all that power..." His voice was sarcastic. "What else *could* I want?"

"I don't know."

"I haven't got *you* Danny. I'm never going to have you while Ian's got anything to do with it."

"That's not tr..."

John's hand pressed over his mouth. "No, don't lie."

Danny lay quiescent. John took his hand away.

"I'll make you a deal." John's voice was close to his ear. "I'll kill Henderson if you kill your brother."

Danny felt as if everything in his body stilled. His heart, the blood in his veins, *everything*, slowed like a film running down. "No." It came out on a breath, hardly a word at all.

John laughed, a little low sweet sound in his ear. "You don't surprise me."

"Why are you doing this?" Danny could still feel his heart going dully, pulsing on reflex. No heart for it, he thought. My heart has no heart for it. Listen to its feeble aching.

"Fun."

Danny shook his head.

"He betrayed me," John said as if he'd spoken.

"He wouldn't."

John laughed. "Your loyalty is heart-warming, but misplaced. I want those little succubus teeth out your skin, once and for all. Feel..." John put his hand on him. He was hard as iron, still sticky from Rab.

"I don't believe you, you sick bastard."

"What's wrong, love him too much? You should be glad." John was crushing his hand down on his cock.

"You don't want to kill him."

"I'm not going to. You are."

"No."

John let him go. "No Ian, no Henderson."

"But I *told* you, Henderson's going to..."

John grabbed his face, gripping it tightly, cutting him short. "Henderson's going to do *nothing*. You think I'm stupid?" He pushed his head away violently, dropping onto his back. "You make me *sick*."

Danny lay there, squeezing his eyes shut, but he still felt them burn with tears. They slid out, escaped like blood oozing out of a wound. John turned towards him then felt them with his thumb, one eye, then the other, delicately. "Crying?" he said softly.

Danny said nothing.

He kissed Danny's eyes. His tongue licked out the corners, licking the tears away like an animal healing a wound. "Cry a few for me Danny." His voice was still gentle, hardly John's at all.

He felt John shift away, then roll back. He felt the blade of it, long against his stomach. His eyes sprung open.

"Jump like that again and you'll eviscerate yourself." John's voice was sharp.

"This is your night for knives, isn't it?" Danny said, feeling himself begin to sweat, feeling it turn cold on his skin.

"When the mood's on me Danny, what can I do?"

The blade was lying flat, but the point dug in slightly just above his navel. It was warmer now, but felt sharper, more uncomfortable. Danny held his breath.

"You or him Danny - which is it to be?"

Danny kept breathing. His sluggish heart woke up, decided it didn't want to stop after all, now that it no longer had a choice.

"It's got to be one Danny, and I'd rather have you. But if you won't then maybe I'll just have to surrender. Are you ready to die for him?"

The point felt sharper now. How would John know when to stop? Point first into the soft flesh of his belly, when would he stop? When it met the bed at the other side?

"*Which* Danny?"

"Don't John." Danny closed his eyes to say it, to not see John's face looking down at him, reading his fear.

"Afraid? Danny finally really afraid of me?"

"Yes, I'm fucking afraid."

"Uh-uh, don't move." The blade bit. "What is it your boyfriend says? Easy, Danny... that's it. Could be talking about you."

Danny relaxed his muscles but the blade still bit. He could feel it piercing his skin. He was impaled on it like an insect, John driving it through him slowly, quarter inch by quarter inch.

"Think I'd be safe coming with a knife in my hand? With it pressing into your belly?"

"No."

"Shall I try it?"

"*No.*"

"I think so."

"John... don't... please stop," Danny begged.

The knife bit again. It was worse this time. Danny's eyes flew open.

"You were *crying* for him."

"I was crying for *me*."

"You were crying for him." John climbed up onto his knees, keeping the knife pressed into him. He straddled his thighs and slapped his head. "You wouldn't give anything for me, would you? Not a tear, not a drop of blood, not a drop of fucking spunk, if I didn't make you." He slapped him again, grabbed his face. "If you only had

the guts you'd cut my throat as soon as look at me, wouldn't you? *Wouldn't you?*"

Danny shook his head.

The knife slid in, definitely this time. Danny stared down in horror. "Oh Jesus, John."

"Why don't you love me?"

"John, take it out, please." Danny gripped his hand. "*Please.*"

"Tell me why."

Danny yelled at him, pulling at his hand. "What can I tell you, that I do? You won't believe me. What can I tell you John? Tell me, 'cause I don't fucking know!"

He burst into tears. He let John's hand go, wanting him to do it, wanting to stop expecting it, living with it in his mouth - the taste of death on everything he touched.

John withdrew the knife slowly then sat over Danny's body with it lying limp in his hand. It glittered dully in the faint light coming through the curtains. Danny's head was turned away, straining against John's weight, trying to bury himself in the pillow. He was crying like someone grieving, someone lost with nothing to live for.

John took his hands, pressed them to his face, bent over them, kissed them.

Danny didn't feel the wet of his tears, but it was there.

"I'm sorry," he said gently, lifting Danny's hands above his head and putting them on the pillow, as if to stop him covering his face. "Danny, I'm sorry. Love me Danny, please. You're all there is. Love me Danny."

And he brought the knife down in an arc, pinning Danny's left hand to the bed.

Rab heard the scream and shot bolt upright, riveted for an instant with shock.

He jumped out of bed and ran for John's room, terrified that it would be locked, wondering if he was capable of destroying the old door. But it was open.

The room was lit only by a streak of moonlight. He could hear Danny's panic-stricken voice saying, "*No*" over and over again. He felt a horrible cold revulsion at the sound of it. He was petrified by the idea of putting on the light. He groped for it, not wanting to find it. When it came on he was momentarily dazzled. Then he saw John, bleached by the light, dead-faced, whiter than a corpse, staring at him as if he had no right to be there. Then he saw Danny, grey with shock, staring at his hand, pulling at it by the wrist as if he couldn't lift it off the bed. And then he saw the knife, the fucking flick knife, sticking clean out of his palm, buried right through into the bed, pinning his hand there like an impaled insect.

"Oh fuck." He moved quickly. "Danny, don't touch it, don't pull it, leave it where it is." But Danny wasn't hearing him. He skirted round John like he was a dangerous dog. John watched him, close-mouthed, flat-eyed. Rab wondered if he was going to snap at him.

Ian appeared in the doorway. "What the fuck's going on? Who screamed?" Then he saw Danny's hand, watched as Danny finally pulled the knife out of the bed. "Oh Jesus." He turned away, but not before Rab saw him change colour.

"Go and phone for an ambulance," Rab almost shouted at him.

Danny looked up suddenly, stopped struggling with his hand, held it there like it didn't belong to him. "No."

"Christ Danny, talk sense. Look at you."

"It's alright," Danny said ridiculously.

John moved suddenly, like a mannequin come to life. He got up, began pulling his clothes on. He turned his back on them all as if they no longer interested him.

"Just take me to casualty." His voice was pleading. "I'll be fine." He sounded coherent, but his pupils were huge, his colour nauseous, his skin shiny. He started to shiver.

Rab looked at him for a long moment then turned to Ian and nodded. When he turned back John was facing them again, fastening his shirt. Rab spoke to him with a mouth that felt as if it was tacked shut. "Help me dress him."

They put Danny's clothes on, wrapping a blanket around his chest, leaving the arm out. Rab saw that Danny wouldn't look at it. He was no longer trying to pull the knife out.

Throughout it all Rab felt John's eyes on him. They were flat and implacable now, but Rab remembered them in that moment when he first came into the room, like the startled eyes of a snake, something feral, crouching over Danny like something interrupted at its feed.

They took him downstairs and into the Range Rover. Rab put him in the front seat and then got in. John didn't attempt to come with them. Ian didn't offer. Rab put the heater on full. Danny looked worse. Rab hoped it was only the reflected light from the dashboard. "You okay?" he asked.

Danny grunted. He had his eyes closed.

"We'll be there in no time, stick with it." He winced at his choice of words.

He drove the way he always did, fast and a bit more dangerously than he should, but they got there. They saw Danny quickly, frightened he'd either pass out in the waiting room or perhaps start a nauseous chain reaction, like sea-sickness. The knife looked bad, sticking out both sides like a joke shop trick.

They took him away, leaving Rab to answer questions. His name, his address. The nurse wanted to know how it happened.

"An accident."

She looked at him disbelievingly.

Rab flushed betrayingly. "They were fooling around."

Her mouth folded. "It's a stupid thing to be fooling around with." She looked at him as if it was his fault.

"I couldn't agree more."

She gave him another look.

"Can I sit down now?" he asked finally.

She nodded curtly, her face telling him what she, as the hospital, thought of people like him. She watched him walk down the corridor. The hair, the too-tight jeans. She blew down her nose. Too good-looking for his own good, and didn't he know it? She felt over her desk for her pen and forgot about him.

They gave Danny an anaesthetic which didn't work fast enough. They took out the knife and then hurt him some more. The doctor was civil, quick and heartless. He did not care how the wound had been made. He did not ask.

He was X-rayed by a stout black woman who brushed the hair off his forehead and told him to keep his chin up. He fell asleep twice and twice they woke him up. They left him sleeping finally on a bare examination couch behind a curtain while they checked X-rays. They woke him a third time so that a different doctor could reopen the wound, but this time Danny felt nothing.

He winked at Danny and asked him how it had happened. Danny shook his head. The doctor asked him if he was in a fight. Danny shook his head again. He fell asleep again with the doctor feeling his forehead.

"Lovely hair."

Danny knew he had seen her before, but couldn't place her.

She had no accent at all. Not black, not local, nothing. She smiled and Danny suddenly remembered her. He smiled back.

"Aha, you *are* alive," she said just as Rab materialised beside her.

"Okay?" he asked him. He looked thin and cold.

Danny said yes and smiled again at the sound of his own voice.

Everybody smiled.

It was a very happy moment.

Rab drove slowly, glancing occasionally at his face. "He said you were lucky. Thin blade, sharp, a nice clean cut."

Danny closed his eyes momentarily as if he was going to be sick.

"Sorry." Rab looked at him again. He licked his lip. "He says you might lose the feeling in one finger for a while, but if it doesn't come back they might be able to fix it."

Danny looked at him. "By opening it up again?"

"I don't know. I suppose so."

"No thank you." He laid his head back again.

Dawn was breaking in the sky ahead of them. The traffic was already getting heavier. Rab took a breath and plunged in with both feet. "Why did he do it?"

"I don't know."

Rab risked another glance on the straight. "Honestly?"

"God's honest truth. Like a bolt out of the blue."

"What were you doing?"

"He was sticking it in my stomach."

"The knife?"

Danny laughed shortly. "No, his dick." He opened the blanket and pulled the skin out from under his belt.

Rab glanced down. A small scabbed wound showed brown and dark on the white skin. He grimaced. "Oh God Danny, you can't keep this up."

"What do you suggest?" He wrapped himself in the blanket again.

"Get away from him."

Danny turned his face away. "Go with you."

Rab shook his head. "Not necessarily, just go."

"Don't you want me to go with you?"

"Would you?"

"Sorry."

Rab looked at him again then pulled out past a long container lorry, accelerating hard. "Why not? Why put up with it?"

"I told you, maybe I like it."

Rab swung on him. "You fucking don't."

"Watch the road."

"I don't believe anybody enjoys being sliced open."

"Okay, I'm a liar."

"Then why?"

"Because."

"Because *why?*" Rab said furiously.

"Just *because.*" Danny's face was white, angry, drawn.

"Oh fuck, why do I bother?" Rab pushed back into his seat, glaring ahead.

Danny was quiet.

Ten minutes passed in silence then Rab chanced another look at him. His eyes were closed, his face drawn. "Hurting?"

Danny nodded. "I think the anaesthetic's wearing off."

"They gave me some painkillers for you, and some antibiotics."

Danny nodded again.

"You've got to go back, to see how it's healing."

"You mean to see if I can move my hand."

Rab looked at him, wanting to reassure him, but could think of nothing to say.

Danny felt as if his whole arm was on fire. A dull throbbing started in his hand like a hammer landing on his palm. He bit his lip and tried to go to sleep.

Rab didn't speak to him again.

When Danny woke up next they were home and the cows were already milked.

Rab found John in the milking shed. Ian saw him come in and walked away without speaking. John leaned against a stall in the darkness and waited. Rab walked down to meet him.

"Where is he?" John looked in his eyes. John was never afraid to look in your eyes. Not ashamed, or embarrassed, or afraid.

"In the house."

John nodded.

"That's it? Don't you want to know if he's alright? If he lost a hand? If he'll ever play the violin again?"

"You would tell me fast enough."

"Oh very smooth and slick. With any luck you'll slide in your own grease and break your neck."

"You don't love me any more."

Rab closed his eyes and opened them again slowly. "The hospital will report it."

John's face became wary, hard. "Why didn't you tell them it was an accident?"

"I did. I covered up for you very nicely, just like I always do, but it's a knife wound, and it didn't look much like an accident. More importantly, the nurse didn't believe me, or like me, so she'll report it. You can bet on it."

"It doesn't matter."

"No, of course not. Police wandering around, two missing parents, suspicious knife wounds. Why don't you give Danny a black eye or two before they arrive? See if you can't finish us off quickly, spare our sufferings."

John folded his arms slowly, deliberately. It was a threat and Rab wasn't in the mood. He brought his hand up out of his pocket and the knife clicked open.

John moved his eyes briefly towards it then back to Rab's face. "They gave it back to you."

"That's right."

John's eyes moved again. "Surprising."

"It was an accident, remember? Anyway, I said it belonged to Danny's father, said it would get him into even more trouble if it was missing."

"Hearts and flowers."

"That's right."

John glanced at the floor then back up at his face. "Are you going to use it or what?"

"Would you like to fight with a knife in the game?"

"Touché." John smiled but said nothing more.

Rab brought it up to his cheek. John did not move. The blade pressed against the bone. "An eye for an eye John."

John looked at him then lifted his hand, curling it round his. He held it there, warm and dry, like your father's hand, a safe haven, until it squeezed too hard and crushed the life out of you. "You haven't got it in you Rab."

"Leave him alone John."

"You haven't got it in you."

270

Rab moved it quickly, flicking the point upwards, gouging the skin out of his cheek.

John's hand tightened immediately, forcing his hand away. "Drop it." He squeezed Rab's wrist, twisting the skin.

Rab dropped it, down into the thick muck of the runnel. The blood ran down John's face in a thin black line, like he was crying ink. He still held Rab's hand tightly by the wrist. After a moment or two he let him go. "One I owe you," he said. The blood ran into his mouth. He licked it away as if it was water.

Rab felt sickened. "Next time it won't be your face," he said, but his voice was weak.

"Maybe you won't get a next time." John bent down and picked up the knife. He cleaned it on the sleeve of his shirt, both sides. It flashed dully between them. "Maybe you won't live long enough," he said.

And he clicked it shut and walked away.

THIRTY-SEVEN

Henderson looked out of his living room window. Outside it was cold enough to snow. Inside he was warm and snug.

He was sitting in his pyjamas and dressing gown, alone on the vast settee. He looked at the phone. It felt almost like a craving, like an ache in his groin. He could feel the needles of it crawling over his back like claws.

He felt himself through the silk of his pyjamas, watched his hand shaping the bulge of his crotch in the dark window. He slid along the couch to the phone and lifted the receiver. He dialled the operator and slid his penis out into his hand. He asked her for Hope House Farm, Brixby. He watched himself masturbating while she found it. He felt a sudden conviction it would be unlisted. It wasn't. He wrote the number down and hung up. He looked at his erection sticking out the fly of his pyjamas and adjusted his position to make it bigger. He slicked it with two fingers as he had seen Danny do then he dialled the number.

The phone rang and rang. He said to himself, Another six rings, that's it. He counted, moving his hand in time to the tone. He let it ring another eight times and then a strange voice answered.

He asked to speak to Rab. The voice asked who he was. He told it. There was a pause then he heard the phone being put down. There were strange hollow noises at the other end, a sound like wind, a door, then Rab was speaking to him. He said, "Hello?" Henderson looked at himself and realised he could get off just listening to his voice. He let go.

"I want you to come round."

"Now?"

Henderson could hear the irritation in his voice. He said, "Yes." Rab said, "No." And Henderson knew he would have said it no matter when he'd asked him to come round. Well, that was too bad.

There was a pause. Henderson filled it by saying, "We got a night sheet from the Victoria casualty department today."

There was another pause. Henderson heard another door banging and the sound of a dog barking before Rab replied, "What time?"

Henderson said as soon as he was ready. Rab told him it wouldn't be for another hour. He said, "Fine" and prepared to hang up.

"Why me?" Rab's voice sounded very close suddenly.

Henderson began stroking himself again, gently, encouragingly. "I'm in the mood for a blonde."

Rab hung up without saying goodbye.

"Why you?" John was leaning against the banisters, watching him. The hall table was between them. He had a blue plaster on his face like the kind meat-packers wore. It should've looked ridiculous. Instead he looked faintly sinister. Much the same kind of effect as an eye patch.

"He's in the mood for a blonde."

John lifted his eyebrows. "Your lucky night."

"They know about the hospital."

John looked at the living room door then back at Rab. "And so you're going there tonight."

"Unless you'd rather go yourself."

"He's not my type."

"Things too equal?"

"Miaow."

Rab walked past him and went up the stairs.

"Rab..." John called after him, his voice level, uninvolved. Rab paused. "Don't go falling in love."

His smile stretched on long after Rab had stopped looking at it.

Danny was lying out on the couch, his injured hand palm-upwards across his stomach. Ian was sitting in the armchair watching the side of his face.

Danny was spacey with painkillers. He felt as if he were floating slightly. Any part of himself that he moved seemed to move slower than the rest of him, and with a kind of distinct detachment. He was not aware of Ian. The television images seemed deeply real, the room removed from him.

John came in and pushed his feet off the settee. Danny adjusted his position. He still lay flat out but at a slight angle, his feet on the floor, head and shoulders propped up against the corner of the settee. Ian expected to be thrown out, but John said nothing.

He found the remote control and changed channels without asking anyone. Danny moved his head slowly and looked at him, then back at the television. John looked at him. "Christ, you look like a hophead."

"They're a bit strong," Danny said. To himself he sounded strange but to John and Ian his voice was quite normal.

John looked at him a long while then put his hand on his thigh.

Ian felt his mouth go dry. John usually kept this stuff private. He knew he ought to just get up and go because he knew that sooner or later John would chuck him out anyway, but the hell with it, he might as well stay and watch Danny being mauled about while he could - free entertainment. He looked at the TV, but kept a covert eye on John's hand.

John spoke suddenly. "Put your leg up."

Danny looked at him blankly. John lifted his leg for him, irritably pushing his knee against the back of the couch. Now Danny lay with his legs spread open like a woman ready for delivery. John reached out and pulled down his zip. Danny seemed to tear his eyes from the TV with difficulty. He frowned at John's hand as if he wasn't sure what it was.

Ian felt as if the whole thing had suddenly shifted from mildly sadistically entertaining to something much more threatening. He felt his face burning. What was John playing at?

Suddenly John pushed his hand in. Danny lifted his injured hand up his chest as if moving it away from a dangerous insect.

Ian watched in a confused state of resentment and something more elusive. When John pulled Danny's cock out he realised it was excitement, an incredible, intense excitement.

John said, "Lift your backside."

Danny lifted it slightly, still frowning. John pulled his trousers down with a yank, exposing his lower belly and genitals.

"Ian's here," Danny said, as if introducing him to his brother. He sounded very young. Ian knew the odd quirk. It made him feel uncomfortable.

Danny turned his head, his eyes moving as if trying to trace him. They finally landed on Ian's face. Ian looked away. "Ian's here," he said again, turning back to

John.

"So? Give the little fag something to wank over on his long, lonely nights." John never looked at him once. Ian felt himself redden, but he didn't get up.

Danny said, "Don't," in that same childish voice. He put his good hand down, but John pushed it away easily, without violence.

Danny felt suddenly as if he was made of lead. He felt very, very tired. He watched John toying with him and knew he would not get an erection. He felt as if someone had given him an unexpected present. He couldn't feel his fingers, or his face, but he knew he was very happy.

John unfastened his shirt, telling him to hold his arm out the way. Now he was laid bare from neck to groin.

Ian looked at the dark red nipples, the hollow of his belly, the fine red-gold hair running from his navel into the thick thatch at his crotch, his cock lying white and soft in the middle of it, and felt his erection burning inside his clothes. It was difficult to argue about Danny's sheer exoticism, no matter how much you hated him. He didn't look human.

"Like it?"

Ian realised John was talking to him. He looked up and saw his eyes, dark on his, the mouth smiling contemptuously.

"He isn't stiff." Ian didn't know what instinct made him say it, but he saw it strike home and knew that Danny's flaccidity was an insult, not something John usually had to deal with. His elation was brief and bitter, poisoned.

John's face tightened. He looked back at Danny. "You're letting me down Danny. Think about your reputation."

Danny shook his head slowly. "No good," he said cheerfully. "Stoned out my head." It was inaccurate in detail, but the same in effect.

John stopped fondling him, stared at him for a moment, and then said, "We'll see."

With an abruptness that made Ian choke on his own spit, John kneeled up between Danny's legs and exposed himself. Ian was silenced, immobilised, unprepared for the extravagance of him, the sheer size. John spoke to Danny like someone cajoling a dog or a cat. "There, look. Look at it Danny."

Danny was looking at it, still smiling vacantly, but John definitely had his attention now. He began to masturbate ostentatiously, like the star of a hard-core movie, displaying its size, holding the blood in it, swelling the veins. Everything done for the viewer's pleasure and not his own.

Ian had a horrible second's fear that he was going to climax right in front of them, just watching. His skin burned. He breathed through his mouth, trying to draw enough oxygen in not to faint. But Danny remained unmoved. He lay there, beautiful, flawless, self-contained, with that stupid half-smile, crippling everyone with frustration. No wonder John hit him.

John let go suddenly, and Ian could see the clenching of his leg muscles, his white lips, as he held his orgasm back, willed it down.

"Take it out."

Ian didn't realise he was talking to him until he turned and swore at him. "Come on, you stupid little fuck. It's up, isn't it? So take it out."

Ian flushed angrily but John's derision didn't kill his desire. He tore his eyes away and fumbled with his zip. He finally managed to undo it and struggle his over-excited penis out.

"Don't just sit there, you dumb bastard. Here."

Ian got up, penis swaying ridiculously, like a girder in the wind. John pushed him forward when he moved to stand beside him, making him stand level with Danny's face.

Danny looked up at him slowly, eyes pausing briefly over his cock before they reached his face. Ian felt an overpowering urge to piss on him, defile him. He squeezed his cock fiercely, shoving it out at him.

Danny's penis came up leisurely, languorously, like a man watching a slow erotic show. He was intent on the expression in Ian's eyes, seeing it in very fine detail, like he had the television. There was someone's dick, red and excited, and behind it the hungry eyes looking down on him.

John bent down and began to lick Danny's cock. Ian could hardly bare to watch. Danny lying there like an exquisite piece of living pornography with John licking him like an ice-cream. He watched John's thick tongue wrap itself round the head, saw his wide mouth slide down over the shaft. Danny was huge, not even looking at John, just looking up at Ian's face.

Ian felt as if he was basking in his adoration. He stopped touching himself, wanting it to last, wanting to see John work his magic. John was sucking the head. He had it peeled back and was sucking it up, swelling it till it was purplish, then squeezing it between his fingers.

Danny shifted his weight slightly, spreading his legs wider, lifting his pelvis. John stopped, lifted his head to look up at him. Danny brought his eyes down finally to meet his. Ian saw them look at each other and felt as if he had been wiped out of the room, as if he'd never existed.

John spoke softly. "Want to see him come?" But his eyes never left Danny's face.

Ian croaked something in reply. He felt his cock jerk as if someone had touched it.

John crouched up and squatted over Danny's body, one knee up close by his side, the foot wedged down the side of him, his other foot on the floor. His position was awkward, ungainly and obscene. He pressed his cock against Danny's, held the two together as if he was comparing them. He outstripped Danny by enough to make Ian's orgasm threaten to spill over.

John began to work them together, both hands, one clockwise, one anti, like a huge phallus being ritually milked. He jerked his hips like some kind of filthy animated toy.

Ian watched Danny's eyes travel up to his face again, then grabbed his own cock, pushing out his stomach, wanting to be part of it.

John tried to speak. He got as far as "Fuck…" before his eyes opened with a jerk, looking down at his hands.

Ian saw it come out in huge squirts, unnatural, larger than life, like John himself.

He felt his own orgasm come up through his arse with a suddenness that made his legs buckle. He saw his hand flailing, saw his come jerk out, high in the air, sluicing over them. He kept pulling his penis, excited beyond belief.

John was reaching forward, his hand crawling into Danny's hair, his fist still slowly milking them. Semen dripped down between them. Ian saw his hand pull Danny's hair slowly, tighter and tighter. "Now Danny," he demanded.

Danny closed his eyes against the pulling pain of John's hand… and came, exquisitely, in juddering arcs, his whole body twitching.

Ian watched him and felt his cock surge painfully, still iron-hard under the stickiness of his hand, trying feebly to relieve him of what wasn't there, and knew right then he was dead.

Henderson was drunk. Henderson was *really* drunk.

Rab stood shivering, moving from foot to foot, hands shoved into the armpits of his jacket, looking at the sky, wondering if it was going to have the nerve to snow in October. He muttered to himself, "Come *on*."

He rang the bell again. This time Henderson answered. It seemed to take him an age to buzz the door. Rab pushed in, letting the breath out of his body, into the glorious heat of the hallway. He felt like rolling in the carpet.

He went up the stairs slowly only because his legs were numb. Henderson had left the door ajar. Rab went in and shut it.

The hallway was dark. He had his hand on the living room door when Henderson's arms snaked round him. "Give us a kiss."

Rab ducked his head, avoiding Henderson's mouth. He felt silky and warm under his hands, shifting like water. He reeked of drink.

"Christ, you're drunk." Rab peeled his hands off, only to have them stick on again like pins to a magnet. Finally he pushed open the living room door and pulled himself through, tugging away from Henderson at the same time.

Henderson stood leaning against the door jamb. He was playing with himself through the fabric of his pyjamas. "It's hard," he announced with glee as if he'd done something awfully clever.

"I can see that."

Henderson grinned vulpinely. His mouth seemed immensely wet, blood-stained.

"Most people as pissed as you are wouldn't even know they had a dick let alone be able to get it up."

"It wants you." Henderson was squeezing it now. Rab wondered when it would occur to him to just pull his prick out and get his show on the road.

Rab moved abruptly and went into the kitchen. As he passed he picked the rum bottle off the floor. Different brand - Pussers 100% Proof. There was only about a third left in the bottle. He took it with him into the kitchen and poured it down the sink. It was probably a waste of time but he did it anyway.

Henderson bounced in behind him. If he noticed the waste of his rum he did not comment. Rab wasn't sure how to go about sobering him up. In his own experience puking up was probably the most effective method, followed by a gallon or so of cold water. He doubted if Henderson would agree to puke just to please him, then the solution came to him. "What sobers you up?"

"The news."

Rab looked at him. "What *really* sobers you up?"

Henderson sat on a chair with a heavy drop of his body. "I told you, the news. All that senseless violence. Gets to me, really does."

Rab tried again. "When you get drunk, and you want to be undrunk, what do you do?"

"I *never* want to be undrunk." Henderson said it very seriously, shaking his head portentously.

Rab tried a third time. "Okay, supposing you're still drunk in the morning and you've got to go to work, what then?"

Henderson considered this. "Never going to work again. You an' me..." he fished in his head, "...are going away together. Going to fuck like ducks." He laughed at this, immensely taken with the idea. "Fuck like ducks," he said again, "with our arses in the air." He laughed inordinately, slapping his leg and missing.

Rab stared at the clock above his head till Henderson had finished sniggering then tried again. "Supposing you *were* going back to work, what would you do?"

"Kill myself."

Rab shifted his backside on the counter. "That's the best idea you've had all evening."

Henderson looked up at him. "You don't like me."

"Not while you're drunk."

"I'll be sober." Henderson tried to sit up.

"Good idea. How are you going to do it?"

"Think great thoughts."

Rab laughed in spite of himself. "And that'll do it?"

"Of course." Henderson seemed outraged by his doubt.

"How about coffee, help it along?"

"Yuk," Henderson said, adding apropos of nothing, "and I don't like grapefruit either."

"Water then?"

"Nope." Henderson shook his head. He looked at Rab suddenly. "Want to fuck?"

"I doubt if you could."

Henderson nodded enthusiastically and began pulling at his dressing gown.

Rab pulled it back on, holding the two halves together. "Not until you're sober."

Henderson looked at his face warily. "Will you?"

"When you're sober." And if Henderson remembered Rab would be very surprised indeed. "Now, how are we going to sober you up?"

"Fruit juice."

"What?" This was a new one.

"Lots of orange." Henderson went to the fridge and pulled the door open. It swung wide, taking Henderson with it. Rab stood up and caught him. Henderson immediately started clinging all over him, feeling his body as if he was searching him. "Nice shape."

Rab pulled the orange out and ripped the carton open with his teeth. Henderson was trying to unbutton his shirt. Rab prised him off and took a tall glass out of the cupboard. Inside there were four more bottles of the same brand of rum. He half filled the glass.

"More 'n that," Henderson said, nodding his head. "Fill it up."

Rab filled it up. Henderson took the glass and held it with both hands, draining the contents.

"*This* is going to sober you up?"

Henderson nodded, "Fill her up."

Rab made a face and filled it up again.

Henderson drunk it down again.

"Again," he said, holding the glass out.

"You'll be sick," Rab warned.

"That's right," Henderson agreed.

Rab filled it up again.

Henderson drank the last one a little slower then put the glass down on the counter. "Going to be sick now," he said and bounced back out the kitchen.

Rab followed him, wondering if he planned being sick on the nice white carpet or off the balcony, but Henderson disappeared bedroom-wise. Rab followed him and saw him go into the bathroom. Within seconds he was loudly and ostentatiously sick. Several times. Then there was quiet. Eventually there was a sound of running water.

Rab looked into the bedroom. He flicked on the light curiously. More mirrors. And the famous black sheets. The room was unnaturally tidy, no clothes lying around. The only discordant note was video boxes scattered across the bed. At least a dozen of them. Rab crossed to the bed and lifted one up. It was blank-faced, the title photocopied in German or Dutch. It was something '...and black'. Those with photographs were 'gay'. What Henderson needed was a police raid. He put them back down. He wondered if he had a video in the room. He looked round but couldn't see one.

Henderson came out the bathroom. He saw Rab in the bedroom and came through, standing in the doorway.

"Alright?" Rab asked him.

"So-so."

He certainly sounded more sober. His eyes still didn't look too good, but being sick didn't really qualify as a miracle cure, just a helping hand.

"I need some water."

Rab nodded and moved to the door, pushing him ahead of him. Henderson went quietly. Back in the kitchen he stood by the sink and drank several glasses then he sat down again. His hair was wet, as if he'd stuck his head under the tap. He had lost his dressing gown and pyjama top. Rab marvelled all over again at the body hair, like a fucking ape. "How we doin'?" he asked.

Henderson shrugged, his head back against the wall, his eyes closed. "Preferred being drunk."

"Why?"

Henderson didn't open his eyes. "It's easier to make passes at you."

Rab smiled, but said nothing.

Henderson opened his eyes eventually and asked for another drink of water. Rab filled his glass slowly, wiping the bottom on a dish towel.

"You've got a lovely arse."

Rab handed him the glass. "You're doing fine sober."

"I'm not sober yet."

"That explains it then."

Henderson drank half his glass and put it down. "How's Danny?"

Rab took a snatched breath, as if he'd been holding it. "Last seen he was hurting and knocking back pain-killers. By now I expect he's in happy-land or asleep."

"What did he do?" Henderson drunk the last of the water.

"Hurt his hand on a knife."

"Come on." Henderson wiped his moustache with his hand.

"What d'you expect me to tell you?"

"The truth."

"That is the truth."

"In a pig's eye."

Rab shrugged.

Henderson looked at him then absent-mindedly pushed down the waistband of his pyjama bottoms to scratch his belly. Rab saw the thickened hair, looked away. He knew that Henderson had done it deliberately. He'd done it too often himself not to recognise it.

"I'm going to nail him."

Rab looked round at him. He didn't sound drunk now. He didn't even sound tipsy. "Who?" he said carefully.

"John the Barbarian. I'm going to get him put away."

Rab felt himself swallow as if the saliva had been gathering all night for the moment. "You can't," he said.

"I'm going to."

"Listen, believe me," Rab said it carefully, licking his lips, "if you start anything the whole thing will come down like a pack of cards."

"What whole thing?"

Rab tried to meet his gaze but he wanted to punch him in the mouth, smash the glass in his teeth. He let his eyes slide away. "Me, Danny, John - the whole lot."

"Why should it?"

"Because John will *make* it happen."

"Then he'd land Danny in it."

"That's the point."

"Deliberately?" Henderson sounded sceptical, as if it was unlikely, illogical, simply

not done.

Rab shook his head at him. "You don't understand him. You don't even *begin* to comprehend him. He's not in your league, not in anybody's league."

"You mean he's nuts."

"If you want to put it like that."

"Tough shit."

Rab looked at him. He really meant it. He had his revenge in his hands and he wasn't going to give it up.

"It won't get you Danny. He'll just drag you in too, lock stock and barrel."

Henderson smiled. "I doubt it."

Rab launched across the floor at him, pressing his hands on the table to keep them out of harm's way. "You fucking dumb bastard. What are you trying to do?"

Henderson's face tightened. "He threatened me."

"And you're going to throw everything away, maybe even do time yourself, just because he threatened you?"

"I won't do time, and he won't touch Danny... or you."

"Oh *Christ*." Rab stood up, dragging his hand through his hair. "How can I make you *understand?*" He turned suddenly. "How are you going to do it?"

"I've got contacts." Henderson looked self-satisfied.

"Like?" Rab jabbed the word at him.

"I have a friend in high places, knows your family from way back."

Rab stared at him.

"Turns out Big-boy has some history after all."

Rab listened with a sinking horror. He felt the frantic anxiety of insecurity. He said desperately, "But it still hinges on Danny. You would have to get Danny to stand witness."

"I will."

Rab laughed, folding his arms. "Oh no, you won't."

"There's the hospital report."

"That means nothing."

"It's evidence."

"Of *what?*"

Henderson smiled. Rab couldn't believe it, but he saw it.

"Then I'll get them to drag the water at Yardholm."

Rab blinked. He knew the colour had drained from his face. Henderson looked at him and Rab saw the odd expression on his face and he realised at that moment that Henderson had never really seriously considered murder, had never really connected anything with Yardholm, other than some dirty wanking games, because that's how his mind worked. You wanted to play dirty games you played them. If the boys wouldn't play you paid them. Nobody needed to *kill* anybody. Whatever he thought they'd done, it wasn't that. Rab wanted to laugh.

"My God," Henderson was almost whispering it, "she's in there, isn't she?"

But Rab had recovered. He laughed. He just let it go. He stood back from himself and admired that laugh. It was the finest laugh he'd ever heard. He shook his head with becoming merriment and watched the relief flood Henderson's face. Oh gosh, he was *so* glad now he didn't need to *arrest* anybody. Rab laughed again. He heard an ugly little note of hysteria in it and put it under his heel.

Henderson had already forgotten Rab's expression, the shock, the fear, because it didn't fit. It was never going to fit in Henderson's world. And Rab could see this go on forever. For as long as he thought it was just some jealous little quirk on John's part he wouldn't take him seriously. And if he knew the truth, then what? All too deep and dirty, and Rab was afraid to tell him because Henderson might just dump them all.

Nothing there he could buy. Safer watching videos, even buying toilet boys. Much safer.

Rab waited. He waited because he didn't know what else to do.

It was then that the door buzzer went.

John got up and squeezed the worst off himself. He wiped his hand on the leg of Danny's jeans and went out the room without looking at either of them.

Ian looked at Danny. His stomach and chest were covered with sperm. Theirs, his. He knelt down beside him, leant over his face and kissed him. He kissed him like a man tasting a new fruit, unsure if he will like it, trying it in small pieces.

Danny did not open his eyes, nor did he kiss him back.

Ian lifted his head, looked at Danny's face, then down at his body. He reached down and put his hand in the come. He slicked it over Danny's stomach, coating him in it. He licked his lips. He could feel his cock pressed against the sofa. He kissed Danny again, a little harder this time. He wanted to push his tongue in. He kept his eyes open, looking at Danny's face, the non-existent pores, the silken lashes. Not a man, a dark angel, something fallen from the skies, stomach still wet with his sin.

He pushed his tongue in between Danny's lips and saw Danny's eyes open slowly. He pulled away, flushing guiltily. He wiped his hand on the sofa without thinking.

"Ian," Danny said, as if he was surprised to see him there. Ian saw his tongue as he wet his mouth, just a vagrant hint, a glimpse. He wanted to feel it in his mouth more than anything in the world.

"Where's Rab?" Danny asked.

Ian looked at his hair and said, "If you kiss me I'll tell you."

Danny frowned for a moment then his face cleared. "That's okay," he said, as if Ian had apologised for something.

Ian said it again because he wanted Danny to understand, be quiet, *let* him. "I'll tell you if you kiss me."

"Yes," Danny said, as if to say, Well, go on.

Ian hesitated then kissed him again. He closed his eyes because Danny's were open, looking beyond him. The lips were too pliant, too unresponsive. This was the real thing and he could find no satisfaction in it. But he wanted it again. "Danny," he whispered, keeping his mouth close, "kiss me properly."

Danny moved his head slightly but said nothing.

Ian tried again. "I won't tell you unless you kiss me properly," he threatened. He didn't know what Danny was thinking or even if he cared. He kissed him suddenly, quickly, with frustration. He felt Danny's good hand touch his head, then unexpectedly his mouth latched onto his, began drawing him in.

Danny kissed him mouth to mouth. It was closer than real. Beyond real.

Danny let him go. He pulled Ian back by the hair. It was a slow movement, but strong enough. "Now tell me."

"Kiss me again." Ian was pressing against him, trying to climb on top.

"No." Danny said it incisively, drugged or no.

Ian looked down at him and hated him for his 'No's' and his 'Maybes' and his come-on eyes. "He's with Henderson, that's where he is."

"Why?"

Ian didn't have a clue why but he knew how to goad Danny. "Why d'you think?" But Danny lay there, unresponsive. If he was thinking Ian couldn't see it. If he had hurt him it wasn't showing.

"Little poof," he hissed close to Danny's face. "Miserable little poof." He lifted his hand and slapped Danny's balls viciously. He dug his fingers into the soft flesh. "Ugly

little pig." He began to gather spit in his mouth. "Stinking little *pig*." And on the 'pig' he spat in Danny's face, just as John came back in.

John lifted him by the back of his sweater, dropping him, back first, onto the ceramic coffee table that sat under the window.

Danny sat up slowly, wiping his face with his one good hand, using his shirt tail. "Don't," he said stupidly.

Ian lay winded, tears of pain coming out his eyes utterly without control.

John picked him up again. Not a word, nothing. The silence was terrifying. Ian tried to speak. John half-lifted him to the fire. Then held him over it. Lower, lower.

Danny got up slowly.

Ian whimpered, struggling violently. He could feel the pain start, the burning. He was going to wet himself.

John let him go. He fell back on the hearth with a thump, banging his head on the floor. John kicked him with his foot, a gentle nudge in the small of his back. "Get out."

Ian's trousers were half-way down his thighs. He tried to pull them up, dragging himself across the floor.

John kicked him again, a little harder. "I said, get *out*."

Ian scrambled to his feet, pulling his clothes up with one hand.

He got out the door. It was barely closed before he let out a moan and felt the piss run down his leg. He stood looking down at himself in the hall. Slowly he walked up the stairs, crying without knowing it, ungainly, like a man who'd wet himself.

John wiped Danny down with a handkerchief and threw it in the fire. "You whore," he said matter-of-factly. But Danny knew it was alright. John wasn't angry. Danny could tell by his mouth.

John stroked his hair gently and said, "You're not going to make twenty, are you?" It was an old game, like the baths, the fighting, the pain.

"No," Danny said.

John smiled, patted him some more. Good boy, the pats said. "They just won't leave you alone, will they?"

"No," Danny said again. He knew all the answers.

John gazed at the fire. "You shouldn't have messed with the old man."

Danny sat watching John's hands. Big, powerful.

John looked at him slowly. "And you should *never* have involved Ian." His hand ran down the side of Danny's face, feeling the delicacy of the bone. "How like an angel," he whispered, "and so far fallen."

Danny reached out his hand to John's mouth, running his finger over John's lips. "I love you," he said.

John looked at him, his eyes unreadable. "Too late Danny. Lifetimes too late."

"I love you," Danny said again, pulling John's hand to his heart, pressing it hard to the flesh of his chest.

John pulled his hand away and stood up. He spoke directly, as if they had said nothing else. "I'm going upstairs. You stay here."

Danny looked up at him. He shook his head.

John pushed him back against the couch. "You stay here and shut up."

"John..." Danny tried to catch at the leg of his jeans.

"Shut up Danny. Just fucking shut it."

He crossed to the door then stopped and turned. "Be here Danny."

And that was that.

As soon as John went out the door Danny stood up and fastened his clothes. He listened at the door until he could no longer hear John's footsteps. He heard an upstairs door close. He crossed to the window and took two tablets from the bottle on the table. He added a third and swallowed them dry. It took him a few moments. When the last was down he climbed awkwardly out the front window using his one good hand.

Danny took the Rover.

He swung the car out into the dark road, driving one-handedly. He wondered how long the painkillers would take. The last lot were beginning to wear off. He could feel his hand protesting at being used, however minimally. The stitches seemed to be dragging his skin together from an inch apart. They felt as if they wanted to burst open. His head was still woozy, half free-floating, but the pain was there behind it, waiting to surface.

He was driving too fast. To him the road seemed to hurtle under him like film of a roller-coaster. The bends seemed to sweep at impossible angles. He felt as if he were driving a Dodgem, having to turn the wheel vastly to move the car at all. He kept wanting to follow the white lines, kept pulling himself off them back into lane. The other cars seemed to jump out of the darkness, vanish. He wondered if he was hallucinating them, building them out of the occasional street lights, his own reflections.

He slowed at the entrance to Jerrett's then realised he wasn't going there. He accelerated in a burst, throwing himself back in his seat. He thought he heard a car blare. He saw headlights flash, but he didn't know if it was at him.

He drove on through the town and onto the coast road. He slowed too early and was tooted at again. When he speeded up he nearly missed the turning. He stopped without checking and reversed the car without looking. He was lucky.

He turned down towards the harbour.

He did not try to park near the basin itself, realising he might well end up in it. He simply stopped the car where he was. He sat a moment, watching the lights, so white and pure. He wanted to wash. He scrubbed his mouth violently with his hand. He began to feel the same sensation of weightlessness and realised dimly the tablets were beginning to take effect. *You've got to go Danny.*

He slid his legs out of the car. The road felt soft underfoot. When he stood up he felt as if he were standing on marshmallows. He bounced slightly on his toes then closed the car door. He walked towards Henderson's house, watching the white marshmallow road. He couldn't smell them.

He did not feel the cold.

He got to the doorway and looked at the bells. None of them said Henderson. None of them said anything. He looked at the lights, cut-out, large, flattening the black, and thought about the bells. He pressed one.

Not the right one.

After some time the owner told him Mr Henderson was in Flat 6. Danny looked at them again. *Got to throw a six Danny.* He pressed another. He fell to watching the lights again.

Henderson spoke to him.

Danny said, "It's me," and knew there was more. "Danny," he added.

There was a long elastic silence where Danny fell in love with the dark, the feel of the cold glass against his cheek, the feeling of no feeling at all, then Henderson woke him up.

"Come up," he said, and a vicious bee began buzzing at Danny's head.

He stood a moment then leaned against the door. He fell straight through and down the rabbit hole.

Henderson looked at Rab. "It's Danny."

"I heard."

They stood waiting for him to go through the door. It seemed to take him an age. Finally the tone stopped.

Henderson felt a dull excitement in his stomach. He opened the door and peered out, leaving it on the latch. Rab was watching him from the living room doorway.

They stood for several minutes, not speaking, then Henderson said, "Where the hell is he?"

Rab walked past him and looked out. "I'll go see." And he went out.

He found him sitting on the second floor landing, head against the window, gazing out into the dark. He called his name.

Danny looked up.

"What the hell are you doing Danny?" Rab hunkered down beside him.

"Watching the light."

Rab shook his shoulder. "How many tablets have you had?"

Danny's eyes were huge, all pupil. "Don't know," he said finally.

"Where's the bottle?" Rab held out his hand. "Have you got the bottle?"

Danny shook his head.

"Where is it?"

Danny looked out the window again.

Rab shook him again. "Where is it?"

"John's got it."

Rab frowned. "Did John give you the tablets?"

Danny nodded.

"How many? Can you remember how many?"

"Bundles." And he had an odd private little laugh to himself.

Rab was leaning on his knees. He dropped his head onto his hands for a moment muttering, "Shit" under his breath.

Danny reached out and stroked his hair. "Love you," he said.

Rab looked up into his face. It was oddly flushed, an unhealthy white with two streaks of red, like powder. "Now you tell me."

He stood up. "Come on, *up*." He pulled Danny up, putting his arm round his shoulders.

But Danny stood up easily. "I can walk," he said shirtily.

"Can you?" Rab said and took a step back. "Well come on, let's see you then, get moving."

Danny climbed the stairs slowly, watching his feet as if he were judging the distance.

Maybe he was.

Henderson saw them coming along the corridor. Danny looked dishevelled, his face flushed. Close up Henderson could see that his eyes weren't quite focusing. His bandage had a small bloodstain on the palm.

"He's doped out his head." Rab pushed Danny past him. "John's been feeding him pain-killers, and I'm every kind of fucking asshole in the book."

Henderson shut the door. "Why would he do that?"

"I don't know." But Rab could feel his skin crawling at the possibilities. John wanted him quiet, subdued, maybe out of the picture. And with John it might be for anything. But if Danny had got away it meant John hadn't been with him. So where was he?

Danny had plonked down on a settee. Rab sat down beside him. He felt Danny's hand. It was deadly cold. "Where is he Danny?" Rab chafed his hand between his own.

"Who?"

"John. Where's John?"

"Home."

Danny began worrying at the leg of his jeans. Rab could see the white stains. He lifted Danny's hand off them.

"Why did you come here?"

Danny looked at him, frowning, then said quite lucidly, "I'll get it in a minute." He scratched his eye with a jerky movement then said, "Ian."

For some reason it made Rab's stomach drop. He felt some horrible irrational foreboding.

"Is that his other brother?"

Rab's head jerked round to look over his shoulder. "Yes," he said. He'd almost forgotten Henderson. He turned back to Danny. "What about Ian?"

Danny looked at him. "He wanted to kiss me."

It was Rab's turn to frown. "When?"

Danny began picking again. "Afterwards."

He moved Danny's hand off again. "After what?"

Henderson sat down on the other side of him. He looked at the stain on Danny's leg. "What's been going on?"

Rab could hear the edge of excitement in his voice. More second-hand debauchery. Tell me the details. Save on Sunday papers.

"How the fuck should I know?"

"Have they doped him up to fuck him?"

Rab could almost hear the little registers clicking them up. More evidence against John, more cheap thrills. Tell me everything about you and your brothers Danny. I understand.

Rab looked at him. "Why don't you shut up?"

Before Henderson could speak Danny suddenly leaned back, closing his eyes, and said, "He's going to kill him."

Both men looked at him. Rab's stomach turned right over. It was true. He knew it with absolute conviction. And if he'd gone to do it when Danny had left it was probably already done. And Henderson, Danny had announced it neatly in front of Henderson.

Danny spoke again. It was like words coming out of a medium. "You've got to stop him." He opened his eyes suddenly. "I've only got one hand." And then his face crumpled.

It was a fantastic thing to watch. It seemed to fall apart, or dissolve, like something melting. He slid sideways, trying to bury his head behind Rab's body. Rab could feel his sobs shuddering through his body. Worse, he made no noise.

He looked down at him in stupefaction.

He didn't know what to do. He didn't have the first fucking idea in hell what to do. And Henderson was looking at him.

He was quite sober.

John went upstairs to his own room and changed all his clothes from the skin out. He did not replace his underwear. His jeans felt cold and hard against his skin. He

crossed the hall and went into Ian's room.

As he had expected, Ian was not in his room. He went to his wardrobe and began searching through the drawers. It was an old-fashioned wardrobe, the oldest in the house. It had three drawers on the right-hand side, a shelf for hats, two shirt drawers, a tie rack, a collar-stud bowl shaped like a soap dish. On the left it had a hanging-rail and a shoe-rail.

It was not in the drawers.

He found it eventually on the top shelf. There were no hats there, only a green combat sweater, large and bulky. It was behind that, a ludicrous cardboard box like something you would keep a pet mouse in, an injured bird. John took off the lid. They were there. Hundreds of them. He took a handful out, turned them over. All neatly labelled on the back in Ian's cramped handwriting.

Nobody ever thought about the obvious thing.

"Found it?"

John put the lid back on carefully and said, "No" without turning. He put the box back on the shelf. He did not disguise it again with the sweater. He closed the wardrobe door.

When he turned Ian was standing watching him with John's knife in his hand. It lay, open and relaxed, down his thigh. He had changed his clothes.

"Always the good boy-scout." John was looking at the knife.

Ian nodded imperceptibly.

"And what's it for?"

"I don't want to go the same way as him and her."

John laughed. "Not him Ian, not at this late hour. Don't be modest."

Ian said nothing.

"What was it? The photographs? Did he finally find some unacceptable limit?"

Ian just watched him.

"No, not the photographs. Not really important enough. What was it?"

"Ask Danny." Ian's voice was calm. His face was white, strained, but calm.

"I lied over and over again for those three lousy photographs. I'm still not sure why."

"No-one asked you to."

"Why did you put them in my room?"

"I wanted you to see him as he really was."

"You mean you wanted me to see how tight you held him. But why photographs? That's what I don't understand. So elaborate, so dangerous."

"Why d'you think?" Ian's face was flushed, resentful.

"Anything was better than having sex with you, eh?"

Ian looked away. "I never asked."

John laughed. "He said no, and you accepted defeat, gracefully of course."

"He always said no. Yes for everybody else, no for me. Does that make you feel better John?"

"Give the man an Oscar." John stared at him for a long moment then said, "So you learned how to get your fix without his knowing. Good job he sleeps like the dead, isn't it?"

Ian smiled at his own cleverness.

"So why did you kill the old man?" John asked.

Ian smiled wider. John watched it with a slight unease. The knife hadn't moved.

Ian was shaking his head slowly. "You always were a sucker for his lies."

John pushed his hands into the pockets of his trousers. "And the truth is?"

"I told you, the old man had gone to the bath about ten minutes after I'd gone upstairs. I was in my room, minding my own business, when I realised I could hear

someone speaking to him through the bathroom door. Very quietly. I looked out. There was no-one there. I went down the hall, listened against the door. The old man was drunk. He didn't have a bottle in with him when he went in so I assume he'd gone in to sober up."

He paused for a reaction but John just stood there, expectant, listening.

"There was a silence, no sound of any kind, then I heard Danny's voice. It was low, odd." Ian hesitated. "It was..." He hesitated again, seemed to change his mind and went on, "He told the old man to open his mouth and close his eyes. The old man never said anything... nothing... during the whole thing. The only way I knew he was in there was from the odd little splash, that creaky noise the bath makes when you move in it." He stopped again as if he could hear it.

"Then I heard a grunt - I think it was Danny, not him - and a sudden splashing. Then it stopped. I didn't hang around. I hadn't liked the noises, but the silence was worse. I got back in here and locked the door. A moment or two later I heard the toilet flush. The cistern had refilled by the time he actually came out. He closed the door behind him and went downstairs. I didn't go in. I didn't go anywhere near it. I didn't even use it before going to bed."

"You must have known he was dead."

"No. And I didn't think about it. It was between Danny and him, not me."

John was silent. He nodded thoughtfully.

Ian watched him then said suddenly, "Why didn't you say something, about the photographs?"

"Like what?"

"You could have given them back."

John smiled faintly. "No way."

"You knew it was me?"

"Who else would be nutty enough?"

Ian flushed. "At least I don't cut people up for fun."

John's smile disappeared. "Who said I do it for fun?"

Ian bit his lip and looked away. John moved suddenly towards him. Ian's hand shot out. John stopped just outside sweeping distance, held his palms up. "I just want out."

Ian moved back from the door, keeping his distance. John walked past him, disinterested, deep in thought, looking the other way.

Ian didn't even see him move till it was too late. John's hand was around his wrist, immobilising it. "Drop it." He was crushing him. "I *said*, drop it."

Ian dropped it.

John kicked it away with his foot, but he didn't let him go. Instead he pulled him back against him, twisting his arm up his back, talking into his ear. "You're a dirty, lying little cunt and I'm going to wipe the floor with you."

"No," Ian said, denying everything, anything, that would save him.

"You've got dirty, sticky little fingers and a dirty, sticky little mind. Who's next?" John was pushing his arm further up his back. "Me?"

Ian yelped as John rammed his arm up higher. He could feel the tendons straining and knew with certainty that John intended to break it. "I'd never hurt you," he said desperately.

John yanked his arm. "No? What about the contents of that fucking box?"

"Stop," Ian said. It came out imploring.

"Oh no, I'm having fun. I think maybe I'll just finish it."

"Please... " Ian was crying. He could feel the tears sliding down his face, dripping off his chin. His arm was screaming. One more push.

The back door slammed.

"*John!*" The voice roared in the silence.

John froze. Ian hiccuped with surprise. He felt John's grip slacken. Fresh pain shot up his arm.

"John, where are you!?"

John let him go. Ian's arm came down like a deadweight, falling uselessly to his side. John moved away from him, bent, picked up the knife.

They heard Rab go into the living room, the front parlour, then come out again. Ian wiped his face with his sleeve. John held the knife in against his stomach, poised. Ian wiped his eyes again, sniffed.

Rab came up the stairs. "John?" His voice was quiet now, cautious.

They heard him open the bathroom door. When he closed it again John moved to the doorway. He saw Rab disappear into his room.

When Rab came back out he saw John standing there. He saw the knife. He stopped where he stood. "Where's Ian?"

John jerked his head to indicate the room behind him.

"Call him," Rab demanded.

"You call him."

"Ian?"

Ian tried to speak but nothing would come out.

Rab said his name again. "Ian, are you in there?"

Ian came forward, scrubbing at his eyes. When he appeared in the doorway he saw Rab visibly relax. It made him warm to see it. Warmer than he'd ever felt in his life.

John was looking at Rab. "Where's Danny?" he said, but he already knew the answer.

"With Henderson." Rab's voice was as hard as his eyes.

John could read it between the lines: *And out of your way, you murderous bastard.* "Safe and sound?" he asked, his voice dry.

"That's right." Rab's lips were tight.

"Which one?"

"What d'you mean, which one?"

"Which one's safe, which one's sound?" Rab could see his smile, grim, ugly, as if it had been forced on him, like a man laughing at a funeral joke. "He's going to kill your policeman."

"Don't fucking give me that. Who drugged him up?"

John shook his head. "What will we do with this one? Push him off a cliff? Maybe we could chop him up and burn him in the Aga." John wiped his cheek, dragging the skin as if he had toothache. "Bags-I the Mercedes."

Rab threw himself at him, knocking him back into the room. Ian jumped out of the way just in time. John had Rab in his arms. They were embracing like two sumo wrestlers. Then Ian saw Rab stiffen. Everything stopped. John's face was over his shoulder. Ian saw the smile. "That's it Rab, nice and easy, and we won't push it in any further."

"Oh Christ." Ian let the words slide out, expecting to see Rab slump to the floor. But John was holding him up, bear-hugging him.

"Much as I like the position, I'm going to let you go. Let's have it nice and easy." John moved back. Rab stood there white-faced. Ian saw the knife hand, then the knife.

"That's it. Now we'll take it out, shall we?" He tugged. Rab's face seemed to go slack, dull with shock. The first half inch of the knife was stained, no more.

Ian felt his body go limp. "I thought you'd killed him."

John laughed, short, derisory. "My right-hand man? Just a little flesh wound, remind him you don't fight with a knife in the game."

Rab swallowed slowly, painfully, looking down at himself. He reached for his shirt. Ian saw his hands were shaking. He pulled the fabric out.

"Don't be squeamish. Let's see the damage." John dragged his hands away. "Nothing. Fixed in no time." He slapped Rab's face lightly, a friendly pat made vicious. He walked out the room and crossed to his own.

Ian went over to Rab, looked at the wound. It was bleeding badly, running down his side and soaking the waistband of his jeans.

John came back in. He swabbed the wound roughly, making Rab wince.

"Here," he spoke to Ian, "hold it shut." The wound was a small gaping slit, filled with blood. Ian pressed it shut, holding the nausea down by sheer effort of will. John put a long piece of elastoplast across it to hold it closed then taped a lint pad over the top. "Good as new."

He moved round in front of Rab. "Now, shall we go and see what's left of Mr Henderson?"

Rab looked at him. Ian saw the defeat in his face.

John smiled. "Good man. I'm sure we'll have no trouble getting him in the Aga."

They went out, leaving Ian all alone in the house.

Henderson sat beside him, running his hand over his hair. Danny's face was marked from crying but he was still lovely. Henderson marvelled at him afresh. Nothing ever spoilt him. He pulled him in tighter against him, kissed his hair, breathing him in. He wondered if he was asleep. His breathing was heavy, regular. His eyes were closed. He put his other hand on his thigh. Danny shifted. "You awake?" he whispered into Danny's hair.

Danny nodded.

Henderson felt it thrill through him. The erection came back. The same erection that had plagued him all day. "Want to go to bed?"

Danny didn't say anything.

Henderson curved his hand up higher, nestling it into the warm space between his legs. "Come to bed."

Danny opened his eyes slowly.

Henderson got up and looked down at him. "Come on."

Danny continued to stare up at him for a long moment, his face oddly blank, then he got up. He went first, Henderson moving behind him like a sheep dog herding him in. He didn't put on the main light, just the down-lighters on the vast velour head board.

Danny looked at the huge king-sized black satin bed.

Henderson swept the tapes up in a bundle and dumped them on the floor. He pulled the quilt back. The same black pillows, but the sheets were scarlet, bright vivid scarlet against the black.

Danny shut his eyes and said, "It's difficult with one hand."

Henderson wasn't sure what he meant but he made sympathetic noises and began undressing him. Danny doped was better than himself drunk. It dealt with all the shame while he had all his senses. He was going to enjoy this. My God, he was going to enjoy it.

He pulled Danny's clothes off, careful of his hand. He herded him back to the bed, lay him down. He wasn't even properly on it before Henderson was on top of him. Danny could feel the silk of his pyjama trousers against him, the coarse friction of the fur on his chest. Henderson's erection was almost painful, digging into him. It was definitely painful to Henderson.

He looked at Danny's hair on the black pillow, felt his cock dragging stickily on the

silk. He wanted to come in his pyjamas, feel it smear inside his clothes.

He stopped moving, lay there breathing heavily.

Danny lay there looking at the ceiling. He wasn't erect but Henderson didn't seem to have noticed. He was too far gone. "I've got some good news." He kissed Danny's face, far away from his mouth. "That ranking guy I told you about... he knows things..."

Danny felt the moustache getting closer. He felt Henderson dig his cock in again and knew he wasn't going to hang in much longer.

"Things that are going to lock your brother up and throw away the key..." he breathed, and then his mouth was pressed over his. Danny felt him grunt into it, then his tongue pushed in and he started forcing his cock into Danny's belly with hard grunting thrusts.

Henderson felt it come out slick onto the silk. He visualised it creaming white onto the black, soaking the fabric. He sucked Danny's tongue, hung onto his hair. He could feel it squidging beneath him, thick and oily in his clothes. "Oh…" he said, letting his weight drop limply onto Danny's body.

"Ohhh..."

Danny got up on the pretext of going to the toilet. He went into the kitchen. The room looked vast. The clock seemed to tick and whirr, tick and whirr. The red hurt his eyes. He looked round the room. The knife rack was hanging on the wall. It was red. In it, evenly spaced, were half a dozen black-handled knives. Danny took the second largest out of the slot. The blade went on for miles. The edge was rippled like the fine edge of a feather. Across it sped the legend, '*LAZER Guaranteed 25 years.*'

Danny pressed it to his throat then walked out of the room.

John took the road at a speed that took Rab's breath away. He watched the hedgerow hurtle by and felt fear grow in him till he thought he was going to scream. "Slow down for Christ's sake."

John ignored him, and Rab knew it was true, because otherwise this didn't make sense. This rush, the whole thing, none of it made sense. Rab watched another road flare past. He spoke to him as much to distract himself as anything else. "Did he tell you he was going to kill him?"

John grunted a denial.

"What then?"

"He wanted me to kill him." He clicked on the indicators. "Come on, you stupid fucker," he cursed the driver in the other lane.

Rab looked at him. "You never had any intention of killing him."

"Do I look stupid?" John hurtled down the harbour road.

Rab held onto the door. "Christ, you led me a dance."

"You wanted to be led."

Rab didn't answer that, instead he asked, "Why does he want him dead?"

John's laugh was fast, over and done. "Don't ask me. Who knows how Danny's mind works? Don't assume I know him any better than you do. Only God understands Danny."

The car jolted over the aggregate, stopping in front of Henderson's flat. John got out first. Rab followed him, trying to move faster, but feeling as if he were swimming through water.

John came to a halt like a buffalo running into a wall.

"What's wrong?" Rab came up behind him.

"How do we get in?" John looked at the glass as if it was a steel wall. "How the

fuck do we get in?"

Danny walked into the bedroom. Henderson was lying on his stomach. He looked as if he was asleep.

Danny lay down beside him and pressed the knife into his neck. Henderson's eyes opened. He frowned, feeling the prick of the blade, seeing the handle. "Danny?"

"Got to shut your mouth."

Henderson's hand came up onto his. Slowly, carefully.

Then the door buzzer sounded for the second time that evening.

"I told you," John said grimly.

"Ring it again," Rab urged.

John grabbed the collar of his jacket. "If Henderson's fucking dead he can't answer the fucking door."

Rab dragged his hands off. "Unless Danny's fucking dead too, he *can*."

John pushed him away. "I should've got rid of you years ago."

"Then you'd really be fucked."

John turned away.

Rab pressed the bell again. It was answered immediately. "Yes?"

They looked at each other. Rab moved first. "Henderson?"

"Yes."

"It's Rab."

"Come up." The buzzer went.

They pushed in and took the stairs two at a time. They had to knock to get in.

Henderson stood, grim-faced, in the hall with a carving knife. They both saw it.

John spoke first. "Where is he?"

"In the bedroom."

John pushed past him.

Rab followed Henderson into the living room. "He tried to..." He stopped, unsure what Danny had tried to do. "He threatened me with this fucking thing." He threw the knife down on the table beside the sofa and sat down abruptly, as if his legs had given way. He said it the same way he had spoken of John's threats, as if it was the sheer audacity of the thing that upset him, not the threat itself.

Rab looked at him, at the wet patch on his pyjama trousers, wrinkled, sticking to itself. He hadn't wasted much fucking time, had he?

John came back through. "He's getting dressed." He didn't look at Henderson.

Henderson stood up. "He isn't going with you."

John looked at him. "He was going to cut your throat."

Henderson shook his head. Rab saw the conviction in it, looked at John. John was staring at him, eyes searching his face. "I don't know whether you're a moron or a cretin. I can't decide."

Henderson's face flushed. "You're in big trouble Moore."

"Really?" There was no anger in John's voice - yet.

Henderson went up closer. "He isn't going with you. He's staying with me. You're in for the biggest surprise of your life."

John's mouth worked. He was biting the inside of his cheek. "What? You going to show me your cunt?"

Henderson said nothing, flushed a little darker.

"Go steal someone else's brother Henderson. You're not having mine."

Henderson pushed up to him. "You dirty, incestuous bastard. I'm going to..."

290

John shoved him squarely in the chest. He went back in a heap onto the sofa. "Shut up." John looked away from him, dismissing him, like a man standing in a garage forecourt waiting for his tank to fill.

Henderson was struggling up when Danny came in. Rab noticed he was cradling his hand against his chest. No more painkillers. His face was white.

John jerked his head at him. Danny walked past him, going towards the door, still without looking at him.

Henderson got to his feet and grabbed him. Danny stopped like a mechanical toy, waiting for the next command.

John dragged Henderson round by one arm. "Let him go."

But Henderson didn't let go. He dipped swiftly, bringing the knife up from the table. "No, *you* let him go."

John's arm dropped. Rab could almost hear him say it. He wasn't going to fight with a knife in the game.

"Now get out."

John moved round Danny. Rab moved towards the door.

"Go on." They weren't moving fast enough for Henderson. "Get out."

Danny looked startled. "John…?"

But John didn't turn.

"*John...*" he said again, more desperately.

Rab watched John's expression as he moved in front of him, saw it sitting hard in his throat, like something he couldn't swallow. He stopped suddenly. "You were right Danny. I should have killed him sooner."

Henderson looked at him, then at Danny, his face pained, confused. John lunged across at him, grabbing the knife hand. Rab saw his thumb slice the blade. Blood seemed to gush out immediately. It dropped in bright splashes onto the sofa. Rab yanked Danny back against him, out of the way. Henderson staggered back under his weight and collapsed on the sofa. John kneeled on his stomach, squeezed the knife out of his hand like a pip out an orange. It dropped. John grabbed it with his other hand.

Rab saw it too late.

John's hand came up quickly into the side of his neck and across. It stuck. Henderson's eyes bulged. His legs kicked. A dreadful gurgling came out of him. Rab watched the blood pulse in red jerks onto the cream leather. He cried out something. He didn't know what.

John sat there, pinning Henderson down while his body twitched. The whites of his eyes rolled up.

It went on and on.

And then it stopped.

John got up stiffly, as if he'd been sitting that way for hours. Henderson's hand fell palm-upwards onto the sofa. Blood immediately began to fill up the palm, then trickle in thin rivulets between his fingers. The blood pumped a little longer, grew sickly, then just seeped. The black handle stuck out from his neck. There was red everywhere. John was covered in it.

John put his hands flat on the crown of his head. He stood like that for a moment, like a workman considering a problem, then said, "Oh good." He backed away, still looking at Henderson and sat on the other sofa. He leaned his head back. "Very good indeed."

Rab spoke but nothing came out. The next time he managed to say, "Now what?"

John didn't look at him. "I'm thinking."

Danny sat down on the floor, suddenly, where he stood. He rested his head in his hands, fingers pressed into his eyes.

John looked at him. "What's wrong Danny? I thought it would please you."

"Christ, do we need to have this discussion now?" Rab snapped.

But John ignored him. "Why so squeamish? It was good enough for the old man. Or is it the blood that bothers you?"

"I didn't kill the old man," Danny said.

John laughed shortly. "Ian doesn't agree with you."

"*Ian*," Danny said and dropped his head again, like a sick man exhausted.

Rab interrupted before John could reply. "Are you going to sit here bickering all night?"

"You're right." John shot up out of his seat, almost cheerful. "Let's go." He headed for the door.

"*Go?*"

"Yup." He turned back suddenly and took out a handkerchief. He wiped the handle of the knife. Rab looked away when Henderson's head slid, revealing a gaping red hole.

John went towards the door again. "Right troops, out. Last one to the murder bus takes the rap."

"What about him?" Rab almost shouted it.

John turned. "What about him?"

"We can't leave him here."

"Why not? They'll take time to discover him. They've no reason to associate us, and even if they do they can't prove it."

Rab looked at Henderson and looked away again quickly. When he didn't move John said, "You know, I'm beginning to think you really enjoy the challenge of disposing of the bodies. Are we going or not? Maybe you'd rather stay here and keep him company?"

Rab flared up at him, "The whole fucking family's in here. What if we've been seen coming in or going out?"

"We never got in. He didn't answer the door."

"Then how did we get in the building?"

"Mickey Mouse let us in." John's voice was suddenly ratty. "We'll worry about that later. Now are you going to get out or not?"

Rab stared at him then moved forward. Danny followed him out.

John said, "Wait a minute" then doubled back into the room. They waited for him in the hall. He came back wrapped in an overcoat miles too short in the sleeve.

They all filed out quietly. As they rounded the corner they heard the women's voices. John smiled fixedly, his eyes warning. Danny kept his head down. Rab looked at the women. It was the same two. They went quiet when they saw him, then Danny. They looked at John keenly. He kept his hands pushed well into his pockets, hunching himself inside the coat. He smiled. The women looked away.

The Jackson Moores filed out.

Rab closed the door quietly.

They got in their car and went home.

John put Danny to bed and went back downstairs. Ian had undoubtedly heard them come in but he did not materialise. He found Rab in the living room. He was kneeling on the hearth, listlessly dropping coal into the fire.

"You look tired."

Rab lifted his head up to look at the clock. "I've had a busy day."

He opened the fire up to make it catch. He watched it for a moment or two then said, "So we found the outer door on the latch and went up but couldn't get an answer

from the flat?"

John nodded.

"And hope like hell nobody saw us or saw how long the car sat there."

"In places like that they don't care." John sounded indifferent.

"If you say so."

They were silent then Rab spoke again. "You know, he has, *had*, a fucking enormous Porsche." He looked up, but John just sat watching him, waiting for him to go on. "We went out in it once. I keep thinking about it sitting there in the dark and him dead upstairs." He stopped.

"You're making me cry." John's voice was dry.

Rab threw another lump of coal in irritably. "You know, I half liked him. I think being stuck like a pig by you is probably the worst death he could have had."

"Oh dear."

"And you know something else?" Rab looked up from the fire. "I don't think I like you. I think I stopped liking you a long time ago, only I didn't realise it."

John looked at the fireplace, the fire tools, the fire itself, and said nothing.

"You didn't kill him in temper at all, did you? You'd shelved him for the right moment. Tonight wasn't it but you thought, What the hell, there might never be another, so you did it." Rab shifted his weight onto the fender, leaning back against the surround and studied John's face in the firelight. His eyes had disappeared into blackness. "What I don't understand is, why? I don't flatter myself but even *I'm* a bigger threat than him. Why not me? Or am I just in the pending file, awaiting actioning?"

John slid down onto one side, head propped on one arm. "Go on," his voice was sleepy. "I'm enjoying it."

"You've fucked me, humiliated me, used me. I don't rate any more, so why am I hanging around swelling the numbers? Maybe it's economics. Maybe you don't want to have to hire help, or are you afraid the help might be vulnerable to Danny's charms? Or is it a question of timing? You can't afford to do us all at once, that would be just a little too, too."

John didn't answer. He scratched his cheek and was still again.

"Come on John, tell me today's truth."

John lay down on his back, hands behind his head. "Today's truth, let's see..." His voice was low. "I'm saving you for Ian."

"You what?"

"Ian's going to kill you." He sucked his teeth contemplatively. "It's all a question of pushing him hard enough, stirring up that bitter green blood." He swung up again suddenly. "There, today's truth, how d'you like it?"

Rab managed to get the words out. "It fits you."

John nodded thoughtfully. "Come over and sit by me."

Rab crawled over the rug and leaned his back against the sofa. He could feel John's presence behind him. It was like putting your head in the lion's mouth. John lay his hand on his head and stroked his hair slowly. "The pain always charges me up."

Rab frowned, listening to him.

John slid the words out. "You want to?"

"Why don't you use him? That's what he's there for."

"He's out of it."

Rab heard his pulse counting itself. "Why not do what you usually do?"

John slid his hand under his hair and squeezed his neck. His hand was dry and warm, rough. Rab remembered there was blood under his nails. He'd seen it when they were driving home. "You're here, they're not."

"Sad."

"Not for you."

"You conceited fuck."

"Maybe." John lapsed back into momentary silence, his hand still caressing Rab's neck, then said, "I want to get inside you."

"Oh, thanks. You want to fuck, you can't fuck him, and you can't be bothered going out." Rab ducked his head away from John's hand, turned round to face him. "Or maybe not. What's the problem John? Won't he let you?"

John took Rab's hand and pressed it over his own crotch. "Shh..."

Rab tried to pull his hand away but John pressed it down. "No, call me what you like but just leave it there."

Rab left his hand where it was but it sent his brain to mush. Everything seemed to fall apart into pointlessness. "John, you cut a man's throat tonight. You cut it for the boy upstairs because you can't bear to share him, and now you're down here with me, telling me you want to fuck me after you've run a little fantasy where you get Ian to kill me. What are you about John?"

"Ten inches." John wrapped his arms around him, trying to pull him up. Rab pushed him off.

"It's you who thinks with his dick, not Danny."

John wasn't even listening. His eyes watched him hungrily, but he wasn't listening.

"What's the use?" Rab said wearily.

"Fuck me and I'll show you."

"Alright John," Rab began pulling his shirt off, "you show me. Make me understand." He stood up, pulled his trousers off. He dumped his clothes where he stood. "Right, now what?"

John undid his trousers.

Rab looked at him. "No underwear?"

"Less to burn." He handed Rab his trousers. They were darkly stained. It looked like varnish. "Put them in."

Rab hesitated a second then took them and put them in the fire, using the poker to lift them and let in the air. When he turned John handed him the shirt.

The shirt was stiff and dark-looking. Rab said, "Do it yourself." He could see smeary marks on John's chest, like the blood had soaked through. He looked away.

John got down on his knees and threw the shirt in the fire then came down beside him and pulled him to him.

"You knew you were going to do it," Rab said hoarsely.

"No." John began kissing his throat. Rab could smell the sweat off him, different, unfamiliar. The sweat of death, or maybe just blood. He could feel John's erection against his abdomen. John held his buttocks, pressing him up against him. He spoke to him suddenly. "Lie down."

They moved down onto the rug. John climbed on top of him then kissed his mouth in the way only John could. It always left you limp, stunned, like being injected by the spider before it eats you. *You'll feel no pain, only the prick of the needle.* John lifted his legs.

"What are you doing?"

John looked at him. "I want to watch your face." He knelt up, taking Rab's weight onto his thighs. He licked his fingers, covered his own cock with spit.

Rab watched him, tensed for the feel of it.

John wet him with one finger but didn't penetrate him. He adjusted himself then guided it in. It was awkward, painful. Rab gritted his teeth.

John got far enough in to rest. He sat a moment. They listened to each other's breathing, felt the fire, hot, burning their skin, then John reached down for Rab's shoulders and began to impale him on it. It seemed to slide up in painful jerks, an inch

more each time.

"Play with yourself."

Rab touched himself, felt it firming under his hand.

"It looks like mine." John was smiling.

Rab looked down. His penis stuck out flaxen from John's groin. He saw the blood smears behind it. He began masturbating, quickly, vigorously, before he couldn't do it at all. John moved him effortlessly, thrusting up under him.

"You're hole's always so tight."

Rab slowed his hand, began to feel the hugeness of heat in himself. He closed his eyes tight. He didn't want to see John any more; mad, bloodied, dangerous.

"Don't hide from me."

Rab felt the heat in his face. "I'll come."

John laughed. "I'll cool you down. Want to know when I last did it like this? I mean up the arse, front on."

Rab opened his eyes. Neither of them was moving. His cock, huge and red, was sticking up between them. He kept his hand away from it. "You've done this before?"

"There's nothing I haven't done before."

"Danny?"

"Hell no, way before Danny's time. I was thirteen."

"You never did this with me. We always fucked from behind."

"I said thirteen, that was before your time too." John moved into him again, his mouth jerking with the effort of it. "It was how you and I got started."

Rab felt a pang of jealousy, a moment's intense distress. "Who was it?" he demanded.

John smiled, "This will kill you."

"Who?"

John lifted him, pushed in hard. "My mother."

Rab felt his heart stop. Absolutely dead. He shook his head.

John laughed quietly. He lifted him and pushed in hard two or three times, grunting with effort. Rab felt his shoulders burn with the drag. John took a deep breath, let it out slowly. "You are so fucking *tight*." He moved again, gently this time.

Rab shut his eyes tight. "You're lying."

John laughed. "You want details?"

"You're lying. There's no way. She'd never have come near you in a million years. She detested you. You're lying."

Rab struggled suddenly, trying to get off him, but John gripped his shoulders, pushing himself in deep. He was smiling. "You want proof?"

Rab went limp. He closed his eyes. He had lost his erection, but he made no effort to get it back. He didn't care.

"She had a mole on the inside of her thigh," John offered.

Rab opened his eyes. "That doesn't prove anything."

"Only if you've never seen her naked."

John watched his face flush, rocked gently inside him. Rab felt himself grow stiff. He tried to make it go away but it seemed to surge up without him.

"She liked to leave her skirt on, just flip it up. Did she like it that way with you?" John was watching him keenly now.

Rab turned his head away. "You bastard."

John began to bump into him hard.

"Get off me."

John shook his head. "Not until I've finished."

"You told me you never wanted her."

"I think it would be safe to say that might have been a fib."

"Christ, how could you kill her feeling like that?"

"Feeling like what?"

"You loved her."

John laughed. "She was a thorn in my side till the day she died. She stole every single thing I ever wanted. But in the end it didn't matter, did it? Because Danny shat on us both. All my life I'd sat on the sidelines, waiting to be noticed, and there she was, crawling all over him."

He'd stopped. They lay there in their obscene coupling and did nothing. Then John smiled, hugely. "You're so fucking gullible." He lifted him with a violent jerk, impaling himself. Rab winced. "If it hadn't been for the fuck that brought us all Ian she'd have died a fucking virgin."

Rab felt him swell inside of him, stretching him. His own cock responded in kind, even while he stared at him in numb disbelief. "You rotten, lying... wait a minute, what d'you mean the fuck that brought us Ian?"

But there was no answer. John demanded, "Come on, I'm going to shoot it any second now, pull your dick..."

Rab watched his face, taut with concentration, his stomach hard and muscled with tension. He could see sweat on his chest. It had appeared suddenly, as if something in him had changed gear.

Rab found himself close without warning. John sensed it, lifted his backside up clear with his hands, not caring about friction-burning him, dragging him down on it, trying to get further in. He bent forwards, dropping his head, bracing himself against Rab's shoulders and began thumping into him.

Rab felt himself do a funny little gasping crescendo. It seized him painfully, making his cock jerk in his hand. He saw his semen shoot inconceivably high in the air.

John pulled Rab down onto him, burying it deep. Rab's body produced another brainless spurt and John began grunting like an animal, digging his fingers in, bruising him, using Rab's twitching body to bring himself off.

Rab felt it slick his arse, felt himself grow wet and oily as John's penis continued to slurp in and out obscenely, drawing the last of it out of himself.

"I'm empty," John whispered and suddenly dropped back, spent, on his heels.

Danny was lying under Henderson. He could feel the slick, wet fur of his body.

He wriggled under him, trying to get out, but Henderson kept saying, "No, trust Grease. Grease will sort everything."

Danny tried to push him off but he was too slippy. The sheets were soaking, wrapping themselves tighter and tighter around him the more he struggled. Then he saw that Henderson had a poker sticking out his neck. Ian was pulling the other end of it ferociously, like a dog worrying a stick. Henderson was saying, "Grease *is* the law." But Ian kept pulling it, a small blood-soaked demon of Ian, grimly grunting, "Bash his head in. Bash his head in." There was blood everywhere, warm, stinking, metallic. The bath was slowly filling up with it while Danny suffocated under the gored body of Henderson, the madly determined Ian. Danny knew he had to get out of the bath, out from under Henderson's body, before he drowned, but he couldn't because Henderson was still fiercely alive, insistent. He could feel the blood filling his ears. Their voices were suddenly deadened, distanced, then he could taste it in his mouth, salt as sweat, thick and cold, like oily snot being pushed down his throat, and he started to scream, only no words could get out, and the blood was roaring into his lungs, and he couldn't breathe, and he tried to scream but no-one could hear him, and he was choking, and he screamed, *Help me, help me, HELP ME...*

He sat up with a jerk, his heart hammering. He hung there for a moment, still

caught in the dream's reality, then flopped back down on the pillow. He wanted to put the light on but was afraid to reach for it. The blackness felt alive around him, breathing.

"John...?" He whispered his name, reaching for him. There was no-one there. He felt his heart pound with fresh fright. He lay another moment or two, telling himself it was a dream, only a dream, and that he was alright. He peered round the room, trying to recognise shapes. He was home. Safe. He reached out and put on the light. John wasn't in the bed.

He needed to pee, suddenly, badly. He needed a drink of water. He had a thirst like an itch in his throat.

He sat up, holding his head a moment, then swung his legs out of bed. He went out into the hall.

The light came on. He stood there blinking, momentarily dazzled, then John and Rab appeared round the corner. John was naked, Rab dressed only in his jeans, carrying his shirt. John spoke first. "What are you doing out of bed?"

"Needed to pee."

John stared at him a moment then said, "Well, why don't you go?"

Danny walked down the hall towards them then stopped in front of them.

"Don't bother." John's voice was hard. "Just get in and do what you got up to do."

Rab looked away. Danny went in, slamming the door behind him. John stared at it.

Rab went into his room without speaking. He stood a moment behind the door, locking it, then heard the bathroom door open.

John had followed him in.

Danny didn't look at him. He watched the golden arc without seeing it.

"Well go on, let rip, piss it out all over me."

Danny flushed the toilet, turned on him. John could see his chest moving. He was white with something. Pain? Anger? He walked across to John with a strange tense walk, like a hunting cat. "I hate you," he said, and he slapped him, an awkward back-handed blow that nevertheless made John's head ring. He gave a small involuntary grunt then touched his cheek tenderly, cooling it with his fingers.

"What's his charm John, make you feel more *male?*"

"Oh shut up Danny, you sound like a parakeet."

Danny hurled himself at him, punching, biting, scratching. He was using his wounded hand, not even aware of it, just wanting to hurt him.

John couldn't hold him. He elbowed and clawed. He felt him rip skin on his shoulder, again on his cheek. He punched him, once and hard to his belly, trying to wind him. But he had to do it again before it slowed him, and once more till he stopped.

Danny sat down on the floor. John could see the blood seeping through his bandage. "You've opened your stitches, you stupid little bastard."

John looked at the scratches on his own shoulder then crossed to the mirror. A long dull red streak oozed from his eye to his chin. His face was beginning to look like a battlefield.

Danny was sitting on the floor, head in his hands. John went over to him and picked him up. Danny shrugged him off, holding his stomach.

"Going to be sick again?"

"Fuck you." Danny wiped his face on his free arm, the other still tight around his middle.

John straightened up and turned on the shower. When he turned back Danny was

staring at him.

"Does being inside him stop you feeling like a girl?"

John looked at his injured hand but said nothing.

"I hate you."

"So you've said." John stared back at him, both waiting, neither knowing what for. John spoke first. "Come to the shower with me."

"Get stuffed."

"You want me to make you?"

Danny transferred his hard stare to the wall.

"Well that's too bad, because tonight Danny you can go to hell. I'm too tired to play games."

Danny flicked a quick glance at him then away again.

"So how about it Danny, you want to come or not?"

"You were on your way in here with him, weren't you?"

"That's an old, ugly jealousy you've got there. You should have grown out of it years ago."

"It's true though, isn't it? I'm only here because without me you haven't got a hope in hell."

John laughed. "Don't flatter yourself."

"At least I don't have to threaten him."

"And I never have to seduce him."

Danny turned his face away abruptly but John pulled it back. "Can you kill him now?"

"Shut up."

"What horrible deaths did you think up for him? You and Ian?"

"Shut *up!*" Danny shouted it, covering his ears with his hands.

John pulled them away, holding him to him. His lips were against Danny's ear, talking close into it. "You know, I've never made love to anyone in my life. Come to the shower with me."

Danny stood there smelling the sweat and sex off him, someone else's flesh and blood. "You *stink* of him," he hissed.

John sagged as if he had hit him. Suddenly he grabbed Danny's hair, dragging him backwards into the shower cubicle. He pushed him hard up against the wall, wrenching the taps on, the water scalding down over them, then slammed the door shut. They were confined in the tiny space, already thick with steam. John could see his hair turn to blood in the water. His eyes were like green stone, staring at him.

"Turn round."

Danny stood there, unmoving.

"I *said*, turn around." John grabbed him and swung him round, shoving his face against the wall. He prised Danny's buttocks apart then took the soap and pushed it between them, mauling him as he lathered it between his cheeks, pushing the bar into his anus. Danny moaned softly.

"How often have you dreamt this scenario?" John dropped the soap, slid an arm round him, squeezing the breath out of him. "Big brother takes you into the shower, up hard against the wall, and starts brownholing you." He held Danny's waist tightly, pressed himself against him, whispering into his ear, "Act that one out too?"

He lifted his cock and placed it between Danny's buttocks, nestling the length of it along the crease. He pressed the buttocks together, drawing back to see it. He looked at it, long and hard and red, between the soapy white curves. "Think tonight is going to be your lucky night?" He began sliding it up and down in the cleft, pressing Danny's buttocks tight around it. "Well you're wrong. Not tonight or any other night, not until you tell me the truth."

He pushed a hand in between Danny and the wall. "Well fuck me, what a surprise, Daniel has a strapping great hard-on. There, now when I fuck, you fuck, and we'll all come together when we come."

John pressed against him hard, butting him against the wall, hoping the tiles would hurt him. He saw Danny's wounded hand, soaked, pink, against the wall above his head.

"What do you want Danny? Come on, it's a day for truths, share a few of yours. I killed him for you. Need to see blood to prove it? There, look, that's the very hand, the one you're trying to pretend isn't pulling your dick. See the blood under my nails? Isn't it enough? Doesn't it prove anything?"

Danny took John's hand and pressed it tighter around himself, rubbing his head back against him like a cat.

John felt his body respond in spite of himself. "Oh for fuck's sake..." His own voice was dull with weariness and despair.

Danny struggled round suddenly and faced him. His eyes were half closed, his mouth red and wet. The hair clung to his forehead in bloodied strands.

John looked at his parted mouth. "No."

Danny reached down between them and caught at John's cock, exposing the head to the jet of the shower. John sucked a breath in. When he opened his eyes again he saw Danny was half-squatting, reaching round awkwardly behind himself, obviously cramming his finger up inside his body. He looked up slowly to meet John's eyes.

John shook his head as if he were in pain and, utterly without warning, felt himself start to climax, tried to go limp and stop it but knew it was too late. He fell against him, reaching round to catch his hand, frantic to push it up inside him, but he was weak with the force of it, could only cling to him as he felt Danny thrust his finger up deep with an odd little gasp.

It was the closest to him John got.

THIRTY-EIGHT

Danny went back to hospital, was told off and stitched up again.

They sat that week and waited. Ian watched them and waited with them. They told him nothing and he didn't ask. But he guessed it was Henderson because Henderson had suddenly become the invisible man.

A full week went past. Everybody got up early and went to bed early, especially John and Danny. Rab did not bother to hide from it any more. He lay on his bed and listened, waiting for it, then he went to sleep. Once he thought they woke him doing it again at two in the morning, but he wasn't sure if he dreamt it.

The second week came and still nothing. Rab began to have nasty daydreams where he pictured Henderson sitting there in his warm, centrally heated, flat congealing like rotten meat. He pictured the Porsche locked in the dark like an abandoned animal, starving to death.

Then it was the end of the month.

Danny's birthday.

And they all had fun.

John lay on the bed, naked, watching him. Outside the wind whistled round the windows, howling like a banshee. "Looks like you're going to see twenty after all Danny."

"Mm."

"What would you like for your birthday?"

"What are you offering?" Danny kept his back to him.

"That sounds like a loaded question."

"No, just curious." Danny threw his shirt over the chair.

"Don't turn round. Take them down as you are." John watched him as he pulled down his jeans and underpants in a oner. "Your body's getting broader. Turn around."

Danny turned to face him. He grew hard under his gaze.

"That can't last." John shook his head, smiling. "Sooner or later it's got to stop."

Danny said, "You still haven't told me what you're offering."

"Bribery?" John cocked an eyebrow, eyes still between his legs.

"If you like."

"Bring it over here and bribe me then."

Danny walked over and sat down beside him. John reached up and rubbed his cheek. "More beard too."

Danny smiled.

"Sit on me where I can see you."

Danny straddled his chest. John began playing with him idly, feeling the peculiar silk of his cockskin, pressing the flat of his stomach. "Well, what do you want? Whose head on a platter?"

Danny looked away from him, no longer smiling.

John looked up at him. "What's wrong, too near the mark?"

"Get rid of Rab."

"Get rid? Don't be coy Danny, it doesn't suit you. Why don't you just ask me to kill him?"

"Don't be stupid, all I'm asking is for you to send him packing."

"I can't send him packing. For a start, I need him. We're short-handed enough with

the death rate around here. Secondly, he lives here. It's his home."

"He gets on my nerves."

"Oh tragedy. Unfortunately that doesn't mean he's not entitled to live here. He works as hard as the rest of us, harder. If I throw him out where does he go?"

"I don't care."

"Not strictly true. Why do you want rid of him?"

"You know why."

"Because he can't get enough of my dick?"

"You conceited shit."

"Then why?"

"You know."

"I don't *know*, so why don't you tell me?"

"You *do* know, you just like to torture me."

"Oh, don't be so bloody melodramatic. It won't happen again."

"Yeah, right."

John began to get ratty. "I *said*, it won't happen again."

Danny climbed off him in one movement.

John lifted himself on one elbow to look at him. "What's this, withdrawal of bribe if I'm not going to co-operate?"

"You got it."

"Why don't *you* kill him, if you're so keen?"

"Will you stop that? I don't want *anyone* to kill him. I just want him out of here."

"You mean you're afraid to kill him, afraid that one more death around here is not only tempting fate but inviting it into the house. You mean you *would* kill him, or better still get *me* to kill him, if you thought you could get away with it. I bet you've killed him before, lots of times, haven't you?"

"No."

"Oh, don't be shy. Don't hide your light under a bushel."

Danny threw back the blankets and climbed into bed, turning his back on him. The window rattled.

John pinned an arm round him. "Why do you want to kill him?"

"I fucking *don't*. Leave me alone."

John laughed, letting him go suddenly. "Well you'll have to settle for a tube of Smarties baby. So sorry."

"Fuck off."

"Listen to its temper, not getting what it wants." John rolled the covers out from under him and climbed in beside him. He put the lamp out. The room was velvety black. The wind whistled like a howling cat. He heard Rab come up the stairs, go into his room.

"Maybe I should go to him tonight. I'm in the mood now."

"You do that." Danny's voice was muffled.

"Okay."

Danny felt the blankets being thrown back, John's weight shifting off the bed.

"You bastard."

"Thank you."

"I hope he tells you to piss off."

"He won't."

"You cunt."

John made a noise as if he'd been burnt. "Such envy."

And the door slammed shut behind him.

Danny lay there in the dark praying that Rab would send him packing. He heard John knock on his door. *Send him back with his tail between his legs. Make the ugly bastard suffer. Humiliate him.*

Rab opened the door. They didn't even speak to each other. The door closed.

Danny threw himself on his back.

He'd go to Ian. Better still, bring Ian in here. Let John worry about that one.

Danny yanked the blankets up around his neck, hurt his hand and winced.

He went limp. He wouldn't go to Ian. He *couldn't* go to Ian, not if his life depended on it.

He needn't have worried. In the event Ian came to him.

Rab closed the door behind him and looked at his back, heavy, powerful. How the hell had the old man produced such a monster?

John turned, smiled broadly at him. "Can I stay the night?"

"Danny throw you out?"

"Lover's tiff." John's voice was mocking.

"What about?"

"I wouldn't give him what he wanted for his birthday."

Rab flushed.

John's smile widened. "You have a dirty mind."

Rab sat down on the bed. "Why wouldn't you?"

"Too expensive."

"I didn't think you were mean."

"I'm not, he's greedy. Can I get into bed? I'm frozen."

Rab nodded without looking at him.

John didn't move. "Want to go to the old man's bed? It's bigger."

"You can, why don't you?" Rab felt suddenly irritable.

"You're not in it." John was watching him.

"What makes you think I'm glad to take your seconds John?"

"Aren't you?"

"No, I'm not."

"But you will anyway"

Rab got up suddenly and crossed to the door again, opening it. "Get out."

John pushed it shut.

Rab held his gaze for a moment then went back to the bed. He climbed in and lay back against the wall.

John climbed in beside him. "I've missed you."

"I'll bet."

"Almost two weeks since you've fucked anyone."

"Well, tonight's my lucky night, isn't it?"

"That's right. How would you like it?"

"Suck me off."

John looked at him and smiled. "Tit for tat."

"That's right."

"And if I say no?"

"Then you can fuck off."

John nodded. "It's a big bad world out there. Three hundred million bastards eating dirt."

Rab looked at him. Nothing moved inside. He said, "Suck it or walk."

John pinched his cheek, hard, then slid down the bed.

Danny woke abruptly.

At first he thought the wind had blown something over in the yard then he realised John had come back.

He ignored him, pulled the blankets up tighter.

He heard him lock the door then felt him get into bed. Then he knew.

Ian's hand came down over his mouth. Tight. "It's a knife." He was hissing the words out, almost incoherent in his excitement. "*His* knife. I'm taking a leaf out of his book Danny, how d'you like it?"

But Danny couldn't reply because Ian didn't take his hand away.

"I'm going to let go and like they say in the movies, I want you to be very quiet. Not a cheep, okay?"

Danny lay still.

The knife dug in. "I asked you a question."

Danny nodded.

"Good." Ian's hand came off and went straight to Danny's stomach. He flinched. The knife dug in again. "Lie still."

Ian's hand slid down, feeling him. "Stark bollock naked. I'll bet you always sleep naked with him, don't you?"

Danny felt the hand crawling over him like a spider.

"Remember this Danny?"

Danny shook his head.

"No, you wouldn't. It didn't mean anything to you, nothing but an ordeal to get over with as soon as possible." The knife dug in again. "Well?"

"Yes."

Ian seemed to relax. "Well tonight's going to be different, tonight you'll be Mr Hard-on for me, and not because I'm pretending to be John either, just me."

He moved the knife, running the blade down Danny's neck to the hollow below his Adam's apple. The point dug into the soft skin. "Say you love me."

"Fuck off." Danny bit it out.

The knife immediately dug in, pricking the skin, suffocating him. "Say it or you'll never say another word again."

"You wouldn't dare."

"Oh no?" The blade pressed harder against his throat. "Just try me."

Danny swallowed. It made the blade pinch. "I love you."

"That wasn't very convincing."

"When John comes back he'll break you in half."

"I won't be here."

"You better pray."

"No, *you* better pray, pray that it's nice and stiff, because if it isn't I'll cut the fucking thing off."

Ian's hand pushed between his legs. He moved the knife suddenly to Danny's side, climbing on top of him. He moved like a dog in heat, rutting against him, fervid, using his nails. "Kiss me."

Danny turned his head away. The knife dug into his side. "I said kiss me or I'll stick it right in you."

Danny brought his head back and kissed him. Ian's mouth seemed to slobber all over him. He made little groaning noises. Finally he broke away. "I'm going to come. How d'you like that? More food for your greedy little ego. But first I want to feel it stiff, so you better make it stiff - pronto."

"How the fuck am I supposed to do that?"

"The way you usually do, just let it happen."

303

Danny closed his eyes, racked his brains, but nothing happened.

"Come on Danny, let's have it."

Danny moved beneath him, trying to ease the knife point's bite. He could feel the panic growing inside him. "I can't."

"You better."

Danny tried again. He tried to forget Ian, the knife. He was thinking determinedly of the girl in the timber yard when suddenly, without warning, he had a vivid memory of a night almost six years ago to the day. John in his room, Danny trying to provoke him with that stupid jumper, and suddenly John pushing him back against the wall... no, it was the wardrobe, up against the wardrobe... and putting his tongue in his mouth.

"*Danny...*" Ian was whispering his name, masturbating him feverishly.

Danny felt his stomach turn, felt the start of his withdrawal, quickly checked it, went back to remembering... away, far away, to the river.

The river two weeks before that night. Rab and John sitting talking, watching him without seeing him, just part of the landscape, always wrapped up in each other, never seeing him. John always treating him like a kid, patronising him. The sudden urge to scream, '*Look* at me.' John so big and adult, lying there in his swimming trunks. Danny chronically aware of him, his state of undress, but John not seeing him, turning to Rab and laughing at something he said, then the two of them looking at him in a moment of silence... and he pulled down his trunks, took them off without looking at them, as if he just wanted to skinny-dip, and then turning to look at them and knowing they'd seen. They were watching him and his prick was half-hard and he knew suddenly that he was going to get a cock-stand and turning away, embarrassed by himself, and getting into the water, still tingling from the feel of John's eyes on him, like he looked at his mother. And then they were fighting, yelling at each other, and Danny had got in between them and prised them apart, but not before John had broken Rab's hand, and Rab screaming and John telling him to shut up and then turning on Danny and saying, "Christ, you stupid little *whore*..." And slapping his head. So hard it had given him a cauliflower ear for two days. But he had jerked off that night thinking about it, and somehow the pain had become part of it, and when he came he called himself a stupid little whore, feeling the words somehow excite him. He'd hung over the edge of the bed, jerking it out onto the linoleum, whispering, "You stupid little whore." It had almost hurt.

Danny jolted back into the real world again as Ian shifted against him. He felt his erection immediately start to deflate. He said quickly, "Call me a whore." His voice was rough, thickened.

"What?" Ian was thrown by the suddenness of his speech, the unexpected sound of his voice in his otherwise absent silence.

"I said, call me a whore." Danny opened his eyes and looked directly in Ian's face. "You want me to come, don't you?" he jibed.

Ian blinked stupidly for a moment then the penny dropped. He got the words out, resentful, but not resentful enough to refuse.

"That's it," Danny whispered.

"You fucking pathetic little whore."

Danny closed his eyes, saw John's face again, saw him looking at him, at his nakedness, and there it was, underneath the anger and the shame and the confusion - the hunger.

"You fucking stinking little whore."

And he was in the middle of it all over again, that delicious forbidden thirteen year old's climax, spent groaning and moaning all over his bedside floor.

Reprise.

"Are you taking the piss?"

"What?"

"The post-coital cigarette." John gestured at it, smiling.

"No, I just need a cigarette."

"Don't I get one?"

"Do you need one?"

"Yes. My need is greater than yours. Give."

Rab rolled one up for him. He was sitting cross-legged against the wall. "What time is it?"

John stretched round. "11:30. The night is yet young."

Rab licked the cigarette, sealing it.

John took it off him. They bent their heads together, lighting one from the other.

John looked up. "What pretty eyelashes you have." He was smirking.

Rab flushed. "Fuck off, you prat."

They sat silent a moment or two then John pushed the pillow up under his head, lay flat out. "Let's talk."

"What about?"

"Anything."

"You mean Danny."

"If you like."

Rab took a deep drag on his cigarette, holding the smoke deep in his lungs, letting it roll smoothly out. "No, let's talk about the past."

John scratched his ribs slowly then rubbed them with the pads of his fingers. "What about the past?"

"Why so cagey?"

John shrugged. "The past's full of holes. Everyone remembers it differently."

"You mean it's like a minefield, trying to remember the lies you've told."

John smiled and rubbed his ribs some more.

"You want to talk or not?" Rab demanded.

"Okay."

"Right, let's play Twenty Questions."

"Which is?" John looked at him.

"I ask you twenty, then you ask me twenty."

"Straight up?" John smiled.

"Of course. No lying."

"You trust me?"

It was Rab's turn to smile. "Implicitly."

John looked at his cigarette. "I hate the taste of these."

"Don't procrastinate."

"I wouldn't dream of it. Fire away."

"When did you first make it with Danny?"

John looked at him sharply. "That's not the past."

"Isn't it?"

John's look this time was level. "No."

"Answer the question."

"About two months ago."

"Ever touch him before then?"

"Once. If it counts."

"Why, what did you do?"

"I kissed him."

Rab looked at him and realised his heart was racing. Suddenly he knew how the character with three wishes felt in the fairy tale. Three down, seventeen to go. He must make every one pay. "When?"

"On his fourteenth birthday."

"Did you ever touch him when he was a kid?"

Rab saw his face tighten

"No."

"Who did?"

"Pass."

"You can't do that."

"I just did. You didn't say that I had to answer, only that I had to tell the truth."

"You cheating bastard."

"Are we playing or not? You've got fourteen more to go."

Rab took another drag. He could still get something out of it. He already had. "Did someone else?"

John hesitated. "This is Danny."

"He was a *kid* John."

There was a pause then, "I'm not sure."

"Then guess."

"I think so."

"Why?"

"I caught them."

"*You* caught them?"

"That counts as your twelfth question and yes, I did."

Rab stopped. Thinking, planning what else to ask. "Did the old man take the photographs?"

"Pass."

"Oh come on."

"Next question Rab."

Rab fumed silently for a moment. "Did *someone* take the photographs? Do they exist at all?"

"That's two questions."

"Well fucking answer them both then."

John shrugged as if to say, They're your questions, waste them if you want to. "Yes and yes."

Rab paused, taking a breath. He felt a muscle twitching in his leg and moved, rubbing his thigh. He tucked the blankets round himself. He was shivering slightly. "How many am I at?"

"Five left."

"When you caught them how old was Danny?"

John hesitated again. He was going to say pass.

"Six or seven."

"Was someone else there?"

This time he was going to say it, this time.

"Yes."

"The old man?"

Sixty million dollar question. John smiled at him. "Pass."

Rab banged his fist on the bed. "You *bastard*."

"Keep your voice down." But John was grinning. He took another drag on his cigarette, enjoying himself. "Only two left Rab. What are they going to be?"

"You've got to promise not to pass on them."

"Go to hell."

"Come on John."

"No. Get on with it."

Rab glared at him but John only smiled. Only two left, they had to be the right two.

"The day you kissed Danny, who really kissed who?"

John hesitated. Rab got in quickly before he could speak, "I mean, who *really* kissed who?" He found he had his fingers crossed, tucked under his leg like a superstitious twelve year old. *Don't let him pass on it.*

"Danny."

Rab's breath sighed out of him. "There was something going on between you two, wasn't there?"

John was silent.

"I've been turning it over in my head, putting it together. I can remember lots of little things, things I should have seen at the time, but didn't. Like that day at the river. I thought he was just showing off, but it was something more than that, wasn't it? That's why you took it so seriously, wasn't it?"

"No... and that's your last question."

"It fucking *isn't*, I was being rhetorical. Answer the question John, don't be so fucking chicken. There was something going on, wasn't there?"

John looked at him and his smile was grim. "Alright, I'll answer your question." His smile widened, but it didn't improve. "Pass," he said and stubbed out his cigarette.

Ian came in his face. He watched Danny climax, pouring abuse on him, and then climbed up over him and finished it. He rubbed it in his eyes then forced his cock into Danny's mouth.

Danny took it, fighting down nausea.

"Just like old times, eh?"

Danny's eyes were shut because he couldn't open them. The bitter salt was making them stream. The knife was still there, under his ear. He had been terrified when Ian had come, visualising the knife jerking into his ear canal. An image of Henderson jumped into his head. He felt his stomach roll. He pulled his head free and managed, "I'm going to be sick."

Ian hit the side of his head with the heel of the knife hand.

But the urge was too strong. Danny pushed him off and bolted for the sink. Most of it went in. He threw up again. And again. He kept throwing up until there was nothing left to come.

He was spewing up lies.

All the lies that had been stuck in his throat for almost fifteen years.

He hung onto the sink and looked at them, the salt blinding his eyes, then he turned on the tap and washed them away.

Rab pulled the blankets tight around himself, hugging his knees, trying to keep warm. "Well, do I get my grilling now?"

John smiled. "You sound almost keen."

Rab shook his head. "No thanks. I can do without it."

"Okay. In that case I'll tell you a story."

"A story?" Rab looked at him as if he'd gone off his head.

"Yes a nice bedtime story, packed with thrills and laughter. They say confession's good for the soul." John looked at him steadily. "Are you ready to be my confessor?"

"What are you going to tell me?"

"Ah, no guarantees. Will you hear it or not?"

"Will it be the truth?"

"The pure unadulterated truth which, of course, is never pure and is always adulterated."

"Okay, but let me put a shirt on first. I'm frozen."

"Lie beside me."

Rab looked at him uncomfortably. "There isn't enough room."

"You mean you don't mind touching me when it's sex but otherwise... not macho."

"Something like that."

"Come on, be brave, come lie beside me. You used to be glad enough to do it."

Rab shifted over and got in beside him. John lifted his arm. Rab hesitated, looking at him.

"Go on, put your head down, it's only sweat."

Rab lay down and felt John's arm underneath his head, holding him close to his body. He felt like a child. He felt scared shitless.

"Jesus you're hard as a board. Relax, your mother can't see you now. Snuggle in, get warm, have a nice time. Comfy?" John asked.

"Mm." It was the best Rab could do.

"Then we'll begin. Once upon a time..."

"For Christsake... "

"Don't interrupt, you're cramping my style. Once upon a time there was a young boy and his name was Daniel. Daniel was the youngest son in a family of three brothers - Big Brother, Middle Brother and Baby Brother - and into the family came Goldilocks." John looked down at him. "That's you in case you hadn't guessed."

"Gee."

"Now Goldilocks was a poor relative. He had no mummy and no daddy."

"Aww... "

"Please, no pathos. Goldilocks was the same age as the middle brother..."

"I'm older."

"Only a year, don't nit-pick... and he was *very* beautiful." John paused. "I notice you don't deny that."

"That's because it's true."

"He was modest as well," John said dryly.

"Get on with it."

"Anyway, the brothers and Goldilocks... oh, the hell with this, the *cousin*, lived on a farm with their parents. Now their parents had not married for love but to escape the wicked sins of their past."

Rab leaned up on his elbow. "Is that true?"

"This part's fiction."

"You said it was all true."

"It is, in essence."

Rab looked at him and lay back down again.

"Not long after they were married the wife fell pregnant. Immediately the whispers started. He had never tupped that mare, his seed was going elsewhere. Then another son was born, such a sour little slip of a thing everyone nodded and offered it as positive proof the first devil was never his. But it was not until the last was born that those gossips really went to town. Oh rumours flew around that village; that the child was not his, that the young wife was not pregnant at all and the child was some changeling put in amongst honest folk to disrupt their peaceful lives. But then he was a wealthy man, what else can we expect?

"Anyway the sons grew up. The eldest was a great ugly creature and he soon learned that in order to survive in this world he had to eat people before they ate him, while the middle brother, pale and sickly as he was, soon learned that he had to be

cunning and devious to survive. But the youngest brother soon learned that he was beautiful and that the only way for a beautiful thing to survive in this world is to sell itself to the strongest protector.

"Now into this came the cousin, who didn't think about surviving at all. He just walked into the lion's den and stuck his head in their mouths to see what was in their stomachs, and when he saw that they were eating each other he simply said, That's fine, then they won't eat me. So he stayed and found his own way of surviving.

"Now the eldest brother grew up and as each year passed he seemed to get bigger and uglier but then a curious thing happened, he noticed women lusting after him. He was only a boy but already he looked like a man, and he was full of hungers. So one day..."

John paused and Rab found himself swallowing, realising he'd been holding his breath.

"...So one day he let someone, much older than he was, do something that was to put him beyond the pale forever…"

Rab looked at him. "Are you serious? Like what?"

John laughed. "You want to hear that you have to pay extra. Anyway something in him was lost, never to be found again. He felt real loneliness for the first time, so he turned to the cousin. The eldest brother knew that he was lonely too and only too willing to please and so, like in the best fairy tales, a 'marriage' was arranged, and he taught his cousin dark things, using him with the voraciousness of an animal, tearing him with rage and pain. But the cousin made no complaint, thinking this was what love was like.

"Anyway… Daniel was the youngest and suffered like all youngest sons from being in the way. And people would say, 'Go away Danny, I'm busy', 'Not just now Danny', things like that. Now the bad lion, the devious lion, offered to take Danny under his wing. He didn't mind Danny being landed on him. Everyone thought him a saint. He might look sly, untrustworthy, but obviously they were wrong and they were relieved to be shot of Danny so they'd say, 'Thank you, please take him.' And he did."

John wiped his face. Rab thought he might be crying, was afraid to look, but John went on and his voice was normal, unmoved.

"Anyway, one day when the eldest brother was fifteen he was working with his father on another farm they owned. It was high summer and they were sitting having lunch in the heat of the day. The youngest brother had been making a nuisance of himself and the devious one had offered to play with him to distract his attention. It had been fine enough for a while but it was soon time to go back to work. They called and they called but there was no reply and the father began to get angry. He said to the eldest son, 'Where is that fucking boy?' or words to that effect, and the eldest son said, 'They were playing in the hayloft.' And the father swore a great deal and stomped off to find him. The eldest boy followed him because he felt a terrible foreboding, like a thunderstorm oppressing him, and he wanted to say to his father, 'No, let sleeping dogs lie, don't find him.' And afterwards he was to remember that with great guilt. So they went up into the loft, father first, and there they were. The devious one was fucking the youngest brother's face. The little boy was crying, but sucking away as if his life depended on it. The devious one must have heard them, but he was in an ecstasy of lust and didn't care. Well, the father tore him off and started laying into him. The eldest brother jumped on his back and pulled him off, afraid he would kill him, so the father turned on Daniel and picked him up, thundering off down the ladder with him. The eldest brother ran after him and saw his father throw him in the back of the truck. He jumped in with him. He held him close, tried to comfort him, but at the other end..."

John paused again, wiping his face again and this time Rab realised it was sweat.

He could smell the anxiety come off him in waves, like he was reliving it.

"...at the other end, when they got home, the father dragged him away. The eldest brother fought him and they pulled the crying boy between them like a sack of feed. Eventually the father hit him. The eldest son was big, but not big enough. So he lay on the ground where he'd fallen and watched his father take his baby brother into the shed. He scrambled up and hammered on the door and then he heard the shears going, the ones they had for sheep-shearing, although no-one had ever sheared a sheep on that farm. And he screamed and cried and begged, thinking that the father was killing him. And the mother came out and he implored her, but she did nothing." John's voice seemed to grow very hard. "She did nothing at all because somewhere inside she was glad this had happened. She'd wanted it to happen. He turned his back on her that day and never loved her again."

He paused again, slowing his breathing. "And when they finally did come out all the little boy's beautiful hair was gone. And you might think that was the end, but it wasn't. The worst part was yet to come. Everyone pretended it hadn't happened. The father treated Danny with shame and contempt, as if he was to blame. He had tempted his brother, brought ugly truths to light. And so the devious one was still allowed to dress him and bathe him, because nothing had happened, and anything that might have happened was Danny's fault anyway. Oh, the devious one was warned off, and they watched him after a fashion, but they didn't *stop* him. And the eldest brother thought, the eldest brother *knew*..." John stopped, tried again, "The eldest brother *believed* that he still did those things to him but he pushed his baby brother away from him and ran away because everybody has to survive and that was how he did it."

He fell silent.

"That's not the end," Rab said when he didn't go on.

"Yes it is."

"No it's not. What about the old man's bender?"

"Different stories, different people, different times."

"Tell me then."

"Christ, I'm not telling you all that."

"Just one then."

"What?"

"The day at the river."

"Ah, the romance. A tale of human loyalty and absolute stupidity. Alright, let's see. It was six years since Daniel had shamed his family in the hayloft and he was now twelve years old. He still hero-worshipped his brother but he couldn't get his brother's interest, because his brother was too wrapped up in his cousin. They were *great* friends, spending all their free time together. They could go to pubs. They were grown men. They sat in each other's rooms and had earnest conversations. With the doors locked, mind you, because in reality they were actually lying head to arse. Only Danny didn't know that. He thought they were true *friends,* not just a pair of rabid little bastards with hot hands.

"Anyway his eldest brother shunned him worse than ever, even when he was desperate for his friendship. The only attention the two young men ever paid him was to take the piss out of him. But none of it mattered, because he had learned lots of useful things about people. Soon the eldest brother noticed a change in his behaviour. Suddenly he wanted in to pee every time the eldest brother was in the bath. He wandered into his room half-dressed, once or twice with no clothes on at all. He used any excuse he could to touch him; fighting and tussling him like a boisterous pup, sitting on him when he lay out on the couch.

"One night when he was thirteen he came into the eldest brother's room and said

he had had a nightmare, could he come into his bed? The eldest brother made a lot of noise about it, but his young brother did look cold and white and badly upset, and besides, it flattered his ego that he should turn to him. And, of course, he had a double bed so it would cost him nothing. It's easy to give when it costs you nothing. So he said, 'Yes, get in, you stupid little cunt,' and the boy climbed in. The eldest brother put out the light and asked the boy what the dream was about and he said, 'A man was kissing me'. The eldest brother felt a tingle of apprehension, like a burglar witnessing a theft, and said, 'A man?' And the boy said, 'Yes', but he wouldn't tell him any more and the eldest brother didn't want to know anyway because he believed in letting sleeping dogs lie, especially when he thought one of the dogs might have been his."

John took a deep breath. "So they lay there in the dark, but the eldest brother suddenly felt wide awake, disgruntled by the conversation, and by the unfamiliarity of sharing his bed. Daniel, however, appeared to be sliding into sleep. He snuggled up to his brother, quite unconsciously, and perhaps the eldest brother was a little touched in the loneliness of the night, because he knew he couldn't even cast the last stone let alone the first, so he put an arm around the boy and held him close. Or perhaps the eldest brother was a little hungry that night in the dark, and his brother's hair smelt nice, and his skin felt soft under his outgrown pyjamas. Perhaps it was nothing but a little comfort, or perhaps it was something dirtier.

"Anyway he stroked his brother's hair a little and listened to his breathing and lay there, wide awake, thinking about himself and his brother, only he soon got bored with soul-searching and began to think about sex instead. And lo and behold, there he was lying in bed with his brother, stroking his hair, with a raging hard-on. Boy, did the eldest brother feel *bad*. But the worst thing of all was it didn't make the hard-on go away. No sir. He looked at young Daniel, and he could see him dimly in the darkness, and that made that hard-on worse because Daniel was getting to be a very tasty piece indeed. So the eldest brother had to lie there and suffer his hard-on till it went away and he could go to sleep. And in the morning Daniel watched him getting dressed from under his lashes, trying to see his nakedness, and the eldest brother swore, Never again. From now on he stays out. And he did. Daniel tried harder than ever to get his attention, but the eldest brother ignored him and sent him to his middle brother and said, 'Go play with him'. And the middle brother did play with him, you bet he did."

John stopped again, shifting Rab's leg slightly, then went on, "So this went on until the second week of October in Daniel's thirteenth year. It was an Indian summer, a freak, almost a full week of glorious sunny weather. It was warm enough to swim, and the brothers had a Saturday off, so they went swimming. There was an odd kind of tension in the air that day, and suddenly, during a lull in the conversation, the eldest brother looked up and saw his little brother slowly and purposefully take his swimming trunks down. That was bad. It was bad that the cousin should be there and see this, bad that the boy was betraying something about himself that the eldest brother didn't even understand. He was frightened and it made him angry, but worse was yet to come. He looked at his cousin and saw his eyes roving over the boy's body. And the brother looked back at Daniel and realised his brother wasn't really a little boy any more. He'd been magically transformed. There, in that incredible fairytale day, with dragonflies in the air, he was suddenly very beautiful indeed. And Daniel turned and looked directly at them, and the eldest brother saw his cock was thickening, ready to stand up, and he saw the nest of thick red hair it was growing in, and how flat his chest was, and how lean his buttocks had become, and it was like he'd metamorphosed right there in the water, and there was no little boy left at all. And the eldest brother grew stiff, and the cousin saw it in his skimpy little trunks and said to him, teasing, not meaning anything serious, 'You can't John, it's incest.' Smiling because he found it funny, not thinking it important, because of course it wasn't, really. But guilt jumped up

and turned his words into monsters and the eldest brother jumped on him and beat him as if he was trying to beat his brother's beauty out of his eyes, and broke his best wanking hand. Ah, a hard rain was gonna fall."

John put his free hand under his head. "So, two weeks later Daniel's birthday arrived. It was Halloween. It was cold. They had stopped working at six o'clock in honour of the occasion. They had given Daniel some beer for a laugh and they were all a little drunk. Daniel had gone upstairs, dragging his eldest brother with him, ostensibly to show him his new sweater. The sweater was pink. A terrible colour, bizarre with his red hair. He'd put it on, still drunk, saying, 'What do you think?' And John, laughing at him, said, 'You look like a girl in it. What colour's pink for a boy?'. And Daniel had said, 'I do not look like a girl', most put out, and the eldest brother had said, 'Yes you do, watch out or the lads will be after you', and Danny had looked at him suddenly and said, 'Think I'd fool them?' And the eldest brother had seen what he was doing and said levelly, 'No problem', and Danny had come up close against him and said, 'Give us a kiss', camping it up. And the eldest brother thought to himself, Cheeky little fucker, I'll nip this in the bud. And he picked him up and pushed him hard against the wall and kissed him, like a terrible screen lover, shoving his tongue half-way down his throat. He could feel the boy panicking and he was laughing to himself thinking, This will cure him. Only he forgot about the law of survive how you can and Danny knew its rules as well as the next man, so if the eldest brother was going to use his strength then he would use his. He stretched up, pushed himself against him, and wrapped his arms around his brother's neck. He began to kiss him back. He didn't know how, but he was doing a good impersonation. And God spare the angels, didn't the eldest brother find it was himself who had bitten off more than he could chew? He hadn't had sex in a long time and here was this beautiful boy offering himself to him, kissing him with more abandon than anyone had ever kissed him in his life. His dick was sticking into the boy's stomach like a pole. He knew that the boy must be able to feel it and it was that that broke it. He pushed the boy off, shocked at himself. The boy was frightened, but elated too. After all, he'd got what he wanted. And the eldest brother said... mark this, this is the best part... 'Don't do that again' as if it was the boy's fault. And the boy took it, as he'd been taught to do, and the eldest brother went away happy in himself that he'd got his jolly big hard-on, and all free of charge, at no cost to his conscience. After all, the boy had kissed him, hadn't he?"

John stopped. He was quiet so long Rab wondered if he'd finished, but he hadn't.

"After that it was different. Daniel stopped all the rough house and pretend play. Now he would just catch his eye and then look away. He still wandered around half-dressed, but more subtly. He learned very quickly. And he kept this up for two years, two long, hot, hard, hungry years, until he was sixteen, and then it stopped." John snapped his fingers. "Just like that. Only by now the eldest brother was besotted, in too deep. It was as if his life had been all starters and no main course. Oh he wanted him very badly now that he was gone. And Danny didn't care. Unkindest cut of all. So the eldest brother died of a broken heart, because this one's a sad story."

Rab struggled round to look at him. "Not true. The eldest brother carried him off to his den and ate him."

"I hate that version of the story, it shows him in such a bad light." John pulled his arm out suddenly, pushing Rab away abruptly. "That's enough for tonight. I think you've got more than your money's worth." John swung his legs out the bed, pulling on his shorts.

Rab sat up on one elbow, watching him. "Why did you tell me?"

"A repulsive urge for self-justification. I get tired of being hated. Even Attila the Hun needed somebody to love him."

"Why don't you stay?"

John turned and looked at him. "I'm flattered, truly flattered, but you were right, I must finish up the leftovers back in my den."

Rab stared at him. "You bastard."

"That's more like it. That's the kind of language I understand."

"He told me you did it."

John stopped. "What?"

"He told me you'd molested him when he was a kid."

John sat down as if he had no muscles in his legs. Rab looked at him closely. "When?"

"A couple of weeks back, in the barn."

John shook his head then said, "You're sure he meant me?"

"He named you John."

John shook his head, looked away, then said, "He thinks I did."

Rab stared at him. "Are you telling me he genuinely believes you did it?"

"Yes."

"Then he's fucking nuts."

John slapped his mouth. Rab didn't even know it was coming. It appeared out of nowhere. He lay back on the pillow, blinking.

"Don't ever say that again."

"I didn't mean it like that."

"I don't care how you meant it. Don't dish out blame like you were someone's fucking sainted aunt."

"What are you doing John? Letting him blame you so you'll feel better? Heap blame on me Danny. Make me suffer. I was wrong, you're a closet masochist."

"Like you're a closet queer."

Rab's mouth shut tight. "Thank you John, and fuck you too."

"Any time Rab, just whistle."

"Why don't you crawl the fuck back to him, you're making the place smell bad."

John picked up the ashtray and emptied it over his head.

John went back to him.

He could smell it as soon as he walked into the room.

"Danny?"

There was no reply. He put on the lamp at his side of the bed.

Danny was lying like a turtle under the covers, only his hair showing, dark in the light. John reached over and shook him slightly. He could feel by the tension in his body that he wasn't asleep. "Danny stop playing possum. You've been sick. It stinks in here."

Danny still said nothing.

John climbed into the bed. "Wake up you little fucker or I'll pulverise you." And he pulled him round to face him.

Danny's eyes were flat and hard, dull as a snake's. His face was a sickly yellow pallor.

"Jesus, what's wrong, don't you feel well?" John felt his forehead but it was dry, if cold.

"Ian was in here." Danny's voice was as flat as his eyes.

John felt a surge of irritation. That little bastard was asking to be sliced up. "What did he want?"

"Just what he took."

"Took?" John looked at him, feeling his heart do a trip and bump. *Keep on going*

heart. I'm too young to die.

"Yes. He had a nice wank in my face then went back to bed."

John stared at him.

"But it doesn't worry me, I'm quite used to it. I no longer find it offensive. I was thinking of asking him back again tomorrow."

"Shut that."

"Don't worry about it John, rest easy. After all you invited him to take it up again."

"Again?"

"Again." Danny's gaze was level.

"Say what you mean Danny."

"I am saying what I mean."

"You're saying he's done it before?"

"You know he's done it before."

"I know he's done it once."

"Once my fucking fairy aunt. Try a hundred. Two hundred. Try six years worth, eight, fourteen."

John didn't know what to say. He'd waited so long to hear it and here it was and he didn't know what to say. All he could come up with was, "You told Rab it was me."

"Screaming betrayal? Tell him I lied. Should be easy for you."

John looked at him, trying to read it, but his eyes might have been glass, nothing there. He looked away, face hot. "I'll get rid of him."

"Don't bother. Only you might ask him to leave off with the knife. I'm fussy about knives."

"A knife?"

"You're beginning to sound like an echo. Yes, a *knife*. Yours, as a matter of fact. And why so surprised? Of *course*... you're right, you should see the hard-ons Ian gives me. Oh boy, original and best. The master's hand."

"Don't."

"No, seriously, think how much of his come I must have drunk over the years. I'm half built out of him. Reared on brother's milk."

"I said, don't."

"Why? Sorry I wasn't a virgin?" He put a hand over his mouth in an exaggerated gesture of error. "What am I *saying*? I *was*."

John reached over and clamped a hand over his mouth. "For Christsake, shut *up*."

Danny's eyes looked at him over his hand. John closed his eyes tight and listened to the wind. He was waiting for Danny to speak, waiting for the noise of it when he took his hand away. Hail rattled suddenly at the window, sharp, vicious, spitting, hissing in the warm sour darkness. He lifted his hand off without opening his eyes.

"You can't let him go, can you?" Danny demanded immediately. "You can't let a single part of your empire go. Is that why you're hanging onto me?"

John opened his eyes and looked at him. Danny was crying, silently, as Danny always cried, as if he'd taught himself how to do it without inconveniencing anyone. Nothing but the wet on his face to show it was happening at all.

John didn't answer.

He climbed in beside him. He was icy cold. Danny felt feverish beneath him. "Let me love you."

Danny pulled away from him, rolling to the edge of the bed. John grabbed at him, pulling him back. Danny tried to get his legs out but John's force was relentless. Danny was always half-beaten by the knowledge of it before he even started.

Danny struggled beneath him, felt John inch over him remorselessly, as if he was heavily drugged. His movements were slow, unnatural, and still Danny couldn't shake him off.

314

"That night Danny, what did you want?" John's voice held the catch of excitement. Danny stopped struggling, breathing heavily from his exertions. "What night?"

John's hands and body kept moving, inching over him, pulling himself on top like a mollusc, something underwater, slow, determined to consume him. "Your birthday, your fourteenth birthday. You took me upstairs. What did you want?"

"Piss off." Danny shoved at him. John never even felt it.

"The jumper was just an excuse. I knew it and I still went with you, and it wasn't just curiosity. I've lied hard, to myself, the worst lies of all. What did you want?" John was on top of him now, holding him there, lying face down into his shoulder like a man spent after sex.

"I don't know. I don't remember."

"I thought it was just the excitement of your birthday coming up, but it wasn't. Going up those stairs I could feel it. What did you want? How had you run it in your head? What was I going to do to you?"

John could feel his hesitation and knew suddenly he was going to tell him, had been itching to tell him. He could feel the revelation tensing him.

"You weren't going to *do* anything John. You were going to make me understand what was so fucking great about having you grunting and heaving away up his bloody hole. I wanted to know why he got so bloody hot and *pathetic* about it."

John still felt the shock of it hit. "You *knew*."

"Of course I fucking knew." Danny jerked beneath him, trying to wriggle free. "I fucking saw you."

"You couldn't have."

"No? You were bending him over a fucking truck in broad daylight in a field, for Christ's sake. I was looking for a place to pee and practically fell over you. One minute you were arguing, next there was all this fumbling and shoving going on. I could hear his moans and groans where I stood. I was so naive I actually thought you were hurting him. You were holding him by the neck, like he was a cat or something, shoving up against him. Suddenly he practically screamed, and then I saw you grip his shoulders with both hands, your arse going jig, jig, jig, and it was *then* I realised what was going on. During your little performance I'd been trying to hold it in. Suddenly I felt all this hot wet soaking through the lining and this weird feeling like I was going to pass out or something. I didn't even dare look at my hand, take it out my pocket, I was so scared. I was so used to Ian frigging me for hours before I got there that I didn't even connect what had happened to me. You know what I did then? I threw up. I actually physically chucked up. That's how sick-making you were; sexy little Rab and gorgeous super-stud John. And that's what I wanted, a bit of your gentle persuasion, and you know what, I still haven't had it, because you still haven't fucked me, have you? Because you pissing well *can't*."

There was a moment's silence. John could feel his heart beating sluggishly. Danny stared unseeingly at the ceiling, looking at the pool of golden light, feeling the tickle of John's hair against his face, feeling the difficulty of breathing under John's weight, feeling the fear of John's words. But when he did speak it was the last thing Danny expected him to say. "Why did you run away?"

"Because I'd put all of this shit behind me. Only you wouldn't let it go. Now it was bigger, uglier, dirtier, like something we'd hidden in a cupboard for twenty years that had come back twenty times the size and fifty times as mean. I was *scared*."

"Did you even want Rab?"

"Oh, don't start."

"What about her?"

"Grow *up*."

"So why did you let her?"

"Why not?"

"You wanted me to see."

"Yeah, right."

"Just like you wanted me to see you with Rab."

"That was his idea."

"But it was you who wanted to be caught."

"Fuck off." Danny began to struggle again.

"You've wanted me all along. You've never *stopped* wanting me."

Danny bit his shoulder, sinking his teeth in. John roared, grabbing at his head, but Danny wouldn't let go. John swore at him, pulling free, clutching his shoulder. Danny squirmed out from under him. John caught his leg as he rolled across the bed. Danny flung out at him with his arm, catching him in the eye. John let go, his eye flooding with water. "*Shit.*"

Danny was up out the bed and into the hall. John ran after him. He saw Danny disappear down the stairs. He went down behind him, hissing his name. Danny plunged into the kitchen. John went in, feeling for the light. Danny's hand closed over his wrist. The knife went in under his arm, almost into his armpit.

"Don't." Danny's voice was edgy with adrenaline.

John left his hand on the light switch, hung there.

Danny ducked under his arm, moving the knife slightly. His free hand came round John's stomach, flat, feeling him. Now he was pressed against John's back, but only lightly, giving himself room. "This body..." That was all he said, but the words were hoarse, dry. "Always the hero John. That was my first mistake. The big, strong, powerful ones are always heroes. I was wrong."

"Danny..."

Danny dug the knife in. John felt the skin break. "Shut up. Just shut the fuck up. I'm sick of you lying to me." Danny moved the knife. John felt pain start in the cut. "Tell me why I shouldn't kill you."

"You tell me."

"There isn't any reason."

"Alright then, go ahead."

Danny's arm tightened round his waist, slid down inside his shorts. "Maybe I'll just cut you, mark you ..." He didn't get any further.

John clamped his arm down over the knife. He felt it slide and cut across his skin, running painfully across his ribs like a breath of cold. He heard Danny gasp. The knife hit his foot harmlessly. He turned and thumped Danny against the door frame, trapping him. He lifted his hand and hit him. He hit him again, feeling the fear flare up inside him because he didn't think he could stop. He punched Danny into the room. He pushed the door shut. He felt icy with rage and pain.

He hit Danny again, open-handed this time, slapping him back towards the table. He could see Danny backing away from him. He couldn't see his face, couldn't hear anything from him, silent with Danny's loaded silence.

"Always knives. It's all that talks to you Danny. You've got a death wish, know that?" John slapped him again.

Danny finally came to rest back against the table. He put his hand on the edge. He looked almost relaxed, except his shoulders were too hunched.

"Know what the psychiatrists would make of that?" John slapped him again. It came hard and fast across his face as if he'd been saving it.

This time Danny made a noise like a whimper, small and intense.

John held his face. He could feel the skin swollen and burning under his hand. It felt wet. "Let's not talk about it. Let's just give it to you, my knife in your guts, right now. Turn around."

Danny tried to move, but his movements were stiff and slow.

John grabbed his hair and tugged it viciously, dragging him up and round. "Down over the table." John pulled his shorts down with one movement. He slapped Danny's leg. "Step out of them."

Danny lifted his foot slowly and cleared them from one leg then the other.

John lifted them and threw them into the corner of the room. There was the sound of their soft fall.

"Spread your legs. *Wider*. Never going to get John-boy up that." John pushed his legs wide apart. "Right, *down*. I'll show you who can't." He pushed him forwards with a quick punching shove.

Danny dropped down onto his arms. In the same instant he felt John push against him. It felt unreasonably dry and hard. The clock chimed in the hall.

"Realise this is your birthday? Gone half past twelve. Here's your present." He pushed hard. It went in, dragging, dry, unlubricated. "Just what you've always wanted, by your own admission."

Danny grunted a denial. John shoved. Danny felt as if the whole thing went in at once; John's whole length in one ripping motion.

John made a noise that sounded like '*Hunh*', half grunt of effort, half something else. Danny had the distinct impression it was meant to be a word only John had lost control. But he pushed again. There was more. Danny felt more go up. Inconceivably more.

He shook his head. He hadn't known, never imagined... It hurt like hell. It burned and itched, felt so tight it was like a knife scraping his insides away. He moaned.

John heard him and felt it crawl over his skin. He held Danny's arse tighter, pulling it up to him, and gave a sharp thrust, pushing the last of it in.

Danny hissed between his teeth, reared his head and dropped it again, lay there sweating, panting, waiting.

John felt his own heart hammering. "That's it Danny, the whole thing, every inch crammed up inside you. Think you could have taken it at fourteen?" He felt no movement.

And suddenly he needed to know. He couldn't bring himself to touch him but he needed to know. His voice was fractured, bleeding, his body still as stone. "Like it?" He could hear his own desperate breathing, the whispery voice that spoke the words. Not his surely?

Danny was silent.

Don't make me ask it again, Danny. He could feel the sweat start on his skin. The kitchen was bitterly cold, the stone floor icy under his feet. He felt Danny reach round awkwardly and take his hand and slide it under himself.

It was like some living thing burning John's hand; huge, gorged on pain. John gripped it tight. "Does that hurt?"

Danny dropped down again. His voice, when it came, was muffled against his arm. "Fuck... *you*."

John felt the words run through his blood like alcohol, felt his cock expand a little more inside him, excited by his stillness, like a dog pulling at the leash. "All I'm giving you is pain and all you can feel..." he squeezed the thick meat of Danny's erection, "is that."

Danny bit down on his arm.

John loosened his hold on his penis, holding it so lightly it could afford Danny no pleasure, only reassure himself.

Then let it go entirely.

Danny felt it hanging there in mid-air, a heavy aching weight, pulling on his groin miserably. His arse was throbbing, longing to be free of this massive obstruction.

John stayed tightly pushed in, not allowing himself to retract, and Danny realised suddenly what he was going to do. He was going to bring himself off without him, quickly and flavourlessly.

He was making little rapid thrusting movements, barely twitching the head of his penis inside him.

Danny knew it for what it was. He lifted his head. "*Coward...*" He hissed it into the dark, felt John's pause, loss of momentum.

"Lie still." John's voice held an edge of frantic anger.

Suddenly Danny shoved back against him, forcing him to take a step back. When he tried to push forwards again Danny pulled himself against the table, making a space between them.

John tried to pull him back against him, shorten the distance, but Danny kept evading his manoeuvres, always managing to keep that space and, in the process, lengthen John's strokes. In short make him fuck him, properly.

"Don't," John said between gritted teeth.

Danny began to talk to him. Danny who always had sex in silence began to tell him things that John suddenly didn't want to hear.

"Don't," John said again, but Danny went on disgorging everything, letting it all pour out; things John had forgotten, things he'd never wanted to remember, sick things that drove him out of his head, and all the time Danny thrust and writhed underneath him, like fucking a snake.

John desperately tried to cover his mouth with his hand. Danny immediately took the opportunity to make their bodies slide in slow deep thrusts together, pushing back hard, pulling away slow. John grabbed for his shoulders, trying to restrain him and only succeeded in freeing his mouth again.

Danny immediately started again. "I know what you wanted, with your big stiff prick fucking my navel. I know what you wanted to give me for my birthday, cocksucker, arse-licker, *shit-eater.*"

"Shut up, fuck you, shut *up.*"

But Danny went on. "Because you told me, your tongue licking out my ear, wishing it was my arse, breathing your slimy spunk-breath all over me, creaming your knob up against that pink sweater that was so fucking *fag.*"

"*No,*" John said, feeling it come up ready, knowing it was going to destroy him.

"*You* kissed *me* John and what were the first words you said when you were finished sucking my tongue out my head? Where were your hands? What were you *thinking?*"

"Shut *up,* shut *up.*" John grabbed his shoulders and started ramming it into him, wanting it, no longer caring, just wanting it.

"Tell me what you *said.* I want to hear it again. I want the right to *believe* it." Danny grunted fiercely, thrusting back on him, "*Tell* me."

"I was drunk," John said frantically, almost pleading.

"Not that drunk."

"You were offering it."

"Oh, it's coming John..."

John lunged into him hard, wanting the release of it.

"You were holding my arse John... up against me... both hands..."

Suddenly John grunted, pulled out with an odd dreamy slow motion, then *shoved.*

His whole body convulsed in one huge spasm. It held him there quivering, trembling like a sick dog, swamped with the most gut-wrenching sensation he'd ever felt in his life. He cried out like a child and jolted forward, his cry offering a sudden release from that frozen rapture, making him ram Danny against the table savagely, his body folding with the annihilating power of it.

He was home.
Inside his little brother.
At *last*……

John got off him with difficulty. He felt rigid with cold and exhaustion. He couldn't look at him.

Danny spoke to him. "Look at me."

But John couldn't meet his eyes, didn't want to see him.

Danny spoke to him again. His voice was low, heavy, familiar.

John turned to him in the dark and saw him, legs apart, cock curving upwards. John came towards him.

Danny's hand came out, stopped him as he reached out. "I want the knife."

John's hand dropped.

Danny reached round behind him. When he turned back the knife was in his hand. He threw it up, caught it blade-first, like a circus performer, then held the handle out to him. It glinted in the window-light. He leaned back again, opened his legs. "Take it."

"No."

"*Take* it." Danny's voice was so low it sounded like vibration.

John began to shiver. The cold, the fear - everything. He took the knife, made to put it down, but Danny moved forward quickly and clutched his head, drawing it down to his mouth. He felt Danny's hand round his own, drawing the knife between his legs. He pulled free and looked down. He could see the point digging into the shallow valley between Danny's balls, indenting the skin. Danny began to masturbate. Every time he pulled, the knife dragged on the skin. John kept the knife steady, pressing just enough.

Danny pulled his cock up, holding it tight against his belly, pulling it up as if he were trying to drag it up his chest. John could see the knife bite. Danny pulled harder. John moved the knife. He watched himself slowly drag the point up the long curving length. He saw Danny lean his head back. He knew he was watching his face. The knife moved teasingly, reached Danny's fingertips. John inserted the knife underneath them gently, like a man levering a tin open. Danny let go. The knife point held his cock in place. It must hurt, John thought, but he didn't move. Danny opened his legs wider, braced himself with his arms. John sensed that he wanted to move, was only holding his thrusts in check and no more, only preventing himself from impaling his cock on the knife by the skin of his teeth. The foreskin began to slide back, a slow peeling roll as his cock swelled then jerked. John reached up slowly and gripped it, holding it tight around the shaft. He took the knife away and peeled the skin right back, then gently he ran the point over the head, tracing its outline, under the ridge.

Danny thrust once and winced as the point pressed in. It didn't break the skin. He thrust again, impatient. John was careful, held the knife lightly so that he couldn't hurt himself on it. It seemed to frustrate him. John pressed the blade against the length of him. Held it on the broad flat side, the cutting edge safely away from him. Danny immediately rubbed against it. John tried to move it - it wasn't *that* safe - but Danny said, "No," and pressed the knife hard, tight, holding it in place. He began to thrust against it in earnest. John watched it in horrified fascination, saw the head press down over the point, expected it to catch, but somehow it didn't. Danny's movements grew faster. What if he slipped? He held John's hand tighter as if sensing his fear.

John lifted his eyes slowly, unable to watch it. Now no-one was watching the knife. He looked at Danny's face, rapturous, with a faint curving smile. "You're crazy," he said. "You're a crazy perverted little…" He began to sweat. He could feel the knife handle grow moist, slippy, dangerous. "Stop it."

Danny's eyes were half shut. He shook his head.

"Danny..." John knew it would slide eventually, soon, and slice him open. But Danny kept moving. "No," John said suddenly, pulling away from him.

Danny gripped the knife hard. "Go on. It's what you want." His face was contemptuous, challenging.

John put the knife down, carefully, at arms length. He held Danny's cock lightly. His hand was cramped. He flexed the fingers. "No," he said, watching Danny's face.

Danny smiled slowly, broader than broad. "We're not finished yet." And the threat was big and ugly in the dark.

"We're finished."

"There are other things I remember."

John stood there, feeling sick now, not cold, still watching his face. "Such as?"

"Once, playing hide and seek..."

And John remembered too.

"...me, you... hiding from Rab. The two of us shut in the linen cupboard."

"What do you want?"

"Oh no, you're too late John, I'm enjoying myself now. It wasn't very long after that night. Maybe a week or so at most. You didn't hold out long, did you? It was raining. I can remember the noise of it on the skylight."

John moved his free hand into Danny's pubic hair. "Why don't you shut up?" He could feel himself trembling. He was sick of this, sick of these games. But Danny went right on.

"Rab went past, calling out suddenly, right outside the door. You were behind me, pulling me against you in the dark to hush me, your hand over my mouth. But you didn't let go after he passed, did you John?"

"I didn't hear you complaining."

"You whispered in my ear..."

John slapped him.

Danny went on as if nothing had happened, "...'Maybe now Danny' and suddenly there was something hard between us that hadn't been there before."

"Crap."

"You slid your hand over my belly and felt my fourteen year old prick..."

John slapped him again. "For Christsake, why don't you just shut up."

"...copping your sly little feel, rubbing your face in my hair, little *moan*... "

John grabbed the knife and pressed it into his belly with a jerk. Danny looked down at it, then up at John's face, black and white in the dark. He took himself in his hand and began to masturbate. "Maybe you could pass that off as the second time John..." He thrust himself up towards him, feeling the knife, hard in his stomach, watching John's face. "But it certainly wasn't the last."

John pushed the blade hard against him. "I'm warning you Danny, you're going to push me too far. For the last time, shut *up*."

Danny smiled suddenly, soft, spreading. John saw his teeth in the darkness, then he bent forwards, his body curving over the knife as if he intended to disembowel himself, and gave an odd grunt, biting his lower lip.

John felt something wet on his hand and looked down in time to see the thick white glutinous milk slide down over the blade of the knife in heavy warm spurts.

THIRTY-NINE

They found Henderson's body.

It appeared as a stop press in the evening paper.

None of them had even looked at it, except Ian. "It looks like they've found Danny's boyfriend," he said.

They all stopped what they were doing and looked up. It was a rewarding reaction.

John spoke first. He pushed his plate away, the food half-eaten. He dropped his cutlery into it as if its weight was intolerable. "What does it say?"

"Not much." Ian folded the paper. "The stop press, there. Read it yourself."

John read it twice. Name rank and serial number, murdered in his own flat. Nothing else. He looked up. Danny was watching him, his eyes restless. Rab was looking at the table, puddling crumbs with a knife edge, squaring them, resquaring them. He didn't look up.

"Let me see." Danny reached across the table. John gave him the paper. He read it and offered it to Rab. Rab shook his head without answering, his eyes fixed on Danny's face. John wanted to punch him in the mouth.

"None of you look very surprised." Ian was trying not to smile, but it was hard work.

John looked at the dog stretched out on the floor. "Why don't you take the Buffalo back to Ostler?"

Ian's face became sulky. "That's Danny's job."

John looked up at him. "Well, now it's yours. Move your arse."

"I've only just eaten."

"Get going."

Ian stared at him a moment, aware of the other two studiously studying the table top, then he got up, pushing his chair back with a tooth-aching scrape. "I hope they get you."

John just stared at him.

"I really hope they nail it on you."

"Fuck off Ian, there's a good lad."

They waited till he slammed out, but after he'd gone no-one spoke. No-one had anything to say.

FORTY

It was two days after Danny's twentieth birthday. He and John moved around each other like skittish horses.

Ian watched them, trying to make sense of their behaviour, waiting for John to do something, but nothing happened.

Everybody's nerves were raw. Rab smoked too much. John lit too many cigarettes. Danny stood under the shower for hours at a stretch until John came in and took him where he stood, wet and aching, chilled through.

And then it was three days after Danny's birthday, three days of his twentieth year gone, never to be reclaimed, when the car drove up.

The rain was slashing down almost on the diagonal, like the eaves of a house. Separate grey rods all moving together like someone had shaded the world in.

The car was long, low, and vividly red in that grey world. It came nosing gently into the farmyard. Rab saw it through the rectangle of light and stopped. John was waiting for him and looked up to see him standing rigid, facing the doorway, watching intently. John couldn't see out from where he stood. "What is it?" he asked.

"The car." Rab's voice was light under the noise of the rain. "Henderson's car."

John came forward. "There's more than one Mercedes in the world. The vet owns a silver Mercedes."

"No…" John moved beside him and saw the sleek red monster pull to a halt, "…it's his Porsche, the red Porsche."

"You're sure?"

"Of course I'm fucking sure. How many of them have you ever seen? I told you, it's an exhibition car, a one-off."

They waited. No-one got out.

"Now what?" Rab heard himself whispering as if they could be overheard. He looked at John. John shook his head once, sharply, saying, I don't know, don't bother me, shut up, all in one gesture. Rab watched his hand go automatically to his pocket, looking for cigarettes. His eyes were black, lost under the weight of his frown. He put a cigarette in his mouth but didn't light it.

They both saw Danny come out of the house. They thought he hadn't seen it. They waited for him to react, but the passenger door swung open and he crossed to it without hesitation, as if he'd been summoned. They saw him bend down for a moment to speak then he climbed in.

"Police?" Rab asked.

"In Henderson's car? Talk sense."

They waited to see if it would go but it didn't. It sat still, cooling under the rain. They watched it, waiting, as if it might speak to them.

"Yes," he said.

She looked at him. "You couldn't really be anyone else. I'm his sister."

Danny looked at her, vaguely aware that his mouth had dropped open.

"He told you I was his wife, or rather, you assumed I was his wife." Her accent was as distant as Henderson's had been. "You jumped to the wrong conclusion, didn't you?" She sounded almost sarcastic.

"He didn't disinform me."

She looked at him again, carefully. He didn't like the look. He didn't like her. He felt

himself redden. He'd forgotten just how well he did that. She kept staring at him, like a school teacher trying to intimidate him. He wondered briefly if that's what she was. She looked like one. She stared some more.

"Think you'll remember me?" he asked, reddening again, only this time it was anger.

"Oh, I'll remember you alright." And that sounded like a threat, but he didn't have time to say anything or think anything, she went on, "He kept a diary."

Danny let that one sink in. He felt it go right through his skin and into his stomach. It sat there like a lead weight. He let her go on because he knew there was more. Her perfume seemed to come up suddenly into the air between them, rich and heavy, too much of it.

"You figure very heavily in it." She looked away from him. "I found some video tapes. I put them in my car. I did it with about four minutes to spare." She looked back at him. "Another four minutes and you and your brothers would have been prime suspects. Did you kill him?"

Danny shook his head, but his face was red, his eyes averted. He wouldn't even have convinced someone who wanted to believe.

"I took the tapes because I didn't want his friends to see them. The diary was inside one of the boxes. No tape, just a diary. It was the kind of histrionic thing he would do. All effect, like his bloody house, this bloody car, even you." She looked at him. "I didn't know, can you believe that? I never even suspected. A good upstanding police officer, very macho, very male, and all the time..." She stopped, looked away again. "Is it true?"

"Is what true?"

She wouldn't look at him. "The diary, the things he wrote, are they true?"

"I haven't read it."

She looked at him quickly. "You look even less queer than he did."

Danny wanted to smack her in the mouth. He said nothing.

"Was he fantasising, or did you do those things?"

Danny could feel the week's anger come out of him. First the waiting, then this bitch in Henderson's Porsche, rolling up with her coy questions, her outrage. "You mean, did we fuck?" He had the pleasure of seeing her flush, a nice dull angry red. Her mouth thinned to a line. "I don't think that's any of your business," he said.

"Then maybe it's police business."

"If you want them to know he liked boys."

"If you killed him I'd want them to know."

Danny looked out at the rain.

"I don't want anyone to know," she said. "I especially don't want my family to know. And I don't want anyone to see that diary. But if I thought you had anything to do with it then I'd show them. *Did* you kill him?"

"No." And this time it had the ring of truth.

"Do you know who did?"

"No," Danny said again with the same conviction.

He saw her visibly relax and realised how much she had been dreading the idea of sharing the diary. In it he measured the strength of his own safety, John's.

"They found three long blonde hairs in here, on that seat. They think he had a girlfriend, maybe another man's wife, but they'd be wrong, wouldn't they?"

Danny didn't answer.

"The hairs belong to your brother, don't they? They went out together one night in this car and got drunk."

Danny shook his head.

She caught the movement. "What do you mean, no?"

"He's not my brother."

She was confused. "But he went on at great length about his hair." She frowned. "Did he make it up?"

Danny shook his head again. "No, he's real enough, he's just not my brother. He's my cousin."

"I thought he was your brother."

"No."

She was silent, turning it over in her head. Danny wondered how long she would keep him here. He wanted to get away from her. She could have been Henderson's twin. Thick black hair, red mouth, hers glossy with lipstick. She was even dressed all in black, or was that mourning?

"You have an elder brother?" she said.

"Yes."

"That's the one he called the gorilla."

Danny said nothing but he could almost taste the dislike in his mouth.

"He threatened to kill him." She was watching him now.

He kept his face averted, his mouth shut. Why couldn't she come to the point?

"He seemed to have some notion that your brother was 'molesting' you." She put an ugly emphasis on the word that somehow managed to imply he was an inbred little peasant who more than likely enjoyed that kind of thing. Danny kept his silence. "He said a lot of things, all incriminating."

She was beginning to sound like him. Insidious, prying, cunning. Come to the point, Danny said to himself. Come to the point you snooping bitch.

"Don't you care?" she asked when he said nothing.

"Should I?"

"If I take it to the police?"

"You won't."

"You're so sure?" She was ratty now.

He turned to face her. "Your brother was a queer. You do what you like with that. He was your brother, not mine."

She slapped him, a stinging little blow, like something straight out of a bad B-movie, right down to the long red nails.

Danny got out. She shouted after him, "I'm not finished."

He bent down. "Too bad. I'm finished with you." And he slammed the door in her face.

She got out after him, yanking him round just as he reached the house. "I'll be seeing you again."

"Why?"

"Because we need to talk."

"About what?"

"My brother. I want to know."

"You want to know *what?*"

"Why he was what he was, what made him like that."

"I can't tell you that, try his diary." Danny turned away again.

She pulled him back. "Listen. I intend to see you again. And I'm warning you, if you won't help me I'll go to the police."

Danny looked at her, wondering how much of it she really meant, wondering if there was any point in pushing her. "You sound just like him."

Her eyes searched his face. "You didn't like him, did you?"

"I hated his guts." He smiled.

She had never seen a face so purposely malicious, so *attractive*, and she knew in that moment that he could have done it, probably had done it, because the *pleasure*

of it was in him. And she knew she should go to the police because this was beyond her, the whole thing was beyond her, crumbling in her hands like so much rotten wood, and there was no point in seeing him again, in fact it was probably dangerous to see him again, and so she said, "When?"

And he smiled some more, looking into her eyes, and said in a low voice, "Any time after eight."

And she watched the rain drip off his hair like wine turning back into water, then he turned abruptly and left her without another word.

"It's a woman," Rab said when he saw her climb out the car.

"Brilliant." John watched her run after Danny in ridiculous high heels.

"Who the fuck?" Rab murmured.

They watched the belligerent way Danny turned to face her, the way his eyes were fixed on her face.

"He doesn't like her," Rab said, taking the cigarette packet from John's hand.

"I don't like her myself."

Rab looked at him curiously. "Why not?"

"She's in Henderson's car. She's talking him into something. She's more fucking trouble."

Rab turned back in time to see Danny smile, an odd vicious looking thing that seemed to go on too long, then he turned abruptly and left her standing there.

She stood for a moment in the rain. Her hair was very black, dripping. She looked like a female undertaker abandoned at the graveside. She got back in the car and reversed out with a screech of brakes.

"She doesn't drive like him anyway," Rab said wryly.

"Why should she?"

"I don't know, something about her."

"Something about her what?" John sounded irritable.

"She reminds me of him."

"It's the car."

Rab shook his head. "No, something else."

"She's got police legs." John threw his cigarette down and tramped on it as if it had been lit. "Come on, let's move it."

Rab followed him out into the rain.

They came into the kitchen in a bundle. Danny looked up, startled.

John shook the water from his hair and rubbed his arm across his face. "Who was she?"

Danny leaned back against the stove. "Henderson's sister."

They heard Mrs Ostler belt out a snatch of song in the upper hall, then she was dulled by a door closing. Her voice became distant. John rubbed his forehead. Rab spoke. "What sister?"

"He told me she was his wife. He had her photo in his wallet."

Rab remembered his conversation with Henderson about Danny wanting to meet his wife. He looked at Danny now, but Danny was watching John. John, for his part, had turned away and was looking out the window. "And what does she want?" he asked without turning.

"Henderson left a diary."

That brought him round. Nobody said, A diary? But everybody thought it.

"And?" John prompted.

"He wrote everything in it."

"Story of my life. What's everything? Exactly?" John's face was oddly weary.

"Enough to make her suspicious." He paused. "She's her brother's sister."

"Meaning?" John was watching him now.

"She likes to threaten people, be in charge. She thinks she knows how to do things better, cleverer, than anyone else."

"Go on." John was still watching, waiting.

"She wants to see me..." Danny smiled, "to *talk* to me."

John pushed his hands deep into his pockets. "And you agreed." His voice was heavy, slow.

"Either that or the police."

John turned back to the window slowly. Danny watched his back. Rab watched Danny's face.

"She find the body?" John asked.

"I think so."

John was silent again then he asked, "Tonight?"

Rab realised he'd jumped back in the conversation.

"I think so."

John turned back. He licked his lips. "Get her off our backs Danny." It sounded like a threat.

Danny smiled up at him, lopsided, secretive. He nodded once.

John walked across to him, touched his face lightly with one hand. "Quickly, no games."

Danny nodded again.

John moved a little closer. Rab felt his stomach knot. He saw John's other hand disappear between them. His arm began to move rhythmically. He suddenly realised what he was doing to him. He left the room quickly, before he could change his mind.

She did call for him that evening, but unlike her brother she came into the yard, got out of her car, and knocked at the door.

John was in the kitchen with him. They stood still at the sound, like burglars surprised, then John jerked his head. "Don't keep the lady waiting."

Danny moved towards the door. John pulled him back before he could reach it and pressed his mouth hard against his, whispering, "Don't forget me Danny." But it was a threat, not an imploration.

Rab watched the kiss from the hall. Twice the voyeur in one day.

Danny moved away, taking down his jacket and opening the door.

John stood behind him in the centre of the room, hands pushed deep in his pockets, looking at her. She saw him over Danny's shoulder. How alike they were. She was unprepared for the similarity. Jimmy's diary made him sound utterly different, as if he and his brother were chalk and cheese, Beauty and the Beast. She realised she was staring. The brother was smiling. A broad, curving smile, curiously showing no teeth, ugly in its intent. She couldn't see his eyes, hidden in darkness. He looked like a first attempt, a clumsy try at creating his brother's beauty.

She felt herself flush, looked at Danny. He was watching her with the same expression. They seemed suddenly dangerous, both of them, possessed of a misogynistic dislike of her. She turned on her heel. She heard the door close and his steps behind her. He had not said goodbye to his brother.

She waited until he was in beside her and then drove away.

326

"Where are we going?"

"Jimmy's flat."

Danny smiled in the darkness. *Jimmy.*

"I'm living there. I might as well. It's too costly to stay at a hotel." She seemed to be justifying herself.

"I don't give a fuck where you live." Danny's voice was dull and indifferent.

She felt her face burn. She glanced at his profile, lit eerily by the colours from the dashboard. His face was relaxed, disinterested, and almost unearthly in its beauty. "You don't like me any more than you liked my brother, do you?"

"No."

She had expected it but it still felt as if she had been slapped. "No-one ever bothered teaching you any manners, did they?"

"Manners don't impress cows."

And that sounded like an insult. She pressed down on the accelerator and did not speak again.

He did not wait for her when they got to the flat. He got out of the car and crossed to the doorway. She garaged the car. He was standing waiting for her in the light. He didn't look at her. He was huddled deep into his jacket. Black leather, not cheap, not expensive. Middling, like his clothes, as if they'd been bought with an eye to ultimately becoming work clothes. The only distinctive thing about them were the colours. Rich green shirt, almost white denims, black jacket. The colours highlighted his own colouring. He looked stunning in them.

She opened the door. He went in ahead of her, deliberately bad-mannered. She looked at his back. She couldn't see anything very boyish about him. She tried to remember how old he was. Had Jimmy said how old he was? Twenty-one, twenty-two? He maybe looked boyish to Jimmy but he didn't to her.

He moved from foot to foot outside the door, impatient while she found the right key. This time he let her go ahead. She put on the hall light. He finally began to look uncomfortable. He didn't move. He's afraid, she thought. He's afraid to go in.

Danny stood there, frozen.

"It's been cleaned up." She was looking at him now, her face cynical, enjoying herself.

Danny nodded almost absently. *Of course it's been cleaned up Danny. You stupid or something? Think she'd leave his blood all over the house?*

She went ahead of him and pushed open the door.

The floor was red, deep violent red, like a lake of blood. Danny made a noise as if he'd been punched.

She looked back at him curiously and saw his face was grey. She felt her own heartbeat speed as if they shared a common fear. "What is it? What's wrong?"

"Nothing." Danny could feel the reaction in his legs. He moved forward into the blood. It sank beneath his feet. "It used to be white."

He needed to sit, but the sofa was missing, the wall blank, empty without it. Only one stood there, facing the television. He crossed to it and sat down. He was shaking. He clasped his hands between his legs and looked at the floor.

She closed the door carefully then crossed to the blinds and shut them. The room looked long and empty, stark.

"There used to be another of these," Danny said.

"It's being recovered."

Danny nodded again.

"I never liked the carpet anyway, but I always did like the sofas."

Danny looked at her. She looked back at him levelly. "Do you want a drink?"

"Is that the family motto?"

"I beg your pardon?" Half irritation, half incomprehension.

"Nothing. Yes. Not rum."

"There isn't any rum."

Danny looked at her again.

"My brother didn't like it."

It felt like swimming in black water. Danny said nothing, listening to her silence. She waited a moment then went out of the room.

Danny felt the texture of the leather. He had not expected ever to be in this room again. He looked at the space where the sofa should be. The room smelt of new carpet. She came back into the room, handed him the familiar glass. The contents were clear, colourless. Ice clinked against the sides.

"What is it?" He sniffed it curiously.

"Vermouth."

He frowned, tasted it. He didn't like it.

She clinked her glass, stood looking down at him.

Danny looked at the buckles on her shoes. Showy tarnished silver on suede. They looked like fancy dress shoes, only the heels were too high.

"Did you know he kept a diary?"

"No."

"You realise how much it tells about you?"

Danny looked up this time. "How could I?"

"Supposing..." she saw that his eyes really were green, a living legend, the green-eyed redhead, the first she'd ever seen, "...supposing he'd written everything down, every detail of every conversation. Would you expect it to say too much?"

"Anything that told every detail of every conversation would be too much."

Her mouth thinned. "You're deliberately misunderstanding me."

"You're being deliberately confusing."

She saw him rub his palm on his thigh and remembered Jimmy talking about his hands, the way he had undressed himself in the kitchen, with deliberation. She looked away, unsettled by him.

"I don't know any homosexuals." She offered it to him almost as an apology, more to herself as a warning.

He smiled at the implications. "You knew your brother."

"He wasn't..." She stopped, looked away again.

He became aware suddenly that there was something she wanted to know. She was trying to edge round it, sneak up to it. He looked at her curiously. Whatever had prompted her to see him in the first place was now full-blooded, eating her up. He waited, a past-expert in waiting. He drank some of the vermouth, trying to swallow it without tasting it, chemical and petty in his mouth.

"You made him insecure." She wasn't looking at him. He waited some more. "He wasn't even sure if you were really a homosexual."

And now she was waiting. He could see the tension in her shoulders. He leaned back on the sofa, watching her. He saw her grow suddenly impatient. She swung her head round and looked at him. "Well?"

"Well what?"

"Are you?" She barked it out at him.

"Why should you care?"

She looked away again. "I don't, I'm just curious."

It sounded feeble even to her. She felt herself blush, turned her back to him.

He said nothing. He was going to sit there and let her sweat it out. She swung on him. "He was right about one thing anyway, you are a vicious little brute."

Danny put his glass down and stood up. He crossed to the door. She moved to him quickly. "Where are you going?"

"Home."

"I haven't finished with you yet."

"Correction, you haven't started with me yet."

She stood in front of the door, blocking his way. "*Are* you a homosexual?"

Danny laughed. He scratched his neck, eased his collar. She could smell the faint scent of something sweet from him. "What do you think? You've read his diary."

She looked at him for a moment. "How old are you?"

Danny frowned at the change of direction. "Twenty." It sounded odd to him, like he was lying.

She remembered now. She looked at him critically. "He said you were only nineteen."

"I was." Danny still watched her.

"You're too young."

"Too young for what?"

"Too young to really know."

He laughed again, once, mirthlessly. He looked at her face, set, angry, and couldn't help laughing again. She really meant it. He turned abruptly and sat back down.

"What's so funny?"

He shook his head.

"He was obsessed with the idea that your brother had raped you." She was watching his face for a reaction. He gave her one. He smiled. She frowned and went on, "Then he discovered that your cousin..." she looked at him as if checking accuracy "...that your cousin was doing it too. It confused him, that you went to it willingly." She stopped. She looked confused herself. Danny picked his drink up, finished it.

"Would you like another?" The politeness was ludicrous, risible.

"Not this crap."

She flushed. "You really do have the manners of a pig."

"Thank you." He handed her the glass.

She took it and went out the room. On impulse he stood up and followed her.

She jumped when she saw him there. He came in and sat on the table. He saw her remember something. He didn't know what she was remembering, but that didn't matter. She gave him whisky this time, without ice, without water. She handed him the glass without options or decorations. "You did it in here with him."

Danny nodded, knowing now what she was seeing.

She seemed startled, as if she hadn't really believed it. "You are queer."

"If you say so."

"You must be."

"Alright."

She banged her glass down. "Stop being so bloody complacent."

He drank the whisky down in one long fiery belt. It sang in his head, his blood, his gut. "What would you like me to do?"

"Do?"

He was drunk. Just a little tasty part drunk. It made him happy, here among the knives. Behind him one was missing from the rack. He knew it was missing because he had taken it down. "Do," he affirmed.

"I don't want you to do anything." He heard the edge of panic in her voice.

"Take off my clothes?" He saw that hit the mark. Oh yes, she would.

"No."

Too quick, sister of Henderson. "Curious to know if I look the way he said?"

"I don't know what you're talking about."

"How did he say I looked?"

"I don't remember."

Danny laughed. "You're a bad liar." He began to unbutton his shirt.

"What are you doing?"

"You wanted to know the truth. How will you know if he was fantasising if I don't show you?"

"Stop that."

Danny went on. She went on looking. He undid his shirt and slipped it off. "So far so good?" He started to unbuckle his trousers. "Did he tell you about the marks? They'll heal. John never leaves scars." He unzipped his trousers.

She turned her back to him quickly.

He stopped. "You must have seen a nude man before. Or are you just disappointed? Perhaps I'm not as beautiful as he said."

"Get dressed, I want you to go." She kept her back to him.

"I'll go with pleasure, but you must look first." Danny's voice began to sink into it. "You wanted to see the truth, hear the truth, *know* the truth. Well ask and thou shalt receive."

Danny got up. She heard him and spun round. He trapped her hard against the counter with his body. "Now you're going to feel the truth." Danny took her hand.

She pulled away, but he pressed her back, hurting her.

He took her hand and put it inside his jeans. He watched it register on her face, the shock, the disgust, and underneath it the same thing that was always underneath it. "Look at it then. Go on." He let her hand go and pulled his shorts down enough to expose himself.

She did it slowly, even reluctantly, but she did it anyway. The flat white belly, the thick red hair, the long smooth erection. She looked away quickly, struggling away from him.

He let her go, pulled his shorts back up. He picked up his shirt and slid it on. He started to fasten it, watching the side of her face. "Everything he wrote you can believe. My cock looks just like he described it. I look just like he described me. Fabulous."

She did not reply.

"You knew it was true all along. You just wanted to feel it for yourself. Well now you have." He tucked his shirt in, fastened his jeans. "Only you're not any the wiser, are you? You still don't know. Queer or not? And it's so important to know. Everybody always wants to know. A little exclusivity, are you one of *us?* Only trouble is, I let him feel, and I let you. I let my brother, and I let my mother. So who owns me now?"

She turned, her face white. "You're disgusting. Your whole family's disgusting. I'm sorry he ever got mixed up with you. You're degenerate."

"And didn't you get a wet cunt finding that out."

"*Get out!*" She screamed at him as if she'd suddenly become unhinged. "*Get out!*"

Danny went out quietly.

He walked into the town centre and found a phone booth. It began to rain.

Rab answered the phone. He told him where he was. "Tell John to come and get me."

He waited in the booth, the light spilling down over his hair. A red Porsche went by but Danny was looking the other way.

It wasn't her anyway.

He had to move out the booth before John arrived. A woman and her poodle wanted to make a call. He stood across the road in a shop doorway, watching for him. He saw the Range Rover come up the hill. He went out into the rain and waved. It pulled in. The passenger door opened as he dived through the headlights.

He scrambled in, shaking the water out his hair, then saw who was driving. "Where's John?"

"I think I'm insulted."

"Where is he?"

"He went out in the pick-up."

"Where?"

"I've no idea."

Danny turned and looked out the window.

Rab looked at him a little longer, a little harder. He made no attempt to start the car. "What happened?" he asked.

"I gave her what she wanted."

"And she threw you out? Are you sure you gave her what she wanted?"

Danny closed his eyes and leaned his head back. He smiled suddenly, turning his head to look at him. It was a difficult smile to read in the darkness. "Positive."

"Want to go home?" It fell into the air like a swallow in winter, an impossible possibility.

"No."

And then there were two.

Rab started the car. "Where then?"

"Where you went in the Porsche."

Rab slid the car out from the kerb. "No problem, Danny-boy."

Danny closed his eyes and slept.

He woke in absolute darkness, surrounded by the rich, sweet scent of liquorice. It breathed in his mouth. There was a sound of shifting leather, the warmth of a hand on his thigh, the smell of strange rich soap.

The mouth moved over his again. He tasted the tongue, felt the lighter weight of his hand on him. He lay there passively tasting him, letting the hand squeeze where it wanted. He opened his legs.

"You feel different." Rab's voice sounded strange, alien.

He took Rab's hand in his own and pressed it down over himself. "No, just the same."

Rab's lips felt hot and dry. They moved across his face into his hair. "I'm creaming in my fucking pants."

"Go ahead and get it out your system."

"Not yet."

Danny felt his hand tug at his belt. He breathed in, giving him room.

"You're wearing them tighter."

"Maybe I'm just getting fatter."

Rab brought him out. Danny breathed out slowly.

"Maybe you're getting bigger."

Danny grabbed his hand, holding it still. "I wouldn't."

"I want to taste you."

"You nuts? I won't last two minutes."

"Good." There was the sound of leather moving again.

Danny felt Rab's weight shift onto his thigh, then his mouth closed over him. He ran his hand over his hair. "Go easy." He felt the weight of his pony-tail, pulled at the tie.

It came undone in one fluid movement. He spread the pale hair with his fingers, saw it white in the black pool of his lap. He tried to push his cock up harder, closed his eyes against the sight of the hair.

He said Rab's name.

Rab eased off, brought him out, and flicked it with the tip of his tongue.

Danny pushed his head down, suddenly thrusting himself up into Rab's face, knotting his hands in his hair. "Harder," he hissed, and he began to come, pushing it up, feeling Rab's mouth come down over him deep. He heard himself grunt. And then the inevitable happened.

Rab creamed in his pants, just as he'd promised.

John almost missed him coming out. He hadn't expected him to be alone. He came out, pulling his jacket tight around himself, his face closed, expressionless, and turned into the wind as if he intended to walk home. She didn't appear. Danny didn't see him.

John didn't move. He felt himself sit there and thought, What are you doing John? Are you going to let him walk the five miles home?

He watched Danny disappear into the darkness. He sat a moment, like a man waiting for divine intervention, then got out. He locked the pick-up door. It was not something he normally did.

He looked at the row of buttons. He pushed number six. There was no reply. He pushed it again. The wind came whipping round his head. Danny would surely phone for a lift. A voice spoke in his ear. "Yes?"

"Miss Henderson?"

There was a pause. John thought, Maybe she isn't a Miss.

"Who is this?"

"John Jackson Moore." Would she know the name?

But she answered quickly. "What do you want?"

"I'd like to talk to you."

There was another pause. The wind tore at him again.

"Is Danny with you?"

"No." John felt the first spits of rain on his cheek.

"Come on up."

The buzzer sounded. He leaned against the door and was swallowed up by the warm carpeted hall.

She answered in darkness. She filled the doorway, blocking his way. Had she changed her mind already? But she stood back abruptly, inviting him in without speaking.

He closed the door behind him, feeling oddly aware of her in the dark. It nettled him. This wasn't the time.

She pushed open the living room door, turning to look at him. He couldn't see her face. She was a silhouette against the light. She could see him clearly, his face powerful, bordering on ugly. She began to understand what Jimmy meant. It helped to make sense of those odd remarks, the contradictory stains.

He didn't react. His eyes glanced over the floor. She saw him seeing it, but that was all.

She stepped back. He came in.

"New carpet."

"You've been here before?"

He looked at her, a tiny smile dirtying his mouth. "You must know that."

She coloured.

"Would you like something to drink?" She saw his odd expression and remembered his brother's cryptic remark. Jimmy and his drink, looks like it was a standing joke. "And there's no rum before you ask."

John laughed. She looked at his teeth. So many of them, like a crocodile.

"I wasn't going to ask. Anything will do."

"Even Vermouth?"

Whatever Danny had said or done, it wasn't a satisfactory result. She was spitting like a cat. "Especially Vermouth."

She found herself taking a step back from him before she turned away. She went out of the room quickly, escaping from his smile.

John turned round, looking at the place. The sofa was missing. He looked again. And she'd moved the television. What else?

He crossed to the windows, looked at the blinds. He found the cord, pulled it. Nothing happened. He pulled it again. They opened. That was it, something like that.

She came back in. He dropped the cord.

"Do make yourself at home."

He crossed and took the drink from her. She looked at his hands. They made the glass look tiny. She had never seen hands that size before.

"All the better to fondle you with."

She jumped, flushed again. She turned away without speaking. She sat down on the sofa and immediately regretted it. Now he had the advantage. She began to wonder why she had ever let him in at all.

John sniffed his drink before swallowing. Whisky, straight. She was drinking it too, by the looks of it, but watered down, iced. He looked at her. The Henderson colouring sat better on her, and she had missed the mean little eyes, but otherwise she was almost his double. He looked at the downy hair on her arms, the thick eyelashes, the heavy brows. Even the same luxuriant body hair then. He felt the thought move in him and let it go.

"What did you want to talk about?" she asked.

"You."

"Me?" She looked startled.

"What you want."

"I don't understand you."

"And I don't understand you. Why didn't you take the diary to the police?"

"That's my business."

"Don't you want his murderer caught?"

"Of course."

"Then surely you should give them the diary, and the tapes."

"I couldn't do that to him."

"You couldn't do it to yourself."

She held her teeth tight shut. "What exactly are you implying?"

"I'm implying that the diary didn't begin and end with Danny. I'm implying that there are other things in it and you couldn't give them half a diary, could you?"

"Other things like what?"

He could see the drawn lines on her face. "I've absolutely no idea. I'm just making this up as I go along." He paused a second, watched her relax, then said, "Why didn't you just destroy it?"

She held the glass half-way to her lips.

"Did it make tasty reading?" He saw the colour stain her face. "Detailed?" She didn't look at him. "Accurate?"

"I wouldn't know." She snapped it out.

"You've seen me, you've seen Danny. What do you think, was he accurate?"

She struggled to get up. "I think you should leave now."

John pushed her squarely in the chest, feeling the silk of her shirt beneath his fingers. She went straight back down again. "I think you should sit nice and tell me what's in the diary."

He could see the shock on her face. Whatever else Miss Henderson was used to, she wasn't used to being manhandled. She didn't even manage a how dare you. She looked afraid. He wondered if fear would loosen her tongue or clam it tight. You could never tell. He'd always preferred to deal in fear. It made him real, brought him out in three dimensions. He could talk in fear. It was something he understood.

"What was in it?"

"Nothing that would mean anything to you, and nothing I'd particularly want repeated." She looked up. "He was very thorough, very meticulous. That's what made him a good policeman."

"He was a crap policeman, that's why he's dead."

She flushed. Not used to taking that either, only her fear keeping her mouth shut.

"So why didn't you destroy it?"

"It didn't seem right." She looked at the floor then slid her eyes away sideways as if she didn't even want to see his feet. He smiled. This was his land, his territory. He knew every inch and twist of it.

"Observant?" he asked.

"That's one word for it."

He let her own words hang in the air. "And that's why you had no problem recognising Danny?"

She didn't answer.

"Did he sound good? Too good maybe?"

She looked at him now, eyes dark, angry. "What are you getting at?"

"Did it make you hot?"

She took a moment to answer. When she did it was forcibly calm. "Your brother is a homosexual. There wouldn't be any point in me pursuing him, would there? That *is* what you're hinting, isn't it? That I decided to make a play for him myself?"

"Did your brother say that?"

"What?"

"That Danny's queer."

Her eyes met his levelly. "Yes."

"You surprise me."

He watched her begin to lose it.

"I don't see why."

"Your brother must be the only person in the world who's ever been sure what Danny is."

"He had sex with another man, what would you call it?"

"I'd call it Danny's Law of Eternal Adaptability."

She blinked.

He said, "And did *you* think he was a homosexual?"

"Who?"

"Danny."

And this time she flushed, an ugly betraying red. "Of course he is. What else could he be?"

"So you didn't."

Her mouth opened. She shut it again with a snap then surprisingly leaned back in the chair and closed her eyes. "No, I didn't. And no, my brother didn't think so either. Now please go away."

"You won't see him again."

She opened her eyes slowly. "Is that an order?"

John nodded slowly.

She looked at him keenly. "I see that part's true too."

"What part?"

"You and him."

He let his eyes slide over her. "Give you a thrill?"

And she surprised him again. "What if I said yes?"

He smiled in spite of himself. "Your honesty would flabbergast me."

"Yes."

"I'm flabbergasted."

"Good. Now will you go away?"

"How old are you?" he asked.

She looked at him. "Why do you want to know?"

"I'm being sociable."

"It's a bit late to be sociable."

"I always do everything in reverse."

"I'm thirty-four."

"Married?"

"No."

"Boyfriend?"

"Yes."

"Would you take your clothes off for me?"

She stared at him.

"If I took mine off for you?" He smiled.

"*No.*"

"If I promised not to touch you?"

"No."

"If I let you touch me?"

She stopped. "This is absolutely, utterly absurd. What are you saying to me?"

John's eyes seemed to rest on her with the weight of stone. "I'm saying I'd like to see you undressed. I'm saying I'm prepared to pay for the privilege in kind."

She remembered those short intense passages about him in Jimmy's diary. Surely just an overheated homoerotic fantasy? She shook her head.

"Then you'll never know."

"Never know what?" She looked at him sharply and he knew he was right. Like he knew Danny and how he would rub Henderson's face in it. And Henderson dutifully wrote it all down.

"If what your brother said about me was true."

"And how do you know what my brother said about you?"

"I don't, I'm only guessing."

"Why do you want to see me undressed?"

"For obvious reasons."

"They're not obvious to me, believe me."

John didn't answer her. He took off his jacket. He smiled as if he was indulging in a practical joke. He pulled his sweater, crackling, over his head and began to unfasten his shirt. She sat there tight, not moving. She was going to sit it out. He stopped.

"Do go on." It was supposed to be sarcastic but he noticed she drank the rest of

her drink before she said it.

He bent down and pulled off his boots, then his socks.

"Lovely feet." She was smiling, but it was fragile, thin.

He finished unbuttoning his shirt and slid it off. Her smile slid a little. He undid the button of his jeans.

"Alright, you can stop right there."

"Why?"

"Because that's enough."

"Enough for what?"

"Enough for me. Put your clothes back on."

"Why?"

"Because you've proved your point."

"You're afraid."

"That's right."

"What of?"

"Just put them on."

He pulled the zip down. "Make me."

"You know I can't."

"Then you'll just have to watch, won't you?"

"You're enjoying this," she said furiously.

"Every inch of the way." He took his jeans off and stood there in his shorts.

She closed her eyes. But she was too late, she'd already looked, and she felt an odd surreal moment, wishing Jimmy could be here too, saying to herself, He didn't lie to you Jimmy, all your fantasies were true.

She opened her eyes. He hadn't moved. She could still see it there, heavy under the fabric. "Please put your clothes back on."

"Only if you take yours off."

"No."

"Then I stay like this all night."

"Do you expect me to take that seriously?"

"What do you think?"

"And I'm supposed to be coerced into taking my clothes off, just like that?"

"Standing on your head if you like, so long as you take them off."

She stared at him for a long moment then said, "Alright, two can play at that game," and began pulling her shirt out from her skirt, unbuttoning it as she did so. She slid it off, wishing perversely she'd put on better underwear. She didn't look at him. She slipped off her shoes. And now she would have to stand up. She got up carefully, still not looking at him, but her face burned. He was closer now. She could smell the farm from him, from his discarded work clothes on the floor. She slid off her skirt, felt painfully aware of the hair spreading down her inner thighs. She slid down her tights knowing he'd see it, hoping it didn't repulse him, wondering why she cared. She stood there finally in her bra and pants, facing him down.

"Go on," he said. "One more to be equal." His voice was thick. That surprised her.

She looked up at him and said it without thinking. "Make me."

His arms were immediately around her, undoing her bra, tugging it open, his hands huge on her breasts. She felt his thumbs, sharp with calluses, rubbing the nipples.

"Don't touch me," he whispered.

"What?" she said blankly. She was hanging onto him. She didn't even know how she got there. She appeared to be trying to climb onto his penis, pushing her belly up against it.

He buried his face in her hair. "If you touch me I'll come."

She pulled his shorts down and wrapped her hand around him. She felt her cunt

tighten with anticipation, like cramped muscles wanting to be stretched, relieved of their tight aching. "Lift me onto it," she commanded.

She had never, ever done this before. "Against the wall," she demanded, pulling him over.

He lifted her, using the wall to support her weight. Her legs caught at the backs of his thighs. She felt something touch her between her legs for the briefest of seconds, then he quite literally shoved her onto it. She went down over him in one drop, like a cork rammed into a bottle. Her eyes flew open with the jolt of it.

"*Shit*," he said.

"I'm too heavy," she grunted, feeling the tension lock his body. She clung to him furiously.

"No. I'm going to come."

She felt frantically relieved, ridiculously. "Come," she urged him.

He held her for a moment. He was trembling very faintly. He looked at her suddenly and it was as if he'd never really looked at her before. She felt his back move like a rock shifting and saw his eyes were green. She watched him slowly incline his head and then kiss her. He did it closed-mouthed. He lifted her slightly, held her there, then let his mouth open. As he did so he dropped her suddenly onto him, ramming every inch home hard. He did it again, shoving her hard against the wall, his tongue deep in her mouth. It was like two of them fucking her, buffeting her between two immovable masses. She could taste, feel, breathe, nothing but him. Then his head jerked free of her. He lifted her almost clear, brought her down hard, buckling under her weight. He started pounding up her, his teeth bared, swearing, "Fuck… fuck… fuck… fuck...." And every time he said it, forking up into her body, spreading her wider, bruising her thighs with his grip.

"Oh *Jesus!*" he cried and she felt it, hot and wet, come running down her insides like all the trashy soft porn she'd ever read, soaking her and probably ruining the new carpet.

He leaned against her, heavy with exertion, suffocating her against the wall.

"Bring me off," she whispered to him, struggling off him with difficulty.

He opened his eyes, looked at her, his face unreadable.

She took his hand, curved it into herself, thrust her crotch against it. "Please."

He slid his fingers in. She was soaking. She leaned against the wall, spreading her legs, thrusting up against him, watching his face. "Kiss me again." She pulled him towards her, his mouth wide, carnivorous. She felt it sink over hers. She reached down and grabbed him, found him still hard. It was enough. She jolted against his fingers. When she started to come he pushed his tongue into her mouth, effectively silencing her. She groaned deep in her throat, her legs buckling, hanging onto him, feeling the huge swollen sticky length tight in her hand. He kept her coming till she pushed him off, moaning and whimpering into his body.

She stood with her weight against him, smelling his strange smell, feeling the odd contours of him, and wondered what she was doing. She decided she didn't care. Whatever it was she wanted to do it again.

"These still taste like shit."

Rab watched the glowing tip of Danny's cigarette, laughed gently, and knew exactly what he was going to say next. He could no more have stopped it than not scratch an itch. "You want to do it again?" He tried to keep his voice level, but it came out lumpy as dough.

"No." Danny's answer was flat, soul-destroying. Rab felt it stick in his stomach.

"Why not?" he asked.

He heard the movement, sensed Danny's shrug. He saw the cigarette move. "I don't know."

Be satisfied with that Hardman, it's all you're getting. Rab wanted to slap his face. Why was it Danny brought out the worst in everybody? First you fuck him then you thump him. What was it about him? And why didn't it stop you coming back for more? Even in the dark, when you couldn't see him, he got you hungry, itching to lay hands on him. That indecent fur-lined voice, unnatural as all hell. Listen to him talk into the small hours. Say rhubarb to me Danny and I'll show you an erection that could knock holes in walls. Face it, you're infatuated with him. Everybody is. He's a disease. I've caught Daniel-Disease doctor. Sorry, there's no known cure, let him rip.

"You know something Danny?"

"Mm?"

Rab could hear the ugliness in his own voice, felt the stomach-sinking anticipation of saying the words. "I don't think I've ever liked you."

There was a silence, and into it came rushing a million desires to take it back, exactly those words, no more God, just those. But the door was shut in his face. You said 'em, you live with 'em. "I'm sorry."

"Don't bother."

He couldn't even read anything into that. No inflection, no anger or hurt, or anything. He grabbed him before he even thought about it, got a handful of jacket, some shirt. "Fuck you." And he pushed him away from him. He heard Danny bump against the door, a silent thump.

He seemed to sit still for a moment then he shifted in his seat and rolled down the window. He pitched out the cigarette, closed it again. "I'll make a deal with you." His voice sounded disembodied.

Rab looked at him in the darkness, could see nothing but the dimmest dark of his eyes. He rolled down the window and threw out his own cigarette, closed it again. "Which is?"

"Fuck her."

Rab was silent for a moment, not getting sense from the words. "Who?"

"Henderson's sister."

Rab was fishing now, feeling his way, beginning to understand. "Are you telling me you *want* me to fuck her?"

"Yes."

He felt it like a struck match flaring up in his head. He could feel it in his blood, taste it in his mouth. He could almost see it. "Why you..." He got hold of him with both hands and banged him against the door, knocking his head on the glass. He liked the sound of it so he did it again. Danny was inert under his hands. He could feel the warm weight of him, the sleek warm flesh of his jacket.

He dropped him, found he was kneeling over him, right across the seat. He could see his face, so close to his own, saw Danny's tongue moisten his lips. "You brought me down here for that?"

Danny said nothing.

"Or is that a stupid question? What's your latest fear, that he's going to run away with her?"

Danny looked up into his face. "Either do it or shut up."

Rab grabbed his face, digging his fingers in. "What's the problem? Make the mistake of telling her about his dick? Think she's decided she likes the ugly version better? Know what you are Danny? A sick little boy obsessed with his brother's sex life. You want to grow up."

Danny pushed him off with a sudden shove. Rab lost his balance and let go, bracing himself against the dashboard.

"Let's go." Danny reached out for the ignition.

Rab knocked his hand away. "Let's not. I want to know just once, straight from the horse's mouth, what goes on in your pretty little head. Why d'you want me in her pants?"

"Because it keeps him out of them."

Rab digested it slowly, letting the insult sink in. *You're low Rab. You don't even rate.* "What makes you think he would?"

"He would."

"We know that part, what makes you think so?"

"I just know it."

"He isn't interested in women."

Danny laughed. It was a big ugly laugh, full of bitterness, and said, "Oh *yeah*."

Rab digested that one too, slowly, trying not to crowd his head with it. "Okay then, she isn't his type."

"She's Henderson with a cunt."

"Meaning what?"

Danny was silent.

"Meaning what?"

"Meaning…" Danny took a tight breath. Rab heard him try to unknot the words but they came out chipped and hard anyway. "…she's got an extra hole so she gets extra Brownie points."

"Don't blur it Danny, you're still not saying what you mean."

"Alright, I once saw Henderson look at John's hands. I've seen you look at them the same way. Well, she's part of the same club."

Rab was silent.

"That's a nice quiet sound Rab. You're speaking to me. Henderson rubbed him up the wrong way because he wanted to rub him up the right way. All fucks lead to John. You, me, John. And you can bet your boots the diary tells her so, in glowing fucking Technicolor. The first time he ever saw you it was with John, and it was John he wanted, even if he didn't know it himself. She's just the same."

"Bullshit."

Danny didn't respond.

"You're fucking paranoid Danny. You think everybody wants him. You're seeing it where it doesn't exist."

"She wants him and he'll always want her."

"And that's what really gets to you - like some little kid locked out of his big brother's birthday party - the idea that you won't be there. Danny doesn't figure. Think he might fall in love?"

"Don't talk stupid."

"So you're just afraid he might spare her an inch or two of what's rightfully yours, is that it?"

"I just don't want him near her."

"I don't understand this."

"No-one's asking you to."

"Alright, what's the rest of this 'deal'? You've told me what you want me to do. What do I get out of it?"

"Anything you want."

"Then come to me."

"No."

"That doesn't sound like anything I want."

"You wouldn't want that, believe me."

"How do you know what I want?"

"You'd be a fool if you did."

"I was a fool the day I ever laid a finger on you."

"Then stop."

"I can't, I'm addicted."

"I'm poison."

"I know."

"You stupid bastard. What are you hoping for?"

"A miracle cure. Handle you enough and I become immune."

"Think you can do it?"

"There aren't enough years left. I can't satiate myself on rations."

"Do what I want and you can stuff yourself with me till you puke, with my blessing."

"And how the hell would I manage that, with John breathing down my neck?"

"I'd find a way."

"Odd minutes here and there when you can squeeze me in? No thanks."

"Four times a fucking day if you want it. I told you, I'd find a way."

"He'd kill you if he found out."

"I'll take that risk."

"He'd probably kill me too."

"That's your problem."

Rab shifted back suddenly, away from him. "And what if she doesn't want to have anything to do with me?"

"She will. He's fired her curiosity with his dirty little boy talk. You won't even need to go to her, she'll come to you, just like he did."

"If she really wants John, why should she?"

"She's greedy."

"And? There's an and in there."

Danny hesitated. "And she'll find John hard work."

"How?"

"That doesn't matter. She'll come to you, that's all that matters."

"And what if I can't do it?"

He felt Danny's eyes on him. "Is this a confession?"

"Maybe." He could feel the heat of his face in the darkness, glad Danny couldn't see it.

"Imagine she's someone else. You've done it before, I'm sure." Danny's voice was sharp with malice.

Rab turned to him. "I think you're the most vindictive little shit I ever met."

Danny laughed. A sweet, low sound, warm and rich as chocolate. He felt Danny's hand on his leg, sliding up along his thigh. "Want to do it?" he whispered.

"What if I say no?"

"Then there'll be no hands, no mouths, no magic. Nothing to catch onto. Poor, bitter, lonely Rab, all alone in the dark..."

Danny's voice seemed to spiral down into it. Rab listened to him, thinking, He'd make a good hypnotist, almost wondering if that's how he did it, hypnotised you into thinking you needed him. And even while he thought those thoughts, his cock was already stiffening, ignited by his own humiliation, knowing he would sell himself out just to be sucked off by a pretty boy in a car, fuck some strange woman so he could be masturbated by a deceitful little slut with the face of an angel. Knew he would give anything just for a quick grope in the dark. There was no signing in blood, no grand dramatic blinding lights. It all came down to your soul for a quick jerk in a dung heap.

And that's what he wanted.

He felt Danny's hands under his shirt, Danny's hair against his neck, Danny's voice velvet against his mouth.

That was what he wanted more than anything else in the world.

She was aware of him putting on his clothes, completely without self-consciousness and with an unpleasant air of detachment. He did not look at her. He did not even seem to be aware of her. She didn't get dressed again. She went into the bedroom and put on her dressing gown. When she came back he was sitting on the settee pulling on his boots. She watched him in silence, wondering if he was going to say anything at all. He stood up and picked his jacket up off the floor; a repulsive aged waxed cotton thing. She saw that it was ripped under one arm.

He looked at her finally, then smiled. It was smug. "I wish now I'd had your brother."

"Are you being insulting?"

"I meant it as a compliment."

"What for? A comparison study?"

He smiled.

"Are you all like this?"

"Like what?"

"Sexual chameleons."

He began fiddling with his collar, making it comfortable. A man ready to be away. If it was affected indifference he was damn good at it. "I thought they called it bisexual," he volunteered.

"Oh no, that doesn't do you justice. It doesn't begin to describe you. It's too simplistic, too uncomplicated."

He did up the zip, watching her now, smile gone. "And we're not?"

"That's right, you're not."

"Why so angry?"

"Are you serious? You walk in here, have sex with me as if it meant nothing, and now you're going to forget it. It isn't very flattering. It isn't even polite. Manners aren't your family's strong point, are they?"

"You got to feel my cock. I don't have to tell you jokes too."

"You conceited..."

He lifted a hand, shaking his head. "No, don't. My temper's stomach-churning. You wouldn't like it. We fucked, leave it at that. Animals do it all the time, without the chat."

"Don't patronise me. I'm not your brother, or any other one of your stinking little brood. Don't try your little toy tyrannies on me, they won't work."

"Is that what your brother called them?"

"No, it isn't, but the idea's the same. He saw through you and your pathetic threats."

John pushed his hands in his pockets, studying her. "You're very like him."

"In lots of ways, so don't try to frighten me."

"Why should I try to frighten you?"

"Because it's second nature to you. You're so used to bullying your own family you think you can try it on anywhere you like."

"Do tell me more about myself."

"Why did you come here?"

"To talk to you."

"You wanted to humiliate me."

"Would you like me to humiliate you?" He smiled at her insolently.

"You're disgusting. You're as warped as he said, worse."

"And just as big."

"Get out."

His smile was showing teeth now. "What else did he say about me?"

341

"I wouldn't give you the pleasure."

"That good is it? Immortalised by PC Plod's glowing pen."

"He thought you were an ape. A foul, loud-mouthed bully. He considered you the lowest form of life, ugly and degenerate."

John tutted softly. "And he still wanted to play with me? Terrible how a man's lusts can drag him down."

She sat down, suddenly deflated. "Get out."

"I'm going but there's something you ought to understand first..." He didn't move any closer, he didn't turn away, and yet something about him changed. He shifted into the realms of the dangerous as tangibly as if he'd taken out a knife, punched her in the head. "People are people. I don't care to label them. I don't believe in the fine distinctions and I don't cover up what I think with pretty manners..." He paused. "Let me put it another way. It would give me just as much pleasure to punch you through that nice big window as it would have given me to do it to your brother, just as it would have given me as much pleasure to fuck him as it did you. Do you get my point?"

"Yes." She nodded slowly, her eyes narrowed. "I get your point exactly. I get the point that you're threatening me, and I've already told you what I think of that, so why don't you just get out?"

"You really are a lot like your brother, aren't you?"

"More than you think."

He smiled with lots of strong white teeth. She could even remember the incredibly erotic feel of them. "Watch you don't end up too like him."

And he went out before she realised exactly what he meant.

John was back before them. He shouted Danny's name up the stairs and received no reply.

Ian came out of the living room door, stopped when he saw him, pretending surprise.

"Where's Rab?" John asked and felt the words like sawdust in his mouth.

"He went to pick up Danny."

"When?"

Ian shrugged. "An hour ago... maybe a little longer." His little yellow smile inched out at the sides. John felt a sudden conviction that it had yellowed from always being kept in the dark. Ian's smile never saw the light of day.

He walked towards him. Ian's smile slipped a little. John pushed him back into the room. It was his turn to smile. He closed the door and took off his jacket. "Talk to me Ian."

Ian looked at him, nonplussed. Now what?

"Entertain me. Tell me your innermost secrets. You're not someone I talk to very often. In fact, I don't even look at you if I can help it. Now there's a dangerous oversight, eh? Nevertheless you've been a big influence in my life. Talk to me."

Ian sat down on the sofa, at the far end, as far away from John as he could get.

John sat down on the armchair and looked at him expectantly, almost as if he really meant it.

"What do you want?"

"I've told you, I want you to talk to me."

"Don't fuck me about John, just say what you want to say."

John spread his hands in a gesture of innocence. "Straight up Ian, I want you to talk to me."

"What about?"

"Whatever you like. What would you *like* to talk about? Everybody always likes to

talk about Danny."

"I don't have anything to say about Danny."

"One man amongst thousands."

"I hate his guts."

"It doesn't seem to keep you away from him."

"This is what it's about, isn't it? I've been waiting for this."

"What?" John's face was clear, a caricature of innocent guile.

"Don't what me, you know what."

"Did you enjoy it?"

"Yes." Ian's lip curled when he said it, half bravado, half vindictive pleasure.

"I didn't give you laissez-faire Ian. It was strictly by invitation only. I thought I'd made that plain."

"You've always given me laissez-faire John, that was the deal."

John's face went white. Where everyone else's went red John's went white. The eternal warrior, blood to his guts, ready for the fight.

"Well it's finished. That night in here was by way of a parting gift. Don't touch him again. Don't even dream about him."

"Or?"

John shrugged, the colour coming back into his face.

Ian said it for him. "Or you'll add me to your list? You wouldn't get away with another and you know it."

"I don't know, some people manage twenty or thirty before they get caught. I'm well within the limits."

"You don't have much trouble with your conscience, do you?"

"I don't keep a conscience. I can't afford it."

Ian shifted in his seat, then the lights went out.

"Shit," John said in the darkness.

Ian blinked for a minute or two, his eyes blinded by the sudden plunge into pitch.

"Where are the lamps?" John asked irritably.

"Under the stairs, I think." He heard John stand up, saw him move in front of the fire. He was opening it to create more light.

"Get them, will you?"

Ian got up and came level with him. John's size, like Danny's beauty, was one of those things you forgot about until you were brought up smack against it again and you wondered how you could ever have taken it for granted in the first place.

John put his hands in his pockets and looked down at him. "I wouldn't if I were you."

Ian flushed in the dark. His foxy little eyes shifted with surprise. "Wouldn't what?"

"Dirty little shit."

"Why? What's so dirty about it? Coming from you, what's so dirty about it?"

"I don't want it, that's what's dirty about it."

"And Danny always did?"

John didn't answer.

"Aren't you glad you've got the strength John? Aren't you glad you can flatten anyone who says no to you?"

"Aren't you sorry you can't?"

"Too fucking right I am. Then it would be me who had him, not you."

"Then why are you standing here in front of me, drooling?"

"Nostalgia."

"And a little bit of lust."

"There's always a little bit of lust. People like you always incite a little bit of lust."

"You mean people this ugly?"

343

"Yeah, your ugly soul, it fascinates people."

"I don't see you fascinating anyone, and souls don't get much uglier than yours. Must be something more, hm?" John's voice was suggestive, insulting. "Must be my hidden assets. Better even than my ugly face or that fascinating ugly soul. Must be something about the way I wear my trousers."

"You're so fucking charged up on yourself I don't know why you need Danny."

"I've got to have someone to worship it, besides myself."

"You're obsessed with your own dick."

"No, I grew up with it. It took me a while to realise everybody else was. That's what's so captivating about me, I've got *scale*. They tell you size doesn't matter, but they only say that to reassure themselves. When it comes right down to it they all wish they had one just like mine. It might even make *you* popular. Size doesn't matter like money isn't everything. Now, how about those lamps?"

Ian didn't move. "Let me."

"Why should I?"

"Because it wouldn't cost you anything. Nothing touches you."

John was watching him, but Ian couldn't see his face, too heavily shadowed in the dark, silhouetted by the fire behind him. His voice was bland, giving nothing away. Ian didn't know how far to push him, didn't even understand why he was pushing it this far. The same old urge of the outsider to have crumbs from the cake everyone else ate.

"Once, here in the dark. No-one would know."

"I wouldn't care if they did."

"Well then, why not?"

"Sheer spite."

"Why? What have I done?"

John laughed. "What have you *not* done? Years of your dirty fingers all over his body, your dirty habits in his head. Fucking him every way you could."

"Like you wanted?"

"Six year old boys don't interest me."

"No? Six year old Dannys used to."

"You watch your fucking mouth."

Ian took a step back, out of his reach. "He always was a beautiful little thing. That must have been a temptation John. Such a touchy-feely kid, and hard-ons are so easy to get."

John took a step towards him.

Ian stepped sideways. "Maybe *you* should talk to *me*, get all those hot lustful thoughts out of your system. Sorry you missed out now? Sorry you can't turn the clock back and get a few more years in?"

John lunged at him. The two of them went back on the couch in a heap. Ian let him hit him twice, considering it money well spent, then grabbed him. John felt Ian's hands on him, tried to push up off him and instead rolled flatter against him into the angled softness of the settee. No leverage.

Ian whispered in his ear, "Violence always turns you on, doesn't it?"

John pulled the sticky hands from between his legs and rolled off the settee. But he could see Ian's expression and knew he'd lost it. He'd been out-manoeuvred. The dirty little bastard had got exactly what he wanted.

Ian whistled, a low indecent leer of approval. "Only half-up too. I should've let you hit me some more."

The back door slammed. John turned his head towards the sound but Ian continued to stare at him. He could feel a dull ache in his stomach where John had punched him, but it was worth it. Now he had the feel of him again. Now he could flesh

out his fantasies with a point of reality.

"Get up." John's voice was a hard whisper. "Get the fucking lamps."

Ian swung his feet to the floor. He moved to the door almost like a crab, keeping John within his sights.

If only he could have kissed him too.

John met them in the hall. Ian was carrying lamps to the kitchen to fill them. One already burned on the hall table. A dull sickish yellow glow, flickering, smoky.

"Where've you been?" He addressed Danny. Rab might not have been there.

Danny looked at his face and knew he was in the shit. "You know where." Playing for time, hoping John would give something away.

"Then where?"

And Danny knew that he knew. How he knew was of no importance. Even if it was only a wild guess, a jealous imagining, it wouldn't make any difference. The fact that it was the truth only made it harder to fight. "We went for a drive."

John moistened his mouth. "Very romantic."

Danny couldn't answer that and didn't try.

John jerked his head towards the stairs. "Go up."

Danny went on up.

John called after him, his voice low, "Don't wash."

John and Rab stood in the hall.

Ian came out the kitchen with a lamp. He didn't bother to say anything. He went past them, giving John an odd look which made him look away angrily. Rab noticed he waited till Ian was upstairs before speaking.

He stood there watching the little eye-play, feeling the irritation mount. Report in, report out, who the fucking hell did John think he was?

"Where did you take him?"

"Where he wanted to go."

"Which was?"

"Down to the sea. By Layton."

"What did you do to him?"

"How do you know he didn't do something to me?"

"I'm sure he did, but first things first."

"Fuck off John. Go take a flying fucking jump."

"Then he'll tell me."

"Oh, I'm sure he will, by the time you're finished with him."

"You could save him a little grief."

"I couldn't save him anything. You just like to be doubly sure of your own righteousness."

"Fucking gay boy."

Rab stared at him. "Christ," he said slowly, wonderingly, "you've really got it bad, haven't you?"

Rab stepped back and avoided the blow by inches. John came after him. Rab ducked into the kitchen and put the table between them. John stood there, moving his head from side to side like a broad-headed snake looking for the right place to strike. Rab knew there was something extra in here. He thought of Ian's unpleasant little smile and decided that was the source of it.

"Whatever Ian said or did sort it out with him. I'm not going to play whipping boy for him."

John's face twitched as if a sudden itch had grabbed it. "I hope you enjoyed it Rab, because it's the last you're ever going to get."

"The sound of your voice gets very boring John."

"Then leave."

"You'd miss me."

"Like a hole in the head."

Rab was silent. John was smiling now. Nothing even of malicious pleasure in it. It was just there. "What's wrong? Frightened there'll be no more gazing at his pretty face over the breakfast table? Christ it's a miracle any female ever got anything out of you, you fucking queer."

Rab closed his eyes. Damned by faint truths.

"Hanging around waiting for him to notice you, eating shit, you puny little fart."

Rab squeezed his eyes tight shut against him.

"That's it, curl up tight in a ball and maybe Big Bad John will go away. Shame you haven't got the guts to kill me. Or have you still got the hots for me? Danny's all very well but you like a nice big length occasionally. Well? All is silence."

Rab opened his eyes. "Just leave me alone."

John looked at the black and white of him, the hair almost glowing in the bright cluster of light from the lamps on the table, his features chiselled by their underlighting, those unnatural dark eyes. "You're almost as beautiful as he is."

Rab shook his head. "Christ, your head's like a roundabout John, faster and faster, throwing everything off with the sheer momentum of yourself."

"I'd like to have you." John's eyes were intense across the space, black caverns. His face seemed heavy, saturnine, as if a child was holding a torch under his chin.

"Oh, give it a break."

"I'd like to have you. Right here. Now."

"Before you go up to Danny."

"Before I go *up* Danny."

Rab knew he'd got high on abusing him. He would bet that he was already stiff in his pants. "Go give it to Danny."

"I want you."

"You can't stand there dragging me through the slime then say, I want to have sex with you."

"I don't want to have sex with you, I want to rape you."

"Then why ask me? That isn't rape."

"You haven't felt it yet."

John's eyes seemed to be squeezing the top of his head. He rubbed his face. "Then there's no point in me saying yes or no to you, you'll just do it anyway."

"Say yes."

"Why?"

"Just say it."

Rab swallowed, felt his own breathing, hard and fast. "Yes."

John smiled and began blowing out the lamps one by one. The room seemed to grow colder, become more sickly, as each lamp was extinguished.

Rab stood transfixed, watching his face change, like a smoky veil was being drawn over it. He moved round the table slowly. Finally Rab felt him move up against his side. He nudged him back against the table. It was the nudge that starts a fight.

He pulled Rab's shirt out. He took no clothes off himself. Rab could feel him hard as iron against him. His breath was on his face. He thrust himself against Rab's leg with sharp jabs like punches, an assault, the mouth breathing on him.

John's hands undid his trousers, pulled them down. One sharp tug, exposing him. He clutched his buttocks, thrust himself harder, the stiff fabric of his jeans friction

burning Rab's leg, still breathing on his face, not uttering a word, making no attempt to kiss him - all nails and thrusting and dirty heavy breathing.

Finally he stopped and unzipped himself. Rab heard it in the silence. He stood back. "Go down on me."

He made no attempt to force him, cajole him. He didn't touch him. The ultimate degradation. John says, Go down on me, you do it. Jump boy, jump.

Rab could suddenly smell it, alien, pungent.

"I *said*, get down on me."

Rab went down on his knees on the kitchen floor and took him in his mouth. His senses were invaded with it. *You're too late Danny. He's already had her.*

"Smell it?"

That was all he said, nothing more. He took Rab's head and pushed himself in, almost choking him. Giving head to John was a dangerous operation at the best of times. Now he pushed it down Rab's throat.

When he came he made sure Rab kept his mouth over it, holding his head tightly in place, like giving a cat a pill. He came silently, only a distant little grunt giving it away before Rab's mouth was filled with him.

Eventually he pushed him off.

Rab didn't look up.

John hunkered down beside him and lifted his head. "That's the closest you'll probably ever get to a cunt Robbie. How did it feel?" John's smile showed all his teeth.

He got up and went out of the room.

Danny woke with a start, his heart thumping.

He turned over on his back, staring into the dark.

John was watching him from the foot of the bed. He was taking off his clothes. He didn't say anything. Danny hated his silences worst of all.

John got into the bed beside him. "Lie on your side."

Danny curled away from him, rigid, afraid. He felt the knife above his left kidney.

"Your favourite, playing with knives. You're very close, you know. Tonight you're very close indeed. I don't know why. Maybe I'm tired." He laughed. "Maybe I need a tonic. Where did you go?"

"The sea."

"What did you do?"

"Talked."

"What about?"

"Henderson's sister."

"Fancy her?"

"No."

"What did you do with him?"

"I told you."

The knife point jabbed in. Nothing hesitant about it, an immediate sharp jab. Danny gasped.

"I've no time tonight Danny. I'm tired and I want the truth."

"He sucked me off."

John made a noise as if he'd just bitten into a favourite confection and found it full of spiders. It came out of him unwillingly. "Did you watch?"

"It was dark."

"That doesn't answer my question."

"For a while."

"Why only a while?"

Danny didn't answer him. The knife dug in again. Danny struggled away from it. John pulled him back.

"John, don't."

"Answer my question."

"I don't know."

This time the knife was sharper.

"*Shit*, John."

"Wrong answer."

"It was turning me on."

"He excites you." Danny hesitated and it cut him some more. "You're a slow learner."

"Okay, he excites me."

"He excites me too."

Danny was silent.

"In fact I had him before I came up here. I saw him standing there with that fake hair of his, that slick dirty mouth, and decided to have him right there. Like that?"

"No."

"Tough, because you haven't got any rights baby. What's good enough for you is good enough for me. You have her too?"

"No."

"I did."

The silence was fraught. Danny lay there feeling his insides detach themselves in a boiling mass.

"I'd forgotten how good that felt. How about you?" Danny didn't answer but the knife lay still. "Why don't you have her? I'm sure she'd be happy to oblige."

"I don't like her."

"You don't have to *like* her."

"I don't want to."

"Feeble."

"Okay. She reminds me of him."

"She reminds me of him too."

"I know."

"What's that supposed to mean?"

"Just what it says, I know."

The knife moved this time, but it was different, the point tracing slow patterns over his rump. "Lift your knees."

Danny pulled them up.

"Higher."

Danny tugged them up into a ball.

The knife point slid into the crack of his arse. "What do you mean, you know?"

"Henderson fancied you, she fancies you."

The knife point lay still, a sharp little nick, gentle against his anus. He tried surreptitiously to move forwards. John's hand immediately pressed his stomach. "Lie still."

Danny lay still. He felt the knife jerk as if a muscle in John's arm had jumped. He squirmed away, yanking his legs down. John pulled him to him with both hands. The knife came round, cold against his abdomen. He could feel its entire length against his stomach. John's head was over his.

"I had her and even while I was doing it I knew it wouldn't keep her away from you. Nothing keeps them away from you. I should have drowned you that day at the river, but I thought I could beat it. Ian can deal with this, I'm too damn tired."

Danny struggled round, trying to face him. John held him tightly, the blade digging

in like a thin steel ruler.

"So now you're giving him permission?"

"That's what you do Danny, not me."

Danny lay in his arms like a rag doll. "I hate you."

John dropped the knife out the side of the bed. It hit the floor with a dull thunk.

"I hate you" Danny said again, flat, unemotional.

John rolled him onto his back, climbed on top of him. "No, you don't."

"Cunt," Danny said, staring into his face.

John felt himself begin to go from him. He kissed him before he could say it again.

FORTY-ONE

In the event Danny was at least half-right.

She rolled up two days later.

Maybe two days was long enough to forget her humiliation at John's hands, maybe she didn't care, but she wasn't looking for John anyway.

And in that event she was also lucky. Rab had just come in for lunch. He climbed down out of the tractor as the red Porsche came round the corner of the yard.

It was a bright sunny day, cold outside, but the sun through the glass had made the cab warm. He was pulling his sweatshirt back on, chilled by the change in temperature. She saw his armpits as he reached up to pull it over his head. She remembered Jimmy's description of his hair. It did look dyed, unnatural. He reminded her of those petulant, lean-hipped rock stars, heavy with mascara in ghost-white, night-life faces. What an odd exotic creature to work in such a place. He looked across at her directly, closing the tractor door. He was attractive, if somewhat predatory looking. He walked towards her. And vain with it, she decided.

His hair wasn't quite as white as Jimmy had described it. He probably had been bleaching it after all. He bent down to the car door. The window slid down with electronic ease. She saw his face quirk with amusement at that. She wasn't sure if she was going to like this man. "You must be the cousin," she said.

He half-smiled, disconcerting her, his face plainly saying, Yes? What do you want? She was annoyed to feel herself flushing, decided she didn't like him. And yet her brother seemed to have liked him best. She felt an irrational disappointment in him. He was just another vain little smart-alec.

"I'd like to talk to you."

Rab laughed and looked away from her. Like brother, like sister. They even used the same lines.

"What's so funny?" She glared at him, feeling her self-control slip.

"Nothing."

"Get in." She reached over to release the passenger door.

Rab stopped smiling. "Go fuck yourself."

She stared at him in a moment's surprise, then felt her face burn up with anger. "None of you have any manners, do you?"

"Yours don't exactly have high visibility either."

He saw perplexity fighting anger. She beat Henderson for arrogance anyway. "Nobody likes being told what to do on their own property," he elucidated.

"It isn't your property."

"Well, it sure as fuck isn't yours, so why don't you fuck off?"

Her eyes hardened just like her brother's would have done. They were brown, not that clear psychopathic blue of his, but the effect was just the same.

"Alright. Both your cousins seem to think they can afford to ignore me, you too, well we'll see." She revved the car up, looked behind her preparatory to reversing out, then abruptly stopped. Rab looked at her face, then tried to peer through the car to see what she'd seen. He straightened up.

Danny had come out of the tractor shed. He was crossing the yard, head down, lost in thought. He looked up, saw the car. Rab saw his mouth set.

He moved purposely towards the house. He was going to ignore her. Rab grinned, bent back down to her. She was furious. "Looks like Danny doesn't like you either."

"I'm going to take it to the police." Her voice was low, intense. "I don't care who

knows. You had something to do with his death and I'm going there to tell them so, right now. God help the lot of you."

Rab stopped her quickly. "Wait."

She was fuelled up with her own indignation and he realised he had pushed her too far. He wasn't sure he could placate her now. "You wouldn't want me in your car, smell that."

She frowned then sniffed. She hadn't really noticed it but he was right, the place stank.

"I'm spreading muck. Believe me you wouldn't want it in there. I'll talk to you if you like, but not here."

She could see the tension in him. Now he was trying to be 'nice'. Did he think she was stupid? She felt an overpowering urge to tell him where to go, just the way he worded it, wipe the condescending smile off his face. "No," she said and had the pleasure of seeing his face slacken, pale slightly. "I think I want to see Danny."

Rab felt an urge to laugh. He could feel it tugging at the corners of his mouth.

"I want to see Danny tonight. You tell him that. And he can bring himself, I'm not running a bloody chauffeuring service. You tell him that too. Eight 'o' clock. Or he can go to hell. You can all go to hell."

She slammed the car into reverse and reversed out of the yard.

"I hope John isn't on his way in," Rab muttered, frowning, expecting to hear a crump.

But nothing happened. He saw Ian watching him from the shed doorway. When Rab moved towards the house Ian followed him.

Rab went in to give Danny the good news.

"What did she want?" Danny's face was angry.

Rab smiled, enjoying it. He didn't know why, didn't try to analyse it. "To see you, tonight, at eight."

"She can get fucked."

"I expect that's what she intends."

"I don't see anything funny in it."

"Don't you? She threatened to go to the police. How about that for amusement factor? Whatever you said to her you haven't made it any better. If you don't go to see her..." Ian came in, undoing his jacket and looking at them both. Rab turned back to Danny, shrugged. "...I'd say we're fucked."

Danny turned away. "Fucking cow."

Rab laughed and sat on the table. "You *do* like her, don't you?"

Danny was saved the bother of replying by John coming in the door. "What did she want?"

"Question of the day. Who knows the secret of the woman in the red Porsche?"

John frowned irritably. "What did she want?"

Rab took out his tin and extracted a cigarette. "She wants to see him," he used it to point at Danny, "tonight."

"Why?"

Rab shrugged and began patting his pockets.

Mrs Ostler came in, effectively silencing the conversation for the full ten minutes it took her to explain the lunch arrangements, the laundry, and half a dozen other things. Rab watched John's impatience grow. He smiled some more.

She went eventually.

"Someday I'll wring her fucking neck," John muttered when she'd barely closed the door.

Ian began serving up food like some well-paid butler. It was as good a way of blending as any; a lethal, silent eavesdropper.

John sat down with a thump, saying aggressively, "She threatened to go to the police."

Rab laughed. "How *did* you guess?"

"There wasn't anything else *to* threaten."

"And she knew she'd have to?"

John looked at Danny. The look was speculative. "I expect so."

Rab was surprised to see the spark of anger in Danny's eyes. John's face was bland. The two of them looked at each other the way they always did, precluding the rest of the world.

Rab felt a sudden urge to shake them up, drag them back into the real world. "Don't go."

John looked at him. "Don't talk stupid."

"Why not? Leave it, see what she does."

"You fucking mad or something? You know what she'll do."

Danny piped up. "So now you want me to go?"

"What I want doesn't enter into it. You have to go." John fixed his eyes on his face again. Danny stared back at him. Rab looked at them both, suddenly confused by the animosity between them. What the fuck was going on?

Ian handed him a plate. He took it absently, burning his fingers. He watched John take his then push it away. He got the feeling he'd like to push it right off the table. He watched Danny take his and got the feeling he'd like to push it in John's face.

Rab began eating slowly, watching the by-play.

Danny began to eat, head down, ignoring everyone.

John sat and looked at him and did not make any attempt to eat. Rab realised he had lost even more weight. Perversely, it made him look bigger, showing his bones, paring him down.

Suddenly he attacked his food, wolfing it down in the time it took Rab to eat two or three forkfuls. Equally suddenly he pushed it away, cutlery on top. Finished. He had not cleared his plate.

No other reference was made to Henderson's sister. John drank three cups of tea in rapid succession then went out without speaking.

When Rab spoke to Danny he received a monosyllabic answer. He saw Ian studying him, smiling.

Suddenly Rab realised he was waiting for him to leave.

He got up, unsettled.

John wasn't that nuts.

He went out and climbed back into his tractor.

Was he?

Ian cleared the table, leaning against Danny's shoulder as he lifted his plate. Danny tugged away from him. Ian laid his hand on his hair, feeling the tangles with his fingers.

Danny squirmed from underneath him. "Don't do that." His temper was in shreds, his face white with it. He could feel his heart thumping.

Ian licked his lips. Danny's emotions had long associations. Hard and happy, they were tattooed into the palms of his hands. "Touchy," he said, picking the plates up again, aware of his own erection as he moved towards the sink. He put them in and filled up with hot water.

Danny watched his back, wondering how long it was going to take the greasy little

bastard to make a move. He got up and put his jacket on.

"I'll be out in a minute," Ian said, smiling at him.

Danny zipped it violently. "You can stay here all fucking day for all I care."

Ian's smile broadened. He turned back to the sink.

The pans on the rack rattled as Danny slammed out the door.

John was waiting for him in the shed.

He hadn't expected that. He didn't even see him.

He was thrown against the tractor with a force that nearly broke his back.

John was dragging him back into an upright position only to bang him back against it again.

Danny made an ugly grunting sound as John dragged him up again. "Get *up.*"

He pulled Danny up, pinning him, panting, against the machine. "Now you listen to me."

Danny's face was turned away, scrunched up with pain. John spoke in his ear, teeth bared, lips bloodless.

Ian slid in noiselessly through the open door and moved silently into the dark. He could hear Danny's breathing, hoarse, rasping.

"I want to feel *nothing* in you Danny. When you come back you better be pristine. You hear me?"

Danny nodded.

John punched him back again. "I asked, did you *hear* me?"

Ian could see Danny's face now, white and sickly. Even his lips looked pale and pained. This was their ultimate intimacy, hidden from everyone. Ian squeezed himself through his pocket.

John pulled Danny's head back by the hair.

"Yes." Danny's voice was thick. "I hear you."

"I'll kill you Danny, that's a promise."

Ian saw Danny push himself upright, palms flat against the tractor, bracing himself. He dropped his head back exhaustedly. Ian watched him do it, could see it even from where he was, could feel it even though it wasn't directed at him. He squeezed himself tighter, enviously, offering his soul to anyone who would listen. But he stayed where he was, only a fixed point in their distant orbit.

"You bloody heartless little thug..." John's voice was low, pained.

Ian watched him hesitate, start to say something more, and then he bent forward, breathing the words into Danny's mouth.

The kiss changed, grew. There were surreptitious fumblings which became feverish movements. John never stopped kissing him. It only lasted a couple of minutes. Danny made no noise, but Ian saw his hands clutch at nothing on the side of the tractor, saw the urgency of John's movements, then it was over. John pushed up off him. Ian waited in a pitch of excitement to see how he would finish it.

He didn't.

He stood back, watching Danny get dressed, obscuring Ian's view. Danny moved slowly, pulling his trousers up, picking his jacket up off the floor. He put it back on. John dried his hand on a tissue, scrunching it into a ball and throwing it onto the floor with a savage energy. It was as if he had only skimmed the surface of his temper off to leave the heart of the fire still raging below. "I meant what I said."

Danny just watched him, saying nothing.

"You come back here intact..." his voice changed, sounding just as violent as before, "or I'll slit your fucking throat."

"Alright." Danny's voice was hard, unexpected in that silence.

Ian saw John move forward to kiss him again and then slap him hard across the mouth. He heard Danny's head bang on the door of the tractor. "Just to fucking remind you." And he turned and went out.

Ian stood there a moment, aware of his own raging pulse. He watched Danny slide down the door and crumple on the step. He could see the flare of red on his face where John had slapped him. He took a breath and let it out slowly, then moved towards him out of the gloom.

Danny looked up. He was holding his ribs as if they ached.

"Been bad to you?" He wasn't smiling.

"Get lost."

"Why do you put up with it?"

"Why don't you mind your own business?"

"You're just a possession. Droit du seigneur."

"Leave me alone."

Ian came over to him, stood by his side. He began stroking his hair. Danny pulled away from him, but Ian simply followed. Danny lost the energy to struggle and lay still under his hand.

"I could love you." Ian's voice was rough with excitement. He felt his face burn.

"Leave me alone." Danny pulled his head free again.

Ian followed relentlessly, letting his fingertips delve slightly into the red silk of his hair, rubbing it between finger and thumb, feeling the soft illusory heat of him against his skin. "I've always taken care of you. What's he ever done?"

Ian felt the change in him, as if he was becoming unravelled. All his magnetism seemed to leave him. In that moment he became human, something vulnerable, weak.

Ian coaxed his head in against his leg. Danny lay there, cheek against his thigh, unresponsive. Ian wiped the warm tears with his hand. He could feel the fine stubble on Danny's skin, the bone of his cheek. He stroked Danny's hair, pressing him tight, encouraging him, murmuring to him.

Danny suddenly buried his face in his leg, wrapping his arms around it. Ian looked down at his head, held it gently in both hands, rubbed Danny's shoulders.

He could feel himself aching with it, but his hands remained gentle, his voice soft, consoling.

Danny clung to him like a man drowning, desperately alone.

Ian's hands soothed on.

The evening meal was strained.

It was obvious to Rab that Danny and John were not friendly.

Danny picked at his food a little and then left to get washed. John perversely ate everything in sight, even attempting two portions much as he had done in the old days, but Rab saw that he couldn't manage it any more. He pushed the second plateful away half-eaten.

Danny was ready promptly at twenty to eight. He obviously intended to arrive on the button.

"Take the Rover." John threw him the keys.

Their eyes met momentarily then Danny went out the door.

Danny stood outside, watching the clear peppermint moon above his head. November always seemed to be like this, still and bitterly cold for a week or two, and then the winter gales started.

The buzzer sounded. He pushed in and went up the stairs. He had to knock for admission when he got there.

She opened the door and looked at him. He looked back, his face hard and unfriendly.

He began to wonder if she was going to let him in at all when she suddenly stood back. He went in and stood there. The hall was in darkness. She closed the door. He felt her pass him and the hall became light. She was holding open the living room door. He went in.

The room was half-lit, very warm. The other sofa was still missing. She had moved the framed poster of the man and baby. The blinds were gone. Instead thick velvet curtains hung there. They were drawn, making the room even darker, redder. She had placed a long, low table in the centre of the room. There were bottles and glasses on it and what looked like an ice bucket.

She was wearing a red silk dress, very ostentatiously feminine. She looked like an advert for five star brandy. She came over for his jacket. He took it off and handed it to her.

She felt the residual heat of him as she took it out to the hall, the faint animal smell from it. He was wearing an old grey sweatshirt, jeans. Clean work clothes. She felt sure he'd done it deliberately. She smiled dryly to herself. He was wasting his time. He was the male equivalent of Marilyn Monroe - he'd look good in a potato sack.

He watched her come back into the room and felt sure she wasn't wearing a bra. He looked away.

"What would you like to drink?"

"Nothing." He didn't look at her.

She stood there, trying not to be angry. "Be friendly," she said, keeping her voice level. This time he did look at her.

"Why?"

She forced a smile. "Because it's pointless being enemies."

"You blackmailed me into coming here, that isn't exactly friendly."

"Would you have come if I hadn't?"

He shook his head.

"Well then." She smiled again, a little warmer this time. "What would you like to drink?"

He looked at the table, saw the rum, looked up at her. "Rum."

His eyes had that same vindictive glint in them she'd seen before. She made up his drink, trying to ignore the feel of them on her. "Want anything in it?" she asked without looking up.

"No."

She shrugged and handed him the drink. She saw that he kept his hand well away from hers when he took it. She felt a spurt of irritation. "I'm not planning an assault, you know."

Infuriatingly, he stared at her, saying nothing. She poured herself a whisky and drank it. She poured herself another and felt the warmth hit her stomach. She sat down beside him, curling her legs beneath her and looking at his profile. He looked dead ahead, like a surly schoolboy waiting for the lecture.

"Why do you dislike me so much?"

"Why should I like you?"

That seemed unanswerable. She was silent a moment then tried again. "Look, we don't need to be friends, but you could try to be civil."

He turned and looked at her quite suddenly. He didn't speak. Instead he took a long drink of rum. He wiped his mouth with the back of his hand. "What do you want?"

She felt as if he'd pushed half a grapefruit in her face. She opened her mouth but

nothing came out. She looked at her glass.

Danny drank the rest of his drink. He had to get this over with. He put his glass down.

She watched his hands, long, white. She saw the fine red-gold hair on his arms.

"You're causing me a lot of grief. My brother doesn't like this." He could see her faint outrage at the words, and the faint interest, the sly, tell-me-more urge to hear all the dirty little details. "He doesn't like me being here."

She found her tongue quickly enough. "Are you saying he's jealous?"

He could hear all the petty morality in it, and the hot, itchy crotch. "I'm saying that he doesn't like me being here. Tell me what you want and I'll do it. Then I'll go. This has got to be the last time because..." Danny stopped, looking for the right way to phrase it and realised there wasn't a right way. He knew it wasn't going to work. She was used to getting everything her own way, just like her her brother was. Nobody ever said no to them. She would no more understand than he had.

"I don't want anything." Her voice was frosty.

Danny wanted to slap her. He wanted to slap the lying, devious little bitch into next week. "You can't just say it, can you? Think your tongue will shrivel up? Think I give a fuck what you want or why?"

She was shocked to see he was raging angry. It seemed to have come out of nowhere. She felt panicked by it, fearing he would get up and stalk out like he did last time. She reached over, held his arm. "Please, don't go." She sat there holding him.

Danny looked at her, wondering how much it would take to keep her quiet. Abruptly he relaxed.

She got up.

He watched her making up new drinks. If he walked out on her now she'd pester them to death. If he gave in she might do the same.

She sat down again, looked at him cautiously. He took some of his drink then surprised her by asking, "What do you do?"

"Do?"

"Yes, do... for a living."

"Oh," she said as if she had suddenly grasped an ornate problem. "I don't work." She looked at him and smiled. "Family money. Didn't Jimmy tell you?"

He shook his head.

"Jimmy liked being a policeman. He didn't *need* to do it."

"Did you find him?"

She looked at him, momentarily confused, then her face tightened. "Yes, why?"

"Must have been a shock."

"Yes," she said again and he noticed this time she had paled a little. He let it drop.

He looked at her long red nails. "Are you wearing red underwear as well?" He smiled at her.

She looked up, startled, then she smiled back. "As a matter of fact, yes."

"Just like your brother."

"What?"

"He liked his underwear to match as well." He couldn't keep the contempt out his voice.

She looked at him and he knew what was coming. "You really don't look queer."

"You said the same about him."

She tilted her glass, looked into it as if she expected it to tell her something. "Yes..." she stopped, picking her words, "but in retrospect... the moustache, the job. And he was always very anti, overreacting if it came up in conversation. I don't see any of that in you..." she paused again, "or your brother." She didn't meet his eyes.

Danny looked at her. *I'll bet, you dirty bitch.*

She looked at him now. "Did you really have sex with your brother?"

"Wouldn't you like to know?" Danny smiled at her.

"I think Jimmy just wanted to believe it. It was his excuse for taking you away. I think he was justifying himself." She paused, went on, "You're not really queer at all, are you?"

Danny shrugged.

"Don't you care what people think?"

"You mean what you think."

"Alright then, doesn't it bother you if I think you're queer?"

"No."

"Not even if you aren't?"

"No."

She laughed without humour. "So I'm back to square one, none the wiser, and that's the way you intend to keep me."

Danny drank a bit more. "It makes no difference what I say to you. If I say yes you won't believe me. If I say no you can't really trust me, because the diary will always be there, at the back of your mind, calling me a liar. Either way you'll never know for sure." He lifted his sweatshirt and rubbed his belly with deliberation. "Will you?" He let it drop again.

He saw her eyes flick quickly over him. "Tell me anyway."

He smiled and tossed back the rest of his drink. He licked his lips and looked at her levelly. "Yes, I am, and women don't interest me." He watched the words sink in, could feel her balancing them up.

"I don't believe you."

He handed her his empty glass. "See?"

She got up and refilled it and handed it back to him. He felt pleasantly drunkish. Just warm, happy, relaxed. She was amusing him. The whole thing was amusing him.

"I can't believe you."

"Why not? Why should I lie to you?"

"I don't know." She looked genuinely perplexed. She looked at him suddenly, her face lit by something almost like cunning. "Is your brother a homosexual too?"

Danny felt a fresh surge of anger, spoiling his mood. *Oh very crafty Miss Muffet. Armed with prior knowledge, WPC Henderson makes a daring foray for information.* "No." *Eat your heart out, you devious bitch.*

She looked disappointed. Danny wasn't sure if it was because she would have preferred the thrill of having seduced a homosexual or because her ploy had failed. He felt happy again, enjoying her discomfort. She was looking at him again.

"Have you ever had sex with a woman?"

"No."

Her face lit up, just as he had expected. "How can you be sure then?" Then in a lower tone, "You're a virgin."

"Technically."

"You are."

"I said yes."

"You can't be sure then."

"I am."

She shook her head.

He looked into her eyes, holding them. "Why is this so important to you?"

She didn't answer, tore her eyes away.

"Do you want me?"

"No," she said, looking up at him too quickly, pink as a picture.

"Why shouldn't you? I'm not that bad."

"You're gorgeous. As you damn well know."

"Thank you." Danny heard himself in surprise. *Quite the polished performer Daniel.* It had the desired effect.

"No seriously, you are. You must know that."

"Must I?"

"You must have been told before now."

Danny shrugged.

"You're beautiful, quite unreal. I've never met anyone so attractive." She was warming to her subject.

"I think you're embarrassing me."

She laughed. "I suppose it's too late now to admit that I do fancy you a bit."

"Go ahead, admit it." Danny's voice was doing it again. He could no more stop it than stop the dumb seduction lines.

"I think you're very sexy..." She stopped.

"And?"

"And I wouldn't mind making love to you." She laughed and drank some of her drink.

"I thought you didn't want me?"

"I lied." She looked at him, face suddenly intent.

He shook his head. "I couldn't do it."

"You could try."

"You've wanted this all along."

She didn't answer. She slid along to him and slid her hand inside his sweatshirt. He could smell her perfume, strong as Henderson's aftershave. She kept her head down. Her hair was thick, jet black. She pressed against him. He felt her breasts, full and warm, against his arm. She lifted her head suddenly and pressed her lips to his mouth. He could feel the fervid excitement in them. Danny closed his eyes, but did not kiss her back. He had not yet decided.

He knew pleasing her would be a mistake, but he must be unsatisfying in a way that she would not want to try again. He simply did not know her well enough. He didn't know *how* to fail her. Maybe, God willing, he'd fail anyway out of sheer ignorance.

She was getting frustrated at his lack of response. She unbuttoned her dress. He looked. He was right, no bra. She had huge, dark red nipples. She had intended to lift his hands and put them on her breasts, but she did not need to. Danny took hold of them. His cock came up like there was no tomorrow. He let go, but she put them back, moving his hands over them, showing him how to rub the nipples.

He knew she was afraid to touch him, afraid he would be flaccid, unmoved by her. He was careful not to look at her face. He tried to slow his own breathing.

She pulled his sweatshirt off, rumpling his hair. She pushed her breasts in his face, straddling him, pulling her dress open.

He took a nipple in his mouth and clutched her backside, pulling her against him. *What the fuck was he doing?* He felt her excitement at his sudden interest. She held his head, clutching at his hair, feeling it in fascination like they all did.

She pulled her breast from his mouth and unexpectedly sat down on his lap.

He met her eyes, like Perseus and Medusa, not thinking, and saw her hunger for him.

She saw his face change and knew suddenly that somehow she had the upper hand.

She pressed her mouth onto his, felt him invade it. She reached down quickly, grabbing at him as if he might disappear. It was there, huge, beautiful, hard as iron. She kissed him feverishly and felt herself lose it. She felt him push her dress off, push

her back on the couch.

He climbed onto her, pushing his hand inside her knickers. She felt his fingers in her, not trying to do anything, just exploring, curious.

She undid his trousers, pushed them down. He was exquisite, sculpted, smooth, just as Jimmy had described him, just as he'd looked in that brief moment in the kitchen. His cock was long, carved, beautiful in the deep red hair. And big. She felt herself surge at the thought. The second one in so many days, both brothers.

He was pushing between her legs. She looked back up at his face. His eyes seemed deeply, unnaturally, green "I want to fuck you."

His voice was incredible. So deep as to be... she stopped. What?

Supernatural.

He was, everything about him was. He was a fantasy. The corrupt angel; exquisite, vicious, irresistible.

She opened her legs wide. "Go on," she urged him. She helped him guide it in, yanking the leg of her knickers to one side to give him entry.

He pushed it up slowly, his face strained, intent, as if he was practising something difficult.

She pushed down on him, thrusting him up. He looked outrageously surprised. She laughed.

He looked down at her, then smiled too. He lay still. "I never guessed it would feel like this."

"How does it feel?" She wanted to hear him praise her.

"Like a vast blow-job, sucking me all over."

She laughed again. He looked down into her face and began to move, slowly, tentatively. She was smiling. Slowly he began to thrust into her. Her smile slid off her face. He was burying it deep, encouraging her to lift her hips. He watched her face. She knew what he was doing and wondered if he had lied to her. He was so knowing, so slow and strong.

"Will you come?" he asked, further disconcerting her.

"Not like this."

"Can I do it so you'll come?"

"Yes." She closed her eyes She couldn't bear to see his face.

"Show me how."

She took him out and struggled onto her knees. Again she helped him in. "Gently," she warned and began fingering herself.

He was gentle. She didn't want him to be gentle. Suddenly she was up there. She pushed back against him. He pushed in harder. "More," she said.

He did it again, pulling her hips onto himself.

She pushed back, wriggling, feeling it hard against her insides as if it was pushing into her stomach. She thought she was going to wet herself.

He started to drag her onto it. She heard herself whimpering and couldn't stop it. He groaned.

She felt him stiffen slightly, then he started to pump into her furiously, his "*Jesus....*" coming out long and grindingly.

She came, her fingers sliding off herself, soaking wet. He almost lifted her bodily onto himself. He threw his head back, arched into her.

She kept coming, every thrust a new wave. She felt her bladder let go a little and set herself off again. She said, "Please…" over and over again, begging him. She didn't know what for. He marvelled at the way she came. So long, so intense, so different. The smell pungent, so unfeminine, nothing delicate about it. Like an animal in a cage, strong, hot, feral.

He wanted to stay here forever, buried in her cunt, drowning in her smell, feeling

her orgasm clutch at him. He reached forward and felt her breasts, lying on her back, spent. She moaned at the feel of his hands, squirmed on him.

"I love you," he said, feeling the incredible release of the words. "I *love* you."

John sat in the living room. He had the fire built up high, blazing in the darkness. He had been trying to read but had abandoned it. He put out the light and lay watching the firelight dance on the walls. He didn't know where the others were and cared less.

He felt the same way as he felt when he'd first seen Rab and Danny together. That same blind, head-aching hatred. The thought of food made him sick. He couldn't sleep. He couldn't read. He couldn't even think.

The door opened and closed again. He felt a hand on his hair. He frowned, trying to look round.

"Is he fretting then?" Ian moved round in front of him. "Your hair looks just like Danny's in the firelight."

John stared at him, willing him to go away.

Ian toasted his backside at the fire, letting his eyes roam up and down John's body. "Very seductive." His voice was treacly, unpleasant, as if it might stick to your skin.

"Isn't it a bit late to take a crush on me?"

Ian shrugged. "You just look good."

"You spastic little queer."

"Couldn't agree more." Ian was smiling. He looked almost pleased by the insult.

John turned back to his meditation. "Go away."

"He wants to be alone."

John ignored him.

There was a long, warm silence. John had almost forgotten he was there when he spoke again. "Missing him?"

"I told you to go away."

"Hurting?"

John closed his eyes and re-crossed his ankles. He rubbed the bridge of his nose, put his arm back behind his head. For some reason he could see vividly the way Danny undid buttons; a strange little lift and push, always one-handed. He couldn't chase those buttons from his head.

"What are you thinking about?" Ian asked.

"The way Danny undoes buttons." John felt the dangerous build-up of it. A longing to confess, to unburden - in the darkness, over a phone, to a face you couldn't see. Ian wasn't the man for it but John couldn't raise himself. It was like being doped.

"What about it?"

"He has an odd quirk, one-handed."

Ian nodded. "He always watches you while he does it."

John thought about it. "Yes..."

"He's a natural performer, our Danny."

"He's a whore."

"Uh-huh," Ian agreed, satisfied with that, happy to hear John say it. He sat down on the fender.

John felt the anger run up behind the thought. He wanted to dirty-mouth him. He wanted to sit here and spew out his hate.

"He's a lying motherfucking little whore. He'd mount any stinking bitch that pushed her crack in his hand. He's a rabid stinking little goat, a festering degenerate little..." He ground to a halt, tripping over his own emotions. He could feel tears pricking at the corners of his eyes. His throat was a single convulsive lump. He couldn't swallow. He couldn't breathe. He opened his lips to suck in air as if he'd been crying.

Ian watched his face working, was stupefied to see the intensity of his emotion. Something more than anger. Loss? God, even grief? Ian hugged his knees quietly, saying nothing.

"He's been putting on the performance of his life, saying he doesn't want her, pretending he doesn't even want to see her. He's dreamt about this one for years. He's been biding his time and now the first bit of cunt he sees and I can..." He stopped, hearing himself almost voicing it.

And you can fuck off, Ian thought. Big bad John is scared shitless, like the elephant and the mouse. Ian laid his head on his knees and hugged his happiness into himself.

John lay there feeling the cold sweat on his skin, his guts churning. He put an arm over his eyes, blocking out the light, hiding himself.

Ian crawled over to him, put his arm across his chest. John pressed both arms tighter across his face, like a saint penitent under the extremes of guilt.

"He isn't worth it." Ian's hand soothed up and down his ribs like a woman easing a child's colic.

John let the words wash over him. They were telling him what he wanted to hear. He let the hand ease him, giving him what he wanted to feel; a little pity, a little love.

Ian luxuriated in the hard feel of him under the thin shirt. His body had the flavour of everything destructive about it. If death was a man with a scythe he looked just like John. No skinny skeleton, but big and powerful, destroying souls without either pleasure or pain, just soaking up numbers - ugly as sin and twice as enticing.

Ian could see his mouth under his arms like a fetish, like the lips in the credits of that spoof horror film, the only visible part of him, full, broad, the edges of his teeth showing, his breathing harsh.

He watched the lips, waited to see them speak. John's tongue moistened them. Ian felt his cock swell. He wanted to kiss him. If only there was a way. Without being punched in the mouth.

Time was fragile. Ian could feel it trickling through his hands as he kept one hand moving on John's chest, lulling him, easing his pain, knowing it would ease out of him entirely soon, be replaced by sleep or irritation before he could do it.

There must be a way.

"He doesn't love you." He heard himself murmur the words, *so* softly, saw John move his head, burying it deeper under his arms. "He isn't ever going to love you. He doesn't know how to." Ian leaned over him, running both hands up over his chest.

John's hand came down suddenly, clutching Ian's, holding it.

He'd fucked it. Time had shat on his head.

John lifted his hand and pushed it down over his crotch. He held it there a moment, his face still hidden by that one arm, then he let go and covered his face again.

Ian was afraid to move. Did he actually want him to...? He wasn't erect, just a little warmed-up perhaps, vaguely desiring, nothing more. Ian squeezed him tentatively. John didn't move. He was still breathing through his mouth.

Ian knew that all he wanted was the sensation of it, the consolation, something to take his mind off the pain. He wasn't going to ask, and he wasn't going to allow any talk. Either Ian did it with his mouth shut or he wouldn't get to do it at all.

But John would owe him.

And John would know he owed him.

Ian unzipped him carefully, one eye on his face, waiting for any sign of displeasure. He undid the buckle of his belt, equally slowly. John did not move. He could see the rise and fall of his chest. He pulled his jeans open, saw the thick brown hair of his belly. He pulled his shorts down. He was coming up under Ian's gaze. He knew he was being looked at, knew he was going to be touched. Ian took the weight of it in his hand. He looked at it minutely, pulled the soft skin down, squeezed the head, feeling

the way it stuck to his fingers.

Ian was so stiff it was hurting him.

He stroked it slowly, soothingly. He thought of everything he could to give him pleasure. John stayed deep inside his arms, only the speed of his breathing giving away how he felt.

He grew massive. Ian marvelled at the sheer mind-boggling dimensions of it. The veins stood up in heavy relief. He seemed to be overfilled with blood. It looked almost painful.

Ian took longer, stiff strokes, squeezing the blood out, only to let it swell up again.

John began to push up into his hand and Ian knew he was near.

"Love me." John's voice was a whisper. Ian looked at him, wondering if that was what he'd said.

He said it again, clearer this time. "Love me."

He began to thrust up into Ian's hand. Ian's grip was so greedy he felt it come up from his balls, watched fascinated as the first spurt struggled out. He felt it, hot and glutinous, slide over his hand.

"Love me," John urged with each ejaculation, and Ian knew he wasn't talking to him, knew he wasn't even with him. He was seeing something else in the red darkness of his buried arms, seeing some*one* else, talking to someone else, urging someone else.

Ian didn't need to ask who because John told him.

His voice died on a whisper. *"Danny..."*

Ian put a hand firmly down over John's mouth, held it there like a hand pressing a pillow over his face, while John's body twitched under his suffocating hold.

Finally he went limp.

"Good boy," Ian murmured then pressed his mouth thirstily to his belly.

Danny went into the mirrored bathroom to wash. He washed without soap. He stood under the shower and let it wash away the perfume, the sweat, the smell of her.

He had locked the door. He didn't want her in with him. He felt trapped.

Intact...

He closed his eyes, washing his face under the water. He could smell her off his hands. He took the soap from the dish and scrubbed his hands twice. He rinsed them, ran them through his hair. He stood under the shower till he felt like a prune.

Eventually he got out. He wrapped himself in a towel. *JH was here.*

He went out.

She was waiting for him in the bedroom, standing opposite him when he looked up. The black satin was still there. She smiled at him. "I thought you'd drowned."

"You're hard to wash off."

She stopped smiling. She didn't say anything.

Danny went into the living room and found his clothes. She followed him through. He turned his back to her, not wanting her to see.

She looked at the long white lines of him. He was so beautiful it almost hurt to look at him. No wonder Jimmy had wanted him. "Are you going?"

"Yes." He didn't turn to her, but she knew he was aware of her, uncomfortable. He wasn't his brother, no ice-cold detachment here.

She crossed to him and put her arms around his waist. She kissed his shoulders. He was still damp from the shower, his hair dark with water, an outrageous burgundy red. "Why don't you stay?"

He stood still, tense under her kisses. "I can't."

"Why not?"

"I just can't." He took her hands and prised them off, stepping away from her to get his sweatshirt. He pulled it the right way out.

"Your brother, right?"

He didn't say anything.

"What's his problem?"

Danny pulled the sweatshirt on.

"I'm talking to you." She came round in front of him. "Why don't you answer me?"

Danny looked at her for the first time. "He doesn't like you."

She wanted to say, Oh no? Well he was fast enough getting into my knickers. But she knew she couldn't. How could she tell him she'd slept with his brother only two days before? How could she convince him it was him she wanted after that?

He sat down and began pulling on his socks and shoes.

"You really are going to trot off back home."

Danny tied his left shoe.

"Just because big brother says so."

Danny tied his right shoe.

"What's wrong with him? Is he afraid someone's getting what he isn't?"

He smiled suddenly, a little thing. It looked odd on that tense face. "You could say that."

She frowned, twice as irritated by that smile as she had been by his silence. What the hell did that mean?

He moved to get his jacket.

"Your hair's wet."

He froze. She said slowly, "You can't let him know, can you?"

Danny stood undecided, only half hearing her, wondering what the hell to do about his hair.

"You've been a dirty boy and now you've got to keep the awful truth away from him. Isn't the washing a bit much? Just a tiny bit paranoid?"

"Have you got a hair dryer?"

She nodded, tight-lipped.

"Well, could I use it then?"

"So you can leave."

Danny didn't answer. There was nothing he could say. "Can I or can't I?"

She went out of the room without answering him. He picked the towel up and rubbed his hair. She came back in and plugged a hairdryer into a socket beside the settee. "Come sit down."

He sat down. She started to dry his hair, running her hands through it.

"I can do it myself."

"God, do you never comb this?"

"There isn't any point." He was enjoying the soporific feel of her hands in his hair. "It just tangles up again."

She ran her fingertips through the soft corkscrew curls at the back of his neck. "You've got natural ringlets."

"So?"

"Most women would give their eye teeth for hair like yours."

"I'm not a woman."

"No, you're not." She pulled his head back against her stomach while she worked on the front. She felt him tense then saw him close his eyes. She looked at the lashes on his cheek, the smooth white skin. "Stay with me."

He opened his eyes. "No."

She pushed his head to one side. "Please."

"No, I can't."

"You could if you really wanted to. You needn't ever go back to him."

Danny pulled forward, tugging away from her. "Don't start that, you're as bad as he was."

"What?"

He was struggling up onto his feet. "Your fucking brother." He impersonated his voice, "Stay with me, you're so lovely." He turned on her. "He made me fucking sick to my stomach."

"And I do too, is that it?"

"Yes." Danny nodded. "That's *exactly* it."

"I see."

Danny turned suddenly and went out into the hall. He pulled his jacket off a peg then realised it was one of Henderson's. He almost dropped it. She put the light on. He hung the jacket back up with unnatural care and put on his own.

"When will I see you again?"

Never, Danny thought. "I don't know."

"I see." Her voice was hard. "What do I have to do, buy you each time?"

"Probably."

"And should I see your brother? Does he do the arrangements?"

Suddenly he was tired of it all. "Yes. There isn't any point in asking me because I don't have any say in the matter. You deal with him." He was yanking his jacket on. Now he turned to the door. "I wish you luck. You're going to need it." And he slammed it shut behind him.

John pushed his head off him. He kept his eyes covered, almost as if he were ashamed or couldn't stand the sight of him. "Get out."

Ian wiped his mouth, could taste the odd bitterness of him. "Don't I get anything?"

"I said, get out."

Ian got up slowly. John was still hugely swollen. Ian knew it hadn't satisfied him, only left him wanting more. It had been little more than solitary masturbation for him and now he was regretting it.

He stood there looking down at him. Let the great ugly bastard come out of there. Let him look him in the face. If he wanted him out he could get him out.

John's arm came down finally. His eyes blinked in the half-light. He looked at Ian's face but would not meet his eyes. He pulled his shorts up, not bothering to dry himself. Not that Ian had left him much to dry. He pulled the zip up. Ian watched him still.

"Last time Ian, get the fucking hell out."

"Enjoy it John?" Ian was back in front of the fire, out of distance.

John looked at him this time. "You putrid little creep."

"Did you enjoy being wanked by a putrid little creep?"

John swung up, feet on the floor.

Ian got ready to move.

But John didn't stand up. "Out." Just the one word.

Ian went. Smiling all the way.

John sat there, unmoving, looking into the fire, remembering the feel of Ian's mouth on his stomach.

Like a leech.

He stood up to fasten his clothes. He sat down again.

He lit a cigarette and closed his eyes.

Danny looked at the house. It was in darkness. All in bed, unless they were sitting in the kitchen.

He drove the car up into the yard and switched off the engine. He sat for a moment, listening to it ticking, then got out. He locked the door. The yard light had been left on for him.

He went and closed the gate then went into the house. He felt for the kitchen light. The dog wuffed and got up to greet him. He scratched its head absently. He felt suddenly ravenous. He stuck his head in the fridge and found a piece of leftover pie. He took it out and ate it with his fingers, washing it down with a swig of milk from the bottle. He threw the last bit of crust to the dog and wiped his hands on his trousers. He put out the kitchen light and went into the hall.

The living room door was open and John was standing in the doorway. He was backlit by the dull red of the fire. "Come in."

Danny walked down the hall and into the room. John caught him to him and buried his face in his hair. He smelt of the night. Damp, cool. The night and cold leather. John kissed his hair, inhaling him, then pushed him into the room.

He closed the glass door.

Danny could hear the clock ticking, the sound loud in the stillness of the house.

John came over and slid his hands inside his jacket, buried his face in his neck. Danny knew what he was doing. Under the lips, the feel of his mouth, he knew what he was doing.

John came up for air and suddenly pushed him backwards. Danny sat down on the settee with a thump.

"Tell me everything you did, everything you said."

"What?"

"What did she say when you went in?"

"Christ, I don't know. Hello or something."

"And when you fucked her, how did that feel?"

Danny looked at his face. Zero to sixty in four seconds. He was livid.

"I..." But the denial dried up in Danny's mouth, evaporated under the heat in his eyes. It was as if the fire emanated from him instead of a source behind him.

"You *what?*" His voice was scraped across the floor like dogshit off a shoe.

Danny shook his head hopelessly.

"You know what I'm going to do to you Danny?"

Danny shook his head again.

"I'm going to kill you."

"John... listen...."

John didn't reply.

Danny sat there, looking at him, transfixed by despair. "John... don't."

"Don't what?"

"I didn't..." Danny stopped again.

"Don't fucking lie to me. One lousy look at her rabid little face and you'd have been out there like a poker." John came for him suddenly, grabbing his sweatshirt. "Out there like a fucking poker, aching to get it up her hole."

He dropped him again, pushing him back. "How did she do it then? She sit on you? I could see her, the pushy bitch. Not quite old enough to be your mother but old enough to teach a sweet virgin like you what it's all about. Daniel loses his cherry. Ha, bloody, ha."

Suddenly he sat down in the armchair. His voice changed. "Take your clothes off."

Danny looked at him, not sure what to do.

"Get them off."

Danny bent down and undid his shoes, pulled them off, his socks. He took off his jacket, stood up. His legs were shaking. He pulled off his sweatshirt.

"Stop." John looked at him, wearing nothing but his jeans, the firelight on his hair, his chest, turning him molten. "Go on. The rest."

Danny unfastened his trousers. He pulled them and his shorts down together, pulled them off. The room was warm, the fire hot on his skin, but he felt terribly, icy cold. John studied him intensely, as if he'd never seen him before, as if he was memorising him. The thought made Danny want to puke. Memorising him for what?

"Lie down. Full out."

Danny lay down on the sofa.

"Hands behind your head."

Danny did as he was told. He felt naked to his bones, like a man on the rack. He had never felt so vulnerable in his life.

"Right, now tell me what you did with her. I want it all. Don't skip a thing."

Danny told him. His own voice sounded alien to him, flat, dull. He sounded like someone reciting bad verse, uninterested, uninvolved. He heard the fire slide down once. He paused but John said, "Don't stop."

John wasn't interested in what he did. John was listening for how he did it, little pointers, the give-aways. John was reading him for signs of excitement.

Danny was careful. He did not tell John about his asking her how to make her come. He told him that he changed position, nothing more. Danny was afraid, so afraid his teeth felt as if they were glued together.

Eventually it ran out. There was a tensile silence then John said, "That it?"

Danny nodded.

"And you washed it all away, so that I wouldn't know."

Danny nodded.

"And she wants to see you again."

Danny said nothing.

"And you want to see her again."

"No, I don't." Danny heard the frantic note in his voice and tried to bite it down.

"Fucking liar."

"I don't."

"Get up."

Danny sat up, looked at him, couldn't see his eyes, only blackness.

"Come here."

Danny got up, crossed to him.

John didn't move. He jerked his head. "Kneel in front of the fire."

Danny knelt down.

"Closer."

Danny moved in closer.

John looked at the beauty of him, finely etched in the firelight, so perfect. No matter what you did to him, always so fucking perfect.

John pulled himself slowly upright and picked up the fire tongs. Danny watched him uneasily.

John put them into the heart of the fire and lifted out a small glowing coal.

Danny moved quickly, but not quick enough. John had his hair, pulling him forward. "Just sit *right* where you are."

Danny dragged against his hand, trying to twist away, but John held him until Danny felt as if his scalp was going to be torn off. "John don't... don't."

"Sit *still*."

Danny stopped struggling.

John tugged him back.

The coal had lost its glow. He threw it back in the fire. Danny watched him uneasily. He reached into the fire again. "Open your legs."

"No!" Danny almost shouted it. He started to struggle again.

John dropped the tongs and back-handed him. Even sitting it came at him with force, breaking his lip against his teeth. "I said fucking *sit still*."

Danny started to cry with an inevitability that made him sick. He didn't want to cry and still he did, as if his body was crying without his permission.

"Now open your legs."

Danny closed his eyes and opened his legs. He knew that when it touched him he'd wet himself. He knew that he'd be lucky if that's all he did.

John took another coal from the fire, looked at Danny's face. He could see the tears dripping off it, two long tracks of silver down his face, his eyelashes sparkling with it. "Open your eyes Danny." His voice was a whisper.

Danny opened them. John held the coal inches from his cock. Danny could feel the heat of it. Its colour was dying but it was still very hot. "Please..." he begged, the word coming out in a desperate hiccup. "Please don't John."

John brought it closer. Danny tried not to move.

"I'm tired of sharing you." Suddenly John put the coal against his lower belly, just above the hairline.

Danny screamed, twisted. He could smell his own skin burning.

John pulled it off again, clamped his hand over Danny's mouth. Danny squirmed underneath his hand, whimpering in pain, almost ripping the sleeve off John's shirt.

"Shh...." John got down on the floor beside him, pulling his head against him. Danny was crying in earnest. The sobs went right through John. He began to feel sick. "Danny, Danny..." He rocked him, stroking his hair. "Don't cry."

But Danny went on crying, and Danny went on struggling against him. It was like trying to hold an unwilling cat.

The door opened. Rab saw the two of them sitting there; Danny naked, struggling fiercely, John glaring up at his interruption with that same mad dog look. "What the fuck goes on here? Who screamed?"

Danny gave a sudden convulsive lunge, breaking free and scrambling to his feet.

"Danny!" John roared.

But Danny was already out of the room.

John got quickly to his feet but Rab barred his way. "What's going on?"

"None of your fucking business."

John made to push past him but Rab caught his arm. "I'm getting tired of this." John looked down at Rab's hand on his arm, waiting for him to move it. Rab kept it where it was. "Even if he isn't, I am."

John's look was black and dirty. He enunciated every word clearly. "Take your fucking hands off me."

"I mean it."

John mimicked him. "I *mean* it." He pushed Rab's hand off and shoved past him.

Rab stood there seething, watching him disappear upstairs into the darkness. He followed him up but John didn't even stop outside the bathroom. He didn't try the handle or knock on the door. He went right past it and slammed into his room.

Rab stood in the hall a moment then tentatively tried the bathroom door. Danny hadn't even locked it.

Rab went in quickly and locked the door behind him.

Danny was the colour of oatmeal. Rab saw the mess on his stomach. "Jesus, how the fuck did he do that?"

"Coal... hot coal."

Rab realised he was in shock. He was shaking like a leaf, his eyes darting about.

"I don't know what to do," he said helplessly. Then he said, "It hurts." And his face fell apart.

Rab sat him on the stool and put two towels round his shoulders. "Sit there, I won't be a minute."

He went into the old man's room and clicked on the light. He saw himself electrified in the mirror, stripped to the waist, ghostly white. He opened the wardrobe. There were still half a dozen bottles in there, untouched. He took one and went back to the bathroom.

Danny was still sitting there. Rab twisted the top off and poured some in the tooth mug. "Here."

Danny held the glass in both hands, trying to stop it shaking. He drank it down, coughed. Rab heard John's door opening. He crossed the floor and locked the door quickly.

John tried the handle.

Danny's head shot up.

"Fuck off John, leave him alone."

There was a silence. Danny's eyes were huge. Rab said, "Drink up."

Danny drank it, but Rab saw him watching the door.

"Let me in Danny."

"You heard me the first time John, why don't you?"

The door buckled suddenly with the impact of John's shoulder. Danny's hand jumped, spilling the whisky. Rab looked at the tiny bolt. No way. He crossed the floor and unbolted it before John could hit it again. "No..." Danny said. But John was already in the room.

Rab hit him, with an intense and satisfying pleasure. John's eyes widened with surprise.

Rab hit him again, once more in the stomach. This one backed him out into the hall.

Rab kneed him in the balls. John crumpled up, still managing to wheeze, "You fucking bastard."

Rab lifted his head by the hair and punched his face. He felt John's mouth spread under it, felt the hardness of his teeth, realised he'd grazed his knuckles. He could do this all night.

John was leaning against the wall, holding himself around the middle. His mouth was bleeding, his eyes were like coals. If he could breathe I'd be mincemeat right now, Rab thought. "Had enough John?"

John went on glaring, his breath coming in harsh gasps as if every one hurt him.

Danny was standing in the bathroom doorway looking at John. His face was unreadable. Rab spoke to him. "Want to sleep in your own room?"

Danny looked at John again. Rab wondered what was going through his mind. Danny shook his head.

Rab felt as if he'd kicked him in the mouth.

Danny looked at him. "I'll be alright."

Rab shrugged, turned away from him. He felt suddenly superfluous, as if he'd interrupted a domestic quarrel. John was still staring at him. He could feel Danny behind him, waiting for him to go.

He crossed the hall and went into his room. He locked the door.

Fuck him.

He dragged off his jeans and climbed into bed.

Fuck the stupid little bastard.

He heard John's bedroom door close. He punched the pillow savagely, buried his face in it.

That's probably exactly what he is doing.

Fucking the little bastard.

Right now.

John covered Danny's legs and fetched a bottle from the cabinet above the bedroom sink. He poured some directly onto the burn, not handling it, not using cotton wool. It smelt like sour wine.

Danny felt a slight cooling, but the pain was so intense it didn't seem to matter. He had never felt pain like this.

"It'll help."

Danny wouldn't look at him. "It's going to mark me."

"This'll help."

"You've scarred me."

"I'm sorry."

Danny looked at him now. " No you're not."

"It's better than dying, isn't it?"

"Is it?"

John brushed the hair off his face.

Danny pulled away from him. "Don't touch me."

John got up and soaked some gauze in the same liquid. He taped it loosely over Danny's burn.

It made it hurt worse to be covered.

"You won't be able to sleep unless it's covered." John was looking down at him.

Danny pulled the blankets up and closed his eyes.

It raged. His whole body felt alive with it. He could feel muscles jumping in his legs. He kept an arm along his side, turning slightly to keep the blankets off himself.

John got in beside him, putting the light out.

They lay there in the dark, awake, knowing the other was awake, not speaking. Danny felt as if his whole body was made of pain.

John touched him. Danny flinched away from him.

John came over against his back, kissing his shoulders.

"Leave me alone John. For once just leave me alone."

"Let me ease your pain." John's hands ran over his hips. His mouth kissed his neck. Danny felt him hard against him. "Danny..." his voice was hopeless, "ease mine."

Danny felt the hairs stand up on the back of his neck.

John was rubbing against him. "Ease mine Danny..."

He had one leg over Danny's. Danny was tense, afraid he would brush against the burn. John clung to him. Danny had never felt him so desperate. He felt the faint curl of his own excitement feeding off the hunger in John's voice. He tried to prise him off.

"Please Danny."

"Go to Rab." Danny felt pleasure just saying the words.

"He can't help me."

Danny hugged it to him. *He can't help me.*

John pushed against him. "Just lay your hand on me."

Danny pushed the blankets off, turned over.

John rolled onto his back, lay there waiting. "Jut put your hand on me," he whispered again.

Danny palmed his cock with his hand, knew he'd had sex, could smell it.

Danny was startled to feel his hand on his face. John's thumb moving over his lips.

"You hate me, don't you?"

"No."

John's fingers traced his face in the dark. Danny lightly traced the outline of his cock. He could feel his own growing heavy against his thigh, his stomach on fire beside it. Pain and pleasure. All John ever gave, pain and pleasure.

"Love me Danny?"

Danny felt the veins, thick, painful under his fingers. "You've got a fucking cheek."

"Don't leave me." John's hand came round the back of his neck. He was tight as a spring. Danny could feel him holding himself in check. "Don't ever leave me."

Danny lightened his touch. He felt a muscle jerk in John's arm.

"Danny?"

Danny squeezed him, peeled him back slowly. "What?" Skimmed him gently.

"When you were young..." John pulled in a sharp breath, stopped Danny's hand with his own.

They waited a beat or two. A board clicked on the floor. John lifted his hand, kneaded Danny's neck with his other. "We did some things..."

Danny didn't say anything.

"Do you remember?"

Still Danny said nothing.

"We shouldn't have..."

Danny began to masturbate him with a sudden determined strength, like some kind of frantic displacement activity.

"I didn't mean it to go so far, I swear."

Danny's movements became savage, constricting. He was hurting him now.

John moaned, took it without a word.

Suddenly Danny swung upright, guided John's cock up against his arse and impaled himself on it, all in a second.

John grunted a fierce negative, but he pulled Danny down hard onto himself.

Danny took his own barely-hard erection in his hand, felt it pull agonisingly tight on the burn, didn't care. He worked it determinedly, trying to encourage it beyond the ferocious pain. He thumped up and down on John's penis with no thought for his discomfort or injury, riding it wildly. "I don't forgive you John." His voice scraped out of him, breathless and harsh. "You think all you've got to do is ask and I'll forgive you. Well I don't."

John pulled him down, trying to still those mad movements.

Danny pistoned his cock fiercely. "I *hate* you. Understand?"

"You're right..." John gasped "...hate me."

He seemed suddenly oblivious to the pounding Danny was giving his body. Out of nowhere *he* was using Danny, like an overgrown sex toy, something he could plunge into until he was delirious, something he could finish all on his own, with no help from Danny.

Danny jerked himself frantically, knowing John had somehow turned the tables on him, icily determined not to be cheated by him yet again, not sure he could make it through the pain. But John's erratic jerking fervour, his sweating determined up-thrusts into Danny's worn-out body, were doing things he couldn't have explained. When it came it came suddenly and he cried out with the strength of it.

John heard it through an odd disembodied shimmering of almost pain-like cramping. It wasn't an orgasm, it was his body telescoping, folding itself so small every last hair was buried in Danny's flesh. He wanted to die. He wanted to die right now and never have to explain himself again.

"I love you..." His hand was buried in Danny's hair, Danny who was bent over him, head down, trembling. "I've always loved you..." He pulled Danny's mouth down to his

own. "Little *brother...*"

FORTY-TWO

Danny was woken by a cramp in his foot. "*Shit.*" He jumped out of bed and pressed his toes down on the floor. Then he felt the pain gnawing at his stomach. He put a palm close to it. He could feel the heat coming off it.

"What is it?" John's voice was muddy, anxious.

"Nothing, just cramp. Go back to sleep."

Then the alarm went off. He heard John swearing in the darkness then its noise was silenced. The light clicked on. John was looking at him, rubbing his face. "Okay?"

"Fine." Danny climbed back into the warmth of the bed. Just five minutes, to heat up. All his limbs felt stiff and sore. He had been sleeping awkwardly. He felt like shit.

John lay on his side, facing him. "Stay in bed, we'll manage without you."

Danny closed his eyes thankfully. He didn't argue. He jumped when he felt John's mouth on his, his eyes coming open. John's kiss was brief but intense, curiously disturbing. It made Danny feel itchy, irritable.

John got out of bed and began to get dressed. Danny closed his eyes again and pulled the blankets over his ears. Finally he heard John go out.

He spread himself across the bed, feeling the residual warmth of John's body. He pushed his face into John's pillow and found it surprisingly difficult to get back to sleep.

Dawn was just breaking, making the room greyish. Danny heard the movement and lifted his head. There was someone moving around the room.

"Awake?" It was John's voice. Danny dropped his head back onto the pillow. John came over to the bed, sat down. He began unbuttoning his shirt.

"What you doing?" Danny frowned at him.

"Coming back to bed."

"Back?"

John stood up and pulled his trousers off, stepping out of them and leaving them where they lay. "I'll be quick."

"Oh Jesus John, give it a rest."

"Shhh..." John ran a hand down his flank.

His hands were icy. Danny winced away from him. "Your hands are fucking frozen."

"Lie on your side."

Danny turned away from him irritably. John came up against him. He was half hard already. He kissed Danny's shoulder lightly. He pulled himself into place, neat against Danny's arse. He made a small sound of satisfaction.

"This is why you wanted me to stay in bed," Danny said sourly.

John held his hips lightly, pinning his legs down, giving himself long tugging thrusts against Danny's backside. "Shhh..." he said again.

Danny lay there letting him use him, trying not to feel anything. It was only minutes before he felt the tempo of John's movements become faster, the strokes shorter. John held himself away from him to get better leverage. His cock was digging in hard now. He adjusted it slightly so that it pressed into the soft flesh of Danny's buttock. He groaned softly.

Danny dragged himself away from what he was doing. The others would be at breakfast by now, sitting there knowing where John was, what he was doing. Mrs Ostler would come in soon. She'd probably arrive in nice time to hear him come on him.

Danny gave up. His body had given up long before. He curled backwards into John's body, half turned his head towards him. John broke away, panting. Danny felt his hot breath in his ear, grunting. He started bucking against him, holding his hips fiercely, bumping Danny into the bed with each thrust.

Danny heard the deep groan come out of him, felt his cock ride slickly against him in its own moisture, spreading it across his back. John thrust twice more then stopped, flopping against him, his head against Danny's shoulder.

"Better?" Danny asked dryly.

John laughed. "Uh-huh."

They heard voices in the hall. Ostler hanging up her coat, already chattering away.

"You better mop up and move," Danny said.

"Let her come in. I'd like to see her face, confirm her worst suspicions."

"The sheets do that already. Anyway, you'd only have to find someone new."

"They couldn't be any worse." But John rolled off him and pushed the blankets down.

Danny heard him pulling tissues out the box then felt John's hand gently wipe him down, the fingers tracing, looking for damp patches. "Okay?"

Danny assented and snuggled into the blankets. He felt better too, warm, comforted. His cock felt pleasantly swollen, pleasantly aroused, not wanting.

John covered him up and sat on the edge of the bed. There was the small silence of someone else's quiet industry. Danny could visualise him handling himself, drying up, his spent lazy concentration. He felt John shift off the bed, knew he was getting dressed again.

Danny became pleasantly drowsy. He felt John's hand on his hair, knew John was speaking to him, but he didn't reply. With any luck John would think he was asleep.

John moved away again. Danny heard the door close quietly.

He went back to sleep. And dreamt his body was full of flames.

Mrs Ostler stuck her head round the door. She had knocked but had received no reply.

She got a nasty turn when she saw him. The little devil was lying there in his bare skin. She felt her face flame up, then she realised he must have pushed the blankets down to keep them off his stomach. Robert was right, it was a nasty mess. How in the world had he done that?

She crossed the room quickly and opened the curtains a fraction to let in a little more light then looked at him again. She could see the starts of the hair on his privates. It was the same colour as his head. She felt embarrassed by how much of him she could see. Somehow it was worse, a good-looking lad like that. She blushed again, feeling foolish. All the same, she wished he was covered up a bit more. He looked so indecent lying there like that.

She realised quite suddenly he was watching her. Not looking at her, *watching* her. He'd come awake like a cat does, without any in-between. She felt intensely uncomfortable under his peculiar gaze. "Morning," she ventured.

He did not answer her.

She wondered if he were not really awake, sleeping with his eyes half-open - some people did that - then he stretched himself, letting the blanket slide down another couple of inches, enough to show her the starts of his thing, distinctly swollen, lying in that red hair, then he pulled the blankets up slowly as if nothing had happened.

"Morning," he answered, still watching her, smiling now, but there was nothing natural about his smile either.

She turned away, completely flustered, briskly opening the curtains. When she

turned back she knew he was still watching her, but she didn't dare look at him again. "I came up to see if you wanted a cup of tea, seeing as you're poorly. It's ten o'clock."

"Yes," he said and his voice didn't sound quite right either. "I'll get up," he added. She felt an irrational urge to bolt for the door. He made it sound almost like a threat. She visualised him standing there naked before her, like one of those flashers, his thing poking up at her.

She went over to the door quickly. "I'll go put the kettle on."

She went out, closing the door thankfully behind her.

Seductive.

The word sprang into her mind unprompted as the door shut to. *Of all the silly...*

She went down the stairs. She was 70 years old. She was definitely getting senile. Seductive indeed.

She put the kettle on, and saw that her hand was shaking.

Danny got up and had tea. He put on a pair of ancient track suit trousers that were too short and comically droopy. They were the only thing he could find that wouldn't aggravate the wound. He took some painkillers without much hope. He saw in the bathroom mirror that his lip was cut. He couldn't remember how it had happened. It was a little swollen and itchy, like an insect bite, but any pain it possessed seemed irrelevant. He didn't look at the burn. He didn't want to see it.

Mrs Ostler came across him once as he lay on the couch, with his belly exposed, reading. After that she stayed out of his way.

John came in first and found him in the living room. Danny hitched his trousers up gingerly and struggled up.

John gave him a dry look. "You'll have to get something else to wear. You look like the arse end of a panto cow. Go in with Ian this afternoon."

"I can't go into town looking like this."

"Well send him then, but make sure he gets something that fits you. Have you had lunch?"

Danny shook his head.

"Come through then."

Everybody seemed to find Danny's trousers amusing.

There was a moment of uneasiness when Ian asked him how the hell he'd managed to burn his stomach, voicing Mrs Ostler's thoughts to such a preciseness she looked up at him. "Implausible or what?" he said when Danny told him. He was smiling his tacky little smile.

"Danny's always damaging himself in implausible places," Rab said, but he was looking at John. John looked back at him steadily. Danny didn't say anything. Mrs Ostler pretended not to be listening.

John got up from the table, breaking the moment. "Go in and get him something to wear Ian."

"What do I use for money?"

John gave him some and went out. Mrs Ostler went home.

Ian sat waiting, and Rab knew what he suspected was true. He got up slowly from the table and stopped beside him, laying a hand on his shoulder, bending down close to his ear so that only Ian could hear him.

He straightened up.

Danny looked at Ian's flushed face and wondered what Rab had said to him.

Ian smiled at him across the table. Danny decided he didn't want to know.

Danny went with him. He disguised the trousers' shortcomings by wearing wellingtons.

He had not bought sports clothes since he was fifteen. He found the options bewildering. Eventually they bought him two pairs of black sweat pants, plain as he could get them, but he still couldn't escape two vertical slashes of acid green on the legs. It was the best they could do.

"They're going to look fucking amazing with wellies."

Ian smiled but said nothing. In fact Danny did look fucking amazing, but then Danny wouldn't see that. He wasn't Rab.

Danny flung them in the back seat and got in, wincing slightly as he sat down. He knew the bandage had stuck to the wound. He wasn't looking forward to taking it off.

"We don't need to go home," Ian announced abruptly.

Danny looked at him. "Where else would we go?"

"World's your oyster."

Danny sighed, just enough. "Let's just go home Ian, huh?"

Ian shrugged, started the car. After a moment or two he asked, "Hurting?"

Danny looked out the window and nodded.

Ian pulled into the traffic. "How did he do it?"

"What makes you think he did?"

"Come off it."

"With a hot coal."

Ian sucked in a pained breath. "What was it for this time?"

"None of your business." Danny turned and looked at his face. "Why don't you just drive the car?"

"Okay. Don't shit your knickers."

They were silent until Danny noticed they weren't going the right way. "Where are we going?"

"Picturesque route. We're not in any hurry, are we?"

"What are you trying to do, avoid work?"

"Why not? Not often I get the chance. We don't all get preferential treatment."

Danny did not rise to the bait.

"You seeing Henderson's sister again?"

"Not if I can help it."

Ian shot him a quick glance, but the edge of Danny's face told him nothing. "What's she called?"

"I haven't a clue." Danny smiled suddenly, realising he didn't even know her name. He was living a cliché.

"What's so funny?"

"Nothing."

Ian thought it was a good job he was good to look at because he certainly wasn't a dazzling conversationalist. Maybe it was the pain. "Does it hurt much?"

"What do you think?"

"I haven't seen it."

Danny heard the slight lascivious feel to the words and looked at him. "Would you like to see it?"

Ian flicked a glance at him out the corner of his eye.

"You're a fucking sicko Ian, know that?"

Ian flushed but he kept a smile pinned there. "Only curious."

"Yeah."

They drove the rest of the way in silence.

FORTY-THREE

John had expected her, but not so fucking quickly. He didn't expect the silver Mercedes either. She had timed it nicely, probably from Henderson's diary. John could imagine that precise little dick taking a note of their comings and goings.

They were all in the milking shed, finishing up. Rab spoke to him over the backside of a cow. "You've got a visitor."

John looked up and saw her standing against the car. She was wearing a yellow outfit. Yellow from top to toe. He wiped his hands on his trousers. "She looks like a fucking banana."

Rab smiled and smacked the cow's arse till it moved. "She's going to wait there till you come out."

"Fine, let her wait."

Rab went out of the shed. He smiled at her but she didn't smile back, instead she said, "Is he in there?"

"Big one or little one?"

"The ugly one."

"Yes, he's in there."

"Would you tell him I'd like to speak to him?"

"Tell him yourself." Rab looked her up and down. "You've got feet like the rest of us."

He moved towards the house, feeling her eyes burning on his back.

She didn't go into the shed. She'd be damned if she would plough through a load of cow muck just to talk to him. He had to come out some time.

She looked into the shed. Its interior was lit brightly with bleaching white work lights. She could see him throwing buckets of water about at the back, then he moved out of view again. He knew she was here. He was just making her wait. Arrogant swine.

She caught herself tapping her foot and stopped it. For a start it was ruining her shoes. What was he *doing* in there? She had the sudden horrible thought that there might be another door and he'd simply escaped out it and left her standing there. She felt her stomach sink. It would be just his idea of a joke. She felt anxiety climb inside her then the lights started to go out. Finally he emerged at the doorway. He looked at her then turned his back to her and pulled the door shut.

She stood there, unsure if he would simply walk past her. She wondered if she ought to cross to him now, meet him half way, but he turned and came over. He was encased in torn yellow waterproofs. His walk was heavy, impeded by outsize wellingtons.

He smiled, big and wolfish, as friendly as a punch in the mouth. It started to rain slightly, as if the sky were just descending on them, grey and damp, like low slung cloud around their faces.

Surprisingly he took a cigarette out. She had not seen him smoke before, had not noticed signs of the smoker about him. No scent, no stains on his fingertips. She remembered Danny had the faint marks of an occasional smoker.

He put it in his mouth without offering her one. He didn't light it. It made him look odd, somehow less sure of himself. She felt her confidence climb a little. "I've come to ask your permission."

He looked at her then took the cigarette out of his mouth. "Not his hand in marriage?"

"If I thought you'd give it to me."

"I wouldn't."

"Then no, not his hand in marriage."

"What then?"

She watched as she saw him fold his cigarette in half and throw it away. He brushed rain out of his eyes. She was being slowly soaked through. "I just want to see him, that's all."

He shook his head. "It's not all, you want to fuck him."

"Must you always be so coarse?"

"I'm only saying it, you did it." He was looking at her now, his face set in that odd carved way, as if something had damaged his facial muscles and he could not express emotion.

"He told you?" She couldn't keep the surprise out her voice. Why all the elaborate covering up if he was going to tell him anyway?

"He always tells me." Delivered in that same flat voice.

"Why?"

He looked at her and now there was a faint hint of a smile ghosting round his mouth. "Because he loves his big brother."

The distaste showed in her face. There was something so claustrophobic about him. No wonder their relationship had triggered off Jimmy's fantasies. At this moment she could have half-believed it herself. She brought the conversation back to the point. "What exactly do you have against me?"

He smiled some more. It seemed to grow worse with each viewing. "Nothing."

"Then why?" she said, feeling her patience slip and trying to hang onto it.

"I don't like sharing him."

She looked at him, frowning. Was he being funny? The smile was like a disguise. She couldn't tell the depth of anything he said. It was like a sheet thrown over every word he spoke. "Why can't you tell me the truth and be done with it?" She could hear the brittle irritation in her voice. The rain was running down her neck. She was beginning to shiver. He was even keeping her out here in the rain deliberately. The man was a pig.

"I have just told you. You weren't listening."

"This is going to go round in circles all day."

He said nothing. His hair was beginning to flatten into dark coils. His face looked oiled. He looked like one of those heavily fanged flat-headed snakes. The smile didn't help.

"Give me a straight answer just this once. I'm tired of this bickering, it's degrading. Why can't I see him?"

He looked at his feet and suddenly she felt the irritation in him, the anger just boiling away under the smile. "Because I say so."

"But *why?*" And this time she stamped her foot in sheer exasperation.

"Because..." he said it slowly, enunciating clearly, "...he's mine."

And this time she did look at his face, really looked at it. "You mean that, don't you?"

He laughed. A small dry sound of cynicism.

"You really are jealous of him having relationships with other people." She saw his face quirk at the words. It infuriated her. "No wonder James thought there was something funny about you. There's a nasty little element of truth in all his sick fantasies, isn't there?"

"I wouldn't know."

"You're obsessed with your own brother."

He was looking at the ground again as if he were bored, impatient to be away. He

wasn't even angered by her accusations. No embarrassment, nothing.

"This is the strangest damn family I've ever met."

"No-one asks you to come here." He looked at her again.

"I *will* see him again."

"I doubt it."

"You can't stop me."

"Don't bet on it."

"What about Danny? Why don't we ask him?"

He smiled then, a nice big new one. "If you think you can afford to put it to the test."

She glared at him then looked away. He was right. Danny was obviously thoroughly intimidated by him. She looked back at him. "I could go to the police."

John shook his head. "You're too late with that one. You're in it up to your neck now. You've hidden evidence, fucked the suspects - no way."

She turned away, face flaming.

John ran his hand over his face, wiping moisture off.

The rain was getting heavier. She could feel the shoulders of her jacket cold against her back. Her hair would be a mess. She was thoroughly fed up. To hell with it. To hell with him. "I'm *going* to see him, whether you like it or not."

He smiled but said nothing. Suddenly he walked away from her, leaving her standing there, threatening the air. "I will!" she shouted to his retreating back.

He disappeared into the house.

She stood there a moment, almost steaming with the heat of her anger, then she brought her fist down on the roof of her car.

"I will," she said, crossing round the front and climbing in. "I bloody will." And she slammed the car back out the yard as if all the fiends of Hell possessed her.

Danny was against the work surface in the kitchen. His trousers were pulled down very low on his belly, leaving him just decent and no more. He held his sweatshirt bunched up in front of him. John could see the curve of his backside against the counter's edge. Old Ostler was stealing surreptitious eyefuls. Rab was sitting at the table smoking, an empty plate in front of him, watching the performance through narrowed eyes. Danny was oblivious to them all, looking down at Ian and cursing him.

"Shut up, it's not my fault."

Danny winced and called him a few more names.

John shut the door with a bang, bringing heads round. "Couldn't you find anywhere more public?"

Danny blinked then looked at Mrs Ostler. She became suddenly occupied at the sink.

John walked into the room and took a deep breath. He hung up his jacket, aware of the tense silence he had created, aware of the old bag listening and recording.

Danny was watching him tightly, his mouth angry. Ian stood there looking into Danny's face, not turning round.

Danny said, "Hurry up, finish it."

Rab watched his eyes challenging John. *Say something you great fat bastard. Go on, say something.* John sat down noisily and concentrated on filling his plate.

Ian began tugging at the bandage again, trying to ease it off. "It's well stuck."

"Shit," Danny hissed again. "You don't say."

"You should have taken it off before now."

"Stop lecturing me, just pull the fucking thing off."

"I can't just pull it off, unless you want half your belly with it."

John got up suddenly, the chair making an ugly scraping sound.

Mrs Ostler stood behind Rab, watching him. Danny was the only one who hadn't looked up. He was watching the tension in Ian's body.

"Let me." John's voice was low, almost oily. Danny looked up and met his eyes. Ian backed off. John took a hold of it with one hand, sliding the other inside Danny's waistband and holding his flesh taut.

Danny tightened the muscles, knowing what he intended to do. He bit on his lip. It was no good, he squealed regardless.

John pulled it savagely, smiling even as he did it. Mrs Ostler moaned out loud at the sight of it.

Danny looked down at the wound, the blood welling immediately. Half his skin was left on the bandage. It began to hurt like all hell. He looked up. "You fucking bastard." It was quietly spoken, but his face was white, drawn with pain.

Rab coughed suddenly, startling himself. He'd been holding his breath. He hacked away convulsively, effectively shattering the moment, but they had all heard it.

Mrs Ostler started banging about, convinced more than ever that John had had a hand in the damage.

John was putting fresh aloe vera on the wound. Danny looked beyond him. Every once and awhile he closed his eyes momentarily under a fresh onslaught of pain. Rab kept watching him, taking any kind of pleasure he could from the animosity between them. He felt like a lovesick teenager, consumed with a desperate longing. He despised himself. He couldn't dress it up. He began to doubt everything he'd ever believed about himself. All those stupid lies to John. He felt like a fake.

He got up suddenly and went out to his tractor. He reversed it up, filled the spreader, went out, but none of it touched him. All he could think about was Danny standing there showing them his neat white belly, the sweet line of his arse, utterly oblivious to their devouring eyes. Daniel in the lion's den.

If only he'd pulled them right down.

He'd kept thinking that even when John had ripped his skin off. Still been thinking it even when he started to bleed.

The worse thing was, another few inches would have done it.

John made them both so uncomfortable they finally got the message and went, Ostler first, Ian last. He put some gauze on the wound and covered it lightly. Danny had let go his shirt and stood waiting with his hands on the counter. John pulled his trousers down, would have hauled them to his knees if Danny hadn't caught at his hands, intercepting him.

John said. "Why not? It's what they all wanted."

"You're full of shit."

"And you're a dumb fuck, standing there practically giving them the full show while they're drooling their guts out, willing you to get them down just an eensy bit more, like kids in a playground."

"Bullshit."

John grabbed his shirt front suddenly with both hands. "And I'm telling you it isn't. Don't you ever put on a performance like that again, not ever, you hear me?"

Danny pulled his trousers up carefully, ducking his head away from John's hands as he bent to retrieve them. "I hear you."

John let him go. "Why is it a bare inch of flesh on you looks like total nudity on someone else?"

Danny said nothing. His expression said it all.

John took a hold of his chin. "You know exactly what I mean, don't you? Standing there looking at me as if you think I'm nuts. You know exactly how it's done. You could

write the book. The Art of Seduction by Daniel Jackson Moore. People would pay a fortune for a fraction of your skill. But of course you have a natural aptitude, don't you? Would you say whores are born, not made?"

Danny kept his mouth shut. John was doing quite well enough for both of them.

"It's being male that does it. People don't expect it. They think they're imagining things. How do you do it without looking like fairy of the month? That's what mystifies me. Even the women, it works just as nicely on them." He shook him, getting angry again. "How did you learn to make it unisex, practice on your mother?"

Danny looked away. "Isn't this a bit past tense John?" He pulled his hands off him. "And she was your mother too."

"You've been leading Ostler on, haven't you?"

"Oh come on."

"Suddenly you're her little pet."

"She's always been like that."

"You must think I'm stupid. You've been winding her up."

"I haven't."

Inevitably it came, as Danny knew it would. John slapped his face. Danny touched his cheek. He felt icy cold.

"What's been going on?"

"For Christ's sake, she's ancient John. What the hell's wrong with you?"

"You're what's wrong with me. What have you been doing?"

Danny looked longingly at the door then got it over with quickly. "She came into the bedroom, day after. She thought I was asleep. She had a look, that was it."

"What did you do?"

"Nothing."

John slapped him again, harder this time.

"Okay, so I teased her a bit."

John stood expectantly.

"Showed her a bit of dick, two second flash, nothing more, I swear."

"Unbelievable."

"She wanted it."

"I'll fucking bet."

"It was no fucking big deal."

John hit him again. "Absolutely fucking anybody."

Danny said nothing. His face was red from the slaps, his right ear singing. His stomach was one big burning wound, the blood slowly seeping through the bandage. It felt as if it was pounding out of him.

"I'll bet you fucking well had it up, didn't you?"

Danny kept on saying nothing.

"Didn't you?"

"She didn't see it all, just an inch or two, that's all."

"But it was up, wasn't it?" he went on relentlessly. He pulled him up against him in a sudden jerk that flared through Danny's stomach. "*Wasn't* it?"

"Yes, it was fucking up. What d'you fucking expect? It was up, okay?"

John pushed him away in disgust, thumping him back against the counter. "You revolt me." Danny closed his eyes, held onto the edge of the counter. "You stinking, lecherous little whore…" *Not in the stomach. Please don't let it be in the stomach.* "You filthy, lying, bitching little whore." And he punched him in the stomach, just as the telephone began to ring.

It was the diary that provided Katherine Henderson with the idea. If it merited the

description of idea. Urge was probably a better word.

Jimmy had meticulously recorded the details of buying his flat or, to be more accurate, the details of the solicitor who had done the conveyance on his flat, one Mr James Conley.

Jimmy had quite literally picked him up. He had been in the high street and had seen a car double parked. No ordinary car, but a 1950's Mercedes. There followed much lyrical prose on this black Teutonic creation, then on Conley himself.

If Jimmy had recorded their conversation accurately then it was a strange one indeed. Conley cool and unfazed, Jimmy... well, Jimmy frankly rather excited by the man's arrogance. When he had let him off with a warning Conley had rather bizarrely given him his card, like some period gentleman, to let him return the favour. And when Jimmy had found this flat he had let Conley return the favour.

Jimmy had seen him often during the house purchase but Conley had resisted all attempts at friendship, perversely, according to Jimmy, unimpressed by either his wealth or his background. He had half-heartedly pursued Conley until the occasion on the road when he had discovered John Jackson Moore and the pretty-boy cousin in flagrante. After that he had other fish to fry. Conley appeared only once more when Jimmy had bumped into him by chance and indulged that evening in more confessional and revelatory prose.

Oddly, about the man himself there was precious little. He was, according to Jimmy, over-educated, whatever that meant, and a snob. Tall, thin, old-fashioned. There was nothing more about his physical appearance other than a lot of incoherent, obscure ramblings.

She closed the book. No long detailed descriptions. She could only deduce, therefore, he was not good-looking, or if he was it had been over-shadowed by his personality, which seemed to consist of arrogance, snobbery and coldness in equal proportions.

However he was clever, and shrewd. Jimmy had been struck by both to the point of repetition, saying constantly that he couldn't understand why he was stuck in a place like this. Conley appeared to have irritated him once by saying he couldn't be a barrister because he had too much sympathy for the criminals and when Jimmy had said, 'Even the murderers?' - she could almost hear him say it - he had said, 'Especially murderers.'

It was the maverick potential of this remark that aroused her interest. She felt that here might be a man who could help her get what she wanted without moral judgements. She needed someone with a dispassionate view of social conventions, a smart, knowledgeable outsider who could run rings around John Jackson Moore.

And buy her Danny.

Or steal her Danny.

After all everyone could be bought… or stolen.

She picked up the phone and traced the numbers off the pasted-in card.

"Hello, Conley, Whymper and Sheard."

"Can I speak to Mr Conley please?"

"Just one moment, I'll see if he's in."

Music came on the line. She pulled a face. She expected this in New York, not here.

"Who's calling please?"

"He wouldn't know me. Katherine Henderson."

"One moment please."

More elevator music. She was trying to identify the much bastardised tune when a voice spoke to her, clear and close in her ear the way telephones sometimes do. "Hello, Miss Henderson."

She made a noise, momentarily thrown.

"James Conley here. I was very sorry to hear about your brother. What can I do for you?"

And that was how it began.

Mrs Ostler was lying on John Jackson Moore's bedroom floor. John Jackson Moore deceased, that is. His bedroom was directly above the kitchen. She had her ear pressed to the floor trying to hear what they were saying, but she could catch practically nothing. Once or twice, when one of them raised their voice. Once John saying something like, 'What have you been doing about it?' and then a bit later shouting very clearly, 'Anybody.' And then Danny shouting, 'Yes it was fucked up...' Then something else she couldn't hear. Then he started getting heavy handed with him again. At first just that mean, low way he spoke to him sometimes then the unmistakable sound of him hitting him. She heard Danny's muffled grunt, then the phone went.

Her heart was hammering as she tried to get up, panic struggling with self-preservation. She went out the door and down the stairs fast as she could go, tugging at her overall, praying she could get to it before he came out.

But he was already standing in the lower hall, hand on the receiver. He picked it up, frowning, looking up at her flushed face. She felt as if it was written all over her. *Eavesdropper.* She felt sure her face must be marked by the carpet. Her hand went up to her cheek.

"Yes?" He frowned harder. "Who wants him?"

She raised her eyebrows. He really could be an obnoxious boy sometimes.

He clunked the phone down without saying anything more and returned to the kitchen.

A moment or two later Danny emerged. He looked terrible, his face red with slap-marks. She had seen too many in her time not to recognise them. He was walking awkwardly, bent, as if his stomach hurt. He looked at her once, face saying nothing. She moved away in the direction of the front parlour. He picked up the phone and slid his back down the newel post until he was sitting on the bottom stair, watching her disappear into the inner hall. "Hello?"

He heard John slam out the back door. He looked at the door to the inner hall standing ajar, then slid his hand inside his sweatpants and began to coax up his little star.

Danny got up and adjusted his trousers. His penis tented obscenely under the loose black fabric.

Mrs Ostler dived quickly into the parlour, her heart racing.

Danny crossed the hall and followed her in. He smiled at her. Her face turned beetroot. He closed the door, leaned against it and pulled his trousers down. His penis came out like a fold-down bed. It should have been funny but it wasn't.

"What are you doing?" She had meant to sound stern but it came out wavery.

"Letting you see it properly."

"Put it away."

"You shouldn't peek."

"I wasn't peeking."

Danny smiled at that. He nodded to the armchair. "Sit down." He touched himself lightly.

"Stop that. Stop it right now."

He ignored her, using both hands to ease the foreskin up. He was much bigger than her husband and growing alarmingly larger. She looked meaningfully at the window, "I could shout for help."

"Go ahead."

Danny began sliding it up and down, watching her all the time. She moved purposefully towards the window, eyes on his hands.

"Why don't you watch me first, then scream?"

His voice sounded so old, way beyond his years. *He's only a boy, he's only a boy.* She kept saying it to herself, chanting it like a mantra.

She stood in front of the window.

"Come on, sit down. It won't hurt you to watch a little."

His smile was so seductive, so *easy*. It warmed your stomach, like taking a drink.

"That's it. You sit there and relax, let me do all the work."

He was one-handed now. She had never seen a man masturbate himself. They had always done their business in the dark, her and her husband. It was better that way. You couldn't see all the silly, ridiculous stuff, all unsightly parts and posturing.

"Let's have some of these off." He stopped a moment and had stripped his clothes off before she had even grasped what he intended to do. He was standing naked in front of her now, cradling his testicles in one hand and that monstrous thing in the other. He opened his legs and braced himself, like the Colossus of Rhodes. "Your very own private performance. Come as close as you like."

She swallowed, didn't look at his face.

"Look, just for you." And he turned side-on, showing its dimensions off. "No, come on, look. It's just between you and me. Want to touch it?" He brought it a little closer.

"*Don't*..." Her voice was almost a shout. "They'll see you. They'll see you at the window." She was seated right before it.

"Well that'll be their lucky day, won't it?" He was squeezing it up and down, painfully tight. "Want to touch it?" He tried to move a little closer again.

She shrank back from him

"That's okay... don't worry... it's okay." He moved back. "See how fat my balls are? I can't even move my dick they're so tight. I'm going to spill all that for you in just... two seconds, in close up. Come closer. Can you see? Christ, it's coming... here it... watch... watch... *watch*..."

She moved forward slightly in her seat, not even blinking. It was all he needed, all he ever needed. The first one hit him like a blow. He swore, thrusting his hips forward, trying to jerk it right up in the air. He pulled his cock violently.

Mrs Ostler felt her face burn, her stomach clench, as she saw the odd spinning streamers of white forced from his hand. He seemed to climax again and again, his face transfigured by it, his whole body working to get it out. He was a monster, a perverted, unnatural monster, not a boy at all.

She lifted her arms to cover her face.

He moved forward to take her hands.

FORTY-FOUR

The rain continued the following day, but it had become sharp and cold with the feeling of sleet or hail following close behind it. A keen wind coming off the sea made it worse.

Katherine Henderson looked out between the curtains at the grey harbour. It was the same colour it had been an hour ago. It was going to be the same colour all day. She left the curtains shut and turned the thermostat up.

She went into the bedroom to dress. She rummaged through the wardrobe and came out with her cream cashmere outfit. It softened her, made her look younger, and was so bland it could offend no-one. She did not want to make statements to Mr Conley, no prejudices. Truth to tell she was rather nervous. She pulled the long sweater on briskly, then the leggings, socks. She rummaged in a cupboard. Flatties.

She spent another twenty minutes choosing and rejecting jewellery.

When she was finished she surveyed the effect in the mirror. She decided she should have worn a bra - the sweater was a little too clingy - but she wasn't going to change now. She looked at her watch and picked her bag off the bed.

She turned the lights off, but left the heating on, and went out.

James Conley had not given much thought to Katherine Henderson since he had spoken to her last. He never conjectured with unknowns.

She had told him practically nothing other than that she wanted to arrange a marriage settlement. He was really too busy to take on a new client but the Henderson family was wealthy. Besides, he was curious. He was a lost cause when he got curious.

He looked at his diary now and thought about Henderson. He got up and crossed to the window, looked down at the river below. Full spate.

His door opened and his secretary came in. "Miss Henderson's here."

He nodded and she went back out. A moment or two later she opened the door again and ushered Katherine Henderson in.

Katherine Henderson looked at the man by the window. His head almost touched the ceiling. He was standing on a step in front of a floor-to-ceiling window which appeared to be French doors leading to nowhere, other than straight down to the river. He smiled. "Loading doors. The crane's still on the wall there to the left. The building used to be a mill."

"Oh," she said, which could have meant anything.

"Sit down." He gestured to the chair opposite him.

She realised she was staring. She flushed and sat down. He came down off the step. He didn't look any shorter - the ceiling was too low for him - but at least his head wasn't brushing the roof any more.

He was quite the oddest looking man she'd ever seen. Thin to the point of cadaverousness, cancerous-looking, with colourless dirty blonde hair and dirty blonde eyes. Yes, tawny, dirty blonde eyes. He reminded her of those little sand shrimps you don't see till they dart away from under your foot. Only he wasn't little.

He was even wearing a sand gold waistcoat with a gold watch chain against a funereal black suit. Both watch chain and waistcoat looked as if they might be antique.

"Sorry?" He'd asked her a question and she hadn't been listening.

He smiled. His teeth were spacey, unhealthy looking, as if he smoked too much or

drank too much coffee. They were crammed with fillings.

"What can I do for you?" he repeated. His hand was toying with an ornate pen lying on the desk, gold and tortoiseshell, another antique. Mr Conley was either an antiquarian or a poseur.

"It's rather difficult to explain," she began and realised it was a bad way to start.

He looked at her in what was probably his version of encouraging. Unfortunately, it merely looked cynical.

"I've.." She stopped again. She had been going to say, fallen in love, but it was neither true nor the kind of thing you said to a man like him. She tried again. "I've met someone I want to marry. However, his family disapproves and won't give consent."

Conley smiled again. She noticed only one side of his mouth moved. It made him look supercilious. Jimmy's lurid imaginings took on a warped kind of reality when she saw it. It made her uncomfortable, as if she knew something secret about him.

"Unusual, isn't it? The man having to get consent? Is there an inheritance involved?"

"No," she said carefully. "But he's very young."

"How very?"

She flushed. "He's just turned twenty."

"Old enough to make up his own mind I'd have thought."

She bit her lip, stopped herself. "His brother thinks he's too young for me, and frankly he's afraid of his brother."

"His brother?"

"Yes, there's no father, he's disappeared."

"Disappeared?"

She frowned. Conley sat up, realising he was echoing everything she said. "I'm sorry, it just sounds odd. Do go on."

"What I want to do is settle some money on my..." she hesitated again, "on the young man."

He looked up at her quickly then down at his desk again.

"So that he doesn't have to be beholden to his brother."

"I see." He said the words but he doubted if he did. It all sounded highly unlikely and she was too uncomfortable. He cleared his throat. "Forgive me asking, but you're quite sure you're not being ripped off?"

She looked at him blankly.

"You've considered the possibility that the elder brother is withholding consent deliberately in order to increase the settlement?"

She surprised him by laughing, genuinely, as if she found the idea incredibly funny. "Quite sure. His brother wouldn't take a penny from me, supposing he was dying of starvation."

"Really?" He looked sceptical.

"Oh yes, really."

"I take it they're wealthy in their own right then?"

"I very much doubt it. They're farmers."

"Farmers..." He said it almost speculatively, as if trying the sound of it. Behind it she could detect a faint note of something indefinable. "I take it your fiancée knows you intend to settle this money on him?" He took nothing of the kind but he wanted to hear it from her.

"No, he doesn't. He's been forbidden to see me."

He looked at her, wondering what kind of life she expected with such a husband. Of course, maybe she didn't actually intend to *marry* him. Maybe he was good in bed, or maybe she just liked paying for it, added a frisson. Either way it was her business. "How much do you intend to give him?"

"As much as it takes."

He smiled up at her again, the same lopsided smile. "To get him away from his brother?"

"Yes."

"You're sure you couldn't buy the brother instead?" His look was level.

She flushed slightly at his choice of words but she met his eyes. "I'm positive."

"It could be preferable, certainly easier."

"No, he won't part with him."

He quirked an eyebrow, studied his pen again. An odd expression to choose. "But you think your fiancée will be more amenable?"

"I hope so."

She didn't sound any too confident.

"And if he isn't?"

"I'll have to think of something else."

"Do you want any conditions on the money?"

She looked at him perplexedly. "I don't know what you mean."

He shrugged. "He has to marry you within a certain length of time, or make out a will naming you as legatee, that sort of thing. Or that if you separate he forgoes all claims on the money."

She thought about it. "No, other than that he must come and live with me immediately and not see his brother again."

He looked up at her. "Will he agree to that?"

"Why shouldn't he?"

He smiled. "I take it then that there's no love lost between them?"

She hesitated. "He's afraid of him."

He studied her face. *And that doesn't really answer my question, does it?* Still, it was her business.

He swivelled his chair suddenly and picked up his pen, pulling open a drawer and dragging out a large battered diary. "Well..." He scribbled something like a doctor writing a prescription. "We'll see what we can do. First we'll have to talk to him, see how best to approach him."

"He won't come to you."

He looked over the desk at her. The pen in his hand may have been an antique, but his desk was split new. "No?"

She shook her head. "Absolutely not. You'll have to go to him."

He raised his eyebrows. "I'll be frank, that's very inconvenient. Do they live nearby?"

"Brixby. It's on the Carlisle road, just outside Ellenport."

He grunted. Almost an hour's drive.

"I'm quite happy to pay extra for any inconvenience," she said coolly.

He smiled at her, rubbing the bridge of his nose. "Of course, let's see..." he flicked a few pages, "we'll make some time." He looked up again. "Have you got a phone number, for your fiancée?"

"Yes." She rummaged in her bag, gave him the number.

He jotted it in the diary then on one of his own cards and slipped it into his pocket. "I've got business of my own in Carlisle tomorrow. We'll see if we can't kill two birds with one stone, see how the land lies, before you spend any more money."

"Thank you."

"Ah, almost forgot, what's your fiancée's name?"

"Daniel Jackson Moore."

He frowned. "Now, that rings a bell." After a moment he shook his head. "No. It'll come to me. With a hyphen?"

"I really don't know."

He grunted again, jotted it down. "It's definitely familiar." He shook his head again. "Not to worry, it'll come." He wrote down some more bits and pieces in what looked like shorthand and then shut the diary with a whump. "Okay, that's fine. I'll let you know what your fiancée says a.s.a.p. - have I got your number?"

"I left it yesterday, with your secretary."

"Right-ho." He stood up then came round his desk to show her to the door. She half expected him to bow and click his heels.

He said goodbye again, rather formally, but noticeably without offering his hand, and ushered her out.

It was still raining as she climbed into her car and backed out of the car park.

He reminded her of someone. She turned it over in her head, reversing out of the tight space. "Of *course*," she said out loud.

She had once seen a soft porn film set in a brothel during the war complete with debonair Nazi officers. That's what he looked like, Hollywood's idea of a decadent Nazi.

She laughed to herself and flicked on the indicators. Well let's hope he behaved like one too. Give Piltdown man something to think about.

She turned onto the coast road and switched on the radio.

Danny was sweeping water down the central drain when John came back into the shed. Everything was shiny and dripping wet. A hose lay coiling water in an arc on the floor.

Danny turned it off. The rain became audible again. Heavy, bad-tempered bursts broken by soft pattering silences. John slid the door shut. Only half the work-lights were on, creating an odd illusion as he moved up the shed towards him. He seemed to appear and disappear as he passed from light to shadow, like a ghost flickering in and out of life. "When's your appointment?"

"Two." Danny leant the brush against the wall.

John moved forward, put his hands inside Danny's jacket. "You fell asleep on me last night." His hands were pulling his shirt out of his sweat pants.

"Don't act it, you've had yours."

"One bleary-eyed effort at half-six?" His hands were cold inside his shirt. Danny came up in goosepimples. "Hold your trousers."

Danny kept a hold on the waist band of his sweatpants as John slid them down to his thighs. The air was chill on his skin. John was undoing his shirt. "I like these pants, quick and easy."

Danny laughed, a low sound.

"Only you could look good with your trousers round your arse, in wellingtons and a filthy old jacket, in the middle of a stinking cow shed."

Danny smiled some more.

John kissed his mouth gently. "Why didn't she come in today?"

Danny didn't bother pretending not to know who he meant. "I don't know."

John was fondling him idly, without any real intent, occasionally pressing against him, more often stepping back to admire him. Twice he kissed his neck with an odd soft threatening pressure. "I phoned old man Ostler. He says she's 'Not well'."

Danny made a non-committal noise.

"She wouldn't get up this morning. In fact, Ostler says, she lay in bed crying. First time he'd seen her do that in years, he says."

Danny finally met his eyes. "What's it got to do with me?"

"You tell me."

"She left yesterday as normal, that's all I know."

"You said she went early."

"That's what I meant."

"And she said nothing to you about feeling ill?"

Danny's mouth grew tight. "I wouldn't be making it up."

"Wouldn't you?" Danny could feel the hot grip of John's hand. He was being rough with him, warning him. Danny felt it curl in his stomach. He outstared him.

John smiled suddenly. "Don't mess with her Danny, she's an old woman. You ought to have some scruples, even if you've no taste."

"I didn't touch her."

"Oh, you never touch anyone. You make them touch you. It's a trick you learnt years ago. It keeps your conscience bright and shiny."

Danny looked away.

John laughed softly. "Why do you always treat me as if I'm stupid?"

Danny didn't answer. John's hand was moving on him relentlessly, a steady pistoning rhythm. Danny made a small sound in his throat, saw his own knuckles white against the black trousers.

They stood in the shadows, but when Danny looked back up into his eyes, even in the half-darkness, he could see it there, knew that he could have reamed Ostler with a cucumber and John would still come crawling back to him.

"Always fucking smiling Danny. Think you've got us all taped up, don't you?"

"I know it." His voice was a caress in the dark, like a brush of heat across John's face.

John kissed him, deep and hard, one hand pulling his head to his. He freed his mouth and whispered, "Come in my hand."

Danny laughed softly. "I can't just do it on demand."

"You know damn well you can. Do it."

"Right now?" The words slid in John's ear like hot black poison.

He managed to grunt something like yes.

He felt it almost immediately rise up under his fingers. He grabbed Danny close. It was too soon. *Not yet.*

"For you," Danny grunted and John felt the first hot seep of it surge over his hand.

"*Wait...*" he said fiercely, gripping him angrily, almost as if he was trying to stifle it before it started.

"You can't..." Danny gasped as another suffering pulse forced its way between John's fingers, "stop..." Danny's voice cracked, John's hand was already slick with it, "...*me.*" And the last one made him drop his head back, weight slack in John's arm.

John devoured his throat, stabbing against him. "You liar, you cheat, you mean little..." He humped against him, "Fuck... Oh *fuck*..." holding Danny like a rag doll, riding against him, feeling it jolt out of himself, his hand feverishly rolling Danny's penis across his sweater, smearing Danny's semen over himself, wishing he could bathe in it.

Danny stood there, still holding his trousers, utterly ruined by the speed of it. He had not touched John once. He had done nothing.

They heard the door rumble back. John's head jerked up. "*Shit...* just a minute!"

Danny stayed as he was and looked over John's shoulder. "It's okay, it's only Ian."

"Christ, the fright..." John half-turned, trying to hide himself. Danny stood there, not attempting to cover up.

Ian peered up the shed at them, half-hidden in the darkness, but not hidden enough. Danny was still standing there with it hanging out. And fucking John, look at him, terrified in case he saw something. Jesus what a fucking pair. He felt it gnaw at him like a fat parasitic leech chewing his gut. He looked straight into Danny's eyes.

"You're wanted on the phone."

Danny smiled at him.

John moved in front of him, blocking Ian's view, saying, "Get your clothes on." His voice was hard.

Danny pulled his trousers up. John stepped away from him, aware that his hands were covered in it. It was all over his sweater. He took a handkerchief out. Danny was fastening his shirt. John became aware suddenly that Ian was still standing there, watching them. "Seen enough?"

"I think I should have got here a bit sooner. I missed the best part."

"Don't fucking cry."

"What would I have to cry about? My time will come."

John could almost feel Danny's pause behind him. "Who wants him?" John demanded, making the question carry all the answers he'd like to have given.

"Someone called Connolly."

John looked back at Danny for explanation, but Danny only shrugged, tucking his shirt in, then sliding past him and making his way down the shed to where Ian stood. John stayed where he was, not intending to let Ian see the state of his clothes. No free masturbation material.

Ian stopped Danny by the arm as he made to go past him, inclined his head to whisper in his ear, "You feeble little fuck."

Danny yanked his arm away. "Fuck off."

John saw it but was too far back to hear what was said. He saw Danny move off ahead of him into the house, Ian following a step or two behind, like a vicious dog just waiting for a chance to snap.

John wiped the worst of it off his sweater then covered it with his jacket and followed them out.

Danny lifted the receiver from the hall table. "Hello?"

Bingo, Conley thought, at last. "Hello, is that Daniel Jackson Moore?"

"Yes."

Conley frowned. The voice wasn't right. Too deep, too old. If he was twenty he'd been smoking since he was ten. "I wonder if I might discuss a private matter with you Mr Moore..."

"Jackson Moore," Danny corrected.

Conley swung his chair round to face the window. The rain was running down it in thick green streams of light. It felt like being in an aquarium. "I do beg your pardon," he apologised.

"What kind of matter? Who are you?"

"Well..." Conley picked up his pen and ran his thumb along the skin of it, warm, worn, his grandfather's. "It's rather difficult to explain over the phone. Could I possibly call to see you? I'm passing your way today. Say half four, if that's convenient?"

"What the hell's all this about?"

Tenacious little bastard, and if he's twenty I'm a Tyrolean mountain goat. "It really would be better if I could explain it to you personally."

"Well that's your tough luck because I'm due in hospital today at two..." There was a sudden pause and when he spoke again it was as if he'd had an abrupt change of mind. "I'm leaving here in an hour's time. If you can make it in that time then fine, if not..." He left it unspoken.

Conley looked at his watch. He would have to go like hell to get there. No lunch. Ridiculous. "Fine," he said. "Perhaps I could drive you to the hospital, give us a chance to talk?"

"I've got to get back as well." His tone was almost sarcastic.

"I'd be happy to," Conley heard himself saying.

"Suit yourself." And Daniel Jackson Moore hung up on him.

Conley looked at the receiver and put it down slowly. He picked the pen off his desk and began to doodle on his blotter. No lunch, a surly toy-boy for company, and a whole afternoon wasted in a hospital for *which* he would have to cancel appointments.

He dropped the pen and swivelled in his seat again. God, it was even raining. He flicked on the intercom and stirred up a little discontent.

His car was frozen as always. He'd put his overcoat on, but he was still cold and wet. His secretary was piqued. She'd been left to do the explaining.

He smiled again at his own vagaries. Well, he'd charge Miss Henderson plenty for the privilege. Let's say he was satisfying his curiosity at someone else's expense.

He turned up the antiquated heater. It blasted more cold air into the interior. *Hurry up*.

The engine moved with beauty beneath him.

He forgave his car everything.

Danny went into the kitchen. Ian was opening cans for their lunch. "Who is he?"

Danny shook his head. "Christ knows."

Ian wiped his hands on his trousers. "What did he want?" He looked curiously at Danny's face.

"He wants to talk to me about 'A private matter'."

"Eh?"

"Yeah, but I'll tell you something, you can bet your boots it's that bitch up to something."

"Who? Henderson's sister?"

"Yeah."

John came in. "What about Henderson's sister?"

Ian turned back to his cans, emptying them into a pot and transferring them to the cooker.

"She's got some bloke coming round to see me."

"When?"

"Now. He's offered to take me to the hospital."

John frowned, suddenly angry. "What *is* this?"

"I don't know, don't look at me."

Then Rab came in. "The pick-up's fucked again. You're really going to have to get someone to take a look at it."

"Well that's handy, I suppose," John said.

"What? That the pick-up's fucked?"

"That Danny-boy here's got a lift for this afternoon."

Rab looked at him quickly. He hadn't really expected to go with him, but it was nice to live in hope. "Who?"

"Some tame animal belonging to Henderson's sister."

"*Who?*"

John shrugged. "Don't ask. More bloody twists and turns. Maybe she's sending someone to kidnap him. Maybe my little brother dropped a few hints." John's voice was growing systematically more angry. Ian stopped what he was doing to look at him.

Danny got up from his chair. "Why don't you shut up?"

There was a silence you could have folded up and made into blankets, then John stalked across the room and went out, slamming the door reverberantly behind him.

"Smart work Danny," Ian said.

"Fuck off."

Danny sat back down and realised he was shaking. Ian turned back to the stove.

Rab came round the table and hunkered down quickly beside him. He lifted Danny's hand and kissed the palm.

Danny jerked his hand away. His whisper was sharp and venomous. "Fucking leave off."

Rab straightened up. Ian looked over his shoulder at them curiously.

The soup boiled over, filling the room with the smell of gravy browning.

Upstairs John threw his clothes in the work basket.

Fucking cheeky little bastard.

He pulled on fresh jeans, a clean sweater.

First he fucks with Ostler, now he's got some paid monkey chauffeuring him to the bloody hospital. She'll be sending him fucking flowers next. The cheeky *little bastard.*

He went back out and down to the kitchen. Ian was serving up soup in the sullenly silent room.

They ate their meal as if it was poison, in an atmosphere that was nearly terminal with dislike.

When the front door bell rang they all looked at each other as if they didn't know what it was. Danny couldn't remember the last time someone had come to the front door, unless it was the Mormons.

It rang again.

"*Jesus…*" John said, getting up. "Jesus H. *Christ.*" And he went out to answer it.

When John opened the door Conley could see immediately how she would be attracted to him. He was the archetypal he-man, unusually tall for these parts, and exactly the non-cerebral creature she would take a letch for. "Mr Jackson Moore?"

John nodded.

Conley smiled. "I'm James Conley."

John continued to stare at him. It was a disturbing stare, Conley had to admit, if only because there was such a lot of muscle behind it, all unfriendly.

"I'm afraid I'm a bit early." Conley realised abruptly he was *not* going to get through the door. "I'll wait in the car for you."

The smile when it came was utterly unexpected. It was worse than his dour scowl. All teeth, like a piranha. "You do that." And he shut the door in Conley's face.

Conley turned and pushed his hands in his pockets. They didn't have many visitors, if the path was anything to judge by. Thick moss grew over the stones. No-one ever walked on it. He went out the gate and back to his car.

He turned the engine on to keep the heat coming. He fixed the tails of his coat. Twenty? She must have been drunk when he told her that one. Either that or she simply wanted to believe it. And that being intimidated by anyone was a laugh. His elder brother must be Attila the Hun. She wanted to marry that? It could only be for his looks.

He stopped, tapped his nails on the steering wheel.

Was he good-looking? Could anyone describe that as good-looking?

He rummaged in his pocket for his cachous. He popped one in his mouth, then another.

Twenty. He snorted to himself. She looked too bright for that.

He looked at his watch, wondering how long he'd keep him waiting. He looked at the sky from his side window. It began to rain, slow fat drops, then heavier until it turned into a downpour. Let's hope he'd fixed the leak. Well it would certainly test it. He ran his fingers under the sill. The rough fabric felt cold over the metal. He stuck his head under the steering wheel, felt with his fingers. Seemed okay, all dry.

There was a violent tapping at the window. He jerked his head up and banged it on the steering column. "*Damn.*"

He reached over and opened the passenger door, tears blurring his eyes.

An angel flew, glittering, into his car.

"Jesus, it's fucking *pouring* out there." Danny shook his head, scattering everything with drops of water. He was charged with icy air and shimmering with water. To Conley he almost seemed to scintillate. Some kind of odd trick caused by the thundery light perhaps. He shook himself again, more than half a shiver.

Conley stared at him, rubbed his eyes, trying to focus on what he was seeing, utterly nonplussed.

Danny ran his hands through his hair, shook himself again - this time it *was* a shiver - and then he looked at Conley. He wiped his cheeks with the heels of his hands, fanning them outwards, watching him all the while. The moment grew too long, became uncomfortable. "We going?" Danny frowned at him. Weird, very weird. The car looked like a hearse and its owner looked like an undertaker.

"*You're* Daniel Jackson Moore."

Danny pondered that one. "Who else?"

That voice.

"Then that was your brother I spoke to, who answered the door."

"Yes." Danny was confused, a little irritated.

That voice, it was him alright.

"Are we going or not? My appointment's at two."

Conley jumped as if he'd poked him with a stick. "Of course, yes." He started the car.

The dashboard was a thing of almost rustic simplicity. Danny quirked a brow at it. "Weird car."

"Thank you." Conley pulled out into the traffic.

Danny smiled and looked out the window. He ran his hand along the chair edge. *Real leather seats. Well, okay.*

Conley was angry at himself. She said twenty, she meant twenty. He shot a glance at the real Daniel Jackson Moore. This he could understand. This was the sort of thing you could see someone wanting to buy. Cast him in bronze and he'd buy one too. He looked at him again. No, perhaps not. And that lump was his brother? It got better. He'd missed lunch for this.

"You're from Henderson's sister, aren't you?"

Conley flicked another glance at him. *Henderson's sister? Terms of endearment it wasn't.* "Yes," he said, there not being much else to say.

"What does she want now?"

Curiouser and curiouser. "To marry you." He tried that for news value.

"What?" Daniel Jackson Moore turned to stare at him. It had news value alright. *Oh Miss Henderson, I've got a bone to pick with you.*

"She wants to marry you."

"Oh Jesus."

He seemed more despairing than anything else. Anyone would have thought

Conley had just told him he'd been cut out of a will.

"In fact, she's willing to pay you to marry her." That's what it boiled down to, might as well say so.

"Pay me? *Pay me?* Is she off her head?"

I'm beginning to think so. Either that or I am. He said, "As much money as you like."

"And who are you? What's all this got to do with you?"

"I'm her solicitor." *In more ways than one.*

The boy made a noise that smacked rather uncomplimentarily of disgust, then he was silent.

Conley glanced at his profile again. His face was tense, white, with two hectic spots of red, for all the world as if he'd had a bad shock. Whatever this was it was knee-deep in dirt and complications, like those messy divorces Sheard revelled in. The boy looked at him suddenly. "You can tell her to get stuffed."

"You're not interested I take it?" Conley couldn't help smiling.

"Too right."

"Even supposing she offers you half a million?" Conley had no right naming sums but he didn't think it would matter. Idle curiosity must be satisfied.

"Not even for a full million."

He raised his eyebrows. "And I was told you were afraid of your brother."

Daniel Jackson Moore laughed, an odd deep little sound without much humour in it. "Oh I am."

Conley looked at him sharply but he was looking out the window as if he'd never said it. Conley didn't know quite how to word his next question so he tried, "Forgive me asking, but you're not in love with Miss Henderson?"

He aired that same cynical little laugh.

"I know this sounds very impertinent but I would like to be clear for the sake of my client. It's not a question of you being afraid of your brother but rather an extreme disinclination to go to Miss Henderson, is that right?"

Danny was watching him now, a smile growing on his face. "You've got it."

"And you would like me to tell her to get stuffed?"

Danny laughed. Conley kept the same deadpan face, his educated, almost robotic, voice putting no inflection in the words at all.

"That's it."

"Fine. Now we know where we stand." Conley popped another two cachous in his mouth and concentrated on the road.

Conley came into the hospital with him on the premise that it would be warmer than his car. Danny led him on a labyrinthian trip of the corridors. They spoke very little. Conley suddenly wondered why he'd come to the hospital. He looked indecently healthy. He voiced it, risking that he wasn't being either impolite or tactless. "What are you here for?"

Danny was checking numbers and arrows on the walls. Had he taken a wrong turning? He held out his left hand to Conley. An ugly wound like a tightly pursed mouth sat in the centre of his palm. It reminded Conley of those lurid Indian paintings of prophets with seeing eyes in their hands. Only this might be a talking mouth. "How did you do it?"

Danny veered off suddenly. Conley had to run slightly to catch up with him. "I didn't."

Conley looked at his back. "It's a knife wound, isn't it?" He drew abreast of him.

Danny made a noise that might have been a yes, or then again it might not. Conley

felt he was walking close to the edge of being told to mind his own business. He backed off a little. "Some problem healing?" The wound still looked raw to him.

"No feeling in one fingertip." Danny stopped suddenly and turned to face him. Conley came to an abrupt halt. Danny reached up and brushed his first two fingers along Conley's cheek. Conley went rigid. The boy's face was smiling at him. It looked almost puckish, elfin, vaguely unpleasant. "With this one I can feel you a little..." He held up his first finger. "With this...." he held up his second finger, "I can't feel you at all."

Conley blinked. Danny smiled wider then he turned and went up to a window in a partition wall. Conley backed into a row of seats and sat down. He stared at Danny's back. If he didn't know better he'd say he'd just been flirted with.

Or something.

Danny was called in straight away.

"Well hello." It was the same nurse, the one with the smile. Danny smiled back at her.

She told him to take off his jacket and roll up his sleeve. She made some odd markings with a blue pencil, stood back, and x-rayed the back of his hand. She came back and turned his hand over, holding his fingertips lightly, a little too long.

The doctor came in. It was the same doctor too. He had to be setting some kind of record here. "Hello. It's Danny, isn't it?"

The fatherly approach seemed faintly ridiculous coming from someone who was only about twenty-five himself but Danny said yes it was. The nurse was rolling down Danny's sleeve.

"Let's have a look then. Come through."

They went through to his room and he pulled a chair up so that they sat knee to knee. Danny smiled at him. He smiled back then took Danny's hand, felt it, prodded it, made him wiggle it, told him off for not protecting it properly. Did he want to die of blood poisoning? Finally he pricked each of Danny's fingertips. "Still nothing in that one?"

Danny shook his head.

"Well, we'll leave it a bit longer, see how it goes. But not so stiff now, eh?"

"No."

"You can grip alright with it?"

Danny's mouth quirked. The doctor looked at him, vaguely unsettled. What an odd boy he was. He moved his seat back so they were no longer touching.

"Yes fine," Danny managed.

"Good." The doctor nodded. "Need any more cream?"

"No, I've got plenty."

"Fine," the doctor said again then shrugged his hands. "Well, that's us. Make an appointment for another six weeks time. That should do it, there's no hurry."

"Okay." Danny stood up. He looked the doctor in the face and smiled again. The doctor smiled back uncertainly then looked away. Danny went out.

Conley stood up when he saw him come back out. He glanced at his watch. Not much more than half an hour. Fastest hospital visit he'd ever had. Maybe the Jackson Moores had connections. He put his overcoat back on. A long heavy black woollen undertakers' job. He'd bought it in a Salvation Army shop in Inverness, God bless it.

"Coming?" The boy neither avoided his gaze nor looked at him with any special significance. He seemed quite relaxed, unperturbed. There was nothing there.

Conley moved into step behind him wondering if he'd imagined the whole scenario. But men simply didn't touch each other. They didn't do it - and he wasn't imagining that.

It looked like a different route to Conley but they got out all the same. The rain had momentarily abated but the sky was a dull grey-green, almost as if it would snow.

Danny stopped suddenly by Conley's car, frowning at it. He turned. "It's a Mercedes, isn't it?"

Conley said, "Yes."

"Fucking weird looking Mercedes." He ran his hand along it. Conley found himself thinking, He only has an imperfect feel of that surface. How odd.

"It's an original, German."

"They all are, aren't they?"

"No, I mean it was bought there. I brought it here."

Danny nodded vaguely then looked at him. "Are we getting in?"

Conley was flustered again. He opened Danny's door with the key. He could feel the boy too close to him, invading his space, deliberately ignoring the rules of how much room we leave each other. It was disturbing and faintly menacing. He didn't need to look at him to know he'd be smiling. He backed off and went round the rear of the car to the driver's seat.

Danny was rummaging in his pocket when he got in, once more as if Conley wasn't really there.

"Do you mind if I do a little business while we're here? I'll only be a few minutes."

"Sure," Danny answered, looking out the window. Conley felt sure if he'd said, Do you mind if I kill a few pygmies while we're here? he'd have said sure in exactly the same way. He was really saying, Do what you like. Who cares?

Conley started the car, wishing he'd never agreed to this. The sooner he could drop this psychopathic oddity the better. He decided he'd charge Katherine Henderson double.

"Did you know James Henderson then?" Conley asked, mentally frowning at himself. What the hell was it to him?

"Mm." Uncooperative again. Stay out. Stay off.

"Well?"

"You could say that." He was still staring out the window.

Conley turned the heater up a bit more. What the hell did that mean? "His murder must have been a shock to you."

"No."

Conley looked at him quickly. He was dead serious. "No?"

Danny turned to him this time. "That's what I said, no."

Conley looked back at the road again. "Why not?"

"I'm psychic, I saw his death in a vision. I also hear the voice of God regularly every Tuesday."

Conley laughed, vaguely relieved. "In other words, mind my own business."

Danny turned back to the window and said nothing.

"Is that how you met Katherine Henderson?"

Danny looked back at him. "You don't give up, do you?"

"Lawyers and journalists - it's a sickness."

"You married?"

Conley was thrown by the sudden question. "No."

"How old are you?"

"Thirty-eight... I think."

"Almost twice my age."

Conley laughed humourlessly, not sure what the observation meant. "Thank you."

Danny considered him. "You don't look it."

Conley shot him a glance, but the boy's face was thoughtful, seemingly serious. "You don't look any age particularly," he elaborated.

"You mean I look ageless."

Danny's mouth grew tight. "I mean you don't look any age in particular." He looked away again.

Conley realised he'd offended him by correcting him. He cleared his throat. "Did you like him?"

"Who?" His answer was clipped, still angry.

"Henderson."

"No."

He was certainly emphatic, nothing indecisive about him. Conley wondered if he'd been so certain of everything at twenty. "Why not?"

Danny turned quickly. "What is this? The fucking third degree?"

"Sorry." Conley shrugged. "I've got bad curiosity problems."

"Well keep them to yourself."

"Sorry," Conley said again. He flicked a surreptitious glance at him but he was looking away again. He turned the heater down a notch. He saw the boy's head move a fraction, watching his hand. He drew his hand back and the boy looked away again, but he knew he'd seen it.

He pulled into the car park and waited for the barrier to go up. He leaned out and paid the man, rolled his window back up. He drove up the ramp to the third floor and found an almost empty row.

"Would you like to come with me or would you prefer to stay here?" He was surprised to hear himself offer. It was a day full of surprises, mostly of his own making.

"Where are you going?"

"Surveyors. I won't be long if you want to wait."

"No. I'll come with you. These places depress me."

He swung out of the car and was standing with his hands shoved deep into his leather jacket when Conley went round to lock his door. This time the boy kept his distance.

Conley led the way across the oily concrete. The air was heady, heavily fumed, warm. He felt aware of the head-down figure beside him. He wanted to ask him what he was thinking. He was utterly bemused by his own reactions. What the hell did he care what the boy was thinking? He gave into it. "What are you thinking?"

"What?" Danny looked up at him, eyes wary.

"You seemed very absorbed." Conley tried smiling.

"I was wondering if I had any clean socks."

Conley laughed. "Mind my own business a new way. Right?"

Danny looked at him as Conley held the door open for him. "Why aren't you married?"

Conley blinked, realised Danny had passed through and let the door go. "Why?" he repeated.

Danny nodded. Conley realised he was waiting for him to lead the way. Conley started walking away briskly. Danny followed him.

"I don't know. Because I never met anyone I wanted to marry?"

Danny looked at him and Conley noticed for the first time his eyes were green, a hard definite green, like bottle-glass or emeralds. The boy was hand-painted, that's what he was. The look held. "Did *you* know Henderson?"

"Briefly," Conley nodded. "I did his property conveyance for him."

"And did *you* like him?" There was a nasty, sticky little emphasis on the 'like'.

Conley looked at him. "To be honest, not much. I found him claustrophobic." Well

396

that was one word for it, he supposed. Conley looked at him again. He was smiling. Conley frowned. It was a knowing, disjointed little smile, saying too much too quickly, with no time to read it. Conley realised he was holding his breath, waiting to hear what he'd say.

"Where are we going?"

Conley rubbed his forehead in sudden irritation. The boy's changes of direction were intensely irritating. "Just across the way."

They ducked in and out across the pedestrian precinct until they reached another road. Conley impulsively caught at his elbow as the boy made to step out in front of an oncoming car. He let go immediately and had to fight the urge to wipe his hand on his coat. The boy didn't even seem to have noticed. He could still feel the warm skin of his jacket on his palm. He surreptitiously put his hand in his pocket and wiped it on his handkerchief.

Conley went into the office and was greeted by the receptionist. She looked at Danny and Conley watched with amusement as she did another take. The boy was studying the aerial photographs on the wall. The girl buzzed for Sharpe to let him know Conley was in reception and sat chatting to him, but her attention kept being irresistibly drawn to the boy.

Danny turned suddenly and caught her staring. Conley saw the whole thing with sudden and tremendous clarity. Every single move had been deliberate. She looked away, intensely embarrassed.

Sharpe came in and began talking to Conley. Conley felt almost guilty leaving her victim to the boy's presence. She was like a bird trapped by a hawk. Conley tried to concentrate on what Sharpe was saying to him but he could see the boy out the corner of his eye, performing an almost ritual circling until he was close to her desk. She looked up at him finally and he smiled at her. She smiled back. Conley dragged his eyes away. The boy was a practised seducer, as sophisticated and dangerous as a man twice his age, and almost supernatural in his instincts.

He hurried Sharpe along but he needn't have bothered. The boy had lost interest. He was sitting in the chair, oblivious to the receptionist's blatant attempts to attract his attention again. Conley looked at him with distaste. He had been playing games with her, like a cat testing its hunting skills by slowly frightening an animal to death. He was a mindless predator.

Danny looked up at him suddenly as if he was aware of what he was thinking. This time there were no smiles. He rubbed the palm of his left hand softly against his thigh, holding Conley's eyes all the time. Conley walked past him, jerking his head for him to follow. Danny looked at his back and got up.

He went out without looking at the receptionist.

She surprised everyone by bursting into tears half an hour later, slap bang in the middle of her coffee break.

Conley walked on ahead of him. This one was as dangerous as a cage full of tigers, a born trouble-maker. How Katherine Henderson could even think of having anything to do with him he didn't know. She must be off her head.

"We in a race or something?" Danny interrupted his furious internal monologue.

"I want to get home before the traffic starts."

Danny smiled and moistened his lips.

"What's so funny?" Conley snapped.

"Nothing."

"You get a kick out of treating people like that?"

"Like what?" He was still smiling.

"That girl, you were teasing her."

"It doesn't hurt."

"You maybe, what about her?"

Danny looked at him curiously. "You related or something?"

Conley flushed and clamped his mouth shut.

They got back to the car park in record time. Conley felt furious about feeling furious. He couldn't remember when he'd last been angry let alone furious. Flirting with him, he hadn't imagined it, it's what he'd been doing.

Conley stopped at his side of the car, surprised to be there. He looked across the roof at him. The boy looked back through the thick gloom. The air was headachy, the fumes denser. Now there were no smiles, nothing, just watching. Slowly the boy leaned his arms on the roof, waiting patiently for Conley to come out and say it, as if he knew what he was thinking. Conley glared across at him. He was messing up his head. The boy looked back, unmoving, then scratched the back of his hand. Conley said, "What are you waiting for?" and his voice came out odd and fragile.

The boy didn't smile at him, or crawl over him with those dirty eyes, he simply said, "For you to let me in."

He had no idea how he got him home. They didn't speak a single word to each other. The rain came on again and, worse, it grew dark.

They were enclosed together in that warm dark space, the rain swishing under the wheels, the lights dancing on the road, the water sluicing rhythmically off the screen. Conley felt each moment like an hour. He had never wanted to be free of someone's company as much in his life. And the boy just lay there, low down in the seat, with his eyes half-closed, watching the rain, hardly ever moving, hardly even breathing. Conley wanted to open the door and push him out.

He was mad, bad and dangerous to know.

Finally they arrived at the boy's home.

He sat up in his chair slowly, as if he was half-asleep. He zipped up his jacket and went to open the door.

"Wait," Conley said. He could feel his heart thumping. The boy didn't turn to him. He sat there waiting, unnaturally patient, making it look insolent, as if he was bored with interminable and tedious questions. "Was Henderson a homosexual?" Conley just blurted it out. What else was there to do at this stage?

The boy just looked at him, a long assessing look that managed somehow to say, You dirty little man, then he said, "I wouldn't know." And then he was gone, climbing out of the car carefully and disappearing into the dark.

Conley drove home slowly. The rain was torrential, turning the darkness into something icy-wet and dangerous.

He felt deflated and tired. And embarrassed. Losing his temper was alien to him. What Katherine Henderson did with her money was her business. Since when did he care about other people's morality? What was it to him if the boy humiliated people for amusement? He saw worse things. What was it Lenny Bruce had said? I'd rather someone flashed at me than punched me in the face.

He sighed and turned the heater down a little more. The car was finally warm. He decided to take the back roads, away from the traffic. It would add twenty minutes to his journey but he was sleepy and he wanted to think. He liked to drive in the dark and think. Tonight he needed to think.

He turned off the main road and watched the beams of his head lamps sweep the

trees.

He slowed a little more.

His anger was niggling at him. He couldn't pin it down.

He had started off on the wrong foot. She had told him nothing but a pack of lies and that never helped. How had she expected him to negotiate in those circumstances? He slowed to let another car pass. But why had he got so annoyed?

It had started in the hospital. Conley pushed around in his head. And then again in the surveyors, looking at him like that. Like what? I don't know, just...

He could get nothing that identified it. The boy's unsettling, unblinking gaze, right into your head. *I know what you're thinking.* But he hadn't been thinking anything, that's what was so annoying. That's why he'd got so angry. It was those dirty insinuating eyes. Conley snapped his mental fingers. All those questions about being married. Suddenly he flushed guiltily, because he had unwittingly started it, asking the boy questions about Henderson. The boy had simply misunderstood his interest. He had felt convinced Henderson was a homosexual, and the murder had only made it seem more likely. But this boy, where did he fit in the affairs of Henderson? Not queer surely? But that flirting with him... No, there was the girl. The flirting was just intended to unsettle. He was trying to undermine him. Which was probably just as well. It would be very uncomfortable to be a victim of his... Perhaps he *is* homosexual. He doesn't act like one, not even when he's...

Conley didn't finish that. He felt tired. He sighed again. This rain wasn't going to let up. It was going to be a record wet winter this one.

So what would she do now?

Why should you care? You're dropping it, aren't you?

He let that one sit a bit.

Maybe.

He felt a sudden surge of irritation at himself. Why, for God's sake, involve himself any further?

Because all these pieces fit, but not into anything I've been given.

So what?

He shrugged to himself.

He slowed the car at the junction back onto the main road. The traffic was getting heavy, but he got in eventually.

He'd phone her when he got in. It wouldn't hurt to follow it a bit further. After all, she would be paying well. She'd need to for that boy.

Conley smiled grimly at himself and stopped thinking.

The office was empty when he got in. He went past it, up the heavily woodwormed stairs, and opened his front door.

The place was still cold. He really must alter the central heating clock, it was still on September's setting. He looked at his watch. It had only come on quarter of an hour ago.

He put on the lights. A set of eight metal downlights like pool table lights hung from the heavily veined ceiling.

"Late! You're always late!"

"Hello Mamma." Conley went over to the telephone and checked for messages. There was one from Katherine Henderson asking him to call as soon as possible. Someone was in a hurry.

"Coffee! Coffee! Coffee!" Mamma began screeching at the top of her voice.

"Shut up!" he yelled back at her.

She started mumbling to herself in her corner, fretting and pulling. Now she would

sulk all evening.

Conley went round closing all the curtains. The rain was lashing down so heavily he couldn't see out the windows. He went behind the counter of his kitchen and pulled a microwave meal out of the freezer. He cooked it, cutting up a pear for Mamma while he was waiting.

She pulled it from his hand, chattering at him, ate half of it then threw the rest about the floor.

"Temper," he admonished her.

"Facts Max, facts," she rejoindered, closing one eye and studying him.

He sat down on the sofa and ate his dinner, eyeing the phone. He decided to phone her before he had coffee, then he might be able to relax. He pushed the half-eaten dinner away from him.

He spun the dial through her numbers, enjoying as he always did the heavy feel of the receiver, the smell of the Bakelite.

She answered so quickly she might have been sitting beside it. He raised his eyebrows at Mamma. She stared back at him, a piece of pear held tightly in one foot.

"Hello? Miss Henderson? James Conley here."

"Hi. How did it go?"

"Not very well. Which, I should imagine, is exactly what you expected."

There was a small silence.

"Without wishing to sound clichéd, you haven't been wholly truthful with me, have you?"

She didn't answer that either, instead she said, "What did he say?"

"That you could get stuffed."

Unexpectedly she laughed. He raised his eyebrows at Mamma again but she said nothing. Katherine Henderson spoke to him. "In that case I'd like you to try something else for me."

"Not until you tell me a little more about what's really going on here."

"Don't worry, I'll tell you everything. Can I see you tomorrow?"

"No, I'm really too jammed up. Let me think..." But with today's cancelled appointments it would be jammed up for days ahead. He didn't want to leave it that long. He spoke to her again. "How about this evening? Or tomorrow night if tonight's out the question?"

"No, no," she said, "tonight's fine. When?"

He looked at his watch again. "Say forty-five minutes?"

"Fine, I'll expect you." She checked her address with him and rang off.

He sat a moment then stood up. "Got to leave you again Mamma."

"Facts!" she screamed. "Facts!"

"I won't be long."

She chuckled at him. He went back to the coat rack and pulled his coat back on. The rain was still lashing down. He must be mad.

He rubbed his cheek and shuddered then put out the lights and went out of the house.

He really began to regret his decision half way to her house. He felt so tired he could have slept over the wheel.

He missed the turning to her place and had to ask directions. By the time he got there he was cold, hungry and fed up. He was also quarter of an hour late.

She let him in. He took his first look at the flat he'd bought for Henderson. They never did look the same as they did on the plans. The trees were always missing for starts.

He nodded noncommittally when she saw him looking round. Two large cream leather sofas dominated the room. She told him to sit down.

She brought them a bottle of whisky and two glasses.

"I'm not sure if I should drink this to be honest. I haven't really eaten."

Immediately she brought them sandwiches, saying she hadn't eaten either. Looking at her he could believe it. She looked like someone who had lived on her nerves all day.

He watched her down two whiskies within five minutes. After that she seemed to calm a little. "My brother kept a diary," she announced, watching his face.

He stopped half-way through biting his sandwich and felt ridiculously like someone caught behaving inappropriately at the scene of an accident. He wondered what the hell he was supposed to say. Maybe offer to have it published. He waited, hoping she might give him a clue to what was expected of him.

"He suspected the Jackson Moores of something illegal." She wasn't meeting his eyes now. "I think we could use it to persuade his brother to let him marry me."

He put his sandwich down carefully. "Blackmail."

"I don't think you need to be quite so dramatic." She was smiling, but it was filled with a dull flush of red, her voice tight and clipped.

"I wasn't being dramatic. I just wanted to be quite clear about what you were saying."

"It isn't blackmail, I'm not attempting to extort money. It's not illegal."

"I'd agree it's not technically illegal but it's certainly immoral. I take it that doesn't worry you?"

"The way his brother treats him is immoral. My morality pales into insignificance by comparison."

"But you're asking me to be involved too, and I don't have righteous surety on my side. You may be lying. Your brother may have been lying."

"You would be paid for it. Whatever you considered appropriate to cover the cost of your conscience." Her voice was cold.

He should get up now and tell her where to shove it. After all, he had just been insulted. Instead he sat there and considered it. It was the idea of knowing. He could never resist *knowing*, and Katherine Henderson was holding out the apple.

"Well?" she said.

"One condition." He saw the excitement jump into her eyes. He realised she had expected him to refuse. He didn't know whether to be flattered by her opinion of him or depressed that he had failed to live up to it.

"Which is?"

"I want to read the diary."

"No," she said immediately.

"Then I won't do it," he came back equally quickly. He was aware of the dryness in his mouth. He was bluffing. He would do it anyway, on whatever she gave him, for she *must* give him something, if only a few more clues to put together.

She looked at his face, set, stubborn. Where else would she get his kind of savvy amongst a bunch of provincial solicitors spoon-fed on Rotary Club ethics? "A compromise," she said, refilling her glass and offering to refill his. He accepted, to show a compromising state of mind. Better than he had expected.

"I'll give you copies of all the relevant sections."

He looked at her a moment, pretending to consider. *Much* better than he expected. "Alright," he said. But she didn't smile. Something else was coming. He waited.

"There's one more thing you should know. You're going to find some of the stuff a bit odd." Her discomfort was tangible. She filled her glass again without emptying it first. "I'm afraid my brother had homosexual tendencies."

He almost shouted, Aha! Actively restrained himself from smiling. She was still talking.

"So you'll have to be prepared for the odd distasteful passage of purple prose."

She was genuinely ashamed, he realised, embarrassed to be telling him. He wasn't sure how to reassure her. He said impulsively, "I suspected he might be." When her head shot up he thought he'd said the wrong thing but she was smiling.

"Well it won't be such a shock then."

He smiled back, wondering why the hell he should be shocked. But she was happy, that was all that mattered. Keep the customer satisfied.

She brought him the photocopies. He did not fail to attach significance to the fact that she had already copied the relevant parts. Obviously if he hadn't agreed to do it then she would have found someone else who would.

He skimmed his eyes over them and was relieved to see no signs of censorship. He wondered what was in the rest of the diary. He shuffled the papers together, only a dozen sheets or so, and put them in his pocket. "So, what exactly do you want me to do?"

"Well, it depends a little on what you think of what he has to say. To be honest I can't make anything very much of it. He seems to have used some sort of private short-hand. Perhaps they might mean more to you."

"And when I've read them?"

"Then we'll agree on something to..." she hesitated "persuade them with."

He noticed it had become 'them'. She was no longer bothering to pretend the boy was held against his will. "Do you mind if I ask you something?"

"Depends on what it is." She smiled at him.

"Don't you find this humiliating? He seemed very definite that he didn't want you today."

"No." Her mouth was set defiantly. "He isn't really sure of anything. If you knew him better you'd see that. He would be as happy with me as he would with his brother."

Conley nodded but the logic of that defied him. As happy with her as he was with his brother? Good God, there wasn't any comparison surely? If he preferred his brother's company to hers then he was either indifferent to her or was too dependent on his brother. Either way it wasn't going to be a good marriage. It wasn't going to be any kind of marriage at all.

"Do you actually intend to marry him?" he asked.

"If I can."

It surprised him. "Why?"

He expected her to look at him aghast, exclaim, It's obvious, isn't it? Instead she said, "Anyone would want him if they could afford him." She looked at him, half smiling. "Wouldn't you?"

He returned the look steadily. "I may not be married Miss Henderson, but I assure you, I don't share your brother's tastes." She had the decency to blush. "But aside from that no, frankly, I wouldn't."

"No?" She seemed genuinely surprised.

"I'm afraid I didn't much like him."

"Like him?" She repeated the words as if she was searching for their meaning, then she laughed. "I don't think I've ever thought about *liking* him. I'd have said he was a love or hate job. I can't imagine anyone ever talking about *liking* him."

He felt slightly uncomfortable under her gaze, knowing that at least to some extent she was right. He smiled suddenly, showing her a fine collection of gold fillings. "I should be more honest, I found him repugnant."

She laughed. "That I can understand. But not physically surely?"

"Physically?" He was perplexed.

"You surely didn't find him physically repugnant?"

"His physical attributes weren't really under consideration," he said, watching her. What was this in aid of?

"Consider them now then. Did you find him attractive?"

He listened for insinuations but the question seemed quite genuine. "Objectively I'd say I found him..." he paused, looking for the right words, "I suppose the word is beautiful. Handsome seems inappropriate, and pretty is quite out of the question, but attractive he definitely isn't. He's repellent."

"Not to my brother."

She was drunk. He saw it quite suddenly on her face. He looked at the bottle and realised just how steadily she'd been knocking them back, probably before he got here too. "Nor to you," he said.

She nodded. "Do you think he's queer?"

She was watching him fixedly. He tried to cover up his surprise. "I think it would be presumptuous for me to say," he said carefully. "Your brother said something?"

"No," she said. Too abrupt, too definite. So there *was* something there then.

He answered her question. "To be honest, I don't think so."

"No, I didn't either."

He noticed the tense. "Have you changed your mind since?"

She shook her head. "Would I be marrying him if I had? I *know* he isn't." She sounded very sure.

"What made you wonder if he was then?"

She looked away, evasive again. "Just the way Jimmy talks about him."

"I thought you said he never mentioned him?"

"I didn't say that." She hadn't of course.

"It worries you?" he asked, half-smiling.

She laughed dryly. "Wouldn't it worry you?"

He smiled. "If I were marrying him I suppose it would."

They were silent a moment then he said, "Well, I must go." He stood up. "I'll read these and get back to you a.s.a.p."

She stood up, a trifle wobbly, and came with him to the door. He put on his overcoat.

"You must find some way to get him." She caught at his arm as he was going out the door. She looked suddenly overwrought, drawn. Perhaps it was the drink.

"I'll do my best," he said, trying not to shrug her off, feeling the sweat start almost immediately, his stomach clench.

She let him go. "I've got to have him." Her face was clear again, just someone determined to win, nothing more.

He went out the door quickly. For the very first time he felt vaguely sorry for the boy.

Conley's house was at least warmer when he got back. He bolted the door behind him and took off his coat. He unfolded the copies and laid them on the table, smoothing them out, resisting the temptation to read them immediately.

Mamma didn't speak to him. She was still sulking. She looked at him levelly, head burrowed down into her shoulders, and flexed each foot carefully as if to say, See how my old limbs suffer when I am left alone here day after day?

He went over to the kitchen and put coffee on. He put all the lights out except the two above the sitting area. The rest of the vast room was in darkness. The coffee filter light gleamed redly in the dark. Mamma shuffled and stirred in her corner.

He took his shoes off and pulled off his tie. He looked at the first sheet. October

8th. It contained nothing but one reference to 'A beautiful blonde' Henderson had seen in the middle of that night's duty. Conley didn't know what sex the blonde was. Long blonde hair and face like... and here someone was mentioned whom Conley had never heard of, but it was a man's name, so assumably the blonde was a man. Why had she given him this?

The coffee machine buzzed. He got up, his legs aching, and realised how really tired he was. He poured it and added four spoonfuls of sugar and took it back to his seat. He sat cross-legged in shirt and satin waistcoat, for all the world like a regency crow, and looked through the sheets.

The next entry jumped on a bit. It was a heated description of two men he'd caught on the A596 rolling around in the front seat of their car. Conley read it again. The physical description was clear, concise. It had to be the boy's brother. He felt a pulse in his neck. *That?* Rolling around in a car with another man? Henderson said that they'd claimed to be fighting, but he hadn't believed them. Conley felt sure that his analysis of the situation was a piece of wild fantasy. Frankly fighting seemed a lot more likely. But it was the same blonde that he'd referred to on the previous page. Conley almost shared Henderson's excitement at the discovery. Already it was like watching the miraculous rows of his Mamma's tatting forming, cobweb spinning out of nowhere. Henderson's excitement was evident, finishing with the rather unsettling declaration that he would 'have him'.

And then there was too much missing. Conley looked at the dates and knew for sure she had left out too many entries that should have been there. It had jumped forward to discussions with "Rab" who, it couldn't be a coincidence, had long blonde hair. One and the same? Had to be.

Conley read through them all with a growing fascination. It was like the slow unveiling of an iceberg. Rab was a cousin to the Jackson Moores and Henderson had tried, unsuccessfully, to have sex with him. He seemed equally, and dangerously, obsessed with the older brother, insulting him with a kind of masturbatory relish which seemed to focus rather too much on how well-endowed he might be.

It was not until the second last page that the boy made an appearance, and when he did Conley realised she'd censored it. She'd put a sheet of paper over the lower half of an entry, effectively blanking it out. She'd even done it quite well, faking a full-stop to lend it authenticity.

He threw the sheets down on the table. Why so coy? Her brother had more than 'tendencies'. He had actively attempted to blackmail the cousin into having sex with him. He obviously intended a lot more, but when Daniel Jackson Moore entered the scene all became silence. Only one thing was apparent, and that was that he was besotted with the boy. He obviously had about as much discrimination as his sister.

He sat there for a while, hands behind his head, and thought about it. He doubted if she had even given him everything pertaining to their alleged criminal activities. And what was that about? They had driven down to the nature conservancy at three in the morning - there followed some cryptic and encoded notes - and they were very keen not to have this disclosed - more notes. Obviously they'd been up to something, but what? It could be a poaching offence for all he knew. The only other suspicious circumstance was their father disappearing some time afterwards on a drunk.

Conley sat up suddenly as if he'd been struck by an invisible hand, whispering, "*That's* it."

He got up quickly and crossed the floor and went down to the office. He rummaged in his pocket for the key and opened up. He put the lights on and stood blinking for a moment. He took the cabinet key from Molly's desk drawer. J or M? He tried J first. Nothing. Who *was* it had asked him about missing persons?

Whymper.

He went through to Whymper's office. The damn thing was locked.

He banged his fist on the door then went back through to Molly's desk. He rummaged in the desk turtle's belly and came up with two keys attached to small plastic hamburgers. He took them back. The second fitted.

Whymper's desk was suffocated with files. It stank of stale pipe-smoke. He wrinkled his nose in disgust and began rifling through the desk debris. It took him almost ten minutes to check everything.

Nothing.

He pushed a pile of files onto the floor with a vicious swipe. "*Damn.*"

He heard himself and saw what he had done with surprise. He ran his fingers through his hair. That was twice he'd lost his temper in one day.

He looked at his watch. Almost one. He bent wearily and picked up the files. He put them back, hoping Whymper would be too hopelessly muddled to spot their incorrect sequence. He got up and went to the window. Only the desk lamp was on and he could see the river down below. The rain was off and a huge clear moon hung in the sky. He thought of the boy and Henderson.

Did you know him well?

You could say that.

What else was in the diary?

He turned and looked round the room, wishing sincerely that Whymper might be suffering from indigestion at this very moment. An old briefcase sat on the chair behind the door, one of Whymper's many. He never appeared with the same ones twice. He used them as some kind of elaborate rotating filing system.

Of *course*.

He crossed quickly to it, opened it and pulled out the files. There it was - Jackson-Moore, John.

He kissed it and took it upstairs.

The dates were the same. The mother had 'disappeared' on the same date as their nocturnal visit to the conservancy. The brother had actually *given* the same date. Whymper had even scribbled something about a car in pencil and circled it, a claim of some sort, because John Jackson Moore was obviously claiming ownership of everything. Mother missing since October 8th. Father missing not long after. He was going to have a long wait to get his hands on his property. Conley couldn't believe that no-one had questioned it. The mother runs away then the father goes missing on a drunken bender? Maybe if you knew them it fitted. Maybe it was even true. But maybe that was why they were so touchy about the police investigating the night at the nature reserve. Why would they murder their mother though? Perhaps she inherited after the father's death? Conley looked at the will again. She didn't. On the father's death the eldest son stood to inherit everything, not so much as a penny to the others. The plot thickened.

Suddenly he was irritated by it. He pushed the file across the floor, away from him, and climbed onto the sofa and lay out. He looked at his watch again. Quarter to two. God, he really had to get to bed.

He got up slowly and walked to the screened-off section of the room that provided his sleeping quarters. The floor-length venetian blinds were already down and closed. He put on the wall lamp above his bed. The glass beads clicked musically with the movement of his arm. Mamma coughed and shifted her weight. He pulled his clothes off and dropped them on the floor.

He went to sleep with those green eyes looking straight through his head.

FORTY-FIVE

Danny's stomach was healing well. John was hunkered down in front of him, cleaning the wound, putting a fresh dressing on it. "It isn't going to scar too badly."

Danny's smile was fleeting and derisory. John looked up at him then straightened up. "What's wrong with you?"

Danny shrugged.

"You've had the hump for about three days now. What exactly is bugging you?"

Danny fixed his clothes and turned away. "Nothing."

John pulled him back. "Don't nothing me. What's wrong?"

"I don't know."

"Sickening for someone?"

Danny glanced at him quickly and was horrified to feel himself colour.

John laughed as derisively as Danny had smiled. "And he is. Who? Henderson's sister?"

Danny wouldn't look at him. John pulled him round. "Who is it? Her?"

"Oh leave me alone."

"Not until you tell me."

"I don't have to tell you anything."

John took his face in an iron grip. "You know what? You're getting too fucking cocky Danny. This is my house and while you're in it you'll do as I say."

"You're not my fucking father." Danny tried to pull his hand off but John held tight.

"No, I'm something a whole lot closer and don't you forget it. I *own* you Danny, body and soul."

Danny stood glaring at him.

"Know what I think? I think you're not getting enough, that's what I think. I think I ought to keep you more thoroughly fucked then you won't have the energy for bugging me. Or maybe I should just kick you around a bit, cure your hot little itch. It's for that bitch, isn't it? Every night you're getting it up with that bitch when you make it with me."

Danny kept glaring at him.

Then the phone rang. John frowned. "Who's that at this hour?"

"It's only ten," Danny said, pushing his hand off.

"Rab still up?"

Danny nodded.

The phone rang on, then it stopped. A second or two later Rab's voice came up the stairs, "Danny, you're wanted!"

Rab stood at the bottom of the stairs waiting, taking bets with himself. Sure enough John came out. "Who is it?"

"Mr James Conley," Rab said, feeling a smile threaten.

"Tell him to fuck off."

Rab looked up at him. He looked furious. Guess was they'd been fighting before the phone went. When weren't they fighting? Rab shrugged and went back to the phone. "Hello?"

"Yes."

"Mr Jackson Moore says to tell you to fuck off."

There was a moment's silence while Conley digested this. Rab was enjoying himself. He looked up the stairs, but John had gone back in, probably to beat hell out of Danny. Probably till he came on John's feet. *J for Jealousy Robert.*

"Perhaps you'd care to tell Mr Jackson Moore that unless his brother makes an

appearance on the end of this line he might care to explain what exactly happened to Mrs Margaret Jackson Moore on the 8th of October."

Rab stopped smiling. "Is this a joke?"

"Does it sound like a joke?"

Rab didn't push it. "Hang on." He put the phone down and went upstairs. He knocked on the door and stuck his head round. Danny was standing stripped to the waist, face fixed and angry. John wheeled round when Rab came in. He had something in his hand but Rab couldn't make it out. "What the hell is it now?"

"He wants to speak to Danny or else, I quote, you'll have to explain exactly what happened to Mrs Margaret Jackson Moore on the 8th of October."

John went completely still then said, "He's bluffing."

Rab shrugged.

John stood a moment longer. Rab could see it battling on his face. Suddenly he jerked his head at Danny. "Go and see what he wants." Danny moved to go past him. John caught at his arm. "Remember, you don't see her."

Danny just stood there. John let him go. Danny went out.

Rab stood facing him a moment or two. There was something wrong, something drastically wrong. John looked tight as a spring, vicious, dangerous. "Doesn't he love you any more?" he asked, watching him.

John came across at him like a buffalo, knocking him back into the hall and into his own door. "You shut your dirty mouth...." John held him bunched up by the clothes, "or I'll shut it for you."

Rab shut it. Oh boy there was something wrong.

Question was - who with?

Danny answered the phone. "Hello?"

"Hello, Daniel?" Conley felt awkward using his Christian name but he didn't know what else to call him.

"Yes." Danny saw Ian watching him from the living room and turned his back to him.

Ian looked at his back. It was almost as good as his front. The view was good, period. He kept watching, and listening.

"Miss Henderson wishes to make a proposition to you."

"I told you to tell her where she can stuff her propositions."

"Well..." Conley's voice sounded odd over the phone, different, "let's say she has a new offer to make to you which it would pay you to consider."

"I don't want to consider it."

"I think you should." Conley's voice got harder. Danny had been waiting for it.

"Why?"

"Because she knows something that might be detrimental to you."

"We've been through all this before."

"Not quite. I've been perusing James Henderson's diary. He seems to have been under the impression that the acts which were committed at Yardholm Bird Sanctuary might have been sexual in nature. I think they might have been more in the line of getting rid of evidence."

Danny felt it run down his back like iced water. He instinctively hugged himself with his free arm.

Ian watched the movement curiously.

"Are you still there?" Conley's voice sounded almost edgy.

"Yes."

Danny thought he heard him let out a breath.

"Shall we meet to discuss it?"

"Not with her," Danny said quickly.

"That's no problem," Conley said smoothly. "Tomorrow suit you?"

"It'll have to be in the evening."

Conley shifted on the settee, unsettled. He'd have to take him somewhere. "Alright. When?"

"Any time after seven."

Conley heard the defeat in the boy's voice and felt a momentary qualm. He quashed it. "Seven thirty?"

"Sure."

"Tomorrow, seven thirty then."

"Fuck you," the boy said succinctly, and hung up.

Conley stared at the phone a moment then slowly put it down.

John was relieved. If he had to see anyone let it be the deadhead. He was as safe as anyone could be with Danny. It wasn't her, that's all that mattered.

Danny told him what he had said. It sounded bad, but it was probably meant to. It could still be so much shit. Henderson had once half-decided they'd murdered her and dumped her in the lake. It was probably in his diary and Conley was using it for a bluff, that's all.

He took Danny to bed and used him dry, made Danny sit astride him, take him hard, do all the work.

Now Danny was fast asleep beside him, curled into the sweat of John's body, breathing John's air, part of him.

He wasn't going to give him up. Not to a cunt.

He kissed Danny's mouth hard, trying to wake him, but Danny groaned fretfully and curled up tight against him.

John held him tight, suffocating him.

Not to a fucking cunt.

Rab shifted in his bed. He was hot and irritable. He had been thinking about Danny and had succeeded in giving himself a hard-on.

He lay on his stomach, pressing it desultorily against the bed.

Danny had had his hair cut the day before. The barber had savaged it but he still looked beautiful. He was always fucking perfectly beautiful.

His door opened. Rab turned over on his back and sat up. "Who is it?" he said in a stage whisper.

"Me. Ian."

Rab lay back down again, inexorably depressed. Hope didn't keep you going. Hope killed you. By inches. "What do you want?" He clicked on the lamp.

Ian moved into the light.

His erection was huge. He was stark naked.

Rab blinked.

"He doesn't care any more what we do. He's proved his point with you. You're yesterday's flavour."

The sentences came out disjointed. Rab didn't say anything. He couldn't see Ian's face above the circle of light, only his excitement. In the dark what else was there?

"I'm desperate. Look at me."

Rab looked at him.

Ian waited, watching Rab's face, bright white hair dazzling under the light. He saw

him push the blankets down, the foxy stripe, the faded remnants of his tan. His erection was just as hard, just as lonely. "Get in," he said and clicked out the light.

FORTY-SIX

Mrs Ostler finally phoned to say she would not be coming back. She had decided the job was too much for her. She was sorry to let them down. John put the phone down and banged his fist on the banister.

Fucking Danny, in everything he shouldn't be. Now he would have to go to the shop, put in another card, go through the same bloody long, boring rigmarole. *Jesus.* God, let it be quick. He couldn't stand another tin of soup, and they were fast running out of clothes.

He went to look for Danny and found him mucking out. "Ostler isn't coming back."

Danny wiped his hands on his jeans and looked at him. He was smiling. The little faggot was *smiling*.

John punched him. Right smack, beautiful, in the mouth. Never had he enjoyed punching anyone so much.

Danny went back like a poleaxed ox.

"Smile on Danny. Fucking smile on."

Danny lay in a puddle of dirty water in the pen. His lip was bleeding. The cut in his mouth never seemed to quite heal. It never really got a chance, and as long as John was alive it never would.

"Right place for you, lying in dung in an animal pen. Right at fucking home, you are."

Danny moved backwards, gently easing himself into a sitting position.

John continued to watch, waiting for him to get up so he could hit him again. "You couldn't keep your fingers off her, could you? Doesn't matter what it looks like, how decrepit it is, you're dipping into it. What did you do, think of Henderson's sister while you shoved it home?"

Danny wasn't getting up from the sitting position because he could see a beating written all over John's face. He was running his tongue over his teeth. They felt loose to their roots, numb, but there didn't seem to be any broken. He could feel the side of his face coming up, and he'd jarred his neck badly. A sharp sick ache was crawling up his spine to prove it.

"Get up."

Danny sat where he was.

"Get up, fuck you." John made a lunge for him.

Danny rolled to one side and scrambled into the next pen. John swung underneath the bar and grabbed his leg just as he rolled through to the next. He dragged him back, climbing along his body. They were half-suffocated in the drifts of fresh straw. They rolled like animals locked together for the kill. John was hitting him harder and harder. This was it, he was just going to beat him to death, here in the filthy black muck of an animal's pen. Danny struggled harder. John had one hand on his neck. He could feel his other arm round him, trying to squeeze the life out of him. Then something happened.

Something seemed to shift.

He realised John was no longer swearing. No, that wasn't it. He was still swearing. It was his tone that had changed. He was saying something familiar. It sounded afraid. No, not afraid, panicky, like a man watching his blood flow away from him, the water closing over his head. He suddenly froze and grunted an '*Oh*' that sounded more like '*No*'.

Danny looked at him, saw the shock on his face, felt the slackness of his body, and

realised what was happening.

Danny watched him as he climbed off him. John wouldn't look at him. He was grey with shock. His hands were smeared with blood, his jacket ripped beyond repair. He'd have to buy a new one now. No excuses.

Danny didn't move. He hurt too much. His mouth felt as if it was filled with blood, but his body was worse. John had simply lain on him and used him as a punch bag. Until he'd come of course. Until he'd got so fucking turned on hitting him he'd finally come in his pants. Danny watched his nervous movements, his eyes darting, never quite making it to him.

"You okay?" John's voice was strained, frightened. Danny had never heard him like that before.

He didn't answer. Make the bastard look at him.

John looked. He came apart. "Oh Jesus Danny, I'm sorry."

"For what?"

John looked away again, but Danny knew the answer. He wasn't sorry for coming on him. He wasn't even sorry for hitting him. He was sorry for giving himself away. "I'm sorry," he said again.

Danny got up slowly. He hurt in places he couldn't describe. John stood with his back to him, like a man turned away to give another privacy. Danny came round in front of him. His hair was covered in shit. He could feel it in the cuts in his hands. It had even soaked through his clothes. Straw stuck to it. John still wouldn't meet his eyes. "I didn't mean it," he said.

"Why are you apologising?"

John looked at him quickly, said nothing.

"You've been doing it for years." Danny's eyes were boring into his head, not letting him go. "You've been doing it since I was just so high, since you first slapped my mouth and called me a whore. My life's been one long wank for you John, and you just came."

"I said I was sorry." Danny saw the snap of temper in his eyes, then something in him seemed to give. "I love you," he said and it sounded stripped to the bone.

Danny said nothing.

John reached up and touched his damaged mouth. Danny could see the cuts on his knuckles. He saw, for the first time, two long scratch marks down his face.

I must have done that, scratched like a girl. You were really panicking Daniel. Really gone there boy.

Danny brought the tip of his tongue out, still stained with his own blood, and licked the palm of John's hand. Dirt, blood. "You came trying to kill me." His voice was sliding away from him. He could hear it himself.

John shook his head.

Danny nodded, touched John's face this time, tracing the scratches with his nails, matching them up curiously. "You were trying to kill me."

"I lost my temper."

Danny looked at him. "It was the best, wasn't it?"

John moved back a pace.

"It was the best you ever had. I *felt* it. I saw it in your face."

"No."

"It was the best fucking spunk you ever had in your life, wasn't it?"

"I said *no*. Why don't you fucking *shut up*."

Danny smiled. John watched it in a kind of fascinated horror. One half of his mouth beautiful, smiling; the other half pulped, covered in blood. Like Beauty and the Beast

in one animal. "Wasn't it?" he said again, cajoling, thick, honeyed.

John had his eyes closed, his head turned away. He swung his head back round savagely, eyes blazing. "Yes. *Yes.* Alright?" And he took Danny's hand and pressed it against himself.

He was rock hard.

Twice Conley had lost track of what clients were saying to him. Once he had forgotten someone was on hold for him and had disconnected them.

He felt nervy, raw. He'd eaten his way through a whole box of cachous in one afternoon. His teeth ached.

He claimed a headache and off-loaded his last two appointments onto Brian. Sheard had moaned at him and taken them with ill-grace but Conley didn't care, out was out.

He went upstairs and stripped off his clothes. He had his shower with Mamma watching him disapprovingly. It was a ritual she couldn't comprehend. She threw apple peelings at him, jumping from foot to foot as she sang Deutschland, Deutschland über alles. She sang it well. It was her favourite.

He felt better. He flicked water at her, sending her into a flurry of swearing and demands for coffee. "I nee-eed coffee!" She screeched.

"Don't we all?"

He put some on and lay down on the couch for a while. He had finally altered the heating clock this morning and the flat was warm, relaxing.

He went over to the window and watched the sun setting. It had been a bright day for a change, but it was bitterly cold. The sky looked bruised; streaks of green and plum mingled, pink, violet, the red edge of the sun itself. Oddly, the river looked dark and unfriendly, still very full from the rains. He watched it running over the steps of the gardens opposite. They must feel nervous every winter. He felt safe high above it.

He closed the curtains, then the coffee machine buzzed.

He poured it and on impulse added some brandy. It had been there since last Christmas. He knew he should eat but couldn't face it. He took his coffee back to the settee, stopping to give Mamma a biscuit. She scattered crumbs in a wide arc around her perch, watching where they fell and charting their positions. "Jude!" she screeched. Then she settled down to eating what was left.

He sat down and faced his anxiety. He knew the cause of it. He was going to bring the boy home. There was, after all, nowhere else to take him. A pub was out of the question, and they couldn't sit in the car in this diabolical cold.

You could take him to the office Max.

No. Here.

And he couldn't face that one, or what it meant, except it was like the agoraphobic going to the shops, or the arachnephobe picking the spider out of the bath - a killing cure.

It would be here.

Or not at all.

Danny washed and dressed. John stood in the bedroom watching him. "Sometimes I feel as if I've spent my whole life watching you walk away from me."

Danny turned away quickly so he would not see his irritation. "I'm only going to talk to the man."

John laughed sourly and lay down on the bed. "The day you '*only*' talk to someone will be the day your dick falls off. And your hair's a mess. What the fuck did he do to

you?"

Danny looked in the mirror and frowned. John didn't like that either. It was out of character. He watched Danny ruffle his hair with his fingers.

"You leave him alone Danny."

"I told you, he isn't interested. He shits himself if you touch him."

"Well don't touch him."

Danny kept his back to him, but his voice was gritty. "I fucking won't, okay?"

"Turn round, let me see your mouth."

Danny turned. John smiled sleepily. "You won't be giving him head anyway." Danny turned away again, quickly. "One look at that mess and he won't want to."

"Did you do it deliberately?" Danny's voice was light but his back was still turned.

"What?"

"My mouth. Did you do it deliberately?"

"And if I did?" John's voice was lazy, and Danny knew instantly he had. He had come out there purposely to hit him and had thought he'd kill two birds with one stone.

Danny turned to him. "Want to slice me up a little and come on it before I go?"

John's face went white. "You little bastard."

"No worse than you."

"You *evil* little bastard."

"Why? Isn't it true then? Isn't my big brother a fucking perv who gets his rocks off hurting me? Doesn't it make you come in your pants without touching it John?"

John swung his legs to the floor. "Shut up."

Danny turned away again before he could say anything else. He could feel John's rage at his back.

Rab's voice suddenly yelled up the stairs. "Danny!"

"Okay!"

He picked his jacket up off the chair. John took his hand as he went past, kissed the mouth in his palm. "I'll be waiting."

Danny looked at him then pulled his hand away and went out the door.

Conley had come up to the front door again. Danny went through it like someone leaving a strange house, not quite sure of his footing in the dark. "Listen..." he said. Conley turned to look at him, trying not to stare at his damaged face. "There's a back door, round there, in the yard. No-one uses this one."

Conley nodded, wondering why the boy expected to see him again. Maybe he didn't. Maybe he was just being helpful, or polite.

They got into the car. The boy busied himself with his seat belt. Conley glanced at him again. He looked up at him. "Why don't you just ask me and get it over with?"

Conley smiled. "Okay. What happened to your face?"

"A cow kicked me."

"A cow?"

"Yes, they do."

"What?"

"Kick."

"I wasn't going to ask that."

"No?"

"No, I was going to ask if you always used the same excuse when your brother hits you."

Danny looked at him for a long moment then laughed shortly, looking away again.

Conley nodded then started the engine and drove away.

He was aware of the boy looking at him covertly. It felt odd, but not unpleasant. His face was merely curious, nothing of that unhealthy maliciousness about it. Yet. He spoke suddenly. "Your clothes are weird."

Conley laughed. "My car's weird, my clothes are weird - wait till you see my house."

"Is that where we're going?" The boy's voice immediately changed.

Conley looked at him curiously. "Yes, why?"

And now the eyes were on him again, just like before, that from-under-the-brows stare, unblinking, too far-seeing. Then he turned away, as if he'd read you dry and you disgusted him.

"What is it?" Conley demanded.

"What?" The boy looked at him again and now there was nothing there, just blank polite inquiry.

"What's wrong with going to my house?"

"Nothing."

"Then why did you look at me like that?"

"Like what?"

"Oh forget it." Conley looked back at the road, feeling the irritation build. *Already he's aggravating me, and I'm going to let him into my house. My God.*

The boy slid down in his seat a little, pushing his hands deep into his pockets. "It moves nicely."

Conley blinked. "What does?"

"The car." The boy's voice was deep, sleepy.

"Even though it's weird?"

"I like it."

Conley looked at him, oddly pleased.

The boy nodded as if to say, Yes, I'm not making it up.

Conley smiled at him.

The boy jerked upright suddenly, pulling his hand from his pocket. He rubbed it furiously on his thigh, then he groaned softly as if he were in pain and laid his head back again. "How this fucker itches."

Conley looked away from his rapt expression, but he could still hear the sound of him rubbing it on his thigh.

"If only I could scratch it."

Conley glanced at him again. His face was intent, pained. He was biting his lip. His eyes were closed. He looked like a man on the point of ecstasy. Suddenly he jerked his hand under him and sat on it.

"Whatever are you doing?" Conley asked.

"Stopping myself. Have you got any ice at your place?"

"Ice?" he echoed stupidly.

The boy looked at him now. "For my hand."

"Yes… yes of course."

The boy went back to his suffering. Conley could see him willing it to stop. After a while it seemed to pass, but he remained sitting on it.

Conley felt as if he had been charged up with electricity. His skin was jumping. The boy's face… did everything come out of him like that?

Like what?

As sex. Did it all come out of him as sex?

Oh God.

He watched the road.

414

"This is where you live?" Danny was peering upwards, trying to see the back of the building in the darkness.

"And work."

Danny looked at him.

"My office is on the floor below. There's three of us share the practice. The two floors below that are rented by an antique market. The top floor's all mine."

They got out the car. Conley locked the doors. Danny was standing looking up at the building. "What was it?"

"Flour mill. Then it belonged to a bible society. They rebuilt it. When I bought it it had been sitting empty for years."

"You own the building?"

"Yes." Conley pointed into the shadows. "We can go in the back way if you want, up the fire escape, my normal route, or do you want to see the other floors?"

"No, the back way's fine."

Conley led the way up the iron stair case. "Actually, this staircase is the most unusual feature the building has. It's far too ornate for a fire escape. It was probably recycled from somewhere else to save money."

Danny didn't say anything. Conley didn't even know if he was listening.

"It's high, isn't it?" The boy's voice spoke suddenly behind him.

Conley stopped and looked back at him. "Are you afraid of heights?"

He could see the boy's smile in the darkness. "No, just an observation."

Conley went on climbing, suddenly uncomfortable about the boy being behind him. He wished they were indoors where he could put space between them. "It is high. Tall ceilings." He thought of his office and corrected himself. "Well, on three of the floors. Our office floor actually has low ceilings. It was the original top floor and when the Templars added their bit they cropped it. Here we are."

It was an ordinary metal fire door. Conley unlocked it and pushed it open. It opened quietly. He obviously used it. Danny stepped into the darkness. Conley put the lights on. Danny looked across the huge floor. He looked back at Conley. "No walls."

Conley smiled. "No walls."

Danny walked out across the floor. It was made of polished wood, very old and wormy, darkly stained. There were two sofas on a rug in the middle of the floor. A long counter, with a sink and cupboards, ran along the back wall where they had come in. It was separated from the room by another counter with gadgets on it. There was a large section screened off by venetian blinds.

"Bedroom," Conley said.

Nearby there was a glass cubicle with ornately engraved walls.

"Not very private." Danny looked at the shower.

"I don't need privacy."

"Bathroom?"

Conley put on some more lights, lighting the bottom half of the room. The bathroom was built entirely of glass bricks. "You can't see in," Conley said

Danny shrugged. One wall was curtained. The other, excluding the 'built' parts, was entirely stacked with books. There were a pair of fancy doors, assumably leading downstairs, at the bottom of the room.

"Jude! Jude!"

Danny jumped. "What the hell was that?"

"Mamma," Conley said.

Danny watched as he crossed to a scruffy crow standing on what looked like half a tree by the window. Danny hadn't seen it against the jungle curtains. It was chained by one ankle to its perch inside a sand pit. He followed Conley over. It wasn't a crow.

"What is it?"

"She's a mynah."

"Jude," the bird said again, cocking an eye at Danny.

"Judy? Is that its name?"

Conley laughed. "No, she's calling you a Jew. It's her favourite insult." Conley scratched the bird's neck, not something Danny would have cared to do.

"Come and sit down." Conley led the way over to the settees. He put some of the lights out, making the vast room look less daunting. "Do you want some coffee?"

"Okay." Danny sat down and looked at the furniture. Most of it was old, strange. The settees were covered in some kind of stiff sculpted velvet. He saw little cigarette burns in the fabric. He looked around, couldn't see any ashtrays. There was no smell of cigarettes.

The table was equally weird, brass-edged with an inlay top. Danny could make out some serpents, and what looked like a decapitated head, but the rest of it was hidden by an old-style black telephone, a great ugly thing that looked like it weighed half a stone. "That work?" Danny called over to him.

"What?" Conley asked, turning.

"The phone."

"Yes, but there's another over there." He gestured at the bookcases. "A modern one with an answering machine."

Danny nodded. Conley went back to his coffee. The whole place was weird, even the curtains. The fabric was full of black faces peering through leaves. Danny didn't know how Conley lived with it. Still the place smelt good. Danny inhaled. Like a bakery and a library mixed; waxy, woody, sweet. "It smells like a bakery in here."

"That's because we have a bakery downstairs, next door. Their venting pipe comes up the back of our building."

"Must make you hungry."

"It does. I've got a sweet tooth."

Danny remembered his teeth. His sweet tooth was well-filled.

The bird began singing. It was nothing Danny could recognise, but the voice was incredible, not really like a bird's at all. It wasn't like a parrot sang, this really sounded human. "It sounds very real."

"What? Mamma?"

"Is that its name?"

"Yes."

"Well it sounds very real, like a real person."

"They're good mimics."

"What is she singing?"

"The German national anthem."

"She's singing in German?" Danny turned to watch her. The bird was stepping from foot to foot almost as if it was marching. Danny laughed. "Does it understand what it's saying?"

"No, they don't."

"It looks as if it does."

"That's their appeal."

"You teach her to talk?"

"No. She belonged to my grandmother. That's my grandmother's voice."

Danny turned back. "Belonged? Past tense?"

"Yes."

"Is she dead then, your grandmother?"

Conley nodded.

Danny pulled a face. "Spooky."

"Not really."

Danny looked sceptical. It was spooky to him.

Conley brought the coffee over then went back and returned with some biscuits. He offered them to Danny, who shook his head. "Well if you change your mind tell me, otherwise I'll eat the lot."

Danny looked at him. He was sitting on the opposite sofa. "You ought to be fat."

"I cheat, I don't eat anything else."

"What, other than biscuits?"

"And cakes."

"No wonder you look so…" Danny stopped.

"So what?"

"I was going to say dead."

Conley laughed. "Well at least it wasn't weird."

"The clothes, the waistcoats, where d'you get them?"

"I inherited a chest full from my grandfather, others I've bought myself. Antique shops, fairs…" He shrugged.

Danny nodded. He was wearing a heavily brocaded item in bright scarlet. It made his suit look very black, his shirt look very white, himself look very colourless. "Henderson would have liked that."

"What?"

"That outfit. He was a great fan of red and black. You ever see his kitchen?"

Conley shook his head.

"The whole room's black with splashes of red, bedroom too." Danny looked at him then, something flickering in his eyes. Conley didn't stop to watch it. He picked up his cup and studied the steam rising from its surface.

There was a silence. When he looked up the boy was looking round the room again, cup cradled between his legs. "You collect furniture or did you inherit that too?"

"No I acquired most of it. These…" Conley patted the sofa, "are from a Victorian hotel. They were demolishing it. It had been sitting intact, boarded up, since the war, I got these as salvage. Most of the stuff's salvage of one sort or another, even the curtains. They're from an old drama school, hand-printed, 1930's."

"Gruesome."

Conley laughed. "But not weird?"

"Definitely weird."

"I do a lot of redevelopment projects. That's how I get most of it."

"Handy." Danny's tone was sarcastic.

Conley didn't rise to the bait.

The boy put his cup down suddenly and clutched his hand as if he'd been bitten. "*Shit*. Have you got that ice?"

Conley looked blank for a moment then said, "Yes, of course, what do I do?"

"Just shove it in a bowl with some water." He was rubbing his hand across his chest this time, to and fro across the buttons of his shirt. If anything it looked worse.

Conley brought the ice back, putting it down on the table and sitting down again.

Danny smiled to himself, watching him keep his distance.

Conley saw the smile and felt like slapping it off his face.

The boy put his hand in the bowl, making noises between his teeth then groaning with relief. "Oh that feels good."

After a minute or two he took his hand out and flexed it, examining his palm. Conley sat up to see it. The wound still looked raw and sore. It was grazed slightly, as if he'd come off a bike. "You've hurt it again."

The boy nodded.

Conley looked at his cut mouth. "Same fight?"

The boy nodded again without looking up. "The smallest graze and it itches like all hell."

"If you're not careful you'll get blood poisoning."

"You sound like the hospital doctor. He likes to hold my hand and lecture me on the dangers of blood poisoning."

And there it was, that slow lascivious smile touching you across the room, distance no object. Conley wanted to get up and move far away from him, but the boy had looked away again and was putting his hand back in the bowl. "So what am I here for?"

He came out with it so abruptly and unexpectedly Conley just stared at him. When he looked up Conley was still staring at him.

"Well?" The smile was back, dirty, crawling over his mouth. Conley looked away.

"Katherine Henderson still wants to marry you." He couldn't disguise the disapproval in his voice.

"You think she's nuts."

"I'm sorry?"

"You think she's nuts, wanting to marry me."

Conley said, grim-mouthed, "It's hardly my place…"

"I think she's nuts." And the boy grinned suddenly, infectiously.

Conley smiled in spite of himself.

"She doesn't really want to marry me at all. You know that, don't you?"

Conley looked at him reluctantly. He put his cup on the table, trying to avoid his eyes.

"She just wants to fuck me."

He was being deliberately offensive and Conley knew it. He kept his eyes off the boy's face. "Well she's prepared to marry you for the privilege, and she won't be the first person to do it either."

There was a silence so intense Conley could hear Mamma pulling at her feathers. He knew that whatever was coming he didn't want to hear it. It was spider in the bath time.

"Why do you always flinch when someone touches you?"

"Who says I do?" He kept his head down, well away from the boy's eyes.

"Every time I come anywhere within two feet of you, you act like a canary the cat's circling. Is it me or what?"

"I don't know what you're talking about."

The boy got up suddenly and came round the table. Conley jerked his head up. "No don't," he said, keeping the panic out his voice by inches.

"Don't what?" The boy stood there smiling

"Okay, I don't like to be touched. You've proved your point, you can sit down now." *Oh very cool Max. If only you don't vomit on the floor you'll be fine.*

"Is it just me or anyone?" He still stood there. Why didn't he sit down?

"Anyone. The clinical term for it is haptephobia." *Please sit down. Please.*

The boy backed off and sat down. Conley wiped his face with his hand. He could feel the film of sweat on his skin.

"Bad?" the boy asked him.

Conley didn't answer. What could he say? Yes it's bad. It cripples me. Every day is a nightmare. Sometimes I can't even go into a supermarket for fear someone will brush against me. It's bad alright, worse than you'll ever know.

"It can't do your sex life any good."

What sex life? Was he joking?

"How long have you been like that?"

Conley finally answered him. "I've always been like this."

"How long's always?"

"Since I was young."

"How young?"

Conley shrugged. "Ten… twelve. I don't remember."

Danny looked at him. Then no-one had been able to touch him for more than twenty years. He had touched no-one for more than twenty years. He was probably a virgin.

He looked at Danny slowly, as if waiting for a verdict, waiting to hear what he would say. The boy was watching him without expression. Conley couldn't tell what he was thinking.

"So what do you want?"

Conley looked at him blankly, watching something moving in the boy's mind, absolutely unreadable. "I don't know what you mean."

"You brought me here. What do you want?"

Conley realised suddenly he was talking about Katherine Henderson. "I told you, she wants you to marry her."

"And?"

"And what?"

"What's the threat? Because the answer's no, as you well know, so you might as well threaten me."

Conley watched him this time, wanted to see his face when he told him. "I think you, or a member of your family, murdered your mother and father - that's your threat."

It was effective alright. Even though he must have been half-prepared for it, the boy still went white. In fact he paled so suddenly Conley wondered if he might faint.

"Is this some garbage from his diary?"

"No. He doesn't strike me as having been a particularly astute or curious police officer."

The boy's eyes flashed quickly in temper. "He didn't need to be astute or curious. He had enough for what he wanted."

"Which was?"

"None of your fucking business."

Conley watched him and waited. The boy jumped up suddenly. "I'll be fucked if I will. I'm not fucking marrying her. You can't prove a thing."

And Conley knew it was true. He realised he should feel something, but nothing came to him. No outrage, not even a healthy fear that he might be alone with a murderer. He was still the same boy, if now potentially more dangerous. He watched him pacing like an animal. He realised what he was seeing was frustrated rage. The boy paced some more, swore some more, then sat down. He laid his head back and closed his eyes. Conley watched the moisture trickling down the side of the bowl of ice. Mamma made a noise like knitting needles. *Clickety-click, clickety-click.* Conley waited.

The boy's eyes opened and looked directly at him. "No."

"Is she that bad?"

The boy shook his head. "It's nothing to do with her."

"What then?"

"John won't let me."

"Your brother? Why not?"

"He just won't."

"Even when he realises what's at stake?"

"He doesn't care about that."

"If he cares about you he will."

"*No,*" the boy said as if exasperated. "You don't understand."

419

"Then tell me."

The boy looked at him a little longer. "Have you read Henderson's diary?"

"Yes," he lied.

The boy shook his head. "You haven't."

"Okay," he admitted, "only some of it. She wouldn't let me see all of it."

The boy nodded then he said again, "I can't," and closed his eyes once more.

Now was the moment. "Can I ask you something?"

"What?" the boy said without opening his eyes.

Conley looked at his swollen mouth. "Did you sleep with her to keep her quiet?"

The boy nodded.

"Not enough for her?"

"It never is."

Conley turned that one over. "And her brother, what did you give him for his silence?"

The boy's eyes opened now, slowly, filled with knowing, damning him. "It always comes down to this, doesn't it?"

Conley didn't answer him, didn't know what the boy was seeing in him, accusing him of.

"The same thing."

Conley didn't realise at first he was answering his question.

"I gave him exactly the same thing."

Conley took a breath, slowly, carefully, pulling it in, then he told him. "Katherine Henderson doesn't know you're here tonight."

The boy was watching him now, keenly, eyes wary.

"She doesn't know anything about your father or mother and, as far as I can tell, she never will. Your secret died with Henderson." Conley heard that and it gave him pause. Why hadn't he seen that possibility sooner? He saw the boy still studying him and pushed on. "I won't be telling her."

The boy licked his lips and looked at the ceiling. What was he thinking? "Unless?" His eyes had come back down and were on Conley now.

"No unless. I won't be telling her."

"What do you want?"

Conley fought the urge to say, Nothing, but he hadn't come this far to give it up now. "I want you to help me."

"Help you?" The boy's voice bordered on sarcastic.

"Yes." *Go on Max, go on.* "You could help me."

"How?"

"You don't care what you do." Conley swallowed. "You've got no moral scruples. It would be easy for you to..." But he couldn't think of the right way to phrase it.

The boy unfolded his arms, spread them wide, palm-down on the settee. "Why don't you just say what you mean? You think I'm some kind of professional fuck who can screw his way in or out of anything, no cost to me. That's what you mean, isn't it?"

"I wouldn't have put it like that."

"Is there another way?"

Conley said nothing.

"And now you want me to fuck you."

"What?" Conley could feel the immediate panic. "Good God, no, nothing like that. I only want you to help me with this... problem of mine, that's all. With ordinary people I can't... What I mean is most people get too involved, take things personally."

"And I won't?"

"I don't think so, no."

The boy stared at him, too long, too intensely. Conley wanted to tell him to stop it.

420

"So you want me to 'help' you," he made it sound filthy, "in return for you not telling Henderson's sister about your 'discoveries'."

Conley shook his head, frowning. "No. This isn't blackmail. I'm not threatening you."

Danny looked at him, his turn to frown. "Odd, you sounded like you were threatening me earlier."

Conley said nothing.

"Okay, so what if I say no?"

"Then I carry on as I am."

"And you don't tell Katherine Henderson?"

"That's right."

"You just nurse it to yourself, in case it comes in handy."

"No." Conley began to feel angry. "I forget it, like I forget the whole sordid affair."

The boy smiled at him. Conley wanted to hit him again.

"Alright then," the boy smiled wider, "the answer's no. The answer's fuck you Mr Conley."

Conley felt the disappointment like something physical inside him, like he'd swallowed lead pellets. He had an overpowering urge to lie down and go to sleep. He felt ashamed, as if he'd asked him to prostitute himself, just as Henderson must have done. He felt dirty, and very old.

He could hear the wind steadily picking up outside. The lights had been flickering for the last hour, always a sign of high winds. He better get the boy back before the weather deteriorated too badly. "I'll drive you home."

He got up and tucked his shirt in at the back. He pulled his jacket back on. The boy stood up too, not looking at him, and pulled his jacket on.

Conley fetched his overcoat from the peg and crossed to look out the window. At first he couldn't understand what was wrong, then he realised the air was so thick with snow he could not see through it. He must have spoken out loud because the boy said to him, "What is it?"

"Snow. God knows how long it's been falling."

The boy came up behind him, brushing against his shoulder, making him pull back. He peered out the window.

Conley had moved further away, close to the wall. "It should be alright. It's only been..." he looked at his watch, "well, a couple of hours at most. It can't be too deep."

The boy came back in, closing the curtains. "We'll soon find out, let's go."

Conley nodded and led the way.

When he got to the door he opened it before putting out the lights. The snow was so thick it was almost like a white fog. "Be careful on the stairs."

They struggled down the staircase like old men and made it to the car. It was now a white Mercedes. Danny measured the depth against the tyre. "Christ, it must be a foot deep already. It must have started literally when we got in the door." The wind was tearing at their faces, whipping his words away. They got inside and sat in the white box. They could not see out the windows.

"Jesus," Danny said, shaking his head.

Conley turned on his engine without much hope.

It didn't catch.

Danny looked at him.

He tried again. Nothing.

"I don't know what to suggest. I don't think we're going to make it tonight," Conley said, already feeling panicked at the idea of the boy staying in his house, trying not to let it show.

The boy said, "Try it once more."

Conley tried it twice more. Finally they went back up to the house.

Conley let them back in in silence.

Where the hell was he going to sleep? It was all he could think about: where was he going to sleep?

"Can I use your phone?"

"Sorry?" Conley looked at him blankly.

"I'm going to have to phone home. Can I use your phone?"

"Yes, of course."

Danny perched on the edge of the sofa and dialled the number. It felt odd. The damn thing weighed half a ton.

Conley went to make himself coffee. He found himself listening to the boy, curious to hear him talking to his family.

"It's me. Is John there?"

Conley busied himself washing cups. After a moment or two John obviously came on the line.

"Listen, I won't be back tonight, we're snowed in... Oh come *on* John, listen to the news if you don't believe me, it's about a foot deep... No, his car won't start, it's a fucking antique."

Conley grimaced at the description.

"No."

One word, in answer to what?

"As soon as I can, I didn't do this deliberately. You think I like being stuck in... Alright... I *said* alright... Yeah... and fuck you too." And he slammed the phone down.

Conley busied himself in a cupboard, pretending great preoccupation. When he turned the boy was still sitting there staring at the phone, face set and angry.

Conley crossed and put a mug of coffee in front of him, more biscuits. "Take your jacket off."

Danny looked up at him. "I'm starving, could I have something to eat?"

"You mean *actual* food? Well, yes and no. Come over and see if there's anything you'd want."

Danny looked in the fridge. There were two half-cut gateaux and a six-pack of fruit mousse. The freezer yielded more cakes, frozen strawberries and a TV dinner. "Can I have the dinner or do you want it?"

"No, go ahead. I hardly ever eat them. Give it here." Conley put it in the microwave and dug out a plate, knife and fork while they were waiting.

Danny watched him moving about the kitchen. He moved very economically, purposefully. Lovely mouth though. He even seemed to suit the gold fillings. Like he suited the clothes. They fitted him well at any rate. Conley became aware of him watching and looked over at him.

"How have you managed to live so long without it?" the boy asked.

Conley didn't need to ask what 'it' he meant. He flushed as if he'd been criticised and shrugged.

"That would kill me. I couldn't go two days without it."

He realised the boy wasn't exaggerating, he was just stating a fact. His voice was slightly wondering, perplexed at Conley's oddity. Conley felt irritated, like a man who's been told he has no sense of humour. "Not everybody feels like you."

"Or you."

Conley said nothing.

"Do you know when I had my first blow-job?"

Conley came to a brief halt then went on with what he was doing. He'd found some

half-edible bread. He was buttering it. "I hadn't given it any thought."

"I was six."

"*Six?*" Conley turned now. The boy laughed, enjoying his expression.

"That's right. I was six when I first gave one too."

"I don't believe you."

The boy shrugged, completely indifferent to whether Conley believed him or not. He was studying the top cupboards, searching his memory. "I was ten when I had my first orgasm. I'd seen plenty of orgasms before, but I'd never managed one of my own. I nearly fucking fainted when it happened."

"My God," Conley said.

"What's wrong?"

Conley shook his head.

"I enjoyed it more when I could join in, get something out it myself. And of course they enjoyed it too." He smiled.

"They?"

"Just a figure of speech. Nice and anonymous." Danny gestured with his head. "I think that's ready."

Conley took the meal out of the microwave. "D'you want it left in the dish?"

Danny nodded.

They carried the food over to the sofa. Danny balanced his plate on his knee. He began eating then looked up at Conley. Conley was watching him. "Want some?"

Conley shook his head and took another biscuit.

Danny gestured with his fork. "You're lucky you've got any teeth left."

Conley shrugged. "Was it another boy?"

"What?" Danny looked up at him, fork arrested.

"When you were a child did you do it with another boy?"

"Don't most men?"

"I expect so."

"Well then." Danny went on eating.

"A friend of your brother's?"

Danny looked at him again.

"I assume he was older than you, quite a bit older. I thought it might have been a friend of your brother's."

"You mean because I was giving head at six." Danny smiled, wiping the corner of his mouth.

Conley nodded.

"Well that depends who's talking. My brother would claim that he was." He laughed suddenly and bent his head to his food.

"Did your brother know?"

"Better than anyone."

"And he didn't do anything?"

The boy put his fork down carefully inside the plastic dish then laid the dish on the table. He took a mouthful of his coffee then leaned back. "Well, I suspect he watched."

"He *watched?*"

"Probably." The boy was grinning at him now.

"You're fabricating this, aren't you?"

He grinned some more but said nothing.

"Is any of this true?"

"All of it." And he made a cross over his heart with his finger.

Conley looked at him but could read nothing there to help him. He didn't know him well enough to know if he was lying.

The lights flickered again.

"I hope you've got plenty of candles."

"Why?"

"Looks like you might lose your lights tonight."

Conley looked up and saw them flicker again.

"Do they go out often here?" the boy asked.

"Never."

"Lucky you. Ours go all the time. External power lines, pain in the arse."

They were silent a while then the boy spoke again. "You never do anything like that then? No messing around in the shed after school?"

"I didn't go to school."

"How come?"

"I had a private tutor. I first attended school when I was twelve. In Kent."

"Are your family rich?"

"They're all dead, but no, they weren't especially rich."

"Not like the Hendersons?"

"No, nothing like the Hendersons. My family lost all their money before the war. In fact if it hadn't been for the war I'd be a lot poorer than I am. My family gained from the war."

"Weapons?"

"No." Conley looked at him levelly. "Theft."

"What kind of theft?"

"My grandfather was a looter."

"A looter? Where did he manage to loot up here?"

"Not here. He was a Nazi officer in a provincial town."

"A Nazi? In Britain? You mean like that whatsisname, Moseley?"

"My grandfather was German."

Conley was gratified to see surprise on the boy's face. At least something could penetrate that thick layer of indifference.

"You mean you're German?"

"Half German. I came to this country when I was twelve."

"Can you speak German?"

"Yes. I can even sing Deutschland, Deutschland über alles, just like Mamma."

Danny looked at the bird. She was asleep, head tucked under her wing. He looked back at Conley. "You look German."

"Well so much for that because the German side of the family had dark hair, just like Hitler. They looked like Jews, just like he did. It was probably a good job my grandfather had a title and a pure Teutonic lineage otherwise he'd have been on the trains with them. It's my father to whom I owe the Germanic looks. I think that's why my mother was allowed to marry him, get some Aryan blood into the family."

"Wow." Danny smiled. "Somehow you always think of the Nazis as something distant, not anybody you might know."

Conley nodded. The lights flickered again.

"I think you're going to lose them," Danny said, looking up.

"I'll go and see if we've any candles."

He went over to the kitchen and rummaged in the cupboards. He straightened up. As if to prove the urgency of the matter the lights went out completely for a moment then came back on again. "Nothing." Then he snapped his fingers. "I'll be back in a sec'." He moved down the room to the front doors. "Just nipping downstairs."

Danny got up and went across to the bathroom. He felt inside for the light pull, found it and tugged it on. The glass room flooded with light. There was a chandelier in the fucking roof. Danny circled beneath it. It sparkled like diamonds. It was obviously very old. Then he realised it wasn't lit. The lights were on the ceiling above

it, shining through it. The chandelier was full of candles, pristine, unlit. He laughed.

There was a bath in here with more engraved glass panels. These matched the ones on the shower cubicle outside. A large mirror was fixed to the wall above a double sink. The toilet bowl and the sink were decorated with fish and water lilies. Danny smiled. Poor fish, how many people had pissed on them? He joined their ranks then zipped up. When he flushed the toilet it thundered down from an overhead cistern.

Danny ran his fingers over the mirror. Enamelled fish were set into the corners, swimming across the room. They felt slick to the touch, almost like real ones.

He heard the front door close.

Conley couldn't see him. "Danny?"

Danny heard him call out his name. First time he'd heard him say it. Beat Daniel anyway. "In here, in the bathroom." He stuck his head round the door. He was sure he saw relief on Conley's face. He looked at him, wishing he'd caught it better. "You've got a whole room full of fucking candles here."

"Where?" Conley came over.

Danny stepped back. "Up there, in the chandelier." He moved back a little further, realising Conley wasn't going to come any closer.

Conley smacked his forehead with the heel of his hand. "I forgot."

"You've never lit them," Danny said, looking up at it.

Conley shook his head.

"You should. It would be something to take a bath with that lit."

Conley smiled at him. "You're a sensualist."

"And you're not? You own it."

Conley stopped smiling.

"And the clothes you wear, the cakes you eat?"

"I don't see what you're getting at."

Danny smiled. "Neither do I." He moved forward, making Conley back out of the room. He put the light out.

"Anyway," Conley said, "I got some in Whymper's office. Our Charles is a traditionalist. Wood panelling, marble fireplace. All fake of course, but complete with Regency trimmings." He lifted a pair of three-branched candelabras.

They were bright silver-plate with turned scarlet candles. They looked like something off a Christmas card. "Gruesome," Danny said.

"I am forced to agree with you, but then so is Charles." Conley put them down between them on the table, one at each end. "I even purloined some of his matches."

"You must have been a boy scout."

Conley shook his head.

Danny laughed. "No, me neither."

Conley straightened up. "I'm having more coffee, want some?"

"How much of that stuff do you drink a day?"

Conley shrugged. "I'm a coffee junkie."

Danny grunted and bent down to undo his shoes. Conley went behind the counter and put some more coffee on. The lights flickered again. He hoped the machine would have time to do its job.

He turned and saw that the boy was lying flat out on the sofa, a cushion under his head. He was wiggling his toes, looking at them thoughtfully. Conley repressed a smile.

"You gas or electricity?" the boy said suddenly, turning his head.

"What?"

"Your central heating."

"Gas."

The boy regarded his feet again. "We won't freeze anyway."

"I never thought of that."

"You can tell you don't have to do without electricity very often." The boy sat up suddenly. "Where's your television?"

"I haven't got one."

"You're joking."

"No."

"Why not?"

"Never got round to it."

He lay back down again. The buzzer went and Conley poured himself a cup, adding sugar and bringing it over. "Sure you don't want any?"

The boy shook his head. He looked at him suddenly. "Doesn't it keep you awake?"

"Sometimes."

The boy studied his face. "It looks as if it does."

"Thank you."

"Bags under your eyes."

"Thank you again."

He grinned and looked back at the ceiling again. "What do you think about?"

"What d'you mean?" The boy had a mind like an eel.

"In bed, when you're lying awake. How do you pass the time?"

"Work usually."

"Sex?" He was looking at him again.

"No."

"Why not?"

"No point."

"I'll bet sometimes you think about it anyway, even if it is pointless."

"Occasionally," Conley conceded.

"You jerk off?" He was up on one elbow now, watching him.

Conley didn't know how to answer that. He opened his mouth then closed it again.

The boy smiled and lay back down. "Well, you're not dead yet anyway."

Conley laughed in spite of himself. The lights went out.

Danny sat up. They came back on. He lay back down again. "Thought we'd had it there."

"I don't know where you're going to sleep," Conley said.

"Here will do," Danny answered.

"I have exactly one quilt, and it's on my bed."

"That it?"

Conley nodded his head.

"I'll use your coat, that great bat cape you wear, that'll do."

"You're going to be cold when the heating goes off."

"Can't you leave it on?"

"I can but it's got a three hour gap. I've never understood quite why. It's to do with the little levers that mark the time. They're too wide or something."

Danny looked at him in consternation.

Conley shrugged. "Sorry, mechanics isn't my thing."

"Obviously. Our central heating's coal. It works if the fire's lit, period. Well, I'm sure I'll survive."

Conley nodded.

They were silent. They could hear the wind buffeting round the side of the building. The fire door rattled and was still again. "I wonder if it's still snowing?" Danny said.

Conley felt he should get up and look but he couldn't be bothered. He was warm and content.

"Shall I go look?"

Conley said, "If you really feel that energetic."

"Snow's a novelty for me." He swung his legs down. "We're at the coast. We never see it." He padded across the floor.

"Why not?"

"Why not what? Fucking hell, it's bucketing down."

"Why doesn't it snow at the coast?"

"The salt."

Conley looked at his coffee. He wasn't sure if he understood that but he let it pass.

"Come and see this."

"It's quite alright."

"Come on, come and see it."

Conley sighed and got up.

Danny held the curtains open for him, moving back a little, giving him room. Conley looked out. "You're right, the town's disappeared."

Danny closed them again. "Just you and me in our ivory tower." He was kidding. At least he started out that way, but Conley was standing very close. He reached out his hand.

Conley jumped. It was the only word to describe it.

Danny said, "Sorry."

Conley shook his head. "No, my fault."

What for? Danny wondered. Looking too tasty?

Conley turned away from him and went and sat down. Danny followed him, lay back down on the couch and closed his eyes. He couldn't remember this happening to him in a *long* time. Conley didn't fancy him, wasn't what it was about. Fuck, he thought. Fuck, fuck, *fuck*.

"What are you thinking?" Conley asked.

"I'm thinking fuck, fuck, fuck."

"Why?"

"Because it's late and I'm tired."

Conley was immediately solicitous. "Sorry, you want to get to bed." He made to get up.

"For Christ's sake sit down."

Conley sat down.

"There's no point in me trying to sleep now. I'm not tired enough and it's a strange bed."

"I'm sorry, I wish I could offer you something better."

Oh you could. Give me your body for ten minutes and I'll sleep like a lamb. "Forget it." He sat up. "Do you have anything to drink?"

"Alcohol?"

"Booze of any description."

"Half a bottle of brandy, maybe some dribs and drabs of other stuff. I can go look."

Danny watched him cross to the kitchen. Pretty nice arse too. *Oh Jesus Danny, forget it, can't you? What the fuck is wrong with you? He asks you to touch him up and you say no, but now you've changed your mind?*

"Half a bottle of brandy, third of vodka, a third of whisky and an almost full sherry."

"No sherry, bring the rest."

"I've nothing but water and ice."

"Well, we'll drink it straight then."

Conley dumped them on the table then went off to get glasses. "What are you going to do, get drunk?"

Danny sat up. "No, I'm giving you a free treatment."

Conley looked at him.

"On the art of touching."

"What d'you mean?"

"Just what I said." Danny watched the fear come into him. "Relax, I'm not going to touch you, I promise. Just trust me."

"You're joking." Conley smiled back with difficulty.

Danny said, "First we get drunk. I learned this valuable lesson from James Henderson." He poured two drinks. "Vodka first. The vodka's the worst of the three." He looked at the bottles. "Whisky last I think. It looks good."

"It is."

"Right the whisky last. To your health."

They chinked glasses. They both took a drink, and both grimaced then laughed. Conley looked at it. "I must have got it free with something."

"Think of it as medicine. Drink up."

They finished the first glass and Danny poured another. He sat back and sipped this one slower. "Alright?"

"Alright," Conley agreed.

They were quiet a moment then Conley said, "What did Henderson teach you?"

Danny frowned at him.

"You said Henderson taught you a valuable lesson."

"I just told you, if you have difficulty getting your act together get drunk first. Henderson couldn't make a pass at you without being drunk."

Conley looked at him. "You think I'm a coward?"

Danny shook his head. "No."

Conley drained his glass and held it out to him.

Danny filled them up again. "That's the last, may the gods be praised."

The lights flickered again, then dimmed. They didn't brighten again.

Conley looked round the room. "That looks rather sinister."

Danny nodded.

"Shall we put them out?" As soon as he said it they went out.

They waited a moment or two. Danny spoke. "Looks like we've finally had it. Light the candles. That usually brings them back on."

He could hear Conley groping on the table. The bottles chinked. "Where are the matches?"

"Hang on..." Danny bent forward and groped for them. Inevitably he brushed Conley's hand. It was pulled away sharply. Danny heard a bottle go over, Conley swearing, "*Damn!*"

"Broken?"

"I don't think so."

Danny found the matches and lit one of the candles. Conley's face bloomed across from him. "Sorry," he said.

Danny shrugged and lit the other two.

Conley found the bottle. It was the vodka, empty, intact.

Danny lit the other candelabra. "Very Christmassy," he announced. "Hang on." He got up and walked over to the bathroom, carrying one of the candelabra.

"What are you doing?" Conley called after him.

"Lighting the illuminations."

Conley followed him. He was standing inside the bathroom, on a chair, lighting the chandelier.

"I hope you realise I'm going to have a hell of a lot of wax to clean up."

Danny looked down at him. "Problem?"

Conley shrugged.

"Well stop moaning then. You may never get another chance."

It took him almost five minutes. Once it was lit they both stood beneath it, admiring it.

"Jesus fucking Christ, have you ever seen anything like that?"

Conley looked at his rapt face. "I don't think I ever have."

"Fan-fucking-tastic." Danny walked round it.

Conley retreated and sat on the edge of the bath, watching him. He nodded. Not that anyone was watching him to see it.

The boy's hair was outrageous. Even chunked off badly as it was, the colour looked faked, a dark blood red. His skin was suffused with colour. The soft candlelight disguised his swollen mouth, making him look more like he had when Conley had first seen him. Maybe Katherine Henderson was right. Maybe he was worth it. Art for art's sake.

"And to think you've never seen it like this." The boy looked at him suddenly. "How long have you owned it?"

Conley shook his head. "Forever. One of the few things in this place that belonged to my family."

"And you've never seen it lit?"

"Never. I should imagine my grandmother is probably spinning in her grave right now knowing that someone's *dared* to light it."

"Is that why you put it in here?"

Conley smiled at the notion. "Perhaps you're right. Perhaps it was unconscious, just to piss her off, if you'll excuse my language."

"*Piss* her off, like it."

Conley laughed.

Danny picked up the candelabra. "Come on, back to the drink."

Conley followed him out. The place looked much brighter with the incandescence coming from the bathroom. The glass bricks glowed green, like watery gemstones.

Danny poured them some brandy, passed Conley his glass. He watched Conley take it, carefully avoiding his hand. Henderson's law of alcohol was going to be sorely tested tonight.

Conley looked at him. Had it really never occurred to Katherine Henderson that this boy might have killed her brother? Or did his face wipe out everything? Or his body? Conley considered his body for the first time. You couldn't really tell when someone was dressed but he was beautifully proportioned.

Oh, you noticed that Max?

Conley drank some more brandy in a gulp and coughed.

Danny laughed at him and realised he was getting tipsy. He was laughing too easily. It felt good to laugh at all. He finished his glass in one mouthful and coughed himself. He stood up. "I'm going to take a bath."

"What?" Conley looked up at him.

"This is going to be the only opportunity in my whole life to have a bath by the light of a thousand candles. I am not going to laugh in the face of fate." He began pulling his shirt out as he wandered towards the bathroom. "Come and keep me company. Bring the booze."

Conley looked at his retreating back, heard the taps go on.

He was pulling his jeans off when Conley got to the bathroom. Conley fought the urge to go right back out again and resisted it. He went in and carefully put the bottle on the wide ceramic surround of the sink, then the glasses. He glanced in the mirror, saw him pull his shorts down, the whole length of his body pure pale gold. Conley looked away, concentrating on the glasses.

"Bubble bath, that's what we want."

"You're out of luck."

"No bubble bath?"

Conley kept his back to him. "Sorry."

The water was sloshed around. Conley glanced in the mirror again. He was climbing in. He sank down under the high sides. "Jesus, that's hot." He leaned forward and put in some more cold. "That's better. I think I'll sleep in here, just keep the water topped up."

Conley took his drink over, careful not to look down at him, but he was aware of the dark shadow between his legs, intense in all that pale gold whiteness.

"Sit down."

Conley sat down on the edge of the bath, as far away as he could, so that he could only see his face and chest.

"This is living, brandy in the bath. I'm drunk."

Conley laughed. He was a bit drunk himself.

"Want to come in?"

Conley heard it in his voice. He was careful not to meet his eyes. "No thanks."

The boy laughed quietly. Conley flushed.

"Not even want to look?"

"I'm sorry?"

"Go on, prove you're not scared."

"I don't know what you're talking about."

"I'm talking about you looking at me, lying here in this bath. Why don't you?" His voice was odd, smooth, a little too deep.

"Why should I?"

"Why shouldn't you?"

"I'm not queer, you know."

"All the more reason. I haven't got anything you haven't. Go on, look."

Conley stood up and turned round.

He had only ever twice seen another man's erection. Once in a photograph and once in a shower room. He looked away again quickly, blushing furiously.

The boy laughed at him but said nothing. He didn't need to say anything.

Conley sat back down on the edge of the bath and looked at his glass.

"There, first part over. Not as bad as you thought. You haven't turned to stone."

Conley took a mouthful of brandy and didn't speak.

"Look at me."

Conley turned and faced him.

"Relax, smile. What's a little nakedness between friends? Put it down to experience."

Conley let his body relax, tried a smile.

"Better. Now pass the soap."

Conley leant over and got a bar from the soap dish at the foot of the bath and threw it to him. The boy caught it and began soaping himself. "Two baths today." He began to hum to himself. The room filled with the scent of violets. "Nice smell, what is it?"

"Violet."

"Smells like those fucking sweets you eat."

"Same scent."

The boy pushed under the water suddenly, rinsing himself. He washed the lower half of his body. Conley got up to put a towel over the rail. When he turned back he saw the boy stretched out, watching him. He no longer had an erection. Conley looked away and sat down again. The boy pulled out the plug and stood up. Conley got up too, moving away.

"Pass us the towel, would you?"

Conley had to walk back with it. He did it as best as he could, but the boy was standing there above him, everything on show. He handed him the towel and left the room.

He heard the boy humming to himself.

He poured himself another brandy and drank it in a oner.

The boy came out wrapped in a towel, clothes bundled under his arm. He dumped them on the couch and sat down. He took up his freshened glass. "Nice brandy."

Conley nodded.

"Or maybe it's just the bad vodka."

Conley looked into his glass then said, "I noticed you have a dressing on your stomach."

"Mm?"

Conley looked up at him. "What is it?"

The boy was watching him. He had his legs crossed underneath him, the towel gaping alarmingly, drawing your eyes into the darkness. "Burn."

"Strange place to burn yourself."

"I was belly dancing."

"Mind my own business?"

"And the marks here..." the boy pointed to a row of small scabbed cuts on his chest, "are where a vulture got me."

"Does your brother do all this?"

"Do you never keep your nose to yourself?"

They stared at each other across the table. Conley broke it first by taking another drink.

The boy stood up and took the towel off. Conley looked away quickly.

"Why does it bother you?"

"What?" Conley studied the floor.

"Me naked."

Conley was silent, aware of the boy's movements. He was towelling his hair, moving leisurely.

"Upbringing. I know it's stupid but I can't help it."

"I'm not going to assault you."

"I know."

"Well look at me then. If it doesn't embarrass me why the fuck should it embarrass you? You're never going to cure it if you can't even look at someone. Come on, look at me."

Conley turned slowly. His face was scarlet. Danny looked into his eyes. There was nothing there. He wanted to smash every bottle on the table, take Conley by the throat and throttle him.

Danny turned away and began to get dressed. He saw Conley visibly relax when he put his shorts back on. He left his shirt open. He'd had the bath water too hot. His head was thumping slightly. He salvaged a couple of flakes of ice from the bowl and put them in his drink.

Conley grimaced. "Ice in brandy, I'm sure that's bad form."

"Who gives a fuck."

Conley looked at him curiously. The boy was in a temper. He seemed to have irritated him. Maybe he thought he was a prude. Well he's probably right. I probably am a prude... *Danny.*

"What?"

Conley looked at him blankly.

"You said my name."

"Did I?" Conley shook his head, retrieved the moment as best he could. "I don't

know what I was going to say."

Danny looked at him curiously then took another drink. It was nice cold, easier to drink too. "How was I going to help you - exactly?"

Conley's head came up. The boy was rubbing his hair again, not looking at him.

"They call it desensitization therapy. You face the object of your fears gradually, in increasing doses, until it goes away. Or at least until you can cope with it. I doubt if it ever goes away, completely."

Conley watched the boy turning it over in his mind. "Why me?"

Conley was glad of another chance to explain. Maybe this time he could make a better job of it. "I've always been put off trying this sort of thing with a woman, too many... complications. I always felt a man would be better, no sex to confuse the issue. But you can see the difficulties. I wanted to get rid of a hang-up, not develop a new one. You seemed ideal."

"Meaning?" Danny was watching him, twirling his glass between his palms.

"I'm not quite sure how to say it without offending you. I insulted you earlier I know..."

"Just get on with it."

Conley licked his lips. "You like to be touched. You invite it." Conley glanced at him quickly. "And I think you may be bisexual."

The boy didn't say anything, just sat there stony-faced, listening to him.

"Anyway, it seems to mean nothing to you, no feelings involved. You're the sort who could have sex and forget it, so I thought..." He paused again. "There really isn't a good way of saying this... I thought if you could do that then you wouldn't have any problems with something as simple as what I wanted, and it would help me to get past this barrier without complications, I mean emotionally. An ordinary man would be outraged at being asked to be physical with a another man. People are so fraught about touching. It seems to carry so much emotional baggage. I'm sorry, I think I may be over-explaining this. What I'm saying is, if you're afraid of spiders you can practice picking up little ones. If you're afraid of touching you can't just fondle people in passing. It's difficult. Do you understand?"

Danny nodded. He understood alright. "You thought you could use me."

"Yes." Conley was pink with embarrassment.

Danny looked at him in surprise. He'd admitted it. He refilled his glass.

"I used Katherine Henderson too. I couldn't think of any other way to get you here."

"You could have asked me."

"What?"

"To come here."

"Would you have agreed?"

Danny nodded.

It was Conley's turn to be surprised. "But why?"

"I like your face." The boy was smiling at him again. That same dangerous smile.

Conley blushed and looked away. "Why do you do that?"

"What?"

"Flirt like that."

"Maybe I enjoy it."

Conley looked at him. "You mean you enjoy unsettling people. You have a sadistic streak."

"Everyone has a sadistic streak."

Conley thought about the marks, the burn. "Including your brother?"

"Curiosity killed the cat." Danny fished some more ice out the bowl and covered it in brandy. He stood up and carried his glass round the table.

"What are you doing?" Conley watched him edgily.

"Sitting beside you." And he sat down, leaving only a foot or so between them. Conley began to sweat. He tried to move away.

"No don't." Danny stopped him. "I'm not touching you, am I?"

Conley shook his head.

"And I'm not going to, okay?"

Conley nodded.

"So you can relax."

Conley took a breath and sat there watching him from the corner of his eye. The boy sat quietly beside him, drinking. Conley let the breath out slowly.

Danny was aware of him sitting there like a coiled spring. What would he think if he knew what he wanted to do to him? How much more would he have to drink to drown this? Putting out a fire with gasoline.

Danny looked at the candles, half-down. He yawned, half-swallowing himself. He felt suddenly bone-weary.

"Tired?"

Danny nodded. "Suddenly."

"Want to go to bed?"

"Is that an offer?" Danny smiled at him.

Conley looked away, felt irritated at himself. Couldn't he take a joke without turning into a maiden aunt? He was filled with a sudden curiosity, the curiosity of someone who can only imagine meeting someone who does. "Would you?"

"What?"

"Go to bed with me."

"Are you offering?" Danny felt his heart miss a beat in the time honoured manner.

"No, that's not what I mean. I mean, *could* you?"

"Have sex with you?"

"Yes." Conley tried to stop it but his face burnt anyway.

The boy laughed. "Of course."

Conley looked at him, startled. "Don't you even have to feel attracted to the person?"

Danny put his glass down slowly and clasped his knees to his chest. "No, I don't." *But I do anyway Mr Conley*. He watched Conley digest this.

"Have you done it with many men?"

"Depends on your idea of many."

"And women?"

He shrugged. "More than you."

"Do you have a preference?"

Danny thought about it. "Some days I think so, some days not." He thought about it some more. "But I don't think so, no, if I'm honest. It's all sex. I like it." He smiled. "I need it."

Conley scrutinised his face, caught by the way he'd spoken the last words. "You mean like an addict needs it?"

"I wouldn't know."

"How do you feel when you can't have it?"

Like I feel right now, Danny thought, like killing for it. He said, "Wound up." He almost laughed out loud at the inadequacy of it.

Conley nodded. Danny wanted to punch him in the mouth. *Don't nod at me you fucking patronising bastard. You don't fucking understand anything.*

Conley bent forward to fill up his glass. Danny looked at the fabric of his shirt. Some kind of silk. He looked at Conley's thighs in the close-fitting black trousers. He stood up. "I really must get some sleep."

Conley was startled by his sudden movement.

"Of course." He felt oddly disappointed. He'd been content, sitting close to someone without feeling threatened. "I'll see what I can find amongst the coats."

Danny went over to the other settee and cleared the cushions to one end. He looked at the curtains thinking, They'd make good bedding. If you could stand to sleep in them.

He crossed to the window and looked out. It was still snowing. It looked just as heavy, but the wind had eased a little.

"Still coming down?"

Danny closed the curtains and turned. "Yes."

"I found another one that might help, and a disgusting jacket you can put over your feet. I can't think why I ever bought it or why I haven't thrown it out."

Danny looked at it and said, "See what you mean."

"Tomorrow it goes in the bin." He threw them on the couch. "Will you be alright?"

"Sure."

"Okay. Just shout if you want anything."

How about you? I want you. Should I shout that? Danny nodded without looking at him.

Danny sat on the edge of the couch and fastened his shirt. He could hear Conley in the bathroom running water. He hung the wet towel over the edge of the table. He blew out the candles and lay down, pulling the coats over him. He could smell him. Violets, the scent of something else off the lining. Deodorant, aftershave maybe. Jesus, of all the things to have to lie under. The room began to grow darker. He realised Conley must be putting out the candles in the bathroom. He smiled grimly. Should shag the fucker out blowing that lot out. He turned over and curled into the back of the sofa. This was going to be one long fucking night.

Conley came out of the bathroom. "Danny?" he called quietly as if he feared he might already be asleep.

"Mm?"

"Goodnight."

Danny curled further into the back of the sofa. "Fuck off."

He heard Conley laughing then the light moved away.

Danny woke up bursting to pee. He was also bitterly cold. He lay in the dark listening to the room, trying to place where he was, then he remembered.

He half sat up and felt his legs. He had lost the jacket from his feet and one of the coats was half off his legs. How the fuck did people sleep rough? He could hardly feel his feet.

He swung them to the floor, pulling Conley's overcoat up to his chin. He sat a moment, waiting for his head to stop thumping. He felt slightly sick and very thirsty.

He stood up and slipped his arms into the coat, pulling it tight around himself. It almost touched the ground. Conley must be a good bit taller, at least as tall as John.

He padded over to the window and pulled the curtains open. An eerie white light came into the room. The snow had finally stopped. The moon shone on it like some kind of odd negative of daylight: dark sky, white earth. It was incredibly beautiful, hushed. Danny shivered.

He left the curtains open for light and padded over to the bathroom. He looked into the bedroom. Conley had not let down the third set of blinds. He was surprised. He would have expected it to be the first thing he did.

He went on into the toilet, absent-mindedly feeling for the light. He cursed silently to himself when the click sounded without effect. "Fucking lights."

He made out the dim shape of the toilet and aimed, hoping for the best. He flushed

it without thinking. The noise thundered into the night. "Oh, for Christsake." He put his hands over his ears. When it finally stopped the place was eerily quiet. That odd muffling effect of snow, as if the world held its breath.

He came back out.

"Danny?"

Danny turned to Conley's room. "Yes."

"Everything okay?"

"No, I'm dying of fucking hypothermia." He could make out Conley's shape in the dark, moving under the quilt. He seemed to sit up and reach for something. Danny walked over to his room.

"It's half three, just gone. The heating's been off for a couple of hours now."

"Great."

There was the flare of a match. Danny saw his face suddenly illumined, his hair tousled, then the candle caught. He only lit two.

Danny said, "Sorry I woke you. I forgot about the thunder closet."

Conley said, "No, it wasn't you, I was awake."

"Too much coffee."

Conley didn't answer him. He was running his hands through his hair. "I saw you at the window. Is the snow off?"

"Yes." Danny stepped into the room. "What the *fuck* is that?"

Conley followed the direction of his eyes. He was looking above the bed. "Crucifix."

"Jesus."

Conley laughed. "I hope so."

"Where the hell did you get that?"

"It was in the building. That and four thousand bibles and a lot of rats. I think the Templars must have confiscated it from some heathen papists. It doesn't look very English, does it?"

"It doesn't even look Christian. How can you sleep under a thing like that?"

"To be honest I don't even notice it." Conley was looking at him, lost inside his giant coat. He was right, it did look a bit like a bat cape. He could see him shivering.

"Does it look as bad in daylight?"

Conley craned round to look at it. "Worse actually. He's greyer in daylight. The candles are putting a bit of colour into him." Conley considered this new phenomenon. "Maybe it was meant to be seen this way. I never thought of that."

"The blood looks almost wet."

"It does, doesn't it?"

Danny slapped his arms round himself. "Fuck me, if I get any colder I'm going to freeze to this fucking floor." He hugged the coat tight about himself. He noticed Conley's bed for the first time. It was huge. "You've got a double bed."

"Yes."

"You bastard, you let me freeze out there and you've got a fucking double bed." Danny walked round it.

"I don't see..." Conley stared in horror as Danny began pulling his coat off then his jeans. "What are you doing?"

"Getting in."

"You can't come in here."

"Try and fucking stop me. I'm not going to freeze to death just because you've got touchy-feely problems. You sleep on the couch if you like."

Danny left on his shirt and socks and climbed in. Conley squirmed over the other side of the bed.

"Fucking ecstasy. Heat."

Conley lay there, heart thumping, knowing he was going to be sick. *Knowing* it.

"You can't stay here."

"Look there's at least two feet between us. At least. That's more than there was on the settee, remember?"

Conley said nothing.

"I'm not going to touch you. I just want to sleep. I'll stay here, you stay there. Everything will be just hunky dory... and you won't have a corpse on your sofa in the morning. Okay? Now relax, smile." Danny smiled at him.

Conley looked at his head, blood red against the pillow, his mouth smiling, and nodded.

"Good. Great. I love you too."

Conley watched the boy close his eyes.

FORTY-SEVEN

Conley knew there was something wrong as soon as he woke.

He turned onto his back, heart thumping, then turned slowly to face it.

There was someone in the bed with him.

He scrabbled away, almost falling out of the bed.

He could see the corner of his cheek, the back of his head. He was lying half on his back, still safely on his side of the bed.

Conley lay there for a moment watching him, taking deep breaths. *He's not going to move. You're safe, see? He's quite still. Asleep and quite still.*

Conley felt behind him for the clock, not taking his eyes off Danny's back. He found it and brought it round. Just before eight. He put it back and eased round onto his back. He lay there looking at the ceiling. The room was lit faintly from the open curtains at one end of the room. He could tell from the light that the snow was still there, thick and white.

"What time is it?"

Conley jumped as Danny's voice came clear out of nowhere. He sounded wide awake.

Conley turned and looked at him. He hadn't moved but he was turning over now. He yawned slowly, like a cat. He looked up. "Jesus, that thing's gruesome."

Conley relaxed a little. It was fine, okay.

Danny pushed the quilt down and stretched his arms above his head. Some time during the night he'd taken off his shirt. Conley could see the thick red hair under his arms. All his hair was an identical shade, no variations, like something synthetic, perfect, just like him - except for the man-made damage. He was a human battlefield.

"No point in asking you for breakfast I take it? Unless I want cake." Danny smiled at him.

"I can nip out and get something from the bakers. That's what I usually do."

The boy's smile was something. It changed his whole face. Conley wished suddenly he could show him he was sorry, that he'd appreciated the things he'd tried to do for him. More than that, show him he was human. But he couldn't reach over the vast distance that separated them to make that fragile contact.

"What time do you start work?"

"Nine-thirty, but I'll take you home first. I'm in luck today, cancelled appointment, so I'll have plenty of time to get you back."

"We'll have to dig your car out first."

"Let's hope not." Conley began to feel vaguely unreal, lying here in bed talking to someone. This must be what being in a relationship was like, waking up beside someone, chatting. And more of course.

Conley caught himself blushing and turned to get up. He swung upright and paused on the edge of the bed, wondering about getting dressed. He felt very naked. He felt sure the boy was watching him. He stood up.

Danny watched his back, saw how thin he was, waited for him to stand up. He got up eventually, long and pale and smooth. Danny whistled at him. "Nice arse."

Conley heard him and flushed to the roots of his hair. He pulled his underwear on quickly, then his trousers. Anything to cover up. He was such an easy target, blushing like a virgin every time he looked at him.

He went past the bottom of the bed en route to the wardrobe and glanced at him. He was lying on his back, following him with his eyes, smiling. "No-one ever told you

you had a nice arse before?"

"Obviously not." Conley despaired at his own brusque tone. He shot the boy another glance but he was still smiling.

Danny was looking at his chest, but the light wasn't good enough to see by. "No hairy chest?" he asked.

"It's very pale." Conley blushed again and rummaged for a clean shirt. He pulled it on and fastened it, tucking it inside his trousers.

Danny watched him rifling through waistcoats. There must be about four hundred in there. He finally came out with something in green. Danny caught a sparkle off it. "Turn round, let me see it."

Conley turned, fastening it.

"Come here."

Conley move a little closer. Danny sat up on his elbows. "Fish?"

Conley nodded. Danny lay back down. "You're a fish freak."

"How so?"

"Your bathroom, your waistcoat. Is that what you've got tattooed on your wrist too?" Danny saw him stand still a moment.

"No."

"What is it then?"

"As you would say, none of your business."

"Me? Never. I would say, None of your fucking business."

Conley said, "Why d'you swear so much?"

"Why don't you ever?"

"There's no need."

"Like there's no need for sex?"

Conley didn't answer.

"Or do you mean you've never let the need come out?"

"I don't see the connection."

"You wouldn't."

Conley turned away. There was a tense silence. Breakfast, he thought, that's what we need. "What do you want?"

"Your body."

Conley stood still for a long moment then realised he was teasing him. God what a fool he was being. "Very funny. What do you want for breakfast?"

"Whatever you're having."

"I usually have doughnuts and black coffee."

"Oh Jesus Christ..."

"You did say..."

"Make it a roll and cheese or something."

"They do bacon rolls."

"Fine. Two bacon rolls."

"Two?"

"That's right, two, I'm a growing boy." *Like right now I'm growing a hard-on.*

"Anything else?"

"Give me a kiss before you go."

Conley looked at his face. No smile, not a trace of one. He was joking, wasn't he? Conley gave him a last quick look and went out to put on his coat.

Danny heard the front door close and rolled over onto Conley's side of the bed. He buried his face in his pillow. *Wonder what he'd do if I suggested we jerk off together? Okay Conley, no problem, we don't need to touch, just me in my hand you in yours.*

I'd like to see that, as John would say.

Danny pushed his hands under Conley's pillow and kissed it. It hurt his mouth. He kissed it again, slowly at first, then harder, humping himself against the bed. Eventually he stopped, panting. Wouldn't do to come in Mr Conley's bed. Wouldn't do at all. *Sorry Mr Conley, but while you were out I dry-humped your bed, figured it's the closest I'd ever get to you.* Not polite behaviour.

He rolled on his back, arms spread across the bed. *What the fuck are you doing Danny-boy? What the fuck next?*

The front door slammed. Danny watched the lights flicker on through the slats of the blinds. "Danny?"

"Yeah."

"Power's on again. You want some coffee?"

"Okay."

Conley took the rolls to the kitchen and put them in the microwave to reheat. He put the doughnuts in beside them. He liked them hot.

He put the coffee on and washed the cups. He went over to the bedroom. Danny was sitting on the edge of the bed pulling up his shorts. He looked up in time to see Conley change colour for the umpteenth time.

"Sorry." Conley turned away.

"Oh for fuck's sake." Danny lost his temper without being sure why he was losing it. "You can turn round now. It's safely locked away."

But Conley didn't turn round. It hadn't looked like that last night. Not sticking up like that, with no visible means of support. Or had he just been too drunk?

"What's wrong? Never seen a boner before?"

"Not for a long time."

"Lucky you," Danny muttered, pulling on his shirt and fastening his jeans. He wondered what Conley would say if he added, Jerk it off for me Conley, seeing as John's not here, there's a good lad. Act of Christian charity, otherwise I'm not fit to know all day.

Conley turned finally and said, "Look, I'm sorry, you must find me a pain." He shrugged. "But I'm not used to having people around me, let alone people like..." He stopped.

"Like...?"

"I'm sorry, I'm making things worse."

"No, like what?"

"Like you."

"And what am I like?"

Conley turned his head, looking around him as if he might see the answer written somewhere. "Very..." he paused, "well, very sexual I suppose."

"You mean *over*sexed."

"I don't know, what's oversexed?"

"Me. Me who'd fuck anything. If it moves, fuck it, that's my motto. Think I'd fuck you?"

Conley's eyes darted away as if he was looking for an escape route. "I don't know."

"Oh, but you could make a guess surely." The boy took a step towards him. It was all he could do to stop himself from stepping back.

"I suppose so." He flushed again. It felt like conceit to say so but the boy had confessed as much last night.

"Think I'd like to?"

"I can't answer that."

"Try."

"No."

439

"No, you don't think so or no, you won't even try?"

Conley didn't say anything.

The boy took another step towards him.

Conley stepped back this time.

"You don't know what you're doing, do you?" Danny circled him, right round, like a great cat pacing round its prey, then he came up behind him, so close Conley could feel his breath on his neck, and whispered, "I want to pull your dick."

Conley shot forward, away from him. But when he turned back the boy hadn't moved. He was still standing there looking at him, his eyes like dull metal. He was waiting for Conley to say something, but he couldn't think of a thing to say.

The coffee buzzed, suddenly, loudly. Mamma squawked, berating them in German.

The boy turned away and walked over to the window. Conley watched him lean his head against the glass and push his hands deep into his pockets. He went to the kitchen and poured the coffee. He took the food from the microwave and loaded it onto a tray. He crossed back to the window. Outside the world was vast and white. He reached out his hand and touched the boy's arm. Danny's head came up. Conley kept his hand there by sheer effort of will. He could feel the heat of the skin on his fingertips. He was going to be sick. He was going to die. "Come and have breakfast," he said.

And he took his hand back and turned away.

They didn't leave Conley's house till after ten o'clock. It took them almost an hour to dig the car out and get it started. But it didn't particularly matter because the roads were untraversable anyway. Most of Conley's clients had either not appeared or rung up to say they wouldn't be appearing. Sheard had agreed to do any business that *did* turn up. Whymper went home and Conley went out to help Danny. They avoided looking at each other. "Everything okay?"

Danny nodded.

"Have you got everything?"

Danny nodded again and got in the car. Conley climbed in beside him.

They drove slowly through the snow. Huge banks of it had been swept up onto the sides of the road. Half way there they caught up with the snow plough. They followed the huge tail-back following the monster.

"It's going to be a slow haul," Conley said as they crawled forward then came to a halt.

"It doesn't matter."

Conley turned the heater up. It was only just beginning to make an impression. He glanced at the boy. He looked cold and pinched. He wanted to apologise again but sensed it would only annoy him. Conley looked out at the sky. It was grey. It was going to snow again.

"Listen..." Conley jumped at the sound of his voice, "about this morning."

"It doesn't matter."

"Fucking shut up and listen." Danny's eyes flashed at him.

Conley shut up.

"I get like that sometimes, if I don't..." He hesitated. Christ, this stupid dick was getting to him. "I get like that if I don't get my rocks off. I can't think straight, everything goes to fuck. I'm like a werewolf, you know? Full moon and I don't know where I am." Danny glanced at him. "I know you can hardly comprehend this, but you're right, I am like an addict I suppose, have to go a day without my fix and I'm not fit to know. I'm sorry I put the wind up you."

Conley blinked. "Do you mean you need to have sex *every* day?"

The boy was looking out the window again. He laughed shortly and turned to him. "Is that so unusual?"

Conley wanted to say, But who with? But how could he? What business was it of his?

"In fact, I usually do it two or three times a day. Now do you see why I'm so ratty? I haven't even got a cigarette."

Conley looked at him. He really did look like an addict going through withdrawal symptoms. "That can't be normal."

Danny turned on him. "And you are? Just get off my fucking case, okay?"

Well done Max. You handled that very nicely. You'll be telling him next it's not nice. "I'm sorry, I spoke without thinking."

"Yeah, but you still thought it."

"I'm sorry."

"Oh fucking shut up."

"Can't you... I mean, couldn't you...?"

Danny looked at him.

"What I'm trying to say is, couldn't you relieve it yourself?" Conley felt himself flush with sickening predictability.

"You mean wank?"

"Yes."

"No." The boy turned away, conversation finished.

Conley stared at him. "Why not?"

"It makes it worse." He didn't bother to look at him. His voice was flat, disinterested. Conley saw him lean his head on the window. "It only makes it worse."

There was a silence then the boy asked, "What will you tell Katherine Henderson?"

Conley dragged his mind back. "I don't know yet." He shrugged. "That I couldn't find anything. That there's nothing there to find. That you weren't impressed. I'll think of something."

"What if she doesn't accept it?"

"Then I'll think of something else."

Danny looked at him.

"I got you into it," Conley said.

Danny shook his head.

"Well anyway, I'll think of something."

There was another silence. Danny was looking out of the window. From this side you couldn't see the damaged mouth. His beauty was flawless. This morning Katherine Henderson would probably sell her soul for him. He was charged up with sexual energy. He emanated it. He reminded Conley of standing beneath heavy electrical pylons. That feeling of being near intense energy. Your brain begins to come apart, your nerves to jump. You can feel the vibrations of it right through you.

"I'd really fuck you up. You know that, don't you?" He hadn't moved his head.

"Yes," Conley admitted.

The boy laughed, dry and humourless. "I'm not normally so nice you know. Usually I just fuck people up for the hell of it. I don't know why you should be an exception."

Conley said nothing.

"I'm lying to you. Truth is, I can't cope with you." The boy closed his eyes then said meaninglessly, "Oh *boy.*"

Conley wished he could reassure him, but there was nothing he could say, nothing he could offer. They didn't even talk the same language.

Conley put a cachou in his mouth and looked away.

Danny got home at lunch time. There were pockets of snow on the ground as he went up the lane.

Only Rab and Ian were in the kitchen. Danny looked at them as if they were aliens. He felt as if he'd been away for months.

"Ah, the snow-bound hero returns." Rab applauded languidly.

"Where's John?"

"Straight to the point. Your brother has gone on a rescue mission. We were reprieved. Have you eaten?"

"No."

"Well come in, sit down. We all love you here." Rab's sarcasm lasted as long as it took Danny to smile.

It was a provocative smile. In a league of its own.

Ian watched it work its magic with an anger so intense he could have ripped the table in half. He only had to walk in the fucking door...

Danny went past them and out into the hall. Ian reached for the biscuit packet, watching Rab out the corner of his eye, wondering how long it would take him.

It took him exactly as long as it took Ian to eat one and a half custard creams.

Ian sat alone in the kitchen and stabbed the table.

Forty-eight times.

Danny had left the door open. He had taken his jacket off and was leaning against the sink.

Rab came in and shut the door. "You have such a nice way of wording your invitations."

"I didn't say anything."

"You didn't need to."

Rab sat down on the bed and began rolling a cigarette. Danny watched his hands, always so deft, so precise. He licked it, eyes on Danny's face, then put it in his mouth. He began patting his pockets. Danny threw him a packet of matches, Conley's matches. Rab looked at them then lit the cigarette. He carefully put the matches in his pocket.

"Don't I get one?" Danny asked.

"No."

There was a pause.

"What's he like?" Rab asked.

"Tall, thin, frigid."

Rab said. "I thought that was a woman's disease."

"Who told you that?"

"John."

"Oh, well that would be right then."

There was a silence.

Rab put his head back and exhaled smoke down his nose. The room was scented with it, sweet, smoky, rich. He looked at Danny, eyes narrowed. "You feel absolutely sweet f-all for me, don't you?" He took another quick drag. "In fact, you've always felt sweet fuck all for me, isn't that right?"

Danny didn't answer him.

"Thank you Danny, message received loud and clear." Rab looked down at the floor. "How do you know he's frigid?"

"How do you think?"

Rab looked at him quickly. "You're some kid, you know that?"

Danny didn't answer him.

"How old is he?"

"Thirty-eight."

"You like them mature, don't you?"

Danny looked away from him, sighing deeply. "You come up here to fuck me Rab, or just to talk?"

Rab got up and crossed over to him, leaning hard into him to stub out his cigarette in the sink behind him. "You've got a fucking dirty little mouth Danny. No wonder John likes to punch it."

Danny looked into his face. His eyes were so black Rab could have drowned in them, but his voice was blacker. "I don't love you Rab, I'm never going to love you, but right now I want my cock in your mouth more than life itself."

Rab grabbed him, trying to kiss him, but Danny pushed him away. "Go down on me," he insisted.

There was a moment's hesitation then Rab knelt down in front of him and undid his clothes.

"I'm going to last exactly thirty seconds." Danny spread his legs a little wider, holding the edge of the sink tightly. He looked at Rab's mouth, his lips going over the head of his penis like a condom unfurling. "Not even that long."

He thought of Conley watching him take his shorts down in the bathroom mirror. "Now," he grunted suddenly, grabbing Rab's head and grinding his hips in his face.

And his legs buckled beneath him.

They did it again, slower this time.

Rab moved over him like a man intoxicated, drunk with loneliness.

They did it on John's bed, coming on each other in magnificent displays of prowess, enjoying their mutual combined beauty, knowing they were poetry in motion, lust made human.

Ian came up the stairs quietly. He stood in the corridor and listened to them murmuring together. Then their silence.

He hated every silken strand of hair, every hollow inch of belly, every curve of their hard little backsides, every sliding glossy inch of their cocks. He could see them smiling, bodies entwined, heard Danny say, Harder, heard Rab plead, Slower.

He went downstairs and took their shoes from the rack in the kitchen, a pair each.

He arranged them on the floor, Rab's between Danny's, and then he urinated on them.

He stood in the kitchen watching his urine fill up Danny's shoes, splash off the soles of Rab's trainers.

When he was finished he stood where he was and masturbated. His orgasm was intense, spinning out of him like a spasm of pain.

He wiped himself with a kitchen towel and went out of the house.

Danny washed himself at the sink. Rab lay on the bed smoking, watching him. "I love the way you handle yourself."

Danny said, "How's that?"

"As if your cock was something sacred."

"It is."

Rab laughed. "You really mean that, don't you?"

"You better believe it."

Rab watched him dry himself with equal care. "You're getting another hard-on."

Danny didn't say anything to that. After a pause Rab asked, "Do you ever not feel like it?"

Danny shrugged.

"Not very often, huh?"

Danny smiled back at him and shook his head.

"And tonight you'll do it again with John. How do you keep it up? The pace, that is. Come to that, how do you keep *it* up?"

"Easy, I think about you."

Rab's smile became fixed. "Not funny."

"It wasn't meant to be."

Rab closed his eyes. He didn't want to fight with him, not now. "So Mr Conley isn't seducible?"

"No."

"Not even by you? He must be a hard man to please."

Danny made a noncommittal noise.

Rab studied his face. "Your ego hurting? I didn't think you had one."

Danny said nothing.

"Well, well. Danny's professional pride has been injured."

Danny turned on him but he had no time to reply. They both heard the back door slam.

Rab got up and went out of the room.

Rab went into the kitchen.

John stood looking down at the floor. "I take it Danny's back?"

Rab coloured guiltily, damning himself. John looked at him. "I was referring to that."

Rab looked at the floor. His trainers had been arranged between Danny's in a parody of fucking feet.

"Someone's pissed on them." John picked up the kitchen towel and opened it. "Amongst other things."

"Christ, that dirty little..."

John looked at him and dropped the kitchen towel back on the floor. "Clean it up."

Rab stared at his disappearing back. "Shitty bastard," he whispered.

He wasn't even sure himself which one he meant.

Danny lay on the bed and listened to him come up the stairs. He felt tired and depressed out of nowhere.

John came in and looked at him. The window was closed tight but the room was frozen. "Very efficient Danny."

Danny followed his movements with his eyes.

John came to rest at the foot of the bed, his hands deep in his pockets. "Well, you've written Mr Conley an excellent character reference anyway."

Danny frowned. He couldn't understand what he was saying. He waited because it would get there eventually.

"I suppose if Rab hadn't been here you'd have had the dog. I mean Ian *is* somewhere below the dog, isn't he?"

Danny understood. "I didn't..."

John held up his hand. "Please. Ian left me a little note. Roughly translated it read, Rab is upstairs fucking your little brother. I'd like to piss in his face. Signed Ian. Love and kisses of course."

Danny watched him uneasily.

444

"You both look as sleek as cats. Well, Rab does. You never do look quite fed. The little sexual carnivore - eat it up as soon as you get it, don't even taste it going down."

He looked at him again and Danny saw it in his face, like skin-writing, demonic possession, all written there in black and white. "It's a sickness with you. You're like a compulsive eater. Every dick, every cunt, every body, and still everybody loves you. No matter what you do to them they all love you. Even me."

John took his jacket off. The smell of animals was strong on him. "Think you can take me and Rab in one afternoon?"

Danny sat up slowly and began taking off his clothes. John waited till he was finished before taking off his own. Danny lay back on the bed and watched him. He never grew tired of watching him.

John came over and straddled him, knees on either side, pinning down Danny's arms. It was uncomfortable but not yet painful. He wasn't erect. His cock hung, slack and heavy, inches from Danny's face.

John looked down at him then reached a hand back to feel for him. His smile was slow and wide when he caught it. "You're a pleasure to do business with Danny." He squeezed the swollen flesh. Danny looked back at him, said nothing.

John let him go and lifted his own cock, gently peeling back the head.

Then he pissed in Danny's face.

Danny took a moment to register what was happening, then he yelled. His mouth immediately filled with it. He coughed and gagged, squirming under him, unable to escape it.

John was speaking, low and intent. "Oh yes, I can see what he sees in it, exactly what I needed. The release is just right." He was erect almost immediately, before he had properly emptied his bladder, the erection choking the flow.

Danny was coughing beneath him, hair soaking wet, eyes stinging. He couldn't even free his hands.

John held him there and began to masturbate. It didn't take him long. It spattered onto Danny's face like spat phlegm.

Danny's eyes were closed tightly. He might even have been crying. John really couldn't tell.

And he really didn't care.

Conley went home and went back to bed. He couldn't remember when he'd last gone back to bed during the day. He felt completely drained. He hoped he wasn't coming down with flu.

He had put up all the blinds so that he could see the windows, the rapidly greying light.

The flat felt empty. Mamma's chirruping sounded hollow in the huge room.

He touched himself cautiously. The boy had been wrong about one thing. He never masturbated, because he couldn't get an erection to masturbate.

He ran his hand over his chest.

Two or three times a day? It must be virtually his sole recreation. There was no real reason why not he supposed, but *every* day? It felt so... determined. The boy hadn't really wanted him, just some kind of release from his frustrations. *He can't do without it and I can't do it at all. Two sexual cripples together.*

He let himself remember the boy standing there, white-faced and intense, telling him he wanted to touch him. No-one had ever wanted to touch him, not really. Nothing but passionless fleeting interests. His own coldness... no, be honest, call it what it

was... his own frigidity keeping them away.

He touched his face, remembering the boy touching it in the hospital.

He would have to phone Katherine Henderson.

What the hell was he going to tell her?

He suddenly saw a red hair on the pillow. He moved closer to it and picked it up. He found another and laid them side by side.

He slept here, beside me. Someone else slept beside me, wanted to touch me. I don't care why, he did want it.

He pressed his lips against the hairs, holding his breath. A dull, nerveless kiss. A parody.

What am I doing?

He pulled away onto his back. He couldn't even do that properly. His body was soft and limp while inside his heart was raging hard.

He got up suddenly and went to the kitchen. He ate both the half gateaux with his hands, cramming them into his mouth. He stood naked, leaning back against the fridge, heart hammering, face flushed.

Better. That was better.

He went to the bathroom and stuck his finger down his throat and threw it all back up. A brightly coloured sweet sticky mess.

He watched it swirl down the sink.

"Turn round."

Danny turned to face him.

John washed his belly, picking the hairs clean. He eased the dressing off and washed round the wound.

He washed his genitals, as reverentially as Danny did himself. Danny grew erect in his hand. John ignored it and turned him back again, washing his backside. The soap stung in the cuts. Danny winced. Blood started afresh and ran pinkly down the backs of his legs. He braced his arms against the wall and parted his legs as he was told. He felt John's hand slick between the cheeks of his arse. His erection came up again. John washed his legs.

Eventually John let him out. He threw a towel at him. "Here, dry yourself." Obviously he was tired of playing dolls today.

He sat down on the linen basket and watched Danny dry himself, thinking about how that afternoon must have went. Danny had obviously come home after a failed attempt to seduce Conley. The poor little soul had been burning up and only Rab to milk out his pain. What a shame.

You could read Danny's spoor with you eyes shut. Even without Ian he'd have known it. Danny should have been on a flyer, dick like a hot pole, but someone had taken the edge off. A little bird called Rab had caught the early worm. *His* worm.

"Do you really think I'm so blind Danny or do you just not care?"

Danny didn't say anything. He was drying his feet on the side of the bath. John heard the first few flakes of snow flurrying against the window. It was almost dark outside. He would have to go down for the evening milking shortly.

"What am I going to do with you?"

Danny shrugged. He couldn't trust himself to speak.

"I know what I'd like to do with you."

Danny looked at him quickly then away again.

"I'd like to keep you wanked up and hungry, no way of satisfying yourself. I'd like to keep you how I feel. That's what I'd *like* to do."

Danny was standing still, listening to him, back to him so John couldn't see his

face.

"I've wanted to do that for a long time, you know." He wasn't talking about the same thing any more but he couldn't give it its name. Even the thought of having done it was stirring up something unimaginable in him.

"I know."

"I saw Ian do it to you once."

Danny nodded as if that answered him.

"You think I enjoy it, don't you?"

Danny was securing a towel around his waist, back still turned stiffly against him. John could see tiny spots of blood soaking through it. "Yes."

"You think I do it because it excites me, just like you think I cut you because it excites me."

"Yes."

"You think all my talk about crime and punishment is just an excuse to hurt and humiliate you."

Danny turned to him finally, face set and white. "Yes John, I do."

John smiled as if it was the most exquisite joke he'd ever heard. He smiled at him forever, eyes lingering over his mouth. "Too fucking right it is Danny-boy."

And he got up and pulled off Danny's towel.

FORTY-EIGHT

Conley phoned Katherine Henderson two days later. He was immensely surprised to hear a recorded message telling him she was away from home and would be back the first week in December. He looked at his calendar. Next week. He felt as if he'd been reprieved without really knowing why.

Twice he asked Molly to put a call through to Daniel Jackson Moore and twice he stopped her.

He had a bad time with his clients. They seemed suddenly difficult and irritating, obsessed with trivialities.

At five o'clock he tried again. This time by sitting on his hands he managed to let the call go through. He listened to it ringing. Eight rings, that's all he'd give it. It rang eight times. He stared at it, still sitting on his hands. On the twelfth ring someone answered it. Conley couldn't be sure who it was. All they said was, Hello? No number, no identification. "Can I speak to Danny please?"

"Speaking."

Conley sat there, heart thumping, utterly unable to speak.

"Hello?"

His voice didn't sound right on the phone, too deep, not matching his face. Conley said, "It's James Conley."

There was a silence. Danny stood in the hall in his work clothes, looking at the mess his feet had left. The insistent sound of the phone had pulled him from the milking shed. He sat down on the stairs. "What do you want?"

How could he answer that?

"I want to see you again." He felt his heart stop. He hadn't meant to say that. The words were terrible, all wrong. He longed to take them back. The silence seemed to go on forever.

"When?"

Conley reached out his hand and touched the phone, wishing he'd taken it off speaker, not had their voices loud and stark in the room. "Tonight?"

"When?"

"Anytime you like."

Danny rested his head on the banister. "Seven o'clock."

"Yes," said Conley. "No problem. I'll be there at seven o'clock." He wanted to say something else - I'm glad, I'm looking forward to it - but he was too late, Danny had already gone.

The dialling tone filled the room.

Danny moved back along the shed. John reached out his hand and pulled him to him, Danny's back against his front. "Who was it?"

"James Conley."

John's arms held him tight round the waist. He lifted his head, momentarily stilled. "What did he want?"

"He wants to see me tonight." Danny willed himself to relax. *Be easy, don't make him think*.

"Will that fucking bitch never give up? I thought you said they had nothing?" John pulled him round to face him, looking into his eyes.

"They don't. I don't know what he wants. I'll find out tonight, won't I?"

John's eyes searched his face. Danny kept his eyes level. *Don't look away, otherwise you won't get out the house.*

"She won't be there?"

Danny almost smiled. "No, just him."

John laughed. "Poor baby." He kissed him, softly, exploring his mouth. "Don't worry, I'll be waiting for you."

Danny kissed him back, filled with a sudden desire for him. He reached inside John's jacket and fumbled at his clothes.

John's face became bright with amusement. "One for the road?"

"I need it," Danny said, knowing he would, knowing he was going to need it a whole lot worse when he came back.

John's face lost its smile as he felt Danny's hand, tight and demanding, inside his clothes. "It's okay baby," he whispered. "It's okay."

And they leaned up hard against the wall.

Conley turned up quarter of an hour late. He had been so afraid of being early he was late instead, and when he realised he was going to be late it shot his nerves to pieces.

Rab was in the kitchen with Danny. Danny knew he was watching him and tried to relax. Where *was* he?

"Think he's stood you up?"

Danny jumped guiltily. He turned round, face flushed. "Fucking shut up."

Rab looked at him, only his eyebrows saying what he thought, then he looked at the table, moving crumbs with his finger. "John finds out Danny and you're in big trouble."

"Finds out what?"

"Just how hot to trot you are for our Mr Conley."

Danny looked away, disdaining to answer him.

"How have you managed to cover it up?"

Sheer fucking mind over matter, Danny thought. But he said, "Stop talking shit." He was amazed at how genuine he sounded, as if he really meant it. *Danny you're great. You're a hero. Hell, we really admire you - a liar amongst liars.*

"You lie beautifully Danny, very persuasive."

It was too close. Danny walked over to the window, away from him.

Someone knocked on the back door.

Danny stood there, riveted with something approaching stage fright. Rab got up and went past him. It was time he had a look at the competition.

He opened the door.

A tall, thin corpse stood there, cold and soulless as the grave. His eyes were like brackish water. His hair was flaked with snow. He had a huge black coat on. A flash of bright gem-blue came from between the sides, otherwise there was no colour on him at all. He was incredibly, outrageously erotic. Rab turned from him and said, "Danny..."

But he needn't have bothered, Danny was already there.

The ghoul smiled past him, face flickering into brief life, then they had passed out into the snow.

The car smelt of violets. Red leather and violets.

You can't smell a colour, Danny thought. "What colour are the seats?" he asked. He couldn't remember. He must have seen them but he couldn't remember.

Conley smiled. "Red."

"I thought so, they smell it."

"Smell it?"

"Uh-huh."

Conley shook his head and let it pass.

"Henderson would have loved this car," Danny said.

"He did. That's how I first met him, drooling over my car."

Danny looked at him. "I thought you'd worked for him."

"I did. But I met him in the street. He was going to book me for double parking, but he let me off when he fell in love with my car."

"More likely with you."

There was a silence.

"I don't think so," Conley managed.

"Huh, don't you believe it." And Danny looked out the window.

Conley read the signs. End of discussion. He'd seen it before.

Danny took in a deep breath, aware of him there beside him, smelling like a confectioner's. He wondered how long he'd get before it started.

Once, when he was a teenager, he had been standing in the only late-night shop the district had. It was part of a garage. He had been in a queue behind a man and his son. The boy must have been ten, eleven, years old. He was sleepy and dirty-faced and Danny had had an intense desire to touch him. Once it had started it wouldn't stop. It spread to the boy's father, and then the girl behind the counter. He wanted to feel the heaviness of her breasts, curve her heavy hips into his hands, stick his tongue in her mouth, taste the metallic oil of her lipstick. He got a cock-stand that frightened him, instantaneous and painful. He had got back into the van and stopped Ian's hand on the ignition and unzipped himself and offered it, just like that, with huge work lights lighting them up, and cars coming and going, people passing within yards of them. Ian thought it was his birthday.

"What are you thinking?"

About my brother giving me head in the middle of a petrol station. "Nothing in particular, why?"

"You were very thoughtful."

"I'm always thoughtful when I'm thinking."

Conley laughed. Danny realised that he liked the sound of his laugh.

The snow was coming down thicker and faster. "Looks like another heavy one," Danny said.

Conley nodded and they both thought, Maybe we'll be snowed in again. Conley could feel a distant panic and Danny a distant desperation. They were both silent, the tension starting.

Danny laid his head against the glass and took a deep breath. *Forget it, be calm.* "So what did she say?" he asked suddenly.

"Who?" Conley glanced at him.

"Katherine Henderson."

"I haven't spoken to her yet. She's away."

Danny felt as if someone had told him the earth was flat. "Then why...?" He paused, catching at the threads before he said anything else. Conley knew it and was dreading it. "Then why am I here?"

The truth Max, go on. "Because I don't care if you..." he stumbled before the hurdle then leapt it, "fuck me up, I still want you to try and help me." He glanced at him quickly. "I think if anyone can, you can. I want you to try." His face was scarlet. He was glad of the dark so that the boy couldn't see him.

Danny lay there blinking. Then he said slowly and carefully, because this was

Conley's last chance, "You don't seem to understand." His voice was hard and clipped. Conley felt his heart sink at the rejection in it. "I don't want to help you. I don't give a monkey's fuck about helping you. All I want from you..." and Danny heard it himself and couldn't help it, his voice sinking into the deep intoxicating mire of it, "is contained in those two fat little bags between your legs."

Conley could still feel the deep vibrations of it going through him.

"Let me near you and I'll try my damnedest to suck them dry, believe me."

Conley turned to him and smiled, tentatively at first then more confidently. "I'll take that risk."

And suddenly, out of nowhere, they both burst out laughing.

The flat was warm and enveloping. Danny felt as if he was coming home. The feeling frightened him. It wasn't his home. He didn't belong here, and he never would. He was afraid to let himself enjoy it.

Suddenly the bird began to talk, its voice low and inviting, eerily human. Danny turned to Conley who was shaking out his coat. "What's she saying?"

Conley smiled. "She's telling you a story. Once upon a time there was a beautiful prince and the prince's name was Rose Red. She doesn't understand what she's saying. She mixes the stories up..." Conley looked at him. "Then again..."

Danny grinned. "Hey, that sounded suspiciously like flirting."

Conley flushed, lifted his hands, denying. "Only an observation, not an opinion."

Danny looked at him. He was wearing the same black suit and a brilliant blue waistcoat. A gold chain went across the middle, assumably a watch. He wasn't wearing a tie. The white shirt stood open at the neck. He was standing with his hands in his trouser pockets.

"You look very fuckable."

Conley watched that same dirty, hungry expression on his face. He turned away. "You want some coffee?"

Danny smiled at his back. "No, I want some hard alcohol."

Conley went over to the kitchen. "I've been shopping, in honour of your visit."

"You were very sure of yourself."

Conley flushed. "Don't pick on me, I'm sensitive."

Danny smiled. "Okay, what have you got?"

Conley rattled them off. "New whisky, although we didn't drink the old, some beer in the fridge, and two kinds of rum."

"You're a mind reader. Another bad habit I picked up off Henderson. Give me rum." Danny rubbed his hands and sat down.

"White or dark?"

"Dark."

Conley began pouring drinks. Danny watched a heavy dull lock of fair hair falling over his eyes. Periodically he swept it back only to have it fall back again. Danny wondered how his hair felt, wondered how he could get a chance to find out.

Conley handed him his drink. Danny saw that he still kept his hand away from him. He sat down opposite him.

"Sit beside me," Danny said.

"Not yet, let me have something to drink first."

Danny smiled. "Okay."

There was a silence then Danny said, "This feels weird."

"What?"

"Being out the house without a reason, sitting here not having to wonder what you're after, when I'm going to fall in the shit." He laughed. "I don't think I feel right

without something to worry about."

"Well, when Katherine Henderson comes back you can start worrying again."

"Thanks, you've really cheered me up."

"Sorry."

"Let's talk about something else, huh?"

"Okay? Who do you sleep with?"

"What?"

Conley knew it was a mistake as soon as he said it. "I'm sorry, I shouldn't have asked."

Danny shrugged.

Conley had apologised but he still wanted to know. He *really* wanted to know. "Is it a man or a woman? Just tell me that."

Danny stared at him till he flushed with embarrassment and looked at the table. "God, you don't give up, do you?"

"I don't suppose there's any point in apologising again?"

"No. Let's just drop it, okay?"

"Okay."

They were silent and Danny knew it had started already. He wanted to climb over the table and rip his clothes off. He wanted to say, I fuck my brother, get off on that. He took a swig of rum. It was a different brand from Henderson's but it was still good, strong and dark. He hoped it pissed him right out his head, beyond it all.

Conley poured them some more.

Danny looked at him and knew this was a mistake. He ought to go home.

And suffer there instead? Might as well go hungry here as there. At least you can see him here. At least he is *here.*

Conley was aware of him staring at him, his eyes making a mockery of the distance between them. He wished he'd stop it. He thought he could handle this, but he couldn't. He'd never been on the receiving end of anything like this and it scared him. It scared him shitless. He laughed.

Danny looked at him in surprise. "What is it?"

"You're having a bad effect on me."

"How?"

"I just told myself I was scared shitless."

"Bad language."

"Deplorable language."

Danny held his eyes for a long unnerving moment then said, "Let me touch you."

Conley shook his head. "I can't, I'm sorry."

Conley watched his tongue come out and moisten his lips, then he got up. Conley shook his head again.

Danny came round beside him and sat down. "See? Just the same distance as last time. No sweat."

Conley watched him, felt the dull thumping in his chest.

Danny looked at his mouth, the dull heavy hair. "You won't die."

"No, honestly, I can't."

"You brought me here. I warned you."

You brought him here Max.

Mamma began a violent screeching. Conley jumped. Danny put his hand on his thigh.

Conley went rigid. He looked at Danny's hand as if it was a tarantula crawling up his leg. He wanted to ask him to move it but he couldn't. He couldn't say a word.

Danny felt the heat come through the fineness of the fabric, the hard leg beneath. He was close enough for his first real scent of him. He slid his hand along his thigh

and felt the terror in Conley's body. His face had changed colour. He was sickly grey with fright. Just one quick feel, then he'd let him go. He ran his hand over his crotch.

Conley went apeshit.

He scrabbled out from under Danny's hand and was across the room in about thirty seconds. Danny sat there bemused, wondering how he'd done it. He was standing braced against the far wall like a man awaiting execution by firing squad.

Danny lay down and put a cushion under his head. "Come and sit down," he said quietly. "I won't touch you again."

Eventually Conley came back and sat down opposite him. He picked up Danny's glass and emptied it in a oner. When he filled it again Danny heard the bottle rattle against the side. His hand was shaking and he couldn't stop it.

"This isn't going to work," Danny said. He felt immensely depressed. Suddenly he wanted John; arrogant, demanding, crushing the very life out of him, fearless to the point of lunacy. That's what he wanted, John's fearlessness.

"I'm sorry." Conley's voice was barely a whisper.

"*Don't...*" Danny took a deep breath. *Be calm.* "Don't fucking start apologising."

There was a brittle silence then Danny tried again. "Face facts, you're trying to do something you don't even like. Underneath all those hang-ups you're one hundred per cent straight. You wouldn't touch a boy in a million years. You just aren't interested. You're trying to do something doubly impossible, relax while you're feeling revolted. It's stupid. The whole idea's stupid. What we need to do is convince Katherine Henderson she fancies you. *I'm* going home. This is the last time I'm going to see you, okay? No more stupid games. You dying of fright, me dying of frustration. This is it, finished, the end of a beautiful big nothing." Danny stopped talking because he could feel tears in his throat. He couldn't believe this was happening to him. He put his arm over his eyes, blotting out the light. He breathed slowly and carefully, making the tears go away.

"Danny?"

"What?"

"You're wrong."

That was all he said, nothing more. They lay there, each wrapped up in their own silence, not knowing what else to say.

Right or wrong Danny wasn't going through this again. He couldn't cope with it.

"Danny?" Danny didn't answer this time but Conley knew he was listening. "Stay and talk to me."

Danny took his arm off his eyes. He turned his head in time to see Conley get to his feet. He saw the buckle on his waistcoat glint as he walked over to the light switches, looked at the neat folds where the blue fabric tucked down over his back, then the lights went out.

There was no sound of him coming back. The dark was complete, velvety. The thick drapes cut out all the light. It was like floating. Then Danny heard the brush of fabric as he sat down, cushions being moved, then stillness again.

"You alright?" Conley's voice seemed closer in the darkness.

"Mm."

Conley seemed to hear the difference too. He was silent. Danny asked him, "Scared?"

"No," he said, and it sounded true.

"Why the dark?" Danny asked.

There was a pause. "I don't know, it seemed right."

"Let's hope we don't fall asleep."

Conley laughed. "I hope we do then you'll be here when I wake."

Danny turned that one over but couldn't fit it in.

"You were only here one night but I missed you after you went. Like every cliché in the book, the place felt empty without you."

Danny laughed quietly. "Sounds like a song."

"It probably is. I'm probably unconsciously quoting."

They were silent again.

"Danny?"

"Mm?"

"I lied to you. I didn't want to avoid women because of the sexual thing... What I mean is... What I'm trying to say is... Oh, to hell with it. I'm impotent. I can't get it up. I haven't been able to get it up for years, that's what I'm trying to say. I couldn't face a woman because I couldn't face that, that's what I'm saying. I thought a man would be better... I thought... Oh, I'm sick of explaining this."

There was another silence. Conley lay as still as glass. *One wrong word and I'll shatter.*

It seemed to go on forever, that long empty silence, then Danny said, "Do you want me to do it for you?"

Conley didn't understand, but something inside him did. It was like an engine roaring into life, starting up and leaving him standing.

"I can pretend to be you and do all the things you're afraid to do."

Conley said, "I don't think I could."

"Yes you can. It's a spectator sport, you don't have to do anything. You can't even touch yourself, can you?"

Conley didn't answer.

"So let me. Tell me what you want and I'll make it happen."

"Even the idea of that scares me."

"Just tell me what you want."

There was a long pause then Conley said quickly before he could change his mind, "Lie on my bed and do... just whatever you would do. Just pretend you're alone on the bed. I'm not even here..." He paused. "Danny?"

"What?"

"My name's Max."

"What?"

"My real name's Maximillian... Max."

Danny tried it. "Max." He said it again. "Max. I'm not sure I like it. I think of you as Conley."

"Then call me Conley, just don't call me James."

"Have I ever?"

Conley didn't answer that. He got up and crossed to the bedroom. Danny felt the air stir as he passed. He sat up. He felt tension knot his stomach. It was almost stage fright. A light came on in the bedroom. He got up and crossed the floor.

Conley was standing by the open wardrobe. He looked quickly at Danny then turned away, consumed by embarrassment.

Danny spoke to his back. "Take the chair out there to the shadows where I can't see you. And get yourself something to drink."

Conley moved past him, still avoiding his eyes.

"And Max..." They both stopped at the unfamiliar sound of his name, Conley turned. "For God's sake, smile."

Conley smiled and went to get his drink.

Danny crossed to the wardrobe and looked inside. Plenty to choose from. He was shorter, and possibly broader in the shoulders, but he could always leave a button or

two undone. He heard Conley move behind him in the room, taking the chair out, but he didn't turn to him.

He took a shirt out - they appeared to all be the same white silky stuff - then a suit. There were two or three black, a couple that might have been navy, and an odd green-grey. He took a black.

Then the waistcoat. He knew which one. The green with the embroidered fishes. He knew because the colour was his and he wanted Conley to be excited by him.

He began to strip off his clothes. He realised he had none of Conley's underwear. Too bad, he'd do without. He could feel Conley watching out in the darkness. He kept his back to him then he began to put on Maximillian Conley's clothes.

Conley sat in the chair holding his drink. He felt unreal. He also felt incredibly perverse, but he let it go. He let it go to Danny, let him carry the weight of it, let him worry about it. He watched him pull down his jeans. His body was far better than his own. Better fed, healthier, more muscled. His skin fresh, smooth. Then he saw with a shock that he had fresh cuts, slashes across his buttocks, shallow, red-raw, barely healed. My God, what did his brother do to him? Strip him down like a prisoner and torture him?

Danny was putting on his shirt. It was too tight for him. He could see it strain across his shoulders. It was also too long, but the silk looked magnificent on him, taut and shiny. He pulled on the trousers without underpants. Conley felt a tug of excitement at the idea of that. It came out of nowhere, twisting his guts. He sat there, slightly surprised by it, then took another drink. The trousers fitted well, better than he would have thought. He saw Danny bend to adjust the legs. Too long? He couldn't see for the bed.

Then he put on the waistcoat. It, too, strained across his back. He was wearing the green. The colour looked dazzling on him, better than it did on Conley. His head was bent, doing up the buttons. He gave it a final tug then half-turned to see himself in the mirror. Conley could see his face in profile. He looked oddly right in the clothes. Conley hadn't expected it.

He watched him in fascination as he slid a hand down inside the waistband of his trousers and shamelessly began masturbating, utterly without self-consciousness. Conley flushed, felt a deep and intense embarrassment. He took another drink. Then he saw Danny had withdrawn his hand, was unzipping the flies.

Conley's glass was arrested half way to his mouth. He watched Danny slide his hand in then slide his penis out. He was hugely erect, just as he had been that morning, only now it looked even more strident, darkly red and curving in the air.

He let it go, just standing there looking at it in the mirror, then he turned to face him.

Conley felt himself blush bright red. *He can't see you.*

Danny crossed to the bed and lay down, arm under his head. He was so much closer now. Conley could see the detailed rich green and gold embroidery on his chest. The top button of the waistcoat was undone, the shirt half-unbuttoned, but his erection was the thing, so dazzling against the black of his trousers. Conley's trousers. *An erection in my trousers*. He felt it turn like a knife in his stomach.

Danny was tracing his fingers up and down it, holding it with one hand while the other circled it, teased it. Conley could almost feel it, so painstaking were his movements. He saw him squeeze it and momentarily close his eyes as if the feeling was too intense, too delicious. And then he said his name, whispered it. *Max.* Conley hadn't expected him to speak. He remembered Danny saying he couldn't relieve himself because it didn't work. It was working for him now.

Danny lay there, eyes half-closed, and began masturbating, slow and hard, whispering his name, watching himself, and Conley became instantly erect. Perfectly, beautifully erect. It came into being in a nanosecond. No half-arousals, no little hints, no warnings, it just happened.

He sat there knowing it was there, feeling the slight ache of it, the unfamiliar urge to ease it. It felt hard and alien. He felt like laughing, crying, everything.

Danny was doing it two-handed now, head reared awkwardly off the bed, the lines of his body tense, and Conley knew suddenly he was going to finish it, knew he'd excited himself beyond the point of no return, saw him try to check it without success. He was whispering to himself, jerking his erection in a way Conley wouldn't have dared.

"Beautiful... fucking *beautiful*. Look at it... *look* at it."

Conley felt the words in his groin like something caressing him. He wanted to hear him say it again, willed him to say it again, and then he saw the first spurt of it, saw Danny's body arc exquisitely as it curved out of him.

"Look at... it..."

Conley touched himself.

"God... look, look... oh...."

Squeezed himself.

"...*God.*"

And felt himself come.

He sat there in his chair watching Danny stroke himself into quietude. His eyes were closed, his lips parted, his skin flushed.

Conley sat there like a glass man, crystal clear, fragile beyond belief, knowing what had just happened, not believing what had just happened, feeling the barely remembered sensation of an erection, the imperfect orgasm, a wet dream waking. He heard himself speak.

Danny turned to him immediately. "What is it?" Eyes wide open, looking into the darkness, searching for him.

"I should never have..."

Danny sat up on his elbows. "What is it, what's wrong?"

Conley could only shake his head.

Danny got up, pushing himself inside Conley's trousers. He crossed over the few feet to where Conley sat. He was afraid to get too close.

"I got excited..." He stopped.

Danny stared at him, trying to read his face. "You were supposed to get excited, what's wrong?"

"I'm... it's..."

"Oh Jesus," Danny laughed. "You've got a hard-on, is that what you're trying to say?"

He nodded. It was the best he could do.

"Let me see."

"I can't."

"I just tossed off for you," Danny reminded him. "Let me see."

"I *can't.*"

"Course you can. Come on or I'll come over there myself."

Conley closed his eyes and unzipped his trousers, knowing it would shrivel up before his gaze, before Danny the Living Embodiment of Sex.

"Jesus Christ you've..." Danny's voice was a surprised whisper. "Dirty fuck, *now* you need a good lick and polish."

"I..."

"Come on, let me, before you lose it."

"Danny, I..." But Danny was already kneeling between his legs, hands on his knees, spreading his legs, pulling open his clothes.

Conley looked down and saw himself, bigger than ever, covered in slime, inches from Danny's mouth. "No," he said.

Danny's mouth closed over him, began to pull him in, deep and hard. He felt a wave of repulsion. "*No*," he said again, shaking his head. "Oh God... *no*." Danny's red hair like blood in his lap. Danny's face pressed into the sweat of his groin. Sucking him. So hard.

He laid his hand on Danny's head. The touch of his hair was like an electric charge up his arm, galvanising him. "*No!*" he cried, lifting himself out the chair, clutching him with both hands, pushing.

Pushing.

Pushing...

John didn't trust him an inch. He decided to drive to Henderson's flat and see if they were there. He felt sure Danny was lying to him.

He waited until he had been gone half an hour and then followed him out.

He drove slowly. When he got there he sat for a while watching the snow whirl round the lights then he got out and crossed to the doorway.

He pressed the bell.

Nothing happened.

He pressed it again.

He stood there a moment then tried a third time.

She wasn't in.

He went back through the snow like a blind man, hearing nothing, seeing nothing.

The little whore.

He slammed the car into reverse.

The fucking little whore.

Ian found Rab in the living room. As usual he was lying flat on his back in the dark watching the television with the sound turned down. It was a talking head show. Ian closed the door. "You can't possibly get any pleasure out of that."

Rab strained to look over his shoulder at him then turned back to the screen. "Don't bet on it." He took the cigarette out of his mouth and lifted his arm, letting the back of his hand rest on his forehead. The smoke rose from the cigarette like a halo uncoiling from his head.

Ian crossed to the window and looked out between the curtains. "Snowing again."

"Bully for it."

Ian came back in and crossed to the fire. He stood in front of it, looking at Rab stretched out on the settee. "I don't know what he sees in him."

Rab didn't ask who he meant. "I do."

Ian smiled slightly. "Fancy him?"

"No, but I can see why he does."

"I haven't seen him, what's he like?"

"Cold, colourless and thin."

Ian laughed. "Doesn't sound too sexy."

"You haven't seen him."

Ian looked at him a moment longer then said matter-of-factly, "You're queer as fuck

Rab."

Rab put the cigarette in his mouth again and took a long slow draw, held it for a moment, then let it out equally slowly. The smoke furled down his chest, disappeared.

"Aren't you?" Ian persisted, still no malice, no malintent.

Rab looked at him finally. "What do you think?"

Ian's mouth laughed but no sound came out. "Still can't say it?"

"Can you?"

"Easy. I'm queer, a faggot, a poof. I like doing it with little boys."

"Alright, shut up, you've proved your point."

"And Danny ain't." Ian was watching him closely.

Rab glanced at him then back at the screen. "We've had this conversation before."

There was a silence and Rab felt he could hear all their words, angry and brittle, settle around them like ash, falling onto the dull carpet, burnt out and meaningless. Like men arguing about the universe, time, motion - utterly pointless. Discussions on Danny, an exercise in futility.

Suddenly Ian said, "And John isn't either."

"What?"

"Queer."

Rab laughed dryly.

Ian said irritably, "Stop deluding yourself. You think it's all legend?"

When Rab didn't answer him he went on. "Know what Danny is for him? An obsession. John's an obsessive and Danny's the obsession. If it wasn't sex it would be something else. They're two halves of one whole. They should have been twins. They *are* twins, they just happened to be born ten years apart."

"I've heard it all before Ian, it's bullshit."

Ian shrugged, indifferent to what Rab thought.

"Does Danny fancy him then?" Ian asked suddenly. His voice was strangely inquiring, as if the answer really mattered to him.

"Who doesn't Danny fancy?"

"You're looking at one of them. Does John know?"

"What do you think?"

"He'll find out."

"Of course he'll fucking find out then maybe you'll get your wish."

"Why?" Ian frowned. "I mean, why this one?"

Rab shrugged.

"What's so special about this one?" Ian insisted.

Rab threw himself back down on the sofa. "Oh give it a fucking break."

Ian looked at the ill-temper on his face and decided he wanted to see Mr James Conley.

He got up and crossed over to Rab. Rab looked up at him. Ian smiled down at him. "Want me to kiss it better?"

Rab looked at his thin yellow smile for a moment then closed his eyes.

"Let me go." Conley's hands were on the chair arms.

Danny looked up at him slowly. "I'll be fucked if I will."

Conley closed his eyes. Danny could see how white he was. "Please."

Danny let him go, pushing back out of his lap and standing upright in one repressive gesture. He wiped his mouth with the back of his hand.

Conley looked at him standing there in his clothes. What looked sartorial, if eccentric, on Conley became almost threatening and war-like on Danny. The green waistcoat was almost iridescent on him. It caught the odd fragments of light, glittering

458

back angrily at him. He looked furious, eyes sharp, hair aflame.

Danny turned from him and began pulling the clothes off, stripping them off violently, throwing the stained trousers on the floor, undoing the waistcoat with a haste that might have made Conley worry about the buttons if he hadn't been worrying about anything else.

Conley pushed himself back inside his clothes, not daring to look. He tried to ignore the impossible sticky flood on his stomach. He just wanted to cover it up, pretend it hadn't happened. He was desperate to wash it away but knew it would only compound his crimes in Danny's eyes. He looked at Danny's white back turned firmly against him. He was pulling his own clothes back on. "Danny..."

"Shut up."

"Look, Danny, I'm sorry..."

Danny zipped his trousers up violently. "I said shut the fuck up."

Conley got up slowly and went into the bathroom. He closed the door, locking it behind him.

Danny sat down on the bed and put his head in his hands. He could hear water running in the bathroom.

He swung round suddenly and swiped the entire contents of Conley's bedside table onto the floor.

He got up and went to get his jacket. He stood for a moment looking at the room, in darkness except for the lamp, the light from the glass bathroom, then he turned and went out the door.

The hail spat viciously in his face. His eyes began to run. Danny went down the stairs quickly.

It was just the cold.

Rab was on the brink of coming when the phone rang. For a second he thought it had pushed him over the edge. He felt the dull throbbing ache of it threatening to spill over, then it receded.

Ian lifted his head. "*Shit*," he whispered as if they might be overheard.

Rab's laugh was dry. "Shit indeed."

"Who the fuck could that be?"

"I don't know. Why don't you answer it and find out?"

Ian got up grudgingly, giving his cock a squeeze. "Keep it warm for me."

Rab looked away. He didn't want to see himself. *Time was you couldn't get an erection with Ian. Yeah, well, time was a lot of things. Know what they say - beggars can't be choosers*.

He fastened his clothes and sat up, tucking his shirt tail in. He picked his sweater off the floor and pulled it on. He could hear Ian's voice as a faint murmur.

He stood up and lit a cigarette. He opened the fire up a little and put on some more coal. Ian came back in. "It was Danny."

"Danny?" Rab stopped rubbing his neck.

"He's in Caldermouth. He wants someone to pick him up."

"What happened?"

"He says it's none of my business."

Rab moved to go out. Ian caught his arm and shook his head. "I'm coming with you, Captain's orders."

Rab looked at him and shook his hand off. "Christ, you're a sick bastard."

Ian smiled. "Now now, share and share alike."

Rab gave him another look and went out of the room.

Danny went into the pub and got himself a drink. He'd have to make it last because he had brought practically no money with him.

It was a trendy pub with little booths and cul-de-sacs. It was the middle of the week and deserted. Danny found the darkest corner he could and sat in it. The barman looked at him curiously, but when Danny looked up and caught his eye he moved away, unsettled at being caught staring.

Danny pushed himself back further into the seat, deeper into the shadows. He laid his head back and rested it on the padded bar that ran along the wall.

In the corner of the room, facing him, a one-armed bandit sent courses of lights in an elaborate sequence. Twice round, then three broken rounds, then back the way it had come, then flashing **WIN...WIN...WIN** over and over, orange, blue, red, green. It was hypnotic. Danny lay there, half-lidded, watching it. Round it went again. **WIN...WIN...WIN........ THREE PLAYS........ WIN...WIN...WIN.**

Danny slid gently into sleep.

The barman had forgotten about him and was shocked to look up and see him lying there looking so dead, half-hidden in shadow. "Asleep," he muttered, hand clasped with unintentional drama to his chest.

"What d'you say?" His wife looked at him.

"Lad there," he nodded his head. "Came in about fifteen minutes ago." He lowered his voice slightly. "Looked as if he'd been crying."

His wife came over closer to him and narrowed her eyes, trying to make him out clearly. "Looks very young."

"That's just his colouring."

"Think he's alright?"

The barman wrinkled his face. "I don't know."

"I'll go and have a look," his wife said. She moved towards the end of the bar.

Her husband stopped her. "No, I'll do it."

He thought at first she was going to argue but she stepped back and let him pass saying, apropos of nothing, "Nice looking lad."

The barman passed her without looking at her.

He crossed the floor and stood in front of the table. The boy's arms lay slackly at his sides, palms up. It was that odd position that made him look so dead, so murdered. That and the white skin, so pale against the dark upholstery.

The barman looked at his face, the lips slightly parted, then at his chest. He couldn't tell if he was breathing or not.

The barman turned suddenly, aware of his wife watching him. He gave her a black look as if to say, Go away, you're making me nervous, and she moved away, busying herself at the other end of the counter. The barman looked back again. The boy hadn't moved, just the same slack face. Maybe he was a druggie or something. "Son?" he said in a whisper as if he were afraid of waking him. "You alright lad?"

The boy didn't answer. The barman eased into the seat beside him, one knee on it, the other on the floor. He bent over him and slid his hand inside the boy's jacket, over his heart, and immediately felt the heat of his body. He felt the relief unlock his muscles. Last thing he needed was a corpse in his lounge. He looked at the boy's face, now heavily shadowed by his body, oddly down-lit by the low-watt picture light above his head.

The barman didn't move his hand. It was perfectly happy where it was, caught between the warmth of the boy's skin and the heavy skin of his jacket, here in the secret dark. Then the boy's eyes came open. Instantly. No blinking, nothing, wide

awake. Even in this light he could see they were a startling shade of green.

He snatched his hand away. "You alright?" he asked, face flushing with embarrassment. Suddenly it all seemed too much fuss over nothing. The boy kept staring at him.

When he spoke the barman wasn't sure he'd actually heard him, the voice was so deep and low. He began to wonder if the boy was quite right in the head, maybe drugs right enough. "Are you okay?" he said again, still caught in the boy's eyes, and this time he did hear him, deep and low alright, but clear enough.

"D'you want it?"

The barman looked at him blankly then he felt the boy's hand on his thigh, moving unmistakably upwards. The shock riveted him.

The hand moved onto his crotch, softly cupping his balls. *Holy Nora, a fucking queer.* The boy's hand was squeezing gently, his face still, not smiling, but his eyes were dark and intense, something worse.

He jerked away, struggling out of his kneeling position in the confined space. The boy kept staring at him.

He turned and moved across the floor quickly, getting back behind his counter. He was white-faced.

His wife looked at him. "Was he alright then?" She peered past his shoulder.

"He's fine."

His wife looked at him curiously, studying his face. "What's up, what happened?"

"Nothing happened. I told you, he's fine. Someone's needing served."

She raised her eyebrows at him but went to serve the customer.

The barman stood filling the sink, watching the bubbles swirl. *I should throw him out. I should bloody throw him out, making a pass at me in my own bloody pub.* But he couldn't go near him again.

The boy sat there for almost another thirty minutes, every one of which burned hot and cold on the barman's back. He moved from outrage and disgust to confusion and uncertainty, then back again, knowing he should throw him out and castigating himself for a coward.

When he saw the tall blond boy come in and look around he connected them immediately. He watched him angrily and saw him seeing the redhead. He watched him smile at him and knew he was the same. Another fucking queer-boy. Another fucking fairy.

The redhead came out into the light. The barman turned his back to him, willing him to get out. He wanted to call out after him right there in front of everyone - let him deal with that, the crafty little thug, coming into his pub with his dirty perverted antics - but he wouldn't look at him.

At the last minute he turned briefly and looked over his shoulder. They were just going out the door. The redhead stopped and turned, looking him full in the face. He felt himself go red and turned away quickly, but not before he saw that smile. The first time he'd smiled, the only time he'd smiled. It was the worst smile he'd ever seen.

"Why the smile?"

"What smile?"

"Oh don't act it Danny, for the bruiser behind the bar."

"He had nice hands."

Rab pulled his arm, directing him towards the car. The snow had died to a gentle fall of flakes. "One of these days you'll get your teeth kicked in."

"Smiling at people?"

"The way you do it, yes." Rab glanced at him again. "I wouldn't have thought he

was your type."

"Everyone's my type."

Rab didn't answer that. He looked up as they were about to turn the corner. He slowed. Danny was aware of the change in his step. He looked at him. "What's up?"

"Isn't that your Mr Conley over there?"

Danny looked in the direction of his gaze.

Conley stood across the road, hands pushed down into his pockets, coat collar up. He was covered in snow. He was looking around him as if he was lost.

Rab saw his expression and grabbed his arm. "Come on Danny, we haven't got all night." And he pulled Danny, unprotesting, around the corner into the side street where they were parked.

Danny allowed himself to be pushed into the back seat. He lay with his face against the glass, listening to Ian and Rab arguing, listening to the intense angry noise of it. After a while Ian got in the back with him.

Rab slammed the car out of the street with his usual high-speed style. Danny looked out of the window, knowing he would be there, and he was. He still stood there like someone stood up, waiting for someone who was never going to arrive. The tears began to slide down Danny's face, lukewarm, slow, silent, hurting his throat, making his head ache. Ian slid his arm around him and pulled him in against him. Danny curled into his side as he had done so many times before.

"Shh..." Ian hushed him.

Rab watched him in the rear-view mirror with a mixture of anger and frustration. He could see Ian's other arm moving, the awkward angle of his body, and knew what he was doing. "You fucking pervert, leave him alone."

But Ian didn't even look up, he went on soothing him the same way he always had.

Danny curled into his side and let it wash over him.

Conley knew he had gone as soon as he stepped out of the bathroom. It was that same silence, only Mamma rustling to herself. "Danny?" he called.

He walked towards the bedroom. "Danny?" he said again.

He walked round the bed. The clothes lay scattered where Danny had dropped them. A glass which had contained water lay broken on the floor, the water spread in a puddle around it. Half of it had soaked into the book he had been reading. He picked up his clock. The face was smashed. He put it back on the table. He picked up his pen and the notepad and put them back too, then he sat on the bed.

After a moment he got up and put on the rest of his clothes then he went across the room and put on his coat.

He went out without any idea of where he was going or what he was going to do. Danny must be outside somewhere so he'd find him. He tried the taxi ranks first, then the two taxi offices. All the time he kept his eyes open, searching through the thick snow for him.

By the time the snow had thinned to a delicate flutter he was left numb and dead by the side of the road, looking around him vainly, like a man who has forgotten his own address.

For a fleeting moment he saw a redheaded boy in a dark leather jacket turning the street corner, but it couldn't have been Danny. He was with another boy, tall, blonde.

He went back to the flat.

He sat on the sofa until he grew tired and then he lay down. He lay down with his coat folded over him like giant wings.

When he next opened his eyes it was time to get up.

Rab could hear the faint noises Danny was making, Ian crooning to him obscenely.

"For Christ's sake," he muttered under his breath. He pulled out round a huge lorry. It spat snow up at them, covering the windscreen. He pressed his foot down on the accelerator.

"That's it." Ian was whispering. "Come on." Then he heard nothing but breathless little grunts as Danny delivered himself into Ian's hand.

The truck blared at them, a loud aggressive bellow, as Rab cut in front of him, driving blind, everything a blur of lights.

"Fucking *dirty* bastard." He watched Ian kissing his hair. "You *dirty* little shit."

Ian smiled at him suddenly in the mirror. "He feels better now." He kissed him again possessively then he disappeared from Rab's view.

Rab looked quickly over his shoulder. He was bent over him, eating up what he'd spilt. He caught a brief glimpse of Danny's face, smooth and wet as stone, and Ian's body crouched over his lap like a giant spider. "For fuck's sake Ian, leave him alone."

But the gritty little noises went on, clearly audible, like a cat licking up spilt milk, until Ian was satisfied. Rab heard the deep little grunts of pleasure, then silence.

Ian reappeared in the mirror, head bent, fiddling in his lap, industriously cleaning himself, then the brief blast of cold air as he threw the soiled tissue out into the dark.

Rab looked in the mirror again. Danny was slumped back, eyes closed, face slack. Ian was smiling at him.

"You smug little shit."

"J for Jealousy." Ian's smile grew a little wider.

"Any time his defences are down you're right in there, aren't you?"

"Just like you would be. All that's bothering you is it isn't you in the back seat."

"You fucking little spastic."

"Only giving him what he likes."

"What you like."

Ian shook his head. "That's where you're wrong. Believe me, I can remember times without number being woken by your little paragon of virtue climbing into bed with me wanting to be 'comforted'."

"Comforted - is that what you call it?"

"It's what he calls it."

"You fucking pederast."

Ian shrugged and looked out the window as if the subject bored him. "Believe what you like." He moved to lean against the door and disappeared from Rab's view.

When Rab shifted his eyes again he saw that Danny was watching him in the mirror, unblinking and awake. Rab looked into the flat black of his eyes then away again quickly.

He drove home without looking in the mirror again.

John was waiting there when they got in. He had heard them come into the yard and was leaning against the cooker when they came into the kitchen.

Rab came in first, shaking off the snow. It had started to fall again, heavy but soft, the flakes falling like huge feathers. It melted as soon as it landed. It always did. Too much salt.

"Where the fuck have you been?"

Rab was just in the mood for this. Sometimes it was like living in the fucking ape house at the zoo, surrounded by fifty bull apes during the mating season. "Out building fucking snowmen, where do you think?"

The others came in behind him; Danny looking cold, his skin glazed and taut, as if

he were made of porcelain, fragile, breathtaking. John looked at him as he crossed the room. Everyone looked at him as he crossed the room. He ignored them all and went upstairs.

"What happened?" John asked Rab's back.

"He phoned about an hour after you went out. He wanted a lift home."

"What happened?"

"I've no idea, you'll have to ask him."

"Where was he?"

"Caldermouth." Rab turned to him. "Where the fuck else would he be?"

"With Danny you never know."

"You're fucking paranoid John."

"Who drove back?"

Rab turned finally to face him. "I did. Want to examine my hands?" He held them out towards him. "Maybe you should ask to see Ian's, they might tell you a different story."

John never stopped looking at him. "Ian's always got dirty hands. I don't need to look at them to know that."

"Christ, you're a magic pair, y'know that? A winning combination, you and your fucking pimp."

"You watch your mouth." John's face had set into hard white lines.

"Take a running fucking jump John." Rab pushed past him, daring John to lay a hand on him, but John stood back and let him pass.

Rab went up the stairs two at a time, pounding his fist on the wall as he went. *Fucking bastard. Fucking dirty, ugly bastard.*

He went into his room and slammed the door.

Danny took off his clothes and got into bed. The room was cold and he felt like ice. He curled tight into a ball under the blankets. He wished he had a hot water bottle. He lay there shivering. He didn't hear the door. He only knew John was with him when he sat on the bed.

John pulled the blankets off him. "Come out."

Danny uncurled and brought his head out. He clutched the blankets back and pulled them tight around himself.

"Cold?" John asked. You could always tell by that transparent look he took on. He really did look as if he was made of porcelain, like a doll.

"Frozen."

John took his clothes off, dropping them on the floor, and climbed in beside him, curling round his back. He was vast and warm. Danny snuggled back in against him, grateful for the heat.

"Where was she Danny?" John spoke into his back, mouth against the nape of his neck.

"Who?"

"Henderson's sister."

"How should I know?"

"Uh-uh," John said.

Danny felt the first warning prickle on his skin. "What do you mean, uh-uh?"

"She wasn't at home."

"You went round there? What the fuck for?"

"Curiosity."

Danny tried to pull away from him but John held him tight. He half-squirmed round, trying to see John's face. "Curiosity fucking nothing, you thought I'd lied to you. You

thought we'd gone round there, didn't you?"

"What I thought is none of your business. She was with you, wasn't she?"

"Fuck you."

"Wasn't she?"

Danny elbowed him viciously in the side, struggling round to get at him, swearing continuously at him, pouring it out. The whole night's disaster coming out in a burst of violence, like throwing up. "You fucking bastard. You fucking lousy ugly bastard. I fucking hate you." He was punching John's head, kneeing any part of him he could reach.

John caught at his hands two or three times before he managed to snare him. Once he had the hands the rest was relatively easy. He rolled Danny over, pinning him down with his weight. They lay sandwiched together, Danny half-crying, John's face stinging. He licked his lip. The little cunt had cut him.

"Where was she?" John's voice was hard and dry in his ear, full of 'last time' final warning. John lifted his head and looked into his eyes, waiting for the answer.

"Between my thighs John, giving me fucking head."

John was still a moment, face like a death mask, then he rolled off him lightly. Danny blinked at the unexpected freedom. Suddenly he was pushed out of the bed. He hit the floor violently, landing on his side, banging his head on the table leg. He felt John shove him flat on his back.

He lay there unable to pull a breath into his lungs, trying feebly to get up on his elbows. John's foot came down on his face. "Stay there fuck-face, just stay there."

Danny opened his eyes and saw John squatting above him, prick in hand, knees spread before he directed it at his face and blinded him. Danny tried to pull over onto his side, pulling his arms over his head, but he couldn't escape it. The hot urine ran through his hair, into his mouth.

When he was finished John wrenched him over onto his belly, spread his legs and stuffed his cock up inside him, face pushed down into the sodden carpet.

Second time, and counting.

FORTY-NINE

Rab came into their room next morning. He stood for a moment watching Danny at the wardrobe then he sniffed. "Christ, it stinks in here." He sniffed again. "Somebody wet the bed?"

Danny kept his back to him. He'd clean it up, get rid of the rug. He'd had to clean it up last time. *Part of the fun, Danny.*

Rab looked at him, listening to his silence. He pushed his hands in his pockets. "Christ, if he wants to play water sports why doesn't he do it in the bathroom?"

Danny closed the wardrobe and crossed the room. Rab looked at his face. "It's not your idea, is it?"

Danny shook his head.

"So what's going on? Is he making you watch or something?"

Danny smiled at that. "You could say that - worm's eye view."

Rab caught at his arm. "What? You mean he's...?"

Danny looked at his hand then up at his face. "What's your problem, you keeping a little black book or something?"

Rab let him go, mouth closing into a thin line. "Why won't you let me help you?"

"I don't need your fucking help."

"Like hell you don't."

Danny moved up close beside him. His voice was low and intense. "I don't need your help or any other fucker's help. I'm sick to death of you and your whining, why don't you just fuck off?"

Rab looked at him for a moment longer, afraid to move, then he backed away from him and out of the room.

Danny stared at the doorway then kicked the door shut. He sat down on the bed and stared at the rug.

He lay down on the bed and curled into a ball. "Fuck," he whispered, digging his nails into his palms, pulling his hands over his head. "*Fuck.*"

James Conley came down with flu. He woke on his settee and tried to sit up. His head weighed twice the weight of his own body. The inside of his chest, his throat and his ears was on fire. They itched, they flamed. His eyes streamed hot blood.

When someone came to his door he rolled off the couch and practically crawled to the door. When he opened it his secretary, worried and faintly shocked, helped him back to bed.

She knew he was very sick because he made no protest when she touched him. She could feel the iron rigidity in him but he didn't protest. She put him to bed, only helping him off with his shoes and topcoat. He got in meekly.

She sent for the doctor.

"Flu," he announced brusquely. "Give him these, we don't want him developing pneumonia."

She protested that she was only his secretary, not his wife.

The doctor gave her the benefit of his gimlet eye and replied, "Well, let him die then." She assumed it was a joke. She hoped it was a joke. She accepted the tablets and showed him to the door.

She sat on the edge of his bed and, on impulse, stroked his hair off his forehead.

He didn't open his eyes. He was very hot. He spoke to her in German, repeating

the same phrase over and over again, speaking to her from deep in his dreams.

When she went downstairs she borrowed Dorothy's German dictionary. Dorothy asked her why she wanted it.

"James is talking in his sleep."

"What, in German?"

Molly nodded. "He's got a fever."

"And what's he saying?"

They looked it up together. They looked at one another. They smiled sheepishly.

James Conley had been saying, Touch me.

Just that, over and over again.

Dorothy leaned back in her chair and wiped the sugar off her hands. "Maybe our James has been up to something we don't know about."

Molly laughed. "Well, whoever it is must have something magical if they've managed to lay hands on him."

"I still say he's a fairy."

Molly shook her head. They'd been over this before, many times. "He doesn't touch anybody. He never even shakes a client's hand."

"Cold fish."

"Not really, not when you know him."

Dorothy pulled a face. "Don't know how you can work with him."

"He's a nice man, really."

"He's a zombie. Give me Brian any day."

"Hah," Molly jeered, "now there *is* a fairy for you."

Dorothy laughed and leaned forward confidentially. "Cedric, Prince of Softies." She spoke with a heavy lisp. They both fell about laughing. It was an oldie but a goldie.

Upstairs James Conley turned over in his bed and began his nightmares again.

Mamma screeched and was still.

Danny went about his work like an automaton.

Twice Ian collared him in the barn. Once without speaking a word either before or after; the second time, when Danny tried to push him off, saying, "You wouldn't want John to know why his little playmate is so broken-hearted, would you?" And Danny let him do it, not because he was afraid that he would tell but because he had no energy left to wrangle, not with Ian and not with John.

Worst of all he was tormented with dreams. The same fucking one, over and over. Him upstairs, trapped behind a huge plate glass window, and outside in the snow, head down, his mother walking towards an unseen door below him, about to disappear beyond reach. Danny beating his fists on the glass, screaming for help, but his mother couldn't hear him. And every time he disappeared Danny would wake up with a jolt, sometimes crying, and John would be looking at him, the light on, face still heavy with sleep, but intent, watchful, even when he would dry his eyes for him with his thumb, movements so gentle, as if he cared.

He would always say, 'Nothing, just a bad dream' when John asked and bury himself in John's body, diverting him. But he could feel the thin line of tension in him, the suspicion.

John, for his part, guarded him like a gaoler, setting Ian to watch him. He saw him exact his fee, just once, a brief glimpse through the shed door, his punishment from God, having to watch Danny stand there like an animal, enduring, uninvolved. He moved on, leaving Ian to it, but wondering what he'd cajoled him with, threatened him

with.

Just wondering.

Molly cleaned up the flat for him. She had nothing else to do now anyway.

She put the clothes away that lay scattered on the bedroom floor. Someone had changed in a hurry last night. She smiled to herself. Maybe it was a heavy date after all.

She picked up the trousers and tried to pull the legs the right way out to hang them up but the fabric was stuck to itself. She tugged it free and saw the stains.

It hadn't been that long that she couldn't recognise semen stains when she saw them. She looked at the man on the bed. She flushed guiltily at her own conclusions. He muttered something and turned over, pushing the quilt off again.

She crossed to him automatically and pulled it back up. She'd been doing it all morning. She put the trousers in the linen basket.

When she found the two used glasses she realised it hadn't been the euphemistic solitary pleasure after all, there had been someone else here. They simply hadn't had time to get his clothes off. She smiled to herself at the notion. Our James in the throes of passion, that would amuse Dorothy. She felt a paradoxical twinge of jealousy. She'd worked for him for years and he'd never so much as patted her back and now he picks up some unknown female and... The fastidious James soiling his own clothes in his haste. She laughed at herself, shaking her head.

She went downstairs and phoned for her daughter. They could spend the night here, this once, bring their sleeping bags. Jackie would enjoy it. She had a bit of a crush on James anyway, give her a kick to spend the night in his house.

She was right, Jackie was suitably thrilled. Her mother warned her there would be no TV. She said she would gaze at James instead. Her mother laughed and told her she'd pick her up then hung up.

She told Dorothy about the trousers. Dorothy covered her cheeks with her hands. "I'm blushing." Then she laughed and clapped her hands together. "Who'd have thought it? No wonder he's got flu, it's probably the shock."

Molly laughed and immediately felt disloyal. Dorothy teased her unmercifully when she told her she was staying over. Molly told her Jackie was chaperoning.

"Some chaperone. The way Jackie's always after him she'll be climbing into bed with him herself."

"Oh no she won't," Molly said firmly.

Dorothy laughed at her. "Oho, mother-daughter rivalry rears its ugly head."

"Give over."

"No, go on, admit it, you're jealous. First some fast and loose hussy playing around with James' equipment, now your daughter jeopardising your chances. You should leave her at home."

"I can't do that."

"My God, she doesn't trust herself."

Molly smiled sheepishly. "Actually, you know, I don't. He's bloody tempting lying there, all unresisting and helpless."

Dorothy cackled wildly until Brian Sheard came in demanding to know what the joke was. "Ah, you wouldn't understand Brian."

Dorothy looked over his shoulder at Molly going out the door. Molly winked broadly. Oh no? the wink said.

Dorothy covered her mouth and began to cough violently.

Jackie and her mother stood looking down at James Conley's flushed face.

"Doesn't he look yummy?"

"Jackie, for goodness' sake."

Jackie reached down and felt his chest. It was soaking with sweat.

"Jackie!" Molly pushed her hand off.

"God, he's boiling hot."

"You don't need to paw him to find that out."

"Got to take your chances as you find them Mum." She grinned unrepentantly.

Conley pushed the quilt down further. Jackie made saucer eyes at her mother. Molly pulled it back up. "Get out of it, go on, go and make us something to eat." Her mother shooed her out of the bedroom.

She had taken his shirt and socks off earlier. He had wrung them round himself like ropes, soaked them with sweat. She would have to rummage in the cupboard for a clean quilt cover for tomorrow, freshen his bed a little.

She felt his brow again. He tugged his head away even in his sleep. She would feel better about him if his temperature would come down a bit, and if his breathing would sound less harsh. He had woken very briefly in the afternoon and asked for a glass of water. He seemed quite lucid but she suspected he was utterly disorientated. He had fallen asleep again almost immediately. He had accepted her presence there in a way that wasn't so much flattering as distressing. It was obvious he hadn't even had the energy to consider it. If she hadn't been there he would simply have gone back to sleep again thirsty.

She went out to find Jackie in the seating area.

"Some place."

Molly nodded. She picked her plate off the table and began eating. "I told you it was stylish."

"He's like a rock star or something."

Molly laughed. "He's a solicitor Jackie. I doubt if you could get further away."

Jackie pulled a face. "Well he doesn't look like one."

Molly conceded the point. He didn't really.

"This bird's really cool." Jackie was feeding Mamma the remains of her apple. Mamma took it and hurled insults at her head. "I wish it spoke English."

"You're probably better off, it sounds like abuse to me."

Jackie turned to her. "You think he's taught it to swear in German?" She turned back to it. "Wonder what it's saying?"

"It's saying, Who is this nosy little cat?"

"Charming."

Jackie wandered over to the bookshelves, peering surreptitiously into the bedroom.

"Jackie..." her mother said warningly.

"I won't go anywhere near him, just looking."

Molly wondered if he'd managed to uncover himself again but decided he hadn't. Jackie wasn't interested enough.

Molly picked up her book and curled up on the couch. After ten minutes or so Jackie settled down opposite her. Her mother looked up. She was very intent. "What are you reading?"

Jackie held it up, colouring slightly. Her mother frowned. The Complete Works of the Marquis de Sade. "Right Jackie, get it right back." Her mother jerked her head.

"*Mum...*" Jackie pleaded.

"Now. Back on the shelf. Find something else."

Jackie slammed the book down. "It's not *fair!*"

"*Shh,* keep your voice down."

"It's not fair," she repeated stubbornly, voice lowered.

"I don't care, put it *back*."

Jackie stared at her for a minute then flounced back to the shelves. Trust Jackie to find that, of all things. It was probably the only dirty book in the whole place. Kids' homing instincts were incredible. After a moment she came back again, this time with a large old volume of fairy-tales.

Her mother smiled at her. Jackie glowered back and curled herself into a ball with her book.

They lapsed into quiet reading. Half an hour or more had passed before James began to talk in his sleep again. Molly looked up, then Jackie. She looked at her mother.

"He's talking in his sleep," Molly explained.

Jackie frowned. "That's not English."

"German."

"What's he saying?"

Molly shrugged. "I've no idea."

After a moment or two he stopped again. They went back to their reading. Then he started saying it again, repeatedly. Molly coloured when she realised what was going on. She wished now that she hadn't looked it up. When you knew what it was it sounded different.

"What's he saying?" Jackie asked again.

"I told you, I don't know," Molly snapped.

"Touchy."

Molly said apologetically, "Sorry."

"Wish Baby-Lou was here."

"Who?"

"Gemma, remember? I told you, she's changed her name to Baby-Lou."

Molly remembered. Well, vaguely. "Why?"

"Because she thinks it's more..."

"No," Molly interrupted. "Why do you wish she was here?"

"She's great at German. She's got a German aunt. Or is she Austrian?"

Molly nodded absently, glad that Baby-Lou, nee Gemma, was not here. She could imagine the fun the two of them would have had with this one.

He was muttering brokenly now. Then silence again. Jackie was back in her book, deeply immeshed in what must be Rose Red and Snow White to judge by the illustration.

Molly got up and went over to the bedroom. She clicked the lamp on. He'd pushed the quilt right off himself this time, his underpants clinging to him with sweat. He had his arms wrapped round himself as if he was frozen cold. For the first time she felt embarrassed by his absence of clothes. She covered him up quickly, tucking the quilt round him. A man so ill shouldn't look so good, she thought. But it was the fever that was responsible, flushing his skin and improving his normally dead-white pallor. She smiled to herself. When this fever passes and he has a runny nose he'll look different, just haggard and horrible like the rest of us.

He opened his eyes. It startled her slightly with its suddenness. "Hello," she said, smiling at him.

He looked at her, unrecognising. She wondered if he were really seeing her. "Where's Danny?" he asked clearly.

Danny? Who was Danny? "He's not here," she said, hoping it was the right answer.

He looked at her for a moment then closed his eyes and turned his head away. She realised he was sleeping again - if he'd ever been truly awake.

She sat down on the edge of the bed and could smell the sweat off him. He must

be losing gallons of fluid. She must remember to give him something to drink next time he woke.

He started to talk again. Half-words then what was obviously one half of a conversation. She could catch none of it, even if she could have understood it. How odd to dream in one language, speak in another. Especially as he'd lived a lot longer here than there. Did he think in German? Surely not.

He brought an arm out and threw it above his head - he was arguing with someone - then he went limp and was silent again.

She eased his arm back under the bedclothes. It was hot and sticky. She could see his eyes moving under their lids. He started talking again, this time low and desperate, as if he were pleading with someone, then he said it clearly, Danny, the English name odd amongst all the alien words. She listened carefully.

He pushed the quilt down again. She brought it back up. Then he said, "Please Danny" clearly, and in English.

She felt his forehead again. He was burning up. She laid her hand on his cheek. He flinched almost as if he could feel it and said almost those same first words - almost but not quite. Unmistakably this time he'd said, *Don't* touch me. Had he felt her hand on him? She wiped it on her skirt and looked at his face. He was still deeply asleep, eyes jerking.

Jackie spoke to her from the doorway. "Is he alright?"

Molly nearly jumped out of her skin. "God, the fright you gave me."

Jackie looked at her curiously then smiled. "Why, what were you doing, feeling him up?"

"*Jackie.*"

"Only joking." She came into the room. "What's up?"

"Nothing, he's just over-hot. I think the fever's a bit worse, that's all."

"Maybe it's going to break. Isn't that what they do, fevers, get worse before they break?"

Molly nodded. "I hope so. I hate the way he talks in his sleep."

Jackie looked at her. "Spook you?"

"My mother used to sleepwalk. I've always hated things like that."

"What, Gran?"

"Yes. Any time she got too het up she would go for walks, wake you up in the dead of night, standing in the doorway."

"Boogie, boogie." Jackie wiggled her fingers.

"Alright for you, she used to scare me half to death."

"How could you be scared of Gran?"

"Oh, they're not like the people you know when they sleepwalk. They don't see you or hear you, they're somewhere else. She used to say really strange things. It used to terrify me."

"Like what?"

Molly thought. "I remember once she woke me up standing at the foot of my bed. She was staring at me then she said, I don't like sausages."

Jackie burst out laughing.

"*Shh...* for goodness *sake* Jackie."

"Sorry." She made snurkling noises behind her palm. "It was just so funny."

"Only to you. You weren't there." Molly looked at James again. "I don't like the way he talks either, or the things he says. He doesn't sound like himself."

"I thought you said you didn't know what he was saying." Jackie was watching her shrewdly.

"The odd word, that's all."

"Fibber." Jackie pounced. "What's he been saying, something dirty?"

"Jackie, you really are the limit."

"No, tell me, what did he say?"

"He said, Get the hell out of it and get back to your book."

"Aw Mum, go on, tell us."

"Out."

James began turning his head from side to side, pushing the quilt down again, diverting Jackie's interest. She watched him. "He really is nice-looking, isn't he?"

"Out."

"I'm going, I'm going." She looked back over her shoulder. "No taking advantage now, while he's asleep."

"Out!"

"Temper." And she disappeared round the edge of the blind.

Molly pulled the quilt up again. He promptly pushed it down again. She tutted, trying to push his arms back under, but he held them rigid, resisting her. He began talking again, rapidly, that same pleading, and there was the name again - Danny. She frowned, trying to catch any of the words, but they skittered past her meaninglessly. Then the name. By itself. And he pushed the quilt down off his hips.

"Oh dear," she whispered, momentarily nonplussed by the sight. He began moving his hips in an unmistakable way. She wanted to cover him up again, but the erection was so obvious, the soaking fabric clinging to it, that she was loathe to touch him.

He held the quilt tight underneath it, pulling it across his thighs. She looked away. This was terrible, positively the end. What if he'd done this when Jackie was here? She heard him with something like horror when he started talking again. *Touch me.* Her face was scarlet. It was like when a friend's dog started rubbing on your leg. You didn't know how to politely stop it, but you couldn't pretend it wasn't happening either. And let's face it, she hadn't seen an erection in a while and that didn't help any. He was pushing it up insistently, still saying, Touch me. Then she had a worse thought. He wasn't going to...?

She looked desperately at the living room. *Stay where you are Jackie.* She grabbed at the quilt, felt the brush of him against the back of her hand. He held the quilt in a death grip, his head thrown back. He was grunting it out now.

"Mum?"

"Yes?" Even to herself her voice sounded odd, high-pitched.

"He okay?"

"Yes, he's fine, just feverish."

"Want me to get anything?"

"No, stay where you are." Oh God, what a stupid thing to say. Now she'd be over here like a shot. She yanked the quilt out of his hands and up his body.

Jackie appeared in the doorway. "What's wrong?"

"Nothing, I told you. Will you go and sit down?"

Jackie looked at him curiously. Molly's action had disturbed his sleep and he was muttering, tossing his head again. The obscene movements had stilled. Molly blessed the disguise of the fluffy quilt.

"He looks a bit odd."

Molly felt like someone in a nightmare. "Jackie, bloody well go and sit *down*."

Jackie looked at her mother, managing that unique combination of hurt and surprise that only children can create for their parents. "Alright, keep your pants on." She went out the room reluctantly.

He started it again, pushing the bedding down. Molly felt his forehead. God, he was actually getting hotter. It really must break soon, surely. She pulled the quilt back up. He muttered savagely and pushed it down again. He was saying something different this time, an angry demand, something with 'me' in it, but that's all she could

make out.

She reached for the quilt again but he pushed it down further, holding it down as he had before. Good lord, was he going to do this all night? She began to wish she had left Jackie at home. She could cope with this, just, but not with Jackie likely to arrive at any moment.

He started thrusting again, more insistently this time, and then he was back on the same old refrain, only this time the tone had changed, not pleading, but demanding, his face streaming with sweat and exertion. And now she just watched him like some kind of helpless spectator, half-fascinated, half in dread.

She caught herself beginning to wish he'd hurry up and do it. Sooner or later he *must* do it. She could almost hear Jackie listening. He was so obvious that even Jackie, young as she was, must suspect what was happening. Suddenly she saw the humour in it. Her trapped with her boss in his bedroom, him deep in a wet dream, her daughter listening fervently outside. God, this would amuse Dorothy. She could hear her now. *You should have pulled his drawers down and had a look.* She glanced down quickly then away again. There wasn't really any need. The state his pants were in, they might as well be transparent. He had stopped speaking again, lulled for a moment, his movements sinuous and stretching, his head moving slowly on the pillow. Whatever she's doing to him, he likes it slow. Inexplicably she flushed at that.

"*Danny...*" he whispered suddenly and clearly.

She looked at him. *Danny?*

He said it again, thrusting up higher, but holding the moment longer, then, "Suck me" very clearly and precisely in English.

Oh God, and Jackie was listening to this as surely as God made little green apples.

And then he rolled his head back and arched up and she saw it jerking on his face and looked down and saw it jerking there too, spasming in a dreadful taut silence. She hadn't seen that in a while either.

When he was finished she covered him up, glad at least that he'd kept the finale quiet, but when she came out Jackie wouldn't speak to her.

She didn't speak to her again until the following day. Which only goes to prove how much silences tell people.

FIFTY

Molly only had to spend two nights with him. On the third day he was rational enough to be by himself. The second day had not been so fraught. His fever had peaked at that point on the first day. In more ways than one, Molly thought. She didn't tell Dorothy. She was still trying to cope with Jackie's sullen silence. She felt like saying, It wasn't my fault, but that would be admitting something had happened and neither her nor Jackie could cope with that. It would pass soon enough. She wasn't sure if it had cured Jackie's crush or made it worse, but she refused to come back the second night saying sullenly, "You can have him to yourself." To which Molly made no reply.

Jackie had a friend round who was probably regaled with tales of how her perverted mother had sat and watched a sick man 'doing it' while forbidding Jackie the same pleasure. Molly even felt villainous. Maybe she was.

By the third day he was sitting up. He looked like a washed-out rag, so thin it was almost painful, but slowly she coaxed him into eating again. Nothing but fruit cheesecake but at least it was food.

He had flinched away from her touch from the first moment he became half aware of her. She hadn't touched him since. Half of her was sorry, the other half glad they had re-established the old status quo. She made no reference to his fever and he seemed not to have realised what it might have entailed. Maybe he was too washed out to think. His amnesia was just fine as far as she was concerned. She had been afraid he might remember and then their relationship would have been spoilt. She knew he would be mortified by it. Anybody would, but him more than most.

The 'Danny' had worried her until it occurred to her it was very possibly a Danielle. She couldn't think of one off-hand but no doubt she'd pop up sooner or later. It was difficult to keep a thing like that secret.

Time for his lordship's lunch. She phoned upstairs and smiled as he asked for more cheesecake. "You'll turn into a piece of cheesecake," she said.

He laughed. He'd always had a lovely laugh. "I'll take that risk," he said.

She hung up and put on her coat.

Katherine Henderson came home on the fifth of December. She arrived tired and ill-tempered at eleven o'clock at night on the third day of James Conley's illness.

She got in and threw her coat on the chair. The flat was frozen. She lit the pilot light and turned the heating on. The damn thing would take hours to heat up. She closed the curtains. At least there was no snow here. Scotland was knee-deep in the damn stuff as usual. She was sick of the sight of it.

She put the kettle on and sat down to listen to her calls. Two. One from her brother and one from her opticians. Nothing from James Conley. She frowned. Still, could be he didn't like leaving messages on machines. She'd phone him in the morning.

She looked around the flat. She felt an intense and irrational urge to drive to Danny's house. She looked at her watch. They'd all be in bed by now. She could hardly wake him up. She smiled. She'd rather climb in beside him anyway than get him up. She smiled again. Not that she'd mind getting him up either. "Dirty girl," she said out loud.

She got up to make her coffee. *A bath then bed Kathy, that's what you need. Time enough for screwing tomorrow.*

"Dirty bitch," she said this time, and went out into the kitchen.

FIFTY-ONE

On the fourth day of James Conley's illness Danny was driving a hedge-trimmer round their hedgerows. It was monotonous. What wasn't monotonous? It was all fucking monotonous. He reversed and began working the other side.

Face facts Danny, you aren't going to see him. You walked out on him, remember?

I don't want to fucking see him. Why should I want to see him? He was a fuck, a bad fuck. Why the hell should I care?

He crested the hill, looked at the sea spread out before him. He stopped the tractor dead and sat there in silence. The landscape glittered with bright hard frost. The sun was painfully white, strobing between the hedgerows as he bumped across the field. Now it was stilled, huge and icy white above him. A crow cawed harshly then was quiet again.

He closed his eyes. *Never, ever, did I think this could happen to me.*

He banged his fist on the steering wheel. *"Fuck."*

He is just another dick in a long line of dicks. Just one of the three million and eight you were destined to eat in your life. You get that right in your head.

He hit the wheel again. *"Shit."*

At that moment Katherine Henderson phoned James Conley at his office. She was told that he was ill and was not expected back until next week.

She asked if he had left any messages for her. The secretary checked but informed her there was nothing for her.

She put the phone down on a wave of irritation. She had expected to come back to a fait accompli. That was, after all, the point in employing the supposed legal whizz kid. How dare he be ill?

She laughed tensely at herself and ran her hand through her hair. Well, she could at least treat herself to the pleasure of seeing Jimmy's little protégé. If she could *get* to see him, that is.

She got up and changed her clothes.

Danny started up his tractor and went down over the hill.

Katherine Henderson was on the point of overtaking when she realised who it was. She had glanced at the tractor briefly before pulling out. Now she slowed and pulled back in again.

Danny saw the movement and looked in the wing mirror again. The car was too close. It was riding right up his fucking arse in fact. He looked at the road ahead, it was clear, what was the fucking problem? This was all he needed. He looked back at the road, face sour with ill-temper.

Danny. It had to be. That hair, the jacket, or did all farmers wear jackets like that? He'd had his hair cut, but it was him.

She overtook him suddenly.

Danny glanced to his right and saw the silver car pull round him. At last. It drew in front of him and braked.

Danny slammed on his brakes, swearing violently. *What the hell?* He came to a stop right up its rear end, almost on top of it. He swung out the cab, ready to destroy someone, then he saw her standing there. He stopped dead. *Thank you God, make my fucking day.* "You stupid bitch."

She raised an eyebrow. "Lovely way to greet someone."

"Smart fucking way to get yourself killed." He jerked his head at her car.

"You look beautiful when you're angry."

He looked at her. She was smiling. He stood there a moment then he burst out laughing. He leaned back against the tractor and let rip.

She watched him with an indulgent smile. "It wasn't that funny."

He rubbed his face, still chuckling. "Struck a nerve."

"Obviously." He was looking away from her, trying to straighten his face. Huge trucks thundered past them, looking at them with the curiosity of accident-gazers. "We've got to stop meeting like this," she said.

He turned, frowning at her, then saw her smile and burst out laughing again. He coughed violently. "Shit..." He coughed some more.

Another truck passed them. "Let's pull into the lay-by," she said.

He nodded.

They drove along the road together, making a strange convoy. He got out the tractor and joined her in her car.

"Miss me?" She looked at him.

He looked away from her, mouth set.

"Well, that answers that." She watched the side of his face. "You haven't changed your mind then?"

He flicked his eyes up angrily then down again, staring straight ahead. "What do you think?"

She braced her arms against the steering wheel and looked out her side window. "Did you hear from James Conley?"

"Yes."

"And?"

"And what?"

"What happened?"

"Ask him, you're paying him." *And while you're at it see if you can help him with a little problem he has.*

"You're always angry at me," she offered finally.

"Oh for fuck's sake." He looked at the roof of the car. "What the hell do you expect?"

"It would be nice if you tried to like me. I mean, you could try."

"There wouldn't be any fucking point in me trying. Christ, are you stupid or something?"

"John," she said in the tone of someone who's heard it all before.

Danny took a deep breath. "That's right, John. I told you before, see him."

"Christ, he's your brother, not your owner. You're not a pet."

Danny said nothing. If she didn't know a pet when she saw one he couldn't help her. Maybe he ought to bark.

As if she'd read his mind she said, "What are you Danny, some kind of bloody dog?"

He turned to her slowly. "Woof, woof," he said. He wasn't smiling.

She blinked and let herself go limp. He looked away again. She looked at his hands lying in his lap, fingers knotted together with tension. They were stained green, as if he'd been cutting grass. He smelled good, fresh. Maybe he had been cutting grass. His clothes looked incongruous in the luxurious interior. He was probably ruining the seats. She swallowed. "Danny..." Her hand touched his arm.

He didn't need to turn, he could hear it in her voice. *You took it up the arse for this three nights ago Danny-boy.*

Her other hand moved onto his thigh. *He pissed in your face for this Danny-boy. You don't owe her anything.* He closed his eyes. When he spoke he knew what his

voice would sound like. "Here," he said. And there it was, the old familiar sound.

There was a pause. She was thinking, considering.

"Here or nowhere," he said. *Listen to that boy sink.*

"People can see," she said finally.

"They've got to come in first."

"We could go back to the flat."

He still didn't turn to her. "Here or you can forget it." His voice was low and hard but he could feel it picking up in him. *Don't let her say no.*

"Alright."

He turned to her and smiled. She saw it and knew it would be alright. He opened his jacket, still watching her, then unzipped his trousers. She glanced down. He was already erect. He never took any coaxing or persuading. He was the most perfect compliment anyone ever gave her.

"Sit on it," he smiled. He held it up and leaned back his head. "Go on, sit on it."

She climbed over him awkwardly and pulled her knickers to one side. He went up embarrassingly easily. She rested her head on his shoulder. He held her hips and bucked into her gently. He slid his hands up inside her skirt, down the back of her knickers. "Jesus," he whispered. "You feel good." He pushed her down on it, impaling her.

She bit her lip, trying not to speak, not to be too obvious.

"Oh Jesus," he said again.

She moaned this time.

He slid his hand round and pushed in between her legs. She was slick and swollen, painful to the touch. He brushed his thumb over her clitoris and lifted his head to look at her face. "It should've been you," he said.

She frowned at him, not understanding. He brushed her clit in soft circles. She moaned again, his words forgotten.

He slid his free hand up and brought her head to his.

His mouth was soft and warm, as voluptuous as she remembered it. He was so bloody hard inside of her and the rest of him soft and moving, like silk over steel. Beauty's only skin deep - her mother always said that. Here that was made real. A fragile layer of beauty over something hard and dangerous.

He tugged at her clitoris gently. He was too young to be so knowledgeable, so good. How could he have learned it so fast? Was it some kind of sixth sense with him, automatically giving you what you wanted? Like a dream lover, never doing the wrong thing.

He kissed her again then flipped her skirt up and watched his hand in the thick black hair. He was moving deep in her, his breathing heavy. She didn't dare to look down. He pulled her down on him, hard. One hand round her waist, the other insinuating, teasing, pleasing himself on her pleasure. She still didn't look down.

"Look at yourself," he said. He pulled her down harder. "Go on, look at yourself."

She could feel two fingers sliding gently round her, parting her, exposing her, while he teased around it, above it, easing it, pleasing it.

"Go on, take a look at it." He thrust into her deeper, watching her face, pulling her down. "Let me see it on your face, go on."

She moaned desperately.

"Let me see." His face was almost vicious with it. He licked his mouth, his eyes trying to see inside her, remorseless. "Show me," he said, low and deep as a growl. "Look at it, fuck you."

She looked down and saw his stained fingers moving in the moist pink of her, and he got what he wanted. She threw her head back and began to moan like a bitch in heat, pushing herself down on it, embedding it.

478

Danny watched her writhing on him, felt it grip at him. No man alive, not a fucking man in the whole world felt like this.

He dragged her clear, trying to hold her still while he drove his own into her. It was like some kind of exquisite torture, the two of them driving it out of themselves in desperation, until she fell on his mouth, aching for it to stop.

He kissed her long and slow and elaborately, tasting the softness of it. "I love you," he said when she finally let him go, dropping her head exhaustedly on his shoulder. He looked down at her for a moment then lifted his eyes, looking out into the lay-by.

The driver looked back at him.

Danny smiled.

The driver looked away then hid behind his newspaper.

Danny went right on smiling.

It was the only thing to do.

"Come off nice and easy, we're being watched."

She froze. "Seriously?"

"For the last five minutes."

"Oh God." She flushed bright red.

He grinned at her. "He enjoyed it, don't worry."

She looked at him, furious.

She came off him as neatly as she could. She thought desperately, No-one could actually see anything. They were dressed. They might only have been fooling around for all anyone knew.

Danny was zipping himself up. She looked out the windscreen. A man was sitting in a truck directly facing them. He was eating an apple, a paper spread in front of him over the wheel. He glanced up at them, then down again quickly.

"He's hoping for seconds," Danny grinned.

"How could you?" she said, her face scalding, not knowing where to look.

"If you're going to fuck in cars it's the risk you take," he said. He was fastening his jacket. By some grace of God he hadn't marked his trousers. "And I'm going." He opened the door.

She grabbed his arm. "Wait a minute."

He looked at her. "Why?"

He might as well have slapped her face. She dropped her hand.

He smiled at her lazily. "Don't hang about after I'm gone." He got out then stuck his head back in. "Unless you fancy a trucker too." And he slammed the door.

She sat there, watching him cross the lay-by and swing up into his tractor, her eyes a blur. It roared into life and he pulled out past her. He didn't look at her. He didn't wave.

She blinked and scrubbed at her eyes. It would be alright. *Oh yes Katherine, it was alright, alright.*

She saw the trucker watching her. She turned on the engine and pulled slowly out of the space.

The trucker rolled down his window and threw out his apple core. *Dirty little buggers.* He briefly adjusted his underpants then picked up his paper and began to fill in the crossword.

When Danny got in he washed his hands at the kitchen sink.

"What happened to you?" John asked.

"Blades got caught again," Danny said without turning.

"Fucking thing should go back," John grunted.

"No, it's okay, it just got fouled up."

John said nothing more but he was watching him steadily when he turned.

Danny went upstairs and took a pee then washed.

He looked in the mirror. He smiled at himself. "A-OK Danny-boy," he whispered. He was getting to be a good liar.

Hell, he was getting to be a great liar.

FIFTY-TWO

James Conley lay in the dark and listened to Mamma singing. He had been ill for almost a week.

He conjured with the days. Five? Six?

Saturday. It must be Saturday. Seventh of December or thereabouts.

He coughed suddenly and violently for several minutes then lay back exhausted on his pillows. Mamma was still crooning away quietly to herself.

Other than feeling half-suffocated and as used as a washed-out condom he felt fine. Alive, in one piece, fine. Except he didn't feel fine, he didn't feel fine at all. Mr James Conley was suffering from an unusual condition that usually only afflicted teenage boys.

He laughed to himself uncomfortably and turned on his side. No, that was worse, now he couldn't breathe at all. He turned back.

If only it were spots.

He stuck his feet out from under the quilt. Why were they always so hot?

His problem was erections. Embarrassing public erections. Suddenly, after God knows how many years, he was waking every morning... *come on Max, it's only been three days.*

Only?

Every morning he woke with an erection, an unpleasant throbbing one at that, like something interrupted, and he lay there, hardly breathing, waiting for it to subside, and it took so long. Too damn long.

He could remember flashes of those fever dreams, rampant, brightly-coloured. They were like something that had happened to him, as if he'd been there, lived through them, and he couldn't shake them off.

Mamma began counting. Ein, zwei, drei... ein, zwei, drei. Why had she never learned any further than three? Cursed, awkward bird, twisted like the woman who'd reared her.

He stretched his arms above his head, hearing his bones creak. He yawned, making his ears pop. What time was it? He reached over and looked at the clock. Eleven o'clock.

It would be too late soon.

There, he'd admitted it. It had only been digging at him for half the evening. He looked across the room. He'd put the blind partition up so that he could see out the windows during the day. *It's still there Max, no-one's stolen it.*

It's too late.

For what?

He'll be in bed.

It's Saturday night. He won't be in bed. Go on, before it is too late.

He sat up and pulled the quilt round his shoulders. He had to use the toilet. He got up off the bed slowly and pulled the quilt around him like a cloak. He padded across the floor.

He went in, did a precarious juggling act, then flushed the toilet. The Thunder Closet. He smiled.

He came out and looked at the phone.

Go on Max.

He crossed to the settee and looked at the phone some more.

Go on.

He sat down and pulled it towards him. Just to hear it ring. Just to know he was listening to it.

Oh dial the damn thing and shut up.

He dialled Danny's number, feeling the finger-holes in the dark. He listened to the whirr of the dial, then it rang.

He counted the rings.

Ein... it paused ...zwei... drei... veer... funf... se.... Someone picked it up.

"Hello?" a voice questioned him.

He had lost his tongue.

"Hello?" the voice said again, louder this time.

"Danny," he said.

There was a silence, then that dreadful pause, that space of time where you know the other person's hanging up, the slow death it takes to return the receiver. He waited for the click.

"Who is this?"

It was Danny's deep unnatural voice, always that slight edge of temper.

James Conley, his brain said. James Conley, remember me? "Max," he said and he felt the sweat start. He pulled the quilt tight round him. The pause went on too long. He had to fill it before Danny ran away. "Did I get you up?"

At the other end Danny stood alone in the hall, watching the patterns of the TV move on the frosted glass. John was sitting behind there, lost in someone else's story. For how long? He caught it in his hand and held it, the space of time he could take from him. He watched it tick away. Then Conley said to him, "Did I get you up?"

Danny laid his head back against the banister, closed his eyes and smiled, and the smile hurt his face. He never wanted to smile again. *Yes you got me up, and you've got me up again, and every time you speak to me you'll get me up.* "No," he said, "I was already up." And he heard Conley laugh, close to his ear. They might have been lying side by side in the dark.

"What are you doing?" Conley asked.

"Standing in the hall talking to you."

There was a pause.

"Danny?"

"Yes?"

"I'm sorry."

Danny felt it move in him, right up and into his eyes, as if the fucking words had been born there.

"I'm really sorry."

Danny blinked then said, "What are you doing?"

Conley laughed again. "I'm sitting on the settee, wrapped in a quilt, talking to you. I've had flu." *Otherwise I'd have phoned you sooner.*

"Just a quilt?"

Conley could see him smiling. He lay back against the sofa. "Just a quilt," he said.

"You'll catch your death of cold." Danny's voice was still smiling.

"I've already caught it."

There was a pause again. Danny stood there watching the door, the colours sweeping over it, feeling the cold round his feet, listening to the relentless, spiteful ticking of the clock.

"Danny?"

"Yes?" he said again, feeling the desperation well up in him.

"Will you..." Conley stopped, tried again. "Could you..." He stopped again.

Come on, Danny begged. He turned and leaned his forehead against the banister, pressed the phone close to his ear.

"Danny, come and see me."

Danny groaned with the relief of it.

Conley listened to the intense silence at the other end, thinking, now he would hear it, now the click, or Danny's voice, hard, vindictive, saying fuck off in the way that sounded as if the words lived in his mouth.

"I don't know when." It was almost a whisper. Conley stared into the darkness, not believing it could be this easy. "I don't even fucking know how." And then Danny saw the movement in the room.

Time's up.

The Angel of Death is on its way.

"I'll come," he said, and he hung up.

Conley put the hand-set back slowly into its cradle. He pulled the quilt tight around him. He knew without looking that it had happened again. He sat and waited for it to subside before getting up to go back to bed.

Thump, thump, thump, it pounded - his head, his heart, his hard-on.

He would come.

Conley smiled. He might at that.

John watched him walk down the hall into the light. "Who was it?"

"James Conley."

John stood back a little to let him pass. Not much, just enough. "What did he want?"

"The usual. Katherine Henderson's thought up something new."

"What?" John's voice was impatient. He pulled Danny round.

"I don't know, he wouldn't say."

John searched his face for a moment then let him go. "Let me guess. He wants to see you."

Danny nodded.

"And you agreed to go."

Danny turned on him. "What the fuck do you suggest?"

"I suggest you tell him to go fuck himself."

Danny looked at him. "I've already said I'd go. And before you ask, she isn't going to be there."

"No?"

"No."

John looked at him a long moment. "The last time Danny."

Fuck you, Danny wanted to say. Instead he nodded once, brusquely, keeping his mouth shut. He moved round him and sat down on the settee, looking at the TV. He saw nothing on the screen. He felt John sit down beside him. John pulled his arm. Reluctantly Danny came to rest against him.

"You don't like it Danny, do you?"

"No-one likes being told what to do."

"No, there's something more to it than that."

Danny pulled away from him, but John wrapped his arm round his shoulders, pulling him back across his body. His arm was hooked across Danny's chest. A little higher up and it would be round his throat. "Are you going there to fuck her?"

"No," Danny said.

"Prove it."

"How can I fucking prove it?"

"You can't," John laughed. "That's what you like about this. No-one can prove anything."

Danny lay there rigid against him, knowing what he was working himself into.

The back door banged. John's arm tightened on him. Danny started praying silently. *Let it be Rab. Please God, let it be Rab.*

John kissed his hair like someone saying, Wait till you see this. Just wait till you see this.

The door opened. Danny smelt the cold air, the distant smell of beer.

"Come in, we were waiting for you."

Danny turned his head.

Ian was standing there, still in his jacket.

Danny's eyes were flat, dark. John's had that distant, inward look, lost inside his own head. Ian felt his heart go a little harder, the dry-mouthed ache start up in him. He moved in front of the fire and warmed his hands.

"Rab not with you?" John asked.

"He went off with Tam Johnstone."

"Where?"

Ian shrugged eloquently. Who knows? Who cares?

John kissed Danny's hair. Ian watched his mouth with a trip-start. He could see the rigid lines of Danny's body.

"You ever ream him Ian?" John wasn't looking at him when he asked it. Only Danny's eyes, flat and black, watched him standing there. The question hung in the room. An insistently cheerful advert bounced out at them.

"No." It came out half-strangled. He sounded as if he had a sore throat.

"Never?" John's voice was incurious, just going through a formality. He knew the answers already.

"Never."

John slid his hand inside Danny's shirt. "Would you like to do it to now?"

Ian saw Danny's shoulders jerk, trying to pull away, and watched John's arm come up under his chin, forcing Danny's head back, locking him tight. "Easy Danny," John whispered to him, then louder to Ian, "Want to?"

"Yes," Ian said. It didn't come out much better.

"What if I let him go, think you can hold him?"

Ian shook his head. John didn't see it but he knew. "He's easy, all you've got to do is squeeze him a little. After that he's butter."

"He won't let me," Ian said. He watched Danny's chest. It was moving heavily with suppressed anger, maybe fear. His feet were braced, ready to bolt, his hands pushed down against the cushions.

"You managed to convince him three days ago in the barn."

Ian licked his lip. He saw Danny go completely still. His breathing stopped. John was waiting. Everyone was waiting.

"How did you convince him Ian?"

Ian swallowed. "I didn't need to."

John smiled. John even laughed a little. His thumb began describing little circles on Danny's cheek, his fingers laid lightly over his mouth almost as if he were gagging him. Danny jerked his head away. "No marks for that one Ian, he's never *let* you do anything in his life. For someone like you he's always got a reason. What was it?"

Ian could see the change in Danny's breathing. It was shallow now, tiny breaths, just keeping him going. His face looked drawn, white. "I don't know," he said. "He was walking around like a zombie all week. I was just chancing it. Ask him why. I don't know."

Ian watched John turning it over. There was so much truth in it, it almost was the truth. Maybe... just maybe...

John smiled and Ian knew it had worked. "Want a hand?" And this time he looked

at him.

Ian nodded.

"I'll hold him, you fuck him."

The words acted like a starter's gun. Danny squirmed out of John's grip like an eel. John grunted and made a lunge for him, grabbing his thigh as he came off the couch. Ian watched it as if it was slow motion. Danny snarling, then turning and swiping at John's head full stretch. John's head jerked sideways like a recoil. He let go.

Danny ran for the door. Ian got to it as he did. The two of them crashed against it, the glass bending under their weight.

Danny tore at his arm.

Then Ian saw John come up off the couch. It reminded him of those animations of the Earth being born, great mountains splitting up out the earth. He grabbed Danny from behind and almost bodily lifted him off the floor. His face was like stone, emotionless with rage. There was a dull aching noise like a silenced gun, a muffled thud that hurt your bones just to hear it.

Danny folded. John held him up and half-pushed, half-threw him on the couch. Ian could see the marks on his face where Danny had caught his head. John was staring down at him, curled up tight against the pain. "You..." It was all he got out. It seemed to be all he wanted to say.

Ian stood watching him, unsure what to do.

John turned to him. His smile was full of teeth. "Go on, take him, or haven't you got the guts?"

Ian went over to the couch and sat down beside him. He put his hand on Danny's hair. John's voice spoke close beside him, standing above him. "Don't talk to it, just fuck it. You wanted to fuck it, fuck it."

Ian stood up. "I can't do anything when he's lying there like that. He's curled up tighter than a hedgehog."

John stared at him, his whole face sneering. "You want me to spread it out nice and clean and put a fucking frill on it?"

Ian felt his face burn up.

"Okay, let's make it nice and easy for you."

He bent down and pulled at Danny's arms. Danny jerked them back, trying to keep his face covered. John pulled them down again and slapped him. "Lie still you little faggot."

He rolled Danny onto his back and began unfastening his clothes. Danny laid one arm over his eyes, the other hand pressed to his stomach. Ian watched as John roughly pulled off his trousers and shorts. He simply pushed his sweater up his chest. "Enough on show?"

Ian looked down at him. All he could see was the heavy red puckering on his stomach where John had burnt him. There were more burns under his left ribs that looked new. The rest was white and smooth, beautiful as always. He nodded.

John smiled back, ugly. "Front or back?"

"What?"

"Are you going to fuck it from the front or the back?" John enunciated each word clearly as if he was talking to a cretin.

Ian looked down at him. "I want to see his face."

John smiled. "Then go ahead, he's all yours."

John sat down in the armchair and crossed his ankles. He stretched out comfortably, hands across his stomach like a man relaxing after a hard day's work, but he was tense as a spring. Ian could see it in his jaw. He looked back at Danny. He was heavily flaccid, shrivelled almost. He still hid under his arm.

Ian sat down beside him and ran his hand over his belly. Danny didn't try to stop

him. Ian circled his finger round the burn then softly across it, fascinated by the violence of it. He saw Danny's stomach muscles clench. He ran both hands up Danny's ribs onto his chest, felt the goosepimples under his fingers, the tense hardness of his body.

He laid himself down over him and heard John undoing his zip. He didn't look round. He kissed Danny's exposed cheek, making his way down to his mouth. He kissed Danny's mouth, felt it soft and utterly lifeless beneath his own. He kissed back towards Danny's cheek then into his ear. He whispered to him, so softly that he wasn't sure if Danny could even hear him, "Kiss me Danny, please."

But Danny made no sign, no movement.

"Danny, kiss me."

But there was nothing. He moved back to his mouth and kissed it again. Sheer, warm, soft nothing. Ian lifted his head and pulled Danny's arm off his eyes. It came away easily, like something dead. Danny opened his eyes and looked at him.

"I want you," Ian said, trying to reach him.

Danny closed his eyes again, with finality.

"You little bastard," Ian hissed at him. He heard John laugh.

He pushed between Danny's legs and unzipped himself. He pushed his penis down underneath him, feeling with his hand. He saw Danny's jaw set. "I'm going to poke you in half, you precious little prick."

He knelt up and found his target. He nudged forward, getting under Danny's arse. It was tight and resisting. This was what Danny kept exclusively for him - every fucking bastard and his whippet welcome except him.

He pushed in hard. He saw Danny's jaw tense and knew he'd hurt him. He pushed in again, lifting Danny's legs higher. Danny lay there, still, breathing hard.

"Look at me," Ian said.

Danny kept his eyes shut.

"Look at me you little bastard." Ian pushed in again. "Come on, look at me."

Danny opened his eyes and looked at him.

Ian smiled. "See it?" He thrust into him. "Fucking feel it Danny." He pushed hard, right up.

The two of them stared at each other, breathing like wrestlers exhausted in each other's arms, a temporary truce.

And then it happened, the same way it always did. Danny came up, slow and sure, his eyes narrow and filmed like something before the kill.

"Oh Jesus," Ian said, watching it. He heard John grunt heavily behind him. "Oh sweet Jesus, look at him." And Ian started to come, without even trying. His body took over. He lifted Danny's legs and slowly squeezed himself into him, each spasm quivering in his body like a feverish sickness.

And behind him he heard John, his movements frenzied, violently jerking himself off.

"Bring him off." John's voice was affectedly lazy, nothing of the kind.

Ian looked over at him. He could still feel a dull throbbing, almost like a pain in his groin. Danny's sphincter was trying to push him out, but he kept it in. Let the little bastard suffer.

Ian looked back at Danny. He was looking up at him, his face implacable, expressionless.

"Hurt him."

Ian looked at John again, frowning. "What do you mean?"

"Use your imagination."

Ian saw that he was still caressing himself, his erection barely diminished. It was wet and shiny but still a hard, angry red. He looked back at Danny. This was above his head. *The water's too deep for me, John.* "No," he said.

John laughed, but it had no humour in it. "Chicken." He said it like he was saying bullshit.

Ian eased out of him. He looked down and saw blood on himself. He frowned, looked at Danny again. There was too much blood. He looked at it in distaste.

"What's wrong?" John was watching him, smiling, his hand never losing pace.

"He's bleeding."

John quirked his face. *So what?*

Ian looked at Danny again and made a tissue-paper guess, push your finger through it it's so fragile. John's been putting things up there that shouldn't go up there. John's been fucking him with everything but himself.

Ian stood up, pushing himself inside his clothes, trying not to touch it. "I'm going to wash."

"Sit down." John's voice was immediate, menacing.

Ian looked at him.

"I said, sit down." And now his hand had stopped, waiting for obedience.

Ian sat down. John's hand began stroking again. Ian watched it, fascinated by the long, sleek movements of it, passionless, tender, like someone caressing a child. Danny lay there, still, arms rolled into the front of his sweater as if he'd been told to keep it up out of the way. His erection lay there quiescent, like some tensed but obedient animal waiting for the command. He watched everything as if he were listening to it.

"You've got two options Ian - hurt or be hurt."

"You're nuts."

John watched his own cock with a lazy but complete absorption, as if hypnotised by his own movements. It was fully hard again, no sign that he had done anything to it, other than nurse it. "Choose."

"Get stuffed."

John waited a beat then said, "If you don't choose you're it. I'm going to give you five seconds."

John began to count. Ian could feel Danny watching him. Steadily John got there. "...five."

"Alright." Ian blurted it out. "What do you want me to do?"

"To Danny." John was smiling. Repeat it Ian, let's hear it.

"To Danny," Ian said quietly.

Ian wouldn't look at him now. John was smiling, anticipatory. "Anything you like Ian as long as you hurt him."

"Christ!" Ian exploded. "I'm not a fucking sadist."

"No?"

"No."

"Never wanted to hurt him? I thought everybody wanted to hurt him. I thought that's why God had had put him on this Earth, to give us all something to hurt."

I've only ever wanted to own him, Ian thought, *be* him, not…

"Never?" John repeated as if he'd read his thoughts.

"No," Ian said again, clenching his fists.

"Liar," John said amiably. Then he said, "Tell you what, I'll let you off lightly. You do something for me then you can go. Okay?"

Ian swallowed, wary.

"It's no big deal. No violence, no pain, I promise you. Okay?"

Ian nodded.

"Once…" John said, and he laid his head back and closed his eyes as if he were commencing a story, his hand still pulling leisurely in his lap, "we were out working late in the evening. You and Danny were in the back field, below the horizon. I had stopped the tractor below the crest and come down on foot, silent and unseen. I could say I don't know why I did that but I'd be lying. You'd been needling him all day. You'd been needling him all summer. The poor bastard couldn't wait to get back to school. You remember this Ian?"

John looked at him suddenly then smiled. "He was almost thirteen, so you must have been about seventeen, and all day you'd had your hands on him, pinching him, tickling him, groping him when you thought no-one was looking. If I saw him blush once that day I must have seen him do it fifty times, and now you had him alone. You had him up against the tree. You know the tree. You'd used it before. You used it again. I was too far away to hear what you were saying, but you were pressed up against him, sandwiching him against the tree. You had his arms above his head, your other hand stuck down inside his trousers."

John laughed. "Christ, he was dirty-mouthing you. He even managed to wriggle away, but you caught him again, pushed him down onto his knees and forced yourself in his mouth… and he bit it."

John laughed again then his face went still. He moistened his lips. "Remember what you did then Ian?"

There was no answer.

"Do what you did to him then."

Nothing moved in the room. The television talked on almost like a silence, irrelevant. Nobody heard it.

"I'm waiting," John's voice was tight, "and I feel very…" he paused, looking for the word, "…*jumpy*." And suddenly he looked as vicious as a rattlesnake.

Ian stood up. "Get down Danny." His voice sounded odd, even to himself.

Danny lay there, watching him, making no attempt to move.

Ian lunged at him, grabbing his hair, dragging him off the couch, just like last time, grabbing his little brother's hair, pushing his half-naked narrow body, sweet with sweat, between his legs.

"*Shit*," Danny said. "You crawling little shit."

And now it was just the same, the same Danny who'd bitten him, who made him fight tooth and nail for every crumb he got. He took his cock out and pulled Danny's head back, remembering the boy squirming, tears rolling down his face as he let himself go in it, the urine streaming down his chest, and the release of it, almost like coming.

He did it again, not watching it, just feeling it, the release of it.

And he heard John come.

From very far away.

Ian had left quickly. He had looked at Danny's face in almost comic surprise and let him go.

Danny stood up and pulled his sweater off. He rubbed the dry part of it over his hair, wiping the worst of it off.

"You're beautiful." John's voice was almost hushed, reverential.

Danny didn't look at him. Very little of it had gone on the carpet. He had taken most of it. There wasn't a lot of it. Ian must have gone for a pee before he left the pub. Hooray for him. He picked his jeans off the couch.

"I love you," John said as if he were repeating it. "Come here."

Danny stood still, naked, chilling rapidly.

"Come here Danny."

Danny went over to him. John took his hand and kissed the wounded mouth in his palm. Danny glanced at him and looked away again. John's hands were warm and dry in spite of the flood that was congealing on his exposed belly.

John pulled him towards him. "Kiss me."

Danny turned his head away.

"Come on, I want to."

"Not with this shit all over me John. For Christsake, let me wash it off."

"No, kiss me." And John pulled his arm again, tugging him down.

Danny bent down quickly and brushed his mouth, but John grabbed his head and held him close, his mouth hard, demanding.

Danny felt his stomach turn. He pulled away. "I'm gonna fucking throw up John." His face was screwed up tight with revulsion.

"You taste good." John's voice was low, caressing.

Danny's eyes flew open. "Yeah, I'll bet I taste good. I taste of fucking dirt and defeat. I'll bet I taste really good."

John smiled at him as if he were giving him benediction. "You never taste of defeat Danny, that's what makes you so fucking irresistible. That's what keeps everyone trotting back for more. There's a little hard core inside you that no-one ever touches. Not me, not Ian, not even her. You're as tough as nails under there Danny, no matter what we do to you. Even that day in the hayloft you didn't let it touch you, did you?"

Danny looked away, trying not to listen.

"You saw, I know you did."

Danny didn't answer.

"He didn't really want to cut it at all." John reached inside his breast pocket and held up something which looked like a small twist of sewing thread. Danny didn't want to look but he dragged his eyes round.

John nodded. "It's yours. I found it tucked inside his will." John looked at him again. "Was it before or after? You can tell me."

Danny's face jumped like an addict's, as if he couldn't control the muscles.

John sighed. "It was after. It had to be."

Danny turned on him, pushed beyond endurance. "It never *happened*. I was *six* fucking years old John!"

John looked at him, gently sceptical, as if the age meant nothing. "You like it?"

"Nothing *happened*."

"Bigger, harder, hairier. Bet you couldn't even get it in your mouth, could you? Could he get it in your mouth Danny?"

"Shut the fuck up." Danny put his hands over his ears.

John stood up and pulled his hands down, held them tight. "Did he do it in your mouth?"

"No."

"Where then?"

Danny's face coloured up furiously. He tried to pull away. John tugged him back, chin up hard. "Where?" he demanded.

"*Yours*."

John's mouth opened. After a second or two he wet his lips, but he couldn't seem to close them again.

"You fucking twisted cunt. What was the ritual? He get you all naked down in the hay and rub himself off on you?" Danny stared at him. "Up above you like he was doing press-ups, so he didn't have to touch you? That how he did it?" Danny glared into his face. John wet his mouth again, stood back a step.

"He lick it off you John? Tell you he loved you? Were you as big a disappointment

to him as I was to you?"

"You were never a disappointment to me."

Danny snapped in a strange tight voice, "*Stop* changing the *subject*."

John sat down and looked up at him. Danny stared at him for a long moment then said wearily, "Why did you do it?"

John stared at the floor for a long time then said, "I had no choice."

Danny was silent so long John finally looked up. Danny's face was flat, dead. "Yeah John." He bundled his clothes up tight against himself. "Exactly."

And he went out the door.

FIFTY-THREE

Rab stayed out all night.

Danny was first into the kitchen in the morning. He was pouring himself cereal when Rab came in. He looked bright and alert. Wherever he'd been he'd got some sleep.

Danny looked at him curiously and was startled to feel a shift of something irritable in him. "Where've you been?"

Rab was hanging up his jacket. He turned and looked at Danny, smiling amiably. "And why should you care?"

"I don't. I'm curious, that's all."

"I went to a party."

"With Tam Johnstone?"

Rab looked at him, smiling a little more. "Your informer is correct, with Tam Johnstone."

"Any good?" Danny asked casually. He looked at the cereal and wondered suddenly how he was going to eat it.

"Meaning, did I get off with anybody?"

Danny looked up. "Did you?"

And Rab looked back and said, "Yes."

Danny blinked and looked away. "Bully for you." He pushed the cereal away from him.

"What's wrong?"

"I'm not hungry." Danny wouldn't look at him.

"Bit sudden, isn't it?"

Danny flared up at him, "Do me a favour, drop dead."

Rab raised his eyebrows. "What's wrong, didn't you get your rocks off last night?"

Danny glared at him.

"Only asking." Rab shrugged and looked away as if to say, Be like that, see if I care.

John came in. "If it isn't the Playboy of the Western World. Whose bed did you sleep in?"

Someone was in a good mood. Maybe that's what was wrong with Danny, John had fucked him legless. "Wouldn't you like to know?"

"Not Tam Johnstone's surely?"

"Give me a break."

"Come on, give, who got The Royal Length last night?"

"I don't kiss and tell."

"His sister."

Rab shook his head.

"His mother."

Rab laughed. "Give up, you'll never guess it."

John snapped his fingers. "That fucking rabbit he keeps."

"You bastard, you guessed."

Danny pushed up from his chair suddenly and pulled his jacket on. John watched his back with a vicious little smile on his mouth. Rab saw it and tasted something sour in his mouth. Even John's good moods threw dirt about. Danny went out slamming the door.

Rab pulled Danny's cereal over and added more milk to it. He began to eat it. John

sat down and poured himself some tea.

"What's biting him?" Rab asked without looking up. When there was no answer he lifted his eyes to look at him.

John shrugged. "Who knows?"

"That's almost an admission of failure."

John shook his head. "I don't try, so I can't fail."

Rab was surprised to see him take out a cigarette. He put it in his mouth. "I'm seeing a woman tomorrow for Ostler's job."

Rab pushed Danny's bowl away half-finished and took a cigarette out himself. "Not before time. What's she like? Have you spoken to her?"

John nodded then added, "Only on the phone." He paused. "She's not very old."

Rab laughed, blew smoke down his nose. "So what? The last one was ancient." And a fat lot of difference that made, were the unspoken words between them.

John nodded again.

"What you want..." Rab blew smoke up to the ceiling, "is someone tough as old boots... or a dyke."

John grunted out a laugh. "I don't think even a dyke could resist Danny."

"He's not superhuman you know."

"You could have fooled me."

And me, Rab thought.

"You get off with someone?" John was watching him now.

Rab smiled. "Jealous?"

"Depends."

"On what?"

"Who it was."

"You mean what it was."

"What was it?"

Rab inhaled his cigarette. "A rabbit."

John grinned suddenly and said, "Watch you don't cut yourself." He pushed up from the table. As he went past he bent down and whispered in Rab's ear, "I'll bet he had red hair."

Rab smiled in spite of himself.

He was right - he did.

Katherine Henderson bumped into the Selsdon sisters on the second landing. She liked them. They were eccentric and droll, filled with old-fashioned acerbic humour.

They talked for a while about Katherine's trip home before the eldest sister took her arm and bent close towards her ear. Katherine was amused. This always heralded some interesting snippet about their neighbours, full of malicious confidences.

"While you were gone dear, I must tell you, that man was around here."

Katherine stiffened. "Who?"

"The one who knew your brother, dark, saturnine face."

Katherine looked at her. John Jackson Moore, who else could it be? "A big guy, built like a house, with dirty brown hair?" she asked.

"That's the one," Miss Selsdon agreed with relish. She almost smacked her lips.

"Was he actually in the building?" Katherine asked. The idea disturbed her.

"Oh no, dear," Miss Selsdon said on an intake of breath. "No, I spotted him from our window. He rang your bell a few times then went away again. I hope I'm not being rude dear, but he really is a terrible looking chap... so *voracious* looking."

Katherine Henderson nodded absently.

"Voracious," the other Miss Selsdon repeated, nodding.

"They were here that night, you know," Miss Selsdon the Elder said, her tone dropped even lower.

"What night?" Katherine asked.

"The night your brother was..." She let it tail off, patting Katherine's arm as if she might burst into tears at any moment.

"They?"

"Yes, the big one... and the two others." She said 'the two others' as if it was a dirty word, lowering her voice still further.

Katherine felt her heart begin to race. "What two others?"

Miss Selsdon the Elder looked at the Younger and there was an indefinable closing of the ranks. They moved closer to Katherine and she had a bizarre image of them like the three witches in Macbeth, standing on the stairs concocting some hex on the residents.

"Ann and I saw them once..." she paused, looking over her shoulder, "...embracing." She said the word with an exaggerated movement of her lips, like someone talking to the deaf, making practically no sound.

"*Embracing?*" Katherine said, emphasising the word in an unconscious parody.

"Yes." She paused. "You know... *kissing*." She did the same performance again, opening her lips and eyes widely, mouthing the word as if Katherine couldn't hear it and was only reading it.

"*Kissing?*" Katherine echoed again.

Both the Misses Selsdon nodded sagely, folding their hands almost in unison. "Didn't we Ann?" the Elder said swiftly. They nodded again, together, like marionettes.

"When was this?"

"Oh," she paused then said airily, "weeks ago."

"What did they look like, the two who were kissing?"

"Oh, very handsome. We have to give them that, don't we Ann?" She said it as if fairness in all things was essential.

"*Very* handsome," Ann echoed, nodding vehemently.

"Was one of them a redhead?" Katherine asked.

"Ooh yes, a redhead," Ann said quickly, pre-empting her sister.

Elizabeth Selsdon looked at her sister sharply and said, "Yes dear, definitely a redhead. Very..." she looked for the word, "...striking." She patted her midriff as if she'd eaten something good, well-satisfied with her selection.

"Was the other blonde? Very..." It was Katherine's turn to look for a word.

"Petulant," Miss Selsdon finished for her as if she'd just found the right word in a crossword puzzle.

Maybe not the word Katherine would have chosen but she knew what she meant. His mouth did have a slightly petulant pout to it. The perpetual cigarette didn't help.

Miss Selsdon tugged her arm tightly, leaned across her. "They didn't look... you know, *that* way... well not the redhead anyway. It gave us a shock. She turned to her sister again. "Didn't it Annie?"

"A terrible shock," Ann offered but her eyes glittered happily. Whatever kind of shock she'd had it hadn't been too terrible, Katherine thought.

"And they were here, all three of them, on the night my brother was murdered?"

"Oh yes," Miss Selsdon said. "We passed them on the stairs dear."

"You didn't tell the police?" Katherine asked, mystified.

"Oh no, definitely not. They were friends of your brother's."

Katherine blinked at that one and bit back the retort, What the hell's that got to do with it? Then she saw the message clear in Miss Selsdon's eyes. My dear, they were homosexuals - these 'friends' of your brothers were *homosexuals*.

Katherine met her eyes for a moment and then said, "Thank you." Message

received and understood.

Elizabeth and Ann Selsdon smiled, nodding.

They departed, their duty done.

FIFTY-FOUR

Danny was swinging the shed doors open when Ian came out of the barn. It was barely light. "I'll come with you," he said.

Yeah, so you can sit behind me up against my rump, Danny thought. Then he saw John come out the house. He shrugged.

He got on the field buggy. Ian swung a leg over and sat behind him, arms round his waist.

Danny pushed down on the accelerator and took them down the lane. The traffic was non-existent. They cut across the road and down into the field access road. Ian's arms tightened around him as they bumped over the rough ground. "Jesus Danny, you drive as bad as Rab," Ian grunted in his ear.

They came to a halt and unloaded the feed. They worked in silence. When they had finished the light was a little stronger.

Ian looked at him. His face was all hollows. His hair looked almost black, just the barest tinge of colour. His breath was puffing out of him like smoke, clouds of it misting before his face. He stopped and blew on his hands, his eyes coming up to meet Ian's.

"I'm sorry," Ian said.

Danny stopped and looked at him then bent and picked up the empty sacks, folding them roughly. He moved back towards the buggy.

Ian caught his arm. "I am." His voice was earnest.

Danny watched his face.

"I was sorry the first time and I'm sorry now."

Danny shrugged it off. "Forget it." He climbed onto the buggy.

Ian could feel the frustration welling up in him. "Can't you believe me, just once?"

"Get on and shut up." Danny sat there with his back to him, waiting.

Ian climbed on and slid his arms round his waist. Suddenly he pressed up against him, burying his face deep into the back of his neck.

Danny could feel his mouth breathing hot over his skin, his hands pulling at the zip of his jacket, trying to get inside. Danny peeled his hands off. "For Christsake Ian, it isn't even seven o'clock yet and you're crawling all over me. Give it a break."

"I love you."

"And stop fucking saying that." Danny turned on him, giving him a violent shove that almost dislodged him. They sat there in the middle of the field with the sun coming up and their breath clouding round them, their hands numb.

Ian reached out and touched his face gently.

Danny looked at him for a long moment then turned away, saying abruptly, "Go on then."

Ian moved up against him and slid his arms round him, warm into the secret darkness.

"For not telling him," Danny said as if he'd asked him.

"I love you," Ian said again.

Danny felt his hand slide in. He sat still and let him do what he wanted.

He wished he'd hurry up.

He was beginning to freeze.

James Conley woke up on Sunday the eighth of December and felt better. He had slept without dreaming and the sun was shining. He touched himself briefly and

shuddered. As soon as that went he'd get up.

He put his arms behind his head and wondered when he would see Danny. Maybe that should be *if* he would see Danny.

He brought his arms down and swung his legs out of bed. His head began to pound immediately. He held it in his hands, elbows on his knees, eyes closed. *Easy does it*. He opened his eyes and saw how swollen he was, flaccid, but only just.

He looked away and got up carefully. He pulled his track suit on, then a pair of thick white socks. He looked at himself in the mirror. Very elegant. He smiled gingerly.

He went to the bathroom then came out and phoned the time. Ten thirty-two. He'd slept straight through till ten thirty-two without waking once. This called for some serious breakfast.

He went over to the kitchen and rummaged in a bag for his last doughnut. He put it on a plate and licked the sugar off his fingers.

The phone rang.

He looked at it as if he didn't know what it was. Mamma yelled, "Telefon! Telefon!"

He crossed as quickly as he could to answer it, socks sliding on the floorboards. "Hello?"

They'd hung up. Damn and hell.

"Hello."

Conley sat down. "Danny?"

"Uh-huh."

"Where are you?"

There was a deep laugh, soft. "At home, where do you think?"

I don't think Danny, I just live on my fingernails.

There was a pause. Conley was aware of the ridiculous pounding of his heart, the excitement in his stomach. Like being in love, he thought, amused by the absurdity. Danny spoke to him again.

"Can you phone me in an hour or so?" There was a pause. Conley could imagine him looking at his watch, maybe a clock. "About twelve o'clock?"

"Why?"

"I've told John you've got Katherine Henderson on your tail again, that you want to see me." And I've already paid for the trip, Danny thought, and I'm fucking well going to have it.

Conley smiled. "Isn't this a bit elaborate?"

There was an infinitesimal pause, delicate, fraught, heavy with unspoken words. "No," Danny said. Then, "Will you do it?"

"Of course," Conley said, no longer smiling. Then he added, "How soon can you come round?"

Danny laughed again. "You're very eager." His voice was deeper.

Conley said nothing. *Don't flirt with me Danny, please.* Then Danny was speaking again. "About three I think. I'll try and talk him into three, be there for four, okay?"

"Alright," Conley said.

"Don't burst a gut. I preferred you eager."

Conley laughed. "I shall look forward to it," he said with heavy politeness.

"Oh *boy*," Danny drawled.

Conley flushed as if he'd said something obscene. "You know Danny..."

"Mm?"

"I don't know how you've managed to live this long."

Danny laughed again, low, dirty. "Sheer luck, mein Führer."

And suddenly the dialling tone was in his ear.

John was staring at him. "You're getting very attached to that phone."

"Wrong number," Danny said. He kept his eyes straight. *No flinching Danny-boy.*

"I didn't hear it ring."

"You probably weren't listening."

"Don't smart-mouth me," John snapped.

Danny shrugged, pushing his hands in his pockets.

John leaned against the door-frame. Danny could feel himself begin to colour under his scrutiny. "Don't fuck with me Danny."

Danny looked up at him quickly then back at the floor. His mouth was a thin line, sullen, angry.

"I'm warning you."

"I hear you."

"Yes, but you're not listening." John came down the hall until he stood in front of him.

"I'm listening."

John pushed him suddenly, hard against the banister. "You're fucking not Danny-boy." He was leaning into his stomach, pinning him there, pressing the air out of him.

"Fighting again?"

John came up off him, turned to look up the hall. Rab was there, standing where John had stood minutes before. "What's wrong, you run out of work?"

Rab held out his hands, a pleading innocent gesture. "Just passing through."

"Why don't you pass then?"

"I'm already gone, but when you've finished beating up your little brother maybe you can help me with this fence. You know, the one that was so important half an hour ago?"

"Where's Ian?" John's voice was irritable.

"Humping sheep, where the fuck else?" Rab's voice was irritable too.

"Everybody wants to be funny today."

"It's Sunday, the day of rest. We're allowed to be funny on a Sunday."

John gave Danny one last look then moved off.

As soon as he disappeared Danny made a violent gesture at his back, and then he hugged himself tight, and smiled.

The phone rang at exactly quarter past twelve. They were all sitting at table.

As soon as it rang John looked at Danny. He looked at him long and hard, putting his fork down carefully and dangling one arm over the back of his chair. Rab watched the performance curiously. Ian kept on eating, his eyes lifting no higher than to watch John's hands.

"Well, well... if it isn't the phone." John wiped his mouth with the back of his hand.

Rab put down his cutlery. "Is anybody going to answer it?"

John pushed up slowly from the table and went out of the room.

Rab looked at Danny. "What the fuck's wrong with him?"

Danny said nothing. Rab sighed and went back to his food.

Danny stared at the table.

"Hello."

"Hello? Can I speak to Danny please?"

"Who is it?"

James Conley shifted position in his chair, hearing the hostility in the voice. "James

Conley."

"Then the answer's no."

Conley digested this slowly. "I take it I'm speaking to John Jackson Moore," he said carefully.

"You take it right."

"Any reason why I can't speak to Danny?"

"Several."

Conley looked at Mamma. She pulled a feather out and beat it to death on her perch. "And they might be…?"

But John Jackson Moore didn't answer him, instead he said, "What has Katherine Henderson dreamed up now?"

The question was unexpected. Conley came back as best he could. "I'm sorry, I can only discuss that with Danny."

"Like fuck." The voice was hard, brittle, full of aggression.

"I'm sorry, only to Danny," he repeated.

"He's Mr Jackson Moore to you, okay?"

Conley moved the hand-set slightly, uncramping his fingers. He said carefully, coolly polite, "I apologise for my familiarity."

There was a long pause then, "Will she be there?"

Conley almost said, Who? biting it back before it left his mouth. "No." He felt sweat prickle his skin. Now why did he say that? He was suddenly convinced it was the wrong answer.

"When do you want to see him?"

Conley took a deep breath. "Today, if that's not inconvenient."

"It's Sunday."

"If you would prefer some other day?" Conley risked it.

There was a pause.

"He'll be there." There was another pause then, "But this is the last time, and you can tell Miss Henderson that, you hear me?"

"Yes," Conley said.

"It'll be sometime after three," John said abruptly, and the dialling tone sounded in Conley's ear for the second time that day.

Danny came out into the hall.

"He wants to see you today." John was watching his face.

"Can I take the pick-up?"

John nodded then said, "Last time Danny."

"You've already told me that."

"So I'm telling you again."

Danny just looked at him. After a moment John reached out and pulled him to him. He said close to his ear, his breath warm on his cheek, "I'm not stupid Danny." He moved a little closer. "Don't treat me as if I am."

He put his lips over his and held his mouth briefly, then he squeezed Danny's backside and pushed him away. "Do some work." He walked down the hall back to the kitchen. "That's what we pay you for."

And he went back to his meal.

Danny managed to finish work by two-thirty. He pulled off his jacket and boots and took the stairs two at a time.

He ran smack into Rab on the hall landing. Rab grunted under the impact and

grabbed Danny's shoulders. "Someone's in a hurry."

Rab was smiling at him. He didn't let go of him. He could feel the coiled excitement of Danny's body under his fingers. "Is he that good?"

Danny might have smiled. Rab couldn't read his eyes in the dark shadows of the hall.

"I wouldn't know."

"Yeah." Rab began kneading his hands into Danny's shoulders. God, how long had it been? It felt like years. "Are you fucking him?"

"No."

"I don't believe you."

"Believe what you like, it isn't any of your business anyway."

"You wouldn't be interested in anything you couldn't fuck." Rab saw the faint glimmer of his smile again, but Danny said nothing. Rab bent his head and kissed him.

Danny felt the kick of it, like poking a stick in John's eye. They backed up against the wall, Rab kissing him as if it were going out of fashion.

Eventually Rab let go. "Jesus," he whispered.

Danny stood silent, breathing heavily, head back against the old floury-scented paper, listening to the clock ticking. He made no effort to move, to start anything, to finish anything. He stood with Rab's body pressing gently against his, tasting him in his mouth, smelling the spice of him.

"Danny," Rab began tentatively.

"Oh shut that." Danny pushed out from under him suddenly. "Why do you always have to start this same fucking thing?"

"What thing?"

"Oh, don't act it. You're not fucking married to me Rab." Danny glared at him in the dark.

"*Married...?* Christ, I wouldn't fucking marry you if my life depended on it. You've got about as much loyalty as a praying mantis. Nobody in their right mind would fucking marry you."

"Listen to what's talking." They were almost shouting, oblivious to anyone overhearing, both suddenly outrageously beyond themselves with anger. "Who were you screwing last night?"

"I didn't *screw* anybody." Rab's voice dropped, became suddenly contained, low, contemptuous. "I *fellated* him."

Danny stood still. This wasn't what he wanted to hear.

"In the back seat of Tam Johnstone's car."

Danny came out of it. He didn't need to listen to this. He stalked towards the bathroom, but Rab caught his arm and yanked him round. "Oh no you don't. I want to make a full confession." He held Danny's arm tightly, the fingers digging into him.

"Let me go you twat."

"We took him down the beach. Tam was in the front, drinking beer, pretending not to listen, probably watching in the rear-view mirror."

"Christ." Danny tugged away violently, but Rab held on.

"He had red hair and his name was Stephen. He said he was fifteen. He's going to be sicker than a skunk this morning when he remembers what he did. He even let me kiss him. That's really going to cut him up, don't you think?"

"You lousy bastard."

"Why? For seducing minors or because I'm supposed to hang around waiting for you?"

Danny punched him but it was a wasted blow, barely winding him, merely startling him. He heard Danny slam the bathroom door and lock it.

Rab went over and leant against it. If it hadn't been so dark you could have seen

him smiling. "What's wrong Danny, don't you like being on the receiving end?" There was no sound from inside the bathroom but Rab knew he was listening. "If you're going to hand it out Danny, you better learn to take it."

There was more silence, long, angry. They stood there, back to back, with the door between them. "He was sweet Danny," Rab whispered finally. "So very sweet."

When the shower came on full blast it sounded like a thunderstorm in the still of the afternoon.

Rab pushed up slowly off the door and went downstairs.

His smile was as hard as glass.

Danny looked at John sitting on the bed and felt like spitting. This had started with Ian this morning. They were all in the mood today. *I'm like a fucking stud bull servicing a herd.*

Danny yanked off the towel and began to get dressed. John watched him in silence. He was smoking a cigarette, actually smoking it, not just dangling it unlit from his mouth. Danny hated it when he smoked. He only did it when he was wound up and it always brought grief with it. "Do you want something John?" he asked, trying to keep it light. It didn't work very well. It came out hard and irritable.

"Nothing I could get."

Oh happy fucking shit. He hadn't even left the house yet. *Right, okay John-boy, you win.*

Danny looked at him for a moment. He was standing there in his jeans, shirt unfastened, socks in hand. He threw them down, crossed over to the bed and knelt down between John's legs. He was surprised to find him already erect. He looked up.

"Watching you dress," John said. His face was utterly still

Danny changed his mind, pushing him back on the bed and climbing on top of him. He took John's cigarette and stubbed it out then lay back on top of him again. John slid his arms around him. Danny could feel him pressing up into him. "What's this Danny, conscience money?"

"Why don't you shut up?" Danny began kissing him, pushing up his sweatshirt, kissing his chest, nuzzling into his armpit. He slid his hand down between them and caressed him with his hand, trying to ease the temper out of him.

John rolled him over suddenly and reversed their positions. He leaned on his elbows and studied Danny's face. "You think this answers everything, don't you?"

Danny stopped his movements. He lay under him, waiting for the rest. He might as well hear it because John wasn't going to be appeased any other way.

"I love you Danny."

"So *fuck.*" It came out of Danny without warning, in an instantaneous flare of temper. Oh Jesus, what was he doing?

John looked at him, face setting like something fast-drying.

Oh Danny-boy, you've really done it now.

John rolled off him. "Get dressed and get out." His voice was barely repressed. He pushed himself back inside his clothes.

Danny got up slowly and finished dressing. John watched him in a tense silence.

When Danny was finished John threw him the car keys. The gesture was oddly light, casual, coming out of that huge furious coil of emotions.

Danny caught them and pulled on his jacket. He went to the door, hesitated, then turned to speak.

John's eyes were like dead black stones in his head. "Have a nice time." He almost opened his mouth to get the words out.

Danny pulled his jacket shut and slammed out the door.

Danny took the drive at breakneck speed, hurtling down the road, working his anger out. By the time he got there he felt exhausted. He drove to the back of the building and saw Conley's car, huge, black, ominous. He slid in beside it. He pulled the sun-visor down and sat for a moment looking down at the river. The violent white light was already dying, although it was only just past half three.

He took a deep breath and got out, locking the door carefully. He went up the fire escape, feeling the frozen rough railing under his hand. When the sun went down it was going to be *really* cold, make no mistake.

He thumped on the iron door with his fist. He heard the bars being knocked up, then the door swung open. Conley stood there smiling at him, mouth full of gold. Danny grinned back. "Your teeth are terrible."

"That's the nicest thing anyone's ever said to me." Conley stepped back and Danny went past him into the room.

Everything looked just the same. Big, empty, airy. Danny looked back at him. He was wearing a sloppy black track suit with thick white socks wrinkled round his ankles. It made him look taller and thinner than ever. His nose looked red and sore, his face thinner, but otherwise he looked just the same.

"Where did you get it?"

"What?" Conley was looking at his face, his hair, renewing his memory.

"The track suit. When I tried to get one they all had fucking headaching patterns on them."

"Ah," Conley looked down at himself, "this is ancient, goes back further than the fashion for coloured stripes. Don't they say that? Keep your clothes long enough and they'll come back into fashion again."

"Well..." Danny looked round the room some more then unzipped his jacket, "wellingtons never date, so I'm alright."

Conley took his jacket from him and Danny didn't fail to notice the same care not to touch, not to brush fingers. He went and sat down.

"Want some coffee?"

"Sometimes you sound like the bird, always saying the same fucking thing."

"Well do you want something else then?" Conley smiled.

"No, coffee would be nice. I'm frozen."

Conley padded over to the kitchen and started assembling cups.

"Did you miss me?"

Danny's nearness made him jump. "*Shit.*"

"You swore." Danny pointed at him gleefully.

"You gave me a fright."

Danny looked into his eyes. "Guilty conscience." And his voice was a little deeper.

Conley flushed and looked away. *You don't know the half of it Danny.*

After a moment Danny said again, "Well, did you?"

"What?" Conley kept his back to him.

"Miss me?"

"I've been too sick to miss anything. I didn't know where I was half the time."

Danny moved closer behind him. "I missed you." He could feel hot excitement come up inside him just at the nearness of Conley's body, the thick faded blonde hair.

"Danny..." Conley stopped pretending with the cups. His hands stilled. His voice was breathless, urgent.

"Mm?" Danny wanted to touch him. He'd never wanted anything so much in his life.

"Please don't pressurise me. Don't..." he wanted to say flirt with me, but he couldn't bring himself to call it what it was, "...toy with me," he finished lamely.

Danny was silent behind him.

Please don't let him be angry with me.

He felt Danny move back, as tangibly as if he'd heard him or seen him. "Okay."

His voice sounded fine. Conley turned slowly to look at him and suddenly everything they'd done that night was there between them, in full glowing Technicolor, the shame and perversity of it.

Conley felt himself go bright red as Danny's eyes looked right through him, seeing everything.

"It was no big deal," Danny said quietly. His hands were pushed in his pockets. "I've done much worse." His eyes were too knowing. "Forget it."

Conley finally managed to look away, but he couldn't forget it. His body couldn't forget it. Every night the dreams reminded him. Every morning the evidence stood rampant on his body.

Danny had moved over to a stool at the counter. When Conley turned round he smiled at him and said again, "Relax."

Conley smiled and tried to relax.

Danny sat there and ached. If anything Conley was more uptight now than he had been before. Everything was a threat. Every overture, every suggestion of an overture. Danny wanted to go and jerk off right now, hump his spunk all over Conley's nice toilet seat. He smiled to himself. *Thought you'd passed all this by, didn't you? Thought this shit was for the birds.* He wished he'd had Rab and John before he'd come out. A nice set of three under his belt might have taken the edge off this. *Yeah, like fuck, Boy Wonder. Your tongue's hanging down to your knees.*

"You're being thoughtful again."

Danny snapped his fingers. "Goddamn, so I am."

Conley smiled. Danny smiled. Everyone was happy.

John sat there for half an hour after Danny left, turning it over in his head. He smoked two cigarettes and lit a third. As soon as he lit it he stubbed it out again, mashing it into the ashtray.

He got up and went to look for Rab.

He found him eventually, in the tractor shed.

He was attacking wheel nuts when John went in, one foot braced on the giant tyre. He looked up. "Ah, just the man I want. See if you can loosen this fucker."

John took the spanner from him and put all his weight on it. Rab watched the muscles come up on his arms. The nut gave. Rab took the spanner back off him. "No wonder it hurts."

"What?"

Rab stroked the biceps of his arm. "This."

John pulled his arm away. "Pack that in."

Rab pulled a face but said nothing. John took out another cigarette and leaned against the tractor. "What's Danny up to?"

Rab dropped the wheel with a dull thud. He grunted. "How the fuck should I know?"

"You know," John said. He smoked a little more, letting that sink in. "You know and Ian knows."

"Then ask Ian."

"I've asked him."

"And?"

"He won't say."

Rab hunkered down beside the wheel shaft, peering up inside.

"What's he up to?" John asked again.

"I told you, I don't know."

John caught Rab's hair and yanked it back hard. Rab came down on the floor with a yelp and a blow to his tail that made his stomach turn nauseously. John was still holding him by the hair. He wrapped the weight of it round his fist. "What's he up to?" He was bending down, breathing in Rab's ear.

"Fuck off."

He suddenly pulled his fist up sharply so that Rab's upper body weight was pulled off the floor by his hair. Rab pressed his hands to the floor, trying to support his weight. "Tell me or I'll rip every fucking hair out your head."

Rab gave a pained little grunt of effort but said nothing.

John hunkered down beside him, momentarily easing the pressure. "This little agony not enough? Want me to give you a *really* good excuse? I can give you one, no problem, but let's not lie about it, eh? You've been aching to tell me for days, so why don't you just get it off your chest?"

"I told you to fuck off." Rab tried to get round onto his knees but John jerked upright, leaving Rab hanging there in mid-air. He couldn't help a yell coming out. He felt as if the hair was being ripped off the back off his neck.

"Alright, suffer then," John said amiably and then kicked him. Rab had been supporting his weight with one hand, the other trying to pull John's hand free. The kick went into his unprotected side like a steel toed boot into bare flesh. He made an unintelligible noise.

"We could do this all day, couldn't we?" John kicked him again, harder this time, catching Rab's protecting hand as well.

"No, don't!" Rab yelped, jerking to one side, ripping more hair out.

John came down beside him again. "Then tell me."

Rab lay there and saw Danny's face as he came up the stairs two at a time, felt his body under his hands, coiled up with excitement. "Conley," he said.

Rab felt John's hold slacken. He pulled his head experimentally. It slid out of John's hand easily. Rab got up slowly onto his knees. He held his side, feeling it gingerly. It was going to look like a fucking rainbow.

He dragged back across the floor on his rump and rested on the other tractor's wheel.

"I don't believe it," John whispered.

"Well you better. He's got a hard-on for him that goes right to his feet and back. He's so fucking itchy for him he doesn't know where to stick it first." Rab licked his lips.

"I thought it was her." John's face was still pale, as if he'd heard bad news. Rab watched it, feeling the resentment. *Tough tits Danny. I'm tired of taking it for you. Now you can see what it's like to be on the receiving end.*

"I thought it was Henderson's sister," John said again.

"Well now you know."

"He said he was frigid."

"Maybe he is but your little brother will thaw him out soon enough, or die in the attempt."

"Little *fuck*."

Rab looked up, startled at the sudden change in his voice. John was pressing his fingers to his temples. "I'm going to kill the little fuck."

Rab watched him anxiously, a frown forming on his forehead.

"I'm going to rip the little bastard apart."

"John..."

But it was too late, John had already left.

Rab sat there for a moment then said, "Shit."

He got up slowly and stood uncertainly against the tractor.

"Shit."

Conley got up and shut the curtains.

"What time is it?" Danny asked.

"Five," Conley said, checking his watch.

"Don't put the lights on yet."

"I confess I wasn't going to." Conley sat back down opposite him and smiled at him.

They only had one lamp on, red-shaded on the table between them. The antiquated phone sat under it. The whole thing looked very quaint, like some dated Father's Day card.

Danny was lying stretched out on the sofa. Half a bottle of rum sat on the table in front of him. Danny balanced a glass on his stomach. It was empty.

"Want more?" Conley offered.

Danny shook his head. "I'm happy."

Conley refilled his own glass and leaned back again.

"This is the last time," Danny said.

"What?" Conley frowned.

"That I can come here."

Conley put his glass down as if he was afraid he was going to drop it. "Why?"

"John won't let me come here again."

"How can he stop you?"

Danny looked over at him suddenly. He grinned. "He can beat the shit out of me."

Conley looked at him for a long moment then said slowly, "The burn... your hand... they're all his."

Danny nodded.

Conley slumped back. "I knew it." He lifted his head and looked at him. "You can't let it go on."

"Tell me how to stop him."

"Well..." Conley searched frantically. "You don't have to stay there, do you?"

Danny looked at him closely. "Is that an offer?"

Conley flushed, shook his head.

Danny laughed dryly. "I didn't think it was."

"I'm sorry."

"What the fuck are you apologising for?"

There was a silence. Danny swung up suddenly and refilled his glass. He took a long drink of it then sat back, nestling the glass between his legs. He looked at Conley through half-lidded eyes. "You know, I took my punishment for coming here today."

"Punishment? What kind of punishment?"

Danny shook his head. "That's not important. What is important is do you want me to come here again?"

Conley nodded once.

"Then we'll have to think up something."

"God!" Conley exclaimed, exasperated. "We're not having a bloody affair."

Danny looked at him then, eyes dark, mouth smiling, and said quietly, "Aren't we?"

Conley swallowed. "No." Then more firmly, "No, we're not."

"That's the saddest thing I ever heard," Danny said, still smiling.

"Danny, don't start this."

"What?"

"You know what." Conley took a breath. "Look, we're fighting again. I don't want to fight with you."

Danny shrugged.

"Why does he act like this? Why so possessive?"

Danny shrugged again. "He thinks he owns me."

Conley took a deep breath. "Forgive me Danny, but he really doesn't seem quite right in the head."

Danny laughed, a delighted shout of it. "Oh Jesus, that's great." He looked at Conley's surprised face. "Not quite right? He's a fucking maniac." He laughed again. "Not quite right, that's a good one."

"Look, I could help you get away. It would take a little organising, that's all."

Danny said, "I could come here."

"No." Conley shook his head.

"I could stay with you."

"No Danny, you *can't.*"

They stared across the table at each other. Danny looked away, took another mouthful and said casually, "Why not?"

"You know why not."

"You think I'm going to suck you into a cesspit of homosexual desire?"

"Don't talk nonsense."

They were staring at each other again then Danny said, "I enjoyed it." His voice was low. He was smiling again. Conley said nothing. "I enjoyed sucking you into the cesspit of my homosexual desire."

"Danny..." Conley said warningly.

"I've wanked myself stupid over you all week."

"Stop it."

Danny took another drink and waited, watching Conley's face.

"I don't know why I did it," Conley said.

Danny said nothing, just kept on watching him.

Conley looked at him frantically. "I didn't mean it to happen."

Danny smiled widely, leaned his head back. "Maybe, but you *wanted* it to happen."

"That's not true."

"Oh yes it is. Sitting there in the dark you were dying for the whole thing to go wild. It was all you could think about."

"That's absurd, I can't even bear to be touched."

"You didn't think you were going to be touched. You thought you were just going to watch. Only your little secret itchy-boy decided it wasn't enough, the greedy little sexy-boy you've locked away all these years. *You* maybe didn't want to be touched, but *he* did."

"I'm not queer."

Danny laughed. "Jesus, it always comes down to this, the naming of names." His face became hard, angry. "What does it fucking matter? What fucking difference does it make what hand's doing it, what mouth?"

"It matters to me."

"Why, for Christsake?"

"Because I don't know who I am if I lose that."

"You can still spunk over women, what's your problem?"

Conley was silent. Danny looked at him curiously. "You can, can't you?"

Conley shook his head reluctantly, eyes fixed on the table.

"What then? Have you started thinking about men?"

"Don't be stupid." It was almost sullen.

"What then?" Danny laughed. "Dogs or something? Surprise me."

"It's you." It would almost have been a whisper if he hadn't sounded so angry.

Danny blinked. He opened his mouth and closed it again. *You asked him Danny*

and he did it - he surprised you.

"I don't mean *thinking* about you," Conley added hastily. "I keep dreaming about you."

Danny could feel his heart racing.

"And they're filthy, worse than you could imagine."

I doubt it, Danny thought, I seriously doubt it. He said carefully, "It still doesn't mean anything. You've just gone without too long. It doesn't make you a homo. I mean, Christ, it must have been practically your first time, wasn't it?"

Conley nodded.

"Well then, meaningless. It doesn't make you queer."

Conley looked at him. "There's more."

Danny moistened his mouth. "Go on."

"I enjoy the dreams. I want them to happen." Conley closed his eyes. "And you're right, I did want something to happen that night, although I swear it was never formulated in my head." He paused. "But what you did to me..." He turned his head away. "I enjoyed it, even though I didn't want to."

Danny took a breath, long and slow. *You hear what this man's telling you Danny? He's saying he wants you. He might not know it yet but he's saying he wants you.* He said, "Let's try it again."

Conley opened his eyes. "What?"

Danny leaned across the table at him. "I want you, you want me, for Christsake let's have it."

"I can't."

"Why not?" Danny banged his glass down. "Now?"

"Because I'm *afraid*. Can't you understand that? I'm afraid of what I am, of what I might become. Once I start with you how will I know when to stop? Every time I do it in the dreams it's like falling from a great height, going down into blackness. It terrifies me."

"Oh come on, it's a blow job."

Conley's eyes flew open again. "To you maybe. I don't know quite what you are, not one thing or the other, but to me it's my whole identity."

"Bullshit." Danny swiped his hand across the table, sweeping books and papers onto the floor. "You're full of shit Conley." Danny gestured with his hand. "Well, fuck you. I'm not going to hang around, bursting a gut, waiting for you to give up the poor virgin act. I'm not going to take beatings for something I don't get. It stops here. I've had it." Danny moved to get up.

"No, Danny, wait. Look, couldn't we be friends?"

"*Friends?*" Danny's voice was incredulous. "I've never had a friend in my life. I fuck people, I don't make friends with them."

Conley looked at him. Danny looked back, then he went limp. He ran his hand through his hair. "I'm sorry," he said. He looked at the floor. "I don't know why I said that." He looked up and laughed shortly. "I'm beginning to sound like John." Then he said quietly, "Come and sit beside me." He smiled gently. "Come on," he patted the settee, "let's prove I can keep my hands off you, like a real man." He smiled a bit more.

Conley got up and came round the table. He sat down close to Danny. Danny smiled again. "Very brave."

Conley moved closer. Their thighs were touching. Danny looked at him. "You're touching me."

"I know," Conley said. "It's scaring the daylights out of me."

"Relax," Danny said. "Enjoy it. It's good for you."

"What is?"

"Touching. Necessary to all primates. I read that somewhere. Apparently apes

have nervous breakdowns if they don't get cuddles." Danny smiled suddenly. "So if you don't want to go nuts, hang loose brother."

They sat there a moment, companionable. Danny refilled their drinks. He lay there enjoying the warmth of their two bodies, close, trying not to enjoy it too much. Conley said, "I like this."

Danny said, "Good," and tried to remember the names of the seven dwarfs.

Conley said, "Put the light out."

Danny said, "No." He could only get five. There were two more.

"Why not?"

"Because you know what happened last time."

They were silent again.

"Danny?"

"Mm?"

"Trade me a secret for a secret?"

Danny thought about it. "Alright."

"You first then."

Danny said, "Okay, tell me the dream."

"I can't," Conley said immediately.

Danny shrugged.

There was another silence then Conley said quietly, "I'm just a young boy, about fourteen or so. I'm on a merry-go-round. It's a real one - organ music, garish paint - you know the kind?"

Danny nodded.

"Well it's only just starting up, picking up speed, and the roustabout is gathering the money. He's moving over the undulating floor with that expertise only years of practice can give. There's something compelling about him, the way he moves. I can see him very distantly, as if he's miles away. Part of me is glad, but part of me wants him to come closer, even though I'm full of anxiety at the thought because I haven't got the money to pay him and now I can't get off.

"Everything's colour and light, so much red and gold, and he's getting closer. Suddenly I realise he's red and gold too, red hair, gold skin, like some gilded Victorian acrobat. He's wearing a money bag slung across his chest, resting on the front of his hip. His hand's hidden in it. It looks sly and suggestive. I start to feel excited by the way he's advancing on me because I know I can't pay, and I know he's going to want money from me, and all the time his hand's fumbling in there.

"Suddenly he looks up, right at me, and I see he's not very much older than me, only about eighteen, and just when I do I become aware of the horse going up and down on its pole and I can feel myself riding against its neck, legs clamped around it, going up and down with it, and he's still creeping closer and I know I've no money.

"Finally he's right there beside me, so close I can smell him, and he reaches his hand out and suddenly grabs hold of the pole and I cry out, 'Don't!' But it's too late because somehow I've grown into it, the horse's pole is part of my flesh, coming up between my legs, almost as red as the paint, the boy's hair, the grinning horse. And I can smell hot oil on the air, sweet, and the boy's pressing against my leg, and I can feel this strange shifting flesh where his money bag should be and the fierce grip of his hand. And, of course, now it's going up and down on *me* and I can't stop it, or the excitement that's threatening to overwhelm me, and I find myself saying, 'Touch me, touch me' and I want it to go faster, harder, I feel as if it's going to burst, and I say his name... and then I..." He stopped, swallowed. "Well, you can guess the rest." He paused again. "Sick, isn't it?"

Danny shook his head. "Sounds alright to me."

"You haven't felt it." He was quiet a moment then said with forced briskness, "Now

507

it's my turn."

Danny waited.

"Who do you sleep with?"

Danny flushed. He felt himself do it with a kind of horror. He glanced at Conley. Conley had seen it. He was watching him intently. "Anyone I can get." He smiled awkwardly.

"Don't cheat Danny, you know what I mean. You told me you were having sex every day. Who with?"

Danny opened his mouth and shut it again. "I can't tell you."

"Why not?"

"You're too young."

Conley laughed. "I'm almost twice your age, remember?"

"No," Danny said. "You're nowhere near my age. Don't ask me, I can't tell you."

Conley looked at him. "Why? What's so terrible about it?"

"Look, drop it, can't you?"

"No, I can't."

Danny turned to him. "Why do you need to know?"

"I don't know, I do. It matters."

"It fucking doesn't."

"Then tell me."

"No."

Conley moved away. It was only a tiny movement, but it was there, a perceptible withdrawing.

"It's a man," Danny said quickly, offering it as a compromise. It didn't work.

"Who?"

"No-one you know."

"Why are you lying to me?"

"I'm not."

"The hell you aren't. Who Danny?"

"I said a fucking man, leave it at that."

Conley looked at him suddenly and said, "My God..."

It hung there, immense in the room. Danny said nothing, he simply closed his eyes and laid back his head.

"...it's your bloody brother."

The silence seemed to stretch on forever. Danny watched Mamma pull out her feathers slowly and methodically. She was singing quietly, crooning to herself. He drank his drink. It tasted like warm metallic water. Finally he broke the silence. "I warned you."

"Is he employing some kind of coercion?"

Danny laughed harshly. "I'm beginning to think I've got doormat stamped on my forehead." Danny looked at him, eyes narrowed, mouth sour. "No, he isn't, unless we have a little altercation and he's pushing my face in the carpet at the time. I fellate my brother willingly. I masturbate him willingly. Alright?"

Conley's face was scarlet. He opened his mouth and closed it again.

Danny caught himself wanting to apologise, to beg for forgiveness. He bit down on it. *Damn you to hell if you do, Danny.*

"Did Henderson know about this?"

Danny looked at him again. "You should've been a detective."

"That's how he got leverage over you?"

"Some."

"What does that mean?"

Danny turned on him. "None of your fucking business."

Conley nodded, pacifying him, "Alright, okay."

There was more silence. Mamma stuck her head under her wing and went to sleep.

"That's why he doesn't want you to come here. That's why he's so possessive."

"Brilliant."

"And probably why he..." Conley hesitated then nodded his head at Danny's wounded hand, "does that."

"Have an award."

"How long has he... have you been..."

"Fucking?"

Conley nodded, flushing again.

"Six months maybe."

Conley looked at him, at his hand lying scar-up on his knee. "That's a long way to go in six months."

"It was a long time getting there." Danny looked at him levelly. Conley didn't dare ask him to explain, but he guessed... at least a little.

"Well?" Danny asked.

"Well what?"

"Does it bother you, knowing what I do? Knowing the kind of person I am? Knowing I come hot from his hands to you?"

Conley considered. "I don't like it..."

"But?"

"It isn't going to stop me."

"Stop you what?"

"Wanting you myself."

Had he just said what Danny thought he had said? Suddenly he became intensely aware of him again, of his thigh against his. He felt suddenly as if a huge weight was pressing on him, pinning him down. He wanted to move and couldn't. But Conley was moving. He leaned forward across Danny's body, not touching him, and put out the light.

Danny was blinded by the sudden darkness. "Why did you do that?" he asked. He felt Conley settle back beside him.

"I don't know," Conley said.

Danny let the back of his hand drop down to rest against Conley's thigh. Conley tensed. Danny rubbed the back of his hand against his thigh. He had an erection like a tent pole. He swallowed.

"Danny?"

He had to clear his throat before he could say, "Mm?"

"Do you make love to him?"

"I don't understand you." Danny slid the back of his hand as far down Conley's thigh as it would go, then back again... slowly.

"I mean, do you get into bed together? Do you indulge in... well, kissing, foreplay, that sort of thing, or is it more a matter of quick convenience?"

Danny laughed. "I sleep with him." He knew Conley wasn't grasping it. "We share the same bed." He could almost hear him taking it in.

"You sleep in the same bed?"

"Yes, a double bed."

"Oh."

Danny smiled in the dark. "And yes I do," he said, "kiss him and 'make love' to him in the way you mean."

"Every night?"

"Most nights." If he isn't cutting me, burning me or pissing in my face, Danny thought. But he said nothing. Let Conley cherish a few ideals.

"Is it good?"

"Yes," Danny said. "He's good." *Scary as hell but he's good alright.*

"What..." Conley stopped.

"Do we do?" Danny finished for him. "You want to know what we get up to? Want to know how two brothers make it together?"

Conley said nothing.

Danny turned his hand over and laid it on Conley's thigh, quietly, no sweat, dead still. Conley felt tense as a spring. "Well, we get undressed. Sometimes he does that for me and sometimes he lies on the bed and watches. He usually sits down when he's undoing my jeans because he likes to kiss my stomach. He's got a love affair going with my scars."

Danny began stroking his leg with his thumb, tiny *relax* strokes. "Sometimes he takes me in his mouth, and occasionally he gets carried away and goes the whole hog, but he's usually too greedy for that, so it's usually just for a minute or two, for the taste of it. After he's had enough of that he lets me get in the bed and he undresses. I have to watch because I'm supposed to think he's fucking irresistible. He *has* got a good body, really powerful. Well, you've seen him. Anyway, then we get down to it. He usually leaves the light on till he's got the first load off his wrist. He likes to see his own dick in action. If he's feeling energetic he'll sit on my chest, bolster my head up with pillows, and use my mouth. He can make that last for ages. If he's sleepy he sometimes just rubs off on my arse, tossing me off if he feels like it, not if I've been a bad boy. Other nights he just lies on top of me and kisses me, barely nudging his prick against me. That can go on for hours, just kissing and kissing until it seeps out of him. Sometimes I don't even know it's happened, I get so fucking sweaty and doped up with it. I always feel like a wrung-out cloth the next day. He swears when he comes and he likes to watch it come out. He's fond of his own fireworks. He's fond of his own dick. You should see the loving way he tosses off."

Danny took a breath. His whole tone changed. "There, that's a brief résumé of John's sex life. Please you?" It should, Danny thought. That's all the nice stuff. We've missed out the other two thirds.

"It just sounds obscene."

Danny laughed. "It is obscene. That's what makes it so good." Danny slid his hand up slowly towards his crotch. "Want to try it?" he asked quietly. "You just lie there and let me." Danny's hand was almost there.

"You haven't said what you do to him," Conley said quickly, not quite managing to keep the panic out of his voice. "Doesn't he like you to do anything to him?"

Danny smiled. "Of course he does." His voice became very soft. "Nights he practically begs for it..." There was a soft laugh.

Conley heard him shift a little, could feel something change in him even through his own blinding sensations.

"Sometimes I get in there first, before he can start anything. I feel him up through his clothes..." Danny slid his hand so gently over his target. "It frustrates the hell out of him, his poor stiffy only getting half-rubbed." He ran his fingertips over the length of it. Jesus, he hadn't imagined it. It was real. "It's big and thick and hard." He laughed softly. "Sounds like him, doesn't it? But he is always *really* hard. I squeeze it..." Danny squeezed it. He could hear Conley breathing through his mouth. "...and tell him I love him - he gets off on that - then I kiss him."

Danny bent his head and pressed his mouth onto Conley's, tasted it instantly, hard, sweet and strange. He moaned, grabbed him tight and ran his hand into his hair. He

pushed his tongue into Conley's mouth. He could taste the rum, rich in his mouth.

Conley lay there, hot and aching beneath him. Danny could feel him wanting to give, utterly unable to do anything, ignorant, not knowing what to do.

Danny lifted his mouth. "Touch me," he urged. "Go on, anything you want, just touch me." And he felt Conley's hand right there, not on his face or his hair or any other damn place, but right where it mattered - straight to his cock. He laughed. "My man, Maxie. Go on, do what you want."

Danny eased him down so they were lying side by side. He felt Conley's hands at his belt, pulled his stomach in to help him. He fumbled but got there. Danny lay still, letting him touch him, explore. He could feel how tentative he was. "Go on, don't be shy, rough as you like. It takes a lot of beating, believe me." He laughed again.

Conley squeezed it, suddenly, tightly. Danny gasped. Conley released him immediately. Danny caught his hand. "No, that was pleasure, not pain. Go on, do what you want, pull it about as much as you like."

Conley took Danny tightly in his hand and began masturbating him.

"Jesus..." Danny whispered. Conley was intense and violent with him. Danny was up there in seconds. He caught at Conley's hand. "Don't, I'll come."

"Then come," Conley whispered back.

"You want me to?"

"Yes." And Conley attempted to kiss his mouth, awkwardly, very unsure of himself. Hell, he doesn't even know how to kiss, Danny thought.

Danny let his hand go and Conley started masturbating him again, jerkily, hard, edged with pain. Danny said quickly, "If you want me to bring you off you're going to have to slow that down."

"No, I want to feel you." Conley pushed a leg in between his, hard up under Danny's balls. That made it worse.

"Christ, man, what are you trying to do?"

"Make you come."

Danny laughed but it caught in his throat. His hands grabbed at Conley's shoulders. "Oh Jesus," he whispered.

"I've dreamt this... " Conley was saying.

"Oh Jesus," Danny said again.

Conley jerked his hand faster.

"Oh Jesus," Danny said for the third time. He went up to meet it, raising himself off the settee, moaning like a stuck pig, begging for it, as Conley kept jerking it out of him panting, "I've dreamt this..."

And then it was over.

"If this makes me a homosexual then so be it." Conley was tracing his finger over Danny's face in the dark, mapping it out.

"Christ, if I've heard that once I've heard it a million times. Don't worry about what you are, just be it."

"I think I'm in love with you," Conley said, experimentally kissing his mouth.

"You *are* drunk," Danny said pulling him down again. "Here, you do it like this."

When they broke apart Danny said, "I'm hard again."

"I've never been anything else," Conley laughed. "I think I've had half a lifetime's erections in one week."

"Keep 'em coming," Danny said.

"I wish you would."

"Want me to?" Danny's voice was low and dirty.

"Yes."

"Alright, but on condition I suck your dick. And this time I swallow."

Conley put a hand over his eyes.

Danny slid down his body. "Lift your arse."

Conley lifted it. Danny pulled his tracksuit trousers down. He could understand what John meant about their attractions. "Hey, you're cut," he said.

"What?" Conley tensed, half sat up.

"Hey, relax. Cut, as in no foreskin, that's all."

"It's not cut, I was born this way."

"It's neat, I wasn't criticising. Anyway, they only do that to Jews."

"Well God saw fit to do it to me."

Danny could hear the tension in his voice. "I like it," he said placatingly. "Gives you a big knob." He lowered his head and ran his tongue all over the swollen head.

Conley gave a little grunt. "Danny..."

"And what a knob." Danny licked into the opening.

"Maybe this isn't such a good idea."

Danny laughed. "It's a beautiful idea." He pushed his tongue into the distended opening in Conley's penis again. "Let me put the light on, I want to see this."

"No." Conley stopped him quickly. "No lights."

"Okay, relax, no problem." Danny licked him again then lifted his penis gently and sucked the head in.

Conley grabbed his hair, tight. "Danny..." His voice was warning.

Danny sucked it in further.

"Danny, no..."

Danny let it go, holding him in place only with his mouth, and slid his liberated hand under his arse. Abruptly Conley pushed up into his mouth whispering, "I'm fucking your mouth."

Danny smiled to himself. *Well, well, getting off on talking dirty - what next?*

Conley pushed up again. "I had no idea how much I really wanted this." He pushed up again. "I had no *idea*." He was thrusting up gently now, undulating. "Since the first day I saw you, I think. From that first moment you flew into my car, wet, scintillating, so..." he pushed, "so..." he pushed again, "...animalistic. That's what you're like, a greedy little animal, eating me up... oh God, no... I'm going to... oh God, eat me... eat me... eat *me*."

And it was out, flooding into Danny's mouth, Conley pushing into his face, fucking it fiercely, giving like Conley never had before.

And possibly never would again.

They sat at opposite ends of the bath. They had lit all the candles and were watching each other in the golden glow.

"You've got to buy bubble bath."

"It's not manly."

"Who cares? I've always had bubble bath. I'm not changing my habits just to suit you."

"I thought you were an all male household?"

 "We are."

"Then how did you get started on bubble bath?"

"My mother." Danny started rooting for the soap.

"Do you miss her?" Conley asked.

"No."

End of discussion Max, hear it? "I lied to you," he said.

Danny smiled at him. "Of course you did."

"About why I wanted to see you, right from the start."

"I know."

"You conceited little tyke."

Danny grinned, unrepentant. "You wanted your rocks off and thought I might force you to do it."

"Something like that."

"Rape," Danny said and he wasn't smiling.

"Perhaps," Conley admitted.

Danny laughed. "Be honest, you wanted to be raped. No responsibility."

"Alright, I admit it."

"You picked the wrong person."

"Oh, I don't think so. I got my rocks off, didn't I?"

Danny threw the sponge at him.

"You know," Conley said, "I really never have wanted another man before this, and that *is* the truth. I've never been attracted to a man in my life."

"But you have fancied a woman before?"

"I don't know. My sexual feelings have been dead for so long."

Danny smiled. "Maybe this is just your delayed adolescence then."

"So *that's* why I've picked someone so young."

"Not that young."

"You're underage. I'm committing an offence."

"You villain."

Conley laughed. "You really don't care, do you?"

"Not a monkey's fuck."

"What are you going to tell your brother?"

"About what?"

"Tonight."

"Nothing."

"Those marks are fresh."

Danny didn't look at them.

"Cigarette burns," Conley said.

"Shrewd man."

Conley smiled briefly. "Kinky fun?"

Danny raised his eyebrows.

"What then?"

Danny splashed the water with his hands, to and fro, to and fro. "They're punishments." He didn't meet Conley's eyes.

"For what?"

Danny looked up and he was smiling that familiar smile, old, sly, *knowledgeable*. "Being a whore. His word, not mine."

Conley looked at the burns again. "Are you promiscuous?"

"He thinks so."

Conley looked at him intently. "He's wrong?"

Danny smiled it again. "Not any more."

"Often?" Conley asked without looking at him.

"Isn't that what promiscuous means?" There was a pause then Danny said, "There's been two of you today, and there could have been two more if I'd tried. Four different people in one day, that's a good batting average."

"You're joking."

"Why should I be?"

"Oh Danny."

"I'm not the faithful type, don't expect it."

Conley said nothing.

"Don't start climbing on my fucking back Conley." Danny stood up.

Conley looked up at him.

Danny smiled suddenly, impulsively. It was hard and ugly. "Know what really turns me on?"

Conley saw his tongue tip come out, moisten his lips, disappear again. Conley shook his head.

"People making it with little kids." And Conley watched him come erect instantly, in front of his eyes. Huge, slick with water and lather. "Now there's something else you can dislike about me."

And he climbed out of the bath and ripped a towel from the rack and disappeared out of the room.

Danny was standing at the kitchen sink when Conley came out. He was naked to the waist.

"What are you doing?" Conley asked.

"Washing my shirt." He pulled it into shape. "Anywhere I can dry it?"

"There, over the radiator."

Danny arranged it carefully over the kitchen radiator. "What time is it?"

"Twenty to eight. When will you have to go back?"

"I'll have to leave about ten, latest."

They were not looking at each other, the atmosphere slightly strained between them.

"Want something to eat?"

Danny laughed. "What? Cake?"

"No. I got food in for you, remember? In the freezer. See if there's anything you want."

"What are you having?"

"Same as you."

"What? Not cake?"

"I'll have that after."

Danny rummaged in the freezer and found something half-decent. Conley took it from him, avoiding his hand. Danny grabbed it suddenly. "I've kissed your mouth, sucked your dick, when do I get to hold your hand?" His face was intent, no humour in it.

"Sorry." Conley forced himself to relax.

Danny let him go, dropping it as if he didn't like the feel of it.

Conley walked to the microwave, aware that he was trembling slightly.

"You know, you and Henderson had a lot in common. He needed drink to do it too."

Conley slammed his palms down on the counter. "I *said*, I'm sorry."

Danny walked over to him, slid his arms round his waist, started rubbing sinuously against his back. "Scares the shit out of you sober, doesn't it?"

Danny kept insistently rutting against him. Conley could see his naked arms, muscular, lean, tight round his chest, the hands splayed over him. "Like it?"

"Stop it Danny."

"Oh, he *doesn't* like it." Danny shifted so Conley could feel the hard heat of his erection. "Big penis likes you."

"Stop it!"

Danny dropped his arms, but still leaned into him, not moving now. "You need the drink and the dark and someone else to carry the can, don't you?"

Conley didn't answer him.

"Don't you?"

"Yes! Alright? *Yes!*"

"That's fine." Danny moved away, sat down. "That's all I wanted to hear."

Conley put the food in the oven. He stayed there, leaning against it.

"Look at me Max." Danny's voice was seductive.

Conley turned slowly. Danny was sitting there on the stool with his legs wide open and his penis in his hand. His smile was broad, leering. He pulled his penis aggressively. It was beefy, swollen, red, and he was aiming it at him.

Conley turned away.

He heard Danny laughing, low, amused. "That's what I do thinking about you."

"Put it away."

"Not until I jerk off on this nice expensive middle-class floor."

Conley whirled round. "Danny, fucking *stop* it!"

But Danny wasn't doing anything. His clothes were neatly fastened. He was smiling. "See? Even in the light you can't tell the difference."

Conley looked at him, utterly baffled.

Danny jerked his head. "I think that's ready." He got down off the stool. "And it's not nice to swear."

John disappeared off the face of the Earth, until seven o'clock.

When he came in Rab and Ian looked at each other. They heard him go upstairs. "He sounds pissed," Rab said.

"He probably is."

"Stop looking at me like that. When did you earn your fucking sainthood?"

Ian looked back at the television.

"I'm going up," Rab announced.

Ian said nothing.

Rab crossed the room and went out. "Fuck you too, sweetheart," he muttered and shut the door.

The hall was bitterly cold. It must be freezing outside.

Rab went upstairs like someone being sent for punishment.

The toilet cistern was filling but a light was on in John's bedroom. Rab knocked on the door.

"What is it?" John's voice was a growl.

Rab went in.

John was stretched out on the bed with his shoes on. He had two bottles of whisky on the floor. They were from the old man's stock. Rab looked at the bottles. "What are you going to do, drink yourself to death?"

John looked at him. "Unless you've got a better idea."

Rab shut the door and sat down on the armchair. John watched him from the bed. A half-full glass sat on the table. Only the bedside lamp was on. This is how it must look. He could visualise Danny bending over him, John lying there stroking his hair.

"What are you seeing Rab, ghosts?"

"Something like that."

"What is it going to take for you to understand he doesn't want you?"

"Him to tell me."

John took the glass and had a drink. He put it back. His hand was meticulous, rock-steady. Only his eyes showed how much he'd had to drink. "Was he good?" he asked suddenly.

"Who?"

"The boy you had."

"You mean the rabbit."

"Was the rabbit good?"

"He was drunk."

"And you took advantage."

"That's right."

"Good man, keep up the family traditions." John paused then asked again, "Was he good?"

"Yes."

"Well, well."

John took another drink then lit a cigarette. No waver, no three attempts. He threw the pack over to Rab. Rab caught it and lit one. They were better than his usual, no menthol-mild. He threw them back. "You waiting for him?" He picked a shred of tobacco off his lip.

John looked at him, said nothing.

"What are you going to do?" Rab persisted.

"What do you think?"

"What good is it going to do?"

"It doesn't do any good, I *like* it."

"For fuck's sake John."

"Spare me the lecture Rab." John drank a little more. "*You* told me."

"Yeah... I told you."

They were silent. John scratched his thigh absently. Rab watched his hand as it eased the itch.

"Do you want it or something?"

Rab looked up. "What?"

"Your tongue was hanging out."

"Old habit."

John showed some teeth in a smile that wasn't. "Well now... you can have it if you want it."

"No thanks."

John shrugged, Your loss. "Want to talk about him?" He looked at him enquiringly. "He's like a hobby. You've got to meet a fellow-enthusiast to appreciate him properly. What do you like best about him?"

Rab shook his head slightly. "I don't know. Physically?"

"That's as good a place to start as any."

"His hair... his mouth... his eyes."

"His belly, his backside, his dick." John laughed. "You might as well."

"So I like all of him, physically."

"And for the rest?"

"None of it."

John laughed again. "Are you saying you don't like him?"

"Sounds like it."

"And if he loved you?"

"I'd love everything about him."

John smiled slowly. "I wonder if I believe that?"

Rab asked, "How about you then?"

"Physically..." he paused, "I like his skin, the way it feels to touch, the way it feels touching me. I like the way it bleeds, the way it bruises, the way he feels naked beside me."

"You're making me hard."

"No, he is."

They were silent again then John said, "Most of all though I like the way he hates." He re-lit his cigarette, put it in his mouth to forget again. "He hates like other people love. He hates like still water running deep. They're old and hard, his hates. He never forgives. He's remorseless, full of revenge. It's the only thing I've got, and it gets me up there every time." John licked his lips. "When you're hurting him it's in there, living in his eyes, looking out at you. It makes me so fucking hot sometimes, I come on him without even trying."

"That's sick." Rab's face was a picture of distaste.

"Of course it's sick. What did you expect? Walt Disney's Snow White?"

"You're going to fuck up like that John. It's a dead end, a big road to nowhere."

John smiled. "Killing Danny, the ultimate orgasm."

"Don't talk like that."

"Think I would?" John was looking at him over his cigarette.

"I don't know. You scare me sometimes."

"I scare myself." John took another drink. "I did that. Week ago. First time ever."

"What?"

"Got off on hitting him, no sex involved."

Rab was silent.

John laughed. "I got back into the house, locked myself in the bathroom, and threw up. You should have seen his face. He looked like he wanted to spit on me. He's the whore and he makes *me* ashamed." John took a deep breath and stubbed out his cigarette. He topped his glass up. "I creamed in my pants hitting my little brother... well, well, well."

"You're drunk."

"It's the only way to be." He looked at Rab suddenly. "I'm not going to kill him Rab, believe me." He rubbed the back of his head against the headboard almost sinuously, closing his eyes. "I'm just going to hurt him a little."

"What's a little?"

"As much as it takes to cure him."

"How will you know?"

John laughed. "When I can toss him off three times in a row and he's still hard, I'll know."

"What if it isn't curable?"

John stopped his odd little head massage and looked at him for a long moment. "What are you saying to me?"

"What if he gets so hot for someone you can't knock it out of him?"

"Is he?"

"What?"

"So hot for Conley?"

Rab held his eyes. "I think so."

John looked down at his hands. "Why are you telling me this?"

"Because I don't want you to beat him to death trying."

John's eyes flicked up quickly. "Sure?"

"What the hell's that supposed to mean?"

"Sure it isn't something quite different? Maybe you want to see him take a little punishment. You don't mind sharing Danny in the family, but outside - no way."

"That's crap."

"Too near the knuckle?"

"I don't like to see him hurt John."

"I don't like to see him any other way, *Rab*."

Rab punched the chair arm then turned his face away.

"Easy, Rab." John smiled and took another mouthful from his glass. "If you're a good boy I might even let you watch."

Danny only ate half his meal. He got up and went over to the radiator, felt his shirt. Almost dry. He put it on.

"Is it dry?" Conley asked. Danny saw he'd only eaten half his too.

"Enough." He fastened it slowly and tucked it in. Conley was watching him. When Danny looked up he looked away.

"I wish you smoked," Danny said. He sat back down.

"Why?"

Danny smiled. "Because I need a cigarette."

"I didn't know you smoked."

"You learn something new every day."

"I've got some if you want them." Conley got up and went to the kitchen. He began rooting in cupboards. "Someplace..."

He found them eventually. "Catch." He threw Danny a pack of two hundred.

Danny laughed. "I'm a little tense, not suicidal." He looked at them curiously. "What the hell are they?"

Conley shrugged. "Gift from a grateful client, from the duty-free. Try them. If you don't like them you can nip out for some."

Danny pulled the wrapper off. Sobranie Black Russian. They were packed flat, like cigars. When he opened them they were long, thin and black. "Fucking hell."

Conley laughed. "Maybe they're more me than you."

Danny took one and caught the matches Conley threw to him. Danny lit it, took a drag, held it. He took the cigarette out his mouth and let the smoke out. "They're alright."

"They suit you." Conley watched his movements as he smoked it. Like everything else he did it was vaguely erotic.

Danny laughed. "You can't suit a fucking cigarette."

Conley shrugged.

Danny pulled his feet up under him and sat cross-legged. He balanced an ashtray on his kneecap. Suddenly Conley could feel his eyes tight on him. "What are we doing here?"

Conley looked at him, vaguely startled. "What?"

"What are we doing? What's this for?"

"I don't know what you mean."

"You can't fuck unless you're drunk."

Conley glanced at him quickly then away again. "Give me time."

"The whole thing horrifies you."

"No."

"Face facts, you're just lonely. You don't really *want* this. It's not natural for you. You're trying to be something you're not."

Conley didn't know what to say.

"This is just one big stiff pain for me. You get me up hard and as soon as you start to come down out of that hundred per cent proof cloud I'm out of it. I need more than that and you won't give it."

Conley was still silent.

"It's not a quick snack for me - sex. It's like..." Danny searched for a way to express it. "It's like I've got to stuff myself with it, feel really sick of it before I can stop. It's like you and your cake. I don't know how you can eat like that. Well I don't know how you can fuck like this either. When I'm here I want to be at it all the time, get right up you

518

and just stay there till I work my dick soft."

Conley looked away, embarrassed.

"See what I mean? You can't even stand the thought of that."

"You've done that?"

Danny inclined his head. "Got the T-shirt."

"I couldn't."

"I know you couldn't, that's exactly what I mean. I come here, get a sweat up then I've got to go home and..." He stopped.

"What were you going to say?"

Danny looked at him steadily. When he spoke it was flat. It sounded curiously like a lie. "I've got to go home and get John to finish the job."

"Was he the other?"

"What other?"

"The other you had today?"

Danny paused a second before answering. "No."

"Who was it?"

Danny laughed shortly. "How did I know you were going to ask that?"

"Who was it?"

"No-one you know."

"Where do you find the people to do it with? In a village that size? How could you manage four in a day?"

"You learn to make opportunities, to take what's offered."

"Anyone?"

"Sometimes."

"How can you?"

"Don't go fucking moral on me." Danny's voice was angry.

"I'm not. I just don't know how you can do a thing like that." Conley's voice was full of distaste.

"Not everybody's as frigid as you."

Conley's face tightened. "Thank you."

There was a tense silence. Danny stubbed out his cigarette and picked up the box for another. He threw the box back down on the table and lit the cigarette carefully, put the match in the ashtray, then the ashtray on the table. He looked across at Conley then said, "Either give me what I want or forget it."

Conley wet his lips.

Danny went on, voice low, "One drunken hand-job doesn't cut it. I want more. If I don't get more then I don't come here, that's final."

Conley's face seemed paler than ever, his mouth almost white. He sat with his hands between his knees, tensely knotted together. "I'm not like this deliberately. I can't help it. How can I promise you anything?"

"I don't care how you do it, that's your problem. Get permanently drunk. Get the doctor to give you tranquillizers. I don't care, just as long as I get what I want."

Conley felt a surge of anger. "Why don't you just get a damn sex doll? What do you need me for? A bloody doughnut would probably do you."

Danny smiled, dragged on the cigarette, blew the smoke out. "Oh no, it's got to be you: fucking with Death, making it with the Dark Angel, the Man with the Scythe."

Conley could feel the goosepimples on his arms at the sound of his voice. How did someone so young get so twisted, so perverse and downright rotten? Abruptly he asked, "How did you start with your brother?"

"How d'you mean?"

"How did you get started with him? Did you suddenly decide you fancied him, or what?"

Danny leaned forward to tip the ash off his cigarette. He looked up slowly from under his brows. "I'd wanted it for a while."

"Wanted it?"

"That's right."

"How long?"

Danny leaned back again.

"How long?" Conley persisted.

"Long as I can remember, but don't tell him I said so."

"Your own brother?"

"Well he's no-one else's." Danny tilted his head sideways as if considering. "He was always so fucking..." he lifted his head suddenly "...*big*." He laughed at Conley's expression. "I mean powerful, indestructible. He wasn't *ever* going to die." His eyes snagged Conley's again and Conley heard his voice grow even deeper. "He was a challenge."

"How?" It came out hoarsely.

"Because he wanted me and didn't dare admit it. Because he had the itchy hots for his little brother and hated himself for it. The last thing in the world he wanted was to give in to it but I was going to make him. I was going to make him if it killed me."

Conley looked at him with a kind of horror. "And did you?"

Danny laughed. "No, I gave up trying. But he'd gone hungry so long that the first time he saw someone else take a bite he went bananas." Danny closed his eyes as if he was remembering. Maybe he was. "Fucking ape-shit." He was smiling. He opened his eyes suddenly, grinning at him. "Be thankful it isn't John that fancies you. If you want raped he's your man."

Conley shook his head.

"John *prefers* girls. Me, I'm just a hobby, but I'm sure we could persuade him to try you out." Danny laughed. "But I warn you, he's hung like a horse. Better get your Vaseline out."

"Danny, for Christsake." Conley rubbed his forehead.

"What's wrong? Too coarse for you?"

"No," Conley snapped at him. "It's not too coarse for me. It's the way you talk about it, as if..." He stopped.

"As if what?" Danny was smiling but it didn't reach his eyes.

"Oh, I don't know, as if it didn't matter. As if it was just some kind of bodily function, like scratching an itch or something. You make it sound revolting."

Danny smiled. "It *is* revolting."

Conley looked at him in a kind of surprise. "Then why the hell do you do it?"

"Because I like it. It's only fuck my hole but I like it." And he grinned again.

Conley closed his eyes and rubbed his face. Danny stubbed out his cigarette. After a moment or two he said, "Well?"

"Well what?" Conley said wearily. Suddenly he was feeling the drink, the flu, the sex as one big emotional disaster. He felt wrung out.

"Do you give me what I want or do we forget it?"

Conley looked at the floor.

"Well?"

"Stop bloody saying that!"

Danny made a tutting noise. "Language."

"No," Conley said.

"Look at me."

Conley looked up at him.

"Now tell me."

Conley saw Danny watching him. "No," he said again, feeling his heart sink. "I

won't debase myself for you Danny."

"*Debase* yourself?" Suddenly he sat forward, making a violent gesture at him. "Well *fuck* you." The finger stayed there, like a threat. "You can play with yourself in the frigging mirror, that should keep you happy." He started pulling on his shoes and socks.

"*Shit*," Conley whispered.

"Don't debase yourself swearing James." Danny crossed the room and yanked his jacket off the peg. "Just get yourself a stiff drink and then you can give one to Mamma there." He jerked his head contemptuously. "Motherfucking's just about your level, you fucking faggot."

He opened the door with a wrench and slammed it shut behind him.

"Was that the door?" John asked. The sound had been quiet, not Danny's usual bang or even more usual slam.

"I don't know, what time is it?"

John turned the clock. "Not quite half ten, earlier than I would have expected."

Rab shrugged. "Want me to go see?"

John smiled broadly. "I want you to take your fucking arse back to your room gorgeous."

Rab's face became taut. "I thought I was getting to watch?"

John's smile broadened further. "You wouldn't like it, believe me."

"John..."

John held up his hand. "Spare me Rab, otherwise I might just punch you in the mouth. Now piss off, there's a good lad."

Rab got up and walked over to the bed. John lay beneath him, looking up at him, still smiling, but there was nothing friendly or amiable about it. "Don't do anything to him John."

"Don't threaten me Rab." And still the smile went on.

"I mean it," Rab said.

John reached out and took Rab's hand. He kissed his palm, closing his eyes, putting everything into it with that same frightening intensity. He opened his eyes. Rab felt the hairs on his arm stand up. "So do I," he whispered.

Rab pulled his hand back and wiped his palm on the thigh of his jeans then went out of the room.

Rab stood by his bedroom door, hearing Danny moving below in the hall. He hesitated.

"Don't bother baby."

Rab turned round. John was standing behind him in the bedroom doorway. He grinned shortly. Rab hadn't even heard the door open.

Rab opened his bedroom door and went in. He closed it and locked it almost as if he was locking himself in, like a man unable to resist temptation.

He didn't go to bed, instead he sat down in the armchair and stared at the door. Slowly he made himself a cigarette. He was waiting.

He didn't have a clue what for.

Ian sat in the next room and listened to John dismissing him.

He sat down on the end of the bed. The rest of it was completely covered in photographs, overlapping slightly, like fish scales.

He got up and walked round it, looking at them closely. He had laid them out in chronological order. He picked one up from the centre, close to the left-hand side. He slid it out from between the others and felt the smoothness of the photograph's surface between his fingers.

He sat down again and looked at the back. Almost fourteen. He'd had to start stealing them not long after that. Danny had his eyes closed, his back up against the tree, trousers round his knees. The front wheel of the tractor was there, his own shadow. He looked so white, so bleached, in that morning light. It had been cold. You couldn't tell that he'd been crying. He looked composed, almost, by some trick of the light, rapturous. His hand was wrapped around his own shaft, pulling his penis tightly. He was close to coming. Ian remembered because he had done, literally seconds after he had taken it, but you could see it in the photograph, the tension, the slight blurring of his hand.

Ian undid his zip, slid his hand in. He put the photograph down and selected another, a year or two earlier. Danny standing in the bath, wet and smiling - how rare those smiles became - pissing in the bath. A beautiful thick arc of it, his body bowed out slightly, showing it off.

Ian grunted, took his hand away. This had to last. He had to hold it in till they came upstairs. If he could just synch it up...

Ian bit down on his lip, let go, hands well away from his body. That was close, too damn close. He was going to spoil everything. They had to be up here, where he could hear them. One night he was going to go out there and do it right up against their door, watch the white spunk slide down the dark varnish, leave it for John to find.

Ian lay down carefully on top of the photographs, could feel their slick, cold surface under his cheek, could see elliptical Dannys, white and turgid, stretching along the line of the bed. He reached out and picked one up at random.

He was about eight - He looked at the back. Yes, eight. - standing in the old Dutch barn on a bale of hay. He had his shorts leg pulled up and his little dick hanging out. His T-shirt was dirty, the neck torn. His hair was too long. It was always too long.

Ian could almost smell him, sweet and dusty with hay.

After he'd taken it he'd pulled his shorts down and suckled on him till his dick came up then frigged it till the poor little bastard had cried. He'd spunked on him then made him sit on his face and licked it off him like a salty little pork sausage. It had been good that day, hardly any tears at all. Danny had been hot and tired and happy enough to lie in the cool hay with him. He'd been happy enough to have his dick sucked too, at first. Maybe he'd been too rough.

He'd watched Ian come with that greedy curiosity he had. He always wanted to know why he couldn't do it too, and when would he be able? Ian had promised, 'Soon'. It was too. Danny was an unnaturally quick developer, in everything. He'd been fated to be a whore. It's what he was. He'd been born to it.

Ian took the photograph and wrapped it carefully round his cock. He held it in place and began masturbating into it. He looked at the others taken that day. They had played at who could piss furthest. It was easy to get him involved, and a great excuse if you got caught. He'd been a gorgeous kid. They said the beautiful ones never kept it. Well they were wrong, Danny just went from strength to strength. He'd always been so eager to please. Shame he'd never kept *that*...

He stopped abruptly and rolled over, face down, panting into the bed. He could feel saliva sticking one of the photographs to his cheek. He closed his eyes and pressed his mouth against it in a futile kiss, then he lay still, not thinking of anything, just seeing that one image of Danny, red shorts round his ankles, tiny dick sticking up in the air and him there, sniffing round it, dying to take it in his mouth and Danny smiling, always smiling.

As if he knew.

John found him in the living room, sitting by the fire. He was sitting in his mother's armchair and leaning towards the heat. He'd opened it up and piled it high with coal. It was a dull, lifeless black, the heat blocked by the new coal, but underneath sharp deep orange glowed, ready to lick up. The room was dark, chilly.

"What are you doing, sitting here alone in the dark?"

Danny turned briefly, then back to the fire. John felt his heart wrench as if a hand had twisted it. *God damn the whoring little bastard to hell.*

Danny shook his head. The gesture was full of defeat.

John put his hands on his shoulders and began kneading them. Danny let himself go limp against the strength of them. "What's wrong, didn't he give out?" He felt as if he could feel the adrenaline flood the body under his fingers, as if Danny had become electric beneath him.

Danny licked his lips, head knocked brainless, no idea what to say or do.

"Why do you keep doing it Danny? If you want to fuc k more we can fuck more." John could feel his shoulders moving. He was breathing as if he'd been running.

"He looks like fuck Danny. Christ, at least she looks like something. I could understand her, but him?"

Danny tried to say something, but nothing would come out. He watched the fire begin to curl round the coal. Yellow tongues, spiteful, crackling, licking up over the hard black rocks.

"You spent the night with him, what were you doing?"

"Nothing." Danny managed to get it out. "Nothing," he croaked again.

He felt John's hands dig into him, hurting. "No shit Danny..."

"It's true. He's frigid. I..." His courage failed him.

"What did you do?" The hands were kneading again, just below pain. Suddenly they seemed too close to his throat. John was sitting on the chair arm, pulling Danny back against his knees, one digging into his back.

"I sucked him off."

"And for you?"

"Nothing."

John laughed, short, ugly. "Not exactly red hot, is he?"

"He doesn't like it."

"Well, our roving whore has finally met his match, and what does he do? Decides he's in love with it and kills himself trying to get into its pants."

"I'm not in love." Danny's voice had an edge of panic in it.

"You've been lying to me, fixing things. For someone who's frigid he does a lot of chasing."

"I haven't been fixing..."

John's hand jerked his chin up, snapping his mouth shut and making him bite his tongue. "Don't fucking lie any more Danny. Don't make it any worse. The fucking phone going every two minutes, full of sly excitement. Just don't fucking lie to me any more."

Danny sat still. Eventually John dropped his hand.

"I'm not going to see him again," Danny said.

John's hand yanked suddenly at his hair, jerking his head back. "Too fucking right you're not. Maybe you won't walk for a few days. Maybe you won't ever walk again." He tugged his hair. "I feel just like that Danny."

Danny swallowed awkwardly, hurting his throat. John's grip eased. "Alright, up." John let him go suddenly. Danny sat there a moment. John's knee nudged him

ungently forwards. "I said, get up."

Danny stood up.

"Up the stairs."

Danny glanced at him quickly, feeling his anus tighten in some obscene Pavlovian response. A dull ache started inside as if John was already shoving up him.

John followed him out the door. When they got to their room John put his hand out to stop him. "Keep on going."

Danny felt something begin to crawl into the pit of his stomach. John shoved him. "Go on."

Ian realised too late. When the door opened he was lying there in something like paralysis.

Danny was standing there looking at him, then John. John pushed Danny in then came in himself and pushed the door shut. He looked at the bed, at Ian trying desperately to push himself back inside his clothes.

"Why don't you fucking knock you bastard? Who the hell do you think you are?"

John pushed his hands in his pockets. He was grinning from ear to ear. "Well now, look here Danny, it's a meeting of your fan club."

Ian stood there dying. He didn't know whether to scream or cry.

John circled round the bed, looking at the photographs. They had slithered awry under Ian's hasty rising. Some had fallen to the floor. John bent and picked up a handful, slowly looking at each one. "Cute." He looked at Danny. "*Small*, but cute."

Danny stood there watchful, no other expression. Ian couldn't look at his face. He began gathering up the photographs, hastily pushing them into a bundle.

"You don't mind if I keep these Ian, do you?"

Ian stared at him. He did mind, he minded like hell, but he couldn't say so. Not with Danny standing there.

"Oh he does mind. Look at his face, he minds plenty. Here you are then." John held them out to him. When Ian went to take them John pulled them back. Ian flushed.

"Oh look, he's angry. All because his big brother has taken his toy away."

Ian stood there, fists clenched by his sides.

"How would you like to spend the night with him Ian?"

Ian looked at him. The silence was like someone scratching their head irritably.

"Not fancy?"

"Don't muck me about John." Ian's voice was small and tight with mortification.

"Me?" John held the photographs over his heart then suddenly pressed them into Ian's hand. "I am desperately sincere. How would you like to spend the night with him, just you two alone?"

Ian looked at John then quickly back over his shoulder at Danny. He was white as a sheet. He had his hands across his chest, gripping his shoulders, as if he was cold. Ian turned back. "Even if you meant it there'd be no point. Look at him."

John laughed. "Oh don't worry, he'll be good." John's face became hard and cold, a muscle twitched at the side of his mouth. "He can give it to everyone else, he can give it to you. Can't you Danny?"

Ian glanced back again. Danny said nothing.

John bellowed suddenly, making them both jump, "*Can't you Danny!?*"

Danny nodded, eyes on the floor.

John smiled, sudden and carnivorous. "Good boy."

Ian looked at him and thought, Christ, he's off his fucking head. He's right out of it. He looked at Danny again and was surprised to see an appeal in it, something that urged him to go along with him. He looked away.

"Well Ian?" He was smiling again, his face picking up a little more colour. "Want to spend the night with him?"

"Alright," Ian said, glancing quickly at Danny again.

John laughed. "*Alright?* Is that the best you can do? Christ, if you don't want him there's plenty that do. Your cousin, Miss Katherine Henderson..." John's voice took on a sharp edge, "Mr James Conley. No doubt there are more we don't know about, people he picks up whenever he's got five minutes to spare." He looked suddenly at Ian. "You'd be doing him a favour Ian. Who knows what he's going to catch otherwise. Keep it in the family, eh? Do you *want* him Ian?" John's face was no longer smiling.

"Yes," Ian said. "I want him."

John smiled again, patting him on the back. "I'll spend the night in here with these lovely photographs, reminisce, while you give your brother a good time." John crossed to Danny. He walked round him, came to rest behind him, sliding his arms round his waist, and breathed in his ear, "You see and have a good time Danny, you hear me?"

Danny nodded.

John thrust suddenly against him, his arms snaking tighter. Ian could see Danny straining under them. John thrust again, obscenely, insulting him. "Anything he wants Danny, you understand?"

Danny nodded again. Ian watched the thrusting, feeling himself grow hard, hating himself for it.

John pulled up Danny's shirt, undid his jeans button. "I don't want him coming in here and interrupting me, coming in here and telling me you're not playing nicely."

Ian watched his fingers move over Danny's stomach, the zip sliding down. He saw them find their mark then trace gently over the healing burn. Suddenly he tucked his nails down under it, like a man levering off a tin lid, and pulled.

Danny's face distorted. Ian felt a sick clench in his gut, a pain in the backs of his legs.

"Be good Danny."

Danny's mouth was open, sucking air into his lungs. Ian saw the blood start, oozing out from under John's nails, the torn scab.

"Be very good to your brother." John was humping him harder, slowly peeling off the scab.

"Stop it," Ian said, taking a step towards them, but John was digging his chin into Danny's neck, holding him there, fingers convulsively embedded in his bleeding belly. Then Ian saw his head drop forward, lips parting with a gasp. His face twitched. He gave an odd little grunt, muscles straining, hips jammed up tight against Danny's rump.

Ian stood transfixed. He looked almost like he was climaxing, hiding it in that tortured stillness. He was rubbing the blood over Danny's stomach. His face was slack, filmed with sweat. His eyes were closed. Danny's face was a cheesy grey, shiny. He rubbed his nose with a violent jerky movement, using the back of his hand. He was breathing through his mouth. Ian could see his hand shaking.

John pushed him away, suddenly sending him jolting towards Ian. "Take him." His voice was rough. "Take him and get out."

Ian could see the erection, still massive under his trousers.

"What are you looking at?" John wasn't smiling. His face was flushed.

Ian shook his head.

"Go on, get out, before I change my mind."

Ian opened the door, taking Danny's elbow and guiding him out.

"Ian..." John's voice was low behind him. Ian paused without turning. "You make him bleed."

Ian turned and looked at him then closed the door on his stony face.

Danny went into the room and heard Ian lock the door behind him. The room stank of cigarettes and liquorice. The ashtray was full of ends. A whisky bottle, a third full, sat on the bedside table. There was only one glass.

Danny went to the sink and tried to clean up his stomach. John had taken the scab right off and the damn thing was bleeding like a well. The pain was savage, throbbing. He'd been itching to fucking do that. Always fingering it, running his hands over it, dying to get off on it, frightened it would heal and leave no trace of him behind.

Ian came in and stood beside him. "Let me see it."

"It's fine."

"I *said*, let me see it." *Or I'll tell John*, it was implied. It hung there between them.

Danny turned. Ian looked at the weltering mess. Why did he look so right bleeding? What was it about the warped little bastard?

Danny turned away again and put a piece of lint over it. It would stick like hell but it would stop the blood.

Ian took the glass to the sink and rinsed it out. He filled it with whisky and brought it back to him. "Here, have some."

Danny took the glass from him, drank half of it and gave it back.

Ian smiled. "Where did you learn to drink like that?"

Danny wiped his hand over his mouth, coughed a little. "Henderson." He sat down on the bed.

Ian sat down beside him and sipped the drink experimentally. Christ, it was vile. He wondered how they managed to drink it. He put his hand on Danny's leg.

Danny looked at it then reached over and took the glass from Ian's hand. He drained it then refilled it from the bottle on the table. He drank half of that then gave it back to Ian. He could feel it working, distantly. A bit more and he would be able to just close his eyes and float away.

He looked up and found Ian watching him. Maybe it was something about his expression but he had a sudden startling image of waking one morning last summer and finding Ian in his room, just standing there in the half-dark, staring at him like a trapped rabbit. He knew he'd been touching him. The blankets were too far down. He was looking at him the same way now. It was elusive, gone before he could decide what he'd seen, just like it had been that morning.

Ian was looking at the floor now, the colour high in his cheeks. He'd taken his hand away and was drinking from the glass. Danny took it away from him. "You don't need that."

Ian looked at him, confused.

"You don't need that to get it up." Danny's face was set.

"Of course I don't."

Then Danny smiled, incredible, unmistakable. "*Are* you up?"

"I wasn't," Ian said, still looking at him.

"And now?" Danny asked, still smiling.

Ian nodded.

Danny stood up in front of him, pushing between his knees. Ian's face was level with the blood soaked lint. He could smell his skin, something floral, alien. Someone else's soap, he guessed. Danny pulled down the rest of his zip, slowly, then he stopped.

Ian looked up.

"Go on then," Danny said.

Ian took hold of his jeans and pulled everything down to his thighs. It was there, right before his face, long and thick, hanging out from his body, swollenly soft.

"In your mouth," Danny whispered. Ian saw it fatten a little as he spoke. He lifted it and put it in his mouth.

"Bigger now," Danny whispered again, hands light on his shoulders. "Better than any vintage kiddy-porn."

Ian moved forward to get more of him in.

"Feels better, looks better, performs better. All-round new improved model."

Suddenly Ian felt Danny's hand on his hair, lightly stroking him. He was massive in his mouth. He was excited, not just erect.

"But maybe you don't like that..."

Ian slid him slowly out of his mouth. "I like it." He rubbed the head over his cheek, inhaling him. "I like it Danny." And he slid it back into his mouth, worming his tongue under his foreskin.

Danny caught the back of his head and forced it in deeper. Ian swallowed it greedily.

"You know, you're good at this." Danny held his head tightly, eyes flickering shut momentarily. "You know what I like." His eyes slid closed more definitely this time. He pushed a little further into Ian's mouth grunting, "Want me to dump this in your mouth or would you like it somewhere else?"

Ian took him in deeper in answer. Danny gripped him tighter, pushed into his face. He opened his eyes and looked down at his head moving backwards and forwards on the length of him. "You're a professional Ian." He opened his legs a little, braced himself, began to buck into him, buttocks clenching. "A real cocksucker. A real beautiful cock..." and he bent suddenly at the knees, jamming it into his face. "Cocksucker... cocksucker... cocksucker..."

On and on he went, pounding into him, watching Ian take it unresistingly, never losing a stroke, never cramping his rhythm. He felt something huge inside himself suddenly let go, beyond the orgasm, beyond where he was or what he was doing. He cried out with the sheer force of it and suddenly he was down there, crawling through fire on his belly, sinking low into the slime of it, wallowing in Ian's fabulous all-consuming need.

It was wonderful.

And John wasn't even there.

Ian woke first and rolled over and looked at the clock. Early. Another ten minutes yet. He lay back down and pulled the covers carefully away from Danny's face. It was buried in his arm. He could only see half of it. He reached down under the bedclothes and ran his hand down and under him as far as it would go without pushing.

Danny was lying face down, half on his side. Ian felt the lint dressing, stiff and hard with blood, down a bit more into the nest of hair, then the soft satiny heaviness of his prick. He squeezed it then squeezed it again. He felt it fatten. His pulse quickened.

He wormed his hand in gently and palmed his penis out from under his body and squeezed again. It grew harder. Danny still lay there, breathing heavily, deeply asleep. Ian looked at him searchingly. His hair was growing in, not be too long till it reached its former glory. Look at him, what a perfect thing he was.

He was masturbating him gently, his hand a loose sheath around him. Danny grew steadily to fill it until he was fully erect, adhering to Ian's palm. It felt like silk-covered wood. Fantastic. Fucking fantastic. Had he known he was going to turn out like this? He felt as if he had, but maybe that was only hindsight. How could anyone foresee this ethereal creature lying beside him? This ethereal creature with a distinctly non-ethereal dick. Christ, he was something.

John had wanted him to use Danny last night but it was Danny who had used him. He'd outdistanced him two to one, easily, no sweat. Christ, it would be something to have this in your bed every night, using you up till you were nothing but a pair of dried-up balls and a smile.

He squeezed Danny's penis with more purpose, riding his hand up and down it. He'd do anything, suffer anything, just to have him, warm and hard like this, stiff even in his sleep. Suddenly the alarm went off. "Jesus Christ!" He jumped guiltily.

Danny rolled over on his back and reached for it, eyes still shut. He battered it with his hand till it went off. "Fucking noisy bastard," he muttered, then rolled back onto his side.

Ian lay there, heart thumping with fright. Danny opened his eyes, suddenly and clearly, and said, "Why don't you sit on it?"

Ian laughed shakily and said, "What, the alarm?"

"My cock," Danny said. There was no smile.

Ian managed to half-shake his head. "I couldn't, not with you that size."

Danny curled one arm languidly over his head. "You'll like it, trust me."

"I don't think..." Ian swallowed. Danny's eyes were relentless, seething with something unwholesome.

"Get on me." Suddenly Danny licked his fingers, slowly, purposefully. He reached over Ian's body and slicked them in the crack of his arse. Ian tensed immediately.

"Open up," Danny said and his voice was sluggish, as if he were falling asleep again, but his eyes were alert, unwavering.

Ian tried to relax. He felt Danny's fingers slide down, surprisingly gentle with those hard eyes staring. He brought them out again and spit on them this time, carrying it down. Ian could feel the slick of it. Then Danny's finger slid inside. He clenched.

"Don't do that." It was a snap but he smiled briefly and added, "It won't hurt if you relax." He turned on his back and pushed the quilt down. "Get on." He didn't even look at him.

Ian swung over him slowly. "I'm scared," he confessed.

Danny smiled properly this time. He said one word. "Good."

He spat on his fingers again, working more of it inside him. Then he did the same to his cock, lubricating it. "Get up on your knees."

Ian knelt up. Danny lifted himself up like a pole. He was hugely erect, the foreskin pulled back. Christ, he was getting to be as big as John. Too big. Ian stopped looking at it.

"Now down on it. Gently."

Ian didn't move. Danny flicked his eyes up angrily. "Come on." He caught Ian's buttock with his free hand and pulled.

Ian eased down, feeling it nudge into him. He tensed.

Danny smiled, slow and easy. "That's it." He pulled him again. Ian felt it shoving in. It felt weird, uncomfortable and way too big. Definitely too much like John.

"Come on, don't be so fucking timid." Danny's face was chiselled, sharp; his eyes colourless; his hair dark and bloody. He pulled.

Ian felt the head suddenly poke in. The sensation was unpleasant, disturbing.

He tried to climb off but Danny caught him round the waist, digging his fingers in. He pulled him down, simultaneously pushing himself up. It went half-way up in one swoop. Ian cried out, trying to wriggle free, but Danny held him tight. "Good enough for me Ian, good enough for you."

Ian looked down at his face but he couldn't read it, only the eyes were alive.

"Sit right down on it."

"I can't," Ian whispered.

A door opened in the hall.

"Do it." Danny pulled him down. Ian resisted, easing himself down as gently as he could. Danny was pushing up slowly to meet him. Their bodies met. Ian felt crammed, his body howling in protest. He had an unpleasant distended ache below his belly-button. They sat there, hugely still, listened to whoever it was going into the bathroom.

"Good," Danny whispered as the bathroom door closed. His voice was deep and slightly tremulous. He closed his eyes and licked his lips. "You're the first man I ever fucked Ian, what d'you think of that?"

Ian looked at him, unbelieving.

Danny nodded.

Ian felt a dull excitement start somewhere inside him.

Danny smiled at the sight of it. "Now you'll like it." He reached down and started playing with Ian's cock, slowly teasing the little excitement up. Ian thrust involuntarily, felt the huge wedge of Danny move inside him. It felt distantly arousing, like needing to pee. Ian flushed with it. His cock jerked.

Danny smiled again. "See?"

They heard the toilet flush.

Ian thrust forward into Danny's pulling hand. He felt Danny's cock come out of him a little. He sat back on it deliberately. Something happened low inside the pit of his stomach. He gave an involuntary grunt.

"I told you." Danny began to masturbate him, one arm supporting his head so he could watch. "Come on Ian, give it a good fuck."

They heard the bathroom door open.

Ian began to lift himself off him. Up slowly, then back down again. "Oh..." he said.

Someone hammered on the door. Ian felt a totally unexpected orgasm come up close, clutch at him, then recede again.

The door handle rattled. "Okay Danny, your time's up. Out."

Danny smiled up at him. Ian raised himself, lowered himself.

The door handle rattled again. "Danny... I said, *out*."

"He's just coming." It was a gasp.

Danny smiled up at him again. He clutched Ian's buttock, thrusting up into him, other hand working on Ian's cock.

"*Now* Danny." It rattled again. "What's going on in there?"

"What do you think?" They were both grinning now, fixedly, breathing through their mouths.

Ian groaned. He tried to keep it in but it came out anyway.

"Danny!" John pounded on the door, no pretence now. "Danny, you get the hell out of there."

"Just doing what you said John..." He was having difficulty getting the words out now. "Just... brown... holing... my... big..."

The door buckled under a sudden slamming blow. Danny grunted in shock. Ian said, "Oh God..."

Danny looked up at him, could see his face working silently with the approach of orgasm. Outside he heard Rab say, "What the hell's going on?"

Another blow buckled the door.

Ian said, "Oh *God*."

Danny gripped his thighs, feeling his whole body twitch.

"For Christ's *sake* John!" A skirmish, a half thump to the door as if Rab was trying to manhandle him away from it.

Danny said, "Go on, ride me... ride me." And watched as Ian, head dropped forward, hands clutching at Danny's chest, plunged his backside up and down on Danny's shaft, grinding down on it, gasping out, "Listen... listen... listen..." as his cock slimed and twitched in Danny's hand, giving little jerky convulsions of fluid, while outside Rab watched John slump back against the door and push his fists tight into his eyes.

John went down the stairs, hurtling down them three at a time. Rab went down after him, convinced he was going to do something stupid, but he had come to a stop in the kitchen. He stood there in the middle of the floor, hands over his ears as if he could still hear them. Rab realised abruptly he had only been putting distance between himself and them.

Rab pulled his hands down. "Has he been in there all night?"

John nodded, wiping his face.

"What the fuck for?"

John laughed shortly. He laughed again and slammed his fist into the wall. "*Jesus*, I should have known better."

Rab stared at him and realised he was finally out of his depth. Whatever had been going on he didn't understand any of it. "Are you saying you *sent* him into Ian?" He looked at him in disgust. "You tacky bastard."

"Looks like he's learned to love his oppressor Robbie. I wouldn't let it worry you."

"Jesus John, you really are the pits." Rab turned away from him.

Upstairs they heard the bathroom door bang.

John turned and went out as quickly as he had come in.

John slammed him up against the door. He locked it, slammed him up against it again. "You are going to pay for this, you little cunt."

Danny looked at him and smiled.

John slammed him a third time for good measure.

Outside, Ian tried the door handle. John roared, nothing but a warning noise.

"My clothes..."

"Fuck *off!*"

There was a silence.

"So you decided you'd play games with me?"

"You told me to give him what he wanted."

"You shut the fuck *up*." John slammed him again. It was beginning to hurt. He pushed him back violently onto the bed. "I heard you Danny. I fucking *heard* you."

Danny looked up at him.

"He didn't have to ask you for anything. You almost fucking milked him dry. Oh *God*, why don't I just kill you?" He shook Danny violently.

Danny dropped back onto one elbow. The response seemed to outrage John. He clambered on top of him and began slapping his face.

Danny felt the old cut on his lip open again, his mouth fill with blood. He covered his head with his hands.

John stopped eventually, panting with exertion.

Danny wiped his mouth carefully with the back of his hand then said quietly, "You're turning into a caricature of yourself John."

John's face was still for a moment, almost serenely composed, then it fell apart, transforming into something snarling and vicious. He began punching into Danny savagely, slamming blows into his body. But it didn't last long.

When it hit him it was blinding white.

No sex involved.

James Conley went back to work on Monday morning. He felt like shit.

He got up and looked in his bathroom mirror and said, "I feel like shit." He looked at himself once more and said, "I feel like fucking shit." But Danny's technique didn't help, he still felt like shit.

He got washed and dressed and went downstairs. Molly smiled nicely at him and made him feel worse. *God Molly, you wouldn't smile half so well if you knew what went on in my head.*

"Molly, I need a sugar jag. Please go and get me something so sweet it makes you feel sick to look at it."

"This is really bad for you James. Honestly. I was reading about it. It's an addiction you know, every bit as bad as heroin or cocaine. It gives you a high but when you come down..."

"Molly, Molly..." he held his hands up to stem the tide, "it's not even nine o'clock yet. Mercy. Lecture me later, but not now. *Please*." He looked at her plaintively.

Molly relented. "If I was really your friend I wouldn't do this. I might as well be giving you heroin."

"If you don't get me some sugar soon I'll need heroin. *Please*."

"Alright, alright, I'm going."

"I love you," he said.

She laughed, getting up and putting on her coat. "Cupboard love."

"Better than none."

She looked at him quickly but he was smiling. "Who's Danny?" she asked on impulse. She was surprised to see the change in his face.

"Danny?" He had definitely paled. She watched him intently.

"Yes." She felt slightly uncomfortable, aware that it was somehow delicate territory. "You were asking for someone called Danny when you were sick. With the fever," she added. She wished now she hadn't asked.

"He's..." He hesitated, licked his lips. "He's a friend."

"He?" She stopped struggling into her coat, looking at him.

Conley looked back at her, worried now, feeling something uncertain gnawing at his stomach. "Yes, he. Why?"

"Nothing," she said airily, smiling, trying to cover her surprise. "I thought it might have been a woman, that's all."

"Why?" he persisted, face unsmiling.

"Just a silly notion. You know how you do that sometimes, get an idea in your head. I really don't know why I thought that. Okay, one gooey cake coming up." She smiled again, not quite meeting his eyes, and was gone.

He looked at the closed door. He didn't believe that, not one word of it. She knew. She knew he was a pervert, a faggot. That's what Danny had called him, a faggot, and she knew.

He sat down at the desk and stared at the phone.

Danny was sick on the floor. He simply hung over the side of the bed and threw up. He felt sure there would be blood in it, but there wasn't. It was mostly bile. There was precious little else to come up. He lay there panting for a moment then pulled himself back onto the bed. Breathing hurt. Breathing hurt worse than he could ever remember. All he could smell and taste was vomit. He knew John was just lying there where he'd rolled off him, unable to move. Not like last night's performance. Last night was toy stuff, not serious business. This was like the time in the shed, only worse. John had shuddered and heaved like he was throwing a fit. Danny had felt him try to stop it, heard him bite down on it, so that it ground out from between his teeth, a grim, suppressed grunt. Then the same words, begging for an end to it.

Danny had felt it through his pain, and he knew that now John was lying there, utterly spent, unable to move a muscle.

"Danny...?" John's voice was a hoarse whisper.

Danny grunted.

"I'm scared."

Danny rolled painfully onto his side towards him. John was lying on his back, arms over his eyes, blocking out the light.

"I'm here," Danny managed, feeling a white-hot needle go in under his ribs. *Christ, he's broken my ribs.* He eased himself over a little further. The pain subsided a fraction.

"Don't make me kill you."

Danny eased over towards him slowly, pulled against him. John pulled his head to his, rolled over to face him. He began kissing his face feverishly. Danny winced but he didn't pull away.

"Don't drive me to it." He stopped suddenly, almost as if he'd heard something. "Danny?"

Danny lay quiescent, breathing shallow, trying to minimise the pain of each breath.

"Feel me." John took his hand, pressing it against his front. His jeans were soaked through. "It feels like I've wet myself." He laughed, a short unhappy noise. "Maybe I did."

But they both knew he hadn't.

"I feel so frightened..." He pressed his face against the wet skin of Danny's cheek. "You've got to help me."

Danny reached up and put his fingers over his lips. It was the best he could manage. "Shh..."

John seemed to soften against him. "Don't put me through that again."

"Shhh..." Danny said again.

"Love me," John said, taking his head in both hands.

Danny nodded gently.

It was the only thing left to do.

Rab came in to see him at half past nine. Danny had been physically unable to get up. He had crawled back under the bedclothes and fallen into a tight, sweaty sleep. His breathing was painful and woke him repeatedly.

Rab sat on the bed beside him.

Danny opened his eyes.

"He hasn't marked your face." Rab touched the swollen cut at the corner of Danny's lip.

Danny rubbed his eyes, felt pain shoot up his back when he moved his left arm. "He never does." It was a croak.

Rab pulled the blankets down, looked at his body. "Ian heard him."

Danny said nothing.

"Jesus, what a mess." Rab felt his ribs gently. Danny flinched away from him. "I hope he hasn't cracked any."

"Cheerful fucker you are," Danny grunted.

Rab felt the other side. "Not so bad?"

"He's a right-hander." Danny smiled thinly.

Rab pulled the blankets back up. He began patting his pockets. When he had his cigarette lit he asked casually, not looking at him, "He get off on it?"

Danny didn't answer him. Rab looked down at him. Danny was studying his face. Rab took the cigarette out his mouth. "Ian heard that too," he admitted.

"Then why ask?"

Rab shook his head. "That's way out of line Danny - *way* out. He'll get so he can't get there without it, then what? Are you going to let him kill you for a better sex life?"

"We've been through this before." Danny closed his eyes as if he wouldn't hear him if he couldn't see him.

"And we'll keep going through it till you wake up."

"Oh, leave me alone." Danny laid an arm over his eyes. He sounded so weary, so defeated, that Rab let it drop. When Danny realised he wasn't going to say any more he took his arm away.

"Want a puff?" Rab offered him his cigarette.

Danny shook his head.

There was a small silence then Rab said, "He's got someone coming here today for Ostler's job."

Danny smiled a little. "Clean shirts."

Rab looked at him. "What did you do to scare her off?"

"Nothing."

"Why do you lie about these things? It doesn't make sense. I mean, you don't care what you do, so why lie about it?"

Danny looked back at him. "Maybe I get sick of being called names."

"Okay then, I won't call you any names. Tell me."

"I fucked her."

"*What?*" Rab couldn't help it.

Danny was looking at the ceiling. "You heard me."

"Why, for Christsake?"

"I felt like it."

"Jesus, you're really..."

"No fucking names Rab, remember?" Danny's eyes were on him now.

"You actually got it *up* her?"

533

"You know how it's done, don't you?"

"Jesus..." Rab said again. "How in hell's name did you manage that? I'd have thought she'd run screaming from the house."

Danny only shook his head, smiling faintly.

"If it comes to that, how did you manage to get it up *for* her? Christ, she's about seventy if she's a day."

Danny shrugged then winced at the movement. "It isn't any problem for me."

"No, it fucking isn't, is it?"

"You asked."

"Jesus, I thought you'd been hassling her. John thought you'd been hassling her." He ran his hand through his hair. "We don't know you at all, do we?"

Danny said nothing.

"Maybe you should leave the new one alone, eh? As a special favour to our household comforts if not our reputation."

"Ostler won't say anything." Danny was smiling again.

"Christ, stop fucking grinning. Everything's one big entertainment to you, isn't it?"

Danny's smile slid away. "Drop dead."

"Think you can leave her alone? Think you can do it?"

"If she leaves me alone."

"He's right, you really are a little whore, aren't you?"

"Get out."

"A driven little whore."

Danny got up on his elbows. "Get out."

"Don't worry, I'm going. I don't like the company." Rab stood up and stubbed out his cigarette. He looked down at Danny, his face dark with dislike. "Dirty little cunt."

He slammed out of the room.

Katherine Henderson pulled the phone over onto her lap. She pushed the buttons then stopped and pressed down the bar, disconnecting the line. She sat a moment, staring out the window, then dialled again. She asked to be put through to James Conley. Molly told her Mr Conley was with a client but could she get him to phone back? Katherine Henderson said yes, refraining from informing the stupid bitch he was supposed to have contacted her more than a week ago. She left her name and number. She put the phone back down.

She waited.

James Conley saw his client out and sat back down. He rubbed his head. It hurt.

Molly came in with a pile of letters to be signed. "Fed up?"

"Headache."

"Want me to get you something?"

"Please."

"Miss Henderson phoned again for you. That's the third time. She wants you to phone her back."

Conley rubbed his head again.

"Is she that bad?" Molly asked.

"No." He shook his head. "No, it's my fault, I keep putting her off. Okay, I'll do it now, but get me something for this head, would you?"

"You should have taken another couple of days off."

Conley lifted the phone and asked Dorothy to get him Katherine Henderson's number. He covered the mouthpiece with his hand. "The boredom was killing me."

Molly smiled and went out. The number connected. It was answered on the second ring. She must have been sitting right by it.

"Hello, Miss Henderson?"

"The elusive Mr Conley."

"I'm sorry I didn't get back to you sooner, I've been ill."

"I heard."

Conley grimaced to himself. She was in a foul temper. He swivelled his chair round and looked out the window. "I'm afraid we won't be able to do anything with the material you gave me, there simply isn't enough there. I spoke to Daniel Jackson Moore," he felt himself blush inanely, *You did more than speak to him Max... faggot*, "but I'm afraid it failed to impress. Frankly I don't know what else to suggest."

"I do." Her voice was clipped. "I have something new for Mr Jackson Moore. I have two witnesses who saw the three of them here on the night my brother was murdered."

Conley felt it clutch at his heart. It was true then. Something inside him had known it all along. It wasn't shock he felt. It was so obvious. And if they'd had to murder him to cover up then chances were it was something equally bad they'd covered up. More murder. Nothing else could have that same relentless logic.

"Did you hear me Mr Conley?"

"Yes... yes I did. This certainly puts a different complexion on things."

Katherine Henderson laughed. "It doesn't half," she said unceremoniously.

"But it still doesn't prove anything." *Fast with the plaster Max. Over the cracks with ease, with comfort.*

"I don't want to *prove* anything Mr Conley. I don't give two hoots for proving anything. I just want Daniel Jackson Moore to realise I'm serious."

"Of course," Conley said lamely.

"Now can you help me or should I settle my bill?"

"No, no. I'm sure we can try something with this."

"I want something a damn sight better than try Mr Conley. As the Americans say, I want results."

"Yes of course, we'll see what we can do. I must see you, discuss this properly."

"This afternoon?"

"No, it'll have to be tonight. May I come to you?"

"By all means."

"About..." he paused for thought, "about sixish, or is that too early for you?"

"No, six will be fine."

"I'll see you at six then."

"Fine," she said and hung up without another word.

Molly stuck her head round the door. "Finished?"

Conley nodded.

Molly put his tablets down in front of him. "Are you alright? You don't look very good."

"Head's just a little worse than I thought, that's all."

"Well take your pills then."

Conley obligingly pushed them out of the foil and swallowed them down. Molly took the glass back from him. "No appointments till ten thirty. Have a rest, let the tablets work."

Conley nodded. "I will, but do me a favour Molly, bring me Katherine Henderson's file, would you?"

"Sure." She went out of the room.

Conley laid his head back against the headrest of his chair.

Molly came back in. "On the desk?"

"Mm."

Molly withdrew again quietly, leaving him to it.

Rab got a brief glimpse of Jean McEvoy. She was a big square-built woman with grey-blonde hair. He had passed her walking her dog but he didn't know her. She was a relative newcomer to the village. Several of its residents were. Everybody knowing everybody else in a village was a myth, like all the other myths in life. He didn't see her face but she couldn't have been more than fifty.

Rab climbed into the tractor and pulled out of the yard. Maybe this one would be immune.

Christ knows, somebody must be.

Rab helped himself to another slice of bread. Ian passed him the butter. The dog tried to stand up on his knees but he pushed it off.

Danny had already eaten and was sitting behind the evening paper, feet up on a chair. All they could see of him was his hands.

"Well?" Rab asked. "How was she? Can we look forward to something better than cold meat and soup?"

John nodded. "She's fine. She doesn't have much to say for herself."

Rab smiled. Ostler's endless chat had driven John up the wall.

"And she can stay till two instead of twelve. No-one to go running home for. She's divorced."

"When is she starting?"

"Monday coming."

"God, a whole week."

"We've managed this long. She's got a lad, sixteen next month, looking for a job. I thought I might take him on, see how he goes."

"Here?"

Danny finally emerged from behind his paper. Ian looked up.

"Well, it wouldn't be at fucking Westlands, would it? We're a man short, remember?" Come spring we're going to feel it and I can't afford a farmhand proper. We'll let him live in, give him his keep. It'll do."

"You're going to have him *here*, living in?" Rab asked.

John looked at him levelly. "Any reason why not?"

"Oh no, none at all, only you'll have to watch your volume at night, won't you?"

There was a silence. John's face was hard and set. "Ostler knew we shared a bed."

"Yeah, and let it be known too."

"Meaning what?"

"You know damn fine. You've got a reputation John." He jerked his thumb at Danny. "And he's got worse. People talk. Maybe she won't be so keen to let her innocent stay here when she sees how the land lies."

"If people talk Rab," John's voice was hard, "then she'll have already heard, won't she?"

"Seeing's believing."

"We sleep in the same bed. We wouldn't be the first brothers to do it."

"With a room sitting empty?"

"It was being kept for hired help. Ostler knew that. Now we've got it, end of gossip."

"Yeah, if you learn to bite the pillow."

"Fucking shut it."

Rab pressed his lips tight together, his face a picture of irritation. *Jump boy and we*

jump.

John picked up the teapot and poured himself a cup of tea. Danny watched his hands, listening, edgy.

"Anyway, I'll see him tonight. He's coming round..." John peered over his shoulder at the clock, "...in half an hour. I might not like him."

Rab let it out. "He might not like you."

But John only shrugged. "Then everything's fine." He looked directly at Rab. "And I won't have to learn to bite the pillow, will I?"

Danny smiled and looked down at the table. Ian busied himself cutting more bread.

Rab glared round at them all then got up and stalked out of the room.

Stephen McEvoy arrived promptly at half past six. His mother had told him to go to the back door in the yard. He felt very nervous. He knew John Jackson Moore by sight. He had a reputation for using his fists to settle arguments. But there were even worse things hinted about him. All kinds of stuff. About his dad disappearing one night when he was drunk, and his mam running off with someone, and about his kid brother, the redheaded one. Not that he was a kid. Real glamour boy he was. He'd heard some really nasty stuff about him, but chances were it was all made up, no-one could be as bad as he was supposed to be. There was supposed to be another brother and a cousin too, but he couldn't have told you who they were, he'd never seen them.

The yard light was on, bright as daylight. He could see his breath puffing out in clouds. He knocked on the door. His heart was thumping. A dog hurled itself at him on the other side. Stephen stood back a step, heart now faster than ever.

A voice snarled something unintelligible and the dog stopped, then the door opened.

John Jackson Moore smiled at him. Stephen couldn't see his face clearly, but he saw the smile. Jesus, he was big.

He stood back and told Stephen to come in. The redhead was sitting at the table, reading a paper. He looked up and smiled. Stephen smiled back at him uncertainly, feeling his pulse pick up again. There was another bloke there who had to be the cousin. He had mucky-brown hair and acne marked skin. He didn't smile. He looked Stephen up and down briefly, oddly, then away again. He got up and began clearing plates. John Jackson Moore was talking to him. The dog was snuffling at his hand, tail pluming from side to side. The redhead leaned forward and tapped ash off his cigarette. Stephen noticed that his lip was swollen, as if someone had thumped him. He looked up and caught Stephen's eye again. Stephen looked away, feeling flustered.

"Come on through, where we can get peace."

John led him through into the hall. The living room door was open, Rab was coming through it. He stopped when he saw them.

"This is Robbie... Rab," John said, then he saw Rab's face. He looked perplexedly at the boy. He'd paled visibly, his freckles looking dirty against the pallor of his face.

"We've already met," Rab said. "Hello Steve, small world." Rab was smiling, but it was forced, too slick, all show. John knew him too well. He always became a grease-ball when he felt out of control.

Rab passed them and went on up the stairs.

John led the way into the living room and closed the door. "Sit down." He spoke to the boy's back. "You've met Rab before then?"

"Yes." It came out faint and the boy tried again. "Yes, at a party in Pithouses. I went with some of my mates. I didn't know he was from here." He was bright red now.

Oh Jesus. John pushed up off the door. *With that hair this has got to be the rabbit.*

Fucking great.

John sat down on the armchair and said, "Relax, I'm not going to eat you." He almost slapped his forehead when he heard what he said. *Lovely choice of words John, couldn't have picked better.* He went on quickly, "Your mother says you've got permission to leave school this Christmas if you've got a job to go to."

"Yes."

John told him about the work involved, watching his reactions. He seemed keen, and he was strongly-built for his age. He could even drive. His mother said his uncle had taught him. But this business with Rab was bad news. Chances were he wouldn't want to live in the same house as him. This kid was no faggot. And even if he could cope with that they'd have to be doubly careful. He'd be suspicious of everything.

Maybe it wasn't such a good idea, only they needed the help and this was a gift horse.

Well, maybe the boy would turn it down, but if he didn't one thing was for certain, Rab could fucking well leave the hired help alone.

John let him go, seeing him to the door and telling him the job was his if he wanted it, to talk it over with his mother and let him know. He almost laughed when he said that.

The boy promised he would.

They parted amiably.

John closed the door and shouted, "Rab!"

Then went upstairs to find him.

James Conley was half an hour late. The car decided to play up. When he got to Katherine Henderson's house he was cold, tired and thoroughly pissed off. When she answered the door the first thing she said was, "What kept you?" She said, "Ah, the antique" when he explained about his car and he realised at that moment he was never going to like her.

She took his coat, saw the flash of dull garnet under his jacket, and felt he was altogether too much a poseur for her taste.

They passed into the living room and it was then Katherine Henderson began to tell him the remarkable tale of the Misses Selsdon and the homosexuals.

John went into Rab's room and shut the door. Rab had been waiting for him. He was half-way through a cigarette.

"He's the fucking rabbit, isn't he?"

Rab nodded.

"What's the fucking idea, shitting in your own nest?"

"I thought he belonged to Pithouses."

"He thought you did too."

"Looks like we were both wrong."

"I hope you realise this has probably fucked everything."

"I didn't do it deliberately John. I was just sucking off boy unknown in the back of a fucking car. I didn't ask him for his frigging life history."

"It would have saved us a lot of grief if you had."

"Well he isn't going to tell anyone."

"Oh praise the fucking Lord."

Rab dragged on his cigarette, saying nothing.

"He'd have been ideal. Hard-working, keen..."

"Cheap," Rab interrupted sourly.

John looked at him. "Something wrong with that?"

Rab said nothing.

John pointed at him. "*If* he comes here," he jabbed again with his finger, "*you* stay away, okay?"

"Why? Want him for yourself?"

John crossed the room and lifted him by the front of his shirt. "Don't fucking smartmouth me." He dropped him back into the chair. "Don't touch him."

"I've no intention of 'touching' him. He was drunk... *I* was drunk."

John nodded. "Good. Just keep it that way."

Rab took another draw. "I don't think you'll see him again anyway." He let the smoke down his nose.

"Why not?" John pushed his hands in his pockets.

"He cried. I mean, afterwards. That's too much humiliation for anyone to face."

"We'll see, it's amazing the humiliation people will endure for money."

"He's still at home. He can't need the money."

"No, but his mother does."

Rab nodded then looked up at him and said, "And Danny?"

John looked back at him. "Danny will stay clear."

"He might not be interested."

John opened the door. "Yeah and tomorrow James Henderson will be risen from the dead."

He went out and closed the door quietly behind him.

Stephen McEvoy lay on his bed, face down, and felt the shame flood through him again.

How *could* he have?

With a *bloke*.

What would his mam say if she knew?

He couldn't take the job. How would he tell his mam? Oh God, what a flickin' mess.

His mam was never going to believe this. He'd pestered her stupid for this job. What was worse was she'd taken a liking to John Jackson Moore, came home and told him he'd be a good influence.

He hadn't exactly *liked* him but you couldn't imagine anyone taking a loan of him. Nothing would put the shit up him. But he couldn't go to work for him. Not now.

They'd make him stay on at school until summer now. Oh no they flickin' wouldn't, no way. He would find something else, anything else. *Like what? Like flickin' what Steve-o? Worst flickin' unemployment in the area.*

The front door banged. "Stephen?!"

"Up here." He sat up and swung his legs to the floor.

His mother came into the room. "How did you get on?"

"Okay."

"Okay? What's wrong, didn't he like you?"

Stephen nodded. "He offered me the job. He said I can live in, all my grub and everything, plus thirty quid a week. That's exactly the same as they get, his brothers and him."

"Well, that's great." His mother looked at him. "What's wrong? Aren't you pleased? Don't tell me you've changed your mind?"

"It's not that."

"Well, what's wrong then?"

"Nothing... just a bit... you know," he finished lamely.

"Scared?"

He nodded.

She cuddled him. "Well, of course you are." She kissed his forehead. He put his arms around her awkwardly. "I'll only be ten minutes away."

"I know I kept saying to you... but living in..."

She smiled over his shoulder and rubbed his back. She felt an odd lump in her throat. "After all your complaining?" She laughed. "You'll see me every day and I'll be living here, ten minutes down the road. It's just because it's new. You'll love it, you'll see. Two weeks there and you'll forget who I am. It's time you got in with some responsible lads. One of them's not much older than you, he's only just turned twenty. He seems a nice lad, always ready with a smile, and *very* popular with the girls." She laughed again. "You want to get in with him." She rumpled his hair.

He sat there, awkward against her, longing to confess, share the awful weight of it, but he couldn't tell her. Because no-one had forced him. He could've said no. If only he hadn't been so drunk.

Oh Mam, you wouldn't want to touch me if you knew.

Oh Mam.

James Conley looked at her as she got up and went into the kitchen. He felt vaguely bemused. She really had no idea. She really hadn't thought that far, or she pretended she hadn't. Maybe she'd rather not consider the possibility that her prospective husband had murdered her brother. It was just leverage, a business deal. Do something with it Conley, don't bother me with the fine detail. This calls for a drink, she had said, and now she was bringing it in. Let's drink to my husband slitting my brother's throat. Conley shuddered.

She looked at him, smiling an enquiry.

"Someone just walked over my grave," he said.

"Here, take this. It's probably the after effects of your flu."

Conley took the whisky from her and sipped it. He wasn't a fan but it was good whisky nevertheless. The sudden image of Danny's cousin kissing him came unbidden into his head. He was still trying to grasp that. He'd felt sure these sisters must have been mistaken but Katherine Henderson said not, said that her brother had said as much in his diary. She said there was a lot of exaggeration but obviously there was some element of truth in it. Conley knew she was fooling herself. There was a lot more truth in that diary than she realised, or wanted to realise. He was itching to get his hands on it. He had a sudden conviction that, far from exaggerating, Henderson had told precise truths. He felt sure that Danny would be laid out in its pages clearer than he was in real life. No confusions, no deceptions. His brother, his cousin. Who else? Danny didn't seem to balk at incest. Or murder. Conley had always wondered how anyone could have been fooled by the Lucrezia Borgias of this world. Now he knew. A pretty face and an animal lust covered a lot of dangerous ground. *Oh, what the hell am I doing in this?*

"So, are you going to confront him with it?" she asked.

"No, I'll go to his brother. He may not like me but he likes me talking to Danny even less."

"He doesn't like anyone talking to Danny, don't let it worry you. He's jealous of him."

He had an overwhelming urge to say, No, he's screwing him, but he didn't. Instead he asked curiously, "Don't you find their relationship a bit odd?"

"Very odd," she said, then she looked up at him. "What are you implying?"

He gestured with his hand. "His brother just seems too intense about him, that's all."

She looked at him over the top of her glass. "Don't let my brother's perverted notions run away with you Mr Conley, Danny has a perfectly normal sex drive."

Normal? That's *normal?* God, who was she fooling? But she wasn't finished.

"You do understand what I'm saying to you, Mr Conley?"

He looked at her. "To be quite honest I don't."

She laughed. "I'm not exactly promiscuous but I have had other partners and Danny wipes the floor with them."

Conley stared at her.

"You seem surprised. In this day and age I'd hardly have thought I'd shock you. I know there's an age difference but it's still less than the average one for older men and younger women. Are you sexist about age Mr Conley or is it just the idea of unmarried people sleeping together?"

Conley took a breath. "I'm sorry. Your relationship just hadn't occurred to me."

She laughed. "He claims not to be particularly experienced but he certainly has a natural instinct. He does things with his fingers a pianist might envy." She laughed again. "Now I have shocked you."

He shook his head, smiled faintly. *Shocked me? No, I'm just lying on the floor in a dead faint. So you're one of several. It's getting to be quite a party.*

Conley put his glass down. "I really must go, this headache of mine's getting worse. This flu seems to have left me more fragile than I realised."

"Of course." She got up. "You will phone me?" she asked, and her tone was slightly sarcastic.

"Yes. Sorry about last time. I'll phone you straight away, as soon as I've seen him."

She went out into the hall with him, gave him his coat. He shrugged it on.

He stood, stretching black leather gloves between his fingers. She watched him. There was something sexy about him - not attractive, sexy - in spite of all that frosty coldness. She wondered if he'd shake hands this time, but he didn't. He kept his distance, as aloof as ever.

He said goodbye, correctly polite, and went out.

"Lie on your side."

"It's too sore."

"Well turn the other way then. Wait, come over this side so I can get round the back."

Danny slid across the bed and turned over, John clambering over him. When they were arranged John eased up against him gently. "Okay?"

Danny nodded.

John looked at the back of his head. His hair was still warm from the fire. It smelt of coal smoke, like frosty air on a winter's night.

John held his hips lightly and pushed slowly against him, kissing his shoulders. "That okay?"

"Mm," Danny murmured.

John reached round and felt for him. "Want me to?"

"Maybe later."

John squeezed his penis and let him go, let his hand rest on his hip again.

"The boy coming here then?" Danny asked.

John slid his erection slowly up against his buttock until it tugged, held it a second then said, "God willing," letting it ease down again. He shifted it slightly, further onto the hard flat of Danny's back. He needed more friction. "Hands off Danny," he warned. He felt down between Danny's legs from behind, feeling the damp heat of his tightly squashed balls, still moist from the bath.

"He isn't even sixteen," Danny said.

John was amused to hear the outrage in his tone. "So?"

Danny said nothing.

"I mean it Danny." He pushed harder, resting his forehead on Danny's back, looking down into the warm dark between their two bodies and watching himself pulled tautly against his back.

"I said I wouldn't touch him. I won't."

"You say a lot of things." He thrust again, lifting himself up a little higher, further onto the small of Danny's back.

"When does he start?"

"Friday, end of term. They're closing early, decorating or something. He can't wait to leave. He reminded me of you." John moved a little slower, held each moment a little longer, pressing hard.

"The hair?"

"Jesus, no, he's like a carrot. I meant wanting to leave school."

"I don't blame him."

John laughed, let himself reach round and feel him again. He laughed again, differently this time. "How do you do it? You lie there talking about Christ knows what, not even thinking about sex, and your dick feels like a fucking red-hot poker."

"How do you know I'm not thinking about sex?"

"You're talking about Stephen McEvoy leaving school. That's not anywhere near sex."

"Try me."

John held still a moment, almost suspended. He could feel the uncomfortable pressure of his heart. He was nearer than he realised. "What d'you mean?"

"Time me, see how long I take." His voice was thick, almost aggressive.

"Reckon you can beat me?"

"You know I can."

John whispered in his ear, "I've never met anyone that could touch excitement the way you can. Never."

"Go on," Danny urged again.

John reached round and gripped him, began to move against his back. "I thought you were having this later?"

"I'll have another."

John laughed then moved hard against him. He made no effort to masturbate Danny, just let his hand pull him as he jerked against him, following his own rhythm. He pressed his mouth against his shoulder. Rab had been right about that pillow. He bit lightly on Danny's back. He intended to hide it if he could, beat Danny to the draw. No way he was going to make it in thirty seconds, and that was about as long as John was going to last. He should've let it rest. Now look at him. He bit harder and heard himself groan, giving the show away.

Oh do the damn thing.

He began to buck.

It came up out of him in almost painful spurts, like milking an over-full cow. He let it rip, then he felt Danny, unmoving beneath him, quiet under his onslaught, his heavy breathing the only sign as the hot creamy liquid spilt over John's fingers. "You little bastard," he gasped, half laughing.

"Keep going, don't stop," Danny grunted.

John rubbed his face in his back, pulled on him with slow, powerful strokes.

Danny let his eyes slide closed and smiled slowly. Now they would really have some fun.

It was Rab who answered the phone. It was half past eight.

"Can I speak to Mr Jackson Moore please?"

"John?" Rab asked.

"Yes."

"Who's calling?"

"James Conley."

Rab held it a moment, wondering if he should just hang up then he said, "Hang on, they've gone to bed." Let him worry about that one. "I'll see if he's still up." And that one. He put the phone down before Conley could reply.

James Conley shoved the coffee table hard with his foot, making the bottle on it tilt perilously. He jerked forward and snatched it upright again, steadying it. He dropped back weakly.

Jealousy, that's what that was Max. A juvenile, jealous tantrum. He's in bed with him and he let you know it. He let you know it because he knows what's going on.

Going on? Don't you mean past tense? There isn't anything going on. It's finished. You killed it.

He lay there and looked at the phone, deep in its pool of light, and listened to the hollow sound of the house at the other end.

"John?" Rab knocked on the door. John was going to love this. "John, you're wanted on the phone."

John lifted his head from Danny's body. "Tell them to fuck off."

"It's Conley."

John looked down at Danny.

Danny shook his head, nothing to do with him.

John frowned. "Christ, talk about timing." He swung up off the bed, wiping his mouth, and pulled on a seldom-used dressing gown then unlocked the door. Danny pulled the blankets up.

John went out, glared at Rab. "What the fuck does he want?"

Rab took a step back to let him pass. "Why don't you ask him?"

John pushed past him muttering obscenities. The dressing gown looked almost comic on him.

Rab looked round the door frame then moved into the room. Now he could see Danny's face. It was flushed, eyes half-lidded. He had his hands behind his head. Rab could smell it, see the sweat spiking the hair in his armpits.

"Looks like he called at a bad time Danny."

Danny smiled and pushed the blankets down. His dick was gorged with blood. Only someone going down on you for half an hour brought the veins up like that.

Rab's face flooded with heat.

"Why the embarrassment? You've seen it before." Danny's voice was half-way down the slippery slope already.

"I wasn't expecting it Danny, you know?" He turned away.

"Then don't make suggestive remarks Robbie."

After a second Rab glanced back. It was still there. "Cover yourself up for Christsakes."

"Why? You can always leave if you don't like it."

Rab looked at his body spread out on the bed. All the scars, the burns, the bruises; they only made him seem more vulnerable with that hard dirty mouth of his. He was full of contradictions, everything about him.

Danny lifted his cock up. "Help me out?"

Rab looked at him. "You cannot be serious."

"Come on, just let me finish it in your mouth."

"While he's out the room?"

"Be fucking stupid with him in it."

"Christ, he made a mistake leaving you like this. You're like an animal on fucking heat."

"Come on Rab." Danny's eyes were alive with it, his tongue flicking out, his cock jerking up, lifting his hips, offering it.

Rab crossed to the bed, knelt on it, then bent over him and slid it into his mouth.

Danny sighed like a man sliding into a hot bath. "My load was just coming up..." He grunted, listened to John talking distantly in the hall, pushed up, then reached for Rab's hair. "I'm going to come."

Rab jerked up off him but Danny's hand snarled in his hair, yanking him back down. "You've got to swallow it. Don't leave anything..."

Rab heard the phone go back down, oh so clearly, the cessation of John's voice, his feet on the stairs.

Danny lifted himself up off the bed with it, silent, tortured. Rab could feel it convulsing him. He'd forgotten what this felt like. He swallowed it down quickly, as if he was taking medicine. He heard John reach the landing. He wriggled out of Danny's grasp, frantically scrambling off the bed and wiping his mouth. His face was burning, his heart thumping. He had a hard-on like nobody's business. Christ, he must be mad.

Danny pulled the blankets up with seconds to spare. His face was flushed with excitement. He was breathing heavily, spunk still pulsing out of him, his balls crawling. John came into the room. He looked at Rab but he didn't see him. "Get out," he said. He began taking off his dressing gown.

Rab went past him quickly, not looking at Danny.

John shoved the door shut and hung up his dressing gown. He went to the bed and sat down heavily. He slapped Danny hard across the face.

Danny brought his head back slowly. John slapped him again, pulled the blankets down. Danny's cock was barely softening. It looked red and used. John lifted it, squeezing it tight. A long string of semen joined his cock to his belly like saliva.

"The come's still leaking out of you. Am I supposed to think it's just over-excited?" John dropped him as if his touch contaminated him. "I think you want to die."

Danny licked his lip.

"*Do* you want to die?"

Danny shook his head. John looked away. "So why did you do it? I'd really like to understand."

"I needed to shoot my load. He was there..." he paused, "and you weren't."

John washed his face with his hands then said, "Move over."

Danny slid over the bed. John climbed in beside him, put out the light. "You wear me out." His voice was weary in the darkness. "You wear me right the fuck out."

There was a silence then Danny asked, "What did he want?"

"To see me."

There was a moment's pause. John smiled hard to himself in the darkness. "You?"

"Yes me, Danny. Not you. Disappointed?"

"No."

"Liar."

There was another pause then Danny asked, "Why does he want to see you?"

"We were seen, coming out of Henderson's the night he was murdered."

Danny took it in slowly, painfully. "Those women?"

"Probably."

Danny felt as if a fist was squeezing his heart. "John?"

"What?"

"Let me do you."

John laughed shortly. "What's this, a peace offering? Or are you still feeling randy?"

"Let me."

"I haven't got your stamina."

"You've only come once, let me."

John was silent.

Danny climbed over him, upside down. John could feel his penis, sticky and silky, brush across his face. He could see its pale shape hanging above him.

Fuck him. Let him do all the work, he wasn't going to lift a finger. The whoring little bastard, he ought to kill him.

Danny was trying to tease him up, alternating between the gentlest licking and cramming him half-way down his throat. John reached up and pulled his body down closer, pressing his face into his balls. He could smell his dick, that curious sour saliva scent of clean sucked flesh. Already Danny felt stiffer, hardening against John's cheek.

No, fuck him, let him go hungry.

He pressed his face into Danny's thigh. His mouth went dry.

It's you who's going hungry John-boy.

John caught the dangling cock in his hand and brought it down awkwardly into his mouth, felt it try to right itself almost as if it were fighting to get away. He pulled Danny's arse down closer, forcing him to spread his legs. Danny sucked him harder.

It was like it was giving you sustenance. You could almost feel it in your stomach, it was so fucking satisfying, so right, as if it belonged there.

Yeah, and in fifty other mouths.

He bit him, hard, heard the sound of his own distress over the grunt of Danny's pain.

I bite him and I suffer.

He used his teeth again, dragging over the head of his cock. He felt Danny shiver.

He likes that. The little fucker likes the pain. For all his contempt he likes that edge of pain.

John dug his nails into his arse and heard Danny moan, a little suppressed noise. He forced Danny's cock down hard with one hand, pressing it uncomfortably into his mouth. He felt Danny tense with excitement. Danny was a little masochist. That's what kept him coming back, the kicks he couldn't get elsewhere.

Well, I can give you that Danny. I can give you plenty of pain.

Danny began sucking on him feverishly. It felt almost like gratitude. John felt his excitement double instantly. He could feel his heart pounding. He sucked savagely on him until he felt like a piece of thick fleshy wood in his mouth, knotted with veins, and then he trapped it in his fist, holding the blood in, and began to scrape it gently between his teeth, dragging on the turgid head, tighter and tighter as Danny grew more and more excited. He felt his own orgasm boil up.

Danny groaned, definitely and audibly. John kept right on, harder and harder. Danny simply stopped, seemed to go limp, boneless. John pushed into his slack mouth. He didn't need it anymore anyway. He was going to make his own pleasure. He worked him faster, in and out his mouth, his jaw aching. Danny clung to him, arse working in time to John's frantic pace, face rubbing over John's penis like a demented dog, then he whispered, "No..." plainly begging. "No, don't..."

Harder, faster...

"John don't... I'm going to..."

But he didn't get any further.

Danny slammed it into his mouth, almost choking him, dragged it back out, scraping it along John's teeth, then slammed it in again. It spurted out, hot and acid down John's throat, Danny grunting like an animal, not like some silent beautiful god, but like some craven animal cramming his cock into the pain of John's mouth.

And then it was John's turn, just nudging against Danny's writhing distorted face, feeling Danny's noise vibrate through him. An animal's noise. A fucking rabid little animal.

Which is exactly what he was.

FIFTY-SIX

John had insisted on seeing Conley during the day. The earliest Conley could fit him in was Friday. When Conley told him the address John said nothing, but he knew it, and he sensed in the sound of the silence that Conley had expected him to know it. He was looking forward to meeting Conley. Conley owed him. Conley was still taking from him. He could feel it in Danny's unnatural hunger, his perpetual demands, his tempers.

Draggingly Friday came round and John, somehow, had forgotten about the boy. Rab looked at him across the table and said, "You hadn't forgotten?"

John looked at the floor. "Looks like I fucking had Robbie, doesn't it?"

"What do you want to do?"

"Hang on, let me think."

Ian came in, hung up his jacket and sat down at the table.

"Just go on as planned. Ian can take Danny's work and Danny can see to the boy."

"Danny?"

"That's right, Danny. He's the only one here who hasn't shown a preference for jail-bait. Any objections?"

Rab shut his mouth.

John looked back at the clock. "Is that right?"

"I think so."

"Well, he's due at ten so Danny'll have time to wash the car. The windscreen is so dirty you could plant it, and I need it this afternoon."

"For Caldermouth."

"That's right." John looked at him. "Problem?"

Rab looked away.

John smiled. Danny came in, huffing warmth into his hands.

"Daniel, see to our boy Stephen when he comes, show him round. Christ, his room..." John slapped his forehead.

"It's clean," Danny said.

"Well turn the bed down or something. He can have a hot water bottle tonight, keep him warm in bed." John's eyes were on Rab. His smile got uglier every day, less like anything human.

Danny sat down. "When's he due?"

"Ten. Wash the Rover for me before he comes. Ian'll take your work."

Danny nodded. He poured himself some cereal, added milk.

"Don't show him too much at once, okay?"

Danny didn't look up. "Give me some credit."

Ian glanced quickly at John then away again. John was staring at Danny fixedly. Danny kept his head down. John reached out across the table and held Danny's hand, forcing it back down as he tried to lift the spoon. Danny looked up slowly. "Watch your mouth," John said slowly.

Danny dropped his eyes and stared at the table until John let go then he went on eating.

Rab watched the interplay with his opinion written all over his face. John saw it. "Something bothering you?"

"Not a fucking thing John-boy."

John nodded. "Good."

They ate the rest of their meal in silence.

Danny's hands were raw from the hot water. He was rubbing Vaseline into them when the door went.

"Shit."

He rubbed his hands on the towel, grimacing at what his mother would have said, and went downstairs.

He opened the back door. Stephen McEvoy stood there, red-faced with the cold, looking almost obscenely healthy.

Come in," Danny smiled. "Dump your bag on the table."

The boy did as he was told.

"I've got to show you round this morning, but we'll take you upstairs first, show you your room, okay?"

Stephen smiled back.

"Follow me." Danny stopped, looked at the table. "Don't forget your bag."

The boy flushed and went back and picked it up.

Danny pushed open the door. "This used to be my room."

"Yeah?"

Danny nodded. "Youngest always gets the shittiest."

The boy laughed.

"It's the smallest, but it's warmest in winter, and you can see out onto the green. It's nice in the summer." Danny looked out the window for a long moment then realised the boy was watching him. He crossed to the wardrobe and opened it. "Piss, I'd forgotten some of my stuff's still in here. Just heave it out. These shirts don't fit anymore, shove 'em in the bin, okay?"

The boy nodded.

"The third drawer sticks - it comes off its runner if you pull it out too far - and the bed leg works loose if you bounce on it." Danny looked at him then laughed. "But I don't suppose you'll be bouncing on it, eh?"

Stephen laughed too. "No, not straight away." And they both laughed again.

What white teeth he had, Stephen thought. He didn't really look like a farmer. Not *not,* but not like one either. He realised Danny hadn't introduced himself. "What's your name?" he asked, although he already knew the answer.

Danny looked at him. "I thought John had said. I'm Danny. Come on, I'll show you the rest."

They went back out into the hall.

"Next door here's Rab." Danny looked round at him. "Have you met Rab?"

The boy nodded, colouring up faintly and looking momentarily uncomfortable. What was wrong here? Rab making him feel unwelcome already? He knew that one of old. He'd been at the receiving end of Rab's three's-a-crowd for most of his life.

"The other side's Ian's. You met Ian?"

"Brown hair, the same colour as..." the boy stumbled over calling John by his first name.

"John's. That's him... except he's uglier. Ian's the runt of the family." Danny smiled to show he was joking.

The boy smiled back uncertainly.

"Across here are the two big rooms. Me and John share this one and this is my parent's room."

The boy became obviously silent.

"I suppose you've heard about them? Both 'disappeared'. That's the polite way of

saying he's gone off on a five year drunk and she couldn't get away fast enough." Danny shrugged.

The boy nodded.

"And this..." he threw open the door, "is the bathroom that we hope your mother will put right for us. We, as you can see, live like pigs." Danny picked a towel up off the floor. "Well almost." He shut the door again.

He showed him the downstairs parlour and the front hall. "We don't use them, that's why they're so bloody cold."

They went back through to the side passage. "We call this the hall, and this is the living room."

Danny sat down on the settee. "Sit down, rest your legs. We'll go outside in a sec'." He looked at the boy. "Have you lived here long? I've never seen you before."

"Two years, a bit more."

Danny shook his head. "I must have seen you sometime." He rubbed his palm absently on his thigh. Washing the car had irritated it. It was itching like hell again. He saw the boy looking at his hand, the small exit scar on the back, and stopped.

The boy looked up. "I've seen you," he offered. "Up and down the road, y'know?"

"Yeah, all fucking day," Danny smiled.

"Half the girls in my year fancy you," the boy said, utterly unexpectedly.

Danny blinked.

Stephen blushed. Now why did he say a stupid thing like that? *God, what a flickin' stupid thing to say. Now he thinks you're a flickin' nutter.*

But Danny laughed, looked away, catching his lower lip between his teeth. He was embarrassed, could feel himself blushing. He was faintly amazed at his own reaction. Well, at least it proved he still knew how to blush. "Shit," he said, and he laughed again.

He got up suddenly. "Come on, I'll take you round outside."

Stephen was mortified. Maybe he didn't realise that girls went for him. You got folk like that. Look at Claire Shepherd, half the school after her and she never even noticed. He wished he hadn't said it.

Danny slid the heavy door of the milking shed back and reached round for the lights. He rumbled the door shut behind him. The cattle moved restlessly in the stalls.

"They're inside just now. We put them out again in May."

The smell was very strong. Stephen wrinkled his nose.

"Bit rich for you?"

Stephen nodded his head. A couple of the cows were lifting their tails, letting rip. The noise was like vomit pouring out. Danny laughed at his expression. "John said you'd worked at Westlands last summer."

"I did." The boy was defensive. "But I worked outside most of the time, on the crops, not with the beasts, like, you know?"

"Don't worry, you'll get used to them."

The cows watched them as they moved up the shed. Stephen narrowly missed being pissed on. "Watch..." Danny tugged his arm, grinning at him. "Now you know why we wear wellies."

"Sorry." Stephen pulled an apologetic face.

"Don't apologise to me. Just keep away from rear ends, and look out for rising tails."

He showed him how the milking equipment worked, told him how big the herd's yield was, explained the collection times, showed him where and how the tankers hitched up. He explained the silos, the slurry, the midden, the barns. Showed him the implement shed, the tractor shed. "Only two in just now. Ian and Rab are out in the others. Rab's got the big Ford. John usually drives that."

He went back out and shut the shed door. "Come on, it's fucking frozen. Let's get some tea or something."

They went back into the house.

"We've got almost half an hour before that lot are due in for lunch. What do you want, tea or coffee?" Danny was filling the kettle.

"Tea please."

Danny looked over his shoulder. "A man after my own heart."

Danny leaned back against the sink and waited for the kettle to boil. The boy was looking at the table. He looked uncomfortable.

"It hasn't put you off?"

"No." He jerked his head up. "Not at all."

"It's not as bad as it looks. You'll learn it easier than you think, and you won't have to drive the tractors for a couple of years yet. Maybe in the fields occasionally, that's all, so John can't exploit you to death." Danny filled the teapot and brought it over.

Stephen smiled at him. "Just a bit nervous I think, you know?"

Danny nodded. He pushed a packet of biscuits over to him. Stephen looked at his hand curiously. "What happened?"

Danny looked down at it, turned it palm up. The boy gazed at the scar, much bigger, uglier on the palm. "It was a knife," Danny said. "Right through and out the other side." He laughed at the boy's expression. "It was an accident. We were fooling around, and that's what happened." He rubbed his index finger. "I still can't feel properly with this finger. It damaged a nerve."

The boy shuddered. He looked at the fine red-gold hair on Danny's arms. It made his skin a funny colour, like the cream on top of a milk bottle.

Danny scratched his palm, shattering Stephen's reverie. "It fucking itches. It really does."

"It looks like a mouth."

Danny looked at it. "It does, doesn't it?"

John came in the door. "Hello, skiving off already?"

Stephen flushed.

"Give the boy a break." Danny smiled at him encouragingly.

John asked him what they'd been doing. Danny told him. John sat down and pulled off his boots. "Where's Ian?"

Danny looked at the clock. "He should be in, in a minute."

"I'm starving. I suppose it's fucking soup again."

Danny nodded.

John turned to Stephen. "I'll be glad when your mother moves in on us. I hope she's a good cook."

Stephen nodded enthusiastically.

"Well, she can't be any worse than Ian," Danny offered, getting up.

"Or more boring than Ostler."

Danny laughed.

Ian came in, then Rab. Rab caught the boy's eyes briefly then looked away.

Danny saw it, saw the boy's blush. What the hell was this about?

They sat down to eat, talking intermittently. Eventually Rab and Ian went back out. John went upstairs to change. Danny and Stephen cleared the table, washed the dishes.

John came back in as Danny was rubbing his front with a towel. He was laughing, the boy laughing with him. Danny looked up and his smile faded. John was watching him, hard-faced. The boy looked from one to the other confusedly, then John Jackson Moore said, "I'm going. Shall I give him your love?"

Danny stared back at him. Suddenly they both seemed intensely unfriendly with

each other. "Don't bother."

John laughed and walked across the floor. He patted his brother's cheek, let his hand lie there a moment. "Be good Danny."

"I'm always good, John."

He patted him again. It was almost a playful slap, that wasn't very playful. Stephen watched him go out the door. He suddenly felt terribly homesick.

And stupidly, irrationally afraid.

Danny took him out in the field buggy. Stephen hung onto his back as they hurtled over the frozen fields. The churned ground was frozen solid and they thumped and bumped like a fairground ride, the balloon tyres taking the worst of the impact. They bumped up to the crest of the last field and stopped, looking down over the sea.

"This is the extreme western edge of our land. We've got more to the east, not so much to the south, and only a few fields at the back." Danny looked down. "You can let go now."

Stephen pulled his hands off. "Sorry."

Danny got off the buggy and stretched his legs. "Come here." He pulled Stephen in front of him, hands on his shoulders. "See over there?" He pointed directly along Stephen's left side. "At the foot of the mountain? That's Abbeytown, that white beach. This is the only point in the village where you can see it."

"Where?"

"There... no, there... to the left, see?" Danny turned his head with his hands. Stephen could smell soap off him, feel the heat of his hand on his cheek. Now he couldn't concentrate at all.

Danny let him go and said, "Come on, let's get back."

Danny got on and waited for Stephen to climb on behind him. Stephen held his shoulders lightly with a new and uncomfortable awareness.

Danny smiled and pushed down on the accelerator. Stephen yelped and grabbed him tight, hanging on like grim death.

Within minutes they were laughing again, hurtling back over the fields.

John parked the car, got a ticket from the machine, peeled off the backing, and slapped it on the windscreen. He crossed the road and went up the worn steps.

Dorothy smiled at him in recognition. "Mr Whymper?"

"No, Mr Conley."

Dorothy looked nonplussed. "Oh..." She turned in her seat. "Well you want the room at the end. His secretary's just in there. Go right in."

John went along the small passage and opened the door. Molly looked up, smiled. It felt like smiling at a grizzly bear - faintly unnecessary, probably provoking.

"I've got an appointment with James Conley, for two o'clock."

"Ah yes, Mr..." She glanced at the diary but he furnished it for her.

"Jackson Moore. John Jackson Moore."

"I'll just let him know you're here, Mr Moore." She got up and went through another door.

John looked round the room. The ceilings were so fucking low he was practically scraping his head on them.

Molly knocked and went in. She closed the door behind her as if she was keeping out the advancing hordes. "Mr Moore's here."

James smiled at her. "Funny how I could tell that by your face."

"He's eating the furniture in my office right now."

Conley threw his head back and laughed, choking it off abruptly. "No, don't, I've got to deal with him. How am I going to do that if you start giving me flak?"

"Where did you *find* him?" Her eyes were like saucers.

"He found me... sort of. You know, I'm not really sure now you come to mention it."

"If I hear disembowelling noises should I try to save you or phone the police?"

Conley smiled again. "Just show him in and less of the comedy. Oh, and Molly, his name's *Jackson* Moore. He doesn't like people abbreviating him."

She made huge eyes at him and went out again. A minute later she reappeared. John Jackson Moore came in behind her and smiled at him. Molly withdrew.

Then he reached out his hand.

Conley looked at it.

His hands were huge, disproportionately big, even on him.

Conley felt sweat start under his arms. John Jackson Moore was grinning at him, challenging him. He knew. Danny must have told him.

Conley reached out, made himself do it. He saw his own hand, dead, white, like something going to the slaughter.

John Jackson Moore took it, grasped it like a snake, fangs down and in, clamped it in his jaws.

Conley panicked. John Jackson Moore held him rigid, gripped tight, grinning at him. "Let go," Conley hissed. "Let go of me."

He let go and sat down, leaving Conley standing there, grey and shaking like a fool. He fumbled back towards his seat and slumped down.

"You *are* frigid."

Conley wasn't sure he'd heard him properly. He had stopped smiling, hidden his teeth. "I beg your pardon?"

"You could try, but it wouldn't work."

Conley looked at him blankly. He felt as if they were talking a different language. "I'm sorry?"

This time John Jackson Moore said nothing. He just sat there and waited. Conley took a deep breath. He'd been nicely out-manoeuvred. Alright, the battle wasn't lost yet. But before he could speak John Jackson Moore said, "Whatever she wants the answer's no."

Conley looked at him and finally broke the surface, dragged the air and life back into himself. "Then why did you bother to come here today?"

"To see you." And he was smiling again. "To see what it is Danny finds so fucking irresistible."

Conley felt himself go under again, being dragged down. He looked at John Jackson Moore's hands, and could almost see Danny under them. He could imagine the two of them, wrapped in that intensity, consuming each other like big cats mating, teeth embedded in each other's necks. He felt his skin flush horribly.

"Maybe you've got something I can't see, is that it?" And he looked down at the desk top as if he could see right through it. And Conley saw something even more disturbing, a glimpse of Danny in him, a faint resemblance about the eyes, the way he looked at you. They were the same startling colour, he noticed. He was like a child's bad drawing of Danny, a rough ugly sketch, full of broad lines and energy.

"*Have* you got something I don't know about?"

"I don't know what you're talking about." Conley forced it out.

"Oh, but you can guess surely?"

"No I can't. If you've got something to say I'd appreciate you saying it and then you can get out."

John Jackson Moore's smile faded as quickly as if it had never been. He leaned across the desk. "I'm talking about you and Danny. I'm talking about you and Danny

fucking. Ah, you know what fucking is I see. Frigid or no, you're not too sodding refined to know what fucking is. I'm talking about you playing the fucking Christmas fairy with my young brother, who's still underage." He paused and dropped his voice a little further. "And I'm talking about making you eat your own dick if you ever see him, or talk to him, or even *think* about him ever again. Do I make myself quite clear?"

Conley stared at him, pinned to his chair by the icy determination in his voice. He felt as if the office was closing in on him and at any moment he'd lean over and grab him. Those huge hands choking the life out of him.

"Say yes Mr Conley then you and I can part forever."

"Yes." Conley whispered it.

"Good. And you can tell Miss Henderson from me that if she doesn't get off my back she'll be joining her brother at the Policeman's Celestial Academy."

He stood up. "Don't bother to shake hands Mr Conley, I'm fussy about who I touch."

And he grinned once more, briefly, in case Conley had missed all the other times, and went out the door.

Danny went for a pee then went along to Stephen's room. It didn't feel right to be knocking on his own door.

Stephen opened it, smiling uncertainly.

"Okay?"

"Yeah." He looked around the room. "My clothes don't even fill one drawer."

"You're going to need more." Danny looked in the wardrobe. "I told you you could get rid of these fucking things."

"They're alright. I don't need the room, honestly."

Danny looked at him consideringly. "They'd maybe fit you. They're only work shirts after all. Or do you hate wearing hand-me-downs?"

"No." Stephen spoke too eagerly and tried to tone it down. "I don't mind."

"Well, try them on then." Danny threw him one over. Stephen pulled his jumper off and unfastened his shirt.

"Jesus, this needs the fucking bin," Danny muttered and came out with a faded denim shirt. Two huge green-brown stains marked the front. He looked at Stephen. Stephen blushed, suddenly ashamed of his white hairless chest, his lack of muscles.

Danny looked away, realising it was embarrassing him. He threw the shirt in the bin and started rummaging again. He dispensed with one more. "These all look okay. That's four."

He turned back again. "How does it fit? Hey, not bad. You must be about the same size I was at your age." He looked at him critically. "No, you're definitely broader. I was skinnier."

Stephen looked at Danny's narrow hips and immediately wished he was skinnier too. He'd like to have been exactly the same size.

"Here, have a look in the mirror." Danny swung the wardrobe door back. Stephen stood in front of it and looked at himself. The shirt was a good fit, warm brushed cotton. The red looked a bit vivid on him, but the others would be better.

"Same colouring, that's why you suit them." Danny smiled over his shoulder at him in the mirror.

Stephen looked at his face, the white teeth, the deep red hair and said, "Mine's ginger, it's pathetic."

"It's not that bad."

"I hate it, and the flickin' freckles." He looked back at him. "You haven't got any." He said it as if Danny had done it purposely.

"I get them in summer."

"Yeah, well, I'm stuck with them all year." *And I don't have your green eyes, or the white teeth, or any of the rest of it either. Like I don't have half the flickin' women in the village panting after me.* "All I've got is this joke-shop ginger mop. I hate it, " he said again.

Danny laughed. "For God's sake try the others on, you're depressing me."

Stephen blushed again. "Sorry," he mumbled. Danny took the red shirt from him and hung it up.

Only one of them proved a little too tight. Danny threw it in the bin. "Well, that's saved you a few quid. Have you got any money to get some stuff?"

Stephen looked at his feet. "Not really, my mam's a bit short just now."

"No sweat, we'll get John to sub you some. You can pay it back as you go, little a week or something. That be okay?"

"Great."

"Good. We'll see if we can worm him into giving us tomorrow off and we'll go into Carlisle."

"Great," Stephen said again.

Danny closed the wardrobe. Stephen fixed his collar and asked, "How old are you?"

"Twenty, why?" He came round scratching his nose.

"You seem older."

Danny shook his head. "Nope, I'm definitely twenty. Only just had a birthday a month ago so I can't have forgotten it."

Stephen smiled at him. "You seem older though."

"It's working in this place. By the end of the week you'll be getting grey at the temples."

Stephen laughed again.

"Let's go down and make soup for the multitude," Danny went out the door, Stephen following, "...or maybe cold meat."

The door closed on Danny's old room.

After dinner that evening Danny took Stephen upstairs to show him how the shower worked.

Danny had asked John if they could go into Carlisle tomorrow for some clothes. He'd agreed irritably and lapsed back into a sullen silence. Danny knew he'd have to wait till they were in bed before John told him what had happened - if he told him.

"It's a real cracker, isn't it?"

Danny looked at it. "I'm used to it, although we haven't always had one. It makes a big difference with so many people to wash, and all stinking."

"We don't have one at home."

"Well, you'll have to get used to going last, unless you want your arm broken. It'll be a nice change for me to move up the pecking order." But Danny knew that was no longer true. Moving into your big brother's bed changed your status in life, especially when he was calling the shots. He pushed his hands into his pockets and felt irritable for no reason he could pin down. Something like guilt made him say, "I'll let you skip the queue tonight, go ahead of me."

"You sure?"

"Yeah, no sweat. Ian's had his and Rab's already gone out."

"Don't you go to the pub then?"

"No." Danny looked over at the door and added, "I need my beauty sleep."

Stephen nodded as if he understood but he didn't. He wished he could go over and

have a drink like everybody else did. Danny said, "Okay then?"

Stephen nodded.

"I'll leave you to it then." And he went out.

Stephen locked the door and took his clothes off, laying them over the chair. He got the shower just right and climbed in. He altered the controls, tried the different sprays, but went back to the fine needle.

He rubbed his face then looked at the soaps. He picked each one up and smelt it. Why three bars? There was only ever one at home. He liked the brown one, it smelt of spice-cake. He rubbed it over his chest. It was strong and pungent, vaguely familiar.

He washed twice and stood under the spray. God, he was probably using all the water up - his mam went daft when he did that - and Danny hadn't had his yet. He reached for the shampoo. Only one bottle this time. He looked at it. Oil of Almond. He grimaced, poured some on his hair straight from the bottle. Too much as usual. Mm, not bad.

He lathered it up then rinsed it out. Once would do. He showered down again briefly then regretfully turned off the taps.

He opened the cubicle and found a half-dry towel. He rubbed his hair with a none-too-clean hand towel. He wished suddenly that his mam wasn't coming here and immediately felt disloyal. He scrubbed his hair vigorously. He was still living away from home, wasn't he? She wasn't going to live here. He lived here. He smiled, knotted the towel tighter, picked up his clothes and went out.

Rab was standing with his hand on his bedroom door. He looked at him and took the cigarette out of his mouth. Stephen stood there like a sick sheep.

"Come in a minute." Rab pushed open his door.

Stephen looked at the open doorway as if it was the gates of Hell. "I..." It was all he managed. He didn't want to go in there with him and he didn't know how to say it.

Rab looked at him and said stiffly, "I'm not a fucking rapist you know."

Stephen blushed deeply, intensely embarrassed. He went into Rab's room, head down, plunging into the breach.

Rab shut the door and sat down on the bed. "Take the armchair, then you're nearest the door."

"I didn't say anything," Stephen blurted out, face hot again.

"You didn't need to, it was written all over your face." Rab stubbed out his cigarette and wiped his hair back off his face, rubbing his temples.

He started rolling a fresh one. Stephen watched the deft movements. Rab lit it and looked up. "You've been using my soap."

Stephen flushed all over again. Now he knew where he'd smelt it before. "I didn't know, it was just lying there."

Rab shook his head. "Don't sweat it, it hasn't got my fucking name stamped on it. Use it if you want."

"I won't use it again." The boy's face was tight. Rab knew what he was telling him. I wouldn't use it again if you made me, not if it's anything to do with you.

"Listen..." Rab looked at the floor. Stephen was starting to shiver, the towels were wet. "What happened last Saturday, it was my fault." Rab looked up, saw him clenched and shivering. "For God's sake, put your shirt on."

Stephen looked blank for a moment then pulled the shirt from the bundle in his lap. He slipped it on and immediately felt better.

"Like I was saying, it was my fault. It was a stupid thing to do." He looked up but the boy wouldn't meet his eyes. "Look, what I'm saying is, you must have done stupid things in your time, put it down to experience. We've got to work together. We don't

need any aggravation. Are you listening to me?" Rab finished in exasperation.

Stephen picked at a loose thread in the towel. "It was my fault too," he said, stung to honesty. "I got pissed."

"Everybody gets pissed sometimes. It was just a different way of putting a lampshade on your head. It only feels worse because it's not the sort of thing you're supposed to do. It didn't mean anything, okay?"

"Okay," Stephen murmured.

"No, don't just say it, is it okay? Or do you want to call me names or something? Whatever it is get it off your chest."

"I knew what I was doing."

Rab looked at the top of his head. "Now you're feeling sorry for yourself. If you'd been sober you wouldn't have done it, would you?"

Stephen shook his head.

"So okay, no sweat."

But the boy still wouldn't look at him.

"Look, what's up? The sooner you tell me, the sooner we can forget this."

"You'd done it before. You said to me..."

Rab held up his hand. "No, don't tell me what I said. Look, Steve, I was drunk too. Can't you just leave it at that?"

This time his head did come up. "You said I was to get it off my chest, now you don't want to know." His face was accusing.

God spare us adolescent trauma, Rab thought. "Alright," he kept his eyes level, "so I had done it before. I have. So what?"

"Jeez." Stephen rubbed his face. "How can you do all that queer stuff?" Then his eyes slid away again. "Are you?"

"Am I what?" Rab's voice was clipped.

"Queer." Stephen kept his head down hard.

Say yes. Say yes and really put the shit up the little fucker. "No," he said. "It's just something that happens sometimes. When you're pissed it seems as good a way of getting your rocks off as any. A farm, it's like the army, or prison, you know?"

Stephen nodded, met his eyes finally. Rab could see the relief in them, the subtle alteration of trust. He was no longer the enemy. Not a friend - he wasn't ever going to be that - but not an enemy. "Okay now?"

Stephen nodded. He stood up.

Rab smiled at him. It cost him, that smile.

Stephen smiled back, tentatively.

A truce.

Stephen put his jeans back on then one of Danny's shirts. It looked better on him than the red one. He decided he didn't like new clothes. He liked them worn like this, washed-in. This one was great. The cuffs were soft, slightly frayed at the edges. The inside of the collar was faded as if it had been scrubbed too often. He peered inside the pocket. The fabric was a different colour inside, a nut brown with deep blue lines making the check.

He looked in the mirror. Now it looked like fudge, the blue lines almost grey. He'd never had a brushed cotton shirt before. Why had his mam never bought him one before? He looked alright in it, older. They were warm too. They all wore them, except Rab. He seemed to wear everything in denim. How many others had he done that with? God, how could he? Putting another bloke's tool in your mouth. Yuk.

He turned and looked at the back. God, why was he such a short-arse? They all outstripped him by a foot or more. Well, John did anyway. He'd never get used to

calling him John. Like those teachers you got that wanted to be called by their first names. Maybe once he knew him better. He was a moody sod though, smiling one minute then scowling the next.

He opened the curtains and looked outside at the green, the lit pub. He wished he could go over for a drink. He wondered briefly where Danny was. He ran his fingers over the chest of drawers then saw that Danny had carved his name on the top. It was almost worn away. He smiled. He'd done that once too. His mam had nearly killed him.

He opened the other drawers, tugging the last when it stuck and causing one corner to fall on the floor. "Shit," he grunted as it dropped on his foot. Well, Danny had warned him. He struggled and finally got it back in, but not without trapping his fingers first.

He stood up. He wanted to go downstairs, maybe watch TV, but he was scared. Maybe he wouldn't be welcome. *Oh come on Steve-o let's go, go, go.*

Stephen opened the door and headed downstairs.

Danny sat down on the armchair and looked at John. John kept his eyes on the screen. "Come and sit." He patted his stomach.

Danny got up and crossed to the settee and knelt astride him. John shifted slightly to let him on. "Now you can't see the TV," Danny said.

"I can, but I want to look at you anyway. Where's the boy?"

"He's in the shower."

John slid his hand inside Danny's shirt and began rubbing his stomach.

"Well?" Danny asked.

"Well what?"

"You know what. What did Conley say?"

"Nothing."

"Nothing?"

"Nothing."

Danny looked at him, trying to read his face.

John smiled. "Ask me what I said."

"Alright then, what did you say?"

"I told him to leave you alone. I told him I'd make him eat his own dick if he so much as thought about you."

"Oh Jesus, John." Danny climbed off him.

John caught his arm. "What is it? Frightened I upset him?"

"I'll bet you fucking upset him. What about this Henderson business?"

"What about it?"

"What's she going to do?"

"Nothing, if I know her."

"Didn't he say?"

"He didn't get a chance."

"Christ John, it's important. She could tell someone, *do* something."

John's hand was rubbing Danny's wrist. "Want me to slit her throat?"

Danny pulled his hand away.

"Oh not squeamish Danny, surely not squeamish?"

"If you didn't go around cutting people's throats we wouldn't be in this fucking position."

John yanked his arm, bringing him half-down on top of him. "No, if you didn't go getting your dick into everything you met we wouldn't be in this position."

"Your fucking temper John."

"Your fucking whoring."

They glared at each other for a moment then John pulled him down and kissed his mouth. After a moment Danny pulled away from him. "You're going to have to pack this in."

"What?"

"You know what. Just grabbing it when you feel like it."

"Why?"

"You know why."

"I thought you said he was in the shower?"

"He probably is, but he might not be. Or he might finish quickly, or change his mind, or a hundred other things."

"I'll do what I want, when I want."

"Oh grow up John."

John yanked him down again, this time shoving him back flat and pinning him with his weight. By the time he was finished they were both breathing heavily. John slid his hand down between them. "Want to?" he whispered.

Danny thought about how long it took to shower then reached down and started to unfasten John's jeans.

John held them together at the final moment, watching them boil out simultaneously, beautifully synchronised. Danny watched John's face, narrow-eyed, intense with his own pleasure. They were kneeling on the floor front to front, cock to cock.

John sucked briefly on Danny's bottom lip. "Good?"

Danny smiled. "It's dripping on the fucking carpet."

John laughed. "And the paper hankies are out of reach." He rummaged in his pocket and brought out his own handkerchief. "I hope someone buys me some of these for Christmas."

"Unhygienic."

"It's wiping you up, smart-alec. Anyway, the paper ones rip."

"You're disgusting."

Danny watched him mopping him up, the callused hands roughly gentle.

John kissed him again, perfunctorily. They heard a door close upstairs.

Danny got up, pushing himself inside his clothes. John grinned and sat back on his heels. Danny bent down and shoved him back inside his clothes, grabbing the hankie and throwing it in the fire.

"Hoi!"

"Christ, you can't put it in the bloody wash John… and zip up."

"Why not? I'm sure she's seen spunk before."

"On a hankie? Zip *up*."

John got up and zipped up his jeans, dropping back heavily onto the settee. "The rabbit probably does it in a hankie every night."

"The rabbit?"

But John didn't get a chance to say anything because the door opened and Stephen came in. He smiled tentatively.

Danny smiled back at him. John stood up, stretching stiffly. "Must take a piss." And he went past him and out into the hall.

Danny was standing in front of the fire tucking his shirt in.

Stephen looked at him curiously. All round his mouth was red, as if he'd been scrubbing at it with something rough.

"Something wrong?" Danny asked.

Stephen flushed. "No, I was just wondering how you cut your lip," he lied.

"John hit me."

Stephen gaped at him.

Danny smiled. "Kidding." And he smiled some more to show that nothing really bad ever happened in this world.

"He's big, isn't he?"

Danny smiled oddly. "Very. It doesn't do to annoy him, you know?" He was teasing but Stephen took it quite seriously.

"Oh I won't." He almost said, I'll be good, but managed to stop himself in time.

"Does he frighten you?" Danny asked.

"No." Stephen looked up. Danny was smiling at him, knowingly, as if he could see right through him. "Well, maybe a bit," he conceded.

"Don't let him worry you, he's not as bad as he looks." *Christ Danny, how can you lie like this?*

"When I told my mates I was coming here one of them, Jammy we call him, said, 'Watch out Steve-o, he did away with his Da'." Stephen laughed, a little uncomfortably.

Danny kept the smile there somehow, even although he felt his gut clench violently.

Stephen looked at him and sensed that maybe he shouldn't have said that. Maybe they were frightened their dad was lying dead in a ditch somewhere. He realised he'd been tactless... yet again. "Sorry, maybe I shouldn't have said that."

"No, he's got a reputation to maintain. I'll tell him. It'll amuse him."

Stephen looked relieved.

John came back in. He was shrugging into a jacket. "I've got to go down the back fields. I want to check out that gate. It's supposed to be fixed but knowing Armstrong's sub-contractors I fucking doubt it. D'you want to come?"

"No, I'm staying put. It's too fucking cold out there."

John looked at Stephen briefly then went out again.

Danny restored the volume on the TV. "Anything you want to watch?" He threw Stephen the remote control. "Here, you pick. I never really care what I watch."

"No, me neither, it's all a load of rubbish." But Danny saw that he knew exactly what he wanted. Well, he'd be watching a lot less television in a few months time. He might as well make the most of it now.

The phone rang.

"Your mum?" Danny asked.

Stephen shook his head.

Danny went out to answer it.

James Conley had a bad day. It had been bad before John Jackson Moore arrived and it was worse after. He was glad it was a Friday. He finished up early and went upstairs. He locked his front door as if he was barricading himself in, or the world out.

He went into the kitchen and poured himself a glass of rum. He cut himself a piece of cake and took them both through to the living room. He sat down and looked at the phone. He ate the cake slowly, breaking the pieces with his fingers, enjoying it in his mouth. He washed it down with rum. Afterwards he felt a little better.

But not much.

He should have realised of course. He'd been so naïve to imagine that he would have behaved any other way. He was so jealous of everyone he'd imagine - Conley balked at the word affairs - relationships, situations, everywhere. But to let him humiliate him like that. He felt so stupid.

How could Danny tolerate him? That made love to him? How could he ever aspire to anything that wasn't rutting or raping? *God, I sound like a bloody old queen.* He ran his hands through his hair. *Is that what I've become, a middle-aged closet queen?*

He looked at the phone again. He might as well phone her, get it over with. He might as well tell her to scrub his fee too. She'd probably refuse to pay it anyway.

He bent forward and dialled Katherine Henderson's number.

She took her time to answer. "Hello?" She sounded breathless.

"Hello, Miss Henderson, it's James Conley here."

"Hello... I've only just got in... hang on... let me sit down." There was a scuffling then she said, "Okay, fire away."

"No go, I'm afraid." He was amazed at how calm he sounded. "He said that whatever you wanted the answer was no and he threatened that if you didn't leave him alone..." he hesitated.

"Go, on, surprise me, what did he say?"

"Well, I can only say he threatened to kill you. I don't know how else to interpret it."

"Shit," came succinctly down the line at him. You said it, he thought.

"Do you want to take it to the police?" he asked. The question tasted like oily gun-metal in his mouth.

"What the hell for? That would get me exactly nothing. Less than nothing."

Conley felt the relief go through him and recognised it for exactly what it was. Relief that he would not have any blame in Danny's downfall - and relief that it might keep him within sight. "I'm sorry Miss Henderson, but I don't believe he ever had any intention of listening to me. His visit was purely to tell me where to get off, I'm sure of it."

"Oh, I believe you Mr Conley. Don't worry, I don't blame you. I know him."

Conley felt the rest of his anxiety fall away. He wasn't going to lose her or his fee. *Or Danny*, a little voice whispered. "So what will you do now?" he asked.

She sighed. "I'm not sure, to be honest. I'm beginning to wonder if I want him that much after all. A new dress might be simpler."

He said nothing.

She sighed again. "Never mind, I'll be in touch. If nothing else you make an effective go-between. At least he doesn't hate you the way he hates me."

Conley said nothing to that either.

"I'll speak to you again. Let me know if anything crops up that you think might be useful."

"I will, of course. Bye then."

"Bye." And she was gone.

Conley went to the bath and lay there watching the room outside get darker and darker. He'd taken to bathing with the candles lit. It was like a sickness, lying here, his excitement plain on his belly, and not being able to do anything to about it. Yet he kept doing it, like someone picking the scab off a wound, taking another look. It was almost like being ill all over again.

He got out of the bath and drained the water. He wrapped himself in a bath sheet and blew out the candles. Another rum or maybe some more cake, that's what he needed.

Other people went out on Friday nights, had a good time, ended up in cars, against walls in back alleys. Him, he sat at home and ate cake.

He went over to the kitchen and got some more cake, the rum bottle and a glass. He went back to the sofa. He threw Mamma a glacé cherry. She came down off the perch and began scuffling for it in the sand.

He poured himself a glass.

He looked at the phone. He turned and looked at the kitchen clock. Half eight. What would he be doing now? In bed with his brother? Maybe his cousin? A stranger?

How could you tell with him? How would you ever be able to tell?

Phone him.

He'll make you eat your own dick, remember? He probably knows how to do that.

Phone him.

What if it isn't him?

Hang up.

What if it's his brother?

Hang up.

Conley reached over and dialled the number slowly, listening to each whirr like bullets spinning in the chamber of a gun. He could feel his mouth getting drier and drier. He wanted to take a drink but knew there would be no time.

The number connected. Conley closed his eyes.

He began to replace the receiver, heard the rings grow more distant.

"Hello?" He heard the voice, tiny, distant, half-way across the room. "Hello?" it said again. He brought it back. "Hello?" Danny said in his ear.

"Danny," he said quickly before he could change his mind.

Danny didn't answer him.

"Danny... it's James Conley."

Danny said hello for the third time, but there was no reply. A wrong number maybe and yet he could sense someone at the other end of the line, almost feel their breathing. He was about to say hello again, once more, for luck, just to let them know he knew they were there, when someone said his name, clear and soft in his ear.

There was a pause, long, hissing, then the voice said, "Danny... it's James Conley. If I said it didn't matter..." he paused, "If I said that none of it mattered." He took a breath and tried again. "If I said I would... would you reconsider? If I promise to do whatever I need to... to give you..."

"Don't say anything else," Danny said and could feel his heart climbing up into his throat. He stood for a moment watching the colour on the door, always fascinated with it. There was an absolute stillness at the other end, like the sound it makes when you wait for the stone to hit the bottom of the well. "I shouldn't have asked," he said finally.

"Danny..."

"No, listen, I was... well, never mind what I was, I shouldn't have asked."

"Come round."

"I can't, you know that."

"I saw your brother today. He told me he was going to feed me my own dick if I so much as thought about you."

"So you phoned me?" Danny smiled.

"So I phoned you." He paused. "Danny, please."

"Listen, it's a physical impossibility. I can't even get out the house. You're lucky he's not in at the moment."

"When then?"

Danny laughed shortly. "Convincing you, amn't I?"

"*Danny*," Conley said pleadingly.

"Okay, I'm going to Carlisle tomorrow. I can take a detour, but I can't stay."

"Danny... Katherine Henderson..."

"What about her?"

But Conley didn't say it. He pulled it back. "Nothing, it'll keep. When tomorrow?"

"I don't know, expect me when you see me."

"Danny?"

"Yes?"

"How do you bring yourself off?"

Danny went back into the living room. Stephen looked up from his programme briefly then turned back. He didn't ask who it was, but then why should he?

Danny sat down beside him and stretched his feet out to the fire. They were like lumps of ice. He sat there thinking about Conley, about what he had offered him, and he couldn't think of a single motherfucking way to do it.

"It's good, isn't it?"

"What?"

"This," Stephen said, pointing at the TV.

"I wasn't watching it," Danny confessed.

Stephen looked at him curiously.

"I was thinking," Danny offered.

"What about?"

"John."

"Oh," Stephen said and looked back at the TV again.

He would have to tell the boy, think of some plausible reason why he shouldn't tell John where they'd been. Jesus, it was all so fucking fragile. *One wrong move and you're in shit street Danny. There isn't a fuck alive worth this.* Oh yes there is. There's Conley, mouth full of violets and gold. Imagine lying under that bleeding Christ, impaling him on your shaft, so shit scared and trembling. The long polished ivory of his dick, bare like that, always peeled back, poking up hungrily in that pelt of dirty blonde hair. His hollow stomach, the thin hard ribs, the nipples dry and brown. The robotic voice, the dead eyes. God if he wasn't a fuck worth dying for nobody was. He might never pass his way again. There had to be a way, and the boy would have to help him. The boy *would* help him or Danny would die.

Just die.

FIFTY-SEVEN

Stephen spent his first morning milking half asleep. When he had asked Danny how he coped with getting up at this time every morning Danny laughed and told him it was an hour earlier in the summer. Stephen looked at him aghast and hoped he was joking.

They went back into the house and had breakfast then John took him out with him in the pick-up.

Danny went into town with Ian to pick up wood for shelving. They went in the tractor, Danny standing on the back, Ian driving.

They were waiting in the workshop for the wood to be cut.

"You seem to have hit it off with our Stephen."

"Mm," Danny grunted. He was absently watching some joiners selecting panels of laminate.

"Fancy him?"

Danny turned slowly. "I'll pretend you didn't say that."

"Oh come on, you going to tell me you never got a letch for some kid?"

"I haven't as it so happens."

"You should try it."

"You should shut up."

"Maybe I should have a taste myself, seeing as how Rab has."

Danny looked at him. "What d'you mean?"

Ian smiled, a repulsive half-born thing that disfigured his face. "Ask him."

"Yeah, right."

Ian smiled again and followed his eyes as he looked away. "Danny?"

"What?"

"Let me fuck you again."

"*Jesus*..." Danny hissed under his breath. "We are in the middle of a fucking lumber yard Ian, in case you hadn't noticed. Keep your frigging voice down."

Ian looked at the joiners. "What's so fascinating?"

"Nothing."

"Which one?"

"Fuck off."

"Come on, which?"

"The young one… there."

Ian laughed softly. "You've got a curious weakness for blondes Danny. Summertime John?"

Danny didn't answer that.

"Reckon you could make him?" Ian asked curiously.

"I'm not going to try."

"Who would you rather have, him or the girl?"

"What girl?"

"Oh ha ha, the brunette that stakes you out every time we come in here. The one you were drooling over till he distracted you."

Danny said quite seriously, "Neither. I would never have sex with anyone I didn't love."

It took Ian a second then he laughed loudly. The joiners turned and looked at them. Danny turned away.

"Would you?" Danny asked.

Ian laughed again then said dryly, "I'm a faggot, remember?"

Danny smiled then, slow and lazy. It curved over his mouth like an oil slick. "How could I forget?"

And he turned away, still smiling, and leaned back against the counter and folded his arms.

"Why don't you have a try?"

"What?" Danny grunted as he pushed the wooden planks onto the trailer.

"With the blonde."

"Give over."

"No seriously, I'd love to see you in action."

"So you could report back to John?"

"If you like."

Danny shot him a sharp glance then said irritably, "Anyway, how the fuck would I get off with him in five minutes in a lumber yard?"

"I don't know. You're the expert, you tell me."

Danny leaned, palms down, on the back of the trailer. Ian was looking away from him, watching the joiners carrying the sheets of laminate out to their truck. "Ian, what is this about?"

"Let's call it an experiment. Everybody thinks it's your looks, but I don't think that's what does it. You've got something more, something that makes people forget who they are. He looks straight to me."

"Can you tell by looking?" Danny was sarcastic.

"Takes one to know one, right? I mean, I'd never pick you out." Ian looked him straight in the eye.

"My my," Danny said in a low voice.

"What d'you think, straight?"

Danny turned slowly and looked at the blonde boy. He nodded briefly, turned back again.

"Go on then, see if you can do it."

"Ian, there is no magic in what I do. You know that. I pick the right time, the right place, the right people. None of those things are right here. What do you want me to do, get my head kicked in?"

Ian moved closer, turned to face him. "Don't give me that. You take plenty of risks. You take them all the time. That's what keeps John in line."

"Yeah, but not when they outnumber me four to one."

"He keeps looking over here."

"I'm not fucking surprised the way you've been eyeing him up since we got here. Come on, let's get back in."

They went back into the yard. The brunette told them the rest of the order wouldn't be long. Danny smiled at her. She smiled back.

"You could have her," Ian whispered as she moved off.

"Shit Ian, give it up."

"You could."

"Yeah, if I took her out somewhere, not in the middle of the fucking workshop."

"Ask her out then."

"Don't talk fucking stupid, and have John make me into jam?"

"You take the same risk with Conley."

Danny looked at him, gaze steady. "Not the same, no how, and I *want* Conley."

"But not her?"

"Not enough."

"And the blonde?"

"Not enough."

"He appeals more though, doesn't he, than her?"

"Christ, what a relentless little bastard you are."

"Doesn't he?"

"*Yes,*" Danny hissed in his face. "Okay? Yes."

"Why?"

"Because I could have her any day of the week. He's different, okay?"

"Do it then."

"*No.*" Danny banged his fist on the counter.

The joiners looked up at them again. Ian smiled at them. Danny turned away hissing, "Now they think we're a pair of loonies out for the day. Give it a break, will you? Or I'll wrap a plank round your head."

Ian smiled and ostentatiously closed his mouth.

The joiners came over to the counter with a stack of wooden beading. Danny slid one way, Ian the other, to let them in. Danny found himself standing next to the blonde boy. He acknowledged him briefly then looked away but the boy turned to him and said, "You don't know if they've got a toilet round here?"

Danny nodded, turning his head to show where it was. "There's one straight through that door there, next to the petrol pump, just round by the stairs. Just turn left..." He looked at the boy's frown. "I'll show you, it's faster."

"Ta, I'm bursting for a leak, been drinking ale all morning."

Danny got up off the counter and walked ahead. The boy said to his back, "Do I know you?"

Danny looked over his shoulder. "Do you think you do?"

The boy looked away, discomfited by the sudden odd expression in the redhead's eyes.

"I saw you looking at me a couple of times. I thought maybe I should know you."

Danny laughed. To the boy it sounded off-key but he couldn't have defined it. "My brother was playing guessing games. Here it is..." Danny pushed the door open, pulled the light toggle. Nothing happened. "Light's gone."

"Piss," the boy said.

"Yeah, on your shoe."

The boy laughed. "Can you hold the door open for me?"

"Sure."

The boy went into the cubicle, leaving the door open. Danny heard his zip in the closed stillness, then the sound of him urinating. He looked out into the tiny yard beyond the iron stairs.

"Guessing what?" the boy called out suddenly.

"What? Oh, about your sex life."

The boy laughed. "My sex life?"

"Yeah."

"What about it?"

"Whether you'd ever done it with a boy."

"You mean homo?"

"I said no. You'd never have the nerve."

The boy was coming out, zipping up his jeans, looking at him. He moved towards the sink.

"Can I let this door go now?" Danny asked.

The boy nodded.

The door hissed slowly shut, plunging them into deep gloom lit only by two square panes of yellow plastic high in the wall. The boy tipped soap into his hand from a ball

above the sink. "What d'you mean I'd never have the nerve?"

"You're like everyone else in this place, a good solid Methodist boy. You'd never have the nerve."

"I'm not a Methodist, I don't even go to church, and for your information I did once, so looks like you were wrong, doesn't it?"

"When?"

"What?"

"How old were you?"

"Thirteen."

Danny laughed. "That's what I mean, solid Methodist through and through. You can't undo a man's background. What did you do, piss in the bushes together?"

"No, you know, just a bit of feeling."

"You mean you didn't even jerk off?"

"No. What d'you think I am?"

"See, I was right."

"Well I'm not a bloody poof, am I?"

"No, that's what I said." Danny grinned. The boy could see his teeth in the dark. "Anyway, you won me a fiver."

"You put money on it?"

"Of course I did, you're a safe bet."

"Fucking cheek."

"Aren't you?"

"No."

"Prove it."

And at that moment the boy became aware of the exact distances of the room, the smell of it, the exact face of the boy looking at him, the complete absence of noise from the yard.

"Here, now, prove it."

And the redhead's voice was curiously deep and thick, like it would stick to you or something, and the boy felt his heart start to gallop like he was being offered something, the chance of a lifetime maybe, if only he would jump across a bottomless chasm. Like those times when you were a kid and you knew you could jump the gap in the pier, the distance between the two graveyard walls, but still the fear froze your legs, and you wanted it, knew you could do it, knew it would give you a high all day, but the fear got to you, killed it dead. The boy swallowed.

"You can't, can you?"

"It's nothing to do with that."

"You're scared."

"I'm not."

"Well do it then." And the redhead came up to him, moved all those careful distances, got too close, until the boy found himself backing off, up against the sinks.

"See, you're scared shitless."

"I'm not. I'm not a bloody poof, that's all."

"Neither am I, but you don't see me running."

The boy licked his mouth. Danny gestured with his head to the cubicle.

The boy shook his head. "I cant, my mates... I've been gone too long as it is... they'll be waiting..."

Danny put his lips to the boy's ear. "*Chicken*..." he whispered.

The boy jerked his head away, turned abruptly and marched into the cubicle.

Danny undid the boy's zip, leaning into him just enough to keep him there.

He pushed his hand in. He wasn't erect. If anything he was the opposite, shrivelled into himself.

Danny smiled. "Relax, you might as well enjoy it."

"I don't think I can." The boy's voice was a thin whisper.

"Close your eyes," Danny said. "Come on, close them."

The boy closed his eyes.

"Right, now pretend I'm someone else, anyone... that's it... now you're getting it." Danny wet his mouth and whispered, "Now we'll do something really *dirty*." And he bent his head and kissed him.

The boy made a noise in his throat and tried to break free, but Danny pushed his body against his and kept kissing him. The boy went limp. Danny took his mouth away, began kissing the boy's throat. The boy had his head back against the wall. He was panting. Danny could feel the panicked pulse in his neck. Slowly, surely, just as Danny had known it would, the boy's penis began to blossom in his hand, in the aftermath of shock, in the relief of being free of Danny's mouth.

Danny went on kissing his neck, like thistledown, getting further into his flesh, his scent, until he could taste him. He began to move back towards the boy's mouth and this time the boy turned his head a little, moving towards the approaching kiss, lips parted, cock now monstrously swollen in Danny's hand. Their mouths met. He tasted of bitter ale and peppermint. His teeth were cool and hard. His tongue came to sudden life, pushed against Danny's, then into Danny's mouth.

Danny squeezed him gently, never taking his mouth away, making the boy giddy from lack of oxygen, and Danny knew with a sudden intense gratification that he wasn't thinking of anyone else. He was right there in the tiny stinking cubicle with him, pushing up into Danny's hand, enjoying the taste of Danny's mouth.

Danny jumped when he felt his hand on him. He felt the hand instantly withdraw. *Shit*. He kissed the boy gently, coaxing him back. He broke away from his mouth and began kissing his neck again, smelling wood shavings off him, other people's cigarettes.

The hand moved back again, cautiously. Danny pressed into it this time, gently, not forcing it. He felt it move up to his zip. He felt his own stomach do a slow flip of excitement. The zip was pulled down, the hand went in.

Squeezed him.

Danny almost came on his feet. He caught the boy's mouth again, kissed it with gratitude. He could smell the salt sex, damp in his hand, so hard it must be ready to blow its works. "Wank me off," he whispered. He felt the boy's cock jerk excitedly in his hand. "I'm going to bring you off while you do it," he promised.

The boy could hardly stand it. It was like a pain. He was so excited it was like it was stopping it getting out. He was going to burst, right here in this icy-dirty little toilet.

"Like it?" the voice whispered.

He chased after the redhead's mouth. His cock felt huge in his hand. He must be hung like a bloody horse. He felt him greedily.

The redhead evaded him again, whispered in his ear, "Tell me you like it."

The boy nodded.

"Want to come?"

The boy nodded again.

"Say please then."

The redhead was holding his cock tight round the base now, kissing round his mouth, but not *on* it. He tried to move his head so that he would kiss him but he kept moving away, and his prick was bursting he was holding it so tight. Why didn't he just wank him?

"Say please."

"Please."

"Say, please make me come."

"Please make me come."

As soon as the words were out the redhead began to pull him in long hard strokes. Immediately he could feel it locking his legs, stitching his belly. He moaned out loud. He could hear himself but he couldn't keep it in. Shaking like a leaf, he started to climax. But it wasn't until he felt the surge of the other boy's penis, the liquid suddenly sliding and slipping over his fist, that he moaned fitfully and cried out predictably, "Oh... *God.*"

And that was that.

Danny had marked his jeans. The boy had fared better. Danny pulled some of the hard shiny paper from the dispenser and did the best he could. He could see the boy trembling, his hands not working properly. Danny smiled and lifted the boy's chin. The boy looked at him, eyes trapped.

"Cheer up," Danny said, then winked. "*Now* you're a poof."

He unlocked the cubicle and went out leaving the boy alone in the dark.

Ian looked at him as he came across the floor. "The wood's on Danny. You ready to go?"

One of the joiners saw him and shouted, "Is our lad still out there?"

Danny nodded.

"He wants to stay off the bloody vindaloo." The joiners laughed.

"Let's go," Danny said.

Ian went out and got in the tractor. Danny climbed up onto the back, straddling the back bar. He could feel the slight tremble in his legs. It had been a strong one. He wiped his mouth.

Ian pulled out into the traffic. "You fucking did it, didn't you?"

"Talk sense Ian."

Ian pulled up to the traffic lights, turned in his seat. "You bloody did Danny, there's come on your frigging jeans."

Danny smiled.

"Jesus, I was only winding you up."

"Then you succeeded."

"Jesus," Ian said again.

Danny nodded, "They're green."

Ian pulled out, still muttering 'Jesus' under his breath.

Danny used the stand pipe in the milking shed to take off the worst of the marks before he went in. He could tell John he'd spilt ice cream on them, if he noticed.

But John wasn't in the kitchen.

"He had his lunch early," Rab said. "He's gone back out."

"Did he leave the keys?"

"They're hanging up." Rab nodded at the board.

Stephen was smiling at him.

"Did he remember to give you money?" Danny asked him.

Stephen nodded, a grin splitting his face in half. "He said I didn't need to pay it back."

Rab jerked his thumb. "Listen to this."

Stephen grinned some more.

Well, whatever had been wrong between these two was patched up. "We'll go as soon as I've eaten."

"I've finished."

Danny laughed. "Yeah, well you'll have to fucking wait."

Danny ate his meal rather faster than he would have normally. He couldn't stand the soulful face regarding him across the table.

He went upstairs to wash. He put his jeans on top of the over-full linen basket and put on his last clean pair. He ran his hands through his hair. *Don't you ever comb it Danny?* He smiled and did it again. At least it was growing back in.

He got his leather jacket out the wardrobe and pulled it on. Inside he found a matchbook from the Caldermouth pub… the barman with the wandering hands. Shame he hadn't bitten. He'd probably have melted like butter.

He smiled to himself, tucked the matchbook back in his pocket, and went out the door.

They pulled out into the Saturday traffic. It was quiet, almost as quiet as a Sunday, but the town would be busy. Too near Christmas for it to be anything else.

"Do you know what you want?"

"Yes." And Stephen rattled off a list.

"You forgot thermal vests."

"What?" Stephen looked at him.

"When you're out on the open tractor you'll need them, believe me. You'll wish you had fucking thermal everything. We've still got a David Brown, you know. John's got you earmarked for it already."

"No way."

"Trust me, buy a couple."

"Do you wear them?"

"You bet, look." And Danny undid his top button.

"That's a T-shirt."

"No it's not, it's a cunningly disguised thermal vest. Good old Damart."

"You sound like an advert."

"I am, they're sponsoring me. I get them free in return for getting all my friends to buy two each."

Stephen laughed. "No."

"Okay then," Danny shrugged. "On your tits be it." Then he added, "John wears thermal long-johns."

"You're joking." Stephen gaped at him.

After a moment Danny grinned.

"You bastard," Stephen said and looked at him again. "Rotten bastard."

The town was packed. Fortunately the army surplus stores were not. Stephen got what he wanted relatively easily and they went to an in-store restaurant for something to eat.

They drank a pot of brown hot water with a string hanging out the side and had two pieces of unidentifiable 'fruit' tart.

Stephen found he'd never had so much female attention in his life. He knew it was because of Danny, but somehow just being with him seemed to make a little of his aura rub off on him. He saw a side of Danny that he certainly didn't show at home, appraising every woman that went by, saying things about them that made Stephen

blush and laugh guiltily, even winking at one middle-aged woman in the queue. Danny was a flirt and maybe something a bit worse, although Stephen couldn't have told you exactly what. He went a bit over the top sometimes, as if he didn't know when to stop.

Danny sat forward suddenly and said, did he realise it would be the last time he'd eat in a restaurant until his clothes wore out? Stephen laughed but he suspected he might have been serious.

They went back down through the city's castellated walls to the car park. Danny got in and peeled the ticket off the screen. It took almost ten minutes to get out of the city centre.

They'd been on the road about twenty minutes when Danny said, "I'm going back via Caldermouth. I've got to see someone, okay?"

"Sure," Stephen said absently.

"I'll not be more than fifteen, twenty minutes, if that. Do you mind waiting in the car?"

"No, that's okay."

There was a pause then Danny said, "Listen Steve, this bloke I'm going to see... John doesn't like him."

Stephen looked at him.

"I'm not supposed to have anything to do with him, you know what I mean?"

Stephen nodded. He had friends like that too, that you couldn't have round at the house, that your mum didn't like.

"Well, don't let on to John where we were today. We just went to Carlisle and back, okay?"

"Sure."

Danny grinned. "Thanks."

Stephen felt the warm glow of being an ally, sharing a confidence. Already he knew something about Danny that John didn't. He smiled to himself and looked out of the window again.

He wished he could meet Danny's friend.

He'd probably like him too.

Danny parked round the back.

"This is private Danny," Stephen said, looking round him. "Jeez, look at that fucking car."

"I know, the guy I'm going to see owns it."

"Jeez, flickin' brilliant." Now he really wished he was going to meet him too. He wondered if he dare ask, but it was a bit soon. He didn't really know Danny that well. He'd better leave it.

"I won't be long," Danny said, reaching over the back for his jacket.

Stephen looked at the high line of his cheekbone as he turned and stretched back behind him and said, "You should get your ear pierced."

Danny laughed. "Yeah, right."

"No seriously, loads of my mates, well, my uncle's mates, have got theirs done and they're roofers. There's nothing poofy about it, loads of blokes do it. You'd suit it."

Danny shook his head. "I'm scared of needles. Anyway, John would have a fit. Okay, I'll be quick as I can."

"See you," Stephen replied.

Danny slammed the door and was gone.

Conley had told him to use the front door. They were having the fire escape

painted while the snow had cleared. Danny saw the signs propped up against the step.

He'd never used the front entrance. He took the stairs two at a time. The antiques market was busy with Christmas shoppers. He went on up to the floor where Conley worked. As he rounded the corner a woman came out of the office door. She looked at him strangely. "I'm afraid the office is closed. Were you looking for someone?"

She had to be one of Conley's secretaries. She had interfering bitch stamped all over her. "No," Danny said and let his eyes drop to her chest. When he saw her put her arms up, pretending to fiddle with the bow on her blouse, he slid past her and went on up the stairs. He heard her shout, "Excuse me!" behind him.

Molly shouted again but he ignored her. She went back quickly into the office.

Conley's phone rang exactly as the door went. He jumped, almost spilling his glass. He put it down and picked up the receiver. "Hold on..." he said tersely then went to answer the door.

He opened it. "Come in, I've just got someone on the phone. I won't be a sec'."

Danny followed him in and shut the door.

"Hello?" Conley said.

"Hello James, it's Molly. I was just on my way out but I've just passed the weirdest little creep going up your stairs. I tried to stop him but he just barged by me..."

Conley's face split into a huge grin. Danny watched him, wondering what was so funny.

"... I just thought I better warn you."

"He's a friend Molly."

There was a silence. "Oh."

Another silence. "Oh, I'm sorry James. It's just that... well, it is Saturday and... well, he was rather rude when I spoke to him. I'm terribly sorry."

"Don't worry about it."

"I feel terrible."

"No, honestly, it's okay."

"I would normally have been gone by now. I really am sorry."

"Forget it."

"I'll see you Monday then," she said lamely.

"Of course, bye."

"Bye." She hung up.

"Your receptionist," Danny said.

"What did you say to her?" Conley was still grinning.

Danny opened his arms. "Not a word. No, that's not true, I said no."

"Just no?"

"That's right." Danny smiled his dirty smile. "They prefer me to say yes. But I'll say this for her, she's got a pair of tits on her."

"Sometimes Danny you're in poor taste... and conceited with it."

"If you've got it, flaunt it."

"You're quoting."

Danny smiled but said nothing else. He looked round the room, breathed it in, smiled some more.

"What are you doing?" Conley asked.

"Getting high," Danny said.

"What on, floor polish?"

"The smell of you."

Conley felt the blood go straight to his face. "You say the damnedest things sometimes." He tried to smile. "And at the damnedest moments."

"Secret of my success."

They sat down on opposite settees.

"Want some…"

"Coffee," Danny finished.

They both laughed.

"No, I can't stay, I've got someone waiting outside."

"Who?"

"New boy, son of our new daily."

Conley felt the worst possible urge to say, And have you had him yet? He didn't even know why.

Danny looked over at him then said, "You can phone me, between seven-fifteen and quarter to eight. John's always out. But not Fridays."

Conley smiled, rubbed his head. "This isn't really happening to me."

Danny held his eyes. "Until we can work something out."

"This is pathetic. It really is."

"You wanted it. Quarter past seven to quarter to eight. Not Fridays. Will you remember that?"

Conley nodded.

Danny looked at him, the bottle on the table. "You drunk enough?"

Conley flushed, shook his head.

Danny kept looking at his face, trying to read it. "Do you want to do anything?"

Conley shook his head again.

"Fair enough, then I'll do what I want." And the same old voice was there.

Conley looked up sharply.

"Don't panic, I won't touch you. Go and put on one of your waistcoats."

Conley didn't move.

"Go on, hurry up. I haven't got all day."

Conley got up finally and drained his glass then went over to his room. When he came back he was tucking his shirt into his black trousers. He had on the garnet waistcoat that Katherine Henderson had so disliked.

"Sit down," Danny said.

Conley sat down.

"Velvet?" Danny asked.

"Of a sort."

"Are those beads on the buttons?"

"No, they're cut glass."

"Nice," Danny smiled then added, "You're too thin."

Conley asked, "What are you going to do?"

"I'm going to solve one of the world's great mysteries."

"What?"

"I'm going to show you how I bring myself off."

"That wasn't…"

"You wanted to know."

"I didn't mean that."

"Well watch and you might learn something." Danny undid his jacket, spread it wide, then he unfastened his shirt and slowly rolled his T-shirt up his chest. He slid down the seat a little.

Conley had been glancing over then looking away again. Danny nodded his head at the bottle. "Have some more of that."

He waited until Conley had poured himself some more rum then he began to unfasten his jeans. He pulled them open and tugged them down to his thighs.

Conley's mouth went dry.

Danny didn't touch himself, not for a full minute. He just lay there getting high on

Conley looking at him. Not that Conley *was* looking at him. Conley couldn't look at him. Conley was altogether too wrapped up in looking at it.

Danny began to masturbate, lightly, easily, no real involvement. Conley watched the slim white hand loose on its hard red heat.

"First today," Danny said. "It's hot to trot. Can't you tell?"

Conley didn't answer. Danny suspected he couldn't.

"Very hard for you Maxie-baby. See what you're missing? All this look and no touch makes Max a sad boy. You'll be hard all tonight, and all tomorrow, unless you let me ease it for you." Danny was doing it slow and hard now. It felt like it had a heart of its own and all it wanted to do was bleed to death. "You're as stiff as a board Conley. I can see that big ugly hard-on from here. Want me to come over there and lick it for you?"

Conley lay there rigid, not answering, mouth as dry as paper, watching that hand sliding against his tense stomach, stubbing against the fold of his body, peeling the sticky skin back. And that voice, like some sick madness in your head, going straight to your belly, right into your blood, making you swell till you ached to rub it on something, anything, but most of all on that pale cream-gold skin, that hair, that face, *that* mouth.

"Take it out for me. You don't need to touch it, just take it out, then I can come for you, just work a fat palmful here into my hand. After I'm gone you can get down on the floor and lick it up. Just take it out and let me see it." There was a tense pause then Danny said, "I'm *asking* you."

Conley slowly, painfully, watching his own hands as if they were someone else's, undid his trousers and pulled the front of his clothes open. It lay there exposed, vulnerable, the head swollen and angry and as bruised red as his waistcoat.

"Suck on that," Danny whispered. Conley didn't dare to look, could only keep staring down. "Suck on that fucking fat meat." And then he hissed at him, hard and urgent, "*Look* at me, *fuck* you."

Conley tore his eyes away from himself and saw Danny's hips pushed up off the settee, his hand strutting his penis up, pushing it out at a painfully obscene angle.

"Look at *me* Conley, not at my dick."

"I can't," Conley whispered.

"Look at my face, look at what really brings you off."

Conley lifted his eyes and looked in Danny's face. "Now..." Danny whispered, and Conley could see the tendons in his neck straining, "...I can see *you*, Conley."

His eyes closed and his head rolled back and Conley could see his teeth biting his lip as it began to pump out. Conley watched the first burst tensing his stomach as if he were being punched.

Danny suddenly slid forward, eyes springing open, furiously riding his balls against the settee, squirming forwards and pushing his cock down hard, angling it at the floor. He was making little panting grunts, focussing fiercely on himself as he continued to work his climax. Conley watched a jerk of it suddenly spin through the air in a long dancing thread. Danny moaned loudly, a tic working in his face with sheer effort.

Conley continued to watch him, even though it was nothing but a dying slump now, his hand slackly pulling on something already over, his eyes closed again, that intense concentration on his own hand gone. His own cock was aching, pleading for release.

But his hands might as well have been tied.

Danny got up unsteadily and made his way to the bathroom, hitching his clothes up.

He came back out.

Conley was standing looking out of the window, hands pushed deep into his pockets.

Danny came up behind him. "Still hard?" And he slid his hand round and felt him. Conley went rigid.

"Hard all over," Danny laughed quietly. He squeezed it. "Want me to do it?"

Conley couldn't speak.

"I reckon I've got about five minutes."

"Please Danny..." Conley could feel his stomach churning.

"Is that please do it or please leave me alone?" Danny squeezed him again, breathing deliberately against his neck. He moved closer. "You always smell so fucking good. Why do blonde men always smell so good? I had one this morning smelt of wood shavings. He had this weird shaft, felt like it grew out of a hollow in his belly. I've never felt anything like that before."

"Let me go Danny."

"No." And Danny slid an arm round him, pressed up against his back, and squeezed again. "Through your trousers, just squeezing, how long will you take? You'll have to be quick. I haven't got all day."

"Danny, I'll be sick."

Danny laughed. "Go ahead, I've had worse done to me." He squeezed it harder.

"*Danny*..." Conley gritted it out between his teeth.

"You want it."

"No."

"You need it."

"Let me go."

"It's an errand of mercy Conley. I'm relieving the sick and needy. You're sick and your cock's needy." Danny laughed again. "I'm a fucking saint. Can't you see the holy light in my eyes?"

Conley moaned, in desperation, in fear, in excitement. He could feel the sweat soaking his armpits, itching his hair. His bowels felt liquid. He needed to pee, but still Danny went on. "I can't," he moaned.

"You will." Danny kissed his neck, rubbed his face in his hair. Conley could feel something very like an erection being thrust against his back. Danny was half-masturbating him now, squeezing it tight then rubbing the heel of his hand along it. It dragged inside Conley's clothes.

"Feel good?" Danny's other hand pressed his stomach, opened the buttons on his waistcoat, slid into the silk of his shirt, remorselessly went on through the layers until it reached his skin.

"I asked you a question." Then he laughed again as he touched Conley's naked flesh. "You're trembling."

His hand moved over Conley's stomach, up his chest, found his nipple and caught it tight between the nails of his fingers. Conley felt a flame of excitement lick at his belly.

Danny smiled into his back. He was as sensitive as a woman. "Does that feel good?"

"Yes," Conley whispered.

"I can't hear you."

"Yes."

Danny chafed his nipple with his thumb. Conley leaned back against him.

"That's it," Danny whispered. "That's my boy." He gripped the length of his cock between his fingers, sculpting the fabric to it, squeezing him with an insistent remorseless rhythm. He dragged his nail over the nipple... slowly... then twisted it sharply.

Conley said, "*No...*"

"Going to dirty your pants..." Danny whispered.

Conley was filled with an intense excitement at the image.

"Going to *dirty* them..."

"*No...*" And suddenly it was like those delicious moments as a child when you couldn't wait any longer, the perfect panicked flooding release of it, and Danny pulling him higher… higher… *higher*…

Danny left him standing there against the wall, shaking like a leaf.

He stroked his cheek and said, "The right people, the right place, the right time."

And he kissed him briefly, and left.

Danny went downstairs with an uncomfortable hard-on jagging at him. With any luck he'd meet Conley's possessive little woman, see if he couldn't convince her that she had an itch she needed to scratch. Christ when had he last wanked off in a pair of tits like that?

Christ, *fuck* John.

He pulled his jacket shut and smiled grimly.

If all else failed he always could.

"How did I do?"

Stephen all but wagged his tail to see him back. He looked at his watch. "Twenty-four minutes and forty-two seconds."

"You were counting," Danny accused.

"When my mam says she'll be fifteen minutes she usually means half an hour."

"Oh ye of little faith, it was only twenty-four minutes."

"Almost twenty-five. Did you get him alright?"

"Yes." And Danny smiled as he turned on the ignition.

"What's he like, your friend?"

"Too old for you."

Danny saw the boy's puzzled frown. *Bad mistake Danny. Not thinking.* "I mean too old to interest you, he's thirty-eight."

"God that's nearly as old as my mam, she's forty-two."

"She'd thank you for giving her secrets away."

They waited patiently, indicators ticking, to get back into the flow of traffic.

"Nah, she doesn't care."

"No boyfriends?" Danny asked, sliding in front of a car full of grinning girls. He grinned back. Stephen watched him with an already familiar twist of jealousy and pride.

"No."

"Why not?"

"She's not interested."

Danny looked at him, smiling faintly. "You sound very sure."

"She isn't."

Danny laughed this time. "You just don't like the idea of her getting hitched again."

"I don't care," Stephen said defensively.

"Or is it the idea of her getting laid?"

Stephen tutted as if to say, Don't be gross.

Danny glanced at him then grinned and elbowed him in the ribs. "Fancy my chances?"

Stephen looked at him, openly repulsed. "She's too old for you."

"I like them mature."

"You make her sound like a cheese."

Danny snorted a laugh. "Think she'd fancy me?"

"I told you, she's not interested."

"I could make her interested."

Stephen looked at him. "And how would you do that?"

Danny tapped his nose. "Ah, trade secret."

"No," Stephen said with finality. "You couldn't."

"I think I'll try." Danny smiled at him.

Stephen looked out the window and hoped he wouldn't.

Conley peeled the sticky clothes off and climbed into the shower.

He held his face up to the spray, cauterising it, trying to wash the feel of his mouth off. He scrubbed his neck. He could still feel the breath there, warm, moist, insidious in his ear, saying filthy things, like a needle straight into the nerve. His hands reading your body like someone had printed your soul there in Braille. It wasn't holy light in his eyes, it was damned. Everything that touched him was damned.

Conley laid his head on the cold glass fish.

Oh God.

His come was still on the floor.

Conley got dressed again, shoving the dirty clothes inside the basket without looking at them, trying not to touch them any more than was necessary.

He walked over to the window and looked out into the dark. One by one he pulled the drapes shut, the faces leering at him. He stopped and scratched Mamma's head. He went to the kitchen and made himself a cup of coffee. He looked at it and poured it down the sink.

He got a fresh bottle of rum from the cupboard and filled a glass. He kept his back to the living room and drank it down.

He poured another glass and drank that too.

He took his third to the couch. He sat down. He looked at the ceiling.

Half way through the third glass he looked at the floor. At first he couldn't see it. It was obscured by the table. He had to slide along a little to place it. But it was still there. He hadn't imagined it.

He would have to clean it up. He couldn't leave it there.

He got up and walked round the table. It was like a pattern on the floor, a Celtic rune. Some of it was dry, almost all.

You can get down and lick it off the floor.

Conley sat down where Danny had been sitting and opened his legs. He looked down between them, remembering the impossibly cruel angle of Danny's penis, forced into leaving his spoor on the floor, oily and warm on the polished wood.

You can lick it off the floor.

Conley sat there looking at it, feeling a pulse in his temple. He hadn't ever...

He closed his eyes and lay down on the couch.

He knew. Danny *knew*.

He turned over on his stomach, felt himself pressed hard into the couch. It was like a pain. He was sick and this was the pain.

He slid over to the edge and looked over, feeling the twinge of pleasure the movement gave him. He rested his face in his arms. He was very close. He could touch it if he wanted to.

Max, don't.

Conley let his arm trail over the side.

He did it deliberately. There's no magic, it's all sleight of hand.

Don't do it.

He trailed his fingers over the dry marks. They felt powdery, flaky, like coarse talcum powder.

Max, no. No.

He closed his eyes and ran his finger into it, following its trail, powdery, then sticky and finally wet. It was cold and gelatinous. Cold and dead.

He opened his eyes, looked down.

Max...

Then he lifted his finger to his mouth.

The essence of Danny, bitter and salt, like electric metal on his tongue.

His mouth flooded with saliva.

And he threw up.

Only Rab was still in the kitchen when they got home.

"Anything left?" Danny asked.

"Tonight's your lucky night, big brother bought us a Chinese take-away. Yours is over there, and if you don't like it moan at Ian, he picked it."

"Who's moaning? Beats the hell out of cold meat."

Danny and Stephen agreed to shove everything together in a frying pan and reheat it. "Gross," Rab offered when he saw it.

"It tastes good," Stephen said. It did.

Rab asked Stephen about where they'd gone, what they'd bought. Stephen gave him a blow by blow account finishing, "We came back through Caldermouth. You should see this bloke's flickin' car - brilliant." Then he realised what he'd said. He looked at Rab, but Rab was already looking at Danny.

Danny wiped his mouth with his hand.

Stephen's face was a picture of distress. "Sorry."

Danny forced a smile. "No sweat."

"I won't tell John, I promise. It came out without thinking." Stephen saw Rab's face tighten and realised that he'd only made it worse.

Rab said, "Steve, do me a favour. Nip upstairs and get my fag papers, will you?"

Stephen got up. He knew he was being got rid of. Not for your ears. He'd put Danny in the shit. He could kill himself.

He went out of the room.

Rab sat forward and spoke quietly. "You little bastard, dragging the boy in."

"Oh leave off."

"You went to see him, when you knew the risk you were taking, and you dragged the frigging boy in. I don't believe you. I really don't." He dragged his hand through his hair.

"I said, leave off. It's none of your fucking business."

Rab leaned across the table and grabbed the front of his shirt, straining it upwards. Danny closed his eyes. "You fucking think with your dick Danny. Ian told me what you did this morning, in a fucking *toilet* for Christsake. Now this."

Danny grabbed his hand, eyes flaring open. "What's wrong? Jealous?"

Rab let him go, pushing his chair back, standing up. He looked down at Danny, his face white and pinched with anger. "One of these days Danny you're going to catch something, something as nasty and dirty as yourself, and it won't be your fucking brains it rots either."

Danny gave him the finger, a vicious jab.

"You too sweetheart," Rab said, going out the door. "You too."

He walked smack bang into Stephen in the hall and knew he'd been standing there listening. Question was, for how long? Answer was, he didn't give a fuck.

He didn't even bother to smile. He took the papers off him, went on into the living room and slammed the door.

Stephen went into the kitchen cautiously.

Danny was sitting there digging the point of a knife into the table. The table was covered with marks just like those. Now Stephen knew where they came from. He was completely absorbed in what he was doing, his movements neurotic and disturbing.

Stephen had just decided to sneak back out again when Danny looked up and saw him. He threw the knife down, washing his face with his other hand. "Come in." After a second he smiled.

Stephen went in. "I'm sorry Danny."

"Don't be. I only told you not to tell John. You weren't to know."

"He was really pissed off with you."

Danny looked at him.

"I heard you arguing," he confessed.

Danny looked at the floor. "He doesn't like him any better than John does." He managed a laugh. "But he's more worried that John will find out, for your sake."

"Me?"

"Yeah, piggy in the middle. I'm sorry I took you along now, it was out of order."

"No," Stephen said quickly. "I'm glad. I mean..." he rephrased it quickly, "I didn't mind."

Danny smiled then stretched out in his chair. He yawned widely, finally saying, "Well fuck 'em. Fuck 'em all, that's what I say."

Stephen smiled back, then nodded agreement.

Danny went upstairs to wait for John. The ache felt like a lead weight in his belly. Putting on a performance for Conley had only made him worse. Wanking him off without getting anything in return had just finished it. He paced up and down the room.

Where *was* he?

He stopped pacing abruptly and leaned his hands on the bed end, staring into space, lost in whatever thought had just struck him. He looked down suddenly and ran his hands along the old wood of the footboard then pressed against it absently. After a moment or two he turned and went out the room.

He knocked on Rab's door.

Rab grunted something unintelligible from inside.

He went in.

Rab was lying on the bed reading. He laid the book on his chest when he saw who it was.

Danny closed the door and moved to the side of the bed.

Rab looked up at him. Danny's face was oddly shadowed, up-lit by the bedside lamp. He looked faintly sinister. "What d'you want Danny?"

But Danny didn't answer him.

Rab began to feel a faint trickle of fear. Hard on its heels he felt ridiculous. Danny wasn't someone you were afraid of. Which was probably part of most people's problem with him. You ought to be afraid of him.

Rab got up on his elbows then tried to sit up, but Danny bent suddenly and pushed him back down, all in the same dreadful silence.

Rab gave a small grunt of surprise then Danny was on top of him, hands deep in his hair.

Rab tried to push him off. Danny punched him.

It wasn't a hard punch but the shock of it took Rab off-guard. Danny was moving against him, pushing insistently, whispering in his ear, "Come *on*."

To Rab he felt almost drunk, intoxicated with some bizarre emotion. Part of him was still trying to come to terms with the fact he'd just hit him. Danny didn't seem to have any sense of what he'd done.

"Danny what is this?" He was trying to wriggle free, unaccountably frightened by his violence.

"I want you to love me."

Rab felt something fire up inside him at the strangeness of the words, his voice detached, curiously level and emotionless, like he was saying something utterly removed from what he was doing.

"Want me," Danny urged, and he took Rab's hand and pressed it against himself.

Rab slid his arms around him. *Want* him? Was he joking? "I do," he said.

Rab pressed him back on the bed, half climbing over him. He felt Danny's stillness. He had his eyes closed, his face almost pained. Rab pulled his clothes off, then his own. The two of them rolled naked between the sheets.

"Christ, that feels good," Rab grunted.

"Love me."

Rab looked into his eyes, all pupil and blackness in the pale light, his hair rich red-gold, his skin flushed pink by the lamp. He bent his mouth to Danny's and kissed him then he said, "I will." And he buried his face in Danny's hair.

Danny had disappeared. Stephen sat in the living room with Ian watching a film. He had seen it about fifty times already and he hadn't enjoyed it the first time.

"Where's Danny?" Ian asked him.

Stephen shrugged. "Dunno. He went upstairs a while back."

Ian smiled. Stephen didn't like his smile much. To be honest he wasn't sure he liked Ian much.

"You like him, don't you?"

"Who? Danny?"

Ian nodded.

"Yeah," Stephen said. He felt faintly defensive, as if there was something bad about liking Danny.

"A lot of people like him," Ian said, but he was still smiling that horrible half-smile. It made everything he said sound as if he meant something quite different.

"He's nice," Stephen said, and felt even as he said it that the word seemed somehow inappropriate for Danny. He added, "He's different." And the word kept coming to him so he let it out. "Exciting."

Ian looked at him now, as if before he was just making chat and now he wasn't, now he was concentrating on what Stephen was saying. "He's more than exciting," he said. "Sometimes he's downright terrifying."

Stephen didn't say anything but he had an idea, a feeling, of what Ian meant. He'd felt it himself in Carlisle. Being with Danny was like being on a roller coaster. You knew

you couldn't stop it. You knew if you fell off or died on it it wouldn't stop for you. It had a circuit to do and it was going to do it. You didn't rate.

"Doesn't he frighten you a little?" Ian persisted.

Stephen shook his head, small rapid shakes.

"John?"

Stephen smiled this time, on safer ground. "Sometimes."

"And don't you find them alike?"

"Who? John and Danny?"

Ian nodded.

"No." Stephen was almost outraged. "They're nothing alike."

"Not even to look at?"

"Danny's nice looking."

Ian laughed this time. "And John's ugly?"

Stephen flushed. "I didn't mean that."

"Oh, don't worry, he'd agree with you."

"You're not going to tell him I said that?"

"You didn't say it."

Stephen looked at him but he was just smiling that irritating smile again. The answer told him nothing. Maybe Ian would tell him.

"I've got some photos of him when he was young, want to see them?"

"John?"

"Danny. Want to see them?"

Ian seemed keen to show him them. It wouldn't hurt. "Okay." Then he added out of curiosity, "Have you got any of him when he was my age?"

"Fifteen?"

"Nearly sixteen."

Ian smiled. "I don't know, I'll see. Hang on, I won't be a sec'."

Ian went out, leaving Stephen alone with the TV, alone with his thoughts.

He was a funny bloke, Ian. You felt as if he was talking round everything all the time, like he wanted to tell you something and was sounding you out. He was like those people who only talk to you to find out things, not to give anything away, always picking at your brains. Schoolteachers were like that, never really interested, just snooping, dying to know if your mother was a whore and your father a drunk.

He shrugged to himself unselfconsciously and settled down to watch the boring film.

Ian heard them in Rab's room.

He pressed his ear against the door, heard one of them say something suspiciously like 'Turn over', then there was silence again. Was it finished? Had he missed it? Was this the post-coital cigarette? Then he heard Rab, too low, but the tone was unmistakable, an endearment. How fucking sweet.

He leaned his forehead against the door. The *dirty* little bastard…

He pressed his ear to the door again and heard Rab saying clearly and unmistakably, "Not so hard Danny, for Christsake."

He couldn't believe this. John was due home any moment and he was…

Ian got up off the door and went to his room. He opened the wardrobe and took out his box of photographs. He'd let Stephen see a few alright, let him see a little of the excitement that was Danny.

He closed the wardrobe door.

Let's see you worship this Steve-o.

John came into the kitchen while Ian was listening at Rab's door. He took his boots and jacket off and padded into the living room.

Stephen looked up, expecting Ian.

"Hello, all alone? Where is everybody?"

"Ian's upstairs," Stephen said then added, "and so's Rab. I'm not sure where Danny is. He did go upstairs a while ago but he hasn't come back down... I don't think."

"All upstairs?" John said, and Stephen saw that faint glimmer of ill-temper about him that always seemed to be so near the surface. Stephen was ashamed to admit he was frightened of him, but he was a big man and when he got ratty he looked savage. Stephen would have defied anyone not to be frightened of him.

Stephen watched as John stood there a moment then turned suddenly and went out of the room.

John didn't bother to go to his own room. He went straight to Rab's and opened the door.

Rab was up inside him.

He froze, almost comically, mid-thrust and stared at John standing there above the headboard. Danny glanced up quickly then put his head back down on his arm. "Shit," he said, quite clearly and without emotion.

John said, "Get out of him."

Rab pulled out and rolled off back against the wall. His cock was pulsing unpleasantly. He'd been near coming when John had come in. Danny stayed where he was, face down in the pillow. John reached over and yanked the blankets down. Rab clutched at them too late. His cock was exposed, dwindling rapidly from fright and humiliation. Danny's back and arse were spread there, smooth, white, untroubled.

John unzipped his trousers. Rab closed his eyes. "Oh Jesus John, for fucksake."

But John stood there, legs slightly apart, pulling himself violently into erection, then he climbed into the bed fully dressed.

Rab was pinned hard against the wall by his shoulder. His face was level with his. He swore and tried to get up but John put his arm over him and said, "You get up out this bed and I'll break every bone in his body."

Rab lay still.

He took his arm away again and started prising between Danny's legs. Danny grunted but did not move. His eyes were shut, his face colourless. He almost looked asleep, but not quite.

John lunged suddenly. Rab saw Danny's face work. It was almost surreal. Danny's face with John's on top, all three face to face, so close they could have kissed, but none of them looking at the other.

John settled his weight. Rab saw him take a breath, knew he was too excited already. Danny hadn't even spoken, John hadn't even seen his face, yet here it was, all ready to come spilling out.

"Kiss him." It was virtually the first words John had spoken since he had gotten into bed. "Go on, kiss him. I want to see how you do it, what it is you've got." John was barely moving inside him, just keeping up the boil.

Rab kissed him, gently, closed-mouthed, wanting him to know he was sorry. Danny didn't kiss him back.

Rab broke away, feeling miserable and angry.

"Kiss me," John said.

Rab looked at him.

"Come on, kiss me." And John inclined his head towards him.

John's mouth was only two inches away. It was easy to do, painless. It was like being sucked into the mouth of Hell. Eventually John let him go.

Rab opened his eyes and saw Danny looking at him. And now there was something there - anger, hate - and he wasn't even sure what for. For kissing John or for being kissed by him? Danny's jealousies were as elusive and confusing as singing in a dark room.

"He doesn't like that." And John jolted into him suddenly.

Rab saw Danny's mouth quirk with pain.

"He doesn't like us kissing Robbie. Only which one doesn't he like?"

Rab bent forward suddenly, impulsively, and kissed Danny again. This time his mouth was a firm, hard line.

John was grinning at him. "No luck, he's a closed shop."

Rab made a dive to get up again but John stopped him. "You want me to hurt him?" And he pulled Danny's hair, yanking his head back savagely.

Rab lay back down, heart pounding.

John let Danny go, but slowly, as if he was reluctant to do it at all. He kept his hand in his hair. "Did he come in here?"

Rab didn't say anything. John pulled Danny's hair again, letting the pain mount slowly this time. Rab could see the skin tugging at the side of Danny's face. He nodded. John eased off.

"Ask you for it?"

Rab hesitated.

"Yes or no."

Rab nodded again.

John smiled and said, "And why didn't you say no? Why didn't you say no when he belongs to me and you know it? Why didn't you say no when chances are he was using you and you know that too? Why Rab?"

"I don't know."

John pulled Danny's hair again. Danny's eyes opened involuntarily, seeing nothing. Rab could see them watering.

"Because I didn't care. I wanted him."

John let Danny go again, slowly. He pushed up inside him two, three, times in hard succession like a man scratching a sudden itch. "That's better. Now it's your turn Danny." And John began kissing his cheek.

Rab had never seen him do this before. He felt himself grow erect and was horrified. John must be able to feel it against his leg. He closed his eyes, willed it to go away, but he could hear the small quiet sounds, so close to him. His erection didn't go away.

"Why did you come in here?"

Danny didn't need any more pain. "I was tired of waiting."

"For what?" John went on kissing him.

"You."

Rab opened his eyes. *Oh Christ Danny, do you have to be so fucking truthful?*

"So what did you ask him to do?" Danny felt the threatening pull on his hair.

"Love me."

John laughed. "Oh he does that anyway, every day from fucking afar. I wouldn't have thought you needed to actually get him in bed to prove it."

Danny said nothing.

"You certainly have a novel approach." John was moving now, long, slow, steady strokes. They were pulling against Rab's erection. He tried to surreptitiously ease away, but John pushed his leg hard against him, pinning him there. He knew. He was

doing it deliberately.

"And what was the order of business?"

"Blow job..." he paused, "...then what we were doing when you came in."

"Ass reaming."

"Yes."

"Like I'm doing now." And John thrust in viciously.

"Yes."

"And you're enjoying."

Danny didn't answer.

"And Rab's enjoying."

Rab felt his face flush.

"He's got a hard-on Danny. It's right against my leg. Know how he got it? Watching me kiss you." John looked at him but Rab couldn't meet his eyes. "Everybody's got a secret little letch to see us together, noticed that?"

Danny still didn't reply.

"So how did you get in this state?"

No answer.

"Being with the boy?"

"No."

John pushed in hard. It was like a slap. "Want him?"

"No."

"Well too bad if you did, Rab's already had him. Haven't you Rab?"

Oh shit, Rab thought. *Shit*.

"Come on Rab, don't be shy. Our Stephen's the little rabbit Danny, the fuck in the car, the jail bait, the white meat off the chicken. Isn't that right Rab?"

"Shut the fuck up," Rab snarled at him, pushing hard against him, but John rolled into him, full of vicious anger.

"You hypocritical bastard." Danny said, low and intense, and Rab knew exactly what he meant. It threw everything he'd said back in his face.

John looked at them, frowning. "What gives?"

"Fuck off," Danny snapped, trying to shrug him off.

John bit his back with a sudden breathtaking savagery, breaking the skin and drawing blood. It oozed from a small flap of loose skin. John had blood on his teeth. He pressed his mouth to the wound, staining his lips red.

"Oh Jesus John, stop it. *Stop* it." Rab pushed at him, but John was too far into himself. He began heaving into Danny, mouth trying to hold onto the wound and failing as he ploughed on as if in answer to some inner command.

Suddenly he raised himself up on his arms and rutted in deeply, moving Danny with the jolt of his body. His head was thrown back, his chin smeared with blood.

Rab watched transfigured as he thrust into him, each spasm clenching the muscles of his shoulders and arms. He felt the dreadful ecstasy of it begin to catch at him, the leg tugging worse than ever, and still John kept going, even though he must have finished coming. God, was he going to stay in there and do it again?

He had his head down now, pounding into Danny's back, then Rab realised what he was doing. Danny's hands were dug into the pillow. Rab could see sweat on his face. John's movements were riding him against the bed, faster and faster. Rab could feel his own orgasm begin to build. He was going to come on John's fucking leg if he didn't stop soon.

He suddenly realised Danny was fighting it when he saw him twist his head away and his body begin to tremble. He watched him try to rein it back in but as John lunged once more, with an odd twisting motion, it was like a switch being thrown. Danny's body bucked furiously, filled with rabid intensity, almost throwing John off. His hands

were clawing at the pillow, his armpits wet with sweat. Rab felt him thumping against the bed.

Gasping, helpless, Rab clutched John's leg with both hands, dragging it against himself to give himself more pleasure. He heard John grunt, "Together..." then "...*sweet.*"

But Rab was past caring.

Ian went back downstairs with the photographs. He had not heard John go into Rab's room.

He came back into the living room and said, "Shift over."

Stephen moved along the couch and Ian sat down beside him. "There," he said and handed Stephen a small pile of photographs.

Stephen looked at them closely. The first showed a very small redheaded boy about six or seven standing in the nude. Stephen laughed. "He'll be mad when he knows you showed me this."

Ian smiled.

"You can see it's him, can't you?" Stephen looked at the photo again. "His hair's lighter though, more like mine."

"It got darker as he got older," Ian said and felt something almost like pain.

Stephen slid the photo off, looked at the next. He was a little older, naked again, this time from the back, standing by a river. His skin looked almost transparently white, except across his shoulders which looked an angry red. He was looking back over his shoulder, smiling faintly at the camera, as if someone had shouted his name and he had turned - click. Stephen grinned. "How old is he here?"

Ian held the top of the photograph, looked at the back. "Eight."

Stephen looked at it again briefly then slid it off too.

The next one jumped a couple of years. Danny looked about ten, but the photo was disturbing, vaguely unpleasant. Danny had his trousers pulled down around his knees, his T-shirt still on. His hand was shading his eyes as if he had been facing the sun, so Stephen couldn't see his face. Stephen felt intensely embarrassed by it. The boy - he looked almost a stranger - was too old to be photographed like that. And it was so deliberate.

Ian spoke in his ear, making him jump. "Danny always was an exhibitionist. You couldn't get him to keep his clothes on."

Stephen let that pass and slid it off the pile. The next was almost as bad, about the same age, obviously pissing against a tree, again looking back over his shoulder, legs slightly apart. This one didn't look deliberate, it had that faint air of surprise about it.

The next one was worse. It was Danny standing in the bath. He looked about twelve. He was naked except for a towel round his shoulders. His hair was darker, longer and already he had a plush, deeply-coloured nest of pubic hair. He was smiling and it was horribly reminiscent of the way you sometimes saw him smiling now, like he'd done today in Carlisle at the women.

"Looks more like him, doesn't it?" Ian's voice was low, thick.

Stephen turned to him. "Are they all like this?"

"Like what?" Ian was still smiling.

"You know." Stephen blushed.

"You mean Danny showing it off?" Ian smiled. "Look and see."

"No." And Stephen held them back out to him.

"What's wrong?" Ian didn't take them.

"I don't know why you're showing me these. There must be photos of him dressed."

Ian quirked an eyebrow and immediately Stephen felt as if he were overreacting, seeing more in them than there was. Ian was his brother, after all. He wasn't going to find Danny nude very unusual. They were probably just a laugh to him.

He flicked through the others quickly until he reached one where Danny must have been at least fifteen and he was standing outside somewhere against a tree. He was fully dressed, with his arms round behind him, wrapped around the trunk, and his cock out. Just his cock. Hanging there.

"Jesus," Stephen said in disgust. "What kind of flickin' photos are these?" And this time he did push them back at him.

"You haven't seen the last one yet. Look, just before his eighteenth birthday."

Stephen took it from him slowly.

It was dark, taken in a bedroom in bad light. Danny was lying in the bed asleep, naked as in all the others. And erect. Hugely erect.

Stephen pushed it back at him.

"Good, isn't it? We took it for a laugh one morning when he was asleep. Well, Rab took it."

"Rab?" Stephen said.

Ian laughed. "The two of them together, two of a kind, you know?"

And the way he said it, the way he looked at Stephen, made him feel sure he knew what Rab and him had done.

"They were great friends this summer, but Danny gets bored easily."

Stephen could hear him talking round it, not saying it, whatever it was, and he was afraid to ask.

"Well, I hope Danny knows you show everyone these," Stephen said stiffly.

"Not everyone."

And even that meant something. What was that supposed to mean? "Why did you show them to me?" It was the best Stephen could manage.

"I thought you'd like them... being a fan and all."

"What do you mean, a fan?"

"Of Danny."

"I'm not a fan. I hardly know him."

"Oh, you will be."

Stephen began to lose his temper. "What are you up to?"

"Up to?"

"Yes, up to. You show me these bloody weird photographs then drop a lot of hints."

Ian shook his head as if to say, Not me.

"Well just come out and say it if you've anything to say."

"I haven't. I'm sorry if I've offended you. They're just photographs. I thought they'd give you a laugh." Ian was managing to smile and frown at once. He looked genuinely puzzled.

Now Stephen felt stupid again. "Forget it," he mumbled and turned ostentatiously to the TV. Ian smiled and got up, giving Stephen's knee a squeeze as he went.

Stephen only realised how tense he'd been when he heard the door close behind him and felt himself go limp. He looked at his knee then rubbed it fiercely and crossed his other leg over it.

John got off Danny and told him to get dressed.

He zipped himself up and stood watching while Danny pulled his clothes on. Rab lay on his back looking at the ceiling.

"Now get out," he said to Danny.

Danny went out and met Ian in the hall. Ian pushed the photographs into his pocket

but Danny hadn't seen them. Danny hadn't seen him either. He went on into the bathroom. Ian pressed his ear to Rab's door.

John was in there. God, when had he come in? He must have caught the little bastards red-handed.

He listened again. John was reading him the usual. Get off, stay off, or certain death will be yours. *Why don't you just kill him John? One less to worry about. And yourself while you're at it, then I can chain him to the bed and have him while your poor ghost watches and suffers.*

He didn't stay to listen. He'd heard it all before.

He went back to his room and put his photographs away.

Danny got washed and went back downstairs. He went into the living room and immediately regretted it. Stephen was there. He didn't feel like being sociable. His arse hurt.

Stephen looked at him and looked away again quickly, blushing.

Danny saw the look and frowned. Now what? Had he been upstairs and heard something? That was all he fucking needed.

He went in and sat on the armchair. "Any good?" he forced himself to ask.

"Don't know." Stephen was almost sullen.

"What's up?" Danny asked. Might as well get it over with.

"Nothing."

"Tell me Steve, come on."

Stephen picked at imaginary fluff on his trouser leg. "Ian was in here."

Oh great, I might have known Ian would appear in it somewhere. "And?"

"He showed me some photos of you."

Danny felt his heart turn to stone inside him.

"They were..." But Stephen got stuck there and Danny couldn't help him, not without fucking up, because he had no way of knowing what he'd shown him.

"What were they?" he asked.

"They were all... well, a bit funny, you know?"

No, Danny thought, I don't know. I can imagine. I can imagine all night, way beyond anyone else's possibilities. "How many?"

Stephen shrugged. "Half a dozen maybe."

That narrowed it down. "Me as a kid?"

"Some. Nearly all. Except one when you were about fifteen... and one when you were... older."

"The older one," Danny didn't soften it, "I had a hard-on?"

Stephen nodded, watching the floor.

"Ian's a cheeky bastard." Danny managed to work up a smile. "He likes to embarrass me with those things. One day I'll get the whole lot and burn them."

"He was really tacky about it," Stephen said, looking at him intently. "Trying to make out you were a bit weird, liked doing it or something."

Danny smiled. "He would. Ignore him. He likes to wind people up."

Stephen looked at him and said with a sudden honesty that belonged to his fifteen year old self rather than the sixteen, "There was a lot of them Danny, and pretty strange."

It was Danny's turn to look away. How the fuck did he explain this? He shrugged. "It was my way of getting attention when I was young. Like everything you do when you're young it ends up embarrassing you."

Stephen seemed to relax a little.

"Ian's a trouble-maker, ignore him. Don't believe anything he tells you." Especially

as it's invariably the truth, Danny thought.

Stephen smiled a little now. "When I was young I used to fake fainting fits."

Danny laughed. "See? Me, I just took my dick out and waved it at people."

Stephen laughed then looked away again, blushing all over again. "Can I say something?"

Now what? Danny thought. "Go on."

"You're a hell of a size."

It took Danny a moment to realise what he was talking about and when he did he let out a shout of laughter. Stephen grinned up at him, embarrassment forgotten. "Like a flickin' horse."

Danny looked at him, grinned again and winked.

Stephen grinned back.

FIFTY-EIGHT

Monday rolled round.

Mrs McEvoy came to work and blitzed the house. Danny met her for the first time and smiled at her. Stephen was with him and watched her smile back. She didn't seem unduly impressed, but then Danny only gave her an ordinary smile.

She stayed until two o'clock, managed to get Stephen alone and quiz him about the work. She was pleased to see he had settled in so well but had to admit he'd settled in a little too well. She'd known the dear-Mother-I'll-miss-you wouldn't last, but still... She smiled to herself wryly and thought about all those disgusting verses about birds leaving the nest.

She cleaned the house with gusto, made them a scratch meal, told them they'd get better when she was better caught up, and promised to do some laundry the following day.

By Wednesday everybody was in their stride. John sent Danny and Stephen anywhere there was a two-man job. He trusted neither Rab nor Ian with him.

Danny was glad of his company, and Stephen enjoyed being with Danny. His strangeness - it was the only word he could think of - exhilarated him. Being with Danny was like being drunk. He was always so full of repressed energy, tempers too. He'd go from strange, almost sullen, silences to euphoria just like that.

But John saw the restlessness and knew it for what it was.

He took him to bed and wrung him dry, but it didn't make any difference. Danny always fucked looking over his shoulder.

And he waited every night.

And Conley didn't phone.

On Thursday John sent them both to a tractor dealers outside Carlisle. Rab had ordered two spare parts for the big Ford and they were 'available to be collected'.

They went off in high spirits, relieved from the monotonous work they had been doing.

Danny knew what he was going to do. He didn't even try to fight it. Stephen would just have to come along for the ride.

Hold tight now.

James Conley spent the rest of Saturday getting drunk.

On Sunday he washed the floor and threw away the floor cloth.

He went for a long walk, following the course of the river, and did a lot of thinking.

He went home hungry and tired and frozen through and burnt Danny's telephone number over the bathroom candles.

That night he had a virulent nightmare. He was being fondled by Danny in front of the window, just as he had been the night before. He could only see Danny's hands, perfect, accurate, except they were laden with large, garish women's rings. He could see them wrapped around his erection. Danny was talking in his ear, telling him to look down, but Conley didn't want to look down. He was afraid. Danny told him he must look, and finally, desperately excited, frantic for the release, he'd looked down and the window was gone, and he could feel the cold wind gusting round him and the sheer terror had made him come, like some awful unintentional release of his bladder. It had

felt scalding as it spun out of him, thick and white, dropping down into the sickeningly churning waters below, and then Danny had said, "Lick it up. Go on, lick it up." And he'd pushed him, suddenly, out into space. It had been like coming again, that clutching spasm of terrified release, and he woke up with a muffled cry and had lain there, not knowing where he was, bathed in sweat, and his stomach covered in a sticky flood.

He'd gone back to work on Monday with a headache. Molly had given him more tablets without saying anything, but she had looked, and Conley felt guilty of crimes he hadn't even committed. She had refused to bring him cake and said he could have a sandwich or lump it. He'd lumped it and she had finally relented and brought him the plainest bun she could find. He ate it with no enthusiasm. Somehow he got through the day.

On Wednesday, beaten into submission by sheer misery, he had asked Molly to go out with him. To the theatre. She had accepted with an alacrity which almost embarrassed him.

Conley took her out to the theatre and then for a meal and then took her home.

He didn't touch her, he didn't kiss her goodnight, but he felt better.

She felt great.

On Thursday Conley felt he just might shake it off, until he was out and saw a redhead ahead of him in the queue at the post office. His heart turned over, then he realised it wasn't Danny, wasn't even a man, and the hair was bottled.

Then he knew he wasn't as well as he thought.

He went back to the office and asked Molly to come out with him again on Friday. She said yes.

He sat after lunch, consisting of two custard slices, and looked out of the window. The river was in spate and it made him think of the dream. He had an erection, the first he'd had in two days.

He turned back to the folders on his desk. He picked up a brochure on unit trusts. It proved to be an excellent cure.

Danny glanced at Stephen and said, "Steve-o, I want to go see my man again."

Stephen knew who he meant straight away. "Okay."

"Sure?" Danny didn't look at him because he didn't want to see anything there. No doubt, no disapproval.

"Yeah, sure." If Danny had looked all he would have seen was mild pique. Stephen felt sure that Danny liked him but he knew he wouldn't risk the wrath of his brother just to see him.

"What's he like, your friend?"

"How d'you mean?" Danny indicated and turned into the huge forecourt of the tractor service centre.

"What's he like?" Stephen shrugged. "You know."

"What does he look like?"

Stephen nodded but added, "What sort of person is he?"

Danny parked the car half into the space. He always did. Stephen smiled at it.

"He's tall, thin, wears weird clothes. Looks like the man with the scythe."

"Who?"

"Death."

Stephen pulled a face. "Sounds charming."

"Oh, he is. He could charm the pants off you."

"What's he called?"

Danny hesitated then said, "Max."

"Funny name."

"German."

"Is he German?"

"Yes, but he doesn't sound it."

"Where did you meet him?"

"Long story."

"And you're not telling me?"

Danny smiled to soften it. "That's right. Now let me go get these bits. You coming?"

"No, I'll stay here."

Danny climbed out without saying anything more. He suspected Stephen was throwing a sulk. Well tough shit.

Danny had to wait ten minutes while they found the parts then listen to another five minute lecture on why one of the parts wasn't exactly what they'd ordered but how it could be adapted.

He took them back out to the pick-up and pushed them in at Stephen's feet. He leaned across his lap to do it, his forearm on Stephen's thigh. Stephen looked at his hair and wanted to touch it. It was a sudden intense urge.

Danny straightened up.

Stephen was left feeling slightly breathless. He felt his face, hot, and a half pleasurable excitement in the pit of his stomach, then he was ashamed, confused. What a weird way to act. He looked firmly out of the window.

Danny climbed in and glanced at him. Still sulking. Let him.

Stephen thought about that night in the car with Rab. It was the first time he'd thought about it since moving into the farm. He remembered he'd touched Rab's hair.

He felt himself blush in earnest. He stopped thinking about it.

Danny said, "What are you thinking about?"

He replied, "Nothing" but wondered what Danny would have thought if he'd known. He'd probably never speak to him again. *I let Rab suck my root in the back seat of a car.* Jeez. What would he say to that?

Danny left him alone.

They turned down the back roads to cut onto the Caldermouth road. Finally Stephen said, "What time is it?"

Danny looked at the dashboard and muttered, "Wrong car. I don't know, about two I should think."

"Won't John wonder what's kept us?"

"We had to wait for the part to be made up." Danny looked at him.

"Rather you than me," Stephen said.

"What?"

"Lying to him."

Danny felt irritated. He shut his mouth tight before he said anything he regretted. He changed the subject. "When's your birthday?"

"Hah!" Stephen snorted.

"What is it?"

"You'll shit yourself when you hear."

"When? Go on." Danny was curious now.

"Twenty-fifth December."

"No kidding?"

Stephen shook his head.

"What a shit. Only one lot of presents, huh?"

"You got it."

"Never mind, I'll get you a box of hankies."

"Thanks a bunch."

"What would you like?"

"Serious?"

Danny nodded.

Stephen thought about it. "A leather jacket."

"How about your mum?"

"Can't afford it."

"Drop hints to John."

"You're joking, I wouldn't dare." Stephen pulled a face.

Danny laughed. "Then I will."

"No, don't Danny, I've only been here a week."

"Is that all? Feels like I've known you years."

Stephen smiled, felt considerably more cheerful, until they pulled up at the junction and he saw the road sign for Caldermouth. He looked away again.

"What time is it?" Conley asked Molly as she came in.

"No watch?"

"Forgot to wind it."

"Half two."

He altered his watch. She offered, "Want a cup of coffee?"

"I'm going to charge him for this appointment, that's the third time he's cancelled a half hour appointment."

"Forty-five minute."

Conley looked at her. "Then I'll charge him extra."

She laughed. She hoped he'd ask her to stay and talk to him but he didn't. In fact he more or less sent her out with a, "Go and send out a few bills Molly, cheer me up."

She went out.

Conley turned round in his seat and stared out the window again.

Danny parked in the car park this time.

"How long are you leaving me for this time?"

Danny bit down his reply and said, "Not long."

"How long?" Stephen looked out the window.

Danny said, "I'll be as fast as I can, but I don't know how long I'll be, okay?"

Stephen said nothing.

"Steve-o..."

Stephen turned reluctantly.

Danny smiled at him, that dirty up-and-under smile, and said, "Trust me."

Stephen grinned in spite of himself. "Stupid fucker."

Danny climbed out and slammed the door.

Danny met Dorothy.

Dorothy looked at Danny and couldn't place him.

Danny said, "I'd like to see James Conley."

"Ah, you want the office at the end of the passage, just through there. You'll find his secretary in there."

Danny smiled briefly and went through the door.

Dorothy thought Molly had all the luck.

Danny went in without knocking. Molly looked up. It was the lecherous little pig. Same boy, different clothes. Now he was dressed like a farmer. In fact she could smell

animals off him.

Danny smiled. It was as dirty as Molly remembered. This time he looked at her face though. "Can I help you?" she said. She could hear the frost herself.

"I'd like to see Conley," Danny said.

No 'please'. He wouldn't, the ill-mannered little pig. "These *are* working hours."

"Just tell him it's Danny."

Her eyes jerked up to look at him, her affected cool shot completely. "Hang on," she said, her professional front slipping a little more.

She went into James' office. He turned from the window.

"James, that boy's here again, your friend, the one I met on the stairs."

"Danny?" he asked without thinking and immediately wished he could take it back.

She looked at him then said, "Is it the same Danny?"

"As?" he asked, knowing damn fine.

"The person you were asking for when you were ill."

He nodded. *Max, you should have said no.*

There was an odd little silence then Molly said, "Shall I show him in?"

No, Max, don't. Don't let him in. He felt his palms begin to sweat. He nodded. "Yes." It came out roughly.

She went out. A moment later Danny came in. He stood there leaning against the door, looking at him. The tiny room filled with the intense hay and dung smell of animals.

Danny didn't manage a smile. "Miss me?"

Conley said nothing.

"Why didn't you phone me?" Danny paused, licked his lips then said, the words coming out like caresses, rolling off his tongue, "You low, spineless bastard." Then he stood there, eyes narrowed and black, waiting.

Conley sat there unmoving then finally said, "Because I can't stand to have you do that to me every time you see me."

"What?"

"Humiliate me."

"And what the fuck do you think you do to me? Looking at me like I was something the fucking cat dragged in."

"Keep your voice down."

"Fuck her," Danny hissed, and this time he came up off the door and stalked straight round the desk. Conley stood up to face him, keep him at a distance. "And fuck you, you lousy, two-faced, chickenshit bastard."

"Did you come here just to call me names?"

"No, but I'm enjoying it now I've started."

"Get out Danny. Now." Conley's face was hard, no longer edgy.

Danny looked at him in surprise.

"I mean it," Conley added.

Danny stared at him for a long moment then backed off. "Alright," he said. "Fine." He turned and slammed out the door.

He stalked past Molly's surprised gaze. She watched him stop and turn. He came over to her desk. He leaned on it, palms down. He was smiling, but it was vicious and threatening. When he spoke his voice was low and intense. "You've got the hots for him, haven't you?" But before Molly could answer he went on, "Well let me let you into a secret. Your Mr Conley likes to do it with boys. You understand what I'm talking about, don't you?"

Molly's mouth was a hanging 'O', her face slowly reddening.

"Better stick to fantasising about me," he said and he wheeled around and slammed out the door.

Molly sat there for a long minute, staring after him, then got up and went into the office.

Danny was in a blind rage.

He climbed into the pick-up and sat there.

Stephen looked at him. He started to say, Quick work, but didn't get any of it out. "What's wrong?" he asked instead.

Danny shrugged and looked out the window.

"You have a fight?"

"Shut it Stephen, okay?"

Stephen pulled back as if he'd been slapped. Danny turned immediately and caught up his hand, kissed his palm and curled the fingers shut around it. "Sorry," he said. He did the whole thing without once looking at him.

Stephen looked at him, eyes like saucers. Now he didn't know where the fuck he was. If Danny had been trying to shut him up he couldn't have done it more effectively.

They sat there in silence. Stephen looked at his own hand lying clenched in his lap as if he was keeping the kiss in, as if he'd been given it to hold. He wanted to uncurl it but felt somehow that he would unwrite it if he did. It was the sort of intense thing people did in books. He wanted to keep it, prove it had happened to him.

"Shit," Danny muttered under his breath. Then, "Shit, shit, *shit*." The last he punctuated by thumping the steering wheel with both fists. Then quite suddenly he went limp. He laid his head on the steering wheel like a man in the depths of despair.

This was beyond Stephen's capabilities. "Danny..." he said hesitantly, putting an arm around his shoulders.

Danny did not respond. Stephen left it there, tightening his grip slightly, feeling curiously warmed by Danny's need.

After a while Danny sat up. Stephen dropped his arm and looked at him curiously, but his face was dry. He looked quite normal except for his eyes and they weren't red, they were alive. "Steve-o," he said, turning on the ignition - he backed out with a screech - "let's go *fuck* something."

Danny drove like a maniac, full of something pent-up and dangerous. Stephen didn't know whether he loved it or hated it.

Stephen knew they were not going home. He felt they were on some kind of hell-bound adventure. He was terrified and exhilarated at the same time. "Where are we going?"

"I told you, to fuck something."

"Seriously."

Danny glanced at him for the first time since he'd got into the car at Caldermouth. "I am serious Steve-o. You ever fucked anybody?"

"You mean..." Stephen felt himself blush stupidly.

"Yes. You ever actually fucked?"

"Not really."

"Which means no, right? Today you will. You and I both. Together. Three in a bed. What d'you say?"

"Who?" was all Stephen could think of to say.

"Or we could take turns, but I think I could convince her easier for the other."

"Who?" Stephen asked again.

"You'll see. A very tasty lady. Like fucking chinchilla. Owns a Porsche and a Mercedes. Classy enough for you?"

"You're taking the piss Danny. What are we really doing?"

Danny laughed. "I told you before Steve-o." And he reached over and pinched Stephen's cheek. "Trust me."

Stephen watched as they pulled down into the harbour development. "You know somebody who lives here?"

"Uh-huh." Danny parked the car with dangerous finesse on the edge of the dock.

"You know some folk Danny."

"Uh-huh," he said again. He turned off the engine, took out the keys then he turned to Stephen. "You okay?"

Stephen smiled. "I think so."

"Want to do it?" Danny asked and his smile was only faint now, his eyes searching Stephen's face.

Stephen swallowed. "You really serious?"

"I've been serious all along. I always am about fucking. Fucking's a very serious business. Fucking screws you up." Danny laughed. "You ready for it?"

Stephen nodded.

"Come on then." And Danny opened the door.

At first Danny didn't think she was in - after all it was mid-afternoon - then her voice answered sleepily, "Yes?"

"It's me."

"Danny?" she said, her voice sounding more alert.

Danny winked at Stephen. "Yes. I've got a friend here would like to meet you, another handsome redhead, can we come up?"

There was a pause. Both of them were smirking at each other. The buzzer went without her speaking. Danny pushed in.

"Some place," Stephen said in hushed tones.

Danny smiled at him.

They got up to the door. She was waiting for them. She looked at Danny, then Stephen. "Not in your class."

"He's young yet," Danny answered. She was wearing a red towelling robe and matching mules. That appeared to be it. "Did we wake you?" Danny asked.

"Yes. I was out Christmas shopping and wore myself out." She took their coats. "You smell like a barn."

"Just the way you like me."

Stephen was confused by the way they spoke to each other, as if they didn't really like each other. Danny had definitely been joking. Definitely.

She showed them into the living room. "And to what do I owe the pleasure of this visit?"

"Purely social," Danny answered.

"You're paying me a social call?" And she looked at Stephen oddly, as if it meant something.

"That's right." And Danny's look back seemed equally meaningful.

"I see, well in that case we better have something to drink."

"Good idea... and his name's Steve." He nodded his head at Stephen. "And he drinks too."

"He doesn't look old enough."

"He is," Danny said and smiled at her.

She raised her eyebrows but went without saying anything else.

594

Stephen whispered to him, "What are you doing Danny?"

"What I told you Steve-o."

"What did she look at me like that for? I don't think she likes me."

"Christ Stephen, what are you, doubting Thomas? Stay here, I'll be back in a minute." And Danny followed her through to the kitchen.

She looked over her shoulder briefly as he came in, then went back to what she was doing. "Who is he?"

"New boy, works for us."

"Why did you bring him?"

"Because without him I couldn't have come at all. Besides he gives me a good alibi."

She looked at him then. He met her gaze levelly. She went back to what she was doing.

He came over behind her and put his arms around her waist then undid the dressing gown. She did have something on underneath, a one-piece thing like a swimsuit. Danny eased his hand into the gusset.

"God, you stink," she breathed but she didn't stop him.

He kissed the back of her neck. She turned quickly and put her arms round him. He pressed up against her, eating her mouth.

Eventually she broke from him. "Turning up here at all hours is one thing but bringing some kid in tow is another. How can we do anything with him here?"

"Easy." He kissed under her ear. "We take him with us."

"What?"

"You heard me."

She pushed him away. "You must be mad. You are mad. Mad, bad and bloody dangerous to know."

Danny pulled the poppers apart on her underwear. It rolled up immediately, revealing the thick fur. Danny looked down at it. "I've missed that." He brushed his hand over it lightly.

"Thank-you," she said dryly, but she still felt the kick of it, hating herself for it.

He began kissing her again, pressing his leg between hers.

"No," she said. "*No* Danny." And she pushed him away.

Surprisingly he let her go. Worse, she hated it. Everything inside her was up there, screaming for him, and he'd put two feet between them. "Think about it," he smiled.

She looked at him and felt a kind of slow crawl go over her skin. "Are you giving me an ultimatum?"

"Let's all have a drink and you can think about it."

"No," she said again, but Danny only smiled over his shoulder and pushed out the door.

Stephen jumped when he came in. He was looking at the TV. "It's a cracker, isn't it?" he said.

Danny looked at it and shrugged.

"Jeez Danny, nothing ever impresses you," Stephen said petulantly.

"It does. The rum you get here is impressive. Ever had rum?"

Stephen nodded. "My uncle drinks it."

"Well you're a step ahead of me. I'd never tasted it before."

Katherine Henderson came in with a tray of drinks. Stephen saw there was three glasses. She'd brought Coke as well. He supposed that was for him. Some had been poured from it. She handed them the drinks. Stephen sipped his. It was rum alright. He smiled, pleased.

"You didn't cough." Danny sounded almost accusatory.

"What?"

"I did when I first drank it. In fact I nearly choked."

"There's Coke in it," Stephen said as if that explained everything.

Danny laughed. Stephen laughed too.

Katherine Henderson looked at the boy. There was a fleeting resemblance to Danny and it wasn't just the red hair. He was heavier-set but there was something about his mannerisms or something, fleeting but there. There, like that, she'd seen that before... She lost it again before she could identify it.

He was a nice looking boy, but not Danny, nowhere *near* Danny, and never would be - and she wasn't taking him to bed. He was lucky if he was eighteen, lucky if he was seventeen. What the hell was Danny playing at? "How old are you?" she asked him.

"Eighteen this Christmas," Danny answered quickly. He smiled crookedly at her expression.

"That right?" she said to Stephen.

He felt Danny's eyes on him and nodded. It wouldn't have fooled anyone.

She downed her drink, refilled her glass.

Stephen looked at her, the thick black hair, the dark eyes, the scarlet dressing gown. He swallowed. Danny wasn't really serious, was he?

Danny watched Stephen sitting on the floor, looking up at her, wondering, and smiled.

She looked over at Danny.

He leaned back and smiled at her, his eyes black with it.

He didn't wonder - he *knew*.

Danny drank the least - Danny always did - but Stephen got drunk.

"Uh-uh," Danny said putting his hand over Stephen's glass when Katherine Henderson went to refill it. "He's had enough."

"I think you should let him decide," Katherine said, smiling at Stephen.

"No," Danny said. "He's had enough. I've got to get him home."

"I'm alright," Stephen said petulantly, but Danny wouldn't take his hand off the glass.

Katherine Henderson refilled her own alone. "Come sit beside me," she said to Danny.

Danny got up and crossed to the other couch.

"You too Stephen."

Stephen crawled over to the settee and sat on the opposite side. She smiled. Danny smiled back. She put her hand on his leg and held her mouth out to be kissed. Danny laughed and kissed her. She sank back into the sofa. Danny said, "Where's Stephen's?"

"What?"

"Kiss."

She smiled and turned to Stephen, inviting him to kiss her just as she'd done with Danny. He blushed and kissed her awkwardly, breaking away and saying suddenly, "I need to pee."

Katherine Henderson laughed and Stephen blushed all over again. "Sorry," he mumbled.

Danny stood up. "I'll show you."

"He could hardly lose it Danny," Katherine said, looking up at him.

Danny looked back at her. "So I'm frightened he'll fall down the toilet."

"I'll manage," Stephen said, struggling to get out the depths of the sofa.

Danny pulled him up. "Shut up." And he propelled him out the room by one arm.

They walked along the dark hallway. Danny propped him up against the doorjamb and pulled the bathroom light toggle. The room floodlit into a million mirrors. Stephen whistled.

"You okay?" Danny asked.

"Yeah, sure." Stephen pushed into the bathroom, mesmerised.

"Well don't piss on your foot."

"Fuck off," Stephen said. Danny shut the door.

He went across to the bedroom, switched on the light. Just the same. She had hardly changed it. There were more clothes lying around. She wasn't as maniacally tidy as Henderson had been. He wondered if he could do this after all. Maybe he should stick to the living room floor.

"Cor," Stephen said unimaginatively. He staggered slightly as he came in.

Danny laughed and caught him round the waist, pulling him back unresisting into his arms. Stephen lay there passively. "There, now you can stay upright while you survey the wealth of the few."

Stephen looked round. "She got a lot of money?"

"Enough."

"Cor," he said again.

Danny looked at the top of his head and realised he could smell his hair.

"Danny?"

"Mm?"

"How d'you know her?"

"I knew her brother."

"Do you like her?"

Danny laughed in his ear. "No."

"Why d'you come here then?"

"To fuck."

Stephen struggled out of his arms to face him. "Someone you don't like?"

Danny laughed again. "You don't need to like them."

"Them?"

"The people you fuck."

"Have you..."

Danny raised his eyebrows, Go on.

"Have you fucked a lot then?"

Danny patted his cheek. "None of your business."

Stephen pushed his hands into his pockets. He went to the bed and sat down, bouncing on it slightly. "*Alright,*" he said with emphasis.

Danny sat down on the opposite side then stretched out full length. It felt fine. He sat up suddenly crying, "Shoes!" and pulled them off without untying them.

"Jeez Danny, what if she comes in?"

"I've slept in it before." Danny smiled at him.

Stephen made to stand up. Danny caught his arm. "Try it."

Stephen shook his head.

"Come on, don't ruin my master plan. Lie down," he urged.

Stephen lay down gingerly. Danny caught his legs and pulled his shoes off. Stephen yelled.

Katherine Henderson appeared in the doorway. "Having fun?"

Stephen sat up. Her expression was odd when she looked at him. He stood up.

"Come and join us," Danny said.

"No thank you."

"Come on. We promise not to ravish you. See if we can make three in a bed." Danny rolled onto his stomach. "It is king-size, isn't it?"

"You know it is."

Danny smiled into the pillow. "Come on then, come lie beside me." He lay there listening to the silences of the room. After a moment he felt her weight on the bed, then her head was beside his. He smiled at her then rolled over. "Come on Stephen, last man on."

Stephen hesitated a moment but Danny grinned at him, challenging him.

Stephen lay down beside her.

"See? Easy." Danny propped himself up on one elbow then he leant down and kissed her, long, slow and hard.

Stephen looked away, felt his heart racing. He wanted to get up, go out.

Danny eased off her again. Her face was flushed. Danny smiled down at her. "Now it's Steve-o's turn. Come on Stephen." And Danny looked at her, his eyes saying, Give the boy a break. It surprised her.

Stephen lay there numbly, not knowing what to do.

She rolled to face him and took his face in her hands, then she kissed him, gently, teasing his mouth open.

Stephen lay there drunkenly, letting her do it. He felt himself grow hard.

While they were kissing Danny reached over and turned down the lights. He thought of Henderson doing exactly the same thing. The methods of slow seduction.

Katherine was enjoying it, teasing the boy. He was so passive under her hands it made her feel powerful.

Danny lay on one elbow watching her. He reached his free hand over and undid her dressing gown. She didn't stop him. He slid his hand up and squeezed her breast. She went on kissing Stephen.

Stephen reached his arm out cautiously and put it on her hip. She moaned as Danny's hand slid inside the cup of her bra. Stephen was encouraged by the sound. He kissed her back. She was kissing his face. She smelt of expensive perfume and hair stuff. Her skin was soft and silky.

Danny eased her dressing gown up at the back and slid his hand in between her legs. She closed them tight, stopping him. He let it lie there and began kissing the back of her hair, rubbing his face in it.

Katherine Henderson briefly let her hand pass over the boy's crotch. She was elated to feel the erection there. She could feel him straining towards her, wanting to press it against her. Danny had pulled her dressing gown off one shoulder and was leaning into her back, but only his top half. She could feel nothing against her hips, only his hand there, jammed between her legs.

She wriggled her backside towards him. He pushed it away, towards the boy.

Stephen felt the movement and moved in closer, felt a kind of desperate pounding in his chest.

Danny reached over suddenly and took her hand and pressed it against Stephen's front.

Stephen closed his eyes tighter.

She resisted then relaxed, letting her hand cup him. It felt good, locked in there, wanting her. She could feel him pushing up against her. She squeezed it.

Danny's hand slid between her legs again. She let him. She squeezed the boy again.

Danny slid his hand round and pulled the crotch of her underwear apart with a quick tug. She held her breath, ready to stop him, but nothing more happened. She undid the boy's zip, his belt. She slid her hand in.

Danny's fingers slid in between her legs. She was soaking.

She moaned again. The boy was so hard he felt curved.

Danny's fingers moved in her. He kissed her neck, breathing on her, then he whispered to her, the words sounding huge in the heavy breathing silence, "Let him fuck you."

Stephen heard it. Her hand stilled. *Don't stop,* Stephen begged silently. *Don't stop.* Danny said it again, louder this time.

Stephen opened his eyes and saw Danny leaning above her, looking down at her, smiling. "Go on." And he kissed her face, tiny soft kisses. Stephen watched his mouth moving over her skin. He was pulling her round now, still leaning over her, pulling her away from him. She still had a hold of Stephen's cock.

Suddenly she turned and looked at him and smiled and said, "Come on then." And she invited him over on top of her.

Stephen scrambled over her, between her legs, saw briefly the thick black hair as he tried to insert himself. She caught at him when he pushed too soon. "Whoa..." she laughed, then she said, "...now do it."

Stephen pushed again and felt it slide in. He saw her face change, an expression flit across it of something elusive, like the girls in the magazines, only softer, more genuine. He felt his cock surge. He pushed in again and this time he really went up. She opened her legs for him, letting him in further. He pushed again. She kissed him, deeply, different this time, kind of begging, grateful, a bit of both maybe. He pulled free and buried his face in the pillow. Danny was lying beside him now. He turned to look at him, braving it, and Danny smiled, so close Stephen could have kissed him. Stephen looked into his eyes, pushed into her. She was squirming beneath him, kissing his ear, making little noises every time he went in. He kept looking at Danny, the black eyes, the ivory skin, then he felt Danny's hand on his arse, making him push in. "*Don't,*" he gasped.

"Why?" Danny said, smiling, his hand shoving his bum, and Stephen thought how like a kiss it looked when his mouth formed the word and suddenly it was there. Just like that. The urge. The *need.*

He put his hand out and touched Danny's hair. It felt like silk

"Nice?" Danny asked and Stephen knew he meant what he was doing to her but he nodded and felt Danny's hair under his fingers and wondered why Danny was letting him do this, touch him like this.

Danny brought his face closer, only an inch apart, pushed Stephen's bum again. "Up her," he urged.

Stephen could feel his breath on his face. Katherine had wrapped her legs round his and was pushing up hard against him.

"Shove it up her."

"*Don't,*" he gasped again. He lifted his head quickly and buried it in the pillow at the other side of her head, away from him.

Danny brought her head round to face him. "God, you're beautiful Danny," she whispered. He kissed her, hard, pushing into her mouth.

"Me next," he said when he broke free.

She grunted, "You next."

Stephen heard them, brought his head up to stop them talking. She caught Stephen's head in her hands, kissed him again. He wanted to come so much it was hurting him. He'd been ready to come for ages and now he couldn't make it, couldn't push it over.

He hid his face again, on Danny's side, keeping her away from him. He didn't look at Danny but he could feel his hand light on his flank. Every time he pushed Stephen felt it come up ready to spill out then it stopped short.

Stephen opened his eyes, looked at him. He moved his hand off the pillow and

tentatively touched Danny's face. Danny only looked at him. Stephen let his hand trail down over his cheek. Danny just kept watching him. Suddenly he took his hand off Stephen's rump.

Stephen pushed in harder, charged with desperation now Danny had let him go completely. He ran his fingertips down over Danny's mouth, no clear idea of what he was doing. He could feel the silk of it, the slightly drawn dryness of the bottom lip, the rough stubble above his upper lip. He pushed one fingertip between Danny's parted lips, felt the slight moisture inside. Danny wasn't smiling any more, just watching him.

Stephen begged him with his eyes. *Let me go Danny. Let me go.*

Suddenly Danny sucked his finger in. Stephen could feel himself boil up furiously. He dragged into her fiercely, said, "*Shit*... oh shit," and began to come, thumping it into her, levering himself up on one arm, eyes riveted on his finger deep in Danny's mouth.

"Come on Casanova, roll over," Danny said into his ear.

Stephen opened his eyes and looked at him.

"Off." Danny jerked his head. "The lady needs attention."

Stephen looked down at Katherine Henderson as if he'd forgotten her. She laughed and said, "You're an expert."

Stephen blushed and rolled off her, pulling out too quickly. He collapsed at her side. He saw Danny look down at her then bend his head to kiss her, then he realised Danny was playing with her. Stephen lifted his head slightly. He could see Danny's fingers rubbing in and out between her legs. She was squirming her crotch up onto his hand. Then he realised he could see Danny's cock, squeezed up hard against her hip He could see the top of it, red and shiny, obviously sticking out the fly of his jeans. He blushed, looked at Danny quickly to see if he'd seen him looking, but they were still kissing, Danny intent on his hand, her mouth.

Stephen glanced down again, watched as Danny thrust it up against her. He'd never seen another man's erection before. Somehow it looked even bigger than in the photograph. It made him feel inadequate.

She was moaning now, worse than she had been before. She opened her legs wider, throwing one over Stephen's legs. Stephen looked at her spread crotch in fascination. So thick and hairy, right down her legs. He could see how wet and red she was, realised it was his come that Danny was rubbing all over her slit. He could feel himself start to get another erection.

Then she started to growl, actually growl, a low deep sound which slowly turned into anguished cries. She thrust her hips up at Danny, squirming on his hand.

Danny was urging her on saying, "That's it, that's it." Stephen stared at her and realised abruptly she must be coming. Oh crikey, he thought, and his erection swelled up fully. It seemed to go on forever, much longer than his did, until she finally grabbed Danny's hand and pushed it off saying, "No more."

Danny laughed then eased himself over on top of her. Her thigh moved up hard against Stephen's body. He could feel Danny's weight in it. She reached down and guided him in as she had done with Stephen but Danny went up in one slick violent movement. She grunted. Stephen thought to himself, I bet that thing of his hurts, but she was clinging onto him, holding his bum, pushing him into herself in a way she hadn't with Stephen. Danny held himself above her and fucked her slowly, watching her face as if he was searching it for something.

Stephen lay there and watched him moving obscenely on top of her. He wanted to touch himself but didn't dare. What would Danny think?

She kept saying Danny's name in little breathless gasps. It excited Stephen to hear the way she said it, as if she was getting off on it. Danny just went on, same pace, like

a fucking machine, then he spoke to her. "Want it?"

Stephen had never heard his voice so deep.

"Yes," she said with a little grunt.

"Say you want it up you."

Stephen looked at Danny's face. He looked almost cruel, something bad in his eyes. She said what he wanted her to say.

"Now ask for it."

She did it.

"Again."

She said it again, and Stephen knew that right now he wasn't even there as far as Danny was concerned. It was just him and her. "Please," she whispered, then, "Danny *please*." And Stephen watched Danny close his eyes, his head go back... and then he started jerking his hips, just his hips, like a dog fucking. Stephen watched the movements hit some kind of strange trembling peak and knew at that precise moment he'd put his load inside her. She let out a wavering moan and proved it. Danny hung there for a moment, his hips still doing that filthy little doggy thing, and Stephen thought he looked beautiful.

Outlandish and really, really beautiful.

And quite unreal.

When Danny rolled off her she followed him across the bed, cuddling into him and throwing a leg over him, erasing Stephen's brief glimpse of Danny's wet, used penis. There was a long silence then Danny spoke, quietly. "Steve?"

"Uh-huh?" Stephen could hardly trust his voice. Danny seemed incredibly distant now, half-shadowed in the low light on the opposite side of the bed.

"Go clean up and wait for me in the living room. I won't be a minute."

Stephen lay there a minute, felt oddly like crying, then he swung his legs up off the bed. He held his clothes shut, keeping his back to Danny. He picked up his shoes and went out of the room.

In the bathroom he was faced with hundreds of himself, red-faced and dishevelled. He stared at himself for a moment then pulled his trousers and pants down with a jerk.

He tweaked his erection up to full size. In seconds it was red and angry, sticking up in the air. Without thinking about it, he braced his legs and began to masturbate, rubbing it hard, watching his hand. *Look at my big red prick... look at it... look at it...*

He came up to it immediately, eyes fixed and glazed, mind jumping with images. Her thick wet cunt... Danny's fingers rubbing in and out, smearing his come over her slit... his cock squeezed up hard against her hip... the fat wet plum sticking out the fly of his jeans... his wet mouth... putting his finger... putting his fat... wet... finger... *oh shit... SHIT...*

A hundred Stephens spurted thinly into the sink.

Danny whispered in her ear, "I told you, you would."

He laughed when she said nothing. "Enjoy it?" he asked.

She wouldn't answer him. He laughed again then eased himself out from under her. He swung his legs to the floor.

She looked at his back. "Did you come here today to do this?"

He was fastening his shoes. He stopped and turned to her. He trailed a finger up through her cunt. She closed her legs, pulling her gown round herself.

"What if I said yes? " He smiled that hated smile, too smug, too knowing.

"You're a bastard Danny."

"Why? Because you enjoyed it even better than usual?"

She pulled her dressing gown shut. "There's no point in asking when I'll see you again, I suppose?"

He only smiled. Too right, it said. Maybe next time I want to bring someone else round to share you. Maybe not.

"You're a shit." Her voice was low, tremulous with tears or anger. She heard the bathroom door open.

He didn't even turn to her when he spoke. "And you're a two-faced bitch," and he went out, closing the bedroom door.

Danny came into the living room, winked at him.

Stephen looked at him and looked away again.

"Cheer up Steve-o, you just lost your cherry."

Stephen pushed his hands in his pockets but didn't speak. Danny turned him round, held his shoulders. "What's up? Didn't you like it?"

"It was okay."

"*Okay?*" Danny laughed.

Stephen pulled away. "Let's go Danny, huh?"

Danny looked at his averted face a moment then led the way out into the hall. They put on their jackets.

Danny opened the door and let him go out before him.

They went down the stairs in silence and got into the car. Stephen realised he was still a bit drunk. He felt giddy and his balance was all fucked.

Danny reversed out of the space.

"What are you going to tell John?" Stephen asked.

"Fuck knows."

Stephen looked at him in alarm. "He'll be mad."

Danny looked at him curiously. "Why? He isn't going to know."

"But we've been gone for hours."

"No sweat, we'll think up something."

There was a silence while they sat waiting to cut into the home-flowing traffic.

"Does John know about her?"

"Let's say yes and no." Danny's eyes were on the oncoming traffic.

Stephen looked at him. "He wouldn't like you going there either, would he?"

Danny turned to him this time. "Smart little fucker, aren't you?" And there was something in his eyes that made Stephen colour up hotly. He shut up and looked out the window.

They drove in silence for a while then Danny said, "We ran out of petrol. Just after Thurston. We had to walk back and get some, alright?"

Stephen nodded.

"He doesn't know I filled the tank this morning. It was me that went back and got it. You stayed in the truck, okay?"

Stephen nodded again. They were silent again.

"Danny?" Stephen said without turning.

"Mm?"

"Did you enjoy it?"

Danny rolled down the window a little and kept his eyes on the road. "I always enjoy it, Steve-o. Always."

They arrived back in time for milking.

602

John looked at him, tight-faced, and said, "Where the fuck have you been?"

Danny told him. Stephen watched him lie smoothly and without effort. He couldn't have faced John and done it. When he was finished John looked at Stephen then Danny and said, "This better be the truth Danny or I'll ram my fist up your arse and rip your guts out."

Stephen swallowed, face burning. He felt intensely embarrassed. He wanted to be somewhere else, anywhere else. He'd never heard John talk like that before. It scared him beyond his normal fear of him, as if he was about to do something unhinged, but John only turned away and moved off.

They went back to work without speaking, going their separate ways. Stephen passed him crossing the yard to the house but Danny didn't look at him.

Stephen worked alone and in silence, letting the animals butt him harmlessly, thinking about what had happened.

He hadn't imagined the first time being like that, a woman like her, a place like that, and with someone else watching. Had Danny really enjoyed it? He said he didn't even like her. Stephen couldn't understand why, she'd been nice to him, and she was sexy, but he really *didn't* seem to like her, although he got a big enough stiffy for her, Stephen had noticed *that*. What made it worse was she obviously preferred Danny. It was obvious, the way she acted with him. Trouble was, he didn't have Danny's experience. Danny must have fucked loads of women. He'd probably had at least six. He knew what he was doing. God, he hadn't even been able to put it in properly.

Stephen blushed suddenly, remembering a hundred things that showed up his inexperience, while Danny had said the right thing, done the right thing. He'd even made her come. Stephen hadn't. He didn't even know how to. Hell, he hadn't even thought of it. He shouldn't have done it. Getting drunk always landed you in the shit.

He stood still a moment, staring into the darkness, lost in feeling.

Oh, but it had been good too. Much better than he'd imagined and much better than the time in the car.

He smiled suddenly, cheered. He'd done it with a woman and it had been *much* better than the time in the car.

It was alright after all.

John got him in the hall and pushed him through the house into the front parlour. It was three hours later and the room was frozen, sealed against the early nights and chilled deeply with its winter neglect.

John pushed him up against the wall. "What happened?"

"I told you."

John hit him, deep into his stomach. Danny's face jerked with pain.

"Have you been at him?"

Danny's eyes flew open. "*No.*"

John grabbed his front. "The truth Danny."

"It is the fucking truth, ask him."

John let him go, stared at him. "Then what did you do? He was hunched up like a scalded cat."

"He's frightened of *you*. Is it any wonder he looked like a fucking scalded cat?"

John watched him rub his face. He looked tired, weary, close to tears. He said angrily, "Frightened of me? What the fuck for?"

Danny looked at him, laughed like someone crying, and said, "Because you're scary John."

John took a deep breath and moved away from him.

Danny began to shiver. He slid silently down the wall and sat on the floor, head

resting on his knees.

John turned back and was momentarily thrown, then he saw him on the floor. He went over and hunkered down beside him. "Come up to bed."

Danny didn't look up. "It's only half seven."

"So?"

"They'll go out, leave him on his own."

"You're not his fucking keeper Danny." John began to get angry again.

Danny looked up, equally angry. "I didn't say I was, but he might wonder where we are, might even come looking, comprendez?"

John stood up. "Then let's go now, before the others go out, and he won't know whether we're in at all, will he?"

Danny looked up at him, letting his head lean back against the wall, then John reached out his hand. Danny transferred his gaze to the work-roughened palm.

Then stretched out his hand and took it.

Rab was putting on his jacket. He opened the living room door and found Stephen sitting there by himself. He had the TV on but he was staring at the fire. "On your own?" Rab asked.

Stephen nodded.

"Where's Danny?"

Stephen shook his head.

Rab went in and shut the door, sat on the arm of the armchair. "What's up?"

"I don't know," Stephen shrugged. "Fed up, I suppose."

"Want to come over with me?"

"I can't."

"Sure you can. You're sixteen, good as. Have a Coke or something. They'll let you, everybody else does it."

"Seriously?"

"Course. I'm surprised you never have before. Come on, go and get changed."

"I won't be a minute." Stephen hared out the room.

Rab smiled to himself and started to roll a cigarette.

Stephen ripped off his clothes and put on a clean shirt, the fudgy one Danny had given him. He put on his new jeans and ran a comb through his hair. He pulled his good jacket off the chair.

He went out of the room and heard an odd noise.

He stopped, listened. There it was again. Grunting. He moved towards it. It was coming from John and Danny's room.

He held his breath, moved a little closer. There it was again... then an exclamation... more grunts... then a rising moan.

Suddenly Stephen realised what they were. He went bright red. Jesus. *Jesus.*

He tiptoed away from the door, down the hall. He began to smile. By the time he got downstairs he was grinning.

"What's so funny?" Rab asked.

Stephen laughed. "You're not going to believe this. I just heard John tossing off."

Rab almost slapped a hand over his mouth, managed to turn it into a disbelieving chin-rub. "You what? Where?"

"In his room. You should have heard him. He sounded like a little kid who'd just wet his pants, doing all these whimpers and everything. You'd have thought he was fucking God's gift instead of pulling his dick." He laughed again, letting some of his

fear of John out in derision.

Rab smiled back at him, pushing it, and thought, He probably was Stephen. That's probably *exactly* what he was doing. "Come on," he said.

Stephen followed him out, still grinning.

FIFTY-NINE

Stephen didn't see much of Danny during the weekend. He was working with John mostly. When he did see him he seemed quiet and self-absorbed. He looked like someone with a hangover, or who wasn't getting enough sleep. John was taciturn and silent too, hardly talking to anybody but Danny, and only communicating with him by odd little nods and gestures.

Ian ignored him which pleased Stephen just fine. Rab was silent when John and Danny were around but fine the rest of the time. His mum didn't come in Sundays, but he didn't miss her.

On Monday the snow started again. Rab looked out the window and said, "Maybe we'll have a white Christmas."

"Only *six* more shopping days to go," Stephen trilled in a sweet falsetto.

"Jesus, is it? And I haven't bought a thing." He clutched his brow dramatically.

Stephen laughed. "Don't you buy each other anything then?"

Rab snorted. "You must be joking. Margaret used to buy everybody presents. This year we'll get zilch."

"Bit dismal," Stephen suggested.

Rab shrugged. "Who needs it? We'll get a good dinner though. Your mum's going to provide it."

"Really?" Stephen looked up, surprised.

"Really. John fixed it up with her. I assume you're staying?"

"John hasn't said."

"Then you are. Your mum's cooking it, isn't she? Consider yourself invited. You work here, food provided. You're entitled. John's just taken it for read."

Stephen smiled. "As long as John says it's okay."

"He will."

"Ask him first Rab, promise."

Rab looked at him. "Relax. I'll ask him, okay?"

John came into the kitchen. Rab promptly said, "Stephen's staying for Christmas Day, okay?"

John grunted, frowning, "What the fuck are you asking me for?" And he walked over to the teapot.

Rab grinned at Stephen. Stephen grinned back.

John sat down and said without looking up, "Give Danny a hand with the hen-house, will you Stephen? That run's a fucking disaster. The fence looks like it's held together with spit."

Stephen said, "Sure."

John turned his attention to Rab and began outlining his proposed shelving of the interior of the implement shed. They lapsed into a discussion on lengths of wood. Stephen poured himself another cup of tea and watched the snow.

It took them all morning and the best part of an afternoon. By the time they were finished they were filthy-dusty and tired. Danny rubbed his neck and said, "Let's go have a cup of tea, we missed this morning's."

"You've got shit on your nose."

Danny grimaced and wiped it off, holding his face up for inspection. "Okay?"

"No, bit there."

"Where?"

"No, to the left... no, there."

"Oh for Christsake, get it off me," Danny exclaimed.

Stephen used his sleeve, rubbing it off. Danny looked at him for approval.

Stephen smiled back and nodded.

They went into the kitchen. Danny opened the cooker door and pulled a chair up. "My hands are so cold I can hardly feel anything." He put a kettle on then sat down.

Stephen pulled a chair up beside him. They held their feet up to the fire.

He glanced at Danny. He was slumped down in the chair, head on the back, eyes closed. There was something hypnotic about his face. If you got to looking at it, you kept looking at it, like holding a stone up to the light, watching it sparkle. "You've got a nice face," he said quietly.

Danny opened his eyes almost with a jerk. "Pack that in." His voice was tight, angry.

Stephen looked at him, the surprise plain on his face. What had he said?

Danny ran his hand through his hair and muttered, "Sorry."

Stephen said nothing. Danny sat up. "Look, I said I'm sorry."

"Forget it."

"Oh come on..." He stopped then said, "Look I am terribly, genuinely, bottom of my heart sorry." He smiled at him. "Okay?"

Stephen said, "Okay." But it wasn't really.

Danny settled back down again. They were silent. Gradually the kettle came to the boil. "Shit," Danny grumbled.

"I'll get it." Stephen stood up.

Danny opened his eyes and smiled lazily at him.

Stephen smiled back and went to fill the teapot.

"Bring it over here. Put it on the back of the plate there."

Stephen did, sat down again. "Danny, about last Thursday..." He glanced quickly at him, watching for another abrupt change of mood, but Danny looked just the same, perfectly placid.

"Mm?"

"You took me along just because you didn't know what else to do with me, didn't you?"

Danny opened his eyes, fixed him with them. He wasn't smiling. "I took you because I thought you'd enjoy it, because it was better than bursting a Durex behind a toilet somewhere with some stupid little slag you don't even fancy, that's why I took you. I'm sorry if it was miserable for you."

Stephen swallowed, opened his mouth, shut it again then said, "No it wasn't, honestly." He shook his head. "It wasn't." He looked away. "It was good. I just thought maybe I'd been a gooseberry, you know?"

Danny laughed. "Well you weren't. If anybody was the gooseberry it was me."

Stephen stared into the small bright square of the fire, trying to understand that, then said, "*Did* you like it?"

"Mm-hmm." Danny's voice was deep and sleepy.

Stephen felt something slow turn over in his stomach "All of it?" He breathed it out, still not looking at him.

There was a faint pause this time. Stephen waited, heart thumping, then Danny said in the same slow, sleepy voice, "Mm-hmm."

"So did I." Stephen almost whispered it.

"Good." And Stephen could hear the smile in his voice. "Now why don't you pour the fucking tea?"

Stephen laughed and got up and poured the tea.

The snow got heavier and the wind picked up. By evening it was almost gale-force.

John and Rab went out to check the livestock, Ian to secure things in the yard. Stephen and Danny were left with the washing up. "Better than being out in it," Danny said, watching it slide down the window. "It'll lie," he added.

"Think so?" Stephen peered out between his hands. Danny nodded.

They finished up and the lights went out.

"Classic," Danny announced into the dark.

"Shit, it's dark," Stephen whispered. There was a crash, Stephen swore.

"What was that?" Danny asked.

"Chair, I think."

"Where are you?"

Stephen laughed nervously. "Fuck knows."

Danny reached out towards his voice. "Talk to me."

"Come in Red Four, come in."

Danny caught his arm. Stephen hung on to him, doing another one of those nervous laughs.

"The shipwrecked waifs cling in the storm," Danny said. "I wonder where the lamps are?"

"Where are they usually?"

"I don't know."

They both laughed this time. It was a moonless night and the dark was very intense, like being blind. A faint red line showed round the cooker door.

"Poor Ian, it'll take him half an hour to find his way back. He'll probably end up in the back field."

They laughed again. Danny was aware that they were becoming faintly hysterical but he couldn't seem to stop it.

"Christ it's dark, isn't it?" Stephen's voice was awed.

"Like ink Steve-o, like ink."

"It feels like the room's huge, doesn't it?"

"No walls," Danny agreed.

They held each other a little tighter.

"We can't stand here like babes in the fucking wood all night," Danny said. "Let's try for the living room. The fire will give us a bit of light."

"You lead, I'll follow."

"Hang onto my shirt tail."

Stephen took a fistful of Danny's shirt and let himself be led. They walked into another chair and the edge of a counter before they made it to the door. They knew they were in the hall by the rush of cold air but otherwise it seemed exactly the same.

"Jesus, this is creepy," Danny said. He found the side of the staircase and followed it along. They bumped into the hall table. "Fuck," he cursed.

Then the phone rang. They grabbed each other. Danny pushed him off. "It's only the fucking phone."

It rang on, loud and insistent. Danny groped on the table for it, knocked off the receiver, swore again, and finally succeeded in picking it up. "Hello?"

There was a silence at the end of the line. "Hello?" Danny said again. The silence crawled inside him like a slow death.

Stephen held his arm, hissed, "Who is it?" He could sense Danny's fear like it was something tangible, a primeval instinct.

"Who the fuck is this?" Danny said.

The phone cut dead. The purring was worse. Danny put the receiver back down

quickly, pulled Stephen's arm in against him. Stephen said, "What is it?"

"Nothing, given myself the willies, that's all." He laughed unsteadily.

"Who was it?"

"Fuck knows. Wrong number, weirdo, who knows?" Danny pushed him away again. "Come on."

They passed the terrifying openness of the stairs, then the worse gap where the hall turned into the front parlour. They could see the glass door now, very faintly golden. "Salvation," Danny said. He opened the door.

"Come on, let's open this fire." He did it himself, sure-footed now in the faint light. He could make out dim shapes of furniture. "There, sit down." He pushed Stephen back onto the settee, sat down beside him then laughed, obviously shaken. "Jesus, that phone really put the shit up me." He laughed some more.

The fire began to glow brighter. Stephen looked at him, desperate to see something he recognised. He could only make him out dimly, the dark holes of his eyes, the white of his face. "Me too," he confessed.

They were sitting close together, thighs touching. Stephen felt the sudden warmth of it, safe here in the light, no longer blinded, laughing about it, chasing away the demons. The fire glowed up bright, filled with heat. Stephen looked at him. "Danny?"

Danny was thinking about the phone call, his mind jumping with it. "Mm?" He looked at him suddenly, as if he'd just remembered him.

"Can I ask you something?"

He nodded vaguely.

"You ever do it with another boy?"

There was a small silence then Danny laughed, properly this time.

"Why are you laughing? I'm serious."

"Sorry," Danny coughed. "It just struck me as funny. Why do you want to know?"

"Just wondered." Stephen looked into the fire.

"Yes," Danny said.

Stephen looked at him, searching his face. "Really?"

Danny nodded.

"When?"

"When? That's an odd question. Tell me why you want to know."

"I told you, I'm just curious."

"As to when?"

"No, I just mean if you'd ever done it, that's all."

"Have *you*?" Danny asked, already knowing the answer, suspecting that's what this was all about.

"Once."

Danny nodded. "And did you enjoy it?"

Stephen hadn't expected the question, couldn't seem to understand it. "Enjoy it? No, of course not."

"Why did you do it then?"

"I was drunk," he said as if that must be self-evident. There was a silence then he said slowly, as if he'd never thought of it before, "Did you enjoy it then?"

"Of course."

Stephen stared at him. He thought he saw Danny's mouth quirk in the dull light. "You're taking the piss."

"I'm not."

"Seriously? You really liked it?"

"Yep."

"How old were you?"

Ah here we were, back at when. "Old enough..." Danny looked at him, Stephen

could feel him looking at him, "... to know what I was doing."

Stephen blushed, hoped Danny couldn't see it. "You ever wanted to... well, you know, do it again?" He looked away again.

"Why? Do you want another try?" He felt Stephen's shock, felt him move his leg away from his.

"Don't be funny Danny."

Danny said nothing. Slowly the leg relaxed against his again, softly, like something melting. There was a long silence. The fire grew steadily brighter, flames flickering. Danny's face seemed to dance in it.

"Would you ever do it again?" Stephen asked.

"If I fancied whoever was offering."

"*Fancied...?*" Stephen tried again, lowering his voice. "If you *fancied*... what, a bloke? D'you mean a bloke?"

"That's what we're talking about, isn't it?"

Stephen stared at him. Danny wasn't looking at him. He seemed perfectly relaxed, even disinterested. He was watching the flames.

"Did you fancy the bloke you did it with then?"

Danny said, "I thought so... at the time."

Stephen wet his lips and said, "What was he like?"

Danny turned this time. "What was yours?"

Stephen looked at him then blushed and looked away. He was silent for a long time before he said again, "Danny?"

"Mm?"

"I was old enough to know what I was doing too."

"Mm?" Danny prompted.

"I feel really bad about it sometimes."

"Don't," Danny said flatly. "Do it, forget it. That's the motto."

"But don't you think it's a bit sick, that? It's not exactly normal, is it?"

"What's normal? No-one's normal. Normal's bullshit."

Stephen didn't know how to answer that but he felt better. Danny didn't disapprove, didn't even seem to mind, and he'd done it too. He said, "I liked it much better with her... you know, your girlfriend."

Danny laughed, said nothing.

Stephen smiled. He leaned his head back beside his on the settee and turned to look at Danny's profile. What thick eyelashes he had. He said, "Your hair looks like tarry blood in this light."

Danny smiled slightly. "You're a poet Steve-o."

Stephen laughed, pleased. "You ought to get your ear pierced."

"Get stuffed."

"No seriously."

Danny turned his head and looked at him. They were suddenly very close, their faces near enough to kiss. Stephen blinked, felt his heart stop. Danny moved his head towards him...

Then sat up. "I wonder where Ian's got to. He should have made it back by now."

Stephen lay there feeling his heart thumping. His face was flushed with heat. He was painfully, intensely aware of the stirring in his belly. He felt excited, disappointed and sick at once. He swallowed, his mouth full of saliva.

Danny stretched and stood up. Stephen watched him silhouetted against the fire. He felt suddenly heavy, drowsy, unable to move. He wanted Danny to sit back down, not be so fucking energetic. He was afraid Danny was going to dash off and look for Ian.

Danny turned and looked at him. Stephen looked back, willing him.

Danny sat back down.

Stephen sighed. He was further away now, but still there.

Danny put his arms behind his head. "Poor John, stuck out in that," he said.

Stephen grunted. He didn't care about John. He wished Danny would sit close again. He was sleepy. He felt envious of John sharing with him, curling up beside him in bed.

He suddenly felt a cold trickle of something run through his head. He chased it. He didn't want to look at it. He wanted to go on being warm, comfortable. No worries, no guilt. He heard himself say, "Did you kiss him?"

"Who?"

Stephen heard the sudden tenseness in his voice, wondered if he was overstepping the mark. "The bloke you did it with."

"No," Danny said, and Stephen could hear it now, the flat anger.

"Sorry," he offered. "I'm bugging you."

"No," Danny said. "It's alright." But Stephen knew he had been.

"Think Ian's alright?" he asked, not caring a monkey's, but he asked anyway.

"With any luck he's fallen into something."

Stephen laughed. Danny looked at him, smiled. It was okay, they were friends again. "It's nice here like this, isn't it?" Stephen said, looking at the fire.

"Mm," Danny agreed.

"Cosy."

"You're a romantic Steve."

"Me?" Stephen looked at him, surprised.

"Yes, you."

"No I'm not." He was faintly outraged by the suggestion.

Danny laughed. "Yes you are, an out and out romantic."

"Rubbish."

Danny laughed again, quietly, then lunged at him, tickling him fiercely.

Stephen shrieked, unprepared for the attack. He grabbed at Danny's hands, flailing helplessly. They rolled off the couch in a tangle, thumping down painfully onto the floor, but Danny went on tickling, relentless.

Stephen finally begged him to stop. Danny heard the panicked pain in his voice and let him go. They lay there side by side on the hearth rug, panting with exertion. "You bastard," Stephen gasped, half-laughing, half-agonised.

Danny laughed, choked on it, coughing violently, then subsided onto the floor again.

Stephen dragged himself up onto one elbow to look down into Danny's face. Danny lay there, eyes closed, chest rising and falling evenly, still breathing heavily from the skirmish. His hands were folded on his stomach. His face was bright, incandescent with the fire. Stephen lifted his hand and slowly brought his fingers close to Danny's mouth.

Danny's eyes opened suddenly. "Don't," he said sharply.

Stephen dropped his hand, swallowing, suddenly outrageously close to tears. "I wasn't going to do anything."

"I know," Danny said and his voice was soft. That made it worse. Stephen could feel his mouth trembling. He lay back down quickly, biting his lip, berating himself. *Don't you dare, don't you dare.*

Then the lights came back on.

Danny got up without looking at him and said, "I'm just going to see where Ian's got to."

Stephen said nothing.

When Danny left the room he got up into a sitting position. He could feel the lump

in his throat as if something was wedged there. He swallowed, but it didn't go away. All it did was make it hurt.

He dropped his head on his knees and for the second time in so many weeks felt the tears, slowly, and for absolutely no reason, start to run down his face.

Danny's front was thick with snow in the short distance it took to cover the space between the house and the milking shed. The lights were on inside. "*Ian?!*" he shouted, sliding the door shut.

"Here," Ian answered right beside him, making him jump.

"What the hell are you doing lurking in here?"

"I came in out the snow to await your imminent rescue, then I remembered there was a lamp in here." He jerked his head at the wall. "Then I realised I had no bloody matches anyway." He smiled. "But by then the lights had come on, so what did it matter?"

Danny looked him up and down curiously. "Is everything okay?"

"Fine," Ian smiled.

"Then why the fuck are we standing out here? Why didn't you come back in?"

"I wanted to talk to you… without the little shithead in tow."

Danny put his hands on the aluminium guard rail. "He's not a little shithead." He gave him a hard look. "And don't start messing with him. He told me about you showing him the photographs."

"It's Rab that likes lookalikes Danny, not me."

Danny started sliding his hand to and fro on the rail restlessly. "Say it, whatever it is, and let's get back inside."

Ian kept silent until Danny was forced to look at him then he said, "He's got a crush on you."

Danny rubbed his face irritably, as if something had bitten him. "Bullshit."

"Don't be so sure."

Danny put both hands back on the rail, arms braced, then dropped his head, looking over his arm at him. "Look, what's it to you?"

"Nothing. I just wonder, how long are you going to be able to resist?"

Danny stared at him, arms rigid, knuckles white on the bar. "It isn't any problem. It isn't *ever* going to be any problem."

"Someone drooling over you, right in front of your eyes, every day? Come *on*. You get so fucking turned on at other people's want you can get your little penis into white-out just thinking about it."

"Shut up."

Ian was smiling thickly now, one on top of the other. "Fuck, he *wants* you to do it, even if he doesn't know it himself yet, and you're pushing him away. Remind you of anyone?" And now his face was bright with it.

"I said, shut up." And Danny dropped his arms, stood there loose, waiting.

Ian held up his hands. "Uh-uh. Not me. Not my scene." He paused then whispered, "Want me to take him off your hands?"

Danny stood there for a moment, blinking, feeling an intense sinking déjà vu.

"Mm?" Ian's persistent whisper, close to his head.

Danny looked down at his hands. They were clenching gently at his sides as if he were kneading fur or thick velvet. "You've done this before," he said. His voice had no substance. He looked up slowly into Ian's face. Ian simply smiled.

Danny looked round. "In here? No, this wasn't built. The tractor shed… or was it the old Dutch barn?"

Ian rubbed his own cheek, flat-palmed, half-smiling, lips parted, watching him.

Danny moved closer. "Did you use those very same words? Was it? Word for word?" And Danny grabbed him, pulling him up close.

Ian pounced on his mouth, dragging his head towards him, pushing his tongue in.

Danny shoved him off, scrubbing at his mouth. "Christ you're low. Unbelievably..." but he couldn't finish it. "You leave him alone," he said, backing away from him, moving sideways towards the door.

And he pulled the door open and disappeared into the snow.

When Danny got back into the house Stephen had disappeared from the living room, assumably gone to his room. He wondered if he should follow him but decided to leave it. He was probably sulking or feeling sorry for himself. Danny could cope with neither.

John and Rab came back in, blue with cold, their clothes running with melting snow. The air was thick with curses, the dog running wet round the room. "Put the kettle on," John said.

Danny did it while they pulled off coats and boots. "The power was off," he said. "You just missed it."

John grunted, "I know. The whole village was out. We saw it coming in." He grunted again, pulling another boot off. "Where's Ian?"

"Still outside somewhere. He was in the milking shed five minutes ago."

"Doing what? Jerking off to increase the yield?"

Danny saw Rab smirking across the table at him. "Probably."

The kettle boiled. Danny made tea and sat back down again.

"Where's Stephen?" Rab asked.

"Upstairs I think."

John looked up at him briefly then away again. There was a small silence then Ian came in.

"Where are the lamps these days?" Danny asked him.

"Under the stairs, where they've always been."

"Be nice to be told. We had to sit in the dark like a right pair of tits."

"Plenty to do in the dark."

There was another silence. It was John who broke it. "Meaning what?" he asked Ian, but he was looking at Danny.

"Just an observation," Ian said. He sat down and pulled the teapot over, helping himself to the first cup.

John kept looking at Danny. Danny was staring at Ian, mouth tight. Rab sat there, head cocked to one side, running his finger along the table, back again, listening.

John poured tea for himself. Only Rab and Danny, sitting facing each other, remained motionless. The clock's ticking seemed intolerably loud. The dog sat up suddenly and scratched, subsided before the cooker again.

John stood up abruptly, taking his mug with him, and crossed the room. "Danny," he commanded as he got to the door.

Danny wanted to say, What? just to piss him off, but he got up and followed him out. Ian smiled at his disappearing back.

As soon as they were out the room Rab said without looking at him, "You little turd."

"Boo-hoo, I'm hurted."

Rab leaned across suddenly and grabbed the mug out of his hand just as he was lifting it to his mouth. He turned it upside down in Ian's lap. Ian yelled as the scalding tea soaked through his jeans.

"Big fucking wet dream Ian." And he banged the empty mug down and went out.

John pulled Danny down beside him on the settee. He had the television on, up loud, no lights. "What was he getting at?"

"You know what he was getting at."

"What goes on with you and the boy?"

"Nothing and he knows it."

"Nothing on your part maybe. You think I'm blind? He thinks the sun shines out your arse."

"So? What am I supposed to do about it?"

"Stop encouraging him."

"I don't encourage him."

"Then *dis*courage him."

Danny was silent.

"You hear me Danny?" John pulled his face round. "I'm sick of him trailing round after you."

"Then why the fuck do you keep shoving us together?"

John held him a moment, face angry, then let him go.

"Look, just give it a break for a while. Put me with Rab or something."

John turned on him. "Yeah, you'd like that, wouldn't you? What's wrong, kid's blind adoration not enough for you?"

Danny rubbed his face. "Oh for fuck's sake John..."

"I *bet* you'd like that."

"Listen..." Danny sat forward, half round to face him. "I don't want to go anywhere with any of them. Not him, not Rab, not Ian..." *and not you*, he wanted to add. "They're all a pain in the fucking arse, but believe me, he's the best of the bunch. At least he isn't always trying to stick his hand down my pants."

John made a small noise of disgust. "Yeah, right."

"Jesus John, he's only fifteen. The idea hasn't even occurred to him."

"I don't believe I'm hearing this. He was playing cocksuckers with Rab in the back seat of a car not three weeks ago. He's probably been fucking since he was ten and sucking dick since he was twelve."

"Christ John, what do you think this is, the re-enactment of your life?"

John slapped him. "You dirty-mouthed little shit. Why don't you keep your trap shut?"

Danny got up and sat in the armchair, away from him.

John glared at him. "Get back here."

"Fuck off."

John lunged up but Danny was faster, half-ready for it. He went over the chair arm and put the settee between them. "Fucking *leave* it John. I'm sick of you thumping me about."

"Danny..." John growled it, low, imperative, like warning a dog.

"No."

"I'm gonna mark you Danny..."

"If you even try I'm going to yell the fucking place down, then you can explain that to Stephen and his mother and the whole fucking village."

John stared at him, unable to believe his ears, then he turned, took a step towards the door, and with a grunt of anger put his fist through the plate glass door.

Danny stared at it. Heavy shards hung down from the top of the frame like a jagged curtain, icicles. The bottom had caved in completely and lay on the floor. John's fist was hanging by his side. Blood dripped off the knuckles onto the carpet. He was

grinning, manic.

"You shit," Danny said in a slow whispery voice. "You stupid mad shit."

Rab came down the stairs at a run. "Danny? Danny are you okay?"

Danny jerked out of it, white face flushing up with anger. "Yeah, great." He looked at John. "Why don't you open the door Godzilla? Or are you just going to bleed to death on the floor?"

The door handle turned from outside. Danny yelled, "Hold it! Don't open it yet. There's glass everywhere." He stepped over and bent down and began picking up the pieces. He tried to ignore the steady drip of blood on the floor beside his head where John stood watching him.

Rab hunkered down at the other side and peered through the shattered door. "What happened?"

"Get me the bin," Danny said then added, "Hurry up, he's bleeding like a pig." He saw Ian's feet come out of the kitchen and stop at the far end of the hall then Stephen's, in stocking soles, come running down off the stairs.

Rab came back and passed the bin through. Danny cleared the biggest pieces and passed it back. He used the hearth shovel to clear the last of the blockage and opened the door. Rab came in, looking at John, face curling with disgust. "And what's this supposed to prove?"

John smiled at him, nodded faintly and said, "Go crawl up your arsehole queer-boy."

Danny went out, pushing Stephen back into the hall, but he saw in an instant that the boy had heard the exchange. His face was white, frightened. Danny sent him to get his trainers. "Go on, it's covered in fucking glass in here. Jump to it."

Stephen went back up the stairs two at a time. Ian still stood there at the kitchen door, watching. Danny walked up the hall towards him. "Someday Ian, if God's good to me, it'll be your fucking head he puts through it."

Ian smiled. *Nothing touches me Danny. Nothing.* He turned and went back into the kitchen.

Rab and John came out the living room. Danny stood back to let them pass then stood in the kitchen doorway and watched Rab shove his hand under a running tap then attempt to pick the glass out with tweezers. "Fucking animal," Rab said, but John was watching Danny over the top of his bent head. He might as well have been saying, Rhubarb. John wasn't listening.

Danny turned away, hearing Stephen come back down the stairs. He went out to meet him. "Come and give me a hand to clean this up."

They picked the rest of the glass up then Danny hoovered the floor for splinters. "Come on," he said, pulling out the flex and dropping it where he stood. "I've had enough of this, let's go."

"Go?" Stephen looked at him.

"Yeah, go." Danny looked out the window. "Snow's off. Go and get our jackets. Hurry up, chop chop."

Stephen went up the stairs two at a time again. Danny waited in the living room doorway, watching their shadows moving in the kitchen, listening to the sound of their voices.

Stephen came back down. Danny grabbed his jacket, taking his arm and propelling him into the front hall. "Come on, out the front," he whispered.

They went out quickly through the front hall and out the front door.

The snow crunched underfoot. The air was icy cold, dry as peppermints. It caught in their throats. "Jeez," Stephen whispered.

"Come on." Danny went down the path and over the grass to the road. "We'll go to the pub."

Stephen called out after him, running to catch up, "They'll wonder where we've gone."

"Let them."

They went inside, feeling the blast of hot air come out to meet them. Danny hadn't been inside in months. He was greeted like a long-lost son. He bought a double rum and a Coke. The publican ribbed him about his drinking elsewhere.

Danny endured the banter and took the drinks over to the farthest booth. Stephen was hiding in the corner. "This do?" he asked

"Couldn't be better," Danny said.

The pub wasn't particularly busy. Monday night regulars. Danny poured half the rum into the glass of Coke. Stephen smiled up at him. Danny topped his own rum up with what was left in the Coke bottle. "Okay?" he asked.

Stephen nodded.

Danny sighed and leaned his head back against the wall.

"What happened?" Stephen asked after a minute.

Danny opened his eyes, looked at him, then into his drink. "Listen Steve-o, he's got a shitty temper. I mean, you know that, don't you?"

Stephen nodded, feeling an odd kind of relief to finally admit it.

"Yeah, it's not exactly secret, is it? You've heard all the rumours." Stephen wanted to say, What rumours? but Danny was talking to himself. "He lost it, put his fist through the door, that's all."

"He could really hurt himself doing that," Stephen said earnestly.

Danny laughed. "Not John, he's indestructible."

"What were you arguing about?"

Danny shrugged. "Nothing important. He just sees red sometimes. It doesn't take much."

Stephen made a puffing noise, letting his breath out in disgust, amazement.

Danny sat forwards. "Listen, don't tell your mum, okay?"

Stephen looked at him.

"Tell her we were just larking about, otherwise she'll think you're living with a maniac or something."

Stephen nodded, feeling oddly irritable.

"Good lad," Danny smiled and sat back, taking another drink.

He stretched his legs out suddenly, digging in his pocket. Stephen watched him cramming his hand in. "These are getting tighter than fucking Rab's." Finally he pulled out some change. "Here, go and put something on the jukebox, something loud. I don't want to think." He gave Stephen the money.

Stephen went across and put the money in, selected three tracks. He came back and sat down. It came on almost immediately, loud and wild. Danny laughed, pulled him in against him, whispering in his ear, "Visualise their faces, behind here." He jerked his head back in the direction of the regulars' cubby-hole.

Stephen slid along the seat and stuck his head round the partition. He came back in almost immediately, pulling his face into an impromptu impersonation. Danny barked a laugh.

Stephen could feel excitement bubbling inside him.

Danny got up and bought another round of drinks. Same again. "Are we going to stay here till closing?" Stephen asked.

"You bet."

Two girls came into the bar. One of them turned, saw Danny, and came to a standstill. She blushed and turned away again. The other turned a moment or two later, but she took longer to look away. Danny took a drink. He hadn't smiled at them. Stephen said, "D'you know them?"

Danny shook his head. The second girl looked over again. Danny looked away till she turned away again, bending her head to her friend's ear. "D'you want them?" he said abruptly.

It took Stephen a moment or two to realise he was speaking to him and another to truly understand the question. He might have been asking if he wanted a packet of crisps. "They wouldn't even look at me. It's you they fancy." He paused "Do you?"

Danny shook his head. "I'm too tired to make the effort."

Stephen felt relieved. He didn't know why.

Danny drained his drink and said suddenly, "I've never liked a woman in my life."

Stephen looked at him, feeling a heavy dullness creep into his chest. "What do you mean?"

"What I say."

"You liked your mam."

Danny laughed. "Christ, especially not my 'mam'."

"But why not?" The idea was inconceivable to Stephen.

Danny looked at him. "Forget it."

But Stephen couldn't forget it. How could anyone really dislike their own mother? She was blood. You loved her no matter what. "You don't really mean that," he said finally.

Danny laughed shortly. "Okay, I don't really mean it. I loved my mother, okay?"

"Where do you think she is?"

"Dead."

Stephen gaped at him. "But how d'you know? How can you be sure?"

"A little bird told me." And horribly Danny grinned.

Stephen took some of his drink. Danny got up again and got another. Stephen watched him standing along from the girls, not looking at them, yet somehow aware of them, his body subtly conveying it, as if he wanted to turn to them but didn't want to be caught doing it.

He brought the drinks back. Stephen felt slightly tipsy already but Danny seemed completely unaffected. "Hang on a sec' Steve, I'm going to make a phone call, okay?"

"Who?" Stephen asked.

Danny smiled crookedly at him. "Nosy little fucker, aren't you?"

Stephen blushed.

Danny squeezed his shoulder. "Be back in a tick."

He disappeared out into the hall.

Danny went into the small alcove that served as a half-private phone booth.

He checked through two pockets and picked up the phone. He fed the coins in, punched out the number. He rested his head on the wall, looking at his feet in the darkness. The phone purred in his ear.

Purr-purr

Purr-purr

Purr-purr

Purr-

Someone lifted it. "Hello?" The voice was slightly breathless, as if they had run a distance to answer it.

Danny didn't reply.

"Hello?" they said again.

Danny lifted his head and leaned back against the wall, deep in the dark, closing his eyes.

"Hello?" the voice said again, angrier this time.

Danny hung up.

Smiled.

"Get them?"

"Yep."

Danny wasn't going to tell him any more, that was obvious.

"*Danny...*" Stephen hissed suddenly. "Look, it's Rab."

Danny was half way to sitting down. He finished the action. Rab saw them. Danny smiled at him, slow and somehow dirty. It gave Stephen goosepimples when he did that, like watching a flick knife spring to life.

Rab didn't smile back. He went over to the bar and bought a beer and brought it over. Stephen saw the girls turn and look at him as they did at Danny, although not with the same recognition. He realised with a sudden feeling of incomprehension that Rab was good-looking too. Somehow it had simply passed him by, as if Danny had blinded him.

"So this is where you went." Rab took a mouthful, wiped his hand over his mouth. "He's going apeshit."

Danny smiled. "Good."

A strange look passed between them and Stephen suddenly felt acutely aware that he wasn't wanted there, that Rab had more to say and wasn't saying it because he was there. He shifted in his seat, suddenly irritable. Why did Rab have to come in anyway and spoil things? Why couldn't he mind his own flickin' business? Danny was old enough to do what he liked.

"You're being a party pooper Robbie, give us a break." Danny was still smiling at him, but Stephen could feel the animosity between them. He felt glad Danny had said it, felt his heart zip up a little. *You tell him Danny.*

Rab leant across the table. "And when you go back?"

And now Danny stopped smiling. "That's my problem."

Stephen didn't understand what they were talking about, but he felt suddenly afraid for him. "Maybe we should go back," he said.

Danny smiled at him. "Relax. We'll go back when we're ready and not before. It'll give him a chance to cool down." But Stephen could see the corner of Rab's averted face, the hand tight on his glass, and knew Danny was feeding him bullshit.

Danny squeezed his arm. "Relax."

Stephen forced a smile. Danny finished his drink and got up to get another.

They didn't leave till closing time.

All three went back together. Stephen was drunk. Rab was drunk. Even Danny was drunk.

Outside the cold hit them for six, making them all feel even drunker. "Ho boy," Rab drawled, "are *you* kids drunk..."

"Listen to who's talking," Danny said.

Stephen tripped over the kerb. Danny caught his arm and dragged him upright. Stephen laughed inordinately, as if it was the funniest thing that had ever happened to him. Danny put an arm round his waist. "Lean on me, little brother, and I shall guide you safely through the night."

Stephen felt ecstatically happy. It had been the best night of his whole life and now Danny was calling him his little brother.

Rab walked slightly ahead of them. They safely navigated the road. Danny suddenly announced, "I'm going to take a piss," and let Stephen go.

Rab caught at him, saying to Danny's back, "Wait till you get in. You're only thirty yards from the fucking house Danny."

"No, I'm going to take a piss in the bus shelter. I've always wanted to piss in the bus shelter. Everyone else does it, why not me?"

"Because you live right next door to it, you fucking idiot." But Danny had already disappeared inside.

Stephen looked at Rab's face and began to laugh. Rab could feel him shaking with it. He looked down at him and began to laugh himself. Danny was singing something loud and tuneless over the sound of his urination.

"Come *on* Danny," Rab said, peering inside after a minute or two.

"Go 'way."

"Christ, what are you doing, pissing a lake?"

"I've had a lot to drink."

Stephen could hear it splashing on interminably. He started laughing again. Rab propped him up against the wall and went inside. "Go *away*," Danny muttered.

"What are you doing, having a quick wank while you're at it?"

"You wish."

Stephen grinned some more and moved round to the front of the shelter. He could see Danny now, back to him, looking down between his legs. A dark stream flowed down and out over the bottom of the shelter.

"You're a dirty bastard Danny," Rab was saying in a low voice. He was leaning against the wall, watching him.

"You're watching."

Rab laughed. "I'm not stupid."

Stephen felt his smile slide, felt his brain dully start to register what they were saying. He stood there in the dark, four feet away from them, listening to it change; the sound of the words, the tone, what was between the lines becoming the lines, until the lines themselves disappeared.

Danny was fastening up. He turned half-way to face Rab. Stephen could see both their profiles in the light from the street lamps, orange, dull, shadows and headaches.

Rab said quietly to him, "You don't get any harder to look at Danny."

Stephen felt his heart thump hard, so hard he could feel his skin jump under his hand. His shirt felt fragile with the heavy pound beneath it.

"Look on, it's free."

They were talking softly so they wouldn't be overheard, by him, because he was supposed to be tucked away round the side, wasn't he? Not round here, watching them, listening to them. Then Stephen saw Rab move towards him, the light slide along his face, showing his cheekbone, the underside of his chin, all sharp, and Danny's hair, suddenly deep, flaring blood into the light, and Stephen knew they were kissing, arms by their sides, not touching, just their mouths, kissing in the dark, standing above Danny's piss kissing, and Stephen was watching them.

And he felt his heart rip. Right up the middle.

Stephen got round the shelter, going back the way he'd come, hanging onto the half-wall then moving up round the side. He staggered painfully up the grass and onto the farm road.

Inside the shelter Danny broke away and said, "Where's the boy?"

"Outside," Rab said and tried to pull him back.

Danny pushed him off. He went outside, saw Stephen disappear round the side of the house and knew he'd seen them. He went after him, hearing Rab call out his name behind him.

He caught up with him outside the back door, pulled him round. "Hold it... whoa."
Stephen pulled his arm free. "Let me go." And Danny knew he had, no mistake.
"Wait... Stephen."

"I won't say anything, you needn't worry." Stephen kept his face firmly away.

Rab came round the corner. "What's up? What's everybody running away for?"

Stephen pulled away violently, saying again, "Let me go." He sounded as if he was close to tears.

"What's wrong?" Rab persisted.

Danny turned on him. "Let it go Rab, eh? Just give us five minutes. Go and tell him we'll be in, you left us coming out the pub. Five minutes." Danny kept a tight grip on Stephen's arm.

Rab pushed past Stephen and went into the house, slamming the door.

Danny tugged Stephen's arm. "Look at me Steve." But Stephen kept his face averted. "Come on Steve, it was just fooling around."

That moved him. He whirled on him and Danny could see the silver tracks going down his cheeks, his eyes lustrous with unshed tears. "You *kissed* him!"

"Shhh..."

"You fucking shoved me off when I wasn't going to do anything and you were standing there *kissing* him. I heard what John called him. He's a fucking poof and you let him kiss you!" And he burst out crying in earnest, pressing his face hopelessly against the wall, hands above his head, sobbing his heart out.

"Shhh..." Danny said again, and he put his arm around his shoulders, trying to quieten him, but he turned violently, pushing Danny away.

"Are you one too? A fucking queer-boy like him?" His face was distorted with rage.

Danny slapped him. Stephen flew back against the wall, hiccuping into silence with shock.

Danny grabbed his jacket. "Who was it got in the back seat of a fucking car with him, eh? Who was it let him suck his knob like a lollipop until he shot his wad? Who Stephen?" Danny pushed him away.

Stephen stood there against the wall, face so white he looked ill, greenish. "Danny..." he said, almost like a cry, then he doubled up and threw up.

"*Shit*," Danny cursed and jumped back, missing the worst of it. The yard light came on, hugely bright. The vomit looked dreadful, a bright repulsive splash in the snow.

Danny turned away. Stephen retched some more. Danny put his hand on his back. "Hang on, I'll get something to clean you up. Stay here."

Stephen nodded dumbly.

Danny went into the kitchen. John got up.

"Save it John, he's been sick. Let me clean him up first." Danny didn't look at his face. He knew what it would be like. He went back out.

He wiped Stephen's shoes down with some rag and told him to move back a bit. He swilled the vomit away with a bucket of water.

Stephen went into the kitchen. He could feel John staring at him, but he was past caring. He sat in front of the stove where Danny had put him while he refilled the bucket. Numbly he heard Danny go out, come back in, lock the back door. He heard Danny say, "Give me ten, just to get him to bed. I'll come up, okay?"

John didn't answer but he went out of the room.

Danny hunkered down beside him and unfastened his jacket, took his hands and rubbed them between his own. "Okay?"

Stephen didn't answer, couldn't. If he sat here long enough, still and silent, he might die without waking up.

"Steve-o, come on, snap out of it. It's not the end of the world."

Stephen kept his eyes shut.

"Come on." Danny pulled him up. "Let's get you to bed."

Danny kept a hold on his arm all the way upstairs, as if he was going to run away or something. He stopped outside the bathroom. "Want to pee?"

Stephen shook his head. They went on into his room. Danny opened the door and put on the light. He propelled him in, shut the door again, sat Stephen on the bed. He closed the curtains and put on the bedside lamp, put out the overhead light. "You manage?"

Stephen nodded and continued to sit there.

Danny made a sharp noise of irritation and came over. He pulled Stephen's jacket off and began unfastening his shirt, easing him out of it. He pulled his jeans and shoes off and eased him into bed, still in his pants and socks. Stephen didn't protest. He curled up into a tight, cold ball.

Danny brushed his hair with his hand. "We'll talk tomorrow, okay?"

Stephen didn't answer him.

"You be alright?"

Stephen didn't say anything.

Danny stood up. Stephen heard him move away and wanted to ask him to stay, to make everything alright again, but Danny had already gone.

Stephen began to cry.

All over again.

John was smoking.

Danny shrugged his jacket off and hung it in the wardrobe.

"You stink of puke."

Danny said nothing. He took his clothes off slowly and methodically. John watched him. He was sitting fully dressed in the chair. When Danny was down to his shorts John stopped him with a curt, "Come here."

Danny walked over. Before he had registered his intention John had pulled him down and pushed the cigarette into his stomach, grinding it in.

Danny felt his bladder let go with fright and pain, but there was hardly anything to let go of. Nevertheless John pushed his hand inside his shorts and said, "What's this, a heavy dew?"

Danny lay there, passive, like some overgrown schoolboy sprawling in his lap, and felt the slow, itchy pain start to flare out across his skin, an angry vicious bee sting of it.

John's hand squeezed him, tangled tight in his pubic hair, squeezed his balls, always verging on pain. "You left me here all night, for that."

"No."

"For that little shit," he insisted as if Danny hadn't spoken.

"Don't talk fucking stupid."

He dug his nails in deep under Danny's balls. "I don't talk stupid, not ever."

Danny gritted his teeth, waiting for it to stop. Slowly John let him go, began gently squeezing again. "What did you do?"

"We just went across the road. We were with Rab. Ask him... ask the boy. You know he couldn't lie to save his life. We got drunk, came home. That's it."

"Why did you do it?"

"You annoyed me. All that fucking macho strutting gets up my nose."

John became intensely silent, over-still. "You prefer our resident queer-boy, or maybe Mr Conley, Mr fucking Nice, is that it?"

"No, I just don't like being punched about."

"Like fuck you don't." He pushed Danny off, dragging his shorts down. Danny

half-sat, half-fell on the floor. John dropped down beside him and crammed him into his mouth, like a hungry man swallowing meat wholesale.

Danny saw the entirety of his penis disappear inside his mouth. He dropped back limply, closing his eyes. He went over the numbers of his library tickets, tried to remember the months in French. He had learned that once, a hundred thousand years ago.

John pulled him out of his mouth, then trailed his tongue over it. "Beautiful," he said, his voice ragged, and then he took him in again, slow and deep, like a ship sliding down a slipway into water.

Danny let a breath out as quietly as he could. John did it again, withdrawing his head, then that slow, slipping slide in again. He kept doing it till Danny pushed his head away, face flushed, nerves jumping.

John looked up at him, holding his thickly veined cock in one hand. "He couldn't do it Danny. He doesn't understand what you need. He wouldn't know where to start."

Danny looked down at him, licked his lips. "I told you, he's of no interest." The sight of his own cock sucked into unnatural engorgement was exciting him, John down there holding it like he was worshipping it. He'd seen it all before, a million times, but it never failed to twist his guts.

John looked at him, smiled knowingly. "Want to come off on it? I'm willing."

Danny shook his head.

"You think I can't?" John smiled.

He began to talk to him, holding his cock lightly between his hands, only occasionally doing that slow slide into his mouth to bring him up into full relief again. Then he'd start talking again.

It poured on and on, a slow masturbation with words, John hardly touching him, and when he finally said, "Just my tongue..." and he did it, "...here," it was then Danny realised he'd had his hand shoved inside his own trousers all the time he'd been talking.

Danny lifted his head, saw what he was doing, saw his other hand start to slowly pull his foreskin down, further and further, peeling him back tighter and tighter, until his hand was down against Danny's balls, turning Danny's shaft into a huge totem, an object, nothing more. Suddenly there was no more movement, just that frig, frig inside John's pocket. Danny hung there, watching John kneel before him, his fist performing his obeisance, and he felt like his whole body was inside his cock, standing up there as John's altar.

"You're nothing but this lousy lump of meat. You know that, don't you? But God, don't we love you for it? Every last fucking miserable bastard of us. Look at me grovelling in front of you, like I've been grovelling since you were twelve years old. It's pathetic." And he let Danny go, dragging his own zip down and pulling his penis out into his hand saying, "Look."

Danny's cock lay there, abandoned. John took no more than two pulls on himself before he began to come, staring at it spurting out whitely between his fingers, whispering, "Pathetic..."

Danny felt something surge up inside him. He gasped, dragging his legs up, spreading himself wide, making a grab for his genitals, wanting to feel the warped satisfaction of whatever climax he could achieve.

John dropped back onto his heels and watched Danny's face twitching helplessly, unable to hide it, as the aborted mess boiled out from under his weakly grasping hands.

John smiled and pushed between his legs whispering, "Got you," then lowered his head and took the final pulse of Danny's writhing penis deep in his mouth.

Danny woke at two in the morning with a raging thirst and bursting for a pee. He groaned.

He would have to get up. Shit.

He rolled onto his back and dragged his arms out of the blankets.

Shit again.

John grunted beside him, rolling over to him and putting his arm across his chest. Danny picked it up and laid it gently alongside John's body, shifted his legs to the edge of the bed.

"What's the matter?" John rolled it all into one word.

"Got to go pee." And Danny swung his legs out.

John grunted something unintelligible and pulled the blankets over his head.

Danny caught the edge of the bedside table and cursed.

"What is it?" John grumbled.

"Oh fucking shut up and go back to sleep."

John turned over and appeared to do exactly that.

Danny got out the door and closed it quietly behind him. The hall was intensely dark, except for an oblong of light coming out from under the bathroom door. Just what he fucking needed; someone was in the bathroom and he was bursting. He padded along, shivering.

He tried the door handle. It was open. Maybe someone had just left the light on. He peered round. Stephen was sitting on the toilet, still in his shorts and socks. He looked up, startled.

"It's me," Danny said.

He was sitting on the closed lid, using the toilet as a chair. One hand rested on the basin. "You been sick again?" Danny asked.

He nodded. Danny went in.

Stephen looked up at him, long and whitely naked. He had a horrible puckered scar on his belly and what looked like an angry little burn above it. There were tiny marks all over his chest. Stephen's eyes went down between his legs.

Danny pulled a towel off the radiator and wrapped it round his waist. "I need to pee Stephen, like nobody's fucking business. Can you sit on the chair?"

Stephen got up and sat on the chair, slowly, like an old man.

Danny lifted the toilet seat and the towel and let go. "Sheer fucking poetry."

Stephen watched his back, just as he'd watched it earlier that night, doing exactly the same thing. He felt dreadfully ill. He was bitterly cold and his head thumped.

Danny flushed the toilet and turned to him. "You look fucking terrible. Do you feel as bad as you look?"

"Worse."

Danny smiled and crossed over to him. "What's wrong?" He sat beside him on the edge of the bath.

"Everything. My stomach, my head. Everything." He shivered violently.

Danny put a towel round his shoulders. "Better?"

"No," he said dismally.

"Get back to bed."

Stephen shook his head.

"Why not?"

Because I'm so lonely Danny, that's why. Because I can't stand lying there all alone in the dark. But all he said was, "I feel too crappy."

"Come on, let me take you back. You'll catch your death of cold in here."

Grudgingly Stephen let himself be led back to bed. He felt like a chunk of ice.

"What you need is a hot water bottle."

"I'm alright."

"Let me get you one, okay?"

Danny moved to get up. Stephen caught his hand impulsively. "No, just sit here with me for a few minutes. I'm a coward, I hate being by myself when I'm ill." He did his best at smiling.

Danny looked at his face, felt the icy chill of his hand, and said, "Roll over."

Stephen looked at him.

"Come on, roll over, there's room for two. I'll heat you up."

Stephen kept on staring.

"Come on, *shift* yourself."

Stephen rolled over against the wall. Danny climbed in. "Face the wall, curl your back into me. Come on, this is what they do when people have exposure or are stuck in the Arctic wastes. That about describes this room."

Stephen laughed. He knew Danny was trying to make him feel better about it, but he was intensely uncomfortable, lying in a bed like this with him.

"Relax Steve-o, go to sleep."

Sleep? Was he kidding?

Danny pulled him in tight against him, cuddling up like spoons. Stephen could feel the heat seeping back into him. He could feel Danny's arm loosely around his waist. A faint smell of sweat came off him, that, and something else that made Stephen think of beds after you'd lain-in too long, like on Sundays. It was an odd smell, disturbing. He could feel the hair on Danny's legs against his own, his smooth chest against his back. He was glad for no reason he could explain that he had his shorts on.

"Better?" Danny's voice was heavy in his ear.

"A bit," Stephen said. He knew it wasn't quite true but he didn't want Danny to go just yet.

"I'll stay till you go to sleep, okay?"

Stephen nodded. That could be ages yet. A long time. As long as he could make it.

Danny shifted slightly and Stephen curled imperceptibly closer. Danny didn't seem to mind. Suddenly Stephen thought, If he got a hard-on right now I would feel it up against my bum. He tensed, terrified by the thought.

"What is it?" Danny asked immediately.

Stephen spoke as if his lips were cardboard. "Nothing, just a pain."

"Where?"

"It's alright, it's gone now." Jeez. He wasn't going to get a hard-on. *Jeez Steve-o, sometimes.*

He relaxed again slowly. He felt Danny sigh, noiselessly, and realised he was keeping him up. "You can go back to bed now Danny, I'm okay."

"You sure?"

"Yeah, I'm fine," and then he shivered, charged with misery again, and spoilt the whole thing.

"Crap," Danny said succinctly. "Go to sleep." And he rubbed the top of Stephen's arm briskly with his hand, the other still wrapped around his waist, trapped under Stephen's body.

They were silent a moment, Stephen enjoying the slow flow of heat, then he said, "Danny?"

"Mm?"

"Why d'you let him do a thing like that?"

Danny was silent for a while. Stephen felt sure he was angry with him, like when

he'd slapped him. He didn't even want to think about that.

"I thought we were going to talk about this tomorrow," he said finally.

"Okay."

"You want to talk about it now?"

"As long as you do."

"Okay. I let him kiss me because he wanted to."

"Just because he wanted to?"

"Is that so weird?" Danny sounded ratty.

"You're always fighting with him. Some days you hardly even talk to him."

"Yeah." Danny paused. "Well, he annoys me sometimes."

"Ian said you used to be really good friends."

Danny snorted.

"Weren't you?"

"Not in my lifetime."

"Why did you fall out?"

"We didn't."

"Was it because he's queer?"

Danny was silent then he said, "Just because John says a thing doesn't make it true."

"He came in there to watch you, that's pretty queer. He said he liked to look at you."

"He didn't say that."

"Well something like that, I heard him, then he kisses you."

"He was drunk."

Stephen swallowed and said quickly, "What about me then? What about what he did to me?"

Danny was silent again then he said, "It's his business. If I don't mind him kissing me when we're both pissed why should you? I kissed you when you were making it with Henderson's sister, didn't I?"

Stephen was silent.

"Didn't I?" Danny insisted.

"It wasn't a kiss."

"That doesn't matter, I did it because you wanted me to. No, don't try to pull away, you know that's true. It doesn't make you or me or Rab a fucking queer, okay? You don't light a match and become a pyromaniac. Well you don't kiss a man and become a homo, okay?"

Stephen nodded.

Danny was quiet again for a while then he said, "I don't know what Rab is or isn't. All I know is when he gets drunk he sometimes does stupid things. Big deal. End of conversation."

They were silent again.

"Did he tell you what he'd done with me?" Stephen asked.

"No, he wouldn't talk about a thing like that. I found out by accident."

"Does Ian know too?"

Stephen felt Danny grow tense. "I don't know, why?"

"He seems to. He drops a lot of hints, you know?"

"Tell him to go crawl up his own arsehole."

Stephen laughed. Danny went on, "I mean it. Don't give him an inch or he'll take a mile. If he starts trying to fuck with your head tell him where to go. Promise me."

"I will."

"Promise."

"I promise." Stephen felt as if the words were some kind of sacrament between them, almost a bond of allegiance.

"Good. You better now?"

"You said you'd stay till I was asleep."

"I will, don't panic."

Stephen shifted closer then cautiously risked laying his arm along Danny's arm, the one round his waist. He could feel the hair tickle the delicate skin on the inside of his arm. "I'm sorry I yelled at you Danny."

"Forget it, you were drunk."

"I was jealous." It came out thick with embarrassment. He felt Danny go tense again. "You know, stupid kids stuff... he's your best friend, I'm not... you know."

Danny nodded, seemed to relax again. They were quiet for a moment or two.

"Where d'you get all those marks Danny?"

"*Jesus*, if you don't ask the most impossible questions."

"Sorry."

"I'm clumsy, okay?"

"Okay." Stephen lay there, suitably chastened, then said, "Did John chew you out?"

"A bit."

"Not too bad?"

"No."

Stephen felt better about that. He felt better about everything. Danny shifted his arm under his body. "Let me take this out, I'm getting cramp."

Stephen lifted himself. Danny slid it out and put it under Stephen's neck instead, pulling him down further into his armpit. "Okay?"

Stephen had his face buried in the hair of Danny's arm. It smelt of salt and soap. He nodded as if he was getting comfy and let his lips brush over the downy hair, then he laid his cheek against it, breathing it in deeply until he became giddy with it.

"What are you doing, relaxation exercises?" Danny's voice sounded above his ear.

Stephen blushed. "No, nothing, why?"

"It's alright, you must have been dozing. Sorry I woke you."

Stephen subsided again. He pressed Danny's other arm into his stomach as he curled up. "You always sleep in the nude?"

"Usually."

"My mam always makes me wear pyjamas. She says in case the house goes on fire during the night."

Danny laughed. "Cheerful fucker."

"Don't you like her either?"

"I don't know her Steve-o. Don't pay so much attention to things I say when I'm drunk."

But you meant it, Stephen thought. "Why d'you fall out with your friend?"

"Christ Stephen, you really are the limit."

"Sorry. I'm sorry."

"So you bloody ought to be. You don't half go on."

Stephen was silent.

"Go to sleep, for fuck's sake."

"You want to go back to bed?"

"Yes."

Stephen pulled away, turned to face him. "I'm better now, really I am. Feel." And he put a warm hand on Danny's face.

Danny smiled at him.

Stephen didn't smile back. He was lost somewhere in the green blackness of Danny's eyes. He let his thumb, just his thumb, fan out and slide over Danny's mouth. He watched it, his heart thumping painfully. "Can I?" He actually said the words. He heard them.

Danny took his hand away, curling the fingers shut gently like people did when they gave you a coin, something to keep, like he'd done with the kiss.

"No." Danny swung out of bed.

And was gone.

SIXTY

On Tuesday morning James Conley stood shaking and cold in the middle of his bedroom floor. He was up an hour too early, eaten alive by nightmares. Unable to face sliding back into sleep and into another one he got up.

He made himself coffee, had nothing to eat.

He showered and walked back to the bedroom. He walked past the clothes he had put out for work. He went to the wardrobe and pulled out a new set, everything in black - the shirt, even the waistcoat - black, rich and heavy with jet, uncomfortable to wear, like armour almost. He looked in the mirror. He looked tall and emaciated, like something reanimated. He looked the way he felt, like the living dead.

He sat down and put on shoes and socks. He pulled a notepad over and scrawled a message. He got up and shrugged into his coat. He looked like a gold-crested crow.

He went down the front stairs and left the note on Molly's desk.

Outside it was snowing so faintly it felt like soft rain. He pulled his collar up. It wasn't quite light yet. He went round the back of the building and got into his car. It started beautifully, God bless it.

He turned the heater on and put up with cold air for the first fifteen minutes.

Ian was irritating him, then some. Twice he had tried to grope him as he had passed him. The third time Danny caught his hand. "Do that once more and I'll break it."

Ian had smiled at him and said, "Careful." He nodded his head almost imperceptibly to where Stephen was working further down the shed.

Danny said, voice low, only for him, "Careful be fucked Ian. I mean it, keep your hands off."

Ian moved away, slowly.

Danny got out the shed as soon as he feasibly could.

John told him he was sending him out with Ian.

"Oh no, not Ian, not today."

John looked at him a moment then said, "Take the boy then. Ian can manage the feeds."

"Can't I do the feeds or something?"

"No."

"Why not?"

"Because I say so. And don't start on the back-chat, I haven't got the patience." And John walked away, leaving him staring angrily at his back.

He went into the kitchen, told Stephen and watched the boy's face light up. He felt like slapping him. He turned away to hide his irritation.

After breakfast they went out together.

They had driven half-way down the road when Stephen leaned over Danny's back and shouted in his ear, "Isn't that your friend's car behind us?"

Danny looked in the mirror. Conley's car. No two like that.

"Isn't it?" Stephen yelled at him again.

Danny nodded. He waited for it to overtake. It didn't.

They trundled along to the field. Danny pulled into the verge and Stephen jumped down to open the gate. Danny turned in his seat and watched the car go past. He felt as if a hand was pulling him inside out. Then the car pulled in and stopped.

Stephen came back.

Conley got out the car. His coat billowed out behind him like a black sail, his heavy hair blowing up off his face.

"Is that him?" Stephen asked. His voice was almost a whisper, as if Conley was close enough to hear him.

Danny nodded. Stephen looked at him. Danny was biting his lip, his eyes shifting. He was pale, his skin odd, transparent-looking.

Stephen looked at his friend again. *Jeez, what a zombie. And those clothes, flickin' weird man.* He reminded Stephen vaguely of Rab; the pale hair, the high cheekbones. Or maybe it was the walk, long legs sliding along like a flickin' guy in a western or something. But he wasn't as good-looking as Rab. He looked too sick.

He came up close finally, hands pushed tight in his coat pockets, huddling into the coat like a vulture. He brought a hand out and swept the hair off his face. He was wearing black leather gloves, shiny tight. They made his hands look false, like robot's hands. "Hello Danny."

Stephen stared at him. He even sounded like a robot.

Danny nodded. The man looked at Stephen. Danny said, "Stephen, this is James Conley."

The man smiled at him, small, tight, as if it hurt him.

Stephen shot a glance at Danny. He'd said his name was Max. It didn't seem very polite to point it out right now though.

Stephen tried to smile back but the whole thing was so weird, standing here at the side of the road like this, and this freak with his huge coat, and his hair and skin and eyes all the same colour, like dirty straw, and the way they were both standing, so tense.

The man brushed the hair off his face again. "Can you come and talk a minute Danny?" He glanced over his shoulder. "In the car?"

Danny looked at him then said, "Sure." He turned to Stephen. "Go back inside. Take the tractor in. I won't be long."

Stephen looked at the man. The man was watching Danny, waiting for him. Stephen nodded.

"I won't be long," Danny said again and moved off into the wind.

Conley had left the engine running. The car interior was warm, smelling of him. Danny breathed it in, holding it tight inside himself. Conley got in beside him. Danny looked at the waistcoat, thick and shiny-black, as if it was made of thousands of hard beetles. He looked up at him and said, "It was you who phoned, wasn't it?"

Conley nodded and said, "And you who phoned back."

Danny nodded.

Conley looked out the window and said, "The boy looks like you."

"So they say."

"Or maybe it's..." he hesitated.

"What?"

But Conley turned and looked at him and said, "Danny, I'm here because..." But he didn't finish that either.

"Because what?"

"I think you know."

"I don't until you tell me."

Conley looked out the side window, hands tight and shiny-black on the steering wheel. "You asked me once to let you come and live with me..."

Danny was silent.

"Would you still want to?" he finished.

"No."

Conley closed his eyes. Danny said, "I've got the boy here now."

"What?" Conley turned to him, frowning.

"I've got the boy now."

Conley was searching his face. "Are you and the boy...?"

"No, we fucking aren't," Danny snapped.

Conley pushed the hair off his face again. It needed cut. "Then what's he got to do with it?"

"You wouldn't understand, just leave it at that."

"I can't bloody leave it at that, I need you." Oh *God*, what had he said? Stark, ugly, like a stain.

Danny felt a quick excitement flare up, like a match in petrol, a curving, black-smoked thing, blowing right through him. He leaned forward and put a hand on Conley's leg then right up, smooth and fast, onto his crotch. He could feel the bottom of the waistcoat, rough and impenetrable, cold with a dull warmth behind it, like Conley himself.

He ran his hand over him. His movements were quick and light, touching everywhere. "Jesus, you're a real turn-on. You look so fucking *good*."

Conley watched his hand in open-mouthed fascination. He could feel the strange frozen tremble of his own excitement pinned down by the fear of that hand, but he didn't want it to stop.

"Jesus," Danny said again. He looked back quickly. Stephen had gone inside the field. The tractor was nowhere in sight. He pulled Conley's head to his and kissed him. It felt like a hand squeezing his guts. It felt alive in him, *need*.

He pulled away, lewdly cupping his own genitalia. "My balls are turning blue."

Conley understood that tiny thrust of his hips, the way his tongue slicked over his lips. "We can't," he said, thinking, Talk me into it Danny, make it right, give me permission.

Danny said, "Come on, quickly, no-one can see. Have you got a map or something?"

"A map?"

"Oh don't be so fucking dense."

"In the compartment, there."

Danny took the map out, hastily unfolded it, spreading it across the wheel and covering his lap. "Come closer, get underneath. That's it." And even as he spoke his hand was unzipping Conley's fly and worming in with an urgency that left Conley breathless. Danny immediately began pulling his penis up and down, the map rustling.

"Do mine. Hurry up," Danny said.

Conley didn't move.

"Come on Conley," and Danny looked at him sharply.

Suddenly Danny felt him fumble unseen below the map. His hand slid in, cold and clammy. "Oh Jesus," he whispered when Conley's fingers touched his flesh. "I've got to see this." And he pushed the corner of the map down.

Now his penis was up over it, red and erect, sliding up and down in Conley's leather-gloved hand. A truck roared by, shaking the car. Danny closed his eyes. "That is the best fucking thing I ever felt in my life."

"Danny, cover up..."

"I am going to cream all over those fucking gloves, right now." And he started to thrust his hips up.

Another truck went by.

"Don't stop... keep going... don't..." Danny ground his teeth and said slowly,

draggingly, "Oh... *shit*." And Conley saw it come out like a slow pulsating throb, sluggish, heavy, dropping like white paint onto the black leather, oozing down it, while Danny's hand jerked uncoordinatedly in his lap and Conley felt a release so intense it was like dying. Worked up into a frenzy, it spent itself in one glorious jolt... right into Danny's hand.

Slowly Danny looked down at them. They were both still hard, red, covered in thick strings of it. It was all over the map. "Shit," he laughed. "What a frigging mess."

Conley laughed too. "You should worry, they were my favourite gloves."

Danny wanted to do it again, was nowhere near satisfied, but he pushed it down, locked it away. Let big brother deal with it. "We've got to fix something. I'm sick with wanting it."

Conley nodded. It was the best he could manage. "When? I mean, how?"

"I don't know." Danny looked away. He was silent. "Listen, I've got to go. When I think of something I'll phone you."

Conley nodded dumbly. He felt like a starving man watching someone take his food away.

Danny squeezed him, hard. "Next time we'll lubricate my arse."

Conley flushed, tried to wet his lips.

Danny opened the door. "I'll phone you." And then he was gone.

Stephen was sitting in the tractor waiting for him.

Danny checked the front of his jeans. Nothing anybody was going to notice. The map had taken most of it... and Conley's gloves.

Danny climbed inside. Stephen moved off the seat and sat on the sill, leaning back against the windscreen. "Have a nice time?"

Danny looked at him sharply. Stephen's face was set, sulky. "What the fuck is that supposed to mean?"

"Nothing. It was just an innocent question. Sorry I spoke."

"Okay." Danny rubbed his face. "Let's have it. What's bothering you? "

"Every time he's about I get shoved off like I had a disease or something. What have you got to say to him that's so flickin' private?" Stephen stared at him belligerently.

"I don't believe I'm hearing this." Danny's face was hard and angry. "I've known you two weeks Steve-o. You don't fucking own me, okay?"

Stephen looked at him, blinking.

"What do you think you are, my fucking mother or something? Think you're bloody married to me?"

Stephen's face went white. He pushed open the door and jumped out, but he had nowhere to go. All he could do was stomp off a few paces and stand there with his hands in his pockets.

Danny stared straight ahead then hit the steering wheel. He sat there some more then said, "Shit."

He climbed out of the tractor and walked across to him, said his name. Stephen didn't respond. He tried again. "Stephen, I'm sorry."

Stephen turned suddenly and threw his arms around him. Danny stood there, nonplussed, with Stephen clinging to him. "Hey," he said, trying to prise him off gently. "What's wrong? Come on, let go."

Stephen lifted his head and said, "Just once." Danny could see tears spilling out his eyes. Christ, his hormones were on overdrive.

He looked at the raw emotion on his face and shook his head. "It's bad news Steve-o. Don't keep on about it."

"I won't ask again, I promise."

Danny tried to prise him off again, not gently this time, but Stephen clung to him like a limpet.

"On the mouth."

"I said *no*."

"It's not a sex thing. I just want to try it. Just once... please."

"Fucking leave off Stephen." Danny pushed him off violently.

Stephen looked as if he'd slapped him. His face was like putty.

Danny said quickly, "Look, I lied to you. Rab's queer. With you it would be different. You can see that, can't you?"

Stephen just stood there like a dumb animal, face slack. Danny took his shoulders in his hands. "Honestly, believe me, it would."

Stephen said dully, "I don't know why I... I'm sorry." His body felt like lead underneath Danny's hands.

"It's okay. It was my fault. Now let's do some work, eh?" Danny let him go and walked back to the tractor. Stephen followed slowly. Danny jumped up on the trailer and unfastened the gate. He jumped back down, went back to the tractor and tipped the load. It went up slowly. Stephen stood there, numb, watching it.

Danny looked at him, bit his bottom lip. He went round to stand beside him. "Steve," he said softly, his voice low.

Stephen didn't answer.

"Come on Steve, look at me."

Stephen looked round at him slowly... and felt everything inside him slide away like water.

Danny bent his head and kissed him on the mouth.

Danny broke from him and said, "Okay?" His voice was lower, deeper. It sounded different.

Stephen felt as if he was on fire. His lips, his skin - *all* of it - burned.

Danny said again, "Okay?" He was holding him away from him slightly, their bodies not touching. They never had. Danny had kissed him distantly, closed-mouthed.

Stephen said stupidly, tongue-thickened, "I wasn't ready for it."

Danny laughed quietly. "Did you need to be ready for it?"

"It was over so quick."

"It was only a kiss."

Stephen looked at him.

Danny felt his heart sink.

"Do it again properly."

"What do you mean *properly?*" But Danny knew what he meant.

Stephen came up against him. "Again, properly."

Danny looked at him. Now what? Now the fuck what? Why had he started this? "This is the last time Steve," he warned.

Stephen nodded.

"I mean it."

Stephen pushed against him.

Danny bent his head again and this time felt Stephen strain against him, push against his mouth, trying to open it. He felt his arms slide round him. Danny could feel himself slide out of control. He was going to come up in a minute. He pushed Stephen off, but Stephen wouldn't let go, his mouth clinging to him. Danny heard him make a faint sound against him, felt the vibration of it, and felt himself go like an over-stretched elastic band. One sharp sting... then nothing.

He pulled Stephen sharply against him and thrust into his mouth. His hands moved over his back, down over his backside, the tight hard little bum. Danny pushed into him, tongue deep in his mouth, exploring the taste of him. He tasted of salt tears and fruit chewing gum. His mouth was like a kitten's tongue - soft and pink - his skin faintly furred, like a peach.

Danny came up harder than iron, pulled Stephen's hips into it, letting him feel it.

Stephen pulled out of his arms, suddenly intensely frightened. He was panting.

Danny stood there, eyes black, smiling faintly at him, looking like he'd like to eat him. Stephen didn't even recognise him.

"It's not a sex thing," Danny mimicked unpleasantly, his voice so deep it sounded like someone else's dubbed over his face. His hand snaked out and cupped Stephen's crotch. "And what the fuck is that?"

Stephen pulled away, humiliated, frightened. "Why did you have to go and do that?"

"Do *what?*"

"You know what."

Danny laughed, a horrible noise. His mouth was red from the force of his kiss. "Maybe now you'll listen to me."

Stephen looked at him, wanting him to be Danny again. "Please stop this Danny. Please. I'm sorry."

Danny looked at him, slowly wiping his mouth. His arm dropped to his side again and somehow Stephen couldn't help it. It was almost like he was being directed towards it. He looked at Danny's crotch. He couldn't seem to tear his eyes off it.

Danny took a long, deep breath then turned away, breaking the spell, letting him look away. When he looked back he seemed more normal, more his own self. When he spoke he sounded like Danny again. "Now you've had your turn. It's finished, okay?"

Stephen nodded, relieved.

"I mean it, it's finished, okay?"

Stephen nodded again.

"And no more stupid games."

Stephen nodded one more time.

Danny smiled, and here at last was the old Danny. "Right then, let's get some fucking work done."

The four of them - Stephen, Rab, Danny and Ian - sat in the living room that evening. Ian was in the chair, the other three on the settee. Rab was in the corner, then Danny, then Stephen. They were sitting drinking beer. They had been given a rare reprieve from John's company and were making the most of it.

They had been there an hour and had sunk quite a lot of beer when Stephen noticed that Rab had his arm casually along the back of the sofa behind Danny's head, and that Danny was leaning back on it. He felt as if somebody had stuck a knife in his stomach.

He looked away and caught Ian smiling at him, smugly, as if to say, Think you're his little chum? Look at those two and think again.

He wondered again for the hundredth time if it was Rab that Danny had done it with. Half of him felt sure it was and the other half couldn't bear the thought. Maybe they'd done it more than once.

He glanced along the back of the sofa again. He couldn't believe his eyes. Now Rab was stroking his neck, fly little kitten strokes, just his fingertips, hidden behind Danny's head. He wanted to get up, go out, so that he didn't have to watch it, but if

he did he knew he would imagine worse. He sat where he was.

Suddenly Danny said, "Shift up a bit Steve-o, I want to stretch out."

Stephen moved along to the end of the couch. Danny lay down and put his head on Rab's lap, his feet on Stephen's.

Stephen saw that Rab had one hand cupped under his head now, just like Danny was a girl or something.

He could feel Danny's feet, heavy on his thighs, the warmth of them, the wrinkly white socks worn thin at the toes where his boots rubbed. He felt suddenly languorous and warm, like he had that night on the sofa when the lights went out. He wanted to stay like this forever.

Danny moved his feet slightly, curling them round his thigh. Emboldened by the drink and the liberties Rab was taking, Stephen slid down further into the settee and brought Danny's feet up into his groin. He opened his legs, just a little to get more comfy, and Danny's feet slid neatly down in against his balls. He closed his eyes and let the sleepiness wash over him.

"Hey, you nodding off Steve-o?" Danny's voice came to him through the dark. Stephen shook his head.

"He is," Rab's voice said. "Look at him."

Stephen didn't contradict him. He put his hand carefully across Danny's feet and pulled them to him. Danny did not attempt to move them. Stephen held them with both hands and slid deeply and effortlessly into sleep.

Rab said, "Ian, see what's on the other side, this is boring me to death. Look, it's sent Baby Bunting here into a coma."

Danny smiled up at the ceiling.

Ian flicked the channels until he found a film. It was Danny who stopped him with a "Hold it." The hero and heroine were getting undressed. "Just in time," he said. It was the usual coy prick-tease stuff but he felt himself grow hard anyway.

Rab said, "Is he enjoying that then?" eyes flicking to his crotch. He was smirking.

"Leave it out," Danny said, shifting a little to ease the pull of his underwear. They were doing the slow hand down the unidentified curve bit now. "Fuck that," he said in a low voice.

"Would you like to?"

"And then some."

"Dirty little bastard," Rab laughed.

They started humping. Tasteful humping but humping nevertheless. Danny covered his eyes. "Sometimes I feel as if my whole life's sex."

Rab laughed again. "Listen to it complaining but look at its dick. Christ, what a hypocrite."

"Shut it," Danny said but he was smiling under his hands. "Have they finished yet?"

"They're just heating up."

Danny gave a soft grunt.

"Come out you coward."

Ian said, "She's got her legs wrapped round him. Christ, she's rippling like a ferret."

"Give it a rest."

"Now it's the slow haul up her snatch while he gazes into her eyes." Ian's voice seemed to drop in pitch. "Nice arse."

Danny opened his eyes. The arse belonged to the hero but her nipples were on show now, stiffly erect. Danny's cock did another press up. "I would pay *money* for that."

He dropped his head suddenly, grinning up at Rab. He grabbed round behind him. "Hey, listen to this fucker carping at me. He's got a hard-on like nobody's business."

"Yeah, but it's for you, not her." Ian's voice was sharp, no humour in it.

Danny's smile slid off. The music reached a crescendo. Rab watched him, not denying, not saying anything.

Danny got up, pulling his feet out of Stephen's hands. Stephen woke up with a jerk, giving a small grunt of surprise. "What's up?" he said.

Danny rumpled his hair. "Nothing. I'm going to bed, that's all."

Stephen said, "Oh," and rubbed his face.

Danny stood up, stretched, then tucked his shirt in. Ian licked his lower lip. Rab looked at the fire. Stephen yawned. "I'll come with you," he said and stood up. He scratched his back awkwardly.

They went out. The door closed firmly behind them. Ian looked at Rab and said softly, "Want me to work it off for you baby?"

Danny and Stephen brushed their teeth together in silence.

Danny rinsed his mouth and said, "I need to take a leak, make yourself scarce."

"Goodnight," Stephen said, going out the door.

"Night," Danny answered absently.

He did his business, listening to the noises of the house. He flushed the toilet and went out.

Rab came along the hallway. Danny stood with his hand on the door, waiting for him. Rab drew level with him and said without preamble, "Sooner or later he's going to want to get into bed with you."

"Yeah, right."

Rab spoke low. "It's true. You know it is."

"Hero-worship."

"Yeah, but you're no hero. If he gets a taste of you you'll fuck him up for life."

"What are you saying? That I corrupt little kids or something? You've got a fucking cheek."

"All I'm saying is he'll go the same way as the rest of us. You ruin people. After you they don't want anybody else."

"Christ, that's pathetic."

Rab's face tightened. "Have it your own way."

"I'm not having it any way, and I'm not having him. Got it?"

"Alright," Rab said.

"And don't fucking forget it."

"I said alright."

Danny turned abruptly and went into his room.

Stephen lay in his bed and listened to them talking outside.

They were talking in low voices, like heavy whispers. He couldn't make out what they were saying but they sounded angry. He heard Danny's door slam then the bathroom door open and close quietly.

He tried to picture John's room, Danny moving about in it. He'd be taking his clothes off right now. He wondered if he undressed the same way as he had at Katherine Henderson's, everything just dropped on the floor.

Danny wore boxer shorts. They all did, except him.

He undid the button on his pyjama bottoms, pulled them down and off his feet, and kicked them out the bottom of the bed.

He felt a deep curl of excitement, doing something forbidden. Did John sleep in the nude too? Both of them together in the nude? What if you got a boner?

He let his hand trail over himself. Gosh he was stiff.

Just one kiss, that was all he'd wanted, just to see what it was like, but Danny had got the wrong idea. Stephen had felt his cock, stiff as anything, pressed right up against him.

He stopped squeezing himself. His heart was pounding. He took a deep breath.

It had been scary. Fucking her hadn't been as scary as that. Not like you'd stepped off into thin air, nothing beneath you, being dragged over into space.

What would have happened if Stephen hadn't stopped him? What if he'd let him go on?

Christ... imagine if he'd started feeling me up, right there in the middle of the field. *Shit...*

He let go of himself, gulping air in. He lay there for a full minute before letting his head rest back on the pillow.

Imagine if he was though... like Rab. He acted like he wanted to, all that tongues and stuff. He might have if I hadn't stopped him. He might have just stuck his hand in before I could stop him and started...

Oh no...

This time it took him longer to calm his heartbeat. He was stuck to his own hand with sweat and excitement.

What if he'd gone the whole hog? I mean, got down there and... right in the middle of the field. He was dead excited. He could hardly stop himself. He could have, dead easy, if I'd let him. He could've just pulled me out and sucked my... *knob* right down his...

Oh God... no... not yet...

But it was too late. Stephen lay there, moaning softly, as he watched Danny kneel before him and bring him to climax in his mouth.

SIXTY-ONE

The next afternoon John told Danny to go into town and collect their Christmas shopping. He gave him a list that Jean McEvoy had made up for them. "Take the boy to give you a hand."

"I don't need him."

"Take him."

Danny caught his arm. "Listen John, don't keep pushing us together."

John looked at him. "What's wrong? The silver plate beginning to wear off?"

"He's getting difficult."

"*Difficult?* As in the opposite of easy?"

"Don't fuck me about John, you know what I mean. Give me a break."

"I said take him." And he walked away.

"Fuck you," Danny whispered to his back. "*Fuck* you, you bastard."

Danny found him with Rab in the tractor shed. "Come on Steve-o, we're going Christmas shopping."

Stephen grinned and followed him out.

"Go change your clothes."

"Do I need to?"

"Yep. Now fuck off, make it snappy."

Danny sat in the Range Rover and waited. Rab was standing across the yard, smoking in the shed doorway, watching him. Danny rolled down the window and shouted, "What's your problem?"

Rab didn't answer him, just continued to stand there and stare. Danny rolled up the window again muttering, "And fuck you too Hardman," hoping he could lip read.

Stephen opened the door and jumped in. Danny accelerated out the yard. "Hey," Stephen protested, "let me get my seat belt on."

"I've got to get out this dump before I kill someone."

Stephen buckled in and looked at him. "What's wrong? Was Rab hassling you?"

"Everyone's fucking hassling me."

Stephen heard an implication he didn't like. He shut up.

When they drew near the town Danny pulled into the lights and said, "Let's make this fast I want to go fuck."

Stephen looked at him and said quickly, "Danny, I don't want to."

"Okay you can stay in the car." Danny didn't bother to look at him.

Stephen looked at the hard line of his jaw. He remembered the filthy thoughts he'd had about him. He felt sick at heart. Danny would hate him if he knew, and who could blame him? He said tentatively, "If you're going I'd like to come with you."

Danny looked at him. "I thought you didn't want to?"

He said it again firmly. "If you're going I'd like to come with you."

"But you'd rather I didn't go, is that it?"

Stephen nodded.

"Well tough tits." Danny looked out the window again.

Stephen glanced at him. He was in a real bad mood alright.

When the lights changed Danny took off at top speed, and the shopping wasn't much better. He went through it like Attila the Hun.

"There's enough booze here to sink a ship," Stephen said, looking at the trolley.

"John's contribution to the festivities." Danny's voice was dry and hard. "Never know when he might need to fuel some sad girlish fantasy."

Stephen didn't dare ask what he meant.

They loaded it all into the back and got back into the car. "We going to the same place?" Stephen asked.

Danny clicked his belt shut and started the engine. "You're not getting all my girlfriends."

"Is she expecting us?"

Danny laughed. "Of course."

And they took off.

She let them in. She was fully dressed this time, in cream. Stephen blushed terribly when she looked at him. She smiled thinly. "Come for another?"

"That's right," Danny said.

Inconceivably she showed them in. Stephen couldn't put the woman and the things she did together. His mother would have had a fit if anyone had spoken to her the way Danny did.

She got them drinks again. Stephen drank two in quick succession, trying to chase the fear away. She laughed at him. "A bit young to be drowning your sorrows Stephen."

Stephen smiled awkwardly.

Danny was saying very little. He was silent, edgy. Stephen had never seen him as bad as this. He wished they could go home.

Danny got up suddenly and crossed to her chair. He sat down beside her. Stephen had been sitting on the same sofa as him. Now he was alone.

Danny put his hand on her leg and pushed her skirt up, right up to her thighs.

"What the hell are you doing?" she said to him, but she didn't make any attempt to stop him.

Stephen sat there gaping, glass half-way to his mouth.

"I want to see your cunt."

Stephen wanted to die.

Danny lifted her skirt up. Stephen could see the red lacy triangle of her crotch with the black hair showing through.

"That's enough," she said, her voice tight.

Danny shook his head. "Not for me..." he smiled, "and definitely not for you."

He stood up and held out his hand to her. She stared at it for a minute then took it. He pulled her up and gave her a gentle push towards the bedroom.

She walked on ahead. Danny waited until she had gone through and then turned to him. "Come on Steve-o."

Stephen shook his head. "She doesn't want me there."

Danny laughed. "That's where you're wrong. Three in the bed's the family motto. Trust me Steve-o, she wants it. Come on."

Stephen got up and went towards him.

As Stephen knew she would she said, "Not this again" when the two of them appeared in the doorway.

"Your lucky day," Danny answered. He was unfastening his shirt, peeling it off. He unbuttoned his jeans then bent down to pull off his shoes and socks. They watched him, both of them. Danny was completely unselfconscious about undressing.

"What have you done to yourself now?" she said when she saw his stomach.

638

Danny didn't answer her. He was pulling his shorts down. They both looked. He grew steadily erect in front of them.

She held out her hand. He walked into it. She was sitting on the bed so it was easy for him to catch her head and direct it onto himself.

Stephen stood rooted to the spot, slack-jawed, watching Danny's penis disappear into her mouth. She was still fully dressed. It made it look worse somehow - Danny naked and her dressed.

Danny stroked her hair in some kind of soft encouragement then turned and looked at Stephen. "Come on then, take them off Steve-o. Let's see you." His voice was low, coaxing, like the hand in her hair. There was something eerie about him.

Stephen began unfastening his clothes. He felt heavy, detached from himself. Danny watched him absently, barely smiling, repetitiously stroking her hair like someone stroking a cat. Noises came from her. Wet noises.

Stephen hesitated at the last. He was ashamed of his erection: for having it in the first place, for the diminutive size of it.

"Come on Steve-o, get them off."

Stephen pulled them down, hating the way it bobbed out, so indecent, harder than anything but still miles too small.

Danny jerked his head.

Stephen went over. Danny pulled him into his side. The heat of their bodies touching was instant, like plastic melting on a stove. Stephen's cock jerked. He wanted to die with shame.

Danny eased her off him. She looked up at him. "His shot," he said.

She looked at Stephen briefly then she just did it, sucked him in, deep into her mouth.

Danny moved away from him, leaving him feeling cold and exposed. He climbed onto the bed behind her and began lifting up her clothes, pulling off what he could. He took her breasts out so that Stephen could see them, making an obvious display of them. Stephen watched his hands squeezing them. He tried not to be aware of her mouth going up and down on his penis. The feeling was so intense it was almost painful.

Danny whispered something into her ear and she stopped. He pushed her down on the bed and got the rest of her clothes off. Stephen couldn't stop looking at her. She was so naked.

Danny told him to lie down on the bed. He positioned her between Stephen's spread legs so she could suck his cock while her backside was stuck up in the air. Stephen knew what he was going to do. He could see everything.

Danny knelt up and took his cock in one hand and simply slid it up her from behind like he did this kind of thing every day of the week. He was looking right at him now, smiling, his face saying, Watch.

He began to fuck her. His cock seemed to be going in deeper every time he thrust inside her. Stephen could feel it as he bumped against her, her arms on Stephen's thighs transmitting each jolt into his body. And suddenly Stephen knew absolutely that he was doing it deliberately. He was smiling at him and fucking her and he was saying, Eat this Steve-o, eat *this*. Stephen dropped his eyes so he couldn't see him, and felt his cock deflate. Utterly.

She stopped and looked up at him perplexedly - he saw her head come up - and all the time the bed kept jolting. Danny the fucking machine, going on and on... watching him.

"Stephen?" she said, but he squirmed out from under her and got off the bed. He heard Danny laugh.

She called his name again but Stephen grabbed his clothes off the floor and

slammed out the door.

Stephen got dressed in the living room.

He was going to sit in the car before he realised that Danny had the keys in his jeans' pocket. Then he decided he would take the bus back but couldn't face the thought of all the questions. Danny would have to explain where he'd been and Stephen would probably lose his job.

He bit his nails, wiped his eyes again as fresh tears threatened. He heard her cry out.

He was making her come. They had gone on fucking as if nothing had happened and he was making her come, and then he would come in her while Stephen sat out here and cried like a baby.

He got up and switched on the television. At least he didn't have to listen to them. He sat down right in front of it.

You'll ruin your eyesight Stephen.

Fuck off Mam.

He hoped he'd go blind. And deaf. And dumb. And he would never need to see or hear or speak to Danny again.

The television ran in bright coloured blurs all down his face.

"Why did he go off like that?" She was running her finger down his face, lying on top of him.

"He's shy." He had his eyes closed.

"You get more beautiful every time I see you."

Danny said nothing.

"You're getting to be like a demon lover, turning up when I least expect you."

"Secret of my charm."

"Marry me."

"No."

They were silent for a while.

"It's not fair, using him to come here."

His eyes opened. "Want me to stop?"

She shook her head.

"Well don't carp then, he got his chance."

"Is that what I am? Payment for his silence?"

Danny smiled at her, slow and dirty. "Would you like to be?"

"Yes," she said, holding his eyes.

"I'll tell him, he'll be flattered."

"You're never jealous, are you?"

"Why should I be?"

She rolled off him, sullenly silent. He took the opportunity to get up. She grabbed at him. "Don't go."

"I've got to."

"Stay a while."

"No." He peeled her hands off and got up and got dressed.

"You still don't like me, do you? You only come here when the urge for sex gets too much for you."

He didn't answer her.

"Well?" she demanded.

"That's right," he agreed.

She rolled flat on her back. "Bastard," she whispered.

This time he went out without even returning her insult.

Danny went across and turned off the television. "Let's go."

Stephen didn't look up. He got up slowly, legs cramped, and followed Danny out into the hall.

They put on their jackets in the dark and went out.

Danny didn't speak to him on the way home and Stephen couldn't think of anything to say.

When they got home he helped Danny in with the food. No-one was in the house.

They unpacked in silence until Stephen, unable to stand it any longer, blurted out, "Why did you take me?"

Danny put a tin down on the shelf and said, "What else could I do with you?"

Stephen watched him put the rest of the stuff away, numb with hurt. Danny glanced up at him. Stephen felt the tears spill out of his eyes.

Danny said, "Oh fuck..." so quietly he might only have thought it. He crossed the floor and put his hands on his shoulders. "I'm sorry," he said, and for the briefest of moments he laid his face in Stephen's hair.

Stephen clung to him, desperately burying his face in his jacket. "What did I do?"

"Nothing. You didn't do anything." And Danny squeezed his shoulders, letting Stephen press in tighter against him so that he could smell the leather of his jacket, a faint smell of sweat, her.

Danny looked down at his face, brushed the hair off it. "Don't cry, come on," and he tried to ease him out.

"I'm not crying."

Danny laughed. Stephen listened to it inside his chest. "Not much. Come on, that's enough." He tried to prise him out again.

"Not yet."

Danny let him hide there a while longer then said, "Come on Steve-o, let go."

"Why?"

Danny heard it, felt the tension in it. *Christ, here we go again.* "Off," he said, pulling Stephen's hands out.

Stephen let him go reluctantly. Danny stared at him. Stephen flushed. Danny turned away. "Come on, help me put this lot away."

They worked in silence, but it was oddly companionable. Stephen felt curiously content and Danny seemed in a better mood, more relaxed. He was always like that after he got his rocks off, Stephen thought, looking at him covertly.

Danny was hunkered down beside him putting dog food into the lower cupboard. The tins were on the floor beside him. Slowly, licking his lip as if he were threading a needle, Stephen reached out and laid his hand on his hair. Danny became still under it. Stephen stroked it, gently, as if he were stroking a sleeping cat, afraid of waking it.

Danny looked up at him.

"It's lovely," Stephen said.

Danny straightened up. He looked at him, shaking his head slowly. "You've got to stop this."

Stephen swallowed and said slowly, finally admitting it to himself, "I don't want to." And he was breathless with it, the sheer enormity of the discovery. His face was pink.

"*Stephen*..." Danny ground it out, looking up at the ceiling as if he was at the end of his tether.

"I'll say it if I want to."

"That isn't it and you know it."

Stephen held his eyes with difficulty.

"Well is it?" Danny insisted. "It's more than that, isn't it?"

"No it's not."

"Yes it is." And Danny lifted his head with his hand. "If I said right now, Come on, no-one's home, let's go upstairs and do it, you'd do it, wouldn't you?"

"Do what?"

Danny looked at him, long and hard, until Stephen was forced to look away, unable to meet his eyes any longer.

Danny said suddenly, "Come on." He grabbed Stephen's arm and hauled him out the room and up the stairs.

"Where are we going?"

"Just walk."

Danny pushed him into his room then closed and locked the door.

"Why are you locking it?" Stephen asked, beginning to feel panicked.

Danny came over to him, began nudging him towards the bed. "You wouldn't want anyone to catch us, would you?"

"Danny, don't mess me about. What are you doing?"

Danny pushed him flat on the bed. "This is what happens Steve-o when two boys make it together. This is what you want."

Stephen pushed his hands off, tried to sit up, but Danny brought them right back, began pulling his shirt out.

"Danny, don't, stop it."

"It doesn't stop at a kiss or two. This is how it ends up. You might as well know it and cut out all those boring warm-up exercises."

Danny was half on top of him. He tried to push Danny's hands off. "Let me go."

Danny ran his hands into his armpits, into the small nests of damp hair. He could smell it off him, sweat and a faint hint of fear. *Enough*, he told himself, but he didn't stop.

Stephen said "No" again then suddenly went limp. Danny pushed him back easily, barely noticing, and climbed on top of him. He looked down at him, saw that his eyes were grey, looked at the fine freckles across his nose, the heavy red hair spread out under his head, his mouth slightly open, and thought, *Oh Jesus*, and began to pull away.

Stephen's arms came round him, strong, definite, pulling him down.

Danny sank into him, kissing his mouth, his face, his hair, as if he didn't know him, didn't recognise him, had forgotten who he was. Stephen clung to him, letting him do it, almost as if he had unconsciously engineered the moment.

Danny ran his hands over him, under his clothes, feeling the hollow boyishness of his chest, the smooth hairless skin.

His hand went down inside Stephen's jeans.

Stephen breathed in hard, held his breath until Danny touched him, then he groaned into Danny's mouth, pulling him onto him, thrusting up towards him, hands gripping Danny's back, and Danny felt it jerk, hot and wet into his hand.

Stephen lay there, heart roaring in his ears. He'd come like a wet-dream, all up here and nothing down there. He felt terrible, as if he were made of stone.

Danny pulled off him, dragging his hand out, and stood up. He looked at Stephen lying sprawled on the bed, shirt pushed up, trousers still fastened, face hot, eyes drugged. He shook his head and said, "No way…" then turned abruptly, unlocked the door and slammed out.

Danny went out the house and down past the old barn. He climbed the gate and vaulted over to the other side.

He went down the back field, striding down it, jacket open, bitterly cold and not feeling it. He climbed over the stile at the bottom and went across the next field. It was ploughed and heavily rutted, solid with frost. He walked in strides over the waves of earth, leaping from crest to crest like a man crossing stepping stones. He climbed another gate, hands burning on the cold rusty metal.

The sky was streaked with pink across a darkening duck-egg blue. He saw the river. It looked almost black. A burst of birds flew up at his approach. He slowed his pace then stopped.

He sat down on a rock and buried his hands under his arms.

That was the last. John could do what he liked. He wasn't going anywhere near the boy again. There were going to be no more scenes, no more dramas.

It was his own fault. Crushes can't survive the stink of sex. Fat lot of shit he knew.

Christ he came on your hand, you stupid fucker. At the first touch. You, the expert. If John had come onto you like that you'd have smeared all over him too, is it so surprising?

But I'm different.

Looks like you're not that different. Looks like there's another pair of hands out there in the dark.

A hush seemed to come over everything; the landscape, the river, the birds, all sliding rapidly into blue darkness. A deep hush, listening, waiting, then he heard it, that little silent voice.

You liked it.

No.

You liked all that little-boys-together spunky fun. Get one of your own to take into the shed, suck his little dick.

Danny jumped up and pulled his jacket tight around himself. If he was quick he could get back before any of them got in.

He turned and started the slow climb back up over the fields. By the time he reached the top field he was out of breath and sweating. The yard light wasn't on so it was still short of half-four. He went over the gate and past the barn. No-one there. He went into the kitchen.

Stephen was sitting at the table. Danny didn't look at him.

Stephen waited for him to speak, but all Danny did was take a key from the board and go out again.

Stephen sat there, afraid to go out, afraid to stay in. He heard a car start up, then the sound of it pulling out. He bit his nail.

He sat there a full ten minutes before anyone appeared.

John stuck his head round the door and said, "Come on Steve, what the fuck are you sitting there for? Where's Danny?" Then he came in and looked at him and said again, "Where's Danny?"

"I don't know," Stephen said then added, "I think he went out."

"Out?"

"In the car... I heard the car."

John stared at him so hard Stephen looked away then he asked, "What happened?"

Stephen didn't know what to say. He could feel his face go scarlet. Why had Danny left him like this? He could have yelled at him or something, thumped him even,

instead of leaving him like this. What was he supposed to tell them?

"Well?"

"Nothing."

"Don't give me 'nothing'." John's voice was hard. He'd never spoken to him like that. The others yes, but never to him.

"We had..." Stephen hesitated. "We had a fight."

"A fight?"

"An argument."

"What about?"

"It was stupid."

"And he stalked off?"

Stephen nodded.

John looked at him and knew he was lying. Whatever had happened it wasn't that.

"He didn't say where he was going?"

Stephen shook his head.

"He say anything?"

Stephen shook his head again. He heard John sigh then he said, "Well don't just sit there, get out and get the fucking cows milked."

Stephen got up and pulled on his coat and boots. He was glad to be doing something, getting away from John. He went out, John following him.

They went into the shed and joined the others.

Conley was getting ready to go out.

He was taking Molly out, to a pantomime of all places. He didn't feel like going.

What if Danny phoned while he was out? The idea of Danny getting his answering machine, a dead voice on a tape, made him sick with anxiety. Anxiety he might not phone back, might not even make the effort. What if he wanted to see him that evening?

He laughed and rubbed his face.

Chance would be a fine and very wonderful thing.

Come on Max, get out, you're running late. You've got to go out there and prove yourself, live down Danny's slander, show everyone how normal you are. Come on.

He turned the taps off and got out the shower.

He dressed carefully. All in black again except for a white shirt this time. No tie. The hell with the tie, she could do without. Every man his rebellion.

He brushed his hair back with his hand. He really would have to get this cut. He was beginning to look like a mad Bavarian. He looked at himself again and smiled. Or a deranged concert pianist.

He went round putting out lights, scratched Mamma's head, spoke to her in German and was roundly abused for his efforts.

He took his coat off the peg and turned out the last light.

It was a bitterly cold night, the snow hardening into hail. Conley pulled his collar up. He pulled his gloves on and felt a slow heat in his belly.

Stop it.

As usual the car wouldn't start. He tried it again. This time it caught. *Hoo-bloody-ray.*

He reversed out carefully and nearly lost an irreplaceable tail-light as he was blinded by headlamps. He slammed on his brakes. "Bloody idiot," he swore. "Turn those bloody lights off."

The car obligingly cut its lights as if the driver had heard him. Now Conley couldn't see anything. Could he reverse out or couldn't he? Where was the stupid fool? What a bloody insane way to drive, and what was he doing in a here anyway, couldn't he read?

He got out the car with a slam. Someone was standing there, his car hemming him in. "Would you move your car please? I'm trying to get out. And this is a private car park."

"Tough tits."

Conley saw red. He stalked over. "You've no business driv... ."

Danny was standing there smiling at him, snow settling on his hair.

"Danny," he said ridiculously. Then, "What the hell are you doing here?"

"I've brought you a Christmas present."

Conley moved closer, looked down at him. He was carrying nothing, just as he stood.

Danny smiled, teeth showing, and said, "Aren't you going to take it upstairs and unwrap it?"

"Make her some excuse," Danny was saying as he took his jacket off, shaking the snow off it.

"Like what?"

"Car won't start."

"She'll bring her own."

"Then you're ill." He turned suddenly and walked towards him where he stood by the phone. "You've had a relapse, then you won't have to go into work tomorrow either."

"Tomorrow?"

Danny nodded. "Christmas Eve, remember?"

"It's a half day. We don't see anyone, just tidying up."

"Good."

"Are you saying you're going to stay overnight?" Conley asked, slightly breathless just with the idea.

Danny nodded, smiling his slow, dirty smile. "And the next day, and the next..."

Conley sat down.

"Phone her."

Conley looked at the phone. "She'll want to come over if I'm ill."

"Tell her you're not that ill. No, wait, give it to me." And Danny sat down beside him and took the phone from him.

"What are you going to do?"

"What's her number?"

"Danny, what are you going to do?"

"Maxie... her number."

Conley told him. He dialled it. A kid answered. Danny asked to speak to... he looked at Conley.

"Molly."

"Molly," Danny finished.

"Hang on," the girl said.

She came on the line.

"Hello, is that Molly?"

She said it was. Danny smiled and put a hand on Conley's hair, ran his fingers through it. Conley swallowed. Danny said, "I'm phoning from James Conley's. I'm afraid he isn't going to be able to make it tonight."

"What's wrong?" Her voice was concerned.

"Nothing serious," Danny said and ran his hand down Conley's neck and inside his shirt. "Touch of flu again."

"I'll come over," she said immediately.

"No need. I'll be with him. I'm staying over Christmas. He'll be fine."

There was a pause then Molly said, "I'm sorry, I didn't catch your name."

"Danny," he said, undoing the top button on Conley's waistcoat. "We've met." He undid the next. "Remember?"

Conley watched him. He was enjoying this. He felt ashamed that he had let him do it to her. He put a hand over Danny's, halting the unfastening of his clothes.

"I will," Danny was saying, then he said goodbye.

"You didn't need to do that."

"It got rid of her, didn't it?"

"What is she going to think now? Especially after what you told her. I think you enjoy dropping me in it."

"You don't need her."

Conley looked at him and said slowly, "You're jealous."

"She acts like she owns you or something."

Conley smiled. "I would *never* have believed it. You're jealous."

"I'm not."

Conley laughed. "God I'm made. He's actually jealous."

"Shut up."

"Admit it."

"Give over."

"Come on, admit it."

"No."

"Come *on*."

"*No!*" And Danny stood up, glaring at him. "If you don't fucking chuck this I'm leaving."

Conley lifted his hands, placating.

Danny sat down on the other sofa and glared at the table.

"Friends," Conley said.

Danny said nothing.

"Come on Danny."

Danny looked away and mumbled, "Friends."

Conley stood up. "I'm going to have some coffee, liqueur coffee, with gallons of booze in it. Want some?"

"Have you got something to eat? I'm starved."

Conley laughed. "You're always starved, but there's practically nothing here." He paused. "If you're staying we'll have to get some food in."

Danny said nothing. Conley asked quietly, "Are you staying?"

"I'm staying."

"How long?"

"Till Boxing Day." And it was Danny's turn to hesitate. "If you want me."

He waited, listening to his own heartbeat, waiting for Conley's answer.

"I want you," he said.

Danny laid his head back and smilingly closed his eyes.

Danny drained his cup and said, "I've got to take a shower. I stink." Then he added, "These are the clothes. Have you got anything that will fit me?" And they both thought of that first evening, Danny dressed in his green waistcoat, lying on his bed, doing

646

what he did.

Conley said quickly, "My tracksuits will probably fit you. They okay?"

"Fine," Danny nodded.

"Shower or bath?"

Danny looked at the shower cabinet's pale green glass walls. Like being a fish in a tank. Suddenly he didn't want it. He wanted to lock himself away, just for half an hour, alone. "Bath," he said.

Conley smiled and said, "I'll run it." He got up and disappeared into the bathroom.

Stephen was sitting watching television.

When Rab came in and turned the sound off he looked up at him as if he might burst into tears at any moment. Rab sat down beside him.

Stephen said, "John's gonna kill me."

Rab smiled reassuringly, shook his head. "Not you."

Stephen pushed his hands between his knees and hunched forward. "Oh God, that's worse." And the tears began to spill over.

Rab leaned forward and put an arm round him. Stephen turned awkwardly into his shoulder. "I didn't know he'd do that. Why did he do that? God, what if he's run away?"

Rab would have laughed if the boy hadn't been so distressed. He was crying in earnest, hiccuping the words out.

"For God's sake Stephen, he hasn't run away. What happened?"

He burrowed into Rab's armpit.

"It can't be that bad," Rab said, beginning to worry.

Stephen shook his head fiercely. "It is. It's worse. God, I hate myself."

"Tell me."

"No, I can't."

"You've got to tell me. How can I help you if you won't tell me?"

"I can't."

And he sounded so panicked, so near hysteria, Rab said, "Alright... shhh... for God's sake stop crying."

Stephen straightened up immediately. Rab gave him a hankie out the box. He blew his nose noisily then laughed shakily. "I think I've cried more in the last few days than I have in my whole life."

Rab frowned. "Why? What's been going on?"

Stephen looked away, shrugged. "Just Danny... you know."

Rab looked at him keenly. "Has he been messing you about?"

"What?"

Rab said it quickly. "He hasn't tried anything... you know, like I did at the party?"

Stephen flushed and looked away again.

Rab saw the blush and thought, Oh Danny, you never could resist it, could you? "So what did he do?"

"Nothing. I told you."

"Come on. He tried something, didn't he?"

"No, I've *told* you."

Rab heard his voice raise dangerously high again. "Okay. Alright. Here..." He reached round. "Take a clean one, chuck that."

Stephen threw the sodden paper in the fire.

"Listen," Rab tried again, using a different tack, "John's gone looking for him but I don't think he's going to find him, and neither do you. He's going to come back soon, only this time he's going to want to know the truth and he isn't an easy man to lie to, especially in the mood he's in."

"Oh Jesus," Stephen said. "He'll kill me."

"No he won't, not if you listen. You don't have to face him at all. All you've got to do is tell me what happened and I'll tell him. But if you don't..." He let it hang.

Stephen moaned. He lay down suddenly and buried his face in the couch. "What am I going to *do?*"

"Tell me what happened."

There was a silence then Stephen spoke, muffled under his arm, hiding his face. "He took me upstairs." His voice sounded dead.

Rab looked down at him. *Oh shit.*

"He got me on the bed and... and..."

He was silent so long Rab said, "And what?"

"He put his hand inside and... you know."

Rab waited but he said nothing else. "Is that it?"

Stephen nodded. Rab frowned down at him. "Did you threaten to tell or something?"

"No, I wouldn't tell," he said vehemently, then realised what he was saying. "I mean, I wouldn't have told, not if he hadn't gone off like that. Oh God..." And he started weeping again.

Rab said sharply, "Stop that. How the hell can we sort this out if you won't stop that?"

The boy made an effort and checked his tears.

"Something's wrong here Steve. You're not telling me everything."

"I am."

Rab reached over and tried to pull him round. Stephen tried to hide his face under his arm but Rab pulled it away. "Then why did he go off like that?"

"I don't *know.*"

"Tell me," Rab demanded, shaking him.

Stephen yanked his arm free, sat up, face white, eyes red and swollen. "Because he *fancies* me, that's why!"

Rab looked at him and saw something else under there, something sly hiding beneath the misery, and then Stephen dropped down again and covered his head with his arms.

When John came back in Rab met him in the kitchen. He knew by his face that he'd found nothing. John looked at him briefly, pulling his boots off. "He hasn't turned up, I take it?"

Rab shook his head.

"Surprise, fucking surprise. Where's the boy?"

"Bed."

"At this hour? I want to talk to him."

"I've talked to him."

John looked at him sharply. "Have you indeed? And?"

"Danny tried it on with him."

John sat back. Rab was shocked to see how badly he'd taken it. He really hadn't expected Danny to do it. Jesus, you'd think that he'd know him better by now.

"You sure?"

"I more or less had to prise it out of him with a crowbar. He was telling the truth."

"So why the dramatic exit?" John ran his hands through his hair. "Christ it wouldn't be the first time he'd stuck his dick in something he shouldn't."

"I reckon he thought he was onto a safe bet. The boy's got a crush on him."

"Tell me something I don't know."

"I reckon the kid's been going along with it then somehow he's put the shit up him. I think he's wanted to do something heavy and it all went pear-shaped."

"You sucked him off for fuck's sake, what gets heavier?"

"He was pissed out his head then. He was sober this time."

John shook his head. "Bullshit," he said succinctly.

"Why?"

"It just is."

"Okay, suppose he's got the kid down on the bed and he's resisting."

"Why the fuck should he be resisting?"

Rab said irritably, "Because he doesn't want it? Danny can be pretty scary sometimes. You've seen him up there. It's like fucking a wild animal."

John didn't say anything

"Suppose he wants to ream him..."

"Good *Christ*." John rubbed his face.

"That would scare the boy and the scare scares Danny. After all, he might cry rape on him. It wouldn't be the first time, would it?"

John was quiet, staring at the floor.

"Where did you go?" Rab asked.

"Town."

"Henderson's sister?"

John nodded.

"Not in?"

"Oh she was in alright. He wasn't there."

"You speak to her?"

"Only over the bat-phone."

"Then how can you be sure?"

"I was sure. She would have been expecting me if he'd been there."

Rab was quiet.

John said, "Think the boy went willingly?"

Rab shook his head. "Not for sex, no way. It's the male bonding bit he wants, lots of intense emotion but no groping."

John laughed without humour. "He picked the wrong person. He should get himself a dog."

"He'd stand a better chance of getting something out of it."

John made a small derisory noise then said, "So what you're saying is Danny got fed up being crowded, 'gave in', took him upstairs for a little love opportunity session, got carried away, brought his big dick into play and started squeezing it up the boy's crack. The boy starts squawking and Danny realises he's misread the situation, bails out and pisses off."

"That's it."

"So he'll be back, that your theory? Leaving me to placate everybody."

Rab nodded.

"He better be." John looked up and said, smiling, "But if he isn't how would you like to come to bed with me?"

"I wouldn't."

John stood up. "Well there's always the boy." And he grinned and went upstairs to wash.

Danny came out wrapped in Conley's bathrobe, a voluminous thing in white towelling.

Conley looked at him and felt his mouth go dry. Danny's hair was wet. It curled in

thin dark spirals. His skin was flushed from the hot water. He grinned and rubbed his hair with a towel. "Now I don't smell like a sheep."

"You never smell like a sheep."

"Huh, you ain't smelt nothing." Danny sat down opposite him and pulled his legs up under him. He disappeared under the towel again, emerged and ran his hands through his hair. It was brighter now, the curls less tight.

"I wouldn't like you as an enemy," Conley said.

Danny laughed. "What a fucking thing to say. Why d'you say that?"

"I don't know. Just looking at you. You wouldn't be a good enemy."

Danny threw down the towel. "There's no such thing as a good enemy."

"Some are worse than others."

"But no worse than friends."

"Cynic."

Danny shrugged.

Conley was sitting there in his shirt sleeves, waistcoat half-undone, long legs crossed in front of him.

"You look very relaxed," Danny said.

"Meaning I usually look petrified." He held up his glass. "I've been cheating."

Danny laughed. "I might have guessed."

"Don't say it like that."

"You don't need it."

Conley shrugged.

Danny said, "Come over."

Conley put his glass down carefully and got up. He walked round the table. Danny looked up at him. "Sit down."

Conley sat down beside him. Danny looked down at the robe he was wearing then back at Conley. "Unfasten it."

Conley wiped his palms on his trousers then pulled at the knot round Danny's waist. The gown hung there loosely, still covering him.

"Go on then, open it."

Conley took the sides and opened it, almost like a man disrobing a statue.

Conley looked at him. Hard narrow chest tapering down into the flat, almost concave, stomach and then the thick red hair and his cock, heavy, thick, pale, lying plumply on his folded-up feet.

"Touch me," Danny said.

Conley reached down and touched his penis with his fingertips.

Danny laughed quietly. "Always straight there, no messing. Steve-o wouldn't like you."

Conley withdrew his hand, looked at him.

"He's a romantic, believes in the gentle art of sex."

"How do you know?"

"He tells me. Frequently. About forty times a day."

"What are you saying?"

"Nothing." Danny lifted his hand and kissed the palm then pressed it to his face.

Conley leaned forward slowly, so slowly it felt as if he wasn't moving at all, and pulled Danny's head to him.

Danny felt it and couldn't believe it, was afraid to breathe in case he broke the spell. Conley's mouth came close, breathed violet against his own, and then touched.

Danny went up.

Way up.

In flames.

At half eleven John came into Rab's room. Rab hadn't locked the door. "You awake?" he asked quietly into the darkness.

After a second the light clicked on. John went in and shut the door.

Rab sat up and pulled the blankets up over his lap.

John sat down on the bed, looked at him.

"I was wrong, huh?" Rab said.

"Oh, maybe."

"Throw me my shirt."

John got up and brought his shirt over. Rab slipped it on, not fastening it.

"He's not coming home tonight," John said.

Rab didn't say anything to that.

"You know where he's gone, don't you?"

Rab looked at him.

"He's gone to Conley," John said for him. "The boy's lying." He looked up suddenly. "No, *you're* lying."

Rab didn't say anything to that either.

"You're full of shit," John sighed and slid back across the bed to lean his back on the wall. "Let's start again. What happened?"

"I don't know, he's closed tight."

"Then guess."

Rab reached over for his tin and started rolling a cigarette. When he finally had it in his mouth he started talking round it while he felt in his shirt pockets for matches. "I don't know how they got upstairs. Maybe the boy tricked him..." He paused and struck a match, lit the cigarette. "Maybe he made a pass at him. Either way, something went wrong and Danny got pissed off. He left the kid in the shit, deliberately. He's in the wrong and knows it, the kid I mean. He's suffering from a bad case of guilt and self-satisfaction. Whatever happened he got some response out of Danny 'cause he's living off it." Rab gestured above his head. "He's way up here with the taste of success until he remembers Danny's gone off likely, he thinks, never to return." Rab smiled suddenly and took the cigarette out, grinning at the end of it. "He thinks he's shocked him." He laughed shortly and put the cigarette back in his mouth.

"Think he got Danny hot then refused to give?"

"Maybe. It's the kind of emotional jag that might turn him on."

John sighed again.

"He's giving you a warning John."

"I'll kick his fucking head in when I get him."

"Great idea." Rab blew smoke down his nose.

"Who the fucking hell does he think he is?"

"Oh shut up. You can be a real pain in the arse, you know that?"

Rab expected fireworks but instead John rubbed his temples and said, "Okay, I'll kiss and forgive."

"Well it's better than kicking his head in."

"Now I'm going to have to get rid of the boy."

Rab burped quietly and said, "No you don't, just keep him off Danny's back, that's all."

"He was useful."

"Yeah, so fucking useful Danny's with Conley right now."

John punched the bed. "On second thoughts, I think I will kick his fucking head in."

"You're only making it worse."

"What d'you suggest?"

"Let it run its course."

"Oh *right*." John turned his face away.

They were silent then Rab said, "He isn't going to change. Not ever. It's too late now."

"You mean until he loses that fucking pretty face I'm going to have to share him with anybody he gets itchy for."

"When he loses that pretty face you won't want him any more anyway."

John laughed. "Is that what you're waiting for? Incipient old age?"

"Aren't you?"

John shook his head almost imperceptibly. "He's *twenty* years old Rab. He isn't going to *have* an old age. He isn't going to have a *middle* age."

"You going to make sure of that? What's it going to be, internal injuries?"

John looked at him. "You're not getting it, are you? Danny doesn't *want* to live. He doesn't want to get old. It terrifies him. He's living all his life now because he knows not a fucker will want him when his face goes."

"Oh yeah? Maybe he wants to die because he knows it's the only way he can get away from you. You ever think of that? When d'you ever see him look at himself, give himself more than a glance? He doesn't give a fuck about the way he looks. If he wants to die it's because he wants to be free of you. How about that?"

"Shut up."

Rab laughed. "Scary, isn't it? Knowing he's running around out there somewhere looking for his way out. Maybe someday he'll find it, then what? Think you'll be able to stop him then? He comes back here of his own free will. He doesn't know it but he does. He's well-trained - will give anything in exchange for unqualified love. Think he stands a chance, with that face, that body? He's beaten before he starts. And *that's* why I'm still here, like you're still here, vultures feeding off the carrion." Rab stubbed out his cigarette.

John stood up. "What was all the piffle about Danny seducing the boy?"

"I didn't want you to get rid of him."

"Why not?"

Rab shrugged.

John stared at his face for a long moment then said slowly, a smile spreading, "Christ, you want him, don't you? You want the bloody boy."

Rab said nothing.

John laughed. He was still laughing when he went out the door.

Rab rolled another cigarette, lay there thinking. A knock sounded at his door, so quiet he wondered if that's what he'd heard. It sounded again. "Come in," he said.

Stephen stuck his head round. Rab said it again then, "What's wrong?"

"I heard John in here. It was John, wasn't it?"

Rab nodded at the bed. "Sit down."

"What did he want?"

"Just to talk."

"About Danny?"

"Yes."

"Oh shit. Is he in trouble? I mean, real trouble? You didn't tell him anything, did you?"

"No. No to all of it. It'll be alright."

Rab watched him go almost limp with relief. He began to shiver. "Jesus, I'm so cold."

"Want to get in?" Rab offered.

Stephen looked at the floor.

"Don't worry, I won't touch you."

"I know you won't. I didn't say anything."

"In or out?"

Stephen scrambled in beside him. Rab moved over to let him in.

"Danny sleeps in the nude," Stephen said.

"Does he? And how would you know?"

Stephen flushed. "He said he did."

"Don't believe everything he tells you."

"Think he'll come back?"

"Don't be daft. Of course he'll come back."

Stephen snuggled down under the blankets. Rab looked at the red hair, heavy and bright on the pillow, as different from Danny's as black or blonde, then he realised Stephen was looking up at him, lying on one side, hand under cheek. "D'you think I look like him?"

"A little."

"The hair?"

"No, not the hair."

Stephen looked almost comically disappointed.

"Something about you, I'm not sure what."

"Tell me."

"I'm not sure, I told you."

"You must have *some* idea."

Rab studied Stephen's face. "Same face shape but not so..." he searched for it, "...fine-boned. Similar build now but I think you're going to be heavier when you're done growing. Mostly though I think it's something about the way you move. I noticed the first time I saw you."

Stephen looked up at him, up and under. "At the party?"

"Yes."

Stephen looked away then he said, "Don't you think my mouth's a little like his?"

"No."

Stephen's eyes looked up again. "I think it is."

"It isn't. It's wider for a start, and not so well-defined."

"You mean not so nice."

"Okay, I mean not so nice."

There was a silence then Stephen said, "I saw you kissing him. In the bus shelter."

Rab squeezed his eyes with his hand then dragged it down over his face. "Did you indeed? Well you shouldn't have been looking."

There was another small silence.

"Why did you do it?"

Rab looked down at him. "Why do you fucking think?"

"You fancy him."

"That's right."

Stephen was silenced by the absoluteness of it, the *admission* of it. He hadn't even tried to hide it. "But he's your cousin."

"So what? That isn't illegal."

"It's incest, isn't it?"

"No it isn't, cousins can marry."

"You couldn't."

"Right." Rab leaned over and stubbed out the cigarette. "I don't know what the fuck you're playing at Stephen but you can get out. Now."

Stephen said quickly, "I'm sorry. I won't say anything else."

Rab looked at him and sighed. "Okay," he relented, "but no more shit, alright?"

"Okay."

They were quiet again.

"Rab... if I tell you something will you promise not to tell John?"

"Depends what it is."

"No, you've got to promise."

"Alright, I promise."

"Swear."

"I fucking swear."

"I think Danny's gone to stay with his friend in Caldermouth."

Rab looked at him. "What friend?"

"Well, Danny calls him Max..."

"Max?" Rab asked, frowning.

"That's what he said his name was but he introduced him to me as James Conley."

"Conley? You've met him?"

"Yesterday. He stopped to talk to Danny. In his car. Have you seen his car?"

"Where was this?"

"The field beside the sub-station."

"What did they talk about?"

"How would I know? Danny and him went off to the car together. I had to sit in the tractor."

Rab looked at him curiously.

"Every time he sees him I get shoved out the way. I don't know what's so fucking secret they can't share it."

"How often have you seen him?"

"That was the first time actually, but we've been to his place in Caldermouth a couple of times." Stephen looked up suddenly. "Don't tell John this, promise."

"I won't."

"Promise."

"I promise."

"I think Danny's gone to spend the night there. What if John finds out? Danny's not supposed to go there. And John's right, he looks flickin' weird to me. His legs go right up to his chin."

Rab laughed in spite of himself.

"Have you seen him?" Stephen asked.

"Once."

"The clothes, all in black. Even black leather gloves. Hey, wonder if he's lost his hands? Maybe they're false."

"Jesus, you've got some imagination."

"They looked false."

"How was Danny with him?"

"They had a fight."

"What, yesterday?"

"No, before. Last time. They were awkward, you know? I think Danny was still angry."

"What was it about?"

"Fuck knows. He doesn't tell me anything. I just get to sit and wait about. He doesn't trust me enough to tell me anything." Suddenly he said, "What are we going to do?"

And Rab had to bite back, What do you mean 'we'? and realised the boy had been dying to tell someone. It had been too much responsibility for him. Danny was a no-good little shit, leaving him with this. "I'll think of something."

"Couldn't we go and get him?"

"Maybe. I'll think about it."

"Tonight?"

Rab nodded and felt Stephen settle down heavier beside him.

"You ever sleep in the nude?" he asked suddenly.

"Sometimes... in the summer," Rab answered abstractedly. He was turning over what Stephen had said in his head. Danny was like a cat. You thought you knew his life and then you discovered he had another one, another four, tucked quietly away.

"Rab, can I ask you something?"

"What?"

"You ever do anything with Danny?"

Rab looked at him. "What kind of anything?"

"You know."

"No I don't. Play cards, go swimming, what?"

"Sex," Stephen said with sudden bluntness.

"No."

"Would you like to?"

"No."

"I thought you said you fancied him?"

"That doesn't mean I want to fuck him."

"But you kissed him."

"I kiss the dog but I don't fuck it."

"I bet you don't kiss it like you kissed Danny."

"Stephen, pack this in, alright?"

Stephen lay quiet. Rab said, "How about you going back to bed? I'm cold up here."

"Not just yet. Come down beside me, under the blankets."

"No."

"Don't worry, I won't touch you." Stephen was smirking up at him.

"You cheeky little bastard." And Rab laughed in spite of himself.

"Come on down."

Rab slid down under the blankets and put one arm under his head. Stephen lay on his side, looking at him. "The hair under your arms is a different colour. Is your hair dyed?"

"No, it fucking isn't, you cheeky sod."

Stephen grinned, unrepentant. He moved a little closer. Rab stiffened when he felt his body brush against him. Stephen said, "Can we put the light out?"

"Why?" Rab looked at him without turning his head too close.

"It's hurting my eyes."

"That's because you should be asleep. If you turn it out you'll fall asleep in my fucking bed, then where'll I be?"

"Lucky," Stephen said, watching him.

Rab opened his mouth and closed it again. What was going on here?

Stephen turned suddenly and clicked it out.

"*Stephen*, put that on again."

Stephen laughed in the dark.

Rab reached over him, swearing, and felt his arms come up round his neck, pulling him down sharply.

Rab came down on top of him. Stephen kissed him, missing his mouth at first then finding his way to it.

Rab rolled back off him. "Jesus, have you gone mad?" he hissed.

"No," Stephen whispered. "I want to do it. You did it before." He moved over against him in the dark, pinning him against the wall.

Rab pushed him back. "What *is* this?"

"Please Rab."

"Why the sudden change of heart?"

"I want to know what to do."

"You want a girl for that, get off."

"No, not that. What you do... you know."

"This is stupid. Have you forgotten?"

"I know what I'm doing. Come on."

And Rab realised with sudden blinding clarity, *This is for Danny. He thinks he can learn how to seduce Danny.* And then Stephen put his hand between Rab's legs and said, "In the car, that first time," he ran his hand over Rab clumsily, but hungrily curious, "I knew what you were doing. As soon as you put your hand on my leg I knew what you were up to. I was dying to know what you were going to do... I never really guessed... I mean... but it was alright. Once you got started, it was alright. I was scared at first, but when you took me in your mouth it felt really good. Do it to me again. I want to see. Do it..."

But by then it was an academic question.

Because Rab was already half-way there.

SIXTY-TWO

Danny woke early on Christmas Eve.

He was still tired. Maybe it was just too many years of training. He sighed.

Conley's voice spoke in the darkness. "What's wrong?"

Danny turned his head to him. "Nothing, habit, sorry I woke you."

"You didn't, I was awake anyway."

Danny rolled onto his side. He reached out and ran his fingers over Conley's face in the darkness. Conley said, "I think maybe I'm not used to having anybody in bed with me."

"In one this size I'm surprised you can tell."

Conley was silent, half-drowsy under the feel of Danny's stroking hand. "Maybe it's you. Maybe I'm too aware of you."

Danny laughed quietly. His hand traced down Conley's chest and onto his stomach. Conley's cock came up to meet him like a friendly dog. Danny laughed again. "Maybe you are at that." He traced it lightly with his fingers, feeling the tension in the body under his hand. "You're still frightened of this, aren't you?"

"Yes."

"Why?"

"I don't know. Habit, like you waking up early."

They were silent a while. Conley barely breathing under Danny's absent stroking. "Danny?"

"Mm?"

"Something's bothering you, isn't it?"

Danny's hand stilled. "Like what?"

"I don't know. Are you regretting it?"

"No." But he had answered too quickly.

"Do you want to go back?"

Danny didn't answer.

"Do you?" Conley persisted.

"I don't fucking know, don't go on at me."

Conley was silent.

"I'm sorry," Danny said almost immediately and he rolled over against him, kissing his mouth hard. "I'm so sorry," he whispered.

Conley reached up and held his head, let his hand run over his hair, down his back. He did everything tentatively, like a man trying to remember something new he's been taught. Conley knew it was the age-old problem. Now Danny had him he no longer wanted him and Conley knew, even as he felt Danny grow hot and hungry against him, even as Danny began to move over him like a slow fire, that this would be the last time. He wasn't going to see him again.

Es ist alles aus.

The end.

Stephen felt tight with excitement. He didn't know why, he just did. He looked at his watch. Not quite nine yet. If Rab was too scared to go get Danny back he'd just have to tell John and risk it.

He didn't think about what he'd done last night. He wasn't going to think about it. You had to know these things, do them once. It didn't count.

He would go in for breakfast in a minute.

He found himself blushing. His mam would be there.

Less of that. It didn't matter. Once, just to know.

Suddenly he felt very sophisticated, adult. He'd done something a lot of blokes wouldn't because they were too scared, even if they wanted to. You had to live life.

When Danny came home he'd tell him it was okay. He didn't mind. There was nothing to be ashamed about. It wasn't his fault he needed sex so much. If it happened sometimes that was okay. He would still like Danny no matter what. After all, it didn't mean anything. They had no girls here, just like prison.

Everything was okay.

Or it would be - as soon as Danny came home.

They did it again in the bath, steamy and pungent with the scent of violets. Conley hung onto him, face to face, kneeling together, and wanted it to go on forever. But the white heat burnt up, faded and died, and Danny's eyes became green and veiled again, full of secrets, closed to him. Danny kissed his mouth with almost cruel detachment, dried himself, and then told Conley he was beautiful with one of his sudden frightening flares of intensity and disappeared out of the room.

Conley felt sure he'd go without saying goodbye but when he went out Danny was there, fully dressed in his work clothes, looking out of the window, hair still wet. He turned and smiled, held his hands up. "See? I'm a stinking liar." And he stopped smiling.

Conley shook his head and stood there looking at him.

Danny said, low and quiet, "I don't know what's wrong with me. Looking at you..." He hesitated. "I've got to go back home." He turned away suddenly. "Jesus, what melodramatic shit."

He stared out the window. "Will I tell you something?"

Conley said, "Go on," watching his back.

"I like women..." He stopped and said in a voice so quiet it was barely there, "I've got a heat for them sometimes that feels like a disease, but afterwards I feel so guilty, like I've done something beyond bad, something scummy, traitorous, like I've betrayed..." He stopped and said suddenly, "I talk too much."

He turned and scanned Conley's face as if he was looking for something. He said again, "I talk too much."

"Betrayed what?" Conley looked at him intently, and Danny unexpectedly grinned.

"See what I mean? Always fight the urge to confess. It isn't good for the soul at all."

"No, tell me, betrayed what?"

But Danny shook his head and said, "I've got to go. What time is it?"

Conley looked over his shoulder at the kitchen clock. "Just after nine." He looked back. Danny was looking at him oddly.

He took a step forward and said, "Listen. You're not queer Conley, don't let this scare you into thinking you are."

"You told me it didn't matter." He didn't want Danny to say any of this because he was telling him what he didn't want to hear. No more. Finished. That's what he was saying - longhand.

"It does if you're going to get fucked up over it." Danny laughed. "You're cured, remember? That's what you wanted."

Conley nodded. *That's what I wanted. Only I expected painless surgery.*

Danny came over to him. Conley could smell the animals off his clothes. He liked the smell of it, sour, unmistakable, like Danny.

"One for luck," Danny said and kissed him gently.

But Conley grabbed him and kissed him back hard.

Stephen and Rab finally met in the milking shed.

No escape.

"I think we should get him back."

Rab felt inexplicably and intensely irritated, as if he'd known all day this was what was going to happen. "Do you? And what if he doesn't want to come back? What if he's gone to Conley because he doesn't want to see you ever again?"

"He hasn't," Stephen said. His voice was sulky, surprised by Rab's inexplicable hostility. "He does want to come back."

"How the hell would you know? You've barely known him two weeks. What are you, his fucking Mother Superior?"

Stephen blinked at him. "Just because you've known him longer doesn't mean you know him better."

"I know him better than you ever will."

Stephen's face flushed up angrily. "You're jealous because you didn't even know where he'd gone. He didn't tell you anything about James Conley, did he? You're not his friend. All you want is to get into his pants."

"Just like you."

Stephen coloured up hotly. "I do not."

"Like fuck you don't. Think I don't know why we got the little performance last night? You wanted to learn how to suck dick... his dick."

"Shut up."

"You little queer."

Stephen launched himself at him, knocking Rab backwards with surprise. The two of them ended up in a heap on the floor, Stephen flying into him in a fury.

"What the *hell* is going on here?" Hands pulled Stephen off bodily, dumping him unceremoniously on his back.

"Get up." John yanked him upright, pushing him against the wall. He turned to Rab who was already climbing to his feet. "What the hell are you playing at?" he demanded.

"Cluedo." Rab wiped his hands on his jeans.

John grabbed his front and shoved him against the pen. "Fucking smartmouth. What was it about?"

"Ask him." Rab jerked his head at Stephen.

"I'm asking you."

Rab pushed his hands off. "Yeah, well as you can see I'm not telling you."

Stephen said suddenly, vehemently, "He knows where Danny is."

John stood back a pace, looked at Stephen. "Does he now? And do *you* know where he is?"

Stephen nodded.

"Well suppose you tell me."

But Rab interrupted before he could say anything. "Suppose you ask him yourself." He looked past John's shoulder to the shed door. John turned, following his gaze.

Out in the courtyard Danny's hair flared in the morning light. Rab smiled and began to walk towards the door. "Christ, your faces, anyone would think you'd seen a fucking angel."

The fucking angel went into the house.

Rab got to him first but only with minutes to spare. "John's on the war path and

Stephen's ready to lay down his life for you."

Danny smiled. "Nice to know I've been missed."

"Christ, you're trouble Danny."

Danny smiled an odd smile but before Rab could identify it, say anything else, the other two came barging in. It was almost undignified. The moment, whatever it was going to be, was effectively halted in its tracks by the unexpected entry of Jean McEvoy. Rab couldn't have told you how but Danny somehow made good his escape with her. It was almost comic.

Rab turned to go back out, as much to hide his own amusement as anything else, and caught sight of Stephen's pale, angry face.

He felt recognition clench at his stomach.

He turned abruptly and went out the door.

Danny went shopping with Jean McEvoy.

They made small talk, meaningless chitchat.

Danny felt afterwards as if he'd been to sleep. He was almost sorry to drop her off at her own house. They wouldn't see her again till the twenty-seventh. She told him to send Stephen packing if he became a nuisance over the holiday. Danny said he would and wondered what she'd say if she knew exactly what kind of a nuisance he was likely to be.

He went into the house with the last cardboard box. He kicked the door shut with his foot.

"Alright Danny-boy, let's hear it."

Danny put the box down on the table. John was leaning, arms folded, in the kitchen doorway.

"Where are the rest of them?" Danny asked.

"Over the hills and far away."

Danny nodded. "Want me to unpack these or do you want to punch me about a bit first?"

"I'm in no hurry, unpack them."

Danny began to unpack the boxes. He saw the turkey, neatly foil-wrapped on its roasting tray, sitting on the draining board. It made him want to laugh. *A happy Christmas to you too.*

"Where did you go?"

"Conley's." Danny kept unpacking.

John marvelled at the ease of his admission. So easy for him, so smooth. Didn't hurt a bit. "While you were gone Rab had the boy." He watched with intense satisfaction as Danny halted for a moment then slowly went back to what he was doing.

"How do you know?"

"I heard him go in. He didn't come back out again."

Danny turned slowly to him. "You *let* him?"

"Why should I stop him? It's their love affair. Not as if it was the first time." John was smiling.

Danny turned and slammed the cupboard doors shut. He began breaking up the cardboard boxes, pulverising them.

"What's bothering you Danny?"

Danny didn't answer him. He just kept flattening the boxes until they looked like something that had been baled by a machine. Eventually he ran out of steam. He sat down heavily and looked at the boxes. He wasn't seeing them.

"How often did you do it?" John asked.

"What?" Danny's voice was dull, disinterested.

"How often did you do it with Conley?"

"I don't know."

That hurt worst. The way he just said it. I don't know. Don't bother me. Who cares? It didn't even fucking matter to him.

"Think then Daniel, to please your big brother."

Danny heard the menace in it, the lumbering anger.

"Two or three times."

"Think again Danny, I like precision."

Danny looked out the window. "Five. Three last night, twice this morning."

"Jesus, you've reformed him."

Danny didn't say anything.

"What do you think I should do? I mean, if you were me and had a stinking little whore to keep in line what would you do?"

Danny looked over at him. "I'd get rid of him."

Their gaze locked, held for a long time, became almost challenging. *You go first. No, you go first.*

"Is that an invitation?" John said finally.

"No, just a statement of fact."

"What if you couldn't? What if you needed him too much?"

"I wouldn't ever need anyone that much."

"Not even Conley?"

Danny looked at him and said with an odd weary contempt, "Don't be stupid."

John had never expected to hear it and yet when he did he felt only as if something had been taken away from him, and for the first time in as long as he could remember he wanted to cry, while all the time those stupid words of Ian's were going through his head. *And a splinter of the mirror entered the boy's heart.*

John went over to him and hit him across the face, slapping him mechanically, getting it over with.

Danny didn't even try to protect his face. He just accepted it, like going to the dentists.

John stopped.

He looked at Danny's face, red with streaks of pain, his eyes closed. "*Danny...*" he said, hard, intense, pleading.

Danny looked at him.

"*Love* me, damn you." And he punched him, hard in the mouth.

SIXTY-THREE

Danny woke up on Christmas Day to feel John hard against him. He stretched his legs.

"I love the way you do that," John murmured into his neck. He rubbed softly against him, not trying to do anything, just enjoying the feel of it. He felt as if Danny had been away from him for weeks. That one long night, alone, while Danny had been wrapped up in someone else's sweat, not even thinking of him.

He pushed hard against him, suddenly wanting to hurt him. Danny spoke sleepily. "Is this my Christmas present?"

"No, that's when you get my load in your face."

"You sound like you'd rather hit it."

"I would."

"I've only just woken up, for Christsake. Now what have I done?"

"You torment me."

"How?"

"You just do." And John rolled back off him suddenly, not wanting to touch him any more.

Danny sighed and rolled over to face him. He looked at John's profile, dark and heavy in the feeble light. "What do you get out of me John?"

"Nothing but fucking pain."

Danny reached out and traced his heavy brows with his finger. They were thick, silken. His hair felt beautiful in the dark. Only the crappy colour let it down. In the dark he felt as beautiful as Danny himself. "Why do you do it then?"

"I don't know."

Danny ran his finger down over his cheekbones, solid, almost Neanderthal. "I don't understand you," he said finally.

"No-one's asking you to."

"Can I ask you something?"

John grunted.

"How old was I when you first fancied me?"

"Twelve years, two months and three days."

Danny laughed. "You can't remember it that clearly."

"I remember it exactly, to the day. Third of January."

Danny said, "Rab's birthday." And he placed it with a sudden clarity, like seeing something that had been there all along only you never noticed it before. He said, "I had toothache."

"A wisdom tooth."

"You came in and asked me what was wrong. You brought me clove oil and put it on my tooth. I remember that, the horrible dry feel of the cotton wool... and that horrible taste."

"It made you taste like Rab."

"You kissed me." Danny said in an odd hushed voice.

"You were half-asleep by the time it started to work. You were exhausted with pain, lying there, your face dirty with tear marks. You felt as soft and bruised as a peach, all cried out. I sat with you a while, untangling your hair, just to soothe you. Nobody ever bothered to make sure you got it cut. After a while I asked if you felt any better. You didn't answer. I thought you were asleep, so I kissed you. A go-to-sleep kiss. It didn't mean anything. I'd done it a thousand times before, but this felt different. You didn't

look like you. Close up you weren't my brother at all. You looked sexless, like that proverbial angel we're always accusing you of being, so I kissed your mouth."

John paused, remembering. "You kissed me back, drowsy, not really with it. I think somewhere inside I knew you would. You tasted of cloves. Suddenly I was kneeling on the floor with an erection like nobody's business. I told myself it was because you tasted like Rab. Even then I knew I was lying. You brought me nothing but trouble. You turned Ian into an unpredictable little shit, brought out the worst in everyone. You made me guilty and angry by turns. Then in that one instant, feeling you kiss me back..."

He stopped then went on again more slowly, "I didn't kiss you again for two years, although I wanted to so often it was like living with an illness. I was a pervert, a child molester. Can you sink any lower?"

They were quiet for a long time. Finally Danny said, "I thought maybe I'd imagined it. It was nice, that's all I remember. You didn't shove your tongue..." Danny didn't finish the sentence, instead he said, "Christ, I worshipped the ground you walked on but you were always ashamed of me."

"I was ashamed of *me*," John said. "I *loved* you."

"It didn't feel like it."

"I know."

They were silent again then John said, "We'll have to get up." But they didn't move. Suddenly he said, "You never did want it, did you? It was just a way to get my attention."

"No," Danny said quickly.

"You just wanted me to notice you."

"That's crap."

John rolled over suddenly, on top of him. "I destroyed every bit of love you felt for me that day in the hayloft, didn't I?"

"John, I don't even remember it."

"I do everything I can and all I end up with is nothing. I get everything except what I want, because you can't give me it. Because you don't fucking *feel* it. You don't fucking love me Danny, do you?"

"Shut *up*."

"*Do* you?"

Danny slapped him. Hard across the face. Then again, slapping him back down on the bed, John with his hands over his face, curled up against the blows as if he was a tiny frail thing. Danny slapped him again, more savagely than before, then dropped back on the bed.

He lay there panting, staring up at the ceiling. John lay curled in a ball beside him then his voice came out, fragile in the darkness. "Fuck me."

Danny pulled a breath in, wanted to say, What? in a big outraged voice, wanted desperately to pretend he didn't understand. He said, "No" and was horrified to hear how scared he sounded.

There was an aching black silence then John again. "Give me that if you can't give me anything else."

Danny got up on top of him like a man drugged and pushed him flat on his face, climbing between his legs, heart racing.

"Danny, listen..."

Danny tried to get inside him. But it was so dry it hurt, squeezing the head of his cock so tight it felt clamped, dragging in, resisting every fraction of the way.

"Danny, wait, listen..." he said again, as if he had changed his mind and was too frightened to tell him.

Danny went in suddenly, with an odd lurching lunge onto his back, grunting with

surprise and effort.

John's hands came up and clutched the pillow. His back felt huge under Danny's body. He realised suddenly he'd never even wanked on him like this. John had never asked and he had never offered. He pulled back off him in a kind of frightened revulsion. "*Fuck* you," he hissed.

John moaned.

"Fuck you, you grabbing, greedy shit." He kept his body off him, pushing his pelvis up harder, tighter, getting deeper in. It was like fucking a wall, something huge and unyielding as stone. "How long have you wanted this? How long have you wanted me to fuck you like a bloody woman, you spineless shit? You didn't dare ask before, did you? You bloody tight-arsed, chickenshit..." And suddenly Danny was crying. "It wasn't *ever* Rab, was it? It was always some bloody woman. This week, last week, next week. God I hate you... I fucking hate you..."

Danny went up on his hands, as if he couldn't bear to touch him, while his body determinedly crammed every inch inside his body. He was crying, couldn't breathe, gasping out on the point of climax, "It *hurts*. Don't you *understand?* It *hurts!*"

And he rammed it up inside him, and let it all come out.

They milked the cattle as normal, John and Danny staying well away from each other, filled with an uncomfortable awareness. Too much admitted too soon, too openly. Danny worked by Ian, finding his presence oddly comforting and strangely without pressure.

Afterwards Danny volunteered to help him with the Christmas dinner. He sat at the table peeling vegetables, feet up on the chair. He was humming to himself. Ian watched him curiously for a moment or two then asked, "What are you thinking?"

Danny looked up, startled. "What?"

"What were you thinking, right then?"

"Nothing." But Danny did something he very rarely did nowadays. He blushed.

Ian smiled. "Tell, I'll keep your secret."

"I was remembering."

"What?"

"The boy in the toilet."

Ian remembered too. "What about him?"

"Just his mouth."

"Doing what?" Ian's voice was insidious.

Danny ignored it. "He had a beautiful mouth."

"You're a mouth man. That's why I do nothing for you."

Danny didn't answer him. He got up and put the veg into pots, filled them with cold water.

Ian watched him moving about. John had bought him a present. He was wearing it. A plain black sweater. Expensive. John wasn't fooling anyone that it was an altruistic gesture because Danny looked like something someone had dreamt in it. It was a present for the whole family really. They could all enjoy it. He had the sleeves pushed up. It made the skin of his arms look like pale gold, his hair almost ruby.

"You're indecent Danny."

Danny turned and looked at him.

"So fucking beautiful you're indecent."

Danny turned away, utterly uncaring. Ian could visualise him looking at himself in the mirror when John had given him it, appreciating distantly his own beauty then forgetting it. It didn't matter. In fact, Ian suspected he'd rather do without it, and everything it brought him, except perhaps his big brother's adoration. "Have you got

anything on under it?" Ian asked his back.

"No." Danny was adding salt, putting on lids.

Ian looked at the wide shoulders, narrow waist and hips. "You've grown," he said. Danny made a noncommittal noise.

"You're shoulders are broader. Another year or two and you're going to look like a god. You're going to be so fucking good to look at people will think we built you."

Danny turned and leaned back against the counter, folding his arms. "You did."

Ian nodded. "Is your mouth still sore?"

"Yes."

Ian didn't move any closer. "Would you let me hold you, just once, since it's Christmas?"

Danny looked out the window then put his hands palm-down on the counter, spreading them out from his body. He nodded briefly.

Ian crossed to him and went up against him, felt the fine warm wool under his hands, the warm hardness of Danny underneath, buried his face in his neck and hair. "Hold me," he whispered.

Danny put his arms around him loosely.

Ian kissed his neck. "I love you, you know."

"Don't." Danny started to push him off.

"No." Ian held tight, moving his hands over his back, poker-hard with the sheer sensation of it. "Don't take it from me. You're the most beautiful thing I've ever seen. You get more beautiful every day. I wish you were dead, mutilated, then I wouldn't have to look at you any more."

Danny stood tense under his kisses, keeping his face averted, feeling the hands, now up inside his sweater, listening to the fevered words, wishing he'd hurry up, get it out of his system.

"I'd sell my soul for you, commit murder for you. If I thought I'd get you I'd kill anyone who got in my way... *anyone*." Ian's hands slid down over his buttocks.

"Enough," Danny said, pushing him off violently. "That's it."

Ian stood where Danny had pushed him and said, "Feel." He took Danny's hand and pressed it to himself. "Look, the little mouth is doing me. Your wound is giving me head. I'm fucking your wound."

Danny tugged his hand away. "Jesus. Shut up Ian. You're really sick sometimes."

He hugged himself as if he was cold. Ian's excitement always turned his stomach. It was the bed-mate of masturbating till you dry-ached, swallowing every kind of filthy slime till you threw up, being woken when you wanted to sleep. "You make me ill," he said suddenly, watching Ian's twitching face. "I ought to hate your bastarding guts and all you do is make me ill."

Ian smiled at him, hand pushed obscenely in his pocket. "I love you," he whispered hand jerking, picking up tempo.

Danny pushed up off the counter and went out the room.

Danny went upstairs and lay down on the bed. He wished they had an upstairs extension. He could phone Conley, tell him everything, unburden his whole fucking ugly life.

The room smelt strange and sweet. Jean McEvoy had put bowls of potpourri in every room. She had made it herself and given it as a Christmas present. It smelt spicy, like Conley's bakery, like Conley's breath; sharp with coffee, sweet with violet. Sometimes he smelt of cinnamon, like gingerbread. He ate too much garbage. All those fucking gold teeth. A mouth like a Jew.

He remembered an instant - one single moment - lying above him late at night and

Conley tight-stretched beneath him, eyes closed, head straining like the crucifix above them, in an ecstasy of pain, as emaciated as the Christ spread out in his tortured pleasure.

Someone knocked at the door. Danny lifted his head and looked at it as if he could see through it. He shouted, "Yeah?" and sat up on one elbow.

Stephen came in. Danny had known he would appear sooner or later but he'd hoped it would be later.

"Can I come in?"

Danny nodded.

Stephen came in tentatively, like someone entering a sacred shrine. Danny saw his eyes move quickly round the room, avoiding the bed.

"Sit down," Danny offered, looking at the armchair.

"I brought you this." And Stephen handed him a tiny package still wrapped in its fancy paper bag, neatly taped. He retreated and sat down. Danny sat up cross-legged on the bed to open it.

Stephen watched him, his throat aching with those utterly inexplicable, exasperating, unshed tears. He looked so good in his new jumper. Stephen thought he'd never seen a man look as handsome as Danny did without even trying.

Danny finally managed to extract the tiny box inside. He opened it. Inside was a pair of gold hoops the size of his smallest nail. He picked one up, smiled. "Determined, aren't you?"

"You don't need to, but if you wanted to you'd have them. They're good ones. Not cheap ones."

"I can see that."

Stephen got up, crossed to him. "They're hinged, see?"

Danny shook his head despairingly, smiling up at him. "Steve-o."

Stephen looked at him, felt the tears come up, perilously near. "You're not angry?"

And Danny knew he wasn't talking about the present. "No." He put the lid on the box.

"You don't need to get them done."

"I'll see."

"If you didn't like it you could always let it close up again."

"I hope you never decide to hurt me Steve-o, you'd make a hell of an enemy."

"I wouldn't ever want to hurt you," Stephen said earnestly, eyes fixed on the cut on Danny's lip.

"I was joking. Joke. Okay?"

"Sorry."

Danny could see the tears threaten again. The boy was so overwrought everything was making him overreact. Danny put the box down and put his hands on his ankles. "I've got something for you too."

Stephen looked at him, eyes alight.

"In the wardrobe. Go on, go look. That's it... down the bottom... in the revolting cheapo paper."

Stephen brought the package out and brought it over to the bed.

"Well, go on. Don't just stand there, open it."

Stephen opened it. Inside was Danny's leather jacket. Stephen looked at him.

Danny smiled. "It doesn't fit me any more. It's getting too tight across the shoulders. You said you liked your things worn. Well it's fucking worn. Any use to you?"

"*Danny*," Stephen exclaimed, rendered almost speechless.

"Try it on, it might not fit you."

But it did, with a little room to grow in. Stephen strutted up and down in it, admiring

himself, smelling the leather. "What about you?" he asked.

"I'm getting a new one. John's given me money for it."

"You're his favourite, aren't you?" Stephen said with a sudden childlike naivety.

Danny laughed. "One word for it."

"He shouldn't hit you like that."

"Drop it Steve-o," Danny said warningly.

Stephen dropped it. "Where *is* John?" he asked after a moment and his voice was too casual.

"I don't know." Danny glanced at the clock and Stephen thought there was something odd about it, as if he was trying to avoid doing it, like biting your nails.

"Is he still angry with you?"

Danny shook his head. "His anger doesn't last. Bang and it's finished."

"He seemed a bit funny this morning."

Danny shrugged. "Probably pissed off because I didn't buy him anything after him forking out for this." He smiled as he plucked at the sweater. *Actually Steve-o, it's because we both discovered a nasty little truth or two. He's got a tacky little streak of masochism and me... well, we won't bother about my problems.*

"You really suit it."

"John's got good taste."

"It's only a plain jumper."

"He'd massacre you for that. I'll have you know it's a very expensive plain jumper. Cashmere wool, no less."

"What?"

"Cashmere. Feel." And Danny held out his arm.

Stephen stroked it, felt Danny's upper arm beneath it, steely hard under the fine soft wool.

"Most expensive wool you can get. I knew someone... Katherine Henderson's brother..." Danny looked at him to be sure he knew who he meant. Stephen nodded. "All his sweaters were like this. I told John once, One day I'll own one. Now I do." He laughed. "It's probably the only one I'll ever own."

"What happened to him?"

"Who?"

"Katherine Henderson's brother."

"He died."

"Was he your friend?"

"No."

"How did he die?"

"John cut his throat."

Stephen gaped at him for an instant then saw Danny smile. "Jeez Danny, you had me fucking going there for a minute." And Stephen crumpled the Christmas paper into a ball and threw it at him.

It hit Danny painlessly in the chest. He caught it and began tossing it softly in the air.

The door opened and Rab stuck his head round. "This a private party or can anyone attend?"

"Come in, join the group," Danny said, without breaking his rhythm.

Rab came in and shut the door. He went round the other side of the bed and sat down, back against the headboard, legs stretched out.

Stephen stared at the floor, irritated by his arrival.

"If I'm not mistaken Steve-o is wearing your leather jacket."

Danny threw the paper up and batted it across the room. It landed on the chest of drawers. "My *ex*-leather jacket. I have been given financial resources for a new one."

Rab looked at Stephen. "It's a good fit."

"He's about the same size I was when I was seventeen. That's when it was bought."

Stephen smiled to himself. Danny went on, "It's too small for me. It's beginning to rip under the arms."

"You're getting to be a big boy Daniel."

Stephen looked up at Rab and saw the smiling look that passed between them, full of double-meanings. He wished he'd go away, leave them alone. He was so obvious. Couldn't Danny see it?

Danny slid back up the bed and leaned against the headboard beside Rab, legs stretched out alongside. Stephen wanted to climb in between them, wanted Danny to come back where he was. He felt like an outsider, sitting alone on the bottom of the bed.

"Aren't you warm in that?" Rab asked, smiling at him, and Stephen could hear the snide dig in it. He had hardly spoken to him since their fight yesterday and now look at him, pretending to be nice to him.

"No," he said, tight-mouthed.

"I won't steal it, I promise." Rab did more of his smarmy smiles.

"Leave him alone," Danny said. But he was smiling too, looking at his hands and trying not to enjoy the joke. Stephen could see him.

He got up. "I'm going to watch TV." And he slammed out the room.

As soon as he did it he regretted it. What a stupid thing to do. Well, he could always go down and come back up, say there had been nothing good on. He went downstairs reluctantly, feeling the starts of a headache. He hoped Rab would die, preferably of something nasty.

And soon.

Rab laughed.

Danny stretched out in the extra space, flat out with his hands behind his head as he had been before Stephen had come in. "You shouldn't tease him," he said.

"I wasn't."

"Yes you were."

"He bugs me."

"He's a baby."

"Some fucking baby."

"So I've heard." And Danny closed his eyes.

Rab looked down at him and said quietly, "Ian?"

"John."

"He came into my room." As an explanation even he knew it was pathetic.

"I'll bet."

Rab put a hand on his hair. "He wanted me to teach him how to seduce you."

Danny pushed his hand off. "That's worse."

Rab was quiet. His stomach felt as if it was full of stones. "He reminds me of you," he said.

"Poor kid."

"Don't say it like that."

"Why not? You're not even fucking him for the right reasons."

"You can shove that shit Danny. Why the fuck was *he* in bed with *me*? Not for my good looks anyway."

"He's only fifteen."

"Sixteen... today."

"You're still ten years older."

"So?"

"Christ." Danny opened his eyes and looked up at him. "What do you think?"

Rab looked at him then looked away. Danny rubbed his face.

"Okay so I shouldn't have done it," Rab conceded. "I didn't do it deliberately and it won't happen again. Satisfy you?"

"I don't care what you do."

"Not much you fucking don't."

Danny put his arm over his eyes and crossed his ankles. They lay together in silence then Rab said, "Danny?"

"Mm?"

"Why did you come back?"

"What d'you mean?"

"You know what I mean. You didn't intend to come back, did you, when you left? Just like all the other times. Yet you always do."

Danny lifted his arm and looked at him. "And where would I have gone? What would I have done?"

"What you did do, go to Conley's."

Danny put his arm back. "How do you know I went to Conley's?"

"Don't be a dumb-fuck."

"Okay. So supposing I did, why should he keep me there?"

Rab made a noise, half laugh, half derision. "Why would any of us keep you? Because you look nice about the place. Because there's always a chance you might take your clothes off. Because you look the type who might indulge in mindless sex at the drop of a hat. They would do for starters."

Danny didn't say anything. Rab asked again, "Why did you come home?"

"Because it *is* home. No place like it and all that shit."

"Yeah, sure."

"Okay then, you tell me. Why d'you think?"

"Unfinished business."

Danny seemed to take on an incredible stillness, like someone afraid of spilling water, balancing the glass, biting their lip. "What unfinished business?"

"I don't know, it just fits. Stephen."

Danny laughed shortly.

"It is Stephen, isn't it?" Rab persisted.

"*No.* Christ!" And Danny rolled up into a sitting position, feet firmly on the ground.

"Then it's John," Rab said with absoluteness. "It isn't me and it isn't Ian so it must be John. But then it always was John, wasn't it?"

"Oh for Christsake, shut *up.*"

"Maybe you missed the way he punches you about."

"Right..." And Danny moved to get up, but Rab caught at his sweater, pulling him back down.

"Hoi..." Danny went down on one elbow. Rab pulled him back against him, locking one arm round his neck and whispering in his ear, "I wish it was me. I wish you came crawling back to me like you crawl back to him." And he pushed him away, getting out from under him and going out the room without another word.

He met Stephen on the stairs coming up.

Stephen kept his head down, intent on snubbing him, but Rab stepped in front of him. When he moved to pass him Rab moved too.

"Get out of my flickin' way," Stephen said looking up at him.

Rab smiled, dirty, malicious. "He's in a bad mood Steve-o. You'll never get into his pants now."

Stephen's face went white. "You're a dirty bastard."

Rab laughed and came down a step to stand beside him. He squeezed the boy's crotch. "Poor baby," he said and went on down the stairs.

When Stephen knocked at the door Danny felt like pretending he wasn't in, but he was afraid he'd simply stick his head round, then how would he explain it?

He shouted for him to come in and Stephen went in. "Nothing good on," he said, unable to meet Danny's eyes.

Danny was sitting on the edge of the bed. "Come and sit down then," he said. He sounded tired.

Stephen sat beside him. "Ian's putting the dinner on. Do you think John will be back in time?"

"He hasn't missed a meal for it yet."

Stephen felt vaguely disappointed by his answer then realised he didn't really understand it, but the moment had passed to ask him what he meant so he said instead, "Where did you go?" then blushed at so direct a reference to what had happened.

"Caldermouth."

"I knew you had."

Danny glanced at him, at the sound of so much certainty. "Did you?" he laughed. "Looks like I've no secrets."

Stephen blushed again, sure that Danny felt now he couldn't be trusted. Rab had probably lost no time telling him that it was him who'd blabbed. "About what happened..." he said, and he wished he could die. His face was beetroot. Danny didn't say anything, didn't make it any easier. "I'm not upset about it. I mean, I don't think you're..." He stopped, tried again. "Well, I don't think you're queer or anything just because you did that."

He was shocked to realise Danny was laughing. In fact Danny was helpless with laughter. He had rolled his face into the pillow and was lost in laughter, which he'd obviously been trying to keep in. He wasn't keeping it in now.

"I don't see what's so funny," Stephen said stiffly.

"It's not, it's just..." But Danny was off again in a convulsion of fresh laughter. It was beginning to hurt him. He clutched his sides in pain.

"What's so funny?" Stephen demanded more belligerently, beginning to get genuinely annoyed.

Danny wiped his eyes on the counterpane and said, "You came on my fucking hand Steve-o." And he started laughing again.

"Jeez..." Stephen said, face flaming, and Danny wasn't sure if it was embarrassment or exasperation.

Danny wiped his face again and sniggered, brought it under control, sniggered again. "I didn't come on you Steve-o, *you* came on me. Don't forget it." And there was an edge to his voice now. He was still smiling, chuckling a little, but it was edged with hardness, like someone laughing at something that wasn't really funny because it was the only thing left to do.

Stephen looked at him, beginning to feel vaguely unsettled, as if he was getting into water that was too deep for him. "You..."

"I what?" Danny prompted.

"Nothing."

Danny lay back down on his back. "Right. Exactly. Nothing. Don't get too innocent

Stephen, it's bad for you."

Stephen didn't know what he meant, all he knew was he felt angry, hurt. It hadn't been his fault. *He* hadn't dragged Danny upstairs. *He* hadn't stuck his hand down his pants. It wasn't fair. "You don't need to be so fucking nasty about it," he said, giving full vent to his hurt. "How do you think I feel?"

Danny looked at him, steady, unsmiling. "I don't know Stephen." And his voice was low. "Tell me how you feel."

Stephen went scarlet and turned away. "I feel really bad."

"Shame." And Danny laid his head back and closed his eyes again, dismissing him.

Stephen looked back at him, blinking away tears, wondering how the hell the conversation had got like this. Everything had been fine before Rab had come in. "Danny..."

"What?"

"Let's not fight."

Danny felt the unintentional familiarity of the words wrench at him. *You bastard, he's only a kid*. He opened his eyes, looked at him... then smiled. "Let's not," he said after a moment.

Stephen smiled back and reached across eagerly for the earrings to see how Danny would suit them.

John came back with twenty minutes to spare before lunch.

Ian was being chef, filling the kitchen with an outrageous number of dirty dishes, enjoying himself. Stephen was whipping cream, being commandeered as the only person who admitted to knowing how it was done.

"Where's Danny?" John asked.

"Living room," Ian said then, "Where've you been?"

"Walking," John answered and went out the room.

Stephen saw Ian's surprise before he went back to what he was doing. "Walking," he muttered and said nothing else.

"Where've you been?" Danny said when John came in. He was sitting on the couch, Rab on the chair.

"Out," John answered.

Danny gave him a look then went back to the television.

"Anything good?" John asked.

"Shit," Rab said succinctly. "So Stephen says. He's seen it all before... as he keeps telling us."

Danny gave a small, soft laugh.

John looked at him and said, "You look good in it."

Rab looked at him perplexedly then realised he was talking about the sweater. Hadn't he seen him in it then? No fashion show without panties this morning? Bloody weird considering he'd obviously bought the bloody thing as a prick-tease. Buying Danny that was like buying a woman black lace underwear - it couldn't be for anything else. He wasn't going to spread fucking muck in it.

John sat down beside him and stroked his arm. He did it as if he wasn't thinking straight, or was past caring, or was hurting so much he couldn't help it.

Rab was aware of his own mouth dropping open. He was shocked to see how vulnerable he looked. John stopped suddenly, head coming up, as if he'd suddenly realised someone else was there. Danny had sat through the whole brief interlude taut

and icy, uninvolved.

Rab got up and went out without John saying anything. He couldn't stand to be near the pair of them. They were like live electric wires together. They made his teeth hurt.

He left them to it.

"Driven out?" Ian asked.

"He's in a mood," Rab said.

"He's been out *walking*."

"Walking? Him?"

"That's what he said."

"Screw *and* walk, that's a new one."

Ian looked at Rab sharply, making Rab look at Stephen. He had been following the dialogue. The trip in it didn't escape him. Rab ostentatiously changed the subject. Stephen wondered what he wasn't supposed to know. Whatever it was they could relax, he didn't know it. Did John have a girlfriend? Was that where he'd gone this morning? Who the hell would go out with John? He wasn't *bad* looking, it was just that he'd probably split any girlfriend in half if he tried to fuck her. The idea was oddly disturbing. Stephen chased it away.

"Right, clear the decks." Ian shooed them off the table and spread it with a large paper cloth. They set everything out, including candles that his mum had bought.

Rab whistled. "Better than when the old bastard was alive."

Stephen saw it, an instant face-whitening look of fear, both of them, then Ian said, "Go call them Steve, will you?"

Rab was still standing there, looking green, when he left the room.

The meal was good.

John and Danny seemed slightly more at ease with each other and therefore everyone else was too. John ruled the house like an emperor. When his majesty laughs, you laugh.

They even pulled crackers and wore party hats. Danny, as usual, managed to look good in one while it only succeeded in making John look worse. Anything short of leather armour seemed inappropriate for John.

They drank three bottles of wine and got happily drunk. Stephen got the wishbone and shared it with Danny. Stephen got the wish.

Danny smiled at him as he made it. Rab drawled, "I hope it comes true Steve-o." But Stephen knew he wished nothing of the kind.

They took some beer to the living room and all squeezed onto the couch so that no-one had to take the chair. It was stupid but it seemed logical at the time. Danny was sandwiched between John and Ian. Rab beside John at one extreme and Stephen beside Ian at the other.

Everyone was finding everything inordinately funny. They even found the TV funny, although it wasn't meant to be.

Danny squeezed out and went upstairs for a pee. Stephen noticed immediately how empty the place seemed without him, as if he was the pin holding them all together.

When Danny came back he sat in the armchair, stretching out luxuriously, sighing, "Space..."

John protested that he was being anti-social but Danny demanded his right to it as a Christmas present. John said he'd had enough Christmas presents, but Danny

returned promptly that you could never have too many and if John didn't like it he could lump it.

Rab laughed at that.

Stephen realised suddenly something was rubbing his leg. He looked down and saw Ian's fingers tracing up and down under his thigh. He jerked his leg away, face pink. Danny suddenly announced, getting up, that he intended to sit beside Stephen and promptly did so, squeezing in between him and Ian. Stephen felt ecstatic.

So did Ian.

They got very drunk.

Enjoyably drunk.

They had never liked each other more and fought less. Looking at them it might have been a good idea for them to be permanently drunk.

Rab ended up lying on the floor in front of the fire, John across the armchair, Ian and Stephen still on the settee with Danny, only with more space now.

Ian kissed Danny's cheek and told him he loved him, which seemed to amuse Danny oddly.

John told him he was drunk to which he replied, "Not enough." And proceeded to drink some more.

By the time the evening came they were all beautifully drowsy, lying in the warm dark, watching the hypnotic light of the TV.

Stephen and Danny had their heads together, talking softly. Ian was half-dozing in the corner of the settee, feet on Danny's lap. John was watching the TV through half-lidded eyes and Rab was gracefully asleep, hair streaming across two cushions like Sleeping Beauty, an empty beer can on his chest.

"This is the best Christmas I ever had."

Danny laughed sleepily. "Why? Because you've been allowed to get drunk?"

Stephen laughed too. "No, it's just been good. Nice, warm... you know."

"Nice? Warm? Not words I associate with our happy home."

"*You* are."

"Me least of all." Danny shifted his head a little, easing it into Stephen's shoulder. Stephen could feel his hair on his cheek. He half wished Rab was awake so he could see him.

Ian came to suddenly and said, "What are you two whispering about?"

"You," Danny said, lifting his head to look at him then laying it back again. He settled it further into Stephen's body.

"I'll bet," Ian said and started rubbing Danny's leg with his foot.

Stephen looked at the foot sliding up and down Danny's thigh and frowned. Danny put his hand on it, slowly, as if it was no great bother, and held it still, saying quite amiably, "Chuck it Ian."

"I still love you."

"Of course you do."

"I'm your brother."

"We know."

"And I love you."

"Go to sleep," Danny said and squeezed his foot.

"Give us a kiss."

Danny lifted his head and said clearly, "Go to sleep or I'll knock your fucking teeth in."

Stephen laughed. Danny put his head back down and smiled. "He's drunk," he said.

Stephen didn't say anything. He was thinking about asking Danny for that very same thing. He had been a hairsbreadth from using the very same words. But then, they would be, there weren't any other words. A kiss is a kiss is a kiss. Stephen said so.

"Very profound," Danny said.

"Why does he want to kiss you?"

"Because he's drunk."

"Because he's *beautiful*," Ian corrected him.

"I thought you were asleep," Danny said in surprise.

Ian didn't answer.

Stephen turned his face slightly into Danny's hair. "He's right, you are."

Danny smiled. "And *you're* drunk too."

"Yes, but you're still beautiful."

Danny laughed. "Outsmarted." Then he said, "Shit, I need something to drink. I'm thirstier than a burnt cat."

"There's more down there."

"No, I've had too much of that. I need water, lots of it." He struggled up. "Water, water..."

Stephen giggled helplessly then said, "Hang on, wait for me."

Danny pulled him up out of the sofa, unceremoniously dumping Ian's feet.

"Watch out for alligators," Ian said then went back to sleep. John looked up at them but said nothing.

Danny rumpled his hair and said, "Easy, old boy."

Stephen laughed some more.

They went out, weaving precariously, and made their way down the hall. Danny stopped by the phone and lifted the receiver. Stephen looked at him, said, "What are you doing?"

Danny looked at him and said, "Hell knows" and put it back down again.

They went into the kitchen. Danny announced that he'd changed his mind. Now he wanted fruit juice, lots of it. He opened the fridge and took out a bottle of apple juice. He twisted the top off and leaned back against the fridge, head thrown back, drinking straight out the neck of the bottle.

Stephen watched him, black and red against the white metal. He brought the bottle down and wiped his mouth. "*Beautiful*..." He pulled the word out long and grinned at him, his teeth white as white.

"Yes," Stephen agreed.

"Want some?" He held the bottle out to him.

Stephen shook his head.

"More for me then." And he did it all over again. He put the bottle back in the fridge. "Want to go out?" he asked suddenly.

"Out?"

"Yeah, see the stars. Christmas stars. We can make a wish."

"Okay."

They pulled on work jackets and went outside. It was very frosty with a full moon, clean and white. "Beautiful," Danny said again. His breath puffed up skywards as he looked up at the stars. He was black and white, perfect black and white. Black eyes, white skin, black hair. No grey. He howled like a dog.

Stephen laughed. "What are you doing?"

"Howling at the moon. I always feel wild when I see the moon."

Stephen laughed again.

"Brings out my blood-lust. Now I want to rape a few virgins, kill a few sheep. Or maybe rape a few sheep and kill a few virgins." He howled again.

It gave Stephen goosepimples, it sounded so real. "Do it again," he whispered.

Danny howled again, long, eerie, unsettling. A dog started barking in the distance. They both laughed.

"See? I'm a natural howler. Primeval man." And he did it again, long and wild and uninhibited, like only someone drunk could.

"Now I feel like raping sheep too," Stephen said and shivered.

"Want to go back in?"

Stephen shook his head.

"Come on then, let's go down the back field."

"What for?"

"See the river, howl a bit, who knows? Come on."

They went down over the back fields, shoes saved by the dry-frozen earth. Their breath came out in long plumes, like horses. They ran down the last stretch to the river, laughing with sheer momentum. "Hey, nice," Stephen said, looking round.

"Never been here before?"

"No."

"I'm surprised. There's no official right of way but the kids use it. I'd have thought you'd have... no, you didn't grow up here, did you?"

Stephen shook his head.

"We used to come swimming here. Not any more though."

"Why not?"

Danny shrugged. Stephen recognised it suddenly and said, "This is the place in the photographs."

Danny looked at him, hiccuped, said, "What photographs?"

"The ones Ian showed me."

Danny grunted then said, "Yeah."

"He's a bit funny, Ian."

"Very," Danny agreed, then he howled again, wild, loud, really letting go. "God, that feels good."

"It gives me goosepimples."

"Try it."

"No, not me."

"Go on, let rip."

But Stephen shook his head. Danny did it again, head thrown back.

"Shit, Danny, they'll be thinking there's a fucking werewolf on the loose."

"There is. God, I feel like ripping my clothes off."

Stephen laughed again. "You'd die of flickin' frostbite."

"I must come down in the summer, strip off, and have a howl sometime. Can't you just see me standing on the rock there, stark naked, howling at the moon?"

"Yes," Stephen said. He shivered again.

"Cold?" Danny asked.

"A bit."

"We'll go back, come on."

"Not yet, in a minute."

Danny smiled, "Okay."

"Would you really strip off out here?"

"Course. Why not? I've done it loads of times."

"How does it feel?"

"What?"

"Taking your stuff off outside, where someone might see you."

"You mean, is it a turn-on?"

Stephen looked at him. "Is it?"

"Sometimes. Depends who's watching you." Danny was grinning, teeth clear and sharp in the moonlight.

"*Did* you used to show off for Ian, like he says?"

"No. It only looks that way."

"How did he get them then, those photographs?"

Danny laughed. "By fair means or foul. This is a boring subject, let's talk about something else."

Stephen wasn't so drunk he didn't know when he was being told to mind his own business. "Let's go back," he said impulsively. "I'm cold."

Danny led the way back over the gate, giving him his hand to help him down. They stopped, panting slightly, at the top of the hill. Stephen felt as if something were slipping out of his hands, as if there were something he should say, do, but he didn't know what it was.

Danny looked at him and said, "Well?" And there seemed to be a world of meaning in it, a thousand million possibilities, and Stephen thought frantically, Well what? and tried to read it in Danny's face. But Danny only laughed, suddenly, as if he were intensely happy, like an impulsive handclap, and said, "Things you can't teach people at all."

And he laughed again and strode on up the field back to the house.

"You never even fucking missed us," Danny said and stuck his hands down the neck of John's shirt.

John let out a roar, waking both Rab and Ian. "*Jesus*, where the fuck have you *been?*" John was pushing his hands away.

"Over the hills and far away." Danny sat down, pushing Ian's legs off the settee. "We went down to the river. It's a lovely night."

"Fucking maniac," Rab offered from the floor. Danny pushed him with his foot. Rab grabbed it and tickled the sole, making Danny panic, kicking like a wild thing to free himself.

Stephen stepped over them and sat beside him. Danny was swearing at him, even while he was laughing, scratching Rab's hand. Finally he let go. Danny yanked his feet up out of harm's way. "I need a drink," he said.

John leaned over the side of his chair and offered him a whisky bottle. It was two thirds full. Danny looked at him but said nothing. John looked back and said nothing too.

"Steve-o, want some of this?" Danny said, tearing his eyes away and breaking the moment.

"Okay."

"Go and get us two glasses then... and bring some lemonade."

"Coward," John said as Stephen disappeared out the door.

"I admit it," Danny replied.

Rab sat up and leaned back against the sofa next to Danny's legs. He half-turned and rested one arm across Danny's knees. John watched him but said nothing. Danny looked down at him and said, "It was lovely out there, you should have come."

"I could say something."

"Well save it," John said sharply.

Stephen came back into the room. He'd brought extra glasses. Rab joined them. Stephen saw the way he was sitting and didn't like it. He took a gulp of his drink without adding lemonade to it.

John raised his eyebrows. "Boy after my own heart, I see."

Stephen flushed, not sure if he was being criticised. "I don't like anything with it."

"Rock on," John said and lifted his glass in salute.

Both Rab and Danny put lemonade in theirs. "Beer drinkers," John said scathingly. Everyone laughed.

Two or three drinks later Danny went out to pee again.

Danny went to the phone and picked it up.

He punched in the number quickly, wishing for the millionth time that the phone was somewhere else. Anywhere else. He lifted it off the table and slid down to the floor, back against the under-stair cupboard, phone balanced on his knee.

It rang.

And rang.

Danny didn't know whether to be disappointed or relieved. He listened to it ringing. So desolate, empty. He suddenly felt depression like something pressing him into the floor. He'd had too much to drink. He sat there listening to the sound of silence.

Then someone answered the phone.

A woman.

Danny thought he must have the wrong number, checked it with her. It was the right number. He wanted to hang up, still could, but he didn't. "Can I speak to Conley please?" he said, using the surname, realising it sounded odd.

"Who is it?" she asked.

"Just let me speak to him, will you?"

He heard the phone being put down in hostile silence, voices distantly, then Conley's voice said, "Hello?" Smooth, flat, emotionless.

"Hello," Danny answered. There was silence and that made it worse. Danny knew silences better than sounds, knew how to read everything people didn't say. "Who's with you?" he asked.

"I wasn't expecting you," Conley said.

"What took you so long to answer the phone?"

"We've just come in. I heard it ringing on the stairs."

"You fucking bastard." Danny laid his head back on the cold wood and said it again. "You fucking bastard." It made him feel better.

Conley was silent.

"It's her, isn't it?" Danny said. "The poppet. Girl Friday. I couldn't do without her." He mimicked Conley's voice. "Have you fucked her already? Or is that coming up for later? If you'll forgive the expression."

Conley was still, silent, listening.

"Jesus Conley."

"Where are you phoning from?" Conley said finally.

"Home. Here in my very own home, that's where."

"I didn't know I was supposed to be hearing from you."

And Danny heard it in there and felt himself colour even here in the dark where no-one could see him. "I know," he said.

But Conley said suddenly, voice warmer, "I'm glad you phoned."

"I love you," Danny said and then added, "That's a lie."

"Yes," Conley said and there was a million other answers in it, all held in one little word.

"Say my name," Danny said suddenly.

"No," Conley said and another million answers came flying in with that too.

Danny closed his eyes tight to stop it hurting and said, "I hope you rot in hell." And he slammed the phone down.

He sat with it there on his knees until Ian found him there five minutes later.

"Not home... or didn't you get that far?"

"Go away."

Ian hunkered down beside him in the darkness and took the phone off him. He put it back on the table. "He couldn't even be bothered to get out his chair. He sent me. Where does *that* hurt?"

"Go away Ian."

"Broken hearts and wounded egos, all catered for. Let me help." He leaned on his knees, a hand on each knee, holding Danny's legs open.

"Go suck yourself."

"I'd rather suck you."

Danny shoved his hands off and pushed back against the wall, levering himself up. He straightened up, head thumping, legs weak and cramped from their awkward position. Ian came up against him. Danny turned his head away. Ian spoke in his ear, hand against the banisters at either side of him, holding him there. "I'll do anything you want. I'll tell him any lie you like. You don't need to give me a thing. I mean it."

Danny flexed his legs, feeling the blood come back into them. "Leave me alone Ian. For Christsake, just leave me alone." And he slid out, shouldering Ian's restraining arm away. He went up the stairs, Ian following him like a dog, still promising the world.

When Danny got to the bathroom he turned and said, "I want to take a leak. Go away."

"Let me watch."

"*No*. I fucking hate this. Why do you keep asking me for something I fucking hate?"

"Because I know you hate it. Because if you won't love me then you can fucking well hate me. I'd rather you hated me than nothing at all."

Danny pushed inside the bathroom and slammed the door in his face, locking it quickly against his pushing. He lay against it for a moment, listening to Ian scrabbling outside then he heard him whisper, "I'm going to grind you down to dust Danny. Fucking *dust*."

Danny moved across to the toilet so that he couldn't hear, turned his back to the door as if Ian could see him. He could hear Ian turning the handle. Just turning it one way then the other, over and over again.

"Fuck *off!*" Danny roared suddenly. The door handle stopped turning.

"Dust, Danny," Ian said clearly through the door.

Danny gave him the finger and felt better. He flushed the toilet, put the lid down and sat on it. He saw a packet of cigarettes on the edge of the bath and crossed to pick it up. He lit one and sat back down on the toilet.

It was a good cigarette. He loved it.

Very much.

Danny lay on the bed and stared at the ceiling.

He had no right to phone Conley up like that, but the little poppet? Looked like it was going to be his day for being second best.

Unfinished business.

Right Rab. Sitting downstairs right now. I gave up Conley for this, sitting downstairs, right now.

Come up here. Let's finish it.

He put his cigarette back in his mouth and looked at the ceiling some more.

What are you looking for Danny?

An answer.

To what?

Where the line starts and finishes.

You're full of shit Danny. There is no start or finish, just the line going on and on, and you've got to cram as much of it up you as will fit because that's your job.

Stephen knocked on the door for the third time that day.

Go away, Danny thought.

"Danny?"

"What?" *Go away, fuck you.*

"John wants to know where you are."

"His legs been amputated or something?"

There was a silence but he hadn't gone away. Danny could feel him outside the door, standing there, waiting. He got up off the bed, stubbing out his cigarette and opened the door.

Stephen started back as if he'd been listening outside it. Danny looked at him then stood back saying, "Come in. It's what you want, isn't it?"

Stephen went in, no longer sure if it was. "You were gone so long John was wondering where you were."

Danny sat down on the edge of the bed, took another cigarette out the packet. "And you volunteered to go look."

Stephen nodded, embarrassment betraying him.

Danny lit the cigarette with a throwaway lighter. Stephen watched the flame colour his cheek, his mouth and cheekbone shaped by it, his eyes downcast. "You don't smoke very often," he said. It sounded like a criticism, although he didn't mean it as one.

"Special occasion," Danny said. "Which reminds me, I haven't wished you a happy birthday yet." He stood up and lifted Stephen's face, then kissed him full on the mouth. Stephen tasted the smoke, felt the instant hot surge of his breath, then it was finished.

"Happy birthday Steve-o." And smoke curled from Danny's mouth. He sat down again and looked at Stephen disinterestedly, as if nothing had happened.

Stephen's face was pale, his eyes large. He didn't know what to say, what was expected of him. "Why d'you do that?" he asked finally.

"A present, something you didn't have to beg for. Anyway, John wanted you to have it."

Stephen flushed to the roots of his hair. He didn't know whether Danny was being nice to him or getting at him. He knew this mood. Danny was restless, attacking and apologetic by turns, saying things you couldn't understand, everything so brittle and nervy about him he made you feel tired after fifteen minutes in his company.

Suddenly Stephen wanted to be away from him. He hurts me, he thought. Just looking at him hurts me. I'd be better off drowning myself, cutting my throat, than being with him.

Danny said, almost as if he was reading him, "Are you going or staying?" And he was watching him with those black eyes - no colour in him, just that bloodied hair, his red mouth - and Stephen wanted to be far away, with Rab, with Ian, even with John, rather than be with him, and Danny took another drag on the cigarette, waiting... waiting...

"Staying," Stephen said and felt his stomach turn to water.

Danny smiled and slowly reached over to put out his cigarette.

Unexpectedly Danny had told him to get his jacket, they were going out.

"Out?" Stephen echoed just like the last time.

"Yes, out. Come on, shift yourself."

Stephen had put Danny's leather jacket on. Danny had smiled at him and said, "Nice touch." And Stephen had no idea what he meant, but that didn't make him like it any better.

They went out, Danny in an ordinary work jacket. They took the Range Rover. No-one saw them. No-one stopped them. Danny left the gate open.

"Where are we going?"

"You'll see."

Stephen was glad that they were heading away from town. At least he wasn't taking him to Katherine Henderson's. But the mood was the same. Wherever they were going it was for the same thing. Another woman perhaps, a different one. Danny could have more than one. Stephen looked at him. Danny would.

Whatever this was, it was going to hurt, he thought again. *You should have stayed home Steve-o.* He looked at Danny, face lit pale green in the dark and said, *No, I want to be here, driving into the dark, frightened out of my wits. I want it.* "Danny, can we stop a minute?"

Danny glanced at him. "Need to pee?"

"No..." he chewed his lip, "I just want to stop a minute."

"You carsick?" Danny looked at him closely.

"Can we just stop, huh?"

"Alright, don't shit yourself. There's a lay-by ten minutes up the road, will that do?"

Stephen nodded. They drove the distance in silence. Danny didn't look at him again.

They pulled into the lay-by. There was another car there, the interior lit. A single man sat in it, looking at a map. Danny left the engine running. Almost immediately the other car's interior plunged into darkness and his rear lights came on. He pulled out slowly, indicator winking bright and orange in the dark.

"Well?" Danny said. And Stephen remembered him saying the same thing earlier, on the crest of the hill, waiting for him to do something, say something, just like he was waiting now, and Stephen still didn't know, felt he ought to know and didn't, but he wanted Danny to like him again, not this cold, hostile hardness about him, as if he was taking Stephen to his execution.

"You're annoyed with me," Stephen said without looking at him. "I don't want you to be annoyed with me."

"Why not?" Danny asked and his voice was lazy, idly curious. Stephen heard him shift in his seat, could see him watching him out the corner of his eye.

"Nobody likes to be disliked," he answered, irritated by the question. "I just want you to like me. There's nothing so strange about that."

"How much?"

"What?" Stephen looked at him.

"How much do you want me to like you?"

Stephen felt as if he was suddenly standing on a huge precipice, a tiny ledge, and it was shrinking. Even as they talked it was shrinking. "I don't understand," he said.

"You do." Danny was looking at him intently. "You understand just fine only you won't listen when it talks to you."

"Stop talking shit at me," Stephen flared.

"How much do you want me to like you?" Danny said again as if they had said nothing else. "Scale of one to ten, that should be easy enough for you."

"I don't know," Stephen said, reluctant to commit himself. "This is stupid."

Danny laughed like people did when they were calling you a liar. "Try. One to ten."

"I don't know." Stephen looked out his window. "Ten, I suppose," he mumbled.

"A lot," Danny said. "You want me to like you a lot, the most I can."

There was a pause and Stephen could feel Danny looking at him. "In *fact*, you want

me to love you." And Danny's voice was soft, low, a tiny fragment overheard, familiar and wrong at once.

"Don't be stupid," Stephen got out, but it sounded hoarse and unconvincing even to him.

"Why stupid? Because we're *men?*"

"Yeah," Stephen said belligerently.

"So you don't think brothers love each other? Or fathers their sons?"

Stephen didn't answer.

"You don't think they can?"

"Course they can."

"Then why is it stupid for you to want to be loved?"

"It just sounds stupid, that's all."

"But it's what you want, isn't it? Me to love you?" He added, "Like a brother?"

Stephen nodded.

"Like John loves me."

"He doesn't love you," Stephen said. He regretted the words as soon as they were out his mouth. "I mean, he's always..." He searched for it. "He's always angry at you. I would love..." He caught it just in time. "I would treat you better than that."

"So we love each other like brothers, no fighting, no pain, just ten on the scale of love?"

Stephen nodded then said, "You're the best friend I ever had. The others were all cowards, scared of everything, not like you."

Danny turned away from him. Stephen reached out a hand and touched his arm. "It's true."

Danny turned and slapped him away. He immediately dropped his head back and said, "*Shit.*"

"What did I say?"

Danny shook his head, not looking at him, still staring up at the roof.

"I'm sorry Danny, all I ever seem to do is irritate you." Stephen looked at his hands on the steering wheel. Danny was braced against it as if to stop himself from throttling him. Tentatively he put his hand over Danny's, slowly, curling it over, willing him, *Like me Danny, like me.*

Danny pulled his hand away saying, "Don't" sharply.

Stephen retreated to the corner of his seat, feeling wounded, wishing he could control this. He could never keep hold of it. It was like a shadow, smoke.

Danny dropped his arms suddenly. "Let's go home," he said and reached for the brake.

Stephen gripped his arm. "No." He didn't even know why he said it. "Not yet. In a minute." It wasn't often he could have Danny completely to himself. He wanted to hang onto it, make the moment last.

Danny cut the engine. The silence was absolute. He sat back in his seat. Stephen heard him sigh. "Am I a bore?" he asked, feeling sick at heart.

Danny laughed. Quiet, sweet-sounding. "No."

Stephen didn't believe him, but he didn't contradict him. "If you could do anything you liked right now, what would you do?" he asked.

"Have a girl I had when I was thirteen."

Stephen felt himself flush. He laughed, embarrassed. "Jeez Danny, don't you ever think about anything else?"

"Often, but right now that's what I want. You asked."

"But *thirteen*, Jesus. What would you do with her?"

"Go down on my bended knees and beg."

For some reason Stephen saw Katherine Henderson standing above him naked,

making him crawl for it. He felt excitement trail over his belly like a hand.

"What about you?" Danny asked. "What would you do?"

Stephen thought then said, "What I'm doing, sitting here in the dark with you, talking."

"That all?" Danny asked and there was an odd note in there, as if he was expecting him to say more.

"That's all," Stephen lied.

Danny laughed. "You're easily pleased."

"Don't you like it?" Stephen asked, knowing it was a stupid thing to do.

"Not as much as being sat on." Danny smiled out his window. Stephen could see it at the corner of his mouth.

"You like it a lot, don't you? Sex I mean."

Danny laughed. "Doesn't everyone?"

"Not as much as you. They don't get weird about like you do."

Danny turned to him, amused. "Weird?"

"You go all weird if you don't get it, like you want to hurt everybody."

Danny stopped smiling. "Do I?"

Stephen nodded.

"Including you, eh?"

Stephen looked away, sorry now that he'd brought it up, but maybe Danny would be more careful if he knew. Danny looked out his window again, said nothing. Stephen looked at Danny's hands, one lying loose in his lap, the other rubbing his cheek as if it ached and asked, "Is that where we were going? To fuck some other girl?" He blushed as he said it.

"Something like that."

"But not any more."

"No."

Stephen took a breath then said, "Don't you want to any more?"

"No," Danny said.

"Why?"

Danny laughed, turned to him. "I don't fucking know, I just don't."

"Is it my fault?"

"Fault? Surely you've done me a favour?"

"I don't know." He looked at Danny and said, "If you still want to go I don't mind."

"Even if I don't take you with me?"

Stephen was silent, heart sinking.

"That's different, eh?" Danny turned and looked at him. "I think you're getting to be a voyeur. You like to watch."

"I don't." But Stephen knew a part of him was lying.

"Don't you like to watch me then? You told me earlier I was beautiful."

Danny was laughing at him. He could hear it. "I was drunk."

"So I'm not beautiful?"

He said 'beautiful' oddly, as if he thought it was the stupidest damn word he'd ever heard.

"You *are*," Stephen said, angered by his tone of voice. "You know you are."

"Well tell the truth then, all your fucking lies get up my crack."

"You haven't got a crack," Stephen snapped back.

"How do you know?"

"I've seen, remember? With a prick like yours there'd be no room for a crack as well."

Danny laughed. "You might not like to watch, but you've got a good eye for detail."

"That isn't a detail, that's the main attraction."

Danny looked at him and said in a different voice, "Think so?"

And Stephen swallowed and said, "Yes."

Danny smiled widely and looked out the window again. The silence suddenly seemed warm, heavy, full of possibilities. Stephen wanted to lie down, go to sleep. Being with Danny often did this to him, made him dozy, half-hypnotised.

"Want to go home now?" Danny asked quietly, without turning to him.

Stephen made a negative sound in his throat, adding, "Not yet." And everything was velvet around him - the car seat; the dark beyond the window; the fabric of Danny's jeans; Danny's hand lying there; the way Danny lifted it, running his hand through his hair. All slow and velvet.

Danny's hand finally came to rest on the side of the seat. Stephen touched it just to see, running his fingers over its back. Danny didn't move, didn't look at him. His skin was warm and dry, but not velvet after all. His hand wasn't rough and cut like John's, but it wasn't velvet. Stephen felt the wound, the tiny scar line - a ridge, that's all - the mouth hidden, pressed against the velvet of the seat.

He turned Danny's hand over, cupped it like a leaf in his own, then brought it over to rest on his knee while he traced the palm with his finger tips, feeling the tight little mouth, the two rough patches on Danny's fingers and the callused heel where he slid the tractor's steering wheel through his hands.

He felt the cuff of Danny's sweater, warm, soft, round the fine hardness of his wrist. He slid his fingers inside the sleeve then slowly turned Danny's hand over and laid it on his leg. He felt Danny's hand slowly curve round him, tighten there.

He felt his erection grow like his heart swelling. He could feel his blood singing in the dark. Danny's hand moved up an inch and rested there, Danny still looking out the window.

Stephen wanted him to do something, but Danny just sat there, waiting. Stephen could feel him waiting, feel the tightness of his breathing. He reached over quietly, afraid that Danny would move, start the car, say something shattering, and laid his own hand on Danny's thigh.

He knew what he wanted, but he was afraid.

He leaned over and pressed his mouth to Danny's cheek. It felt strangely rough, bristled. He moved closer. Danny could have touched him, felt his excitement, but he didn't move.

Stephen brought his head before Danny's face and kissed his mouth, so softly it was hardly there. His lips felt numb, he was so scared. He waited for Danny to yell at him, throw him out, but Danny didn't.

Stephen kissed him again, felt it open up inside himself like a floodgate. He wanted this so much. *Please God, let it happen.*

Danny didn't respond. Stephen began to feel an edge of anxiety. What was he doing wrong? "Danny..." he whispered against his mouth, "it's okay..." He pressed his mouth with his lips again, pushed his hand down between Danny's thighs, not actually touching it, but so close. "I wouldn't mind if you wanted to," he said tremulously. Then, when Danny didn't speak, he asked, "Don't you want to?"

And this time Danny finally brought his face round to his, meeting his eyes, and said, "Do *you* want to?" And his voice was low and deep.

Stephen nodded and leaned over against him, longing to push his hand right up and feel him.

"Then tell me," Danny said. "I want to hear you say it."

"I want to do it," Stephen said, face flaming.

"No, you've got to say what," Danny insisted. "You've got to say exactly what."

Stephen turned his face away so he couldn't see him. "What I did with Rab."

"That's not good enough. Say the words, say what you want me to do to you."

Stephen could hardly recognise his voice. There was something about the sound of him that made him harden in his pants, although he was already so stiff it was hurting. Like doing something dirty with a stranger, someone you've only just met and never will again, all sex and nothing else.

"Suck me," Stephen whispered, dying a death. "I want you to suck my prick." And he pushed his hand deep into Danny's crotch.

Molly looked at him. His face was drawn and white again. She was annoyed. It had taken her all evening to thaw him out and now look at him. "Who was it?" she asked, but she had a pretty good idea who it was. James didn't have many friends and none of them with an accent like that. There wasn't anyone else it could be.

"No-one important," Conley said, making an effort to smile.

"You shouldn't put up with that James. Who does he think he is?"

Conley looked at her, startled.

"I know who it was. It was Danny, wasn't it?" She said his name like an old prophet might have said Jezebel.

Conley smiled, as dry and tight and painful as the skin on a burn. *I might as well have given you the pleasure of your name Danny, it's no secret anyway.* "Yes." He smiled some more, ripping his face open. "It was."

"He really is an unpleasant character. Why do you put up with him?"

Conley held up his hand. "It was nothing, honestly. He just surprised me, that's all. I wasn't expecting to hear from him again."

"He's done more than surprise you. When we came in here you were feeling fine, cheerful for the first time in days. Now look at you."

Conley shrugged. "I'm sorry Molly." He sat down.

"Don't apologise." She sat down beside him, moving back a little when she saw him tense. "It's not your fault."

She looked at him for a moment then said, "Look, James, I know it's none of my business." And Conley felt an immediate urge to say, No, it bloody isn't, but she was already far into her speech. "But what is he to you? Why do you let him march in here, pester you with phone calls? I mean, he isn't a relation or something is he?" And Conley could hear the doubt back in her voice. The same doubt that was always going to be there now. Words spoken could not be unspoken. What she was really wondering was whether the hold Danny had on him was blackmail.

Or something Molly. It's 'or something'.

He said, "He helped me once, when I needed it, that's all."

Molly looked at him, wondering how, wondering for why. "Well, he isn't helping you now, that's for sure. Why don't you tell him where to go?"

Because I don't want to, you stupid bitch. "Molly," he smiled. "You don't just dump people when it suits you."

She had the good grace to blush, but she said anyway, "No, but you don't have to be a doormat either."

Conley laughed, surprising himself. "Am I a doormat? That bad?"

"No. Not really." She smiled. "But you know what I mean."

You mean he's competition. You mean he riles me in ways you couldn't even reach. That's not competition, that's defeat. But Conley only nodded because she was right. He knew she was right, but all he could wish was that she hadn't been here. He'd rather have sat here all alone all day and had that phone call to himself, been able to talk to him even for five minutes, two minutes, than a lifetime of her devotion.

He rubbed his face and closed his eyes. He'd rather have one minute of Danny's loathing than all her love, God help him.

Danny said, "No" and took Stephen's hand away.

"But why?" Stephen said, feeling the tears run down his face as if they had nothing to do with him. "You want to, I know you do." And he pushed his hand into Danny's crotch again, feeling the swollen heat, consoling himself with the irrevocable truth of it.

"Stop handling me." Danny peeled him off again, pushing him away this time.

"I hate you," Stephen choked at him and he curled up, far away from him, against the door, dying of shame - for the rejection, for the child's tears, for the horrible burning frustration gnawing at his stomach.

Danny turned on the ignition and let off the brake. Stephen felt the car move. He felt dry and washed out. His tears had stopped as suddenly as they had come. He felt nothing, just dull and empty. He'd offered Danny everything and Danny had shoved it back at him like it had meant nothing. He pushed his face into the cold glass, the rough bumping making his teeth ache, and wished he was dead.

Eventually, when they were almost home, he glanced once at Danny's face. It was serene and unperturbed. He was watching the road, face still and neon-lit, hands relaxed on the wheel, and Stephen thought he felt his heart break, felt it physically clench and crack inside him.

He hadn't even touched him.

Stephen hadn't touched him at all.

Stephen went straight upstairs. He didn't want to see anybody, talk to anybody.

Danny took his jacket off and hung it up.

John saw Stephen go upstairs but he didn't speak to him. He went into the kitchen. "Where've you been?"

Danny glanced up at him. "We went out for a drive."

"You were too drunk for that."

"I lived."

"Lose your fucking license and as far as I'm concerned you might as well be dead."

"I won't do it again Dad, I promise."

"Don't call me that."

Danny's head jerked up as if he was on the verge of saying something, but he never said it. They stared at each other, the sense of waiting palpable between them, until Danny broke it. He washed his face with his hands, rubbed his neck.

"Doesn't look like it was a very relaxing drive," John said.

"I'm tired."

"What about the boy?"

"What about him?"

"I don't know, I'm waiting for you to tell me. Looked like he'd been crying."

"Maybe Christmas makes him sad."

"So what was it about?"

Danny looked up at him, a hairsbreadth from telling him, then said, "Nothing, John."

"Don't take your vicious little habits out on him."

"Is that an order?"

"Yes. He has to put up with enough shit from you without you rubbing his face in it."

"*His* face? Sure it isn't your own you're worried about?"

John closed his eyes as if Danny had spat in them. He scratched his lower lip with

his teeth, whitening it and leaving it reddened. He opened his eyes again, slowly. "I'll never cease to admire your courage Danny, or your fucking brass neck."

"Go suck yourself."

"See what I mean? The boy hasn't got a clue, has he?"

"Just as well or he might wonder why you keep sending him in for it."

John pulled his face round where he could see it. Danny met his eyes briefly then averted them again.

"Too much pressure to bear? Laying it out for you too often? Too hard to refuse?"

"Too fucking easy." Danny pushed his hand away. "No fucking sweat."

John laughed. "You say, but the temper says something else. What's wrong, he make a pass at you that you nearly couldn't refuse?"

"I told you, he doesn't give me any problem."

John smiled suddenly, widely. "Let's see how long that lasts."

"What *is* your problem John? Pissed off that the substitute hasn't been taken for play?"

"Christ, you are one sick little bastard."

"Me? I never thought it up."

"If you're not careful it might be the last thought you never had."

"Is that a threat?"

"Am I laughing?"

They had talked themselves into a silence again, full of the usual tense hostility. Danny sat down again, heavily, staring sullenly at the table. John said quietly, "Let's go to bed."

Danny looked away, eyes flashing with temper. "Let's fucking not."

"Come on, you can sweat it off."

"It's too late for that."

"Try it."

"I said no," Danny snapped at him.

John looked at him for a long moment then said, "You're going to have to learn to ask Danny, just like the rest of the world."

"Drop dead."

"Well I'm not going to so you better just get up those stairs before I have to drag you."

Danny smiled up at him. "So drag me, Big-boy. Let's see you fucking drag me." He suddenly pulled his sweater up over his head and threw it at him. "And you can stuff that up your fucking arse too." And he got up and strode past him like some half-naked fury, oblivious to everything but his own anger.

John stood there holding the sweater, feeling the soft warmth of it, still full of Danny's heat.

He pressed it to his face and breathed him in.

SIXTY-FOUR

December slid away from them. Painless, almost dull.

John kept Danny separated from everyone, holding him tight on that string of want and no reward that he was so good at. It began and ended in that bedroom and it never got any slacker.

December was numb and painless and full of tears, and Danny was tired.

On New Year's Eve they stirred themselves from their torpor enough to go to the pub, and Danny and John had their first fight since Boxing Day.

Danny wanted to go and John didn't, and what's more, he didn't want Danny to go either.

"I'm sick of looking at you John."

"Meaning you want to look at someone else."

"No, meaning I'm sick of looking at you. What's more, if we spend much more time up here Stephen is going to have very serious thoughts about what we do in here… if he hasn't already had them."

"Fuck Stephen."

"No thanks."

"Everything's fucking Stephen with you. It's my bloody house, I'll do what I want in it."

"Yeah, sure, and have him tell his mother and then everyone else, John-boy Jackson Moore sticks it up his little brother Mam, what about that?"

John slapped him. "Your dirty mouth. Your fucking *dirty* mouth."

Danny rubbed his cheek. "It always gets to you that, doesn't it? What's wrong? You do it, what's the problem with saying it?"

"You like that, don't you? Rubbing my face in it?"

"In what? That you're an ugly, incestuous bastard who tossed off for ten long years over the thought of brownholing his little brother again?"

John slapped him again.

"Before you did it, that is." Danny rolled over the bed as John came at him again. "Before you actually did it - more rape with violence."

John came round the bed after him. Danny scrambled back over it, keeping his eyes on John's white face. "Let me out John. Before we kill each other. I'll go mad if you don't let me out. Just tonight."

They stared at each other across the bed then Danny said, " Come on John, please."

John turned away from him. "Alright." His voice was tight. "Get out, go on. *Now. Move* it."

Danny went out, not stopping to change his clothes. He found Rab and Stephen downstairs. "I'm getting out tonight," he said to Rab then smiled so that Stephen would know he was joking.

Rab saw the tension in his face and said, "You and Steve go ahead, I'll wait for Ian."

Danny went out without looking at Stephen. Stephen followed him, feeling embarrassed to be alone with him. They hadn't been alone together since Christmas Day. Nothing had been said about what had happened and Stephen knew it wasn't ever going to be said. He had told his mother the day after that he had just eaten and drank too much and been up all night being sick. She'd believed him. There was no reason why she shouldn't after all, it was true. Only it was shame that had made him

throw up, not drink.

They got into the pub. Stephen wasn't wearing Danny's leather jacket. It had hung in the wardrobe unworn since that night, except sometimes when he was alone he would put it on and just sit there in it, thinking.

Danny bought whisky, no lemonade, and a Coke and a double rum. He put the glasses on the table and left it to Stephen to do what he liked. Danny looked round the pub almost as if Stephen wasn't there. Stephen found himself wishing Rab would arrive so that he could at least become visible.

He watched him surreptitiously, saw Danny's eyes snag on someone, watched him do a double-take then he turned his back, slowly and carefully, as if he was trying not to draw attention to himself. It was just like when you saw someone you didn't want to see.

Stephen looked past him curiously, expecting to see a girl. But it wasn't. It was a group of middle-aged men, still in work clothes. They looked like decorators. One of them, much younger than the rest, glanced over and Stephen knew it wasn't a casual glance. It was checking if someone was still there, if it was who you thought it was. He caught Stephen's eye and looked at him deliberately as if to say, I know you. But Stephen didn't know him. The look was slow, challenging, half-hostile. Stephen said, "Danny, do you know him?" without thinking.

"Who?"

Stephen suddenly remembered they weren't really talking. "The young bloke behind you, short blonde hair." And Stephen knew, looking at his face, that he'd known all along who he meant. "Have a look," he said, just to see what he'd do.

Danny kept his eyes on the table. "I don't know him."

Stephen knew he was lying. "He gave me a dirty look but I've never seen him before. You sure you don't know him?"

"I'm sure." And Danny's voice was hard, and his eyes were hard, and suddenly Stephen wanted to tell him to climb up himself, tell him he'd had enough of being treated like shit, but Rab came in with Ian and somehow the mood changed with them.

They brought their drinks over and sat down, Rab on a stool by Danny, Ian on the bench with him. Ian was drinking beer. He took a long drink then half-lowered his glass, other hand arrested mid-wipe across his mouth. "Friend of yours Danny," he said.

Danny looked up. Ian brought his head down to meet his eyes. Stephen watched them both. "At the next table." And Ian smiled.

Rab said, "Where?" and turned to look. Danny stared at Ian, eyes conveying an unmistakable and unsettling message that Stephen was glad wasn't aimed at him.

"The blonde," Ian said, never taking his eyes off Danny's face, and Stephen saw the cropped blonde head turn and look at them again, then look away quickly under so many eyes.

Rab turned back slowly, looked into his glass.

"The joiner," Ian said.

"I guessed," Rab replied without looking up. "He's got the right mouth."

All of this meant nothing to Stephen. He looked from one to the other and he wanted to say, Who? What? But he didn't because he knew all they'd do was clam up and he'd learn less than if he just sat there silent, being invisible.

Danny finished his drink and got up to get another, and Stephen saw the blonde boy look up to watch him, and he saw Danny glance over at him and them both look away, the blonde colouring, Danny never changing.

Rab said, "At least you can't argue with his taste."

Ian smiled an ugly smile and replied, "Or his nerve."

Rab looked suddenly at Stephen and said, "Everybody's ignoring you."

And Ian said, smiling too, "That's the way he learns things."

And that was how the evening started.

And that was how it finished.

Danny could feel him behind him like something searing his skin. It all came flaring up in him, a week's worth of it.

Like a pet, an animal, a slave.

He drank and he waited. Sooner or later…

Eventually the boy went to the toilet. Rab and Ian watched him go. Stephen watched him go.

But only Danny got up and went after him.

Rab put his glass down and looked at it consideringly. "Shit," he said as if he was saying, Well now.

"Jesus," Ian said. Then, "He takes the fucking biscuit."

"Yeah, right down his throat, where his teeth are likely to follow."

"Maybe we should go see."

Rab looked at him. "Why? Do you want to watch?"

Ian looked back at him coolly. Stephen found he was holding his breath. "I'm never averse, but in this case I mean it. It would be just fine if he beat the fuck out him in our own local, with his reputation."

Rab looked at his glass. "Speak for your own."

Stephen got up. They both looked at him. "I'm going to take a piss."

"Steve-o…" Rab grabbed his arm but Stephen shook him off.

Rab called after him, half getting up, but Ian tugged him down. "Leave it," he said quietly, warningly.

Rab sat down reluctantly.

"If he goes in after him Danny can't do anything. No fighting, no fucking."

Rab stared at him. "Yeah, but what if he catches him doing the fucking not the fighting?"

"Tough tits, let Danny sort it out."

"Oh great." Rab turned in his seat as if the sight of Ian disgusted him.

"Any better suggestions? Maybe go in there and drag him out by the dick? I can see three… no, four people in here that would like an excuse."

"Great," Rab said again but he made no move to get up.

They waited.

For something to happen.

Danny went in and leaned against the wall. The blonde was just standing there, arms loose, waiting for him.

Danny smiled.

The blonde looked at him and said, "What the fuck are you smiling at?" and his voice sounded high, uncertain. He hadn't expected the smile.

"You," Danny said.

The blonde shivered as if someone had walked over his grave. Suddenly he needed to pee, very badly. He said so.

Danny smiled again, but he didn't speak.

The blonde unzipped, self-consciously turning away. The flow of urine seemed to go on forever. He felt embarrassed by the noise of it, vulnerable. Then the door

opened.

A young boy came in, the one at their table, the one who looked like his brother. The redhead smiled again. "Steve-o."

Stephen looked at Danny leaning against the wall. He looked at the blonde standing there urinating, looking at him over his shoulder, obviously startled. Danny had lied to him. They'd been talking when he'd come in. He did know him. "I've come to take a leak," he said.

"I didn't think you'd come for a pint. There's the place you want." Danny nodded at the urinal.

Stephen moved into the next stall. He found he did need to pee after all. The blonde was zipping up. Stephen felt him pass behind him, then the door opened. Stephen turned. Danny was going out behind him. "See you later Steve-o." And his smile was gone.

Stephen didn't see him again.

Danny caught his arm and said, "Let's go outside."

"Piss off." The blonde pulled his arm away.

Danny looked at him and said, "Five minutes, come on."

The blonde went with him. He couldn't have told you why.

Danny took him up to the tractor shed. The blonde followed him in silence, looked round the shed intently then said, "You work here?"

Danny nodded.

The boy looked round the tractors, came back to where Danny was standing and said, "You're lucky I don't punch you in the mouth."

"Go ahead." Danny watched him until he looked away.

"What's the point?" He sounded defeated, flattened.

Danny said nothing.

"Why did you do it?" the boy asked suddenly. "A thing like that, just to win a bet."

"It wasn't just to win a bet."

There was a pause. The boy turned his back to him. "You queer, is that it?"

Danny didn't answer him, forcing him to look at him. When Danny had his eyes he said, "No. I just took a fancy to you."

The boy stared at him, unable to grasp it. "I don't understand," he said finally.

Danny shrugged. "What's to understand? I fancied you... there, then, at that moment." He smiled. There was a tiny pause. "Like you fancied me."

The boy couldn't answer that, couldn't deny it. How could you say, No I didn't, when you'd had a peg on you like a fucking clothes pole? You couldn't. He didn't.

Danny came up and leaned against the tractor beside him. He took the boy's hand and pressed it against himself.

The boy pulled his hand away as if he'd been burnt. "You fucking perv, leave us alone."

Danny let his arm drop and stood watching him. He could see him trying to make it fit. He stood there waiting for his cue, the signal that would give him the key. The boy paced like a trapped animal.

"I'm not doing it again," the boy asserted. "You can forget it. I'm not a bloody poof."

Danny smiled and said, "I wouldn't want you if you were."

The boy stopped his pacing. Danny saw his tongue tip move over his bottom lip, full, oddly pink, as if he were wearing lipstick. His mouth was beautiful, wide and dangerous.

Danny came close to him, reached out a hand and laid it flat on his chest. He felt scalding hot under the fabric. Danny's stomach tightened with anticipation. "I've never

seen a mouth like yours."

And Danny moved his head and kissed him.

The boy stood there tamely under it. Danny could feel his skin flush against his cheek. His mouth felt as if he'd been drinking hot tea. The lying little fucker wanted it as much as he did. More.

Danny walked him back against the tractor with his body. He pressed him up against the wheel and kissed him again, this time with his palms flat against his chest, his mouth pushing the boy's open.

It yielded almost immediately. He tasted of beer, no peppermint this time, just beer. Danny felt instantly moltenly drunk with him. He was surprised to hear himself groan, even more surprised to feel the boy grip his shoulders.

He began to undo the boy's clothes. He felt sure that his body was special, that despite not having seen it that first time it had a lot to do with him risking his neck for it in the first place He pulled his shirt open, his trousers down. "Christ," he said, "you're built."

And he was, thickset and hard with ropy muscle, his cock and nipples that odd shade of chafed red-brown. Dressed he looked squat, too beefy. Danny might have passed him by if it hadn't been for that mouth, something about the scale of him. Now he knew what it was and he didn't even care. It was exciting him too much. The sameness, the difference.

He felt a sudden intense urge to go down on him, grovel before him. If the boy had pissed on him at that precise moment it wouldn't have made any difference. He slid down onto his knees on the dirty floor and took him in his mouth.

The boy looked down at him with his shocked breath still trapped in his throat. His peg kept disappearing down the redhead's throat, slurping back out again. He wasn't sucking it, he was vacuuming it. He saw himself standing shivering, naked, in an oily shed, with another man sucking him, his tongue everywhere.

He touched the redhead's hair, that fascinating hair, and said urgently, warning him, "I'm going to do it." He took a grip on his head, pushing up to meet it as it threatened to overwhelm him. "I'm going to." He pushed tremblingly forward. "I'm doing it... oh no, I'm doing it..."

And he did.

He'd been very quick, too quick for Danny's taste.

Danny got to his feet, knees tingling, and kissed him. The boy pulled back, revulsed by the idea of tasting himself, but Danny held his head until he stopped struggling, eventually relaxed, then began to enjoy it.

Danny unzipped his trousers but didn't ask him, just the invitation of the noise.

Danny kissed him, ran his hands over him. He was so hard it hurt. He heard himself moan again, once more with surprise, then the boy touched him, much as he had done that first time, shyly at first then bolder. Danny kissed him again, waiting until the boy gave in and made a move on his dick, gripping it firmly, before he said, "I thought about you." And he slipped his hand down and felt him. He was already more than half-hard again, firming in Danny's hand. "I thought about you a lot." He felt the boy's cock fatten another fraction. He smiled into his neck. "Kissing your mouth, that's what I thought about. I could taste it."

He felt the boy slide his trousers down, pull his buttocks towards him, feeling them in odd grabbing handfuls. Mr Fucking Straight had done this in his head. Mr Fucking Straight, bent as a frigging hairpin.

"I love the way you hold my cock," Danny said, kissing him again. It did something inside, that kiss. He found himself standing there, suddenly letting the words just go.

"Wank me." He pushed up into his hand. "Pull it." He strained. "Frig it."

But it didn't work.

He'd done this once too often today and now he couldn't get there. How often in his life had he ended up shivering in pain at the point of climax, needing more pain to take the pain away?

Danny shoved him back, held him away from him by the shoulders and watched his bitten, stubby hand painfully pulling his raw cock. That dirty, stained, meaty hand pulling him without any care or refinement. Suddenly it was there. He said in short gasping thrusts, hips jerking up at him, trousers sliding down, "Now... now... now... now."

The joiner's grip was suddenly fierce as a spasm of pleasure gripped him from the jerky workings of Danny's hand. It was an accident, a reflex, but it was enough.

Danny came, with all the cramping pain he could want.

Stephen came back into the bar. Rab and Ian looked at him.

Let them ask. They can fucking ask.

Rab said, "Well, where is he?"

"Who?" Stephen said irritatingly.

"Danny."

"How should I know?"

Rab and Ian looked at each other.

"He went with his friend. I don't know where."

And they all looked away from each other, all at separate things, all pretending they didn't care.

When midnight struck Danny was masturbating a twenty year old joiner. Both of them had left their New Year drinks sitting untouched at their respective tables. Only one set of friends wondered where they were. Only one set thought the joiner was alone.

If asked neither boy would have cared. They were happy, deep in their pleasures, finding their own satisfactions. They could have done worse things. They could have been killing each other.

When they were finished Danny looked at him and said, "You're good at that." And the joiner blushed because he felt the same way but couldn't say it.

Danny kissed his mouth and said close to his face, "But now you're going to fuck off."

The joiner began to feel that same sinking shame as the last time, the feeling of being used. He began to dislike him again; his perfect bloody handsome face, that irritating smile, his smug fucking detachment. He could have said anything, just something friendly, but not him. All he did was smile as if to say, Hop it, I've had you, now you're making the place look untidy.

The joiner tidied himself up as best he could, pulling up his jeans, hiding his swollen sticky flesh from himself. He wiped his hands on his legs, feeling ashamed and angry. What happened to the beating he was going to give him when he saw him again? The way he'd left him standing there in the stinking dark like he was a quick wank in an alley, and now it was happening all over again. "You're a fucking little poof," he said before he could stop himself, but the redhead just fastened his clothes and ignored him.

It didn't touch him.

The joiner blurted out, "Why did you do it with me?" and he felt like shrivelling

under the naked disappointment in his own voice.

The redhead looked up and said, "Because you were there."

And it was like being spat on.

The joiner went out into the cold and walked down the lane back to the pub, where he went to the bathroom and washed his face with cold water, over and over again, till it was numb.

He finally looked up at himself, breathless and half-suffocated with cold, and saw the tears on his reflection, just running there, not on him at all.

He wasn't crying at all.

Danny went home.

He felt good. So good he wanted to smash something. He felt higher than a kite, filled with destructive power.

When he went in John was sitting in the dark watching TV, watching other people party. He looked up and saw the curious play of colour on Danny's face, ribbons and confetti moving over him. He patted the settee.

Danny sat down beside him. He tasted of cold and beer, smelt of oil and sweat, and John could feel it in him, the lassitude, the softness.

Danny kissed him again, seriously this time, kneeling up to do it. John lay there, weak with it, smelling it off him, tasting it, just as he'd known he would. He wondered who'd got it. He wanted to ask but couldn't do it, because all the rest of it was coming at him, all the underside, the soft, secret belly, the part he never saw, was never given, until finally Danny pressed him down, leaning on his shoulders, then unzipped and eased himself into his mouth, coaxing him, whispering like a mother, "There..."

John tasted it, rich and salt, still oozing out of him, still red and silken from the friction, barely soft, and Danny crooned to him, stroked his hair, forcing his head back into the sofa as he fucked his mouth, still dressed, still wearing his jacket, only his trousers undone, and he said gently, "I never even noticed the resemblance the first time. Ian did... but then nothing passes Ian. All those things you told me I should never tell John - he saw them all. You've trained me so well and look what it's got you."

Danny laid his head back and let it roll over him, close, near the edge, knowing any one of them might come in at any moment, catch them, catch *John*, doing him, here in the middle of the room, like any desperate addict, and he loved it, wanted to torture and degrade him more than anything in the world. "Once. That's all it took. He was that good, that hard. *John*..." he whispered his name urgently. "You listening John?"

Danny felt his mouth pulling hard on him, trying to hurt, succeeding, but he didn't care. He knew his wound was deeper. "Does it hurt?" he gasped, pulling his hair, his head huge and hard, like a tiger's, a lion's. "I would have done it ten times if it would have hurt you more. Tell me you're hurting. Show me." But John drew him closer, deeper into his mouth, suddenly softening the pull.

"You bastard," Danny said brokenly. "Oh fuck... you rotten bastard." And he came, out of nowhere. A horrible cold shivering thing that felt like a jerk on a pulled muscle and that barely filled John's mouth with thin acrid flavour.

When the others came in John and Danny were nowhere to be seen. They knew Danny was home because his jacket was lying on the living room floor along with his boots. They had an abandoned air under that harsh overhead light, as if Danny had been swept away and that was all that was left.

They went to bed feeling sour and gritty and too sober. So drunk they could hardly stand and everything around them too clear. Except to Stephen who could only feel it,

like a blind man, knowing it was bad, but not knowing what he could see.

He went to bed subdued, desperately unhappy.

Danny and John lay there in the dark listening to them. John had dragged him up here and fucked him, once standing up, which was difficult and tiring enough, and then again in a position awkward enough to pull muscles and graze his sphincter, which was the intention. John had been enraged by his flaccidity and they'd come to blows when Danny had complained that it was the pain that was causing it. It had been a lie of course. He wasn't even sure why he'd said it.

They'd washed together and now Danny was lying in the dark, with John separating the strands of his damp hair, curling it round his fingers. They were both aching, warm and used and exhausted.

John said, "I wish I could keep this."

Danny didn't answer him.

"I wish there was no farm and no family. I wish there never had been. Just you and me."

Danny lay half-asleep, listening to the noises the others made; doors closing, a murmur, the water running. Gradually they grew quieter. Someone yelled in the street. It sounded very distant from this side of the house.

"Danny?"

Danny grunted gently.

"Did Dad ever actually... "

Danny stiffened, shifted away from him.

John pulled him back. "Okay... just tell me where you went."

Danny wouldn't speak to him, wouldn't answer him.

"You talk in your sleep. For six months I've listened to it. You call him Daddy. I can't remember anyone ever calling him Daddy."

Danny lay there feeling tight and cold and ugly. "Leave me alone," he said.

"If I thought he hadn't... what I did to you..." He stopped and said again, "Just tell me where you went."

"No."

"Why not? It can't hurt now."

"Leave me alone." And Danny pulled away from him.

John let him lie there, feeling the huge distance between them. "I'm sorry," he said and he was apologising for a lifetime - his own, Danny's. "I'm sorry," he said again and he pulled Danny, unresisting, back to him.

Danny lay against him, hidden in the vast security of his chest, and listened to the solid eternity of his heartbeat.

"Shh..." John said and stroked his hair. "Shh..."

Danny went to sleep.

SIXTY-FIVE

January, and Rab would soon be twenty-six years old. He felt like a hundred. He felt that if he had to get through another year of this he'd kill himself.

Maybe it was just the winter talking but for the first time he seriously considered getting out of it, away from here, away from all of it.

He lay in bed on January the second, awake too early, woken by another nightmare of Margaret coming out of the water, and made a New Year's resolution. Better late than never. He would start looking for another job.

Today.

Stephen woke up lying on something cold and hard. He had a pain in his side. He rolled over on his back and felt blindly with his hand.

It was a zip, the tag of a zip. It had been digging into his ribs. He lay there numb, trying to think, his mouth dry and filthy tasting, then he remembered. He made a noise of disgust and pushed the jacket out the bed.

He lay there trying not to think about it, trying to stretch his cramped limbs into movement. John banged on the door again. He acknowledged the summons with a ratty, "Alright!"

He swung his legs to the floor, rubbing his eyes, trying to stop them swimming. His feet stood on the heavy worn leather. He bent down and picked the jacket up. He clicked on the light.

There, inside on the cheap black silk, he could see the stains where he'd worked it out of himself, kissing the pillow, rubbing the sleeve over his backside while he dry-humped the inside of the jacket.

He threw the jacket across the room, down behind the chest of drawers. It could stay there and rot.

He got up and began pulling on his clothes.

Danny met January the second head on.

By throwing up.

John sat up in bed and looked at him, a dim outline bending over the sink. He clicked on the light. "What's wrong?"

"I'm pregnant."

John scowled at his back. Danny threw up again.

John got up and put a blanket round his shoulders. He stood there a while, shivering, until John asked, "Alright?" and Danny nodded.

John washed it away while Danny climbed back into bed. "Stay in bed."

Danny grunted, "I'll be alright in an hour or two, just too much to drink last night."

"And the night before," John said. "And the night before that."

Danny turned over and shivered some more. *Fucking know-it-all.*

John got dressed and went out, banged on all their doors.

He heard Ian curse him under his breath and smiled.

SIXTY-SIX

Katherine Henderson came back on the third of January, Rab's birthday, itching to see Danny again. She felt as if she'd been gone for weeks. She was full of restless boredom. Christmas was a bore. Christmas with her parents was a double bore. Since Jimmy had died they were insufferable with maudlin sentimentality. When he'd been alive he'd been every kind of failure to them. Now they'd failed him. It made her want to throw up. Next year she wouldn't go - the hell with them.

Dying was the best thing he ever did for her - the only thing he ever did for her - leaving her the flat, his car and Danny. Especially Danny.

God bless you Jimmy, wherever you are.

God bless you for that.

On the third of January Danny was second up. Rab was first.

Danny went into the kitchen and smiled at him. "Happy birthday, birthday boy."

Rab clapped his hands with mock glee and said, "You *remembered.*"

"Another year older, another nail in the coffin."

Rab watched his backside as he walked across the room. "I needed you this morning."

"You need me every morning." And Danny glanced over his shoulder at him.

"Don't play camp, it doesn't suit you." Rab could hear the angry edge in his own voice.

Danny went back to what he was doing without comment.

Rab said after a moment, "When are you going to get your jacket?"

"Tomorrow, why?"

"Think John would let me come along?"

"I don't know, ask him." Danny sounded indifferent. Rab tried not to let it hurt, but it did anyway.

Danny looked up from pouring milk into a bowl of cereal. "What's up?" he asked, carton arrested mid-flow.

"You."

Danny put the carton down. "We're not going to fight Rab, tell me we're not." He looked at the dog, put the half-filled bowl down for him. He watched him slurp it noisily. "Every day it's the same old shit. It's all we've ever done." He looked up. "What are we fighting *about?*"

"I don't know," Rab said and at that moment truly he didn't.

"I almost like you," Danny said suddenly. He smiled. "Not many people know that."

"Least of all me."

Danny reached across the table and took his hand, bent down and kissed the palm, folding it shut.

Rab looked at it. "That is the weirdest fucking habit."

Danny sat down and poured himself some tea. "Ask him," he said, delicately picking something off the rim of his teacup. "Maybe he'll let you come with me."

"Not taking the boy?"

Danny shook his head, stirring his tea with the handle of his breakfast spoon.

"Not friends any more?"

"We're friends."

"But nothing more?"

Danny looked at him.

Rab said, "He looks miserable."

Danny looked away.

"Not sorry?"

"I didn't ask him to get a crush on me."

"Maybe you encouraged him."

"And maybe I fucking didn't. What's wrong with you? You determined to have a fight or something?"

"No," Rab said, then added, "Sorry."

"You know, you're not easy to like. I should get a medal."

"I said I was sorry, didn't I?"

They fell silent. Danny drank his tea then turned to look at the clock. "Where the fuck is everybody?"

"Writing last minute cards."

Danny looked blank for a moment then laughed. He stood up and crossed to the coat rack. He shrugged into his jacket. "Get him to let you come out with me and I'll maybe give you a little something."

Rab looked up at him in surprise.

Danny winked and was gone out the door.

At evening meal that night Danny took his first good look at Stephen. Rab was right, he looked like shit. He felt one of those twinges of intense guilt he never felt. He chased it. It was a primrose path to nowhere.

Danny finished up and got first into the shower.

John caught him just as he was stepping in. He came in the bathroom door and locked it behind him. "Put your clothes back on."

Danny looked at him, about to tell him where to go, but John shook his head. "Rab wants to go out with you tomorrow. I'm sure you'd like a change of company. Isn't that what you keep telling me?"

Danny continued to stare at him.

"So why don't you put your clothes back on like a good lad, and maybe I'll consider it."

Danny stepped back out and started to get dressed.

SIXTY-SEVEN

January the fourth was a beautiful day, cold and crystal clear, white sun cutting long angles across the ground. Danny pulled down the sun-visor and adjusted his belt.

"I'm not used to you driving," Rab said as Danny pulled out.

"You mean you don't *like* me driving."

Rab laughed.

"Well hard titties, you'll just have to lump it. You're going to enjoy today or else. It's your birthday treat from me. It cost me a lot, this."

Rab looked at him. "What d'you mean?"

Danny clicked on the indicators, waiting for a break in the traffic. He was looking away from him. "I had to endure golden showers and bathtime with brother John for this. If you'll pardon the expression, this outing comes expensive, enjoy it."

Rab half-turned in his seat. "Are you saying he made you pay for it?"

Danny laughed, genuinely amused. "You don't think I live here rent-free, do you? I pay for everything, through the nose."

"Jesus," Rab said. "Jesus... fucking... *Christ*. Sometimes I feel as if we don't live in the same house."

"We don't. I'm in the master bedroom, you're in the servant's quarters."

"Jesus," Rab said again.

Danny laughed again. "Lighten up. It was no problem. I enjoyed it. Happy birthday."

Rab made a noise of disgust. "I don't know if I want it at that price."

"Hey," Danny was outraged, "I've already paid for it so you'll fucking well like it."

Rab shook his head and looked out the window. Danny smiled at his expression and began to enjoy himself.

It was going to be a lovely day.

Stephen watched them go with a desperate sense of jealousy.

It would be flickin' Rab.

He forked hay with a vicious energy.

He hoped they'd have an accident on the way there and Rab would die in it.

Ian stood watching him for a while in the darkness before he spoke to him. When he did Stephen almost jumped out his skin. "It's only me," Ian said.

"Fucking hell, d'you have to sneak up on me like that?"

"I wasn't sneaking. You were just far away, that's all. Off in the land of green monsters."

Stephen flushed and began forking hay again. "Fuck off," he said tightly.

"That's a nice way to talk to someone who's on your side."

Stephen didn't look at him, didn't answer him.

"I know how you feel."

"You don't know shit," Stephen snapped at him, stopping his movements for a second then going on.

"I know how much Rab wants to push you out."

Stephen didn't look at him, but he was listening. The sentiments fitted his mood.

"He wants to have Danny to himself again." Ian let that one sink in, letting Stephen make his own implications, then neatly, casually, he said, "He's queer, you know."

Stephen kept his head down. He could feel himself blushing. "I guessed," he said.

"He fancies Danny. That's why they fell out."

Stephen looked up at him. "Wouldn't Danny do it?"

Ian smiled. "Not as much as Rab would have liked."

Stephen felt it grip his insides. He'd been right all along. Danny and Rab had done it, and more than once probably. That's what he was hinting. "Is Danny like that?" he asked, looking at him in quick glances, afraid to hold his gaze.

"What? Queer?" Ian laughed, shook his head. "I wish. Danny's a lot of things, but not that."

Stephen felt ashamed all over again. No wonder Danny had got fed up with him. He must have seemed as bad as Rab, telling him it was okay when he didn't really like doing it at all. But he'd really thought...

"Everybody has a bit of boy-meat occasionally," Ian interrupted his thoughts, "especially when there are no women around, but Rab's queer, he doesn't like girls... at all."

Stephen nodded. He didn't want him to go on about it.

"Sometimes I do it myself," Ian said, watching Stephen carefully. "I'm sure you'd like to too." He smiled, and then horribly put his hand between Stephen's legs. "You don't need to go to Rab you know, I can help." And he let go again just as Stephen went to push him off.

"I don't want any help," he said stiffly, face hot.

"Just bear it in mind. He might be good Steve-o, but I'm better."

And it was then Stephen knew that he knew. *I know what you did with him. I'm next door, I heard.*

He watched Ian's back as he walked across to the tractor and climbed in. He turned back to his work as the engine started up.

Oh Jesus, what a mess. What an awful fucking mess.

They stood together admiring themselves in the full-length mirror.

"We look like fucking pimps," Danny said succinctly.

Rab laughed and undid the jacket. The assistant smiled tensely. They had tried on practically every jacket in the place, and they were too odd for her tastes. It felt like being visited by the famous - a little exciting, a lot wearing.

Rab gave her back the jacket, then Danny his. She went off with them. They put their own jackets back on. Rab spoke to him in the mirror, "Look at all that combined male beauty. Doesn't it make you weep?"

Danny looked up from his zip and met his eyes. "You conceited bastard."

"No, go on, look at yourself," he urged.

Danny looked at himself in the mirror then flicked his eyes back to Rab. "So?"

"Properly," Rab said, directing his face with his hands. The assistant kept her distance. The other assistants shot interested glances from their huddle, more convinced than ever they were incognito rock stars. Danny looked again. One of the assistants moved closer on the pretext of organising the racks.

"So?" he said again, this time keeping his eyes on himself.

Rab laughed, shook his head. "Come on, you're a lost cause."

They went out the shop, leaving the assistants disappointed and uninformed.

"Where to now?" Danny asked.

"Down by the station. There's a place where the patchouli and heavy-metal crowd hang out, we'll try there."

Danny looked at him. "You're joking."

"No, come on, they might have something."

"Yeah, with Adolf Hitler's European Tour on it."

Rab looked back at him and jerked his head. "Now there's an idea. Conley might

just go for that."

Danny looked at him in surprise then followed quietly.

"Jesus..." Danny said in a sotto voce that was useless in a place so small, "what a stink."

"Incense."

"Smells like..." He stopped. Rab turned to look at him. He shrugged. "I don't know what but it stinks."

"Oh stop moaning."

Danny looked at him in injured surprise. "Who's moaning?"

"You. Try this."

"Fucking hell."

"*Try* it."

Danny undid his jacket. The girl behind the counter continued to read her magazine. She had not looked up since they came in. The leather jackets were not wired. Danny shrugged the jacket on. "It weighs about fifteen stone."

"Shut up." Rab watched him do it up. "*Shit.*" He whistled. "What a dreamboat."

"Oh fuck off," Danny said, shoving him out the way. He looked at himself in the mirror. "Oh, *no* way." He started to drag it off.

Rab pulled it back on. "Come on, give it a chance. You're just not used to it."

Danny looked at himself again. It had heavy built-up shoulders, making him look ultra-long and lean-hipped. It had an inconceivable arrangement of zips and studs on it.

"Suits you," a voice opined behind them. Danny turned. The girl looked at him, eyes catching his momentarily, then she went back to her magazine.

Danny looked at Rab. Rab looked back and smirked. Danny looked in the mirror again. Rab saw the hesitation, the temptation. "Go on, buy it."

"It's not me, it's more in your line." Danny began to unfasten it.

"Bullshit." Rab caught his hand and spoke to him in a low whisper. "You're just scared because it isn't plain and boring and you can't hide in it. You're fighting a losing battle Danny. There isn't anywhere you *can* hide."

Danny shrugged it off, face set, and hung it back up. Rab gave him a look and said softly, "Shame, your big brother would have loved it." Then, "Let me find something then."

Danny nodded ill-temperedly, without looking at him, and put his jacket back on.

Perversely, Rab bought something understated, not black, no studs, no ornamentation, just worn rich brown leather.

Danny looked at him in the mirror. "Yes," he said, nodding.

Rab looked at him and said, "Do anything for you?"

Danny met his eyes and said yes again, then added, "Spot on" and he didn't smile.

Rab felt it like a match flaring up inside him. Why did he get you harder when he wasn't trying than when he did? Because he meant it, that's why. Because he wasn't hiding it behind that smart mouth. Rab took it off and put his own jacket back on.

"You buying it?" Danny asked.

Rab nodded. He picked it up then suddenly pulled the black space-age creation off the rack.

"Hoi, what are you doing?" But Rab had already got to the counter.

Danny went over, frowning, but before he could speak the girl took the jacket from Rab and began folding it saying, "You're the first person I've seen suited this thing." She made it sound like it was way too weird for anyone normal to suit.

Danny looked at her, then at Rab. Rab was looking away, fighting a grin. "I don't..."

he began.

"Money," Rab said, holding out his hand.

"It's the hair," the girl said. Danny looked at her. Rab put his hand in Danny's breast pocket.

Danny said, "What is?" Rab pulled out the money. Danny grabbed for his hand but missed it. He'd been too caught up in the conversation.

She looked at him, utterly objectively. "It's the colour you've done your hair."

"I haven't *done* it," Danny said irritably.

Rab laughed this time, handed the girl the money. She separated the notes.

"No, I don't..." Danny said quickly. She put them in the till without counting, banged it shut. "Looks dyed," she said, bending down and rummaging under the counter.

Rab rubbed his face and turned away. Danny could see his shoulders shaking. "*Shit*..." he said, squeezing his eyes.

The girl appeared with two huge carrier bags, black and glossy, decorated with what looked like spider's webs made of chewing gum. Rab helped her ease the jackets in and said, "Don't you think he's a pretty boy then?" He looked at Danny and was pleased to see him blush.

The girl looked at him, not in the least thrown, that same objective dead-eyed stare. "I suppose."

"You *suppose?*" Rab laughed.

"He's got a good face," she conceded, much as she might concede a building looked rather interesting.

"Do carry on talking about me as if I'm not here," Danny said, glaring at Rab.

"Fancy a date with him?"

The girl looked at Rab. Danny said, "Jesus Christ..." and looked at the ceiling.

She said, "God, no."

This time Danny did look at her, eyes immediately sharp. Rab felt a little kick at the expression on his face. It did matter to him. It *did*. "Why not?"

"Who wants a boyfriend that outshines you?" She picked up her magazine. "Anyway, you'd always be fighting them off." She looked at Danny again.

Danny looked away, face red, but Rab knew it was irritation, not embarrassment. "Who?" Rab asked.

"Everybody," the girl said and began riffling through the pages, already fading away from them. "He's the sort that attracts everybody."

She wrapped a strand of her long inky hair round her finger and was lost to them.

"You fucking shit," Danny said as soon as the bell tinkled shut behind them.

"Why? Because of the jacket, or because she didn't fancy you?"

"The fucking jacket."

Rab looked at him, smiling evilly. He pushed the jacket into Danny's arms. "Here, you carry it, you paid for it." And he walked on.

Danny caught up with him. "I maybe paid for it, you fucking bought it."

"It was John's money and he'll like it, believe me."

Danny pulled him round angrily.

Rab met his eyes. "Danny, people are watching sweetheart."

They were. Danny let him go and said in an undertone, "You fucking shit."

"You don't like it when they don't go for you, do you?"

Danny didn't answer.

Rab looked at him for a long moment then said, "No. Exactly."

And after that there was nothing else to say.

Danny let himself be talked into black jeans instead of his usual blue. Rab bought blue. When they were finished they stood in the shop doorway. "Okay, what now?" Rab asked.

"There's something I want to do," Danny said, looking away.

Rab looked at him curiously. "What?"

"Get my ear pierced."

Rab watched him blushing. "Oh boy," he said, smiling.

Danny turned on him. "You can shove that right now."

"Jesus Danny, you're going to have to watch that temper. Every day you get more like a traditional fiery redhead."

"You piss me off."

"I thought you liked me?"

Danny said nothing.

"Okay," Rab said, taking a deep breath. "For little Steve-o we shall go and get your shell-like pierced."

"Where?" Danny asked.

"Back there. There's a hairdresser's does it."

Danny followed him as he moved off. "You know, I'm not so sure about this now," he said to his back. "You don't think it will hurt, do you?"

"Fucking agonising," Rab said.

"Thanks."

And Danny glared so hard at him Rab said without turning, "Stop it, you're making my back itch."

"Left or right?" the girl asked.

Danny looked at Rab.

"Left," Rab said.

"Okay." She leaned over Danny, giving him a brush of soft white scented cotton breast. He concentrated on a shelf of shampoos.

She moved back. "Just going to freeze your ear."

"What?" Danny said, pulling away.

"Relax," she said, leaning on him again. "It doesn't hurt."

Relax she says. How can I relax when she keeps pushing her tits in my face? He closed his eyes.

She sprayed his ear. Danny jerked away from her. She laughed. "There, see?"

"See what?" Danny said tersely. "I've shit myself."

The girl laughed and blushed simultaneously. Rab winked at him. Danny scowled back.

She jabbed him. "Feel it?"

"What?"

She laughed again. "Fine. That's okay. Now we'll just pierce it for you."

"Oh shit," Danny said, closing his eyes again.

"You know," the girl said, "every time I get a man in here it's the same thing. Never a murmur out the women, not even the little kids, but the men..."

"Hurry up," Danny said.

She put the needle gun to his ear. Rab said, "Relax, she can only skewer your ear to your head."

Danny's eyes flew open.

"Don't," the girl said. "Or I'll mess it up."

Danny sat as stiff as a board, eyes fixed blackly on Rab's. Rab grinned back at

him.

"There," the girl said. "You didn't even feel it, did you?"

Danny had to admit that he hadn't. The girl threaded one of the tiny hoops through his ear. She told him to wash it every day with warm water and antiseptic and turn the earring a full circle every time.

Danny felt sick.

The girl looked at him. "You really suit that," she said, her cheeks flushing pinkly as she met his gaze.

He looked at Rab. Rab looked away, face flat, unsmiling. They went out.

"One to me," Danny whispered, bending to his ear, gripping his elbow.

Rab pulled his arm away and walked on ahead of him.

"Where to now?" Rab said. It was beginning to rain. The clear morning had turned to a dull midday.

"Home," Danny said. "Via Ellenport."

Rab looked at him. "Why Ellenport?"

"A little detour," Danny said. "I need to pay a quick social call." He turned up his collar and left Rab standing in the rain.

Rab watched the houses pass, rows of identical grey boxes broken only by one wicked pink extravaganza, a suburban rebel. As the houses drifted away to become greenhouses, the odd factory, Rab said, "You going to Henderson's sister?"

"We are."

Rab looked at him. Danny kept his eyes on the road.

"Why?"

"Why do you think?" And Rab watched a slow smile spread over his face.

"You're not serious Danny."

"Why shouldn't I be? It's your birthday."

Rab looked at him a bit longer then looked out the window again. After a minute he said, "How often have you being going there?"

"Often enough…" he smiled again, "…and more than anybody knows." He indicated and overtook a minibus, pulled in again.

"And what am I along for? Or do I just sit and wait like Stephen?"

Danny smiled again, still not looking at him. "Not unless you want to. This is your treat."

"Well I don't want any of it."

This time Danny flicked a glance at him. "Why not?" And he was still smiling, irritating the hell out of him, the smug little bastard.

"I don't like her," Rab said.

"Just her?" Danny asked, the smile coming out in his voice.

Rab coloured. "Does that matter?"

Danny shook his head.

"I'm not going Danny."

Danny stopped smiling. "What if I just take you?"

"Then as soon as you get out the car I'll go."

Danny was silent, face unrevealing, eyes dead ahead. He accelerated again and overtook, pushing the car. "I feel tense," he said while the engine strained.

"Tough."

Danny pulled in too neatly, got the finger for his efforts. He didn't even notice. "You yellow shit," he said, eyes flicking to Rab.

"I don't like being used."

"Yellow shit."

They were silent again then Rab asked, curiosity overriding everything else, "What did you plan to do, get all three of us in a bed?"

Danny didn't answer him.

"Jesus," Rab said, and looked out the window again. After a moment he said, "And how would you have performed this miracle?"

"I'd just let nature take its course." Danny rubbed his injured hand on his leg as if it itched him.

Rab looked at him. "Meaning?"

"She's like her brother. The more the merrier."

Rab watched him rub his palm feverishly then said, "You've done this before."

Danny put his hand back on the steering wheel. His face was implacable.

"The boy," Rab said. "That's why he thought he was safe trying it on with you, he's already shared you with someone else. Christ, you crafty little shit. You let that hard-faced bitch loose on the boy."

Danny laughed, dry, short. "Classic." That was all he said.

"Meaning what?" Rab asked.

Danny didn't answer.

"Come on, meaning what?"

"Me? You? *John?*"

"John hasn't taken him to bed."

"So?" Danny turned on him suddenly, ignoring the road. "And what does that signify? You don't have to screw someone to screw them up."

Rab said, "Mind the road." But only because he didn't know what else to say.

"Face facts Rab, all that bothers you is *what* she is. You wouldn't mind if she was fucking Attila the Hun as long as she wasn't a woman. You're as bad as the old man, fucking running scared, only he had cause. But you, one sniff of cunt and you think the world's coming to an end."

"Shove it."

"No you shove it. I'm sick of people telling me what *I* am. You've fucked him, I haven't. At least with her he's putting it in the right God-given hole."

"Shut the fuck up."

Danny shut up.

After a few minutes he said, "I'll let you off at the house."

Rab felt a sinking in the pit of his stomach. "You going yourself?"

"No, I'm taking the Dearham Brass Band."

"Very funny. And what do I tell John?"

"The truth. You had no problems last time."

Rab flushed. He hadn't realised that Danny knew he'd been the one who'd told John about Conley. "If I tell him the truth he'll crucify you."

"Fine. You can throw a party, invite Stephen."

"Oh can that."

Danny laughed. "Why?" He glanced at him. "It's true, isn't it? You're beginning to get your jollies out of it, just like Ian."

"I said, can it."

Danny took a deep breath and let it out slowly.

Rab rubbed his face. "Is it worth it, just for a fuck?"

"If I offered to do it with you what would you say?"

Rab looked away.

"Well? Would it be worth it, just for a fuck?"

"Alright," Rab said. "I get the point."

"No amount of wishing's going to change me Rab," He slowed the car, looked at him. "And believe me, I'm sorry."

Rab realised he meant it, that he was genuinely sorry, as if he'd somehow failed their expectations. He probably had. "I'll come with you," he said.

Danny looked at him. "What the fuck for?"

"Alibi. He isn't going to believe I went there. John knows me better than that. I'll wait in the car. Just try and make it quick."

"You can come up. She won't mind."

Rab looked out the windscreen. "Maybe, but I will."

Danny glanced at him briefly then concentrated on the road.

Danny's luck held. She was in.

"It's Danny."

"I was going to come and see you."

"Well I've saved you the bother. I've got Rab with me, can I bring him up?"

There was a silence then, "What's this, another threesome?"

"Would you like that?"

"Bring him up," she said coldly.

Danny smiled. "I'm afraid I'm going to have to convince him. When I get up there be nice to him."

"I wouldn't dream of being anything else."

"He's beautiful naked."

She was silent at that. Then, "I won't ask you how you know that."

He laughed. "I'll be back in a minute. I'll buzz."

He walked back to the car. Rab frowned, leaned over and opened the driver's door. "What's up? Not in?"

Danny bent down and kneeled on the seat, door resting on his leg. "Come on Rab, come in."

"No."

"I don't know how long I'll be. You can't sit out here."

"Listen Danny, I'll be fine. Just fuck off, will you?"

"Come on, I said I'd give you a little something, didn't I?" He looked in at him.

Rab shook his head.

"Come on," Danny urged quietly. "It's your birthday, let me shower you in gifts."

"I think that's what she's getting."

Danny shook his head. "I wouldn't do fuck all for her. Come on, make it good for me."

Rab felt his stomach turn over, half excitement, half fear.

Danny backed out the car and locked the door. Rab heard him lock it. He only sat another moment or two then he got out.

Danny smiled at him and threw him the keys.

She was waiting for them, as perfectly groomed and sleek as Rab remembered her. I liked your brother better, he thought. And a little voice jibed at him, *Yeah, but he had a dick queer-boy*.

She brought them drinks just as her brother would have done. For once Rab was glad of them. He still wasn't sure exactly what Danny had in mind and the insecurity gnawed at him. But Danny didn't keep him waiting long.

She went to him like she'd been waiting a fortnight for him. Maybe she had.

Rab looked away but was aware that Danny had his hand up her sweater. She was

groping his crotch.

He turned away. He couldn't go through with this. He didn't even *like* the woman. He put down his glass. "I'm going Danny."

Danny said, "Wait a minute," pushing her off and getting up.

Katherine Henderson watched in fascination as Danny crossed to him, knelt on the settee and kissed him, just the same way as he'd just kissed her. *God*, she thought, and she could feel the unexpected rush of excitement. *Jimmy, eat your heart out.*

Rab lay there letting him do what he liked, not caring why he was doing it, or who he was doing it for, just so long as he was doing it at all. If it was the only way he could have him then so be it.

Danny unzipped Rab's jeans. Rab laid his head back, closed his eyes. Jesus, it felt good.

Danny kissed him some more. Eventually Rab opened his eyes, looked at him.

Danny smiled, then got up and took him to bed.

Rab found himself in bed with them like a foreigner on a cultural exchange. He didn't understand what he was doing but the guide ensured he never felt left out. He realised very quickly that he was seeing a new dimension of Danny, some extra edge because she was there. It made him want to cry, for what he would never have, *could* never have. He was afraid Danny was shoving what he was in his face, and even more afraid that he was genuinely trying to give him something, that essential excitement he never caught with a man and never would. Another one of Danny's secrets, another one of his cat's lives. And it was all pleasure and pain till she came between them, making him break from Rab like a mother answering a baby's cry, brought to it at the last moment by her, not by him. Worst of all Rab came too, just at the sight of him frantically plunging into her, saying things he never said. Rab gripped her shoulders, face buried in her back as he pounded it inside her, as if trying to breach the vast distance of the body that both separated and joined them.

His deflation was instant and complete.

He pulled out of her and got up and went into the bathroom.

Rab drove back. Danny sat beside him, satiated, content. For a change she hadn't fought him. She had accepted his exit with a cold calm. As he'd gone out the bedroom door she'd said, "Don't bring him again, he enjoys you too much."

Danny had turned and smiled at her and said, "You mean I enjoy him too much."

And she had looked away and said, "Don't bring him again. I don't like faggots."

And Danny said, "I won't" and closed the door.

Rab had been waiting for him in the living room, looking as drawn and unhappy as Stephen, and Danny had patted his cheek and said, "Smile." But Rab hadn't smiled and Danny had turned away and said, "Let's go home."

And they had gone home and now Rab was saying to him just as they were entering the village, "You better wake up or John will be down on you like a ton of bricks."

"Let him," Danny smiled, turning his head to him, lazily resting it on the back of the seat.

"You don't mean that."

Danny laughed. "Toy pain, all on the outside. It doesn't reach me."

"It ought to. It's a fucking dangerous toy when he's playing with it. Wise up Danny."

Danny smiled at him. "Drop dead Rab." And he turned away and wiped Rab out of existence.

John didn't spot it because John wasn't in. They changed their clothes and went back to work.

John saw him at evening milking. "Nice time?"

Danny nodded.

"Good." John looked at him hard.

Danny smiled at him and said, "Lighten up John, you'll give yourself a headache."

John said, utterly unsmiling, "I'm going to fuck the arse off you boy."

Danny nodded and moved away to another part of the shed.

On the evening of the fourth of January at 9:47 Danny stood there in his new clothes and felt the pain begin to gnaw at his ear as John held him tight in front of him, running his hands over the jacket and whispering to him, "You did it with him, didn't you?" He kneaded the hard studs against Danny's arms, felt the heavy weight of the leather and said, "You threw my present back at me, but you couldn't wait to trollop around in his. You little faggot." And he pushed Danny down on the bed and climbed on top of him.

Danny could feel how hard he was and knew it was because of the clothes, the strangeness of them, the exotic look of them.

John was still calling him names, groping him through his clothes, but never attempting to take them off. Danny began to feel breathless and panicked by the itchy fever in him.

John rolled him over onto his stomach and pulled the harsh unwieldy jeans down over his hips. Danny tensed, waiting for it, but nothing happened. After a moment or two of soft rustling Danny felt the silky heat of an erection being placed snugly into the cleft of his arse.

John raised himself and began moving against him, watching himself slide up and down between Danny's cheeks. He said abruptly, "Clench on me." Danny, like a well-trained dog, did as he was told. He knew what John was doing. Getting off on the strangeness of it. A whole new boy to play with.

"You're fucking beautiful Danny," John said, low and thick-throated above him, moving faster, muscles in his arms standing out rigid, supporting his weight.

Danny closed his eyes, feeling something else shifting under his words, knowing it wasn't going to be that easy after all.

"A fucking beautiful little *slut*." And suddenly John was down on him.

Danny yelped but John's arm came down hard across the back of his neck, pressing his face into the pillow. John was cursing him, riding ferociously against him, but Danny couldn't hear it because all his energies were concentrated on trying to breathe. Oh Jesus, he thought, he's going to suffocate me. The rotten fucking bastard's going to suffocate me. And his lungs screamed at him, his head bursting with panic, when John suddenly fell on him, going limp, a dead-weight on his back.

Danny struggled his face out by sheer effort and dragged a raw breath into his lungs.

"Fuck," John was whispering. "Jesus, *fuck*..."

After a moment Danny wasted valuable breath, scraping it through his blood-raw throat to say, "You fucking cunt." And then he wasted a little more by starting to cry.

Stephen had seen Danny's ear at the evening meal. He didn't know what to say. He felt a kind of wild elation. Did this mean Danny had forgiven him?

707

He managed to catch Danny's eye. Danny winked at him. Stephen smiled, feeling his face go pink with pleasure. Before he could say anything Ian said, "Come out Danny?" and tugged at his left earlobe.

There was a tense, uncomfortable silence then Danny smiled at him. "That's right Ian."

Stephen had seen Rab smile down at his plate and John look away irritably.

But he didn't get a chance to talk to Danny that evening. He went back out with John immediately after the meal and when they came back in they went upstairs to wash and never came back down again.

Stephen watched the TV and felt vaguely disappointed. He wondered why Danny always looked so tired - John too some days - they went to bed earlier than the rest of them every night.

After a while he became involved in the television and forgot all about them.

SIXTY-EIGHT

Danny cursed as he tried to free his hair from his ear.

"What's wrong?"

"This fucking thing's been bleeding during the night. Look at it. It looks like cow cake." He hissed as it came free.

John said, "Serves you right." His voice was cold and unsympathetic.

"I take it you don't like it?" Danny said to his back, eyes caught for a moment on the magnificence of it, as if he'd never seen it before. It disappeared under a T-shirt then a sweater before he turned.

"You look fucking beautiful in it."

Danny was surprised. He blinked, aware that his mouth was hanging open. He shut it.

"That's why I hate it." And John went out, closing the door behind him with a slam.

They were lucky, working indoors. It was throwing it down outside, battering down on the tin roof. The noise was spectacular. At least to Stephen. It was the first time he'd heard it. "Wow, some noise." He looked up at the joists of the roof.

Danny smiled up at him from the steaming bucket. He straightened up, scratched his ear and winced. Stephen said, "It looks sore."

"It is."

"It does suit you but, I was right."

Danny smiled again. Stephen still wanted to apologise and fought it, knowing somehow that it would only irritate him. A fresh burst of rain made him look up again. "It's nice that."

Danny rubbed his hands on his trousers, shook his head. "You really are a romantic. I don't know why you wanted to work here. There's nothing very romantic about a farm."

"I don't see why liking the sound of rain makes me a romantic. It hasn't got anything to do with romance."

"It doesn't mean that, it means..." Danny had to stop and think about it. "It means you always see the nice side of everything."

"What's so terrible about that?"

"Nothing," Danny laughed. "I never said it was."

"You always make it sound like it's a stupid thing to be."

Danny looked at him for a moment then said, "Sorry. I probably do. It isn't."

Stephen came down off his high horse, charmed by the unexpected humility of Danny's apology. "It's alright," he said. "I'm being crabby."

Danny went back to work. He began whistling then changed it to a hum.

"Did you get a jacket?" Stephen asked suddenly.

"Yeah."

"What's it like?"

"Something out a sci-fi movie, all black leather and odd angles."

Stephen paused in his movements and looked at him.

"Don't look at me, Rab got it. It's his taste, not mine."

"Don't you like it?" Stephen felt outraged on his behalf. Who did Rab think he was?

"It looks good on," Danny conceded. "I got black jeans to go with it."

"I like black jeans. I've got some."

"I've never owned any before."

"Rab pick them too?" Stephen asked. He couldn't help it.

Danny laughed. "He did actually. But I like these."

Stephen bent his head and hated Rab a little harder.

Danny began to hum again. He seemed very relaxed. Stephen wondered what else they'd done yesterday and hated Rab some more.

Danny sat in front of the television. He was alone. Blissfully, entirely alone. He stretched his legs out along the settee, enjoying the luxury of it. The light caught on his earring and winked. As soon as it healed he would forget it, as oblivious to the beauty of that as he was to all the rest.

He found himself wondering where John was. It was stupid, senseless, but an image of him kept running through his head like a film loop, as if it was trying to tell him something. John outside in the summer, stopped for lunch. Rab throwing him a sandwich and him biting into it and spitting it out again like he'd bitten into putrid meat. He'd jumped up, face chalky-white, and gone round the side of the building. Ian had gone with him. Danny had sneaked round after them and found Ian with his arm around John's doubled-up, spewing body murmuring, 'It's alright. You're alright.' They'd claimed he was taken ill because the alternative was barely credible. Their mother had put chocolate spread on their sandwiches. It was absurd, but Danny knew that somewhere in the surreal scene John's Achilles heel had been momentarily exposed for all to see, and instead of comforting him, the impenetrable riddle of it made him depressed and he was glad when Ian came in and said, "All alone?" in a tone that suggested a million things, all repulsive.

"Don't shoot your load Ian."

"You're inheriting John's sweet disposition."

"I've always had it, before I was just too small to show it."

"I think I'm being got at." Ian sat down on the armchair and swung his legs over the arm, facing him. You could watch Danny all night and he never registered a thing. You never knew if it irritated him or not. Like sometimes you could grope him, pretty much do what you liked to him, and he just took it. Oblivious. "The earring suits you."

"Even though I look like a faggot?"

"Especially as you look like a faggot."

"Nice try." Danny hadn't even looked at him. Tonight he was going to be hard and mean. It always made Ian want him more than ever. He had always had a temper and Ian loved it. He loved it even when it scratched and bit him. Danny and his vicious tongue, his black hating eyes. Ian wondered how far he could goad him before he lost it. *If* he lost it.

"You fuck him in the jacket?"

"Who?" Danny didn't bother asking him how he knew about the jacket. Ian would already have been in to see it. Ian probably sniffed the sheets.

"John."

"No."

"Rab then."

"No."

"Come on, which one?"

"Guess fat-boy, why don't you?"

Ian felt the excitement stir up in him. Danny lying there so sleek and self-contained, that tiny sparkle of gold glittering against his hair, hating him in that cold, abstract way. Such a fucking turn-on.

"Maybe you gave it to little Steve-o."

"Yeah."

"Lucky boy."

"Watch your blood pressure."

"What would you do with him, if you could?"

"Fuck off."

Ian heard the edge in it, pressed his hands between his legs. "Will I tell you what I'd do?"

"You don't need to, I know all your routines."

"I've thought up some new ones since then."

"In that case you've redesigned the human body." And Danny finally looked at him. "What have you done? Put in an extra hole?"

Ian laughed. It bubbled out of him unchecked. "I love you," he said quickly, getting it in while he still had his attention.

But Danny had already turned from him, not listening. Ian felt the same familiar desire to slap him into awareness. "John's little Sleeping Beauty, lying there in suspended animation, waiting for him to come home and kiss you back to life."

"Oh fuck off."

"Never mind Danny, he can always rescue you tomorrow."

Danny rubbed his face and Ian knew he'd hit home, penetrated the shell, even if it was only for a moment. Then Danny put his hand behind his head again, recrossed his ankles, said, "I'll form a queue." And he was himself again. Intact. Inviolate.

They sat quietly for a moment or two then Ian asked him, "What do you think about?"

"What?"

"What goes on in your head?"

"The same things as go on in anybody's head."

"You think about little boys?"

"No."

"Big boys?"

"No."

"In that case you don't think about the same things, not as me."

"You're not anybody Ian. You're not even human."

Ian laughed again. "You mean you've never wanted to roll a juicy little dick in your mouth?"

Danny rubbed his face again. "You're beginning to bore me."

Ian smiled. "You mean I'm beginning to irritate you."

"Same difference."

"I'll bet you've thought about it. Abused children always end up being abusers. Don't they say that?"

"I'm an abused adult Ian and any minute now it's going to be your turn."

"Go ahead."

Danny looked at him, ratty now. "Fuck off Ian. I'm being nice to you."

"No," Ian said and smiled at him.

Danny sighed, deeply, and closed his eyes.

"Don't you care about being an abused child?" Ian persisted.

"No."

"Why not?"

Danny looked at him. "Why should I?"

Ian shrugged. "Anger. Resentment. Even plain old pain."

"Lots of things make you feel those. Someone playing with your dick is the least of it."

"Not even if you don't want it?"

"Who says I didn't?"

"A confession yet."

Danny looked at him, managing to convey sharp irritation and weariness at once. "Ask yourself Ian, who's got the power now, me or John?"

"You're the one waiting at home Danny."

"No, he's the one running away."

"Very profound. I didn't know you'd thought about it."

"I didn't think about it, I *learned* it."

"You were molested."

"I still am. What do you want me to do, report you?"

"No, just hate me."

"Easy. I hate you. Feel any better?"

Ian unzipped his trousers and began to play with himself.

Danny looked away. "For fuck's sake, put it away."

"Only pleasure I get."

"Look, I can't be bothered with this. Give me peace."

"Just lie there and I'll look at you."

"No," Danny said, suddenly angry. He swung his legs to the floor.

Ian went on pulling himself loosely, working more of himself out his clothes. "Come on, just lie back and inspire me. I'll be quiet as a mouse. You won't even know I'm here." He licked his lips.

"Christ, I don't know which one's nuttier, you or John."

"Me. Tell me you hate me."

"You sicken me."

"That'll do."

Danny got up.

Ian looked up, the tight movements of his hand suddenly winding down. "Do you have any idea..." he said, voice whispery, insubstantial, "how fucking obscenely beautiful you are?"

It stopped Danny in his tracks. He meant it, meant it to the point of pain.

Ian nodded and said, "Her tonight..." and suddenly, out of nowhere, it began to ooze out of him. He was holding it in check, spoiling his own orgasm. "You tomorrow..." The words shivered out of him and he looked up again, face twitching, tongue flicking at his lip like a snake. "Then maybe he can save me..."

Danny sat down like he'd been shoved. He sat there hunched forward as if he was going to faint, face grey.

After a while he became aware of the sounds of Ian cleaning up, then the sound of him fastening his clothes.

Ian got up and crossed to him. He sat down beside him and laid a hand on his bent head. "Dirty trick," he said quietly, looking at his white face.

Danny was trying to press it back with his fingertips but Ian could see it, held fragile on his face. It really had been a dirty trick.

"Sometimes I get the urge to hurt you so bad I don't know what I'm doing." He bent and kissed his cheek.

Abruptly Danny turned and burrowed into him, face deep in Ian's shoulder. Ian held him, trying not to feel good about it. But he couldn't feel what he ought to feel. When had he ever been able to feel what he was supposed to feel about Danny? "I love you," he whispered into his hair.

He held him like that for as long as he could and then gave into it and began undoing his clothes.

With an inevitability that was almost poetic John caught them.

He came in noiselessly on stocking soles and switched on the light.

Ian's turning was too sluggish, revealing him.

John closed the door and leaned against it. "The boy's in the kitchen. How would you have explained it to him?"

Ian got off him, as fast as his drugged excitement would allow. Danny lay there, blinking in the harsh overhead light, shading his eyes.

"Dry it up Danny, before it gets crusty, there's a good boy." John threw a wadded-up hankie at him.

Ian was standing by the fire. John looked at him. "You sad little fuck."

Ian said nothing. John went on, "How did you trip him up this time?" He looked back at Danny. "Or are you just getting so pathetic you can't say no, even to him?"

Danny closed his jeans and sat up. He felt weak, tired, fragile. Ian had masturbated him too deeply, leaving his groin feeling pulled and uncomfortable.

"Well? Cat got everybody's tongues?"

"It just happened," Ian said. "We didn't plan it."

John made a noise of disbelief.

"It was my fault," Ian added, just late enough.

"It always is. No-one in their right mind would have sex with you otherwise, you ugly little fuck."

"Leave it," Danny said.

John looked at him. "Who the fuck asked you?"

"Leave him alone," Danny said again.

It would be difficult to say who was the most surprised, John or Ian, or maybe Danny himself.

He stood up. "You wear me out."

He went up to the door.

John stood aside to let him pass.

Danny went out and closed the door.

Stephen met him in the hall. Danny smiled. It was a weak one but it was there. "Come and see my jacket," he said.

Rab came out the kitchen door and saw them. He mouthed a kiss behind Stephen's back. Danny pushed Stephen ahead of him, giving Rab a black look.

"Charming," Rab said and went back into the kitchen. Stephen looked back at the sound of his voice and felt glad that he must have seen the two of them go upstairs together. That would show him.

In the bedroom Danny took the jacket from the wardrobe. Stephen whistled. "Couldn't have been cheap."

"It wasn't, feel the weight in it."

Stephen took it from him, hefted it, and handed it back with suitable exclamations over its bulk.

Danny put it on. Stephen looked at him with a kind of dry empty pain that felt like hunger. "It's nice," he said finally.

Danny laughed. "*Nice?*"

"No, it is." Much as it pained him to admit it.

Danny looked at himself in the mirror. He nodded. "It is, isn't it?" He looked different, even to himself. Even less like a farmhand, even further away. Goodbye Daniel Jackson Moore, last seen fading from sight.

Danny took it off abruptly. Stephen said, "Can I try it on?"

"Sure." Danny held it for him. He laughed. "Bit big for you."

Stephen looked in the mirror. It just looked comic on him. He didn't have the legs or the face for it. He turned away. "I'm not you," he said, feeling inadequate and depressed.

"Be happy." Danny helped him off with it. "I wish I wasn't me too."

"Why?"

"I just do."

"But why?"

"But *why?*" Danny mimicked him. "Your curiosity will kill you one of these days, if it doesn't get me first."

"Sorry." Stephen smiled apologetically.

He looked around the room while Danny was hanging the jacket up. The bed always seemed to dominate it. Stephen looked at it - flat, smooth, neatly made up, all its secrets hidden. "Why do you share a room?"

"There aren't any others."

"What about next door?"

"John's superstitious about keeping it empty."

Stephen accepted the answer with a nod. "You'd think he'd make the two youngest share. They usually do."

"God forbid. I'd rather share with John than Ian any day."

"It would be me, not Ian."

Danny turned to him, smiled. "So it would."

Danny didn't look horrified by the idea. Stephen felt relief spread through him almost like contentment.

Suddenly Danny said to him, "Want some dirty books?"

He began rummaging in a cupboard under the sink. Stephen didn't have a sink in his room. There was nowhere to put one. Rab had one in his but Ian didn't.

"Here they are. Look at the fucking things, they're ancient."

Danny handed him a bundle of porno mags. Over the counter stuff, nothing he hadn't seen before, even if not quite so many at once. "There, take the fucking things, I'm sick of the sight of them."

"These yours?" Stephen asked, looking at the large backside on the top cover.

"John's. He isn't going to miss them. Take them."

Stephen took them, staggered off to his bedroom with them. He laid them on the bed. It was like Christmas all over again, a huge new pile of things to look through. He felt vaguely excited. Had Danny tossed off looking at these? He decided to have an early night, make the most of it. It would be nice to be able to read them without having to worry about his mam catching him. She'd done her nut once when she caught him looking at a nudist magazine.

He brushed his teeth and locked himself in for the night. He settled down under the blankets for a good read.

He nestled himself into his pillows and began to sort through them. A couple of them he already knew. His uncle bought tons of these flickin' things. He went through them slowly, flicking the pages, making two bundles. One on the bed that he liked the look of, another on the floor that he'd either read before or that looked too boring. The pile on the bed, as always, was smaller than the one on the floor.

He was two-thirds of the way through sorting the bundle when he found the other magazines. He had opened one of them without somehow taking it in and was flicking through it when he realised something was wrong. His heart did an odd lumpy start in his chest, as if he'd come across crotchless panties amongst his mother's underwear. He lifted it slowly and saw there was another one underneath. There were two of them. He checked. He looked through the second one first, reluctantly, hoping maybe that it wouldn't be what he thought it was. But it was. One of the men looked like

Danny. At first he thought it *was* Danny, the shock of discovery fuddling his brain, but the model was too tanned, too fleshy, and his mouth was different. His hair looked fake. It wasn't the same colour round his dick.

The magazines were American. Half the men were erect, including the ones of the Danny lookalike. Stephen swallowed awkwardly, making himself cough. He went back to the start. He looked through it again slowly, building up the tension of arriving at the same pictures. He looked at Danny's twin again, meticulously studying him. He was as big as Danny down there, but his skin was definitely tanned. That proved he wasn't a real redhead. People like him and Danny never tanned, they just burnt and freckled. He was looking at himself, never at the camera. He was trying to make his dick look bigger, pushing his balls down. He needn't have bothered.

Stephen picked up the first magazine and turned over the pages with a kind of heavy dread. There he was again, almost as if he'd known he would be. Danny all over again. Different photos in the same setting. He had some clothes on in these, if you could call them clothes. A strange leather contraption that looked like a harness. Stephen had never seen anything like it. The man's cock was sticking out stiff through a metal ring. He had black leather gloves on.

The photos were poor and grainy but they still looked like Danny. More so maybe. In a couple of these he was looking at the camera and maybe it was that that did it. He had the same kind of dirty look you sometimes saw on Danny's face.

Stephen went back to the start and worked his way through it again as he had done before. He knew he had an erection, but he was trying to ignore it. It was because of all the stiffies in the book. It was difficult to look at an erection without becoming erect yourself, but it didn't make him feel any better about it. His mouth was dry by the time he reached the Danny section.

He looked at the leather harness, the straps going across his body, the way his hips were thrust out. He looked at the first photo where he was lying on the bed, jeans open and down. He was looking at the camera, his expression saying, Like what you see? Stephen wished he'd had real red hair. The brown pubic hair spoilt it, drew your attention away. You knew he wasn't…

He closed the magazine with a slap and pushed it far away down the bed. He looked at the covers. One was called *Studz*, the other *Stallion*. Stephen stared at them some more. His cock made a thick, heavy weight under the quilt. He could feel his whole body inside it.

These yours?

John's. He isn't going to miss them.

Stephen looked at them again, wanting to pick them up. He bent and retrieved them, laid them on his lap, side by side. He didn't open them. Danny had said they belonged to John.

Stephen could feel something inflating in his chest. He began to shake his head. He could feel a bubble of it inside him, moving up into his throat. "*No*," he whispered.

He shoved the bundle of girlie mags onto the floor. Now only the two gay mags lay there, looking up at him. Coy boys showing their bums, squinting over their shoulders.

Queers.

They were John's and he shared a room with Danny.

Stephen opened the second one again, right where the pictures of Danny were. He wasn't looking out at him. He was only interested in himself. Not like Danny at all. Only the face, the hair, that's all. The rest was someone else. Inside he was someone else.

John had got these somewhere and inside there was a man who looked like Danny.

Stephen looked through the first one, leaving the second open. He looked at the

leather harness. Danny was looking at him now, his cock stuck through a painful metal ring. He turned back a page and looked at Danny undressing on the bed, Danny saying, Like it? Danny with the wrong colour of pubic hair.

Inside these magazines were pictures of a man who really looked like Danny and *John* had gone out and bought them.

There, that was easy, wasn't it? Say it again.

I think, maybe, John went out and bought dirty books to look at pictures of a man who looks like Danny.

Good boy, that didn't hurt. Now try, And they go to bed earlier than everybody else just about every night.

"No," Stephen said, slamming both magazines shut, leaving his palms flat over them as if trying to hide them from his sight.

He shoved them off the bed and threw himself down on his stomach. He pressed against the bed for comfort, squeezing his eyes shut. He reached over blindly and clicked out the light, wanting to be safe in the dark where he couldn't see them. Had Danny known about them? Did he even know they existed? How could John sleep with him if he felt... God, what if he was queer too?

Then the thought came to him. They were Rab's, not John's. Rab had bought them and somehow John had got a hold of them. Maybe Rab had given him them as a joke. No, somehow he just knew John wouldn't tolerate that. No, he must have confiscated them. That means he knew Rab was queer. He could see that now, now he knew John better. John wouldn't give a fuck what Rab did unless he bothered him. John didn't give a fuck about anybody unless they bothered him.

Except Danny.

Stephen lay still, oddly stopped by the thought.

John was really possessive about Danny. Danny tried to cover it up, but John didn't, almost like he wanted you to know. He'd never really thought anything of it, folk were often jealous of their brothers and sisters, it was just one of those things, but it was different in John, like it was more serious somehow. What did Ian call Danny? John's green-eyed boy, that was it. And he had loads of other names like that, all dead sneery, like it was a big joke, like he was jealous because Danny was John's favourite. Even that jacket he'd bought him. He hadn't bought anybody else anything, not even Ian, and he was his brother too. Maybe John didn't even know these mags existed. He bet he didn't know about Ian's horrible little kiddie pics, for sure. Ian was pretty fucking queer himself and just about weird enough to get a turn-on out of looking at shit like that.

Stephen lay still again, breathing ragged. God, he was wanking off against the bed. Well, he wasn't going to, not over these things.

Maybe they were Danny's. Maybe Rab had given them to Danny. Hey, this guy looks like you. For a laugh. That made more sense. That he could see. And Danny would hide them. Hide them from John.

Why didn't he just give them back?

Stephen was still again.

Good question. A very fucking good question. And here's a better one. Who's done it looking at these? Somebody has. Last two pages, where that harness thing is, where the ring is, biting into his cock. That wrinkled paper, like spilled water. The tide mark, where the edges begin to dry first, like salt stains on leather boots. I've seen it because somebody's done it. Who?

It has to be Rab.

They're John's.

But it *has* to be Rab.

He said they were John's.

But it *could* be Rab.
John shares with him.
But I'm sure Rab…
John sleeps with him.
But I *know* Rab...
John's got pictures of him.
But Rab has...
John's seen him.
But Rab...
John's felt him.
But Rab…
John's sucked *him*…
"Shit!"

SIXTY-NINE

Stephen hid them in the bottom drawer, the one that fell on your foot. He kept nothing in it so his mother had no cause to go in there. If she did he'd tell her where to go. She only worked here. She wasn't running the show.

He made sure he put the two magazines down the bottom of the pile, well covered by girls. Those two would really give his mother something to think about if she found them. He wasn't taking any risks.

He went downstairs to breakfast. He never ate till nine. Unlike Danny he couldn't face it. Neither could Rab. Both of them drank tea and watched the others eating.

Stephen was glad they were all too sleepy to do more than grunt at him. He felt as if his discovery last night was written all over his face. He felt that they must be able to tell he had them. Worse, that they all knew he'd shot his load thinking about them. He felt alien in his own body. Somehow it was worse than anything he'd done with Rab.

He sneaked a look at Danny, eating systematically, not really tasting it, just fuelling up. And John, vast and ugly, relaxed, truly relaxed, not just acting laid-back like Rab did, his hands huge on the cutlery, the mug, needing a shave, his face dark with sleep, his own inward thoughts. He always made Stephen think of comic-book gypsies, black and murderous, with too many white teeth and too much temper about his eyes. Except his hair wasn't black of course, just mucky shit.

He looked at them both, Danny and John, their hands only eight, maybe ten inches apart, and tried to see them in bed, maybe touching. He couldn't picture it. They never touched, or at least not any more or any differently from how they touched anyone else. Rab touched Danny. He'd seen him. Like that time before Christmas on the sofa, he'd seen that. And Ian... Ian touched everybody, if they'd let him.

Stephen couldn't see it. He began to feel sick with himself for having thought it. He was seeing it everywhere, like he wanted it to be true. He was getting sick in the head. He'd be imagining Russians next, like his old aunt in Solihull. But it still didn't answer the question, whose were they? Why did Danny and John have them? And how could the fact that they had Danny's twin in them be an accident? It couldn't. It simply couldn't.

Maybe they *were* Ian's.

Stephen looked up at him in sudden surprise. Why hadn't he thought of that last night? It was the next logical step from those disgusting photos. Oh Jesus, because it was sick, that's why. It was really sick.

Ian caught his eye. Stephen, irritatingly, blushed and looked away. He could feel Ian watching him now. God if he knew what he had been thinking. But it was still possible, even likely. Much more likely than any of the others, even if it didn't solve the problem of how Danny and John had got hold of them.

Maybe one of them found them and took them for a laugh. Maybe they do know about Ian and think he's a joke. They certainly treated him like a joke. But it was still sick. Pictures of your own brother. Christ, how gross. How could *anybody* fancy their own brother? God, you grew up with them. It was just *boring*.

He looked at Danny.

Could anybody be bored by Danny? Ever? He blushed again. He was turning into a right little weirdo. A total, creepy, little weirdo. As bad as Ian, worse than Rab.

John got up and spoke to him. Stephen was startled by the sudden sound of his voice. He looked up guiltily, as if he'd been caught out not paying attention.

"Still dreaming?" John asked him, smiling. His smile never did quite reach his eyes. His questions always sounded loaded.

Stephen flushed guiltily as if he had indeed been dreaming. John squeezed his shoulder as he went by. Stephen shivered at the mindless strength in his fingers, as if they were measuring you to see how much flesh you had on you. *Ready for the pot yet? I eat kids like you for breakfast.* John made him feel twelve years old and twice as puny.

He heard him tell Danny to take him out with him again today. He felt a rush of pure pleasure. He pushed last night out of his head. He smiled across the table at him. Danny smiled back and got to his feet.

He looked very tired.

Stephen kept one hand on Danny's shoulder. He moved it closer to his neck. He could feel the hair brush his fingers as Danny moved his head to look in the wing mirror. Stephen looked down at him, enjoying watching him, even if it was a bitterly cold way of doing it. The sky was leaden. It looked like snow again.

"Looks like it's going to snow again," he shouted in Danny's ear. He saw him nod absently.

Stephen felt the tractor begin to slow. He frowned. They were pulling into the big lay-by where the trucks stopped. "What you doing?" he asked. As was often the case the lay-by was deserted at this time of day.

"I want to make a phone call. I won't be long. Come in." Danny gave him a hand into the cab as he climbed over. "Close it, keep warm." Danny swung down out the tractor.

Stephen pulled the back window shut. He watched Danny go along to the phone booth. He knew who he was going to phone. Him, the great fucking friend. Stephen wondered why there'd been so much silence. He had hoped they'd fallen out again, maybe this time for good.

He saw Danny pick up the receiver, ferret in his pocket for change, then feed the coins in. Plenty of it. It was going to be a long call. Stephen watched intently and wished he could lip-read.

Rain began to spatter on the windscreen.

Conley was with a client.

"Then interrupt him."

"That's not possible, I'm afraid." Molly nodded at Dorothy, eyes alerting her. Dorothy raised her eyebrows saying, What?

"Listen, I don't care what's *possible*, just interrupt him, will you?"

"I'm sorry, I can't do that." The smile still held, but it set harder.

"Fine. Right. I'll tell him that when I see him." The boy's voice was hard, unmistakably threatening.

Molly was silent. She licked her lips. "Hang on, I think I hear him coming out." She put him on hold.

"Who is it?" Dorothy asked. James wasn't coming out. He wasn't likely to emerge for the next twenty minutes at least.

"It's him, the one I told you about."

"Let me hear." Dorothy hurried round the desk, pressed her ear to the phone. Molly buzzed James.

"Yes?" He sounded irritated.

"I'm sorry to disturb you James, but your friend's on the line and he's very insistent.

Shall I get him to call back?"

There was a brief silence then, "Danny?"

"Yes," she said and knew he was going to take the call. She felt a dull resentful anger.

Dorothy looked at her, eyes shrewdly searching, then pressed her ear to the phone again.

"Put him through Molly."

She heard him cover the handset, talking to his client. She took Danny off hold. "I'm putting you through," she said. He didn't answer her.

"Hello?" Danny said.

Conley heard his voice. He also heard the tell-tale hollowness and knew that Molly was listening. "Danny..."

"About time."

Conley swallowed dryly and turned to the window so that his client couldn't see his face. "Listen Danny..." *the stupid bitch is listening* "...can I phone you back?"

"No." Danny sounded curt.

Conley tried desperately to think how he could warn him, but Danny was going on. "This is difficult enough without you giving me the run-around."

Don't say anything else Danny, please. But Danny still went on. "I need to see you."

Conley interrupted quickly, "That's okay, when?"

"I don't know. John's doing his let's-pretend-I'm-indifferent act, but he won't be if I say I'm going out. I'm going mad here." He paused then said urgently, "I *need* to see you."

Outside the two women looked at each other. Dorothy's hand was tight on Molly's wrist.

Conley prompted, "When?"

"Tonight," Danny said suddenly. "I'll just go. As soon as I get a chance. I don't know when it'll be."

"I'll wait."

"I've missed you."

Conley closed his eyes. *Danny, shut up. Please shut up.* He said it. There wasn't anything else he could do. "Not now Danny."

He could feel Danny's silence at the other end and hoped he understood. "I'm in the office." *Understand Danny. Understand.*

Suddenly Danny's voice came clear over the line and Conley could hear the smile in it. Danny's slow, evil smile. "Then the stupid bitch shouldn't be listening, should she? Know what they say..."

There was a click. They both heard it. Danny smiled and looked out at the rain. Conley frowned and looked at the rain clouds overhead.

"Tonight then."

"Okay."

There was another click and the tone sounded in Conley's ear.

Danny bolted across the lay-by. The rain was slanting down in heavy icy sheets. Hail spat amongst the drops. Stephen pushed the door open for him.

Danny flung himself up and in, slamming the door shut. He shook his head, shook the worst off his jacket. "Oh boy." He blew air out in a huge cold burst. "Fucking wild." He blew on his hands.

"Was he in?"

Danny nodded absently then turned and looked at him. "Oh, very crafty Steve-o."

Stephen looked away. He heard Danny make a small noise like a man blowing a feather, a small disgusted puff of a laugh, then he was tugging each sleeve of his jacket, shaking water off.

The windows had steamed up. The hail made a deafening racket on the roof. It slid down the windows like melting ice-cream.

"There were two homo mags in that pile you gave me."

Danny had slid into the chair when Stephen had got up to sit back against the dashboard. He looked up at him now. Stephen took a vindictive pleasure in his expression.

"What?"

"You heard me. Who do they belong to?"

Danny shook his head then said, "I don't know." And Stephen knew he was lying. He watched him recover a bit more. "I didn't know they were there."

"There's a guy in them looks like you." Stephen looked away then back again.

Danny looked at him, then unexpectedly smiled. "Get a good look?"

Stephen blushed.

Danny went back to drying off. He ran his hands through his hair, wiped his face with the duster he used to clean the windscreen. Stephen could feel his own nails digging into his palms. He was furious. They weren't his bloody magazines. He hadn't bought them, it wasn't his room they'd come from, and here was Danny making it sound like he was a perv. "*You* gave them to me."

"I told you." Danny sat still suddenly and looked at him. "I didn't know they were there. I've never seen them before. Ask John. Maybe he knows."

"I can just see me, asking John."

Danny shrugged, and Stephen realised he'd out-manoeuvred him again, like he always did.

Danny said, "We'll wait till this goes off a bit, eh?"

Stephen didn't answer him and Danny didn't seem to expect it.

"Aren't you even curious? Two homo porn mags, both with pics of you in them, and you're not even curious?"

"They're not me, and curious about what?"

Stephen looked away, irritated beyond belief. "Curious about who would buy them, read them. Somebody's *wanked* over them Danny."

"Really?" Danny was looking at him as if to say, And was it you?

Stephen blushed anew. "Stop making it sound like I'm the weirdo. It wasn't me, but somebody had."

Danny kept his eyes on him. "Well I hope they had a good time."

Stephen just stared at him. Danny stared back, then he said in that low, crawling voice, "Get stiff at them Steve-o?"

Stephen looked away, hands tight between his knees, misery gnawing at his innards.

"Don't be shy, share it." Danny was trying to get him to look at him. He reached forwards and began rubbing Stephen's thigh with his hand. "As good as coming in my hand Steve-o? Was it as good as that?"

"Danny *don't*." Stephen looked at him imploringly.

Danny grinned, let go of him, stretched back in the seat. "Throw them away, Stevie-baby. Get rid of them. They're poison."

Stephen looked at him and knew he'd known about them all along, known who'd bought them and who'd used them. The only thing he'd forgotten was that they were in that cupboard.

Danny held his eyes, hardly smiling. Stephen nodded. "Okay," he said quietly.

Danny slapped his leg. "Okay, let's move it. Hold tight."

And he started the engine and pulled out into the hail-spattered road.

Danny got his chance just after seven. Or he would have if Stephen hadn't followed him out.

He was opening the pick-up door as noiselessly as he could in the darkened yard when Stephen spoke to him. "Take me with you."

Danny's head jerked up to look at him across the roof. Guilt had startled him badly. He could feel a pulse in his neck. "I didn't hear you."

"Take me with you," Stephen said again, as if he'd misunderstood his meaning.

Danny shook his head. "I'm going out."

"I know, and I know where. Take me with you."

Danny looked at his watch. If he delayed much longer John would discover he wasn't in the house. "No," he said, and got in.

Stephen got in too, slamming the door shut.

Danny braced himself against the wheel, arms taut. "Get out Steve."

"No."

"Out," Danny said, turning on him furiously.

"Take me. I'll wait outside."

"I'm going to be there a long time."

"I'll wait."

"You'd fucking freeze."

"I don't care."

"Jesus!" Danny swore, turning his face away. "Now get out."

"I'll tell him." Stephen said it quickly, heart hammering. He saw Danny turn to him, could feel the anger off him like a change in temperature.

"I didn't hear that."

Stephen said nothing.

"You little shit."

Stephen swallowed, feeling the corners of his mouth pull down. "Please Danny, take me along."

Danny scratched his nose furiously, as if he'd like to rip it off his face. He turned on the ignition and drove out of the yard quietly.

It almost killed him to do it.

Danny didn't speak to him.

Danny didn't speak to him at all.

After half an hour Stephen ventured, "Don't be angry at me Danny."

Danny didn't answer him. He just kept staring ahead. A steady snow had been falling for the last five minutes. It melted as it landed. The wipers swished white blades of it from side to side. It accumulated in the corners of the windscreen then slid off in lumps.

"I can be your excuse. You can say we went for a drive."

"What do you want?" Danny's voice was hard.

"Nothing. I don't want anything."

"You fucking little liar."

Stephen sat there, feeling numbed by the intensity of the dislike in his voice. Eventually he said, "It's true."

Danny looked at him for the first time. "Soon as you feel like telling me the truth Steve-o just let me know." And he looked back out the windscreen again as if Stephen had ceased to exist.

Stephen knew there wasn't any other way he would talk to him, sensed he'd probably never talk to him again if he didn't tell him. He realised he'd made an enemy of himself. He said, "Danny?"

Danny didn't answer.

"I'll tell you Danny. I'll tell you why I wanted to come with you."

Danny was silent then he said irritably, "I'm waiting." He didn't look at him.

"I want to meet him."

"You have met him."

"Properly."

"*Properly*..." Danny's voice was sarcastic.

"You always shunt me away as if I'm too young to hear."

"Maybe you are Steve-o. That never fucking occur to you?"

Stephen looked at him blankly. Danny looked back at the road.

"What d'you mean?"

Danny gave that same disgusted laugh he'd given earlier that day, but he didn't answer him.

"Tell me what you mean."

"What makes you think you're fucking welcome Stephen, hm?"

Stephen blushed.

"Maybe we've got something private to talk about. You do understand what private means, don't you? Or is nothing ever private to you?"

"I'll wait outside," Stephen said stiffly.

"Too fucking right you will, and I hope you fucking freeze to death."

Stephen felt close to tears. If they hadn't been so near their destination he'd have asked Danny to take him home again. He couldn't remember *ever* feeling so bad in his whole life. Danny was livid.

Stephen stared out the window numbly. The snow was heavier than ever; the wipers making two clear fan shapes, the rest a blank white. Danny had slowed his speed.

Stephen risked another glance. Danny's face was set, tight, a pale eerie green. Like the Rat King.

Stephen felt a tear roll down his cheek and drop coldly onto his neck.

Danny left him in the pick-up.

"I'll leave the keys. When it gets too cold turn it on, but don't run it more than you have to." He sounded grudging, as if it cost him to offer that much.

He slammed the door without saying how long he'd be or even goodbye.

Stephen watched him disappear into the snow. He sat in the odd ticking silence, listening to the wind. He shivered although he wasn't cold. Suddenly he felt angry. Angry at himself sitting out here in the cold for God knows how long when he could have been snug at home, angry at Danny for leaving him here, angry at everything he'd thrown away. He'd never, *ever* be friends with him now. *You've fucked it Steve-o, you've really fucked it this time.*

Stephen watched the windscreen fill slowly with snow. He switched the wipers on, cleared it. It filled again almost immediately.

He left it this time.

Why bother?

Danny came in in a flurry of cold and snow.

Conley looked at the outrageous jacket. "That's new, isn't it?"

Danny was staring at him. He nodded.

"Christmas present?"

Danny nodded again.

Conley said in a low voice, "He knows how to dress you."

Danny didn't say anything at all.

In the end it was Conley who moved first, and Danny who tasted of snow and cold and sheer unadulterated pleasure.

Danny took his jacket off and handed it to him with a smile. Conley smiled back.

Danny went into the room while Conley hung it up.

"Coffee?" Conley said to his back.

"Mm."

"It's bitterly cold out there."

"Mm."

Conley looked at him curiously. Danny sat with his back to him. "What's up?" he asked.

He heard Danny sigh. He watched him get up suddenly and walk over towards him. He came round and sat up on the counter top, legs dangling. He smiled briefly at him.

"Well?" Conley asked again, leaning beside the coffee-maker.

Danny looked at his feet.

"What is it?"

Danny looked up at him. "The boy's outside."

Conley looked at him for a minute. "You brought him along?"

"No, he brought himself along. Uninvited."

"Why didn't you get rid of him?"

"He threatened to tell John."

Conley digested it slowly, every ugly word. "Threatened to tell him what?"

"That I was coming here, that's all. All he knows is that John doesn't like me here."

"He'll freeze out there."

"I live in hope."

"You can't leave him out there."

"Watch me."

Conley looked at the hard, set lines of his face. "Why did he want to come?"

"He wants to meet you."

"He's met me."

"Not enough. He wants to play gooseberry."

"Why?" Conley looked at him.

Danny shrugged.

Conley looked at him some more. "Adolescent pash," he said.

"What?"

"He's got a crush on you. Thinks you're the greatest guy alive."

Danny laughed humourlessly. "Not after tonight he doesn't."

"Don't you believe it. The only thing crushes can't survive is indifference. They thrive on anything else."

"Well that theory's going to be sorely tested tonight."

Conley laughed. The buzzer went. He poured the coffee, over-sweetening his own as usual. Danny made a face at it. Conley smiled. "One man's meat..."

"Rots your teeth."

"Too late." Conley offered his smile again to prove it.

"The man with the golden smile."

"You feed off perversity Danny."

"Reared to do it, Mr Conley."

Conley couldn't quite meet his eyes and didn't know why. He said, "Bring him up Danny, be Christian."

"Like fuck I will."

Conley smiled at him. "Go on."

"Maybe," Danny said, sipping from his cup. "After."

Conley pushed his hair back off his face, not meeting his eyes.

Danny smiled to himself and put his cup down. "Max..." He spoke quietly.

Conley looked up.

Danny smiled slowly, jerked his head.

Conley came over.

Stephen looked at his watch and turned on the ignition. He rubbed his hands. He'd been gone almost thirty-five minutes, or should that be *only* thirty-five minutes? Maybe he planned to be two hours. It was twenty-five to nine now. He could easily leave it as late as ten and still be home comfortably. Oh Jesus, he'd die. If the cold didn't get him the boredom would, or the depression. He felt tears prick at his eyes again and pinched the back of his hand.

The door burst open.

"*Shit!*" Stephen jumped.

"Come on." Danny turned the ignition off and withdrew again. All Stephen had seen was his arm and the top of his head. He heard him lock the door. Stephen scrambled out the passenger door, legs stiff. His foot disappeared into about six inches of crisply packed snow, and it was still coming down.

Danny was standing beside him, locking the door. "Go on," he said, without looking at him. "Up the stairs."

Stephen zipped across the park, skidding once.

"Watch the stairs," Danny's voice called behind him.

Stephen climbed the first flight, watched Danny cross the park below him. He waited till he caught up.

"Go on, what you waiting for?"

Stephen went on ahead, aware of Danny behind him. He couldn't sense any anger in him, just a distant irritation. He felt surprised. Happy, but surprised. He hadn't expected it to evaporate at all let alone so quickly.

They got to the top of the stairs.

"Weird place," Stephen said. "Is this it?" He looked at the fire door.

Danny laughed, thumped on the door. It opened.

Stephen felt the warm air rush out to meet them, then the crow was ushering them in.

Danny brushed the snow off his shirt, shook his hair. "Steve-o thinks your house is weird."

Stephen blushed.

"Thank you," Conley said. He was smiling but Stephen couldn't tell if he was serious or not. His voice gave nothing away.

Stephen looked around him. The place was vast, and really *weird*. He whistled then said, "You live here? Really?"

Danny said, "No, it's just a rumour."

Stephen blushed again. "You don't have to be so fucking snipey Danny. I only asked."

"Yes, I live here," Conley interceded. He turned to Danny and said, "Don't be so

smug. You thought it was weird too when you first saw it."

Stephen looked at Danny but his triumph was short lived. Danny was smiling. They were both smiling, like Danny and Rab smiled, that same secret private joke smile. He felt depressed and irritable all over again.

"Want some coffee?" Conley asked him.

Stephen nodded.

Danny had sat down on one of the two huge sofas in the middle of the floor. Stephen peered into the darkness beyond the pool of light, then sat down beside him.

Danny was looking at him. Suddenly he took one of Stephen's hands. "Cold?"

Stephen managed a nod.

Danny moved closer and took both his hands in his and began chafing warmth into them.

Stephen watched his bent head. He wanted to throw himself at him, beg him to forgive him. Instead he sat there, a heavy lump of love stuck in his throat, nowhere to go.

Conley watched the boy watching Danny and thought, I know exactly how you feel. And he turned away so that he didn't have to see it naked on the boy's face any more.

Danny looked up at Stephen and smiled slowly, then said, "Better?"

Conley was banging cupboards, washing cups.

"Danny, I'm sorry," Stephen whispered.

Danny lifted his hands, kissed the palms. First one, then the other. "Another two for your collection."

"Danny..." was all Stephen could manage, his eyes blurring.

Danny let him go and went over to the kitchen.

When they brought the coffee back Stephen was smiling.

Practically.

They showed him round Conley's house - the incredible bathroom; the weird bird; the weird bedroom with the gruesome corpse hanging over the bed.

Stephen looked at the books in awe. He asked Conley if he'd read them all and blushed when he saw them exchange an amused glance as if he'd said something funny.

They got nicely, happy drunk.

He laid his head on Danny's lap and let Danny stroke his hair. It seemed oddly acceptable here when it wouldn't have been at home. Conley never tried to come between them. He sat on his sofa alone and talked to them across the table in that low, flat voice. What his mam would call 'beautifully-spoken'. Stephen smiled to himself. That meant he finished all his words and you couldn't tell where he came from.

"What are you smirking at?" Danny asked, flicking the end of his nose.

Stephen turned his head and smiled up at him, feeling the warmth of Danny's thigh on his cheek. "Nothing."

"You're drunk."

"So are you."

Danny tugged his ear and smiled at him. Stephen kissed his wrist. Danny raised his eyebrows. Stephen blushed immediately, turning to look at Conley, but Conley was pouring himself a drink. He hadn't seen anything.

Stephen let his breath out and relaxed again. Danny had stopped stroking him, lying one hand along the back of the sofa, the other holding his glass. Stephen didn't mind. He'd been stroking him on and off for the last half hour. Stephen didn't mind anything.

"Want some more Stephen?" Conley's voice said to him.

"No thanks."

"He's drunk," Danny said above him.

"I'm not, I'm just happy." Stephen kept his eyes shut, listening to their voices, both beautiful, even if Danny did have an accent. It was deep and warm and beautiful, like Danny.

He felt Danny's belly against the side of his face as he leaned forward to have his glass refilled. Stephen turned into it slightly, enjoying the smell of the new denim, the stiffness of the fabric. He felt Danny sit back again.

"What time is it?" he heard him ask.

Conley's voice said, "Ten to ten."

"We'll have to go in a minute."

Stephen felt his heart sink. "Do we have to Danny?" he asked.

Danny laughed. "Unless you want to wake everyone up, yes. I'll be in enough trouble as it is."

Stephen was silent a moment. Danny's hand came down and rested across his chest, holding him, palm curved around his shoulder, as if he thought he was going to roll off his lap. Safe in his arms, Stephen thought, and smiled at his own stupidity.

"You're grinning again," Danny said. "Tell us all."

"Why doesn't John like you..." He opened his eyes suddenly and turned to Conley. "I don't know what to call you."

Conley smiled. "Call me Conley."

"Conley, then. Why doesn't he like you?"

"You're a nosy little bastard Steve. Don't tell him anything," Danny said.

Stephen closed his eyes again. "Okay, don't then."

"He won't," Danny said firmly. He looked across at Conley and shook his head. *Don't try to explain it.*

Conley smiled at him briefly then looked away. He felt a momentary and intense pang of jealousy for the boy lying there, so complaisant, so sure of himself, having Danny's company whenever he wanted it, monopolising it even here, unselfconscious about touching him. It passed, but it left him feeling depressed, aware of the time, aware that they were no further forward, that Danny would probably add a bruise or two to his collection just for this, just for one... *no, two Max.* Okay, two... But he couldn't say it. Just for half an hour's fevered desperation, and then nothing at all.

What do you want Max? A bouquet of flowers?

No, just time to have him to myself, when *I* want it, that's all.

"Is the snow off?"

Conley looked over at him. Danny was looking at him strangely, as if he'd been listening to him think.

Conley sighed. He couldn't help it. "I'll look."

He got up and crossed to the window. "No, still coming down, but it's not very heavy."

Danny tweaked Stephen's nose, leaned forward hard against his face. Stephen heard the glass chink against the table. "Come on, sleepy-head, time to go home."

Stephen made a groan of protest.

Danny pushed at him unceremoniously. "Come on, *up.*" He slid out from under him, letting Stephen's head drop onto the unyielding cushion.

Stephen felt immediately cold and lonely, over-tired and depressed. He didn't want to go home. He sat up slowly and began searching under the sofa for his shoes.

The bird woke up with the sudden activity and started singing. Stephen smiled, but he couldn't manage a laugh.

Danny was getting their jackets. Stephen could feel Conley watching him. His

waistcoat was hanging open, his shirt unbuttoned half-way down his chest. Stephen could see the thick fair hair on it. He stood with his hands deep in his pockets, smiling at him faintly.

Danny threw their jackets down on the sofa then went for a pee.

Stephen fastened his shoes. Conley was still watching him. "I had a nice time," he said, although he had no idea why he said it.

"Good," Conley said, voice still flat, but his smile looked genuine.

"I don't suppose Danny will bring me again."

He looked at Conley steadily, and Conley knew what he was asking him to do. He licked his lip and said slowly, "He might," and tried to keep the smile there, but it was hard.

Danny came out, shattering the moment. "Come on Steve-o, shake a leg, crucifixion to attend. Don't want to be late for my own."

Stephen shrugged into his jacket. Danny was fastening his. Conley saw that the boy was wearing Danny's old jacket, or something very like it.

They moved over to the door. Danny handed Stephen the keys. "Go down and heat her up. I'll be down in a minute."

Stephen took them, feeling a moment of sullen anger. Here they went again - secrets, private, not for your ears - then he realised he was being churlish. That was his aunt's favourite word. She used it for everything from not eating your peas to an out of order remark about the local choir.

Conley opened the door for him, smiled at him.

"See you," Stephen said, and held his eyes.

It wasn't lost on him. He nodded, his smile holding in there.

Stephen went down the stairs whistling.

Conley closed the door.

Danny said, "I'm sorry."

"Not your fault." Conley couldn't look at him.

"What's wrong?" Danny was close to him, inside his space. He felt no panic and wasn't even glad, nothing, just numb.

He pushed his hands deeper into his pockets. He felt cold, tired, old.

"Tell me," Danny said, touching his face.

"I hurt," Conley said, and felt his eyes sting. "I *hurt* Danny."

Danny took his head, hands through his hair, and brought it to his mouth.

They kissed without touching. When they broke apart Conley said to him, "You know that I love you, don't you?"

Danny stepped back from him. "Not now."

"I do."

"I *said*, not now."

Conley, utterly unexpectedly, banged his fist on the door. "Fuck it Danny, I'm *telling* you."

"And I said, *not now*."

They stood glaring at each other, then Danny put his hand on Conley's chest, flat, almost as if he was pushing him away. "I've got to go."

Conley moved further in front of the door, blocking it. "Why? In case I ask you to say the same?"

"This isn't a picnic for me either."

"Sure. Must be a strain."

Danny pushed him suddenly, a violent shove, hard against the metal door. "It isn't you that gets a knife blade across your fucking balls Conley, alright?"

Conley blinked then slowly nodded, tiny imperceptible nods.

"I'm sorry," Danny said, moving back.

"No," Conley said and moved away from the door.

Danny said, "I've really got to go."

Conley nodded.

Danny pulled him to him hard, suddenly, kissing his mouth tightly, then pushed him away again and was gone.

"What's wrong?"

"It won't start." Stephen was wriggling over onto the passenger seat to let him in. Its surface was cold, the car a lot colder. He shivered.

Danny climbed in. "It's probably just cold. I told you to heat it up."

"I've been trying. It won't start. It doesn't sound right to me."

Danny swore and turned on the ignition. It made a dull unhappy noise like a sick camel's cough then went dead.

"Flat... fucking A-flat." Danny slapped his palms on the steering wheel.

"What?"

"The battery's flat. You running that bloody heater."

"It can't be," Stephen protested. "I hardly had it on."

"On this fucking wreck you've only got to use the bloody indicators to flatten the battery." Danny tried it again. "Why the fuck won't the lousy bastard buy a new one?"

"I thought it had a new one?"

"I'm talking about the truck. Fucking tight bastard. I warned him. This thing was dead before the old man was." Danny tried it again. Nothing at all happened this time. Danny shook his head, ran both hands through his hair.

Stephen looked at him tensely. Danny didn't seem to have noticed what he'd said.

"Oh shit... are we cooked Steve-o."

"Conley can give us a lift."

"Oh, I know." Danny tried it again. "But how do we explain where the truck is when they come to collect it? We'll get home alright, but I don't see how we can fucking lie about it."

They were silent a moment then Stephen said, "Could he jump-start us?"

"That's an idea. Nip upstairs and get him. Hurry up."

Stephen got out the van and slithered at speed across the tarmac. He frost-burnt his fingers on the railing, sending a spray of snow spitting down into the darkness.

Conley came to the door in a towel. His face was startled. "Stephen. What's wrong?"

"We can't get started. Can you give us a jump-start?"

Conley shook his head. "I can't. No car."

"What?"

"It's sprung another leak under the sill. I'm having it fixed. In fact I'm picking it up tomorrow, but that doesn't help you tonight."

"Shit."

"Come in, close the door. Let me get dressed."

He disappeared into the bedroom. Stephen wandered over behind him. He saw Conley pull the towel off. How long and thin he was.

Conley turned and saw him. They both coloured up, Stephen turning and moving away. He went over to stand by the bird, talking to it nervously. After a few minutes Conley came out and crossed the room to pull on his coat.

They went downstairs without speaking.

Danny slid over beside Stephen. "Try it yourself."

Conley did. "It's flat alright. Did you leave your lights on?"

"No. It was the heater."

"Wasn't the engine running?"

"He had it on and off. Every time he's turned the ignition on, one more drib. The battery leads leak or something. Rab's always telling him, but he never listens. Stupid fuck."

Conley assumed he meant John. "Well, come up and we'll get you a taxi."

"Great," Danny said.

"I don't see what else you can do."

Danny sighed heavily and they all filed back out again.

They couldn't get a taxi.

"I don't believe this," Danny said.

Stephen looked at him and chewed his lip.

Conley pushed the hair off his face and pushed away from the phone. "Men short, cars short, impassable roads..."

"What they're really saying is they don't want to make the thirty mile journey back to Brixby stuck behind a fucking snow plough."

"That's about it. I don't know what else to suggest."

"Cunts," Danny said succinctly and dropped down beside Stephen.

Stephen slid a sideways glance at Conley. Danny's language wasn't exactly refined at times, but Conley didn't seem to have noticed.

"Fucking cunts," Danny elaborated and dragged both hands through his hair as if he wanted to pull it out.

He slumped back and closed his eyes. They were both looking at him. Suddenly he opened one eye and said, "Well, looks like you've got two guests for the night Mr Conley." And then he surprised both of them by grinning from ear to ear.

"I don't suppose you've bought any blankets?"

Conley shook his head.

Danny smiled. "Didn't think so."

Stephen felt they were saying much more than they were saying, but he couldn't work out what.

"Think we'll fit three in that bed?"

Conley looked horrified.

"Don't worry about Steve-o here, he's used to three in a bed, aren't you?"

And now it was Conley's turn to be perplexed by the conversation beneath the words.

Stephen blushed and said, "We could sleep on the sofas."

"Hah," Danny snorted. "You only think that. Once the heating goes off this place is as draughty as a fucking warehouse - that being exactly what it is."

"Haven't you got any spare blankets at all?" Stephen asked, obviously confused by this most undomestic of arrangements.

"None," Conley said. "Only what's on my bed."

"I think we could manage it," Danny said. He was smiling, enjoying Conley's discomfort.

"I don't think..." Conley said.

"You'll survive," Danny interrupted flatly.

Stephen looked at them, not having a clue what was really being said.

"I'll sleep in the middle," Danny added, then said, "Warmest spot."

That seemed to make Conley happier. Stephen wondered what his problem was. Did he think he was going to catch something or what? He felt vaguely insulted.

"I've got to take a bath," Conley said abstractedly. He ran his hand through his hair.

"Go ahead."

"Would you change the sheets?"

Danny elbowed Stephen. "We're getting the preferential treatment."

Stephen smiled.

Conley went over to the bedroom. Danny poured Stephen and himself a drink. They clinked glasses. "To three in a bed." Danny smiled at him.

Stephen flushed again and whispered, "Lay off Danny."

Conley called to him from the bedroom. Danny put his glass down and went over. Stephen watched him cross the floor, disappear inside the bedroom.

Conley looked at him and shook his head. "I can't Danny." His voice was low, almost a whisper.

"You can." Danny stood beside him. A fresh quilt cover, sheet and cases sat on top of the chest of drawers. "I've told you, I'll sleep in the middle."

"That's not the point."

"What is?"

But Conley wouldn't say.

"Well, what is? Frightened you talk in your sleep, get a hard-on, have a wet dream - what?"

"*Danny...*" Conley said in exasperation.

"Don't look at me, you're stuck with it. I can think of people who'd be glad to swap with you."

"They're welcome," Conley said irritably, ineffectually pushing his hair back again.

"I think I'm insulted."

Stephen appeared in the doorway. "What's all the whispering in aid of?"

"God, it's The Nose, trying to sniff out secrets again. Come in and help me make up the bed."

Conley looked at Stephen, a single unreadable glance, and went out the room without speaking.

Stephen walked round the room picking things up. Finally he looked in the open wardrobe door. "Jeez, look at these fucking waistcoats. How many has he got?"

"Four hundred and eight."

Stephen stared at him, open-mouthed.

Danny grinned.

"Piss-artist," Stephen said, flushing. He turned back. "Seriously, how many do you reckon there are?"

"Ask him. Come on, stop snooping and help me make the bed."

They stripped the quilt cover off and manhandled it into the clean one.

"Nice stuff. What is it?" Stephen ran his hand over the snowy white cover.

"No idea." Danny was holding a pillow under his chin. He let it go momentarily and thumped Stephen on the chest with the other. "Here. *Do* something."

Stephen began changing the slip.

Once they'd done that they dumped them on the floor and stripped off the sheet.

"It looks clean to me," Stephen said.

"That's because you're a peasant."

"I am not."

"Yes you are."

"I am not."

"Yes you are." And Danny pushed him back on the bed.

Stephen struggled back up.

Danny pushed him down again. "And what's more, you're still drunk."

"Pig," Stephen said. This time he rolled over the other side of the bed and got up.

Danny shook the sheet up into the air. Stephen caught it and they began folding it under. Danny threw him the pillows, then they squared the quilt on top. "Lovely. Looks like a cream cake," Danny said, throwing himself on top.

Stephen climbed on beside him.

"No problem," Danny said, shoving Stephen back towards the edge. "As long as nobody turns over suddenly." And then he did just that, pushing Stephen off the bed.

Stephen landed with a thump.

Danny lay on the bed, consumed with laughter.

"Very fucking funny." Stephen scrambled up and dropped onto Danny's stomach. Danny grunted, laughing, and pulled him down. They wrestled on the bed until Danny succeeded in pinning him into a bear-hug.

Stephen lay there, exhausted, grinning, no longer trying to fight him.

Eventually Danny let him go, limp with exertion, one arm still pinned under Stephen's body.

Stephen lay looking up at the crucifix, aware of Danny warm against him, still giving the occasional chuckle. His eyes were shut, his mouth curved with a sleepy smile.

"How does he sleep under that?" Stephen asked.

"He doesn't notice it any more."

"You slept in here before?"

"Uh-huh."

"With him?"

"Well he didn't spend the night on the fucking bird's perch."

They were silent again. They could both hear the distant splash of water, the sound of taps being run, water moving through the plumbing.

"What's he so uptight about?" Stephen asked.

"Grubby boys in his nice bed."

"I am *not* grubby. I wash every night, like you do."

"Just your neck and ears."

Stephen punched him with his free hand, rolling over.

Danny caught the punch, held it. He opened his eyes, smiled at him. "Sucker..."

Stephen flushed.

Danny looked at him curiously, then let him go, pushing him away slightly. "You've got a dirty mind Steve-o."

Stephen didn't say anything.

"Give me my arm out, you're cutting off my blood supply."

Stephen moved to let him take his arm out. Danny massaged it then laid it across his front, flexing the fingers. Stephen lay on his side, facing him. They were no longer touching.

Danny turned his head and looked at him. "Now what are you thinking?"

"Conley never mentioned your earring."

"Yes he did, you just weren't here at the time."

"What did he say?"

"None of your business."

"Don't forget to clean it tonight. You've got to do it every night."

"Yes Mum. I know Mum."

Stephen threw himself on his back. "I was only saying."

"Yes Mum."

Stephen hit Danny's chest loosely with the back of his hand. "Don't."

"No Mum."

Stephen turned into him and started pummelling him like a cat back-kicking a ball of wool.

Danny started laughing again, trying to push him off. He managed to roll him over and climb on top of him. He pinned his arms to his chest, one elbow digging into Stephen's chest. "Submit," he demanded.

"Fuck off," Stephen grunted.

Danny leaned more weight on his elbow. "Come on, submit."

"No."

Danny dug his elbow in hard.

Stephen yelled in complaint. "Alright, alright, I submit."

"Say, I am a grubby little peasant."

"No."

Danny dug his elbow in again.

"I'm a grubby little peasant..." Stephen rushed it out.

"And a sucker."

"And a sucker," Stephen added, blushing all over again.

"Good boy," Danny said, lying loosely on top of him now, letting the offending elbow slide down onto the bed to support his weight.

"You've got a sadistic streak in you Danny," Stephen said petulantly.

Danny smiled down at him. "Everybody has." He circled Stephen's cheek with his thumb, soft, slow, insinuating.

Stephen began to feel the dull, slow thump of his pulse. He lay there watching Danny's eyes, watching the slow change in them. He felt the thumb move down over his mouth, heard Danny say, "You've got a nice mouth." And he wet his finger and ran it over Stephen's lips.

Stephen felt himself come up and was powerless to stop it. He was intensely embarrassed and excited at the same time.

"Looks even nicer wet." And Danny did it again.

Stephen watched him suck his fingertip then felt the finger, almost unbearably ticklish, over his mouth. He wanted to scratch it, but he didn't dare move.

"I'd like to..." And Danny lowered his head.

Stephen closed his eyes, felt everything inside himself stop, waiting for the first touch of it... and then Danny was gone. Up and off him in one movement. Stephen lay there a moment, feeling foolish, disorientated, then he opened his eyes.

Conley was standing in the doorway in a dressing gown. He was looking at Danny who was standing by the bed.

Stephen looked at Danny. He was smiling, hands pushed into his pockets. It looked almost like a shrug. Conley's face was unreadable. Stephen wondered when he'd got there, how long he'd been standing there, if he'd seen anything, if there'd been anything to see. He didn't know himself. He sat up on his elbows.

"Come on Steve-o, clear out. Let the man get his nightie on." Danny winked at Conley and moved out of the room.

Stephen scrambled off the bed and hurried out after him, not meeting Conley's eyes.

They sat up for another half hour and had another drink. Conley was wearing pyjamas, or at least the bottoms, under a dressing gown. Stephen felt sure they'd been put on for their benefit. They had crease-marks in them like knife edges.

Stephen lay slumped against Danny, half-asleep. Finally Danny pushed him

upright saying, "Go do the ness' Steve-o, before you fall asleep. I'm going to phone big brother. I've put it off long enough."

Stephen got up reluctantly and went to the bathroom. Conley got up and began locking the doors. Danny picked up the phone and dialled. Conley listened to it, trying not to.

"Hello? John?" There was a pause that obviously covered more than a yes or no. Conley saw Danny rub his temple as if he were already exasperated. "Caldermouth... Guess... No I didn't... I can't, we're stuck. The battery's flat... Oh come on, you know it's had it... I tried that, but Conley's car's in for servicing. There's no-one else here."

After that there was a long listening silence. Conley watched his back. It looked tense and angry. He was sitting on the edge of the seat as if he wanted to slam the phone down.

"Look... I know... Of course he's fucking with me. What d'you think I did with him? Shoved him in a snowdrift?... Oh, don't be fucking stupid. This isn't a suicide plea... No don't, he'll only get stuck... Look, I'm not trying to do anything, the roads are.... Well fuck you, do what you damn well like."

There was another silence then a curt, "Yes" then a, "Look John I didn't..." But he stopped half way. John had obviously hung up.

Danny put the receiver back slowly. Conley went over and stood above him. "Unconvinced?"

Danny grunted. It sounded as if he couldn't speak, although whether it was anger or not he couldn't tell.

"Is he going to come and get you?"

Danny looked up at him sharply. "Would you like that?"

Conley shook his head then said quietly, "Although he's welcome to take the boy."

Danny smiled stiffly and said, "Well you don't need to worry. John hasn't inconvenienced himself for me yet. Anyway, think of the fun he can have tomorrow punishing me for his indifference."

"Are you serious?"

"Never more so." Danny stood up. "So we might as well enjoy it," and he slid a hand inside Conley's dressing gown and inside his pyjamas.

Conley drew a breath of surprise. Danny held his penis, squeezing gently. "Maybe we'll get a chance after he's asleep," he said quietly, watching Conley's face.

"Tell me you're joking."

"I never joke about fucking, it isn't funny." But Danny was smiling.

"I never know how to take you Danny."

Danny squeezed him again. "Any way you can get me." He crossed to the bathroom and went in.

Conley stood there until his erection diminished.

It was a long wait.

Stephen was cleaning his teeth with his finger. "What'd he say?" he mumbled through a mouthful of foam.

"Peasant," Danny said, but he squeezed toothpaste onto his own finger nevertheless. "He's going to tear me limb from limb - that's a rough translation."

Stephen bent his head to the tap, sucked water in then sprayed it out. He wiped his mouth with his hand. "Was he really angry?"

"What do you think? He's two short for milking tomorrow. I mean, that's serious."

Stephen stood watching him brush his teeth. When Danny had rinsed his mouth he straightened up and said, "Piss off, I want to pee."

"It's only me."

"Out."

Stephen shrugged. Danny was funny about people seeing him pee. You'd think he was underdeveloped or something.

He went out. He heard Danny lock the door behind him. It irritated him. He wasn't so sick he got his kicks out of watching other men pee for Christ's sake.

Stephen wandered across the huge dark room to the glow of the bedroom. Conley was already in bed. Suddenly Stephen felt very self-conscious. He didn't know what to say or do. It didn't help that Conley didn't speak to him. He was lying there on one side of the bed with his eyes shut. Stephen looked at his face. It reminded him of those marble figures you got on top of tombs in churches, thin and white, somehow different from modern faces. Conley's hair was too long. It looked very gold under the yellow light of the lamp.

"Why are you looking at him like that? Wondering if he's still alive?" Danny came in behind him, unfastening his shirt.

Stephen turned away, flushing. Fucking Danny, opening his big fucking mouth. He heard Conley speak to him, that same flat voice, but he didn't hear what he said.

Danny twitched his hands into Stephen's waist. He laughed when Stephen jumped and elbowed him, full of instant bad-temper.

"Come on Steve-o, last man in makes the tea in the morning. Hell, I'm in the gap between the pillows."

"Good," Stephen muttered.

Danny stuck cold feet on him as he got in.

"Piss off," Stephen grunted at him, trying not to laugh.

Danny moved over closer to Conley to let him in. "Lights out Mr Conley, please."

Conley put the lights out. There was a moment's intense silence in the darkness then Danny blew a raspberry. "Who did that?" he said, feigning outrage.

"Oh fuck off Danny," Stephen said. "Grow up."

Danny laughed. "Listen to this, Pensioner of the Year."

Conley could feel them tussling beside him and suddenly realised there was only four years between them. It was nothing. In a year or two you wouldn't even notice, but his age difference would always show. He was old enough to be father to them both. He felt an intense depression. He suddenly wanted them, with all their flawed perfection, their youth, far away from him, out of his bed, out of his life, as if they'd never been, and as soon as he thought that he felt worse.

He became aware that they were lying still now, Danny curled away from him, facing Stephen. He felt Danny shift slightly and then he felt his hand, sliding warm and dry down his stomach.

Conley froze.

Danny was talking quietly to Stephen while his hand slid down deep into Conley's pubic hair. It had unbuttoned the single button of his pyjamas, laying them open, as stealthy and silent as a snake. Now it moved round him, over him, idly, without intent, simply fondling him, amusing itself. His cock took it more seriously, came up raging hard, like a solid immovable rock in Danny's way.

Danny's hand slid under it, ignoring the hot swollen mass of it lying on the back of his hand, and continued to play with the hair, continued to talk to Stephen.

Conley could feel frustration, lust, jealousy as if it was one emotion, and Danny caressed on, teasing and no pleasing.

Stephen lay facing him, trying to see him in the dark. Danny was lying half on his back, but his head was turned to him rather than Conley. Stephen could feel his breath on his cheek. It smelt of toothpaste and the funny American whisky they'd been drinking, like burnt coconut.

Stephen's sleepiness had left him as soon as he'd got into bed. The bed was

strange, high and very upholstered, more comfortable than his rickety old bed that had once belonged to Danny.

Danny shifted again beside him, slightly further onto his back. It brought his shoulder and thigh into sudden contact with Stephen's body. "That alright?" he asked.

"Yes," Stephen said.

Yes, Conley thought as Danny's hand finally began masturbating him.

"I'm not pushing you too close to the edge?"

"No," Stephen said.

Yes, Conley thought. Jesus, Danny, *stop*.

Conley grabbed at his hand, gripped it tight. He felt Danny's hand resist then lie still. Conley lay breathing hard through his mouth, willing Danny to keep talking so that the boy wouldn't hear him.

Stephen got a hard-on again. He wanted to turn away, terrified that Danny would accidentally discover it, but there was no room to turn now that Danny was lying on his back. "Is Conley asleep?" he whispered. Conley hadn't said a word since they had got into bed.

"I think so," Danny said. "Hang on."

Stephen felt him turn onto his other side.

Conley felt Danny's mouth on his, deep, soft, exploring, so quick it was hardly there, his hand squeezing his cock hard. Conley lay there so close, trembling with tension, not knowing what to do, how to stop it, how to make himself want to stop it. Then Danny had turned away again, hand now a light teasing friction, moving awkwardly.

"Out for the count," he heard him say to the boy. He could almost hear Stephen's relief, or was it excitement?

"I thought he was. He's breathing heavier. You can always tell."

"You cunning fiend," Danny said and Conley could hear the smile in it. Stephen laughed quietly.

Conley turned slightly, closer into Danny's hand, pushing his face into Danny's hair. He risked a kiss, one, soft and dry on Danny's neck. He felt Danny shiver.

"You cold?" Stephen asked.

"Just someone walking on my grave."

Conley smiled and kissed him again. He didn't shiver this time but his hand squeezed Conley tight, warning, Don't, you bastard. Conley smiled some more and began to wonder if Danny had an erection. Could Danny play with him like this and not have an erection? He wouldn't put it past him. Danny was lying almost flat on his back, one hip resting on Conley's side, his hand down back across his body, gripping his penis. One of Conley's arms was trapped but he could easily feel with the other if he just turned a little.

He turned a little. He heard Stephen sigh, Danny ask, "What's up?"

Conley smiled, slid his hand over, felt Danny flinch. He found the back of his shorts, down over his hip, there.

Danny was as hard as he was. Conley squeezed it. Danny coughed, pulling round away from him onto his side, pushing Conley's hand off. Conley grinned some more.

"I can't sleep," Stephen said.

Now Danny's back was turned firmly against him. Conley lay there aching, but still amused.

I can't sleep, Stephen thought, because this hard-on's killing me. If I could only jerk off. It was like thinking of a cold drink on a hot day. As soon as you thought it you couldn't get it out of your head. It became everything.

"Strange bed," Danny said.

"Suppose so."

Danny had turned back onto his side again, so all Stephen could feel now was the brush of his knees. Purposefully he lay on his back in the extra space. It brought his shoulder and arm against Danny's chest. Danny felt very warm, almost hot. Stephen could feel how smooth he was. "I haven't got any hair on my chest either," he said.

"It'll come," Danny murmured. He sounded sleepy.

Conley moved closer to his back then kissed him softly, across his shoulders, running his hands slowly and stealthily over his backside. He could feel Danny's goosepimples.

"I wish it would hurry up."

"Don't wish your life away."

Stephen was silent for a moment then shifted onto his side again. Danny jumped, making Conley jump.

"Sorry," Stephen said.

"It's alright," Danny's voice answered. Conley could hear how low it had sunk, wondered if it was sleepiness or something else, wondered why Danny had jumped and why Stephen had apologised. "Feel it if you want."

And Conley knew it wasn't sleepiness. He felt suddenly wide awake. What the hell was going on? He wanted to pull the blankets off and see who had whose what where.

There was another silence. He distanced himself from Danny's body as if he might be able to hear or feel better what was going on.

"It's soft."

Not when I felt it it wasn't, Conley thought.

"What did you expect, wire wool?"

Wire wool?

"I thought it would be rough. You know, like your..." Stephen petered out.

"Like your what?" Danny asked and Conley could hear that smile.

"Like your pubes."

"Yours are maybe like wire wool, mine's aren't."

"What, your pubes?"

Danny mimicked him. "Yes, me pubes."

"I haven't got any hair on my belly. I didn't know."

"Well now you do."

Conley let his body relax a little. He'd been touching the hair on his stomach. He wasn't sure whether he felt any better about that than if Stephen had been feeling him more intimately. He put a hand on Danny's lower back, felt Danny move back slightly, encouraging him.

Stephen felt the hair again, running it under his fingertips. It was as silky as the hair on his head, well almost. Was his pubic hair really like that? "Is it really soft like that?"

"Yes."

Stephen was silent then said, "That's weird."

Danny laughed. "I don't see what's so weird about it."

"I thought everybody's was curly."

"It is curly."

"You know what I mean, coarse, rough, like a dog."

Danny laughed again. "I've never felt a dog's pubic hair. I wouldn't know."

"Oh give over Danny."

Stephen left his hand against Danny's stomach, enjoying the intimacy of being allowed this close. He began to play with the hair, running his fingers through it. He let his hand trail up his body until he found a nipple. He brushed it once, expecting Danny to tell him off. He lay still, cock jerking, but Danny didn't say anything. His body seemed relaxed. Stephen went on feeling him, slowly tracing his way over to the other nipple. He wondered if he dare rub it, like Rab had done to his that night in bed. Rab

had licked them and bit them too. It had felt good, embarrassingly good. He stopped thinking about it. He shouldn't be doing this - he knew he shouldn't - but he felt such an urge, such a *need* to do it, he couldn't stop himself. He didn't want to think about it. He just wanted to touch him. He'd wanted to touch him right from the start. He fascinated him. He loved him.

He stopped.

He didn't *love* him, love him. Not like that. He swallowed.

Danny didn't seem any more aware that he'd stopped than of what he'd been doing. He wondered if he'd fallen asleep. He whispered his name. "Danny?"

Conley heard him and lay waiting to see what Danny would do. He knew he was awake. Only a second before he had reached behind him and started squeezing Conley's penis again. He lay still now, hand deep inside Conley's pyjama trousers.

"Danny?" Stephen whispered again, then he was silent.

Conley reached over and carefully slid a hand up inside the leg of Danny's shorts. Danny lay back slightly towards him, letting him in. Conley eased him slowly and with difficulty out the leg of his shorts. Danny made a noise like a man moaning in his sleep.

Stephen had laid his hand flat against him and let it slide, just a little, slowly down over his nipple, rubbing it with the heel of his hand. Danny moaned. Stephen stopped, his excitement quickened by the sound. Could he feel this? He let his hand slide a little further. He was under his ribs now, sliding down to the inward curve of his belly. His little finger dipped into Danny's belly button. Stephen felt the little hollow, perfect and round. He probed Danny's belly with his fingertips, thinking of the scar.

Conley felt Danny's hand clamp his forearm and yank him off. There was a quick agitated fumble.

Stephen felt Danny jerk as if he had jumped in his sleep. Danny's arm brushed his. He was scratching or something. Was he awake? Stephen lay still, his heart hammering, but there was no further movement.

Conley lay there wondering what the hell was going on, filled with suspicion. What was Stephen doing round the other side? He lay still, listening.

Stephen took a deep breath, let it out again. Danny did not move. All was still. Stephen let his hand slide down a little further. Now he could feel hair again, that lovely silky belly hair. Soon he'd reach the scar. He wondered how it would feel.

He reached the waistband of Danny's shorts, sitting low on his hips. He would need to put his hand under it if he was going to reach the scar. He lay there dry-mouthed, willing himself to do it. Just quickly. Danny would never know. Maybe he'd been lying to him, maybe he was as coarse and wiry as the rest of them. Danny had called him a sucker tonight and suddenly, right now, he wished he was. As soon as he thought it he could feel his ears burning, his face and chest hot. His cock kicked at him, alive with indecent shame. His hand pressed into Danny's belly, the fingertips worming under the elastic.

Conley could hear the boy's breathing, ragged, heavy. What the hell were they doing? What was *he* doing? Because Danny wasn't doing anything. He wasn't moving a muscle. Conley still had one arm trapped under Danny's body and he could feel the tense stillness in him. So what was the boy doing? Not...? No, he'd feel that. Unless that *was* what he was feeling. Was he feeling the tension of Danny being masturbated in the boy's hand? He lay there still, waiting like he could feel Danny waiting.

Stephen eased his fingers in slowly then lost patience and pushed his hand in. But he didn't feel the mythical pubic hair because something hot and huge and hard brushed against his hand. He made a noise.

Oh God, I think I'm going to shoot my load.

He lay there feeling it throb in him, so close. He held his breath.

Tentatively he felt him, the length of it, the head on it. He felt underneath and felt the hair, soft and springy. He went on down and felt between his legs, warm, secret, slightly damp. He came back up, trailing his hand over his cock. He wished he could get his shorts off. He took it in his hand and held it, tight. He wanted to...

He bit his lip and pressed his free hand against himself awkwardly. He wanted to wank him.

There, you said it. You said it. Oh God, I don't care, I do. I want to wank him.

He moved closer and pressed his mouth against Danny's. *Wake up Danny. Be awake and know it's me.*

He kissed him again, willing it, desperately. He let go Danny's cock and pushed both hands against his chest.

Conley could feel him moving in the bed. He wasn't attempting to hide it. He saw Stephen's head come up, a bare outline, leaning over his face, and knew he was kissing him.

Conley felt Danny shift slightly, curving towards Stephen and felt like someone plunging down into an abyss. What was going on? Had Danny been having a relationship with the boy after all? He'd seen them on the bed together. He'd been sure he'd interrupted a kiss, or something that looked a hell of a lot like one.

Danny pulled Stephen to him and kissed him just like that time in the field when he'd scared him half to death, but this time Stephen wasn't panicking. This time Stephen was ready for it. He locked his legs into Danny's, pulling him to him.

Danny could feel the uncontrollable heat in him. He was further gone than he had realised. What had been a game to him was obviously a damn sight more serious to Stephen. *Never fuck in the dark Danny, when you can't see their faces.*

He felt Stephen groan in his throat, could feel him thrusting up against him. He wasn't going to let go. *Shit, how the fuck did I get myself into this?*

Conley coughed suddenly and loudly.

Stephen froze.

Conley sat up and put his feet on the floor.

Danny rolled off him onto his back. He could feel his own heart racing.

Conley moved across the room.

Danny turned over, turning his back on Stephen.

Stephen lay there afraid, not sure what had happened. Danny was gone, his back turned firmly against him. Stephen lay listening to Conley coming back across the room, then he felt him climb back into bed. Now Danny was curled up towards him and Stephen was alone. He'd never felt more alone in his life. It was like the feeling you had as a kid when you dropped money down a drain. You watched it fall down into the iron darkness, gone, irreplaceable, and you just sat there and cried.

He got up out the bed, feeling as if he had flu, and went to the bathroom.

"What the hell was going on?" Conley hissed at Danny.

"He was exploring."

"Some fucking exploring."

Danny was momentarily silenced then he said, "That's twice you've sworn at me tonight."

"I've got a lot to catch up on. What were you going to do, let him bring you off?"

"No." Conley could hear the tightness in his voice. "I misjudged it, that's all."

"*Misjudged* it? What the hell is this Danny, a bloody sport?"

Conley heard him sigh, but it was a sigh of irritation, not remorse. No shame for Danny. "You make me sick," Conley said before he could stop himself.

There was a moment's intense silence then Conley said, "Danny..." just as Danny got up. "*Danny,*" he hissed after him. "Where are you going?"

"Fuck off Conley. Go play with yourself." And Danny disappeared out the room.

A second later Conley heard him open and close the bathroom door, then the unmistakable sound of the lock.

"Steve-o?"

"Here."

"Where's here?"

"On the side of the bath."

Danny walked over to him. He ran a questing palm over his cheek. "Not crying," he said. It was almost a question.

"No. Disappointed?"

Danny sat down beside him. He put an arm round him, but Stephen remained stiff and unyielding under his arm.

"What's wrong?" Danny asked.

"You," Stephen said.

Danny felt his heart do a sink and stop. Why did the little bastard always have to be so honest? "What about me?"

"I don't know what you want."

Danny could have said, I don't know what you mean, or I don't understand, but he couldn't do it. *Once too often Danny. Do it another time and you might as well stamp in his face.* He was silent.

"You weren't asleep, were you?"

Danny fought that one too. "No," he said finally, and by the silence he knew Stephen hadn't really expected that answer, although he knew it was true.

"Danny?"

"Mm?"

"Tell me the truth. Would you like to... I mean tonight, did you want to... you know, what I was doing to you?"

Danny dropped his arm. Stephen felt it go. He wanted to pull it back.

Danny cleared his throat then said in a low voice, "You're too young and I was playing stupid games with you. If it helps any I don't like myself. I'm even sorry." And Danny laughed, a short harsh sound.

"I'm not too young," Stephen said in a quick low rush. "I know what it's about."

"You don't. You know all the technicalities and nothing about how you're going to feel afterwards."

"I do. Anyway, how old were you the first time?"

"That's got nothing to do with it."

"Yes it has. You're saying I'm too young, how old were you?"

Danny hesitated and was lost.

"See? I'll bet you weren't any older... or not much older, were you? It was Rab, wasn't it?"

"No," Danny said shortly.

"Who then?"

"No-one you know."

"Now you're lying to me. Why won't you tell me?"

"Because it doesn't matter, you're still too young."

"No I'm not. How old were you?"

"Listen, Stephen, there's more to it than that."

"Like?"

"Like John."

Stephen was silent then said cautiously, "What about John?"

"He wouldn't like it."

"What?"

"You know what, don't act dumb."

"I don't see what John's got to do with this. He doesn't need to know."

"The answer's no."

"Why not? You like me, don't you?"

"Yes I like you, that's why it's a mistake."

"What about her? You don't even *like* her but you're round there every chance you get. I've seen you sneaking off."

Danny was silent.

"You're just messing me about, aren't you? Well I wish you'd leave me alone and stop fucking leading me on and then saying no. Know what?" Stephen said, his voice rising not with anger but with the excitement of discovery. "You're a cock-tease."

Stephen stood up as he said it, Danny following him, trying to placate him. "Keep your voice down."

"Why? He's probably one too. I've seen the way he looks at you. That's why he doesn't want me here. He wants me to piss off so he can suck your dick, just like her. Is that what they all do, suck your..."

He didn't get any further. Danny slapped him, conclusively and definitely across the mouth. Stephen felt it in his ear like a painful popping. His face stung, first with pain, then embarrassment.

Then he was furious.

He came tearing into Danny like an angry cat.

They went down on the floor, Danny jarring his elbow viciously, then Stephen was pummelling him. He had the advantage, a soft landing and a winded and already injured Danny. Stephen went for his face. It was something else Danny wasn't used to. His hand snagged on Danny's newly pierced ear. Danny felt it rip. He covered his face with his hands.

Stephen realised eventually that Danny wasn't fighting back. In the same moment he knew with a terrible conviction he'd killed him. Conley was banging on the door.

Stephen felt Danny's face and felt the slippery touch of blood. "Oh God, *Danny…*" He shook him.

Danny's voice said, "Stop fucking shaking me."

Conley shouted, "Will you open this bloody door?!"

"That's three times," Danny said.

Stephen got up and crossed to the door. He realised suddenly he could see dimly. Conley had put the living room lights on.

He slid the bolt open. Conley came in like an avenging angel. "What the fuck is going on?"

"Four times," Danny said and he rolled up into something like a sitting position.

Conley put on the light. Stephen looked at Danny. Blood was smeared all over his face. A trail of it ran from his ear down his chest. A long thin red line. Inconceivably, Danny smiled. It looked revolting, like broken bones amongst the blood, like a deaths-head rictus. If it was meant to reassure it didn't work. Stephen said, "Oh..." and promptly slid down onto the floor.

Conley said, "I don't believe this," in a flat emotionless voice, and crossed to where Danny was sitting. Danny reached a hand up to him. Conley pulled him up.

"Really, it looks worse than it is," Danny said, and Conley answered, "Good, because it couldn't be worse than it looks."

Danny turned and looked in the mirror. "I see what you mean." He crossed to the wash-hand basins and washed one-handedly. "Arm's fucked. I think your floor

fractured my elbow."

Conley felt it.

"Ow. Shit, don't *do* that."

"Just bruised."

"You say. See if he's alright."

Conley crossed to where Stephen was still slumped on the floor, head between his knees. Conley hunkered down beside him. "You okay?"

Stephen nodded but he didn't lift his head.

Conley looked at his cheek, the only part he could see. His colour looked alright. He was embarrassed, that's all.

Danny was pulling a long streamer of toilet paper off the wall and dabbing his face with it. "See if he's torn my ear, will you?"

Conley inspected it, trying to stem the bleeding enough to see it clearly. "I don't think so. You've lost your earring however."

"It'll be on the floor somewhere."

Conley looked around for it then spotted it. He picked it up. "It's broken."

Danny shrugged. "He paid for it. He's allowed to break it." He looked at himself in the mirror again. One torn and determined to bleed copiously ear, and a row of three lovely scratches right down one side of his face. Possibly a bit of a black eye to come. All told it was about right. Maybe not including the fractured elbow, otherwise it was a pretty fair exchange.

He looked at Conley and jerked his head towards the door, mouthing, Five minutes.

Conley went out without a word or look and closed the door.

Danny looked down at him for a moment or two then said, "Come on Steve-o, it's late, let's get to bed."

Stephen didn't move. He kept his head down and said in a muffled voice, "I'm sorry I said those things."

"Forget it."

"And I'm sorry about the mess I've made of your face."

Danny laughed.

Stephen finally looked up. "What will you tell John?"

Danny was still holding toilet paper to his face. "I'll tell him a wild cat got me." He held his hand out.

Stephen took it and pulled himself up. He looked at Danny's ear. "And I broke your earring."

"At least you didn't break my ear. I've got another. Earring, I mean."

"It'll be difficult to get it in now. It's going to be all swollen."

"I'll bite on a knotted hankie. Now are we going back to bed?"

"What about Conley?"

"What about him?"

"What'll we tell him?"

"Nothing. He won't ask. He's not John."

Stephen looked at him.

"He's got better manners. Come on, let's go."

Danny opened the door and put the light out. The living room was dark again, only the faint glow slanting out from the slatted blinds of the bedroom.

Conley was lying with his face on the back of his hand when they went in. He looked at Stephen briefly, that same flat implacable way he always looked. Stephen looked away.

742

Danny got in, Stephen after him.

"I'll probably bleed on your sheets. Do you want to put on an old pillowcase, or something?"

"No, don't worry about it," Conley said, clicking out the light. "Let's get some sleep."

Nobody said anything else. Stephen lay rigid and unhappy. He couldn't feel Danny beside him. He didn't even know which way he was lying. He heard a rustle at Conley's side. Now he could tell Danny had his back to him. He told himself it wasn't deliberate, but he didn't believe it.

After a while he moved a little closer, more for warmth than anything else. Danny didn't pull away. Stephen tentatively laid his cheek against his back. Danny was warm and soft, utterly relaxed. Stephen felt comforted. He closed his eyes and was soon asleep.

"Is he asleep?"

"Like the living dead."

Conley sighed. Danny laid an arm across his stomach. Uncharacteristically Conley caught it to himself and held it there.

Danny whispered, "Want to dirty the sheets?"

"It'll wake him," Conley whispered back.

"Not unless you yodel."

"I never yodel."

"Bite the pillow if you feel one coming on." But neither of them moved, both sleepy and relaxed.

"Do I really sicken you?" Danny asked unexpectedly.

"Let's not start that."

"No, tell me, do I?"

"Sometimes."

Danny was silent. Conley didn't like the silence so he added, "I'm a hard-line moralist."

"Since when?"

"On some things."

"Like?"

"Cruel games, destructive behaviour for cheap amusement."

"I like him," Danny said and Conley could hear the cold defensiveness in it.

"I think that's worse."

He felt Danny jerk his arm away. He felt irritated. "You asked, now you're going to throw a bloody sulk about it."

"Stop swearing at me. You've done nothing but fucking swear at me all night."

"I'll swear if I want, it's not your exclusive domain."

"I don't like it."

"Now who's being a prude?"

They were silent, the air suddenly hushed without the angry hiss of their whisperings. They could hear Stephen's breathing, long, steady, almost a gentle snore.

Danny put his hand back across Conley's stomach then laid his leg over his, turning into him fully. Conley completely shattered his record by lifting an arm and saying, "Want to come in?"

Danny went in under his arm, pressing his face into his chest. He ran his tongue into the nick of his armpit. In an instant that neither of them had intended they were kissing, mouths ground tight together.

When they finally broke Conley whispered, "I needed that."

"I need more." Danny was pressing against his leg. "Let's dirty these sheets, come on." He reached down and began squeezing his cock.

Conley felt the fervour of his grip and let himself melt into it.

Danny pushed his hand off when he tried to reciprocate. He didn't want Conley to touch him. Instead he just kept pressing against him. They were silent, their mouths busy on each other. Danny's stroking was slow, holding him back, but it still didn't take long. It was as if he'd already jumped two or three stages in the process.

Conley pulled Danny's head back by the hair, gasping, "Slow down."

Danny laughed. "I can't go any slower without falling asleep. Just come."

"Not yet." Conley's restraining grip on his head was like iron.

"Come on Conley, let me have a little spunk." He began squeezing him rhythmically, since Conley had him otherwise immobilised.

"Danny, don't."

"You're gonna come just squeezing? You never told me you could do that."

"I didn't know I could. Stop it."

"No."

"Danny please, I mean it, I'm going to spoil it."

"I sincerely hope so."

"*Shit*... Danny..."

"You're swearing again."

"*Danny*..." Conley said urgently, then, "Oh God, oh no... Danny..." And Conley began to jerk in his hand.

Danny sucked his tongue into his mouth, reducing him to a kind of low animal grunting.

Conley felt as if he were dissolving, breaking away in slow burning chunks. He was sure he felt his ears pop. He felt his own wetness sliding over himself as Danny went on squeezing.

"Danny...?"

Both Danny and Conley froze. Conley felt something drip onto his stomach. His cock spasmed unpleasantly. It was like being startled during urinating, that same flow-choking clench. His foot twitched with a sudden savage itch.

"What is it?" he heard Danny ask. His voice sounded terse and irritable.

"Did you hear a funny noise?"

Conley listened to the perceptible pause before Danny answered him. "What kind of a funny noise?"

"I don't know. Something woke me."

"You dreamt it. Go back to sleep.

"Sounded like an animal."

"It was probably the bird. Go back to sleep."

Stephen was quiet a moment then he said, "I'm cold."

Conley heard Danny tutting in exasperation. "Cuddle up against me," he said then sharply, "No, don't do that, hang on."

Conley felt him turn away from him, first squeezing his diminishing cock almost like an apology. Why are you apologising? Conley thought. It's you that's been left high and dry. He swung up out of the bed, holding his pyjama bottoms up, thankful of the darkness, trying vainly to keep them out of the wet on his belly.

He went to the bathroom. He heard Stephen say, "We've woken him up again" and Danny reply shortly, "Go to sleep" before he closed the bathroom door.

"I'm frozen."

Danny tutted again. "What the fuck do you want me to do about it?"

"Nothing." Stephen sounded sulky.

Danny gave in and turned to face him. "Come on," he said, and if he sounded defeated Stephen didn't choose to hear it.

He moved over under Danny's arm. Danny pulled them close together. "Happy?" he asked sarcastically.

"Mm," Stephen said. Ecstatically, he thought.

Conley came back into bed and realised Danny was facing away from him. He ran his hand down Danny's back but Danny didn't respond. He felt tense and angry. Conley wasn't sure if it was at him or Stephen.

Conley turned on his side, back to his back. He fought it briefly but he was too satiated to hold out long. He fell asleep, filled with a well-satisfied sense of guilt.

Danny could smell Stephen's hair. He turned his face away.

Stephen put an arm around him, pulling himself in tighter. He had gradually insinuated one leg over Danny's. Danny let him. He hoped his body heat would coax him into sleep faster. The little bastard didn't even feel that cold, except for his fucking feet. And Conley was asleep, Danny could sense it. He was too still. Not tense still, gone still. Goodnight, goodbye. *Fuck you Conley, I'll remember this*. But he knew it wasn't Conley's fault.

He felt Stephen sigh, a sliding into sleep sigh. He felt anger twitch at him. His excitement had turned into a dull ache of bad temper. He felt wide awake. His ear was burning, his face doing those itchy little throbs like cat scratches. It felt as if his blood was poisoned. His elbow ached, already stiff. The only bloody thing in this bed that's stiff, he thought, getting progressively more irritated.

He tried to scratch his stomach without disturbing him, but Stephen moved restlessly against him at his movement. He could feel the blood beginning to fade in his supporting arm.

What the hell am I, a fucking charity? Solace for the weak and needy? What about my needs? I should have stayed home, got big brother to offer up his sacred arsehole.

He lost himself for a moment in a sudden memory of the night John had asked him to fuck him, then realised what he was doing. Shit, now he'd given himself another hard-on.

Jesus. Go to sleep Danny. For fucksake, go to sleep.

"I can hear your heart beat," Stephen whispered sleepily against him.

"I thought you were asleep," Danny whispered back. He felt Stephen shake his head, a bare negative. He felt very heavy and boneless against him. If he wasn't asleep he was damn near it. "Well go to sleep."

"I can hear your heartbeat."

"So you've said. That means I'm still alive, you can go to sleep now."

Stephen snuggled up to him, his raised knee coming perilously close to Danny's erection.

"Danny?"

"What?" Danny asked irritably.

"Would you mind if I took my pants off?"

"What the fuck for? I thought you were cold?"

"They're making me uncomfortable."

"And I'm going to feel relaxed? Anyway I thought you were used to pyjamas?"

"Not any more."

"Go on then, if you want to. Hurry up. But you're not cuddling in, understand?"

Stephen levered his arse in the air and struggled them off, dropping them out the side of the bed. He came back into Danny's side, but he was careful to keep the angle

of his hips turned away. "That's better," he sighed.

"I'm so glad."

"I'll go to sleep now."

"Oh super."

They were silent. Danny felt oddly ill-at-ease suddenly, different from his earlier bad temper. He could feel it in his chest, like a bubble of emotion trapped too long.

"Danny?"

"*Jesus*..." Danny's whisper was explosive. "Now what?"

"I was only going to say, if you wanted to take yours off I wouldn't mind."

"Thanks, but I think I'll skip the nudist convention for tonight."

"Don't they irritate you?"

"Immensely, but not as much as you do."

"Take them off if you want."

"I don't *want*." Danny spaced each word hard and clear. "Now fucking go... to fucking sleep."

"Okay."

Stephen snuggled down again, moving his head further into Danny's shoulder, letting Danny flex his arm a little. Now he could smell his fucking hair again.

He sighed, taking the breath in deep and letting it out slowly, using it to relax. Stephen moved his head as he exhaled and Danny felt his mouth on his nipple.

It took him a moment. But that was all it took for Stephen to slide his hand down onto Danny's stomach and throw his leg over Danny's thigh, squeezing his cock up against his hip.

"What are you doing?" Danny hissed.

Stephen ran his hand down over Danny's shorts. Danny's cock obligingly took the hint and became fully erect again. Stephen grasped it through the fabric.

"*Stephen*..." Danny prised his head off his nipple.

"Don't you like it?"

"What the fuck are you doing?"

"What does it feel like?" He was squeezing Danny's cock. His own felt scalding against Danny's side.

Danny could hear the breathlessness in his voice, as if he had no control of his own speech. "Stop it," he said.

"No." And Stephen climbed up him, up to his mouth. "No," he said again and pressed his mouth down on Danny's.

Danny let it go. He didn't even try to stop it. He put his arms around Stephen's body and kissed him back, then kissed him beyond that. They rolled into each other, bodies tightly twined together.

Stephen broke from his mouth, clinging to him, whispering fiercely, "I'll come, I'll come. Don't kiss me."

Danny dropped his head and kissed his neck, his shoulders. "Christ," he whispered, "you're beautiful."

Stephen heard it with an intense emotion, almost like pain. He knew he wasn't beautiful but he also knew Danny wasn't lying. "So are you," he whispered.

"Help me get these shorts off," Danny urged him.

Stephen realised he could hardly move his hands, his excitement was so intense. Suddenly places on his body that usually felt nothing were alive with sensation, while his hands and his mouth seemed numb with overkill.

He fumbled with Danny's shorts, pushing them down. Finally, they lay around one of his ankles where they stayed. Neither of them cared. Danny tried to kiss him again, but Stephen moved his head away.

"Let me," Danny urged.

"I'll come."

"Please." Danny sounded desperate.

Stephen felt it burst like a bubble inside him. He thrust his tongue into Danny's mouth. They locked together, both molten with feeling. It was Danny who broke away with a dull groan. "Christ, *I'm* going to come, never mind you. This is a big mistake."

"No it isn't. I want to do it. I want to."

"It stinks." Danny ran his hands up through his hair to grip his head. His hair felt straight and thick and silky. Wrong.

"No it doesn't. It feels right. It feels great."

"I want you," Danny heard himself say.

Stephen grabbed him and they kissed again, once more welded together, pressing into each other. Danny pulled his hand off when he tried to worm in whispering, "Don't touch me, just kiss me."

Stephen shivered, breaking away from him with something like his old fear, as if something wasn't right.

"Come on," Danny urged, pulling his head back. "This way I can feel your orgasm in my mouth. Put your tongue in my mouth. I love you, come on."

Stephen heard him say it. I love you.

I love you.

They wrapped their legs tight together, mouth to mouth, every inch of them pressed deep into the other. They kissed until they felt suffocated by it. They could both feel it, red-hot and hard, mouths devouring, hip bones grinding.

When it finally happened they clung together shuddering, heaving, both groaning with it, saturating each other, gluing their stomachs together with the flood. Their mouths flew apart like something breaking sparkling out of the water for air, both gasping, deep in their own white heat, one body heaving with the climax of two. They were in love with it.

They lay in a deep and incredible silence, only their own ragged breathing. Conley incredibly, inconceivably, asleep beside them.

"Never," Danny whispered, "have I felt anything like that."

"I love you," Stephen whispered back.

"Steve-o..." Danny sighed and brushed the hair off his face. "I'll be fucked if I didn't actually *want* that." And Stephen could hear the sound of wonder in it, as if Danny hadn't known it himself.

"I love you," Stephen said again.

They fell asleep still pressed together, their mingled semen trickling down between them in a slow, seeping betrayal.

SEVENTY

Conley woke up alone in the bed.

He lifted the alarm clock groggily and peered at it. 5:37.

God bless agriculture.

He turned on his back. He could hear water running in the bathroom. He knew he ought to put the light on but he couldn't be bothered.

He heard Stephen laughing. *Laughing at this hour of the morning.* He rubbed his face and lay looking up into the darkness. He had a sudden unpleasant premonition of wrongness. He shook his head at himself. Mysticism, and it wasn't even six yet, that was worse than laughter. He threw the quilt back and clicked on the light. *Up, might as well, everybody else is.*

He dressed slowly, listening to the murmur of their voices; their silences, which were worse; their quiet laughter, perhaps worst of all.

Danny liked the boy, that much was obvious. How many people did Danny actually *like?* Did he even like Conley? Had he ever?

Oh shut up.

He slammed the wardrobe door, intensely annoyed by his inability to shake the gloom off. He pulled the quilt off over the end of the bed to air, like the good German he was, then brushed the sheet down. That's when he saw it - a lovely clear stain on a lovely clean sheet, the only one on the bed and at a point midway between where they had lain.

Conley heard the bathroom door open. His first urge was to cover it over, then something stopped him, something hard and ugly and cold.

Danny came into the bedroom. He smiled widely. His hair was still damp. He looked too young and too old at once. His teeth seemed too white, his skin too smooth. Everything too fucking beautiful, Conley thought.

Danny looked at him and the smile faded. "What's wrong?"

"Somebody is a filthy fucking liar," Conley said in a voice that didn't belong, using words that didn't belong.

Danny's expression managed to look blank and cunning at the same time. Conley wondered how he'd never seen it before. Maybe Danny had never used it before. Maybe he'd never had to.

"The bed Danny. Look at the bed."

Danny didn't look at it, instead he said, "What were you doing, checking up on me?" And he was smiling faintly.

Conley felt a cold, dead pain in his gut. He said, "Phone for your taxi, then take your boyfriend and clear out. I never want to see you again. Do I make myself clear?"

"Perfectly."

"And I don't want to hear from you either. As from this minute you're dead."

Stephen came into the room, eyes wide, face pale. He'd heard the last two sentences, but even if he hadn't the tone was bad enough.

"Wait in the living room Steve," Danny said over his shoulder.

Stephen went out without a murmur.

Conley looked at the long red scratches on Danny's face. One eye was slightly darkened, as if he'd been wearing mascara and rubbed it.

"You're nothing but an animal. Standing there, marked like some kind of warring male fighting for the next mating, servicing your herd, only rutting with the males to prove your domination. There's too much hormone in you Danny. Too much

something."

Conley's voice had risen. He stood breathing heavily, looking at Danny's pale face, trying to regain his composure. It took him a minute to finally say, "Get out."

Danny went. He jerked his head at Stephen, white-faced and edgy, pretending he hadn't been listening, to get their jackets. They took them and left.

Conley didn't see them go. He heard the door slam like the door to a vault. He stood there for a moment then stripped his clothes off, dropping them where he stood. He climbed into the bed and pulled the quilt over his head.

He hugged himself tight into a ball and fell asleep almost instantly.

Danny tied his shoes on the stairs.

"What happened?" Stephen risked.

Danny shrugged and Stephen knew he was too angry to reply. "Danny..." he said, pulling his arm, but Danny tugged it away. "Don't bug me. Come on, let's find a taxi."

Stephen followed him down the stairs.

It was raining, a vindictive icy spit. It turned their hands blue and their faces red. They found a cab office, warm and smoky, and got a cab within ten minutes. Their driver looked three-quarter's asleep.

As the dawn came up they saw the snow was thawing. Ditches began to run with water. Great wide ribbons of it flowed across the road.

Stephen didn't speak to him again till they were nearly home. He had spent the journey separate from him, not daring to approach him. Now he moved closer, letting his knee lean against his. Danny kept looking out the window.

"What happened?" Stephen asked again.

Danny turned to him and said quietly, "All over the bed Steve-o."

Stephen looked at his face then at the back of the driver's head, then back at Danny again.

Danny smiled. "That's right," he said. "Someone came all over his nice clean sheets." His voice was hard and sarcastic. The driver must have heard him, but he didn't register anything.

Stephen took in the breath he'd been holding and let it out again.

Danny looked away again. No-one said anything else.

"Why this time?"

Danny was sitting on the bed. "I don't know. I got restless."

"Is that this week's euphemism for randy?"

There was no answer.

"Does he always scratch when he comes? A real hot bitch, is he?"

"It wasn't him. It was Stephen. We had an argument."

"What about? Who fucks who first?"

"No."

"Then what about?"

"I can't remember."

"Try."

"He overstepped the mark and I hit him."

"Overstepped what mark?"

"I can't remember."

"You fucking liar."

"Alright, I'm a fucking liar."

"About what?"

"Being a cock-tease."

John laughed. "So? Not so far from the truth, is it?"

Danny snapped, "Oh give it a fucking rest John."

John looked at his hard vicious face. Difficult to believe it was the same Danny. Maybe that was the point. Maybe it wasn't the same Danny. Maybe it wouldn't ever be the same Danny again. "If they could see you now," he said.

Danny continued to stare at him malevolently, the scratches livid on his white skin, the bruised eye somehow dangerous-looking.

"I'd like to hit you." John laughed sourly. "Gratified that I'm really itching to hit you?"

"Go ahead, fat-boy."

John made a noise as if something had jabbed his ribs. "Oh boy, you itch me, you really do."

Danny didn't answer this time.

"Cross because it's always worked before? Run away, John gets mad, gives you a spanking, cries big tears, climbs on, does it, hates himself and you get to forgive him. That's okay, I'm not going to be cruel about this, we can still make up. Suck my dick." John moved forward, pushing between his knees to stand before his face.

Danny yanked his head away, pushing back across the bed, but John caught his shoulder, grounding him like a rugby player. "Get it out and suck it before I break some part you need."

"Fuck off." Danny tried to claw free.

John caught his pierced ear and twisted. He could feel the heavy scab come off, gritty in his hand, and the fresh slip of blood beneath it. Danny cried out.

"Come on Danny-boy or I'll rip it right open. I'll fucking rip it right off."

Danny reached up and unzipped him. John kept a hold on his ear. He could feel Danny's pain like it was his own - he always did - a dull ache in the backs of his knees.

Danny took him in his mouth. John pushed his head onto it, watching it sink in. "Like being sucked by a fucking hyena. Eat my *dick* Danny." And he pushed himself in hard. "Show your true colours, uncover your teeth and *eat* me."

John suddenly let go his ear and grabbed his hair. " Don't you *dare* take me out your mouth. Who the fuck d'you think you are?"

John dragged his head back onto him again. "You lying, secretive little shit. Oh come on, *bite* it, bite it before I wring your scrawny neck. Think your scheming hurts me? Think I care? Think you can wean him away from me? Think again, you stupid little cunt. Bite it. Come on, *bite* it, you chickenshit little whore. Prove you can hurt me."

John was humping his hips relentlessly into his face, making Danny's jaws ache.

"I said, *bite it*. Why don't you really bite it? Go on, bite it. Let's see you hurt me. *Bite it.*" John suddenly yanked Danny's head back and slapped him. Danny felt it like the falls in dreams where the ground disappears beneath you - a black plunge into nothingness. "*Bite* it, fuck you!" And he slammed Danny's head onto himself with a force that felt as if he had been punched in the face

Danny's teeth came down on his penis like a pit bull's into prey.

John jerked, coming violently, boiling and salty into his mouth.

Danny gagged and tore himself out of John's still jerking grasp. He coughed, semen coming down his nose, then doubled up and threw-up violently on the floor.

.

John found Stephen where he was supposed to find him. Alone, as he was supposed to be.

He felt bruised and swollen when he moved. It was partly the savagery of the bite, but more because of the way he'd come, deep and wracking, as if it was trying to pull his balls inside out. He felt slack and heavy, as if he were still half-erect. He felt randy,

mean, vicious.

He watched Stephen for a while until the boy got too nervous and stopped. John could see him working up the courage to face him. He smiled.

Something wrong?" Stephen asked, and it didn't come out much the way he would have liked it.

John shook his head. "No, carry on. I like watching you work."

That made Stephen feel worse.

John watched him some more, giving him time, then he asked him, "You enjoy being sucked off by Rab?"

Stephen stopped, feeling the blood rush to his cheeks.

He turned to him, an urgent denial in his mouth, but John held up his hand. "No, don't. Your mummy went hours ago, no need to lie. Just you and I and a couple of sick animals. Did you enjoy it?"

Stephen shook his head.

"Liked Danny better, eh?"

Stephen looked at him, face ashen.

"Oh yes, he told me."

Stephen stood there feeling it crawl all over him. *Oh yes, he told me*.

John moved closer to him. Too close to him, touching close. Stephen looked at a spot somewhere over his heart, horribly aware of the sheer bulk of him.

"Shall I tell you something secret?"

Stephen couldn't even shake his head.

"Something so black and secret it's like tar, sticking to everything it touches…" And John's hand came up and lifted Stephen's head, holding his chin, the fingers callused and dry, so light, so deft, like iron. Stephen looked into his eyes and saw that they were green, just like Danny's, saw something in them just like Danny.

"At night my tongue goes places it's not supposed to. Want to know where my tongue's been tonight?" His voice was low, almost a rumble, and suddenly he bent forward and pushed his tongue inside Stephen's ear. Stephen tried to jerk away, but he never budged an inch. John was holding him fast in his huge hands. "So far up my little brother he thought it was my prick." The words were a whispered hiss, his lips burning hot and wet against Stephen's ear. "So far up him I tasted his shit." John's body held a faint tremble as if he was wildly excited, barely repressing it. "He squirmed on it to get it up further, took my hand and stuck two fingers up, three, then started begging me, 'Fuck my hole. Oh please, *please* John, fuck my hole.' Every night while you lie dreaming about him he's eight feet away crouched over me, grinding his arse in my face demanding, 'Fuck my *hole*.'"

Stephen felt that John was holding him up, that if he let go of him he'd fall over flat in the muck. He really felt as if all his insides had ripped out and sunk down to his feet. His head was a bubble of dumb pain. An idiot. A stupid idiot. A dumb fucking idiot. *Oh Danny*.

John's hand tightened on his face. "You've got the mouth, the hair, but you're too seamless, a plaster-cast. Pain's carved him into something unique, burnt it into his eyes. Want to feel what he's like inside?"

Stephen stared at him, no idea what he was talking about, terrified of the dull, smiling glitter of his face. John was the animal. Conley was wrong about that, this was the animal here.

Stephen shook his head, bringing his hand up to John's, but he couldn't move it, just held it hopelessly.

"Want to kiss me and feel what he's really like?"

"No." Stephen squeaked it out, amazed that he could voice it at all.

John laughed, light, breathy, as if he was tickled pink by the idea. "Too bad." And

he pulled Stephen's face round to his, the other arm going round him in a huge suffocating grip. Not an embrace, a clamp, pinning him tight.

John's mouth was hot, incredibly sweet. It felt as if it was crammed with teeth. It was like drowning, like when someone pulled your legs under you at the swimming pool. The utter inability to do anything. The feeling of death tearing through you.

He went limp, gave up the struggle. John pulled him to him with both hands. His kiss became gentler, more searching, and it was then Stephen felt it. Oh Jesus, it *was* like Danny.

Stephen pressed up against him, weakly clinging to his jacket. He dug his fingers into the oily fabric and began to kiss him back.

John slid a hand down and pressed the boy's hips up into his, lifting him up against him.

Stephen groaned, clung to him, heady with it. None of Danny's reluctance here. No desperate guilt at the back of your mind saying, He wouldn't be doing this if you hadn't tricked him.

John reached in between them. He unzipped the boy's jeans and slid his hand in.

Stephen felt it, huge and rough on him, covering most of his dick in one grasp. He did something odd with his thumb, moving the shaft while sliding it over his knob at the same time. It felt wonderful. Stephen wanted him to go on doing it forever, the trick with his thumb, dry and hard, rubbing the head of his cock. It's because his hand's so big, he thought dizzily.

John suddenly stopped kissing him, whispered in his ear, "Feel me."

Stephen felt goosepimples go down his back.

John unzipped his jacket, still rubbing his cockhead and squeezing his shaft at the same time. "There." He pulled the two sides apart. "Go on, feel."

Stephen, cheeks burning, moved his hand down hesitantly. At first he didn't realise what it was. Through the fabric it felt like a torch, a blunt-headed mallet, *something*, but not *that*. Stephen felt the unbelievable dirty joke proportions of it. His heart was hurting his chest.

John laughed quietly, bent and nuzzled his mouth gently, then said against his lips, "It's real, don't worry. Go on, open it up and see for yourself."

Stephen pulled the zip down with difficulty and reached inside.

Oh Jesus.

"Look at it, go on."

Stephen dropped his head, letting it lean against John's chest and looked down between the shadowed dark of their bodies, then pulled it out.

John let Stephen's cock go and held his shoulders with one hand, pressing his bent head into his chest with the other. He ran his fingers through his hair. "Wank me," he said, catching a handful of the silky-fine hair. "Wank me off, then I'll give you something you'll never forget."

Stephen didn't know if he could. His hand seemed much too small to give him any pleasure. He wrapped it round him, feeling the thick veins, the steel-hard core of it underneath. The eye was widely distended with the size of his erection. Stephen tried to slide his foreskin up.

"Both hands," John urged. "Use both hands."

It was slow and awkward but John groaned, thrust his hips into his hands. "Like a girl," Stephen heard him say above him. "Like being wanked by a girl." And his hands went through Stephen's hair again, running the heavy silk of it between his fingers.

"Your hair's beautiful." And Stephen felt him bend to kiss it. "You can do it harder, don't be scared." But Stephen could see two nasty swollen lumps on either side of his cock, one of them flaky with dried blood. It looked like he'd caught it in something.

"Harder you little cunt..."

Stephen could feel an odd tension in him, growing with his excitement, but he was afraid to be any rougher with him, afraid of those raw marks, his anger.

Suddenly John's hand came down over his. "Do I have to do it myself? Look, like this." And he took hold of his own cock, trapping Stephen's hand underneath, making him do it with him, and began frigging it up and down so hard it looked mechanical.

He pressed Stephen's head harder against him. "Watch now... here it comes." And he rubbed it frenziedly, his hips thrust forwards, obscenely pulling himself up towards Stephen.

Stephen felt his own cock twitch and jerk then John started to swear, his hand clamped down on the back of Stephen's neck as it started to come out, odd translucent streamers of it ribboning in the air between them like threads.

John's hand never slowed, he just went on pulling it out in that odd mechanical way, as if he was climaxing without feeling it, crushing his head to him. Finally he slowed, peeled his foreskin right down and said, "Good?"

Stephen nodded, no idea if it had been.

"Touch it," and John let it go. It still stood there, grossly engorged, shiny, a drip hanging off the end like spit hanging from the cattle's mouths.

Stephen touched the shaft, feeling the heat of it.

"The head." John's hands began kneading his shoulders. "Feel the head."

Stephen wasn't sure he wanted to. It was covered in come, slimy, still oozing. He'd never touched anyone else's before. Not deliberately.

"Get your hands dirty, come on."

Stephen touched it, felt it slippy and oddly cool on him. It felt shivery, like sticking your fingers in a pot of Vaseline. He rubbed it over the head, between his finger and thumb.

"You're a natural," John whispered.

Suddenly John caught him round the waist and lifted him up, clean off the ground, as if he were a child. He plonked him down on the top bar of the pen gate as if he weighed nothing. Stephen gave a little grunt of shock. John's cock had slid out of his hand. He could still see it down there as he clung shakily to the bar, standing out red and sticky beneath him. He met John's eyes for the first time and flushed a deep embarrassing pink, but John was smiling at him. "Now it's your turn."

He pushed Stephen's legs apart, pushing the pen gate back against the wall. Stephen clung on, almost overbalancing. He bumped against the wall as it made contact, hooking his feet around the bar to stop himself falling forward. John moved between his legs. He spread his arms and put his hands on the bar that held Stephen's feet then bent his head.

Stephen realised what he was going to do. He didn't wait to be asked. He slid his own hand in quickly and pulled his penis out. He tilted himself back on his perch, thrusting his hips out towards him like an offering. He looked down, not at the strong ugly face, but at the mouth, John's incredible hungry mouth, and saw him smile. He thought about his tongue, watched his mouth fervently, itching to see it.

He watched John take hold of him, making it look tiny, like a toy cock, but it didn't matter. John kissed it. Rab hadn't done that. He'd just taken it right into his mouth, deep and quick, as if he was scared he was going to change his mind. John kissed it then peeled it back and licked it. His tongue looked huge and pink.

Stephen shivered, pushing up, clinging harder to the bar. The gate bumped gently.

John sucked him in slowly, so slowly it felt like he was being sucked down a drain. Too much of him disappeared inside. Stephen closed his eyes. He couldn't bear to watch it. Then John began to do things with his tongue, things as torturously delicious as the trick with his thumb on his knob.

Stephen moaned, bit his lip. He wanted to push up and couldn't. He was already

balanced as far out as he could be, his muscles trembling with effort. He couldn't move, take control. He had to wait for John to do it. He couldn't help himself, could do nothing to speed it up or slow it down.

John began to move his head on him, up and down. Stephen watched it, brown, curly, moving between his thighs. He reached forward shakily and touched it. John seemed to open his mouth wider and take him further in, too far in, like he was swallowing him. Stephen could feel something pressing on the head of his cock, like gentle fingers. He gasped, fingers flexing convulsively in John's hair, pulling him into his lap. He had to speak, let it out. "Oh..." he whimpered.

Something strange was definitely happening inside John's mouth. Stephen could feel his teeth far too close to the root of him. He was filled with an exhilarating terror. He was being *eaten*. "Please... no..." he whispered, running his hands through his hair, over and over again like some kind of coaxing plea, encouragement. It felt just like Danny's. With your eyes shut it felt just like Danny's. But Stephen had his eyes open. He knew whose head it was.

"John..." he whispered and felt it immediately, irrevocably, begin to happen. He slipped on the bar, caught at John's head. But it didn't matter. John held him, John had him, safe in his mouth.

And he kept him there - till he was utterly spent.

John lifted him down just as he'd put him up, without effort.

John closed his clothes.

John didn't need to dry him up, but he did kiss his mouth, revolting and exciting him at once. "You'll never ever taste that sweet again," he said, and Stephen watched him, not sure what he meant, as he pushed himself, long and thick and used-looking, back inside his clothes.

Then John left him.

Stephen stood there and realised what he had just done. It was sinking in slowly, like waking and remembering a dream. But he could *feel* what he had done, and it felt like a wall had fallen on him. A stone wall. His legs felt weak, his arms were trembling. He felt bruised and achy.

He sat down heavily on a pile of feed bags, massaged his thighs. He felt bloodless, drained. It had been so intense he felt stupid with it.

He felt terrible.

Guilty and ashamed and terrible.

He didn't even understand why, except John was the common enemy, and he'd taken part actively. He'd actually... but he couldn't quite bring himself to voice it.

Gay-boy.

Stephen dropped back flat on the sacks and let the tears run down his face until they dripped into his ears. When they did that he rolled his face into the cold plastic and lay there.

Waiting to die.

John was waiting for Danny when he came out of the shower. "Into your Daddy's room."

Danny side-stepped him, but John stepped with him saying, "I don't think so."

"Fuck off John, you've had your pound of flesh."

John put a hand flat on his chest. "Nothing like it."

Danny pushed his hand off. "I said, fuck off."

"Get in." John grabbed his shoulder.

Danny slapped at him but John was ready for it, grabbing his hair and dragging him through the door.

Ian stood up as they came in. John shut the door and locked it. Danny looked at Ian, but Ian wouldn't meet his eyes.

John leaned against the door and said, "There you are Ian, hasn't been touched by anyone for at least twelve hours. Purest you'll ever get him. Other than those nasty cat scratches he looks quite attractive, doesn't he?"

Ian did not look at him.

"I asked you a question."

"Yes."

"And how would you know, when you haven't even looked at him?"

Ian turned, his thin mouth thinner than ever. "Because he always does." And finally he looked at Danny, eyes travelling up over his chest onto his face.

Danny continued to stare at him expressionlessly. It was impossible to tell what he was thinking.

"Well, what have you got planned for him?"

Suddenly Danny spoke. "How did he get you into this?"

Ian looked at the sink in the corner.

John laughed. "The pretty child asked you a question."

"He said he knew about the old man." Ian glanced at him quickly, then away again.

Danny said, "You didn't tell him?" He heard John laugh behind him.

Ian shook his head. Danny searched his face for a moment then spoke to John without turning. "What's this for John? Why don't you just spit it out?"

"I want to know the truth."

Danny gave a small laugh. "Forgive my cynicism, but about what?"

"The old man. "

Danny turned abruptly to face him. "I think you could probably tell us."

John licked his lip, glanced at Ian.

Ian responded by moving over to stand by Danny, almost as if he was trying to avoid his gaze. They stood almost side by side, facing each other, like flamenco dancers.

John said in a low voice, "Christ, do you two have a secret handshake?"

Neither of them answered. They stood there unmoving, still in their strange position. John straightened up off the door and began circling them, looking at each of their faces intently. Ian wouldn't meet his eyes, but Danny held his gaze.

"You're a real little hard-nut Danny, aren't you?"

Danny said nothing.

John undid the towel at his waist and took it off. Danny didn't stop him. He didn't move. Ian flicked his eyes over his body then looked away again.

"He wants you," John said.

Danny didn't say anything.

"Can't you feel his heat from there?"

Danny still didn't say anything.

"Tell him Ian, tell him how *bad* you want him."

Ian pressed his lips together. He didn't speak.

John laughed, running one finger down Danny's belly. "He's shy." He ran his finger back up again. "Is this how you paid him? Like this?" And John trailed his finger down again, this time all the way down to his cock.

Danny kept watching his eyes.

"Well? Did you pay for your big brother's lying and conniving with this?" John wrapped his hand around his cock then said, "Come on Danny, you want to keep it dangling there, don't you?"

Ian looked at Danny quickly.

John intercepted the look. "Oh-oh, he doesn't trust you Danny. He thinks you're going to betray him." He laughed. "You don't stand a chance, supposing you fuck him five times a day."

"Why don't you shut the fuck up, you conceited shit?"

Ian closed his eyes, whispered, "*Danny...*"

John laughed again, eyes black as pitch. "That's my boy, always gives me a good excuse."

John slapped him. The scratches on his cheek looked dark and purplish in the mark it left.

Ian came between them. "Leave him be."

"Well now, look at this. Here's the same boy who normally cheers me on. This *is* a surprise." John stopped smiling. "Maybe he's trying to prove something to you Danny Maybe I even put him up to it."

John saw that they'd moved closer still. He stared at them for a moment then said, "The old man - whose idea was it? Yours Danny? Or was the cord of complicity still too tight? Did your big brother think it up for you?"

"Drop it John," Ian said, the words sounding hard and separate.

"Listen to him." John grabbed Danny's face. "No wonder he hates you as much as he loves you. No wonder he doesn't know whether he wants to cut you up or save you in cotton-wool. You've turned him into a fucking lap dog, you devious little shit."

"I said, leave him alone." Ian came between them with a cold definite click.

John looked down at the knife, spoke to it. "You killed the old man for him, didn't you?"

Ian didn't answer him.

"You really scared him Ian. He doesn't know you like I know you baby."

"Shut *up* John." Ian's voice was fraught. They could all hear it.

"Why Ian? What the fuck are you going to do? Cut my throat?"

"If you want." Ian's hand was trembling.

John laughed. "You mean if *he* wants. Am I supposed to believe that?"

Ian didn't answer again. It spoke louder than any words could.

All three stood silent, the knife holding court. Finally John said, "Okay" and he backed off.

He wiped his mouth and said it again. "Okay," then he walked to the door, unlocked it, and went out.

Danny sat down on the bed.

Ian closed the knife and looked down at him. "I never told him anything, I promise."

Danny didn't answer. After a moment or two Ian crossed to the door and locked it. He came back and said, "He's just trying to wind you up. I'd never tell him anything. You know I wouldn't."

Danny dropped back on the bed, feet still on the floor and stretched out, hands behind his head and said, "Remember you used to tell me stories?"

Ian nodded, not as startled as he should have been by the non sequitur.

"I can still remember them."

"Can I suck you off?" Ian said and got down on the floor between his knees.

"There's one I really remember, sticks in my head."

Ian put a hand on the fat curve between his legs.

"It was about this snow prince, lived in the snow forest and this guy, some king, comes along and sneaks in at night and starts shafting him, the whole rape bit, but just as he gets there his servant whacks his cock off, but it's still up there, poking

away, bleeding at one end, come spunking out at the other, until he pulls it out and it lies there writhing on the bed, like a snake. Christ, you've warped me…"

Danny settled his hands more comfortably under his head and looked at the unfamiliar ceiling. He cleared his throat. "He had hair the colour of vixen's blood, eyes as green as sea-stones and skin as cream as…" Danny hesitated.

Ian lifted his head. "Damask."

Danny nodded and said, "Damask. Every day this pansy cunt would ride through the forest on his black horse, dressed from head to foot in black velvet except for golden shoes and a single golden earring." He laughed softly. "Now is that a weird coincidence or what?"

There was a stretching silence. It was marked by the small sounds Ian made filling his mouth.

When it was done Danny cleared his throat again and said, "Anywhere close?"

Ian lifted his head. "Close enough." His hand slid up and down wetly on Danny's swollen cock.

"I never could tell them like you did."

"You never believed in them like I did."

Danny pushed his head down gently and said, "Keep going."

Ian took him in his mouth again. They were silent then Danny said, "You never gave yourself much reward in any of them."

But Ian didn't answer him.

"You must have wanted more sometimes. It's bad to always want the least."

"Not when you've never had it." Ian went back to him.

"I'll come thinking about someone else. I always do."

Ian went on fellating him, never pausing.

Danny said flatly, "I just can't get there without him. I'm sorry."

Ian closed his eyes and ran his hands up Danny's belly, stroking him.

"Truly I am," Danny said. "Believe me, I would if I could." It was almost as if he was talking to himself when he said abruptly, his tone completely changed, "It's the same with everyone you know, not just you."

He was silent for a long time, then he began gently stroking Ian's hair before he said, "Here I am, the prince, taking head from my faithful servant." And unexpectedly it was Stephen he saw sliding down his body, smeared in the filthy gore that was still pulsing from the evil king's dick, lying there severed beside them.

"He's sucking me so beautifully," he whispered, seeing Stephen's head between his thighs, lips sliding over his penis as his own hand fumbled blindly on the bed for the severed organ.

"He's tonguing my knob." His hand brushed against it. He felt his excitement pick up out of nowhere.

"He's drawing me in." He grasped the cock, felt the blood pulse out between his fingers. The thing was monstrous, huge, stupidly familiar, but he was too far gone to care.

"He's spreading…" he said, betraying himself, but it didn't matter, he was already lost in it, hovering on the brink. He saw himself spread Stephen's arse, saw himself thrust the severed prick up inside him, felt himself ejaculate with force. He slammed his hands down on the bed, grabbing the counterpane as if to root himself there and cried out, "*Shit!*"

That was as bad as it got.

But it was bad enough.

John could feel years of frustration and guilt pounding at his head. Danny and Ian,

full of secret whisperings, vices, a private world. Nothing they were ever going to share, either of them. They knew everything that the rest of them could only guess at. All the secret faces, masks off, everything that ever happened in the dark corners of the house.

John smiled sourly at the ceiling. Where was everybody tonight? Where was the beautiful little dumbfuck Stephen? A mouthful of that would do to numb the pain.

He pinched the back of his hand savagely, bruising the skin. The only thing that could numb his pain was locked away in his father's room, deep in the mouth of his only brother.

He pulled his sweater off and unfastened his shirt. He looked down at his belly without seeing it then dug his nails into his flesh. He watched the marks appear as he released the skin.

I'll bet there are things even you don't know Ian. I'll bet there are things none of us knows. He's carrying another man's pain, another man's dirty crummy little soul. That's what eats away at him. He's been given another man's weaknesses to carry.

He undid his trousers and pushed his shorts down. The pain had brought him up hard but now he was there he didn't know what to do with it.

He took a darning needle from the tartan pincushion that still hung on the wall beside his mother's chair. He felt the point of it then experimentally ran it up the length of his penis. He thought about Ian and Danny lying on his father's bed. He thought about the hayloft at Jerrett's Farm and could feel it, his dick, huge, hot, sweating, alive with poisonous pleasure.

He ran the needle gently over the head of his penis and whispered, "You shit..."

He took the needle and pressed the point into the head. His cock jerked. "You dirty shit..." he whispered.

He shook his head then pushed the needle in. His mouth dropped open. He remembered the dust, the smell of the loft, his mouth. His tiny, sweet mouth...

He pushed the needle in again, harder this time. He left it sticking out the top of his penis like a pin and started pulling on the shaft of his cock.

"Not my fault," he whispered, his movements growing more rapid. "Not my fault."

Suddenly he caught the needle between the fingers of his other hand, bent it back then pushed it forward. It went through the head of his penis, trapping a half-inch of flesh like a giant stitch. He grunted, the hand working furiously on his shaft, his other hand still relentlessly pushing the needle through. He closed his eyes to the pain.

There was blood now. He could feel it. He looked down and saw the eye of the needle grow close to his flesh. He was grunting, the masturbating hand working furiously. Sweat stood out on his brow. He pushed the needle through, felt the eye rip his skin open. He cried out, jerking forward in his seat. The needle fell to the floor. White fluid streaked with blood surged over the tops of his fingers.

He fell back in the chair and covered his penis with his hands.

Stephen and Rab had gone out in the Rover.

Rab had found him sitting in the living room looking tense and unhappy. When he'd asked him what was wrong he'd said, Nothing, then promptly burst into tears. After that he could get nothing coherent out of him, so he'd offered to take him out for a drive, get him out the house.

They drove down to the coast and sat there listening to the wind and the rain. Rab had offered to put the radio on but Stephen had said no.

Rab felt as if his skin was alive with tiny needles. He felt too aware of the boy beside him, and the setting was too familiar, with too many connotations. He felt tense and wished he'd taken him somewhere else. I'm not getting enough, he thought to

himself. I feel like a tom cat.

"Know something?" Stephen's voice broke into his thoughts.

"What?"

"Two things I never did before I came here."

"Mm?" Rab said, but he wasn't sure if he wanted to know.

"Crying. All I ever seem to do these days is cry. Everything makes me fucking cry. I'm sick of it."

"Maybe you bottled up too long."

"Is that what the other is too?" And Stephen's voice sounded hard and too old.

"You haven't told me what it is yet."

"Guess."

Rab looked at his profile turned towards the window and said, "No, you tell me."

"I never even so much as *thought* about another bloke let alone touched one."

Rab was silent a second then said, "And now?"

"I'm at it all over the place. First you, then..."

But Stephen didn't say anything else and Rab glanced at him quickly and saw him brush his eyes.

"And now I'm fucking crying again."

"Then who?" Rab prompted. "Danny?"

Stephen nodded. Rab needed to be sure. He had no idea why, but he needed to be sure. "We're not talking about the time you went upstairs with him? This is since?"

"Yes."

"When?"

"Last night."

"At *Conley's?*" Rab couldn't keep the disbelief out his voice.

"In his flickin' bed, with him in it," Stephen said, and Rab thought he heard a certain satisfaction in it.

"The three of you?"

"No." Stephen was emphatic. "Nothing like that." And the implication was that that was too sick even to contemplate. "He was asleep."

Rab took a deep breath and said, "That sounds like Danny." And he couldn't say anything else without thumping the little bastard.

"That's not all," Stephen said in a quiet voice.

Rab looked at him again. "Well? Go on."

"I can't."

"Don't be fucking stupid, you've got this fucking far." *Tell us everything, you smug little bastard. Brag about your successes.*

"I did it with John."

"*John?*" And this time Rab turned in his seat. "But John doesn't... John isn't..." He stopped and said instead, "I don't believe you. When? How?"

"In the shed, this afternoon. He said he'd show me what Danny was really like. I still don't know what he meant."

Rab could see him press his hands to his face and knew he was trying to cool his cheeks. "Did you do it deliberately?" he asked, but Stephen didn't seem to understand the question.

"What?"

"Did *you* want it?"

"Not at first."

"Not at first?" They seemed almost to be talking at cross-purposes.

"I didn't want to do it but..."

"But?"

Stephen covered his eyes with his hands. "I got excited and before I knew where

I was I was doing it with him."

"Jesus," Rab said.

"Don't," Stephen said and his voice had the tremor of tears in it all over again.

"You know why he's done this, don't you?"

Stephen shook his head.

"Because now he can ruin you with Danny. Danny's got this peculiar characteristic. He expects people to be faithful to him while he sticks it where he likes."

"There's something worse," Stephen said.

"What could *possibly* be worse?"

"Him and Danny."

"What d'you mean, him and Danny?"

"They're doing it."

"Doing...?" Rab was silent for a moment, struck dumb, then he laughed. Slowly at first, then more seriously, as if the humour of it was growing on him.

Stephen looked at him as if he'd gone off his head. "What's so funny?"

"You," Rab laughed. "You stupid shit."

"What d'you mean?"

"It was there under your nose all the time only you were too fucking blind to see it." He laughed some more.

"You knew," Stephen said.

"Of course I fucking knew. Grow up."

"Why didn't you tell me? You could have told me. How could Danny *do* that?"

"Oh don't be so bloody stupid. Danny isn't what you seem to think he is. He's a rabid little animal."

"Don't call him that. You're not so flickin' fussy yourself."

"You make me sick," Rab said and looked out the window as if he was disgusted by him.

"Why? Because I like him? Are you the only person who's allowed to like him? Think you own him or something?"

"Listen to what's talking." Rab turned on him. "You all but piss on his leg when you're with him."

"Shut up."

"If you can't take it, don't dish it out."

"Oh fuck," Stephen said, turning suddenly, face into the seat, and he could feel the tears sliding out again.

Rab knew he was crying but had no comfort to offer him. He felt like crying himself.

After a while he heard Stephen ferreting around and then blow his nose, loud and clearingly, then he asked, "Why does Danny do it? With John, I mean."

"I haven't a clue."

"I don't think he even likes him."

"I'm sure he doesn't."

"Then why?"

Rab looked at him suddenly and said, "You've done it with John, what do *you* think?"

Stephen stared at him a moment, but before he could reply Rab said, "I've done it too, and I can tell you why Danny does it."

"You?"

"Don't look so surprised."

"Oh God," Stephen said.

"I'm only a cousin, remember."

"Oh God," Stephen said again.

Rab laughed and said, "Well? What was it like? Was he good?"

Stephen shook his head, looking at his hands.

"Liar. Bet you felt as if your dick was coming off, like he was dragging your guts out."

Stephen didn't reply.

"I knew it," Rab said, and that was all.

After a moment Stephen said, "I've never felt anything like it."

Rab laughed shortly. "I'll bet."

"Not even with Danny."

"Better?" Rab asked, looking at him curiously.

Stephen hesitated. "No, not better, but it was stronger, much stronger."

"Left you legless."

"Yes," Stephen nodded as if it described it perfectly.

Rab looked at him then said in a low voice, "Would you do it again, if you got the chance?"

Stephen said nothing.

"So would I," Rab said.

Stephen looked at him sharply.

"All he's got to do is start eating you with that mouth of his and it's as if you haven't got a bone of resistance in you. I still can't say no to him."

Stephen nodded without knowing he was doing it then frowned and said, "What did he mean about feeling what Danny was really like?"

"Who knows?"

"I thought maybe it was because he was like Danny, in a weird way, but I don't think I really understood now. I don't think he really meant that."

Rab didn't answer him, instead he said, "He'll tell Danny, you know."

"But why?"

"I told you, he can't stand competition, so you better have a good story ready because, believe me, Danny'll take a whole lot of convincing. You haven't seen anything till you've seen someone mess with his brother."

Stephen had an instant of sheer knowledge. They come to us all in crystal moments too few to be useful. "Is that why you fell out?"

Rab laughed. "Something like that."

"You were fucking him… until John told him he'd fucked you too."

"On the nail."

"Oh God," Stephen said. "Who hasn't he fucked?"

"John or Danny?"

"Danny."

"I can't think of anyone off-hand."

Stephen looked at him. "You're not being serious?"

"I'm not joking either."

"Ian?"

"Ask him."

"Are you saying yes?"

"I'm saying ask him."

And Stephen knew he was saying yes. They'd all shared him - both his brothers, his cousin, and now him - they'd all had him. John was still having him and Rab and Ian still wanted him, just like Stephen did.

"Oh God," he said again and it sounded very inadequate indeed.

Danny got up and picked up the towel. Ian tried to kiss him but Danny pushed him away saying, "Enough" in that familiar irritated voice. Ian knew that was it for tonight.

He was going to go running back to big bro. He didn't have any fucking dignity at all.

"Back to the status quo?"

"We never left it."

"You crawling little suck. You're pathetic."

Danny nodded absently and pushed past him. Ian got up and followed him to the door. He watched the long white body go the few yards to their room, then disappear inside. He heard the door lock.

He went along the hall and pressed his mouth to the door. "Little suck," he whispered, knowing Danny could hear him. "I hate you, you sycophantic little suck," he whispered again.

Danny stood on the other side, dressing slowly, listening to his voice.

He was smiling.

He looked quite beautiful.

Danny found John in the living room. His clothes were unfastened, his trousers pulled down to expose his genitals.

There was no needle. John had picked it up, inserted it back in the wound and drawn it through again, savouring the intensity of his own distress, bereft this time of pleasure. Afterwards he had thrown it in the fire.

Danny looked down at him. His hands were cupping his genitals. "Have a good time?"

John looked up. "Great."

Danny sat down on the settee. "Shouldn't you put it away now?"

"Does it bother you?"

"No, but you never know who might wander in John-boy."

"It'll give them a thrill." John took a handful of his flaccid cock and slid it up and down in the stained wet of his palm. "I'm not quite dry," he said.

"You *could* use a hankie."

John shook his head. "Spoils it. I like the tight feeling of it drying on my skin." He looked up at him. "Did *you* have a nice time?"

"No."

"I wish I could believe you."

"You can."

Suddenly John said, "Where did you go?" as if they were in the middle of another conversation entirely.

"Christ John, don't you *ever* stop?"

"Tell me."

"No."

"Why not?"

"I don't want to fucking talk about it, that's why not."

"He's *dead*. What difference can it make now?"

"No."

John punched the arm of his chair.

Danny said nothing.

After a moment John said, "I wonder why you? He never touched the rest of them, why you?"

Danny's mouth was a closed and definite line.

"Just because you were so fucking beautiful? He tried it on with Rab once, did you know that?"

Danny looked at him sharply.

John smiled. "I didn't think you did."

762

Danny was staring at him.

"What does that look say Danny? You jealous that he wanted someone else?"

"I don't believe you."

"Ask him."

"Shithead," Danny said. "Fucking dirty shithead."

"Who?"

But Danny wouldn't say.

John got up and came over beside him and sat down. "Close your eyes."

Danny did it.

"Now lick my fingers."

Danny took his hand and lay back, running the tip of his tongue up each finger, then between them, and finally the palm. If he noticed anything odd about the taste he didn't say.

When it was done Danny turned his head and looked at him through half-closed eyes.

John slid his hand over the crotch of Danny's jeans and felt him. "Why does that turn you on?"

Danny shrugged. "I don't know, the taste maybe."

John moved away abruptly, sitting forward, arms dangling between his legs. "Think you could ever love me Danny? Think if we got out of here, away from this place, you could love me?"

"Oh, come on."

John turned to him. "That means no, right?"

Danny sighed ill-temperedly.

"Why don't you just come out and fucking say it? Don't be such a coward, just come right out and say it. No. Go on, say it."

Danny looked at him, eyes black. "No. Not ever. Not in a million years. Happy?"

John blinked, then nodded and said, "Okay." He took a deep breath then said quietly, "Wonder why I still love you? I wonder why it won't just shrivel up and die?"

But nobody answered him.

He leaned back beside Danny, shoulders touching. Danny reached up and touched his face gently. "Don't cry."

"Why not?"

Danny sat forward and turned to see his face better. Whatever he saw there made him kneel up on the sofa and sit astride his lap. John looked up at him, eyes bright.

Danny bent his head and kissed his mouth, holding his face between his hands.

"It won't work," John said. His face felt numb, frozen. He couldn't have kissed him back if he'd wanted to.

Danny brushed his cheeks with his thumbs. John reached forward and held his hips, curving his hands round his buttocks. Danny moved forward, pressing his knees into the back of the sofa. He whispered his name. John looked at him, trying to guess what he was thinking, what he was feeling, and he could tell nothing, nothing at all.

"Tell me what you feel Danny. Tell me what you're feeling right now."

"Like I'd like to fuck my way right inside your skin."

John closed his eyes as if the words hurt him. "Why? Just because it's something to do? Because you think it'll shut me up?"

Danny shook his head. "Because this distance..." and he held up two fingers the barest millimetre apart, "is still way too far away."

John pulled him to him hard, burying his face in Danny's belly, whispering, "I *want* to believe you."

Danny stroked his hair, hushed him.

They stayed like that, locked tight together, until Danny whispered, pressing his

head, "Let me in."

John looked at him for a long moment, as if he was trying to read the truth on his face, then he dropped his eyes and pushed Danny off. Danny watched him pull his clothes off then lie face down on the rug in front of the fire.

Danny didn't strip. He climbed over him, unzipped and went inside him with no preparation at all. John was aware of just how easy he was to breach. It didn't even embarrass him any more. He was beyond that.

Danny stayed there for a long time, moving restlessly, deeper and deeper, until it felt as if that millimetre wasn't there any more. They lay there like that, still, John suffering gladly under his weight till Danny suddenly twitched and said, "Oh fuck, I'm going to…"

And it was over.

And the distance was back again.

"I don't think I can face him again."

"You mean you're frightened you won't be able to say no if he tries it on again."

Stephen's mouth was tight. "I mean what I said."

Rab felt suddenly ratty. "Well leave then."

"You'd like that, wouldn't you? You're rotten with jealousy because you know he prefers me."

"You conceited little shit."

"He's fucking me, he isn't fucking you."

"No Steve-o, he's *fucked* you. Don't count your Dannys till they're in your bed. He's got a life history of once-ofs, believe me."

"You're jealous," Stephen repeated triumphantly.

"You're asking for a smack in the mouth."

Stephen laughed but he didn't say anything else.

Rab sat fuming, wondering if he should hit him anyway and the hell with it, wondering how he could convince him to get in the back seat and jerk him off.

There was a tense tingling silence then Rab felt Stephen's hand on his leg. Not shy, it rested there briefly then was right up onto his crotch. "Want to?" he asked.

Rab could feel it in his throat, the word yes dying to get out. But he didn't need to say it, Stephen's exploring fingers read the truth even under the castrating jeans. "Do you wear them like that to hide your hard-ons?" he asked, and Rab could hear the sly little grin in it. He didn't answer him.

Stephen's hand went on, travelling up his zip then finally, boldly, breaching it. It was on the tip of Rab's tongue to say, Faithful type, aren't you? But he knew if he did he'd fuck his chances. He could always say it afterwards.

He felt a growing excitement as Stephen's fingers took hold of him, began to feel him feverishly. He'd had Danny then John and look at him, still hungry. Which could mean only one of two things. One: he was turning out to be another Danny, or two: that whatever Danny had done with him hadn't really satisfied him, and that's why he'd been so easily snared by John. Danny had used him, that was Rab's bet. It wasn't sex that Stephen was looking for, it was reassurance. Stephen broke into his thoughts. "Let's go in the back."

Rab said, "Go on then."

Stephen clambered over, Rab following, holding his jeans up.

As soon as they were in Stephen practically clambered onto his lap.

Rab said, "What d'you want me to do?"

"Whatever you like," Stephen said, his voice sounding almost panicky with excitement.

"What did you do with Danny?" Rab asked, trying to keep anything betraying away from his voice. Nevertheless he felt Stephen react.

"Why do you want to know?"

"Just curious. It's nice to know... improve on." He put as much promise into his voice as he could. It wasn't difficult. He was so fucking horny it came out without trying.

"We rubbed off on each other, that's all."

"You mean until you came?" Rab asked. He was holding Stephen lightly by the shoulders. Stephen was making desperate forays inside his jeans.

"Mm." He said it on a little groan as if he was half-way to coming already just from handling him.

"Did Danny touch you? I mean your cock?"

"A bit."

Meaning hardly at all, Rab thought. No more than he needed. He stroked Stephen's hair, felt him worm in tighter against him. "You touch him?"

Stephen shook his head. "We were too close, and moving really hard, you know?"

"Yes," Rab said and his reply came out on a sigh as Stephen's hand moved determinedly in his lap. He lifted Stephen's head and kissed him, thoroughly, deeply, doing it until he felt Stephen's hand slow in his lap then he broke from him and asked, "It wasn't really enough though, was it? Danny, I mean. He didn't really give you enough, did he?"

Stephen began handling him again, like a woman picking up knitting to distract herself. "I don't know what you mean."

"You felt more frustrated afterwards than you did before."

Stephen was quiet so long Rab thought he wasn't going to answer then he said, "I wanted to touch him in the taxi but I couldn't. He was..." He stopped and then said, "It was a bit better after John, even though I felt sick about what I'd done, but it didn't last. It was like eating food when you're watching TV. You forget what you've eaten. I don't know, not really like that, just..." He hesitated. "Well, I can't remember Danny touching me. I can remember feeling him. He's huge. Not like..."

He hesitated again and Rab said, "Not hung like John but a fucking nice piece of equipment nevertheless."

He felt Stephen nod. "But I liked him better. I don't know why."

"Because he's beautiful, not just a hunk of meat."

"Maybe. Anyway, I remember feeling him, being so fucking excited I was finally getting to feel him, but it was through his shorts. He took them off but I still never got to feel him. He was kissing me, pulling me about. I was too excited I think."

"And he knew it."

"What d'you mean?"

"Nothing. Go on, you were too excited."

"It happened so quick. Danny must have been excited too," Stephen's voice held that irritating smugness again, "because he was just as fast."

Rab smiled but didn't say anything. With Danny it meant nothing, less than nothing. Orgasms to order.

"It was late when we went to sleep. In the morning, in the bathroom, I tried to..." He tried again. "I said that we could do it again if he wanted but he wouldn't even let me near. He just laughed and moved away like I was just fooling around. I began to feel really frustrated. It was like we were right back at the start again, him saying no all the time." He stopped as if he'd realised he'd confessed too much, shown too much of his hand, then he said, not trying to deny it, although Rab hadn't spoken, "I kept trying to get him to do it." His voice seemed to sink into nothing.

Rab felt a curious and contradictory wave of pity. "Don't worry about it. At first I was

the same."

"Seriously?" Stephen asked and now neither of them were moving, not even fondling, as if they'd forgotten why they were in the back seat at all.

"Seriously. Anything just as long as I got what I wanted."

"Didn't he fancy you?" Stephen's voice held hope of sorts although he tried to hide it.

Rab laughed. "There isn't a man alive Danny doesn't fancy."

"What d'you mean?" And Stephen's voice was itchy with excited curiosity.

"Forget it. It won't help you." Nothing will, he thought but he didn't voice it.

"Did he make you feel like that? Frustrated?"

"Oh yes."

"What did you do?"

"Kept having him, kept hoping, got mixed up with other people."

"John?"

When Rab didn't answer Stephen said, "You're full of secrets, aren't you? All of you."

"That's what happens when you start doing what you're not supposed to. Maybe you should stop now Steve-o."

"Fuck off." Stephen let go of him. He had been holding Rab docile in one hand, erection slowly softening. Now he let him go, moving away from him.

Rab began closing his clothes, doing it slowly, letting Stephen hear it.

When he began fastening his shirt Stephen's hand stopped him. "Wait..."

"Mm?"

"We can still do it, if you want to."

Rab sat still and laid his head back, feeling the weight of Stephen's hand on his arm. "Because you're frustrated and want Danny?"

Stephen didn't answer him. Rab hadn't expected him to. "Because you feel desperate and lonely and want to know somebody needs it as much as you do?"

"Don't," Stephen whispered, letting go of him.

Rab said quietly, "Poor baby..." he leaned over and kissed him lightly on the cheek, "...come join the club," then began kissing his neck, sliding his hand up under his sweatshirt, feeling the narrow hard chest, smooth, utterly smooth, only those tiny seed nipples.

"Jesus Rab," Stephen said, lying there unmoving, and Rab wasn't sure what it meant until he said, "this is really sick."

"Then we've got the same disease. You can treat me. I'll treat you." His hand slid down Stephen's front and inside his jeans. Stephen's erection was iron-hard and scalding hot in his hand. "Let's play doctors," he whispered.

And Stephen tasted the peculiar spicy taste that was Rab's mouth.

John and Danny went to bed.

They lay in the dark and listened to the same wind and rain that howled round Rab and Stephen, and that Ian was trying not to hear.

John looked at the clock and rolled on his back again.

Danny was lying on his stomach, face pillowed on his hands, watching John's profile in the light from the lamp.

"They're late," John said.

"Mm."

John looked at him. "Not care?"

"Why should I?"

"Not even if they're going down on each other?"

766

Danny shook his head.

John searched his face. He smiled slowly, widely. "Fuck me, you really don't, do you?"

Danny closed his eyes and adjusted his hands without answering.

John laughed. "Christ, they'd probably cut their throats if they knew."

"I doubt it." Danny's voice was sleepy.

John looked at him again, eyes narrowed, but he could read nothing in the smooth sleepy expression. He ran his fingers over the scratches on Danny's cheek. "Little cat, isn't he?"

"Don't play the faggot," Danny said, sounding irritable for the first time.

John smiled. "You really don't like that, do you? What if I am one? How about that?"

Danny opened his eyes and looked at him but he said nothing.

"I do a fucking good impersonation, or hadn't you noticed?"

"I don't want to talk about it."

"Why not? What's so scary? You're not, why worry about me?"

Danny closed his eyes again like someone shutting out something they don't want to hear.

"Can't stand big brother being one of the bad guys..." Danny lay there pleading, *Don't say it, don't finish it*, but John did, "...like your daddy."

Danny turned his head away irritably.

"Come on Danny. He sired three children... although you might have been someone else's for all I can tell, you've got fuck all of him in you."

"Or you," Danny snapped, turning back to face him.

"Oh I'm his alright."

"Then so am I."

John laughed. "So he sired three children. Not bad for a little poof. You knew him better than any of us, would you say that's what he was Danny, a poof? How would you describe him?"

Danny didn't answer.

"Come on, no cost to you, what would you call him?"

"A dick," Danny said, mouth tight, hardly getting it out.

"Is that association? Father - dick. Is that how you think of him? Reckon that's why she married him? I think so. I think she married him for his prick. What a disappointment that must have been. All that flesh and it wouldn't even get up for her. Poor girl, she must have been very frustrated."

"You wish."

John smiled. Danny saw it and closed his eyes. He felt John's fingers moving over his mouth. "So beautiful, this mouth, and listen to the dirt that comes out of it. He hates his mummy. He hates his daddy. He slanders his favourite brother. Such a dirty mouth."

John kissed him. Danny could feel excitement in it again and suddenly felt tired. "Don't look at me," he said sharply, opening his eyes, surprising even himself.

"Why not?" John said, the same surprise stamped on his face.

"Because I want to get some sleep tonight."

John laughed, a quick bark of genuine amusement. Danny smiled too, at his own erratic behaviour. John might just as easily have smacked him in the mouth. He still might.

"Jesus Danny, it wouldn't do to have a fragile ego around you."

"You were getting horny looking at me," Danny said, meeting his eyes.

"And don't you love it?" John said, smile fading. "The day I don't your heart will break."

"Don't bet on it."

John winced ostentatiously and said, "Such a dirty mouth," then he kissed him again. When he lay back he asked, "What about Conley?"

"What about him?" Danny said, closing his eyes.

"He queer?"

"I don't know."

"What d'you *think* Danny? You're the expert."

"He could be."

"Meaning?"

"If he got in the habit of it he might never get out of it again. He'd just accept it."

John's thumb brushed his eyelid, making Danny jump. "Easy..." John murmured. Danny took a breath and relaxed.

"My excellent brotherly perception tells me my favourite brother and Mr Conley are not speaking."

Danny said nothing.

"Right?" John prompted.

"So?"

"What happened? Catch you having the boy?"

"More or less."

John laughed shortly. "An admission and a confession all at once. What's wrong? Normally I have to beat it out of you."

"You've already done that part, you might as well have the rest."

"And what if I feel like beating you all over again?"

"It wouldn't surprise me."

John grabbed his mouth suddenly, fingers squeezing painfully into his cheeks. "You dirty little whore." John shook him briefly then let him go. He threw himself onto his back.

Danny eased onto his side and rubbed his cheek.

John was staring at the ceiling. "You said you wouldn't touch the boy." His voice was rigid with anger.

"I didn't. Conley got me hot then left me high and dry. I used him, that's all."

"Jesus... *Christ*." John said each word slow and hard.

"He pesters me, night and fucking day. He never lets up. What the hell do you expect me to do?"

John looked at him suddenly. "Now you know how I felt."

Danny blinked and felt tears start impossibly to his eyes.

John saw them, green, washed, sparkling, and rolled towards him again. "That's not true. It isn't true." He kissed his forehead, his eyes, his mouth. "Forgive me, that isn't true."

"Yes, it is." And Danny pushed him away.

"No it isn't. You know I wanted it."

Danny covered his ears with his hands, screwing his eyes tight shut.

John pulled his hands away. "No, you'll listen. I wanted it. I used to engineer it, and that's the truth. It wasn't you Danny, it was me. I swear it."

"You're lying.."

"Listen... *listen* to me!" And John pushed his hands down to his sides. "The time in the loft, that first time..."

Danny shook his head furiously, struggling to get up.

John pinned him down with his weight, trapping his arms relentlessly. "I took you up there because I knew we'd be alone. I told myself it was to keep him away from you but it wasn't."

"Shut up!"

"No, you'll fucking listen Danny. I'm tired of carrying the guilt around. I'm tired of trying to be your idea of me. I asked you to do it. I stood there, fifteen years of age and *asked* you. I unzipped my trousers..."

"Shut up, *shut up!*" Danny was almost screaming it. John put a hand over his mouth.

"I took it out and said..."

Danny made a huge effort and caught John a blow to the side of the head. John swore and held a hand to his face. Danny punched him again in the mouth, then on the ear. He struggled up and scrambled across the bed like a terrorised animal, but he didn't get up.

John felt him drop onto his chest, heard the click, then felt it sharp and hostile in his neck. He lifted his head slightly and felt the point immediately jerk up into the soft underside of his chin. He could hear Danny's breathing above him, erratic, ugly. He was afraid to open his eyes, afraid to see his face.

"I told you to shut up," Danny whispered.

John lay there and told himself to open his eyes. He opened them slowly and looked up into Danny's face. He was a pure, icy white with purple patches under his eyes. His eyes were red from crying. The pupils were black, bottomless, as if he were drugged, wildly drunk. There was an ugly oily sheen on his skin. He was trembling. John could feel it. Not through the knife, the knife was steady, held rigid by the force with which he was digging it into John's neck, but his body was trembling, clammy.

John was afraid to speak, afraid to move, because he knew Danny would simply push it through, skewering his tongue to the roof of his mouth.

The door opened and someone came in. John heard it but didn't even move his eyes. He knew who it was. He heard the door click shut.

Well Ian, now's your chance. Danny's got me here on the end of a pin. Say sic him Danny, and I'm sicced.

Go on Ian.

"Danny..."

"Shut up," Danny hissed without taking his eyes off John. John watched his tongue come out, lick his lip, then disappear again. No other movement. No-one else home. Just a little craven monster with a knife inside Danny's face.

Ian wasn't coming over. Ian wasn't even going to try. Why should he? *How often I've wished I could die and now I don't want it.*

John felt tears form in his eyes and hated himself. *I'm afraid. At the last moment I'm afraid. I don't want this. I don't want Danny to kill me.*

"Danny, you're frightening him," Ian said and John wouldn't have known his voice, had never heard it before.

Is it because I can't see your face Ian? Is that it?

"Danny..." And Ian said his name soft and cajolingly, like he'd caught him telling a naughty white lie and Danny wouldn't go to Heaven. "He didn't mean it," he said and his voice had changed again. It was definite, solid, unrecognisable yet again. "Believe me, he didn't mean it. He doesn't know when to shut up, that's all. He's a moron." And Ian said it like an endearment. "Let him go Danny. Don't scare him any more. Let him go."

"He's a liar," Danny said and still his face was chiselled, white, dead, stiff, all the humanity passed away.

"I know," Ian said as if it was old ground, he'd heard it a million times before. "But he's thick, stupid. He can't help it. Forget it. Let him go."

"He's going to tell me one thing, then he'll tell me something else." And this time there was pleading in it, tears, and John blinked to clear his eyes, making the wet trickle slowly down into his ears, and he saw Danny's lip tremble. And then Ian moved

and the knife came back hard, forcing his head up.

"Don't come any closer," Danny hissed, hunching over his body. John heard himself make a small strangulated noise from the suddenness of the movement.

"I won't," Ian said immediately and John sensed his retreat. Imagined it. Prayed for it. Then Danny said, "I'm going to waste his face."

"You go ahead."

John saw Danny nodding but he never moved.

"Do anything you like to him, but not with the knife."

"I'm going to cut him. I'm going to cut the ugly bastard."

And John felt his heart break, watching his empty face, nothing in it but that cold, flat, black hate.

"You can't punish him for someone else's sins Danny."

"I don't care." And John knew he didn't, and suddenly he wished it was over, he'd just do it and it would be finished. He was too tired.

"He's an ugly, lying bastard and I know exactly who he is: John the hero, the impossible dream. I know everything about him. Better than he knows himself. Better than you know him." He fell silent again and it went on so long John opened his eyes, had to know what he was doing.

What he was doing was smiling.

Smiling was what he was doing.

"Ian?"

John blinked, listening to it.

"Mm?"

"Will I tell you something about him?"

"If you like."

"Something you don't know?"

"Go on then."

And John lay there feeling the prick of death at his throat, Danny appropriately in charge, the ultimate blow job, deep throat for the big sleep, and felt more afraid of what he was going to say than of dying.

"Once..." and John watched him wet his lips again, "I caught him in the bathroom, during the day. He shouldn't have been there. He should've been at school. He was cleaning himself up." And then Danny laughed. It was a delicate shivery laugh as if he'd been tickled. He was so white his teeth looked yellow against his skin. "Shit Ian, it looked like shit, smeared all over him. Chocolate, that's what I keep thinking. Just like chocolate." The knife dug into John's throat again.

"Danny..." Ian's voice sounded almost warning.

"Think it was chocolate Ian? How old was he? Fourteen? Fifteen? I've thought about it. Definitely no mistaking it, don't you think Ian?"

"No, no mistaking it."

"You're a sad liar John. You've always been a sad liar." The knife was digging in.

"Danny." Ian's voice held the first hint of panic. Then John heard him let it go. "Don't Danny, it wasn't what you think. We can't afford this Danny, you know we can't. It isn't worth it. I can't cover this up Danny. Don't."

Then the back door slammed.

John jumped, feeling the knife cut his skin. He felt his bowels turn to water and knew that he'd shit himself. The degradation of that was almost as bad as the fear itself.

He could no longer make out Danny's face, because he was crying too much. Really blindingly, silently crying. Real tears.

"Danny, that's them..." And now Ian sounded desperate.

They could hear Rab whistling downstairs.

"You can't drag them into this Danny. Don't."

Don't Danny, John begged. *Don't.*

The knife point eased.

Then slashed painfully across his face.

Ian slapped Danny across the face. The slap was so hard it sent him back off John and onto his backside on the bed. He overbalanced and fell on one elbow.

"You stupid, unhinged, moronic little *shit*," Ian said and slapped him again. Danny darted back, eyes wide, to avoid a third blow.

John was struggling up, hand held to his face, blood flowing freely between his fingers, streaming everywhere. "For Christ's sake leave him alone and get me something."

Ian said, "Let me see," and pulled John's hand away.

"I think I've shit myself," John said and his voice sounded too light, uncontrolled.

"It's not as bad as it looks," Ian said, trying to stem the flow with a tissue.

"Shit," John said sitting down again heavily. "*Shit.*"

Ian looked at him and said tersely, "Don't start fucking falling apart on me, for God's sake."

"Oh Christ no, he just tried to kill me, that's all."

"Yeah, well, maybe he'll have better luck next time."

Ian glanced over. Danny was still sitting on the bottom corner of the bed, knees pulled up tight against his chest. He looked like a child, pressed hard against the footboard, but his face had colour in it. His eyes were wary, alert. Ian saw that he'd put the knife down on the bed, blade still open. He pressed John's hand to the wound and said, "Hold that," then he leaned across and picked the knife up, squeezing it shut. Danny's eyes watched him, like a cat watches you moving round the room.

Ian shoved the knife in his pocket and stood up. "Come on, come over, let's clean it up."

"I can't, I've shit myself."

"It doesn't matter. Get up."

John got up reluctantly. Ian glanced down at his backside and said dryly, "Relax, no tell-tale stains. Your dignity is unsullied."

"In that case I wet myself."

"Couldn't you tell the difference?"

"I had other things on my mind."

John winced, flinching away, as Ian attempted to clean the wound.

"I don't think it'll need stitches, see for yourself."

John looked in the mirror above the sink. "I can't fucking tell for the blood."

"D'you want to go to the hospital?"

The toilet flushed and either Rab or Stephen came out of the bathroom, still oblivious to the scene that had just taken place in virtual silence.

"No, leave it."

"It might scar. It looks just about deep enough."

"So, it'll scar."

"You sure?"

"Mm." John pressed at it some more.

Ian looked at him and said, "Don't you think we've got too many knives in this house already?"

"Don't look at me, they're breeding. That one makes three."

"Then where are they coming from?"

"You tell me. I think they've been here all along."

"Just waiting for a chance to materialise?"

"Something like that."

John kept his back to Danny and Ian realised suddenly he didn't want to look at him. Perhaps he was afraid to look at him. A chance like this didn't come every day of the week.

Ian looked past him and said, "Danny?" He saw Danny tense, listening, but he didn't reply. "You can sleep with me if you want."

John looked at his face, eyes dark, but he said nothing.

Danny nodded. Ian saw it and couldn't quite believe it. He asked again. "D'you want to?"

This time Danny spoke. "Yes."

Ian saw John's mouth tighten, his eyes slide sideways as if to say, Tempt me a little more, go on.

"Go on through then," Ian said.

Danny surprised him again by getting up and pulling his jeans on without underpants, then moving round the bed. Ian watched John listening, his face cold and angry. He was still holding an inappropriately pink tissue to his face. The blood was drying at the edges of it, already changing colour.

Danny went out the door quietly, without fuss.

As soon as it closed John said, "Nicely done."

"Cheap price for your neck I'd say."

"What d'you want, a thank-you note?"

Ian smiled. "From you? I could paper my walls with them."

John turned away from him abruptly and crossed to the bed. Ian looked down his naked back at that high, hard backside. When he turned round to sit, Ian looked between his legs.

John saw his expression. "Enjoying the show?"

"Take it while you can."

"Greedy little sod, aren't you? You want it with fucking jam on it."

Ian shrugged then asked, "What happened?"

"Nothing." John looked away irritably then leaned over for the cigarette packet.

Ian watched him stretch, watched the muscles move. "That's a lie, no matter how pretty you are undressed."

John glanced at him quickly then lit the cigarette. He shivered.

"Why don't you get into bed?"

"Because then you wouldn't be able to see my dick." John was watching him.

"I think I could live with that."

"What if I said I liked you looking at it?" John was still watching him, his eyes narrow over the smoke.

"I'd say to myself..." Ian looked at the ceiling briefly then back down at him, "what is my big brother offering me, and why?"

"He's offering you a long life if you leave Danny alone."

"Now that sounds more like a threat."

"Maybe it is."

"You're very ungrateful."

John leaned back on one elbow, parting his legs and bringing everything between them into show.

Ian looked. After all he was meant to.

"Not completely."

Ian felt a shiver of it, excitement, fear, gratification, all together. "I think I'm flattered," he said finally. "But much as it pains me to admit it, I think you're overestimating my importance."

"No." John's voice was definite. He shook his head. He inhaled smoke from the cigarette and almost immediately let it out again.

"I *am* flattered, but you're wrong nevertheless."

"No," John said again. "You've always been right in there, since that night at Jerrett's. You'll be in there when he dies. The rest of us are just passing through."

Ian laughed. It changed him. It was so rare it always looked like it didn't belong there, an alien in Ian's body. "That's lovely stuff John, heady, but it's bullshit."

It was John's turn to shrug. "The offer stands." And he rubbed his stomach, using the flat of his hand, low down and with deliberation.

Ian watched him then looked up at his face. "It's nice John, it's very nice, believe me. But it still isn't a good exchange."

"No-one's asking you to go away Ian. Nothing drastic."

"I hardly ever get to touch him as it is, why the panic? He doesn't like it, or hadn't you noticed?"

"He says."

Ian laughed again. "Oh come *on*, don't let your jealousy turn your brain to Shredded Wheat. This is *me* we're talking about, Ian, remember? Ugly? Spotty? The runt?"

"And I'm telling you what I know."

"And what *do* you know?" Ian's voice was suddenly hard, irritable.

"You're in there somewhere, somewhere deep, and I don't like it."

"Then it's him you need to see, not me."

John took a breath. "Okay, so I'm lying. I don't care if you fuck him senseless. Think I'd ever have let you spend two minutes with him if I did? I just don't want you to give him anything else. No love, no kindness, no fucking understanding. Fuck him all you like, screw his fucking balls off if you have to... just don't love him."

Ian tried to laugh but his mouth couldn't quite get it out. "I'm not hearing this."

John looked at him steadily, hand pressed low into his belly, a thick wad of pink tissue stuck bloodily to his face, eyes like flint.

Ian stopped smiling, even trying. "No," he said. "That's all I've *got* John. It's all you've ever given me. You're not fucking reneging on it now. No *way*."

"Think about it."

"No, not even for your dick twice nightly."

"Then make it three times."

"No."

John sighed, a quick exhalation, as if he'd been holding his breath. He sat up. He climbed under the blankets and lay down. Finally he looked at Ian and said, "Fuck off Ian, your frantic little face makes me sick." And he reached over and stubbed out the cigarette and had flicked out the light before Ian had even closed the door.

All Ian could see of Danny was the top of his head. He had his back to him, blankets well up, turtle-wise, over his face. "You asleep?" he whispered as he pulled his jeans off.

Danny, predictably, did not answer him. Ian sighed under his breath and climbed into the bed. God he was tired.

Danny was cold and hard as a statue beside him, rigid with unshed tears. Same old Danny.

The ice is still in there Danny. The tiny flake of mirror with all the world's sins lodged in your heart.

Ian put his arm round him. It was awkward and difficult because Danny wouldn't move, wouldn't help him, and he wasn't a scant four foot any more. He was a

strapping, angry six foot. And he wasn't asleep. Very obviously wasn't asleep.

"Danny..." Ian tried again.

"Leave me alone." It came out like a growl.

Well it was a start. Ian reached behind him and put the light out then settled back down again. He cuddled up against Danny's back purely for warmth. The wind whistled drearily outside the window. Not violent enough to be a storm, just irritating, whistling and moaning like it felt sorry for itself. Look at me, poor old wind, stuck out here in the cold.

Outrageously Ian felt himself grow sleepy. He smiled. *It must be late. Lying here with Danny, smelling him, feeling his skin warming up against mine and I'm going to sleep. Incredible. The first night I've spent with him in how long and I'm going to go to sleep.*

Danny turned on his back, pushing Ian back into wakefulness. He moved back a little to give him room. It was a tight squeeze. "Alright?" he asked.

Danny grunted. It still managed to sound full of temper.

Ian laid a hand across his stomach, trying to placate him. Danny moved into him imperceptibly. Ian smiled and pressed his fingers against him, already beginning to slide into sleep again. "Goodnight," he whispered.

Danny didn't answer. Ian felt his silence, the sudden rigidity in his body, like a warning signal. He came awake quickly, as if he'd been startled by a noise.

Danny slid round under his arm and came up against him, mouth breathing against his face. Then it brushed Ian's cheek. Ian moved his head in surprise. Danny kissed him again, quickly, moving over his cheek rapidly, moving closer to him, forcing him onto his back.

"Danny..." Ian said.

"Shh." And Danny went on kissing him, arms going round him, pulling him close, and finally, although Ian did nothing - nothing at all - kissing his mouth. Kissing the thin, hated, cynical mouth.

Ian grunted, lay there like something stunned, holding Danny loosely while he moved over him like a slow fire. It smacked of desperation, like a terror of the dark.

And when Ian finally grasped that it was Danny doing this - Danny making love to him - he slid from Ian's suddenly alert arms and moved down his body. Ian felt his shoulders slide away from him, down low on his belly, then the fingers lifting him, incredibly still flaccid, slow for once to come into his excitement, and Danny kissed him into fullness, peeled him back and licked him into a fervour.

Ian reached for his head, catching it fleeting between his fingers, while Danny writhed and circled round his cock like something deliberately elusive, like a dream of coming, sliding away from you.

Ian's cock began to wrack itself with it, stretched to bursting point, aching to get into his mouth. Ian tried to catch his head, push him onto it, but he kept ducking it, licking, teasing, never drawing him in.

Eventually Ian begged him, driven beyond endurance. "Take it in your mouth," he whispered into the feral darkness under the blankets where Danny hid, nibbling at him. It made him think of the first night he'd ever spent with him, when he'd done exactly the same thing.

Suddenly Danny reared up out of the dark, huge, grown, and straddled Ian's face like a boy made instantly man, cock transfigured into adulthood and Ian squeaked, "Jesus..." half in fright, half in superstitious awe. But Danny with the same child-like arrogance only said, "Lick my arse."

Ian blinked at the change in plot. He could see Danny smiling above him, above that huge supernatural erection. "Come on, lick it." And he suddenly sat forward, right over Ian's face and dropped his arse over his mouth.

Ian licked it, pushing deep with his tongue, the perversity of the feeling utterly new to him, and everything inside him seemed to gallop.

"Push your tongue in," Danny urged, and Ian did, working it inside, making his jaw ache until he heard Danny make a small noise, delicate, half-desperate, and then he was gone again, the blankets pulled with him, and Danny was over his body, squatting over his cock, lifting it.

Ian looked down and heard him spit, felt the wet slip of his fingers rub over his cockhead then he felt him push it in, slowly, easing down onto it.

He dropped his head back on the pillow and closed his eyes. "Oh Jesus," he whispered.

"Like it?" Danny asked from somewhere out in the dark howling space.

"Yes," Ian whispered.

And Danny lowered down further onto it, then further and further, until they touched, rested together, sighing.

Silent.

"Ian?" Danny's voice, insecure, alone, afraid.

Ian opened his eyes instantly, peering through the dark. "What is it?"

"Tell me you love me."

Ian pulled him down, Danny now on his knees, bending forward, Ian rising to meet him, pulling his mouth to his. "I love you." Kissing him, whispering it. "I love you."

Danny broke away as if filled with sudden energy and began to ride him, leaning on his hands, sliding up and down on him eagerly, watching Ian's face.

Ian gripped Danny's knees, moving his hands over them, whispering his name, telling him how beautiful he was, how much he loved him, and Danny let him say it, never telling him to shut up.

Ian reached forward awkwardly and caught Danny's cock in his hand, pushed the pillow and one arm under his head so that he could stay there, watch, and Danny didn't stop that either, instead he said, "That's nice, do it harder."

So Ian did it harder, feeling it all come up in his throat, and he told Danny to slow down, but Danny laughed and said, "No, this is too good. This is the best tonight. The very best..."

Ian didn't miss a word.

The best tonight.

The very best.

"I think I'm..." Ian whispered. Then, "Danny please, just wait a little..."

But Danny rode him harder, faster, throwing his head back, Ian forced to watch the white curve of his body, his neck, feel the hugeness of his excitement in his hand.

Danny came forward suddenly, unexpectedly, dropping onto his hands. "Now," he grunted and forced himself down hard on Ian's cock. "Christ, now... now... *now*." And he shook his head like an animal worrying at something, and then he was up again, right back, digging his hands into his thighs.

And coming.

Incoherent, loud and coming, cock jerking in Ian's hand, backside slamming down on him, hissing as it spurted out of him, driving him on as if he couldn't stop the spasms of it.

"Oh *shit*," Ian said, riveted by the sight of the animal squirming on top of him, his cock impaled inside a wall of grasping muscle.

"Stop it," he pleaded, but Danny couldn't hear him. Danny who was cramming his orgasm into Ian's hand. Danny who was somewhere else in a world of dark noise, then who snapped his head down suddenly and said, pulling Ian's hands off himself, yanking them up over his head and pinning him down, "Give it to me," deep, low, slamming himself down. "Give it to me." Slamming down again. "Give it to me."

Squirming on him, making his cock churn inside him unpleasantly. "*Give* it to me."

Ian watched him, balanced as if he were on the point of a pin, wondering if it had already seeped away from him in the fright and intensity of Danny's orgasm. Maybe it had already happened and he didn't even know. And then he felt it, immense, about to rip him apart, and he didn't want it, couldn't handle it. "Stop," he pleaded.

But Danny slammed down on him, teeth bared.

"Danny," Ian said, trembling on the brink, desperately afraid.

But Danny went on saying it, urging it, thrusting down on him, driving him up harder, demanding, and Ian felt it rip, detach itself, and his body jerked convulsively, and he roared like something in pain. Danny's name. God's name. All in vain.

It was agony, ecstasy, all of him up there, inside him, pounding it out, raging into him.

This is what it felt like, what it was meant to feel like, being one, one single solitary person, together.

At last.

Everybody heard it.

Stephen was woken by it just as he slid into sleep. He listened but there was no other sound.

He fell asleep again, unsettled, unsure what it was or if he'd dreamt it.

Rab heard it. He was closer, lying awake, listening.

He heard them both.

First Danny, grunting, groaning. Then Ian.

Oh Christ, and then some. With a fucking hat on. Yelling like he'd been shot.

Danny really hit the target tonight alright.

He chewed his lip then sat up and reached for a cigarette.

Danny eased off him, legs like jelly. Ian moved over to let him lie beside him.

He moved to hug him but Danny pushed him away.

Ian felt it twist in him. "What's wrong?" he asked.

"Nothing, just don't fuss me, that's all."

"Alright," he said. But it wasn't alright.

They lay in an uneasy silence then Ian asked it. He had nothing left to lose. "Why did you do that?"

"I don't know." And his voice was snappy, edgy.

"Some kind of gratitude?"

"For what? Saving that fat shit's life?"

Ian was silenced by the bitter venom in his voice.

Danny rolled away suddenly and said, "I've got to wash," and he was gone out the room before Ian could say anything.

Danny stared at himself in the mirror.

Who are you shit-face? Yeah, you with the stretched arsehole.

Who are you?

Family whore, that's who.

Danny looked down at the water in the basin and picked up the soap. He raised one leg on the toilet and began washing.

Stephen came in as he was patting himself dry. "What are you doing?" he asked. It was a reflex question, meaningless. His voice was slurred, childish in its

disorientation. He looked at Danny without seeing him.

And Danny saw everything in that red cracked glass, full of sharp edges, slicing everything up. "Washing my arsehole. What does it look like?"

Stephen blinked at him.

Go on, Danny urged to himself, ask why you stupid little cunt. Ask me why.

But Stephen didn't and so Danny said, "Don't you want to know why?" But Stephen said nothing. "Because I've just been fucked up it, that's why." And he crossed to Stephen and pulled him to him, kicking the door shut, squeezing his buttocks in his hands, feeling them small and hard under the fabric.

"Ever had it up the arse Stephen? Jesus it makes you come, it really does. Like me to do it to you? Shall we lock the door and I can do it to you now? We could sit on the toilet and you can sit on my dick and I'll pull you off as I ream you. Would you like that?"

Stephen stared at him as if he was a dangerous animal or an escaped lunatic speaking in tongues.

Danny licked his lips and squeezed his buttocks hard. Hard enough to hurt. "See that toilet? John used to sit on his daddy's knee on that toilet. Toilet training, that's what he used to call it. Know what that was?"

Stephen shook his head, but he wasn't answering Danny's question.

"Know what he used to do?" Danny's eyes searched his face, repeatedly going back to his mouth as if he was going to kiss him, or was watching for a lie to come out. "He used to sit on it with his trousers down, legs wide apart, and hold him over the top of the gap. His dick would be up - you've got to understand that part otherwise this doesn't make sense - " Danny smiled as if he was telling a joke and was about to deliver the punch line, "then know what he did?"

"Stephen doesn't want to know what he did, so why don't you just leave him alone?"

Danny didn't even move. His eyes flicked up, over to the door, but nothing else moved. Stephen pushed against his chest, but Danny didn't let him go, didn't even seem to feel it.

Ian closed the door quietly. "You're really going to have to watch your mouth Danny. One of these days it's going to land you in big trouble."

Danny dropped his arms. Stephen stood there, mouth hanging open. He half turned to Ian as if he intended to speak, but nothing came out.

"You lie like shit," Ian said, voice hard, and Danny nodded.

Suddenly he patted Stephen's cheek, smiled, and he looked so normal. Stephen looked at him and could see none of the other Danny at all. All gone, as if he'd been wiped out.

"He's right, I lie like shit. Self..." He looked at Ian. "What do you call it?"

"Aggrandisement."

"That's it." Danny clicked his fingers. "Self-aggrandisement. The urge to make myself more interesting than I really am. Craving for attention, that's what Ian always says. Isn't that right Ian?"

And for a moment Stephen could see it again, hear it, the black glitter in his eyes, the vindictive little dig in the question, almost like deliberate provocation.

"Take your arse back to bed Danny."

"Oh yes Ian." And the glitter was deeper, harder, flatter.

But Danny went, watching Ian all the way.

"You wanting to go, or have you been, or what?" Ian said, and he wasn't quite the same Ian Stephen knew. He seemed cool, in command.

"Neither. I mean, none. Something woke me and then I must have drifted off again because I woke up again and I felt something was wrong, you know? I came out to see."

"Well go back to bed."

"Is Danny okay?"

"Fine. Him and John had a fight. It always makes him ratty and difficult." Ian smiled suddenly and that was different too. Not much prettier, but more comfortable. "He's like a kid, too much excitement and he's running around bursting into tears."

Stephen smiled back. Ian's smile seemed to deserve that much. "Okay," he said and went towards the door. "Have they really been...?" He had his back to Ian. He barely looked back over his shoulder. "You know... what he said?"

Ian turned to look at him. "I don't know," he lied. "What did he say?"

"He said he'd been..." Stephen rushed it, "doing it up his arse." He flushed violently.

"I wouldn't know Steve-o." And Ian's voice was the old voice, snide, insinuating. "Why don't you ask John?"

Stephen went out, slamming the door violently behind him.

Danny went back into their room and locked the door.

"What makes you think I want you?"

"I don't give a fuck if you do, this is where I sleep."

John watched him climb into bed. Danny turned his back to him.

"What's wrong, he too much for you?"

"Put out the fucking light."

"He'll be sad when he finds out you're gone."

"My heart bleeds for him."

John stubbed out his cigarette and put out the light. He slid down beside him.

Danny jumped as he felt his fingers slide into the crack of his arse. "Keep your frigging hands off me."

But John had already let go. "So he was up your arse. I knew it. When he came like that... Your private sickness, needing meat where it isn't supposed to go." John pushed his fingers in again.

Danny clenched on them, squirming over onto his back to keep him out, but John simply shoved his legs apart and shoved his hand under him instead.

"Don't." Danny forced him off, slapping his arm.

"Why?" John got a hand under again and began trying to get his finger inside him. "You've already had something a lot bigger up there. What's wrong with my little finger?"

"You're hurting me. Fucking pack it in."

"I owe you worse than this. Look at my frigging face, you little bitch." And he pushed his finger in hard, sharp against Danny's resistance.

Danny winced, trying to struggle away from him. "Leave me be. I mean it."

"Let me finger-fuck you and I will."

"No. For Christ's sake, it's almost two in the fucking morning. Get off."

"So? Let me finger-fuck you." John nudged him down with his shoulder, half-lying on him and pushing his finger up harder.

"Fucking pack that in... Get out..."

"Let me. It won't take long the way you're stretched. It's slacker than tripe. Look I'm up to my knuckles and you can't even fucking feel it, can you? I can feel his spunk. It's stuffed right up here. I can feel your shit covered in his slimy spunk."

"Jesus, shut *up*." Danny covered his ears.

John took the opportunity to push a knee in between his legs. "Come on, I'm

already up. Just let me get a couple of fingers up there to feel how deep he's been then I'll leave you alone. Come on, open your legs."

Danny pushed hard against him... and then he went limp, simply lay there.

John pushed his legs apart till he looked like he was giving birth then murmured, "That's it." He inserted another finger, carefully enough, then mounted Danny's leg and began thrusting against it. He was up on one elbow, looking down on Danny's face. He was flaccid. Danny closed his eyes but he could still feel him looking at him.

"Three fingers, easy."

"No." Danny pushed at his hand immediately, eyes jumping open, but John batted it away.

"Yes." Voice icy. "It's going to take three to stretch you. Look at my competition. Be thankful I'm not using my dick Danny-boy." And he pushed another finger up sharply, the nail ragged and snagging.

Danny grunted, trying not to clench, trying not to make it worse. It was hurting badly.

"That's it. Good boy. How does that feel then?" And John punctuated each sentence by pushing his hand up hard inside him. He paced the movements with his own against Danny's leg. He was stiffer now. He made no attempt to kiss him or caress him. He just watched him in the darkness, pushing his hand up inside him.

"I can feel where he's been. You had him right up to the hilt. Couldn't get it any further than this. If you were sick you could probably vomit him. You're going to be leaking his slime all night."

"Why don't you just come John and shut up?" Danny managed between bitten lips.

John laughed, very unfunny. "No, I'm enjoying myself. He's allowed up here to enjoy himself, so am I. You don't like him, remember? Or had you forgotten?" He rammed his hand suddenly, spreading his fingers. Danny swore.

"That'll jog your memory. You don't like Ian, remember?"

"Christ, you know I don't."

"Do I? Didn't sound it. Sounded like everybody had a good time." And he pushed in hard again.

"That hurts, fuck you."

"Shame." And he did it again. "Want to come?"

"No, I want to sleep."

"Too much excitement, or not enough spunk left?"

"I'm tired."

"I'll bet." And he did it again, his knuckles crushing up hard against Danny's balls.

"*Shit*..." Danny hissed.

"That's right, plenty of it up here with his spunk. Right place for him, in beside the shit."

Danny closed his eyes tight as if he could somehow block out the sound of him.

"Your legs are sliding. Lift your knees," John commanded.

"No." Danny refused because it was stopping John getting in properly and that was making it difficult for him to hold an erection. If he stayed soft long enough he'd get pissed off and pack this in.

"Lift them or I'll rip your fucking arse open." And he hooked his fingers inside his body, tearing at his rectum. Danny jerked his knees up high, spreading his legs wide and lifting himself slightly.

"That's better." John arranged his half-hard penis against his shin again. "Feel how much better that is? Feels just like Ian now, doesn't it?" And suddenly John was swinging over between his legs.

"What are you doing?" Danny said, frantically trying to see him in the dark.

"Kneeling here masturbating while I push my fingers up your hole."

Danny sank back, trying not to let him feel the relief, but John heard the sigh.

"Am I annoying you?"

"Yes, you fucking are."

"Right then." And suddenly Danny's legs were pushed up hard against his chest.

"What?" he managed, but all he could feel was the slack relief of John pulling out his fingers. He was so numb at first that unbelievably he felt nothing. It was the slam of John's abdomen that told him what was happening.

"Shit... *John*..." He tried to pull back but he was too late. John was already half up inside him, grasping his knees, pushing. "John, don't." But John was grunting and shoving, cramming it up, and Danny could feel nothing but hot icy pain as it swelled inside him, scraping at his raw insides, burning him. Then it was digging at the inside of his belly. Bigger, harder, deeper.

John was emitting an odd noise - he could hear it, sudden, raw, harsh above him - hurting him so bad it made Danny clutch at the bed, unable to keep the pain in any longer, forcing him to cry out, "John, stop it, you're *hurting* me!"

But John only moved faster.

"*John*..." Danny ground out, trying to bite it down, stop it coming out, deprive him of it.

"You little shit." John was almost lifting him off the bed with the violence of his thrusts, making the last restraint snap and Danny whimper with pain and distress, "Please... John... *don't*..."

"I can't hear you."

"Please," Danny heard himself beg. "*Please*."

"Can't hear you..." And John's grip loosened slightly as he thrust faster.

So Danny said it again, and again, and kept saying it, just to make him stop. "Please, please, please..."

And he'd have gone on saying it if John hadn't suddenly hissed, "Coming..." his body moving light and fast now, barely touching Danny, high above him, so he was free to enjoy his pleasure without him, so he was nothing but a hot hole to take it, and it came out high and gliding, skimming into Danny's body like stones flipped across water.

"Coming..." he said again, and he was lost to everything but the inside of his own joy.

SEVENTY-ONE

Breakfast was very strange.

It was an intensely cold morning, bitterly black outside, as if the windows were covered in black paper. Stephen's hands hurt already just thinking about it. *Nothing too outdoors today John please.*

Ian looked up as he came in. He was raking the ash out the stove, opening it up, refuelling it. The stove was kept going all night but you wouldn't have guessed it to feel the kitchen.

"It's like an icebox in here," Stephen said, shivering, and he found he couldn't quite meet Ian's eyes.

"Not for long," Ian said and his voice didn't sound quite right either. Stephen glanced at him quickly, but he was just Ian, the same Ian he'd always been.

Rab came in next and looked at Ian, hardly even seeing Stephen, and when he did see him he looked as if he wished he was elsewhere, and Stephen knew he wanted to talk to Ian. He felt an irritation mounting in him. He knew it was all to do with last night. All their flickin' secrets.

When John came in it got worse.

First of all he had a horrible knife slash right across his face. Ian had said last night that him and Danny had had a fight, but he'd never thought...

Stephen stared at him, mouth stupidly open, until John caught his eye, and held it. Stephen flushed and shut his mouth. He stared at the table top.

"Nice face John." Rab's voice was slow, drawling, irritating.

"Crawl up it Rab."

"I thought somebody already did. Or was I hearing things?"

There was a silence like a void opening up in the room, splitting it in half like an axe blow, and they all froze in it.

Then Danny walked in.

Everybody looked at him, and you could feel it, like something running through the room, like excitement, or a cold draught, or a wave of fear, everybody's eyes on him like breakfast had just walked in the door. And he looked tired and crabby, and his mouth was tight, and his eyes looked oddly hollow, and he seemed thinner, taller and thinner, and incredibly gut-wrenchingly beautiful.

Another day lit by his light.

Praise the Lord.

Danny wiped his face with his hands. A worm of anxiety had been eating at him all day. Twice he'd had to make emergency bolts to the toilet and had sat clenched up with the runs and spasms of cramping pain, and too much stomach-churning bleeding, then dull, raw throbbing.

He leaned his face on the cold rough stone. He closed his eyes.

"Not sad Danny, surely?"

"Fuck off and leave me alone."

"Like you left me?"

Danny pushed up off the wall and shoved Ian in the chest. "I mean it. Now."

"Spoiling for a fight? Think you can handle me, even if you can't handle your big brother?"

Ian ducked as Danny swung at him, smiled as he came back up. Danny stood

there glaring at him, fists clenched.

"Why don't you go see Conley? Take a break."

"I told you to leave me alone."

"Go on, give yourself a treat."

"Why? So you can tell him? Maybe have him split me right up the middle? Do it once more and haemorrhage me?"

"Ah," Ian nodded, "that's what he did."

"Yes, that's what he did."

"Without the pleasure you got from me." And Ian watched spellbound as Danny flushed and looked away. He felt it sing in his veins. He *had* enjoyed it. No faking. Ian waited for him to deny it but Danny said nothing, nothing at all. Instead he turned to him and said, "Why do you want me to go?"

"Because you're my brother and I love you."

Danny looked at him with a sudden intentness. "You've said that before."

Ian shook his head but Danny was vehement. "Yes you have. You've said that before."

Ian shook his head some more, feeling that familiar dangerous excitement, walking the line. Danny was looking around the shed as if he was searching for something then he turned suddenly and thumped the wall, a dull stony sound. "Why can't I *remember?*"

"Because there's nothing there to remember."

Danny swung on him. "Oh there is. There fucking is. And you know it. Sometimes I lie awake, staring into the dark, and it's like it's just out my line of vision - things I can see but that I can't make out, things I can hear but I don't understand, pieces, fragments - and I keep sliding into sleep, although I don't want to, and when I wake up I don't know what was real and what was a dream, or worse still I've forgotten it all." He paused. "*Jesus.*" Then slammed the wall again. "And you. You make it worse, mixing everything up, sticking in lies of your own, as if his weren't bad enough."

"No," Ian interrupted him. "The lies are all his. They always have been."

Danny looked at him and smiled. "You don't lie, and John doesn't lie, and Rab saw nothing, and the rest are all dead. Who am I going to ask Ian? Who's left? Who can I trust?"

"Me."

"Why should I?"

"Because you're my brother and I love you."

"A bedroom," Danny said suddenly.

Ian watched him.

"We were in a strange bedroom, you and me and someone else..."

Ian said nothing.

"How old was I?"

"How old do you think?"

"Five maybe?"

Ian said nothing.

"Please," Danny said, whispering it. "Tell me Ian. You know. I know you do. Tell me."

"I can't do that."

"Why not, fuck you?" And Danny grabbed him.

"Because you're my brother and I love you." And Ian reached out and pulled him quickly to his mouth.

Stephen saw the kiss.

He managed as far as the house before he threw up.

He hung onto the wash-hand basin and then looked at himself in the mirror, cheesy-faced and sickly, and it made him throw up all over again, like other people's vomit sometimes will.

He washed it away and found he was crying. He could hear his mother vacuuming downstairs. *Oh God Mam, go away, go away.*

Ian. Dirty, slimy, foul-mouthed Ian. Weedy, greasy little Ian. And Danny had moved his head to let him. Stone cold sober. Stephen had seen him close his eyes, like they do in films, as if he was enjoying it.

It had gone on a long time, held in the space between them till Ian had broken it. Danny had blinked as if he didn't know where he was or what he was doing, and then Ian had smiled at him and Danny had pushed past him, looking furious, and stalked off.

Why Danny? Because he didn't kiss you long enough?

Have you had the dog too Danny? Or how about my mam? How come you haven't got it up her yet? And what about me? Where do I fit in?

It was hardly even a grope. Not like what you and John had last night. That's what I heard, wasn't it? You fucking your great ugly cunt of a brother.

What about me?

Stephen scrubbed his face with toilet paper then flushed it away. "What about *me?*" he said aloud and he set his mouth in a grim line and went downstairs.

Danny was in the kitchen with his mother, lounging in the chair, making some joke about John's face.

Jesus Mam, he did it. Look at him. He lies like butter drips off toast. Don't listen to him. He sliced him with a knife. He did it.

Danny reached forward and caught her arm, laughing. Stephen wanted to slap it away. *Don't touch her.* But she broke away from him.

Danny looked over at him and smiled then got up and followed her. He put his arms around her waist and hugged her back into him, hugged himself deep into her neck, nuzzling her playfully. Stephen watched it all, the surprise, the embarrassment, then the slow easy relaxing against him. Danny had been doing this all along, behind his back. That's all that was embarrassing her, Stephen catching them out.

Her smile.

Do I look like that when he touches me?

"Let her go."

They looked at him. Danny smiling, eyes knowing. Her surprised, then angry.

Danny let her go.

Stephen went out the kitchen and slammed the door.

"Whatever is wrong with him?"

"Jealous."

Jean McEvoy looked at him. Danny smiled. "Doesn't like me flirting with his mum."

She shook her head. "I'm sorry about that."

"Don't be, I obviously looked as if I meant it."

She flushed again, embarrassed by something in his steady gaze rather than what he said.

"Mind you, you do feel good," he said, his voice low.

"Very funny," she managed.

"Who's being funny?"

She swallowed. Unexpectedly he pulled her to him again, arms around her, body pressed into her back. He spoke into her ear. "Women always feel good like this, like they fit."

She wanted to prise his hands off but she didn't trust herself to touch him.

He kissed her. Unmistakably. On the back of her neck. Soft, slightly damp, like he'd done it with his mouth open. She could feel it like a brand on her skin. "Sexy." And his voice had slid even lower.

"You're a flirt Danny," she said, finally pushing at his arms, hating the hard silky feel of them, wishing he had his sleeves down. She could smell him. He'd never been close enough before.

"It doesn't hurt anyone."

She laughed, trying to keep it light. He kissed her again. She flinched away from him and snapped, "Don't."

He let her go immediately. He smiled apologetically at her flushed face. "Sorry." And his smile was open and honest and she felt ashamed of herself for overreacting.

"That's alright. It's my fault." She laughed. "It's probably Stephen, making me feel like a scarlet woman."

Danny laughed. "I like the way you go pink when you're embarrassed. You look just like him." And he moved in front of her and dipped his head and she felt his mouth soft and persuasive against her own.

And then he was gone, like the cat's vanishing smile, leaving her pressing her mouth with her fingers and holding her stomach with her hand.

"What's wrong?" Danny ducked under the pen to face him again. "Not like me feeling up your mum?"

Stephen tried to turn away again but Danny swung round in front of him, grinning.

"Shut *up*," Stephen flared at him.

"Touchy, touchy." Danny lifted his chin with one finger. "Frightened in case I prefer her to her son?"

Stephen closed his eyes, feeling the tears squeezing out from under the lids. "I saw you kissing him." He opened his eyes, saw Danny watching him warily. "I saw you kissing Ian."

It seemed to be a long, long time until Danny's hand let him go, even longer till he spoke. "You're getting to be quite a little snoop Steve-o."

"I didn't mean to. I came to look for you."

"Well you certainly found me, didn't you?"

"First it's John and now it's Ian. They're your *brothers* Danny." And Stephen sat down on the floor. Plonk. Just like that. As if the idea was suddenly too vast for him.

Danny gazed down at him for a moment and then said slowly and carefully, "What do you want Stephen? What do you *really* want?"

Stephen looked up at him slowly, frowning, and said, "How do you mean?"

"There's two options." Danny hunkered down beside him, hands on his knees. Stephen could feel them strangely, as if they were on his bare skin.

"What two options?" he said, clearing his throat, distracting himself.

"One: I fuck you."

Stephen looked away, unable to meet the hot feel of his eyes.

"Two: I don't fuck you, but I don't fuck anyone else either. Not even your mother." Danny smiled. "Now that *is* a sacrifice. I've been lining it up for weeks."

Stephen could feel his breathing coming too rapidly. It felt as if he was building up to a scream.

"So, either I fuck you and anyone else I like, or no-one at all, including you."

"You couldn't," Stephen said, hanging onto the only thing he could grasp. "You couldn't go without."

"We can be friends and I'll leave your mum alone. Which is it to be?"

"No."

"Ah. That's the third option. You don't choose you get nothing." He paused then said oddly, "You know, sometimes I've had my prick in someone and forgotten who it was." He stroked Stephen's cheek. "But your mum's next and I'll know exactly who I'm in. Try and warn her. See what she says."

"You wouldn't."

"Watch me. Choose."

"I can't."

"Don't lie to me. You chose hours ago, before it was even out my mouth. You chose the first day you saw me. What you can't do is say it. Say, I want you to fuck me Danny and I'm willing to let you fuck my mother in exchange."

Stephen scrambled upright and tried to shove past him, but Danny caught his arm and pulled him back against him, gripping his arms and thrusting his hips against him lewdly. "Say it." And horribly he licked his earlobe. "Say, I want you to fuck me."

"No."

Danny cupped his backside in his hands and jerked him up against him, grinding his hips against his. "Say it." His voice was heavy, between his teeth. "Let's hear it." He pulled him up against him again. Stephen felt himself get hard with that dirty thrusting, knew Danny must be able to feel it.

"Danny, please, stop."

"No problem." And Danny let him go. Stephen became suddenly intensely aware of how excited he was. His cock was hard, jumping. He was breathing heavily. He felt itchy, like he wanted to rub himself against him. He wanted his body back.

He took a step towards him.

Danny took a step back. "Say it."

They stood there. Danny intact, beautiful, waiting. Stephen disintegrating, dying to say it, get it over with.

"Come on Steve-o, let's hear it." And Danny moved further back into the darkness of the shed. The animals snorted and moved in their stalls. Stephen followed him.

"Come on," Danny's voice disappearing into the dark, "say it."

And suddenly Stephen walked into him, up close against him, and he felt Danny's hand down there, between his legs, and he looked into his eyes and said, "Not my mam Danny, please."

"Your mother Steve-o, oh yes."

"Danny..."

"*Say* it." And Danny's hand was sliding his zip down, and Danny was whispering, "I can go down on you right here, lick your knob, suck your balls, eat your come..." Danny was pulling his cock out, doing things to him. Stephen moaned and closed his eyes, clinging to his shoulders, pushing into his hand. "But first you are going to *say* it. Say, I want you to fuck me. Say it now or, believe me, you're never going to get another chance."

And then there was nothing but Danny's hand, squeezing him, making him want to drip all over the floor, and Danny's body hard and strong against him, every nerve screaming. I want more, he thought. "I want you to fuck me," he whispered.

"Again." And Danny's hand was gripping him tight, bringing him close.

"I want you to fuck me."

And there was a silence, a stillness, just as he was about to spoil it in Danny's hand, and Danny stopped and licked his ear again, only this time he whispered, "What do you want?"

And Stephen clung to him, red-faced, and whispered back, "I want you to..." and he wet his mouth then let it out in a rush, "suck my prick..."

And his voice fell away, all its imperative energy lost, as Danny dropped to his knees and finally did exactly that.

Danny was on a flyer.

Ian could see it, his nerves jumping. He could see them watching him. Rab, predatory, waiting for his chance. John too clinical, stonily-silent.

And Stephen.

Stephen jittery and doped simultaneously, like the cat that got the cream and found it was laced with Benzedrine, bruised-looking, like someone who'd lain in bed all day fucking his arse off, putting his dick through the wringer.

And Ian saw John seeing that too and felt sick.

The house was full of knives.

And Danny was right out his head.

Conley had not thought about Danny.

Until now.

He had dreamt Danny, sweated Danny, fevered Danny, but he hadn't *thought* about him.

He sat chewing his lip, watching the phone. He was still watching it when it rang.

He didn't want to pick it up in case it was Danny. He didn't want to pick it up in case it wasn't.

He picked it up.

"Hello?" He actually said that. He even heard himself.

"Hello. It's Ian Jackson Moore, Danny's brother."

Conley felt his stomach turn over slowly, unpleasantly. The coincidence felt supernaturally repugnant.

"Hello?" The voice seemed to whisper at him.

"I'm still here," Conley said. It was the best he could do.

"Can you come here and get Danny?"

"What?" Conley said and it sounded harsh and sharp in his own ears.

There was a soft laugh. "You wouldn't, huh? Well, it was an off-chance."

"No, wait." Conley said it quickly, hearing the end of discussion note in his voice.

Ian Jackson Moore waited.

"Why?" Conley asked.

"He needs your help, he's sick..." and Conley realised he *was* almost whispering, like an obscene phone-caller, "...he needs to get away for a few days." Then the magic words, "He needs you."

Conley said, "Right now?"

"Couldn't be better. They've forecast snow; heavy, deep snow. Lock him in the Snow Forest with you." And he laughed again, that odd whispery noise, and Conley began to wonder if it wasn't him that was sick, not right in the head. He tried to remember any description of him from Danny and realised he couldn't. Danny talked round him, past him, over him, like a dog covering something in leaves. Ian didn't exist. Conley had thought Danny found him a nonentity, now he began to wonder.

Camouflage.

"Alright," he said and wanted to snatch it back immediately.

"Come to the front door. Park your car up behind the old petrol station on the hill and walk down. Alright?"

"Yes."

"I've got to go."

And the line was instantly dead.

Ian got him alone in the bathroom.

"Which part of me do you want?" Danny asked. It shouldn't have meant anything, cheap and sarcastic as it was, but it did. It always fucking had.

Ian locked the door.

Danny smiled, just barely. "It's going to be that good?"

"Conley's coming here for you, tonight."

"You *what?*" And Ian watched his face begin to close down on him, the doors slamming shut like so many Chinese boxes until he was barely recognisable.

"He wants to see you."

Danny looked at him. "And you never lie to me."

"I don't. He wants to see you."

Danny smiled and said, "You, him and a bottle of wine."

Ian managed to smile back. "Do you love?" He laughed sourly. "I wonder if he realises it's you waiting in that water under the raft, not him."

The smile dropped off Danny's face. He looked round the room as if he was looking for some way to escape.

"Danny..." Ian said, trying to redeem his mistake.

"What?"

Ian licked his lip. "I'm doing it for you. A day or two, that's all."

"Christ, you're not even pretending any more, are you?"

"It's not about that, I swear. Isn't this what you want? Isn't this what he was for?"

Danny gave a short laugh. "Any use he's ever been has gone. I'm not going Ian."

"You need to."

Danny moved closer. Ian felt as if the contempt was coming off him in waves, a palpable chill. "No, *you* need me to. A lifetime spent trying to divide us hasn't got you any closer, but you're still trying. Christ you're pathetic."

Ian took a breath, tried not to lose it. "It's for you," he said doggedly. "How many times in the last week have you lost it? You nearly killed him."

Danny turned away. "You're still in love with him." He turned back suddenly and demanded, "Aren't you?"

Ian stood there, pinned by his gaze, and felt himself flushing. He replied weakly, "Christ Danny, we've been over this before."

"You don't tell me any lies, remember?"

Ian jerked his head away and said, "Oh come on, what do you expect me to say?"

Danny laughed, and then he said in a quiet voice, "How much did you hate me, during those years?"

"Never."

"Two days ago you were hissing it through the door."

"And you know damn fine I never meant it. I never have."

"Oh yeah? And all the times you wished me dead? Said so to my face?"

"I still didn't hate you. I just wanted it to stop, that's all."

"Because you were in love with him."

"No."

"Because he was *your* best friend."

"No."

"*Your* brother."

"No."

"Sex," Danny whispered, coming close. "You wanted to have some of that sex you were so sure we were having..."

Ian could only manage to shake his head.

"I still remember the first time you put it in one of your fairy stories. Good name that Ian, very appropriate. Do you remember? Well... *do* you?"

Ian nodded this time.

"Tell me then."

"This isn't the time."

"Why? It seems like just the time to me. After all this is what we've been fighting about for years, isn't it? Come on, let's see how well you remember. Always tell the truth Ian, because you're my brother and you love me. Come on."

"Three weeks after the first time..."

"Correct." Danny clapped his hands once, sharply. "Go on."

"He was drunk..."

"Couldn't have been, he was too young, don't want to hear it."

"It's true. He'd been out with some..."

"I *said*," Danny was instantly livid, icy-quiet. "I don't want to *hear* it."

"No you never fucking did, did you? You still don't."

"Get on with it," Danny snapped. "The story."

Ian took a deep breath, let it out again. "The servant saved you and earned three wishes."

"First was a royal blue ermine coat. Second?"

"A black horse, like his master's."

"And the third?" Danny asked.

Ian said nothing, couldn't meet his eyes.

"The third Ian."

"The prince, spread out naked on the cloak..." he petered out.

"For him to play with, worship, *adore*. Wasn't that it?"

"Yes."

Danny walked behind him and Ian could feel him looking at his back. "And you took my pyjamas off and laid me out on the bed and a funny thing, I never did feel really adored. I never even really felt there."

"Whose fault was that? I loved you."

"Yeah."

"It was you that wanted it."

"I thought it was a game Ian, dirty senseless games, and it didn't hurt. No cutting or biting or tying up. No blood. It was kindergarten stuff, except it was a little too sophisticated, wasn't it? Because you were how old? Refresh my memory."

"Fifteen, and you know it." Ian's voice was clipped.

"You had some rich appetites. Like the fucking. Remember the fucking?"

Ian swallowed.

"That got a bit odd Ian, you know? Like him really, all that punishment."

"It was only two or three times."

"Once when I was thirteen."

Ian turned on him, suddenly angry. "And a big fucking boy Danny. You were standing there sticking it out saying, 'I bet he'd be green if he could see how hard you make me.' You fucking said that Danny. Then giving me that up and under look and saying, 'How would you like it inside you?' You *said* that. You stood there pulling it and said that. What was I supposed to do? Pretend I was John? Be noble? Say no?" Ian stopped, skidded to a halt. "Alright." He took a deep breath. "Enough of this. This is so fucking stupid." And they looked at each other.

Danny reached out a hand and touched his cheek. "You're such a fucking pathetic

mess."

Ian smiled and said, "You got it all Danny-boy, lock stock and barrel."

"You know I'd give you half if I could."

"I know you would."

"But I still wouldn't let you any nearer. If it came to it, I'd kill you first."

Ian said, "Get your clothes on. He'll be here in half an hour. You're better away from him for a while."

Danny nodded then said, "I had the boy today."

Ian kept looking at him. "I guessed."

"And you never threatened me with it?"

"I knew your conscience would win the day."

"Are you going to tell him?"

Ian laughed. "It was my idea, wasn't it? Anyway, I never waste time talking about you. Now are you going to get dressed? I've got to wait downstairs for him. It's got to be me who answers the door."

Danny nodded. Ian gave him one last smile and went to leave. Danny caught his hand and pressed his mouth to the palm then curled it tight.

Ian smiled again and went out the door.

It had already started to snow when Conley left the flat. He was filled with an intense, almost frightening, excitement. He tried to drive slowly and kept finding his speed rising. "Be calm Max," he whispered to himself.

The drive was interminable. The weather forecast was right, the snow was getting heavier.

He wracked his brain. Ian. Ian. Mentions here, there - little shit and little creep being the two most common - but always irascible, full of contempt. Hate? Maybe. Danny was angry so often you couldn't tell. A sudden cold dread went through him. What if it was simply a vindictive joke? Worse, what if it was in some way intended to injure Danny?

He slowed his speed again. No, it was legit. It had to be.

Conley didn't examine that.

It had to be.

"Where's Rab?"

"Gone out with John."

Ian sat down with a sigh. Better and better. He looked at Stephen, too long.

Stephen shot him a poisonous glance. "My dick hanging out or something?"

"I wish." And Ian smiled that horrible narrow smile.

"Jeez, you're a creep," Stephen said in disgust. After a moment or two he asked too casually, "Have you seen Danny?"

"He's upstairs, in the shower."

Stephen looked at him and the look was so hostile Ian felt as if it could slice his skin open. "Steve-o's got a hate on," he said in a sing-song voice. "Doesn't love his Unca Ian."

Stephen turned on him. "I saw you with him. In the shed. You're disgusting."

"Ah," Ian said and left it at that.

Stephen turned back to the TV but he wasn't watching it. All he could think about was Danny going down on him. At least when John stopped, he stopped. When it was finished it was over. But this went on. And on. He could feel it aching in his balls. He wished he'd never done it while a part of him was desperate to do it again. He'd come

gallons, pulling Danny's hair, squirting it in his mouth, just like he'd imagined it, only much worse...

"Penny for them."

Stephen flushed scarlet.

"Has to be Danny. Danny and dirt - the two go together."

"Shut up."

"He never fucked you?"

Stephen glared at him.

"No, course not. I'd say cocksucking. You look like a cocksucker."

"You dirty pig." Stephen was furious.

But Ian was smiling, unperturbed. "Bet you'd like to suck him, wouldn't you?"

Stephen looked away, heart racing.

"But he didn't even ask, did he? Not even a hint, dear me."

Stephen felt tears sting, tears of anger and frustration, because Ian was right. At heart he'd wanted that most of all. Only somehow he couldn't say it. It sounded so crawling.

"Any time you need a little help with that problem Stephen..." and Ian's dirty eyes slid over his erection, the same unwanted erection that kept popping up out of his filthy thoughts.

"Leave me alone, you little poof." He crossed his legs, trying to cover it up.

Ian smiled. "Don't let him get to you. He'll give in eventually. Relax."

Stephen stared at him, not sure whether to deny everything or ask him for further reassurance.

"Believe me," Ian was smiling again, "with your determination you're bound to succeed. All the sex you can handle."

"It'll never be enough," Stephen heard himself say.

Ian looked at him in surprise but managed to cover it up nicely. "You only think that."

"You've done it with him too, haven't you?" Stephen said suddenly, voice tauter than a wire.

"Once or twice." Ian smiled then told a little white lie. "But not for a long time." *God forgive my almost-truth. I've told too many in my time to worry about one more.* "You can relax, I'm not competition." And that, at any rate, was true.

Stephen visibly relaxed. He closed his eyes and spoke almost hopelessly. "It's just he's so good-looking. It feels like..." But he couldn't think what it felt like. He opened his eyes again. "He makes me feel so edgy, so restless, so..."

"Hungry," Ian supplied.

"Yes," Stephen agreed emphatically.

"You're not alone." And Ian's smile was dry. But before Stephen could ask him what he meant the front door sounded. Ian got up quickly, almost as if he was expecting it. Stephen listened. He could hear voices but nothing else.

Jehovah's Witnesses. Who else would come to the front door? He closed his eyes and watched the red head sink down before him for the fiftieth time that day.

Conley stood in the vestibule and looked at Ian. He looked utterly alien. How could this be Danny's brother? He was small and rather thin with bad skin and die-straight, dirty brown hair. There was a very faint cast of John Jackson Moore about him, the eyes maybe, and of course the hair colour, but that was it.

A runt, that's what Danny had called him, the family runt.

"Not what you expected?"

Conley realised he'd been staring. He flushed and averted his gaze.

"He'll be right down. John's out, so..." He left it unspoken.

"You said he... wasn't well."

"No, I said he was sick. He gets restless, so restless that he ends up like a bomb waiting to go off. Things happen." He looked at Conley as if he expected him to understand. *More* even, take responsibility for it. The implication was there.

Conley knew he meant something precise, it wasn't a vague remark, but he still wasn't sure what. It was too vague for him.

"He pushes everyone to extremes and then they don't know what they're doing." Ian Jackson Moore was smiling at him and Conley finally understood.

He nodded. "Yes," he said.

Ian grinned. It changed him. His teeth were strong and yellow, like a horse's. The discoloration wasn't from bad diet, not like Conley's own, just bad luck. Danny had taken all the cards. But it was a clean grin, strangely the healthiest he'd ever seen amongst them. Conley smiled back.

Then Danny appeared. He looked almost shy, insecure, then it was gone. "My man," he said, voice low.

And Conley smiled at him too.

They went out the door without looking back.

So long and goodbye.

Restless didn't describe it.

Conley watched him out the corner of his eye.

"Does it bother you?" Danny said without looking at him, with an uncanny and goosepimpling perception.

Conley took a breath, feeling an army of dead men walking over his grave. "What?" he asked carefully.

Danny laughed. "Me, here. It was Ian's idea, wasn't it? He called you."

"Yes."

Danny looked at him now, smiling. "Good old Ian." And what that noise meant Conley couldn't begin to guess. All he heard were the words and they meant nothing.

Danny was gone again, back inside himself, body low in the seat, gazing out the side window. Not a flicker, nothing. Like a hover-fly or a humming-bird, something defying the eye. The feeling that he was *so* charged, was moving *so* fast, you couldn't see it. Danny wasn't still at all, he was an illusion.

Conley felt the hairs on his arms go up as if he were close to static.

"Blink and you miss me." Danny's voice cut into the air.

"What?" Conley darted a look at him, not sure if he'd actually said it.

"I don't know, I just said it." And he smiled again.

"You a mind-reader too, in your spare time?"

"Of course, keeps me one step ahead."

And Conley looked at him again and realised he was serious and didn't know quite how to answer that.

They drove the rest of the way in silence. When they got there the ground was thick with snow, and it was still falling, large soft flakes like feathers tumbling through the sky, directionless and muffling.

Danny got out slowly, dreamily. The feathers lay on his hair and slowly melted, spotted his jacket. His face was dyed by the sodium lamp, his hair deep and rusty. His hands were pushed high inside the chest of his jacket.

Everything looked faintly unreal to Conley. Danny most of all.

He went round to where he stood, unmoving, snow floating past him, disappearing from him as if he had a force-field around him. "You look unearthly," he said quietly. If he had shouted it it would still have been quiet, levelled by the airborne layers of snow.

"Unearthly bad or unearthly good?"

"Just unearthly... not of this world."

"It's the light, the snow, the jacket." Danny smiled at him.

"Like hell it is." Conley touched his face.

They stood there like that until Danny said, "Go on then, do it."

So Conley kissed him, separated by layers of coat and leather, numbed by the cold, and still he could feel the heat of it, the instant flare of it right through him. He let go. "I don't know whether that's heavenly fire Danny or something worse."

Danny laughed. "It's my fucking mouth, that's all. No mystique."

And Conley wondered what he felt when he kissed you, if he felt anything at all.

"Come on," Danny said suddenly. "Before we freeze." And he led the way upstairs, Conley watching him climb ahead of him, all leg and shoulder and flaming hair, like some kind of god.

Danny was going to live forever. Perfect, young, beautiful, immortal. Nothing could age him. Nothing could destroy him.

Conley opened the door without looking at him.

The flat was warm and welcoming.

Danny went into the room and did one turn, arms held wide. "I love this place. No animals, no stinking dark, no John."

Conley wondered if they were listed in decreasing or increasing order of importance. He made them coffee and laced it liberally with rum.

Danny sat opposite him, shoes off, feet crossed under him, and Conley decided he definitely did look bigger, older.

"I think you're still growing."

Danny was watching him from under half-shut lids, his coffee cradled Buddha-like between his legs.

"Why d'you say that?" His voice was sleepy, seductive. But then it always was. He didn't know how else to talk.

"You look taller, thinner, broader up here." Conley shrugged his shoulders.

Danny laughed. "It isn't that long since you last saw me."

"I don't know, you look it."

"Well, maybe I am."

"What height are you?"

"No idea."

"Never measured yourself?"

"Not since I was about seventeen. I was almost five-ten then."

"You're taller than that."

"Could be."

"You're a slow grower."

"Childhood runs in the family. Some of us never grow up at all."

Conley heard the hard, brittle sound of that and changed the subject. "How's Stephen?" he heard himself say then felt himself blush.

"He's fine." Danny was still watching him. He lifted his head and took a drink before letting it fall back against the settee again. "And for what it's worth, I didn't lie to you, that was the first time. I'm sorry it happened here."

"I'm sorry I brought it up. I don't know why I said it."

"Yes you do."

Conley looked at him sharply and Danny went on, "You said it because I hurt you and you wanted to hurt me back. Go ahead, make me feel bad."

And Conley could suddenly feel it, like a fish being played out on a line, Danny saying, Come on, you want a fight? You've come to the right place. And he knew this is what Ian meant. He pushes people to extremes and things happen. Danny goes around smashing vacuums, filling them with movement, destruction, anything.

Danny was scary.

Really scary.

Conley was watching him. He was watching Conley. Smiling. Nothing ever made him lose his smile.

Conley leaned back in his seat and forced himself to relax.

Danny smiled some more. "Not in the mood?"

"Not for that."

Danny raised one eyebrow and said nothing else. He drank some more coffee, drained it, then rested the empty cup far from him on the sofa. "Let's talk about the past."

"The past?" Conley said, feeling oddly unsettled by the idea. Danny's expression didn't help.

"I'd like to talk about it. I'm not allowed to at home. It would be nice to talk about it. Don't you want to talk about the past? Got any dark secrets?"

"Everybody has."

"Are yours as dark as mine? Like Pilate's truths, are yours the same as mine?" And Danny looked unearthly again, inscrutable, sitting there like that, watching him, talking about something else, something Conley didn't begin to understand. And he felt as if he were locked in the room with a madman or a rogue animal, something unpredictable, dangerous.

Maimed and dangerous.

Conley frowned. *Maimed.*

"What's wrong?" Danny asked.

"Word association."

Danny looked at him blankly. "Are we going to play it or what?"

No. Conley almost said it, but something else kicked in and he said instead, "Yes." He paused then said more certainly, "Yes, let's, see what we get."

"Oh goody." Danny's voice was heavily sarcastic.

"Blood," Conley said for no earthly reason.

"Come," Danny said back immediately.

"*Come?*" Conley stared at him.

"Yeah, come. You know, spunk, sperm, semen." Danny was smiling at him as if he was an idiot.

"Alright." Conley tried to straighten his thoughts. "Red."

"Glass."

"*Glass?*" Conley said again.

Danny laughed. "We're not going to get very far if you question everything I say."

"Perhaps if you didn't come out with such weird associations."

"Perhaps if you didn't give me such weird words." And there was a hint of asperity in it now.

"I apologise. No more remarks."

"Fine by me." As Danny waited Conley thought again of an ill-tempered animal. Crotchety, unpredictable, razorish.

"Curtain."

"Dark."

"Snow."

"Forest."

Conley stopped, hearing Ian say it. Danny watched him. Conley went on, "Death."

"Blood."

"Knife."

"John."

Conley raised his eyebrows. "He'd be flattered, I'm sure."

"He probably would," Danny replied levelly. "What did you expect me to say? Henderson?"

Conley felt his face muscles go slack. He inhaled his own saliva and coughed on it, looking away from him.

When he'd finished Danny said, "What are you doing, Max?" And the name was put in like an insult. "Playing trap the murderer?"

"Are you?"

"What?" And Danny was smiling at him now, knowing damn well what he meant but making him ask anyway.

"Are you Henderson's murderer?"

"What do you think?"

"You could be."

"My feelings are hurt." But Danny was still smiling.

"You look hurt."

"You can't see how I'm bleeding inside."

And Conley hated the imagery of it, the way he said it, relishing the words as if he was saying something dirty, forbidden.

"I think we'll stop this." Conley drained his cup.

"If you like. What are we going to play now, Ludo?"

"I don't have a set."

"Shame."

And they were right back there again without Conley even knowing how they'd done it. Danny's voice saying, Come on, start something, why don't you?

"Want to fuck?" Danny said it suddenly, with a smile that went nowhere.

Conley looked at him, feeling that familiar frightening skip of excitement, worse somehow, with him like this.

"I mean *fuck*," he went on before Conley could say anything. "As in me putting it up you. Want to do that?"

Conley wiped his palms on his thighs.

"I feel so hard and edgy. I'd really like to fuck. I'd be good. I'm always good like this, really stiff and lasting. Ian'll vouch for me, phone him up and ask him. Would you like to? Tell me you'd like to. Make my day." Danny paused and in that moment his voice seemed to slide down into a pit of something sticky and black before he said, "Come on Conley, help me out." No smile, nothing, just that.

Help me out.

Conley's hair stood on end. He felt it up the back of his neck, scalp prickling.

Danny got up and crossed to him. He sat down beside him and started squeezing Conley's crotch. No kissing, no talking. Like some kind of randy teenager hell bent on the experience no matter who it was with.

Conley sat there, hands pressed against the sofa, saying nothing, heart giddying along. Eventually when Danny began to unzip him he confessed it. "I'm frightened," he said, closing his eyes.

"It's okay, I'll be careful. It won't hurt." Danny's voice was fast and whispery, low and urgent, too eager.

"No Danny, I'm frightened of *you*." And this time Conley managed to look at him.

Danny's face was incredible, in the proper never-used-before pristine meaning of the word. His eyes looked alight. If he'd suddenly sprouted elfin ears he couldn't have looked less human. Conley thought immediately, I can't do this, not with him like that.

794

Who *is* he? I don't even recognise him.

Danny smiled, and his whole face moved with it, became curved and sharp and mouth-drying. "Let me." And his voice was deep and low. "It won't hurt. You know I wouldn't hurt you."

And he didn't even *sound* like Danny, and Conley understood how people believed in possession and evil spirits. He felt as if he was watching a superstition being born. Even as Danny muttered meaningless reassurances, his hands were moving like sensate beings, something he had sent out to do his bidding, until Conley felt himself laid bare, and he could feel the excitement rip-roaring through him. He couldn't even hide it from himself. Danny was pushing him down, climbing on top of him and urging him, "Help me get this off."

Conley did everything he asked until they both lay there, torsos naked, trousers pulled down around their thighs, their cocks like two angry strutting animals, nudging at each other, stretched tight, looking for relief, and then Danny whispered, "On your stomach, roll over." And he lifted himself to let Conley twist under him.

They hadn't kissed, not once.

Conley rolled onto his face, but Danny didn't lie down over him again.

Conley lay there, hung on his own anticipation, before he felt a shiveringly light touch run right down his spine. Danny trailing his finger along it. He felt it again, but this time it was icy cold. It took him a moment to realise it was Danny's tongue.

Without thinking about it he struggled his trousers off his legs, freeing himself. Danny didn't stop him or help him. He felt Danny's hair tickle on the small of his back and knew what he was going to do. He felt his tongue go further and further down and thought, I can't do this. But he lay there, face pushed into the dust of the old velvet, feeling it rough and abrasive on his skin, feeling his cock dig painfully into it, aware of how he was thrusting against it, marking it, smearing small drops of it out of himself like a snail's trail of silver, like Danny's tongue down his back, and now there between his cheeks, licking the underside of his buttocks.

He felt an intense spasm of pleasure across his stomach and instead of clenching as he meant to do, he felt himself pushing up, wishing Danny would go in further. But Danny just kept licking the crease of each buttock where it met his thigh.

Conley opened his legs, ashamed of the transparency of his action, but wanting more. Danny ran his tongue in. Conley opened his legs, flagrantly, pushing his face into the settee, pushing himself against it. He heard himself moan. Danny's tongue went in further. Conley opened wide, one leg down on the floor, spread-eagled, letting him in, rising to meet him.

Danny's tongue went right in.

Conley said, "Oh God..." He lay still, heart pounding, letting it subside. When he relaxed Danny's tongue slid back, soft, pushing, wet. Conley wanted to push down on it. He squirmed like a woman, feeling it climb, almost instantly up there again.

Danny stopped.

On the brink.

Conley felt himself poised in the air for an instant, and then it recede again. So close. *So fucking close.*

He said it again, loving the sound of the word. *Fucking.*

And then Danny was on top of him again, his weight on one arm, his leg thrown over, and Conley felt it nudging at him, wet and silky-headed. Not small and tickling like his tongue, but big and pushy and determined.

Danny lay down over him slowly, hand still pushing it in at him, guiding it. He came down by inches, until his breath sounded in Conley's ear, "In we go..."

And he did.

"Oh God..." Conley said again.

Danny shifted over him and suddenly Conley could feel his weight, lying on him heavily, pinning him down with both hands. He was breathing heavily in his ear. Conley was spread wide open, held there, his sphincter screaming, trying to push it out, but Danny kept nudging it in, going against the tide, forcing it in and whispering, "This is nothing. Wait, this is nothing."

And every time he nudged, Conley's cock, rigid with blood, pressed hard into the sofa, sending pain and pleasure twining together through his body.

"Another inch, that's all," Danny grunted, and Conley found himself pushing up towards it, trying to impale himself on it in spite of the discomfort, and when he did he felt something alien uncurling in his belly, and Danny like some kind of psychic said, "That's it. Feel that?" And he pushed a little harder and Conley felt it move, actually *move* up inside him, past the resistance into his bowels.

He said Danny's name, urgently.

"I'm here. Can't you feel me?" And he pushed. "There. Feel me?"

And Conley wanted him to thrust into him. He was desperate to feel the movement in him, the friction.

He pushed himself up onto it, raising his arse as best he could under Danny's weight.

"Now he wants it," Danny breathed. "And now he's going to get it." And he began to move. Not just that slow upward coaxing, but sliding back out. The pleasure was intolerable.

The thrusting was slow and teasing, barely recognisable as thrusting, just that slow pull out, that gentle squeeze in. It went on and on, slowly picking up momentum till Conley couldn't keep it in any longer. "Oh God..." he moaned, then, "Oh God, Danny..."

And Danny kissed him, finally, softly, on the shoulder, lifting his weight from him and kissing him again. And Conley could suddenly move beneath him. He rose to meet the thrust of his hips and he could hear Danny grunting slightly with effort, pushing it steadily inside him.

Conley hissed, "Harder."

Danny laughed, an odd breathless noise, and began pushing it in hard, lifting his body up and slamming it in, and Conley felt it boil up inside him.

Danny began to really hump it into him and Conley realised he was saying, "*Fuck you... fuck you...*" over and over again, full of aggression, pile-driving it in.

And Conley said, "Yes," and offered himself to it, tried to open himself wider, felt his cock dragging on the settee and knew he was going to come.

Danny lifted himself suddenly, struggling right up onto his knees, dragging Conley up with him, pulling Conley's arse up in the air. Conley struggled up with him, his cock suddenly hanging in mid-air, pulsing on the edge, and he could see himself, see Danny's legs between his own, Danny slamming up against him, obscenely braced. Then he saw his hand come round and close over him and begin to pull.

Conley felt Danny deeper than ever, somewhere in his stomach, forcing him open, and watched Danny's hand pulling his orgasm out of him.

He closed his eyes and opened his mouth, and it came out, pumping, boiling, spurting, spilling all his secrets, spattering the couch, sluicing over Danny's hand, dripping hot and white over everything, while Conley's body jerked like a man electrocuted, an insect on a pin.

Conley left him lying on the couch. When he came back Danny had lost his jeans. He was sprawling, naked and satiated, with one arm behind his head. Conley was aware of the three red dots against the white of his skin. His head, his armpit, his

groin. Like the three of diamonds. "Better?" he asked, smiling.

"Much, but I wish I had a cigarette."

"The ones I gave you are still where you left them. Do you want one?"

Danny struggled up onto one elbow. "Do I? Give."

Conley retrieved the open packet from the kitchen drawer.

Danny took them from him and sat up cross-legged to light one. He inhaled then dropped his head back and let the smoke out. "Nirvana."

"You hardly ever smoke the damn things. Why the sudden desperation?"

"Gets you like that sometimes. Like fucking, you just gotta do it." And he looked at Conley with a steady and unnerving gaze.

Conley was sitting on the coffee table wrapped in a dressing gown.

Danny took the cigarette from his mouth and picked a piece of tobacco from his lip. He looked at it, balanced like a tiny flake of gold on his fingertip. "Enjoy it?" he asked without looking up.

"What do you think?"

Danny's eyes came up. "You made a hell of a fucking mess on your nice sofa."

Conley glanced down at it and smiled. "Who cares?"

"I must go and wash." Danny took another drag on the cigarette.

"No hurry."

Danny grinned at him. "What are you doing? Enjoying the show?"

"I think I might be."

Danny laughed. "This is the man who used to shit himself if you walked too close."

"Long time ago. Different people, different times."

"I've even grown."

"You've even grown," Conley agreed. Then he said, "Do you realise you're not even twenty-one?"

"So?"

"Just a boy."

Danny grinned again, caught his flaccid penis and jigged it up and down slackly in his hand, all the while holding Conley's eyes. "Think so?"

Conley flushed and stood up saying, "I think maybe you *should* go and wash."

"It's your shit." And Danny was still grinning.

"Don't be so gross." And Conley flushed all over again.

He heard Danny get up, chuckling, and disappear inside the bathroom.

Ian watched John pace across the floor. He watched the strong, bullish curve his neck made, saw him turn and measured the width of his shoulders with his eyes.

What they would call a fine figure of a man. No fat, not any more. Gone, never to return. He didn't need it any more. What did he have to hide?

"I don't believe you." John was glaring at him. "I don't believe a single fucking word you've said."

Ian shrugged and smiled.

Stephen watched him and swallowed, wondering, not for the first time, how Ian said and did these things without John disembowelling him.

John turned to him suddenly. Stephen had to physically stop himself from flinching. "You heard them at the door?"

Stephen nodded.

"And you thought it was Jehovah's Witnesses?"

"I just assumed... coming to the front door..."

John turned back to Ian, not even waiting for him to finish. "You lying little spastic. What did you talk about?"

797

"The place of surgery in modern religion."

"Bullshit!" John slammed his fist on the table, making them all jump, even Rab, sitting doing his laid-back bit on the kitchen counter. Stephen heard him mutter, "Shit." He smiled, enjoying his discomfort. Rab caught the smile and gave him the finger. Stephen did it back then realised John had seen him. He blushed as if he'd been caught doing something behind his back.

Ian said, "Can we go to bed now?" distracting John's attention again. Stephen went limp and sat down heavily on the chair.

"They can, not you."

Ian raised his eyebrows but said nothing.

John turned and looked at them expectantly. Stephen got up and scurried out the room, trying not to. Rab got up more slowly, irritated beyond measure, and said, "You know where he's gone, you know this little shit helped him, so what's all this crap for?"

John moved towards him. "I don't know anything. How do I know it wasn't *this* little shit?" He stabbed a finger in Rab's chest.

Rab looked down at his chest, pressing his fingers to where he'd effectively punched him and said, "I hope he's finally fucked off and left you, I really do."

"It'll be you too sweetheart. Why don't you go to bed and have a good cry?"

"Christ." Rab shook his head contemptuously. "The world's first fairy gorilla."

John patted his cheek. "Fuck off faggot, before I pull your pony-tail."

Rab gave him one last venomous look, with nothing left to spare for Ian, and left the room.

"Alright, get all your best clothes on," John said, crossing for his jacket.

"You're taking me out?"

"You bet I am."

"Mr Conley's?" Ian said, getting up with a leisurely stretch.

"I wonder *how* you guessed that?" Each word slow and sarcastic.

Ian smiled and it was his turn to pat John's cheek.

Ian watched John's face as they drove. It was set and pale. Or at least it looked pale in the darkness, flaring white and hollow as each set of oncoming lights swung through the interior then passed on.

"Reading anything?" John asked, voice just a low vibration.

"Not yet, still a blank."

"What do you expect to see?"

"I don't know... intent. You must intend to do something."

"Why?"

"Every action has a reaction. I'm just trying to decide if it's going to be deliberate."

"Or an accident."

That slowed Ian. Slowed him right to a stop. He said carefully, "I don't believe you've done it deliberately yet."

"Who are you trying to convince, me or you?"

"I already know. I was there."

"Don't remind me." John's voice was bitter.

"I did as per your instructions John."

"No Ian, you just butted in."

"Well, it wasn't me who shoved the bar of soap in his mouth. Maybe you should have thought of that first."

"Christ, you cheeky..."

Ian could hear the outrage in it. He smiled into the dark. "Nothing like guilt for breaking a strong man's back."

"Shut up, you little dick."

Ian smiled again and said nothing.

After a moment John said, "You engineered this, didn't you?"

"You always were the brightest star in the family."

"Next to you I suppose?"

"There has to be some compensation for my face John. Be fair."

"You really think you're so fucking smart, don't you?"

"That's right."

"And what's the script? Do I go in here and go apeshit? Is that it?"

"We can always rely on you to go apeshit. World's first fairy gorilla, remember?"

"Jesus..."

"Watch the road. Let's not die before we get there."

"I don't believe you..."

"I've felt the same about you many times."

John shot a glance at him then said, "Meaning?"

"Oh I don't know..." Ian looked out the window for a moment, then turned and said quietly, "Like how it would be to be loved by you. How it feels to be touched by that gentleness." He turned away, voice bright again. "The usual."

John snatched a breath, suddenly aware he was holding it, and couldn't think of a single thing to say. Nothing.

The car suddenly seemed full of a great ugly silence. Full of unspoken thoughts, unvoiced dreams, unfulfilled passions. All dark and deformed and dangerous. Ian's voice sounded oddly chirpy in it, out of place. "Relax John, it's only illegal, immoral and a sin in the eyes of God - nothing our family can't handle."

"Are you saying...?" John finally managed. "I thought..." But he didn't finish that either.

"That it was just a passing phase? A novel idea I picked up a couple of weeks ago? A curious-to-know-what-it's-like urge? Oh please John, spare me. You've known as long as I have. It just suited you to pretend you didn't. We can give up the pretence now. Believe me, I'm not about to tell. I have to retain some dignity."

"Shit," John said succinctly and they fell into silence again.

"This snow is getting worse," Ian said. "Let's hope we can get back."

John said nothing. Ian could feel him, self-absorbed beside him. He knew what he was thinking. He was wondering what kind of a threat he posed now. Ian felt a curious sad elation to realise he really didn't care. Day was when confessing himself to John would have been unthinkable. Not now. And didn't that put the wind up his big brother?

He watched the wipers cut swathes through the snow and thought, Big surprise heading your way Danny-boy. Six foot of solid muscle-bound confused pain.

Wonder if he's gonna kill anyone? *Grrowlll*...

Ian smiled to himself. Well, you never knew. You never knew at all.

Conley looked at him in the mirror. "Want to go out?"

"Out?" Danny asked, smiling.

"Yes, you know, out, like ordinary people do. A drink, a meal, the cinema, anywhere you like."

Danny's smile widened. "Well, what do you know... is that what they do?"

Conley nodded. "Want to join them?"

"Where will we go?"

"Anywhere you like."

"Somewhere with women."

"Only if you promise not to start anything."

Danny looked at him and said, "Jealous or scared?"

"Scared."

"Try it. You'd like it."

"I seriously doubt that."

"We could do it together."

"What are you suggesting?" Conley was half-amused.

"Threesome, foursome, all in together."

Conley looked at him and realised he was serious. "Good grief."

"It's the best of both worlds. I could hold your hand." He was grinning again.

"No. Positively, categorically, no. Out yes, but no group sex."

"Killjoy. How about a quick one then? Would it bother you if I disappeared for a quick one?"

Conley stared at him in the mirror. "Are you *seriously* asking me?"

"Say no and I won't."

"And if I say yes?"

"I will if I can."

"It's none of my business." Conley smiled disbelievingly. "I mean if you want..."

"Want to watch?"

Conley flushed. "Alright Danny, stop it..."

"No, I'm serious. I could hear it in your voice. What is it, fucking by proxy? I mean it, I don't mind you watching. In fact, I think I might even like it, who knows?"

"This conversation's too tacky to be real."

"You *do* want to watch."

"*Danny.*"

"No problem, we'll see what we can do. In the car maybe. You can watch in the mirror."

Conley turned away, feeling a disturbing mix of revulsion and excitement. "I wish I'd kept my mouth shut."

"Where's the best place?"

"For what?"

"Girls out looking for a good time."

"There's a wine bar outside town. Big place. It's new, very trendy and noisy. They tell me it has a disco."

"Then that's where we'll go."

"I'm not sure I like this Danny."

Danny took Conley's hand and ran it over his naked belly, over the scar, down onto his stiffening cock. "You will, trust me."

Then he kissed Conley hard on the mouth, and let him go.

The bar was smoky and loud, packed full of young women in black lycra dresses, older women in shiny fabric that made them look corseted and hard.

Danny and Conley squeezed their way through to the bar. Danny leading, enjoying himself; Conley behind him, amused in spite of himself.

The barmaid took an instant dislike to Danny and served him with a surliness that bordered on rudeness. Danny never even noticed.

After she'd gone Conley tugged his arm and shouted over the noise, "Does that happen often?"

"What?" Danny tore his eyes away from the handkerchief-sized dance floor and looked at him.

"The worm from under the mat, does it happen often?"

"Sometimes."

Conley laughed. "I thought you floored everyone."

It was Danny's turn to laugh. "No way, it's sleight of hand. I just make it look that way. Envy and lust fifty-fifty every time."

"Why should she dislike you?"

Danny shrugged. "Maybe she hates it when her clit gets up for a stretch."

Conley looked away, laughing. "You really *are* gross."

Danny followed his face, smiling at him. "Some people do you know. They'd rather sleep on. Especially if they suspect you wouldn't take it if they were giving it free."

"You would though, wouldn't you?"

"Not from her."

"Why not?"

"She doesn't like me."

Conley burst out laughing again. "I give in."

Danny grinned back at him. "Let's go find somewhere to sit."

They elbowed their way through the standing groups of office parties and tense-faced people desperate to get their rocks off without being too obvious about it, and found two stools by a glass-smothered table. The tables were too small and cramped as usual but nobody was caring.

Coloured lights swooped across the darkened walls and ceiling, throwing the room into a strobe effect that heightened people's movements until they looked almost syncopated in time to the music.

Danny almost passed unnoticed. "I blend," he said, leaning across the table so that Conley could hear him. "I've discovered my natural habitat at last."

Conley looked around him. "It's like someone's idea of Hell," he said.

"That explains it then," Danny smiled back at him.

Conley wasn't sure if that was funny or not.

Danny sat back and looked across at the dancers. He felt someone tug at his arm. He looked down at the hand and realised it was Conley's. When he looked up at his face he knew something was wrong. "What is it?" he asked, knowing Conley couldn't hear him.

Conley shouted but it was still barely discernible. "Katherine Henderson's just come in."

Danny rubbed his face. "Shit," he said.

Conley nodded then he said, looking down at the table, "I think we've just been spotted."

Danny didn't catch the words, but he knew what he'd said reading Conley's evasive gesture.

He watched Conley's eyes come back up and a polite smile fix on his face. He wasn't going to turn, fuck it. He would sit right here, just as he was.

He could read how close she was by the angle of Conley's head as it lifted to follow her advance.

He felt the hand on his shoulder purely by its weight. The heavy padding and thick leather of his jacket destroyed all other sensation. Then he smelt her perfume and something leapt, like it always did. No matter how much he kicked it, it wouldn't lie down.

"Hello Danny," she said in his ear.

Danny turned and looked up at her. She was in a black sequinned sheath dress. She looked like some kind of sinister fish. A shark maybe. She looked liquid, wet.

She had someone with her. Neat, tanned, hair with blonde streaks in it. He looked as if he was made of plastic. He had blue cold-water eyes. Danny knew the eyes but

the rest looked like an aftershave advert - tacky aftershave. No, a watch advert, one of those ugly bastarding things they described as 'Steel and yellow metal'. Too much money for nothing shit. That's what he was, a too-much-money-for-nothing-shit, a member of The Lucky Sperm Club.

Danny stood up. He didn't know why. He just did it.

Conley stayed where he was, which was even odder.

Katherine Henderson was smiling, a well-what-have-we-here smile, smug and unhappy all at once. "This is Robert," she said, stepping back a little to give them a clear view of each other, "my brother."

The music died with a suddenness that was unnerving.

"Robert, this is Danny. And this..." she looked at Conley, "is James Conley. He did Jimmy's conveyance for him... on the flat."

Robert Henderson nodded at Conley, a tight white smile about his mouth. Danny saw Conley nod back, no smile. It was the only German gesture Conley really had, that small bow. You expected him to click his heels. Then Henderson the Second did an odd thing, he turned to Danny and held out his hand. *Big* smile.

Danny actually looked at it for a moment before taking it. It was an entirely unconscious gesture.

Henderson's grasp was strong, confident, like he'd been taught it at the encyclopaedia salesman's school. "Hi." He actually said that. "Pleased to meet you." And the transatlantic twang was there.

Danny looked at his narrow blue eyes and saw James Henderson looking back at him, sharper, meaner, and Danny wanted to smile, so he let it out.

He smiled at Robert Henderson and said, "How d'you do?" *You fucking faggot.*

And he waited until Robert Henderson finally let go his hand.

They joined them.

Fate provided two newly emptied places and they took them.

Katherine Henderson sat beside Danny, her knee touching his. He moved it then let it rest against hers again. What the hell, who cared?

But he could feel it building in the pit of his stomach, almost like a cramp of fear. He'd successfully kept away from her for how long now? A fortnight anyway, and here he was feeling that knee like it was welded to his own. He wanted to put his hand on it, feel the texture of the shiny stocking she was wearing, feel how far up it went. He caught Conley looking at him and knew he'd read it on his face.

He blushed as if he'd been caught stealing.

Like I said Conley, it makes me feel bad, like I've betrayed somebody.

He looked at Robert Henderson, mostly because Robert Henderson was looking at him. What had she told him? Nothing? Everything? He recognised Danny. She had introduced him simply as 'Danny' and he knew who he was so she must...

Katherine Henderson had put her hand on his leg. She was talking to Conley, but she had her hand on Danny's thigh. She was leaning into him. He stood up. "Going to take a leak," he said, and he looked at Conley as her hand dropped away from him.

Conley nodded. *I see you running away Danny.*

Too right, Mr Conley.

Danny was finishing up when Robert Henderson came in.

Fucking faggot, Danny thought again. Which would have surprised everyone who knew him, especially the man himself.

Danny crossed to the roller-towel and dried his hands, taking his time, because

Robert Henderson was not the coincidental type. His life was as clear cut as the fake blonde streaks in his meticulously layered hair. Things didn't just happen to Robert Henderson, he made them happen.

So Danny waited and watched him, smiling faintly, let a little hint of it sit on his face, just to unsettle him.

He talked inanities, all in that odd bastard accent. Not American, not Scots. Like a computer generated voice for a talking watch. It kept coming back to watches. It would be white rabbits next.

"Kathy says you knew Jimmy."

Kathy wasn't a family name, of that Danny was sure. Jimmy might be, but not Kathy. Robert Henderson was an abbreviator, and you can bet when he met with a short name he lengthened it. Jane would become Janey. John, Johnny. It was a handy way to cut people down to size, trivialise them under the guise of friendliness.

"Mm," Danny said noncommittally.

Henderson went over and washed his hands very thoroughly. Plenty of soap, lots of rubbing, as if he'd been handling something dirty. Or maybe he was just killing time.

He came over beside Danny and dried his hands, equally thoroughly, between every finger. "Bet his murder shook you up."

And there it was. Henderson watching him, waiting to hear what he said, because what he'd actually said to Danny across that wet strip of greying cotton was, Bet you didn't give a fuck, did you? You look as if you might have stuck him yourself, that's what I think.

"Terribly," Danny said and he gave a little smile. He looked as convincing as a six pound note.

"I'll bet," Henderson said and the blue eyes went on probing until Danny said, "Your brother said you were a lawyer."

"Not quite, I trained in law. I'm an investment broker."

Danny smiled at him and nodded.

Robert Henderson suddenly put his arm around his shoulder like they were some kind of old football chums. "Guess we better be getting back," he said.

Danny let him stay there just long enough, then he pushed out the door, extricating himself, and went back out into the multicoloured noise.

Conley - who must be drunk, Danny thought - was doing a slow smoochy dance with Katherine Henderson. Danny saw him bend his head to hear something she said then smile at her.

Fucking bitch. What was he playing at?

"They make a cute couple, don't you think?" Robert Henderson was sitting beside him on a velvet covered banquette.

"Beautiful," Danny said, unable to keep the irritation out his voice.

"Not jealous Danny?" He drawled the vowel in Danny's name, giving it the full American treatment. Danny was surprised he didn't call him Dan.

He wondered what he'd say if he said, Yes, I wish she'd keep her hands off my fuck. Instead he said, "No," and left it at that. Let him make of it what he liked.

Truth was he didn't know what way his jealousy was going. He watched Conley's hands on her back, wondering if he'd have the nerve to make a grab for her backside. He looked as if he wanted to.

Well, if you've got a boner Maxie she'll feel it alright. You couldn't get any closer. Looks like it would be him doing the watching.

"Get laid much?" Henderson's voice sounded disembodied, like a voice in his head.

Danny's eyes flicked sideways. He picked up his beer and drank some without turning to him. "Nope."

"Good looking guy like you?"

Danny turned and said, "How old are you?"

Henderson looked startled. "Thirty-two. Why?"

"Consider that middle-aged?"

"No, why?" Now he looked really puzzled.

"Because you're a patronising cunt."

It took Henderson a full minute to say, "Now wait a minute..."

But Danny cut him short. "Drop dead."

He looked back at the dance floor. The music slid into another slow number. End of the evening blues. Conley and Katherine Henderson stayed where they were, his hands marginally lower.

Go on Conley, get a handful of her arse. That's what you want.

"You know my brother was gay?" Henderson spoke again and Danny heard the change in it. Less Americano, harder, more precise. Now he sounded like a no-nonsense Scottish barrister. Let's not beat about the bush.

"Yep," Danny said, still without looking at him.

"Is that what it was about, you and him? Pair of fruits?"

Danny let a beat pass, maybe two. Unexpectedly he could feel his heart thumping. Henderson had been working up to this all evening. Danny had just made it easier for him.

"No."

"That's not what his diary says."

Thumpetty-thump. Thumpetty-thump.

Still going heart, I see.

Yes Danny.

Good lad.

Danny said nothing. What was there to say?

"That why you don't get laid much, because you're a fruit?"

Danny felt it right in there, like a cold current going through him, and suddenly there was no anxiety, no nerves. Heart sweet and calm, working without his knowing. Ian would have recognised this metamorphosis. Ian would have said, Danny's on a flyer.

Danny turned and looked at him, and Conley would have said he looked unearthly. "Want to try me and see?" And he smiled a slow, curving smile.

Henderson who had expected anger, denial, guilt even, looked at him and numbly shook his head.

Danny said, still smiling sweetly, "Suck my big fat dick."

Robert Henderson could see his lips move oddly, too clearly, as if he was enunciating each word for a lip reader, and then his tongue came out, just the tip, pink and living, and wet over his mouth.

Henderson shook his head and the disc-jockey's voice came loud and intrusive into the room and said, The party's over, and his sister came back, flushed and smiling, and the whole moment was flung spinning up into the air, like a clay pigeon, and was blasted out of existence.

Never happened.

The door of the Mercedes had barely closed, Conley wasn't even finished belting himself in when Danny said, "Get you up hard, did she?"

Conley looked at him for a surprised moment before he said, "No." And his answer

was almost a question - What the hell is this?

"I'll fucking bet." And Danny pushed his own belt home with a shove that had probably sealed him in the car for life.

"Danny, at the risk of you throwing another one of your legendary sulks, is this jealousy I'm hearing?"

Danny turned on him, flaring at him, "I do *not* sulk."

Conley laughed. He tried to hold it in but it came out anyway. He looked so furious, like one of those proverbial scalded cats.

Danny started trying to struggle out his seat belt again. Conley caught at him. "Hey, hold it. Whoa. Where are you going?"

"The fuck out of here."

"At one-fifteen in the morning? Come on Danny."

"You were *pawing* her."

"I was *dancing* with her."

Without warning Danny slapped him, savagely. A full-force, lunging crack.

Conley grunted with the impact, sat there for a moment, then slowly put a hand to his burning cheek.

"You dirty fucking cunt," Danny spat at him.

Conley blinked, stared at him as if he'd never seen him before.

Danny suddenly covered his face with one hand and laid his head against the window. "Shit," he said flatly, banging his head against the glass. "Shit, shit, shit... *shit.*"

He stayed behind the hand. After a moment he said, "I'm sorry," and it came out less harsh, more Danny.

There was another silence then he said, still hiding behind his hand, "Say something."

"You've got a hell of a temper."

Danny peeked between his fingers. Conley was smiling. Danny dropped his hand. "Christ, I can't believe I did that. I'm sorry," he said again. "I don't believe myself sometimes."

"Let's go home," Conley said, straightening round in his seat and engaging the engine. He heard Danny whisper '*Shit*' again and saw him rub his head wearily against the glass.

When Conley looked next he was asleep.

And dreaming.

"John, this is fucking ridiculous."

"You wanted it. Shut up."

"It's gone half one."

"I said shut up."

Ian shut up.

John leaned over and turned the engine off. The sudden silence was deafening. The engine began to tick slowly, already cooling. It was a cold night.

Ian watched the snowflakes falling gently earthwards. He tried to remember something from a distant Sunday School talk on angel's souls - or was it babies? - and snowflakes, but it kept sneaking away from him. He smothered a yawn.

"Stop fucking yawning."

"That's the first..."

John cut him short. "Shut it."

Ian muttered something under his breath but John chose not to hear it. Suddenly powerful headlamps swung across the car park, floodlighting them for an instant.

"That them?" Ian asked, sitting up.

"I don't know."

The car stopped and cut its lights. John rubbed the condensation from the screen, switched on the wipers.

They waited in the dark.

Watching.

"Come on Danny, wake up."

Danny was proving very difficult to rouse. Conley wasn't familiar with the if-you've-got-to wake-him-heaven-help-you phenomenon.

"*Danny.*" Conley gently tugged a lock of hair. "Come on Sleeping Beauty, time to get up."

Danny came out of it groggily.

"We're home," Conley said.

Danny groaned then said succinctly, "Shit."

"First and last words."

"What?"

"Shit. You said it before you fell asleep as well."

"How very uninteresting."

"Grouchy in the morning, aren't you?"

"This isn't the morning, it's the middle of the fucking night." Danny undid his belt and dragged himself out.

Conley smiled and pulled out the keys then followed him.

"It's them," John said, watching Danny move gingerly across the snow, huddled into his jacket. Conley was locking the car.

"Now what?" Ian said.

"We let them get in then we go calling."

There was a silence while John watched them.

"John?"

"What?"

"What the fuck are we doing here?"

"You tell me Ian." John finally turned to look at him. "You tell me."

Conley hung up their coats while Danny went to the toilet. When he came back out Conley said to him, "Want anything?"

"Is that an invitation?" Danny smiled at him.

"I meant to eat or drink."

"It *was* an invitation." Danny's smile grew dirtier.

"Smutty little bastard."

"You're swearing too much. I must be a bad influence."

Danny went over to him and started rubbing against him, slow thrusts up against one hip. "You're a nice mover," he whispered up against his ear.

"I think you're being obscene. I mean, quite apart from dry-humping my leg."

Danny laughed. "I am not. You *are* a nice mover. You looked very slick rubbing up against her like that."

"And how did she look against me?" Conley was smiling, enjoying the feel of him, but he was watchful too.

"Very fucking beautiful. How did you keep your hands off her?"

"They were on her. You accused me of pawing her in fact."

"If it had been me I'd have had her arse..." Danny clutched his buttocks in both hands and jerked him up hard against him "...right here."

Conley felt his goosepimples come up. When he spoke it was hoarse. "I don't have your subtlety obviously."

"You really weren't stiff?"

"Really."

"Jesus, is that iron fucking will or what?" And now Danny was grinding his pelvis into his.

"Think I'm queer after all?"

"Who cares?" Danny licked his lip, sliding a hand in between them.

"I mi..."

But Conley never finished it. Someone thumped on the door. They froze.

"Who the fuck is that?" Danny whispered.

"I don't know," Conley whispered back.

The door thumped again.

"You going to answer it?" Danny whispered, lower this time.

"I better." Conley made to move from him.

"Don't." Danny pulled him back, gripping Conley's genitals almost like a threat.

"Why not?"

"Lots of reasons. It's two in the morning, I want to go to bed, I don't like the sound of it. Leave it."

The door hammered again, louder this time. Conley pulled away from him.

"*Conley!*" Danny hissed at his back, but Conley ignored him. He went to the door and shot the bar open.

John Jackson Moore stood there, a knife blade golden and glinting in his hand.

Before Conley could move, even think of speaking, Danny yanked him back. A violent tug at his shoulder, pushing past him. "What the hell are you doing here?" he was snarling at his brother.

Conley thought, He hasn't seen the knife. He can't have seen the knife.

John Jackson Moore walked him back into the room, knife keeping them a precise twelve inches apart, Danny walking backwards, never looking at the knife, John Jackson Moore smiling.

"Well, well, if it isn't the whore of Babylon." He looked Danny up and down. "What, still dressed?"

Danny saw a movement beyond him in the darkness. John said without turning, "Come on in Ian. Shut the door."

Ian came in.

"You told him." Danny almost whispered it. "You fucking *told* him."

John said, "Oh-oh."

Ian said, "I didn't."

John laughed. "There you are Danny, take your pick."

"Well?" Danny demanded, eyes on Ian.

"He guessed."

Danny looked at John. He smiled, knife still standing there between them. "He told me."

Conley watched it as if it was nothing to do with him. He couldn't take it in. People marching around with knives. What was the knife *for?* He kept saying that to himself as if it was the most important thing in the world. The answer mattered to him. He wanted to ask Danny, Why has your brother brought that knife?

John moved closer. Danny stepped back. Conley realised abruptly Danny had been aware of the knife right from the beginning. He was simply treating it like a handler treated big cats. He knew its limitations, knew the risks he could afford to take. The knife didn't frighten him any more than it ought to. Danny *understood* the knife, like Danny understood his brother, part of the same animal.

"Go to fuck John," Danny said.

"No," John said right back.

Stalemate.

Everybody waited.

Danny again. "What do you want?"

"God knows." There was a slight pause. "Maybe your boyfriend."

And now there was a long pause and at the end of it John raised his voice without turning, "That right Ian?"

But Ian didn't answer him. Ian kept his eyes on Danny. Danny in a borrowed white shirt. It looked like silk. It was half-unbuttoned. It looked dazzlingly white with the black jeans he wore. Ian wondered why no-one had ever thought to put him in such a combination before.

Now they were all waiting again. Conley didn't know what for because he hadn't understood a single word. It was like the conversations you often had with Danny. You didn't really know what he was saying, only that he was saying something important and you had better *listen*.

"No," Danny was saying and Conley thought, At least Danny knows what he means. I wish he'd tell me.

"Yes," John Jackson Moore said. "Or I'll cut his fucking throat."

And Conley looked at him and thought, He did it. Of course he did. Probably in a scene just like this one. Slaughtering his brother's lover. That's what you are, another one in the long list. Wonder how many throats he's cut? Did Danny stand by and let him do it? Is that what he's going to do now? Stand by and watch while his brother ruins your favourite waistcoat? Should have worn the garnet, then the stains wouldn't show.

Suddenly John Jackson Moore looked at him, really looked at him, eyeball to eyeball. "Having a nice time?" His voice was deep, oddly like Danny's when he was excited.

That's what he is, excited. It's blood lust.

"Wonderful," Conley said and was amazed at the levelness of his own voice. For the first time in his life he was glad of its flat unemotional tones.

"Very cool," John said. "I begin to see your appeal. Unless of course you've also got a big dick. Have you got a big dick?"

Conley didn't answer him.

"Danny likes them big, but if he can't get big eager will do. Are you an eager little beaver James? Go down on him with enthusiasm, do you? Or am I being unromantic?"

"You're being a pain in the fucking arse," Danny's voice cut in, hard and icy.

John's eyes shot back to him. "You shut the fuck up, Danny-boy. Nobody was talking to you."

"Tough tits, I'm talking to you. You're getting to be a fucking bore John, know that?"

John jerked forward, catching the front of his shirt, and said, "And you're getting to be a mouthy little shit." Suddenly he looked down at his hand, rubbing the fabric between his fingers. He looked back up. "His?"

Danny nodded curtly. John ripped it apart. Conley saw it, not believing it. He'd read that people ripping clothes off was a fallacy of fiction. In reality it was very difficult. Out of curiosity he'd tried it with an old shirt, and it was. But here was this man ripping an

expensive, well-made silk shirt asunder like tissue paper. The buttons spattered on the wood floor.

"Get it off." He pushed Danny away from him slightly.

Danny slid his arms out the sleeves, tugged it out at the rear, and took it off.

John snatched it out his hand and threw it on the floor.

Ian watched them, looked at Danny, saw the tiny curve of softness over the bite of his belt, wondered if John was going to strip him there, at knife-point, in front of them all.

Conley looked at Danny's profile, his chest. He looked angry enough to tear his brother limb from limb. Maybe he was. Maybe he would.

"Now let's try again Danny." John's voice was determinedly patient, as if he was talking to a particularly infuriating six-year-old. "We want to see you doing what you do best with your boyfriend. Make us hot, then maybe you can treat us too. Think you can manage three in one night?"

Conley began to feel a dim flickering of his intent. At least he thought he did. He was hearing it *and* understanding it, only now he didn't want to.

"No," Danny said again.

"He keeps saying no to me." John's artificial annoyance suddenly became more sinister, more defined. It had an itchy quality to it. "Ian," he appealed suddenly, "What should I do?"

"Make him." Ian's voice came back clearly, no hesitation. There was something about the calm volte-face of it that was far worse than any of John Jackson Moore's brutal posturings.

Conley shot a quick glance at Danny, aware of his own shock, wanting to see how he'd take it. He saw him close his eyes, slowly, like someone trying to retain their temper and then John laughed.

It was a humourless noise and it seemed to typify everything that was ugly about the scene that had just taken place. Conley had a sudden conviction that the scene was just starting, that everything that had gone before was just strutting, noise. It was what was about to happen that was important. He wanted to speak, somehow avert it, but he didn't know what to say.

"Do I make you Danny, or shall I just concentrate on Prince Valiant here?" John flicked a glance at Conley then back to Danny again. "Will I cut his face? Mark him like you've marked me?" He looked back at Conley again. "Your little pet prick did this to me. Bet you didn't think he had it in him. Lots of people make that mistake. Looks like an angel, doesn't he? Oh that's not original, believe me. Ian has this notion he's a changeling, inside everything's rotten and black, diseased. Bet when you first met him you didn't want anything to do with him, did you?" John laughed when he didn't answer. "You're just another poor sod who couldn't get out of the way."

He turned to Danny again and said, "Come on Danny, make it easy on yourself, say yes before I cut him."

"No." Danny's voice was flat, hard, no fear in it at all. Which was why Conley didn't see the knife. He thought John had flicked something off Danny's shoulder, that's all. Then he saw the blood running down his arm in a thin, slow seam, like treacle running down a sheet of glass. Conley gasped something, stepping forward.

"Stay *right* where you are." And John had the knife in Danny's stomach, the point no longer visible, dug into his flesh.

Conley stopped.

"Good boy. Now back a step."

Conley took a step back.

"Good, fine."

Danny hadn't even moved. He hadn't even looked at it. Not a whisper, not a

murmur, but his face was white - a horrible, pure putty-white.

"What do you want me to do?" Danny's voice was as still as death, no life in it at all.

John smiled and Conley thought he had never seen so many teeth. "Ian, what do we want him to do?"

And Conley watched as Ian Jackson Moore, the silent brother, moved forward into the light and started to unfasten his brother's clothes.

Ian unfastened the button on Danny's jeans, but Danny stopped him before he got any further. Danny didn't look at him. Ian smiled into his face, close up against him, enjoying the feel of Danny's hand on his, the betraying sweat of his palm, but Danny was looking at John. "Let's go home," he said.

"Let's not." John's voice was clipped, edgy. A man who has been spoiling for a fight too long to let it go now.

"You can't do this," Danny said.

"Just watch me."

"You can't."

John smiled his wolfish smile and turned to Conley. "What does he do with you? Tasty stuff now."

Conley stared at him, not answering.

"Now, now, don't be shy." John's smile got wider. "Otherwise..." And he pulled Danny by the ends of his belt, jerking him forward onto the knife. Danny sucked his stomach in with an audible grunt, but John slackened his hold again saying, "Surely you wouldn't like a thing like that on your conscience?"

Conley shook his head, but he couldn't take his eyes off Ian. Ever since he had moved close to unfasten Danny's jeans he had been running his hand up and down Danny's arm.

Conley watched, fascinated. Danny standing there looking into the middle distance, only a vague tenseness about him betraying his fear of the knife, but letting his brother's hands move over him as if he didn't feel them at all.

"Come on, Mr Conley." And Conley saw the smile harden, Danny flinch back slightly from the point of the knife.

"Mind your own damn business," Conley said, his voice sounding cracked and hoarse.

John Jackson Moore laughed. "He doesn't believe me Danny, sorry."

"Wait..." Conley almost shouted it, seeing the movement in John's body. John looked at him expectantly, smiling.

"What do you want to know?" Conley asked, trying to bring his voice back under control.

"Oh come on," John's smile widened, "you know what we want to know. We want to know what you do with my young brother. What you *like* to do with my young brother."

"Anything," Conley managed. "I don't care what we do." He could feel the heat tidal wave up his face.

"Sounds like an cop-out to me." John looked at Danny. "Is he lying to me?"

"No." Danny's mouth was tight.

"He's so sweet on you he'll take anything you give him? Oh..." John laughed, "big ego trip Danny. No wonder you like it here. Big house, nice manners, loves your sweet little arse inside out. *Big* ego trip."

"Fuck off," Danny almost spat in his face.

John jabbed him with the knife. Danny winced and pulled his stomach in again.

Conley watched spellbound as Ian Jackson Moore perilously caught the blade between thumb and forefinger and pushed it back at him. "Don't," he said shortly. His voice was quiet and threatening. He held his older brother's eyes.

Conley watched a slow flush creep up John Jackson Moore's face. It had an odd effect on him, making him look younger. Perhaps it was the closest he'd ever get to looking vulnerable.

"Don't tell me what to do." His voice was equally quiet, equally threatening.

Conley realised they were uneasy partners, sharing fifty-fifty, both wanting the whole hundred. He wondered how long they'd been sharing him, how much longer it could go on. He wondered what the hell they were all doing here, but Danny answered that one for him.

"Will you two stop dragging me about like a fucking bone!" It was the closest to a shout Conley had ever heard him make. He saw him shove the knife away, slapping John's hand away like a mindless irritation, and then he simply and effortlessly moved out between them. "I'm going home. I don't give a fuck what you two clowns do, but I'm fucking going home," and he marched over to the bedroom.

They stood watching him, Conley forgotten. Conley couldn't decide if they were simply dumbstruck, or no longer concerned now that the game had fallen apart. Maybe it was a bit of both. He saw John Jackson Moore drop the knife hand and casually fold the blade shut. He did it one-handedly, absently, as if it was of no importance. He pushed his hands in his pockets like an actor between scenes. He might have been waiting on a bus. Conley half expected him to wander round the room idly picking things up, like a man waiting on his wife in a strange home, but he did not move.

Danny came back out, fastening his shirt, sweater over one arm. He dropped down on the sofa and pulled on his shoes, temper showing in every line of his body. Everybody was watching him. He stood up and pulled his sweater on, tugging his shirt collar out. Conley began to wonder if he'd forgotten him too. Maybe he'd ceased to exist, the invisible man. But Danny came over to him, straight, direct, past his brothers. He stood in front of him, meeting Conley's eyes. "I'm sorry - yet again."

Conley shook his head and tried to speak. Nothing came out. He cleared his throat and tried again. "Don't be, you're not your brother's keeper."

"No, we left him at the zoo." His voice was spiny with dislike.

Conley glanced past him uncertainly and was thrown to see that it was Ian Jackson Moore who was responding to the insult. John Jackson Moore was just standing there, absorbing everything at one remove.

Conley shook his head again. It was the best he could do. He suddenly wanted to hold him, afraid he wouldn't see him again, but he couldn't do it with them standing there watching, and that unspoken third, the knife, only a thin layer away, only temporarily halted by Danny's freak temper.

Danny held his gaze a moment longer then turned. He crossed the room and pulled his jacket on. He went out. His brothers followed him like policemen escorting a witness, protection that was more a threat.

The door closed with its dull metallic thunk.

Not one of them said goodbye.

Ian sat in the back with him and tried to manhandle him.

Danny slapped him away, not even looking at him. "Fucking leave off."

John glanced in the rear-view mirror but said nothing.

Ian was smiling into the dark. John could feel it without seeing it. He pulled out slowly into the street. There was no traffic. Everyone was safely home in bed. The

traffic lights played to no-one, changing colours meaninglessly, like a dictator proselytizing to an empty stadium. John drove through them at red.

"Smart," Danny said, then in a burst, "What the fuck was all that in aid of?" He turned to Ian. "Did you think this up?"

"Shut up," John said, and his voice was quiet, almost disinterested.

"Not until you tell me what this was all about."

"Ask your brother, he's in charge."

Ian slid his hand round Danny's thigh. "Kiss me and I'll tell you."

Danny pushed his hand off and turned away from him. "You can kiss my arse. Jesus," he said in exasperation, "you're a pair of fucking lunatics, do you know that?"

John glanced in the mirror again. This time he let the sight of him into his heart, let it crush all the light and life out of him. He spoke to Ian. "If you want him, hurry up and have him. He gets home, you've had it."

"And you think he's going to let me?" Ian spoke directly to him in the mirror. Danny looked from one to the other.

"Here." John raised himself and reached into his pocket. He passed his hand over his shoulder. "Let's see *you* try and persuade him."

Ian sat back heavily. The knife sprang perfect and coldly dark in his hand.

"I don't believe this." Danny almost whispered it.

Ian smiled.

"You set me up." He looked at Ian's hand holding the knife. "You sent me there then told him where I was knowing for your help you'd get to... like I was..." Danny didn't finish.

"Not for my help." Ian was unbuttoning his jeans all over again. Danny watched his hand. "Just a demonstration of the trouble I could make. This is payment in advance, that's all."

John's laugh was almost a snort. There was nothing funny about it at all.

"You shit," Danny whispered.

But Ian already had his hand deep inside his trousers. "Now kiss me Danny," and the knife pressed hard through his clothes while Ian's mouth moved determinedly over his own.

SEVENTY-TWO

Stephen and Rab were surprised to see him at breakfast next morning. He looked terrible, so did John, but there were no fresh marks on him. If he was marked it was on his body where no-one could see it. Only Ian looked chipper. A little tired maybe, but not washed out like the other two.

Danny kept his eyes down, not looking at anyone. He didn't eat much. Rab thought he saw John 'accidentally' brush his hair with his hand, and he definitely saw Ian touch his fingers when he passed him a knife, but Danny ignored them both.

Rab saw Stephen watching them. Everybody was watching somebody. Meals were becoming studies in human behaviour.

Rab pushed his plate away with a sudden feeling of disgust. Stephen looked at him curiously. On an impulse he would never understand Rab winked at him. Stephen blinked then tentatively smiled.

Rab got up and went out. Stephen got up and went out after him.

Danny looked up and watched them going then he slowly pushed his crockery to the floor.

John looked up and smiled at him. It was going to be a lovely day.

Danny was haunted by something he didn't understand.

In the car coming back he'd been forced to go down on Ian. Same old story: he hadn't been able to achieve an erection, so Ian had made him do penance.

He had come copiously in Danny's face, drawing out at the last moment to spurt it in his eyes, dirty-mouthing him for his impotency, pulling his hair so tight it left his scalp tender.

Nothing new.

Except...

Now it kept going over in his head, as if there had been something different about it, something about the way John had been watching, something about his eyes in the rear-view mirror.

He worked hard, trying to burn the sensation of it out, numb the itchy restlessness, but it wasn't working, and he knew why. He also knew how to fix it, what he needed.

Who.

He wondered how he was going to pull it off, and he needed to pull it off. He had half a mind to go to Rab, Stephen, even Ian, but not one of them could take this knot out of him. Not one of them was revenge enough.

He caught himself biting his nails, a long-dead habit, and wondered how far he'd gone inside himself to dig that one up.

He walked down the barn and looked outside. The pick-up was there, but there was no way he could get out and back without John knowing.

Unless he was fast.

He might make it. He might not.

Who cares? a voice said inside.

He smiled. Too fucking right.

He walked over to the pick-up, got in. The keys were in the ignition.

Who fucking cares?

Danny tanked along the road in a kind of desperate exhilaration.

It would be too much if she wasn't in, if he'd risked all this for a fuck that wasn't to be. What if she'd gone shopping? A fuck out-manoeuvred by Safeway. Too sad.

He smiled grimly to himself. He remembered her in the black dress up tight against Conley, trying to get him going, sliding all over him, crotch pushed into him. *Did it really leave you cold Conley? Really? You didn't look it. No sir, as Robert Henderson would say.*

Danny smiled again and found it cut off half on his face. Shit, what if the fat little faggot was there, staying with her? Of course he would be. They were Scots, weren't they? *Shit, shit,* shit.

He slowed, wondering if he should go back.

No, fuck it. Go see. You never know, maybe you'll be in luck.

He went round into the harbour too fast, sending a trail of white dust up behind him. He parked too near the edge and sat there, staring at nothing.

Come on Danny, snap out of it, let's move it.

What am I doing here?

Oh please, no fucking soul-searching. Just get out, fuck you.

He got out the car and crossed to the entrance. He remembered suddenly and vividly the sensation he'd had of walking on marshmallows the night Henderson had died.

He looked at the stones underfoot. They felt like that again today and he wasn't high, not on drugs. Nothing was killing his pain today, that's why he was here, but everything was numb around him. He couldn't *feel* anything.

Know why Danny? It's because you've tipped the scales. You're already over.

He rang the buzzer. He couldn't feel it beneath his finger.

She answered.

One up Danny-boy.

"Hello. It's me. Danny."

She laughed. "I felt I'd be seeing you somehow."

He felt an intense urge to punch his fist right through the slitted box of tin where her voice jabbed at him.

"Can I come up?" *I can't even feel my voice. I'm hearing it, but I can't* feel *it.*

"Bobby's here."

Shit. One down. Do not pass go. Do not collect two hundred pounds.

"But I don't see why you can't come up."

"I didn't come here to see him," Danny said. *I came here to fuck.*

"You don't need to see him, just say hello."

And it hung there. So Danny said, because he needed to be clear, because he wasn't thinking very well, "And then what?"

"We can do what you came here to do. Are you alone?"

"Yes."

"Makes a nice change."

"But how? If he's there?"

She laughed again. "He's not in my bedroom." There was a faint pause. "*I'm* not into incest."

Danny let the barb into his flesh, let her have her pain and glory. He leaned his head on the metal box.

"Danny?"

He felt it tickle his skin. He straightened up. "I'm here."

"Are you coming up?"

"What does he do, sit in the living room?"

"Why should you care?"

"I don't," and it was true, he didn't, "as long as I don't have to look at his Barbie-doll face."

"Ken, surely."

"Barbie," Danny said, and he could hear his own metallic voice. *Who's speaking please?*

There was a pause again, no laugh. "Come on up Danny." And the buzzer went. Danny went on up.

"What are you going to do? Take him through and screw him in front of me?"

"Oh don't be so childish. Go for a walk if it bothers you that much."

"He *murdered* your brother."

"Of course he did. You'd know that, even although the police couldn't find a thing."

"You never told the police about him."

"Look, don't start this again. Go for a walk, cool down."

"You mean take a hike."

"If you want to put it that way, yes."

"So you can screw some psycho fruit that murdered your brother."

"If you like."

"My God, if Jimmy could hear you, his own sis..."

"Oh shut up, you pompous little oaf. Who the hell do you think you are? This is *my* flat, Jimmy left it to me, along with everything else, and why? Because he couldn't stand you and your bloody pompous, self-important..."

The door bell sounded. She looked at him. The look was threatening and repressive at once. "Don't start anything Bobby," she whispered. "I'm warning you."

He looked at her and said without attempting to lower his voice. "He must be one hell of a ride."

"He is." She smiled tightly and went to answer the door.

Danny came in, smiling. The old Danny, sweet in the darkness of the hall.

He pulled her to him and kissed her. The first time he'd ever done it, or anything like it. She felt her skin crawl with something almost like panic. He felt charged up. These visits of his were like playing Russian roulette. You never knew whether fear or excitement was uppermost in your emotions.

"No time to wash," he whispered, stroking her hair. "Or change my clothes. You'll have to take me as I am."

"My pleasure," she found herself whispering back.

She slid his coat off. She had to struggle out of his grip to do it. He didn't seem to want to let go. "Come on, come in and get Bobby over with."

He hung back, letting her go ahead. He had wellingtons on. He pulled them off and left them in the hall. He went in in his stocking-soles. Let Mr Orthodontics make of that what he liked.

He hadn't realised how small he was. About her height, not much taller. Smaller than Henderson had been. A good four to six inches shorter than Danny. It pleased him immensely. He smiled. "Hello," he said.

"Hi," Robert Henderson said again, only this time there was no smile. His face looked as if the skin was sore, he moved it so little.

Katherine Henderson didn't bother with drinks. She took one look at her brother and said, "Come on Danny," and pushed him ahead of her into the passage leading to the bedroom.

Danny stopped at the door and smiled over his shoulder to him. "See you."

"Not if I see you first," Robert Henderson muttered to his disappearing back.

Danny kissed her again as soon as she closed the bedroom door. She began pulling his clothes off. He stopped her. "Put on that dress you had on."

She smiled. "Just the dress?"

"The dress and the tights."

"They were stockings."

"Stockings then. Who gives a fuck? Put them on."

She moved away from him and crossed to the wardrobe. He leant against the door, watching her. He watched her undress, only able to see her back, a teasing glimpse of black between her legs as she bent down.

He watched her struggle into the dress, do it up.

She crossed the room again, without looking at him, and took a packet out of the drawer. Assumably stockings, new ones.

She sat down on the bed and pulled them on. She smoothed them up her legs and looked up at him, smiling. "What now?"

"Come here."

She crossed over to him. He pulled her in against him. She could feel his erection pressed hard into her. It was always there on demand, never any coaxing or teasing into being, no insecurity, not about that. He never needed to tell you you were beautiful, his cock did it for him. Every time.

He slid his hands down her back and cupped her arse, pressing her against him. "As good as I thought," he murmured.

"Were you jealous?"

"If I said yes?"

She felt her heart thump. "I'd be amazed."

"Then be amazed." He began to tug the skirt up, hitching it above her hips. He cupped her backside again, kneading the flesh. "I'm going to cream in my fucking pants doing this."

She laughed. He pushed her away and said, "On the bed."

She went over, him walking behind her, watching her backside as she moved. She sat on the bed.

"No, on your knees."

She smiled and climbed on her knees, leaning her head on her arms.

He unzipped and eased himself against her. She reached round and guided him in.

Danny closed his eyes and let it slide in gently. "Oh yes." He sighed the words so quietly she almost missed them.

She felt excitement leap inside her, completely out of proportion, but she couldn't tie it down. He reached under her to masturbate her but she pushed his hand off. "Later. Just do what you want."

"That is what I want."

"No, just fuck me first."

"I won't last."

"Who gives a damn? Come on."

He moved into her slowly, feeling the wet heat of her. He ran his hands over the sharp roughness of the sequins, then down inside to feel her breasts. He squeezed them once and let go. Too far gone.

She was breathing heavily, squirming on him, wanting him to move. He quickened his stroke, easing up against her, straightening up to get in further. She moaned, bit down on her arm to stop any more. He said, "Jesus..." so quietly she almost missed

that too, then he began to jab it into her. Odd sharp movements, fast, pulling her hips onto him. She moaned some more in spite of herself.

"This is for Conley," he whispered, pushing into her with quick short thrusts that didn't go completely home, frustrating her. Then he pushed it in deep, breaking rhythm once, twice, before saying, "And this is for you."

The words seemed to galvanise him. He started to pound into her, dragging her down onto him. "You fucking two-timing *bitch*."

She felt him pull himself back, felt his whole body slam against her. He held it there, his whole body straining against her, his cock jerking inside. She could feel it, leaping, like something alive. He was holding her rigid against his straining body, no longer thrusting, no movement at all, only fiercely repressed twitching. She felt his strangulated climax, his shivering tremors. She struggled against him, frustrated by what he'd done.

He let her go, dropped down out of her to sit on his heels, leaving her feeling cold and bereft.

She rolled over and pulled him down to her. He came down willingly enough but he wouldn't kiss her. "What's wrong?" she asked, utterly perplexed by this new perversity in hm.

"Nothing," he said and then suddenly he smiled and slid a hand over and in between her pubic lips. "*Now* can I have what I want?"

The rule of threes was with Danny that day. He got home without being missed.

He even managed to part from her without fighting. That was twice by his reckoning. Keep this up and he might get to like her.

When he got into the yard there was no-one in sight. He went straight back to the barn and went back to work. He felt as if all his muscles were back in co-ordination. The headache which had threatened was now just a dull feeling of heavy tiredness. In truth, bed was what he wanted most. He wondered absently if going to bed early would be a good or a bad thing.

Stephen wandered through the doorway. Danny paused and looked at him, resting on the heavy brush he had been using.

"Hello," Stephen said, almost shyly.

"Hello yourself," Danny smiled back at him. The smile was relaxed, sincere.

"Feels like ages since I saw you last." Stephen came in a little closer.

Danny could hear the faint tremor in his voice and wondered if he was on the brink of another one of his emotional outbursts. He looked at him closely, trying to read his face against the light.

Stephen came a little closer still. "I've missed you." And Danny knew the tremor was excitement; pure breath-holding excitement. Steve-o was on heat.

Danny didn't want this, any of it. "How did you know I was here?"

"Ian." Stephen came up close, close enough for Danny to see. He looked like a drug addict.

"You should go."

"What?" Stephen's voice was instantly hostile, as if he'd been half-prepared for the rejection.

"Go." Danny saw a flicker of movement at the far end of the barn. He lowered his voice. "Just go."

"Don't worry, I'm going." And Stephen's voice trembled perilously, spoiling the effect of his anger. He heard it himself and turned tail, almost running out the barn. He kept his head down, looking neither left nor right.

After he'd disappeared Danny stood there listening to the silence, then Ian's voice

detached itself from the darkness. "You're cruel to him."

Danny didn't answer.

Ian came out of the darkness in person, walking leisurely towards him, hands in his pockets.

"You brought him home early," Danny said.

"Well somebody did."

"You can tell he doesn't know you Ian. Anybody else would have stayed well away from you doing a good deed."

"Element of surprise. You can't keep it forever."

Danny looked at him for a moment. Ian was keeping his distance, his face all darkness, but Danny didn't need to see it. "Feeling good Ian?"

Ian only smiled and said, "Was she that good Danny? You're looking better."

Danny felt his traitorous heart lurch.

"It's not a lucky guess. The pick-up's still warm. I thought I saw it heading towards town. We were working at the new drain, remember?"

"Gold star for observation."

"No, something a little more I think." And now he did move closer. "It's very valuable information. It's something he doesn't even suspect, and you know, and I know, it's something he'd kill you for." His voice changed, softened. "A woman... He'd be hurt Danny, so sad and rejected. You know what people can do when they feel rejected... you ought to."

"Alright, shut it. You've got your hard-on."

Ian's hand came out and stroked his cheek. "Lots of hush money."

Danny looked down at him. "You always fucking win, don't you?" And he was horrified to hear the catch in his voice, naked, defenceless.

Ian withdrew his hand from his cheek. "Always," he whispered, leaning towards him. "Poor baby."

"You're doing a good job Danny."

Danny looked up at him and pushed his plate away. There wasn't any point in trying to eat any more of it, he could hear the fight in Rab's voice. "What of?"

"Fucking him up."

Danny looked at the table, kicked a pea with his finger. "Stephen, you mean."

"Who else?"

"And you're *deeply* concerned, of course." Danny looked up at him, eyes flashing, A fight? Okay, a fight it is.

Rab sat down opposite him and finger-kicked the pea back. It landed in Danny's lap. He looked down at it, then back at Rab.

"You're an ugly little twat Danny." He tapped his head. "Up here."

Danny picked the pea up and threw it at him. It bounced off Rab's shoulder. Danny pushed up from his chair but Rab caught his arm. "Sit down."

Danny pulled away from him.

"Sit down, fuck you." Rab pulled hard.

Danny sat down. "Alright, say it. Get it off your chest Rab. I'm your captive fan."

Rab's face flushed. "I'm leaving."

Danny's lips opened but he didn't speak. He looked at the table then said carefully, "When?"

"Fortnight."

Danny's head shot up. "You liar."

Rab was thrown by the reaction. All he could manage was, "Am I?"

Danny stared at him, trying to read his face, then abruptly turned away. He said,

"Have you told John?"

Rab shook his head.

Danny bit his lip, pushed his temples with his fingertips. He looked like a man who's been told to decide his life in thirty seconds.

Rab suddenly wanted to ease it for him. He looked like a bee trapped in a bottle. He squeezed Danny's arm. "I was only thinking about it. I mean I hadn't decided…"

Danny turned on him furiously. "You shithead."

Rab pushed back in his chair, letting him go. "Thanks, that helped me make up my mind." He pushed up from the table.

Danny got up quickly, came round to face him. "Wait… I'll fuck you."

Rab laughed, a small dry noise. "You're good Danny, but not that good."

Danny moved in front of him, blocking his exit. "Not a once-of, like we were before."

Rab looked at him. Had they been any different 'before'? He realised he no longer trusted him. Maybe he never had trusted him. "No," he said and pushed past him and went up the stairs quickly.

Before he could change his mind.

Danny came to his room.

It had to happen but he hadn't expected it so quickly.

Rab had locked the door to keep temptation out. As soon as he heard someone try the handle he was unlocking the door again without even asking who it was. Danny hadn't had time to utter a word.

He walked in, not looking at him.

Rab locked the door behind him, mouth dry.

Danny stood there staring at him, face uneasy, oddly embarrassed. "Even if you go," his voice was rough, "I still want to do this."

His eyes seemed unnaturally bright, filmed, as if they were filled with pale green water.

Rab saw the utter resignation in his face, and in that moment it was as if the boy he'd been had been completely wiped out. This man was a stranger to him. It was as if he belonged to some other time, was someone he had known in childhood, years ago.

"It's been too long Danny. Way too long."

Danny closed his eyes. They looked red and sore, his eyelashes dark and spiky. "Don't you want to?" he asked, his voice childish with insecurity, his body limp and heavy with weariness, and Rab knew the answer, could feel it swelling his body like an excess of emotion.

"Want you Danny? I'm practically creaming in my fucking pants."

And in the end, that's exactly what he did.

John didn't miss him because John was out beating up James Conley.

Stephen didn't miss him because he was in the living room with Ian and the conversation was too interesting.

Ian didn't miss him because Ian knew where he was, and what he was doing, and why he was doing it. Go do your stuff Danny, if you want to hold on to what you've got. Maybe that's why Danny was crying. Like Judas.

James Conley was facing John down, knowing in his heart he didn't stand a chance, while Ian told Stephen a few tales.

This is how they went.

"Once upon a time there lived a beautiful boy in a secret kingdom far away, and

the boy was the only beautiful boy in the whole land for all the other people were ugly, and all the people prized him for his beauty, although they despised him too, for what use was beauty?

"The boy had only one fault, he could never resist telling tales about himself.

"One day he announced that his brothers were passing him from hand to hand and using him as they might a woman, revelling in his beauty until they had spent themselves, then discarding him again and telling him to make himself useful, for beauty had no use but this one.

"And his listeners looked at the boy and said, Your brothers? And he said, Aye, and my father too. And they said, Your father? And he said, Aye, and my mother too. And they looked at each other and smiled behind their hands and said, Your *mother?* and they started to laugh. They walked away, shaking their heads and said, That boy, his terrible lies. And from that day on no matter who he told it was always the same. The end."

Stephen blinked. "What the fuck are you on about?"

Ian smiled, watching him struggle up on the settee, television forgotten. "Just lies and shit. Don't you know lies and shit when you hear it?"

"Are you talking about Danny?"

Ian looked at him, stopped smiling. "You know, you're a pretty boy. You're going to be good-looking. Not in Danny's league, but you'll do. It's why John took you on. Know what Danny would have said if I'd told him that story? He'd have said, Stupid little faggot, what did he expect? That's bad. Don't you think that's bad?"

Stephen looked at him as if he were insane, hung onto the one point tenaciously, determined to make sense of it. "This is Danny, isn't it?"

"*Correct!*" Ian cried like a conjurer. "This is Danny."

"Okay." Stephen nodded, taking a breath. "Now I know where you're coming from."

Ian laughed. "Where do you pick these things up?"

"What things?"

"These expressions."

"I don't know. What's this got to do with Danny?"

"Nothing at all."

"What was all that shit?"

"Shit, as you so rightly describe it."

"You're a fucking crackpot Ian, know that?"

"So they say." Ian looked at the fire suddenly. "But only because they're so fucking shit-scared of me they don't know what else to call it." He looked back at Stephen with a suddenness that was unnerving. "That your problem Steve-o? You so shit-scared of me you don't know what else to call it?"

"I'm not scared of you."

"Not so," and Ian shook his head emphatically. "You think I'm more dangerous than a rattlesnake. I think you'd rather face Danny on a flyer than me."

"What d'you mean, a flyer?"

"Up here." He gestured with his hand. "So tightly-sprung he hurts your teeth to look at him. He looks like interference, live wires, water on a hot-plate. Danny on a flyer. Way out there somewhere. Now do you understand?"

"Yes." Stephen understood.

"You've seen it?"

"Yes." Stephen had seen it.

"He goes to her when he's like that, doesn't he? Henderson's sister?"

Stephen looked at him.

"Oh don't worry, no-one's telling. Does he take you with him?"

"Sometimes."

"Still running to his mummy. He never learns."

"She's not his mummy," Stephen said, irritated without understanding why.

"What would you know? Fuck all, that's what." Ian's voice was alien. Stephen had never heard him use that tone before. He looked different, harder, less pathetic. *Scarier*. Ian smiled again.

Stephen frowned. *It's like he's putting on a fucking disguise, that's what it's like.* And in one of those moments of adolescent shrewdness he said, "You're full of shit, aren't you?"

And Ian nodded once, so briefly that it said, *Yes, but I'll deny it if you ever repeat it, ever so much as mention it, but entre nous, as at this moment, yes, I'm full of shit. You better believe it.* And then it was gone. "Always the truth Steve-o, that's me."

"That story thing... you're saying he's a liar, aren't you? Well he never lied to me about John, or you, not when I asked him, so how is he lying?"

"Like an iceberg."

"You're bonkers."

Ian shrugged. "Your privilege."

"John..." Stephen paused, struggling before he managed, "does it with him."

"Definitely. John *does* it with him." Ian's voice was sarcastic.

Stephen flushed, but he pushed on. He wasn't going to let himself be bullied, or side-tracked. "And you do."

"No, I'd *like* to, but I do not. There's a world of difference. Danny doesn't love me. Isn't that sad?"

Stephen looked at him, not knowing whether he could believe it or not, wanting it to be true. "And Rab?" And this time it was a question.

Ian smiled. *They're at it right now Steve-o, right above your head. Can't you feel their tongues thrusting?* "Not for a long time. Poor Rab, he's like me, wants and doesn't get. Just like you, eh Steve?"

"Shut up."

"Danny only puts out for John-boy..." he paused, "and Mr Conley of course."

Stephen stared at him.

"Mr James Conley. Nice long man, nice long di..."

Stephen shouted him down. "You're lying!"

Ian laughed. "Oh no, I'm not. Use your head Steve-o, what else would Danny want from him? What else have you ever seen him want from anybody?"

"What about me? He's friends with me. He never wanted to do anything with..." he petered out.

"Lucky old you." And Ian's face was cold, his smile frozen on, and Stephen had another one of those crystal moments and thought, He's jealous. He's jealous of me because Danny isn't friends with him.

"I don't believe you," he said. "He's just a friend, that's all." And this time he felt more conviction in it.

"If you say so."

"I do."

"Fucking bully for you."

And Ian was smiling again, in such a way that it all crumbled to dust in his hands. He wanted to plead, scream, Tell me the *truth*. Somebody tell me the fucking *truth*. But he sat there, dumb with frustration, while Ian smiled at him, smug as a bug in the proverbial rug.

Stephen looked at the television, not seeing it. Upstairs a door shut quietly. They both heard it but only Ian listened to it. After a moment he said, "Danny turn you down again today?"

Stephen glared at him. "So it was you, fucking snooping."

821

"No, just waiting for my chance."

"To do what, eavesdrop?"

"No, suck his dick."

Stephen flushed, a bright flaming scarlet. "Jesus." His voice was hoarse. "You're really sick, you know that?"

"Why? Because I want to do what you want to do?"

Stephen turned his head away, feeling the heat right at the tips of his ears.

"You look very sweet when you blush," Ian said.

"Shut up you little shit!" Stephen yelled at him, fistfuls of cushion in his hand. He went limp. "Just shut the fuck up, okay?" He was almost crying, desperate with humiliation.

"Don't be upset. I didn't get it either. We're brothers in misery."

"I'm not his fucking brother."

Ian leaned forward, face sharp. "No, but you're still a fucking little homo, aren't you?"

Stephen went white, as if he'd hit him. "I'm not," he said in a voice that was suddenly tiny.

Ian laughed. "Sure. Just a passing phase, that right?"

"I'm not," Stephen said again.

Ian looked at him and thought, No, you probably aren't, but what the hell.

Stephen lay down on the couch and began to cry, face pushed into the cushion.

Ian stood up and ran his hand along the boy's thigh. Stephen didn't even feel it. "Poor baby," he said. And he smiled and went out the door.

When James Conley opened the door and John Jackson Moore pushed him back into the room and stepped in behind him Conley thought, You stupid bastard Max. And like some kind of psychic thread, John Jackson Moore smiled with all those teeth and said in a low voice, "You stupid bastard."

And Conley nodded. He thought so too. It was only polite to say so.

This time he had no knife. Not in his hand. He stood there, hands hanging loose by his sides, almost but not quite clenching, and said, "Aren't you going to ask me in?"

"You're already in," Conley replied, not moving.

John tutted. "Not polite. Not even nice. Let's go in like civilised people."

Conley turned his back on him, feeling as if he was inviting instant death between the shoulder blades, but they got into the room without incident.

Conley stood by the settee. John Jackson Moore stood and looked at him. Nobody talked about sitting down.

"You know, I'll be fucked if I can tell what he sees in you."

Conley felt the bubble of aggression growing in him, slowly, poisonously, as John Jackson Moore went on studying him, looking at him like he was a curious specimen of insect.

"You look old, washed-out. You must be forty at least."

"Thirty-eight," Conley said in a clipped voice.

"You look older."

Conley dipped his head in Danny's pet gesture. "Thank you."

"Don't mention it." He studied him some more then said, "You look like a faded old queen, somebody who chases after young boys. That describe you?"

Conley didn't answer him.

"I asked you a question, faggot."

"Fuck you."

John looked at him, unable to hide his surprise. Conley looked back, knowing John

Jackson Moore out-weighed him, out-muscled him, and most importantly, out-hated him. Conley didn't have the anger he needed. John Jackson Moore was a born fighter, a natural aggressor. He had so much hate inside him he didn't know who to bite first.

"For such a dried up husk you've got a big noisy mouth."

"Not as big as yours."

None of this is very clever Max.

No Mamma, but it's fun, and while we're at it, why don't you drop dead?

John Jackson Moore was clenching his fists now. Conley knew it wasn't to impress either. He didn't even know he was doing it.

"You know, I didn't come here to beat you up."

"No?"

"No. I wanted to see what the fascination was. He takes some big risks for you, you know that?"

Conley nodded.

John Jackson Moore shook his head. "I doubt if you do. Like to fuck me?"

Conley flushed. "No."

John laughed. "Listen to him. You look like someone's maiden aunt. You look as if you've just bitten into something bad. I'll tell you something, only don't spread it about. I don't really go for men." He shook his head. "I've had two in my whole life, and one of them was just expedient..." He smiled abruptly. "Hear that? Big word for a thick peasant like me."

"If you think you're a peasant I won't disagree."

John laughed again. "Saying you're not a snob Mr Conley?"

"You're the one with the inferiority complex."

"Shut up," John snapped at him suddenly, the wolfish smile gone as fast as it came. "You think you're so fucking smart, don't you? With the clothes and the manners and the fancy style."

"Did you give Henderson this same lecture?"

John was thrown for an instant then he smiled again. "Henderson didn't have any style."

"You're the snob." And Conley couldn't keep the malice out his voice. His voice always so nicely modulated, so flat.

John Jackson Moore smiled once more. Slowly. "Getting ratty?"

Conley said nothing.

"Mr Nicely-Bred is getting lower class and ratty. Danny go for that voice in bed? Talk dirty to him in those sweet Teutonic tones?"

"They're not Teutonic."

"No, they're not. You're a fake. Nothing but a posturing, middle-aged fairy preying on young boys."

"Danny isn't a boy." Conley could hear the anger surfacing in his voice and took a breath, trying to push it down.

"He's underage. You a lawyer and you don't know fuck about the age of consent? You a faggot and you don't know fuck-all about the age of consent? Shame on you."

"And you," Conley said, and his voice was his own again, flat, smooth, emotionless. "You bed him too. How about you and the age of consent?"

John smiled, widest yet. "Bed him? Me? I fuck my own brother, is that what you're saying? Jesus, what a sick mind you have. Must be a bit of the Nazi in you after all."

"Did Danny tell you that?"

"What? That you're a closet Nazi? Got it in the blood? Of course he did."

"Under duress..." Conley stopped as if he'd thought better of it. "Oh I'm sorry, perhaps you don't know what that word means?"

The vindictive spite in the words hung there bright as a red slash in the air.

John Jackson Moore responded to it like a piranha to blood in water. He crossed the floor and grabbed the front of Conley's clothes. "You sanctimonious shit, I'm going to make you pay for every time you ever touched him. I'm going to knock every fucking gold tooth down your cocksucking throat." And John hit him, deep into his stomach.

Conley only had time to think, You shouldn't have let him in Max, before John Jackson Moore began killing him.

Ian went upstairs and into their room. Danny was in bed, only the bedside lamp on.

He sat down beside him, stroked his hair. Danny was curled away from him. He didn't move.

"Well?" Ian asked.

"Well what?"

"Did you convince him?"

"I don't know, I didn't ask."

"Confidence or what Danny?"

"What, Ian." And he shrugged away from him.

Ian pulled the quilt off his shoulder and leaned over to kiss it. "Don't be like that."

"Get off me."

"Now that's nice, isn't it? Let's hope your big brother's more grateful."

Danny turned on his back. "Where is he?"

Ian's face was above him, smiling. "He'll be a while. Relax, we've got plenty of time."

Danny pushed at him. "Where is he?"

"Out, I told you."

"Out where?" Danny struggled to get up, but Ian rolled over him.

"Relax." He stroked his face. "Where is he usually? Come on, trust me."

"You're trash Ian, dog-shit, rat vomit. I wouldn't trust you if you paid me."

"I love it when you talk dirty to me." Ian wet his lips, still smiling, and Danny knew he was going to kiss him. He was pinned down under the quilt and Ian was going to start crawling all over him with his wet dirty mouth. He felt an instant intense panic.

"Ian..." he was suddenly breathing heavily out of nowhere, face pale, "I swear if you don't get off me right now I'm going to yell the fucking house down. I mean it. Get... off... me." He ground out the last three words through gritted teeth.

Ian looked at him, smile fading, and eased up off him. Slowly. "You ungrateful little shit."

Danny said nothing, just watched him straightening up.

"Some day you're going to push me too far and I'll throw the whole of your dirty life in your big brother's face."

"He wouldn't believe you if you did. Think I don't know you'd have told him by now if you thought he would?"

"Ungrateful little shit," Ian said again, face working.

"Get out." Danny smiled at him. "Get the fuck out, shithead."

Ian slapped him. Danny's head flinched away. He brought it back. "Out." He smiled again. "Get the fuck out."

Ian stood up and got out.

For some reason Danny told himself he couldn't explain, he became wide awake, all his tiredness gone, replaced by anxiety.

He rolled over and let the word sit there, lumpen and ugly, looking at him. *Anxiety.*

About what? It was just a fucking cheap trick to wind him up.

Danny pulled himself upright and reached over for a cigarette. He lit it, face angled and planed by the bedside lamp, looking as beautiful as he'd ever looked, only there was no-one there to see it.

Danny inhaled, then exhaled. He did it through his nose, head back in an unconscious parody of Rab. He coughed and hugged his knees to his chest.

When someone knocked on the door he jumped guiltily, spilling ash on the bedclothes. "Come in," he said, sounding half-strangulated, brushing the ash off with nervous flicks.

When Stephen opened the door the moment was held in a strange suspended slow motion. He saw the long golden line of Danny's back right down to his buttock, a flash of his underarm hair, somehow brilliantly, intensely red in that dull light, as his hand slowly took the cigarette out his mouth and reached over to stub it out, then his head came round, eyes coming up, vividly green, to finally meet his. It took forever and happened in an instant.

Stephen saw his belly, another tiny glimpse of hair, then Danny spoke to him. "Well, come in, don't just stand there."

Stephen went in and Danny nodded at the bed. "Sit down where I can see you. You look sinister standing there only half-lit. The faceless bloody man."

Stephen sat down and looked at Danny's face, at the distant dry remains of where he'd scratched him.

"Did you decide you didn't want to live any more, or did you know John was still out on his rounds?"

"I knew. Well, I guessed."

Danny smiled and reached for another cigarette. Stephen watched the quilt fall down his belly again. Danny came forward and hugged his legs, hiding it again. "You saw Ian coming in," he said round the cigarette. "You've no idea where John is, have you?"

Stephen shook his head, watching Danny's face in the flare of the lighter. He was so beautiful it was mindless, scary. "I wish you looked like a woman," he blurted out suddenly, not even knowing he was going to say it.

Danny's eyes seemed to suddenly focus on him, like a cat's coming into the light. "Why?"

"Then I'd have a reason, an excuse. But you don't," Stephen said bitterly. "You look fuck-all like one. Even less than when I first came here."

Danny said the only thing that seemed safe. "You've known me hardly any time at all. I can't have changed that much." Suddenly everybody was telling him he'd changed.

"You have," Stephen said emphatically, then he looked at the floor, flushing. "Besides, I'd seen you about the village... before, I mean."

Danny felt something strange and sweet inside him. He said in a low voice, cigarette poised delicately between his fingers, "Are you saying you fancied me before you came here?"

"Sort of," Stephen said. "I think I did, sort of, only I didn't know what it was."

"And what was it?" Danny took the cigarette back to his mouth.

"I was a bit jealous… you know… of the way girls talked about you. But I could see why. I knew why."

Danny laughed. "That's horseshit. You seriously think you're the only boy who ever realised another boy was good-looking? By that definition you've just branded every other man plus some into a raving queer."

"No." Stephen said it very emphatically. "It was more."

Danny looked at him through narrowed eyes. "You know, you sound to me as if you

want it to be more. What are you trying to do, punish yourself?"

"I'm trying to stop lying to myself." Stephen said it tightly.

Danny looked at him in surprise. He was too young for that one, much too young.

"Listen," Stephen said. "There's something else." He looked away again. "Once, last summer, Doug Johnstone..." He looked at him to be sure Danny knew who he meant.

"Tam Johnstone's brother?"

Stephen nodded and went on, "He was talking about your family. We were all sitting in the bus shelter, just out there. He said, 'They're hung like porkin' horses'. It always stuck in my mind." Stephen smiled briefly. "I always wondered what a porkin' horse was." He paused and went on, "Of course everybody wanted to know how he knew, but I was the only one there didn't know that John's dick was a legend. Everybody knew that."

Danny laughed. "I don't believe this."

"It's true, I swear it. It's common knowledge. These things get about. But like I say they were kidding him, wanted to know how he knew." Stephen looked at him suddenly. "It was Doug's big brother... Rab had told him."

"Rab?"

Stephen nodded. Danny laughed again. Stephen went on, "Of course they took the piss, said they didn't believe him, even though they'd all heard the same thing. He swore it was true. He said that Rab had seen it." Stephen looked at him again. "I didn't know it was Rab then. Doug just said his cousin. I didn't know who his cousin was. I never even asked him. Somehow I'd never seen Rab. I still don't know how."

Danny said in a low voice, "Neither do I."

Stephen looked at him quickly, then away again, not wanting to see it or hear it in his voice. "Anyway, he said it was true, ran in the family, your dad was supposed to be the same. I said, what about you?" He looked at Danny this time. "He said, Danny? He was acting like he knew you. That's what was getting everybody's goat, because your family was... well, you know... private, but here he was acting like he was a friend of the family."

"I don't think I've spoken two words to him in my life."

"You know his big brother though."

"Yes," Danny said slowly, "I know his brother."

Stephen looked at him for a long moment then went on, "He said you were. Everybody laughed and said, Sure. He said it was true because you'd once let his big brother see it." Stephen looked at him, but Danny was watching the smoke curl off his cigarette, not looking at him. "When you were fifteen."

"Fourteen," Danny said without looking up.

There was a pause, a long pause, then Stephen said, "It's true then?"

Danny nodded his head, still without looking up. Then he looked up slowly and said, "I blew him. For three dirty pictures of a woman being shafted by two men at the same time, but I'll bet Doug Johnstone didn't tell you that part, did he? That I went down on his brother in the scout hall toilets and that he pestered me for about six fucking months after to do it again." Danny smiled and inhaled his cigarette again.

Stephen watched him for a minute before he realised he wasn't going to say anything else. He said, "He just said his brother had seen it, and that it was bigger than his dad's. Bigger when it wasn't even hard." Stephen blushed.

Danny smiled tightly and said, "Nice to know he remembers. As I recall that's what I was supposed to exchange, a quick look at the Jackson Moore legendary equipment, only once he saw it he got grabby." Danny was silent for an instant then he said, "Good job for him he was bigger than me." He smiled. "I mean in years." He looked up. "And did you believe all this shit Steve-o?"

"Not really, but I got turned on." He looked away, biting his lip. "I jerked off that night thinking about you showing it to him, imagining how big it was."

"And how big was it? Really enormous?"

Stephen could hear the smile in it. "Yes."

"Bigger than the real thing?"

Stephen looked at him and said, "No."

And Danny felt that same sweet dangerous heat in his stomach. He looked away. "Danny, there's more."

Danny gave him a quick glance then said, "I dread to think."

"I'd forgotten this, the way you forget things that embarrass you."

"You mean you hadn't really forgotten it?"

Stephen nodded. "When my mam told me about the job I could feel it here..." He held his stomach. "I'd seen you only the day before. You were in the post office buying lemonade."

Danny shook his head slightly. "I don't remember."

Stephen smiled for what seemed the first time. "No reason why you should, you didn't even see me. I wasn't used to seeing you in the flesh, close up. I thought you were much better-looking than I realised. It made me feel weird, nervous. I felt like that first night I came here and you were sat downstairs reading the paper. I thought it was just nerves then, but I don't think so now. I didn't know where to look. I needn't have worried, you never even noticed me. Not at all."

Danny watched his face curiously. He could see it hurting him, what it cost him to say it.

"When she told me who she was going to work for I nearly shit a brick. I pleaded with her to ask John about giving me a job. I think that's really why I was so nervous at first. I was scared of you. You were my hero."

"Some hero."

"Danny, I think I wanted you before I even came here..."

"No," Danny interrupted quickly, but Stephen went on relentlessly.

"Yes. Stop being nice to me, or whatever it is you're doing. I think I did... and I still do."

Danny stubbed out his cigarette and rubbed his face.

"Know what I want to do to you Danny?"

"Yes." Danny's voice was flat. "I know."

"Let me. Please. Just once."

Danny's eyes came up, hard with anger. "Yeah, like it was one kiss, one cuddle, one tumble in Conley's bed. No."

"Why not?" Stephen slapped his palms on the bed. "Christ you just told me you did it with Tam Johnstone for three lousy porno pictures you probably lost a week later."

"A year later."

"Okay, a fucking year later. Why not?"

"You're too young. How often do I have to tell you? You're too fucking young."

"I'm *not!*"

"And I say you are. Now go to bed."

"*Please* Danny. What's it going to cost you? Do you know what it feels like to keep begging you?"

"Well don't. That's easy, just fucking don't." Danny tugged the quilt as if he was trying to jettison him off it. He lay down, rolling onto John's side of the bed and pushing his face in his pillow.

Stephen got up on his knees and pleaded with his back. "If I swear to you it will be just once? If I promise?"

"No." Danny's voice was muffled. "Go away."

"*Danny*," Stephen begged.

Danny flung himself on his back. "No, no, *no!*"

They glared at each other for a moment then Stephen fell back on his heels. "Alright," he said slowly. "Okay, I'm sorry."

"Don't be," Danny said, rubbing his face. "Just go to bed, okay?"

"A kiss?" Stephen asked quietly, then he smiled when he saw the refusal on Danny's face. "Just one?"

Danny laughed. "Alright, just one."

Stephen leaned over his face and touched lips, very softly, no kiss at all, then lifted his head, six inches, no more.

Danny looked up at him and said, "Call that a kiss?"

"Another?" Stephen asked.

"Scheming little shit." And Danny pulled his head down and their mouths came together, then Stephen was lying on him and Danny had his arms round him, and he was kissing him, hard.

Stephen tasted him, hands pushing down as far as he could get under the quilt, suffocating him, until Danny broke away, coming up for air.

Stephen went on kissing him, determined not to let go, to keep the spell going. Danny was limp, unresisting. Stephen kissed his neck, his chest, moving down relentlessly, pulling the blankets back as he advanced.

Danny lay there and looked at the ceiling, loving the small animalistic feeling of him moving on him, his hot little mouth devouring his flesh

Stephen pushed the quilt down. Danny let him, taking his head in both hands, almost guiding him, and Stephen prayed, prayed so hard he could hardly think. He kissed his stomach and the scar, and then the hair was there, and to the side, just showing, there it was, distended, stiff as all fuck, waiting for him. Stephen grabbed it, wanting it in his mouth just once. He could smell it and then taste it. *Taste* it. *Oh God.* He felt his cock almost ripple with sensation. It spread through his stomach like fire. He could feel heat, *real* heat, inside him, like he'd been plugged in.

He moaned. He tasted the huge salted roundness of it and moaned.

Danny gripped his head and opened his legs, pulling Stephen between them, spreading himself wide, lifting his hips up to meet his mouth.

Stephen panicked. He didn't know what to do. He could hardly get any of it in. He tried to remember what John had done to him... and did it.

"Christ, where d'you learn that, you little shit?" He made it sound like an endearment. "This was never Rab. Rab's never sucked a dick this well in his life." But he pushed Stephen's head down when he tried to lift it. "No, I don't want to know, just keep doing it." He was silent for a long, intense moment, holding Stephen's head rigid, then he eased off again. "Almost had your first mouthful." He clutched Stephen's head and pushed himself deeply into his face.

Stephen gagged, trying not to panic, feeling his cock jerk at the same time, wondering if he was going to spill over and come in his jeans. Danny let him go, withdrawing slightly. Stephen dropped back to slow boil.

"You're going to make me come Steve-o. Just hold me in your mouth. Gently. I'm going to finish it. That's it..."

Danny began to thrust in and out very quickly, a light friction over his glans. "Don't suck... close your mouth... that's it... that's it..." He pistoned his hips faster. Stephen could feel it almost pulling away from him, the movements were so shallow and fast. He was afraid he was going to lose it altogether. He tried to suck him back in, but Danny held his head fiercely and began plunging in.

"God... God... here it comes... shoot my load... shoot it... *shoot*... oh... *shit*." And Danny grabbed him, shoved in hard, jerking each spasm tight down Stephen's throat.

He felt it curdle up in his mouth, hit the back of his throat. It went up his nose. He closed his eyes, trying not to panic, wanting to puke it up and swallow it down simultaneously. It tasted so strong, much slimier and saltier than he would have thought.

I've been spunking this muck for years and I've never even tasted it before.

Danny was grunting on and on, creaming in his mouth like he hadn't come since last year, until he stopped, went limp, pushing Stephen's head off, saying, "No more, it's hurting."

Stephen felt an instant of shame that he'd spoiled it, but Danny pulled his head into his crotch, murmuring, "Christ that was beautiful…" And Stephen knew he'd done just fine.

Just absolutely fine.

"Want me to do it to you?"

Stephen snuggled his face into the soft springy hair, ran his fingers through it. "I don't want to move," he said.

"No sweat," Danny's voice came from above. "Just turn upside down and we'll do a sixty-nine."

Stephen felt a huge kick of excitement. He'd have Danny's dick in his mouth while Danny sucked him off.

"Come on." Danny tugged his hair. "Give it up here."

Stephen wriggled round.

"Turn your hips a bit more." He felt Danny pull him close. "That's it." Then Danny's hands were in at his clothes. Stephen panicked, no idea why. He said Danny's name.

"I'm here," Danny said, a smile in his voice, as if he understood everything. "Lift your bum."

Stephen lifted it. There was the cold rush of exposure then the excitement of knowing he was looking, then Danny pulled his hips into his face and began kissing him, like John had done, murmuring, "Someone's a big boy." He was so excited he thought he'd burst. He looked at Danny's cock lying fat and slack on his thigh and started kissing it, a hundred hungry little pecks.

Danny laughed softly and said, "Nice." Stephen did it some more. Danny pushed it against his face. Stephen could feel it thickening. He couldn't help himself. He reached up and pushed it into his mouth.

Danny gave a soft little grunt then said, "That's it, eat it up."

Stephen immediately started to fellate him again, even though his face ached from the last time. Danny came up hard within minutes. Stephen sucked on him eagerly.

"I'm supposed to be doing you," Danny said, almost as if he'd been daydreaming, then he took Stephen impossibly far into his mouth, just as John had done. Stephen groaned deep in his throat. The fact that his mouth was full, rendering him incapable of speech, seemed to make it worse, more intense.

Danny mouthed him and sucked him and pulled his balls. Stephen could feel the silk of his hair between his legs, tickling his thighs. He lay there stupefied, mouth full of Danny's cock, not doing anything with it, just slackly suckling on it like a helpless baby. He was trembling. So close he could hardly control his muscles.

Then Danny did something so incredible he felt he would die. He sucked his cock further into his mouth, almost as if it was going down his throat, then pulled his buttocks apart, slowly exposing him.

Stephen bucked like a worm on a hook. He made noises he'd never heard before. He imploded.

It came out of him in gut-wrenching jolts. Danny seemed to pull them into him,

grabbing Stephen's hips and making him thrust into his mouth. Stephen went with him, thrusting so hard it must have nearly choked him. Stephen didn't care. It was Danny doing this to him, *Danny*. He couldn't see, smell or breathe anything but Danny.

Danny's cock sprang out of his mouth. Stephen let it go, wanting to give voice to it. He yelled and moaned like he was dying. Suddenly Danny pushed him on his back, swinging over him, all the while his mouth working up and down Stephen's shaft relentlessly. He straddled Stephen's head, spread his legs wide, and began to push his penis against his face, squashing his nose, his balls rolling over his forehead. Stephen grabbed his hips and pulled him down like he wanted him to do it harder. He pushed his face up into Danny's groin, felt his cock grind against his cheek, dragging the skin, butting against his nose, sticking and pulling.

Stephen's cock was hurting, wanting to come more when there was nothing left to come. Suddenly he felt something hot and wet squirting in his face. It went in his eyes, began to slide down into his ear. He could hear Danny making an odd rising moaning sound, although the thrusts against his face had gone oddly slow and boneless.

Danny let his cock drop out his mouth, gave a half-cry. Stephen could feel the ache in his arse, his balls. He hadn't come, he'd fucking given birth. They collapsed on each other, faces and bodies wet with sweat, spit and semen.

Stephen said quietly, compelled by an urge to tell him, "It was John."

Danny squeezed his thigh and said equally quietly, "I know."

Stephen put a hand on his head and said, "I thought I'd never get anybody to do it that good again."

And Danny said, "Me too."

Stephen lifted himself up onto his elbows to look down at him. Danny rolled on his back and met his gaze, but his eyes were strangely veiled, as if he were hiding something, like he was hurting and didn't want to show it.

Stephen dropped back down and closed his eyes and barely wondered why that felt so good.

They lay cuddled together, Stephen tucked under Danny's arm, watching his own hand stretch and pull the slack skin of Danny's foreskin. "We going to do it again?" he asked, watching the soft browny skin wrinkle and furl.

"Sure."

"When?"

Danny laughed, low, making Stephen's stomach turn over. "As often as you want. Every spare minute of every day till you go blind."

Stephen heard the words, the soft easy complacency in them, and hugged them to himself. "Like me?"

Danny turned his face into his hair. "Yes."

"A lot?"

Danny laughed again. "If you want to say it Steve-o, go ahead and say it - everybody else does - don't fish for it."

"What?" Stephen asked but he pushed his face into Danny's armpit, glad he couldn't see him blushing.

"You tell me."

Stephen said nothing, not now. Moments passed. Stephen slid his hand down between his legs, briefly felt his balls, then boldly made for his anus. Danny didn't seem to mind. Stephen grew hard against him almost immediately. "Danny?"

"Mm?"

"Ian said you were doing it with Conley."

Danny's hand came down over his, checking him. "When?"

"Tonight." When Danny didn't say anything to that he asked, "Are you?"

Danny let his hand go again, taking too long to answer, and Stephen knew it was true. "Yes," he said finally.

Stephen burrowed his face into him, pulling his exploring hand away before it had reached its goal. Danny kissed his hair again, but said nothing.

"Will you stop now you've got me?" Stephen asked in a tiny voice.

"No." Danny pulled his arm out from under him. "No, I won't. And you've no fucking right to ask me."

Stephen clutched at him. "Don't be angry."

Danny hesitated then pulled him close again, roughly. Stephen wriggled and nudged until he was under his arm again. He kissed Danny's breast, pressing his mouth hard to his nipple. "I love you Danny," he whispered, half-hoping he would hear him, half-hoping he wouldn't.

Danny heard him. He closed his eyes tight against the sound of it and said nothing.

"I love you," Stephen whispered again, sucking the little nipple into his mouth.

The erection he'd lost to Conley was growing again. Danny could feel it. Suddenly he found the whole thing funny, ridiculous. He smiled and the smile became a grin. *Keep taking them on like this Danny and soon you won't be able to service them any more.*

Stephen threw a leg over him, shoving up against him, and half-climbed over him. "I want to Danny. Can we?" he asked hesitantly, the words completely at odds with his body's actions.

Danny laughed. "You already are. Okay, one more time, for luck."

Stephen pushed his crotch up against him, giving it little doggy thrusts.

"What do you want?" Danny asked, looking up at him.

"You choose," Stephen said, and Danny could hear the excitement in it. *You choose Danny then he'll know you're doing something you want. That's a big turn-on for him - you better believe it - knowing you want it.*

"Wank in my face."

"What?" Stephen was suddenly still.

"Wank in my face."

Stephen just blinked down at him.

"What's wrong? Too kinky for you?"

"No. It's just..."

"What?" But Danny knew what. He was just too beautiful.

"Come on, up, over my face."

Stephen got up and straddled his face, legs wide apart to get over his shoulders.

Danny looked up at him. "What a view, right up your crack."

Stephen's cock was inches above his face. He looked down at him, face pink with excitement. Danny's eyes looked almost closed, the eyelashes thick against his cheeks, but Stephen knew they weren't. He knew Danny was looking up his bum. Suddenly he wanted Danny to close them, not look at him any more. It was too much too bear. "Danny, I don't think I can do this."

Danny looked up at him. "Too pretty to come on?" he smiled.

Stephen nodded hopelessly, not confessing to how exciting he found it.

Danny laughed. "You'll do it and be amazed. Go on, try it."

Stephen slid a hand round himself, watched Danny's face, and started to masturbate.

"That's it," Danny said and Stephen saw his tongue flick over his lips as if he was getting ready to kiss someone. Danny gripped his thighs, forcing him down a little. Stephen could feel his balls bumping Danny's chin. He made a small noise in his throat.

Danny looked up at his face. "See?"

Stephen swallowed. "You're lovely Danny."

Danny smiled, let him go again, so that Stephen knew he could see up him again. "Really, honestly. So beautiful it hurts me inside to look at you."

"Come in my face. Come as hard as you can so that I can see your hole spasm. I want to see how beautiful I am written all over your arsehole."

Stephen made an odd little whimpering noise, breathing through his mouth, movements slowing to a standstill.

"Don't stop, you stupid twat. I'm watching. Go on, do it." Danny pulled Stephen's thighs open wide, making him slide down so that he was practically sitting in Danny's face.

Stephen felt a panicked jerk of it come up, barely recede, too near. "Danny..."

"Come on, I want to see it. It's twitching. Your arsehole's twitching. *Do* it."

Stephen grabbed at himself. But it didn't matter, it was already too late. It had been too late the moment Danny had suggested he sit over his face. He threw his head back and gasped, "Oh..." His hand began jerking it up. "I love you," he panted, harder, pulling it up violently. He wanted Danny to see everything. He looked down, desperate to know he was watching and heard himself say as if from a very long way off, "Oh no... I'm coming. Oh God, help, I'm coming."

His eyes were wide on Danny's face and with that same out of body detachment he could see it foaming over into Danny's hair. He could see nothing of Danny's face but he could hear him. At first he didn't understand it then he realised he was saying, "Soil me, soil me, soil me..." while Stephen went on helplessly pulling it out, feeling as if the orgasm was ripping his stomach out, and all the time Danny's voice urging him to soil his face.

To deface him.

And incredibly, as the wave of his own climax began to pull away from him, Stephen felt the unmistakable twitchings of Danny's body, saw it plainly on his face as he slumped back to look at him.

Danny was coming, silently, secretively, wrapped in his own private world.

And for the first time Stephen was scared.

Really, earnestly, scared.

Stephen climbed off him and dried Danny's face, gently wiping it off his brow, out his hair. His hand was trembling. He could see it. Danny was laughing, saying, "You sting like fuck. Have you got extra salt for added flavour?"

Stephen swung off him and glanced down while Danny was rubbing his eyes and saw it, thin and clear, a long loop of it joining his cockhead to his belly, glistening wet.

He looked away quickly and went on cleaning him with numb fingers, then he realised Danny was watching him, watching him and smiling, a slow, seductive, dangerous smile.

Danny caught his hand and when he spoke it was in that low crawling voice that made your hair stand up. "Aren't you going to ask Steve-o?"

"What?" Stephen said, and his voice was too high.

"How I did it?"

"Did what?" Stephen asked, and he felt as if his eyes were too big, staring, but he couldn't seem to shut them any, blink them, anything.

"What do you think?"

Stephen nodded, his lips moving without him. "It's there," he said. "I can see it." He swallowed dryly. "I felt you between my legs, shaking."

Danny smiled, waiting.

"How the hell did you do that?"

Danny stretched his legs, just as John liked to see him do, and put his hands under his head. "I don't know. I can do it. I don't know how."

"Without touching?" Stephen sounded awe-struck.

"No fucking hands."

"What does it feel like?"

Danny shrugged. "A wet dream maybe."

"Achy?" Stephen asked.

"Yes, sort of achy."

"Not so good?" It was only half a question, and more than half a hope.

"Oh no, it's good alright. It *hurts*. Sometimes I like it better." And his voice had sunk again.

"It *hurts?*" Stephen asked, not really wanting to but doing it anyway.

And Danny stroked himself, still tensely erect, and said, "Yes. It hurts so sweetly it makes you want to cry."

"I don't like it," Stephen said, watching him trace his fingers softly up and down himself.

"Spooks you." Danny's smile was as grating as his voice.

"Don't do it again."

Danny laughed. "I can't promise that. I don't always know I'm going to do it. Sometimes they sneak up on me."

"It's horrible," Stephen said.

"Horrible and fascinating," Danny said, his cock arching up into his tracing fingers. To Stephen it looked over-swollen and sore. "Side effect," Danny said, watching his eyes. "Makes me too hard. Can't get rid of it. That's why it hurts."

"Stop saying that," Stephen said tensely.

"Relieve me Steve-o." Danny's voice was thick. "Take away my pain." His cock was curved, up off his body, deep stained red. It looked as if it had a tourniquet on it. For the first time Stephen was afraid of it, the sheer lumpen size of it.

"Touch it," Danny said, and his voice sounded soft and slimy. "Put your cold fingers on it and ease me."

"I can't," Stephen said definitely, staring at it.

"Then I'll just lie here and do it again, like something dead and unseen is sucking my dick."

"No, don't."

"Then touch me."

Stephen reached out his hand and touched him. It seemed to come up into his palm. It felt hugely hot, like something crammed full of hot gravel, covered in swollen bumps. The head was scarlet, the eye wide open, oozing.

"Hurt it."

"What?" Stephen almost let him go, had to fight the urge to drop it.

"Hurt it."

"Danny, don't say these things."

"Just squeeze it hard."

Stephen squeezed it, feeling it pulse like a held artery.

"Harder..."

He did as he was told.

"Now dig your nails in."

"No."

"*Do* it." Danny's voice was hard, his face tense.

Stephen did it.

Danny seemed to relax, closed his eyes. "Now drag them up. Drag your nails up

my prick."

Stephen did it, biting his lip.

"Harder." Danny squeezed Stephen's hand tight on himself, making his nails dig horribly into his flesh. It felt like pushing your nail into an eraser. Stephen gritted his teeth and held it. Danny flushed. Stephen saw it spread over his face and chest. His mouth opened. He was suddenly breathing heavily. "Now down," he whispered. "Drag them right down till it feels like it's going to rip."

Stephen began to drag the foreskin back down, digging his nails in, watching it peel back. It was suddenly intensely arousing. It looked magnificent, frightening, diseased, all at once. He dug his nails in hard, suddenly wanting to do it.

Danny's eyes flew open. He grunted something, staring at Stephen's hand.

"Like this?" Stephen said and he was aware of his own cock poking up in the air between his legs. Danny's eyes looked glazed, drugged. The flush seemed to be spreading over his body. Stephen watched as his hands moved behind him, clutching the pillow. His whole body was straining upwards.

Stephen drew it down harder, squeezed tighter, then did something he would never be able to explain.

Danny's cock was peeled right back, bent with the drag on it. Stephen was forcing it down into his balls. It must have been hurting. It hurt him just to look at it. It was so dark it looked purple. Danny was staring at it and trembling. Stephen bent his head, wanted more than anything to feel what it would be like to have that tortured lump of flesh in his mouth. He heard Danny say "No" faintly, as if he was expiring from loss of blood.

Stephen closed his mouth over his cock, just putting the whole engorged head in as if it was an overripe plum that he intended to swallow whole, then he began to close his teeth, clamping them down on it, gently increasing the pressure.

Danny went apeshit, grabbed him and began pounding into his head, sperm salting Stephen's mouth, Danny thrashing convulsively on the bed, yelling, actually *yelling*.

Stephen thought, Christ, everyone will hear. Everyone.

But he didn't care.

Danny was coming dry and it was agony. There was nothing in him to come with but his body kept on trying anyway. Stephen could feel the pain in him, but he didn't stop. He was enjoying it too much.

It wasn't till many years later that he realised that it was at *that* moment that he finally sold his soul away.

The anxiety came back with a bang. Immediate, huge, because Danny knew something was wrong. The something that had been wrong all night but he'd been too fucking preoccupied to see it.

No John.

Nowhere.

Danny sat up and looked at the clock.

It was all wrong and it stank.

"What's wrong?" Stephen asked, intensely uncomfortable about what he'd just done, knowing something strange had happened between them, something wrong and ugly and dangerous. He was scared by the sudden edginess in Danny's movements.

"Did you hear John say where he was going?"

Stephen was nonplussed by the non sequitur of the question. It took him a moment. "No, he was talking to Ian. I couldn't hear what they were saying."

"*Ian?*" Danny turned and looked at him. He said Ian's name as if he were saying, You let him kill a baby? An innocent little *baby?*

"Yes, Ian. What's wrong?" Stephen pulled himself upright, crawled over beside him to the edge of the bed.

"He should have been back. He'd never stay out this long, unless he's found fucking nirvana. He should have come in here and caught us fifty times over. We've been lying here rolling around in borrowed time. And where's Rab? Ian? Hear anything? I should have fucked up fifty different ways tonight, and look at us, screwing like a pair of jack-rabbits and not a fucking peep out of them. Where is everybody? What party are they at?"

Danny stood up and started pulling on his clothes.

"What are you doing?" Stephen asked, panicked by something in his manner.

"Getting dressed."

"Where are you going?" He scrambled off the bed.

"To the party."

"Danny, wait..." He started to frantically pull his clothes on.

"You've got two minutes." He opened the door. "I'm going to find Ian." He went out, slamming the door.

Stephen pulled his clothes on urgently, aware of the rumpled mess of the bed, suddenly feeling what Danny meant. He pulled the bed straight hastily. John could have come in at any moment. *Jesus.* He felt cold at the thought. They must have been mad... or desperate.

He stopped as if someone had pushed him in the chest.

He had been, blindly desperate, but Danny?

He sat down on the bed.

He felt hot and cold at once.

He wanted me. He really did. He hugged himself. It was worse than him *not* wanting you.

He stood up suddenly.

Come on, get going.

He went out and down the hall to Ian's room.

Ian was in the kitchen, wearing only his jeans.

Danny could smell drink off him.

"Why didn't you get a fucking stick-on hairy chest, you fucking shithead?"

Ian smiled. It was filled with self-satisfaction.

"Where's John?" Danny demanded.

"Guess."

"No. Where is he?"

Ian smiled and raised his glass at him. Danny slapped it out his hand. The whisky curved in an arc through the air, the glass following it, bouncing twice then smashing on the floor. "*Where?*"

"That was perfectly good whisky Danny-boy." Ian was looking at the glass with an air of genuine loss.

Danny shook him. Ian dipped his head and rubbed his face on the hand on his left shoulder. "The feel of you on my skin," he whispered.

Danny let go and slapped his mouth. "Fuck you Ian, where *is* he?"

"Conley's." The voice was quiet, satisfied, in command.

Danny stared at him.

"Too late now Danny."

Danny sank down into a chair.

"Don't blame me. I *liked* the man. He was sexy."

Danny shot bolt upright. "Shut up. Shut the fuck up before I wring your scrawny fucking neck. Christ, you're the most evil bastard I ever met."

Ian smiled but it didn't quite make it. "You made me Danny, you and your big brother. Look upon me and see that I am good."

Danny closed his eyes tightly then wheeled about and went back out the room. Ian shouted after him but Danny ignored him. He took the stairs two at a time and met Stephen in the upstairs hall.

"He's not there," Stephen said. "Where were..."

"Come on, get your jacket."

"What?"

"Get your jacket, we're going out."

"Out?"

"*Out*, fuck it!" Danny roared. "Now *move!*" And he shoved Stephen hard. Stephen moved.

Ian met them coming down again. He grabbed Danny's arm. "He said you were to stay here." His face was suddenly tense.

"Not part of the great master plan?"

"If he's done anything you'll be in deep shit. Leave it be."

"*If?*" Danny pulled his hand off his arm and threw it away from him. "*If?* Who are you fucking kidding? You bloody sent him there to do it."

"Don't talk shit. You think I'd let him take a risk like that?"

Danny pushed past him, a white-faced Stephen in tow.

"*Danny!*" Ian screamed it so harshly Stephen stood stock still with shock.

Danny dragged his arm. "Ignore him, move."

He was being dragged out, still looking over his shoulder at Ian.

They went out quickly.

"John must have taken the Range Rover." Danny slammed his fist on the pick-up roof, then opened the door and climbed in, reaching over to open Stephen's side. Ian came after them, haring across the yard.

"He's coming," Stephen whispered, climbing in quickly, inexplicably terrified at the sight of him.

Ian was screaming at them. Stephen could only make out every second word. "What's he saying? God, he hasn't even got his shoes on." That seemed the worst part of all. He didn't have his shoes on and he was running through muck and he didn't even feel it.

Danny ignored it all. He tore out into the road muttering, "Come on you fucking beat-up old bitch. Come *on*."

They drove until just before Jerrett's then took a left turn. "We going to Conley's?" Stephen asked.

The noise Danny made sounded like he had a bone stuck in his throat. Stephen looked at him and thought, God, he's going to cry, and he didn't know what to do, or say, or think. He only knew it must be bad, very bad. And John was there. Probably making more bad than Stephen would ever see in his lifetime. Or would ever want to see. And he wanted to say, Don't go Danny, let's go home. Let's go home to mad Ian and let John be bad without us.

I don't want to know.

And he watched helplessly as a tear rolled down Danny's cheek.

Danny drove like a maniac, and every turn he took too fast, every hillock they flew over, made Stephen feel worse, more sure they were speeding towards something dreadful. Terminal.

The end.

The last time he'd ever see Danny. The last time anything. This was going to be the first and the last time all in one.

Goodbye and thanks for all the shit.

They came into the outskirts of the town. Stephen risked a look at him. He looked terrible, almost as mad as Ian. "Danny," he said suddenly. "What are we going to find?"

"I don't know."

"What's he going to do?"

"I don't know."

"D'you think he'll kill him? He wouldn't kill him, would he?"

"I don't fucking *know*. Shut up!"

Stephen shut up, shivering with cold and fear. He wasn't dressed properly, neither of them were, but only Stephen was shivering. Danny looked as if he was already dead.

Shiver Danny, Stephen wanted to shout. *Fucking shiver.*

They came to it.

Conley's building.

Stephen felt somehow they'd never reach it. He realised now it wasn't because it had taken so long, it was because it hadn't taken long enough. He didn't want to reach it. He hadn't wanted to reach it, ever. And now here it was. Traitorous fucking thing, sneaking up on them, full of blood and pain.

"I don't want to go in," he said suddenly, shamed by how young and scared he sounded.

"Wait here then," Danny said and there wasn't a single hint of criticism in it.

"I'm coming with you," he said immediately. Danny didn't say anything.

He parked as badly as he had driven. Stephen saw the Rover as soon as he got out. It looked as scary as the brown dot on your tooth, the one that says, You're going to the dentist sunshine. Rot-down has commenced.

Danny walked on ahead, half-running. Stephen ran behind him.

Why are you running Danny? What's to run for? You want to see it?

Danny took the steps two at a time. It was raining here, cold, icy, stinging. Stephen went up behind him.

Danny was already there, hammering on the door like he wanted in. He began kicking it.

The door opened.

And Rab stood there.

They both stared at him.

He looked at Danny. After a second or two he stood back to let them in.

John was sitting on the couch. He had his head back and a folded cloth pressed to his face. His shirt was covered in blood. When he lowered his head Stephen saw that it was from his nose. It was purple and swollen. So was his lip and one eye, all on one side of his face. He looked as if he'd taken a hammering.

"Where's Conley?" Danny asked. John stared at him. Danny never even looked at him.

"Bedroom," Rab said.

Danny went over. Stephen stayed where he was, looking at John, flicking a quick glance at Rab then back at John again. John was staring at the telephone, eyes black

as thunder. Rab was staring at John.

Stephen began to walk over to the bedroom.

Conley was in the bed, on his face, breathing stentoriously, as if he had a suffocating cold. He was twitching slightly. He was uncovered to the waist. His back was criss-crossed with cuts, thin, red, raw. His hair had been hacked away in chunks. It looked like something had gnawed it. Danny was sitting on the bed staring at him.

"He's alright, isn't he?" Stephen whispered.

Danny nodded.

Stephen sat down beside him and looked at Danny's face. "Are *you* alright?"

Danny nodded again.

"Very touching," Rab said. He was standing in the doorway, licking a cigarette, sealing it. He put it in his mouth and began patting his pockets. He found what he was looking for and lit it. You could smell it almost straight away. Stephen realised again, perversely, how good-looking he was, and felt intensely guilty for it. Here, like this, with Conley all sliced up and Danny falling apart. He stared at the floor, ashamed of himself.

"How did you get here?" Danny asked.

"Tam Johnstone. You want to see his face? Want to see what your big brother did to his face?"

"No. Don't touch him," Danny said when Rab made to move towards him. "You'll wake him."

"No danger, he's well gone. Sleeping tablets."

"He gave him...?" Stephen felt Danny rise off the bed.

"Relax. I gave him them. They're his own." He looked at Danny then smiled. It looked tight and malicious. "He informs me he has trouble sleeping. Nightmares. I think you spread them."

Danny sank back onto the bed. "What's he done to his face?"

"Look and see."

"No, you fucking *tell* me."

Rab wet his lips and inhaled. He exhaled slowly as he spoke. Smoke curled out his mouth, curled round his words. "He carved cocksucker on it. When I got here he was just starting on his backside. First three letters, fag... What's your guess?" He inhaled again.

"Oh Jesus," Danny whispered.

Rab shook his head, caught his lower lip lightly between his teeth. He laughed a small incredulous laugh, like he couldn't believe how naive Danny was being. Stephen wanted to tell him to shut up, but Rab was going on, "He was tied to the bed, face-down. I reckon he was probably unconscious, or very near it, when he brought him in here, but he tied him down anyway, probably because he still had the back to do and he didn't want him coming to and spoiling his fun."

Stephen was watching Danny's face. It was a horrible colour, like nothing human.

"Then, of course, he did his party piece. Can't you just see him striding the bed like the Colossus of Rhodes? Bet that got him off."

"Shut up." Danny said it through gritted teeth.

Stephen swallowed, looked desperately from one to the other.

"How does he normally like it, before or after?"

Danny shot up, shoved Rab hard in the chest. "I told you to shut up."

"Christ! Still fucking defending him, even after this. Still in there rooting for him. When is it going to stop Danny?"

"Leave me alone." Danny pushed past him and went out into the living area.

Rab looked at his cigarette then pinched it between his fingers. Suddenly he looked at Stephen and made an attempt at a smile. "Ruined your love life Steve-o." He said it matter-of-factly, almost as if he was sorry. Stephen didn't know what to say. Rab sat down beside him. Stephen moved to get up.

"No, wait. Give them five."

Stephen sat down again, as surprised by the idea of Rab giving John and Danny time together as he would have been by Jesus coming back for another try. He twisted his hands in his lap and said in an undertone, "Did he really do all that?"

Rab leaned across the bed and lifted the quilt. The letters were there, three of them, just like he'd said, but it wasn't on the first cheek. On the first cheek, clear and complete, the word Nazi had wept and bled. *Nazi fag.* Rab dropped the quilt.

"You didn't say..."

Rab held his finger to his lips. "Not all in one day, eh?"

"Did he...?"

Rab looked at him. "Rape him?" He looked away again, nodded. "It goes with the territory, doesn't it? Cutting him up, pissing on him. I'm surprised he didn't shit on him too and make his humiliation complete."

"What?" Stephen said dully.

Rab turned back to him then, unusually, blushed. "Shit, I thought you knew. I mean the place reeks of it. Christ I wouldn't have told you if I thought you didn't know... sorry." And he looked it. Suddenly he looked tired and strained and sad. Sad most of all. No bright shiny arrogance. No macho and strutting. He smoked another cigarette like it was holding him together, like he'd chew his fingers off if he didn't have it.

"Conley could charge him," Stephen said abruptly, aware of Danny and John's voices, not wanting to hear what they were saying.

Rab laughed. "Conley could put him *away*. This isn't just a violent outburst, it's sick, wrong up here." He tapped his head.

Stephen remembered Ian running across the yard. He remembered Danny urging him to hurt his genitals, his crazy 'flyers'.

"What's wrong?" Rab was asking him.

"Nothing." Stephen shook his head to clear it. Suddenly he was tired beyond belief. "I wish I could go to sleep. Just here, right now."

"Go ahead, lie down, there's plenty of room."

"I couldn't, not with him like that."

"It won't hurt him, he's out of it."

"No."

Rab looked at him keenly. "What you really mean is on this bed."

Stephen nodded his head. Rab rumpled his hair. "I don't blame you. We'll go home soon. Stick with it."

They sat together in silence and watched the clock go round.

John didn't look at him. Even when he moved in front of him his gaze remained fixed where the phone had been a moment before.

"You fucking filthy animal," Danny said. "You fucking dangerous bloody animal."

John moved suddenly, throwing the wet face-cloth at him, hitting him in the chest.

Danny never even flinched. He spoke as if John hadn't so much as blinked. "I wish he'd killed you. I wish he'd fucking beaten you to death."

"I'll bet," John said.

"How did he get you to stop John? How did he tear you away from your meal?"

John smiled with his half-mouth. He looked like a gargoyle. The damaged eye was so bloodshot it looked like it would cry blood if he wept. "I was up him when he came

in. Wasn't ready for an assault to the side of my head Danny-boy. Way live into my pleasures."

Danny could feel his heart hurting his chest.

"I couldn't shoot my load." John closed his eyes. "Ian's right, I make a lousy faggot." He was silent for a moment then he said, "It would have gone on for bloody forever if your fairy cousin hadn't come in to save the day. Should have locked the door, shouldn't I? Shouldn't have got drunk. Shouldn't have been out spilling the seed in the first place."

Danny stood and stared down at him. He looked as if he was listening to bad news, a tragedy, something terrible. Something close to grief was written all over his face.

John said suddenly, "Stop *looking* at me like that." His voice was shot with distress, anguish. He went on, words pouring out of him, hand coming up blindly. "Okay, so I did it. And the night before. And all the other bloody nights. I don't know why any more than you do. Christ, I don't *want* to do it, you fucking drive me to it. Not a fucking word do you say to me, but I can feel it, all your fucking contempt, like I can't control it or something. Christ if you hate me why don't you just say so? You're just like her, with all her patronising bloody acceptance, just turning a blind eye while he goes out and shags some other bitch senseless."

Danny looked at the hand, still meaninglessly held out to him, like John didn't know it was there, and slowly took it. John pulled him down to him. "You could stop me. Just say the word and I'll stop."

"Don't," Danny said, face grey as John tried to make himself small against him.

"Stop me Danny, I'm begging you."

"Christ you sound like Ian. Shut the fuck *up*."

John buried his head in Danny's lap, holding him tight round the waist.

Danny laid a hand on his hair. He could feel John crying silently against him, words still whispering out of him. "I *wanted* to come. He was covered in blood and I *still* couldn't do it. I could feel his pain every time I pushed in. It was like it was in my dick, not in him at all. Jesus, I wanted it so much. I was nearly there. So close. But it wasn't going to happen."

Danny closed his eyes so tightly they hurt, hushed him, but John wouldn't stop. It was vomiting out of him.

"I told him what I was going to do, but I still couldn't get hard. I hacked his hair off chunk by chunk. I kept looking at the back of his head, thinking, I want to stick this knife in him, feel the resistance as it pushes through his skull. I want to dig a hole in him, gouge him open, bleed you out of him like poison. I wanted to squeeze you out of him like so much white pus until his itch was gone, the disease removed from him. I wanted to cure him. I wanted *him* to cure *me*. I did it carefully, kept it shallow. I wasn't trying to hurt him, I just wanted him to bleed. I asked him if that felt better, but he wouldn't answer me. He hardly made a sound. I could hear him breathing, that's all. I asked him if he wanted to come."

John laughed, low and muffled in Danny's lap. "He told me to fuck off."

He turned his face. Danny looked down at him. His own face was streaked with wet but he didn't feel it.

"It was that that finally got me, him swearing at me. I went up him, quick, before I lost it. He tried to keep me out, but he was too spread. He couldn't do anything. He made a noise then. I think that was the only time I felt anything, that little noise of distress. I started cutting him again. He began to cry. I could feel it. Still not making any noise, but I know silent tears. I knew then I wasn't going to get any further. It was like finding myself fucking some woman I didn't even want. I lay still, just twitching it occasionally, sobering up. Fucking sobering up when I needed to be drunk, right out of it. It was then Rab came in."

John suddenly shoved his face hard in Danny's lap, seemingly oblivious to the damage to his face. It made Danny's stomach turn. He prised him off. "Get up John. Come on, get up."

John got up slowly and heavily, like he couldn't bear his own weight. They were facing each other now. John said so quietly it was almost a whisper, "I let him do this to me. I could have stopped him, but I didn't."

Danny shook his head, trying not to let the disgust show on his face. "You're going home."

John moved up close before him. "Don't tell Ian anything. Don't tell him the truth, swear to me."

Danny saw John's hand was pinching his bruised cheek, doing it mindlessly, like someone picking at a scab. He pulled it away from his face angrily, fighting the nausea. "*Stop* that."

Suddenly he saw blood on the neck of his shirt, almost hidden by his sweater. He reached up and yanked it down. John's hand came up quickly and held his, tight, immovable. John suddenly looked lucid. Lucid and clear-eyed and exactly in himself.

Danny breathed it out. "What have you done to yourself?"

John shook his head, kept Danny's hand tight in his own.

"Let me fucking *see* it John," Danny hissed, angry, afraid, icy with foreboding.

"It was an accident."

Danny wrenched his sweater down, pulling a button loose on his shirt. His chest was covered in lines, just like Conley's back.

"His thighs are the same," Rab said behind him.

Danny let him go as if he was infected with leprosy. "Oh Jesus. Jesus *Christ* John."

"It was an accident," John said again.

"How could it be a fucking *accident?!*" Danny almost screamed it.

"Keep your voice down," Rab said tensely.

Danny looked at him as if he'd gone mad, bafflement fighting with anger.

"The *boy*," Rab said, jerking his head. Danny blinked, dropping to his knees on the sofa. After a moment he slowly rested back on his heels, then he collapsed against the back of the settee. "I need to take him home," he said dully.

Rab looked down at him. "I'll do it. You stay here with Conley."

"No." Danny's voice was sharp. "You stay. Keep Stephen here with you."

Rab was going to say, There's no need, when he realised there was every need. Well, Ian would be there if anything happened. Good old fucking Ian, always reliable in a crisis.

As if Danny had read his thoughts he said, "Did Ian send you here?"

"Let's say he thought it would be a good idea."

Danny looked at him. "Didn't you realise what he was doing?"

"I'm not stupid Danny."

Danny looked away then got up. "Where's your jacket?" he said to John, but John was looking at Rab, eyes cold and black. He didn't answer him.

"It's in the bedroom," Rab said. "I'll get it."

He went to get it. Danny said, "You got everything?"

John turned away slowly without looking at him. He never answered that either.

Rab came back and handed the jacket to Danny, not John. Danny carried it over his arm. He pushed John ahead of him. John moved forward with sudden speed, disappearing out the door.

Danny stopped and handed Rab the pick-up keys. Rab said, "We might not make it back in time for the milking."

"It's alright," Danny said, "we'll manage."

Rab caught his arm. "Phone me if he starts anything..." He tugged Danny's arm.

"Promise."

"I promise."

"Take care Danny," and he bent his head and kissed him briefly on the mouth.

Danny nodded and went out the door.

Ian!" Danny shouted his name as he stood shaking water off in the kitchen.

There was no reply.

"Where is he?" John asked.

Danny shrugged and looked round the room. Somehow it looked too neat. He expected to see signs of Ian's outburst. Smashed plates, something.

He went out into the hall and shouted again, "*Ian?!*"

No reply.

He stuck his head round the living room door.

Nothing.

He went up the stairs two at a time, beginning to feel panicky, anxious. He went into Ian's room, saying his name. He clicked on the light, heart thumping.

Nothing. The wardrobe door was wide open but otherwise everything was fine. He came out and closed Ian's door.

John came up into the hall. "Well?"

"He doesn't seem to be in."

"Pub?"

Danny looked at his watch, although he already knew it was miles too late for it. "Shut ages ago."

They checked the other rooms. "Where the fuck *is* he?" Danny said.

"It doesn't matter," John said, then he smiled and said, "Just you and me baby."

Danny wanted to say, No way, you're on your own tonight, but he kept it to himself. He'd provide him with a fait accompli. No arguments. No discussion.

"I've got to go wash," John said, looking down at himself. "I look like I murdered someone."

Danny looked at his smile and wanted to slap him. "I'll go check the animals, lock up." He made to pass him.

John caught at his arm and pulled him to him. Danny could feel the stiff dry blood under his hands. "I'm going to love you tonight. You won't believe what a faggot I can be when I'm with you."

Danny stood unresisting in his arms. John pressed the clean half of his face in his hair then let him go. Danny walked away without looking at him. John watched him until he disappeared from sight.

Danny ran across the dark yard. I should have put the frigging light on, he thought, head down into the rain. He pulled the shed door open and felt for the lights.

He squeaked a useless noise when a hand caught his, pulling him off-balance and jarring his arm.

Ian was soaking wet. Danny could feel the soggy fabric under his hands. He was icy to the touch. "Ian? Jesus. What have you been doing? Put on the lights."

"No."

And then Ian slammed him hard against the wall and Danny felt something cold and stinging along his side. He sucked in his breath, said, "What the hell...?" and felt it again, this time sharp and burning under his arm. "Ian..." he said helplessly.

"I'm going to stick you Danny, right here in the dark."

Danny struggled violently and felt another cut along the back of his hand, sorer, deeper. "Oh Jesus," he whispered.

"No, me. *Ian.*"

Danny felt as if his legs were turning to water. He could hardly stand.

"I'm going to keep cutting you until you do what you're told."

Danny remained frozen where he was.

"We're going in the car... and no tricks."

Danny took a breath, wondering where the knife was, trying not to panic, not to wet himself.

"I'll be right behind you Danny."

"I'm doing it, I'm *doing* it." Danny pulled open the shed door, feeling the cut on his hand screaming at him. He could feel the sticky wet of it between his fingers, the drip of it filling his finger nails. Ian was up close against him. It was like being in the grave with a corpse, he was so cold and clammy.

They got to the Rover, still ticking in the darkness.

"Open the door."

Danny reached in his pocket and got the keys, wishing like hell he'd hung them up.

"Hurry up." Ian pressed the knife into his back.

"I'm doing the best I can." In truth he was trembling so hard he couldn't feel the fucking things. He got it open.

Ian climbed in, pulling Danny in after him. "Now drive."

Oh Jesus, Danny thought. Away from the house. Away from John. What the hell am I going to do?

He started the car. It caught first time. If only it had been the pick-up. John wouldn't even hear it, not in the shower. Oh fuck. *Fuck.*

Danny drove it out carefully. "Where to?" he said. He still hadn't looked at him, didn't want to, not yet. Not until he stopped shaking.

"Due left, Danny-boy."

Danny risked a look at him, a quick glance.

"Keep your eyes on the road."

Danny looked back at the road again, but he'd seen enough. He was drenched through, as if he'd been walking in the rain. No coat on. His hair was plastered to his head. His face was pale, his mouth a tight thin line.

"Turn next left," Ian said.

Danny slowed, frowned, then said, "Jerrett's?"

"Top marks."

"What for?" Danny asked, feeling the panic well up all over again.

"Just do what you're told."

Danny indicated and turned when the turning came. The gate had been shut. Danny slowed the car.

"Get out and open it, and don't try anything stupid."

Danny got out into the rain and crossed the beams of the lamps. He lifted the rusty chain, seeing the blood garishly streaming down his hand, soaking his cuff. He felt his side. Right through the heavy waxed cotton of his jacket. The cuts were painful, wet, but not deep. He got back in, blood on both hands. They drove through. Ian made him stop and shut the gate behind him.

They bumped up the track to the house. Ian reached over and cut the lights, then the engine. They sat there in absolute darkness, the rain drumming on the roof.

"You bleeding Danny?" Ian's voice came out of the dark.

"Yes."

"Hurting?"

"A bit."

Ian laughed then said, "Get out and go over to the house."

Danny did as he was told, making for the dim darkness of the doorway. A torch suddenly shone in his face, blinding him. He turned away from it. Ian moved beside him. Danny was shivering but Ian, soaked to the skin, didn't even seem to feel the cold.

He opened the door. "Get in."

Danny went in. The door closed behind him, plunging him into absolute darkness. Ian pushed him into the living room. "Draw the curtains."

Danny drew them. The lights clicked on with such brilliance Danny shaded his eyes with his hand. When he blinked out from under it Ian was standing there by the door watching him. "Like a stuck pig," he said and smiled.

Danny looked at his side. Blood had soaked right through his shirt and T-shirt. The fabric of his coat gaped open. His hands were red. It looked garish, ugly, but it was only a hot, hard stinging, like bad paper-cuts, all surface pain and glory.

"Now you can light the fire. Everything's there for you. Go on, don't stand there staring. I need some heat and I don't want these lights on any longer than necessary. Move it."

Danny crossed to the fire and began to build it. He could feel Ian's eyes on his back. After a moment or two Ian said, "We have a nice electric immerser now, thanks to your mother. I put it on for us. After you've got that lit we'll go for a bath."

Danny said carefully, without turning or stopping what he was doing, "Were you along here earlier?"

"No, I went for a stroll and there was a heavy dew."

Danny didn't say anything.

"I suppose I should really have carried you over the threshold, but given my gnome-like stature I think that would have looked a bit ridiculous, don't you?"

His voice sounded perfectly rational. He even looked relatively rational, given his drenched state, but something about him was all wrong, off-key, out-of-kilter.

Danny built the fire. He'd stopped shaking. It didn't look as if Ian planned to kill him. At least not yet.

Danny stood up and brushed his knees down. "I need to wash my hands." He held them up, like a child proving he wasn't lying.

Ian smiled. "Upstairs. We might as well, while the fire's catching."

He let Danny pass out before him into the hall. This time he put the light on. Danny hadn't seen the hall finished. He didn't even know it *had* been finished. Who'd done it? On whose instructions? Why? He looked at it curiously, saw the part he'd painted. He felt a shiver of revulsion.

"Go on." Ian pushed his back gently. "No time to get morbid."

Danny went up the stairs and saw it all again, the stuff of nightmares.

"Remembering Danny?" He could hear the insidious smile in it.

Danny said nothing.

At least the bathroom was untainted with memory. Ian turned the taps on. The water ran flaky with rust then cleared. He put the plug in. The room was cold, but there were two clean dry towels there. Danny looked at them.

"I have an eye for domestic detail. Never noticed it before?"

Danny still said nothing.

Ian came over to him and said, "Better get these things off." And Danny watched him unfasten his clothes for him, carefully lifting them away from the wounds, tutting over the damage, then unfastening his shoes, his jeans, stripping him off.

Danny stood there, covered in goosepimples, and watched Ian looking at him.

"Oh Lord," Ian said. "Can I say that? Can I express my wonderment at your captivating beauty?" And he ran his hand down Danny's body.

Eventually he turned the tap off, added a little cold, then said, "Get in."

Danny climbed in, added a little more cold, and sat down cross-legged at the tap end of the bath. He listened to Ian undressing.

Ian climbed in and sat down facing him. "God, that feels good," he said, lifting handfuls of hot water over himself. He picked the soap up and began washing.

Danny watched him, feeling the hot water sting his cuts. Ian passed him the soap. "Now you," and his eyes looked drugged and heavy, his face coloured for the first time. His hair looked very dark. It made him look odd, almost Latin, slicked back off his face and glistening wet, not so much as a wave to break the light on it.

Danny took the soap and began running it over himself. Ian did what he expected him to do.

He watched him and slowly masturbated.

Ian dried him with meticulous care, his erection bobbing out obscenely from his belly. He let it nudge against Danny's leg, stood with it brushing against him, acting as if it wasn't there, making it worse. He made Danny open his legs while he dried between them. He took too long about it, pushing the towel between his buttocks. Danny bit his lip and kept quiet.

Ian finally decided he was dry enough. He began patching up his cuts. The bathroom cabinet was fully stocked. Danny said nothing about that either.

He'd washed Danny's hair for him, running his fingers through it, his cock standing up in Danny's face, nudging his shoulder as he worked. Now he rubbed it dry with the towel.

Danny ran his fingers through it when he was finished. Ian said quietly, "I love watching you do that. You've done that as long as I can remember, only now you look even more beautiful doing it."

Danny looked away, feeling as if he was stretched like a long thin piece of chewing gum. Snap. Broken.

"Come through to the bedroom," Ian said. Danny followed him. He didn't want to go but he went.

The fireplace was still there, the gas fire. He felt his stomach turn over. Ian shut the door and looked at him. "Has to have been here, it's all over your face."

Danny nodded.

Ian smiled. "Don't ever try to lie to me Danny, you're never going to make it."

"I don't."

"Good, don't start."

Danny felt a flush of irritation but said nothing.

Ian stroked his face. "Like the cliché, you're beautiful when you're angry."

Danny pulled his face away, even as he told himself not to do it, but Ian didn't seem to notice or care. Danny realised suddenly the room was warm, curtains drawn. The bed was turned down. It looked like the honeymoon suite.

"I'm going to sleep with you tonight." Ian took his face in both hands. "And no-one will take you away from me. Just you and I. Alone."

Just like John had said, only this time it was more likely to be true.

"I'd take you now but your hair's wet and I know you hate that. Want to go down and eat by the fire while it dries?"

Danny realised he was hungry, very hungry, and tired as all fuck. He nodded.

"Don't get dressed, just wrap a blanket round you, that'll do. Here." And they wrapped themselves in blankets and went back downstairs.

The fire had a good heart in it, although the room was still cold. Danny pulled a cushion off the settee and sat on it, as close to the fire as he could get. He opened the blanket and let the heat reflect on his front.

Ian looked at him and ran his hand through his damp hair. "You look as if you're made of flame."

"I wish I felt it."

Ian laughed and went to get them something to eat. When he came back Danny was half-asleep in front of the roaring fire, head on his knees. He looked soft and vulnerable and young. "Danny..." Ian said quietly.

Danny jerked upright in a quick cat-like movement. "Dozing," he murmured.

Ian gave him a cup of soup and a buttered roll. Danny ate it sleepily, drank the soup in small sips. Ian finished well ahead of him and stroked his shoulders while he ate, occasionally running his hand into his hair. Danny felt utterly spent.

"Almost dry," Ian said and even half asleep Danny heard the catch in it - repressed excitement. His stroking had put Danny to sleep but it had stoked Ian up. Danny glanced down covertly and saw Ian's erection sticking out under his raised knees. He felt a sudden surge of irritation, knowing he wouldn't be allowed to sleep until Ian had worked it off. He said snappily, "Let's get to bed," and he struggled up, pulling the blanket up around himself.

Ian said, "Alright," and closed the fire and put the guard on. He followed Danny out the room, putting off the light.

They went up the stairs quietly on bare feet.

Outside the rain poured on.

Danny climbed into the cold bed. Ian put out the gas fire. There was a bedside lamp. That was new too. A little thing in lavender with a pleated paper shade and a ceramic base. It was very much his mother, her colours. The shade was still in its cellophane. Danny wondered who'd put it there, where they'd found it. Was it another one of Ian's little domestic details?

Ian climbed in beside him, pulling his attention back. Danny moved slightly, trying to ease the pressure on the cuts on his side. Now they were hurting like hell.

Ian came close to him, said his name, then kissed him.

Danny lay there rigid, suddenly wildly, irrationally angry. "Don't you even want to know who died? Who won or lost?"

"No." Ian kissed his forehead.

"What, after all your hard work?"

"I told you, he makes his own decisions. Let him worry about what happens. All I care about is you."

"Oh, not John."

Ian paused before saying carefully, "If you think so."

"He didn't kill anybody."

"I'm relieved."

"You sound it."

Ian sighed. "Danny, don't start a fight with me."

Danny pulled away from him. "Fuck you."

"Yes please. I'd like you to." Ian leaned up over his face. "I can't think of anything I'd like more, other than maybe fucking you, so please don't fight with me, let me love you."

"No." Danny pulled away violently.

But Ian pulled him back. His voice hardened, saying, "I'm going to do it Danny, so you might as well stop fighting me. I don't want to hurt you any more, but I'm *going* to do it, so let's have some co-operation."

Danny lay there, still, sullen. Ian smiled and said, "That's better. Now you can kiss me."

"I'll see you fucking rot first."

Ian slapped his face, much as John would have done. For some reason it took Danny utterly by surprise. His eyes went round with shock, his cheeks flamed.

"Right," Ian said, breath coming tight and hard. "Let's try that again. You'll fucking kiss me and you'll make it convincing or I'll fucking skin you. I mean it."

Danny closed his eyes then reached up and dragged Ian's head down.

"Danny?"

"What?" Danny tugged over into the darkness, grudging being dragged from the brink of sleep for what felt like the fortieth time.

"What did you do with her?" Ian curved into his back, one arm loosely around his waist.

Danny went rigid.

"I mean sex," Ian said. He felt Danny relax again.

"Nothing."

"Don't lie."

"I'm not lying. He caught her feeling me up. We didn't get anywhere. He broke her neck first."

"I don't believe you."

Danny made a small exasperated sound then said, "Alright. She jerked me off, downstairs, couple of nights before. That night I was trying to push it but he came in and stopped it. Okay?"

"She jerked you *off* ?"

"Got a problem with that?" Danny snapped it.

"Oh, absolutely not. Did you enjoy it?"

"I hated her guts."

"That doesn't answer my question."

"It wasn't about *enjoyment*. Now are you happy?"

"I would *never* have believed that. To be honest I'd never have believed you wanted it either, unless it was just to rub John's face in it."

"Give it a rest Ian." Danny moved away from him, but Ian followed him, pressing against him.

"She was panicking about nothing. It wasn't enough that he should find you this time, it was *where* he was going to find you. In his mother's arms."

"She deserved everything she got."

Ian laughed, like he knew something special. "You should have given in sooner then, been better if he'd caught you at it."

"Desperate to add motherfucker to my list of accomplishments?"

"Well you did, essentially."

"No we *didn't* - that's the point."

"Not for the want of trying. Anyway, you shouldn't hate her just because she was stupid enough to let John kill her."

"I hate her because she hated me. Tit for tat."

"Rab never had her you know."

He felt Danny go completely still, hold his breathing.

"So you can forgive her that at least. Rab never so much as sniffed near her no matter what he told you. John just wanted to discredit her in your eyes. The whole idea was fantastic. Only a kid would fall for it. She was just about the most frigid woman you could ever meet. I reckon you probably broke some world record there. The only person in the family who ever got close to her was you, and that's the truth."

"The *truth*?" Danny said. "What the fuck's the truth? It's different every week and

twice on Tuesdays."

"Your privilege," Ian said, just like he always did.

Danny let it sink in then said, "So none of it's true? The girls he used to brag about?"

"None of it. The big myth making machine. He's as queer as I am."

There was a pause before Ian said, "Have you ever realised that John was around for four years before any of the rest of us appeared? Almost school age. Just him and his mum and dad. No brothers. No cousins."

Danny listened in the darkness, holding his breath. At first he thought Ian was changing the subject, now he felt this was even more important.

"He was around for nine years, almost ten, before you appeared."

"So?" Danny prompted.

"He was his dad's favourite boy. Always."

"What are you saying Ian?" Danny asked. His voice sounded fragile.

"Eight years of listening to the old man. Eight years of listening to a homophobic freak who was too chickenshit to admit boys could get him off."

"Don't tell me who he was."

"Nobody's telling you anything, but think about it, eight years of that drivel pouring into his head, day after day."

"What am I supposed to do? Cry for him?"

Ian laughed. "Hard little bastard, aren't you? You've no soul Danny."

"Yeah, sure."

Ian laughed again. "Okay, then let me ask you something. Supposing your daddy told John that one of his brothers *wasn't* his brother?"

"What?" It came out whispery.

"You heard me. Supposing the old man told him one of us wasn't his brother? Supposing he said, Your mummy fucked the milkman? Supposing that?"

"I don't believe you. Why would he do a thing like that? Why would he say a thing like that?"

"Well..." and Ian's voice was low and breathy against his cheek. Danny felt his lips brush against it, his hand circling low over his back. "Suppose he said it because it was true?"

Danny lay there, feeling the pulse thumping in the side of his head. A pain began to dig in over one eyebrow.

"Aren't you going to ask which one of us?" And this time Ian's whispery mouth kissed his cheek.

"Who?" Danny said, mouth full of saliva.

Ian laughed and suddenly grabbed Danny's backside, squeezing his buttocks together like he was in high spirits. "Who do you think? Who looks fuck all like the rest of us? Who does everybody say, How the hell did that ugly old bastard produce *that?*"

"No," Danny said, pushing him off with hands like wads of wet waste. "I look like John."

"A distant family resemblance. Like a *cousin* would look." Ian paused long enough to let that one sink in then said in case he'd missed it, "Like Rab looks. There's only one person in the family you really look like and everybody misses it. Same mouth, same cheekbones, same build, same height, same long legs... just like your daddy's... both of you."

"No," Danny said.

"Yes." And Ian laughed. "You fucked your long-lost brother tonight and neither of you knew it. There, isn't that a fairy-tale for you? A real one."

"You bastard," Danny said, wriggling away violently. "You rotten bastard. You're making this up."

848

"I'm not and you know it, that's why you're so fucking scared. Just like he knows it. I've seen it worry him. Unlike you he can remember his father. Red Jackie, that's what they used to call him, and guess why? Because he had flaming red hair. Not as dark as yours, but red all the same and he was fucking beautiful. I remember him, tall and thin with curly red hair. It's the hair that throws everyone, makes everyone think you and Rab are opposites. It's only Rab that looks at you and sees the dead-spit of his father, and worries. Why do you think he took so long to move in on you? Who knows, maybe she even told him. Maybe the old man told him. Maybe he's known for a while. Maybe he's just come to accept it. Danny's my half-brother. No big deal. Think so?"

"I don't believe any of this, you're lying."

"Fine, I can't prove it. Rab might have some photographs, but I'm pretty sure not. And even if he did I still couldn't prove it, only it's true and you know it is."

"Why d'you tell me this now? Why wait all this time?"

"I just felt you should know."

"Christ, you poxy liar."

"Okay, I want you to tell me where you went with him. And don't bother with 'He left me outside', he must have told you something."

"He never told me anything."

"You must have seen something. He was a drunken bastard and riddled with guilt, he must have let something slip."

Danny shook his head.

"Come on, I told you. Fair's fair Danny."

"Fair's fair shit. You've just ripped my life in half and you tell me fair's *fair?*"

"Who was it Danny? Where did you go?"

Danny suddenly sat up and pushed him back on the bed, covering the lower half of his face in a smothering grip. Ian scrabbled at his hand, scratching it, trying to get it off.

"Want to know Ian? Really want to know? Well, why don't you dig him up and ask him?" And Danny pushed him away, clambering over him and out the bed.

"What are you doing?" Ian was hoarse, trying to inject authority into his tone.

"Getting dressed."

Ian scrambled up, clicking the lamp on. Danny was already in his T-shirt and underpants. He was pulling his shirt on.

Ian shot out of bed, grabbing the knife. Danny turned and caught it slap in his palm as the knife sliced upwards. He pulled it out of Ian's grasp, laying his fingers open.

He never even felt it. He flicked it in Ian's face. "Back off, shit."

Ian stepped back.

Danny took a swipe with it. Ian dived back. "Danny, don't."

"Why? I owe you a few. I might even get off on it, like my *ex* big brother."

"He's still your brother."

"No, he's my *half* brother, and *you* took that away from me."

"It's not important."

"Not *important?*" Danny almost screamed it. "It's the only thing I've got and you tell me it's not *important?* Who the fuck *are* you?"

Ian was backed into a corner. "Danny... I love you. Don't do this to me... please." He was pleading with him, tears beginning to roll down his face.

"I *love* you Danny," Danny mimicked, pushing the knife against his throat. Blood dripped off his hand onto the floor. "I love you so fucking much I'm going to stand by and smile while I rip your heart out."

"Danny... please." The blade was breaking the skin.

Danny suddenly closed his eyes and whispered, "Time to *die…*"

When the lunge came Ian whimpered and felt his bladder let go.

But it was only spit he wiped from his face. And Danny and the knife were gone.

Ian slid down the wall and sat in his own urine.

When John discovered Danny was gone he couldn't believe it.

It took the accumulation of facts to convince him. Danny was gone; the Rover was gone. Worst of all, Danny's clothes were gone. All of them.

At some point Danny had packed up and John never suspected a thing. Nothing. Not a hint. Not a clue.

He couldn't believe it.

He stood for a moment in the middle of the kitchen floor then roared, giving vent to his pain. A primeval roar of thwarted rage. He was blinded by misery and confusion. He couldn't think.

He had to do something, but he had no car, there was no-one there to help him. There was no-one even to rage at.

He ran his hands through his hair.

Rab. He had to phone Rab. He practically ran out into the hall. He tried to remember Conley's number. Nothing.

Come on, come on. Directory enquiries.

He tried to visualise Whymper's business card, remember the address. He gave them Conley's name. No, not the practice, there's a private number there, for Mr James Conley. *Hurry up you bitch, come on.*

She found it. He scribbled it down on his hand and hung up. He had to dial it twice, fucking up the first time.

It rang.

And rang...

And fucking rang.

Finally someone answered it. "Hello?" It had to be Stephen.

"Steve?"

"John?"

"Let me speak to Rab."

"He's in the toilet."

"Then go get him."

"He said he was going for a shit."

John felt an uncontrollable urge to laugh. He said, "I don't care if he's gone for a bath. Get him out of there. Tell him it's urgent. Now."

The phone clunked down. John listened but could hear nothing. Their voices were too far away. "Come on, come on," he whispered.

"Hello?"

"Rab?"

"No, he's just coming. What's wrong?" Stephen asked.

"Nothing. Where is he?"

"What is it?" Rab's voice came clear and dry over the line.

"He's gone," John said.

"Who's gone?"

"Danny."

There was a silence then Rab said, "What happened?"

"Nothing. He's just upped and left. All his stuff is missing. He's taken the car. I need transport. You have to bring the pick-up home."

Stephen stood watching Rab's face, knowing something bad had happened.

"I can't leave Conley here by himself."

"Leave Stephen with him."

Rab looked at Stephen and said into the phone, "Hang on." He said to Stephen, "Now Danny's disappeared."

"Disappeared?" Stephen said, his voice too high.

"Don't worry. He does this all the time. John needs me to go back. I'm going to have to leave you here with Conley."

"I want to come with you."

"We can't leave him here by himself."

"He doesn't even know we're here."

"Yeah, but what if he comes round? Chokes on his own vomit or something?"

"No, I don't want to be left on my own with him."

"You'll need to. I'll be as fast as I can." He turned back to the phone and said to John, "I'll be there as soon as I can."

"Make it sooner."

"Look, don't start panicking."

"He's taken all his fucking clothes Rab. I'm past panic."

"Alright, I'm with you." And he hung up.

Stephen hung on his arm, beseeching him.

Rab peeled him off. "Look, if you were allowed to drive then you could go instead, but as it is one of us has got to go back, and that's me."

"He's alright."

"No he's not. Besides, we can't have him waking up and phoning the cops."

"God, and how am I supposed to stop him?"

"Look, he isn't going to wake up. Just you stay here with him. I'll be back, okay?"

Stephen nodded dumbly.

Rab finished fastening his shoes and shrugged into his jacket. "Right, I'm off." He moved away then stopped and looked back. He crossed back quickly and kissed Stephen's mouth, hard. "That's my thank-you in advance," he said quietly, then he smiled and pinched his cheek. "Now smile for fuck's sake."

And he was gone.

It took Rab just under fifty minutes to get back, breaking the law and the pick-up's back all the way.

John was in the kitchen. The sink was full of half-smoked cigarettes from where he'd been standing by the window watching for him. As soon as Rab came in John was up and pulling on his jacket. Rab pushed him in the chest. "Hold it. Let's stop and think first."

"No, let's not. I've thought so fucking much my brain hurts. I need to *do* something."

Rab looked at him and said almost wonderingly, "Christ, your face is one fucking mess hombre."

"Try not to mess your pants. Give me the keys." John held out his hand.

"I think you enjoyed it. You certainly didn't try very hard to stop me. Sexy, being beaten up by me while you were doing arse?"

John grabbed his front. "Just don't push me Rab, I'm not in the mood. Now give me the keys."

"Want to kill something tiger?"

John let him go as if something huge had just dawned on him. "It's Ian."

Rab blinked stupidly. "What?"

"Ian. He isn't here. He hasn't been here since we came in."

"And you think he's had something to do with it? Why would Ian help him get away?"

John laughed, shortly. "He's *taken* him Rab, he hasn't helped him get away. The little bastard's finally taken him. Clean away."

Stephen woke up, heart hammering. He didn't even know where he was. Then the noise came again, a horrible screech.

Stephen shot upright. What *was* that?

The screech came again.

Oh God, it was the *bird*. The stupid fucking bird. He was on Conley's couch.

He rubbed his face. What time was it?

He got up and crossed to the kitchen and peered at the clock on the oven. Two in the morning. Jesus. Why hadn't Rab phoned? What was happening?

He heard the muttering in the sudden silence. He stopped and listened. That was Conley, talking in his sleep. Oh God, what if something's wrong? What if he's haemorrhaging or something? Puking blood?

He was afraid to go and look, afraid of what he might see, but Conley got louder. He had to go.

He crossed on tiptoe and peered in. The lamp was still on. Conley was on his back now. His forehead was covered in dried blood where it had been bleeding again. He had a black eye.

Stephen went in and leaned over him, tentatively touched his cheek as if he might bite.

Conley thrashed away from him and woke up, eyes staring. "What?" he said clearly.

"Shhh... it's me, Stephen."

Conley stared at him.

Oh God, Stephen thought, he's flipped. He doesn't even know who I am.

Conley lay back down. "Where are the others?" He spoke perfectly clearly.

Now Stephen could read it, crammed and blurred and crude. *Cocksucker*. It looked terrible, deforming.

"Stephen?" Conley prompted.

Stephen said quickly, "It's just me."

"On your own?"

Stephen nodded. "Danny took John home and Rab stayed here, but John phoned about two hours ago and Rab had to go home. Danny's disappeared."

"Disappeared?" Conley frowned then winced, touching his forehead.

"Yeah. I know fuck all else, so don't ask me. I haven't heard a cheep."

Conley closed his eyes. He was tracing the marks on his forehead.

"Is it awful sore?" Stephen asked.

Conley shook his head. "No, just tender. The headache's worse." Conley looked at him suddenly. "What has he written on it?"

"Jesus," Stephen said. "Don't you know?"

Conley shook his head. "What?"

Stephen bit his lip. "Cocksucker."

Conley turned his head away. "Shit." It sounded odd to hear him say it. He'd never heard him swear before.

He kept his face averted. "And on my back?"

"Nothing. But he's written... well, he's written Nazi on your bum." Stephen felt as if he'd just said nigger to a black man. "And he put fag on the other side. Rab stopped him. He really beat him up," he added as if Conley hadn't been there.

Conley nodded. "Anything else?" he asked.

"No, just these long cuts."

Conley looked down at his chest, traced the flaky swollen stripes with his fingers. His ribs felt bruised and he had a lump on the back of his head where he must have hit the floor. That was probably the cause of the headache. His back felt as if it had a particularly bad case of sunburn. What he needed was painkillers, strong ones. "Stephen. Do me a favour?"

"Sure. What?"

"Nip out across the road, first turning after the Midland Bank, there's a chemist there. He should be open for prescriptions tonight. Ask him for the strongest painkillers he has. Have you got any money?"

"No." Stephen patted his pockets.

"You'll get some in my coat pocket. The black one."

"Okay." Stephen got up. Conley called him back.

"And get some plasters. Big ones, to cover this up." He touched his forehead. "I might be one, but I don't need to broadcast it."

Stephen flushed when he met his eyes and went out without speaking.

When he came back Conley was sitting on the bed in a pair of black trousers, nothing else. He had his head in his hands. He lifted it as if it weighed too much. "Get them?"

"Yeah. Hang on, I'll get some water."

He brought Conley the tablets saying, "It says two," and gave him two. They were orange and yellow, like plastic diodes.

Conley swallowed them. He smiled. "See how I trust you? You could be finishing John's job for him."

Stephen shook his head but didn't answer him, instead he said, "Want me to put this on for you?" He held out the roll of plaster.

"Please."

Stephen kneeled on the bed beside him and cut a piece off the roll. Conley watched his bent head, face absorbed in his work. He peeled the backing off, then leaned across Conley's body, trying to make sure the lint went over the cuts and not the adhesive. Conley watched his tongue trapped between his teeth, concentrating. He could smell him, young, powdery, faintly salty. He smelt faintly of sex. Conley averted his eyes from his face.

"There." Stephen rested back on his heels. "That looks better."

"Seriously?" Conley asked, smiling.

"Truly. Now you look interestingly wounded instead of..." He stopped.

"Instead of what?" Conley asked, searching his face.

Stephen flushed again. "I don't know, branded or something." He flushed some more.

"The Nazis used to use a pink triangle."

Stephen didn't say anything. Conley was still smiling at him. "They used to send homosexuals to the camps with a pink triangle on their suits so that everybody knew."

Stephen said, "Will it scar?"

"I shouldn't think so. If it does I'll have to either start wearing a fringe or get plastic surgery done."

"You already have a fringe."

Conley laughed. "That's a side parting. It's not supposed to fall over my face like that."

"It's nice. I mean..." He flushed again. "I meant, it suits you. You've got... I mean

had... Oh shit, I wish I'd never started this."

"Thank you. Compliment accepted." Conley smiled.

Stephen smiled back.

"Know what I would like?" Conley said suddenly.

"What?" Stephen asked nervously.

"A cup of strong coffee. Black, with plenty of sugar."

Stephen laughed. "Tell me how to work that thing and it shall be done."

Conley told him, and behold it was done.

John and Rab searched for over an hour and found nothing.

They woke Katherine Henderson up but Danny wasn't there.

Danny wasn't anywhere.

Eventually, after almost coming to blows, Rab insisted they went back home.

John came into the kitchen and threw his balled-up jacket across the room. It hit the dog who loped off, tail between his legs, and hid under the hall table.

"You're scaring the animals John. Give it a break, eh?" Rab said, hanging his jacket up.

John kicked a chair and turned on him. "You don't want to find him, do you? You think he'd be better off fucking dead than being with me. Or is it just fucking dead rather than be with anyone who isn't *you?*"

Rab put the kettle on and said, "Why don't you sit down and shut up before you say something you regret."

Rab kept his back to him, washing cups. John stared at him, feeling as if something red was washing over his eyes. He even wondered briefly if a capillary had broken in his eye. Maybe he was crying blood. Then he said, voice like nails down a blackboard, "How does it feel to fuck your little brother?"

He waited, letting the smile spread, even though it felt like it was twisting his mouth with pliers, until Rab said, "Say that again?" back still turned to him.

"Your little brother. Danny's your little brother, and don't you just *know* it?"

Rab turned slowly. John grew on the tense white face. God it felt so good. After all these years it felt *so* good.

"That's rubbish."

John just looked at him.

"It's rubbish. Who told you that?"

John laughed, pain shooting up into his eye, making him blink. His face was getting stiffer. "My daddy told me. Who the fuck else?"

"Yeah. When he was drunk?"

"No, before Danny was even born. I wasn't even so high." John held a hand waist-high. "He said, Your mother's a slut, she's been tupped by a slut, and you're going to have a slut for a brother. He knew it was going to be a boy, because that's all the Jackson Moores ever produce, and he knew exactly what Danny was before he was even out the womb - a whore, just like your shit-sucking father."

Rab shook his head, numb with disbelief. "A million times I said to you. I saw it a million times. I *said* to you and you never told me. Christ, you evil bastard. Why didn't you *tell* me?"

"What do you take me for? You come poncing along with your fucking faggy little crushes and expect me to hand over my own brother? To you? I'd see you rot in Hell first."

"Christ, you were *jealous*," Rab said.

John laughed contemptuously then suddenly sat down as if he'd been deflated. "Some other brat's brother, who didn't even *look* like me? What do you think?" And he

closed his eyes and let his head drop back..

Rab looked at him then crossed to him and said, "Oh John, what a fucking mess."

John lifted his head and looked at him. "No-one ever sees it." He laughed shortly. "Have you never watched him smoke a cigarette?"

"I thought he was copying me."

"Yeah, like he's copied your hands, your legs, your shoulders."

"That's new," Rab said. "That's only just begun to show."

John sat up and wiped his mouth. "Yeah, and how."

Rab took a breath and sat against the table. John slumped back in his chair again. "Are you going to tell him?" Rab asked.

"What the fuck for?"

"And if you tell him in temper?"

John looked up, smiling the painful half-smile, and said, "Like I just did to you?"

Rab nodded.

"Then I think I'll cut my throat." And he held Rab's eyes.

Rab bit his lip. He could feel sudden tears, out of nowhere, filling his eyes. "He was a rotten, vicious old bastard," he said.

"Yeah, well, at that age you don't know any better. I was nine years old for Christsake. I didn't question it."

"Then how can you be so sure? I mean, couldn't he be his?"

John rubbed his face, looking at the floor. His eyes flicked up. "You really want to know?"

Rab nodded.

"He never fucked her after Ian. That simple."

Rab looked at him for a moment then said, "Did he tell you that?"

John nodded, not meeting his eyes.

Rab said, "A nine year old kid? How the hell were you supposed to deal with that?"

"The same way as I dealt with all his sexual peccadilloes. With a smile on my face." He looked up and laughed abruptly.

"What did he do with Danny?" Rab asked.

John looked at him. Rab felt a sudden surge of irritation. "Oh come on John, I'm not fucking brainless. Blind maybe, but brainless no. I remember them disappearing out together, regular as clockwork. Where did they go?"

"I don't know."

"Like fuck you don't."

"It's the truth. He won't say. Ask Ian."

"Why doesn't anyone ever ask *Danny*?"

Rab turned so quickly he knocked a cup off the table. It fell, breaking the handle off. Danny stood inside the door. His hands were covered in blood. His hair was soaking wet.

"*Jesus*," Rab said. "What the hell happened to you?"

Danny came in and closed the door. He was looking at John all the way. John hadn't moved, hadn't attempted to get up.

"Well John? Why does nobody ask *me*?"

"I have," John said and his voice was surly, like someone caught out in a half-truth.

Danny grinned, wide with lots of teeth. He had never looked more like John on the one night when he wasn't supposed to look like him at all. "Of course you have. On the strict understanding that I don't actually *tell* you. It's a test of loyalty. How well I can keep my mouth shut. You taunt me, and I don't tell you. That's the way we play it, right?"

Rab looked at him, looked at John. John's face was an odd chalky white.

"Because you don't want to hear it. Because you don't want to hear about what he

855

did, or why he did it, or just how fucking out his head he might have been in case it implicates *you*, right?" Danny's voice was going up and up. He was getting closer and closer.

Rab got in between them, using his shoulder, putting his hands on the tops of Danny's arms. "Alright Danny... easy."

Danny shoved him hard, making him thump back against the table. "Don't you fucking easy me, big *brother*."

There was a moment that felt like a steel blade whispering through the air, then Danny laughed, half-hysterical. "Oh, hilarious. For twenty years I've had 'Kick me' pinned to my pants. Big fucking laugh, huh? Know what his latest one is?" He was talking to Rab now. He went on without waiting for him to answer. "Saying, He's dead Danny, it doesn't matter any more, tell me. Want a rough translation? It matters more than ever. Don't you ever tell a fucking soul. No-one. Not ever. You take this secret to the grave Danny. Well I've got one for you John. Your father was a rabid little homo who couldn't even keep his hands off his own brother."

"His brother?" Rab said stupidly. "Are you saying...?" He grabbed Danny's shirt, shook him violently. "I don't believe you, you twisted little fuck."

Danny laughed, making no attempt to stop him.

"Shut up!" Rab roared and finally slapped him. The sound went off like a fire-cracker.

Everything stopped.

Danny's eyes closed and he went limp, saying, "Take your fucking hands off me," in a voice as old and dry as a dead leaf.

Rab let him go, turning away and pushing his hands in his pockets.

Danny opened his eyes and walked over to the sink. He looked out at the rain-washed yard. The rain was off and a moon had appeared in a clear sky.

There was nothing left to say.

"Staring at it isn't going to make it ring."

Stephen pushed his hair off his face exasperatedly. It stood upright for a moment then slowly slid down again. "I know, I know." He threw himself down on his back. "Why doesn't he ring?" He turned his head and looked across the table at Conley.

Conley shrugged. "He probably thinks you're in bed. He'll ring when he's got something to tell you."

"He's got something to tell me now, like what the fuck's going on."

"He will Stephen, relax."

Stephen glared at the ceiling. "Relax, he says."

Conley sighed and said, "Why don't you just go to bed?"

"I wouldn't be able to sleep."

"We can't sit up all night."

"I told you, you go, I'm alright."

Conley sighed again and got up and crossed to him. He was wearing the white towelling robe over his trousers.

Stephen looked up at him. Conley jerked his head. "Well, sit up."

"Why?"

"So I can sit down."

Stephen sat up. Conley sat down. Stephen looked at him.

Conley smiled a small dry smile. "A little human contact. Do us both good." He patted his lap. "Go on, put your head down. The close shave with death has made me brave."

Stephen looked at him.

"Come on," Conley said. "Before I start finding you threatening."

Stephen lay down and lowered his head onto his lap, never taking his eyes off his face.

"Okay?" Conley asked, and incredibly laid a hand on his hair.

Stephen nodded. He looked into Conley's faded gold eyes and asked quietly, "Are you making a pass at me?"

Conley's mouth quirked at the corners. "No." He ran his hand over Stephen's hair. "Would you like me to?"

Stephen looked away, flushing worse than ever.

Conley ruffled his hair. "Relax Stephen. I want to get some sleep tonight, that's all. Now relax."

Stephen closed his eyes and tried to relax, but he couldn't. Conley's hand felt strangely sexless, stroking him like he was stroking a cat. After a while his fingertips started running through his hair. Stephen felt the warm spread of excitement in his belly. It was giving him a hard-on.

Conley said, "This isn't working for you, is it?"

Too well, Stephen thought.

Conley's hand stopped stroking. "Up you get then."

Suddenly Stephen didn't want to get up. "No, I'm fine. Just don't touch my hair, okay?"

"Alright," Conley said.

Stephen glanced up a minute later and saw that he had dropped his head back against the sofa, eyes closed. He let another minute go by then turned in towards him, laying his cheek on his lap, facing his belly. Conley didn't move. Stephen pillowed his face with his hand, felt Conley's thigh under it, hard and thin under the robe. Conley's arm came down over his shoulder, as if he was holding him on his lap. Stephen snuggled down, relaxed at last.

Conley yawned. Stephen heard him try to disguise it and the small noise of discomfort that followed it. "What's wrong?" he asked, turning his head to look up at him.

"Nothing, it just hurts."

"Where?"

"Every bloody place," Conley said wearily. "But mostly my heart."

Stephen lay looking at the knot in Conley's dressing gown, turning the words over. Finally he said hesitantly, "Why?"

"Why what?"

"Why your heart?"

Conley took a breath, let it out slowly in a sigh. "Because I'm ashamed of myself. Ashamed that I let him in here, ashamed that I let him hit me, ashamed that I let him tie me up, ashamed that I let him..." He stopped.

"That's stupid," Stephen said. "It wasn't your fault. Besides I thought you were out cold when he tied you up?"

"I was."

"Well you can't blame yourself for that."

"But I do. It was so bloody undignified." He laughed shortly. "God, he knows how to make you feel small."

Stephen said, "He makes everyone feel small. He'd make Genghis Khan feel small."

"Danny wouldn't have let him do it."

"Danny knows him," Stephen said surprisingly. "And he takes plenty of beatings off him." He glanced up quickly, suddenly realising he shouldn't have said that.

Conley stroked his hair. "I know, don't fret."

"I shouldn't have said that."

"I already knew. Forget it. I've seen the damage he does."

Stephen knew somehow he was referring to the marks on Danny's body and he felt embarrassed that they'd both seen him, probably under the same circumstances. He closed his eyes and was silent.

Conley was stroking his hair again, gently, absently. Stephen was sure he didn't even know he was doing it. But it was alright. It wasn't worrying him any more. It just felt nice, not sexual. "What does it feel like, making love to Danny?" he asked.

As soon as the words were out his mouth he thought, Jesus, what am I saying? and waited, heart in mouth, for Conley to go apeshit. Conley went still as death, not apeshit, but the effect was much the same.

"Who said I did?" he said stiffly. His voice sounded like a sheet of ice.

"Ian," Stephen said in a small voice, eyes fixed on the knot. Suddenly he felt Conley relax, more than relax, go limp, like he was tired out.

"Good." And his voice was quiet. "It feels good." He paused and then said, "Now you tell me Stephen, what does it feel like when you make love to Danny?"

Stephen could hear something sharp and accusatory in it. He blushed violently and said, "I'm sorry, I shouldn't have asked that. I don't know why I did."

They were quiet, Stephen lying tense in his lap, then he was surprised to feel Conley's hand on his hair again. Stephen began to relax, glad they weren't going to fight, then Conley said in a quiet voice, and Stephen knew he was looking down at him, "You haven't answered my question. How does it feel when you make love to Danny?"

Stephen turned his face further into his lap, then said, "Like I'm dying." He felt Conley's hand slow a second then carry on stroking him.

"That makes me one, doesn't it?" Stephen said, face still hidden.

Conley didn't answer him.

"Doesn't it?" Stephen persisted.

"I don't know," Conley said, his hand slowing again.

"Well I fucking do. It does." And his voice was sad and angry at once.

Conley said, "Shhh..." and began stroking him again, and Stephen was horrified to feel tears, the new constant companion of his life, threatening to spill out his eyes.

He pushed his face into the towelling of Conley's gown and said, "Christ, why does it have to *hurt* so much?"

Conley said, "Shhh..." again, and tightened his arm around him, pressing him into his lap.

"He doesn't care," Stephen said hopelessly.

Conley went on stroking him, completely devoid of any comfort for him.

Stephen struggled up out of his arms, knelt beside him, searching his face as if he knew all the answers, as if he was keeping something from him, but he, Stephen, wasn't going to let him. "He doesn't, does he?"

"I don't know Stephen," Conley said, feeling trapped by his intensity. "I don't know how he is with you."

Conley looked at his pale, drawn face and knew he'd said absolutely the wrong thing. He'd somehow managed to infer that Stephen was getting less than him, being cheated of Danny's affection. He tried to patch it up. "Look, you have to take him as you get him. We all do. It's the way he is. You can't make people love you the way you want. You can only take what they give you and hope for the best."

"I don't want that," Stephen said angrily. "I don't want poxy little bits. I love him, for fuck's sake," he finished in anguish.

There was a stunned silence. Stephen's face took on a slow, dull flush. Conley just stared at him, half-horrified by his naked emotion. He wasn't used to adolescent

outbursts and didn't know how to handle it.

"Oh God," Stephen said, covering his face.

Conley put his hand on his arm, half-heartedly squeezing it. "Don't be upset. You're overwrought, that's all."

"Oh God," Stephen said again and crushed himself against Conley's chest.

Conley looked at the top of his head for an appalled moment then carefully, lightly, laid an arm around his shoulders and patted his back. He could feel the boy crying against him. He felt a fleeting envy for the way he just let his emotions go, then felt immediately guilty because he knew the boy was in constant turmoil, unable to understand anything that was happening to him. He felt angry at Danny. The boy was too young for this.

He held him tighter, one hand stroking his hair. His weight was hurting the cuts on his chest, pressing the ones on his back into the settee. But it didn't matter, he felt useful, needed. There was some kind of comfort in it. He bent his head and laid his cheek on Stephen's hair.

Then kissed it.

Stephen lifted his head. Conley could see the traces of freckles on his nose, the fact that his eyes were grey. Stephen lifted his head and reached up and kissed Conley's mouth.

Conley's heart began to thump. Everything had changed, become frighteningly different, drying his mouth.

Stephen's mouth came off his own, his eyes closed. Conley swallowed nothing, pressed himself back into the settee, intensely uncomfortable.

Stephen settled down against him again, cuddling close, no longer crying.

Conley sat there, rigid, hardly breathing and felt the unmistakable heavy swollenness in his groin.

He couldn't believe it. His body was one mass of burning itchy pain. His headache thumped distantly, just waiting under the painkillers to surface again, and he was getting excited. He felt like a pervert, a child molester. He wanted to push Stephen away and didn't know how to do it. Not without starting him off again. Oh God, how did I get into this? he thought.

You've been wanting to get into it since he knelt across you putting on that plaster, Max.

The voice was cold and precise and undeniable. It spoke in truths. Stephen was lying heavily against him, hands curled under his body. Conley held him loosely, trying not to hold him at all, no longer stroking him, trying to straighten out his breathing, trying to look and feel normal, put everything right again. Stephen spoke to him, making Conley jump guiltily. "What's wrong?"

"Nothing's wrong."

"Yes there is," Stephen asserted, and Conley could hear something too knowing in it. "You're all tense suddenly."

"You hurt my chest, that's all," he said, despising himself for it.

"I don't believe you. You're scared," Stephen said, and the tone was unmistakable now. Elation, self-satisfaction.

Conley dropped his arms. Stephen straightened up slightly and looked him in the eye. "You're scared because I kissed you."

It was Conley's turn to flush. "Alright, I'm scared." And his voice was cold.

Stephen searched his eyes, close enough to kiss him again without effort. Conley watched him moisten his lips with the tip of his tongue. "Want me?" he said, looking at him up and under, voice quiet and seductive. He looked like Danny, a young unpractised version of Danny. He was copying him. Badly. Conley felt as if someone had thrown cold water over him.

"No," he said and his voice was level. He took Stephen's arms and lifted them away from him. "And stop playing stupid, dangerous games. You're not Danny, Stephen, and if you had any sense you wouldn't want to be him."

Stephen's mouth twitched. A dull red suffused his cheeks. "You don't need to be so fucking patronising, I'm not a little kid."

"I can see that," Conley said. "So I suggest you stop acting like one."

"You're just a flickin' coward," Stephen said angrily.

"And you're a spoiled brat," Conley snapped back.

"I am not."

"Yes you are. You think the whole world revolves around you and what you want. Well it doesn't, and it's time you realised it. The only reason you're upset is because Danny is somewhere else and you feel left out. You're not worried a damn about where he is, or what might be happening to him, it's all you, you, you."

Conley knew he was being grossly unfair, but he couldn't stop it. He could see Stephen's face falling apart and he couldn't shut up.

Suddenly Stephen jumped up, headed towards the door.

Conley realised what he was going to do and jumped up after him. Every muscle in his body screamed. He felt as if his skin ripped in fifty different places, like taut tissue paper. "Stephen! Wait! I'm sorry... wait!"

He did his best attempt at a run and managed to push the door shut just as Stephen finally managed to struggle it open. If it had been a conventional door he'd have been gone. Conley could feel the sweat on his chest, under his arms, above his lip, *everywhere*. Sweat and pain. He hadn't realised how much he hurt till he moved.

"Let me go," Stephen said, face working to check the tears.

"No." Conley leaned heavily against the door.

Stephen continued to glare at the floor.

"Look at me Stephen."

Stephen looked at him and saw the bruised eye, his grey sweating face, and the tight look about his bones; saw the way he only took half breaths because full ones hurt, and said, "Oh shit, it's me that should be apologising." He pushed his hair off his face in that already familiar exasperated gesture. "Jeez, I can be such an asshole sometimes. I'm sorry."

"Let's go and sit down," Conley said.

Stephen nodded lamely and walked ahead of him because he sensed Conley was embarrassed by the state he was in.

They sat down again. Stephen said awkwardly, "Would you like a cup of coffee?"

Conley laughed dryly. "Maybe something stronger. There's some rum left I think. Get us both some. You have some too."

Stephen got up without speaking. Conley shut his eyes and listened to him in the kitchen. God, he hurt. He hurt like nobody's business. When was he next due painkillers? He probably wasn't supposed to drink with them. Well too bloody bad.

Stephen handed him a drink and said, "You look terrible."

Conley managed a smile. "Thank you."

"I *feel* terrible," Stephen said miserably.

"Forget it. It's the waiting, that's all. It's given us a short fuse. Sit down beside me. Talk to me."

Stephen sat down. Conley took a long drink and immediately felt better, soothed by the heat in his throat, the warming glow in his belly.

"Think Danny is alright?" Stephen asked.

"Yes," Conley smiled at him, but he was lying. He felt sure that even as they sat there Danny was in trouble again. When was he ever out of it?

"What if he's dead?" Stephen asked.

Conley laughed. "Good Lord Stephen, don't be so dramatic. He's not *dead*." But his laugh was full of dread, a burst of denial.

Stephen didn't seem to hear it. He smiled and said, "Sorry, sometimes I think I got a bit of my aunt's madness."

"Have you got a mad aunt then?"

"Yeah, in Solihull."

"Where?"

"Solihull. It's in the Midlands. She's nutty as a fruitcake. Thinks there's Russians under the bed, that sort of thing."

Conley laughed. "I thought that was a bad TV joke."

"Yeah, well my aunt's a bad joke, so it fits."

Conley could feel the rum beginning to work. The pain of his skin was beginning to recede slightly. Only his head still thumped viciously, that and his ribs.

"Why don't they fucking phone?" Stephen said tensely.

"They probably aren't near one. Now relax, stop worrying."

"I can't."

"You can, you just aren't trying. Do you want to try and get some sleep? It's beginning to get cold in here."

Stephen shook his head.

"It's a clean quilt. I asked Rab to change it."

Stephen looked at him quickly. Conley smiled. "Check for yourself if you don't believe me. The old one's in a black sack in the kitchen. John's never been anywhere near this one, it's perfectly hygienic."

"I thought you only had one quilt."

"I bought it. Brand new and still in its box." Conley smiled some more. "In case anyone came to stay."

Stephen smiled and looked at his glass. "Like me?"

"Like you."

"You told him you never wanted to see him again."

Conley shrugged, still smiling. "I told myself I was buying it for an emergency. I was lying both times, obviously, although I had the emergency."

Stephen laughed. Conley reached out and rumpled his hair. "Want to go to bed?" he asked.

Stephen met his eyes. "Yes."

"Then let's go."

They went.

Stephen lay watching him undress. He looked at his back as he took off the dressing gown. "What a mess," he said.

"You should feel how they hurt," Conley said without turning. "Although I'd rather he'd covered me in them instead of tattooing me."

Stephen saw him touching the raw stripes on his chest. "I suppose I should be thankful he did so little to the front of me. It's difficult to feel grateful though."

He unfastened his trousers and slid them down. Stephen could see spots of blood dotting his underpants where he'd bled again. He'd seen it on the clean sheet too when he got into bed, and his pillow was blotchy with it. He had turned it over while Conley was out the room.

Conley got into bed carefully, sitting down first then swinging his legs in. "God, I feel about ninety." He turned onto his side, facing Stephen, trying to keep off the cuts on his back and breathe at the same time. It wasn't easy.

"Want the light off?" Stephen asked.

"You better leave it on in case Rab calls you."

"We should be so lucky," Stephen said, plumping his pillow up with angry punches. "Did you take your tablets?"

Conley laughed. "Yes, Doctor. Wild horses couldn't have stopped me."

"Hurting?" Stephen had settled down with his hands under his cheek.

"Like fuck, as Danny would say."

Stephen laughed. "It never sounds right when you swear, that posh voice."

"What posh voice? I haven't got a posh voice," Conley said.

"Yes you have, don't act it." And Stephen did a credible impersonation of him.

Conley laughed then winced, pleading, "Don't make me laugh, it hurts."

"Your teeth are incredible," Stephen said, looking at his mouth.

"So everybody keeps telling me. You're a tactful bunch."

"How many fillings have you got?"

"Good Lord, I don't know. I've never counted."

"You eat too much junk."

"You sound just like Danny."

And his name shut them up again, their relaxation chased away by him.

Stephen sighed and lay on his back. Conley looked at his profile, the outlines still soft and childish, not chiselled like Danny's. No stubble, skin still fuzzy. No grainy skin, no lines, not a mark of age on him. He looked almost as if he'd been cast, except he was too fine-drawn. Too fine drawn in a way that told you he wasn't as young as he looked. Nor as innocent. He put his arm under his head, showing a fine silky tuft of red-gold hair. It made Conley smile, although he had no idea why.

Stephen looked at him suddenly over his arm. "Can I come in?"

"What?" Conley said.

"Can I cuddle in?" He brought his arm down. "I feel so fucking jumpy, my stomach's churning."

Conley said, "I'm sure this isn't man-to-man etiquette, but I don't see why not. You'll have to allow for me shifting all the time. I'm afraid I'm not too comfortable on my back."

"I don't care."

Stephen slid over. Conley lifted his arm gingerly and let him in. They arranged themselves as best they could. Conley felt aware of the sweat on him, embarrassed by it. He said, "You haven't got a very fragrant pillow. The pain's making me sweat too much."

"It's okay," Stephen said. "I'm a weirdo, I like the smell of sweat."

"Just as well," Conley smiled, but he felt more comfortable.

He took a deep breath and let it out slowly. Stephen lowered an arm across his chest, well below the damaged part. "That okay?" he asked.

"Fine." Conley had his face in his hair. It felt silky and warm under his cheek, oddly comforting, like cuddling a kitten or a small baby. It wasn't a pleasure he was used to. He began to feel sleepy. The painkillers, the drink, the pain itself, wearing him out. Anyway it was damn late. It was a miracle he'd lasted this long.

He felt Stephen's hand brushing the hair on his stomach, running his fingertips through it. He was aware distantly of the impropriety of it, but he was too doped, too tired. It was just part of a whole weird evening. He made an appreciative noise into Stephen's hair.

"Like that?" Stephen asked.

Conley gave a soft grunt.

"Sleepy?" Stephen asked.

Conley grunted again.

Stephen didn't say anything else.

Conley's stomach was flat, slightly hollow. It reminded him of Rab's, with the thick blonde hair. It was surprisingly coarse. The hair on his head looked soft, what was left of it, but the hair on his body was thick and coarse. It felt like a rough animal.

He felt down as far as the waistband of his underpants. He wished he didn't have any on. Not because he wanted to try anything. He was just curious to feel the rest of it.

He realised Conley was asleep, breathing deeply and regularly. He smiled and cuddled in closer, taking care not to touch the cuts on his chest. He smelt sweet and sticky. *Like he sweats all that sugar he eats. Wonder if it tastes sweet?*

He turned his face into Conley's armpit and licked the crease of his flesh. Salt. He was almost disappointed. He laughed at himself, settled down again.

Conley's flesh was slightly sticky against his face. It made Stephen think of shiny hot-cross buns, glazed in syrup. Conley smelt like that, like cakes and sweets, with the heavy yeasty smell of sweat beneath it. Stephen wished he wasn't all cut up so he could touch him properly without fear of hurting him.

He thought about the kiss he'd given him, the strange feel of his mouth, those odd colourless gold eyes looking at him. It was difficult to tell what he was thinking from his eyes. His voice didn't help. It was colourless too, never anything in it. He'd got a hard-on kissing him. More because he knew he was going to do it than anything else. He hadn't really meant to start messing about with him.

He blushed in the darkness, ashamed of himself all over again, but he hadn't been messing him about for the sake of it, he *had* wanted to kiss him.

Stephen lay still and let that one sink in a little. *I fancy him a bit. Just a bit. There's something about him. He's nothing to look at, especially not now, all cut up and bruised. Maybe it's the way he talks or something, and he moves nice, kind of lazy and elegant, like Rab, but he isn't such a poser. Rab practices, I'm sure he does. He's pretty old though. Did Danny say forty? I can't remember. Oh, who cares? Danny fucks him and he's only twenty, so he can't be that bad.*

Suddenly Stephen realised he had another hard-on. It was all he ever seemed to do these days. Anywhere, any time, the slightest thing. He was like one of the bullocks, running around trying to get it up the others all the time.

Jeez, what an image to pick.

He took a deep breath and willed it to go away. It didn't. It lay there, hard and uncooperative as a morning erection, determined to make itself felt. He'd had one too many and now it was in a mood. He grinned suddenly to himself. *Doctor, my cock's got attitude.*

A small laugh puffed out his mouth. Conley never stirred.

He touched himself, wondering if he could masturbate without Conley waking. He suddenly wanted to, very much. The idea wouldn't go away. He wondered about moving out from under his arm - he was probably cutting off the poor bastard's circulation anyway - but he didn't want to. Conley was sweating again, making his skin moist. It felt sexy.

You're a perv Steve-o.

He laid his hand on Conley's belly, enjoying the damp feel of him, while his other hand gripped his own penis, working it deftly.

Conley spoke.

Stephen froze, listening. He realised they weren't complete words, were barely recognisable. Conley jerked. He's having a nightmare, Stephen thought. Conley muttered again. It wasn't English. Conley shouted something so suddenly Stephen jumped, hissing, "*Shit.*" He wondered if he should wake him. He could remember lots of times wishing someone would wake him from a nightmare.

Conley's body was jerking again. Stephen felt the muscles in the arm under his

head clenching. Conley began saying no in German. Stephen recognised it from the war comics he had read. *Nein, nein, kamerad.* It's all Germans ever said. Then Conley said Danny's name, clearly and distinctly.

Stephen listened, holding his breath. He could feel the wet of Conley's body under his face. He lifted his cheek, trying to ease the pressure, cool him down a little. Conley began to talk in a low, rapid voice, very distinctly, only it was all in German. He couldn't understand a word of it, but he understood the tone.

Stephen slid his hand down and groped the damp fabric of his pants. He found it. Like a ramrod.

Dirty bastard. He was having a dirty dream.

Stephen lifted his head and looked at his face. His eyelids were twitching, his lips barely moving. His voice came in indistinct mutters. He was having a conversation. All the gaps were there for someone to reply.

Then it changed again, swiftly. Stephen saw his neck working. His arm jumped violently. He was saying no again, then he whimpered, actually whimpered, then he jumped about four inches clear off the bed, waking up and scaring the living daylights out of Stephen.

"Fucking *hell!*"

"Danny?" Conley said, eyes wide open but seeing nothing.

"It's me, Stephen," Stephen said, pushing the quilt down off him to give him some air. "You scared the shit out of me." He sat up on one elbow. Conley was glistening with sweat, as if he'd been spread with oil.

Conley slumped back down on the pillow, closed his eyes.

"You had a bad dream," Stephen said.

Conley wiped his face with his hands.

"I'll get you some water."

Conley gripped his arm, opening his eyes again. "No, I'm okay."

And Stephen realised he was scared. He had the heebie-jeebies. "What was it?"

"Nothing, old stuff."

"You were saying Danny's name." Stephen watched his face. He saw Conley flick a glance at him then look away.

"Was I? I don't remember."

Stephen said nothing and thought, Like hell you don't.

"Hang on, there's a towel on the chair." Stephen got out the bed to retrieve it then nipped back in, kneeling up and drying him carefully. Conley lay there with his eyes shut, letting him dry his chest and armpits, dab at his face. He pushed the quilt down.

"Your shorts are soaking," Stephen said. "Take them off."

Conley opened his eyes.

"Take them off, go on, they're wet through. It'll hurt if I try to do it. Hide under the quilt if you're shy."

Conley pulled the quilt up and raised himself on one elbow, sliding them off and dropping them out the side of the bed. "You should have been a nurse," he said. He looked better, less blank-eyed and frightened.

Stephen ran the towel over his groin under the quilt. Conley caught his hand. "I'll do it."

Stephen gave him the towel and lay down again, knowing exactly why he wanted to do it himself.

Conley dried himself and dropped it out the bed. He shifted himself and got comfy again.

"Better?" Stephen asked.

Conley nodded.

"I think I made you too hot, sorry."

864

"No, it's the pills. Painkillers always make me feverish. When I was very young they used to give me aspirins in milk every night to make me go to sleep until they realised they were giving me nightmares. It's like an allergy, but it's either that or the pain. Paracetamol's better but not such a good painkiller. These must be aspirin based."

"You should have told me."

"I know, it's not your fault." Then surprisingly he offered, "Want to come in again? Or am I sweating too much even for your depraved tastes?"

Stephen smiled and went in under his arm again. He felt warm and dry now, less sticky than the first time. Maybe the towel had taken it away.

Conley sighed. "What a night. Bone tired and too sore to sleep. You must be exhausted."

"No, I'm too wound up. I think it must be that coffee of yours."

"And I went to sleep and left you on your own." Conley's voice was gently mocking.

"I forgive you. Anyway, God punished you."

"My, I can see you're a Christian soul."

Stephen settled in, hand across his stomach again. He was glad he was awake again. He'd been lonely by himself. He sighed in contentment.

"Something wrong?" Conley asked.

"No."

"Then why the sigh?"

"It wasn't a sigh, it was pleasure."

"You've got strange pleasures, lying in sweaty armpits."

"You've got to take them where you find them, as Danny says."

"Does he?"

"All the time. Haven't you ever heard him say that?"

"No."

"All the time," Stephen reiterated, and fell into silence. After a few moments he said, "Do you think he's beautiful?"

"Danny?"

"Yes."

"Very," Conley said.

Stephen digested that in silence then said, "I sometimes wonder if it's just his face, the way he looks. It worries me."

"Why?"

"I don't know. It doesn't seem right to love someone just for the way they look."

"*Is* that why you love him?"

"I don't know." He sighed again. "I really don't know."

"Do you think it matters?"

"I think it matters to Danny."

And Conley felt ashamed that Stephen should care when he'd never even thought about it, never really worried how Danny felt about it. "What a lovely boy you are," he said gently, and he squeezed him under his arm.

Stephen said, "Why?" in genuine perplexity, but felt warm at the compliment anyway.

"You just are."

Stephen held him tighter round the waist and smiled.

Conley brought his free hand up and stroked his hair. Stephen felt himself held in the dark circle of his arms, surrounded by the smell of him. He grew hard again, lay there feeling it, deriving a strange excitement from the fact that Conley didn't even know it was there.

Conley asked, "What are you thinking?"

Stephen said, "What it would be like if you touched me."

Conley's arm lay still then came away from Stephen's hair. "I am touching you," he said, and his voice sounded raw, as if he had a sore throat.

"No," Stephen said, and he reached up and took Conley's hand, guiding it down. "There." And he pressed Conley's hand over his erection.

He expected Conley to snatch his hand away, express outrage, but he didn't, he let him press it there then said slowly into his hair, "And how does it feel?"

Stephen closed his eyes. "Beautiful." He pushed his face into Conley, gripped him tight, easing one leg between his. "Please do it," he whispered.

Conley felt it, painfully hot and hard under his fingers, and knew he wanted to do it, had wanted to do it all evening, had wanted to do it since that night when Stephen had looked at him and said, I don't suppose Danny will bring me again, and Conley had thought, You're flirting with me. You're flirting with me and I don't mind, not one little bit. And now he wanted to do it so much and he couldn't think of a single justification, other than that Stephen wanted it too, and he hadn't tricked him into it, so it was alright.

Wasn't it?

And as if Stephen sensed his hesitation he said, "I've wanted to do it since that night we slept here. I think half the reason what happened was because I was so turned on at having both of you in bed with me. Please do it. I feel so wound up. Please." And Stephen kissed his chest, gently at first, then more feverishly.

Conley curled his fingers around him and squeezed.

It was like a signal. Stephen's hand immediately slid down into Conley's pubic hair and took hold of him. "Together," he whispered, straining up to kiss him. "Let's do it together."

And then Stephen pushed his tongue into Conley's mouth.

"He isn't going to tell you anything, save yourself the effort."

"Where the fuck is he? What have you done with him?" Rab pushed him in the chest.

"Nothing, and push me once more like that and it'll be the last time you ever push anyone."

"I don't think I'm ever going to want to touch you again."

"Sure." And Danny smiled. "You've got my well-hung brother... forgive me, *half* brother on tap. You don't need me."

"Jesus, you've got a shitty little head Danny, and a dirty little mouth to go with it."

"I'm crying."

"Where is he Danny?" John said from the table.

Danny looked past Rab to where John was standing. "I wouldn't know sunshine, so don't ask."

"*What* did you call me?"

"Sorry?" Danny's smile was ingenuous, somehow disturbing.

John came charging across the floor like a bull. "You little *shit.*"

Rab swung in front of Danny, taking the full impact of John's weight. "Hold it!" he yelled, grunting. John was still trying to get at him. Danny was just standing there waiting for it, like he wanted the fight.

"*John!*" Rab shouted finally, shoving him back.

John turned away, dragging a hand through his hair. "You should have let me kill the little bastard."

"Book me a ticket," Danny said.

Rab swung on him. "Why don't you fucking shut up?"

"Why don't you fucking drop *dead?*"

Rab grabbed his front and banged him back off the sink. "Where *is* he?"

"He's at Jerrett's," Danny said suddenly, levering Rab's hands off. "And what exactly are you planning to do about it Batman? Or is he Batman? Which one's wearing the tights tonight?"

Rab slapped him without saying anything. Danny took the blow then looked at him slowly, as if he was pleased that he'd done it. "Just about your fucking level."

Rab dragged his hand through his hair just as John had done. Christ, ten minutes around him and he was lashing out, out of control. "You're a fucking magnet for trouble Danny," he said, not looking at him.

"Blame on, it's what I'm here for. The hostess with the mostest. I also give head."

Rab turned away, feeling nauseated by the whole sick show. "Let's go," he said to John.

John stood there.

"Come on John, he can't walk back in this. I mean, Christ knows what he's done to him. Look at the state of him. We need to talk to him."

Danny laughed. "Maybe he's past talking."

John glanced at him, but Rab ignored him.

John nodded suddenly and went for his coat.

"You too," Rab said, turning to Danny.

"No way, I'm going to bed."

"I said you too, supposing I've got to fucking drag you there. Until we see what you've done you're fucking well not getting out my sight. You'll come and finish this. You started it."

"Then what?" Danny demanded belligerently.

"I don't fucking care what," Rab said, giving him an ungentle push towards the door. "Because I'm not going to be here."

And he shoved him again, propelling them both out the door.

Danny sat at the far end of the seat, Rab in the middle, and John driving.

Danny looked at his cut hand. It was stiff and intensely painful. He could barely move it. He realised he felt slightly sick and distinctly light-headed and wondered if he'd lost too much blood.

The knife was still in his pocket. He traced the shape of it through the lining. *Could cut your throats boys, right now.*

He closed his eyes, feeling crushed by the confines of the narrow seat. Just like his bed, with John's heavy weight always dragging him down towards him. One clean sweep and it would be all over. No more tasting his own salt, swallowing his own dirt. Like fucking yourself. Being a homo was fucking yourself, one big long wank.

Life's a wank guys.

He opened his eyes, startled, uncomfortable.

He sat up suddenly, realising he had a hard-on. He looked out the window.

They turned up into the lane, nobody speaking. John drove. He looked calm, nothing like the man who'd sliced Conley up only a few hours before, just a big, ugly, sour looking man, not a murderer or a nut.

The house was in darkness. John cut the engine but left the headlights on. He stretched his hand out without turning. "Keys," he said.

"I haven't got them..." Danny paused then finished, "sunshine."

John shot round in his seat.

Rab pushed at his arms. "*Leave* it! Come on John, forget it."

Rab glanced at him as he pushed John back. Danny smiled back.

John got out, slamming the door shut. Rab spoke quickly to him in a quiet

threatening tone. "Get off his case or next time I won't stop him. I mean it Danny."

"I'm terrified."

"Christ!" Rab thumped the sill with the heels of both hands. "What is *wrong* with you? You want him to kill you?"

Danny's smile dropped away. "Do you?"

"No," Rab shook his head, "I fucking don't."

"If you say so. Are we going in or not? He's coming back. Wonders what two brothers could have to say to each other that's taking so fucking long." Danny leaned forward suddenly. When he spoke his voice was incredibly low. "How does it feel sucking your baby brother's dick?"

Rab flinched away from him, pulling his hand back.

John opened the door. "What the fuck goes on here?"

"Nothing, sunshine. Just coming." And Danny climbed out.

They knocked on the door.

Danny leaned against the wall, huddled tight into his coat, looking bored. No-one answered.

"Now what do we do?" Rab asked.

"Fuck knows." John banged his fist hard against the door.

Danny looked off into the darkness. John scowled at him then snapped, "How about a fucking suggestion from you, it's your mess."

Danny looked at him then suddenly leaned over and turned the door handle.

The door swung open.

John looked at him.

Danny straightened up and walked in.

The fire was still lit.

Rab and John searched the downstairs rooms. Danny said, "I'm going to take a leak," and went upstairs.

He walked to the bedroom and opened the door. It was empty. All his clothes were there, strewn around the room.

Danny closed the door.

He went down to the back bedroom and tried the door. It opened. He went in and clicked on the light.

Ian lay on the bed wearing only a shirt and sweater. He was fondling his penis like a child will, for comfort.

Danny closed the door and bolted it. "Hello sweetheart," he said.

Ian lay and watched Danny take his penis from him. "Where are they?" he asked.

Danny rolled the soft fat slug of it between his fingers. "Downstairs."

"What did you tell them?"

"Nothing. I caught them talking about it. It was like part of the same conversation. I'm almost tempted to believe it was a coincidence." His eyes came up and met Ian's

Ian flushed. "Did John tell you something?"

"Like what?" And Danny rolled his penis again, softly, between both his hands.

"I don't think I'll ever understand you," Ian said, and his voice had a catch in it.

Danny was playing with him like someone who'd never seen a penis before, fascinated by its elastic softness. He pulled it this way and that experimentally. "Don't try, there's nothing in me. What you see is what you get."

"If only that was true."

"Come on Ian, don't get antsy on me now. I need you with me here. One man alone can't support this incredible fabric of lies." And suddenly Danny bent and kissed the soft putty of his cock.

Ian made a small hopeless noise in his throat and grabbed for him, but Danny pulled away, evading his arms.

Ian looked at him, breathing heavily, and said, "What do you want?"

"You to stop trying to force a show-down. He doesn't want it, no matter how much you'd like to give him one."

"And what was this about?" Ian's eyes flicked angrily at the walls.

"What d'you think?"

Ian shook his head

Danny took his hand and smiled as no-one else would have known it. No-one else had ever seen it. The original, the best, not designed to *do* anything. Danny's real smile. "I was saving you from yourself," he said.

"By taking the only bloody thing I had?"

"You didn't have it. That's the point."

Ian stared at him.

Danny said, "Oh come on, you can't have doubts now Ian." He turned over Ian's hand and kissed the palm. "Now we're all brothers together."

Ian pulled his hand away. "John *did* tell you something."

"Don't push it Ian, or you might have to tell me."

Ian coloured and looked at the floor,

Danny stood up suddenly and said, "Come on, get up, they're going to come up here in a minute. Wouldn't do to be caught in the shrine."

Ian got up and began dressing. Danny held out a hand. "The key?"

"On the dresser," Ian said.

Danny crossed the floor and picked it up.

"Danny?" Ian's voice was hesitant.

"Mm?"

"The picture you left..."

Danny cut him short. He didn't turn, didn't move. "I didn't see it Ian." Then he turned and smiled at him. "I didn't see it. I don't know it exists… and you don't need to tell me anything." And their eyes locked - no smiles, Danny's dark and dangerous - and then Ian looked away.

They went out the door. Danny clicked off the light. A thousand curly heads disappeared.

John came in as Ian was folding up and repacking Danny's clothes. His face was an almost comic display of surprise. Danny was leaning on the mantle.

"He expected to find you dead Ian. He thinks I've got blood on my hands."

Rab came in beside him, but he looked at Danny. "You little shit, you did this deliberately."

"Did what deliberately?" Danny asked, smiling.

"You led us on a fucking wild goose chase."

"It was you and Pancho Sanchez here that wanted to come on this little outing, don't blame me."

"How the fuck was he supposed to get back home?"

"In the car, unless it's been stolen."

Rab looked at John. John nodded.

"I walked," Danny said, no longer smiling. "You know the maxim Rab, screw or

869

walk. I'm sure you must have used it on some sweet young meat occasionally."

"You really are desperate for a fight, aren't you?"

"Go suck it," Danny said, no humour in his face at all, not even malice. He was deadly serious.

Rab about-wheeled and stumped off downstairs. They could hear his feet angrily thumping down the narrow wooden stairs, then the front door slammed.

Danny stood smiling at John, looking up at him from his down-tilted head. It was the same look Stephen had tried on Conley earlier, except this one was the real thing. Shiveringly real. "Go and console him John-boy, he's had a hard night."

"I'm not leaving you with him," John said, not looking at Ian.

"How can you be jealous of your own brother? He's more yours than I am, blood of your blood. Trust him John. Be more loving." His voice was as unpleasant as the expression in his eyes.

Ian kept his eyes averted from them both, his movements nervous. He picked his jeans up from in front of the fire, where he'd put them to dry after rinsing them out. They were still wet, but at least they didn't stink of his own fear. He folded them carefully, aware of John watching him, taking in the fact that he had Danny's clothes on.

"I'm going to make you eat your own shit," John said.

"I'm looking forward to it, sunshine."

John lunged across at him, but he was too slow. Ian was there before him, knife in his hand, standing between him and Danny, shaking his head.

John looked at the knife, then at Ian, then finally at Danny. "I think you two are joined at the hip, only the rest of us can't see it."

"Could be," Danny said.

Ian stood tense, poised. John moved back a little. "Looks like it *was* just a phase, eh Ian? Why did you stop him the other night? Why didn't you just let him do it?"

"I wouldn't let him dirty his hands," Ian said, and his voice was unsteady.

"You'd rather have done it yourself and been hung for it, than let him soil his lily-white hands."

"That's right." Ian's face was unmoved, utterly uncaring about what John said or thought.

"You scare me," John said. "You really scare me."

"I've always scared you John. I scare everyone. It's how I stay alive, just like you. My technique's a little different, that's all."

Suddenly Danny said in a pulpit voice, "We are all survivors in this world," and then he laughed. He stopped. "Now fuck off John, there's a good boy."

John backed out of the room, keeping them both in his sights like a pair of unpredictable animals.

They didn't move until he was downstairs, then Danny stepped away from the fireplace and moved behind Ian, sliding his arms around his waist, murmuring, "You were almost believable."

Ian stood there, uncooperative. "You think this sorts everything?"

"Oh, he'll forgive you. He always does."

"I want payment for this Danny."

"You'll get it."

"I better."

"I can do it now if you want."

"A two minute wank? No thanks."

"I know how much it hurts you Ian, believe me. Come on, this one's on the house."

Ian said gruffly, "You better not be messing me about Danny."

"Would I ever?"

Rab stood in the cold dark of the upper hall, feeling the chill come up through his stocking soles, and watched through the crack in the door as Danny reached inside Ian's jeans. He masturbated him quickly and soulessly, like a prostitute with a ten pound commission, until Ian boiled out over his hand.

Not even thirty seconds.

He hadn't even lasted thirty seconds.

Rab looked at Danny's face as he watched Ian spasming and jerking in his arms and thought he'd never seen anything quite so beautiful in his life.

"They coming?"

"Yes," Rab said dryly.

John looked at him curiously, then looked out the car window into the dark and said, "Payment in kind."

Rab turned to him, trying to hide his surprise. "You knew?"

"What? That Danny throws him a crumb occasionally? Yes, I knew." He turned and looked at him. "They act it perfectly. You would never know that Danny's probably done it with him more often than either of us have ever had. We're still trying to catch up. He's had a head start."

"They've been doing this regularly?"

John shook his head. "It's strictly payment on demand. Every once and a while Ian begins to feel left out, throws a sulk, and Danny whips his dick out. It's like giving a baby a bottle to soothe it." John was quiet for a moment then he said, "But I'll tell you, I never realised before how much Danny gets out of it."

Rab said sharply, "What do you mean?"

And John looked at him afresh and said, "Sure it was Ian crawling all over him?"

Rab picked an M.O.T. leaflet off the sill and crumpled it.

John laughed, rubbing his face. "Yeah. Like I said, I never realised just what a kick it was for him. He's killing him by inches, and it sends him right out his head with pleasure." John shut his eyes. "As soon as we get to bed he'll be dry-humping my leg, asking me to ream him, itchy for it. It's a turn-on for him. That's what it is, a fucking turn-on."

"Like you get out of cutting people up?"

John turned slowly. "Alright Rab. Thank you."

"You're a hypocrite John."

"You've already made your point cousin, don't push it."

At that moment Ian came out the house, then Danny. Danny shut the door and locked it. John shouted out, "Leave the pick-up, I'll get it tomorrow."

No-one questioned him. Ian crossed and got in the back.

"What kept you?" John asked.

"Tidying up, putting out the fire."

Danny got in. The car seemed to fill with the cold sweet smell of him, everybody aware of him.

John turned on the ignition and reversed down out the lane. Danny got out and shut the gate. They all watched him, bleached in the headlamps.

"You ever see anything so fucking beautiful?" John asked quietly.

No-one answered him.

When they were almost home Rab glanced in the rear-view mirror. Danny was looking out the side window, utterly self-absorbed.

He saw Ian reach over and put his hand softly on Danny's thigh and Danny, casually, without even looking, push it off again.

He had never seen so much contempt in anyone's face in his life. He closed his

eyes so he wouldn't have to look any more.

But he could see it anyway, acid-etched right inside his head.

"Is there even any point in hitting you any more?"

"I don't know, what do you think?" Danny leaned against the open wardrobe, eyes implacably black in a face that looked worn beyond belief.

John shut the door and walked over to him. Danny watched him, only his eyes moving.

"It doesn't make any difference, does it? It doesn't even really frighten you. I don't think it ever has." John stroked his cheek with the fingers of one hand, thumb lightly brushing Danny's mouth.

"I didn't think it was for me. I thought it was your idea of foreplay."

John gripped his face fiercely. "Christ, you really can't resist it, can you?"

Danny just stared at him, waiting for him to let go.

John let go and half turned away from him, pushing his hands in his pockets. "You make me fight you every fucking inch of the way. No fucking rest. No peace for me."

John turned to face him again. He made a sweeping gesture with his arm. "You know, out there, there's hundreds of stupid bastards who think you really are something. The little boy lost, looking for love. If they only knew. What are you going to do? Squeeze your revenge till it chokes? How long am I going to go on paying? Five years, ten, twenty, what?"

"Long as it takes John-boy."

"For *what?*"

Danny pushed up off the wardrobe and came up close against him, face narrow with malice. "Till I *see* you bleed."

And Danny pushed past him and went out the room.

Rab was in his room, already in his bed. He looked up irritably as he clicked on the light, then lay back down again. He put one arm under his head. "Now what?"

"Are you still going to go?" Danny asked.

"Christ you woke me up to ask me that? Yes Danny, I am."

"Sure?"

Rab laughed without humour. "Give me one single, solitary reason why I shouldn't."

"Because you don't want to."

"Don't I?" Rab was looking up at him, trying to read his face. The light was creating a strange effect shining up under him. It made his face look heavy and coarse, like John's.

"You want to stay."

"No, not even for you."

"Then tell me what would make you stay."

"Nothing."

Danny laughed, soft and low, like he was laughing at some subtle irony. Rab suddenly wished he could see him better, wished he'd sit on the bed. He saw Danny's hands push themselves into his pockets. His head moved, shadowy in the upper darkness. He looked as if he was listening to something. Then he spoke, and it was as low and unpleasant as the laugh had been. "Then I'll just have to tell you something that might give you pause."

"Danny, what *is* this?" Rab demanded. "It is *late*. And why don't you come round where I can see you?"

"I'm fine where I am. I'm not staying. You just listen carefully."

"You are pissing me off Danny."

"How much did he give you?"

"What?" Rab looked startled.

"How much did you get for 'going out with the girls'? I mean he named a figure but he was drunk, and he always was a big liar. How much? Over the years?"

Rab lay still. Danny could see him thinking, the way you always could with Rab, only this time he was thinking like a rat running round a maze. No way out.

"Come on Rab, say something original. Surprise me."

"What did he tell you?"

Danny laughed. "No, you tell *me*. How much? That's what really interests me. How much equals how often, equals what a grabbing little queer you are. You know, I think that's why I like you so much. I admire a really good liar." Danny paused then asked quietly, "Did you enjoy it? Between you and me I always thought he was a slimy bastard but he could work his tongue into places that haven't been discovered yet, don't you think? How about you Rab? Did it work for you?"

Rab had closed his eyes and put his arm over them. Danny looked down at him, no longer talking. Finally he sat down beside him. Now he spoke quietly, his voice different, softer. "Can't hide from it Rab."

Rab shook his head, a small quick emphatic gesture. Danny stroked the exposed underside of his arm. "Come on," his voice was low, coaxing. "How much?"

"Seven thousand, one hundred and seventy pounds," Rab said finally. Danny could see him chewing his cheek, could tell he'd screwed his eyes tight to say it, even under his arm.

Danny let a low whistle escape between his teeth. He'd stopped rubbing his arm. He said, "That must be... how long?" He paused, trying to work it out, but he didn't need to.

"Twice a week for seven years," Rab said. "More or less."

"Which is..." Danny hesitated again, but this time Rab didn't offer it and Danny finally said, "What? Ten pound a go?" He laughed. "Your going rate was ten pounds a go?"

"First time was ten pounds. Last time was ten pounds."

"Last Tuesday."

Rab nodded.

"You never ask him for more?"

Rab's arm came off his eyes, face shot with temper. "I never asked him for any. The first time he gave me the money because I was hard up." His voice was sharp. "Then one night, coming home, we were drunk and it just happened."

Danny smiled. "Tell me what he did."

"It was a wank, nothing more."

"And after that?"

"One Friday night he gave me a lift home when John ditched me. I'd be out there trying to be what John wanted, watching all the others get it right. Sometimes I even had to watch John doing it, like it wasn't anything. It *hurt*... so I did it. The money made it better. I felt like it was nothing to do with me, it was his sickness. Know what I did with that money?" He looked at Danny suddenly, eyes too bright.

Danny nodded. "You opened a post office account and saved it up to run away."

Rab blinked then said, "How did you know?"

"Call it empathic skill."

"I used it to justify myself." Rab covered his eyes again. "Only by the time I hit the first thousand it looked so fucking beautiful in its own right I didn't know whether I wanted it to stop or not."

"Fridays," Danny said. "So when did it become two days a week?"

"Not long after. Tuesdays he used to get money out the bank for his grandmother. He always took an extra tenner."

Danny laughed. "Christ, robbing grandma to pay Paul."

"I knew what I was doing was stupid. I knew it was the thin end of the wedge. I didn't know what he was getting out of it, and I didn't care, I just knew it was poison, but I couldn't stop it." He said suddenly, "How long have you known?"

"Oh, way back."

"When?" Rab was watching him intently.

Danny smiled. "Now it wouldn't do for me to give away all my secrets, would it?"

Rab turned away and asked without looking at him, "You haven't told John?"

"I haven't told John." Danny's voice was silky.

Rab looked at him for a long moment then said, "Are you going to tell him?"

Danny laughed sourly, rubbing his nose viciously like he always did when he was irritated. "Tell me Rab, if it came to my life or him knowing, which would you pick?"

"Don't be stupid."

"No, come on, be honest."

"Right now, I don't know." Rab wouldn't meet his eyes.

"Thanks, that tells me all I need to know."

Rab's head shot up. "You know, you've got a fucking cheek Danny. You've got everything in the palm of your hand and you still throw shit at me for..." he hesitated, but he couldn't find a way to finish it.

"Go on, say it," Danny urged. "For wanting to screw my big brother? For taking me as second best and lying blind about it, and all because you're too fucking proud to go back to him? Too fucking shit-scared to admit what you are? So fucking grabby you want to run away and take me with you because you know what it will do it to him?"

"You conceited little shit."

"Oh am I? Christ, butter would melt up your arse. You think you're going to win this, don't you? By hook or by fucking crook you've been determined to win this all along." Danny stood up. "Well you won't."

There was a silence, then Danny's voice, quiet in the darkness. "Now let's see you leave Rab. I won't tell him anything... I wouldn't give you the pleasure... but it won't make any difference, will it? Because, surprise, surprise, you're not leaving suddenly." And his voice grew a little softer still. "You sad bastard."

And then he left, silently, his face disappearing into the shadow, his turning head a last glimpse, like blood on Rab's retina.

John turned in the bed and looked at him. "You going to tell me?"

"Why don't you get some sleep? You must be tired out after all that bondage."

"Christ, you cheeky little shit."

Danny got undressed, paying no attention to him, face closed, emotionless.

He got into bed. It was so late it hardly seemed worthwhile but suddenly he felt so tired he could hardly lift his limbs. It wasn't a question of wanting to sleep, it was a question of falling over.

He clicked out the light. John's was already out. The darkness was sudden and complete. No moon, no stars. The house was silent. Danny could feel himself plunging into sleep. Soon as my head touched the pillow, he thought, then he smiled and was gone.

John realised he was asleep, so quickly it seemed almost contrived. He listened to him breathing, trying to detect a sign that he was faking it. Nothing. He was asleep, soft, relaxed, heavy.

He felt intensely cheated. He'd rather have fought with him than been left alone. He felt a brief flare of suspicion, wondering if that's what the visit to Rab had been about, but he knew he was deluding himself. You always knew with Danny.

John clicked on his light, wanting it to wake him, knowing it wouldn't.

Danny's face was soft in repose, all the angry, bitter lines out of it, washed away. His mouth was very slightly parted. In sleep he looked like someone else, showing that mystery chromosome X. Awake he somehow became harder.

Oh Danny, what have we done to you? What would you have undone? Tell me and I'll do it. Promise me you'll love me and I'll do it.

He ran his index finger very lightly over Danny's eyebrow, feeling the slightly wiry feel of them, like thin plastic fibres sleek over the bone.

"I love you," John whispered, feeling a lump of misery in his throat. "If you ever try to leave me..." He didn't say any more.

He traced his finger down over his cheekbone and onto his mouth. Danny twitched his face, like a horse pestered by flies, startling him.

John smiled to himself. Ticklish. He always had been. Once, when Danny was seventeen, rolling on his bedroom floor with him - this room when he'd been alone in it - shouting, 'Submit' and them both laughing, and John using his superior weight to hold him down, tickling him till it hurt and tears came to his eyes, pushing him past the limit, never able to resist hurting him, always punishing him for being what he was - beautiful, unavailable - and Danny defeated by it, gasping and panicking, and John going on relentlessly, no longer funny, and looking down at him, seeing his distress, and thinking... He's almost a grown man, and when he is I'm *still* going to be able to beat him like this, and feeling the elation of it, knowing Danny wasn't going to be able to escape him, wasn't going to develop some frightening talent to elude him, and sensing an equal desire in Danny to snare him, make him grovel, defeat *him*.

And they were still fighting, a fight to the death, both determined to win; John to control him, Danny to enslave him. *Oh no Danny, not ever. I'll die first. You think I don't know. You think I'm as dumb as the rest of them, as infatuated as Rab. But some day Danny I'll own you, and then it will be all over. When I've got you where I want you, when you're broken so bad you can't be fixed, when I can finally wash my hands of you, know what I'm going to do? Go on, guess Danny. Bet you'll never guess, because this is a very* secret *secret, a very dark, scary secret. Whisper it. I'm going to love you Danny. I'm going to go on loving you till the day I die because you've already beaten me. You beat me years ago. I was beaten before I started. There was never a fight. I'm nothing without you. Meaningless.*

John's hand was resting on Danny's face. Now he whispered to him again, "You are *going* to love me Danny." But Danny was deeply asleep, not even hearing him in his dreams. His sleep was a wall between them.

"You're a bastard Danny," John whispered, watching his eyelids flicker slightly in deep dreaming. "Sometimes I think you're four thousand years old, the oldest boy in the world, full of rottenness and corruption. I think you live off the stench and stink of it. I think you don't really need food, you..."

John stopped, aware of how cracked he sounded. He let his body go limp and whispered, "I think I love you too much." He smiled. Today's quantitative understatement. Loving Danny at all was too much.

He yawned, suddenly and jaw-breakingly, making his eyes water. He lifted his head and looked at the clock. Jesus, he'd be up again in three hours.

He turned and reached behind him and put out the light. He reached down into the warm dark of the bedclothes and slid his hand between Danny's legs. Danny made a small noise in his sleep and moved in against him blindly.

John tightened his hold and went to sleep.

SEVENTY-THREE

Ian was dispatched to collect Stephen.

He got there at eight-thirty and interrupted them at breakfast.

Stephen had opened the door barefooted and had grudgingly let him in, greeting him only with, "Did you find Danny?"

Ian had smiled and said, "Yes," and resisted the temptation to add, 'dead.'

Conley was still in his dressing gown. He experienced the unpleasant sensation of Ian looking at him. He remembered women referring to being mentally undressed. It was the first time he'd ever *felt* the sensation as opposed to simply academically understanding it.

He was aware of the way Stephen had looked at Ian, a mixture of contempt and distrust, with maybe a touch of fear. He felt sure that Stephen didn't even know the fear was there. Swamped by the dislike he probably just assumed it was just part of it. Oddly, Conley could understand the fear better than the dislike. The day before he'd thought Ian Jackson Moore the most rational of them all. But what if he was wonderfully rational about exercising a personal madness? What then? Conley decided his judgement had gone to pot. Danny and his family had turned his perspective inside out.

Stephen went to finish dressing, leaving Conley alone with him. It was peculiarly uncomfortable. Ian wouldn't sit down, using his work clothes as an excuse, but Conley sensed it was deliberate. He remained standing himself, determined not to let him get the upper hand.

But he did, in the easiest way possible.

He smiled and said, "I thought John might kill you." He said it speculatively, as if the fact that he hadn't was vaguely surprising. Not that he was put out about it. Oh no, he was easy. He kills you, he kills you not, no sweat to Ian Jackson Moore.

"Thank you," Conley said and he could hear the rattiness in his own voice.

The smile became a nasty little yellow grin, hardly showing any teeth, as if his lips had been stitched together, as if he grudged you. Conley felt himself flush with irritation. The little sod had succeeded in riling him.

"What did he write?" Ian asked, searching his face with an ingenuous look, as if John had done something endearingly comic.

"How do you know he did?" Conley asked back.

"These things travel," Ian said, smiling a little more.

"I suggest you ask him."

Ian nodded as if that was *exactly* what he had expected to hear. Conley wanted to thump him.

Stephen came back out the bedroom, stuffing his shirt tail in, shoes in one hand. Ian looked from him to Conley and back again. The look was unmistakable. What made it worse was he was right. Stephen looked angry and Conley felt intensely uncomfortable. They both went red. Conley wanted to hit him more than ever.

Stephen tied his trainers with tugs that should have snapped the laces. He stood up and said belligerently, "Are we going, or are you going to stand there getting your rocks off all day?"

Conley looked away, vaguely surprised at the outburst, even more unsettled by the suggestions in it. Ian only smiled and said, "Poor baby, he didn't get much sleep." He paused just long enough, cutting short Stephen's retort. "I meant from worry, of course."

"You shit," Stephen said. It sounded like all he could manage.

Ian simply smiled and walked across the room and out the door, leaving Conley and Stephen alone and more tense than ever. Even that seemed to have been deliberate.

"Charming character," Conley said.

"He's a shit."

Conley smiled. "I think I have to agree with you."

Stephen glanced at him, then laughed shortly. It was the closest they'd got all morning. He said quickly, before he could change his mind, "About last night..."

"Forget it," Conley said equally quickly. "One of those things." He looked at the floor.

"Listen..." Stephen flushed worse than ever. "Don't... I mean you won't..."

Conley looked at him for the first time. He was smiling faintly, a little grimly. "Tell Danny? No, I won't."

"He wouldn't like it," Stephen offered, as if that explained everything.

"Oh, that wouldn't do, would it?" Conley said with inexplicable exasperation.

Stephen looked at him, aware that somehow he'd offended him without knowing quite how he'd done it. "I've got to go," he said.

Conley nodded, feeling angry and frustrated and full of temper and he didn't have a clue why.

"I'm sorry," Stephen heard himself apologising, and he didn't have a clue why either.

"Just go, will you?" Conley said, turning his back to him.

Stephen crossed the room, looking back once over his shoulder.

Conley didn't answer him when he said goodbye.

"Does he smoke?" Ian asked.

"Who?" Stephen asked just to be awkward.

"Conley."

"No."

"He looks as if he does. Cancerous looking, like he's eating away at himself."

Stephen shot him a venomous look, "Why don't you shut the fuck up?" and then looked back out the window.

"You want to watch your mouth," Ian said. "Otherwise I might just spread that dirty little cocksucking trap of yours right across your fucking face."

Stephen looked at him, aware that his mouth was hanging open. Ian wasn't shouting. If anything his voice was quieter than normal. His face was white and drawn, like John's went when he got really angry.

"You think I don't know what you've been up to with him? Think he doesn't know it's illegal? Think your mother might like to hear about it? She can vouch for you in court."

Stephen licked his lip, shook his head, a tiny denying gesture.

Ian said, "Alright," slowly, colour coming back into his cheeks. "Next time you watch your trap."

Stephen nodded, afraid and ashamed at once.

Ian looked at the road again, Stephen forgotten.

Stephen turned away and swallowed carefully.

Stephen's mother was watching him talking to Danny. He looked tense. He always did these days. She didn't understand why. He said he liked it here. He talked about

nothing else. Danny this, John that, and yet he always seemed tense and unhappy.

What worried her more was the fighting. She knew brothers fought. Families fought, particularly ones that lived in each other's pockets like this one did, but the way they seemed to set about each other. It was real violence, not just arguing and scrapping. John Jackson Moore's face was a fright this morning, and Danny still had marks from where one of them had scratched him, not to mention a mysteriously bandaged hand.

Scratching was such a woman's style of attack. It didn't seem to fit any of them. Maybe it had been a girl. God knows Danny was a womaniser. But he blew hot and cold, make no mistake. He had hardly so much as spoken to her since that time in the kitchen when Stephen had thrown a sulk. Maybe it had put him off. She felt a twinge of irritation then a flash of embarrassment. *God's socks, he's half your age Jean, get a grip. That one is no more interested in you than for the five minutes you attract his attention. All wrapped up in himself.* Not in a conceited sense, that was the strange thing about him. God knows he would have the right to be conceited. No, it was like his head was always full of his own private concerns.

She watched Danny pat Stephen's cheek. It was an odd gesture, too intimate. She'd seen him do it before, his hand lingering too long. She saw Stephen turn his face in towards it then spot her at the window. He hadn't known she was watching. He looked as guilty as a cat with its head in the cream pot.

Danny turned and smiled at her. She saw Stephen say something then turn away. He looked intensely uncomfortable. She could see him blushing from here. What was going on?

Danny was crossing the yard towards her. Stephen disappeared into the shadows of the barn. She bent her head over the dishes again. The door opened. She didn't look up. Danny came in and leaned against the draining board, backside on the edge.

"You'll get wet," she said, still not looking at him.

"I get worse," he said.

She finally looked at him. He smiled a long, slow, lazy smile. "What were you and Stephen talking about?" she asked.

"Private," he said, smile never slipping.

"I'm his mother."

"And I'm his friend. You can't expect me to snitch on a friend."

"Snitch?"

"Just an expression."

She started banging dishes in the sink, trying unsuccessfully to ignore him.

"You know," he said, and his voice was syrupy low. "I do believe you're jealous."

She paused, face colouring, then said snappily, "Of what?"

Danny shrugged - she felt it rather than saw it - then he said, "You needn't be, you're prettier than he is."

She flicked a quick glance at him. "Very funny," she said.

He grinned and said, "You *are* jealous."

"Stop it Danny," she said irritably, beginning to get genuinely annoyed.

He pushed off the draining board and came round behind her in one movement, wrapping his arms around her waist, leaning into her back. She could feel him heavy against her, her front pushed against the sink. "Hey..." she said.

"Mm?" Danny breathed into her ear. She felt goosepimples come up.

"Leave off Danny." She elbowed him half-heartedly, thinking dimly, I need to get a boyfriend. I'm too easy prey for this.

"Want to go to bed?" he whispered in her ear. She felt it clutch at her stomach before she could stop it.

"You dirty little devil," she said, trying to wriggle free, blushing furiously.

He laughed. "Come on, no-one will know."

"Danny. You stop that. It isn't funny."

"Who's being funny?" And although he was smiling, although she could *hear* him smiling, she felt suddenly that he wasn't really, that if she said yes he would, just like that.

His hands had slid up onto her breasts, squeezing them gently. He was unmistakably pushing at her back, little hints of it, thrusting so gently you couldn't be sure he was doing it. But he was. She knew he was.

She clutched at his hands and said, "Don't," sharply, and his hands eased off, slid back to her waist. Immediately and shamingly she wanted to pull them back up.

"One kiss then and I'll let you go."

"Promise?" she said, not giving a damn whether he did or not, but she needed to save face.

"Promise," he whispered.

And he kept it. He turned her round, kissed her and kept his promise.

It was the most miserable day of her life.

Danny made good his escape.

Sheer nerve, talent, and lots of luck.

I shouldn't want this, but I do.

He was dog-tired from lack of sleep but Steve-o's sweet little grey-haired mother had him harder than a fence-post. He *needed* it.

He turned down into the harbour, too fast, too high. Even he knew it.

Not a way to die Danny, drowning trapped inside a fucking stinking dead-beat clapped-out pick-up.

Be calm, be good, live long.

He parked relatively sanely and crossed the wind-torn road. It was stormier down here. Going to be a wild night judging by the sky. *Wild and cold and dark. Sounds like me.* He smiled into his collar, hunching up against the wind, and rang the buzzer.

A man answered.

If a man answers, hang up.

Danny leaned back against the wall. *Looks like your luck just ran out sweetheart.* He asked to speak to her, calling her Miss Henderson.

"She's not in I'm afraid, can I help?"

Danny recognised the twang, felt his frustration well up. A little black bubble burst somewhere inside. "Tell her Danny called, will you?" If he could talk sweetly, he talked sweetly.

"Come up," Robert Henderson said and the buzzer went.

Danny lifted his finger off the button. "Fuck you," he said, and he smiled as it buzzed on unheeded. He laid his cheek against it, feeling it crackle on his face.

"You have to push it," the tanned voice said irritably, and it buzzed again.

Danny straightened up and pushed through into the foyer. The door clicked shut behind him.

Robert Henderson stood back to let him in without speaking. The hall was dark. Danny wondered why none of them ever put the light on. A rich man's foible. Maybe that's how they got rich, saving on light bulbs.

He walked on ahead into the room. She'd changed something again. Danny's eye could see it, but Danny couldn't. He frowned, looking around, trying to place it.

"The painting," Henderson said. He gestured with his head.

She had replaced the framed photograph with a modern abstract nude. Male, scratchy over-endowed genitals, a bright shock of red hair on his head. He lay on what looked like giant sherbet lemons.

"Very nice," Danny said, looking him in the eye.

Henderson coloured. "I didn't pick it."

"Surprising."

Henderson didn't know what he meant and didn't know how to answer it.

"Do I sit down, or do you prefer me standing?" Danny asked, aware of his discomfort.

"I don't think I like your tone," Henderson bristled.

"How sad." Danny sat down.

Henderson remained standing, looking down on him. "And I don't like you seeing my sister."

Danny cocked an eyebrow.

"I want it to stop."

"Do you now?" Danny wasn't smiling. He wasn't smiling because suddenly it tired him. This man tired him. Life tired him. He rubbed his eyes.

"Well?" he could hear Henderson demanding, aggressive as a strutting little bantam.

"Well *what?*" Danny said, looking up at him.

"Are you going to stop seeing my sister?"

"I don't see your sister, I *fuck* your sister."

Henderson's face went a dull mottled red colour. It made him look as if he had measles. Danny wanted to laugh.

"How *dare* you."

"How *British*," Danny mimicked. "Where has California gone?"

"You dirty little yoik."

Danny grinned, genuinely amused. "*Yoik?*"

"Yes, yoik. She gets a kick out of being common, sinking down to your level, fornicating in the gutter. That's all you are to her, a cheap thrill."

"Alright by me."

"You fucking little queer," Henderson struggled out, beside himself with rage.

"Turn you on Bobby? Wish it was you, fucking common little dirty boys?"

"Get out." Henderson looked as if he was going to have apoplexy.

"Come on, try a bit rough trade. You might like it."

"I'm giving you four seconds to get out."

"Then what?"

"One..."

He began to count. When he got to four he lunged at Danny. Danny caught his arms and pulled - a short sharp yank - toppling him over on top of him. He rolled him over, pinning him into the settee. He knew from experience what it was like to try to get out of the soft sinking leather, especially with someone on top of you. He knelt on his chest.

"Well, Mr Macho..." Danny pressed in viciously with his knee. "How do you feel right now? Hot and horny?"

Henderson grunted as Danny leaned more weight into him. "Here we are in your favourite fantasy position, you dominated by a rough working type. I mean, it's jerk-off time."

Henderson grunted, "You little fairy."

Danny pressed in again, harder this time. "J for jealousy Bobby. Jealous of your poor dead brother, because he had the guts to do it. Of course maybe you're jealous of me. That's why you hate to see me with your sister. That's incest Bobby. Dirty,

dangerous stuff, incest."

"Faggot," Henderson grunted this time, wincing before he'd even completed the word as Danny pressed the breath out of him again.

"Tell you what Bobby, you kiss me and I'll let you go. How about that?"

"Get *lost...*"

The knee pressed forward, leaning into his throat, bruising his Adam's apple. "Come on Bobby, be kind to me. I mean, I really fancy you, a sexy guy like you. One kiss. I won't tell. Come on Bobby. Much longer and you won't be able to pucker up."

Henderson managed a slight shake of his head. Danny shifted his weight onto the knee in his throat. Henderson gurgled.

"Say yes Bobby, let's hear it." Danny kept exerting the pressure, suffocating him. Suddenly his eyes flew open. "Yes," he choked.

"Much better. Now say, kiss me."

Henderson barely got it out. His face was purple.

"Say, kiss me darling."

Henderson clawed at his leg.

"Uh-uh," Danny said, pulling his hands away. "Say it."

Henderson said it. The words were barely recognisable.

Danny slid back off, still straddling him and bent forwards, kissing his mouth before Henderson could draw breath.

Henderson gasped, mouth wide open like a fish, feeling Danny's tongue in it. It was a horrible, wet, messy adolescent kiss. It was invasive, raping, squalid.

Finally, many thousands of years later, the redhead got off him, stood up. Robert Henderson opened his eyes. He waited for him to grab his crotch. He waited for the sneer, the mocking derision, but it didn't happen.

The redhead smiled down at him. He looked amiable, friendly. The smile looked genuine. "Fucking faggot," he said and he walked out of the flat.

Danny drove back slowly.

He rolled the window down. Here, inland, it was a brilliant white-lit winter's day. Cold as fuck. The air felt as if it was burning his cheeks. He enjoyed the scouring feel of it, numbing him.

The business with Robert Henderson had had an odd effect on him, nothing he'd ever experienced before. He'd got a kick out of humiliating him - so had Henderson, with his little stiffy filling the front of his pants like a wad of toilet paper, and his little scared eyes begging for more - but he'd felt no answering response in himself. It had nothing to do with not fancying him. He'd screwed a world of people he didn't fancy. This was something else, and he wasn't sure he liked it. He wasn't sure if it would be a very useful habit. He hoped like fuck it wasn't going to become one. He couldn't function without that excitement. It's all he had. Fuck it, it was all he *was*.

Odd, Henderson wasn't bad looking, if you ignored the fact he looked like he was made of plastic. If he'd been physically repulsive it would have made more sense, but he wasn't, he was simply ordinary. So why nothing? Maybe it was because he'd gone to fuck her. Maybe his dick was waiting for the right signal and didn't get it, that was all.

It had spoilt his day, make no mistake. Suddenly he felt depressed. He wished he could go to bed. He was dog fucking tired. Early to bed tonight, give John-boy time to get his rocks off, and then get some sleep.

Sleep, glorious sleep.

He would talk to Ian. Ian would sort it.

Danny rolled up the window again, feeling the immediate warm silence of the

closed car.

Danny found Rab first.

"Have you seen Ian about?" he asked his back.

"No."

Danny watched him working for a moment or two then said, "Well that's definite anyway."

"And I don't want to see him." He kicked an unidentified object into place. "If that helps any." He wiped his hands on his trousers, back still firmly turned against him.

"You'll have to turn round some time Rab."

"I don't think so." He began tightening nuts with a spanner, giving them sharp vicious twists. They looked as if they had already been tightened as far as they would go.

Danny leaned against the tractor so that he could see his face. Rab kept his eyes down.

"You're too old to sulk Rab."

Rab didn't answer that one. He hunkered down lower, sliding his hand under and behind the wheel, feeling for something. He turned his face away, cheek against the tyre.

"Okay, what exactly are you hating me for? Keeping you here? You can go any time you want, you know."

Rab adjusted his position to get further in, but didn't reply.

"Angry you got caught out, that somebody knows? Or is it *me* knowing? I told you I won't tell him." Danny smiled, laid his head back. "Since I'm in a good mood, I'll promise. Listen. Robert, I promise I won't tell John you whored it to the tune of almost eight thousand pounds with Tam Johnstone. There, that's reasonable, isn't it?"

Rab slapped his palm violently against the wheel, brought his other arm out. He pushed against the wheel with both arms outstretched, still hunkering down, as if he was going to be searched. "Danny..." his voice was tight, restrained, "please go away."

Danny dropped his head and looked down at him, still smiling. "I can't bear it when you don't like me."

"I'm *asking* you," Rab said. He was rock still, like a spring held down with one finger.

Danny looked at himself. "Well, as you can see, my legs are paying no attention whatsoever."

Rab came up, as Danny had expected him to, white-faced and furious. "Fuck *off* Danny."

"That's it, that's all I wanted to hear." He pushed up off the tractor. "I love honesty, it's so refreshing."

And he walked away.

He finally tracked Ian down in the hen house, sticking his head into the pungent darkness. "Ian?"

"Here. Hang on, I'm coming out."

Danny reversed back out. Ian followed seconds after. "What's up?"

"Nothing, I just need to talk."

Ian felt his chest tighten. "What time is it?" he asked, watching Danny intently, trying to read him. Danny was looking away from him, hands in his pockets.

Danny turned and said, "Time enough," eyes flicking over him briefly. "Let's go."

They went inside and took off their jackets and boots.

Danny went upstairs without speaking. Ian followed him moments later. Danny's voice came from Ian's bedroom. "In here."

Ian went in. Danny was sitting on the bed, cross-legged. He was smoking a cigarette. The packet lay beside him, along with a clear Day-Glo lighter.

Ian shut the door.

"Lock it," Danny said, blowing smoke down his nose. He was further inside himself than ever. Ian could see it happening, felt the familiar mixture of excitement and frustration. Excitement at it happening at all, frustration that Danny wasn't going to be there when it did, just his beautiful, empty, well-trained body.

Ian walked over to him and took the cigarette out his mouth.

"I hadn't finished that."

"Too bad." He pushed Danny back on the bed with a shove. It was aggressive and angry.

Danny looked at him from where he had landed on one elbow, then he relaxed and put his hands behind his head. "What are you going to do, be John for the occasion?"

"You spiteful little shit."

"I keep my promises and he calls me a shit."

Ian swung over his body, one leg on either side, and pulled his hands from under his head. He held them down against the pillow, pinning them tight by the wrists.

"Going to tie me up too?" Danny was smiling. His shirt was sliding out the waistband of his jeans. Ian could see a small triangle of flesh, the beginning of his navel. The hair was a fine reddish sheen meeting in the middle like an upturned V.

"I'm thinking about it," he said finally.

Danny laughed and closed his eyes. "Something funny happened to me today."

"Mm?" Ian let go his hands and began unbuttoning his shirt.

"I got into a situation with someone and felt nothing."

Ian laughed. "A situation? That's a new one. A fuck and suck situation, no doubt. So? It must happen occasionally, even to you."

Danny opened his eyes. "No, not like this. I wanted to do it. I wanted to see him squirm."

"Him? Another joiner?"

"No. No-one you know."

"Who?"

"Henderson's brother." Danny watched him.

Ian stopped his undressing. "I didn't know he had one."

"He does. Did."

"And how the hell did you meet him?"

"That doesn't matter. All that matters is I did it and felt nothing. I couldn't even get it up."

"Worried?"

Danny chewed his lip and nodded.

Ian laughed. "Reckon it's the onset of early impotence?"

"Don't joke about it."

"For God's sake Danny, relax. Maybe you just didn't fancy him as much as you thought."

"I didn't fancy him at all."

Ian frowned. "Then what are we talking about here?"

"That doesn't matter, you know that."

Ian looked at him. He looked at Ian. Slowly Ian nodded. He felt as if the world was falling right through him. "Of course it doesn't. I keep forgetting. How do you do it? Think about John?"

"Don't start," Danny said warningly.

"Or what? I don't get my overdue payment?"

"Look, why don't you just hit me and get it over with?"

Ian scrambled off him, pushing himself far down the bed as if Danny was contagious.

Danny sat up on both elbows. "Now what?"

"You, that's what."

Danny sighed and dropped back down. "God, all I wanted was to talk about it and now I'm getting the full trauma."

Ian hugged his knees, laid his head on them. He rocked slightly. Danny looked up, feeling the motion. After a minute he crawled down the bed to him. He rubbed his hand over Ian's back. "Come on," he said softly. "It doesn't matter. Forget I brought it up."

Ian went on rocking himself backwards and forwards.

Danny shook his shoulders slightly. Ian came out of his hunched position like a snake striking. He brought the flat of his hand stinging across Danny's face, knocking him sideways, dropping on top of him. He hit him again, the same flat blow, then he just lay there, panting over him, watching the marks come up red and white.

Danny took a deep, ragged breath then let it out again slowly. "Better?" he asked.

"Much," Ian said, face calm and cold and angry.

Danny lay there and waited, face burning from the blows. Finally Ian got up off him and said, "Get your things off."

Danny got up slowly and began undressing.

Ian sat and watched, utterly impassive, that same cold expression.

Danny stood there, feeling cold and oddly vulnerable.

Ian said, "Wank."

Danny did what he was told, finding it frighteningly difficult until he saw the first flicker of change in Ian's expression, then it flowed through him like heat. He felt as if he'd been suddenly thawed. He watched Ian's face and slowly masturbated.

"Faster," Ian said.

"I'll come," Danny said and Ian heard the depth of his voice and felt his stomach do a slow roll of excitement.

He moved closer, unbuttoning his shirt, pulling Danny up against the bed between his knees. "On me," he demanded.

Ian pulled his shirt open and lifted his face, watching Danny's hand moving quickly up and down inches from his face. He could see every vein on its body. He felt as if he was going to burst a blood vessel. It was always like this, no matter what he did to you, how you felt. "Come on Danny," he said urgently.

Danny smiled. His hand slowed. "Want to hear yourself beg?"

"Don't stop," Ian said, glancing up at him warningly.

Danny went even slower.

Ian licked his lips then looked back at Danny's cock. "Please," he said, his voice papery and dry.

Danny's hand didn't increase its pace.

"Please." Ian squeezed a hand between his legs, trying to ease his discomfort. He felt his cock pulse unpleasantly at the contact. "Don't stop..."

Danny laughed. "You're drooling Ian. Let me hear a nice please again."

"Please. I'm saying it... please."

Danny began to slide his fist up and down his shaft, thrusting his body forward towards him, picking up momentum again. Ian watched the white hand skim up and down over the swollen red meat of him. The ultimate vision. He squeezed himself, then did it again. "Now," he gasped. "Do it now."

Danny's hand jerked fast and violent, pulling himself in three hard vicious tugs. He threw his head forward and it came out, silent, hot, pumping onto Ian in long thick

strings.

Ian crushed fistfuls of himself through his jeans, riding frantically against his own hand, frustrated by all the clothes, intensely excited by his frustration. He felt it clutch in a miserable little spasm, a half-tormented wet dream. He moaned helplessly, still panting, "Please..."

Danny's come trickled down his chest, ran down onto his stomach. Ian scrabbled his jeans open, falling back on the bed, and smeared it over his genitals, panting, grunting.

Danny stood there and watched him, hand slowly and rhythmically easing the last of his semen into his hand.

Ian, already dressed, watched Danny pulling on his jeans. He smiled, rubbing the back of his neck. "I don't know how you can doubt yourself."

"How d'you mean?" Danny asked, not looking up.

"You just came, twice in succession, not even pausing for breath. If I could convince you to let me, I could probably make it three times, and you don't even like me."

Danny looked at him, hands arrested. "Who says?"

Ian looked at the carpet. "You don't fancy me then."

This time Danny didn't contradict him and Ian felt the same old surge of bitter resentment. *Why do you keep inviting it Ian? Because I keep hoping some day he'll feel different.* "Do you fancy John?" he asked dully.

Danny gave a small laugh. "Oh come on." He was pushing his shirt in, trying to get it comfortable.

"Rab then."

"Now you're just being stupid."

Ian looked at him in surprise. "Never?"

"That's what I said."

"What's wrong with him?"

Danny tapped his nose. "Yesterday's flavour." Then he sat down on the bed and turned his socks out the right way and began pulling them on.

Ian said, "What about the boy?"

"His name's Stephen."

"Stephen then."

Danny came to a halt. "What does it matter?" He looked at Ian's face.

"You do," Ian said, and hated himself for how transparent he was.

Danny stood up. "You know Ian, this kind of thing is like sticking pins in yourself. You want to watch it."

Ian stared at him sullenly.

Danny unlocked the door. "And it's almost time for milking." He opened it. "So you better move your arse."

And he disappeared, leaving the door wide open, the cold hall air swirling round Ian's bare feet.

Danny had just pulled his boots on when John came in.

John watched him shrugging into his jacket. "Where the fuck have you been?"

"Helping Ian in the hen-house. Why?"

"I looked for you."

"Not in the right places obviously."

John blocked his way. "I didn't look for you in anyone's bedroom, if that's what you

mean. What was he getting, a back payment? Or was it something in advance?"

"I don't have the slightest idea what you're talking about."

"I wish I could understand this thing with you two. I feel as if I'm looking for the proverbial black cat in the dark room. Tell me one thing, do you have any secrets from him?"

"No."

"None?"

"No, I'm not telling you."

John laughed humourlessly. "I should've guessed."

"Are we milking cows or not?"

"Oh we are, most definitely. Just what I've waited for all my life."

"Bit late to worry John, you're stuck with it."

"Not necessarily."

"Forget it," Danny said.

John grabbed the front of his shirt. "Which one's so fucking important?"

Danny gripped his hand, not trying to take it off, just keeping it from making any other moves. "What makes you think it's a person? Why not the place?"

"You'll be telling me next it's the job."

"You wouldn't leave," Danny said scathingly.

"Want a bet?"

Rab stuck his head round the back door. "Any danger of anyone doing any work?"

John let Danny go. "Coming," he said, keeping his eyes on Danny's face.

Rab looked at him for a moment, not once at Danny, then went out again. John followed him a minute later, giving Danny one last unreadable glance.

"Gone?" Ian asked, coming through the door from the hall.

Danny nodded.

They went out.

Danny had promised him he'd spend some time with him tonight and he did.

He came into the living room and smiled an invitation.

Stephen got up with alacrity. "Where are we going?" he asked.

Danny put a finger to his lips and smiled again. Stephen felt a surge of excitement. The same kind he used to get playing hide and seek. That mixture of anticipation and anxiety.

He followed Danny out to the pick-up. "Where?" he asked again as they climbed in.

"You'll see," Danny smiled. "Don't be so impatient."

They drove out onto the main road.

"Where is everyone tonight?" Stephen asked.

"Rab's avoiding me and Ian's in the bath. Where John is no-one knows."

"Why is Rab avoiding you?"

Danny laughed. "Always first in at the bit that matters, aren't you?"

"Sorry."

"He's got the hump."

"Why?"

Danny laughed to himself. "Because I know him too well."

Stephen didn't know what to make of that and was afraid to ask.

He was surprised when Danny slowed and indicated only ten minutes down the road. They turned into a dirt track. "I didn't know this went anywhere," he said.

"Ah..." Danny unbuckled and got out to open the gate, "well now you know."

Stephen watched him in the headlamps. He got back in and took them through.

"Your turn," he said.

Stephen got out and shut it behind them.

They bounced along the tracks until the lamps hit a building, a cream-washed farmhouse. A couple of dark shapes loomed on one side, presumably outbuildings.

"Visiting?" he asked, but there were no lights on.

Danny laughed again. "Only ghosts if we are. It doesn't look like he's home."

"Who's home?"

Danny shook his head.

"Where are we?" Stephen persisted.

Danny cut the lights and the house disappeared into darkness. "Jerrett's Farm," he said.

The house smelt of unused rooms and new paint. It was quaint inside. Old-fashioned and cramped compared to their place, but it was nice, kind of cosy.

Danny took him through to the living room. The curtains were drawn. He saw Danny looking around as if he was looking for something. He put his hand over the ash of the fire then straightened up and put his hands in his pockets.

Stephen walked round the room surveying it. Finally he turned and looked at Danny.

Danny smiled slowly and said, "Well, we've got it to ourselves. Want to light a fire or would you rather go upstairs?"

It took Stephen a second or two. When he understood he flushed bright scarlet.

"Well?" Danny prompted gently.

"Let's light a fire." He walked away and looked out the curtains as if he did this kind of thing every day.

There was a moment's silence then Stephen heard Danny clearing out the fire. He half-turned to check that he wasn't looking at him before he turned right round.

Stephen sat on the settee and watched while Danny lit it. He disappeared twice into the kitchen, second time murmuring, "Just going to wash my hands."

Stephen watched the sticks crackling. They smelt sweet. He was used to the paraffiny smell of firelighters. He jumped when Danny spoke to him.

"Firegazing?" He sat down beside him.

"They've got a nice smell."

"Pine logs." Danny leaned back and crossed his legs.

Stephen looked at his knees. He remained where he was, sitting forwards, suddenly very tense about the whole thing. Danny seemed odd, different, but then, when did Danny ever seem the same? At least for any time at a stretch. "How come we're here? I mean..." He felt himself blush again. "Do you own this place or what?"

"John does. John will... eventually."

"John?" Stephen turned and looked at him curiously.

"Its been left to him. It's part of the farm... our farm," Danny clarified.

"John owns your farm?"

"He will."

"By himself?"

Danny nodded his head.

"Jeez, that's a bit mean."

"He's the eldest."

"I still think it's mean."

Danny shrugged. "It doesn't bother me. I don't give a monkey's fuck who owns it."

"What if John falls out with you or something?"

Danny laughed. "What if?"

"It would bother me. It's like favouritism."

"It is favouritism."

Stephen turned towards him, this time tucking one leg under himself. The coal began to spit as it caught. "Was he your dad's favourite then?"

Danny looked back at him, not saying anything.

"D'you think your dad liked him better than you?"

"Looks that way, doesn't it?"

"But he didn't leave anything to Rab or Ian either. I mean, he didn't just pick you out."

Danny shook his head. "He left them both money. There was money allocated for my mother too. John will get that."

"Unless she comes back."

Danny smiled. "Unless she comes back."

"Your dad might turn up some day too."

"I hope not."

"Why?"

Danny laughed but he didn't answer. He got up and opened the fire, putting more coal on. "Come on, let's pull this couch in closer." They pulled it up close to the fire then sat down again. "Better," Danny said, pulling his shoes off and holding his feet up to the fire. Stephen followed suit.

"Very romantic, don't you think?" Danny said, smiling at him.

Stephen flushed. "Don't take the piss."

Danny said, "Pop the light out."

Stephen got up and put it out. At first the room seemed too dark, but after a while the fire's glow brightened.

They sat side by side, faces lit by the fire, Stephen's hair now the colour of Danny's while Danny's looked almost black.

Stephen watched the flames through half-closed eyes, sleepy with that strange hypnotic quality Danny always induced in him, as if his body was drugged.

"You fuck Conley?" Danny's voice was quiet, without emphasis.

Stephen went rigid, eyes shooting open.

"Well?" Danny prompted.

"No," Stephen said in a small voice.

Danny tugged a lock of his hair. "Tsk tsk, lying to your best friend. What did you do?"

"Danny..." Stephen sat up, hands clenched in his lap. "I didn't mean it, honestly."

Danny laughed. "Of course you meant it. I saw all the eye play. You reminded me of a pair of pigeons, circling each other, puffing up your feathers. I wondered how long it would take you."

To Stephen, who hadn't even known he'd wanted to do it until he did it, Danny's words seemed almost psychic.

"Did you enjoy it?" Danny asked.

"Not really."

"Why not?" Danny was looking at him intently.

"I felt too bad afterwards. It spoilt it."

"How about him?"

"I don't know, but I think he felt the same. I..." he hesitated, "kind of pushed him into it."

Danny laughed some more. "I'll bet you did."

Stephen shot him a glance but Danny didn't seem angry. He didn't seem anything, other than amused. Stephen felt oddly piqued. Relieved too, but piqued nevertheless. He might at least have been a little bit jealous.

"What did you do?"

"Nothing great." Stephen looked at his hands, twisted together between his knees. "Just tossed off."

Danny was silent. It felt like a lifetime. Stephen waited for him to say something, yell at him, instead he asked, "Do you like him?"

"Conley?" Stephen frowned at his hands.

"No-one else we're talking about."

"He's alright. I didn't like him at first, but he's alright."

"Want to do it again?"

Stephen practically jumped round to face him. "No. I don't know why I did it. I think I was just too upset. I needed..." He searched, wondering what it was he had needed.

"Comfort?" Danny suggested.

"Yes," Stephen agreed. "I was scared sick about you. So was he," he added. "He was trying to make me feel better. I felt sorry for him."

"Like a get-well gift." And there was a hint of sarcasm in Danny's voice, ugly, unkind.

"If you like, yes it was," Stephen said defensively.

Danny looked at him searchingly. "You're very old for your age Steve-o."

Stephen wasn't sure whether he was being complimented or not. He said, once more defensive, "Maybe I've had more responsibility than most people my age. No dad and all."

Danny nodded, but didn't say anything. After a while he laid his head back and closed his eyes. He recrossed his legs.

Stephen looked at him then sat back beside him. "You're not angry with me?" he asked.

"Uh-uh," Danny said in his throat.

"I promise I won't do it again."

Danny opened his eyes without raising his head. He pressed a finger to Stephen's lips. "Don't promise me anything."

"You *are* angry," Stephen said miserably.

"No, just wondering why the things you want always taste so bad."

Stephen looked at him, but didn't have a clue what he meant. Danny didn't seem to expect him to know and didn't seem to care that he didn't. He closed his eyes again as if he'd forgotten it already.

Stephen leaned up against him, carefully, letting his body-weight rest against him. It felt almost sexual, the relief of just touching him. Danny eased him off and Stephen felt the rejection as palpably as a slap in the face, then he realised he was putting an arm around him, pulling him in closer.

Stephen cuddled in close, putting an arm around Danny's waist. He felt his erection come up slow and lazy, like it was half-hypnotised too. He sighed contentedly but his heartbeat was already taking him past contentment, urging him for something more. But not yet, no hurry.

Danny pressed his face into his hair and murmured, "I like you. Promise me you'll remember that."

Stephen tensed. "What do you mean?"

"Just what I said. Promise you'll remember I like you."

"I know you like me," Stephen said with absolute surety.

Danny laughed. "That's what I want to hear."

"I love you Danny," Stephen began to say, but he never finished it.

Danny pressed his fingers over his mouth. "Shut that," he said. The words sounded oddly violent, spoken so softly.

Stephen flushed and turned his face down into Danny's body. He felt the sudden

need come tearing up inside him. He pulled himself up Danny's chest and pressed his mouth hard on his. He felt Danny's flinch of surprise. He pushed hard, running his hands behind Danny's neck into his hair, pulling his head to his own. Danny seemed to hold back, making Stephen feel even more desperate. He broke away and said Danny's name pleadingly. Danny caught his arms and unmistakably held him away.

"What's wrong?" Stephen asked.

"I want to do something." Danny's voice sounded odd.

"What?" Stephen asked, his anxiety growing.

"Something to you. Can I?"

"Sex?" Stephen asked, not caring if Danny thought he was stupid.

But Danny only smiled, eyes black in the darkness, and said, "Sex," in that same treacly voice.

Stephen felt his anxiety disappear like a flame bursting into life, a huge red flower of excitement. "Anything," he whispered, eyes moving over Danny's face. "You can do anything you want to me."

Danny smiled and said, "Wait there." Then he got up and went out into the hall.

Stephen heard him go up the stairs. He kneeled up on the couch, feeling the fire on the soles of his feet. His excitement was caught in his throat. He couldn't imagine what Danny wanted to do. Why would he have to go out the room? He immediately imagined the weird harness with the cock ring in the magazines in his room. He felt his chest tighten so hard he felt he couldn't breathe. He took a shaky breath.

"Don't be so fucking stupid, you pervert," he whispered to himself. But his mind conjured up images of weird sex toys he'd seen in magazines, strange depraved things in candy-pink plastic. Surely not? He felt shivery with excitement and apprehension. He heard Danny coming back down the stairs. When he came back into the room he laughed.

"Christ, you look like The Startled Fawn perched there. Here, catch..."

Suddenly he threw something small and heavy. Stephen caught it on reflex. "What is it?" he asked.

It was a small bottle, a jar. Danny hadn't answered him. Stephen looked at it, tilting it towards the light. Then he saw what it was.

He swallowed although his mouth was dry. He looked up. Danny was smiling at him. Stephen said haltingly, "Vaseline?"

Danny nodded and he walked over to the couch.

He took the jar out of Stephen's hand as he sat down. He half-turned and put it on the arm of the couch. "Scared?"

Stephen nodded.

"It doesn't hurt you know. Not if it's done properly."

"But what if I'm not any good?"

Danny tilted his chin up with his hand. "You don't have to be good, that's my job. You just lie there and take it, that's all. You want to?"

Stephen nodded his head. *More than anything in the world Danny. Twice nightly. Into the secret domain.*

"What's wrong?" Danny asked.

"Nothing." But Stephen was twisting his hands again.

"We don't need to."

"No." Stephen's head shot round. "No," he said more quietly. "I've come this far down, I want to go the rest of the way."

Danny looked at him for a long moment and Stephen knew he should never have voiced that. Danny said tightly, "No-one forced you Steve-o."

"I didn't mean that." He lowered his voice. "Can we do it now? Please?"

Danny said, "Don't start hating yourself. You're sixteen. You're having a good time,

trying it out. Two years from now you'll be fucking some six foot blonde Playboy centrefold telling her, You know, when I was a kid I used to go at it hammer and tongs with this boy I worked with. Jesus, talk about kinky, we did it all. Roll over sweetheart, I want to give it to you up the arse in fond memory of Danny. God bless him."

Stephen laughed, half wishing it was true, hoping it would never happen. Two years from now he wanted to be here, with Danny. "I don't like Playboy," he said, still smiling.

"Christ, nobody likes Playboy."

Stephen laughed again. "Somebody must."

"Barbie's Ken maybe." And Danny had an immediate image of Robert Henderson, complete with jointed limbs. He rumpled Stephen's hair. "Are we going to fuck or what?" he said.

Stephen flushed and said, "Fuck. Or what later."

"That's my boy," Danny said and pushed him firmly and smilingly down on the couch.

"Your arse is like a peach," Danny said and he kissed it again. He could feel Stephen shiver. "Cold?" he asked.

"No."

"Excited?" And Stephen could hear the smile in his voice.

"Oh Danny, get on with it before I damage something."

Stephen heard him chuckle then the lid being unscrewed. He jumped when he felt the cold slick feel of it between his cheeks.

"Unclench." Danny slapped him lightly.

Stephen went limp. Danny's fingers slid inside the cleft of his bottom, skimming his anus lightly. Stephen made a small involuntary noise, hid his face.

Danny did it again until Stephen could feel the oily movement of himself when he clenched his buttocks. Danny ran his fingers up and down between his cheeks for what felt like hours, until Stephen felt like he was going to explode. Then Danny slid a finger inside him. It was utterly unexpected, and it went in too easily. Stephen immediately clenched, gasping something foolish.

Danny laughed and said, "Let me go. You've got muscles up there like an iron maiden." Then he said in a lower voice, "Do that when I'm up there and you'll emasculate me."

Stephen took a breath and slowly unclenched, feeling secretly excited that he had something so potent, literally within his grasp.

Danny eased his finger out then slowly inserted it again. He did it twice then started to finger-fuck him, gently, but with an unmistakable rhythm. Stephen wanted to come. Immediately. It felt almost like a pain. "God, I didn't know it would feel so good. I didn't know it felt like anything at all."

Danny laughed. "That's because no-one ever stuck their finger up you before."

Danny stopped, withdrawing his finger. He took a scoop of the jelly and began smearing it over his erection. Stephen turned his head to see what he was doing and was riveted by the sight of it, glistening and oiled, Danny's slippery fingers going up and down it. "Okay," he said, and promptly lay down on Stephen's back.

For some reason it had not occurred to Stephen that he would do that. He was shocked to discover how heavy he was, how vulnerable he felt underneath him. The enormity of what he was about to do suddenly hit him. He tensed.

He immediately felt Danny's fingers probing between his legs, his knees pushing his legs apart. His fingers found his anus, then it was there, something wide, nudging, surprisingly hard. It didn't feel silky and soft like it felt in your mouth, it was just big and

hard. He said Danny's name, some dim idea of stopping him, but Danny only said, "It's just a little, relax. You shit bigger than this. It'll be fine. Relax."

Just a little? It felt like plenty. He could feel the muscles protesting like someone pulling your jaws too wide at the dentist, as if the sides of your mouth were going to split.

Danny lifted himself and pushed, definitely and not gently. It went up, as definitely and ungently as Danny had intended. Stephen did not make a small noise now. He gave an unmistakable cry of pain, but Danny did it again, and then he whispered, "That is so *tight*. God..." and he began to move. But the pain of it going in was nothing compared to the incredible sensation of it coming out. This great thick oily thing pulled out of him the most delicious sensations, like the world's most erotic shit. He shoved his arse in the air, keen to have it back in just so he could feel it pull out again. He couldn't have enough of that.

Danny obliged him, whispering, "Is that nice?" like he was giving a pet dog a treat.

Stephen said, "Put it up me... no, put it up... put it..." But his inarticulateness was explained by the movements of his body. They were perfectly clear.

"Your arse is too tight... too good... I'm going to give you a spunk enema. Shit, I'm going to come..."

"Not yet... not yet... not yet..." Stephen gasped meaninglessly. He wasn't even sure what he wanted. He dragged his erection against the settee, terrified of being left behind.

"I'm coming... I'm coming... Christ, I'm..." And then Danny was heaving it up and out of himself, burying himself to the hilt.

Stephen thrust frantically against the couch, trying desperately to get Danny to pull his penis out so that it would bring him off, but Danny was doing tiny twitchy thrusts into his arse, moaning fitfully.

Stephen writhed under him, spreading his legs wide, shoving one foot against the floor, trying to lever his arse up under Danny's crushing weight. "Oh please... please..." he was moaning, locked in some awful stasis.

Danny grunted in something like pain then started to pull his penis out stiffly, sliding his hand under Stephen's body as it rose to follow him.

Stephen said, "Oh..." as he felt Danny's hand curl round his cock, and then it was *all* out. The sensation was fantastic. Danny pulling out, his hand gripping his dick. Stephen came, body twitching erratically, saliva spreading over the back of his hand as he moaned open-mouthed.

Danny finally pulled free, allowing Stephen's semen to spill like a lake of burning fire.

Stephen felt as satiated and luxuriant as a cat. He felt *fucked*. Danny's exhausted weight was crushing him. It felt great, but not for long. Danny grunted and rolled off of him, down onto the floor. He smiled and kissed the end of his nose.

Stephen felt suddenly embarrassed. He was aware of how soiled and used he was. His arse was covered in Vaseline, Danny's sperm oozing out of him. His face was smeared with saliva. He was soaked with sweat. He felt like a wreck. And he could smell shit.

Danny sensed his embarrassment and said, "I'm going to wash," almost as if he were reading his mind. Stephen closed his eyes, relieved to be alone, and lay stretched in the warmth of the fire.

When Danny came back in he stood above him for so long Stephen opened his eyes and looked up at him curiously. "What is it?" he asked.

"You look very fetching like that. Very fucked."

Stephen turned his face away. It was too close to what he was feeling.

Danny sat beside him, perched on the edge of the couch, and ran his hand slowly up and down Stephen's back. Stephen felt as if he was going to die of happiness. "Can I say it?" he asked quietly.

"Oh Jesus," he heard Danny mutter under his breath. His hand stopped stroking, resting lightly on Stephen's hip.

"I won't if you don't like it, but it's true."

Danny laughed quietly. "You've said it now anyway."

"Yes," Stephen said, smiling into his arm. "I have."

Danny slapped his arse, making him jump. "Go and wash, you dirty little peasant."

Stephen turned over then said, "Yuk, wet patch." He sat up, looking at it. "It's going to leave a mark."

Danny looked at it too. "A nice big mark. You randy little tom, shooting your load all over John's sofa. Tsk tsk."

"Christ, don't sound so happy about it, you pig," Stephen said, taking a swipe at him.

Danny held his nose ostentatiously and said, "Wash, *please*."

Stephen went off grumbling, half-embarrassed.

Danny yelled out to tell him where the bathroom was.

"I'll find it," he called back and went up the stairs.

The rest of the house was frozen. He shivered, wishing he'd pulled his sweatshirt on. Bet there was only cold water. He went into the wrong room first time, a bedroom. He closed the door and tried the other side and found it.

There was only cold water. He washed as well as he could. His arse was slightly raw and tender and incredibly oily. He couldn't get the damn stuff off. He felt like the bottom of a chip pan. He was also aware of how stretched he felt. The sensation was vaguely exciting.

He dried himself and took a leak then went back out. He saw another door further up the hall.

He walked along and turned the handle but it was locked. He pulled a face and went back downstairs.

Danny was still naked, sitting cross-legged on the settee. He thinks *I* look beautiful? Stephen thought and hard on its tail came, I've just had him inside me, shoving his big prick up my bum. He smiled, glad Danny hadn't dressed.

"Hungry?" Danny asked.

"Starved. Is there any food here?"

"Plenty, but it's all tinned. Want to go see?"

Stephen nodded.

"We better get dressed." Danny laughed at his expression. "They come off again Steve-o."

Stephen grinned and began pulling his clothes on. When he'd finished he sat down and watched Danny pulling on socks. He said his name. Danny looked up.

"I love you," Stephen said.

Danny got up and turned away before Stephen could see his face.

Perhaps Danny had been wrong in his assumptions because John and Rab were together, even if they had not set out that way.

John had waited until Rab had come back into the kitchen and then said, not looking at him, "I want to talk to you."

There had been a moment's pause and then Rab had answered with forced casualness, "Fire away."

John looked at him quickly, only just catching his eye, and said, "Not here, let's go out."

Rab had seen the flush on his face before he'd had time to look away. He couldn't remember the last time he'd seen him embarrassed. It threw him utterly. " Okay," he said, just standing there.

John looked at him for a moment then prompted, "Do you want to wash or something?"

"No. No, I'm fine."

"Let's go then." And John had put his jacket on and gone out leaving Rab to follow him.

The Rover was still warm inside. John must have just come in. Rab got in and put his belt on. John was already pulling out into the farm road.

They drove in silence, John keeping his eyes on the road, Rab watching him in sidelong glances.

They turned down onto the coast road. Rab felt a worm of something inside at that. He wasn't sure if it was excitement or unease. He rolled a cigarette, slowly and carefully in the twisting dark. He put it in his mouth and lit it, catching sight of John's face turned towards him at the sound of the match.

The car filled with the sweet scent of his cigarette. Aniseed and woodsmoke, the scent of Rab. John said suddenly, "Have I ever told you I love the smell of those?"

Rab took the cigarette out his mouth and said, exhaling, "You always said you hated them."

"I lied."

Rab laughed and felt better. He saw John smile slightly and felt better still.

The road was quiet. A high wind blew in from the sea, buffeting the car slightly. Rab could see the white horses breaking dimly in the darkness. It was stormy, not the tranquil clarity of the night inland. He wondered if it would move over them during the night.

"Looks rough," John said.

"Mm," Rab agreed, looking out again.

They fell silent again, Rab's cigarette winking in the dark.

Eventually they pulled into the long lay-by which served as a picnic area in the summer, and where James Henderson had once almost broken Danny's nose. The noise changed as they drove in, the dunes sheltering them from the sea and the wind.

There was no-one else there. It was usually only weekends that brought out the fornicators and romantics. Besides, it was too early in the evening for either.

John left the engine running but cut the lights. The heater continued to blow warm air into the car. It was very dark, clouds obscuring what light there was from the thin skliff of moon.

John said suddenly, "Has Danny talked to you?"

Rab tried to frame the right reply but ended up saying, "He talks to me quite often, surprisingly. What did you have in mind?" And it came out sounding arrogant and he wanted to say, I'm sorry, I'm so fucking tense I don't know what I'm saying, but it stuck in his throat like a fish bone, hurting him, but not moving.

"About leaving," John said without even a glance to indicate that Rab had annoyed him, and Rab knew he must be even more anxious than he was himself.

"He told you," he said, colouring up.

John gave a tiny laugh and shook his head. "Ian."

"How did Ian…" But Rab stopped, realising how naïve he was being and said, "He doesn't reckon I will... go, I mean." That at least was true.

"And is he right? Will you?"

Rab couldn't resist it, a chance like this might never come again, and so he said, "Do you want me to?" And he felt as if he was standing on a wire thousands of feet in the air.

And John said, as Rab knew he would, "It doesn't matter to me one way or the other."

Rab sat a moment, feeling it in the pit of his stomach, just sitting there spreading up into his chest, like his soul was squeezing the words out against his will. "You'll never come right out with it, will you? Never admit anything. Never a straight fucking answer. Start the car." He was almost shouting. "I'm sick of this. Let's go." And he leaned over and turned the ignition full on.

John sat there, frowning and looking startled at the same time. "What's the matter?" he said, as if he'd purposely sought out the one thing most guaranteed to annoy him.

"The *matter*?" Rab stared at him. "*You're* what's the matter."

"Hey," John said, frowning harder than ever, utterly lost in his violence. "What the hell's wrong with you?"

"Drive the fucking car John," Rab said, turning away from him.

"Not till we sort this out."

Rab turned on him. "Sort *what* out?"

"This..." John said, moving his hand lamely.

"*What?*" Rab said again, harder this time.

"I don't know," John said finally. "I really don't know."

"So can we go home now?"

"You haven't told me yet if you're leaving."

"Why do you want to know?" Rab continued to stare at him relentlessly.

John paused, wet his lips. "I need to know." Then he said angrily, "Christ, I'm running a farm, although you wouldn't fucking know it. I need to know if my hands are going to be here, don't I?"

"That it?" Rab said, voice like stone.

"Yes." John sounded defensive. "What else?"

"Oh," Rab nodded. "Exactly, what else? No, John. The answer's no. I am not going to be here. I am going to be somewhere else entirely. Happy?"

John stared at him. "Are you saying you're leaving?"

Rab clapped his hands slowly. "Collect your prize at the door, sir."

John turned away from him and said, "And what about Danny?" His voice sounded muffled.

"What about him? Scared he's going to come with me? Well, don't fucking worry, he isn't."

"You asked him?" John kept his back to him.

"John, I've been asking him for six months. I could ask him for the next six years and the answer would still be the same. No."

"Does he know you're going?"

"I very much doubt it. You can tell him, give you both a thrill."

Rab could feel the downer starting. So far he'd been cresting along on his anger. Now he was beginning to realise how far he'd committed himself. He'd burnt his boats. Suddenly he wanted to weep. He wanted to climb under the blankets of his bed, curl up and cry, like a two year old, like how he felt. "Can we go home now?" he said, and his voice was dull and lifeless.

John turned forwards in his seat and slid the car into gear. Rab laid his head against the glass and closed his eyes, willing the tears to stay where they were till he got home. John pulled out slowly then suddenly slammed on the brakes. Rab

895

exclaimed in fright.

"What is it?" He looked out the window, expecting to see someone standing there, worse, lying there. John was just staring straight ahead, hands rigid on the wheel.

"I don't want you to go." It came out almost as one word, fast and pushed, as if he half-hoped Rab wouldn't hear it if he rushed it.

Rab sat there, still staring out the windscreen, not really taking it in, still thinking in terms of corpses and flattened rabbits.

"Rab." John said it again. "Please don't go."

There was no mistaking it this time, what he said, or what he meant. But Rab needed more than that. It could be for anything, anything at all. "Why?" he asked.

"You don't need to fucking *ask* me that," John said tightly, still not looking at him.

"But I do, otherwise I wouldn't ask you."

"I just don't." He hesitated then said, "If you leave me alone with him I'll do something."

"For him, in other words," Rab said, tasting it like bitter pith in his mouth.

"No." John turned. "For *me*. I don't care a damn about him, this is for *me*. I need you to..."

"What?" Rab said when he didn't finish.

John looked away again. "Care... I mean, about what happens." He dropped his voice. "I need you to care about me."

And Rab knew somehow that it wasn't what he'd been going to say. He hadn't been able to say it, the 'L' word, the dirtiest word of them all. Most people couldn't even put it in their mouths, the rest put it in so often it meant fuck all. John wanted him to love him. Fine, great, but where was he?

"What about me John? What do I get out of it?"

"What do you want?" John asked, and already there was implied criticism in it. Grabby little Rab. Greedy selfish little Rab.

"I want to sleep with you." Rab felt a liberating rush of excitement as he said it.

"*Sleep* with me?" John said as if he wasn't sure what it meant.

"Yes," Rab nodded as if he were agreeing with him. "And I want twenty quid a week extra on my wages."

"*Twenty* pounds?" John said, looking at him.

Rab smiled. "Don't you think I'm worth it?"

"What am I doing, paying for you?"

"Yes," Rab said. "That's exactly what you're doing."

John looked at him for a long moment. "Are you serious?"

"About what I want, or why I want it?"

"Both."

"Yes. To both."

"Why?" John asked.

"Because."

"That's not a reason."

"Too bad. Take it or leave it."

John licked his lip and looked out the side window, then he said slowly, "Why do you want to sleep with me?"

"Because Danny ought to try a single bed occasionally. It's good for the soul."

"You mean you want to do it to spite him."

"And if I did?"

"Then I'd say I was being used."

"You're using me John. I think it's a fair exchange."

"I'm not using you," John said, turning to him.

"Prove it."

"How can I *prove* it?"

"By sleeping with me twice a week and paying twenty pounds for the privilege."

"Do I have to pay you?" John said, voice tight.

"What's wrong, think I'm not worth it? Reckon you could get a better fuck in Grampton Road Mens for less money?"

"I don't like it, that's all."

"Spending the money or buying me?"

"Buying you."

"Well it's in your interest. Remember, you've paid for it, you can do what you like with it. Just consider it two nights rest from Danny."

John was silent.

"Well?" Rab said finally.

"The budget isn't going to stand twenty."

"Okay, ten, since it's you. After all it's the principle of the thing."

"Alright." John kept his face turned away from him.

"Only one more thing."

John turned to him slowly. "What?"

"This..."

Stephen turned and threw the balled-up kitchen towel into the fire and said, "How come this place is so well fitted-out?"

"My mother was going to rent it out as a holiday cottage."

Stephen nodded, hugging his knees and looking round the room. His back was burning because he was sitting too close to the fire but he didn't want to move. He liked it where he was, where he could watch Danny, his face lit by the fire. He was playing with a cigarette, trying to blow smoke rings.

Danny looked at him and smiled, holding it out to him. "Want to try?"

"No thanks." Stephen shook his head. "They make me puke."

Danny laughed. "What a quaint way you have of putting things," he said in a strange flat voice.

Stephen exclaimed, "Hey, not bad."

"Sound like him?"

"Close."

"Oh thanks. My life's work perfecting Conley's voice and all you can say is, Close."

"No, it was good, honestly."

"Huh," Danny said then he yawned and stretched and said, "I suppose we better go home."

"It's not that late."

Danny looked at him and said, "What do you want, you dirty little sod, seconds?"

Stephen looked over his knees at his feet and said, "You're the one who said they come off again." He flicked his eyes up at Danny quickly then looked down again.

"Hey, you know, I'm getting on. Some of us aren't sixteen. Once a night is my dead strength."

"You liar," Stephen said. "I bet you do it more than that every night."

Danny smiled, raising his eyebrows. "What, with my big brother?"

Stephen flushed.

Danny's voice changed again. "Does that feel bad?"

"What?" He didn't look up.

"Knowing I do it with him, does it feel bad to you?"

"A bit." Stephen let the understatement go. "If I see you. I mean, if I see something... you know."

"If you catch me actually doing it, like the time you saw me kissing Ian?"

"Yes..." Stephen chewed his lip uncertainly as if he would have said more.

"Go on, say it then," Danny prompted.

"It's worse with John. I mean, you can see you're brothers and somehow that's worse."

"You've never seen me do anything with John though." It was half a question.

"No, other than sometimes he touches you funny, does something brothers don't normally do." He looked up to be sure Danny understood him.

Danny nodded.

Stephen went on, "Mainly it's just the *idea* of him and you. That's enough."

"Do you imagine us together?" Danny's voice was quiet, probing.

"No," Stephen said quickly.

Danny could read something more into his answer, an implication that he had indeed imagined them together - but not enjoyed it.

He stubbed his cigarette out and slowly slid another out the packet, putting it in his mouth while he stuck his other hand between the cushions, looking for his errant lighter.

"Here..." he eventually handed Stephen the cigarette, "light this fucking thing for me."

Stephen turned and touched the cigarette to the flame.

"Draw on it," Danny said.

Stephen put it in his mouth and brought it to life, blowing the smoke out quickly, then handed it to Danny, turning it in his fingers.

"You think it's worse than me doing it with Conley?"

"Much," Stephen said. "It's kind of *dirty*, you know? Like people feeling their dogs things or something."

Danny laughed. "Do people feel their dog's 'things'?"

"Yeah," Stephen said earnestly. "I knew a bloke once used to do it."

"Seriously?"

"Seriously. We used to go round his house when his mum was out, drink cheap canned lager. We all got pissed and he'd start this business, pulling the dog's dick, making it go hard. You know, nobody liked it, but we always used to watch it. It was kind of fascinating and revolting at the same time."

"Turn you on?" Danny blew smoke down his nose.

"No way." He added, "Thank God."

"How about him? What was in it for him?"

"I don't know, maybe he just liked showing off. One of the blokes, Dex, said he was once round there by himself and Millson jerked off after he did it, but Dex was a flickin' liar, probably still is, so you couldn't believe him."

"Think he did?"

Stephen considered. "Well, it wouldn't surprise me."

"And you feel like that, revolted and fascinated, by the idea of John and I?"

"No, it's not the same. It's..." He thought about it then shook his head and said, "It's not the same. I just don't like it, that's all."

"Jealous?" Danny asked, watching him, half-smiling at him over the smoke.

Stephen swallowed before answering. "I suppose so."

"Maybe that's all it is then," Danny ventured.

"No. It doesn't feel right. Like before you're going to be sick, that achy feeling, like that."

Danny laughed. "We make you feel *sick*? For God's sake don't ever come in and catch us on the job. I'd hate you throwing up on me."

"*Danny*," Stephen said repressively.

"What?"

"How can you be so...?"

"So what?"

"I don't know... so cheerful about it, as if it wasn't anything. I mean, it's probably illegal, isn't it?"

"I've no idea. Why shouldn't I be cheerful about it, if I enjoy it?"

Stephen looked at him and moistened his lower lip. "*Do* you enjoy it?"

Danny's smile spread very slowly. He was watching him from under his brows, eyes dark and glittery. "He fucks beautifully," he said finally. "There is no better."

Stephen looked away, pulling his legs tight to his chest. "And Ian?" he asked.

"What makes you think I fuck Ian?"

"Don't you?"

"Not if I can help it."

Stephen looked at him. "What do you mean?"

"Just what I say. I don't fuck Ian if I can help it, but sometimes I *can't* help it, and then I do."

Stephen studied the pattern on the carpet. "Does he make you somehow, is that it?"

"Yes and no."

Stephen looked at him again, knowing he wouldn't get anything else out of him. Danny put the cigarette in his mouth again. Stephen said, "Do you enjoy it with him?"

"Ian? No. Never."

"Then he does make you."

Stephen left a hint of question in it, but Danny didn't oblige him. Instead he asked suddenly, "How about you? Did you enjoy fucking John?"

Stephen looked at him.

"Well, did you?" Danny pushed.

"I don't know."

"You don't *know?* Jesus, that would floor him. Admit it, you thought it was a dirty dream you were having, some kind of porno nightmare. He feels like that, if he's turning it on. Did you feel like that?"

"A bit."

Danny laughed. "You're a lucky boy. Whatever he was doing it for he meant it. He wasn't holding anything back. Don't you want to do it again? Wouldn't you like to?"

"No."

"Why not? Or do you just think I'll be annoyed if you say yes?"

"I mean it, I don't."

"Why?"

"He's scary. Besides, he didn't want me, that wasn't why he was doing it."

"Why was he then?"

"I don't know. To teach me a lesson... to make you jealous." He lifted his head. "To split us up."

Danny looked at him hard for a moment then said, "Who told you that?"

"Ian," Stephen admitted.

"Did he now? The whispering fucking serpent."

"I think he was telling me the truth Danny," Stephen said, strengthening his voice to show he meant it.

"Do you? Why?"

"Because John *is* jealous. Of us."

"And so is Ian. That never occur to you?"

Stephen searched his face, not sure any more where he was in his own line of thought, but Danny went on, "And believe me Steve-o, when Ian is jealous he does

some very strange things. Once, when I was twelve, he caught me in the old cow shed with a girl. He didn't say anything. He didn't do anything. Took one look at our bare arses and walked out again. About a fortnight later I made some joke in his bedroom. I don't even know what I said now, it was nothing important, and he grabbed me right out of the blue. He shook me senseless then shoved me in the wardrobe and locked it. I'm not joking, he left me there for six hours. I nearly ruptured my fucking bladder. And when he let me out he said, 'Don't ever let me catch you doing anything like that again'. I didn't have a fucking *clue* what he was on about, until it twigged later, something he said, and I realised that's what it had been about, me and the girl. He'd nursed it for a fortnight. Sometimes he nurses it longer, and the longer he does the worse it comes out."

"Jesus, what a fucking nut. How old was he?"

"I don't know..." Danny thought. "Seventeen he'd be."

"What were you doing with her?"

Danny laughed. "We were just looking. Don't get excited."

"I didn't know you'd done anything like that."

"Everybody does things like that. I bet you have too."

"I was younger than you."

"Little perv," Danny smiled. "Boy or girl?"

"There were four of us, two of each. We did it on and off all summer."

"Playing doctors," Danny said.

"Yes," Stephen smiled back at him.

Danny stretched his legs out, leaning over to stub out his cigarette. "Okay gorgeous, let's get back."

Stephen caught his ankles. "A quick one?"

Danny looked at him, laughing. "You little creep."

Stephen crawled in between his legs, holding his thighs. He looked down at the V of Danny's crotch. "You don't need to take anything off."

"Stephen McEvoy, you are shocking me."

Stephen leaned up between his legs and kissed his mouth. Danny could feel his hands tugging at his zip, Stephen's mouth still on his, then Stephen broke away.

Danny smiled as he saw him look down at what he had unveiled, trying not to look too eager or too fascinated. Danny wasn't erect, he hadn't had time yet, but it was coming on apace at the expression in Stephen's eyes. Then Stephen further surprised him by dipping his head and neatly taking the whole thing in his mouth.

"Jesus," Danny swore. "You dirty little..." He felt himself leap three stages further on than he ought to be. Well, he wanted a quick one, he was going to get a quick one.

He stretched his arms back above his head and gripped the back of the settee, pushing himself up and out further. Stephen rewarded him by sucking it deeper.

Danny watched his mouth, stretched and sliding over him. He felt a strange, brief moment when he wished he was queer, really, purely, like Ian or Rab, so that it could be everything to him, not just some imperfect experience, at best a blissful release, at worst so bad it made him throw up. But release was all it ever was. Sometimes he felt good afterwards, relaxed, but nothing else. How could you want something so much and be so indifferent at the same time?

He chased it from his head, looked down at Stephen, looked at the boyish face, the child's mouth devouring him, pushed himself up. *Is this how it felt John?* "I want to come Steve-o," he said, pushing up again.

Stephen gripped him tight, rolled his tongue over the head, saying yes with his mouth.

"Give me a hand. Peel me back. Right back till it's really tight. That's it. Now just use your tongue, your whole tongue, flat up and down like this... no, like this." Danny

gave a soft moan. "Now you've got it. I know it's awkward, I won't take a second. A little harder. That's it... just there... harder... that's it..." And then there was a savage grunt. Danny gripped the back of the settee, hips levering up. He said, "Inside... inside... inside..."

Whether it was instinct or not Stephen knew what he meant. He took the whole raw distended penis as far into his mouth as he could and immediately felt the thick white phlegm hit his throat, flooding over the back of his mouth. He made himself swallow it down, thinking of snot even while it was exciting him.

There were a couple more paroxysms, but no more semen, then Danny dropped down whispering, "*Shit...*"

There didn't seem to be anything else to say.

"Want me to return the favour?" Danny offered.

"Do you mind?" Stephen asked, looking at him stretched out beneath him, penis still half-hard and very red.

"I never mind. Come kneel over me."

Stephen climbed up onto the couch and kneeled over his body. Danny slid down a little further until he could push his face in Stephen's crotch. He nuzzled him, holding him tight round the bum. "You're a sweet little bastard Steve-o."

Stephen smiled at the top of his head, touching the curls lightly, listening to him complimenting him. "Tell me more," he said.

Danny laughed and began to slide his zip down. "You suck dick very prettily, you've got an arse like the aforementioned peach, and..." he slid his hand inside Stephen's pants and pulled the elastic down, letting Stephen out and himself in, "one of the hardest, most polished pieces of equipment it's ever been my pleasure to spit on. What do you do, buff the fucking thing up with Cherry Blossom?"

Stephen laughed and said, "Stop admiring it and do something with it."

"No, I've got a better idea. I feel lazy. You do it. Fuck my mouth."

"What d'you mean?" Stephen asked, feeling the familiar surge of intense excitement that Danny always gave him, as if he always knew exactly the right thing to say at the right moment.

"Easy. I open my mouth, you fuck it. I don't do anything, just give you a wet, warm hole to shove it in. You ride my face."

Danny was fondling him as he talked. Already Stephen was far gone. First, giving Danny a blow-job, now this. If he wasn't careful they'd never get that far, he'd deposit his whole fucking wad in his hand.

"But remember, you don't want to choke me, so go easy as you can. That's the fun part." Danny smiled up at him. "They never can."

They. Stephen pushed it away, down into the dark. It was him and Danny, here, now. Nothing else mattered. 'They' could go to hell.

"Come on," Danny pulled his hips towards him.

Stephen took himself in one hand and pushed into the wet of Danny's mouth. He saw Danny close his eyes, drop his arms, just lie there. It was like doing it to someone asleep. God, he wasn't going to last two minutes.

He pushed in and out gently, falling out once with a plop, watching Danny smile at his faux pas, although he never opened his eyes.

He pushed it back in, embarrassed, pushing hard to punish him for that smile. He grunted at the depth to which it sunk, saw Danny flinch, his throat work. He knew he had made him gag, that he'd pushed in too far. It felt good.

He moved gently again, then a little faster. He took Danny's head in his hands and said something he'd long wanted to say. "I'm making you eat me."

He listened to it, trying to feel if it was right. He said it again, softer. "I'm making you eat my dick and you can't say no."

It was slurping in and out now. He saw Danny gag again as he pushed too far. He took a breath, slowed, backed off a little.

"Fucking your mouth Danny," he whispered, fingers deep in Danny's hair. "Fucking your mouth." He pushed in too hard again, but didn't care. He gripped Danny's head. "I'm going to make you eat my come, going to shove it right down your throat. Eat me Danny..." He pushed, ramming it in, feeling Danny struggle back underneath him. But he still didn't touch him. He didn't try to push him off.

It was that that did it, Danny's silent compliance. Stephen cried, "No... *Mam!*" without even knowing he'd said it, and began to push in wildly, pulling Danny's head down onto himself, feeling it in his arse, like a pulling pain.

Stephen couldn't stand it any longer. He pulled out, dropping down onto his heels, gasping, squeezing his balls to stop them aching.

Danny wiped his mouth with the back of his hand. "I said go easy, you fucking rapist." And he pushed Stephen, laughing, backwards onto the floor.

They drove back home.

When they got into the kitchen Danny said, "I'm nipping across the road for fags. Won't be a minute." Stephen nodded and he went back out again.

Stephen took his jacket off then sat down and pulled his shoes off.

He went out into the hall. Someone was watching TV. He contemplated going straight up to bed, but he didn't want to in case Danny was going to sit up. He went in.

It was just Ian, by himself. Just his luck. "Where is everybody?" he asked, closing the door and sitting down.

"Fucking around I imagine," Ian said and the look he sent with it said, I'm not swearing here Steve-o. That's a verb, to fuck.

Stephen promptly and infuriatingly blushed.

Ian looked back at the TV.

For the very first time Stephen sensed something in him. Like the time he lost his temper in the car. Like the dull gritty red glow you got on very hot metal, lasting only a second then it faded. But how hot must it be, even when the red was gone?

That was Ian. Nothing to warn you just how he'd split your skin, sizzling, if you got too close. Like the bars in the metal-work room floor with the chalk circle round them and 'HOT' written underneath, because otherwise you wouldn't know.

Ian ought to have a chalk circle round him.

"Where's Danny?" Ian asked, startling him.

"Across the road, getting cigarettes."

Ian looked at him, as if he expected something more. Stephen bridled, saying, "What's wrong? I got two heads or something?"

"So I've heard. One you give and one you get." He looked at Stephen's crotch.

Stephen crossed his legs as if he had something to hide. It was distressingly automatic. "You're a dirty pig."

"Maybe, but I'll bet you weren't discussing science."

"What's wrong, jealous?" Stephen felt the satisfaction of saying it, of seeing it irritate him, even if it was just a momentary flicker.

"I couldn't care less."

"You say. No wonder he doesn't like doing it with you. It would be like fucking a slimy eel."

"Get it off your chest Stephen, don't mind me." There was no irritation on his face

now, only amusement.

"Oh shut up."

Stephen looked at the television, although he had no idea what the programme was and watching it told him less. He could feel Ian looking at him. Like being watched by a mental subnormal who didn't know it was rude to stare. "Don't," Stephen flared at him.

"What?" Ian said in tones of innocence.

"Keep staring like that."

"I was only thinking how pretty you were. Suddenly I can see Danny's attraction. I just realised who it is you look like."

He searched Ian's face. He looked utterly serious. He didn't know what to say.

"You get it up for me Stephen, know that?" Ian's voice was still quiet, no smile.

"You tacky bastard." Stephen felt his face burning.

"Why? You get it up for Danny too, exactly for the same reason I suspect. I bet you don't call him a tacky bastard."

"I don't fancy you."

"Obviously," Ian said, the amusement surfacing again.

"You like fighting, don't you?" Stephen said suddenly. "I think you like people disliking you."

Stephen saw his words strike home, the tightening of Ian's mouth, his eyes narrowing, becoming even piggier than normal.

"Do I have to pay for this character reference or do I get it free?"

"It's true, isn't it? You like goading people. You're not right up here, know that?" Stephen tapped his head. "You're a crackpot."

"And you're a little poof," Ian said.

Stephen got up.

"You little fairy." Ian's voice was low behind him.

Stephen heard, "Cocksucker..." just as he pulled the door to.

Danny took the change he'd been given and went into the alcove.

He dialled Conley's number, pressed his mouth to the wall, a motionless kiss, tasting the sweet chemical taste of the vinyl paper.

It rang.

He laid his cheek to the wall whispering, "Come on..."

Someone passed the alcove, a shadow unaware of him, like a bird flying past a window. The bar noise opened and closed again.

"Hello?" a sleepy voice answered.

Danny made a tiny noise in his throat, like easing out a sigh. "They could sell the sound of you."

"That has to be you Danny."

"The one and only. How are you?"

"If I said cut up you'd think I was joking."

Danny laughed. "You sound like John."

"You sound guilty."

"Not in my vocabulary."

"Now *you* sound like John."

Danny was silenced as effectively as if he'd told him to shut up.

"Danny?"

"I'm still here... for the moment."

"Don't blackmail me Danny. Remember, I'm the one keeping quiet here and I'm getting tired of it. Why did you phone me?"

"To make sure you were alright. I don't know why I bothered."

"Then hang up."

There was a long silence then Danny said, "What's wrong?"

"I think I was set up. I think I was set up so elaborately I haven't even half unravelled it yet. I don't like being used Danny. I'm not some pawn between you and your brothers."

Danny felt a dull ache start in the pit of his stomach. The same fear he used to get as a child at the barbers, that same mindlessness. He bit the inside of his lip. Someone watching would have said he looked sick with nerves. When he spoke it didn't show. "Set up by who?"

"You."

"Have you gone off your head?"

"Maybe, the day I decided you were a good idea. Maybe then, but not now." He went on quickly, barely pausing for breath, "What if he'd killed me? I take it you don't care if he'd killed me?"

Danny was silent.

"Are you still listening Danny?"

There was no reply.

"John was sent round here. He knew he'd been sent but he didn't know what for and he didn't care. He just wanted to hurt somebody and I would do nicely. Rab comes along, does what he's supposed to do and everybody's happy. You roll up with Stephen in tow. You disappear off with John. Then the phone call, Rab come home. Stephen left alone with me. You knew exactly what he'd do, what I'd do when he did. You're a born psychologist Danny, you've got us all off pat. There's only one part I don't understand. What for?"

But the phone was already disconnected.

Ian pushed him back hard against the alcove wall, deep into the darkness. "Who?"

"Conley."

Ian pushed him again, square in the chest. "What for?"

Danny smelt the whisky, rich and sour on his breath. "Just to see how he was."

Ian pushed him again.

"Ian, we're in the middle of the fucking pub."

"I don't give a boiled monkey's fuck where we are."

"Look, I'm not trying to make trouble."

"Oh no?"

"I was just trying to stop him calling the police."

"Just trying to drop me in it, you mean." Ian looked into his eyes and said, "I've got John's knife, right here in my pocket, and I feel *very* tired."

Danny didn't say anything.

"It's getting to be boring, I know. But nevertheless, here in the dark you could bleed to death before anyone found you. I like the idea of you lying bleeding in the dark. Maybe your hair would go white, all the colour run out it. It always looks like it should bleed when you cut it. Think what a colour you'd be bled dry. Pure white, transparent, dead and white and empty. You couldn't get a cock-stand without blood Danny." He laughed, a small shivery sound, too high. "Although *you* might make it. Now, let's go see where you were tonight."

Danny immediately struggled to get out round him.

Ian's arm shot out, trapping him. It felt like a steel band. "I'm stronger than I look, you know that. The strength of madmen. Remember the matches? He loves me, he loves me not." Ian laughed again. "Did he love you or not? I can't remember."

Danny didn't answer him.

Ian grabbed his hair and yanked. "Did he?"

"*Yes*," Danny hissed.

Ian let him go. "Of course he did. Because I fixed it for you. Poor Danny. Unrequited love. Very tragic. Know how you feel. Was Stephen good? And how good is good? Is it because he looks like John?"

"He doesn't."

"I'll bet that beefy little arse does though, doesn't it?"

"Don't talk shit."

"Feels like it then."

Danny was silent.

"I knew it." Ian laughed once more. "Close your eyes and you might be in Wonderland. Up the rabbit's hole as opposed to down it, and Danny the Cheshire Cat, always grinning." Ian pushed him suddenly. "Let's go."

"Where?" Danny could feel Ian behind him now, and the unmistakable jab of the knife.

But Ian didn't answer, he simply walked Danny out the pub at knife point without anyone turning a hair.

Ian got him out of the farm with five minutes to spare before Rab and John drove back in.

The stormy weather was moving inland. The wind had picked up. Heavy rolling black clouds boiled past the moon, alternately darkening and brightening the landscape.

"Not Jerrett's *again*." Danny was looking out the side window so that his face wouldn't betray him.

Ian laughed. "Nice try Danny." That was all he said.

Danny closed his eyes and thought, Shit. Shit, shit, *shit*.

They got there too fast. Blink and they were there. Ian unlocked the house door, pushing Danny in ahead of him.

They had left the living room door open. Danny mentally kicked himself. But it didn't hurt, not nearly enough.

Ian stopped. He held one of Danny's arms in a vice-like grip. They stood in the darkness of the hall and Danny could feel the anger in him, trembling.

"You brought him here." He pushed Danny up hard against the wall, jarring his back. "You fucking little prick."

"I didn't. John must have been here..."

Ian thumped him back again. "You fucking spineless little shit. John hasn't been anywhere near here tonight. I *know* where John is. Where did you do it?"

Ian just let him go, turning and going into the living room. The Judas fire was burning a dull red. Ian bent down and opened it up. Danny watched him from the door jamb. He always looked better in the darkness. It covered up his bad skin, made his hair look darker, glossier, made his tight insignificant features look small and sharp, more glamorous. Danny had always preferred him in the dark.

Ian turned his back to the fire, legs slightly parted as if he were warming his backside by it. "Did you do it by firelight?"

Danny said nothing.

"You're low, and mean, and bitter as all hell Danny. I hope I never end up like you."

"It wasn't deliberate."

Ian made a small noise that masqueraded as a laugh and said, "Christ, you're like some thug that shouts on automatic, 'I ain't done nuffink' every time he gets caught.

You don't know the difference any more. You've got so complicated even you can't find the end of that black ball of wool that makes up your poisonous little mind."

Danny didn't answer that. He knew that no matter what he said it would end up the same way, a knife to cut himself with.

Ian turned to face the fire again. Danny watched the sloping line of his shoulders, his bent head, and knew exactly how his next sentence would sound, not the words but the sound. Defeated, weary, sad.

"Tell me why. Make me laugh."

"I just wanted somewhere safe, where I wasn't looking over my shoulder."

"*Safe? Here?* You could have done it in the car, the shed. The fucking pavement in broad daylight would have been safer than here. Christ, you'd even have been safe in the house tonight."

"I didn't know that, did I?"

Ian made that same dry laughing sound. "I've never known it worry you before."

"If you stopped lying about it I wouldn't need to do this."

"*Lying* about it? You want me to tell you the truth?"

"It's your fault."

Ian swung on him. "Now what he does is *my* fault? How do you expect me to feel any sympathy for you when you're constantly sneaking about behind my back, trying to fuck everything up, pushing everything to the limit? How would I have squared this with him? How would I ever have got him to believe anything I said after this? How the hell could this feel *right?*"

Danny shrugged. "It did. I don't know why."

"You mean you got a kick out of it."

Danny didn't answer.

Ian yelled at him, "Fuck you, didn't you Danny?!"

Danny dropped his arms, straightened up. "Yes Ian, I did. Both times."

Ian was watching him now, something new dawning in his eyes, some new enormity that had only just struck him. "What did you do?" he asked.

He could see Danny's eyes flick away, then he leaned back against the door frame again. But it was pretend. He was tense, anxious, giving himself time to think.

Ian didn't let him. He yelled again, louder, "What did you *do?!*"

Danny's head shot up. "We fucked. F. u. c. k. e. d." Then he yelled too, "Alright?!"

Ian came tearing across the room at him, his body hitting Danny's like a missile. They went out into the hall with the momentum, up hard against the wooden panels of the walled staircase. The air came out Danny in a grunt. Ian began slapping him. Small hard smacks like you would give a child who had gone too far. Danny held his hands to his face in a futile gesture.

"You filthy little pig. You fucking sick little pig. You..."

It went on and on, the words pouring out, the slaps punctuating them. Anyone watching would not have understood the way they stood there. Ian, a good four inches shorter, hitting his little brother who was obviously bigger and stronger. It looked grotesquely funny. Pathetic.

Eventually it stopped.

Ian moved away from him, panting with exertion. Danny had his body half-turned into the wall. He was silent, arms thrown up protectively over his face. After a moment or two he dropped them. He was leaning there with his eyes closed. It was impossible to see any marks in the darkness.

"Say you're sorry," Ian said.

"I'm sorry."

"Say it again. *Mean* it."

"I'm *sorry.*" Danny sounded harried to the point of anger

Ian came back, swiftly lifting his hand again, but this time Danny caught it, hard around the wrist. "No," he said, opening his eyes. "No more."

"Or *what?*" Ian's voice was tightly furious.

"I don't want to fight with you but I won't take any more Ian, I mean it."

"Who the fuck do you think you're talking to? John? Think you've got rights or something? Think you've got one single right to tell me anything? Who gave you your fucking life Danny? I gave it. I'll take it away."

Ian pulled his hand away in a sudden violent gesture. Danny steeled himself for the blow, but it never came. He opened his eyes again. Ian was standing there watching him, eyes calculating, plain even in the semi-darkness.

"Don't get smart Danny. Don't decide you can run rings round me. And don't *ever* bring anyone else here again." He grabbed Danny's shirt front. "D'you hear me?"

"I hear you."

"Right." He let him go with a push. "You remember Danny, or I'll spoil your face so badly none of them will ever want you again."

Suddenly Ian took a deep breath, dragging it into his lungs then letting it out again slowly. When he spoke again his voice was soft, cajoling, all the hardness gone. He laid his palm on Danny's cheek, could feel it burning from where he'd repeatedly struck him, felt the warmth go right down his arm into his groin, like a current of electricity. "You know I love you no matter what you do. You know that, don't you?"

Danny nodded, bottom lip caught between his teeth.

"Why do you do this? I hate myself after these blow-outs."

Danny said nothing.

"You know I don't mind. But not here. I draw the line at here. I'm not having him fucked over by you."

"I won't."

"Promise me."

"I promise."

Ian took Danny's head in both hands and kissed him, gently. He moved back off his mouth enough to say softly, "Kiss me back." He put his mouth over Danny's again and Danny kissed him back.

Ian moved up against him, kissing him harder, finally pushing his tongue in his mouth.

Danny pulled away sharply, back against the wall, turning his head away. He apologised immediately, as if he were getting it in quickly before Ian could speak. "I'm sorry. I don't know why I..."

"That's alright," Ian interrupted. His voice was quiet but there was no warmth in it. "Too fast, that's all." He pinched Danny's cheek gently. "Trouble is you're too damn beautiful."

Danny could feel the way Ian's groin was crushed into his leg. He could feel the insistent hardness of it. Sometimes he felt like one of those religious icons that people touched to heal themselves, supposedly blessed with mystic powers. That's how he felt, as if everyone in the world thought they could touch him and be different, cure whatever was wrong with them. As if he were a lump of wood that just went on giving out. And he never knew when he was going to feel like this, or why. Mostly it was alright, he could do it, even enjoy it, but sometimes...

Ian was pushing imperceptibly against his leg. Somehow he'd pulled Danny's shirt out and his hands were underneath, one at either side, feeling his rib-cage, touching the cuts he'd made, sliding the tips of his fingers into Danny's armpits, thumbs over the nipples.

"Love me?" he asked.

Danny nodded.

"Say it."

"I love you." Danny heard the words and wondered why he was saying them. Next time he'd refuse. Next time Ian would probably want him to. He liked it better that way, having to work for it.

"You're shivering," Ian said.

"Someone walked over my grave."

"I think we'll go upstairs."

Danny became rigid where he stood. Ian looked up at him and Danny said, "Let's just leave it." He tried to inject promise into his voice.

"Let's not. I don't like secrets. How many have you got, tucked away?"

"None. I swear it."

"You swear too easily, like you lie too easily, and fuck too easily, and look beautiful too easily. Everything comes too easily to you." Ian laughed. "Even coming comes too easily."

He looked at Danny's face for a moment and could feel the tension in him, still there under his hands. He brought them out from inside his shirt. "Come on Danny."

"I don't want to."

"What *you* want isn't under discussion, I'm *telling* you. Now move it." And he pushed him.

Danny straightened up and punched him all in one movement. Ian grunted and folded up. Danny hit him again, this time on the side of the head, then once more on the side of his body, on the top of his right arm, bruising the muscle and jarring Danny's own arm.

Everything was done quickly and silently. Three blows and it was finished.

"I said no, Ian." Danny was breathing fast but only he was aware of it. It made no sound.

Ian stood holding himself together. He felt sickness like a dull rolling ache move up his chest. He bit his lip to try and stop himself throwing up. Gradually it passed.

Danny stood there watching him. After another minute he put on the hall light. It flared eye-wateringly bright after the long dark.

Ian looked at him, still holding his sides. He said in a hoarse voice, each word breathed out separately, as if it hurt him, "You're getting very confident."

Danny shook his head, but he said nothing, no elaboration.

"Think I won't tell him?"

"Not this far down the road. You're too frightened of losing him. Some day maybe. Isn't that why I put up with this, because someday all my dreams will come true? My worst nightmares? Isn't that what you're living on Ian, the promise of one day? The threat?"

Ian took a step back and leaned against the wall, legs pushed out to brace himself, backside half sitting against it. He leant on his upper knees, holding himself upright, taking long, slow, delicate breaths. He was watching Danny, head raised as far as was comfortable, which wasn't much. It made him look saturnine, devious. Maybe that's what he was.

"Very unchristian," he said finally. "Not only is your head dirty and dark inside but you don't believe in anything either. No morals and no faith. How do you keep your body and soul together without one or the other? Or don't you have a soul?"

"It was washed down the toilet years ago, bled out of me bit by bit in little white smears."

Ian shook his head slowly. "You know, if you were Dorian Gray that painting would be in a state of putrefaction by now, and you're hardly anything more than a kid."

"You read too many books. You're beginning to think you can write my life just like one."

"If I could write you Danny you'd be a whole lot different, believe me."

Danny said nothing.

"You know, no-one else would put up with this shit from you, all these speeches. The poor kid so badly used and abused. You seem to forget I was there. I know everything about you. Whoring it to all and sundry. Offering it to the old man. Want me to remind you?"

"No."

"I think you could stand a little refresher. I think you're getting too fucking big for your boots. You seem to have some idea that I ought to consider your feelings, maybe treat you with some respect. Maybe I should pretend you haven't spent your whole life like a stud animal, offering every orifice for someone else's gratification. Think I should respect that? Would you?"

"I want to go home Ian."

"You asking my permission?"

"I don't want to fight. Are we going home?"

"What if I say no?"

Danny looked at the floor. "Then we fight, don't we?"

Ian could still see the marks where he'd slapped him, raised and sore-looking against the unnatural white of his skin. Why was he so white? What was it he'd said that had made him so white?

"Alright," Ian said suddenly. He saw Danny's shoulders drop. "But first I want you to tell me something."

"What?" Danny asked and his voice was cagey.

"Tell me what you are Danny, say the word. I want to hear it come out your own mouth. I want to know that you know."

Ian walked over to him, put his fingers on Danny's mouth.

Danny looked down at him, eyes bright, but nothing else showed in his face.

"Come on, I want to see this beautiful mouth say it. What are you Danny? Let me hear that filthy word in this beautiful mouth."

Danny closed his eyes and said it. "I'm a whore Ian."

Ian watched one single tear run down over the angle of his cheek. He caught it with his finger tip and lifted it carefully to his mouth. Was it an illusion or was it sweet? "Even your own body betrays you Danny," he whispered and he leant forward and kissed him gently on his averted cheek.

Stephen didn't realise there was something actually wrong till he saw the look pass between Rab and John. Danny had been gone a while but he might just have stopped to talk to someone. The look was because Ian had disappeared too.

Rab had gone across to the pub but Danny wasn't there. Stephen had been banished from their presence after that, but he had managed to catch half a sentence from the hall down below, "...go look for them?"

But he hadn't caught John's reply.

They didn't do anything. They sat tight in the kitchen where Stephen could only half-hear them. He sat at the top of the stairs but could only catch the odd word. Mostly it was John ranting and Rab pacifying, so that their voices rose and dropped.

Stephen got rattier and rattier until he wanted to stomp downstairs and march into the kitchen - *then* let them carry out their private little confabs. He stood up and promptly sat back down again as he heard John say, "And where the fuck have you been?" The door banged shut almost simultaneously.

It wasn't Danny who answered. It was Ian talking, John throwing questions at him, accusations by the sounds of it. Nothing from Rab. No sound of Danny.

Stephen hung onto the banisters like a man behind bars, his ear pressed between two posts as if he might hear better, but he only caught the 'fucks' and its variations, always distinct, for some reason, in overheard conversations. It was a carrying word.

He had his eyes closed, as if his sense of hearing might be better tuned that way, when he felt the unmistakable sensation of someone watching him. He opened his eyes.

Danny was standing on the half-landing where the stairs turned. He came up the remaining six or so stairs to where Stephen sat. A slow smile was spreading over his face.

Stephen let go the banisters as if it could possibly help to disguise what he'd been doing at this stage. Predictably he went pink.

Danny sat down beside him and whispered, now almost grinning, "Hear anything juicy?"

Stephen surprised himself by laughing, clamping his hand over his mouth, trying to stifle it.

"You should have seen yourself." Danny was still whispering. They were still arguing downstairs. "You looked like one of those tacky Victorian paintings of chastised children they print like photocopies and sell in reject shops."

Stephen turned away and laid his forehead against the banister, hiding his embarrassment.

Danny reached over and rumpled his hair. "You are something, know that?"

Stephen lifted his head and smiled at him.

"Really something," Danny added, then he bent and kissed him casually on the mouth.

And then it changed, with such speed it was frightening.

Danny seemed to pause a second, mouth in the act of breaking away, as if he'd thought better of it - no, nothing so calculating, nothing you could have thought - then his mouth pressed back down on his, hard, as he pulled Stephen to him.

Stephen was taken by surprise and hung limp in his arms. He felt rather than heard Danny give a small grunt of surprise, as if he hadn't expected it either. The noise brought Stephen instantly erect. From zero to six inches in four seconds.

They actually fell back on the landing, legs hanging down the stairs, and grappled on the floor. Danny was lying on top of him, with one leg pushed between his, devouring his mouth. Stephen lay underneath him, humping himself up feverishly against Danny's body, immediately desperate to climax. They looked as if they were fighting. Small animal noises came from them.

Below the voices had died down, become intermittent. Danny and Stephen were oblivious. They rolled. Stephen was now half on top of Danny, pushing harder against him. He felt huge with excitement. It was as if they hadn't seen each other for months instead of less than an hour ago.

Rab came up the stairs just as Stephen pulled himself up off Danny's body, back arched, holding him by the shoulders, arse pounding against him and saying, "Oh... oh... oh," on a rising cry.

He stood there riveted by the sheer animalism of it. They were both fully clothed but there was no mistaking what was happening, or what they were doing.

And then it was Danny, his hands convulsively gripping handfuls of the arse of Stephen's jeans and using his feet on the top stair to lever himself off the floor so that he could thrust and grind his pelvis against Stephen's rutting body. And the *noise* he was making. Rab couldn't see his face - it was obscured by Stephen's back - but he caught one glimpse of his hair as he thrashed his head from side to side.

Jesus Christ. It must have happened in about four minutes, if that. Rolling about on the fucking stairs. Anybody could have come up here.

Somebody did.

Him.

"Jesus... *Christ*," he whispered as he climbed the last stairs towards them. Stephen flew back off Danny's body as if he'd been shot. Danny lay there blinking blindly, like something unearthed from under a stone, then he climbed up onto one elbow. Stephen was slithering up into a sitting position, backing away.

Rab looked at them, looked at Danny's face. He looked flushed, drugged. He'd never even suspected. This boy, this fucking mealy-mouthed little... *kid* was getting *this*. Jesus. Rab said it again, like he couldn't believe it. "Jesus."

Danny pulled himself up into a sitting position. Stephen had collapsed back against the banisters, eyes shut. He looked like someone who'd been ill. Rab didn't know if it was shock or the strength of his orgasm. He had his legs stuck out in front of him. Rab was surprised to see he had a wet stain on the front of his jeans. Christ, the little fucker must have come a real load's worth. His hands lay palm up on his thighs. He looked like a rag doll. He looked spent, that was the word. But then he was, wasn't he?

Danny was rubbing his face with his hand. He looked up at Rab and scrubbed at his lip furiously with the back of one hand. When he had satisfied the itch he held out his hand for Rab to help him up. Rab felt an instant desire to slap it away. Danny held his eyes, the hand hanging there too long, then Rab slowly reached out and took it.

He pulled Danny up, feeling the warm sweaty grip of his palm. Danny stood, easing down the legs of his jeans, tucking his shirt in. He gave Rab a look as much as to say, Don't say anything, and then he turned to Stephen.

Stephen's eyes were open. He looked up at Danny slowly. Danny winked. It was alright. Everything would be alright.

Danny gave him a hand up, saying in a low voice, "Get to bed. I'll see you later chicken." And he winked again. Rab saw that Stephen's legs weren't steady as he moved away.

As soon as he'd gone, before Danny had even turned back, Rab said, "Chicken?"

Danny looked at him. "It's what he is, isn't it?"

"Does he know what you're calling him?"

Danny smiled. "I doubt it."

"You're a bastard."

"Truthful."

"My arse."

Danny ignored that and said without further deliberation, "Don't tell them, either of them." Then he added belatedly, "Please."

"Tell them *what* Danny?"

"What you saw." Danny tried to keep the irritation out his voice.

"And what *did* I see? You and Steve-o rolling about the floor, coming on each other, no hands? Hardly a surprise to either of them, I would've thought. Nothing that they don't know you're doing. Even if the time and place is a bit unusual." He leaned against the banisters and said, low and quiet, "Or is it that neither of them, certainly not John, realises how far you're into it? He thinks it was a one-off. My bet is it's more like four times a day. My bet is you probably can't keep your hands off him. John know that?"

Danny's face went a dull red. Rab didn't know if it was anger or guilt. Maybe both.

"Does Ian know?" Rab asked.

"No." Rab saw him do something odd with his hands, rubbing the wrists together. It looked neurotic.

Rab shook his head. "I don't get this. He's a kid. What would you, of all people, see in a kid? If you were a faggot I could understand it. So cute with just that little hint of thug to come, a little John clone..." Rab stopped as if he'd just heard himself, then he

said, "Oh, tell me it isn't that."

"He doesn't look fucking anything like John. Why does everybody keep saying that?"

"Christ, what the fuck are you *doing* Danny? What about him?"

"It isn't all *me* Rab. It takes two. I don't bloody seduce him." He paused, trying to pull his temper back. "Swear on your mother's grave you won't tell him."

"Why should I?"

"What do you want me to do, get down on my knees and beg?"

"Is that an offer?"

Danny paused a beat then said, "If you want it to be."

"Okay, what am I getting?"

Danny felt himself flush. It was so naked, like he'd said, How much? "Revenge?" he asked, trying to keep the anger out his voice.

"What am I getting Danny?"

"Whatever you like. Maybe you'd like it in the toilet. Create the right atmosphere." It slipped out, sharp as a razor blade.

Rab nodded, a vicious little smile. "A nice idea. The toilet it is."

Danny took a breath and let it out slowly. He wanted to say a lot of things, big long speeches, but all that came out was, "Now?"

"Now," Rab said, and he walked over to the bathroom door and held it open with a sweeping gesture.

Danny went in, listening to Rab slide the bolt home behind him.

He turned. Rab was standing against the door. Danny, for some reason he couldn't explain or understand, felt like a virgin at his first encounter.

"What's wrong Danny? Worried you won't be able to get it up?"

"Look, let's just do this, huh? Before one of them comes up here."

"You sound nervous."

"Maybe I am."

"Why?" But Rab's face looked as if he knew.

"I don't like it in here."

"Since when?"

"Look, what is this? A fucking cross-examination?"

Rab shrugged, holding out both hands in self exoneration. "Just an innocent question. Harmless curiosity, that's all."

"Do you want this or don't you?" Danny snapped.

"Oh, I want it alright, although you seem to be doing your level best to make it as unpleasant as possible."

Rab pushed up off the door and crossed the room. He sat down on the toilet without putting the lid down and crossed his legs at the ankles. "Here I think." He saw the colour drain out Danny's face like somebody had pulled the plug. "Yes, I think I'd liked to be sucked off sitting on the toilet."

"No." It came out as a breathy whisper. Rab was astounded to see him even take a step back in classic melodramatic fashion. People really did that then. His face was so pale Rab could see faint red marks on his face like stripes. He looked at them, trying to decide what they were.

"I'm not doing it there." Danny seemed to have got over the initial shock. "I'm not sticking my head in a toilet for anybody."

"In that case I'll tell him."

The cool went, utterly. Only skin deep, faked.

"Either you suck me here, now, and have my lifelong silence or I tell him. No

compromises."

"I can't," Danny said emphatically.

"Why not?"

"Because, *fuck* you."

"Shhh... keep your voice down."

Danny was doing that odd wrist thing again, rubbing them together as if they itched. Or hurt. Rab tried to see if they were marked, wondered if they went with the face, but there was nothing there, not that he could see. He suddenly felt vaguely uneasy about him. He didn't look right. His skin was greyish and he was sweating heavily. His eyes were jerking everywhere, like a trapped animal.

"Let's go to your room." Danny was rubbing his wrists again as he spoke.

"I'll give you another option."

Danny stopped rubbing.

"Tell me why and we can forget the whole thing. I'll be quiet, not a cheep, not even if they stick lit matches under my nails, but you've got to tell me the truth. Why don't you want to do it on the toilet?"

Danny suddenly turned his back on him and started talking rapidly, like someone reciting poetry with their back to the class because of a severe attack of shyness. "I used to have to do it in here."

"Who with?"

"Guess."

"The old man?"

Danny didn't answer.

Rab couldn't tell from his blank back what he was thinking. "How old were you?" he asked.

Danny shrugged.

"Was there anyone else there?"

There was another pause, longer this time, then Danny said, "No," and his voice was suddenly calm, controlled. "Just the two of us."

"What did you do?"

Danny shrugged again.

"Danny..."

No response.

"Danny, turn round and show me you're not lying."

Danny turned slowly and met his eyes. He held them. Whether it was easy or cost him hard Rab couldn't tell.

"The truth?"

"Truth," Danny said, eyes never wavering.

Rab got up off the toilet. He felt ancient. "He never did anything to me. It was John, always going on about what a faggot he was. He seemed so sure it was true I let him believe it was. Anything to please him."

Danny said nothing. His face looked utterly cold and detached, as if Rab was telling him about some boring hobby he had. Rab felt a sudden wave of irritation. "Don't worry, your secret's safe with me. You and Steve-o can go on your merry way to Hell any way you like. If either of them find out it'll be because they trip over you tonguing him on the stairs, not because I told them."

Danny finally spoke. "What do you want, a thank you?"

"Might be nice. Try one, see how I like it."

"Thank you." Danny said it utterly without inflection.

"Wouldn't win any prizes Danny."

"Wouldn't try Rab."

"Think I love you Danny?" Rab was watching him intently now.

"No."

"Think I ever have?"

"No."

Rab smiled. "That's what I thought."

He unbolted the door and walked into his room.

John found him still standing there ten minutes later. Still in the middle of the bathroom, looking at nothing.

"What the fuck are you doing?" he said from the open doorway. "Meditating?"

Danny nodded once, the tip of his tongue showing between his lips as if he were thinking. "Meaning of life," he said finally.

"And?" John asked.

"No surprises." He pushed his hands in his pockets. "It hasn't got one."

John came in and shut the door. He crossed to the sink and started brushing his teeth, looking at Danny occasionally in the mirror. He still hadn't moved. "Anything wrong?" he asked finally.

"Nothing," Danny said. "Other than the fact I came in my pants meditating."

John looked at him, frowning. "Say that again."

"I came in my pants. I dreamt..." He turned his head for the first time. "Do you dream when you're meditating?"

"You transcend."

"That explains it." He looked forward again. "While I was meditating I transcended. Three spurts and it was over."

"What were you meditating on, fat women?"

"I told you, the meaning of life."

John rinsed his mouth out and patted it dry on the towel, half-turning. "You been drinking?"

"Just meditating."

"Alone?"

"Just me and my god, our father..." he smiled for the first time, "who art in Heaven."

John leaned back against the sink and said, "Don't bet on it."

Danny nodded and said, "And he isn't 'ours', right?"

They looked at each other then John nodded at his lower half. "Want to show me?"

"What, the miracle that has come?"

"Show me," John said, and he wasn't smiling.

Danny unbuckled his trousers, turning to face him. He pulled them open. The stain showed on the fabric of his shorts, still wet, clear. "Can you see it from there? It's only a small miracle."

"I can see it," John said.

"Praise the Lord," Danny said, raising his eyes. He dropped them again and said, voice utterly different, like someone doing a lightning change of persona, "Want to see another?" And he slid his shorts and trousers down to his thighs, letting his cock drop out, hugely erect, pointing straight up at John. "Lazarus is risen," he said in that same biblical voice.

John felt a shiver of excitement, like cold air blown on the back of his neck. His mouth started to salivate, like a dog's at the sight of food. "Oh Daniel..." he said slowly, shaking his head, "what in God's name have you been doing?" He stared at it, peeled back, larger than life, no visible means of support.

"Having a one-man religious experience. No hands, just heavenly music."

"Who with?" John said, eyes still on Danny's cock.

"God."

914

"And who was God this evening? Exactly?"

"God is God is God John, you know that. He's down your way and up your hole. Tonight he was in my dick, as you can see. This, in religious parlance, is a right royal hard-on. It probably glows in the dark. My come probably imparts eternal life." He smiled a little smile. "Want to try some?" Voice lower still. "Want to take part in tonight's religious experience, tonight's out of the body extravaganza, float your balls on that heavenly cloud? Want to?"

John watched him warily, trying to hear what he was really saying. He couldn't get anything. It was like he was speaking Greek. "Danny, be kind to me," he said finally. "Tell me in English, without the voodoo."

"That you do so well?"

"That's my boy."

"I was thinking about the meaning of life John."

"I got that part."

"And I decided that all it was, all it meant, was come drying on your belly while you stood alone in a room. One half of a million people drying on fifty per cent cotton, fifty per cent polyester underwear. And that's the meaning, the one everybody searches for; one half of a person, like fifty per cent cotton looking for our fifty per cent polyesters on other people's underpants."

John looked at him for a long moment then said, "*What?*"

"Being alone John," Danny said quietly. "Being fucking alone." And he began to masturbate, slowly and dreamily, as if there wasn't another soul in the room.

Danny lay in the dark. He was exhausted but unable to sleep. These days he was always exhausted but unable to sleep. They could put that on his tombstone: 'In life he was exhausted but unable to sleep. Now he has Eternal Rest.' And worms in his eyes, and red hair falling out in handfuls, and his dick never gets hard, and if you try and squeeze it, it will come off in your hand, and not in any way you'd like.

A big bundle of laughs, Eternal Rest. Almost as good as being unable to sleep.

He threw himself onto his other side.

I shouldn't have done that in the bathroom. Him standing there watching, not knowing quite what to do, not knowing whether he even really wanted to watch. Hardly came a fucking drop. Bit of a give-away that Danny. Har-har.

Feel the way he touched you when you got into bed? Like you were fragile, or breakable, or dead fucking dangerous. You spooked him. Didn't appreciate your little hand-job. Didn't appreciate you standing there making love to yourself like you meant it. Nope, did not.

Danny sighed and turned on his back again.

John shifted heavily in the bed, ending up facing him. Danny adjusted himself again. *Every time John moves we all move.*

"What's wrong?"

Danny jumped. "Jesus. I thought you were asleep."

"I was, but some fucking prat keeps turning over in the bed."

"Sorry."

"And sighing. Let's not forget the sighing."

"Sorry twice."

"What's wrong?"

"Would you believe I can't sleep?"

"I know how you feel. What is it, a guilty conscience, or too much cheese at supper?"

"Guilt. I'm remembering the time I stole a three pack from Boots."

"Liar."

"What? That I stole it or that I'm guilty about it?"

"That you stole it. I remember you and condoms. It was almost a phobia."

"Yeah, I remember you and condoms too. Even then you were putting your fingers where they weren't supposed to go."

"Ha, bloody ha."

John gave a long sigh then reached an arm up over Danny's head in invitation. Danny lifted his head and went in against him, in against the solid warm wall of him. John lay his other hand on his stomach, flat, still. Immediately Danny began to feel sleepy. He yawned jaw-breakingly.

"Am I boring you?" John said, but Danny could hear the amusement in his voice.

"No, just tired suddenly. They should bottle you and sell it. Insomnia cure."

"I'm not sure if I'm being insulted here or not."

"You're not. You're good for me."

Danny hadn't known he was going to say that, didn't even know he thought it. It woke him up. He lay there, listening to John's heart slogging on, keeping all that solidity breathing, and waited for him to say something.

John lay there waiting to say something too, but nothing came to mind. Was Danny being sarcastic or what? He stroked his stomach. It was the best he could offer.

Danny felt it and felt something tighten in his chest. He slid his hand down John's body till he found his cock. It was thickly soft. He held it gently. It came to life in his hand. He squeezed it. John pulled him tighter, closer, face in his hair.

Danny went to sleep, sliding slowly down into it, gently squeezing him like a cat rhythmically kneading its paws.

For a long time after John lay listening to him breathing, thrusting gently in the slack warmth of his hand.

SEVENTY-FOUR

The next day was cold and bright and sharp. The storm had never happened. Collected, hung around, and went back to where it came from, hanging over the sea like an ominous warning, a pessimistic threat.

The sun was bright, white and aching. Their breath hung in clouds round their faces as they worked. Everybody was red and blue, no feeling in their fingers.

It seemed a strange, slow day, like being part of a dream. Someone else's.

Danny was working alone, taking the feeder round the fields for the wintering sheep. He had had the radio on but switched it off again. He couldn't stand one more jolly jingle, one more pithy platitude for keeping life's problems at bay.

As soon as he turned it off all he could hear was a cacophony of crows irritable with hunger and cold, seagulls crying behind them. They sounded harsher than usual.

"Bullshit," Danny muttered under his breath, but he wasn't sure what he was muttering it about.

He put the radio back on.

It was better than the crap in his head.

They had ended up fighting, which was inevitable. Rab hadn't missed Stephen's expression when John had packed them off together that morning, and after that it was a downhill slope. Ironically, it was probably made worse by the way they had both tried not to fight - hardly speaking to each other, never looking at each other, doing everything they could to stay well away from each other - creating an icy cold environment just right for a nice raging hot argument.

What was worse, Rab started it. He heard himself start it and went right on and started it anyway.

"Any chance of you doing what I ask or are you going to stand there mooning all day?"

"I wasn't mooning, I didn't hear you."

"What were you doing? Watching the action replay of Danny coming on you all over again?"

Stephen smiled a smile that managed to look narked and exultant at the same time. "Watch out Rab, your face is turning green."

And because it was true it made him twice as furious. "You know what he calls you, you little shit? Chicken. Know what that means? A cheap thrill for satiated homos. A piece of underage jail bait for sickos just like him. That's what it means."

"Shut up."

"That's what you are to him, another kinky thrill in a long line of some *very* kinky thrills. Want me to tell you a few things about what turns him on?"

Stephen made a violent gesture with his hand as if he were ushering Rab on ahead of him. "Go on then, why not? It's about burning a hole in your flickin' gut, so why don't you tell me? You fucking snitch."

It was the last insult that did it. Rab stood there looking at him, thinking, Oh so close. So close to pouring out everything and anything you could lay your hands on. All the rumours and half-truths. Anything. Just pile it all on.

Stephen was staring at him, the anger turning slowly into satisfaction.

Rab turned away so he couldn't see it any more, because if he did he wouldn't be able to keep his mouth shut. He was so fucking *irritating*, so fucking sure of himself.

The stupid little dick. I have to hit him. Just once. Just one fucking time God. Forgive me.

Rab took the two steps he needed and punched him. He did it with all the force he had. He hadn't *meant* to, but he had wanted to.

Stephen was crumpled up against the wall. All Rab's satisfaction disappeared. He stood watching him, wanting to apologise, even while the other half of him said, I'd rather stick pins in my eyes than apologise to that.

Stephen slid down the wall into a sitting position, head lying on the arms loosely linked over his knees. He looked like someone trying not to faint. He looked so helpless, so small, so young, that Rab hated him worse than ever.

Rab wanted to walk out on him, stalk off. After all, he wasn't going to say anything, do anything. What the fuck was he standing here *for*? To gloat? Then he knew what it was he wanted.

He'd been aching to say this for a long time, and when he said it, it came out in that strange choked voice that always marks a feeling repressed too long, as if the speaker's throat aches, as if the words are coming out as helplessly as irrepressible tears, and with as much relief. "Know what Danny's *really* doing to you?"

There was a bubble of silence. A cow coughed, shifted, something dripped, then Rab answered himself. "He's raping your head."

Stephen didn't lift his head but Rab saw him raise it a tiny fraction to let the sound in.

"He's been raping your head since day one but you've been too fucking stupid, too fucking *besotted*, to see it."

Rab looked at his bent head, trying to will him to look at him. "He hates you. We *all* hate you, because you're the one dirty blot on our landscape, the one thing Danny might cross us over. You're walking around with four sticks of dynamite up your arse and you don't even know it. Think he's fucking you for fun? Well here's a new idea, people don't always fuck for fun. The only people those two fuck for fun are each other. The rest of us are just foreplay. You're not even that. You're Spanish fly, bedroom chat."

Rab stood breathing fast and shallow, feeling the exhilaration of letting it go, letting all the hate out, watching him sit there and take it, bowed down by the weight of it. He relished the last sweet drop of it in his mouth. It made him think of peppermint liqueur; green, cold, sweet. He felt it singing through his veins, that icy alcohol of venom, so sweet it made your teeth itch.

Stephen looked up at him and Rab could see the tears spilling down his face. He looked beautiful, first time ever, and he thought, That's how Danny got it then. Someone fucked with his head just like I'm fucking with his now. Beauty with cruelty.

Rab drew saliva into his mouth and spat at him.

It landed on the back of Stephen's hand and slid down it slowly like come.

Rab turned on his heel and left.

Danny tried to eat slowly after Stephen left the kitchen that night but as soon as he was finished he got up and followed him, feeling John's eyes on him every inch of the way.

He went to Stephen's room. The door was locked. Danny knocked. Stephen let him in eventually, taking an age to do it.

Danny said, "What's wrong?" searching his face.

When Stephen saw his expression he pushed past Danny and ran for the bathroom. He threw up, then threw up some more.

Delayed reaction. Better late than never. Rab punches me in the stomach and I

throw up three hours later.

Stephen heard the bathroom door close. The bolt shot home.

He turned the taps on, threw water in his face. His legs were trembling so violently he could hardly stand. He sat on the toilet. Sat was too generous a description. He dropped down on the toilet, holding his head as if it weighed too much.

Danny was sitting opposite him on the edge of the bath. "Can I smoke?" he asked.

Stephen nodded. He heard the click of the lighter, the faint rustlings of him reclosing the cigarette packet. After a moment or two he smelt it, nipping and dry in his head. He took a deep breath. When he looked up Danny smiled and said, "What you doing, passive smoking?"

Stephen found himself smiling back, even if it was only a ghost. He felt a sudden surge of something warm and reassuring. *If he's raping my head Rab it's with a fucking good anaesthetic, because I don't feel any pain.*

"Good," Danny said, smiling some more.

"What?" Stephen asked, surprised.

"You're looking better." Danny smiled.

Stephen laughed and rubbed his face. "I thought you'd gone psychic on me for a minute."

"Can you tell me now?" Danny asked.

Stephen got up and put the lid down and sat down again. "I don't know what to tell you," he said honestly.

"Okay, who then?"

"It was Rab."

Stephen watched Danny stare at the floor for a while then he lifted his eyes, fixing Stephen with an up-and-under look, penetrating. "Throwing his weight around, threatening you, what?"

"He hit me," Stephen said and saw something tight in the way Danny rubbed his jaw. He said quickly, "It wasn't important. I mean, we were arguing. It wasn't that that..." he hesitated then finished, "upset me." He smiled, a small lopsided thing. "It fucking hurt though." He licked his lip, studied the bathroom tiles again. "It was after. He started in on me, telling me how much you all hated me."

"Fucking dickhead," Danny interjected.

Stephen looked up. He rubbed his face again. He couldn't tell Danny what he'd actually said. He wasn't even sure why. Maybe in a while, but right now he couldn't bring himself to repeat it. Danny was watching him. Stephen wouldn't look up and meet his eyes. Danny said, "It must have been bad."

"It was. I don't know why."

There was a silence. A couple of times Danny took drags at the cigarette, letting the smoke roll slowly out of him, as if he were waiting. It made Stephen tense. He knew why as soon as Danny spoke.

"I think you're lying to me."

It dropped into the room like a stone, like when the husband comes through the door and catches them in bed, like when they say, We know you killed him. Stephen shook his head but it was so lame it looked like an admission of guilt.

"I think he said something really dirty and I want to know what it was."

"I can't," Stephen whispered.

"Why not?" Danny asked and Stephen could feel his eyes boring into the top of his head.

"It makes me feel mucky. I don't want to, not yet. Let's leave it Danny. I will tell you, but not yet, eh?"

There was a long silence. He could feel Danny turning it over. He didn't want to look up in case Danny fixed him there, insisted with his eyes, but it went on so long

he did look up and what he saw was Danny burning holes in the face cloth with his cigarette, slowly and purposefully, like he was doing poker work, designing Christmas gifts at home.

"What the hell are you doing?" he asked.

Danny's hand stopped moving then he stubbed the cigarette out in the soap dish, bending back over the bath to do it. When he straightened up again he took the facecloth in one hand and threw it into the wastepaper bin, then he turned to Stephen and smiled, warm, deep, wild inside, and said, "Let's fuck."

Stephen stared at him, wide-eyed.

"Come on," Danny said. "Come here."

Stephen got up slowly, Danny watching him as he walked towards him.

"Take your stuff off. Just the bottom half."

Stephen did what he said, toeing his trainers off without untying them, pulling his jeans and shorts off in one strip. He left his socks on, his shirt tail hanging down. He looked about fourteen.

Danny lifted the front of his shirt and rubbed his stomach. His hand felt rough and warm.

Stephen came up, half embarrassed seeing it stand to attention so close to Danny's face. Danny pulled him closer between his legs then he bent over and picked up a bar of soap and held it under the hot tap. He looked back over his shoulder at Stephen.

"What are you doing?" Stephen asked.

Danny just winked at him. After a minute he straightened up again and turned the bar between his hands, lathering it, then he reached round and pulled Stephen close, close enough that Stephen's cock was resting against Danny's chest. He pushed his hot soapy hands between the cheeks of Stephen's arse. Stephen's mouth fell open. He put his hands on Danny's shoulders. Danny worked one finger inside him, began easing it in and out. Stephen let him, no resistance at all.

"Nice?" Danny asked.

The soap stung but he still said, "Yes." He put his hands inside the neck of Danny's sweater, feeling the spread of his shoulders, the warmth of his skin.

"Back off a minute," Danny said, pushing him back. He let Stephen go and unzipped his own jeans. He undid the buckle then slid the whole lot down to his thighs. His cock was standing straight up. Stephen looked at it with the same awe it always inspired.

"Sit astride me," Danny said. "Come on, over my lap. Going to see Santa like it never was before."

Stephen opened his legs and walked over him, knees on either side, up hard against the bath. Danny had to move forward a little to let him on. Danny held it up in the air, right up, like a pole, and said, "Now sit on it... slowly."

Stephen did it, bending his knees, tongue trapped between his teeth. They guided it up between them. Stephen only moaned once, Danny not at all. They smiled at each other, trying to outdo each other's cool. The most laid-back fucker of them all award.

Stephen slid down a little more. "It's..." He tried to look for the word. "It feels *more* like this."

"More?" There was a slight grunt in it. Stephen smiled into his eyes to show he hadn't missed it.

"Mm." He slid down a little further. "Wider feeling than last time."

"Must be the depth of my angle."

"You sarky bastard," Stephen said, letting another small noise escape as Danny did a quick unexpected thrust upwards.

"Jesus, I think my balls are going up."

"You're splitting me."

"Another inch."

Stephen nodded and let him pull him down the last inch in a jerk. He felt it push hard against the back of his intestine, like a dull stretching behind his navel. It made his cock jerk violently. Danny laughed, watching it.

Stephen took two long slow breaths then another one and said, "Now what?"

Danny leaned back carefully, placing one arm behind him on the rim of the bath, then the other like he was making a bridge. It made his cock poke up further, let Stephen come down closer. "Shit Danny," he said, "that hurts."

"Well, ease off then."

Stephen did, easing himself up a little then, slowly at first, sliding himself back down on Danny's shaft like obscene knee bends. He could feel the slight vibration of Danny's body from the awkward position he was in, could see the muscles straining in his arms, across his stomach. It made him look more beautiful than ever, tortured, exquisite. Stephen took a hold of his own cock and began pulling it in time to his bobbing motion on Danny's body.

Danny watched Stephen bite his lip then toss the thick hair out his eyes. "Going to pip you at the post Steve-o." And he felt the trembling in his arms change, felt his cock take over, start thrusting up to meet him of its own volition.

"You bastard," Stephen gasped. "Don't you dare. I'm not ready."

"Too late," Danny said, and his arms strained up taut as bows as he pushed himself up. "Oh fuck... oh fucking..." But he didn't get any more words out, his whole body dissolving with it, locked in that tight smooth flesh.

Stephen only had to see his face, see his arms corded with the strain of it, and it started to pump out of him, arcing up as he held it peeled tight down, not moving it, just shafting himself on Danny's cock, letting Danny bring himself off in him. He watched it shoot up and land on Danny, run down his own hand, make a glorious, thick mess. He laughed with sheer exhilaration as Danny swung upright and grabbed him hard round the waist, grinning and pushing his face into his chest. He spoke.

But what he said was lost forever.

He remained sitting on Danny's lap, his cock still hard inside him. Danny kissed the underside of his jaw. "Good?" He slid his hands down over Stephen's back.

"Mm."

"Don't 'Mm' me, you little cunt. Tell me how good it was." He squeezed Stephen's buttocks, pulling them open a little, pushing up a little.

"Fucking amazing. Will that do you?"

"No, I want more."

Stephen rubbed his face in his hair. "What am I supposed to tell you?"

"How beautiful I am."

"You're beautiful, gorgeous, fantastic. You know it."

"That's more like it."

"Rab's right, you are a conceited shit, even if you do have a big dick."

Danny laughed against his chest, a low warm vibration, then thrust into him again. "That's not hurting, is it?"

"Uh-uh," Stephen said. His own cock was barely at half-mast. Danny's ability to stay up always made him envious. He needed at least five or ten minutes to get stiff again. Sometimes a lot longer. If he'd come properly, that is. But then, he always did come properly with Danny, whether he wanted to or not.

"How d'you do that?" he asked.

"What?" Danny was fingering between his cheeks, feeling where he was up inside

him, wishing there was a mirror so he could see it.

"Stay up like that."

"No idea." He went on tracing the stretched perimeter of Stephen's sphincter.

"That's turning me on."

"Good."

"You mean you don't know how you do it?"

"That's right. Sometimes they go, sometimes they stay. Nothing to do with me."

"You dirty fucker. I bet you were born with a hard-on."

"So Ian says."

"How would he know?"

Danny was pulling his cheeks apart, trying to thrust up further, gently but insistently. "Used to play with it in my pram." He felt Stephen tense under his hands, even felt the clench on his cock. "Joke Steve-o, relax."

"You had me going there."

"You'll have me coming in a minute."

"You know, if someone wants to take a leak we're going to have problems."

"No, *they* are. We're inside."

Stephen laughed. "Nothing scares you, does it?"

"Wrong. *Everything* scares me. This is just a front."

"Danny, what the fuck are you doing?"

Danny was holding him open with both hands, pushing faster.

"Bringing myself off up your arse. What does it feel like?"

Stephen bent his head and kissed Danny's mouth. "It feels like fuck," he said quietly, and they kissed again.

Danny broke it, saying, "Bit of alright you are, Stephen my lad. Could ream you all night."

Danny was hardly moving, teasing them both. He was handling Stephen's cock, playing with it idly. Somehow that was worse. Stephen could feel blood pounding in his ears. He was suddenly aware of how ragged his breathing was.

Danny pulled Stephen's bum apart and jolted twice to please himself.

Stephen wriggled, trying to push it up further. Danny pulled on him earnestly. Stephen held his shoulders tightly, fingers digging into his back, then he whispered into Danny's ear, "Tell me something secret."

Danny was close, very close. "What kind of secret?" He could feel his heart going too fast.

"I just want to hear something secret, something you wouldn't tell anyone else."

Danny slowed a little. "That's going to bring you off?"

Stephen nodded, a reluctant admission.

Danny pulled him tighter, skimmed his cock soft and fast, then said, "Okay, I'm going to tell you something John likes to do."

There was no answer, but he could feel the tension in Stephen's body, feel the overfull rigidity of his cock. He went on, voice low, "Some nights he'll be on his own and feeling sorry for himself, so he starts drowning his sorrows in the old man's whisky supply. Like a lot of drunks he wants you to get drunk too - misery loves company - but instead of making me drink it he lies flat on his back and pours it over his prick, then makes me lick it off. It burns. That's what a lot of these dick creams are, alcohol. It makes your prick burn and swell, and the stiffer it gets the more it burns him. He really enjoys it, bathing himself in all that pain, watching me get drunk on sucking it off. It's like I'm getting drunk on him. But that isn't the real secret. Know what the real secret is?"

"No," Stephen said and Danny could feel his nails digging into his back. Danny wasn't even certain that it was an answer.

"I enjoy it, that's the secret. I *am* drunk on him. That's the real secret."

Stephen gave a panicked grunt and suddenly started to grind himself down on Danny's cock. Little wet spits of fluid spattered Danny's stomach. Stephen pressed his whole body back onto him, legs splayed, as if Danny's cock couldn't be far enough up to please him. Somehow more came out of him. He panted, shivered.

Danny bore it as long as he could, until Stephen finally dropped against him, a rag doll, wasted by excess.

It was then Danny softly, secretly, let his semen twitch out into Stephen's body.

Like parasites sneaking home.

They got into the shower together, washing each other with too much soap, both ending up with soft erections that didn't really have the energy to do anything, but that felt too restless to be left alone.

Danny was drying Stephen down, whispering in his ear, making him laugh, when John banged on the door. Stephen clutched at him like a stage heroine.

"Danny?" He already sounded ratty.

"What is it?"

"Is Stephen in there with you?"

Danny looked down at him and suddenly grinned. "Don't be fucking stupid."

Stephen tried to smile back but didn't quite make it.

The door handle turned. "Let me in."

"I'm having a shit."

"With the shower on?"

"I'm having a shit, okay? Fuck off." Danny reached in and turned the shower off.

There was a silence. Danny cupped Stephen's balls in one hand and pushed his tongue into his mouth.

"Danny?" John was still there.

Danny sucked on Stephen's tongue hungrily. Stephen stood there tingling from head to foot with dread and excitement.

John's voice was suddenly quieter. "If he's in there with you..."

Danny let go Stephen's mouth, but not his balls. "If he's in here he's a pervert. I don't like people watching me shit, and I don't like talking to people while I'm doing it either. You're constipating me, go away."

He took Stephen's hand and pressed it round his cock. Stephen had immediately gone flaccid but Danny was stiffening in odd little surges. He whispered in Stephen's ear, "Jerk me off, " then stuck his tongue in his ear, making him flinch. Stephen could feel how hot his skin was against his own. It seemed unnatural, feverish.

"You take your time Danny. I'll wait."

Stephen felt Danny's cock jerk again and knew something wasn't right. It wasn't a coincidence, Danny definitely seemed to be getting a kick out of him being there, outside, while they were in here, doing this. He hoped it wasn't anything more, but a little hard knot was forming in his stomach, holding his cock in a cold grip. It felt almost shrivelled.

Danny whispered again, "Faster."

Stephen tightened his grip, felt Danny tremble.

"You still there John?" Danny called out softly.

"I'm here." John's voice was soft too.

"Maybe I could get used to this."

"Don't plan your day around it. Hurry up."

Danny held Stephen's arse in both hands, kneading it so hard it hurt. He was looking down between their bodies, watching Stephen masturbate him. He was jutting

his cock out, hips tilted into his. Stephen wondered how the hell he *got* so big. Didn't he ever get tired? Didn't *it?*

"John?"

"What?"

"Maybe I lied to you." Stephen stopped dead. Danny gripped his hand and forced it up and down, telling him without words, Don't stop. "Maybe I'm really jerking off in here."

There was a pause. Danny kissed Stephen's face repeatedly, hot and fast, then John said, "I wouldn't have said it was your style."

"Maybe it is. Want to hear me come?"

"I already had this last night Danny. I'm not sure I want a repeat performance."

Stephen didn't want to hear this, any of it, but Danny was gripping his hand, not letting him stop. He whispered, "Do it *hard*. Don't worry about it. Hard." And he crushed Stephen's hand, making his grip sadistically tight. If anyone had done that to him he'd have thumped them. After he'd stopped howling, that is.

Danny's eyes slid shut and he said almost in a whisper, "Too bad. I'm going to do it anyway, so if you don't want to hear it fuck off."

There was a pause then, "I told you, I'm staying."

"Dirty bastard." It was definitely a whisper this time. Danny had his hands tight in Stephen's hair now. Stephen could feel how close he was, how taut and ready.

"Let me in."

"No."

"I've changed my mind."

"I'll bet."

"Let me do it."

"I'm doing very nicely myself." And he moaned a little, a small noise. Stephen doubted if John could have heard it, but he did.

"You really are doing it, aren't you?"

A grunt from Danny answered him.

"Is this going to be a new hobby?"

"Maybe."

"What's wrong? Don't I satisfy you or something?"

"I need more John. Lots more." He suddenly kissed Stephen's mouth, wet and hungrily. He felt like a rabidly randy dog, shivering with need. Stephen felt it go through his body.

Danny didn't let go. He kept kissing him, as if he was trying to get up there, push himself over.

John said, "Danny?" But Danny didn't answer. He caught at Stephen's hand, making him jerk it up and down fiercely. Stephen did what he wanted, gripping him roughly, like it was made of rubber or something. He felt Danny tremble, then buckle, then his mouth broke away from his. He threw his head back and stuck his cock out into Stephen's hand. What little there was came out into it, warm and almost clear, but Danny came like it was killing him, nothing but noise, lots of big moany noise, like he was in a porn movie, getting bigger and bigger till he cried out.

It was then he opened his eyes and looked at Stephen.

And then he simply said, "Fuck..." and dropped his head on Stephen's shoulder.

"What are we going to do?" Stephen whispered. "Now you'll have to let him in."

"So I'll let him in."

Stephen stared at him, horrified.

"Best way out is through." Danny didn't even seem perturbed.

"*Danny...*" John's voice was loud, angry.

"What now?" Danny said, equally angrily. They were trying to pull their clothes on. Danny had shoved some toilet paper at him and flushed the toilet while he pulled his suddenly very flaccid penis back into shape. Now the noise of the cistern refilling was helping to cover their hurried dressing.

"I'm not moving till you open this door."

"Have a nice time."

"*Danny...*"

"*What!?*" Danny yelled suddenly, and Stephen saw a flash of real anger in it. No fear, none at all. That scared him most of all. He ought to have been scared, scared was right, anything else was fucking weird.

"Let me *in!*" John was openly yelling now. The door handle rattled.

Danny didn't even pause to make sure Stephen was dressed. He marched across the room, yanked back the bolt and flung the door open. John got in before he got out. Stephen stood there like a refugee, trying to look inconspicuous.

Everything was *wrong*. The mirrors were steamed, there were wet towels, two of everything. Even their hair was wet. He wasn't going to be able to claim it had been some kind of joke because everything was *wrong*, really fucked up and *wrong*.

"Jesus Christ..." John said, taking it all in. His eyes went round the room like he was witnessing some gross act of vandalism. He said it again, slower, harder. "Jesus *Christ*."

His eyes came to rest on Stephen, saw the damp hair, the red face, the bare feet, socks in one hand, and said, "Get out."

Stephen stood there, transfixed by fear.

"I said, get *out*."

Stephen looked at Danny desperately, not wanting to leave him. Danny, incredibly, smiled, even if it was taut and strange-looking. "Go on," he encouraged.

Stephen went, skirting past John, half-expecting him to lash out at him.

The door slammed shut.

And the bolt slid home.

"Right."

The first slap brought tears to Danny's eyes. The second split open the old cut in his mouth. Danny thought he'd seen the last of that. The blow irritated him. He looked at John blackly.

Not smart.

John punched him. Two or three times. When he felt Danny was more pliable he sat him, wheezing like an old man, on the lid of the toilet then he pulled his head back by the hair.

A thin line of blood trickled from the corner of Danny's mouth. It was bleeding heavier than usual. Danny kept his eyes down. They looked closed from where John was standing, although he knew they weren't.

"How long?"

He tugged his head back further when Danny didn't answer him.

"This is the first time."

John jerked his head again. "Unlikely."

Danny winced but said nothing.

John grabbed his throat and banged him back against the toilet cistern.

Danny felt the pain knife under his ribs, half winding him. "*Christ*."

"That's twice you've lied to me. First Conley, now this. Saying one thing to my face, doing something different behind my back. You actually stood in here and did it in front

of him, didn't you? And what the fuck went on in the shower?" He pushed him again.

Danny answered quickly, before he could do it a third time. "Nothing. A bit of feeling. We were too tired."

"From what?"

"Just tired. I swear it."

John let him go suddenly, wiped his hands on his trouser legs as if he was dirty. "He's going tomorrow."

Danny looked at him, not understanding what he was saying. John could see the blankness and twisted the knife. "Out Danny. The sack. I'm not having the thieving little dick here a day longer."

He could see it begin to penetrate, watched him blink once, then again. He sat up, then he said, "No."

John said, "Yes."

Danny stood up and leaned on the sink, head hanging down, then he straightened up and suddenly his hand came up, hurling the glass tooth mug at John's head.

He ducked instinctively.

It flew past him and shattered into a million pieces against the bathroom wall. It looked like an explosion of light. The tiny fragments showered over the bath making an odd tinkling noise. The violence with which it had been thrown must have been phenomenal. John's mouth was hanging open. If it had hit him, square in the face, where Danny had aimed it...

"Christ..." It was all he could get out.

But Danny was growling, a low noise of rage. He shook his head, a small violent negation. "He stays."

"Over my fucking dead body."

And he saw Danny hearing that and accepting it. *Okay, it's a deal. Over your dead body.*

And John knew he'd finally lost him.

And nothing would ever be the same again.

John was afraid to go to bed.

Danny was in there and he couldn't face him. He was utterly lost, no idea where to turn. The pain raged through him. He wanted to maim something. He wanted to break Stephen's door down and disembowel him.

He went to Rab.

He knocked on the door. Rab was up and dressed. He'd heard them fighting - they all had - and they were all sitting tight, waiting.

Rab let him in although the door was open. He said, "What's up?" because John seemed to be stuck. He kept opening his mouth and closing it again.

"It's Danny," he said.

Rab looked at him then sat down beside him on the bed and took out his tobacco tin and fished out a cigarette. He practically had to force it between John's lips and light it. "Now inhale... that's it... right, keep doing it."

John had a coughing fit then wiped his eyes. After that he seemed calmer. "It's Stephen."

"Make up your mind."

"They've been doing it. I mean really fucking *doing* it, not just some quick adolescent wank." His eyes flicked up. He saw Rab's expression and felt all the anger drain out of him. "You knew," he said tonelessly.

"Only yesterday. By accident. I fell over them on the stairs."

"*What?*"

926

"On the stairs, I kid you not, enjoying each other like you've never seen before."

John dropped his head in his hands. "I told him the boy was going tomorrow." He looked up, dragging his hands through his hair. "He went apeshit." He stared ahead blankly then said, "He's going to fucking *drop* me, for that little runt, still hanging on his mother's tit. Christ I'm scared to go into the same room as him. You've never seen anger like it."

Rab looked at him for a moment then said, "What are you going to do?"

"I don't know." He looked up at Rab, almost as if he was asking him.

Yes you do, Rab thought. Throw him out the fucking house, like you should have done years ago. He said, "There's only two things you can do, either lose the boy or chain Danny to the bed. What do you *want* to do?"

"I want to kill him, that's what I *want* to do."

"Well there's always that option."

John looked up at him quickly.

"He'll get bored," Rab said placatingly. "Anyway..." he smiled slowly, "there's always me."

Danny was lying awake in the dark. John knew he was awake. He could feel it. He asked him anyway, just to say something, hear his voice. "You awake Danny?"

Predictably Danny didn't answer him.

"I'm going to put this light on," John said. He did.

He could see only the back of Danny's head. He was humped in a foetal position on his side of the bed.

John took his clothes off and got in. He was bitterly cold. When he touched Danny's shoulder he flinched away from him.

"I'm sorry," John said, and he could have been apologising for anything from cold hands to being alive. "I'm sorry I said what I did. He can stay. Do what you want with him."

He knew he needed to say more, undo the damage, but he couldn't bring himself to do it. He'd given him all he could. He couldn't do anything else to save him.

He lay on his back, rolled onto it as if he were exhausted. He wanted to claw his own eyes out. He wanted to kick Danny out the bed.

He felt Danny turn beside him, onto his stomach first, then round full circle to face him. John turned his head. Danny was looking at him, clear-eyed, very green. John couldn't meet his gaze. He shut his eyes, turning his face away again.

Danny said, "Why?"

"Why what?" John said, but he could feel a dull betraying heat on his skin.

"Why the sudden change of heart?"

"I don't want you to leave."

"You wouldn't let me anyway."

John opened his eyes and looked at him. "What makes you think I'd be able to stop you?"

"You're too scared Rab would follow me. That's why you went crying to his room, wasn't it?"

"Alright. Then maybe I don't want you to knife me in my sleep one night."

Danny looked at him. "Think I'd do that?"

John looked right back at him. "Yes, I think you might."

Danny nodded slightly and his face became veiled, inward-looking. After a while he said, "So you're offering me Stephen in exchange for your life?"

"I wouldn't have put it like that but I suppose that's about it."

"I've got a better idea. Supposing I move out of here, this room, *your* room. That

should make you feel safer."

John felt as if he'd punched him. "Safer? That's your idea of *safer?*"

"Yes."

"You fucking little liar." John covered his face with his hands then took them away again. "I don't believe this. Just because I lost my temper."

"I'm sick of the way you change with the wind John. Maybe this will help you make up your mind."

"No." John put his hands above his head, then thumped the pillow with his fists. "*No!*"

Danny sat up. He turned and looked down at him. "You say you love me, well show me." Danny looked at him for a long moment then said, "Let me go."

John's face was ashen. "I can't... never able to touch you."

Danny laughed sourly. "That's what it's all about, isn't it? You can touch me any time you damn well like. What's ever stopped you before?"

"You know fucking well what I mean," John snapped.

"There's always Rab."

"*Fuck* Rab."

"Keep it down," Danny warned.

"Don't fucking tell me to keep it down. You're telling me it's over and I'm supposed to say, Yes Danny, of course Danny, whatever you like Danny. Well go fucking screw yourself Danny. No." He pulled the arm Danny was leaning on from under him, pulling Danny down on top of him. He crushed him hard to him, not knowing whether he was trying to hurt him or hold him. Danny lay tightly unresponsive against him.

"Danny stop this, please."

"Let me go."

John let him go, just dropped his arms.

Danny flopped back off him.

They were both breathing hard.

"Danny," John's voice was quiet, "tell me one thing, just one thing, truthfully. Have you ever actually felt anything for me?"

"Yes," Danny said, equally quietly.

"But not now? You don't feel it now?" John asked, and the question hung there, like a heavy muffling cushion over their breathing.

"No," Danny said finally. Oh and you could hear hearts breaking just as you sat there.

"Oh Jesus," John whispered. "Then why did you let me *do* it? Oh Jesus Christ..." And he rolled onto his stomach

Danny could feel his pain as if it were his own, wanted to touch him, console him and knew he couldn't, knew he daren't.

After a while he realised John was crying. He had pulled himself over to the far side of the bed and lay there like a wounded animal, face buried in the pillow.

Danny didn't remember falling asleep but when he woke in the morning the bedside lamp was still on and John was nowhere to be seen.

SEVENTY-FIVE

John was going out as Danny and Rab came down together, having met in the upstairs hall. Rab had looked at him. Danny had nodded in greeting, but that was all. They had entered the kitchen in silence.

John got up and put on his jacket as they came in. He gave them their day's work without looking at them then he went out.

Ian came in.

Danny was sitting looking at the table top. Ian thought he looked shitty. Actually he looked ill. For the first time ever something seemed to have marred that flawless beauty, taken the colour and life out of him.

Stephen came in last. Danny looked up at him and gave him a quick smile.

Rab went out.

Ian knew they wanted rid of him. You could see it in the way they sat; two people craving to talk to each other over the obstacle of the unwanted third. He sat tight. Let Danny shift him if he wanted his bum-boy so bad.

Danny looked along at him suddenly, almost as if he'd been listening to him thinking. Perhaps, Ian thought, they're not the only ones giving things away with their body-language. He leaned back in his chair. Stephen assiduously and meticulously buttered a slice of cold toast. Ian wondered what he was going to do with it. He certainly had no intentions of eating it.

Ian smiled at Danny. Danny didn't smile back. Instead he said with a calmness Ian admired, "Piss off Ian."

Ian looked at the table, still smiling. He could see Stephen blushing out the corner of his eye. He looked up again. "Want to talk to sweetie-pie?"

"Something like that." Still that beautiful, seamless, enviable calm.

Stephen wasn't calm. Stephen was angrier than a bee in a bottle.

"What does he fuck like Danny? Tight?"

"Why don't you ask him? He's sitting right there."

Ian didn't even look at him. He could feel Stephen's fury come rolling down the table at him. Danny hadn't even clenched his hand. *I'm going to get to you Danny. Somehow I'll get to you. Just got to hit the right nerve.* "You and John all over again, eh?"

Danny's eyes came up off the table, all the green gone. *Now we're talking Danny-boy.* He said nothing.

Stephen looked at Danny for the first time since he'd sat down. *What?* was plain on his face.

"You told Steve-o here about you and John?"

Ian turned his face to Stephen without taking his eyes from Danny. "Danny had a very close relationship with John when he was young."

"Drop it," Danny said and his voice was threatening.

Ian stood up. "Remind me to tell you sometime Steve-o. Help you to understand the man you love."

"Fuck off," Stephen said, banging his knife down.

"Tsk tsk," Ian said, shaking his head.

He was still smiling when he went out the door.

Stephen jammed the two bits of toast together without looking at them. "What the

fuck was all that about?" He ripped the elastic toast in half and threw it to the dog.

"Forget it."

"How old were you when you started with John?"

And now Danny was looking at him with the same black eyes that had looked at Ian. "I said forget it, alright?"

They stared at each other for a moment then Stephen looked away. "Alright, if you say so," and his voice was petulant.

Danny caught his lower lip between his teeth, twice, as if it was itchy, then he said in a low voice, "Come here."

Stephen looked up at him then got up. He went round the table.

Danny took one of his thighs between both hands, sliding them up slowly to the recess of his crotch. He watched Stephen's face. "I want to fuck you," he said.

Stephen swallowed a sudden mouthful of saliva, but said nothing.

"Want to?" Danny asked.

"We haven't got time."

"My mouth then."

"Here?" Stephen said, already feeling the erection growing.

"Mm," Danny said, hands squeezing Stephen's thigh, hard under his balls, eyes fast on his face.

Stephen said, "What if one of them comes back?"

"Then we'll get caught." Danny waited.

Stephen nodded, reaching out but not quite touching him, not quite making it, letting his hand drop.

"Say yes," Danny said, making no move towards him.

"Yes," Stephen said, licking his upper lip.

Danny pulled him along the table edge a little till he was between his knees then he pulled his chair in, trapping him there. He sat back, hands hanging limp by his side. "Take it out. You can hold it." He kept his eyes on Stephen's.

Stephen felt heat in his face as he unzipped himself and took his erection out.

Danny smiled, so slowly. "Hold it for me," he said.

Stephen tilted it down a little for him. He was really up too hard for this position.

Danny sat forwards in his seat and slid his mouth, wet and strangely cool, over Stephen's cock.

Stephen shivered, watching the back door over Danny's head. "Your mouth feels weird," he whispered. He didn't know why he was whispering.

Danny sank him deep in reply.

Stephen touched Danny's head with his free hand. The feel of his hair, tangled, still vaguely sleep-warm, was mesmerising. Stephen whispered his name, wishing he would take hold of his prick so he could use both hands in his hair, yet at the same time excited by his own frustration. He pushed his backside against the heavy table, thrusting his pelvis up more, spreading his legs. Danny was holding the backs of them, pulling him towards his mouth.

Stephen watched the door feverishly, desperate to come before it opened, wanting it to be finished and wanting it not to stop. He knew the anxiety was slowing him down, keeping him an edge away from orgasm. He felt frantic.

Danny just kept mouthing his glans. Stephen watched his lips, widely stretched, sliding backwards and forwards over the head of his penis and thought, God, he's sucking my prick. Daniel Jackson Moore is sucking my prick.

"Suck my prick," he said, knowing it was going to happen, and he pulled Danny's head onto himself, feeling it finally come, watching himself spill into Danny's mouth, seeing a little creamy bubble of it escape the corner of his lips like there was too much to get in, and it was better - it was *always* better - than the time before, and he heard

the door open just as he'd known he would, and saw Rab stand there a moment then come in, closing the door quietly, watching him helplessly coming in Danny's mouth, right in the middle of the kitchen.

"Oh shit." Stephen didn't even know he'd said it until Danny looked up quickly, wiping his mouth and turning in his chair all in the same movement.

Stephen pushed himself back inside his clothes, feeling humiliated. Danny got up, stood in front of him, almost like a shield. Stephen, feeling a coward to the last inch, let him. He couldn't face Rab, the look on his face, so he let him.

Rab looked Danny up and down.

Danny faced him out, waited for him to say something.

It wasn't necessary. Rab probably couldn't have stopped himself supposing he'd wanted to.

"You've really got it bad, haven't you? Can't keep your fucking hands off him."

Danny said nothing, just kept watching him. Rab said, "We're waiting for you. Or do you want him to return the favour before we go?" Then he looked past him as if he were talking to someone in hiding. "Has he told you the good news yet Stephen?"

Danny watched him, expression unwavering. Rab waited till Stephen stepped out from behind him. Danny knew he had by the change of focus in Rab's eyes.

"Danny-boy is escaping big brother's clutches, finally graduating to a room of his own, so you two love-bunnies can get together as much as you like. Think of all the dick you can eat then."

Danny spoke suddenly, sharply. His voice was hard. "Can it."

Rab's eyes came back to him and he looked suddenly furious. "You dirty bastard, sucking him off in the fucking kitchen. It's not even *light* yet. What if he'd come back in? You don't care what you do to him, do you?"

Danny went tearing across the room at him. They started flying into each other, punching what they could reach. Stephen stood there watching them thud into each other viciously as if they wanted to kill each other. He was blinded by panic, visions of Danny landing on the stone floor, smashing his head in. They were in front of the door. He couldn't get out to get anyone.

He ran across the room and tried to get near enough to pull them apart. He caught at Rab's arm and was elbowed in the face. He recoiled, the yells he was making momentarily stilled.

He came back, yelling even louder, although afterwards he would swear he never said a word.

The back door opened with only a few inches give, all that was possible behind their thrashing bodies. It bumped against them again, this time opening about six inches. Suddenly it flung open violently, sending their bodies ricocheting off it as John put his shoulder to it. He bellowed, "What the *fuck* is this?!"

But they went on fighting, bumping off the kitchen cupboards, rolling round the room. John got in between them, trying to drag them apart and when that didn't work, pulling Rab's hair and shoving Danny hard in the face to separate them.

They came apart like glue unsticking, with a rip and an immediate distance. John turned on Stephen. "Shut the fuck up!"

Stephen was immediately silenced.

"Have you two gone off your fucking heads?"

Danny's mouth was bleeding, Rab's nose. Rab was going to have a black eye as well by the looks of it. They were both breathing like traction engines. Danny was braced half-upright against his knees. Rab stood holding one side as if he had a stitch. Stephen saw Danny wince as he straightened up.

"Well?" John's voice was belligerent.

He looked at Danny, who looked through him. When he looked at Rab in turn he just stared at a point above his head.

John turned to Stephen. "Well, what about you? Cat got yours too?"

"Leave him alone." Danny's voice sounded too breathy still.

John gave Stephen a look that said, This is your fault, isn't it? then turned back to Danny. "Was I talking to you?"

Danny didn't say anything. John grabbed him with a sudden roar. "*Was* I?!"

"No," Danny said, pulling his head away from him.

John let him go, but kept a palm flat on his chest, holding him where he was. "Right, get out, all of you."

He turned to Stephen. "You... move it."

Stephen moved it. Rab came after him, slower.

Ian watched them come into the shed but said nothing.

It was almost fifteen minutes before John and Danny appeared.

They were behind for the rest of the day.

In the late afternoon Danny moved all his stuff from John's room to his parents' old room. Jean McEvoy had packed what was left of his father's belongings into boxes. She had put linen on the bed and aired blankets that morning.

Danny, on some obscure impulse, locked the door and looked around the room. He wondered if moving the furniture would help, change any of it.

He moved away from the door and sat on the bed. The bedding smelt faintly of mothballs, and more strongly of animals from hanging out to air. He ran his hand over the counterpane. It was old, a heavy jacquard cotton with fringed edges. It had been on his parent's bed, one of an alternating pair, for as long as he could remember. This one was pale primrose, the other pale green, the pattern identical. There was a faint brown stain on this one. Washed-out blood.

He lay down on his stomach, face against the rough cotton. Sleeping alone in a double bed. Somehow it seemed inconceivable he'd ever slept alone. But double beds always felt emptier. Unless, of course, he put Stephen in it.

He rolled over abruptly and sat up.

He stared at the open wardrobe, his new leather jacket dull and glittering in its depths.

He stood up and strode across the room and slammed the wardrobe door shut.

He stood there for a moment, both hands against it, like he was keeping something locked inside it, then suddenly pulled it open again.

He took the sleeve of his leather jacket and pressed the studded cuff to his face, felt the odd padded ribbing. He rubbed it over his mouth, inhaling the smell of the leather.

He stood like that for a long moment, eyes closed, then abruptly he pushed the jacket back in, closed the wardrobe door and locked it.

He took a last look round the room and went out.

At the evening meal things were slightly reversed. Danny looked fine; John looked terrible.

He sat down to his meal but never ate it. When he pushed it away Ian thought he looked as if he might be sick. The urgency with which he got up and left the room seemed to confirm it.

Rab looked angry, keeping his head down except for one venomous look at Danny,

and Danny... well, if Ian hadn't known better Ian would have said he looked distressed. Danny openly distressed over John? Curiouser and curiouser. Also very unlikely. If something was distressing him it wasn't that. He was probably worried that John would upset his plans, throw a blue funk and refuse to let him go.

Ian watched him finish his meal like he was forcing himself.

He didn't like this. There wasn't any point in pretending it was just another stage in the same stupid game. Danny was in it up to his neck, out of character. Worse because the boy was available all the time, part of the household. And the little twerp hanging onto his every word. If it wasn't so pathetic it would be funny. And Danny high on the whole thing. So high on it he didn't care what he was doing. Somebody ought to wring the little prick's neck and make everybody happy. Danny didn't even like boys.

Ian looked at him again. Well, he *thought* he didn't like boys.

"Unless you plan to eat all that yourself, pass some up here, will you?" Rab's voice broke into his thoughts.

Ian half stood up and pushed it up the table.

Rab pulled it up towards him. "Anyone mind if I finish this?"

Both Danny and Stephen shook their heads. Ian wondered if they always sat opposite each other so they could play footsie under the table. He felt a sudden curiosity to look.

He ducked his head under the table. They weren't touching.

When he came back up they were all looking at him. Rab cynically, Stephen in irritated perplexity, Danny utterly unreadable.

Ian smiled. "Just checking my dick was where I left it."

"Under the table?" Rab asked.

"Ha ha."

Danny pushed up from his seat. He looked at Stephen, the invitation clear on his face. Stephen got up too, colouring under the eyes of the other two.

Everybody was perfectly silent.

When they got to the door Rab's voice, quiet and ugly, said behind them, "Have a nice time boys."

Stephen heard Ian's laugh as he shut the door.

Danny faced him in the hall. "Coming upstairs?"

Stephen nodded, feeling the excitement that had been building in him all day let go. He went upstairs behind Danny, feeling as if he wanted to throw him on the floor.

John came out his room just as they got to the bedroom door. *Oh Jesus*. Stephen wanted to die.

Danny opened the door and pushed Stephen inside then closed it behind him, sealing him in.

Stephen stood there in the strange room listening to them outside. He didn't need to press his ear to the door.

"You can't fucking wait, can you?"

Danny didn't answer that. Stephen half-expected to hear a blow, but none came.

"What are you going to do? Poke him all night?"

"None of your business."

"Danny..." and John's voice sounded odd, nothing that Stephen recognised. Through the door he might have been a stranger, a vaguely familiar stranger. Danny interrupted him.

"No. Get used to it John. It should've been finished years ago. It should never have started again."

"But it fucking did, and you wanted it."

"Don't start that. The last time I wanted it I was fourteen years old and you fucking know it, so don't start that."

"Fourteen my arse. It went on a lot longer than that and *you* know *that*. Stop kidding yourself Danny. At fourteen you were just flexing your dick muscles. It took another two years of trying to seduce me before you finally gave up."

"*Me* trying to seduce *you?*"

There was a silence. Stephen held his breath. Then he heard John's voice, low and full of some repressed emotion he couldn't identify. "You know, I don't think I've ever hated you quite as much as I hate you right at this moment, and I've hated you plenty, believe me. You've caused me nothing but pain. I hope one day it comes full circle, all the pain you've ever given me, right back in your face, and I hope it hurts like hell because, by Christ, you've earned it. You've lied and cheated and manipulated me all along the line. I hope he sees through you before I did, before it's too late, and when he does I hope you're still wanting. I hope it breaks your fucking heart."

There was a tiny pause, then Danny's voice, trying to sound sarcastic but too angry to make it, said, "Finished?" And then John's, "No," and there was a slight thump against the door and then silence.

Stephen was beginning to panic when the door opened and Danny came in. John was nowhere in sight. Danny was flushed and uncomfortable looking.

"Did he hurt you?" Stephen demanded as he closed the door.

Danny wouldn't meet his eyes. He shook his head.

"What happened?" Stephen persisted.

Danny sat on the bed and shook his head again then he pulled Stephen down beside him, crushing Stephen's hand to his crotch all in one gesture.

In the brief seconds of lucidity before Danny started kissing him Stephen wondered how he'd gotten so hard, then he forgot to care because the whole world was on fire.

"Jesus," Danny whispered. He pulled Stephen up close to him and kissed his mouth, long and slow and exploratory.

Stephen lay on him, a heavy satiated weight, and let him do what he wanted. When Danny had enough and let him go he flopped beside him on his back.

Danny brushed his hair off his face and said, "You're beautiful."

Stephen smiled in an intensity of contentment and said nothing. After a while he spoke to him sleepily. "Danny?"

"Mm?"

"Think we're queer?"

"Christ, you pick the times."

"Sorry." He stretched round and kissed Danny's chest, squeezing him tight in apology. He eased off again. "It just worries me, that's all."

"Yeah. Well, it worries me too." And Danny's voice was hard and unhappy.

"Really?"

"Really."

Stephen digested this. Danny had never seemed worried by it before, had always said it didn't matter.

"Why?" Stephen asked.

"Why what?"

"Why does it worry you? Now, I mean. It didn't used to."

"No it didn't," Danny said slowly. He sounded almost reluctant.

"Well why now?"

"Jesus. Can't you leave this alone?"

But Stephen sat up on one elbow, suddenly convinced this was important. "No, tell me."

Danny closed his eyes. "I don't know. It's just never been so bad for me before, that's all."

"What do you mean bad?" Stephen asked with a horrible sense of foreboding.

"I mean intense. I've never..." Danny paused, not as if he was searching but as if he were being cautious, reluctant again. "I've never got this involved before."

Stephen felt as if there were bands around his chest. "Not even with Conley?" he asked.

"Christ, no."

Stephen held him tight. He felt as if he would burst with happiness.

In spite of himself Danny held him back, not wanting to but feeling some odd intensity in himself. He came up hard again. Immediate, raging. "Can I fuck you?" he whispered into his hair.

Stephen made a small satisfied noise of acquiescence.

Danny rolled over on top of him and immediately, hot and itching, pushed his tongue in Stephen's mouth.

Stephen lay there passively beneath him, feeling Danny's cock grinding against his leg, his tongue raping his mouth. It was beautiful. Heady and poisonous. Like Danny.

Danny slid down his body and sucked his cock, painfully, hurting him. It felt deliberate, but it still managed to make him hard, even although he was half-asleep.

Danny let him go and said, "Turn over."

Stephen turned over on his belly. Danny kissed him and licked him till Stephen thought he'd cream right there on his mum's clean bedding. When his hands began pulling at the cover and the noises started Danny said hoarsely, "Kneel up."

Stephen knelt up, feeling slightly apprehensive. He could see his own dick hanging down, red and angry, stiff as a poker.

Danny greased him with a jar from the drawer, finger-fucked him, but only briefly. He went up. Not slowly - fast and hard and painfully. It jarred inside Stephen's body. He made a noise of pain.

Danny said, "I need to... sorry." And he sounded it.

Stephen felt excitement clutching at him. He said, "Go on." Urging him on even though it felt intensely uncomfortable.

Danny pushed in, holding it trembling at the extreme, then pulling out again. Stephen could tell he was trying to keep it slow but couldn't. Danny didn't attempt to fondle his penis. He stayed up on his knees, holding Stephen's backside lightly, pulling it open, straining at the leash.

"Can I come?" he asked. He'd only been inside a couple of minutes.

Stephen couldn't answer him. He felt choked with excitement, anticipation.

Danny mistook it and said urgently, "Please Steve. Just let me get this load off and I'll let you have anything you want. I'm aching to bury this. Please."

Danny had never begged him for anything, ever, never sounded like that. Stephen felt the immensity of his own power. He reached down and pulled on himself, roughly, wanting suddenly to bring himself off. "Okay," he said, loving the sound of it, the feel of giving it. "But you've got to be really slow. I want to feel you really slow. You're not allowed to speed up."

Danny said nothing but he didn't disagree.

He made it slow. For the first three trembling strokes he made it slow. Stephen pulled on himself furiously, face half-smothered in the pillow. His dick seemed to glide in his hand, oozing and slippery with excitement. He'd had a blow-job ten minutes previously and you wouldn't have known. He felt magnificent, in love with himself, intoxicated.

Danny said, "*Uhh...*" as if someone had punched him and then everything changed. He grabbed Stephen's arse, gripping him half under the pelvis, and almost lifted him off the bed. He started throwing himself into him so fast and hard Stephen had to let go of his cock to keep from smothering. "Shit... Danny..." he gasped, trying to grab hold of the pillow, then compelled by some impulse, he could feel himself straining up on his toes, pressing off the bed, offering his backside and demanding, "Give it to me, give it to me."

And Danny did. Sweating and cursing, almost weeping with effort, he slammed into Stephen's body and jerked it out in half a dozen violent thrusts.

Danny hung onto him, his whole body weight pulling on him as he desperately tried to cram up further, then Stephen felt the impossible happening. He started to come, an odd wet-dream sensation. He watched it fascinated, feeling the half-orgasm torture him, knowing it was from being fucked, from feeling Danny come in him. He moaned, feeling the delicious throbbing ache of it, tortured and perfect.

He dropped his head down, feeling utterly destroyed. He felt Danny, in turn, drop onto his back.

They kneeled there like that for an age, come dripping out of them onto his mum's clean counterpane.

John had crept quietly back up to his room - his now empty room, every scent and sight of Danny gone - expressly to listen to them.

The pain was acute. It reminded him of once when he'd had mumps. The pain had been so bad his whole head had almost turned into a kind of frozen pain, an intolerable agony. It was like that now except it was inside his chest, like his heart hurt. And he knew it couldn't, knew there was no such thing as a broken heart.

He wanted to take the knife out the drawer, cut himself with it, squeeze the wounds, see them bleed. He wanted to stab his dick, sit and stick it till all the pain oozed out, then it wouldn't hurt any more. Like those headaches that made you want to bleed.

But he was afraid to take out the knife, afraid to open it and see the clean sweet lines of the blade, because maybe this time he wouldn't be able to content himself with a few shallow nicks to his flesh. Maybe this time he'd start hacking at his body, cut his own dick off and bleed to death. It was like sex with Danny. Once you started you couldn't stop.

He couldn't stand this, day after day, night after night. People said your imagined fears were worse. Oh no they weren't. This was real and it cleaned everything else away. Nothing he'd ever imagined had been this bad.

Someone knocked on his door. He didn't answer. They knocked again.

"John." It was Rab, voice quiet, determined. "Let me in."

John lay there staring at the ceiling. He didn't reply.

"Come on John, let me in. This is stupid."

Still no reply.

"John." Rab's voice sounded angry. The door handle rattled.

John never answered.

After a while Rab went away.

Stephen and Danny heard him outside John's door. Danny lay tense, listening.

Stephen whispered, "Think something's wrong?"

Danny shook his head.

"Maybe you should go see."

"The hell I will." Danny looked at him, a strange half-smile on his mouth. "You trying to get me killed?"

"How?" Stephen frowned.

"Christ Stephen, use your head." He rumpled his hair. "If he's in there he's been listening."

"You mean he's been listening to us? Deliberately?"

"Looks like it."

"But why?"

Danny shrugged as much as to say, Who knows?

"That's just sick."

After another few minutes they heard a noise in the hall again.

"What's that?" Stephen was whispering again. Danny put his finger to his lips. They heard the bedroom door open and close again.

Then silence.

John heard the odd scrabbling noise and opened his eyes. He tried to place it, then he heard the half-metallic clink of something hitting the floor. He turned his head in time to see the key being pulled under the door on a sheet of paper. He sat up, cursing under his breath.

Outside the key went into the lock, turned, and the door opened. Rab came in. He was smiling. He closed the door. "Well, you're not dead."

"Did you think I would be?"

Rab didn't answer that. Instead he folded his arms and leaned against the sink. "What the fuck are you doing up here? Torturing yourself?"

"That's what I'm doing, torturing myself." John lay back down, hands behind his head.

"*Why*, for Christsake?"

John shrugged one shoulder. "I'm a masochist. I like torturing myself."

"Johnny lad, this is stupid and you know it."

"No, this isn't stupid, *I'm* stupid. There's a difference."

"How so?"

"For wanting such an evil little bastard in the first place."

"You can't help who you want."

"Jesus Rab, you sound like Patience Strong."

"How is Dame Patience on incest?"

John didn't laugh.

Rab got off the sink and crossed the room. When he sat on the bed John's eyes opened briefly then shut again. He put his hand over them.

"Why didn't you let me in?" Rab asked.

"Couldn't be bothered."

"By me?"

"By anyone."

There was a silence. John could feel the weight of it pressing down on him. It was as tangible as the silence from next door. He wondered what they were doing. When Rab spoke it startled him.

"John, I want you to listen to me. Don't say anything till you hear me out."

John listened, waiting to hear what he was going to say.

"You and I could be good for each other. We were once before. I'm not suggesting I move in with you, try and replace him, but at worst, at the very lowest denominator, I'd be company for you. Half of my problem is I'm not putting it anywhere, and now you're going to join me. Why don't we try it? It doesn't need to be permanent. I know

you want him back and I know you'll try and get him, but let's try it."

Rab didn't touch him, sat there looking down at him thinking, just imagining, what it would be like to have him again, and he wanted it. He'd wanted it a long time.

John didn't speak. Rab didn't know if he was thinking or trying to phrase a rejection. When he still didn't speak Rab said, coaxing, "One night then. Let me stay with you just for tonight. We don't need to do anything, but it won't be so..." he hesitated, decided against lonely, "bad for you if someone's with you. Come on John, it isn't going to hurt."

John finally took his arm away and looked at him. Rab could see the green of his eyes and couldn't begin to understand why Danny didn't want him, could prefer that stupid little prick to this.

John smiled. "And do you still want that raise?"

Rab looked blank for a moment then slowly smiled back. "I never did."

And he stood up and pulled his sweatshirt off while John watched unsmiling from the bed.

James Conley had a strange visit from Robert Henderson. Strange because he had not expected to ever see him again. Even stranger because he had James Henderson's diary with him. Stranger still because he gave it to Conley.

Conley had seen the appointment in his book that morning and had buzzed Molly to ask about it. *R. Henderson* was what she had pencilled in. Which meant exactly nothing. The name had not clicked. Here in Border land such a name was not exactly an oddity. Molly could only remember that he was American. It still hadn't clicked, although it should have.

When Henderson came in Conley stood up and had to use a bit of professional recovery. Henderson did not shake his hand this time either. Conley did not feel inclined to cry over the loss.

Henderson sat down when requested, commented on the low ceiling, and then put the diary on the desk and said, "Daniel Jackson Moore murdered my brother and I want him hung for it."

Conley looked at the diary without touching it and said, "We don't hang people any more."

"I was talking figuratively." Henderson cleared his throat then said, "My sister reckons you're smart. Me, I'm not convinced. Strikes me you might constitute yourself a personal friend. Is that what you are? A *personal* friend?"

Conley looked up. "I can assure you I'm not a personal friend." He said it quite calmly.

"Then what were you doing out with him?"

"My associate acts for his brother."

Henderson looked at him for a long moment, assessingly. Suddenly he smiled a dazzling paste smile, utterly insincere, and said, "Fine, then maybe we can do business."

Conley said, "I'm a little perplexed Mr Henderson. It's a matter for the police surely? Why come to me?"

"Because Kathy doesn't want the police involved. She doesn't even know I've got the damn thing..." Henderson paused.

"And because you're not sure she would stand witness against him?" Conley ventured.

"I'm damn sure she wouldn't. I'm lucky she told me the whole thing at the outset or I would never have known at all. She actually expected me to like him. Figure that one out."

Conley said, "I still don't quite see my place in all of this."

"I want you to go on doing just what you've been doing for her, acting as a go-between. He trusts you. I want to talk to this guy."

"Can I ask why?"

"I'm going to get him to admit it, then I don't need Kathy or the diary, I'll have him anyway."

"How?" Conley asked, genuinely curious.

Henderson's face split into a slice of Californian white again. He tapped his nose.

Conley looked at him then reached out his hand to the diary. He looked at Henderson before he touched it.

"Go ahead," Henderson said, sitting back in his chair. "Be my guest."

"...He lay there on the bed and told me to pour the whisky over him. It was turning him on, although I'm not sure why. His hair looks fantastic against my sheets, really vivid. He has these little ringlets underneath, curled in tight against his neck. The idea of putting his hair in my mouth really gets me going. I kept pouring booze over him and supping it up. I was quite drunk at the end of it, hardly knew what I was doing. He just lay there, propped up on the pillows, watching me with that peculiar closed face. I'd love to tie him up and make him do anything I wanted. Finally I got pissed off. I was too far gone and the frustration was killing me so I asked him straight out. 'Why don't you come?' 'I didn't know you wanted me to,' he says. 'Well I do,' I said. 'Right now?' he asked. I just looked at him. I wasn't sure what he was getting at. Then he said in that filthy voice of his, 'Take me in your mouth.' So I did and he's hardly in it before I feel all this slime spilling into it. I've never tasted anything so revolting. He tasted like he'd been pissing grapefruit juice or something. I didn't know whether to spit it out or what, but he was watching me, like he knew and was daring me. I swallowed it. Worst of it was, his prick was so big, filling up my mouth like that, and these little twitches in his body, and the breath gasping out of him while he's trying not to show how hard he's coming, that it was really sending me over, even with this dirty-tasting shit still filling up my mouth. Suddenly he pulls out my mouth and just gets up and slides down in front of me and the whole of my prick disappears in his mouth. I came in four seconds flat. He never even breaks his stride. I can actually see his throat working, gulp, gulp. I'm coming and coming. I couldn't seem to stop. He does everything like a professional, like you'd imagine a real whore would be. I think that's partly what excites me. That and the way he gets turned on. I mean he has to be turned on to get that stiff, yet I don't think he even really likes me, or at least he pretends he doesn't. Afterwards he lay on the bed for a while and let me play with him. His prick was as hard as ever within minutes. It made up my mind for me. I'm going to get him to move in with me. I'm desperate to have him to myself. I'm getting stiff just thinking about it. This is my wanking passport. When I'm old I'll be able to look back and see all the hand-jobs I gave myself. There... that's some of my pre-come. Going to wank now."

The entry finished there, but he had fulfilled his promise. The pages were stained and tide-marked, as many of them were right through the book. Conley avoided them as he turned the pages, feeling a peculiar repugnance.

He looked up at Henderson. "I can see why your sister wasn't keen on letting anyone see this."

"It's probably all fantasy," Henderson said dismissively.

Conley said, "Your sister seems to think the same."

"But you don't." It wasn't really a question.

"I don't see how anyone can be sure. Given Dann... given Daniel Jackson Moore's..." Conley didn't finish that either, but Henderson did it for him.

"Given Jackson Moore's filthy habits it doesn't seem so unlikely?"

Conley didn't answer him. Instead he said, "Is it like that all the way through?" He nodded his head at the diary.

"Pretty much. Worse in places, if anything. It gets pretty kinky, you know?"

Conley didn't but he nodded.

"Gets pretty weird about this older brother too. Wades about in all this pain and humiliation shit. Really cuckoo. Freaked me out."

Conley rubbed his face and swung his chair half towards the window so he could see both the river and Henderson. Now he was looking at the river. "Do you want me to threaten him?"

"No need, just tell him that I'll go to the police if he doesn't cooperate. He'll cooperate."

Conley nodded, thinking, I'm sure he will. He won't take much frightening, not about this.

"Well…" Henderson sounded very hearty, as if they'd concluded a particularly satisfactory business deal, "you game?"

Conley didn't hesitate, no time to think. "Yes," he nodded, turning his chair back. "No problem," he added, and he smiled.

Henderson stood up. This time he offered him his hand. Conley had no option but to take it.

When Henderson went out Conley looked at the desk. The diary was there. It should have been thirty pieces of silver.

He picked it up and began to flick through the pages.

Stephen spent the night in Danny's new room. They masturbated and fellated until they grew too tired to do anything but fondle each other and then they did that until they got too tired to do even that. They climbed under the blankets, naked and exhausted, and fell asleep curled like spoons.

Danny dreamt about someone he couldn't see shaving his body with a straight razor, taking all the hair off in thick suds, leaving his pubic area till last. He was afraid, watching the flat, spatulate knife moving around his cock, but he still got harder and harder as it did its work, until his pubic area was naked as a child's, utterly smooth, not even stubble, and he was massively erect, adult and very unnaturally red. He felt his penis deliciously, aware of how stickily it clung to his hand. He could remember thinking how much John was going to love him like this, then something red started coming away in his palm, sticky and raw, and he could see a deep gash running across his lower belly. He realised he'd been sliced open so cleanly, so sharply, he hadn't even felt it. The cut was beginning to hurt because his erection was getting bigger and bigger. He knew he had to come, just so his guts wouldn't spill out. He squeezed the head of his penis repeatedly until it happened, horrible, thick creamy ropes just oozing out of him, like toothpaste out a tube. He could feel the orgasm jerking at his groin, pulling the cut apart and knew suddenly it wasn't come, it was his guts coming out. He grabbed himself, trying to hold it in and suddenly his father was there, pulling his hands off. Danny kept trying to cover it but his father just kept slapping his hands away, licking his lips and watching his guts spill out over his hands.

He woke up with a start, covered in sweat, their two bodies wet and stuck with it. He reached for the lamp and realised where he was. There was only one in this room and it was on the other side of Stephen's body.

He lay in the dark, heart pounding. Stephen felt very small and densely asleep beside him.

Nowhere to hide now Danny-boy.

He pushed Stephen awake, feeling some awful panic choking inside. Stephen came awake, slowly at first, then more rapidly, saying, "What is it? What's wrong?"

Danny lay there and heard the panic in his voice and said slowly, "Nothing. Go back to sleep."

Stephen grunted and went back to sleep.

Danny lay awake for a long time.

John insisted they made no noise.

Rab wasn't sure if he was being complimented or not. Too good to use against Danny or too temporary to be involved. Which?

He'd probably never know.

The first time was good. Too fast but exciting and violent. The second was even better.

Rab woke in the middle of the night and realised John was crying. At first he lay there in an agony of indecision, then he moved over against him, stroking him, not speaking.

John immediately rolled on top of him, like a rutting beast, full of desperation. He rubbed his face on the pillow, almost as if he were sandpapering the tears away, then he said, "I want to fuck you."

Rab turned over without speaking.

John took enough time to wet him with spit then went in. He went in slowly and carefully, until he was imbedded inside him, and then he rolled them onto their sides and curled Rab's knees up and took a hold of his cock and then fucked him like it was going out of fashion. Deep and silent and thorough. And this time when they came - John first - neither of them was quiet. But no-one heard them. It was after three in the morning and everyone was asleep.

John kissed him afterwards and rubbed Rab's come all over his belly and said, "You always were a good fuck." And he sounded almost as if he meant it.

Almost.

SEVENTY-SIX

Both Danny and Stephen dressed with morning erections.

"You too?" Danny smiled up at him from the edge of the bed.

"Every flickin' morning," Stephen smiled back, then yawned cavernously. He scratched his nose and added, "And they take fucking forever to go down."

Danny pulled him to him by it. Stephen grinned down at him. "You shouldn't do that, yours is easier to grab. I might start doing it to you."

"Promises," Danny said and bent his head and drew him into his mouth.

Stephen swallowed dryly and went with the tide.

And when the tide came he very nearly did.

Conley phoned at the back of nine. He knew they came in then for what Danny called 'A proper breakfast'.

Jean McEvoy answered the phone. He didn't know who she was, and the sound of a woman's voice threw him until he realised she must be Stephen's mother, their 'new woman'.

He asked to speak to Danny, told her who he was.

After what seemed a long time Danny came on the line, said, "Hello?"

He sounded odd, like a stranger.

Conley realised he didn't really know how to do this. He said, "I'm phoning on behalf of Robert Henderson. He wants to talk to you."

There was a pause and he could sense Danny's surprise at the way he had spoken to him, without greeting or acknowledgement. When he said, "Oh," it sounded like an accusation.

Conley went on, "He's going to go to the police otherwise. He's given me the diary for safe-keeping. If you want to attempt to talk him out of it I suggest you see him."

Danny seemed to be considering this then he said slowly, "And why the fuck would he give me an option on trying to talk him out of it? Does he want to marry me too?"

Conley heard him swearing with that casualness and felt his palms start to sweat. He felt suddenly edgy, unhappy, all wrong, but all he said was, "I don't know. I suggest you ask him."

There was another pause, and as usual Conley couldn't be quite sure what Danny was going to say, what way the urge would drive him. 'Yes' and 'Fuck off' were equally likely. "When?" he said finally.

Conley let out a small grunt of relief, although he didn't know why. "Today," he said. "Three-thirty, at his sister's flat."

"Confident, wasn't he?"

"Hopeful," Conley said.

"Will you be there?"

"No." Conley could feel his heart pounding, but whatever Danny had been going to say, was thinking of saying, he never said.

The phone disconnected and Conley was listening to the dialling tone.

Danny didn't tell John, couldn't face telling him, not on top of everything else. He didn't tell anyone. At three o'clock he returned to the house, changed quickly and went out again. He was lucky that one of the cars was there.

He drove quickly because he was a little late. He didn't want to be late because he wanted to get it over with. No aggravation. Whatever it was, he wanted it finished with. Quick and painless.

He arrived there in rain, heavy, sleety, miserable rain. It felt right. Maybe chase the fucker back to the sunny USA.

He rang the bell. Henderson kept him waiting. He rang it again thinking, If this is a run-around I'll break his fucking neck. Henderson answered this time, making him say his name as if he didn't know who it was. He let Danny in almost grudgingly, as if he hadn't arranged it. Danny began to feel nettled and uneasy.

Henderson opened the door. He was wearing some kind of grey marl sweat suit with large pink lettering advertising something American unknown to Danny. It looked expensive in the way everything the Hendersons wore seemed to, as if it had the price tag on it somewhere, probably woven into a gold label.

He let Danny in with a sort of lazy insolence. Something else Danny didn't like.

He stood in the hall and waited. Henderson said, "Go in then. You've been before."

Danny went in. The room was same as last time. No more changes. The painting was still there. He decided for the first time that he preferred the room the way James Henderson had had it, all cream or white or whatever it was, not this red. It made the room narrow, cramped, over-warm. Henderson touched his shoulder. Danny jumped.

"I only want your jacket."

Danny had wheeled to face him. "Am I staying that long?"

Henderson said nothing, just looked at him

Danny eased it off reluctantly, not crossing him. Not yet. Let him say his piece first. "Sit down."

Henderson did, so Danny did.

"You enjoy fucking my homo brother?"

He'd said it for maximum shock value, used 'fuck' for maximum impact. You could tell by the way he said it he didn't use it often. You could also tell he enjoyed saying it.

He'd misjudged his audience. Danny sat there looking at him flatly. He stuck to the truth. "No," he said. *Your ball Bobby*.

Henderson picked a glass up off the table. Danny hadn't seen it when he sat down. The ice in it was still fresh. The drink was amber. There was a bottle beside it on the table. American Whisky. Imported, not brought with him. Danny only knew because they had plastered *Imported American Blend* all over it. Henderson drank some before speaking.

"Diary says something different."

Danny didn't answer that. There wasn't any point and he still didn't know where this was going.

"What *are* you?" Henderson asked finally and he was staring at him, eyes blue and narrow, as if he were trying to read it on his face.

Danny wanted to say, A sheep-shagger, but he knew Henderson wasn't finished. "Gay or straight?"

Danny almost laughed. He shrugged and said, "Your guess is as good as mine."

"Gay," Henderson said immediately.

For the first time Danny felt an irritation at the assumption. He took a deep breath and concentrated on looking like he wasn't annoyed. To Henderson he looked completely impassive, indifferent, almost bored. It annoyed him.

"You're gay and you fucked him because you were getting paid for doing what you liked best."

Danny stared at him then said, "He never paid me for anything - *I* was paying him - and if that diary's telling the truth you know it." Danny paused, looking at him

speculatively. "Where is this leading? Get to the point."

Henderson took another drink, a big one, then looked at him over the rim of his glass without lowering it. "After your little performance the other night I'm curious. I know we're all supposed to have adolescent crushes, guilty flings in the frat, but not me. I've decided I want to know what it's all about and you're going to show me. You're clean, aren't you?"

"*What?*"

"Clean. No diseases? Nothing like that?"

"Jesus..." Danny whispered.

"Well? Are you?"

"Fuck off." Danny jumped to his feet. "Just fuck off."

"Sit down," Henderson said calmly. More calmly than he felt.

"Like hell I will."

Henderson could see he was furious. His face was white with two tiny red spots, almost like a doll's. It made his hair look vividly unreal, his eyes black and glassy.

"You better," Henderson said quickly. "Or it goes to the cops. I don't give a shit who reads it. I'm not my sister. She should never have let you get this far. You're getting a damn good deal lover-boy, so if I was you I'd just sit down and take a breath and reconsider."

Danny stood there. He caught his lip between his teeth. Henderson saw it and said, tone placatory, "Come on, sit down. Let's talk."

Danny wanted to smack him right in the plastic mouth but he walked stiffly back and sat down. He remained perched on the edge of the sofa as if he were ready to make a bolt for it, watching Henderson with an oddly disturbing up-and-under look, head butted down low, like an animal about to charge him.

Henderson recrossed his legs. "Strictly business," he said. "Conley's got the diary. You give me what I want, you get the diary."

Danny felt a lift of his spirits. This was an improvement. Finally he could get his hands on the diary then all this was finished. Burn the fucking thing, wash his hands of the clan Henderson forever. But when he spoke he was careful to keep the anticipation out his voice. "What do you want? Exactly?"

Henderson smiled. Danny tried not to look at his teeth.

"Well, hell, I'm not sure yet. This is new to me." Danny saw him look at the table. "Let's just try a few things. Kind of sexual sushi. Grass is always greener, you know?" He smiled again. "I'm not getting any younger." He laughed. "Don't guys always go fag at forty?"

Danny just kept staring at him until Henderson said, "Well?"

"What is there to say?" Danny looked down his body, slowly back up again. "I'm going to give you a cocksucker's selection box, you're going to give me the diary."

"I want the works." Henderson warned. His face was reddening now.

Danny felt the urge to twist the knife. If he was going to have to suck this creep he could damn well pay for the pleasure. "I suck you, fuck you. Anything else? I'd like to know exactly what my job spec is."

Henderson's mouth tightened. "You'll wash me, bed me and eat my shit if I want, understand?"

Danny listened to the American words come out in a vague and distant Scottish accent, clipped, hard. He smiled. "Just checking."

Henderson took a deep breath then let it out slowly and said, "Now you can answer one last question and I want a straight answer or the deal's off, understand?"

Danny nodded.

"Are you a fruit?"

Danny looked at him and said, "No."

He saw that Henderson believed him whether it was true or not. He felt some kind of wild excitement kick through him. Christ, this one was going to be jam.

"I thought not," Henderson said, and sunk back in the settee, rubbing his glass slowly with his thumb.

Danny watched him and thought suddenly, Jesus, I'm not.

And that was the first time he ever knew.

"Do you want something to drink?"

Danny nodded shortly. It ought to be funny. Even this one, this cocksure bastard, still had to get behind that haze to do what he wanted.

Henderson brought him a glass. Danny took it from him, feeling Henderson brush his fingers with deliberation. It was empty. He put ice in it for him then began pouring in the American whisky. "Say when."

Danny watched his face, not the glass. He said nothing. Eventually when the glass was two-thirds full Henderson stopped pouring and looked at him. "Some problem, or are you just greedy?"

"Just greedy."

Henderson sat down beside him and put the bottle on the table. He picked his own glass back up. Danny eased back into his seat, cradled the glass between his legs, feeling the cold of the ice slowly chill between his thighs.

Henderson stared at the glass nestled there and said, "You didn't like my brother any better, did you?"

"Nope."

"What about Kathy?"

"Nope."

Henderson's eyes came up slowly to his face. "It's an admission of guilt. You realise that, don't you? They've both been too blinded by conceit to care, too desperate to believe in their own ambitions. Me, I don't give a fuck." He swore in the same relishing way as last time, like a little boy saying bum. He was practically handling himself in his pocket. "This is strictly business. I'm buying you." He enjoyed saying that too, really loved it.

Danny kept his mouth closed tight.

"You slit his throat because he knew something, even though he was too besotted to want to find out what it was. You didn't even need to kill him, there's irony for you. He thought he was in love with you... dumb bastard," he finished. His voice sounded singularly emotionless.

After a moment he went on, "He was always a stupid idealistic bastard. Even when he was a kid he used to always say he'd give away his shares when he grew up. Funny, I never saw him part with a penny." He laughed dryly. "No surprises there, eh?"

"Looks like I wasn't alone," Danny said, finally taking a drink.

Henderson watched the glass go to his mouth then seemed to suddenly realise what he'd said. "In what?"

"You didn't like him either."

"He was my brother." Henderson said it shirtily, as if it vindicated everything he said or did - now, later and forever. Amen.

"So what?" Danny said.

Henderson opened his mouth then closed it again. Danny took another drink. He wiped his mouth with the back of his hand.

Henderson watched him then moistened his lips as if he were steeling himself and said quickly, "Can I touch you?"

Danny smiled. It amused him to hear him ask. "You're paying."

Henderson wiped his palm on his trouser leg as if it were wet.

Danny expected him to feel his crotch, straight into the good stuff. He didn't.

Henderson reached out slowly and ran his fingertips over Danny's mouth, feeling the full silkiness of it, the unexpected harshness of the invisible stubble on his upper lip. The contrast was sharp and disturbing, like Danny himself, all steel and velvet, silk and broken glass.

Danny's mouth curved into a smile under his finger. He watched Henderson's body straining at the leash, leaning forward slightly towards him. Danny knew what he wanted, another taste, see if it was as potent as he remembered. He'd already given it some mystical quality. Never felt anything for the past fifteen years of his life because he's been too busy building an image of himself then suddenly he's going to throw it all away for nothing, another image, a chimera.

Good word Danny.

I'm a chimera.

Henderson dropped his hand. His face was flushed. He looked as if he was going to burst something. This was too easy.

"Go on," Danny said, very low and quiet. He let his hands lie out wide beyond his body, throat exposed, legs slightly open, smile softly, neatly in place. "Come on," he urged, turning his head slightly towards him, leaning back into the sofa, limp, available, offering.

Henderson moved slowly and compulsively, not putting his drink down, leaning his body over his. Danny's spread actually made it more difficult, but it made it look easier and that was what mattered. He felt Henderson's body against his own. *Five seconds and counting.* He could smell him now, not as cloying as his brother, just soap and something lemony, presumably aftershave.

Henderson's mouth touched. As soon as he did it Danny let one arm go round him, pulling him closer, turning in towards him slightly, and began kissing him. He could feel nothing. Nothing at all.

He stopped, pushed Henderson away.

Henderson blinked then slowly flushed that deep ugly mottled red that Danny had seen before.

"I don't think..." Danny sat up. "This isn't going to work."

"What?" Henderson was still blinking, looking at him blankly.

"I said," Danny tried to keep the irritation out his voice, "I don't think this is going to work."

Henderson's face grew tight. It seemed almost to become more glossy, like plastic being stretched taut. "What's going on?" he said, voice hard, suspicious.

Danny didn't bother trying to think anything up. He felt too edgy. It was too new to him. Like Ian, that's what it was like.

"Nothing's happening," he said.

Henderson stared at him. "Is this some kind of a trick?"

"I wish it was." And Danny reached suddenly for Henderson's hand and pressed it against his crotch. "Feel. Nothing."

Henderson pulled his hand away. "So? It was only a kiss."

Danny looked at him. "What do you feel?"

Henderson looked blank for a moment then slowly flushed again. He didn't need to say anything.

There was a silence, each trapped alone in their thoughts. Danny was trying to hold it there, catch it, look at it and ask, What's happening? But it shied away from him. Don't come any closer. When Henderson spoke to him he felt relieved. Relieved of the obligation of chasing it.

"Too bad. It still stands. You'll just have to lie back and think of England."

Danny looked at him for a moment, realising what he was saying, and then said, "Grow up, you stupid bastard." And his voice startled even him, all his fear coming out as anger. "We're not talking about faking fucking orgasms here," he heard himself say. "If it won't come up I can't do anything, end of the line. Even you must be able to understand that."

Henderson's face mottled again. His eyes became stubborn. "Fine, then I'll go to the cops."

Danny fought the urge to say, Why? Think they'll have better luck than me? He let out a breath and let his shoulders drop. He reached over and picked up his drink. He took a long gulp, coughed and put it down again. He dropped back into the settee, stared at the ceiling. Eventually Henderson said, "Well?"

Danny said, "Why? I mean, what the hell for? I can't do anything for you."

"No, *I* can't do anything for *you*. You warned me you weren't queer. I don't see what the big deal is."

Danny said slowly and carefully, trying to pick his words, "It'll be poison for you. After ten minutes of that you'll come to hate it, believe me."

"Why should I? I'm getting what I paid for, the best sex there is. I don't do anything, you do all the work. I don't even have to pretend."

"It won't work," Danny risked again.

"Alright." Henderson stood up.

Danny transferred his gaze to him. He knew what the 'Alright' meant. He shut his eyes. He couldn't think. But there wasn't anything to think about anyway. Slowly, without opening his eyes, he began to unfasten his shirt.

It took Henderson a moment to realise what he was doing and what it meant. It was a nice try but this proved that's what it had been. A nice try. His shirt showed an inch of white flesh right down to his navel. He was undoing the cuffs. When he had done that he opened his eyes, but they were downcast, watching his fingers. He was unfastening his jeans. The belt made a heavy clinking noise. It brought Henderson's excitement right back, the sound of it coming undone, so definite, then the zip. When he had finished he lay there unmoving, undressed yet still fully covered. Henderson couldn't remember being so hard in a long time. Maybe because it was so forbidden. After all, he was good looking... and the ultimate unavailable.

When Danny spoke to him it came out almost surly, low and grudging. "What do you want me to do?"

But it didn't turn him off. If anything his reluctance only made him more excited. It reminded him of one of the rare occasions in his childhood he had succeeded in winning a fight. He had made the other boy do fictitious errands for him. He had realised in later years the pleasure it had given him had been vaguely sexual. It was the same feeling now, only it was no longer vague, it was hot and hard and standing right up in his trousers, slavering from its mean little mouth, drooling over this long pale boy spread out beneath him.

"Open your shirt," he commanded.

Danny laid it open. Henderson looked at his chest, looked at the clusters of tiny marks, very faint, as if he'd been peppered with something.

"What are the scars?"

"They're not scars." He still wouldn't look at him.

"Well, what are the marks then?"

"Burns."

"Burns?" Henderson said, aware that his mouth was hanging open.

Now Danny looked up. A strange upwards look, not lifting his head properly. A

cunning unpleasant look. "Yes, burns."

"How did you...?"

Henderson didn't finish it, but Danny didn't tell him. Instead he said, "Are you going to touch, or just look, or what?"

The question seemed hugely erotically charged, way beyond the words themselves. Maybe it was his voice. It seemed to have changed completely. Now it was deep enough to drown in.

"You do it," Henderson said. "You're the faggot."

Henderson was rewarded by seeing his eyes flash black at him. Suddenly the redhead lunged at him. Before Henderson knew what was happening he'd hit him, slapped him viciously across the face. He grunted with shock and pain.

The surprise gave Danny the advantage. He hit him again, yanking him down by the hair, twisting a handful of the neatly held style. He could feel the lacquer or whatever it was sticky beneath his fingers. "Don't you ever call me that again."

Henderson looked up at him blindly, trying to see through the pain. Danny was kneeling on him, half-crushing him, just like he had the first time. How could he have let it happen again? The exact same thing all over again.

"You hear me?" Danny twisted his scalp again.

Henderson managed a noise of assent.

Danny was almost disappointed. He wanted to go on doing it, watching his stupid, priggish little face squirm. He was enjoying it.

He slapped him again, with no provocation, just because he wanted to.

And that was when it happened.

He could feel it in himself, hot and breathy, wanting to do it again. Not just wanting, *needing*, like a sudden mad itch, scratch it or die. And so he slapped him again.

Henderson just lay there, supine with shock, not quite comprehending what was happening to him, and Danny finally recognised it. No longer a vague sensation. No longer a hazy unidentifiable pleasure. It was as real and inescapable as his erection. As stiff and unyielding.

Up and hard, hitting the little bastard.

Just like John.

And a wave of revulsion came just like it should, with a proper guilt and the appropriate shame, but it was all washed away by excitement. An excitement so big he didn't give a damn.

He smiled. "Now I know how to get stiff with you."

And even to himself his voice was too deep. He didn't even recognise it. And way inside, lost inside, he was screaming while the other Danny, big and bad and red, was saying, "All I've got to do is hit you. Look." And he straddled him, keeping his arms pinned down with his knees while he pulled the front of his shorts down and let it fall out, hanging there, a scant six inches above Henderson's face.

"God..." Henderson whispered into the huge silence surrounding them, and Danny luxuriated in the sight of himself, huge and beautiful and *erect*, in control again, no longer afraid, and he knew he'd do anything, *anything*, to keep it like this.

He slid his hand over it, feeling the familiar shape of himself, loving the way it licked his hand, left his fingers moist, because it loved him too.

Henderson had never seen anything like it. The only erections he'd ever seen were his own. For obvious anatomical reasons he'd never been so close to one before. It was so goddamned big. *No exaggeration Jimmy, you were telling it like it was.* And the way he touched himself, like he was communing with it or something. Like he was in love with it.

"I'm going to come in your face. I'm going to fucking blind you."

Henderson wanted to say, No, make all the right noises, prove he had dignity,

self-respect, real *maleness*, but he didn't. He didn't because he wanted him to come in his face. He wanted to be blinded. He watched the skin cling and unfurl itself, roll back like a red wave off the sleek glossiness of the head. When Danny pushed it against his mouth he opened it immediately, but Danny laughed, low and malevolent. "Uh-uh. You'd like that, wouldn't you? In your dreams lover-boy."

He let it salt his lips, let him feel the silken roundness of it, the plushy fat heat, then pulled it away again before he could taste it. He felt as if he was dying of thirst, as if someone had stolen water from his mouth. He wanted to demand, 'Give it back. I haven't tasted it yet,' but he hadn't sunk far enough in his desperation to voice it.

"If you want this," the redhead was breathing heavily, raggedly, "then you'll have to beg. Do you want it?" he demanded, pressing it down, half an inch away from Henderson's mouth. "You said you didn't need it, said all you wanted was me to please you, and now you want it?"

"Yes," Henderson said, wondering if his tongue could reach it.

"Then I'm going to have to hurt you."

"Yes," he said again, pretending he didn't know what he was agreeing to, pretending to mean something else, all the time feeling his own excitement. What would he do? How far would he go?

"You sick little faggot." And the redhead's voice was low and venomous, full of real hate, like the street kids Henderson used to represent in court, the same kind of hate, something deep-rooted and antagonistic.

"Yes," he said again.

And the redhead smiled at him, then took his head in both hands, pulling it back by the hair, and lowered himself till he was sitting over his face, suffocating him, the hard seams of the stiff denim abrading his skin, then he felt the slick stickiness of the boy's cock being rubbed to and fro across his forehead, barely making contact. Dimly he could hear him grunting, calling him a faggot, while he struggled to breathe, head filled with the soapy, fabricky smell of the boy's clothes, and then he felt it, hot and wet, smearing across him, dripping into his hair, and he felt him riding his orgasm against his face, soft balls crushed inside the hard rubbing seams, his body twitching and trembling, grinding himself down on his face and grunting. Grunting like the beautiful little animal he was.

Henderson was embarrassed.

Not so the boy.

He'd slid off him, cock in hand, nice as ninepence, and lay there on the couch, head lolling back, smiling to himself.

When Henderson had finally picked up the courage to look at him he hadn't expected to see that. He should've known better after everything he'd read in the diary.

Danny turned lazily to look at him and said, "Someone's done gone messed up yo' hair, sah," and smiled insolently.

Henderson put his hand to it without thinking and brought his fingers away sticky. Danny laughed at his expression. Henderson sat up, looking at his hand as if he didn't know what it was.

"It won't melt you. Look." And Danny reached over for his hand, bending over it and licking the glutinous mess from his fingers.

Henderson tried to pull his hand away but Danny held it fast. "Patience, don't be greedy. You can have some later."

Henderson went limp, watching that beautiful mouth, and understood for the first time Jimmy's incoherent ramblings over his hair, that incredible red hair brushing now

against his wrist. His erection, momentarily dimmed by embarrassment, came galloping back. With a vengeance.

Danny lifted his head and said, "Here," and began to slowly clean off his face and hair using ragged old tissues from his pocket that looked as if they'd been there since the last time his jeans had been washed. Henderson didn't care. He lay back and let him, looking at the smooth skin on his chest, level with his eyes. He could smell his skin. Finally he gave in and slid his hands over the boy's body. He didn't even flinch, just went on tidying him up, letting Henderson do what he wanted. Henderson felt he could have done anything and he wouldn't have made a murmur. Christ he was so hard.

"So what do you want?"

"Anything," Henderson whispered, running his hands down inside the boy's shorts, feeling the half erection, pulling them away to look at that beautiful red hair. He wished he dared slide down and take it in his mouth.

"Want to suck my dick?" The voice came low above him.

Henderson's face flushed at having his thoughts so transparently read.

The boy pushed his head, coaxing him. "Go on then, have a mouthful, straight from the source." He pushed his head down again, more forcefully.

Henderson slid down, letting the force persuade him. He swallowed carefully, then equally carefully put it in his mouth.

The boy took hold of himself and pulled his foreskin back, flooding Henderson's mouth with the taste of salt. He made a gagging noise. The boy pushed into his face. "Suck," he said, and it was a hard, ugly noise. "Suck or I'll fucking suffocate you."

Henderson sucked.

"That's it." And Danny eased off enough to let him breathe. "But then they say faggots give the best head." And he laughed.

Henderson felt it grow in his mouth, so fast it was indecent. It reminded him of a pantomime beanstalk. Someone should laugh, but he couldn't. It would be rude to laugh with his mouth full.

"That's enough." And suddenly it was gone, out of his mouth with an obscene plop, and the boy was sitting astride his lap, cock pointing at him, and demanding, "What do you want faggot?" And he traced his hand over Henderson's erection. "Got as much down below as your brother? Your brother was very thick." And he smiled an ugly smile.

Henderson didn't know quite what he meant, quite who he was insulting.

Danny unzipped him and slid his hand in. It was oddly cool. Henderson held his breath. Danny took him out and whistled. It sounded genuine. "You've been keeping secrets."

Danny undid his belt and pulled his trousers open fully. He whistled again. "Just as hairy too. I'm surprised. You don't look it. Just as thick too. A little bigger if anything. Are you bigger? Ever get to comparing sizes with your big brother Jiminy Cricket? In bed in the dark?"

"No."

"Come on."

"No. Never."

"Once."

"No."

"Once. He said you did."

Danny smiled, then laughed as he watched the expression change on his face. James Henderson had never even mentioned a brother. "What's wrong? Did he swear an eternal vow not to tell? Well he's dead now, all vows null and void. You should never trust big brothers."

"We didn't."

"Ah, but you did. Your face says so." Danny was slowly rubbing his cock. Henderson was going to surprise him any second now by coming on him but he didn't know how to stop it. He was far too excited and the sensation was too novel, too new.

"I'm going to come," he said, blurting it out.

"Tell me," Danny said as if he hadn't spoken, not even slowing his hand.

"Didn't you hear me?" Henderson was staring at his mouth, trembling on the brink. One more stroke...

"No you won't. Not until you tell me." Suddenly it was true, as if he'd spoken it into being. He felt immediately frustrated, desperate.

"We didn't do anything," he said again, belligerently.

"Come on, your dick'll burst if you don't give. Don't be so fucking shy. Come on." All the time his cool hand soothing up and down, squeezing, teasing, driving him mad. He wanted to spill it, all of it.

He looked at the two erections almost nose to nose - his own thick and sallow, half-swamped in dense dirty blonde hair; the boy's long and red, growing magnificently from the silky auburn curls. He looked at them and said, "We used to play a game called milking the cow. One of us would go down on all fours. The other would sit on the nursery stool and milk him. We used to do it into a milk jug. We were just kids."

Danny laughed. "Now I know why he wanted me. It's the farming connection. I'm surprised he never asked me to do it to him."

"So am I."

"Want me to do it for you? Professional, I know how it's done. Like to feel it? The real thing?"

"No."

"Oh, I think you do. Get down on the floor." Danny swung off him.

Henderson shook his head emphatically.

Danny smiled then slapped him. "Get on the floor."

Henderson got on the floor on all fours, telling himself he didn't want to be hit again, knowing it was because he wanted him to do it, knowing he'd wanted it all along.

Danny sat against him, smiling, and handled him as if he were milking a cow. "That's what it really feels like. Not what you expected, is it? You could take a long time to come like this."

But Henderson was trembling. It was better. God, it was better. "I never..." he began.

Danny kept smiling, kept doing it, as close an approximation as he could, given the dimensions and the equipment. The stupid bastard was so frantic for it he could probably have rubbed tapioca on him and got the same result.

"Oh no please..." Henderson whimpered. "Please no, don't stop... don't stop." And Danny grinned as he started to buckle under his hands. He moved down onto the floor behind him, not letting go, keeping his hand working to keep him coming.

Henderson felt as if he were shaking apart he was trembling so hard. It didn't seem to be jerking out of him so much as leaking.

Danny wondered when he'd last had sex. He pulled Henderson's trousers down with his free hand, then waited till he'd finished gasping and moaning then let him go, squeezing the last of it out into his palm.

He brought the sticky mess round and began massaging it into Henderson's anus. Henderson said vaguely, "What...?" barely lifting his head out of its slump on the floor. But he wasn't sharp enough. Danny had pushed the first inch in before he'd even realised.

"Hey!" Henderson said suddenly, head coming up off the floor in surprise.

But Danny laughed and pulled him back onto his cock, impaling him. "Way to go," he said and he began to pump into him.

Henderson squeaked.

"Shut your fucking mouth," Danny said amiably and continued to move into him. He was very tight. Whatever else Mr Henderson did, it didn't include anal sex, but in Danny's book tight was good.

Tight was right.

Henderson gritted his teeth. He was being raped. *Raped* for Christsake. *Do something*. He said urgently, "You're hurting me."

"Tell me that again."

Henderson felt the boy's cock fill him wider, harder. He realised he had excited him, plain and simple. The boy stuck his hands up his sweater, half-lying over his back. He was feeling his chest, under his arms.

"God, you don't look hairy, but you are. A fucking little ape. The way it grows along your cock like that makes me stiff." He sucked air in between his teeth. "It was the only thing about your stinking, drunken bum of a brother that ever got me going, that cock hair. Jesus."

And he kept pounding into him, clutching fistfuls of his body hair and pulling.

Robert Henderson could feel his arms friction burning on the carpet. His knees too. He could feel something else too. He could feel himself trying to open up wider to him, climb back onto him. He was getting an erection again. He felt as if he were taking a crash course in humiliation.

And then the redhead was saying, "Fuck," hard and vicious. Then again, "Fuck." Then, "Fuck... fuck... fuck..." and he actually felt it inside him, the warm, wet release. He could feel every spasm of his body as it jerked on top of him, pushing him hard into the carpet, could feel him tear at the hair on his chest, ripping out handfuls as his hips worked against him, giving himself release. He sounded as if it pained him.

Eventually it stopped.

Danny pulled out of him almost immediately, completely deflated and wanting to be off him. He'd come with James Henderson's black hairy body alive in his head, moving behind his eyes. He felt shivery and alone. Dirty.

He climbed onto the couch on trembling legs, looked at Henderson's tight little tanned backside in disgust. He laid his hand on his forehead as if he had a headache.

He felt a wave of nausea, big and real and swamping, come over him. He pushed himself inside his clothes, trying not to touch it. He wanted to wash but he didn't want to take the time. He stood up shakily, took a breath. Henderson hadn't moved. Christ, why didn't he cover himself up?

"Had your face rubbed in it enough?" Danny didn't need to inject contempt into his voice, there was plenty there to go round.

Henderson didn't answer.

"You got your 'works'. Hands, knees and fucking boomps-a-daisy. I'm sure you found it a big thrill. Now you can go back to being a happy hetero. I'll pick up the diary from James Conley."

Henderson still didn't say anything.

"Say something, you fucking bastard," Danny hissed.

Henderson said, "Yes," face down into the floor.

"Jesus," Danny said, and before he knew what he was going to do he'd kicked him savagely on the flank.

Henderson went over and curled into a ball.

Danny stared at him in horror. He licked his lips and tried to speak but nothing came out. "Jesus," he said again, but this time he sounded twelve years old, afraid of

the dark.

He went out of the room, got his things and left.

Robert Henderson lay there on the carpet, dry-eyed, wondering how he could have fallen so far in such a short time.

"It was no distance at all," he whispered.

And his fingers went tracing lightly through the dark.

Danny went out, slamming the door, thundering down the stairs, pulling his jacket on. He was shivering, uncontrollably.

Just lying there, letting him kick him like a dog. His fucking dick, stinking and swollen with excitement. *Another couple of kicks and he'd have been climbing up my leg, trying to hump me. Oh Jesus, how do I get into these things?*

He tore open the entrance door and went out into the rain, still bitter cold, cutting.

He hared across to the car, got in, nearly slammed himself neatly into the dock, braked and sat there in a cold sweat saying, "Easy... *easy,*" over and over to himself.

He reversed out slowly.

He would go and see Conley now.

Oh no, please.

Yes, now. Finish it. Come on *Danny.*

Alright, alright. Just let me have a cigarette.

He pulled the car into a piece of waste ground off the half-built road and got a cigarette from the glove compartment.

He smoked it, watching a dog pissing on every lamppost, every boulder, as it moved along the road. By the time it had disappeared he felt better. He threw the remains of the cigarette out the window.

He would go and see Conley and get the diary.

He would give the motherfucking thing to John as a present. In fact, he'd make him *eat* the fucking thing.

Alright.

He took a deep breath, reversed out carefully, put the car into gear.

"Alright," he said.

And smiled.

Danny hit the starts of the teatime homeward-bound traffic. He swore quietly as he got snarled up around the Caldermouth environs. Well, it wasn't going to make any difference now. He checked the time. Conley would be in his office for at least another hour and he wouldn't be nearly that long.

It was alright.

Then why was he so nervous?

He rubbed his face irritably. He looked out the side window and found himself looking into the cab of a huge container lorry going in the opposite direction. The driver was watching him. Danny looked at him curiously then felt the old familiar kick in his groin.

Oh Jesus, this wasn't happening.

He looked away.

The traffic moved. He shot into the space, putting distance between him and the lorry, between him and another face. Another and another and another.

He took a long hard breath, moved forward a few more yards. He tried to calm down.

He was only looking Danny.

Yeah, like he hadn't eaten in twenty years and I was on tonight's menu.

So he was queer.

Oh fuck off. Fuckoff, fuckoff, fuckoff.

The traffic cleared suddenly, giving him a good ten minutes free run before it blocked again, but it was enough to make him feel better. Another ten minutes and he'd be there. He could see the roof of Conley's building in the distance.

He crawled and snaked. It took thirteen and a half minutes.

He pulled into the back car park. It was snowing here, light, crystalline, just frozen rain.

He saw Conley's car, long and black and sinister, and felt something old hurt inside.

He shouldn't have come. This was a mistake.

Come on Danny.

He got out the car, slamming it shut, not bothering to lock it.

He went round the front of the building and went up the stairs quickly, two at a time, getting up them before he could change his mind.

He was past Dorothy before she had a chance to speak. He went in the door to Conley's outer office.

She was there.

He took a deep breath and said, "I'd like to speak to Conley..." He stopped, backtracked, trying to soften his tone. "I'd like to see Mr Conley please."

And the stupid bitch had to say it, didn't she? She knew who he was just dandy but she still had to say it.

"Do you have an appointment?"

He could see her enjoying it. Does that happen often? Conley had asked. The worm under the mat? *Yeah, every time I go into your office Maxie.*

Danny leaned palms-down on the desk. He spoke each word clearly and carefully. "Don't fuck me about, you stupid bitch."

Her face went a dull, dark pink. She said, "He went fifteen minutes ago." Her voice was brittle, trying to enjoy her victory, but too angry to get any pleasure out of it.

Danny wanted to punch her, oh so *very* much.

He kept his palms flat on the desk, gaze fixed on her.

You can't hit her. No way José. Now drop it, there's a good boy.

He stood up slowly. "He's left?" he asked, not even knowing why he was bothering, and then he saw the shift in her eyes. She nodded.

Lying.

The fucking snotty little cow was lying.

Danny's hand shot across the desk, grabbing a handful of silky pink bow, dragging her forward by it. "You lying bitch, where is he?" And he shook her like a dog worrying a rat.

"Upstairs," she said. "Upstairs." And her face was white.

And then, Oh God John, then I did a bad thing.

I kept a hold of that bow, and if I had seen Katherine Henderson that time when I meant to, if I hadn't seen the lorry driver. Oh John, if I hadn't been so fucked up I wouldn't have done it. I wouldn't have done it, you know I wouldn't have.

I went round the desk, pushed her up against the wall, the filing cabinet, I don't know, we stopped moving, then I...

Danny let her go, horrified at himself. "I'm sorry," he said.

She stood there trembling, looking as if she thought he was going to hit her.

"I really am. I don't know why I did that."

He opened his mouth to speak again then shut it. She wasn't even hearing him. She stood there, her blouse hanging out, half undone, eyes blank with shock.

He backed out the room.

He backed out the room and ran up the stairs, hared up them, pounded on the door. Pounded again.

He heard Conley shout, "I'm coming."

It didn't matter. He went on hitting it till it opened, and when it opened he went in and slammed it shut and said, "Lock it," leaning against it, then looked at Conley and said, "Oh for fuck's sake, lock it," and felt tears slip down his face as he heard Conley slide the bolts into place.

"You never just come into a place Danny, you always 'Enter', in capital letters."

Conley's voice was low and dry beside him. Incredibly Danny felt himself smile, felt it begin, slow and warm, like something thawing inside him. Oh I love you, he thought.

He smiled through meaningless tears. He felt them drip off his face, couldn't open his eyes, couldn't let in the light.

He felt Conley's hand, soft, dry, touch his cheek briefly, wiping them away.

"Oh Jesus, I've really fucked up," he managed before more tears came out, swamping him.

His distress began to transfer itself to Conley. "What's happened?"

"Say you forgive me."

"I've told you, you're not your brother's keeper."

"No, not that. Say you forgive me." Danny's hand came out blindly.

Conley caught it, felt how cold it was, held it between both his. "Danny, you're worrying me."

"Say it, fuck you!" Danny's eyes finally flew open, green and huge and lost, filled with childish desperation. He looked so young, so vulnerable. Conley could feel his own eyes fill.

"I forgive you," he said quickly, moving close to him, touching his face, trying to reach him. "I forgive you."

"I raped her," Danny said.

Conley felt as if he'd swallowed lead. "Who?"

Danny looked blank then said, "No." He shook his head, then suddenly banged it back violently against the door. He roared and came up off the door like a wild animal. "I didn't. I fucking *didn't!*" And he put his hands over his ears.

Conley stared at him then said weakly, "Danny?"

Danny stood there, arms up over his head like an autistic child, hearing nothing but whatever was going on in his head.

"Danny..." Conley went over to him slowly. He wasn't sure if he should touch him or not. When Danny didn't respond he did it anyway, preparing for him to lash out.

He didn't.

He stood meekly while Conley pulled his arms down. Nothing. Closed. No-one home.

Conley took him in his arms and held him, kissed his hair, as much to appease his own anxiety as anything else. "Danny, what is it?"

Danny broke down against him, real tears this time, leaning heavily into him, crying his soul out. Conley couldn't stand it, the horrible despair in it. "Danny, talk to me. What *is* it?"

"I didn't rape her. I *didn't.*"

"Who Danny? Who?"

But he simply began crying again. Conley held him and shushed him and stroked his hair. Finally they ran out, stopped as suddenly as they started. Conley heard his thickened voice say, "Sorry."

"Don't be." Conley went on holding him, not wanting to let him go, but Danny pushed him away and said, struggling with a smile, one of his rare old smiles, wiping his nose with the back of his hand, "Now you've seen me at my worst, rotten little soul laid bare. Love me now if you can."

And Conley saw it in his eyes, darting, terrified. He really meant it, really thought it would make a difference. Conley tried to speak but nothing would come out. He pulled him to him again, roughly ignoring Danny's reluctance.

Danny lay stiff in his arms a moment then hugged him so tight it nearly squeezed the breath out him. "Oh Jesus Christ, I've missed you," he said.

Conley caught his face in one hand and pulled it round, grinding his mouth to his, tasting salt tears. He pressed tightly against him, trying to get closer, finally breaking away to say, "Let's go to bed."

Danny pushed away. "No, you don't know what I've done."

"It can wait," Conley said, trying to pull him back.

"No it can't. I've got to tell you. Your secretary..."

Conley pulled back a little. He looked in Danny's eyes, aware of the dirty tracks down his face. "Molly?"

Danny nodded. Conley dropped his arms and said, "What about her?"

Danny said suddenly, "Let's sit down," and went to move away but Conley grabbed his arm and said, "What about her Danny?"

"I..." He licked his lip and tried again. He tried to hold Conley's eyes but couldn't. He looked away. "I messed her about."

"Messed her about? What the hell does that mean?"

Danny turned his back to him and began to speak rapidly. "When I came into your office I was really fucked up. I knew what she'd be like, uppity little bitch. She started messing me about. I grabbed her. Her blouse was some slippy stuff. It came out of her skirt. I could see her underskirt. My mother used to have one like that, same colour." He hesitated then seemed to push himself on. "I pushed her up against the wall and kissed her, forcing into her mouth. Nobody likes that. I don't like it. Squeezing her tits, rubbing up against her. I wanted..." He stopped. Conley could see his back moving.

"That's it. That's all I did. I didn't rape her."

Conley frowned. "You assaulted her. It was indecent assault. Did you hit her?"

Danny swung round. "*No.*" He was genuinely outraged. "No. I didn't hit her. What do you think I am?"

"Given that she provoked you, why shouldn't you have hit her?"

"She's a woman."

Conley laughed. "Woman or not she provoked you. It would have been understandable to hit her. Molesting her was a damn sight more perverse."

"I didn't rape her."

"Why do you keep saying that?"

Danny looked utterly nonplussed.

"Nobody's saying you raped her. Why do you keep saying that?"

"I don't know."

Conley could see the sudden panic in his face.

"Why do you think I'm going to accuse you of raping her?"

"I don't." And this time his voice was hostile. "She might though."

"She doesn't need to. You assaulted her, that's bad enough."

"Fucking bitch."

"She isn't."

"That's right, take her fucking side. And when she reports me, then what?"

"Well you shouldn't have tried to rip her clothes off then, should you?"

"I wanted to show her..." And he stopped, face tight and angry.

"Show her what?"

"Nothing."

"Like hell, nothing. What?"

"That she can't fucking ignore me."

Conley stared at him then said slowly, "Oh Danny..."

"What?" he said belligerently, half-turned away.

"You wanted her to run after you like everyone else and when she wouldn't do it, you were going to make her. Or was it just show her what she was missing?"

"She hates my guts."

"That's her privilege Danny. It doesn't hurt you. She's allowed to hate you if she wants."

"No."

"What do you mean, No?" Conley was staring at him.

Danny's hands went over his ears again. He sat down on the floor. Just plonk. Down, gone, out of it.

"Oh God," Conley said, looking down at him, suddenly contrite. He crossed to him, hunkered down beside him and pulled his hands away. "Danny..."

Danny pulled his hands back.

"Danny... listen... I'm sorry. No more fighting. Come out, please."

Eventually Danny let himself be coaxed out. "I want to wash," he said. He sounded like a fractious child. But Conley saw he meant it, didn't dare to cross him.

"Alright," he said. "No problem. I'll run you a bath."

And he left him sitting there on the floor, head on his knees, like an orphan in the storm.

Only the storm was all in his head.

And Danny was all alone.

Conley gave him five minutes alone then knocked on the bathroom door. When he didn't answer he felt immediately panicked and tried the handle. It was open.

When he first went in he couldn't see him, he simply wasn't there, then his head shot out the water, streaming, throwing off droplets as he shook himself, hair sleek, uncoiling, blood red.

"Lord, the fright you gave me."

"What?" Danny shook his head, trying to clear the water from his ears.

"It's like the first time I saw you, when you came into my car, shaking off water like a dog. I thought I'd never seen anything so beautiful." He sat down on the edge of the bath.

"And now?" Danny slicked the water out of his hair. Curls began to coil up out of it, springing into life.

"Now I know it."

"You flatter so nicely."

"Not flattery."

"Heart-felt love?"

Conley's smile faded. "Don't be cynical Danny, it doesn't suit you."

"Doesn't suit me? I thought it was me." He sank back and closed his eyes. "Sorry, I'm being a dick."

"Forget it." Conley smiled again.

Danny looked at him. "Are you going to go on forgiving me forever?"

Conley nodded.

Danny smiled grimly. "Shit, you sure know how to make me feel bad."

Conley laughed.

"Don't laugh, there's nothing funny about it, because one day you won't."

"Never."

"Oh Jesus." Danny screwed his eyes tight shut. "Don't say that. God, now you've jinxed it. Don't *ever* say never." He smiled again. "I'm a poet and didn't know it."

Conley smiled and made to push the hair off his face in the familiar gesture, but he stopped short.

Danny saw it and said, "That make-up?"

Conley nodded. "Birthmark cream. The chemist got it for me."

Danny nodded. "It looks alright. Bit fake this close up, that's all."

"But better than a huge fucking elastoplast?"

Danny laughed, then he said, "Does it wash off?"

"Why? Want to see it?" Conley watched him intently.

"Maybe."

"Why?"

"It's sick," Danny warned.

"It's you, of course it's sick." And he smiled to soften the words.

Danny swished the surface of the water with his hands, then said quietly, something secret licking at the corners of his mouth, "Something sexy about having that branded on you, like you were... I don't know."

Conley didn't say anything, had the distinct feeling it was only a partial truth.

Danny said, colouring slightly, "I warned you it was sick." And even that sounded like a decoy.

Danny saw Conley's hand sink into the water, waited breathlessly until he felt it on him. He closed his eyes, said nothing more.

"Anything that gives me this isn't sick." Conley's voice was soft, eager. "How can I condemn anything that gives me this? I want this so much I think I'd put up with any depravity to have it."

Danny let his head drop back limply and held Conley's hand still under the water. "You're going to make me come."

"Then let me. You never let me give you anything." Conley smiled at him.

Danny took his hand away and let him. Conley smiled a little more.

"You know, your teeth..." Danny made a soft noise in his throat as Conley took him too close, "...they're terrible, terrible and beautiful both, like what you're doing to me."

"What *am* I doing to you?"

"Making me come." And his head went back as it slid out of him, coiling in white threads under the water, while he moaned in pleasure and Conley watched him, helpless with love, far above him.

"I shouldn't have let you do that."

Danny was sitting on the edge of the bath while Conley attempted to rub handfuls of his hair in a white towel. Danny dodged him irritably. Conley stood above him, smiling, enjoying himself as he caught and held him. "Why?" he asked.

"I'll be picking cooked come out my fucking hair for the next two weeks."

Conley dropped his arms. "God Danny." He laughed in spite of himself. "Must you always be so explicit?"

"Well I will," Danny said, looking up at him querulously. "I mean look at it. It looks like glue. It certainly sticks like fucking glue." He started picking at his pubic hair again, delicately, like a refined ape.

Conley stood shaking his head, laughing silently.

"This..." Danny pulled a tiny thread of egg-white off, "is why I never wank in the bath."

"Now I know."

"You're not taking me seriously," Danny snapped.

Conley laughed outright. "Can you blame me?"

Danny grabbed Conley's balls and squeezed. Conley yelled, "Oi! Let go Danny."

"No." Danny stood up tight against him. "Not till you say, I'm sorry I covered my best friend in cooked jism."

"It's your own cooked jism, you say it," Conley said, half laughing

"Come on, say it." Danny applied more pressure.

"I'm sorry..." Conley laughed and spoilt it.

"Come *on*."

"I'm sorry I covered his celestial master in cooked jism."

Danny let his hand ease off. "I forgive you," he said, eyes on Conley's face, close enough to kiss him.

Conley slid his arms around him. Danny hung teasingly back from him, smiling. "Yes? What do you want?"

"Your body."

Danny ducked his head away from his mouth. "You're one of those dirty middle-aged men who haunts public toilets."

"That's me, give me a kiss."

"No way." Danny ducked again. "You know..."

"Mm?"

"I've never once been propositioned in a public toilet."

"Shall I do it now?"

"This isn't public."

"We could open it if you like, charge a penny."

"Okay, proposition me."

"It's difficult. You're naked in my arms. I think we've already got quite far."

Danny wriggled free, turned his back. "Now do it." And he felt a bubble of unpleasant anticipation inside himself.

Conley came up behind him, pressed his body just close enough so that Danny could feel the brush of his clothes. "You're a very pretty boy," his voice whispered, dry in Danny's ear.

Conley saw the goosepimples come up across his shoulders and realised it was exciting him. He smiled and laid one hand softly on Danny's flank, let it slide. "Very pretty indeed," he whispered and let it slide some more.

Danny felt it come round his front, sliding down relentlessly across his stomach into his pubic hair. "And very big for such a young boy." And Conley moved closer against him, let his other hand touch him, begin the slow slide round. He felt Danny lean back into him slightly.

Conley's hand reached down and caught him. Danny was up hard. Conley swallowed a sudden mouthful of saliva, let his cheek lie against the warm, damp hair. "What's this?" he asked.

He hadn't expected an answer but Danny answered him, "My cock," and his voice was breathless and young. Too young. It sounded odd, off-rote and Conley began to have the strange floating feeling of suddenly treading water, the floor of the innocent sea dropped five hundred feet below you - one of Danny's sudden dark trips into the mirror, taking you with him - and Conley wanted to stop it and at the same time wanted to go on, try and catch something else of him, another tiny, meaningless piece of the jigsaw.

He felt suddenly inhibited, could no longer act the part, didn't know what to say.

He mentally dragged himself round by the scruff and said the first thing that came into his head. "Shall I do it?" And Danny came further back against him and pushed

his hips out, unconsciously enticing, as if he just wanted the sensation and didn't realise how incendiary his own vulnerability was.

Conley began, as slowly and insidiously as he could, to masturbate him, trying to make it sly and devious. Danny surprised him again by moaning. He was trembling slightly.

"Does he like that?"

"Yes." And he thrust himself forward, trying to speed it up, as if the orgasm were everything.

Conley, with some perverse instinct, said suddenly, "Do I get a kiss then?"

He felt Danny's reluctance and knew he was suddenly somehow way out of his depth. Somewhere Danny had taken the long walk off the short pier and they'd been swimming out all along and Conley hadn't even guessed it.

"Do I?" he pushed.

"After," Danny said.

"No, now."

Danny made a noise of frustrated rage and said, low and full of tears, "You *promised* John." It was petulant and distressed at once. A child frustrated by a parent's unfairness.

Conley felt every single hair on his body stand up. *John?* What the hell was he talking about? He wanted to push him away. Instead he held him tighter, hard against him, and said, "Kiss me Danny." And Danny had turned in one liquid-silver movement and slid down his body like an eel and had Conley's trousers unzipped before he even knew what had happened.

Danny had him in his mouth. Danny wasn't *kissing* him, not by any twist of the imagination.

Conley was so unnerved by it he turned soft as butter. Even the determined suckling of Danny's mouth did not rouse him. But Danny didn't seem to notice. His eyes were closed. Tight. Screwed up against it.

Conley touched his hair. "Danny?"

Danny went on relentlessly.

Conley tried to pull him off. He wouldn't let go.

"Danny, stop it. I don't like this."

Nothing. He just went on and on.

Eventually Conley shouted, "*Danny!*"

Danny's eyes flew open, but he only took him from his mouth and kneeled there like someone waiting to be hit, looking trapped, trying to guess where it was going to land first. He was breathing too fast.

Conley pushed himself inside his clothes and hunkered down in front of him, lifted his chin. "Danny, look at me." But Danny kept his eyes down. Conley kissed him softly. "Danny, come on."

Danny said, "You mad at me?" eyes still averted.

Conley looked down at him. His erection was still there, sticking up aggressively between his legs. Suddenly he said, as if he'd seen Conley looking and misjudged his interest, "It's big, isn't it?" And he started playing with himself as if he was trying to tempt him with it.

Conley watched him in a kind of horror. He pulled Danny's hand away. Danny caught at him and tried to push his hand onto it. "You do it. Come on. No-one'll see." And his voice was all wrong, cajoling, whining.

Conley swallowed carefully and tentatively began to masturbate him. He changed tempo abruptly, doing it hard and fast, wanting it over with.

Danny said immediately, "You've got to stop now," real fear in his voice.

Conley stopped but Danny immediately started pushing into his hand again saying,

"Do it fast. Do it fast. I won't tell."

Conley began masturbating him again. Danny had his legs wide open, watching himself in childish fascination. There was nothing adult about it. It was like he didn't know what he expected it to do. Conley wasn't prepared for it when it happened.

"Oh... oh... oh..."

And he kept saying it, more and more urgently until the first ejaculation hit him.

Suddenly Danny's head came up and he swore, a low deep growl, adult, entirely himself. "You fucking bastard. I hope you rot you fucking... you fucking... oh *shit*."

And the come splashed helplessly between them onto the bathroom floor.

The silence was vast and dripping. Danny sat on the floor like a defeated samurai warrior, head hanging down, palms lying face-up on his thighs. The semen lay in clear coils between them on the floor like a runic message, but Danny wasn't seeing it. Conley could feel his pain from where he sat. He touched his shoulder. Danny flinched away from him.

"Danny..."

"Leave me alone."

"You can't keep doing this."

Danny threw himself round violently and hung onto the side of the bath, curled up foetus-like against it.

Conley tried to hold him. Danny scrabbled away like a spider, with surprising agility. He turned on him and hissed like an animal, "Fuck off. Why don't you just fuck off?" eyes black and venomous.

Conley recoiled.

"That's it. Go on, fuck off you bloody pervert."

"Danny..."

Danny suddenly pulled at his own hair as if he was trying to pull it out. "Shut up, shut *up!*" And he covered his head with his hands. But Conley knew at the last he hadn't been talking to him. He had been screaming at something inside his own head. He was hunched there, rocking himself, making an odd crooning noise, half pain, half soothing.

Conley thought, I'm going to die if I have to watch much more of this.

He pulled Danny's hands down and slapped his face. So hard it made his palm sting. Danny made a little noise in his throat, his eyes wide with shock.

Danny stared at him, slack-mouthed, then slowly he nodded. It was the most beautiful sight Conley had ever seen. He pulled him up onto the edge of the bath. Danny began to shiver. Conley brought a warm towel off the rail and put it round him. Danny huddled into it then said, words broken as if they were glass stuck in his throat, "I fucked up again, didn't I?"

"No."

"Yes I did. Don't lie to me." His eyes sparked angrily. "I just opened my mouth and let it all spew out, the same old shit." He tapped his head. Suddenly he started rocking again, eyes closed as if he were in pain. "Ian... Ian..."

"What's Ian got to do with this?"

When he didn't answer Conley shook him.

Danny opened his eyes and looked at him, then he laughed a little dry humourless laugh. "Ian thinks I'm a loony. Ian thinks I should have been locked up years ago. Ian says I can't tell the difference between truth and reality. *Are* they the same? You know what? I *don't* know the difference."

"Danny, tell me, was John doing this to you when you were a child?"

Danny looked at him with a sudden shrewd intelligence. "Doing what?"

Conley slapped him, hard and satisfyingly. The first time ever. He wasn't even sorry. "You patronising little bastard. I've had as much of this as I'm going to take from you. You come in here, use me as an emotional dumping ground, and won't even give me common civility. No more, you hear me?"

Danny was holding his face. "I'm sorry."

"No you're not, you're only sorry you got caught."

Danny licked his lip then said, "Yes."

Conley looked at him, not sure what the 'Yes' meant. Danny saw his confusion and said, "Yes he was."

Conley said inadequately, inanely, "Oh." Briefly, ridiculously, he'd forgotten he'd asked him. He took a breath, watched Danny press his fingers to his cheekbones as if they hurt him and said, "Danny, you sounded as if..."

He saw Danny go still, unearthly still.

"You sounded as if you enjoyed it."

Danny's eyes came up slowly.

"As if..." But Conley couldn't look in those eyes and finish it.

"As if I *asked* him to do it?" he finished for him. His voice was flat and hostile, his expression almost contemptuous. "I was a fucking crawling, sick little pervert even then. I wanted my big brother to jerk me off. I *liked* it. No molestation there. Know what that makes me? I see you do. I see the revulsion all over your face."

"No."

"Don't fucking lie to me!" Danny almost screamed it. "*Look* at you." And he got up and dragged Conley over to the mirror, swiping condensation off it with his hand. "You're revolted."

Danny let him go. Just dropped him and walked out of the room.

Conley stood there a moment, staring at himself in the mirror, before he realised he'd gone. "Danny!" he shouted after him.

When he got out into the room Danny was in his shorts, pulling on his jeans.

"Danny, wait..."

"What the fuck for?"

"You're reading too much into it."

"Am I?" He kept on dressing.

"It doesn't revolt me. *You* don't." He saw Danny's hand fumble momentarily then go on.

Conley grabbed him and yanked him round. "Watch my lips. It doesn't revolt me. I love you."

Danny stood still then he said belligerently, "I don't believe you."

"Alright, fucking don't." And Conley pushed him away, turned his back on him, suddenly at the end of his tether.

There was a silence then Conley heard him pulling on the rest of his clothes. Oh God, his heart was going to break. But he couldn't say anything, didn't know what there was left to offer. He stood there, hands pushed into his pockets. After a while he realised Danny was silent, had been silent for some time.

"Conley..." His voice was quiet, tentative.

Conley turned slowly.

Danny said, "I..." But he didn't get any further before Conley had shortened the distance between them and was kissing his mouth into silence.

"Will I get it? Do you want to read it?"

They were lying in bed watching the last of the twilight slide into darkness.

"In a minute."

Danny lay with his head pillowed on his arms. Conley lay on one side, looking at him, trying to read his profile. "Scared?" he asked finally.

Danny didn't answer him directly instead he said, "Does he mention me much?"

Conley laughed. "Non-stop."

"How bad is it?"

"Like the little girl in the verse, when he's bad he's horrid."

Danny still watched the window. "Like what?"

Conley sighed and lay flat on his back. "He's very claustrophobic about you." He hesitated then said, "He wasn't so much in love with you as obsessed by you."

"Is there a difference?"

Conley turned his head and looked at him. "Of course there is."

"I've never seen it."

"In your house it doesn't surprise me."

Danny turned to him, brought an arm up, ran his fingers through his hair. He smiled. "You know they patched this up quite nicely."

"That's because it was too long when your big brother got creative on it."

Danny said, voice low, "He's a fucking shit."

Conley turned to face him again. "But you love him."

Danny dropped his hand. "Why d'you say that?"

"You do, don't you? Love him?"

Danny looked away. "I don't know any more."

"Come *on* Danny."

"I mean it, I don't."

"Well, did you then?"

"Once." Danny closed his eyes and shook his head gently. "More than you could believe possible." He laughed shortly, as if he was embarrassed by what he'd just said. "I told you I was sick."

"Don't keep saying that."

"Why not? I am."

"Says who?"

Danny was silent.

"Come on, says who?"

"Ian." It came out almost reluctantly.

"Ian seems to be good at feeding you negative self-images. I wonder why he would want to do that?"

"That sounds like textbook psychology shit to me."

"No, what Ian does is textbook psychology shit. You should tell him to take a long walk."

Danny was silent. An uncomfortable silence. Conley watched a tiny muscle jump twice at the corner of his mouth and wondered what it was about Ian. It was like a swamp. Danny started falling apart as soon as he was mentioned, like pins flying off a magnet.

"Why can't you shake him off Danny?"

"Let's drop this."

"Let's not. Why can't you?"

Danny shrugged, getting edgier by the second.

"Come on, why can't you?" Conley pressed.

"For fucksake, leave it out Conley!" Danny snapped away from him, turning his back to him.

"Fine, okay, but if you ever write the story of your life don't forget to send me a copy, then I'll be able to say I knew you. Once I've read up on the subject, that is."

Danny whirled back to him. "If you've something to say, say it."

"Alright." Conley sat up. "I'm tired of all your secrets Danny. I'm tired of them because they mean you don't trust me."

Danny rolled out the bed and Conley had a mad bizarre feeling of here we go again. He knew he had to get up and stop him, do something, but he simply couldn't be bothered.

But Danny didn't go. He unexpectedly came striding back into the room, yanking the zip up on his jeans and demanding, "Alright, ask me then."

"Truthfully?" Conley said warily.

"Scout's fucking honour."

Conley sat up and patted the bed.

Danny sat down grudgingly, staring at the floor.

Conley took a breath and said, "What's Ian's hold on you?"

Danny said without hesitating, "Whenever anything bad happened Ian was there. I would have been in serious trouble if..." He hesitated then said, "He was always there when I needed him. John wasn't."

"I'll bet."

Danny swung on him. "You know nothing from *fuck* Conley."

"Don't I?" Conley said, nodding. "I get the message we don't criticise Ian."

"*You* don't."

Conley stared at him, not believing it. "I'm not hearing this."

"I don't care what you fucking think you're hearing. Leave him out of it. Don't even mention him."

"Don't soil him with my dirty mouth, is that the idea?"

"Yeah, that's exactly the idea."

"Why don't you just marry him Danny?"

Conley wanted to take it back as soon as he said it. Yet as soon as Danny hit him he wished he'd said it sooner.

They rolled on the bed, half in, half out of it, tangled in the clothes. Conley had started out simply trying to defend himself, but it had soon deteriorated into wanting to win.

They slugged into each other in a determined silence, punctuated only by their own grunts and noises, until somehow, subtly, it was as if Danny stopped trying.

Eventually Conley found himself hanging, sweaty, naked and panting above him, saying grimly, "Now apologise, you little bastard," between dragged breaths.

And Danny, mouth bleeding, said, "I'll see you kiss my arse first."

"It could be arranged."

"Try it."

And Conley had looked down at him, at the blood trickling slowly down into his hair, at the flat black eyes, and rolled off him in sudden disgust. At himself, at Danny, at the whole stupid show.

They lay there, side by side on the wrecked bed, listening to each other's harsh breathing. Finally Danny got up and left the room. Conley heard water running in the bathroom. After a while he came back in and stood in the doorway, bathed in the dull light from the lamp, and Conley thought, God, he looks like a statue come to life. The young gladiator. David and his slingshot. Look at him, for God's sake. Too perfect to be real, too beautiful to be safe, even to himself.

"What does that look mean?"

"That no matter what you do..." Conley stopped.

"Go on."

"It's sicker than anything you could ever dream up."

"I said go on."

"I'm as drunk and besotted by your face as Henderson was. I understood

everything he felt when I read that diary. Even my attraction to Stephen was only because he looks so fragilely, elusively like you. I'm in love with your face. So much that when I'm at work I find myself doodling it. I masturbate thinking about you Danny. The first time in my life I've ever been able to masturbate at all and I do it picturing you. That's what it means, this look. It means that underneath everything the reason I wouldn't let you come here that first time when you asked me was because at the back of my mind I thought, What happens when his looks go?" Conley looked over at him and said, "Oh God Danny, don't cry." And he got up off the bed quickly and crossed to him.

"Don't touch me," Danny said, voice cold and hard. Conley could see the two wet tracks down his face. They made him look as if he were cast from metal, even more Grecian than before.

Conley said, "Katherine Henderson once asked me if I wouldn't pay to keep you in my house, like a work of art. I said no, and even as I said it I knew I was lying. She's more honest, that's all. She can face looking hard and acquisitory where the rest of us hide behind friendship and affection."

Conley stood there, a foot away from him, trying to read what was in his eyes. He had a tiny fold of tissue stuck to his lip to stem the bleeding. Conley looked at it, trying to see it as a flaw, trying to humanise him with it, and couldn't.

"And if I scratched my own eyes out? What then?"

"I don't know. I only know what I feel. I feel as if I love you, but it's so mixed up with the way you look that I don't know where it starts and finishes. I don't know Danny."

"I hate you."

"I couldn't go on lying to you," he said hopelessly.

"I hate your fucking guts."

"Danny..."

"No wonder you were prepared to go on forgiving me. It was the least you could do when you were giving me fuck all else."

"Danny..."

"Don't 'Danny' me, you fucking freak. You're so fucking dead you need some absolute of beauty to get you hard. Something perfect. My tough tits it happened to be me. Take a final feel Conley. Go on, take one, memorise it. It's all you're going to have in your old age."

"Danny, please..."

"Go on, feel me. Get fucking high. Or do you just want to stand and stare? You know, Ian once said, If anyone ever tells you you're beautiful Danny keep your eye on their hands. It was the truest thing he ever said."

"Danny, I don't want to lose you again."

"Then take a photograph. You're not the first, you know. Other people, same tastes. You're not unique."

"Who?"

"Oh that matters, doesn't it? You know, love must be the single biggest excuse for personal venom ever invented."

"Danny..."

"Say my name like that once more and I'll ram all those fucking gold teeth down your throat."

"I need you Danny."

"Can't get off no other way, huh?"

"Please, listen to me. I didn't mean to tell you so bluntly. Maybe I didn't say it the way I should..."

"You mean lie about it."

"No, I don't mean that. I mean so baldly, because I do love you. When you cry it

makes me cry too..."

"Sweet."

"Danny, I'm *trying* to explain this to you."

Danny's finger shot out, jabbing him in the chest, sending Conley back a step. "You're explaining nothing to me, because *I'm* not listening." He advanced on him. Conley took another step back. Danny followed him, catching at his arm and saying, "Oh no you don't."

Conley waited for him to hit him.

The blow never came, instead Danny pulled him to him and kissed him, hard, no sympathy in it at all, like he was trying to hurt him. It was angry and condemning.

When he broke away he wiped his mouth. "That's how I'll remember you Conley." And he turned and walked out of the room.

Conley sat on the bed and listened to him dressing again. It was like sitting docilely listening to somebody drowning. He wasn't ever going to make this well again. This was the one where Danny wouldn't come back. The one where he didn't have to ask for Conley's forgiveness.

"I want the diary." Danny was standing fully-dressed in the doorway.

"And if I don't give it to you?"

Danny just stared at him.

"It's downstairs."

"Then get it."

Conley got up and began getting dressed. Danny went back to the living room to wait for him. He didn't want to have to look at him.

"I'll come with you," he said when Conley came out and moved towards the door.

"There's no need. You might as well wait here."

"Why?"

And Conley wanted to say, Because maybe a miracle will happen and I'll think of something between here and downstairs to stop you going. But he didn't, he simply turned away and let Danny follow him.

Conley clicked the lights on in his office and crossed to a small safe in the corner. He opened it and took a black leather book out. He pushed the door shut again. He handed it to Danny.

Danny ran his fingers over the lettering. J.H. 1984. "Long time coming," he whispered.

"Are you going to read it?" Conley asked.

Danny shook his head, still looking down at it.

"What *are* you going to do with it?"

"Give it to John."

"Why?"

"To be free." And now he did look at him. "John killed him and I've been paying for it ever since. Now I don't owe him anything any more."

Conley stared at him.

Danny waited.

"What happened?"

"He knew too much, and was so stupid he used to brag about it. He had all the answers right in his hand and he didn't even know it. He was a moronic bastard. They all are, the whole family, thick as two short planks."

"Your mother's in the lake at Yardholm, isn't she?"

"Down among the fishes, feeding her snatch to the carp."

"And your father?"

966

"Rotting at the bottom of an eight foot hole under the water table. He's swimming too, with the earthworms. And that's only a fraction of my spectacular career to date. What are you going to do now, grass on me?"

"I could."

"You could, and John wouldn't miss next time."

"It would be too late by then."

"It's never too late for the purely pleasurable."

"And would you pretend you didn't know Danny?"

"I'd stand and watch Maxie. Like I watched him kill my mother. Like I watched him kneel on Henderson's body and pull the knife across his throat until it stuck. He went on kicking long after he must have been dead. It was like bleeding a pig. I suppose that's what it was."

"Oh Danny..."

"What? Spoiled your pleasure? Now you can't look at me without thinking of me watching Henderson bleed to death?"

Danny dropped the diary in the map pocket of his work jacket, pressed the studs shut. "Got to go Maxie. Been nice screwing you. Be thankful you lived through it, eh?" And Danny turned and slowly walked away from him.

Conley listened to him going down the stairs and let him go.

"Danny." Stephen jumped up, the relief plain on his face.

Danny held him at arm's length. "Later. I've got to see John. Where is he?"

The rebuff showed on Stephen's face but Danny couldn't care. He couldn't have cared supposing he'd been bleeding to death on the floor.

"He's upstairs," Rab said from the table. "Lighting cigarettes and hating people."

Danny went out without acknowledging him.

Rab turned back to find Stephen staring at the closed door. "Poor baby, big dicks win the day."

John's door wasn't locked.

He was sitting upright on the bed, fully-dressed, back against the headboard, lighting cigarettes and stubbing them out again.

He looked up, ready to tell whoever it was to fuck off. By the surprise on his face it was evident he hadn't expected to see Danny again that night. The surprise dissolved into white-faced anger. "Where the fuck have you been?"

Danny threw the diary, like spinning a stone, into his lap.

John grunted when it landed on his abdomen. He picked it up, looked at it, looked at Danny. "Where did you get this?"

"Conley. He was keeping it for Robert Henderson."

"Who?"

"Henderson's brother."

"You're telling me he has a brother?"

"That's right."

"And why should he give it to you?"

Danny sat down beside him. "Because I gave something to him."

John ran his fingers over the embossed letters then looked up into Danny's face. "Like?"

"What do you think John?"

"I don't think Danny, it gets me into trouble. What did you give him?"

"A little pleasure, a lot of pain."

"Your dick."

"Succinctly put."

"I understood your definition. Anyone who knows you would."

Danny sighed.

"Tired?" John asked.

"No," Danny rubbed his eyes with the heels of his hands, "I'm dead, only no-one's noticed yet."

John eyed him narrowly. "You were gone a long time."

Danny stared at him for a long moment then said, "John, you don't save someone's neck and ream a man's arse in the blinking of an eye."

"Is that what you did?"

"What? Saved your neck?"

"No, reamed his arse."

"That matters more, doesn't it?"

John didn't answer.

"Come on John, that diary there means less than shit to you compared to what I might have given to someone else. Even if all it amounted to was a teaspoonful of night emission and a lot of ugly grunting."

"Never ugly."

"You weren't there."

John shook his head. "Never ugly, not you."

They looked at each other, a long time, in the heavy familiar gold of the lamp, the familiar safe warmth of the night. *Oh John. Things I've done, John. Things I've done.*

Danny felt John's hand on his leg, warm, huge.

They were still watching each other like dogs, not sure if they were hostile or not. Danny moistened his mouth.

"I'm hungry Danny." John's voice was dry, cracked. It made Danny want to clear his throat.

"It's only been one night."

"I don't care. I'm telling you how I feel."

Danny stood up, suddenly wanting to put distance between them. John came up after him, like a snake striking, caught both his arms.

"What's this? Rape?"

"You know I can."

"You'll need to."

"Then I will."

"John, I am really fucking tired. I mean *really* tired."

"Then just sleep with me. I won't touch you."

Danny laughed. "Famous last words."

"Stay with me and I promise I won't touch you. Come on Danny, you owe me. I've been eating my heart out with worry."

John could see the tiredness breaking him. He had no heart for an argument. He pushed him. "Please Danny." And he saw his acquiescence before he'd even finished speaking.

"Alright... but just for tonight."

John smiled, showed all his teeth. He held him, stroked his back, felt Danny give against him, knew he'd won utterly.

Danny lay there, feeling safe, warm, home.

And hated himself.

"Want me to bring you something up?" John asked.

"No, I'll go down."

"You mean you want to speak to Stephen."

"And if I do?"

John said, "I don't want to fight with you."

"Then don't start it. I'm going down to get something to eat, alright?"

"Alright."

"You staying here?"

John nodded. "It's better than watching you foaming at the mouth."

"This your idea of not fighting?" Danny stared at him.

John dropped his eyes. "Go get something to eat. Look, my mouth's shut."

Danny went out, quickly, while his mouth was shut.

He met Stephen coming out the kitchen. He smiled. "Come back in, sit with me while I have something to eat."

"I don't think I'll bother."

"Oh come on Stephen, don't give me any grief. I've had a hard day."

"No thanks." Stephen's mouth was set hard.

"Alright, I'll see you in the morning."

"The morning?"

Danny had already half-passed him, his hand resting on the kitchen door handle. "That's what I said." He looked back at him.

"We aren't...? I thought..."

"What did you think?"

Stephen flushed. "Nothing."

"You thought you'd be sharing my bed again?"

Stephen stared at the floor.

Danny lifted his chin. "Come on Steve-o, come in and sit with me. I can't sleep with you tonight, at least come sit with me."

Stephen went back into the kitchen, meek as a lamb.

Rab was still there. He lifted his mug in mock salute.

Danny gave him a mock smile in return.

"Hey, he sees me. I haven't been struck with sudden invisibility."

"We should be so spared."

Rab made a small noise of distress. "God, he hates me. I'll kill myself."

"Drop dead."

Rab laughed and said, "Come sit on my knee, tell me what dirt you've been doing."

"Just the usual."

"Whose backside?"

"What a low mind."

"About on a level with your crotch."

Danny kicked the fridge door shut, both hands full. "How d'you know it wasn't a woman Rab?" He spread the bits and pieces on the table then crossed to the sink and filled the kettle.

"Was it?"

"Not today."

"Well then."

Danny came and sat down, looked at him, a small smile hovering there. "But it is sometimes."

Rab coloured slightly and looked away. "I'll bet."

"Don't push your luck Rab."

"I'm pushing nothing."

Their eyes locked. Stephen watched, utterly perplexed by what they were saying to each other. He moved into a seat between them, as much to distract them from each other as anything else. He began talking rapidly while Danny ate, pouring his tea for him. He barely noticed when Rab got up, giving Danny a look over his head that said, Doesn't he ever shut up? Only catching Danny's crooked return smile.

"Fuck. Why didn't you shut me up? Going on and on."

"Because I like listening to you."

"I missed you Danny."

"I missed you too chicken. Oops..." Danny covered his mouth in mock horror.

"That's alright. You can call me it if you want."

"Slip of the tongue."

"I don't care." Stephen smiled up at him. "In fact I kind of like it."

"Why?" Danny looked at him curiously.

"I'm not saying. It's a secret. One of my own."

"Hoity-toity."

Danny pulled his chair out and stretched out his legs. He looked at Stephen then patted his lap. Stephen came over immediately, straddled his knee, crotch to belly.

Danny stretched up to kiss him. As soon as their mouths touched Danny was pulling him forward into him, a hand under each buttock, Stephen wrapping his feet round the back of his chair legs, trying to pull himself closer.

Danny eventually broke for air. Stephen immediately said, "Let's go up to bed."

"I can't." Danny knew there was only one way to kill it. "I'm sleeping with John tonight."

Stephen sank back down onto his lap. "What?"

"You heard me."

"But I thought..."

"No, don't say it. It's all arranged. Don't ask me to explain it. It's just for tonight."

"Is he making you do this?"

Danny pressed a finger to his lips. "Stephen, he's the boss. Sometimes it pays to do what he wants."

"What about me?"

Danny smiled, took Stephen's hand and pressed it against the boy's own crotch. "Do it yourself. Think about me."

"I don't want to. I want you to do it."

"Well that's too bad, isn't it?"

"Why can't *he* do without for a change?"

"He will, after tonight."

"Oh yeah? And what'll the excuse be tomorrow night?"

Danny looked at him for a long moment then said coldly, "There won't be one. Don't push your luck Steve-o."

Stephen got off his lap. "Don't fucking worry. I'll leave you to it. I hope he gives you a good time."

"Watch your mouth."

"You fuck off Danny." Stephen marched away, then turned back half-way across the room. "You just fuck off." And he slammed out the door.

Danny slid down low in the chair and dropped his head onto the back. He stared at the ceiling for a long, long time. When Ian came in he was still lying in that exact position, hands folded neatly on his stomach.

When Ian moved into view above him Danny moved his eyes, nothing more. "Why hello Ian," he said laconically.

Ian took one of his curls and twisted it round his finger, uncoiling it again in a perfect spiral. "Hello gorgeous."

"Have you come to shout at me too?"

"If you like."

"I don't like. Be original, say something nice to me."

"I love you."

"That isn't nice."

"Maybe, but it's true."

"I don't love you Ian."

"I know."

"In fact, I don't think I even like you."

"You're making it very hard for me to say something nice to you."

"I didn't think you cared whether I liked you or not."

"Oh, but I do."

Danny sat up. He sighed.

Ian pulled him back into the chair, encouraging him to rest his head against his belly. He began massaging his neck. "Tired?"

"As a fucking dog."

"All wanting their bones?"

Danny laughed. "Something like that, and I've given too many out already today. I am shagged out."

"Literally?"

"Of course."

"Who was the lucky boy or girl?"

"Robert Henderson, James Conley."

They were quiet for a while. Ian reached round and undid a couple of his buttons, slid his hand inside his shirt and went on kneading his shoulders and neck, now against his bare skin.

"You're good at that."

"I know."

"I've always liked it."

"I know."

"Doesn't make me hard though, Ian."

"Don't rub it in Danny."

"Feeling fragile tonight?"

"No, you're just feeling vindictive."

"You can handle that."

"No doubt."

"You don't sound very convinced."

"Maybe I get tired of it. That never occur to you?"

"Maybe I get tired of you Ian. That ever occur to you?"

"Frequently."

"Why don't you get someone? It would be good for you."

"He won't have me."

"Ian, he isn't ever going to have you. What the hell are you waiting for?"

"I don't want anyone else."

"Oh grow up." And Danny pulled away from him irritably.

Ian came round in front of him. Danny looked up at him.

"What were you doing at Conley's?" Ian asked.

Danny could see the tension in his face. He leaned back in the chair again, looking up at him. "Having casual sex. What did you think I was doing?"

Ian's face was a patchy red. "You might have told me. I told John you wouldn't be

there."

"Oh God, your reputation's in tatters."

"Are you going back?"

Danny said yes just to see what happened, just out of curiosity. What happened was nothing - a big, dangerous, ugly nothing. Ian turned his back on him. Danny knew that one. Hiding what he was thinking.

He pulled him round but he was too slow to catch it. "What's the problem?"

"Nothing."

"I thought you didn't care?"

Ian licked his lips, eyes shifting. "You know I don't."

"Oh Jesus," Danny laughed, face incredulous. "Come on Ian, look at you. You look like you've got a hot brick down the seat of your trousers."

"I don't like him."

"Now he says." Danny sat back again, still watching him. "Why not?"

"I don't know."

"Liar."

"I don't like the way you look at him."

Danny looked at him. "This is close Ian, very close. Not like you."

"Oh save your effort Danny, just leave him alone."

"Are you threatening me?"

"I might well be."

Danny looked him up and down, slowly. "You?"

"Yes, me."

Danny jumped up out his seat, grabbing him and yanking him forward. "Don't you fucking *dare*. I'm not cutting my cloth to keep you in big brother's good books." He shoved him hard against the counter then let him go.

Ian pressed a hand to his lower back. "I'm warning you Danny," he managed on a short pained breath. "Next time I'll make sure he gets him. Next time I'll fucking do it myself."

Danny came up close to him again. Ian waited for it, but the blow never came. Danny stopped short, said tightly, "There won't be a next time. Mr Conley and I have..." he paused and Ian saw something strange flit in his eyes, "terminated relations."

"What happened?"

"Oh..." Danny let out a small laugh, shaking his head, "no peace and light for you Ian. I'm telling you nothing. You've been told all you need to know."

"And what if I choose not to believe you?"

"You mean what if you decide to terminate Mr Conley, period?"

Ian just looked at him. Danny smiled then grabbed his scrotum and squeezed. Hard. "You haven't got the guts. Drowning a drunk old man in the bath's more your style. You're too scared big brother might be cross at you." He squeezed again, viciously. "You pathetic little shit," he hissed into his face.

Ian could feel the fine spray of saliva, the heat of his breath. "Alright," he gasped. Danny let him go.

Ian dropped back against the counter, cupping his tender balls in his hands, watching the watery blur that was Danny walk out the door.

John was already in bed. One heavy white shoulder and arm lay out the bedclothes. The other arm was under his head. He was lying on his side, facing Danny. "Long conversation."

"It was three conversations John. Three different people."

Danny spoke to him with his back to him, pulling his shirt out, taking his clothes off carelessly, always full of grace. Not anything you could ever tire of watching. What about him could you tire of watching?

John didn't say anything else. When Danny was stripped down to his shorts he came over to the bed and made a move to get in. John spread a hand across it, stopping him.

"Now what?" Danny said, straightening up again.

"Your shorts, take them off."

"Oh come on John." Danny dragged at his hair, temper fraying dangerously.

"I don't get to touch you, I at least want to see you."

Danny held his eyes for a moment then slid his shorts off. He stood there, mouth a thin line, letting John look at him. After a while he said, "Enough?"

"It's never enough."

"Well too bad, I'm getting in before my balls climb right up into my tits."

Danny threw the blankets back and climbed in. John didn't try to stop him. "Jesus, it's cold tonight," he said, dragging the blankets up round his shoulders.

John lifted his arm in invitation. Danny only hesitated a moment before the cold won out. He squirreled over and in against John's chest, feeling the familiar dry warm heat immediately wrap around him. "You're never cold, are you?"

"Not near you." And John shifted against him with deliberation, letting him feel what his nakedness had done to him.

John felt him sigh, long and slow against him. "What was that for?"

"You said you wouldn't try anything."

"Who's trying anything? It was you wanted a heat." And he adjusted himself with his hand, letting his penis lie heavily against the side of Danny's stomach.

They could both feel it between them, both taking shallow breaths as if they were afraid of pressing on it.

"I knew this would happen," Danny said dismally.

"What?"

"This. I knew you wouldn't just let it rest."

"Then why did you agree to it?"

"I was tired."

"Liar."

The single, almost gentle, word hung there like the heavy heat pressing lightly on Danny's stomach, waiting.

"I called you a liar Danny."

"I heard you John."

John's lips brushed his forehead. "Miss me?" he whispered.

Danny remembered the nightmare. "No," he said.

"Liar," John said again, and now he was running his hand slowly over Danny's stomach, in ever-dropping circles. "I'm going to find out sooner or later Danny. Tell me now, confess it and save your shame."

"Don't be too confident John."

"Telling me it isn't there?"

"I'm telling you that even if it is it doesn't mean anything."

"You've hidden behind that for years, haven't you?"

"If you say so."

"I do." And the hand was brushing his stomach now. "Danny?"

"Mm?"

"I'd give anything if you'd stop this, move in with me again."

"Anything John? An arm? A leg? The farm? My freedom?"

"You don't want your freedom."

"You conceited bastard."

"No, don't." John pulled him tight into him. Danny's fists pressed into his chest. "Stay where you are."

Danny lay still. Anything to breathe again.

"It's true Danny, you know it."

"It fucking isn't. I've never felt like this before."

"You've never been able to fuck anyone right under my nose before."

"*Christ...*"

"You're using him."

"Shut up, you ugly bastard. You bring me in here for *this?* I'm fucking worn out and you start this? I grovelled on a fucking floor, beat up on a cheap little masochist for you John, and this is it, nothing but fucking grief."

John was holding him tight, stifling his struggles. "For me?"

"Who the hell do you think I do it for? Myself? Fifteen years on and you still believe any shit he tells you. You don't even bother to sort it out. I'm every badness there fucking is. You love me in spite of yourself. Big fucking honourable John. Well, what if you're fucking *wrong* John? What if I'm not all bad? I'm sure God must have told you that once. No-one's all bad, probably not even you."

Danny lay pushed into his chest, biting his lip so hard he knew he would make it bleed if he didn't stop. But he wasn't going to cry. He'd cried enough for a lifetime today. No more.

John was tense and silent against him, every muscle in his chest and arms taut. It was like trying to rest against a rock. Danny breathed shallowly. He couldn't do anything else. Eventually he had to say, "Ease up, I'm suffocating."

John eased his arms slightly. Danny pulled a wobbly breath into his lungs.

They lay there in silence. After a while sheer exhaustion began to take its toll. Danny tried to shake himself awake, feeling inexplicably ashamed of himself for simply wanting to let go, but John's voice, low and gentle, said, "It's alright," and he began stroking his hair.

Danny sank into the heavy flesh as the muscles seemed to melt into softness beneath him, sweet, smelling faintly of sweat and cotton waxing.

Must have been doing his jacket tonight, Danny thought distantly, before he drifted finally and irrevocably into a deep and untroubled sleep.

SEVENTY-SEVEN

Danny didn't know what John had done with the diary. The only thing he felt sure of was that he hadn't made any attempt to read it. He had had it now for more than a week, but he gave no sign that he had so much as looked at it. Danny knew that when he did, *if* he did, he'd know.

He'd gone back to sleeping in his father's room without so much as a murmur from John. He'd asked him once, only once, the morning after Danny had slept with him to move back in with him. Danny had said no. John had simply turned his back and not referred to it again. This from a man who would have given him anything.

Danny tried hard not to let it rankle, but it did.

He had slept with Stephen every night since. He could feel him waiting for him to ask him to move in with him, not to bother with the pretence of a separate room, but his mother was in the way and Stephen knew it, and that spared Danny's efforts, and Stephen knew that too.

Danny continued to take so much pleasure out of him it was like he'd rediscovered sex. He couldn't get enough of it and didn't care who heard him. He felt almost driven, like he had to keep hitting higher and higher peaks. It never seemed enough for him. He was always left wanting more.

John was wrong. You couldn't get this much pleasure out of cheap revenge. Anyway, he'd be pushed to get revenge out of John. Danny was out of sight out of mind as far as he was concerned.

Tomorrow would be Sunday. Half day. He would go out somewhere with Stephen where John couldn't watch him, where he wouldn't keep catching those black eyes burning holes in him.

It was like last summer. It was beginning to get to him. But tomorrow was Sunday. Day of rest, even for the wicked.

Anyway, it would give John something to think about.

Wouldn't it?

SEVENTY-EIGHT

Sunday morning was dark. The alarm went off, waking Danny immediately. He pushed the button down and clicked on the light. Stephen grunted and pulled the blankets over his head. Danny pinched his backside, earning himself some more grunts and what sounded suspiciously like 'Fuck off'.

Danny got up and looked out the window. Like pitch.

He peered up at the sky. Snow? Rain? Something, just waiting to come down.

He closed the curtains again, crossed back to the bed. He pulled the blankets off him again.

"Hoi!" Stephen tugged them back. "Don't do that. I fucking hate that." He pulled his head back under.

"I know you do. That's why I do it, just to annoy you." Danny was sticking his arms under, tickling him. "Come on... get up."

"I am up. Why don't you come back to bed and have some?" Stephen wriggled back and peered up at him over the top of the blankets, eyes grinning.

"You dirty little bastard."

"Suck my dick, gorgeous."

Danny pounced on him, this time tickling him with serious intent. "I'm going to wash your mouth out with soap, you dirty little sod."

Stephen immediately started pleading for mercy, half-laughing, half-desperate.

"Alright." Danny stopped, took breath. "Now what do you say? Let's hear it."

"Suck my dick," Stephen said again, diving under the blankets for cover.

"Unrepentant, huh?" Danny began tickling him again, trying to catch hold of his feet.

When he finally caught them he never got as far as tickling them. Stephen screeched, "Don't! I submit! I submit!"

"Apologise."

"I'm sorry, I'm sorry. Just don't tickle me any more." He was gasping for breath, limp with panic.

"Okay, now you can suck *my* dick." And Danny swung up over his face, letting his flaccid penis trail over his mouth.

Stephen looked up at him, smiling. "*I'm* a dirty bastard?"

"Get sucking... gorgeous," Danny smiled back at him.

Stephen opened his mouth and let him push it between his lips.

John lay in the dark, listening to them skylarking around.

He listened to them until they turned silent.

He wondered if he should time them. How long would it take this time for whichever one it was to bring the other to climax? Not very long. It never did.

They got a lot of fun out of it. Good clean boyish fun. Two healthy full-grown boys fucking each other's brains out. It was only sex after all, didn't mean a thing.

He sighed.

Today Danny, you and I are going to spend a little quality time together. Let Stephen mingle with the peasants for a while. I think he's had plenty. Enough to last him.

I should've given into the obvious and slept with Rab last night. But I didn't feel like it. Dick's gone numb. Needs the kiss of life from a certain darkly beautiful boy. Listen.

There he goes. Stephen bringing him off.

Listen to him, in his little ecstasy of pain.

John stretched his limbs, sighing again. *Look at how calm I am. I'm getting too old for this. Nearly thirty. Feel a lot older. Feel as if I've lived here for four hundred years. Feel as if I've waited for Danny twice as long. Wonder what Superboy would do if I ripped in there like the wrath of God and pulled him right out of Danny's mouth and told him to clear out? Probably sit right down on the floor and bubble. It's what I'd like to do right now, sit down and bubble. But it gets harder. The older you get the harder it gets to cry. No release for the wicked.*

Now Ian. You never see Ian crying.

What makes Ian cry?

The same thing that makes Ian breathe. Me on one side, Danny on the other.

I should've dumped him long ago, but I've left it too late now. Never give your children to a nanny, they'll end up calling her Mother.

He sighed again, then swore at himself. "Christ *up*," he hissed fiercely.

He got up. Slowly, wearily.

By the time he had fastened his shirt Stephen was already coming.

John hammered on the door as Stephen was bringing Danny up close again. Danny said, "Coming..." in a tense breathless voice as he hung onto the headboard, working his penis in and out of Stephen's mouth, smiling down at the top of his head.

John stood there looking at the door, wondering if they locked it, wondering why he was wondering.

Danny let a groan out, knowing he was standing there listening. His orgasm followed immediately, pulsing into Stephen's mouth. "Suck me," he gasped urgently, and he could see John's face as he closed his eyes and let it wash over him.

And out of him.

John stood listening to the words.

He hadn't expected to hear words. He'd been able to hear the creaking of the bed bumping against the wall as he pounded into that eager little mouth, but he hadn't expected to hear any words.

He's up on his knees on the bed.

How do you know that?

I know him. Only way he could make the bed play his game. Boy beneath him, everybody in their place. Like chess.

He turned and carefully walked down the stairs, his nails making light tracks on the banister as they slid through the dust.

John waited until the others had gone out in case any of them wanted a fight. If they did they had come to the right place.

Stephen wanted a fight. John could see that. He'd spoiled his day, hadn't he?

"Why?" Stephen demanded. Sharing Danny's bed made him very brave.

John said, "Because I say so."

Stephen's chin jerked up but Danny said warningly, "Man's the boss Stephen," before he had a chance to drop himself in it.

John watched him transfer all his anger to Danny, but Danny only winked at him and said, "Go on, I'll see you later."

977

Stephen got up and stalked out.

Now Danny was watching him. John let him, taking his time to turn back to him, meet his eyes. When he did Danny said, "We bother you this morning?"

John's smile was slow and spreading. "Can you come just thinking about me listening?"

Danny coloured. "Dick."

"Want to see it? Forget what a decent one looks like?"

"Ha ha."

"Nobody's joking."

"That's what's so funny. You're pathetic John."

"No worse than Boy Wonder."

"He's half your age."

"And half my size… but each to their own."

"Maybe I like them small."

"Yeah." And John's voice said, Pig's might fly.

Danny sat down. "So what are we doing today?"

"Going out."

"Where?"

"None of your business."

"Come on John."

"I'm the boss. I say out, I mean out. Any problems?"

"Only you."

"Why don't you do something about me then?"

"Like?"

"Like what you usually do with your problems, fuck them till they go away."

Danny looked at him. "No thanks."

"What's wrong? Scared it shows your brat up?"

"You don't have any problems with your ego, do you?"

"None."

"Okay, we going out or not?" Danny stood up.

"Sure." John stood up.

They got their coats and boots on in silence.

They went out in silence.

Outside it began to snow.

"What the hell are we doing here?"

"Working."

"At what?"

"What a suspicious nature you have Danny. Get out."

Danny got out. John got out too, crossed to the door, opened it. He stood back to let Danny in first.

The hall was dark, John somewhere behind him. Danny knew with a sudden intuition what he intended to do, could sense something repressed about him.

He dodged to avoid him, succeeded in giving himself a brief headway. He heard John's grunt, felt his fingers catch and lose the edge of his jacket. He went up the stairs two at a time. John didn't come after him.

Danny stood in the upper hall listening, breathing through his mouth. *Very clever Danny, up the stairs. Very clever indeed.* He could hear John moving about down below. He wondered if he could get back down and out again without him hearing. But he'd wondered too long. He heard John's steps on the stairs.

He backed down to the centre of the hall where he could choose his room, give

himself at least the pretence of options.

John appeared around the corner. His bulk filled the narrow space. He was a very big man. Sometimes you forgot. It took a small space like this to make you remember again.

"Going somewhere Danny?"

"I haven't a clue John, it's your party."

"Ah, but you're guest of honour."

"And what does that get me?"

"Pick your room."

"For what?"

"Oh I bet you could guess."

"I don't believe you need this, I really don't."

"Then you'd be wrong."

"It's been a *week* John."

"A very long cold week. When was the last time I went week without you?"

"You managed for twenty-eight years."

"What an unforgiving little bastard you are."

"That's right. Now can we give this up?"

"Why?"

"You can't go around acting like some kind of frustrated lover."

"Why not? It's what I am."

They looked at each other like gunfighters, neither shortening or lengthening the distance between them.

"We going to stand here like this all day?" Danny demanded.

"I doubt it."

"Come on then," Danny said, and his voice was low, aggressive.

John smiled, letting it spread into a grin, then he advanced towards him up the hall. Danny backed away from him. John kept on coming.

When they came level with the end of the hall, outside the second bedroom, Danny made a dive for John's left. John moved to cut him off. Danny moved faster and feinted to the right, shooting past him. He heard John mutter, "Shit," felt his hand snag his jacket again, thought he'd slipped him.

He hadn't. The hand held, jerked him suddenly as the jacket stopped giving. Danny felt it tug back.

The noise John made was unmistakable. *Got you.* Half-choking him, he reeled him back in like a landed fish. He pulled him backwards into his arms, pinioning him tight, even spreading his feet so Danny couldn't step on them. "It's Anniversary Time. Scene of our first big moment. Remember how it felt? Remember what it was like to have me finally kill for you? I don't think you've ever been as hard since. Wonder what our little friend Stephen would make of that?"

Danny struggled against him silently, meaninglessly, futilely.

"Or will I have you here, up against the wall?"

"That wasn't what you did John."

"You *do* remember. Was it as good as you thought it would be?"

"Who said I thought it would be good?"

"You thought it would be great?"

Danny didn't ordain to answer that. What could he say?

"Maybe the bottom bedroom. Change of scene. What do you say?"

Danny took a breath, held his silence.

"Okay, bottom bedroom it is."

"No, let's do it here," Danny said quickly.

"Too late, I've a fancy for the bottom bedroom now."

Danny began to panic. "It's locked," he said.

"How do you know?"

And Danny heard it, something soft and silent and predatory.

"It's always been locked."

"Well maybe it isn't now. Let's go see, shall we?"

"John..."

"Come on Danny." And he suddenly let him go, yanking him round, facing him back down the hall. He pushed him. "Move."

Danny stood there like a stubborn cat. John pushed him again. Danny moved.

"Go on then, open it," John said when they reached the door.

"What if it's locked?"

"What if mice were butter knives? Open it."

Danny turned the handle. It was locked. He felt a warm flood of relief go through him. "It's locked," he said, trying to keep it out his voice.

"Well now," John said. "And I don't suppose you've got a key?"

"Why the hell should I have a key?"

"Why indeed? And why, if it comes to that, are you keeping your back so firmly turned against me?"

Danny turned to face him.

"Oh very brave Danny."

Danny moistened his mouth. John went on, "Really you should have said, No, sorry John, but I've got a key at home if you'd like it."

Danny watched the saturnine face, heavy smile, teeth showing whitely in the dark, waited, feeling his stomach turn to water.

"Nothing to say?"

"You're saying it all John." And his voice came out too high and too obviously afraid.

John reached into his pocket. Smiling, he pressed something warm and hard into Danny's palm, curling his fingers round it, like he was giving him a present. "Surprise, I brought it along."

Danny didn't need to look. He could feel the distinctive shape of it. The only key-ring he'd ever owned.

"Go on then, open up."

"John..."

"No Danny, don't bother, just open up." Danny saw his jaw set hard, and so he turned slowly and pushed the key into the lock, leaving the little black bimbo doll hanging there, blinking, in her plastic hula skirt.

"Go on," John breathed in his ear.

Danny turned the handle and opened the door.

John pushed him hard, in the middle of the back.

John was waiting.

He'd put on the light, shut the door, locked it, pocketed the key and now he was walking round the room, looking at the walls, smiling, waiting. Danny didn't even know what for.

After a minute John laughed and sat on the bed. "You're a picture Danny. One of many. These yours?"

Danny nodded.

"Liar."

Danny didn't answer.

"Take a look at them then. Go on, take a look."

Danny looked at the walls, briefly, then away again. He felt it before he saw it. He looked back again, heard John laugh, heard him say, "That's it. Go on, take a good look."

Danny walked over to the fireplace. Something was wrong, but he couldn't place it. He looked at the wall, scanning it with his eyes, then he saw it.

"That's it Danny, now you've got it."

Danny's gaze travelled over the wall, checking every photograph. "Jesus," he whispered. "Oh sweet Jesus Christ..." He turned and looked at John.

"Don't look at me. If I wanted to mutilate you I'd do it. A photograph wouldn't fix it."

"Ian," Danny said.

"Ian," John agreed.

Danny turned back, walked round the room. On every single photograph his eyes had been carefully and painstakingly scratched out. "I think I'm going to be sick," he said.

"Over the basin," John said, pushing him into the corner.

But Danny wasn't sick. He just stood there, stomach heaving without relief, shaking, feeling as if someone had tried to kill him, tasting the bad taste of hate in his mouth.

"You push him and push him," John said. "What do you expect?"

"Not this."

John laughed. "You mean an attack on your sacred image? Christ, you're the limit."

Danny leaned all his weight on the sink, braced his arms against it. "Christ, how long has he spent up here? He must have started the day I..."

"The day you what?"

Danny didn't answer.

"The day you paid him to keep quiet? The day he came *that* close to slicing you open?"

Danny nodded.

"He was angrier than you thought. Doesn't it scare you? To know that any one of those little nicks might have been the one? That maybe they were never meant to be nicks at all?"

Danny nodded again.

"You always underestimate him, don't you?"

"Christ, he must really hate me." Danny's voice was boneless.

John suddenly lost patience. "Of course he fucking hates you. Why shouldn't he? What the fuck else should he feel?"

Danny straightened up. "Not this. Not this fucking..." he waved his arm feebly, "...*mess*. I don't deserve this. He gets what he's owed. Always. More than he fucking deserves. Don't you lecture me John."

"Oh grow up, why don't you?"

"Don't you fucking sneer at me. Who the fuck are you to sneer at me?"

"You watch that mouth. I'm just in the mood to waste it a little."

"Go ahead. Go right fucking ahead."

John slapped his head, a hundred little stinging slaps that herded him back across the room, Danny suffering it till the bed caught him in the back of the knees, making him sit down, and then John pushed him back and climbed over him, breathing hard in his face. "Now I'm up good and hard for it. Want it now?"

Danny glared up at him. "Go on then, fuck me. Let's see you fuck me."

John reached down between them and manhandled their jeans down, then pressed his body against his, the two naked groins locking smoothly together. He began rubbing himself hard into the softness of Danny's belly, watching his face, saying, "Remember how *that* feels?"

Danny spat full in his face. John cursed and grabbed his hair, dragging him round onto his belly. He pushed into him dry and hard, scraping every inch of the way, wiping the spit off on his hair, hissing, "You little cunt. I'm going to rip you open for that." And pushing into him, raw and agonising, until it was all up, then pounding in urgently, no more than half a dozen strokes, before he came, as blind as the eyeless photographs on the wall, hands shoving and grabbing under Danny's body until he found it.

And found it hard.

He grunted thickly, half-elation, half the intensity of his orgasm. It drew the last spasm out of him in an odd gasping moan.

He lay there heavily for a moment then pulled out and rolled Danny over, surveying the sprawled wreckage of his body. "Look at you, lying there on your back with your dick up, spunk farting out your arse, straining your prick up into my hand, trying to lie to me."

Danny shut his eyes.

John went down his body, freeing his jeans from his ankles and shoving his legs wide apart. He jammed two fingers inside the numb slackness of his sphincter then bent and took his shaft in his mouth, peeling the foreskin back and swamping the engorged head in the wet slackness of his mouth. He let it sink in and out twice. On the third stroke he heard Danny's stifled little moan and felt his hands reach up to grip his head. He immediately let his penis slide back deep towards his throat, relaxing the muscles. He felt Danny tremble, just barely.

And then it came.

Danny thrusting beneath him, body twitching into sudden life, his mouth translating each little twitch into a moan, the same moans he made with Stephen, only it wasn't because he let himself, it was because he couldn't stop himself, couldn't help it, and he went on coming until his big brother let him stop.

And it was then Danny surprised him, suddenly saying words they normally only saved for those dark lonely nights when they lost sight of each other.

John came up his body, not sure he had heard them, hungry to hear them again.

He pressed his mouth, his body, his heart into his, climbing into his eyes, letting him shamelessly climb into his, hiding nothing from him, blindly giving him the truth.

That they were nothing but two lost children fumbling kisses in the dark.

John lay by his side, stroking his hair. "I want you back."

Danny nodded.

"And this time I get all of you." His voice was imperative.

Danny turned his face in against him.

"Say you're sorry."

Danny moved his head.

"*Say* it."

"I'm sorry. Alright?" He rolled onto his back.

John sat up over him. "Look at me. No, right in my eyes. Now tell me this isn't going to happen again."

"It isn't."

"Say it."

"It *isn't* going to happen again, alright?"

John caught his chin in one hand. "You missed me. You missed me so bad you had to fuck him and fuck him and *still* his spunk might have been water for all the pleasure it gave you."

Danny said nothing, but there was no anger in his eyes, no denial.

"You can't hide from me any more Danny. It's need, whether you like it or not. Tell

me you missed me."

Danny shook his head to free it. It was almost a denial, but even as he did it he could hear his stupid mouth saying, "Every night I wake up from some bloody ugly nightmare and you aren't there."

John whispered, "*Yes...*" his triumph unmistakable, laying his forehead against his like some kind of exhausted valedictory. After a moment he drew back to look at him again. "Now you can't ever leave me. You rescind on this and I'll kill you. I swear it. Say you need me."

"I need you."

"You're nothing without me Danny. Other people might love you, but I've loved you the longest. I've loved you *best*. I've fought for you, *bled* for you, and that's all the blood we'll ever need. Every time you came to my room, let me into yours, you tied us tighter. Now you can't leave me. You've made an enemy of him, and I'm the only one who can save you. I'm the only one left he's afraid of. He won't dare touch you while you stay close to me. Leave me and you become his enemy. You're safe with me. Say it Danny."

"I *know* it, alright?"

"Say you love me more than your own life."

"Christ, I've died for you a million times John. What more do you want?"

"Every death you've got, all the life left in your body. I want all of you, nothing left out this time. I want it all."

"You've got it all. You've always had it. Christ, all this shit you give me - I can see through you, I know you - and you know fuck all. Think I'm in control? Think again. It's you that I'm running away from, and you that I come running back to. You're the only thing that lasts more than five minutes. Is that what you're calling love? Then fine, I love you. I've always loved you and I'll love you till the day you stick a knife in my back."

"It isn't going to happen."

"Not much it isn't. It's always been on the cards. I'll make you do it."

"You won't."

"No? You think I want this? Think it's all been some plot to get you interested? My whole life tied up in this tangle because I want my big brother's attention? When we were kids you wouldn't let me near you. Now you won't let me go. You wanted to hold me forever, and now you've got exactly what you want I can't shake you off."

"You don't want to."

"Don't I? Just watch me. I'll fuck everything I can until I find somebody bigger than you, someone big enough to blot you right out of my life. I'm going to beat you John, even if I have to die to do it."

"Christ Danny, why can't you just be content with it? We could go away, get out of this place. Why can't you just let it be?"

"Because I don't *want* to. I can't sleep unless you're beside me. I can't even have sex without..." He stopped, said instead, "I just want to stop finding every face I fuck is yours. I don't even feel pain unless it comes from you, like I needed your fucking permission just to hurt. Christ John, I'm not a person, I'm a sickness, a deformity, something diseased."

John slapped a hand over his mouth. "*Enough.*"

Danny grabbed it, but instead of pulling it away he kissed it, repeatedly, until John dragged it away, but Danny held it tight, as if he was trying to press the words into his skin when he spoke.

"It's going to go on and on until you do it in anger. Like this room. I wanted you to see it, to see *me*. *Do* you see me John? Or are you still seeing what you want to see? It was me he shared his secrets with and me he was afraid of. And I *know* you know,

983

and I know you hate me for it, and you're going to go on hating me for it. Because I knew it was a weakness before I even remotely understood why. I had my revenge out of it. I used to flaunt it up and down in front of him. I wasn't his son? Then fine, let's play big boys' games. I wanted you to catch us. Every time you came close it was because I'd engineered it. I wanted you to hurt."

"Why?"

"Because you fucking *loved* him. Your fucking loyalty didn't even go that deep. Look at the walls John. The photographs don't lie. It's all up there in black and white. Every time we left this house I became another secret. I would have done anything to hurt you. Think I'm going to stop now? You *can't* let me live. I'm your enemy."

"No."

"*Listen* to me. You've enslaved me. What else could I be other than your enemy? What slave ever wanted anything other than destruction? Even freedom doesn't mean that much after a while. What's wrong? Want proof? You can have it. I took money off him. Ask Ian how much."

"He never touched you."

"You wish. Listen to me. Take your hands away. Listen. That's why he never left me anything, he'd already paid for me. I'm a bought whore. The real thing. You can only become what you are."

"I don't care."

"I killed him."

"You liar."

"I killed the father you loved."

"No."

"Jesus John, you loved him. For Christ's sake admit it."

"No."

"You weren't the only one, you know."

"I'm not even going to listen to this shit." John rolled onto his back, hands over his head, but Danny rolled after him, yanking his arms away.

"I remember things. Here, in this house. His brother..."

"Jackie was never here." John shoved at him, repeating angrily, "He was never here."

"Yes he was. I remember him with the old man. Something happened. I can remember them together downstairs in the kitchen. Something happened."

"Like what?"

"I don't know. He was here, I'm sure of it."

"If he'd been here he'd have wanted to see Rab."

"I was his son, his real son."

"Rab's his real son, realer than you'll ever be. You're such a fucking conceited little shit. You think the world revolves around you. You think I wouldn't have known if he was here? Think the old man would have kept it secret from me? Where was I?"

Danny hesitated. John could see the struggle on his face. He said, "He was never here. You've dreamt this whole thing up. Some pathetic bloody fantasy to convince yourself you were ever worth anything to any of them. You can't drop allegiances like that Danny. Blood is blood. You don't get to write ideal families for yourself, and I'm not about to be replaced by some fucking notion of your perfect father."

"He was real, I saw him."

"And I'm telling you he was never here. The old man had nothing to do with him. He wouldn't even let him in the house."

"She knew he was here. Ian knew."

"Oh yeah, like she'd put up with that for five seconds. And if Ian knew how come he never told me?"

Danny looked away. John pulled his face back demanding, "Well?"

"He says he was never here."

John's laugh was a small huff of sarcasm. "Right."

"I know where he'd been... in prison."

"Oh Christ, I don't believe this."

"I can remember his hair. It was much shorter than it is in the photograph."

"What photograph?"

"Don't fucking start!" Danny yelled suddenly, jumping to his feet and yanking him over to the fireplace, more or less shoving his face in it. "There, that one, or are you too blind to see that too?"

John turned to look at him, but Danny shoved his face back round.

John looked at it. Black and white, oblong. There were three of them, three young men. His father, looking slimmer, fitter, almost cheerful; another man, foxy-faced, sharp, something arrogant about him; and an almost-Danny. Almost Danny of thirty years ago, tall and straight and handsome, and his father looking at him, and the look so plain it was embarrassing, and John thought, God, do I look at him like that? *Do* I?

"Well?" Danny said beside him.

"He doesn't look anything like you."

"Oh for Christ sake..."

"He's nothing like you."

Danny was looking at the photo. He rubbed his finger over his father's face as if he was trying to slowly erase it. "Something was wrong, I felt it. Maybe he'd escaped from prison."

"Oh for Christ's sake," John flared suddenly, "give it a rest before I smack you in the fucking mouth."

Danny gave him a long look. John held it.

Suddenly Danny turned and went back to the bed. He sat down wearily. "Can we go home now?" He was sitting, hands between his knees, head bowed, staring at the floor.

John was still standing on the hearth, looking back at him. It took him a while to gather himself enough to speak, but when he did all he said was, "As soon as we get in I want all your stuff moved back into my room."

Danny nodded.

"And I want the keys to the old man's room and the keys to here."

Danny nodded again.

"I don't want you going in either place again without my permission."

Danny didn't nod this time. He didn't say or do anything.

"Alright?" John pressed.

This time he nodded.

"And he only gets to stay on condition he understands exactly what the situation is, and I'm going to tell him exactly what the situation is. So much as one longing look at you and out he goes. And if I catch you doing anything, *anything* Danny, he'll be finished. Not so much as a pat on the arse, do you hear me?"

"I hear you."

"And maybe you want to get something fixed firmly in your head, exactly who I am here."

"You're my brother. Don't worry, I haven't forgotten"

"You better not. There's been enough blood spilt, even half-blood, to make you wholly mine and you better not forget that. I'm letting him stay here as a favour, to show you I trust you. Don't forget that either."

John went on looking at him. He hadn't moved. He simply sat there, looking desolate, staring at the floor.

"John, can we *please* go home?"

John looked at him a moment longer then said, "I want you to *understand* Danny, no mistakes."

"I understand."

"You're mine. Not Ian's, not the boy's, not any of the other faggots you let wander inside your life. *Mine.*"

"Yes."

"Then come and show me. Show me you understand."

Danny got up and went over to him. John lifted his chin, looked into his eyes. "Get down on your knees. I want to see you eat your own shit."

"John, please..."

"Now Danny. Everything I have is yours and everything you have is mine, including the shit. I want to know that you understand that. I want to see you eat it. Now move it."

Danny got down awkwardly, as if his bones hurt. He unfastened John's clothes and put his penis in his mouth. He closed his eyes very tight. After a while all he could feel was his own rhythm, the steady pulse of John's excitement, and the sound of John's voice saying I love you, as his hands whispered endlessly through his hair, rocking his cock to keep, safe in Danny's mouth.

Stephen felt John watching him. When he turned and squinted against the light he was just a heavy black shape in the doorway, ominous, ugly.

John started walking up towards him. Stephen turned his back, unable to bear the slow progress of him.

When he got close Stephen could smell the waxing on his jacket, heard his sleeve squeak as he brushed it against something, then the sound of him scratching his head, then silence.

"Long, lonely day Stephen."

Stephen stopped what he was doing but didn't turn.

"Look at me."

Stephen turned slowly. John reached out his hand. Stephen let it touch his cheek, awed as he always was by the sheer size of him. He made Stephen feel like a puny, helpless little kid.

"Danny's moving back into his old room, with me, where he belongs."

Stephen stared at him, feeling the thumb brushing over his cheek, listening to that low voice, so like Danny's, so seductive, warm and deep in the dark. He was the only one who sounded anything like him. The only one who had the same look in his eyes.

"He isn't going to touch you again, and you're not going to touch him, because if you do Stephen, if he does, you'll be off this farm, you and your mother both, so fast it'll burn the soles off your boots. Now, I'm giving you your chance, if you think you can't live with that, and I could understand that, then say so now, because you stay here then you've agreed to stick by the rules. And if I catch you breaking them, even to a *kiss* Steve-o..." and John ran his finger across his throat in the time-honoured gesture. "So say now. I want to hear it. Do you want to stay here?"

"Yes." Stephen practically whispered it.

"And you think you can live with it? Never touching him?"

No, Stephen wanted to scream. Not in a million fucking years. "If I have to." He managed to squeeze the words out.

John laughed. "I knew you were going to give me trouble." And the blow came out of nowhere, sending him down square on his backside in the hay, doubled-up and gasping in pain.

John was a black shape above him, haloed with tear rainbows.

"Just a warning. Just to let you know I mean it. And that was a kid's punch. I'm saving the grown-up ones for when you grow up." And Stephen heard him crack his knuckles as he flexed his hand. A horrible gut-churning noise. He wasn't even showing off, just putting his house back in order, making his hand comfortable after its day's work.

Then Stephen felt himself being lifted, almost gently, picked up effortlessly under the armpits, propped against the pen wall.

"There, all in one piece. Live to fight another day. You know, there's something about you… but there, rest easy. Man of honour Steve-o, even if I don't look it."

The hand was stroking Stephen's face again. "Leave him alone Stephen. Hands clean, eyes forward and you'll be alright. You can live and die here, safe and old in your bed. Look at him Stephen, just once, and I'll rip your body in half right up to your eyes. I can't make it any plainer. Do you understand me?"

"Yes." Stephen rubbed his sleeve over his eyes.

"Good. One kiss, I think, to seal the bargain." And John lifted his chin and pressed his mouth softly against his. It was hardly a kiss, but nevertheless Stephen felt himself climb under it. He felt sick and ashamed, wanted to claw his own eyes out.

"That's it," John breathed against his face. "Now we're blooded." And he straightened up, and Stephen heard him pull a breath in, and then he turned without another word and went out.

A black mass disappearing into the light.

SEVENTY-NINE

James Conley was looking at Molly standing on his living room floor.

"I wish you'd sit down Molly."

"No, I'd rather stand. I want to get this over with."

"I've been expecting this all week."

Molly looked at him, flushing slightly. "You know what it's about then?"

"I can guess."

She looked at the floor. "What did he tell you?"

"He said he'd assaulted you."

"Did he tell you exactly how?"

"He said he put his hands up your blouse, generally manhandled you."

She looked up, surprised, then nodded.

"Did you think he would lie to me?"

"It didn't strike me as impossible." Her voice was frosty. "He's not what I'd call a well-balanced personality."

"Why? Because he finds you attractive?"

"He doesn't find me attractive. It has nothing to do with that and you know it. Since when was rape ever anything to do with that?"

"He didn't rape you."

"He could have. You didn't see him. He could have. Quite easily."

"But he didn't."

Pressed to the point she shook her head.

Conley took a breath and moved round the sofa. He sat down, looking across at her. Finally Molly sat down too. Conley said, "Are you going to press charges?"

"No." Her voice was hard and emphatic. It was Conley's turn to be surprised.

"Why not?"

She looked at him. "Firstly, because you wouldn't like it."

Conley held up a hand. "It wasn't me he assaulted Molly. Please don't give me that responsibility."

"It's not the main reason," she said.

"Then tell me, what is?"

"It was my fault."

"*Yours*? I can't believe that. No-one could apply the she-was-asking-for-it school of thought to you Molly. No judge could find fault with you."

She smiled crookedly. "Thank you for that insult."

"I didn't mean it as one."

She smiled again, looked at her hands. "Well it was my fault." She kept her eyes on the floor. "He's the kind that always make me so cross. They never even give you a second glance because you're not some kind of dolly-bird. I was always rude to him, out of pique. I knew it provoked him but I couldn't resist it. Believe me, there is *nothing* more galling than a beautiful young man ignoring you. Don't get me wrong, I'm not condoning what he did. I believe he very nearly did rape me, and I never want to go through that again, but I know I was partly to blame for it and he was big enough to apologise. It would be mean and petty to pursue it. I know that's what he thinks I am, but I'm not, and you can tell him so." She looked up finally. "In fact, I wish you would."

He nodded. "He'll be relieved. He was scared half to death when he came up here."

"I really can't cope with seeing him again."

He forced a smile. "Nothing to worry about. He won't be coming back. For good this time." And he could feel his own words stick in his throat.

"I'm glad," she said, smiling back at him.

He tried very hard to keep it going but in the end he turned his back to her because there was no smile left inside to dredge up.

Molly looked at his back and faced facts. Time she did.

It was true. For whatever reason, James Conley, her boss, was having a homosexual relationship with one of the most beautiful men she had ever seen, and all she could think about was why it didn't gel.

But she already knew why it didn't gel. Daniel Jackson Moore was why it didn't gel.

He hadn't felt homosexual at all.

His tongue in her mouth felt as hot and eager as any she had ever encountered. More than most. As if it wanted to be there. At that precise moment she *had* felt as if he was attracted to her.

She sighed as the outside door closed firmly behind her.

It was so easy to be fooled. So easy to be wrong.

So very easy indeed.

"Where did he take you yesterday?"

"Jerrett's." Danny watched him across the table.

"And how did he convince you to move back in?"

"Charm, Ian. Personal magnetism."

Ian looked at him then back down at the table. Danny watched him biting the inside of his lip. "You've been in there, haven't you?"

Danny nodded. Ian couldn't see the nod but he knew it had happened.

"I don't know why I did that."

"Oh, for Christ's sake Ian, don't lie about it, don't make it worse than it is."

Ian's head came up fast. "You narcissistic little shit. You drag him through every twist and turn you can think up then you've got the cheek to plaster your ugly little face all over him, blot him out so you can't see anything but yourself, and he doesn't even *notice*. Christ I'll bet that made you hard."

Danny nodded. "That's more like it. I'm surprised you didn't burn them out with a cigarette."

"Think I wouldn't? "

"Well, I'm back in with him so you'll just have to wait, unless you intend to put his eyes out too. Anyway, I saved your bacon. Think what it would have been like if my 'ugly little face' hadn't been there." He smiled unpleasantly.

"I hate you."

"I've noticed."

"What pile of crap did you feed him this time?"

"I just dragged him through every twist and turn I could think up then plastered my ugly little self all over him. Maybe you should be thankful."

"And I'll bet he ate it all up, didn't he?"

"He loves his little brother Ian, of course he ate it all up."

"How can you do it to him?"

"What the fuck is it to you? Be in love with him if you want, just leave me out of it."

"You don't fucking deserve him."

"Too bad Ian," Danny smiled. "It's me Big and Beautiful gets up hard for. Go sharpen your nails."

"Who *are* you Danny?"

Danny smiled. "A beautiful boy with a big dick."

"There's got to be more. He has to see something more."

Danny described an O with his fingers, then poked his index finger through it. "That's me. See me? Nothing there. All body fluids and erectile tissue. You want to fuck? I'll fuck. You want to suck? I'll suck. Come one, come all. Put your life on my tongue, I'll lick it clean."

Ian got up and stood in front of him. "Except me."

"Oh no, even you, beautiful."

"I'm not beautiful."

"To me you are." Danny began rubbing his hand up and down Ian's thigh. "Everyone's beautiful to me."

He got up suddenly and pressed himself against Ian's body. "Want to feel how stiff you make me?" He took Ian's hand and pressed it into his crotch. Ian could feel it, growing under his hand.

"You excite me," Danny breathed in his ear. "Every imperfection, every flaw. Every lank hair, every pitted pore. I want to drink your spit, taste your sweat. I want to cram everything of me inside you, ride you into oblivion, split you open and make you bleed into my hand. I want to love you into the long hours of the night. I don't want anyone but you. I love you more than anyone in the world. I'll never love..."

"*Stop* it." Ian put his hands over his ears.

Danny laughed and immediately let him go.

Ian slowly let his hands drop. "Christ, how can he ever believe anything you say to him?"

Danny shrugged and sat back down.

Ian watched him adjust his underwear, knowing he had an erection. The fact that it was for him just made it worse, because it was fake, like everything about Danny was fake. If you ripped his face off all you'd find was something ugly and black underneath. Only the black eyes and that dirty black voice showed through, the rest was a sham.

"They should've killed you the day you were born."

"Then you'd have no-one to wank over."

Ian watched him sitting smiling up at him.

"Have you ever genuinely liked anyone?"

Danny fixed him there, pinned him with his darkly condemning eyes. "Occasionally. When I was younger. But everyone grows up Ian. It's a luxury I can't afford anymore."

"Even for yourself?"

"Oh I like myself. I like me very much."

"I don't think you do."

"Well that, as you would say, is your privilege."

"I don't think you've liked yourself in a long time."

Danny shrugged again, but Ian could see the tightness round his mouth.

"I think it's what you lie about most of all. You're desperate for someone to love you and all they want is to own you. A little of that face, that body, that *magic*, and you're eating your heart out. You're dying by slow inches because nobody loves *you*."

"Bull." But Danny's face was white. White and tight and unhappy.

"And every time you lie to him it breaks you a little more because really you love him so much it hurts. Just like you loved Rab, and Conley, and Stephen. Probably even James Henderson. That's your whole problem, you love everybody too much, and all the time they keep saying, Gimme, gimme, and poor Danny doesn't know what to do because he goes right on giving, and they go right on taking. Poor, poor Danny."

"Shut up Ian, you're boring me."

Ian laughed. "Oh no I'm not, I'm *scaring* you. I bet some days you've even half-liked me."

"No fucking danger."

Ian took his face in both hands. "I know how you feel. I *know*." Ian's eyes darted over his face. "I mean, you're the one who said it, he doesn't even notice me. I don't even care enough to persecute him any more. With my help he could be eating out your hand. Between us we could have him dancing his dick off for you, and he'd never even know. I've helped you so far, haven't I? And on the promise of what? Look how often I've lied to him. Think I'd have done that if he meant anything to me? I did everything you wanted. We're two of a kind, you and me. I'll take everything you dish out and still come back for more. All your black soul, all the sickness in your head, all the filth and depravity you can dream up - all the things you can't wash away."

He stopped suddenly, bending down to him and whispering in his ear, "All the things he is *never* going to forgive you for. All the things you *can't* tell him. All the things you *know* would kill him if he ever found out. You can never have him Danny, not while I'm alive, I won't let you..." His voice dropped further as his hand dropped into Danny's lap, began its sticky groping. "So why don't you have *me?*"

His voice dropped lower still, the hand worming in, gripping possessively. "Every one of John's secrets... a little of this and you can have *every* one..."

There was a soft grunt behind them.

Ian froze.

"Get away from him... get *way* back away from him..." John's voice was almost insubstantial, as if he'd heard something so unspeakable he couldn't even refute it.

Ian watched Danny's eyes, following John's movements in them. He was too panicked to turn. He took a step back as if trying to cover up what he'd been doing.

John's arm yanked him round, jarring his shoulder. His face was whiter than Ian had ever seen it before. It was fear, trapped animal fear, the kind of dangerous cornered fear Ian would have moved mountains never to see there. He was always so *careful*. He could feel his own heart freezing in his body. He wanted to weep.

"You're never going to tell anyone anything ever again Ian. I'm going to lock every one of your filthy little secrets so *deep* in your throat..."

Ian shook his head, desperately trying to think of a way to explain, make him understand, but he was too late. John had already punched him in the mouth.

Ian felt teeth go, a clear sharp crack. He felt his mouth fill with blood as he went down.

"Jesus Christ... *John!*" Danny tried to pull him back, but John shoved him aside as if he was a feather, had no substance.

He advanced on Ian's prone body.

Ian wriggled back, trying to get away from him, but his limbs were already defeated. There was something in him that Ian had never seen before and he was beaten by it.

John dragged him to his feet and punched him, holding him up to do it. Heavy slugs into his gut. Punches like Ian had never felt before, that had a strength he didn't know John possessed.

John let him go and he went down like crumpled sacking, banging his head on the counter, seeing stars. He began to slip away, like a man under anaesthetic. He could hear the pain, really bad, frightening pain, moaning out his mouth as if he were a million miles away. Danny was screaming. Ian wanted to say something to him, tell him it was alright, but he couldn't breathe.

Danny grabbed John's shoulder and sank his teeth into the fleshy part of his arm, dragging at his ears, his hair, anything he could reach. John turned and shoved his head, prising him off, then punched him. It took only one blow to send him back on the floor in a heap, dazed, blinking up at the ceiling.

John was dragging Ian up again.

Danny managed to crawl upright, dragging himself up the table leg. He felt blindly across its surface until his hand closed over the handle of the bread knife. Long, black, serrated, with a rippling ten inch blade. He yelled John's name.

John went on slamming Ian's head on the work surface.

"*John!*" Danny screamed frantically. "You're *killing* him!"

John turned, slowly, so very slowly. In one of his huge hands Ian hung. Blood was streaming from one eye. His face wasn't recognisable. It was pulp, jam. He was no longer conscious.

"Put him down," Danny said, advancing on him. He was crying, his voice trembling, the knife trembling, obviously shaking in his hand. "Please put him down..."

"For you? You want me to put him down for *you?*"

"I'll run you through John. I mean it. I will." Danny was trying to keep the tears back, didn't seem to know they were already coursing down his face, didn't seem to know he looked like a two year old facing down his father.

"You can't do anything to me. Not any more. I'm finished with you."

"He was talking shit. *Shit* John," Danny cried frantically. "Christ, can't you see? He wouldn't do *anything* to cross you. Ever. He hates my guts John. You *know* it. Christ you said it yourself not an hour ago. Put him down. I'm begging you."

"No." And John took Ian's body and slammed it against the wall. The head flung back against it making a sickening sound.

"*No!*" Danny screamed and dived on him.

The blade went through him. So easily. Straight into his back and penetrating his left lung.

John let him go, both hands coming round his back, trying to pull it out.

Danny watched him struggling, watched him turn.

John's eyes looked at him, blank with disbelief, then the expression seemed to turn into pleading. He managed to say Danny's name, softly, on a bubble of blood, before a dull film glazed his eyes and Danny began to scream.

And scream.

And scream.

The wind was icy. It came along the River Calder creating small waves. They looked cold and grey and vicious. James Conley stood looking down at it, slowly unbuttoning his waistcoat. Another button off it. He'd have to bundle some up for repairing. He pushed his hair back off his face. And he'd have to get this cut. He was getting too old to keep it this length.

He walked over to the bedroom, pulled all the blinds up. It felt like March, not May. It felt cold and grey and wintry. It felt like the bleakest Sunday of all his life. He didn't want to go out, but he would. He would take the car so that he couldn't excuse himself with a mere five minutes walk and back into the warm. He'd drive out somewhere and make himself walk, make himself exercise.

He pulled on a sweater and shoes, laced them up then crossed to the door. Even two years after her death he still kept wanting to say goodbye to Mamma when he went out. He pulled on his black overcoat. He really would have to get a new one soon.

All good things must come to an end.

He took the road to Stapleton for no reason other than he never normally took it. The sun was trying to struggle out. He drove slowly, the Mercedes pulling strongly beneath him. He began to feel better just being out the house.

He watched a tractor pull out into the traffic ahead of him. The car in front pulled round it and he moved up behind it. Same model and colour as Danny's used to be. What a strange thing to remember.

He saw the young farmer driving it had red hair, bright ginger, truncated cut. That's why he'd remembered, like word association. Not even remotely like him.

Danny would be twenty-six years old by now.

If he's still alive.

And Stephen would be twenty-two. Lord.

He shook himself, pulled out and overtook the tractor.

He wiped them all out of his head and forgot them.

He had pulled down the track before he knew what he was doing.

He turned into the vast car park and toured it until he found a parking place. Well, it was certainly busy.

Max, what are you doing here?

I am going to wander about and enjoy a vintage car rally. I should be right at home.

He got out the Mercedes and smiled as the sun came out from behind the clouds.

Conley was beginning to get tired.

I think you've had enough exercise for one day Max.

He stopped to pick up a Mercedes handbook. Not quite his model. He had one for his anyway, but this stuff always pulled him.

"I can do that a little cheaper for you."

"I'm sorry?" Conley looked up blankly.

"Can knock twenty per cent off. I'm clearing my stock."

Conley bought it. The man put it in a recycled bag and said conversationally,

"Fancy owning one some day?"

Conley smiled and said, "Actually I own one already. Mine's a little older."

"You jammy bastard," the man said, flatteringly impressed.

Conley smiled.

"Must have set you back a bit."

"Not really. I've got family connections in Germany."

"You've seen the Mercs they've got here today? Some real classics."

"No I haven't," Conley said.

"Oh you should go take a look, be right down your street. You can't miss them. They're just up there beside the Italian jobs. See that hot dog stand, beside the Michelin tent? That's it, up behind there. Go up and ask, they'll set you straight."

Conley decided he would. One last look then home.

He climbed the slight incline and asked at the hot dog stall. They give him convoluted directions but he simply followed the Italian flag fluttering in the cold wind and got there.

There were ten of them. He went with genuine pleasure from car to car, huddled in his coat like a refugee against the growing wind.

He stood in front of the last, a large black funereal creation not unlike his own, and turned his collar up. He felt suddenly sad, lost in his own grief, for no reason at all.

None.

And when the voice spoke to him it was like something miserable and dead in his own head, haunting him. He didn't even turn.

"Aren't you even going to answer me?" Voice deep and low, no-one else's.

And then he was standing there beside him. Not something from his own imagination, *real*. Tall as himself, face hollow, gaunt almost, older... but *real*.

"Danny..." he said, nothing but a whisper.

And Danny smiled, so white it nearly blinded him.

Conley looked at him and said, "It is you, isn't it?" Eyes going over his face, unable to take in the change in him.

"It's me alright, don't let this throw you." Danny fingered the long scar.

"How did it happen?"

Danny smiled, looked beyond Conley's shoulder. "I tried to gouge my eyes out with a chunk of glass." He looked back at him. "Sorry, not very nice, is it?"

Conley opened his mouth and closed it again. A long thin white line ran from the outer corner of his eye to the corner of his mouth. Other than that his face was as flawless as ever.

"Still beautiful Conley?" Danny's voice broke low and quiet into his thoughts. Even now its mocking tone was still familiar.

"Still beautiful Danny." And Conley could see the discomfort on his face. It wasn't the answer he had expected.

Danny ran a finger down his damaged cheek. "Not pretty."

Conley shook his head. "Still beautiful Danny, no matter what." He smiled. "You trying to tell me they don't still chase you? Looking like that? That's just glamour."

Danny looked away, pushing his hands inside his coat - a large black coat like Conley's - and said nothing.

Conley smiled, looked him up and down. The coat looked like cashmere. "You look like a wealthy man."

"I married money."

Conley felt it hit him somewhere low in the stomach. "You're married?"

Danny turned his back to the wind. He pushed the long hair off his face. Conley

saw the same long slim white hands before they disappeared inside his coat again.

"And divorced all in two brief years. Not my most successful move. I married Katherine Henderson. She paid for the privilege and I married her. For her money of course." Danny laughed. "I wouldn't do it again." His smile faded. "Even although I got to keep the money."

"I can't believe this. I never heard a thing, not a murmur. I tried to see you, you know, when you were in hospital."

"I know." Danny wouldn't look at him.

"They said you didn't want to see me."

"I didn't want to see anyone, not looking like this. It's improved with age."

"You did that in hospital?" Conley was watching him.

Danny laughed. "Kathy was bad, but she wasn't that bad, not bad enough to mutilate yourself for."

"You're divorced?"

Danny nodded. "All she could talk about was who I was fucking. She had me fucking just about every member of her family and friends." He laughed again, looking into the distance. "I gave the dog a bad name before I married her and it stuck."

He sighed suddenly and looked at his feet. "And her brother... Some day I must tell you about the time I ran a bath and came back to find him in it."

He smiled at Conley's expression. "See, I haven't changed. Trouble follows me everywhere. I should've taken out both eyes. All I succeeded in doing was giving myself... what did you call it?"

"Glamour."

"Yeah. All I succeeded in doing was giving myself glamour on top of everything else."

And Conley could hear the familiar vein of self-hate shot through it. Bitter, dark; Danny's trademark. "Come for a drink," he found himself urging.

Danny shook his head and Conley felt his own disappointment like a four year old.

"But I know what you could do for me," Danny said, still looking beyond him.

"Name it."

"Invite me back. I'd like to see your place again."

Danny looked at him and Conley felt the old familiar roll of excitement and he found himself saying, utterly without warning, "The winters are getting too cold for me here."

And Danny was watching him.

"I've been buying some property in Italy, for other people, and I'd been wondering..."

Above them the Italian flag cracked as the wind caught it and Conley looked up at it and said, "But it would mean learning another language. Maybe I'm not up to that."

Danny looked up at the flag too and Conley thought, He's in their colours, red green and black.

Danny looked at him, suddenly smiling, and said, "Maybe you should just bide at home."

Conley nodded and the flag cracked bright and sharp in the brilliant white light.

Like knives flashing in the sun.

THE END

Coming Soon from Poison Pixie

Chancery Stone's

DANNY

VOLUME 2

Please visit **www.poisonpixie.com** for full details
or
if you wish us to keep you informed of developments please email

sales@poisonpixie.com

An exciting trailer for Volume Two follows...

DANNY VOLUME TWO

Danny made himself go back to the gym. If he didn't now he never would. He'd left it too long as it was.

But she wasn't there.

He felt relieved and vaguely disappointed.

He was sitting in the tiny snack bar they euphemistically called The Mezzanine Cafeteria when the policeman came in. Danny had seen him before. He wasn't sure if he was convinced he was a policeman because he reminded him of Henderson - short, dark hair and the ubiquitous moustache - or because he was so obviously scrutinising everyone all the time. Like force of habit.

Danny looked at him briefly, saw his eyes snag on him, not for the first time, and felt the same nagging discomfort he always felt. He wasn't sure why that was either. Guilt? For who? He looked away, crumbled a sugar cube into an abandoned saucer.

"Anyone sitting here?"

Danny lifted his head slowly. "No."

"I think I've seen you before..." The policeman sat down, studying his face with narrowed eyes. It sounded like an accusation.

Danny tried not to let his scrutiny irritate him.

He remembered a fellow-inmate who sat, day in and day out, saying, 'Don't like police' every time someone spoke to him. It was all he ever said. That made it easier to work up a smile.

"...but I can't place it."

Danny said casually, "Here probably. I've seen you."

But the policeman wasn't happy with that one.

"No, somewhere else. Something to do with..." But he didn't finish it. It was almost like some kid's parlour game, as if Danny was supposed to finish it for him. Obligingly his brain immediately furnished, 'My work', 'A crime'.

More guilt talking, Danny-boy.

Danny drank the rest of his tea and pushed his chair back to get up. But the policeman stopped him with a sudden slap on the top of the table. "I've got it," he said, and his eyes seemed to come alive suddenly. "You're the one from Brixby, killed his brother."

Danny was aware that his mouth had come open, like some adenoidal retard. He shut it again, unable to shake off the feeling that this man had known all along, was playing with him.

"I knew I'd get it," the policeman said. "You don't remember me, do you?"

The policeman's eyes shifted over his face, almost eagerly, as if he was looking for something beyond recognition. Then he smiled. One of his front

teeth was noticeably chipped. His nose looked as if it might have been broken too at some time.

"Couldn't forget that hair in a hurry." He leaned back in his seat and crossed his arms. "Tell me," he said. "Are you still married to James Henderson's sister?"

Danny shook his head. It was about all he could manage.

"No?" The policeman scrutinised him, head tilted to one side. "Doesn't surprise me. These marriages of convenience never work. I always thought it was odd, you marrying Katherine Henderson after taking a knife to your brother, what with her brother having his throat cut with a knife, if you get my meaning. Odd, two knives close together like that. Never have liked coincidences."

Danny said, "I don't like strangers who walk up to me and start making a lot of offensive personal remarks."

The policeman smiled. "But I'm not a stranger. I know you, much better than you think. You really don't remember, do you? We shared a common friend, you and I. Our Jimmy didn't have many. Used to talk about you." The policeman dropped a lump of sugar in his coffee, then another. "Wanted to know about the legality of two brothers having sexual relations, penetration, that sort of thing." The policeman sipped at his coffee, watching Danny all the while. "I didn't know it was you then, of course. He just said a friend of a friend, the way people do. Wasn't till you married his sister I put two and two together, given that you'd just polished off two brothers. Seemed a bit *too* coincidental that."

"I didn't polish off two brothers."

"Sorry, self-defence, while of unsound mind. Something like that, wasn't it? Didn't serve much time, did you? Considering."

"Considering *what?*" Danny said, voice hard as nails.

The policeman pushed his cup away, smiling again. "Now, don't go getting upset. A person like you ought not to get upset. Not that you could do much damage with these." And his fingers caressed up and down the round-bladed table knife that lay half-unwrapped from the serviette beside his roll.

Danny pushed his chair back. He stood up then bent down slightly so the policeman could hear him, so they wouldn't be overheard by the other people around them. He laid his palms flat on the table. He looked like a man talking confidentially to a friend.

The policeman smiled up at him, confident but watchful.

Danny said, "Henderson was a cocksucker. Ever suck yours?"

And he straightened up in time to see the policeman's smile disappear, his face colouring slightly, before he walked past him and out of the room.

Danny peeled his shirt off, stripped off his shorts and socks. He got

under the shower, turned it up hot and hard.

Fucking know-it-all. You've made my day you fucking snooping know-it-all.

He used soap to wash his hair, scrubbed at his scalp in a fury, rinsed it out. He sprayed hot water out his mouth, shook his head like a dog. He ran the soap over his body, under his arms, rinsed it off. He soaped his face, held it up to the water. He felt the draught, then the water went cold. Cool then icy. He jumped back out of it, scrubbing at his eyes. He saw the man in the cubicle doorway through a haze of water.

"What...?" He wiped his eyes. He felt the panic of vulnerability, felt that old Psycho-in-the-shower fear. His heart thumped.

The policeman turned the water off. "I ought to kick you in the nuts, sunshine."

Danny looked at him, hearing, with almost perfect recall, Henderson saying that - sunshine. Knew that Henderson had learned it from him, not vice versa. From this ugly, threatening bastard.

"What's stopping you?" Danny said, wondering even as he said it what he was doing.

The policeman looked at his genitals. "Wouldn't want to spoil your sex life."

Danny ran his hands over his hair, squeezing the moisture out. He reached for the towel, but the policeman put his hand on it.

"Oh no, I like you just fine the way you are. Nowhere you can hide a knife on that." And he looked him over again, slowly, trying to embarrass him.

Danny kept his eyes on his face, knowing he was blushing, hoping after the heat of the water it wouldn't show.

"How about it? How about you tell me why James Henderson gets his throat cut just months before you knife your brother?"

"Fate," Danny said.

"Don't get smart."

"If I was smart I wouldn't be stuck in a shower cubicle with a cocksucker."

The policeman's arm shot out, grabbing Danny's balls in a crushing grip. Danny felt the pain like something undigested wedged under his diaphragm. He made a small oomphing noise, clutched at the policeman's hands.

The policeman spoke to him, close to his face. Danny could feel the rough fabric of his jacket against his body, could feel his breath chilling his wet skin, could smell raw onions.

"Now you listen to me sunshine. I don't need to take any crap from you. I'm a bigger man than you are sonny, and don't you forget it. In every way. Get it?" And he twisted Danny's scrotum to make his point. Danny made another involuntary noise.

Then the outside doors swung open and two men, boisterously voluble, came in. They fell silent as they saw the two men close together in the shower cubicle, one dressed, the other naked.

The policeman let go of him, smiled over his shoulder at the two men. They became suddenly industrious, but quiet, listening.

The policeman said under his breath, "I'll be seeing you."

Danny pressed his mouth tight shut, fought the urge to cradle his aching testicles in his hands.

The policeman said, "Be good" in a large cheerful voice then stepped back and drew the shower curtain back across.

Danny stood in the blue dripping echo of the cubicle and watched the seagulls flutter on the damp nylon as the outer doors whooshed shut behind him.

* * * * * *

By three o'clock Stephen knew he would have to do something about his headache. He sat down on a pile of tyres and lit a cigarette. In future, he told himself for the millionth time, he'd lock his door, and it would stay locked. Christ, why now? Why had he started up now, just out of the blue?

He rubbed his forehead.

"Hello there."

Stephen jumped to his feet, head thumping from the sudden effort.

He squinted into the light. The man was no-one he knew. He came in towards him so that Stephen could see him clearly. Middle-aged, heavy-set, with dark oily hair. Everything about him looked vaguely oily. Stephen didn't like him already. "Can I help you?" he asked.

"Just looking for a little information. Name's Greaves." And Stephen was horrified to watch him take out police identification.

He looked at it, at the man, at the navy overcoat and said, "Has something happened?" feeling his heart in his mouth.

"No, relax." The policeman smiled, showing a badly chipped tooth, right bang in the front where you couldn't miss it. Stephen noticed his hands, big and rough and very red, as if he worked outdoors. They didn't look like policeman's hands at all. "Just wondered if you could help me out. I'm looking for a Daniel Jackson Moore."

Stephen stood there and felt his face flush. It was idiotic, frustrating, meaningless. Finally he managed to say, "He doesn't live here anymore. He hasn't lived here for years."

The policeman was watching him intently. "Oh, I know that." He smiled again. "You don't remember me either, do you?"

Stephen looked at him. "I'm sorry?"

"No, I can see you don't. No, what I want to know is where he is now."

"I don't know," Stephen said and he was suddenly glad he didn't.

"But you knew he was back, back hereabouts somewhere?" And the question wasn't a question and it sounded like in knowing Stephen had already committed a crime, tried to cover up evidence.

He nodded.

The policeman pushed his hands in his pockets and suddenly looked round as if he hadn't noticed the place before. "Big." He looked at Stephen. "Own much land?"

"A fair amount."

"How many hands?"

"Four."

"All live in?"

Stephen nodded.

The policeman walked round him, like a dog circling a piece of meat. Stephen fought the urge to turn with him. He finally came back to Stephen's face, still looking round him as if it was all terribly novel.

"Know him, did you?" The policeman wasn't looking at him, then he was. "Did you know Daniel Jackson Moore?"

"Yes," Stephen said.

"Good friend, was he?"

"Look, why d'you want to know?"

The policeman smiled. It was a widening of his mouth, like a sudden rictus, like something ugly he couldn't help. "That's my business, isn't it?"

"Well I don't know where he is so I can't help you."

"And what about Mr Robert Hardman?" The policeman's eyes were deep-set and narrow. His moustache looked stuck-on, darker than his hair, too sleek.

"What about him?"

"Would he know?"

"I doubt it." Stephen lied without a blush.

"Where might I find him?"

"About a mile down the road, going South. He's spreading muck."

The policeman smiled. "Thank you." He held out his hand.

Stephen took it reluctantly. It was as rough as it looked. What did he do, pumice stone modelling?

He held Stephen's hand too long and said, "You've grown a bit, haven't you?"

And then he dropped his hand and simply walked away.

Harry Greaves saw the muck spreader as he went past.

He smiled. *Well, our Mr McEvoy was telling the truth about that anyway. Changed a lot.*

Harry pushed the tape into the player but he didn't switch it on.

Last time I saw him he was attempting to bite a police officer and screaming with frustrated rage.

Harry looked out the window at the tail lights of a passing lorry. Miracle any light got through them. Filthy.

Could almost have been brothers; that hair, the way he was carrying on.

Maybe he thinks I was just going to let go.

Plenty of money, I'd say. Has to have come from the Hendersons. What did he do, nick the family silver?

Harry indicated and pulled into the inside lane to turn down the East Newton road.

I remember Hardman too. Long-haired pretty-boy. Just sat there on the floor holding Johnny's body. I thought he was injured at first. Face the colour of putty, covered in blood. Looked as if he'd done it. He was stroking his hair. Gave me the bloody creeps, that. But our two redheads, spitting and fighting like cats. Must be the red hair. They say that about redheads, don't they?

And they let him off. Stabbed him in the back. How could that be an accident? Unfit to plead. Delaying the trial. Giving evidence doped out his head. I don't think he even knew where he was. And them lying for him. Oh yes, I sat and watched them lying. Just an argument got out of hand. Didn't even know he had the knife in his hand. Big brother was a real bad boy. Violent, unpredictable. Definite self-defence. We were there, we saw it. Loved his big brother, wouldn't do anything to hurt him. No doubt. Loved him so much he stabbed him in the back. And him, I've seen a million of them try it. The nervous breakdown, when they can't face it any more. And what he couldn't face was murdering his brother. I know hate when I see it. It's ten inches long and sharp as a blade.

Harry pulled into the lay-by where Danny and Rab had fought and got out the car and started to walk.

Harry came up round the back of the house. It was a bloody wilderness. Didn't he ever cut the grass? Worse than his bloody hair - didn't look like he ever cut that either.

Harry jingled the loose change in his pocket. Worthwhile looking in the windows? Might come face to face with him. *Wouldn't want that just yet Harry, hm? Let's have a closer look anyhow, take the risk.*

He walked round the side, keeping blind to the window. When he got level he took a quick glance. No-one. He took a proper look, studied the room. Clothes lying on the floor, the remains of food on the table. Messy bugger. Shouted money though, plenty of lovely money.

He went round the front of the house, stood at the corner. He was in

alright. Car parked right out for all the world to see. He lifted his head. No upstairs. Bedroom must be round the other side.

Harry didn't look in any more windows.

He went back down over the fields to his car.

He met nothing but sheep.

* * * * * *

Harry Greaves smiled at the girl in the large floppy-bowed blouse. Why did they always paint their cheeks orange?

"I think you can trust me." He showed her his police identification. He watched the conflict on her face. She was obviously not supposed to go against the rules. On the other hand telling a police officer, a detective at that, where to get off was a bit beyond her. It was tantamount to telling him the force was corrupt.

"The client was very particular about not handing out the keys."

"Ah, but he doesn't know it's to a fine upstanding citizen like me, does he?"

The girl smiled. Cardboard. But Harry knew he'd won.

"Well, just this once," she said to appease her pride.

"That's a girl," Harry said, reaching out his hand. She dropped the keys into it. He smiled and straightened the flap on his pocket. "Have a nice day now."

And he left the shop.

Harry let himself in, breathing deeply.

He could smell him. He could smell the dirty little piece of jail bait.

Money. Sex. That's what he smelt of. Even if Harry hadn't known who he was, he'd have known the smell.

He closed the door. The house was warm, heated by the sun through the glass. But he hadn't been long out of it. It had the feel. Just newly deserted, like it had been abandoned for a holiday, not forever.

Harry went into the living room.

He saw the marks where a hi-fi had been, dimples on the thick carpet. The shelving was still there, dust marks behind the ghost-line of the plastic boxes.

Lots of money.

He wants to sell it quickly the girl had said. Just sales speak or was it true? Moving on? Already moved on?

Harry drummed his fingers in his palm. He was annoyed. Annoyed he'd let him slip so easily, shelved him to the back of his mind, losing sight of

his priorities. *You don't put people like Red to the back. Oh no. Otherwise they slip out the exit door when you're not looking.*

He sat down on the armchair Danny favoured and looked at the phone. He pushed the playback button, then the on/off button. He bent over the table and pulled the flex up. Disconnected. Why hadn't he taken it with him?

He plugged it back in. He pressed the playback again. This time the tape came on. Harry leaned back and listened to him talking. A little too deep, like he'd cultivated it, but natural and easy. A born liar. Smooth, seamless, so good you couldn't see the joins. He played it again. Then once more. He opened the machine and took the tape out. He put it in his overcoat pocket. He got up, jangling the keys loosely as he moved. He whistled between his teeth.

He went into the kitchen. He opened the cupboards. Everything still there, every cup and plate and glass.

Harry took one of a set of six crystal glasses and dropped it on the stone floor. It shattered musically, prismatically, as it exploded. "Oops," he said, stepping over it.

He opened the fridge. Nothing in it. He'd bet his last Rolo it was all in the bin outside, dumped.

He opened the cutlery drawer. Lots of sharp knives. *Not scared of them, are you Red? No hang-ups about knives.*

He closed the drawer again.

He wandered back out to the hall.

There was a postcard on the hall mat, bright, garish. Dutch bulbs in Spring. He wondered how he'd missed it. He bent and picked it up, then turned it over. It was postmarked Amsterdam.

He read it.

You don't answer my letters. All I get is one different address after another. Why are you so unsettled? Write to me. Kobal. P.S. Back Home? For why?

Harry searched his brain. He tapped the card against his nails. It kept slipping over the edge of his mind, elusive. He sucked his teeth then slipped the card into his pocket beside the tape.

He went into the bedroom. He sniffed the air. It was stronger in here, deeper, sweeter. Like the little pervert wore perfume.

Harry walked round the bed. It had been made hastily. He reached and pulled the counterpane back. He looked at the pillow then pulled a loose thread off its edge. He wound it absently round his pinkie as he walked round the room. The wash basket was empty, and so was the wardrobe. In the chest of drawers he found a pencil and a badge, brightly yellow, extolling a hamburger restaurant whose name was unfamiliar. He carefully pinned the badge to his lapel. He got down on his knees and looked under the chest. There was no gap under the wardrobe. There was nothing

there. He got up stiffly and dusted down his knees. He sat on the bed, rubbing his hands over the rough cotton of the counterpane. It looked hand-woven, foreign. It was the only personal thing he'd seen in the place. He picked the pillow up and put it across his knee. He stroked it idly under his fingers. His hand registered the expensive sleek cottony feel of it. Fine linen or something. It felt like the ones his Irish grandmother had had. Hers had been hand-embroidered. This one was plain. Just a line of black piping, like a Victorian mourning card, along one edge.

Harry pressed the pillow to his face. He held it there until he had to breathe again. After a moment he put it down, covered it up. On impulse he got down on his knees and lifted the counterpane. His impulse was rewarded. He reached under the bed.

When he first pulled it out he thought it was a pair of women's knickers. Red silky skimpy little things. He held them up and realised they were men's. Unmistakably cut for a man. He looked at the label. 100% Soie. French. Silk. He rubbed them between his fingers appreciatively, felt something rough and powdery. He turned them inside out. A stain. White, dry, obvious. He'd shot his load in them. Harry smiled as he put them in his pocket. He could have got good money for these.

He went into the bathroom.

Harry stood in the heel bar listening to the odd rhythm of the cutting machine. Whine, stop. Whine, stop. Like a pattern. He looked at the racks of kids Day-Glo laces with horrible turtle faces; dogs with floppy ears; purple ponies with 'real' hair, green hair.

The smell of adhesive made him slightly giddy. It smelt like an explosion in a pear drop factory. Kids didn't need to buy glue, they could come in here and get high for free. He pulled out a stool and sat down. He looked at a rack of shoe cream. Only one or two left in each long slot. They were thick with dust. Olive. Burnt Ochre. Spearmint Pink. When had they last stocked up, 1976? He whistled tunelessly. He turned the key tag over in his pocket. He'd taken it off before he'd given the keys over. It was a huge sloganed chunk of plastic, not exactly generating confidence in Harry's credentials. He realised the older man working on the heel bar was watching him in a long mirror that ran above his head. Harry stopped smiling.

The spotty boy who'd taken the keys brought them back, held out the two sets. The new ones were rough and bright and hot.

Harry paid him. The boy kept chewing, took the money, turned and began heeling a pair of golf shoes like he was on an oiled track on the floor.

The older man was still watching Harry in the mirror.

Harry went out the shop.

Conley called Danny that evening.

"It's me. Your man looked the place over today."

"And?"

"The Great Undecided."

"No, in other words."

"There's something funny about it."

Danny changed hands. His arm was beginning to ache already. "What do you mean 'funny'?"

"Well the girl at Ritsons said he sounded more interested in where you'd gone than in the house itself."

"Where I'd gone? Shit. I'll bet this is fucking Bobby. She didn't tell him, did she? I mean, they don't know, do they?"

"Of course not. But you ever get the feeling that you're only getting half the story?"

"Mm."

"Well, that's what she was like. Hedgy."

"What about?"

"I don't know. But she said he said the place was a mess, things broken on the floor."

"What the fuck is she on about? It was tidy."

"Want me to go check?"

"No, it's aright, I'll go. If this is some nut of Bobby's... if he's paid some arsehole to make a mess of the place..."

"Want me to come along, just in case?"

Danny laughed. "What? Protection? No, forget it. I doubt if they'll still be there." Danny sighed. "Anyhow, it'll be late, late, late by the time I get there. I can always drag Rab along if I get cold feet."

"Well, ring me if you need me."

Danny smiled. "You're a sucker Max."

"I try," Conley returned, and hung up.

Danny stood up and stretched then stifled a yawn. "I won't be long."

"Sure you don't want to go in the morning?"

Danny bent and rubbed his cheek. "What a sweetheart." He straightened up. "Nope. It's bugging me. I want to get it over with."

"I can come along if you want."

Danny squeezed his shoulder. "No. Finish what you're doing then we can..." He bent down and whispered in Rab's ear.

Rab, ridiculously, blushed, pulled his head away. "You're a dirty little pig sometimes Danny."

Danny laughed. "Never done that?"

"Christ, you're sick." Rab ducked away from him.

Danny winked and pulled on his jacket.

He gave Rab one last grin and disappeared out the door.

It felt odd going back. Like he'd lived there years and years ago. Danny opened the front door and clicked on the hall light. The place looked bare. Which was odd considering it had never looked any different from how it looked now. There was no mail, but then, there seldom was. Who did he have to write?

He went into the living room, put on the light. Everything was exactly as he had left it.

He moved into the kitchen. The light flickered into life. He didn't see the broken glass until he stood on it. It crunched underfoot with an odd abrasive squeak.

He frowned, lifted his foot back. He saw the stem and base still intact, the bowl nothing but a glittery powder. It was spread wide on the floor as if it had been dropped from above someone's head. He stepped over it and opened the cupboard door. Five. The sixth was on the floor. They were a good set, bought from a design centre in New York, hand-cut. The figures on them were Bedouin. Kathy had bought them for him. It was a pointless present, but he still liked them. He hadn't broken it, and it couldn't have been Andy. Who else had been here?

Danny walked round it. It looked so deliberate. Like pouring a pot of paint down someone's wall. Like scratching the roof of the car. But not Rab. Not this time. So who the fuck?

Danny felt unsettled by it. If the place had been wrecked... but the one piece, so carefully selected, so ostentatious. Like showmanship. He felt his hackles come up. He wished he'd brought Rab with him after all.

He went back out into the hall. He opened the bathroom door, pulled the light switch. It flooded with light. He went in, half-expecting someone to come hacking out the shower. He remembered the aftershave he'd left. Good old essence of sherbet lemon. He might as well salvage that while he was here. He opened the bathroom curtains. But it wasn't there. The mark of it was there, a nice tidy oval in the white dust, but no aftershave. He'd left it. He knew he had. He had two; one open, one new. He'd taken the new and forgotten the old. He'd forgotten it because he'd stashed it behind the bathroom curtains. He'd been annoyed about forgetting it because he wasn't going to be able to afford any more, and now it wasn't here. He lifted both the curtains as if it might be hiding from him. He dropped them. He looked in the medicine cabinet. Nothing. Nothing at all.

Danny felt suddenly angry. Whoever had been here had nicked his fucking aftershave. Dirty thieving bastards. *You owe me Bobby*.

He pulled the toggle savagely, plunging the bathroom back into

darkness.

He opened the bedroom door and put on the light.

A man sat in the chair pointing a gun at him.

"What the fuck?..." Danny's heart was thundering with fright.

Harry Greaves smiled. "You've gone a funny colour, sunshine."

Danny's eyes flicked from his face to the gun.

"Oh yes, it's real. Come in and shut the door."

Danny shut the door behind him using his incapacitated arm, feeling it protest when he didn't turn his body to help. He pushed it to with his heel.

"He doesn't trust me," Harry said.

Danny had to wet his lips before he could get his next words out. "The glass, in the kitchen."

Harry nodded. "It worked too. You came haring up here, like the good little capitalist you are, to make sure some filthy vandal wasn't dirtying the Wilton. Late, mind you." Harry lifted the gun slightly, eased his elbow a little better on the chair arm. "I thought you weren't going to show."

Danny flicked his eyes to the floor, saw the Thermos, expanded polystyrene boxes. He frowned in disbelief. "You've been here all day?"

"Nothing to an old pro like me. Warm, comfy; all mod cons; good book to read." He moved his eyes to indicate the book hanging over the arm of the chair. Danny could see a black gun and a red rose. He couldn't make out the author's name. Not a best-seller, the title was bigger.

"I like good detective stories. Not bad this one, though I prefer the ladies. They say they have a better eye for detail. Me, I think they're just more naturally deceitful. Don't you?"

"What do you want?"

Harry said, "Don't beat about the bush, do you?"

Danny didn't answer him.

"Where are you living?"

Danny still didn't answer him. Harry lifted the gun, something clicked.

Danny said, "You wouldn't dare."

"Like you wouldn't dare kill a copper. Where are you living? And make it the truth."

Danny licked his lips again. "Back home."

The policeman frowned. "I said the truth, sunshine."

"It is the truth. My cousin took me back. I'm working there. Phone him if you don't believe me."

Harry nodded slowly, consideringly. He lowered the gun slightly. He smiled slowly until his chipped tooth was showing. "So Pretty's lost all his money. Dear, oh dear. What a shame. Right back where you started, eh? Right back in the filth."

"Keeping you company."

The gun lifted again. "Very mouthy for someone looking at death. Nothing to stop me taking my eye and my tooth right now, so maybe you ought to watch what you say, sunshine. What d'you say?"

Danny didn't say anything. His skin felt cold and clammy. He had to fight to stop himself from shivering.

"I asked you a question, sunshine."

"I'm watching what I say," Danny said.

"Good." Harry nodded, lowered the gun again. "And now I'll answer your question." Harry reached carefully into his overcoat pocket. The gun never wavered, nor did his eyes. He held something scarlet in his hand. He threw it.

Danny recoiled, but it landed harmlessly in front of him. He flicked his eyes down, back up.

Harry Greaves was smiling again. "Pick them up. Go on."

Danny bent carefully and picked them up. He wondered where Greaves had got them. He remembered the last time he'd worn them, and who with.

He held them in one hand, loose by his side. Greaves smile was wider. Too wide. Danny waited. Greaves said finally, "Now put them on."

He leaned back comfortably in the chair, holding the gun in both hands.

Greaves watched him undress in absolute silence. Danny's clothes sparked with static.

Greaves said, "All of them" when Danny hesitated momentarily. He rolled his socks off, pulled his T-shirt over his head.

Greaves looked at the underwear he wore. Danny came to a halt again. Greaves said, "What are you waiting for, someone to throw you money? I said, all of them."

Danny slid the pants off. Greaves had to hand it to him. No wonder he'd got away with murder. Cool as a cucumber. "Now put them on."

Danny pulled the red silk briefs on. They felt stiff and cold, dirty. Like wearing someone else's unwashed clothes. They were even more microscopic than the ones he'd taken off. They clung obscenely.

"Turn round."

Danny turned. Greaves saw the thong disappear between his cheeks. There was no bloody arse in them. He looked like a rent boy.

"Back," Greaves said.

Danny turned back to face him.

"You do nothing for me, sunshine. Not a bloody thing."

Danny didn't answer him. What could he say? So sorry. Maybe something in blue? He didn't know what it was for, what Greaves was playing at. He just wanted to keep the gun happy, that was all. Maybe he was going to kill him anyway. This was just the fun part first.

"Why is that, d'you reckon?"

"Maybe I'm not your type."

The gun came up marginally. "Maybe I don't like smart little queers that play at being rent boys. Who d'you perform for in them? They're full of your spunk."

"A girl."

Greaves was momentarily thrown. "Don't give me that. Who was it?"

"A girl. I told you. I picked her up in a bar."

"Name?"

"I didn't ask."

"Describe her."

"Fat hands, too many rings. I don't remember anything else about her. We were drunk."

"Wouldn't she let you get it up her then?"

"We didn't get that far. She brought me off against a wall at the back of the pub."

"Which?"

"The Corn Exchange. In Caldermouth."

"What happened to her?"

"I took her home, she gave me her number. That was it."

"You got it?"

"I burnt it."

"Why?"

"I always do."

Greaves said slowly, "You're a very pretty liar."

"Why should I lie to you?"

"You tell me." Greaves lifted the gun another inch, steadied it. "How many others since then?"

"I don't know."

"Then think."

"Two. My ex-wife and a waitress from a pizza parlour."

"The waitress?"

"She served me in a restaurant. We went back to her flat. We fucked. That's it."

"Did you get her number too?"

Danny nodded.

"Burn it?"

Danny nodded again.

"What was she like?"

"Thin. Strong Irish accent."

"And how was she in bed?"

Danny didn't answer.

"I'm not going to ask you again."

"Not confident enough." Danny didn't say anything else.

"Not as good as the piece from the pub, eh?"

Danny shook his head.

Greaves considered him for a long moment. "This why Katherine Henderson divorced you? Because she found out she'd married a tom cat?"

Danny nodded.

The gun came up. "You're a bloody liar. You divorced her."

"It was still the same reason."

"Mental cruelty, or whatever they call it over there. How did you pull that off?"

"I wanted out and I knew she wouldn't fight it."

Greaves frowned, not understanding his logic.

Danny saw his expression and elucidated, "Better to be thought a neurotic with a devoted husband than a woman who can't keep one. I knew her and I knew she wouldn't fight it."

"Fly boy."

Danny didn't answer.

"You killed her brother, didn't you?"

"No."

The gun came up. Danny bit his lip.

"Didn't you?"

"No."

"One last time then I blow your dick right up your arse."

"I'm telling you the truth. I didn't."

"Then who?"

"I don't know."

"Who?" The gun gave another of those ominous little clicks.

"I don't know."

There was no final warning. The hammer went off.

Danny felt his insides let go.   **DV2**

No text is innocent

www.poisonpixie.com